I0631936

TYBURN DICK,

THE

PRINCE OF THE HIGHWAYMEN.

PROFUSELY ILLUSTRATED

BY

EMINENT ARTISTS.

Publishing Office:

HOGARTH HOUSE, 32, BOUVERIE STREET, E.C.

TYBURN DICK;

THE BOY KING OF THE HIGHWAYMEN.

TAKE ME WHO DARE.

PROLOGUE.

TYBURN DICK TRIED AND SENTENCED.

(From the report of the trial, published in the "London Mercury," one hundred years ago.)

A STRANGE sensation pervaded the court when the judge was heard to give the low order for the prisoner to be brought forward. There was a rustling of silks and lace, as the ladies in the gallery, brought there by their singular wish to be present at the trial of their highwayman hero, leaned over the rails to catch the first glimpse of their daring idol.

Amongst the ordinary spectators, a murmured buzz testified to an unwonted excitement.

Men swayed to and fro; the ushers and

dignitaries of the court looked eagerly towards the bar. There was a slight commotion among the lawyers retained for the prosecution and defence : even the judge, usually cold and stern, and indifferent amidst the cruel scenes of our bloody laws, seemed pale and agitated.

An attempted rescue had been foretold, and the strong doors were guarded by soldiers, whose bayonets were fixed with an ominous click at the order for the prisoner's appearance.

A moment after, the youthful Highway King stepped from amongst the officers. As if by one accord, there was a solemn hush in court, and amidst the breathless stillness of an awed multitude, the prisoner took his place in the dock.

He had scarcely taken his stand, when a lovely arm leaned over the ladies' balcony, and a very beautiful bouquet of choice flowers was thrown towards him. He caught the floral gift with his manacled hands, and raising his eyes—fine dark eyes, fringed by long silken lashes, and thrilling with tenderness and daring fire—sought out the blushing donor from amongst the bevy of fair ladies that surrounded her.

Bowing with courtly ease, he selected one pure white rose, and laying the flowers on the 'edge before him, placed this single blossom in his breast.

Then his small white hands—well-formed as a woman's—and strangely marred by the dull irons above his wrists, fell from view, and while the pens of prosecuting counsel and clerks rustled over their papers, he stood the nosure of every glance.

He still wore his highway attire ; his coat of crimson cloth, with its handsome gold and lace ; his shining black boots, his lace scarf, striped with the crimson stain where the blood had flowed from the wound in his throat, received during his fierce fight to resist capture.

His face was pale and thoughtful, but did not reveal the faintest vestige of fear or nervous excitement. Fear could find no place in the stout heart that beat within his womanlike breast ; his eyes were bright, and his lips curled with proud disdain, as, on confronting the judge and jury, he threw himself into an attitude of haughty indifference.

Once he started, and for a moment his whole frame seemed to throb under the influence of some powerful emotion.

It was when his gaze rested on a lady, evidently of rank, who was seated near the judge.

Her features were concealed by the rich folds of a veil of white lace, but even the light cloak she had about her shoulders did not hide the excited throbbing of her bosom, when the gaze of those clear piercing eyes singled her out with instant recognition.

" My lord," said the prisoner, in a calm rich voice, when formally asked to plead, " it is for you and your jury to determine whether I am guilty or not guilty. Let my trial proceed. I shall offer no delay."

The waving of white handkerchiefs, and the clapping of hands, in the ladies' gallery, followed this speech. Sparkling eyes, as bright as the diamonds on the fair brows or bosoms of their fair owners, flashed admiringly on the unsubdued Boy Highwayman.

Come what might, he was still the popular hero, and many a lady's heart thrilled with the wish that his trial would result in his acquittal.

He stood in a posture of listless graceful indifference while the evidence was given against him ; occasionally he bestowed a careless look of contempt on the villanous visages of the hireling thieftakers, who had helped to hunt him down ; but as if seeking relief from the disagreeable vision his eyes more constantly roved to the fair faces of the ladies above.

Now and then he gave the lady seated near the judge a quick glance, and a strangely grave expression settled on his youthful features, as he saw how she recoiled when some dastardly evidence tended fatally to prove his guilt.

If eloquence could have won him from his doom, he would have been freed. But the arguments and persuasive appeals of his counsel were of no avail against the hard stern fact that he had been guilty of crimes for which the inflexible punishment was death.

He must die !

So every one knew, when, with solemn set faces, the jury returned into court.

The prisoner knew it ; but he did not change from his careless attitude.

Unmoved when his youth, his misfortunes,

the nobility he had displayed in his wildest career, were pleaded for his defence, he was indifferent now, though every bosom thrilled with awe, and sympathising faces blanched, as lovely women, their eyes bathed in tears, bent forward, shiveringly, to catch the terrible words giving him to death.

He roused himself as the judge coldly asked him if he had anything to say why sentence of death should not be passed upon

Roused himself, and fixed his eyes keenly on the ashy countenance of the man whose trembling lips were nerved to speak his doom.

The summing up of that judge had been coldly deliberate, and dead against the prisoner.

Yet all through the trial he had avoided those clear, scornful eyes, which now riveted him with their glance.

" My lord," Tyburn Dick observed quietly, "you who have followed me through life with the malicious hate that is only appeased with the joy of pronouncing my doom, know well what I have to say against this sentence—you know, my lord that, had I my rights, you and your hireling crew would now be debased and grovelling at my feet like slaves. The triumph is yours. I am, indeed, a malefactor —you are my judge !"

The lips of the judge quivered ; his hands in a palsied way clutched at the black cap, kept as yet out of sight; but he was strengthening himself for the final process, when the veiled lady at his side convulsively grasped his robe, and spoke low and hurriedly.

What she said was unheard in court, save by the judge—the hard, stern look deepened in his eyes as he listened ; but the lady's words had something imperious in their power, and he again addressed the prisoner.

" Prisoner at the bar, there is yet time for mercy to be extended to your youth. If you will give the court the information that will lead to the capture of your band, you may be spared."

The youthful highwayman's lips curled scornfully.

" Old man of infamy," he said, " pull the black cap over your brows and mumble the sentence of the law. Do your worst ! But were you to tear me limb from limb these lips should never reveal the secret home of my gallant band. Still, it may interest you to hear that when you captured me my brave night riders were in the very hollow where I fell stricken by the accursed hand of treachery."

The judge uttered an angry exclamation.

" Send soldiers instantly forth," he cried. " Pile burning faggots at the entrance of the hollow —suffocate them if they will not surrender !"

" My lord," exclaimed Tyburn Dick, when the soldiers had gone, " you have sent them on a fool's errand ; it is true I left them there, but they are far away now ; my sacrifice saved them ; not one will be taken. And now, my lord, complete this business."

A breathless hush succeeded his words.

Slowly the judge assumed the black cap.

Slowly and with deliberate emphasis he pronounced the last sentence of the law.

" Abandon every hope of mercy," were his concluding words. " Eight and forty hours alone are left you to seek, by repentance, mercy of your Maker—none remains for you on earth. Your wicked career is at an end ; an ignominious death sends your soul shuddering into eternity. Make the most of the brief time left you. The sentence of the law is that on Monday morning next you be taken to Tyburn Tree, and hanged by the neck till you are dead. At Tyburn Tree, the scene of your desperate career, in your highway dress you shall hang in chains, gibbeted as a warning for your lawless gang to see. Forty-eight hours are mercifully given you—then prepare for a bitter death !"

Forty-eight hours !

The slightest sounds were audible when the judge ceased speaking.

The prisoner stood as before—pale, calm, and unaffected.

Sobs and sighs came from the ladies' gallery, where many a blooming face was pallid and dimmed with tears.

There was a stir amongst the sterner portion of the throng.

The lady who had been seated by the judge rose slowly.

Slowly her veiled face was turned towards the prisoner, and the intense agony of her whispered tones made strong men shiver as she said—

"Madman! what are your worthless companions' lives? Speak, and save yourself."

She clung to the rail of the judge's desk.

A swift shock passed through the prisoner's frame. His eyes blazed fiercely.

"My lord," he cried hotly, "I am tried, convicted, doomed. What woman is this who comes between me and the gallows? If there is any power in your authority, bid her reveal her face."

Before the judge could speak the veil fell.

There was a commotion in court when that face was revealed. She was known to nearly all there. Known by her beauty, her rank, her wealth. Known by the rumour of a mysterious tie which, it was asserted, bound her to the prisoner.

She was superbly beautiful. Deep, anxious excitement was visible in every lineament, and yet, spite of the contrast afforded by the calm, listless features of the boy highwayman, a distinct resemblance, awful if true, could be traced between them.

Fearful, indeed, for with the relentless unsparing fury of a tigress she had hunted that fearless boy to death; her snares had led him to his fate, her money had bribed his enemies, and now only in the last hour did remorse seem to goad her for what she had done—urge her to undo her too fatal work.

"I know you, madam," the boy highwayman observed. "Your presence here is a fitting crown to the ferocity with which you have sent your hireling bloodhounds on my track. Look me in the face! Do I quail? Tell me, inhuman devil! Are my cheeks blanched with fear—blanched like yours and his?"

He glanced towards the judge.

The quivering woman, fierce in her remorseful agony, turned towards the functionary.

"Save him!" she cried hoarsely. "There is time—save him—save him from this cruel death!"

"Save him!" the cry came from the ladies' gallery—came amid sobs and tears. "Save him!" "Petition the King!" "Give another day's grace; let him be saved!"

"Ladies," Tyburn Dick said, "I thank you for your sympathy and interest in my fate. I shall remember you gratefully in my last hour."

He bowed gallantly, and waved his manacled hands.

"For you, madam," he exclaimed, coldly regarding the trembling woman, whose lips, ashy and dry, quivered as she tried to speak, "yours is the triumph of a tigress—I wish you joy of it."

"Speak! a word will save you!" she shrieked. "Withold not that word I implore you!"

"Too late!" His eyes kindled with fiery light. "Oh, madam, I begin to think the triumph is mine. Nature asserts her sway in that breast of yours, which should have been soft in its love to me, but has given me a wolf's ferocity instead; those soft arms of yours, madam, should have been a tender girdle for my throat, round which they have placed instead a hempen circlet, to choke my life out!"

He shook himself at the thought of the degrading noose tightening round his white neck, a flush rose to his cheeks, his voice grew deep and stern, and, fixing his gaze on the cowering woman—

"Look how she quails!" he cried; "she, who from my infancy belied the tie that bound us; whose bitter hate and persecution hounded me through the world; whose snow-white fingers counted out the golden bribe paid to men of infamy, that they might lead me to a career whose end should be death; whose serpent tongue pointed the deadly evidence to damn me on this trial; and now, aha! who shrinks from her black unholy work when it is too late—too late!—shrinks!—shivers at my voice — shrinks from my gaze, that fair devil, who hunted me to the gibbet! that merciless woman, my mother!"

With a wild, fierce jerk he snapped his manacles asunder as if they had been of glass.

His right hand, with the broken irons hanging to his wrist, was outstretched towards the shivering woman—his head was thrown back—his breast heaved with excitement—a faint oozing stream of red trickled from his parted lips.

What a shriek of wild pitying agony rang through the court!

It was echoed from the ladies' gallery

whose fair occupants leaned swooning or sobbing over the rails.

And there, beside the speechless judge, whose head was yet surmounted by the ominous black cap, stood the unnatural woman, who had hunted her own child to a felon's doom. Stood ghastly and shrieking till a strange, awful laugh of mocking triumph came from the lips of the youthful highwayman, when, with a wild agonised effort to spring towards him, she threw her white rounded arms above her head, and fell collapsed and shuddering at the feet of the stricken judge.

CHAPTER I.

OUR HERO'S EARLY HISTORY.

SUCH a night, and such a storm as raged along the sullen coast of Cornwall had not been known by the oldest seafarers of that haunt of fierce smugglers and wreckers.

The waves rolled shoreward in heavy mountainous masses, beating with a harsh roar against the rugged and broken cliffs, down whose sides the rain poured in ceaseless torrents.

The furious gale blew shrieking across the green breakers and whitened foam — loud claps of deafening thunder rolled above the angry war of ocean.

Forked flashes of lightning darted from the blackened sky.

Lighting up the stormy scene.

Lighting up the lonely huts straggling along the coast, where fishermen and wreckers dwelt.

Then leaving all wrapped in a pall of impenetrable blackness.

Once, when a swift ray of fire shot from the lowering clouds, a sad sight was revealed.

A ship, tempest - tossed, riding helplessly in the gale, riding towards the deadly line of breakers, whose foaming eddies, if they drifted there, would dash the vessel to pieces on the rugged reefs.

Awful as was the scene on her ill-fated deck, a more appalling scene was enacting on the black cliffs above, for there, in the storm and torrent, were gathered a murderous gang of hardened wretches, gathered there to try their fiendish arts, and lure the good ship to destruction, that they might possess themselves of her treasures.

Seizing their booty as it came to shore with the pale floating bodies of the helpless beings whose death had been their devilish doing.

Half-sheltered in a fissure upon the summit of the towering peak, known by its ill-name of the Wrecker's Gully, the inhuman gang, gloating over the prospect of speedy plunder, displayed their treacherous light, and laughed when they saw the disabled vessel nearing the hidden reefs.

One of the most fearful peals of thunder had just died away, echoing with a dreadful roar along the rocky coast, when a blazing flash of lightning revealed the form of a graceful stripling clambering his way along a perilous path leading to the peak.

He was drenched to the skin, and the furious blast threatened to lift him off his feet, and hurl him headlong down the broken cliffs.

At times, too, the thunder, seeming to shake the very rocks, almost stunned him, and the swift lightning dazed his bewildered eyes ; but with dauntless perseverance and tireless skill he fought his way higher and higher, till he reached the wreckers' hiding-place, and stood in the midst of the savage men as they plied their infernal vocation.

He was a robust, handsome-looking boy, with fine supple limbs, and free expansive chest.

His throat, singularly white, was bare, and the drenching rain and gusty wind had clustered his rich, dark hair about his fair temples.

There was a look of angry determination in his boyish face, and his dark eyes flashed boldly as he confronted the wreckers.

"Hallo !" one cried with a coarse oath, "here's that devilskin, Dick Wayne—what the fiend's mischief brought him meddling here ?"

"To save that ship !" the boy exclaimed, impetuously. "Murderous cowards, your light has guided them to the reefs !"

"Well, younker, and what the devil if it has ? take your carcase out of the way before we throw you over the cliffs."

"You'll not do that ; I'm armed, you see, and I mean to put out that light. Attempt to display it, and I'll blow your brains out !"

He drew a pistol from inside his coat, and pointed it at one of the wreckers.

"Hell and furies!" cried a stalwart villain; "show the light, Dan. Knock the younker out of harm's way, some of you, or he'll get the life wrung out of his infernal neck."

The boy's bold movement had been received with derisive laughter by some; others gave vent to loud curses at being seen at their diabolical work, and his presence there was critical at all hazards, even if he had been inclined to retire.

But he had come for another purpose.

He had seen from the beach the treacherous light luring the ship, and the wrecker called Dan had no sooner displayed its gleam upon the dark seething waters than he bounded to his side.

"Put down the light, or I'll shoot you!" he said, and his tones evinced his determination.

"To h—l with you, for a whelp!" the ruffian roared, dashing his fist in the boy's fearless face. "Take that, and don't come anear my arm agin."

The boy reeled with the blow.

The next moment his finger pressed the trigger.

The wrecker stood on the verge of the cliff.

Nothing could have saved him had the bullet touched him.

But Dick's ascent in the torrent had wetted the pistol, and it snapped harmlessly in the pan.

The coarse laughter of the men stung the boy's roused nature.

Before any of them could believe he would dare so imminent a danger, he gave a swift bound, and stood with Dan the Wrecker on the brink of the cliff.

His youthful arms held the brawny ruffian in a firm hold, as he cried—

"Drop the light, or I'll jump with you into the sea!"

"Knife him!" yelled the man, trying to struggle back. "Knife the young viper. Curses! have his heart's blood, or he'll drag me down!"

With angry cries the wreckers rushed to the rescue of their companion.

They were not soon enough.

There was a brief wrestle, and then the strong man and the fearless stripling fell together.

It seemed that both must roll down that awful abyss; but, clinging to the rugged ledge, they struggled for the possession of the light.

A furious cry from the wrecker, an exultant shout from Dick Wayne, and the treacherous light was in the boy's grasp, and hurled down the black chasm.

Rude hands seized the dauntless youth, and, as Dan got to his feet, it seemed that the boy's death was certain.

He himself seemed conscious of his fate, but his dauntless gaze displayed no sign of regret as he looked on the excited faces of the wreckers.

"I've a good mind to hurl you after that light, younker," hissed the stalwart wrecker. "And I would, curse you, if our light hadn't done its work. Look, boy, the ship is on the reefs. It is ours. Hark, it strikes! You'll hear the shrieks. Come down and see what help you can give when it grinds to pieces in that white sea."

Quivering with intense excitement, the daring boy looked from the inhuman speaker's face to the storm's dark scene.

A sheeted flash had lighted up the sea, and showed the truth of the wrecker's scoffing words.

Lured by the fatal light the ship had neared the reefs, and was now helplessly plunging amidst the white vortex of its boiling breakers.

An ominous peal of thunder rolled over the darkened sea as the flash died away.

The knell of the vessel's doom!

It struck the heart of the dauntless boy. Loathingly glancing at the inhuman wretches, he dashed from the grasp of the one who held him, and, bounding down the perilous passage, fought his way through the swollen gorge to the reefs at the foot of the cliff.

The leader of the wreckers laughed as his youthful form went out of sight.

"The devilskin will come to something great one of these days," he said; "there aint a bit of the white feather about him; if there had been I'd have wrung his neck for pitching the light into the sea. He's a plucky lad; it's a pity he's so squeamish. Come, we'll descend; there'll be a fine picking from this craft, I'll swear."

At the time of which we are writing the population of the Cornish coast were notorious wreckers.

Fishermen, who on ordinary occasions were content with the takings of their nets, felt their old spirit of plunder return when they heard the signals of distress from a disabled vessel, and were more eager to share in the spoil than to render aid to the helpless sufferers of the disaster.

Their propensity in this respect was too well known, and on board the crippled ship, now driving to the reef, the deadliest consternation prevailed when the light vanished from the cliff and they found themselves in the midst of the frothy breakers.

One brief despairing effort was made to get out of the treacherous whirlpool, then the ship was given to her fate.

A few minutes of sharp agony and suspense; then the fearful crash as the vessel struck, and all knew that their fate was near.

The violence of the storm was beginning to abate.

It had done its fearful work.

When Dick reached the beach he found the fishermen population venturing from their huts, and making their way towards the reefs.

Speeding by them, he bounded to a lonely hut, at the door of which an old grey-headed fisherman encountered him.

"Father," the boy cried, "the ship has struck. Let me get out the boat; we may yet safe life."

"To venture in that sea, my boy, would be mad, indeed. No, no, we'll stay on the beach, something may come to our share."

With a sinking heart the boy turned away.

The signals of distress that had been very frequent had ceased, as the sudden crash resounded above the angry storm.

The boy's cheeks blanched.

Such a cry of women's agony and strong men's despair rang in his ears!

He looked towards the raging breakers.

The ship was breaking up.

Spars—cargo—beams—were dancing in one wild cauldron, and here and there some upturned face showed where the battle of life was already over.

Soon portions of the cargo, followed by some pale corpses, were washed ashore; and then came the fierce struggle for the possession of the booty.

Then occurred fierce and bloody scenes, when the strongest fought his fellow for the spoil, and when the reeking knife, wet with a wrecker's gore, was driven to the heart of some helpless passenger who had reached the shore only to be murdered by those terrible wretches.

In the midst of the tumult and confusion a cry was raised, and every eye was turned to the head of the reefs near the fisherman's hut, where was seen, rolling in the trough of the sea, a solitary boat with one lonely occupant.

It was making for the wreck.

Its courageous occupant was the noble-hearted boy, Dick Wayne.

He was recognised by those on shore, and many a callous heart thrilled with admiration as they saw his boat, almost engulfed in the raging sea, spring forth again to encounter the fury of the waves.

One man amongst the crew on the beach ran hither and thither in frantic excitement.

It was old Peter, the man whom Dick Wayne had addressed as father.

Intermittent flashes of lightning showed the progress of the boat.

It neared the wreck, making its way among floating spars and human forms.

But suddenly there came a large wave, and in a moment the boat and its occupant sank from sight.

A low cry rang along the assembled wreckers; they paused in their unholy work to look across the line of breakers, and see if there was hope of the daring boy's safety.

Thoughts of giving him succour there were none, for none would venture out on such a sea.

The subdued murmur presently became a cry. A solitary form was seen battling with the waves.

The dauntless boy had escaped, and was swimming lustily towards the wreck.

It had gone hard with him when his boat capsized.

The salt spray blinded him, and the gusty wind took away his breath, but he had a stout heart, and he swam towards the reef where the vessel struck.

He had seen there a vision that made every fibre of his frame thrill with the resolve to dare or

A frail, clinging form—the form of a fair young girl. She had been lashed to a spar, and this was still attached, by the tangled cordage, to that part of the wreck which had not yet broken up.

The lightning played in a weird manner around her pale form, the boisterous sea drenched her long white robe, the fierce wind blew her dishevelled hair about, and now and then her wan face was raised to the darkened sky with a sad, hopeless, dreamy look, whose utter misery could be traced when the lightning lit up the scene.

Dick Wayne saw the fair head droop at last, and with renewed vigour he fought his way through the buffeting waves.

A few more sturdy strokes, and he was within grasp of the grinding wreck.

A spring, a brief fight with the hungry waves, yet eager for their prey, and he was clinging with one arm to the broken bulwarks.

He was close to the gentle face now; the soft blue eyes looked wearily into his, the pale lips moved, and a faint moaning voice said pleadingly—

" Save me ! Save me !"

" Save you !" tears stood in the boy's bright eyes. " I will swim with you to land or perish with you here."

The blue eyes beamed gratefully, then the lips closed languidly.

Dick's nimble fingers were already at work. His knife was in his belt, and now its broad blade severed the tangled cords and released the half-conscious maiden.

Her limbs were free only in time.

The harsh creaking of the timbers told Dick that this part of the ship was breaking up.

He replaced his knife and raised the poor girl's head.

She shuddered as she looked on the whitened sea.

" Have no fear," the boy said, " I will swim by your side ; close your eyes if you feel afraid. Now !"

A feeble kiss from her wan lips, a splash, and she was amidst the angry waves.

The buoyant spar righted itself as Dick, who had plunged in after her, came to the surface.

The poor girl seemed quite unconscious, and Dick, with pained heart, looked in her pallid face.

With one arm occasionly guiding the spar he swam towards the shore.

Often the heavy waves washing over him and his fair charge, tore them apart, and threatened to hurl both to a watery grave. But the youthful hero's heart and nerve never failed him, and as often was he again guiding the course of the spar. Near the reef a sickening sensation crept to his heart.

His strength was failing him.

That sign of his weakness was seen from shore, and his every movement was watched with eager interest. Boats had been put off, but the sea's fury dashed them back.

Old Peter Wayne, tearing his gray locks, plunged wildly in the water, but his day of strength was past, and he had to be taken out by his mates.

Suddenly there arose a fearful cry of " They are dashed against the rocks !"

It seemed so, as a huge wave lifted both to its surface and hurled them on to the reef.

Its shower of spray fell over them ; another wave dashed them further in, and as the eddies retired, the two motionless forms were seen lying on the black reefy coast.

There was a rush to the dangerous spot, brawny arms lifted both out of the arms of the furious sea, and as the less brutal unfastened the thongs that bound the fair girl to the spar, old Peter, kneeling beside the seemingly lifeless form of the brave boy, lifted his head, and chafing his cold temples with his hard hands, huskily called upon him to come back to life.

And crowded about them were the fierce wreckers, with hands newly stained with blood, but with their savage breasts so lately full of black passions, now softened to pity for the fate of the daring stripling whom the waves had cast at their feet.

CHAPTER II.

OUR HERO RECOVERS FROM HIS BUFFET WITH THE WAVES AND LEARNS SOME STRANGE SECRETS ABOUT HIS OWN HISTORY.

THEY carried both prone pallid forms to the

rude tenement where old fisherman Peter lived with his youngish wife.

At first it seemed that both were past their aid; but their remedies brought the two sufferers gradually to consciousness, and Lucy Wayne, having had the young girl carried to the inner room, bestowed all her care upon the noble-hearted boy.

Although both had been stunned when thrown on the reef, neither were seriously injured, and when the wreckers left the occupants of the lonely hut to themselves, Dick was sitting up, very pale, and rather weak and shivering, but more of himself than might have been expected. But before morning a dizziness took away his consciousness, and the next day found him in a high state of fever, which speedily brought him to the gates of death.

The young girl whom he had saved recovered more quickly.

She was very quiet and gentle in her manner, though full of grief. Her only relative—her fond old father — had gone down with the wreck on that fearful night, and now she was alone in the world.

But her own sorrow did not keep her from feeling an interest in her youthful preserver.

She nursed him with tender care, and when Dick came back to reason, and the first streaks of health came back to his wasted cheeks, he could scarcely believe that the beautiful being by his side was the maiden he had rescued from the wreck.

Of course, as they got better they went out together, and soon tender words and looks were exchanged between them.

Dick was in love with his gentle nurse, and she was the same with her daring rescuer.

Her name was Grace Merlin.

She had come with her father from Italy. He had claims upon an estate in Cornwall, and was about to prosecute them when this sad disaster deprived her of his protection and love.

Our hero wished all sorts of things when she told him her sad story. He saw how gentle and refined she was, and did not like her to be among the rude population of the coast.

He wished, too, that he was something more than a fisherman's son, for though Grace had told him he was noble enough to be an earl's son, he had bitterly mused upon his humble position.

A little incident occurring some time afterwards added to this bitterness.

At the back of the fishing village, sheltered from the sea by the cliffs that ran along the coast, was the country, fair and fertile.

There were green fields and shady groves, beautiful streamlets and charming dells, with here and there some palatial mansion belonging to the nobles of the land.

Wandering with Grace one day he left her for a moment, while he went to help a little boy across a ford; he heard her scream suddenly, and, springing through a clump of briars that hid her from sight, found her struggling with a well-dressed youth, who had taken her hand, and was trying to kiss her before he let her go.

When this boy saw Dick coming towards him with an unmistakable look in his angry eyes, he released Grace, and, springing out of the way, picked up a whip, which he had dropped on seeing Grace.

"Don't you come near me!" he said, raising his whip, "or I'll thrash you."

Dick was at Grace's side, his right hand was clenched, and his boyish breast swelled with indignant pride, but respect for his girlish sweetheart kept him from punishing her assailant as he deserved.

The other, seeing this, imagined he was afraid of the whip, and coming forward, said—

"I should like to know who you are to be with her; you're only a fisherman's boy, and I am the son of the Countess Aldervale. I'll let you know you're on our estate, and I'll whip you off if you stay here any longer."

He slashed the whip, but did not come any nearer. Dick's menacing movement was too much for his prowess.

The coarse insult had sent the blood tingling through the brave boy's frame.

Grace was afraid to let him get near the other boy. She clung to his arm to prevent him leaving her, and pleadingly begged him to come away, and the young aristocrat, slashing his whip spitefully, stood sneeringly looking after him, until Dick had led his young charge from the spot.

Our hero returned to his home in a high state of excitement, and in angry terms related the affair.

Lucy Wayne nudged the old fisherman when the Countess's name was mentioned, d the old fellow screwed up his face into a aint expression, but said nothing.

"Yes," said Dick, "he's to be an earl, and am only a fisherman's son. He's bigger than me, but if I meet him alone I'll thrash him for what he's done to-day.

"Ha, ha, ha!" laughed old Peter; "ha, ha, ha! What a good thing!"

"He wouldn't think so," the proud-spirited boy cried, his face flushing crimson; "and I'd like to know why you are so fond of laughing at me?"

"Ha, ha, ha!" laughed the old fisherman. "Capital—eh, wife—capital!"

"Peter," Lucy Wayne said quietly, "take the young lady for a walk. I wish to speak with Dick."

The old man looked puzzled for a moment, then seemed inclined to laugh, but ultimately took up his hat and led Grace from the hut.

It was a very beautiful day; the sea was at rest, the waves played merrily in the dancing light, the golden sunbeams shone softly on the steep crags of the Wrecker's Gully.

How different from the fatal night when she had so nearly found a watery grave.

Grace shuddered as the old man led her towards the beach.

Dick looked wistfully after her, and then turned towards his mother.

"Mother, what is it you would say to me?"

Lucy Wayne caressed the boy's gentle brow.

She was a comely woman, and, as we have before stated, much younger and more refined than her uncouth husband.

A very grave look was now on her face, and her voice was subdued with emotion as she said—

"I want you to listen to me attentively, Dick. I am going to surprise you very much. I know you long to be in a higher station than ours, and perhaps the time will come when you may do so lawfully and of right."

Dick gazed up in her face, but said nothing.

"Firstly, you are not our child."

Like lightning, Dick was on his feet.

"Not your child!"

"No, Dick; we have brought you up, but we are not your parents."

"Not—who then?"

Our hero looked at her to make sure he was not in a dream.

True, he had never felt a warm affection for old Peter, but the idea of his not being his father never entered his head.

The wildest thoughts crowded through his brain.

Lucy Wayne had a quiet manner with her that calmed his outbreak, and he sat down again when she desired him to do so, and listened.

"My story will not please you," she went on, "but it must be told. Fifteen years ago a young and beautiful lady, unknown to her friends, married a young officer in the army. Her marriage was secret, and in secrecy their child was born. The lady at first loved her husband, but absence and the prospect of a wealthy marriage prevailed over her love, and she repented having married."

Dick was listening attentively now.

"Her child was born, and she returned to her friends; a brilliant marriage was offered her with an aged peer, the Earl of Aldervale."

Dick started.

Lucy Wayne placed her hand on his brow and continued—

"Her youthful husband, eager to see his bride, wrote asking her to meet him; she was to bring their child. She appointed a secret place of meeting. He went, and from that hour he was never seen again."

"Her child (she had long before grown fearful of that evidence of her weakness proving her ruin) was given to a hireling to be strangled. Six weeks after she was united to the earl, but her love was not his; a young counsellor had overcome her virtue, and the child who was to be the heir, unless heaven gives the rightful one the property, was the bastard child of this gay young lawyer."

"Infamous!" Dick cried, flushing to the temples.

"One year, and the old earl was found dead in his chamber; there was a suspicion of foul play, but it did not touch the young wife, so interesting now with her infant child

Time passed on; the lawyer has become a celebrated judge; the bastard boy has grown to the age of the child of the first husband, for the hired murderer repented of his task and saved his life. The lady is now the Countess of Aldervale, and her bastard son is to be the future earl; but the real heir to the estate is the boy born of the first marriage, and he is *yourself*."

A cry of mingled rage and pain left Dick's lips, and he sprang to his feet.

His brain was in a whirl.

His father secretly disposed of, his mother an infamous wanton, his brother a bastard, whom he felt would also be his bitterest enemy.

Himself, the true heir to the Aldervale estates and an earldom.

His eyes literally blazed with excitement as he paced up and down the room.

"She my mother! that dastard boy my brother! Is this true? Why have you kept this cheat secret so long? My father, too! Why have you told me this? I had better have believed myself a fisherman's son than to be the heir to such a tissue of sorrow and infamy."

The fisherman's wife watched him with quiet satisfaction.

To her it seemed natural that while his thoughts were only of his mother's infamy, his anxiety should be respecting his missing father.

"I have kept this secret," she said, "till you were old enough to understand and act for yourself; but the task before you is a bitter one."

"Your mother will never acknowledge you; to do so would be to publish her shame. Then she has doubtless destroyed the proofs of her marriage with your father, and aided by her seducer——"

Dick interrupted her wildly.

"No more. If she is my mother, let me not hear of her shame."

"He is right," Lucy Wayne thought, then added aloud—"Think your task over, and I will come to you presently."

She left the room and closed the door, and our hero, pacing the floor with fierce strides, tried to realise the position in which he was put by the disclosure of his birth.

When Lucy Wayne returned Dick was seated by the hearth.

His elbows were supported by his knees, and his face was buried in the palms of his hands.

He was in so deep a reverie that he did not hear her light tread, and was unconscious of her presence till she spoke.

With a sudden leap he started up.

She had a parcel in her hand, but hanging across her arm was a small miniature of a young officer.

Instinctively Dick knew that this was his father's portrait.

Snatching it from her arm he gazed at the handsome portrait, and in the excitement of the moment pressed it to his lips.

Very tenderly and wistfully he regarded the miniature.

The likeness was that of a very singularly distinguished young man. A frank fearless depth was in the dark brown eyes, the lips were firm, the brow open and commanding.

A slight moustache adorned the upper lip.

"This, then, is my lost father's portrait?"

"Aye, and so like yours, that where you to stand before the countess, in the dress which was your father's, she would believe the grave had given up its dead, if, indeed, an untimely grave closed over him."

"By heavens! I will fathom the mystery. It shall not haunt me another hour. Give me the dress, I will stand in her sight, I will demand news of my father, if she can outface me—then—Oh, God!—accursed fate—could I be my mother's accuser and judge?"

"Both. You must go. She has lived too long secure in her infamy. Wear this dress, seek her presence, tell her you know the secret of her share——"

Dick stayed her further speech by an excited exclamation.

"Hold!" he cried, "there are others here —I would not have their ears know the dread tale. No, no, not for a king's crown."

Grace Merton and old Peter were on the threshold.

"It must be a vision," Lucy Wayne replied calmly. "The destiny of this young girl is bound up with yours. It was to gain back some part of the Aldervale estates her father took that fatal voyage. The evil agency of the wicked countess would seem to hover in the track of all who cross her. He died, and beware you if she smiles upon you."

"If she does?"

"*Her smile will mean your murder!*"

A loathsome snake seemed to coil about our hero's heart as his foster mother spoke those words.

He gazed at her in a stupor of dismay.

Before either could say more Grace Merton bounded into the house.

She looked inquiringly at our hero and Lucy Wayne.

She looked surprised when she heard he was going out.

An hour later she was still more amazed, when he came into the room dressed in the scarlet and gold uniform of his father.

Dick kissed her tenderly, and bade her good-bye.

His heart was heavy.

She was serious too.

She saw that some mystery was afoot, but, though anxious about him, she made no inquiry, but only told him what a handsome officer he made in his new dress.

Even her softly-spoken compliment pained him; but, mastering his emotion, he passed out, and was soon on his way to the countess's abode.

His heart throbbed quicker when he came in sight of the splendid residence of Aldervale—throbbed with the thought of his coming meeting—throbbed at the thought that those fair acres from which he had been hounded by his bastard brother were by right his property.

His face was flushed, and his voice betrayed his excitement when he asked to be admitted to her ladyship's presence.

He had a cloak thrown over his rich dress, and this was still buttoned over his chest, when the door opened, and the countess was announced.

Our hero's heart gave one wild bound, and then seemed to stand suddenly still.

If Lucy Wayne had spoken truthfully, he was in the presence of his mother.

———

CHAPTER III.

OUR HERO'S INTERVIEW WITH THE COUNTESS, AND ITS RESULT.

LIKE most impulsive and ambitious boys, our hero had dreamed of a peerless being whom he could have worshipped as sister or bride. But in his wildest dreams he had never conceived anyone more beautiful than the lady who now stood before him.

His heart told him, if he could have had his choice, she was the one he would have selected for his mother.

She was just in the full flower of womanhood. Her form and features were faultless in their perfection.

Deep clear blue eyes, flowing tresses of sunny hair, cheeks as fair as the lily, tinted with a peach-like glow; a throat and neck delicately white and exquisitely shaped, arms of living alabaster, lips like chiselled coral, parted now to show her pearly teeth; she was, indeed, divinely beautiful.

Dick Wayne was for the moment dazzled by her queenly loveliness.

He looked at her with speechless fascination.

It was from this lovely being he had been given his existence, and on that rounded bosom he must have lain, if only for a few hours after his birth.

The very thought made his brain dizzy, but the lady's voice called him to his sober senses.

She had entered with a queenly step, and now she addressed him in tones that echoed through his heart with their liquid sweetness.

" I am informed, sir, you have desired to see me on a visit of importance. It is not usual with me to receive strangers; be good enough to favour me with your name."

Dick started.

Her voice awoke the latent fierceness in his breast.

" Madam," he cried, " I have no name to give; yet, I should be no stranger to you. Look, do you know me now?"

He threw aside his cloak and the disguise he had assumed, and stood in a posture of grace, facing the countess.

She had started back at his impetuous speech; but when her eyes rested on his form, clad in that uniform, a hoarse shriek of terror left her lips, and reeling, as if stricken to the heart, she leaned against a marble vase for support, while her jewelled hands were clenched on her brow, as she gazed at the visitor before her.

A shrouded spectre newly risen from the

FROM HIS PERILOUS POSITION OUR HERO LOOKED DOWN UPON THE SLEEPING TOWN.

grave, to confront her with the startling memory of some hideous crime, could not have had a more fearful influence upon her. A chilling spasm went through her frame. All the rich bloom left her cheeks, and the ghastly frozen pallor overspreading her lovely features was the livid hue of death itself. Her jaw dropped gasping in horror, while her ashen lips tried to shape her inarticulate whispers, and her eyes stared with a stony rigidness on our hero's face.

Such was not the effect the visit of the son should have had upon his mother.

Her palpable guiltiness of horror roused him to fierce excitement.

Stepping before her he cried—

"Madam, you shiver as if I were the dead come to life again."

"Back! back!" shrieked the countess. "Who are you?—speak!"

"I am not the father, but the son—your son. Woman, where is my father? I demand him at your hands."

"Help! I know you not; this is some hideous dream."

"No, it is no dream; look on this picture; it is the likeness of my father—your husband. Infamous woman! where is he?'

The lips of the countess moved, but no answer came.

She could not look into those accusing eyes. A bleeding victim seemed before her sight. The dead seemed come again.

Come in the dress in which she had last seen her youthful husband, and when his pale face lay stricken and bleeding at her feet.

In her awful terror she tottered to the gilded bell rope, and clutched at it with her palsied hands.

But Dick Wayne hurled it from her reach.

"You call no aid," he cried, "till I am answered. By heaven! you shall not flee. As I am your son, with your wolf blood in my veins, I swear you shall not stir till I am satisfied about my father."

He placed himself between her and the door.

She was shrinking from him in an hysterical way, her whole frame shuddering in chilling dread, when the door was forced sharply open, and a youth bounded into the room.

A cry of relief escaped her.

"Help me, Edward! help me, my dear son!"

Something of the gleam of a panther was in Dick's eyes as he recognised his foe of the morning.

Lord Edward Aldervale knew him instantly, and supporting his mother on one arm, he extended the other menacingly towards Dick, as he exclaimed—

"Fellow, begone! or I'll have you thrashed from the grounds like the hound you are."

Dick strode towards him.

His hands were clenched.

An angry light burned in his eyes.

"When I leave this house, cur," he cried, "it shall be of my own will; not at your bidding, mongrel."

Lord Edward sprang to his mother's side. The black blood of his nature was roused, and, shaking with rage and fury, he took Dick Wayne by the throat, and the two boys were locked in a deadly grip.

CHAPTER IV.

THE STRUGGLE. —A BRAVE BOY'S THREAT.

THERE was not much difference in the height and general build of the two sons, as the mother gazed upon them in their strife.

But in *physique* they differed as greatly as was possible.

Edward Aldervale had his mother's blue eyes and fair hair, with the same soft regular features, and looked effeminate when contrasted with the bronzed, handsome countenance and fierce dark eyes of his more manly half brother.

In strength and breadth of chest, too, he was Dick's inferior, and it seemed almost without an effort that our hero shook off his hold and thrust him back.

In one thing they both were alike—the equal hate that blazed from the eyes of each.

Dick was the first to speak.

His broad chest swelling with excitement.

"Madam," he said, "as I have thrust your bastard son from my path, so will I hunt him from the title and estates of the Earl of Aldervale; you shall answer, too, mother of mine, for my father's life."

"Mother of him!" Edward's face went ghastly pale. "What calamity is this? Speak, mother, that I may crush the black lie in his heart."

A scornful smile wreathed Dick's lips.

He stepped quickly to the Countess, and holding the miniature before her eyes, exclaimed—

"Speak, is not this your husband's image? Am I not your son, born in secrecy, but born in legitimate right, before that cringing reptile was born to your adulterous infamy?"

"It is false!" the countess shrieked. "You are mad! I have no son but he."

"Minion," our hero cried, besides himself with fury, "seek not to cheat me. I know the woman whom you bribed to strangle me in my infancy; she has revealed all, and in open court I will clear the mystery of my father's death, and proclaim my birth and your infamy."

A cry, more of a laugh than a shriek, left the Countess's lips.

A deadly light shone in her deep blue eyes.

"Then go back to her who told you this tale," she exclaimed, laughing hysterically "bid her produce her proofs; till then intrude not on this estate, or my keepers shall take you to gaol. Impostor! begone now, ere I call them to chastise your insolence."

She seized the cord and pulled violently at the bell.

The veins on Dick's temples rose like writhing snakes.

"Outface me as you may," he said, "your guilt shall be made known, if I fall to the lowest infamy. Base as you are, you yet shall call me son! For you, despicable hound, between us there shall be the bitterest hate, evil blood shall blacken in our hearts when we meet, and shall fester there till one of us shall trample the life out of the other!"

"Worm!" Edward Aldervale exclaimed. "You shall eat dirt at my feet; let him not escape, mother; he shall repent this insolence in goal! Ho, there, help. Bring your guns—a robber! Help! Thieves! Help!"

With a swift bound Dick leaped to the windows at the end of the apartment.

These opened on to the lawn, and as the hurried rush of the servitors was heard outside, he flung the glass doors apart with a force that shivered the frames to atoms.

"Hunt me down," he cried, "if you dare, but beware when you have me at bay, you shall find me as merciless as a tiger fed with human gore!"

He bounded to the lawn and was out of sight before the alarmed servitors could get to the window.

When they were gone to scour the grounds in search of him, and mother and son were left alone, the countess, still ashy pale and trembling like an aspen, laid her hand on Lord Edward's arm, and bringing her face close to his, spoke in a freezing whisper—

"This adder in our path must be removed, or he will sting us both. Be careful in your practice with sword and pistol; his bad blood will cast him in your way, and you must know how to slay him when you meet."

Her voice sank to a fainter breath.

"If you cannot face him fairly, meet him in the dark. Pierce him to the heart, and leave him like a trampled toad by the wayside."

CHAPTER V.

JONATHAN WILD.

GALLED with the treatment he had received, our hero entered an hospitable-looking inn, some distance from the Aldervale estates, and calling for a glass of hot liquor, seated himself at a table and pondered over the circumstances of his reception.

It was a singular fact that even his mother's ravishing beauty had failed to inspire him with love for her, or a desire to be received in her arms.

Still, he had expected Nature to assert herself in their interview, and he bitterly mused over the cold contempt with which she had repulsed him.

It never occurred to him that the abrupt manner in which he had disclosed himself, and the opprobrious epithets he had showered upon her, were scarcely calculated to create in her breast any regard for him, even though he was her own child.

Then again, she could not acknowledge him without branding herself before the world and declaring her son Edward illegitimate, a course she was not likely to take with the offspring of the man she had guiltily loved

Dick did not reason this way, he only reflected that he was an unknown castaway, steeped to the lips in poverty, and compelled to live by the sweat of his brow and at a task repugnant to his nature, while another, reared in the lap of luxury, possessed the wealth and titles that were rightfully his.

With the fierce passions of his nature surging through his breast, he vowed bitterly to wrest his rights from his half-brother, and make his unnatural mother own him before the world.

But how to do this, poor and friendless as he was?

How could he hope to make his tale believed in the face of the cold denial his mother would give him?

"I must have gold," he muttered fiercely, "that I may wrestle with them. I will have gold if I sell my soul to Satan."

A hand was laid on his arm as he muttered these words aloud.

A clammy heavy hand, that seemed to rest on his arm like a coiled snake.

He shook it off with a start, and looked up.

A man was seated at the end of the narrow table.

A man of subtle sinister appearance, with coarse hard features, full of low cunning, a low forbidding forehead, and fearfully vicious eyes.

He was dressed in a buttoned-up coat, with large side pockets.

A five-cornered hat lay before him on the table.

When Dick looked up he nodded in a familiar way, and, lowering his tone that no one else might hear, said—

"Money is to be had without dealing with that nameless personage; and a fine lad like you—a lad of worth and spirit—ought to know the easiest way of getting it."

"I don't know of any mine of gold," Dick answered, petulantly.

"Bah, there's a mine of gold distributed everywhere about you."

"Where, sir?"

"In other people's pockets, in their strong chests; plenty for them and you, and to spare."

Dick's face changed colour.

"Would you have me be a thief?" he said angrily.

"Certainly not—come, come, don't be angry. I only spoke because I overheard your troubles, don't mind what I've said, only remember, those who want gold must take it, or they'll never get it."

"True," murmured Dick. "Who would believe my story while I am penniless."

"Nobody, of course; but don't despair. There's many a bright path open to a lad of pluck, as I take you to be; come, drink with me. Here, Fan, some brandy."

The hostess, with a warning look at Dick, placed brandy on the table, and then left the room.

Dick moodily took the proffered spirit and drank eagerly.

The fiery liquor ran through his blood. He clenched his hands savagely as he thought of his position.

"Accursed gold!" he cried. "It must be mine or they will grind me to the dust."

"Of course they will," his wily tempter said.

"Why not, then, enrich yourself and meet them on equal terms?"

Dick drained another glass.

"I will," he cried. "Point out the way, and if it lead to ignominy, the crime is theirs, not mine."

"Take 'the road' for a way of life—it will maintain you splendidly. Keep yourself masked, no one will know you. Take only from the rich. I will introduce you to the highwaymen. No vulgar set—perfect gentlemen, who mix in the first society unsuspected; daring, dashing fellows, I can tell you, and everyone of them worth a fortune."

Dick's heart thrilled wildly.

There was a course open to him—a course beset with enough danger to make it exhilarating.

He had heard of the dashing riders of the highway, who, on their splendid steeds, and in their rich dresses, took toll from the persons of the aristocracy; fellows who, as the new acquaintance said, mingled in the first society, passing for gentlemen of rank and wealth.

What if he became one of their band?

There was a sure way of enriching himself, and, by always being masked, when on the road, taking spoils enough to enable him to live in the same society as his mother and her bastard son.

His hot blood coursed wildly through his veins.

"I thank you for the offer," he exclaimed, rising from the table. "To-night I will be here to let you know whether I accept it or not."

The man nodded, and he left the room.

At the door the hostess encountered him.

"Beware of that man!" she whispered; "he is the thief-taker, Jonathan Wild!"

Before our hero could reply, the doorway was darkened by the form of his half-brother, Lord Edward Aldervale.

A malicious gleam shot from his blue eyes when he saw Dick, who, on his part, felt equally savage.

But his rage knew no bounds when Lord Edward said—

"So, I have found you, robber! Here, men, the thief is here! Lock him up! I charge him with stealing a gold goblet from our hall. Search him; it will be found in his pocket. no doubt!"

Dick's face was purple with deadly rage, as he stepped up to his half-brother, and, without uttering a word, dealt him a blow on the temple, that felled him to the earth.

"That is how I answer your charge!" he exclaimed, as the young lordling, ghastly from the effects of the blow was raised to his feet.

Dick was preparing for a fiercer onset, when his arms were pinned from behind, and, in spite of his powerful struggles, he was held firmly, a prisoner.

While he was haughtily and undauntedly looking his relative in the face, he was paralysed at seeing the man that was searching him take from his pocket a golden vessel, and hold it triumphantly before them all.

He saw at once the dastardly nature of the trick.

While he was being seized, it had been placed there by one of his half-brother's myrmidons.

His proud nature was stung to the quick, by the foul charge and his helplessness.

He made a terrible effort to get to Lord Edward, struggling so fiercely that it required the strength of four powerful officers to hold him.

They secured him at last, and then his dastardly half-brother crept near, and said in his ear—

" We're going to take that young girl away —*your* dear Grace. She'll be brought up along with me, and that old fisherman and his wife, *your* father and mother, you impostor, will be both hanged for *wrecking* before you come out of jail."

Every sinew in Dick's muscular limbs and chest was strained, as he tried to get at the spiteful young lord.

He was held too firmly. But so wildly excited was he by Lord Edward's goading words, that he dashed his head full in his scoffing brother's face, and sent him reeling, half stunned and bleeding.

While he was being violently maltreated for this by those that held him, a stealthy voice said softly in his ear—

"You must get out of this, or they'll send you to the hulks or the gallows."

He turned.

The speaker was Jonathan Wild.

. . . .

Four-and-twenty hours he lay in the solitary cell where they had thrust him.

Four-and-twenty hours chafing in bitter anguish at his helplessness to resist the indignities thrust upon him.

Bread and water had been placed on the stone bench, but his proud spirit would not permit him to taste either.

Not so much as a drop of water would he take while in that unjust confinement.

No one had visited him since he had been bundled in there.

In lonely misery he had passed those weary hours, never closing his eyes during the weary darkness of night, but pacing madly up and down his prison.

He had asked to have a message conveyed to his foster parents, but this had been churlishly and scoffingly refused.

Had there been a chance, he would have hazarded his escape, though the venture cost him his life ; but the grated window was above his reach, and his hands were securely manacled.

When the door was opened after that day and night of bondage, he turned fiercely on those who came to lead him forth.

They were the goaler, two officers and the beadle.

Dick eyed them savagely, and, determined to make an obstinate resistance, sat down on the stone bench.

This movement created great amusement among the officials.

Then the beadle advanced.

" Come, my young fledgling, none of your gammon here. You've got to come along with us."

" Where am I to be taken, then ?"

" To a more securer place, my nobby kiddy," put in the goaler, " 'cos why, this 'ere crib aint strong enough for you, in case any of your pals wants to get you out."

" Which is very likely," exclaimed one of the officers, " but won't wash. No, no, you've been and begun a pretty stiff bit, felony and 'sault on our young lord, and if you don't get scragged for it, why, you'll go across the herring pond for a sartinty."

" Oh ! he'll cop the nubbing cheat," said the beadle. " Come on, young fellow. No use your squatting there. We'll lug you out in a jiffey, and if you give us any trouble it'll be the worse for your skin."

Dick rose.

The open door had inspired him with a sudden thought.

Escape !

His heart throbbed with the wild hope.

With swift instinct he had counted his

chances, and, as the officers came forward to take him by the collar, he sprang up on the stone bench and dashed his manacled wrists against the sharp edge of the wall where the grating was let in.

The concussion did what he expected.

One of the iron bands snapped, and his hands were free.

Before they could realise his daring act, or raise a cry of alarm, he vaulted in their midst, knocking the two officers against the wall, and alighting on the fat shoulders of the beadle, whom he sent sprawling on his face in the doorway.

The gaoler made a hit at him with his heavy keys, but a blow from Dick's iron-bound wrist crashed into his skull, and like lightning Dick was outside.

Pausing here to shake his manacled hand at the officers, who had hastily snatched forth their pistols and followed him, he cried—

"Follow for your lives. They have driven me to crime. By heavens, they will find me a desperate criminal! I am free now! TAKE ME WHO DARE!"

CHAPTER VI.

CAPTAIN CLAUDE, THE DASHING HIGH-WAYMAN.

Hurrah! hurrah for the Road!
Oh! its daring knights are we;
When pale Oliver leaves the heath,
Then on our silent steeds we'll be.
There's a rumble of wheels—hurrah!
Ho! for the cry of "Stand! Deliver!"
The rumble of wheels—Ha! ha!
Out pistols!—"Stand! Deliver!"
A cry of "Halt! Prepare!"
A smile to ladies fair,
A heavy swag to share
To the tune of "Stand! Deliver!"

Then hurrah! hurrah for the Road!
Its gallant knights are we;
When the moon leaves copse and heath,
On our silent steeds we'll be.

"BRAVO! Bravo, Swig! First-rate! Give him a bumper. Hurrah!"

Cheers and cries of bravo resounded through the highwaymen's haunt.

Glasses rattled on the table, and, amid noisy exclamations, the genius designated Swig was toasted in a brimming bumper for his song.

About a score of high tobymen were seated at the tables, whereon was spread a splendid feast of viands and rare wines.

Gallant, handsome fellows they were—handsome and young all of them, and of a reckless, devil-may-care aspect, with bright teeth which showed merrily as they laughed heartily, and long silky hair that hung in glossy curls almost to their shoulders.

All were dressed in highway costume, gay coats, resplendent boots, and abundance of fine white lace.

Light ornamental swords were at their sides, pistols in their belts.

A few had masks hanging from their sashes.

Swig was the most diminutive of the party.

He was not an inch above five feet in height, and was slim into the bargain, but a glance at his quizzing, impudent face showed that what he lacked in size he made up in conceit.

Near to him was a good-humoured looking highwayman, a perfect Goliath when compared to Swig.

He had a knack of ridiculing Swig's singing, and always put him out if he could in the middle of a song.

He was laughing broad-mouthed at the conclusion of the song, and displayed so fine a pair of jaws, that Swig availed himself of the opportunity to dexterously jerk a pellet down his throat, a process which brought the giant's jaws together with a snap, and his hand so heavily down on Swig's shoulder that the little highwayman was doubled up instanter.

He was up instantly, and faced his big comrade, a mischief in his heroic eye.

"Tell you what, Big Bullskin," he said, "if you come those hanky-panky tricks with me, you and me will quarrel, that's what we'll do."

"Ha, ha, ha," laughed Big Bullskin, "why you titmouse, I'll eat you."

"What, I'll pull your big ugly nose."

Big Bullskin drew himself up to the full extent of his six foot one, and looked down upon little Swig.

Big Bullskin looked an imposing figure when he stood up.

He had a great massive face with a thick dark beard.

His hair hung down to his shoulders.

His immense chest stuck out.

His limbs were of tremendous size.

Each of his boots looked big enough to

stow away a man of much larger size than Swig.

He was too magnanimous to strike his undersized foe.

Putting his huge arms akimbo, he struck an attitude, and looked down upon Swig as a giant might be supposed to survey a pigmy.

Either Swig was in a very pugnacious humour, or Big Bullskin's contemptuous attitude, coupled with his disparagement of his singing abilities, so far excited him, that his ill-temper got the better of his prudence ; and to the infinite surprise and amusement of all, he gave his big comrade such a sudden and vicious punch in the wind, dealt so fairly, that it resounded with a terrible thud all over the place, and seemed for the moment to knock the giant highwayman all of a heap.

What the result of this daring rashness on the part of Swig would have been—whether Big Bullskin would have eaten him at one mouthful, or have divided him into two halves previous to digesting him—cannot be imagined ; that he must have paid the full and fearful penalty of exciting the giant's savage wrath, was evident ; but, fortunately for Swig, fate at that moment interfered to save him from instant and complete immolation.

There was a stir at the end of the subterranean chamber, and in a moment every highwayman was on his feet, to greet the newcomer as he appeared at the entrance.

He was more richly dressed than those at the table, but his costume was of the same nature.

A tall, finely-formed fellow, in the prime of life.

He had a frank, fair brow—proud, gentle, but resolute, and his soft brown eyes beamed with a merry light.

A light rapier was slung by his side, and he carried a pair of gauntlets in his hand as if he had just come off a journey.

A pleased smile was on his features as he was greeted with their welcome.

The moment he had stepped from behind the hangings at the doorway, every highwayman, filling his glass, waved it in welcome, and shouted with one cry—

"Hurrah for our captain ! His health ! A health to Captain Claude !"

The glasses clinked ; the generous liquor gurgled ; and then one deafening cheer rang through the chamber, as Captain Claude gracefully doffing his gold lace hat, stepped amongst his men.

A dozen eager hands proffered a brimming glass.

He took the nearest, and lifting it, so that the bright ruby wine shone in the light of the lamp by which the chamber was lit up, said—

"Gentlemen, your health. Long nights and heavy purses, and may our steeds be always swift, and our sweethearts true !"

He drank, and passing amid his band of gallant followers, each one of whom idolised him, and would have gone to their death in his behalf, retired to an inner apartment at the other end of the chamber.

A far different scene greeted him here.

The chamber was much smaller than the one outside, but was more superbly fitted up.

There were hangings of satin and lace, velvet tapestry, gilded panels round the walls, the richest carpets under the feet.

Brilliant lamps were reflected in the mirrors, and heaps of treasures, each article of which would have won the heart of a *virtuoso*, were literally thrown about the place.

Stranger than all, two lovely birds, evidently brought from foreign shores, were thrilling sweet notes in their golden cages.

But a rarer bird was there—dearer to the heart of Captain Claude than the sacred bird of Paradise.

A fair girl of seventeen.

She scarcely seemed so old—her looks were so girlish—her loveliness and grace so ethereal.

The prettiest of blue eyes, the fairest skin, and the glossiest of mermaid's tresses, added charms to a form that was fragile in its symmetry.

She was standing beside a splendid harp—listening for Claude's footsteps.

When she heard him enter she ran lovingly forward, and tenderly clasping her arms about his neck, glanced up in his face with a look of the truest love and devotion.

"Well, my pet bird," Claude said, tenderly kissing the gentle upturned face, after he had removed his mask, "not weary yet of your cage, nor of your grim gaoler ?"

"Weary, dearest Claude—ah, no—only I feel sorrowful sometimes when you are away. Yours is a life of such danger, you know, and your poor bird has a very timid heart."

"A very true one," Claude said, gallantly leading her to the harp, and seating himself by her side. "Come, Milly, sing me one of our home songs. I am in the mood for music, and your sweet voice can soothe the most unquiet moments of my restless spirit."

"Ah, Claude," Milly said, "if you never had to face those terrible dangers how happy we might be; but when I think of those fearful nights, I am so sad, and wait for your return to still my fears, and give my heart life again. Dearest Claude, will the time soon come when you will leave these daring men, and never venture forth on this career again?"

"Very soon, little one, and then we will leave this land for ever; and perhaps in other scenes we may be as happy as our hearts could wish."

"Ah! I should never be so happy, but my heart would long for more happiness," Milly answered him, sighing, as her delicate fingers ran along the chords of the harp.

Claude sat with his hands toying with her soft tresses, and caressing her fair cheeks as she played him the sweet melodies of her early days.

Her winning voice, and the simple pathos of the words she sang, exercised an unwonted influence over him; his eyes grew moist; the witching spell of her melody stole to his heart, and he was mournfully musing while he listened, when a respectful summons from one of his band aroused him.

Milly ceased playing instantly.

"Is there danger?" she asked, her sweet face growing pale as marble.

Claude's brow clouded.

"Be not alarmed, pet bird," he said, "I am not in the humour to be disturbed. I am under a spell, and could have listened to you for hours."

He walked to the door and answered the secret summons.

Presently he returned with a more clouded look on his handsome features.

Milly, reading every change of his countenance, came anxiously to his side.

"You must retire," he said. "It is a lady."

"Only a lady?" Milly's face brightened instantly. "I feared——"

"That it was a more rude visitor. Don't fear, Milly, we are too well guarded here; only treachery could do us harm."

Only treachery!

Her face went sorrowful again.

She remembered how many a brave band of heroes had been betrayed in the last hour by the treachery of one base dastard.

She shivered slightly; but anxious to conceal her misgivings, kissed Claude on both cheeks, and tripped lightly to her own chamber.

"Poor, timorous lone bird," Claude soliloquised, gazing thoughtfully after her, "a very light breath of danger shakes that gentle breast. God grant that if the worst should come, she may be spared the pain of knowing it."

His face was grave for a while, but presently brightened again.

"Now to admit this lady visitor. Whew—I am not often favoured with their visits. Something is in the wind, or I should not be now. Let's see the fair one."

He placed the silk mask over his face again, and touched a small bell of silver.

Half a minute had barely elapsed when two of his highwaymen conducted in a lady in travelling costume, and retired.

She was veiled and blindfolded. The latter was a precaution adopted by the band, but one which Captain Claude hastened to remedy by removing the scarf.

"I did not anticipate the honour of a visit from a lady," he said gallantly, "or I would have given my men orders to spare you this unpleasant ceremony. Suffer me to remove your veil."

The gloved hand of the lady stayed the act.

"I will remain veiled," she said, in a tone in which could be detected the slightest tremor.

Captain Claude started slightly.

Bowing, he conducted his visitor to a seat.

"It will be in the recollection of Captain Claude," his veiled visitor remarked, when she had waved him to be seated, "that some time since, on a certain night, it was his fortune to stop a coach in which were travelling some distinguished travellers.

"While his band were committing their usual acts of violence, he was gallantly assisting back to consciousness a lady who had swooned, and was about to bend over her, when one of the male occupants of the coach, presented a pistol at the back of his neck, and would have slain him, if the lady, then recovered, had not seen the intended act, and pushed aside her husband's hand, thus saving the highwayman's life."

"Captain Claude is not likely to forget the night or the event," the highwayman said.

The lady continued—

"He did not harm the aged earl. More, he gave the lady back her jewels. He gave her also a ring, telling her where to seek him, should she at any time need his services—the ring is here."

She removed the glove from her left hand.

A blazing diamond signet sparkled on one finger.

"You recognise the token. I now ask you to fulfil your promise of service."

"Command me, madam, I am ready to keep my word."

"The service I ask of you is simple. There is a youth named Richard Wayne, an impetuous hot-headed boy, son of a fisherman, who has committed several outrages against society, terminating in his nearly braining his gaoler, and breaking out of prison, after having committed a felony at Aldervale Hall, and assaulted the young earl."

"Pardon me, madam, if I observe that this youth is very lively for a fisherman's son."

"A headstrong boy criminal—enough—he will seek your band, lured, as I am informed, by the hope of joining in the lucrative exploits of the knights of the road."

There was a slight sneer in her tone as she concluded.

"I understand," Captain Claude observed, "and he will come here, and you will have me instantly hand him over to justice. Madam, I will not disoblige you *when* he presents himself, but I will take especial care that he does not put me to the trouble of handing him over to the clutches of the law."

The lady rose from her seat.

"You mistake me. I would have you re- ceive him with open arms; swear him amongst your band; put him forward in your lawless deeds; let him be steeped in crime—in blood, if needs be; and——"

"Well, my dear madam, and the rest——"

"You may leave the rest to me."

"I will keep my word, madam; but, remember, from this hour my promise of service is recalled. I know the choice between life and dishonour. I will give the lad welcome; for by your account of him, he must have a little of the Tartar in his nature. So far, rely on me; but remember, madam, that whosoever once enters our secret band has a claim for life upon his comrades, each and all of whom are sworn to avenge to the full his fate, should he be betrayed to death. In that oath of vengeance neither age, sex nor tie of nature is respected. The sire is sworn to slay the son, the son his sister or bride—the son, his mother, ay, though he has lain in her arms, and taken his life from her breast."

There was something ominous in his tones; the veiled lady seemed to shiver with an unknown dread.

In silence she listened, and Captain Claude resumed—

"And now, madam, may I ask the favour of your unveiling, that I may see your face?"

"Sir, have I asked you to unmask?"

"Enough, my dear madam, it is not necessary that you should unmask for me to know you. I was curious to see how the charming Countess of Aldervale looked while planning this youth's destruction."

The countess started and reeled as if stricken.

"You know me! Will you betray my visit?" she exclaimed.

"I will not; and more, I will see you safely forth. You will have to pass amidst my gallant band. May I hope that as they do not see your face, you will not see theirs."

"It is not easy to see blindfolded."

"That was a caution on the part of my gallant fellows which I do not deem requisite."

The countess seemed surprised.

"Is it safe to be so trusting? Might I not betray you?"

"Madam," Captain Claude replied sarcastically, "I have never lost my faith in a woman's honour."

"A word more," he continued. "May I know the name of him who has lured this boy to become a highwayman?"

"Jonathan Wild."

"That callous blood-hunter!" exclaimed Captain Claude. "Madam, I give you warning that in me Jonathan Wild shall find the deadliest foe. I will thwart him at every turn—ay, even to the hazard of my life."

He raised the curtains, and they passed out.

Passed through the spacious chamber; passed through the groups of carousing highwaymen; who tried curiously to penetrate the disguise of the white lace veil.

Swig and Big Bullskin, who had long ago made up their quarrel, exchanged knowing winks, indicative of what they supposed to be their captain's little game.

To do them justice, the two staunch-hearted fellows were the best friends in the world; and though very fond of teasing each other, to the delight of their merry companions, would have done anything to oblige each other.

At the exit of the caverned chamber, Captain Claude bowed, and gave the countess to the care of one of his band, who had conducted her there.

Her ladyship paused to bid the dashing highwayman farewell.

After a moment's hesitation, she held out her hand.

Captain Claude took the mere tips of her jewelled fingers.

He did not like those fingers.

For all their wondrous symmetry and transparency they were to him very vulture's —claw-like in their movements.

But his natural gallantry would not allow him to decline the proffered hand.

So he raised the alabaster tips to his lips, bowed, and bade the countess adieu.

He was still thinking of those fingers when he returned to Milly.

"Whew!" he mused. "After my little love-bird's soft caressing fingers, hers seem like stiffened snakes. Who would have thought so fair a face could hide so black a heart? And now, I wonder when we shall have this new-comer here! Dick Wayne—

I've heard of him before, and know a little more about his history than her ladyship thinks, or she would never have trusted me with the task of shaping his future career. Ah! there'll be some curious results from this visit of my lady, the peerless Countess of Aldervale, to Captain Claude, the highwayman."

Little Milly came from her inner room, and crept timidly to the side of her highwayman lover.

Her face was very pale.

"Dear Claude," she said, "I fear that woman. There was a treachery in her cold tones that made me shiver as I listened. Oh, Claude, if she should have come here to betray you!"

"Impossible, love——"

Milly clung closer to him.

"You have often told me there was one woman who has sought your life. If this should——"

Captain Claude started.

A thrill ran like wild-fire through his brain.

A strange and dim suspicion.

There was one woman who he knew if she could pierce the disguise of the silken mask would have no remorse in selling him to his foes—would have rejoiced in giving him to a bitter death.

The wild misgiving was at his heart, and he was doubtingly looking Milly in the face, when the sharp report of a pistol echoing outside caused Milly to leap as if the bullet had tracked its scathing way to her breast, and as she trembling flung her arms around his neck, she shrieked fearfully—

"Claude, Claude, you are betrayed—all is lost—lost!"

With a face white as a sheet she fell sobbing on his breast.

Claude stood erect.

A fierce fire flashed from his dark eyes.

His lips were set to deadly resolve.

Clutching a heavy mounted pistol from his belt, he strode to the doorway, and forced the door.

But here, Milly, trembling from head to foot, flung her soft lithe form between him and the door.

"Claude, Claude, you shall not go!" she shrieked, "they will shoot you down!"

"Stand aside, Milly ; if she has done this, by heavens I will reach her in her infamy, though I fall dead in her sight !"

Hoarse with deadly fear, the pallid girl, tightening her fair arms around his waist, held him back.

He was trying with gentle force to go forth, when a loud, ominous cry of "Treachery !" rose from his band of highwaymen.

There was the ring of steel as their swords leapt from their sheaths—then came a confused shout from without, followed by the sharp rattle of a volley of musketry.

With a deadly cry of rage, Captain Claude put Milly aside.

One bound, and he had sprang to the chamber amidst his men.

And Milly, with a shriek, sank swooning back.

When Captain Claude dashed in amongst his men, he found them armed to the teeth, and prepared for a deadly encounter with those whom they supposed were attacking their secret stronghold.

They were gallant, daring fellows, and the thought of being betrayed, and taken with their beloved leader, inspired each with a fierce resolve to die amongst their foes rather than yield.

They greeted their captain with subdued enthusiasm, and gathered round him as he strode towards the doorway.

The fierce light in his eyes showed them that he suspected their danger, and was ready for the worst.

That they should not fall without making a few of their foes bite the dust, they well knew, even if they came off badly in the encounter.

Captain Claude, a sword in one hand, a pistol in the other, the silk mask hiding his handsome features, led them in silence from the subterranean chamber.

They understood the cause.

He did not wish to have the coming bloodshed seen by Milly.

His suspicion that they had been betrayed by the beautiful demon who had just left him was seen to be erroneous, when they emerged from the hidden entrance of their home.

The rugged and woody nature of the ground gave them ample concealment whence they could survey all that took place in the open beyond, without being detected themselves.

A wave of their leader's hand, and all were crouching in an uneven hollow, spectators of a daring battle for life and liberty— a fight in which they were not as yet concerned.

A first glance had shown to them a party of their natural and mortal enemies—the officers of justice—pursuing a tall stripling, who, fleet as a deer, was bounding from copse to copse, his active movements getting him out of the way of the bullets fired after him at random by the energetic officers.

They were half-a-dozen to one, and the fugitive's chance seemed hopeless, even to himself, for after a fierce run, he came to a stand by a dense copse, and as the evening light revealed his heated features, Captain Claude recognised our hero, Dick Wayne.

He must have fled some distance, and have been warmly chased.

The veins were deeply swollen on his throbbing temples.

He had thrown off his coat, and his broad chest panted, as he strove to gain breath.

He had been stricken in some previous struggle, for a red patch stained the bosom of his shirt, steeping it to his waist, where the oozing stream was yet trickling slowly down.

When the officers saw him pause, not to stand at bay, and dare them to a desperate struggle, but evidently meaning to give himself into their hands, they raised a shout of triumph, and two of the foremost hurried up to lay their hands on their youthful prisoner, little thinking of the sort of reception they were about to get.

Captain Claude, interested from the first in the fugitive's welfare, was wondering how he could best hasten to his rescue, when he was agreeably surprised by the way in which the hunted boy met the sneaking officers.

They had greatly mistaken his meaning.

Hardly had their hands touched his shoulder when Dick's arms shot out like lightning, and the two officers rolled sprawling to the ground.

Dick was upon them instantly.

Snatching each fellow's pistol from his faltering grasp, he dealt them fearful blows with the butts on their hard skulls, and leap-

'ing up, presented the loaded weapons at the other four.

"Now!" he cried, "make me pr'soner if you dare!"

His sudden onset had staggered the fellows and they were not so eager in their work when they saw the expert way in which he placed their comrades in that interesting but helpless position known as *hors de combat.*

Dick was standing now with a foot on the chest of each of the fallen officers, and there was something in his fearless attitude and in the deadly gleam of his eyes that kept his would-be captors for a moment out of his way.

Scoffingly laughing at their cowardly hesitation, the daring boy sprang into the copse.

Then the officers, inspired with a sudden energy, followed after him.

They caught sight of his graceful figure as he was in the act of leaping to the very hollow where Captain Claude and his highwaymen were concealed.

Four pistols simultaneously covered him— four sharp flashes and reports, and Dick, stricken by a second bullet, staggered, reeled, and dropped to one knee.

The officers, with a loud shout, jumped down into the hollow.

"Ah!" they cried; "stay there, my gallows bird, we have you now."

Stunned and bleeding, our hero had sense enough left to know he must make one last effort for his life, but had only the strength to half rise and lift his arms and present the loaded pistols at the officers' breasts, when a dizzy faintness stole over him, and he again fell to his knees.

Then the officers, sure of their prey, hurried to seize him, but were literally petrified to see rising, as if from the ground, a body of highwaymen, who, armed with swords and pistols, stood suddenly between them and their captive, the bright thin sword of the leader stabbing at their chests as they fell back in dismay.

The officers did not have the bravest of hearts beating under their well padded coats.

In a chase of six to one against an unarmed stripling they had been arduous and venturesome enough.

But to be confronted by a body of stalwart highwaymen was altogether a different kind of thing.

They had heard of the awful fate of some of their comrades who had tracked out a highwaymen's haunt, but had never returned to relate what they saw there, and now, a sight of the score of loaded pistols held by the hands of men who would have no scruple as to blowing off the roofs of their skulls, their courage oozed out at their fingers' ends, and in a pitiable state of fear they stumbled over one another to get out of the line of glittering tubes.

"My friends," said the calm, rich voice of Captain Claude, " we have witnessed your courageous chasing of this poor wounded boy, and are extremely obliged to you for coming within our reach."

The officers began to shake in every limb.

Every face went ghastly pale and reeked with clammy sweat.

The glare of the evil one seemed in those two dark eyes gleaming through Captain Claude's mask.

Fervently they wished they had never come there, but more fervently still they wished themselves safely away.

The highway captain's voice made them quake as he said, sternly—

"Cowards! A word from my lips, the uplifting of my finger, and your worthless carcasses would swing from yonder trees with a rope round your necks; there are men here amongst my band who would gladly pay off all old scores by stringing you up like scarecrows in a bunch!"

A good many of the bold highwaymen were glaring upon the trembling officers of justice as if that was exactly the thing they would have enjoyed doing, there and then, and the shaking wretches, who feared the same feeling might influence Captain Claude, began cringingly to mumble for mercy as he spoke again—

"Lay down those pistols. I'll not take your vile lives this time. I give you one chance of escape; but, mark me! if you put yourselves again in our path, or are ever known to attempt the capture or betrayal of any of our band, you shall die a fearful death! Begone, now—flee for your cowardly lives! The last one that reaches that copse

SWIG AND BIG BULLSKIN SCARE THE OFFICERS.

yonder will receive the bullets of my men."

The officers did not wait for him to recant his terms of grace; their pistols dropped as suddenly from their trembling hands as if the butts had been red hot.

They urged their shaking limbs to escape from that fatal volley.

One glance of apprehensive fright they gave at the highwaymen's pistols, then scrambled out of the way.

It was the devil take the hindermost.

They scrambled over each other in their headlong haste, their knees knocking together as they fled.

Awful moment!

They reached the copse.

" Now !" exclaimed the voice of Capt͞n Claude.

The officers gave a yell.

In their sudden fear their legs stuck under them.

The highwaymen laughed as they took aim.

Half-a-dozen bullets sped from the polished barrels with a sudden bang.

The helpless officers were sprawling all of a heap when the leaden missiles came.

Each got a shot.

Each got it in the same place.

Simultaneously, they were seen to clap their hands to the hinder part of their bodies.

Simultaneously, they were heard to yell and scream in pain, and then all rolled head over heels out of the highwaymen's sight.

Captain Claude smiled grimly.

"We've tickled the gentlemen," he said. "I don't think they'll be in a hurry to ferret us out again; and now, my men, let's carry in the wounded lad; lift him gently; we must keep that untamed spirit in his stripling body; he's to be one of our band."

The highwaymen gave a subdued cheer, and Swig and Big Bullskin, with two others, lifted Dick tenderly from the ground, and the rest following, he was carried into the highwaymen's home.

———

CHAPTER VII.

OUR HERO IS GIVEN INTO THE HANDS OF FAIR MILLY—SWORN IN—THE BOY EARL BECOMES A BOY HIGHWAYMAN.

MILLY was waiting with a pale tearful face the return of Captain Claude.

It was marvellous to see how her fair features brightened, when she heard him come safely back again.

Very tenderly she kissed him, and then, with true woman's gentleness, bent over the form of our hero.

He had been carried to their inner chamber, by order of Captain Claude.

The true-hearted highwayman knew that Milly was the best nurse the stricken youth could have.

He himself had trained her to his own skill in surgery, and more than once her own hands had bandaged his gaping wounds.

Never a thought of jealousy entered his noble mind when Milly's delicate fingers laid bare our hero's bosom to staunch his hurts.

Dick was half unconscious from the effects of the last bullet, which had struck him near the temple.

His other wounds were deeper; the bullets were still lodged in his soft flesh, and Captain Claude, producing his case of instruments, set about extracting them.

Our hero lay quiet and passive—oblivious seemingly of his pain—of the dangers he had run—of his brave rescuer—and of the fair young girl, who was using every art to win him back to sensibility.

Milly felt more than ordinary sympathy for him.

He looked so noble as he lay there, with the defiant dauntless look about his bronzed face, that contrasted so strangely with his white throat and chest.

"He is very gentle," she said to Captain Claude; "he looks so noble, too. Is he to mingle with your band?"

Almost tearfully she put the question.

Captain Claude's tones were husky as he replied—

"He will be one of us—he has wrongs to avenge—and his hand must be lifted against the world till his foot is on the neck of his enemies."

"Or on the dreadful scaffold," Milly cried faintly. "Oh, Claude, save him from that!"

"He will not die on the scaffold," Claude cried, passionately; "no, his destiny is sealed."

Milly said no more.

Her heart was throbbing strangely.

She smoothed the matted curls from Dick's temples, and kissed away the clammy dews that stood thickly on his pallid brow.

And her lily hand was locked in his, as with clenched fingers and gnashing teeth, he seemed to be battling with his foes again.

Nature must have proved ungrateful in deed, if such gentle nursing had not prevailed.

Our hero came back to consciousness—came back to look on the fair, girlish face of his nurse—to gaze on the noble form of his daring deliverer, into whose eyes he gazed with a strange sensation creeping over him, a sensation that made him yearn to gaze upon the features of the highway captain.

But Captain Claude, who let no one but Fair Milly see his face, kept his mask on when in the presence of his youthful protége.

Dick got the better of his hurts sooner than was expected, and then was introduced to those who were to be his future comrades in the new life he was to lead.

And one night, in the midst of the band of highwaymen, whose swords were crossed above his head, he spoke his solemn vow.

He took the oath to be one amongst them, and was sworn in to the death, one of their band.

He was not yet well enough to go abroad, but he had his dashing costume, and a magnificent steed was given to him, a superb creature, called Fairy, of pure cream tint from mane to tale, with fleet, lithe limbs, and symmetrical chest and head.

She had been Milly's favourite, and it was at her desire that Captain Claude gave her to our hero.

The doings of the band were kept no secret now that he was a member.

He knew when they went forth on their night rides, on what expedition they were bound, and saw when jewelled caskets, rare gems, and long purses, attested their success on the road.

He saw with pleasure that Captain Claude took no share of the booty, and was more reconciled to the companionship of his fellows, when he found that they often took from the rich to give to the poor, and, their High-Toby occupations excepted, were as noble and daring a set of fellows as could be met with.

Captain Claude had no fear in leaving our hero alone with Milly.

Other highway chieftains might have feared the influences of her soft looks of love on so impressionable a youth.

But Claude loved Milly with a devotion, in which there was not the shadow of a doubt.

He knew that she was pure in heart and soul.

He believed, too, that our hero was not so base as to tempt the faithfulness of her, who had nursed him back to life.

Dick did indeed love his captain's gentle mistress.

But it was with the love of a brother towards a sister.

He loved his own Grace too deeply to allow his thoughts to stray, even if he had been ignoble enough to take advantage of Captain Claude's trust.

He was panting to take his first venture abroad, when one of the band brought him the intelligence that old Peter Wayne, and his young wife, Lucy, had been sent to prison on a charge of wrecking, and that Grace Merton had been taken away, no one knew whither.

Dick's senses reeled when he heard this fearful news.

He understood its meaning.

His malicious half-brother had kept his word.

He loaded his pistols carefully that night.

They were a handsome pair, with long, shining tubes, and heavy silver mounts.

He looked to the point of his sword, and putting saddle and bridle to Fairy, went forth alone, spite of the entreaties of Milly, who had received orders from Captain Claude to bid him stay.

He went forth with a desperate purpose at his heart, and with a whirling brain.

Went on his first night's venture—to lift his hand against the world, and dare the worst in avengement of his wrongs.

CHAPTER VIII.

AN ADVENTURE ON THE HIGHWAY.—STOPPING THE COACH.—A DASTARDLY SHOT.—CAPTAIN CLAUDE HEARS A TERRIBLE MYSTERY.

CAPTAIN CLAUDE rode forth that night alone.

He had left orders for his youthful protege to remain until he returned, and was very thoughtful as he wended his way along the moonlit road.

There had been a marked change in his manner since the countess's visit to him—usually grave and taciturn, he was now moodily absent.

Even his forced lightheartedness had left him.

His gallant band was abroad on their night excursions.

On other occasions it was customary for two or three of them to accompany him, but to-night he had said that he would go forth alone, and many of his faithful followers felt a dim foreboding that danger would that night befall their idolised leader.

But for his stern command many would have followed him, to be ready in case of sudden need

As it was, many a wistful look was sent

after his handsome figure as he rode out of sight.

He was mounted on a horse of matchless beauty, perfectly black from head to tail with the exception of a white star on her forehead.

It was a noble animal, that had borne him safely through many a fierce fight, and had taken him with tireless speed from the hot pursuit of the foes who hungered for his life, and would have shot him down without mercy but for the fidelity of his swift-footed steed.

He had named it Selim, and now as he patted his glossy neck and lightly breathed its name the affectionate animal fondly shook its rich glossy mane and snorted in pleasure.

Docile, faithful, and untiring, a word from its master would control its wildest moods.

No other but Captain Claude had ever crossed its back.

He had trained it, and the sagacious animal would allow no one else to bestride it.

Captain Claude was as usual masked.

It was one of the peculiarities of his nature that he never allowed himself to be seen, except by Milly, without his mask.

His devoted band, who had served him faithfully for years, had never seen his face.

He was riding meditatively on when Selim gave a gentle snort and pricked up her ears.

Captain Claude knew the signal.

Some one approached.

He patted the arched neck of Selim, and sitting still as a statue listened.

Along the still road came the faint rumble of wheels.

Captain Claude backed Selim into the shadow of a clump of trees, and waited for the vehicle to approach.

For about ten minutes the coach, of whose coming Selim's true instinct had given him warning, could be seen lumbering along the uneven road.

It was drawn by two horses.

An officer sat in front beside the coachman; the head of another protruded from the carriage.

He was gesticulating violently, and endeavouring to make the coachman hurry on, and finding his expostulations of no avail, thrust out a large horse pistol, and shook it at the imperturbable John, whom the officer on the box was menacing little less violently.

"Some unfortunate prisoner they are conveying to the sessions or execution," Captain Claude soliloquised. "I shall have to stop the coach and see him—one officer on the box, two, doubtless, inside. Three to one—a mere trifle; Selim, we'll stop the coach."

Selim pricked up his ears and shook his mane.

He seemed to understand what they had to do.

By this time the ricketty old coach had lumbered up, and Captain Claude heard the officer inside bawl, excitedly—

"Whip them cursed beasts of yours, and be d——d to you, or I'll shoot you and take the reins. Them d——d highwaymen are always lurking about the hollow, and we might as well lose our necks as as our prisoners."

"Oh, don't be frightened," Claude heard the coachman reply, "I be a match for any two high-toby men. I've a cracker here ready if they should come, and I'd put a bellyful of lead in their darned skulls like winking, if they tried their tricks at stopping me."

He slapped his huge hand on a cumbrous old wide-muzzled pistol stuck his big coat pocket, and slashed the whip violently at his jaded horses.

Captain Claude, who saw the act, and had no doubt that the fellow's courage would vanish at the first sight of a loaded pistol, at that moment advanced, and put Selim right in front of the two horses, stopping them on the instant.

"My friend," Claude said, laying his hand on the coachman's breast, while with the other he presented the singularly bright barrel of a long pistol at his ear, "I'll trouble you to hand over that pistol, and to give me that whip."

Had the coachman been suddenly confronted by his Satanic Majesty he could not have been more aghast.

He rolled helplessly back, staring openmouthed at his masked interlocutor, who in a trice dispossessed him of his weapon and whip.

The officer on the box no sooner saw the daring interrupter than he drew forth a loaded pistol.

Captain Claude did not give him time to fire it; rapping him sharply on the knuckles, he hurled the weapon from his grasp, knocking it under the feet of the horses.

He then rode round to the door of the carriage.

The two officers inside, finding the coach, suddenly stop, crammed their heads out of the window to discover the cause.

The long shining tubes of loaded pistols, held in the masked highwayman's hands, touched each in the middle of the forehead.

The cold tickling sensation, with the proximity of the leaden bullets contained in those long barrels, sent both their heads in with a jerk.

Captain Claude looked in.

Each hand still held the pistol presented.

He merely wanted to see who the prisoners were.

He expected to see a couple of daring criminals.

He saw, instead, an old grey bearded man, shaking in a deathlike palsy; his sinewy hands clasped together, his clammy head resting on the breast of a woman, whose once good-looking features were haggard and pale, as if with the nervous anxiety of her coming fate.

Both were manacled heavily.

Captain Claude recognised the pair instantly.

They were old Peter **Wayne**, the fisherman, and his wife Lucy.

The highway captain looked angrily on the crouching officers, and then turned to the fisherman and his wife.

"What, old Peter, and you, Lucy! What means this—upon what charge have they dared to treat you thus?"

Lucy Wayne uttered a cry of fierce delight.

"Thank God!" she exclaimed, "I see you before me! I sent messengers to bid you come, but they who put us in that dreadful prison would not let them fetch you."

"Had I known you were confined, my gallant band should have rescued you though they pulled every stone from the prison walls. Unloose those manacles, fellow, or, by the living God, I will blow your brains out!"

"It is too late to help us now," Lucy cried; "do not incur peril for our sakes; we are to die for wrecking and piracy; the was got up against us by the Countess vale; her son has carried off poor Merton, and all this because we know secret of Dick's birth."

"The secret?"—Claude's fine eyes flashed—"has that terrible woman anything in connection with his history?"

The woman's voice sank to a shrill whisper.

Clutching Claude with her manacled hands, she was about to speak, when old Peter Wayne lifted his palsied head, and with his jaws chattering with spasmodic fear, cried, hoarsely—

"The officer! He'll shoot you—hi, murder!"

Lucy Wayne saw the dastard act.

The officer, whom Claude had left in front of the coach, had dismounted from the box and picked up his pistol.

Stealthily remounting the box, he leaned over, and presenting the weapon at the highway captain, was in the act of pulling the trigger, when Lucy Wayne, uttering a quick cry of alarm, thrust Claude aside.

Some conscious instinct seemed to warn her that by saving him she would sacrifice herself.

It was more by the intense look of mingled alarm, horror and resolve in her piercing eyes that Claude was warned of what was about to occur.

The look she gave him was from another world, as, calling him by another name, a name none of the officers—to whom he was well known—had ever heard him called by, she shrieked—

"Beware! He is her son! You are his—Oh, God! Mercy. I am hit to the heart!"

In the midst of her speech, and while she was thrusting him back, there came a sharp report from above his head; a blinding flash passed before his eyes; then the white was hands clutched with a deadly grip on his wrist.

Lucy Wayne gave a hoarse cry of mortal anguish, and with the ghastly dews of death on her features, and her life blood streaming from her breast, fell to the floor of the carriage.

Then came a cry of triumph from outside the coach; the mocking laugh of the dastard who had fired the coward shot, which, aimed at Captain Claude's life, had sunk in the bosom of that faithful woman.

CHAPTER VIII.

HERO'S FIRST NIGHT ON THE ROAD.—TREACHERY AND CAPTURE.

THE very night on which our hero first took to his life on the road, the countess, his unnatural mother, whose only concern about him was the wish to see him lie stiff and cold in death at her feet, gave a grand party at her splendid mansion.

It was a break-up party, for on the following day the countess and her illegitimate son were to leave for London.

They had special reasons for going there; reasons which for the present must be kept secret, but which would have been explained had anyone penetrated to one of the chambers of the spacious dwelling, where, kept close prisoner, a fair young girl, pale and tearful, sat dreading each coming hour.

None of the guests had any idea of the captive's presence, and the feast passed off pleasantly.

One of the ladies, Ruth May, had been the belle of the evening, and now a crowd of young gallants attended her to her carriage, wishing her deceitful old guardian—Judge Gripp—to the very devil, for the way in which he kept her to himself.

The fact was, the shrivelled up old judge had tender thoughts regarding the lady himself.

She was very beautiful, and very rich; that is to say, she was worth a lot of money, which at present the rascally old judge, as her guardian, was taking care of.

He had no wish to part with either the young lady or her money, and it was with ill-concealed pleasure that he saw the mortified looks of the gallants who handed pretty Ruth into the coach.

They had been saying too many tender things to her at the ball, and he was very fidgety to get the door shut and drive off with her all to himself.

Of course the aforesaid young gentlemen were anything but pleased at losing their peerless belle, and as they stood on the steps of Aldervale Hall many were the sarcastic hints they gave the judge.

They touched him on a tender point, when one of them said—

"Keep a look out for highwaymen, or they'll rob you of your treasure."

The rascally old judge had a deadly horror of being stopped by highwaymen.

When on the bench in court he felt himself secure, and passed the severest sentences in his power.

It was said that he had never been himself since the time when a highwayman whom he had sentenced, as he was being led out to die, prophesied with bitter warning that he (the judge) would be waylaid some night and strung up to die on a heath.

He had avoided lonely heaths ever since, and he felt uncomfortable at the thought of having to travel a lonely road that night.

"Coachman," he cried, tremblingly, "are your pistols loaded?"

"Yes, my lord.'

"Keep a good look out on the road, you fellows," he said to the footmen, " if any one attempts to stop us, shoot him dead."

The footmen touched their hats, and tried to look brave.

In their hearts they fervently wished they might not even see the shadow of a High Toby man.

"Highwaymen, indeed," mumbled the judge as he got into the coach, "I'll teach them to stop me—a king's judge."

The door was shut, and the coach rolled away.

Soon the lights of Aldervale Hall were left in the distance, and the road became very lonely and dark.

An hour passed on their journey.

The old judge, shaking in nervous fear, was getting as close as possible to pretty Ruth, and was amorously eyeing her fair bosom, as it was revealed between the light folds of her cloak, when the huge vehicle gave a sudden bump, rolled a little to one side, and then stopped with a jerk that sent old Judge Gripp on his knees, before the fair beauty.

As Ruth gave a little shriek of fright, he scrambled to his seat, and putting his head out of the carriage window, shouted out—

"Go on, go on. What do you mean by stopping here? I'll have the whole of you soundly thrashed. I'll put you in prison. Go on."

He was foaming in the mouth.

"Can't, my lord," exclaimed a muffled, terror-stricken voice, "we're stopped."

"Stopped, d——n you. What is there to stop you here?"

It was a second or so before the answer came.

Then it came in jerks——

"A high—way—man!"

The judge gave a sudden bound, knocking his nose against the bottom of the carriage window.

The old judge tumbled back all of a heap.

His eyes started out of their sockets—his jaw fell—his tongue clove to the roof of his mouth.

He remembered the ominous prophesy of the man he had sentenced to be hanged.

What if his time han come, and he were about to be dragged forth, strung up to a blighted tree, and there left in the agonies of death!

He felt choking with the awful sensation.

Big clammy sweats beaded his brow.

Pretty Ruth, although she went pale, and felt slightly scared, did not display any signs of terror.

She had often laughed merrily at the idea of meeting with a highwayman, and declared archly that she would compel him to bow the knee, and do homage to her beauty.

And now the event had happened.

Here she was stopped by a highwayman.

The frightened look in her eye disappeared as the highwayman looked in—her heart fluttered, and it was with a singular fascination that she met the dark thrilling eyes flashing upon her from the black silk mask.

A very graceful figure, clad in a coat of scarlet and lace, a waist small as a woman's, but the chest broad and full.

He had dismounted from a cream-coloured Arabian of exquisite beauty—one small womanish hand yet held the silver mounted bridle, the other opened the carriage door, and Ruth May had full opportunity to satisfy her romantic wish for the sight of a highwayman.

"Fact is, my lord," said Dick Wayne, for he it was, "your servants were playing with some firearms when I rode up. They had the foolish notion that they were to be used against me—a notion I speedily dispelled by depriving them of their pistols. Here they are."

He laughed, and, displaying three pairs of pistols, stuffed them into the holster of the saddle.

"There they are," he said, as he thrust the last one in, "six, all loaded, and a precious useless lot of hardware they are, too."

For the first time he seemed to notice the lady.

The carriage lamps only afforded a partial glimpse of her loveliness, but the glance of her splendid eyes convinced him she was very beautiful.

Gracefully lifting his gold laced hat, he bowed almost to the ground, and said—

"Do not let my presence alarm you, fair one. I shall not resort to any acts of violence. In my presence you are perfectly safe."

"Safe," mumbled the judge, "safe—you—a—highwayman."

He thought there was nothing very desperate in Dick's manner, and was fumbling for a loaded pistol he had placed under the cushion.

Dick saw the butt, as the judge nervously was rummaging for it.

"My lord," he said, "you need not trouble yourself about the weapon. I shall not suffer you to use it. Don't trouble me to draw mine."

The judge, shaking from head to foot, let the pistol fall.

Dick put his foot upon it.

"Oblige me, if you please," he said, "with that valuable chain you have hanging round your neck. I'll take also the watch attached to it."

The judge stared at him in speechless helplessness.

He was not able to act for himself, so Dick politely relieved him of his watch and chain.

The chain was solid—the watch was set with brilliants.

"Excellent," said Dick. "I admire your taste. That diamond pin, my lord, must be worth a hundred pounds. I'll wear it for your sake. Your rings—thank you. Now your purse—a weighty and full one—exquisite. Your snuff-box next—and that, I think, will be all."

One by one, he took the articles from the trembling judge.

The last one was like drawing the old villain's blood.

It was a massive chased gold snuff-box, set with large opals, and must have been worth nearly a thousand pounds.

"My lord," Dick said, weighing the different articles in his hand, "You have the taste of a connoisseur. When next you travel with such rare and costly articles about you, I hope I may have the good fortune to stop you."

The judge groaned.

"Here, Fairy," Dick continued, "you shall carry these; they will balance the half-dozen 'barkers' on the other side."

He stuffed the valuables into the other holster.

Fairy pricked up her ears, and pawed the ground.

As he was turning to the carriage again, she laid her soft nose on his shoulder.

Dick patted her neck caressingly, but took no further notice, a slight which made Fairy paw the ground more impatiently than before.

As he was putting his head into the carriage, he felt himself gently tugged by the coat-tails.

He turned round, and found Fairy with a bit of his skirt between her white teeth.

"Presently, presently," Dick said, caressing her beautiful neck; "anxious to be off, my pet? We shall start presently."

Pretty Ruth's bosom palpitated quickly.

She was anticipating the youthful highwayman's demands on her jewels and purse.

As he now turned towards her, she commenced slipping the glittering rings off her taper fingers.

"They are prized gifts," she said, faintly; "take them. Please do not touch me."

With gallant deference, Dick drew himself erect.

"I rob not ladies," he said, "except of one thing they possess. A kiss from those virgin lips is the only treasure I will ask you for."

He bent forward gallantly.

Ruth's breath came short and quick.

To be kissed by a highwayman!

She would have shuddered at the idea.

But Dick seemed so gentle, so respectful—and then might he not compel her if she did not yield?

She leaned back, and Dick leant forward.

Their lips touched.

One long, clinging kiss.

His white hand felt the thrilling touch of her fair neck.

Then she pushed him gently away.

Dick's cheek flushed beneath his mask.

The lady, too, blushed scarlet.

"Delicious," Dick cried. "The kiss was Paradise."

A tug at his back jerked the breath out of his body, and cut short his following speech.

Fairy had got him by the skirt again.

The sleek creature's attitude was one of intense beauty.

Her ears were erect, her chest expanded, her mane shook, as she arched her creamy neck, and her snowy feet pawed the ground.

Dick was strange to her sagacious qualities, or he would have known that her movements were the instinct of warning.

Danger was near, and the superb creature scented it.

But our hero only supposed she was eager to be off, and laughingly pulled away his skirts.

"Fairy is jealous," he said to Ruth.

The young girl gave him a glance that thrilled to his inmost soul.

He withdrew his gaze from her fair face, and addressed the judge—

"A fortunate beginning for the first night on the road. May I have many such. My lord, I take my leave. Lady——"

For the first time since the carriage had been stopped, the old judge shook off his palsied lethargy.

A sinister, subtle gleam of malice shot from his half-closed eyes.

Suddenly, as if seized with a spasm, he tumbled off his seat and lay huddled at one corner of the coach.

"Oh—oh—oh—oh!" he gasped.

"Are you ill, my lord?" Dick asked.

"I—I am choking," mumbled the judge.

Ruth bent forward to loosen her guardian's stock.

He was shaking like a leaf, and gurgled as if choking.

Dick stooped lower to assist him.

A shadow, unobserved by him, was thrown across the interior.

Fairy gave a loud snort, and tore the ground with her feet.

Dick loosened the old villain's scarf to allow him to breathe more freely.

In a moment the judge's pretended spasm passed away.

Gripping Dick with both hands by the collar, he cried out, tremulously—

"Seize him—aha!—seize him, the villain, the highwayman!"

With the fury of a young lion Dick tore himself from the judge's hold.

A fierce light was blazing in his eyes.

Had there been no others to capture him, he would have hurled the judge's servitors from him like reeds.

But others were there—more determined men.

Two officers, armed, and eager to capture a highwayman.

They had seen the carriage stopped.

Had crept on hands and knees to get there unperceived.

Fairy knew they were coming, and had tried vainly to warn her youthful rider of his danger.

The old judge had seen them creeping stealthily to the carriage door.

Hence his sudden device of assumed illness; now his trembling lips mumbled and chuckled.

He was intensely delighted at the success of his ruse.

The two officers seized Dick.

The coachman and two footmen hung on his arms.

He was powerless.

A PRISONER!

"Aha!" mumbled the old judge, elate at the success of his dastardly trick, "a fine beginning, a glorious first night's work—your last. Hold him, men. I shall have the satisfaction of ridding the world of one rogue, at least, in the outset of his career."

Dick's frame quivered in every fibre as he tried to wrestle from the grasp of his captors.

Ruth, with tearful eyes, begged her guardian to bid them let him go.

"No, no," mumbled the judge; "we've got him. Aha! he shall swing, aha!"

Poor Ruth, with her pretty face bathed in tears, was compelled to see the youthful highwayman, who had made such a dangerous impression on her heart, pinioned by a scarf by one of the officers, while the rest held him, so that he could not move a limb.

When he was fast bound, one of the officers thought it would be as well to see to the horse.

He took hold of Fairy's bridle.

The queenly creature had been standing as still as a statue of marble, but with every sense strained, as if expecting some signal how to act.

The change of her attitude was marvellous the instant the officer touched her.

Leaping like a fawn in the air, with mane and tail erect, and eyes gleaming, she darted her open mouth at the officer's shoulder, and tore shreds off his coat, shirt, and flesh, down to the waist.

Then, wheeling round, she sent out her hind legs, sharp, straight, and with swift velocity right in among those who held her captive master.

The two footmen she sent spinning on their faces in the mire.

The old judge, who had crawled out of the coach, fell back into it, with his mouth full of broken teeth.

The other officer was sent rolling over the judge.

Having given this specimen of her power, Fairy sidled up to her young master, and arched her graceful neck.

A moment she stayed, as if expecting him to vault on her back.

Then, swift as a flash of light, the creature galloped away.

If Dick had not been bound hand and foot, he might easily have availed himself of the chances of escape afforded him by his sagacious and faithful steed.

But, helplessly bandaged, he could only chafe in bitterness, while his opportunity passed away.

The officers were on their feet first.

Then the old judge staggered forward.

"The horse, the horse," he yelled, "shoot it down. All my valuables are in the holster! A hundred pounds to him who shoots the animal dead!"

The two officers presented their pistols at the fleet animal.

Before they could fire, Dick bounded between them, scattering them aside.

"Hold," he cried. " Hell's power wither your accursed hands for ever, if you fire at my beautiful steed."

They were only a few words he spoke, but they were uttered in such a vehement tone, and with such a lightning flash darting from his eyes, that the officers cowed and for the moment nerveless shrunk back.

And in that interval, the faithful steed had time to gallop out of sight.

Galloped away with six loaded pistols and the judge's valuables in its holsters.

Galloped to the highwayman's home, to tell by its riderless condition, that the new sworn member of their band was a prisoner or slain.

A proud smile wreathed our hero's lips, as the last faint clattering of Fairy's hoofs died in the distance.

"Now," he said, " I am in your hands."

Quiet—patient—and passive now.

His momentary wild energy, that had struck the officers dumb and stupefied with heart-palsying terrors, had left him.

A child's calmness succeeded the storm of angry passions concentrated in his few words of deadly fury.

The old judge mumbled fierce abuse on the officers' heads, then scowled indignantly on Dick.

"To prison with him!" he exclaimed, " to prison, and then—the gibbet."

CHAPTER IX.

TYBURN DICK IS HONOURED WITH A VISIT FROM JONATHAN WILD, BUT PROVES HIMSELF NOBLE IN TROUBLE.

D Judge Gripp's malicious fury knew no unds when he saw Dick's magnificent steed e away with his valuables snugly ensconced n the holsters.

He foamed at the mouth and shook in every limb.

Pretty Ruth shuddered when she looked on his rage-convulsed visage.

His mouth, where Fairy had planted one of her hoofs, was swollen and bleeding. Froth hung about his shaking lips.

His features were green with passion, and

he mumbled the most fearful menace against our hero.

"I'll swing you for this," he cried, " you gallows dog ! I'll swing you. You shall hang in chains, till the flesh drops piecemeal from your carcase."

Dick treated his outburst with lofty indifference, and the old judge, bidding the officers handcuff their prisoner, ordered them to march beside his coach.

When the door was shut upon him, he rolled back in the carriage, yelling by fits and starts at his pain, and the loss he had suffered.

Occasionally he put his head out of the window, with his face buried in a handkerchief, to see that the officers had their prisoner all right, and then Ruth heard him mutter his intended revenge.

It was a hard pang to her when the coach stopped before her door, and she had to look her last on the graceful form of the Boy Highwayman.

Her eyes were swimming in tears, and Dick heard her sob bitterly as he was dragged out of her sight.

He fancied, too, she was pleading with the old judge for mercy for him, and thinking very tenderly of the fair young girl who felt so deep a sympathy for his fate, our hero allowed himself to be thrust into the cell of the town prison.

" There, you young jail-bird," the gaoler said, as he thrust Dick in, we've heard how you got out of the lock-up, but you won't get out of here in a hurry, or I'll eat my head. You'll find them 'ere walls too thick to knock a hole in, and that window's nigh a hundred feet from the ground."

"Shut the door and leave me," Dick said, "I am your prisoner, keep me while you can."

"Hoity, toity, my fine man," cried the gaoler; "so that's your kidney, is it—oho— 'keep me while you can,' that's it now, is it? It was 'Take me who dare,' last time, but you've got took, you have, haven't you?"

"Yes," Dick said, " I am taken, but not for long. I shall escape you, my friend; the prison is not built that will hold me, nor the tree grown that's to be my gibbet."

The gaoler stared at him open mouthed.

"Oho," he cried at length, "it ain't, ain't it, the tree ain't grown to make your gibbet, p'r'aps the rope ain't twisted that's to go round your precious gullet? well, may-be it ain't, but I'll tell you what's made, my fine young joker, an' that's the irons to put on them limbs of yourn, as I'll presently show you, an' I'll give you leave to escape them if you can."

He shut the door with a bang.

Presently he returned with two helpmates, one of whom carried heavy links and chains.

Talking to himself all the while, the gaoler fastened them on Dick's wrists and ankles.

When all was secure he walked round and round his prisoner, to satisfy himself that he had no chance of getting free.

"Yer'll do now, my pippin," he said, standing with both hands akimbo, "an' in case you'd like a passport through the grating, there's a stool I'll put on the bench to accommodate you.

Muttering as he went he left the cell, followed by his assistants.

The door closed.

The ponderous keys rattled in the heavy ks.

Huge iron bolts grated in their sockets

The gaoler's footsteps died away along the stone corridor.

Our hero was alone.

A manacled prisoner.

He did not look very rueful over his position; on the contrary, the first thing he did was to indulge in a hearty laugh at the expense of the ill-natured gaoler.

"One would think," he exclaimed, "I had robbed *him!* to see the airs the fellow put on was comical—he's made sure of me though."

He looked at his irons.

"Here I am at last, bound fast and sure. Not a very charming prospect, I confess; it is too bad for the first night's venture—ah! if I had understood Fairy's warning, I should not have been here now. Faithful creature, now she tried to pull me away. If ever I have the comfort of riding on her back again, I shall know better how to value her warning —ah, well, giving way to laments is useless. I must see what can be done."

He mused deeply, as he paced up and down his cell as far as his chains would allow him.

"That rascally old judge, he laid me by the heels well. 'Twas a neat trick. Poor Ruth, too. How she shivered when she saw me captured. I'll warrant now, highwayman as I seemed to her, that girl would have warned me had she been aware of her guardian's villany. The shrivelled old wretch he is to try me too—sentence me to be hanged.

"Hum. I don't quite like the notion of making my exit from the world in that sort of way. Strung up by the neck like a scarecrow. Something strikes me, too, that Judge Gripp won't have the pleasure of trying me just yet."

He sat down on the oaken bench.

"How changed I am," he muttered, "since the day my own mother hounded me from her chamber. My mother—ha! I often wondered whether Lucy Wayne deceived me. It seems beyond belief that a mother could discard her own son. And yet her guilty looks. Well, well, I'll not think of that. Escape, now, is my first thought; what I shall do when I am free, must be decided afterwards.

"That ill-natured boor." he exclaimed presently, thinking of the gaoler's coarse behaviour, "I daresay the fellow's glad to have me here, and would joyfully witness my execution, if my time had come, which I don't believe.

"One would think I had done him mortal injury. Yet I never harmed the poor fool. It's the way of the world, though. Ah, that world. How men shall curse the hour that turned it's hate against me, and mine against the world. I am tame now, but there's a bitter fury in my heart that makes me feel a very devil."

He was silent for a few moments.

Then thoughtfully he mounted the oaken stool.

This brought his face as high as the grated window.

He could not see below, but at some distance the tall steeple of the church rose before his sight.

Dick took in the anything but cheerful view at a glance, and clambered down again.

"A precious prospect there," he mused, "That confounded old rapscallion was right.

I should want wings, even if I was able to get out of the window. A rather difficult task with these gewgaws on my wrists and legs. I am beaten, and must trust to chance. So come, Dame Fortune, if thou can unscrew these manacles from my wrists, I'll believe even in getting a pair of wings, or as good a substitute to aid me in my flight."

There was a singular light-heartedness about the boy's tones.

The critical position, instead of paralysing his nerves, only inspired his daring spirit.

His eyes kindled, and his cheeks flushed with adventurous excitement, and he remained perched on the tall stool, kicking his ironed legs listlessly against the edge of the oaken bench, and humming a merry carol of the road.

The gaoler meanwhile had gone downstairs, and after taking a glass of something short with the officer, returned to his own quarters.

Half an hour only had elapsed, when a summons at the door announced a visitor.

"More of them High-Toby vagabonds, I shouldn't wonder," he said, rising to leave.

Only one voice however was heard.

A voice well known to him, and he went back to his chair as the new-comer was announced.

With a sinister servile bow and cringing look, the visitor who now disturbed the gaoler's privacy entered the room.

A stiffish greeting passed between him and the gaoler, whose surly looks implied no pleasure at the visit.

But the new comer, not affecting to notice his reserve, entered at once upon the object of his errand.

"I hear, Mark Napper, you've got that young devilskin here—Dick Wayne—took on the highway."

"Yes," growled Mark, in reply, "and safe enough I've caged him; he's in our strongest cell, and he's well ironed, I can tell you."

"Such would be expected. We know, Mark, you are not *too* lenient with your prisoners."

"No, I never lost but one prisoner, and I said he should be the last. No fear of another slipping through my fingers, leastways not till he's took out to be scragged."

The gaoler's visitor took a pinch of snuff.

"Your caution is creditable; but I'm afraid this young dog of a boy highwayman won't grace the gibbet just yet."

The gaoler stared.

"Won't he though? Well, now, I'd like to know what's a-going to get him off—I jest would."

"Fact is, Mark, we want his band—there's a whole gang of 'em; but though I know how to communicate with them, I can't get a chance of laying hands on them—we've one on 'em in our hands, too, but he's too big a cove for us to trust to. He knows that the least treachery would cause him to lose his brains, and they've made him take an oath that's scared his chicken-heart. This boy is new to the business, and with your leave I'll see what's to be made of him."

"Have you got your order?"

"Yes, my friend; I never come on such errands without one."

The gaoler rose and gruffly said—

"Better let him hang; you've time to capture 'em all in time."

"That, Mark Napper, is my business," was the curt reply, as the pair ascended the stairs.

Our hero had at that moment finished the speech wherein he invoked fortune to his aid, and he looked eagerly up as he heard the bolts being withdrawn, and the keys grate in the locks.

Presently the door swung open, a gleam of light shone in, and he saw in the doorway, with the surly-faced gaoler behind him, the crouched form of his tempter at the tavern, Jonathan Wild.

The thieftaker, whose repute was even then great all over the country, entered with the self-complacent air of one who, conscious of his power, had yet no wish to display it to his prisoner.

When his glance rested on our hero, who had slipped from his perch, and now stood erect in the middle of the cell, a grin of malicious satisfaction flitted across his bloated visage, and an ill-concealed triumph lurked about the corner of his repulsive mouth.

Immediately after, his manner changed, and assuming a cringing obsequious attitude, and a fawning look, he closed the door in the

JONATHAN WILD VISITS TYBURN DICK IN PRISON.

gaoier's face and greeted the youthful prisoner.

"Very sorry to see you here, Dick Wayne; the highway robbery is a serious charge—a very serious charge."

"You knew it was a serious crime when you tempted me to take to the road, did you not?" Dick asked.

"Yes; but to be so unfortunate at the onset. Why, many a dashing fellow has been years on the road, and never got into such a fix as you have."

"Then all I can say is, I hope I may be more lucky for the future."

Jonathan Wild looked sharply in the face of the undaunted boy.

For a second or so his searching orb looked into the fearless eyes of the boy Highwayman.

There was no flinching, no hesitation there.

The thieftaker saw he had tough stuff to work upon.

"He'll be great in his fame some day," he muttered to himself, "and will fetch a high reward. I never saw but one who looked so cool and so perfect a devil, and that's the man I want his help to take. I scarcely expected to meet such mettle, but I must try my luck."

"Dick," he said, slapping him familiarly on the shoulder, "do you know what they will do with you for this night's work? they'll hang you."

"Will they? the fact is not pleasant, and might be expressed in a milder form; a prisoner, however, must not be too particular. Still, I don't think I shall trouble them to shorten my passage to Heaven just yet."

"How? do you hope to escape?"

"Chances don't seem much in my favour, Mr. Wild; these walls are, as my friend below took care to remind me, exceedingly thick; the window is well barred, and outside the wall is too steep for a cat to scramble down; besides, I'm heavily pinioned. Altogether appearances are not in favour of my escape."

"They are not," Wild replied, "and yet it might turn out that you *have* a way to escape —a clear way out of this place—a royal free path to liberty."

Dick laughed, very much to the thieftaker's surprise.

"Mr. Wild," he said, "you tapped me on the shoulder just now, I should feel inclined to do the same for you if these irons would permit me.

"Why?"

"Because just before you came I called upon Fortune to help me out of this mess. You don't present a *very* lively picture of the Dame, but you've come in answer to my appeal, and that's something."

"It is; and what is still more, although I'm not Dame Fortune, I am able to set you free —able to restore you to the 'road' again; there, what do you think of that?"

"Think! why that it's very pleasing intelligence. You're quite a wizard, but as a sample of your power perhaps you wouldn't mind knocking these irons off. I should have more faith then, you know."

He held out his ironed wrists, and laughed sarcastically, as if he thought Wild had come there to fool him.

Jonathan Wild hardly knew what to make of his customer, but he stepped quickly towards him, and said—

"I can do that. More—*I will.* See— here's the first touch of the wizard's magic

He took a bunch of keys from his po and fitted one to the manacles on Dick's

A turn, and they were free.

The irons on Dick's wrists were next fastened.

He withdrew the key, and the heavy links fell, with a ringing clatter, to the floor of the cell.

Dick shook himself, and, with a glad cry stepped free of the glittering manacles.

"Excellent!" he cried. "Now, sir, what next? Am I to direct? If so, I say, let me take your arm, and accompany you from these walls."

Jonathan Wild stepped in his way.

"Not yet, Dick. I'm your friend, as you perceive, and I'm anxious to free you, for I admire your pluck and coolness; but there must be some little agreement made between us, before you breathe the air of liberty again."

"Ah, yes!" Dick exclaimed, stepping back, "There is always a compact to be made, if you have dealings with the devil."

"I'm not the devil, Dick. Come, sit down —you're a young fellow of sense as well as nerve, and can well weigh what I have to say."

Dick handed Wild the stool to sit upon, and squatted on the bench.

Jonathan Wild edged himself closer, and putting his bloated face close to our hero's, laid his brutish hand on Dick's knee, and began—

"It's very hard for a young fellow like you to be put out of the way at the first start. Of course you are quite willing to escape, and of course you know freedom can't be bought without some sacrifice. Captured highwaymen don't expect to be let off."

"The price, huckster, the price," Dick cried; "freedom is at all times a cheap bargain."

"Especially with the black cap and the gibbet in the distance. I thought you would think so. Well, now, Dick, I am able to deliver you out of the gaoler's hands—to set you free, to begin anew your dashing career; but before I do so, you must promise me by every oath you hold sacred—every binding vow, that you will serve me in whatever I require—and once swerve from your oath to me, and, mark my words, in the hap-prest hour of your existence, I would bring you to a malefactor's doom."

"Softly, softly, Mr. Wild; I am not free yet, nor have I taken any oath to serve you."

"But you will—you must—life is to be purchased, and the terms are not high. There is a man whose capture I am resolved upon—betray him to my hands—I ask no more."

"I see—to escape myself, I must put another neck into the noose for you to stretch. Well, well, the name of this unhappy substitute."

"You know him well—he is called Captain Claude."

Dick started.

Backing from the thief-taker as if he had been a venomous snake, he dashed his clenched hands on the hard bench.

"Betray him!" he cried. "Why, you dastard, I would rather a thousand times have my neck wrung like a blind puppy's, than lift a hand to set the hounds of the law on his track."

"It is to save your life. Do not reject my terms—be wise, and take the oath."

"Jonathan Wild," our hero said, rising and looking fixedly in his visitor's bloated face, " when I joined the band of highwaymen, do you know that I took a solemn oath to be of them, flesh and blood; to resist all efforts of their capture; to die, rather than disclose their secret abode; to take the traitor's life, if one should prove false; think you, if I took that oath, I should keep yours, even if I soiled my lips by repeating it after you ?"

"I can make it your interest to do so. You are one of a band of highwaymen—Claude is over you—excepting him, who is there but you who could be king over those men? Remove him from your way, and I can prophesy that time will see you KING OF THE HIGHWAYMEN!"

His tones were low and stealthy.

He had risen, and was now anxiously facing our hero.

Dick stood on his feet also.

While Wild was speaking an angry light gleamed from his dark, expressive eyes, and his voice was stern as he replied, hotly—

"Jonathan Wild, you have set these limbs free, and I'll not make first use of them by knocking you senseless at my feet, as I would have done, had you, under any other circumstances, made this dastardly offer."

"Boy—don't be rash—think well."

"I do—and I refuse. If I am to be King of the Highwaymen, it shall not be by betraying my leader. And hark you, Wild, you could not take a surer means of making me your deadly foe than by seeking to injure Captain Claude."

"Tut, tut, Dick, you are not yourself."

"I am as you will ever find me."

"You're a fool—if I may speak my mind Now listen, Dick. If you refuse, I shall certainly leave you to your fate, and as surely as you stand looking at me now, you will be dead meat on a gibbet before forty-eight hours are over your head."

"Very well; but, Wild, I distinctly refuse—and now relieve me of your company. You have kindly released me of these irons, I thank you. Let them lie there, I shall not allow them to be placed on again."

Jonathan Wild's bloated visage was livid with passion.

"Do you see this ?" he cried, drawing a pistol from his breast pocket. "It is loaded. Make resistance, and you shall have a skull empty of brains."

Dick laughed lightly, as he replied—

"So be it. I may as well be shot as strung up, and I am quite certain that if once those irons shackle me again I shall without doubt be hanged. No, Dame Fortune has granted me my prayer, and I'll not throw her gifts away—I would rather be at your feet, Jonathan Wild, a senseless corpse."

For the first time in his life the thieftaker was puzzled how to act.

There was no mistaking the boy highwayman's determined energy.

His limbs were free.

He meant them to remain so, or to die.

A pause of a few moments ensued, during which the practised man and daring boy looked into each other's eyes.

Slowly and surely one was gaining the victory.

That one was Dick.

The pistol held in the thieftaker's hand, after going so close as almost to touch our hero's forehead, was lowered

athan Wild, with a furtive glance at the fetters, slowly replaced the weapon in his pocket.

He had made up his mind to try a different way of gaining his object.

He would work upon the generosity of the sud-spirited boy.

"Dick," he said, speaking in a more subdued and conciliatory tone, "I should be sorry if your hot-headed obstinacy forced me to act against my wishes. You mistake me. I am still your friend. To prove it, I will leave you for this night unfettered. As to my offer, I'll not take your answer now. Think it over—in the morning I shall be here. I hope then you will have made up your mind to save me the unpleasantness of seeing you marched off to the gallows."

He gave Dick a warning, sinister look, and left him.

The door closed.

Once more our hero was alone.

As soon as he heard the last bolt shot in the socket, Dick removed his feet from off the iron manacles.

"That was a hard fought victory," he mused, "but it turned in my favour at last. The slimy reptile, to urge me to betray my true-hearted captain. Come in the morning, will he? Hope I will have made up my mind to save him the unpleasantness, etc. I hope I may spare him the trouble of seeing me at all. Now to act swiftly. Dame Fortune, you have freed my limbs—it is for me to find my wings and take to flight before the morn."

CHAPTER X.

TYBURN DICK MAKES UP HIS MIND TO ESCAPE. —A PERILOUS POSITION.—OUR HERO LOOKS DOWN UPON THE SLEEPING TOWN.

TWELVE o'clock chimed from the church tower as the footsteps of Jonathan Wild died away.

Dick wasted a whole hour, expecting to be visited by the gaoler; but the thieftaker had evidently satisfied him, for one o'clock rang with startling abruptness on the night air, and still our hero was undisturbed.

The sounds in and about the prison had all died into silence by this time.

Watchers, gaoler, and warder seemed locked in sleep, or quiet on their rounds.

"I must make the most of my time before I am interrupted," thought Dick, as he gazed once more round the bare walls of his prison.

He had taken its bearings before.

There was nothing in its appearance to excite any new hopes in his breast.

The walls were of solid thick masonry, floor was of impervious stone; the door massive, and iron-bound.

There was only the window to give hope.

That small iron grating had been his thought from the moment his limbs were free of their shackles, and now, as if by instinct, his gaze rested on the iron links and chains lying at his feet.

Up to twelve o'clock his cell had been in complete darkness; but since that hour the faint star-gleams had lighted the place dimly, and now the moon rose full, round, and brilliant in the sky, and began to flood his cell with its gladly welcomed light.

Its white glimmer fell upon the shining fetters.

To Dick it seemed as if the rusty bars of the grated window guided the moonbeams on to those irons, to point out to him what useful implements they might be made in effecting his escape.

He picked them up from the floor.

"They are not the best things in the world to help a fellow out," he soliloquised; "but there's nothing better to hand, so I'll try their virtue."

Planting the stool firmly on the oaken bench, he mounted to the loop-hole window, and perching himself in a position that gave him the fullest power, inserted one of the largest iron links under one of the grating bars, and used it as a prise to force it from its socket.

All the strength of his lithe body he threw into the effort; but the grating had been well-fitted, and though he strained every nerve, it resisted all attempts to dislodge it.

In one of his persistent attempts, the bright link snapped suddenly like a bit of glass.

An exclamation of vexation escaped Dick's lips.

He examined the remaining links.

They were all of the same temper, evidently, and appeared likely to go the way of broken one, if he tried them in the same manner.

Pondering what to do next, our hero, scarcely heeding what he was about, picked at the end of the bar with the sharp end of the broken link.

At the first tap, a cry of delight escaped his lips.

A bit of the mortar where the bar was imbedded in the solid wall tumbled out.

The inspiration roused his faculties anew.

Here was the way to overcome his difficulty.

Digging at the dried mortar, he crumbled piece after piece, and at length had the satisfaction of laying bare the end of the bar.

Dick could have laughed outright at this first instalment of success.

Pausing in his work, he wiped the moisture from his brow, and throwing off his coat, he renewed his labour, till a final wrench brought the bar out of its place

Another desperate try, and it came away at the other end.

The boy highwayman flourished it above his head, and gave utterance to a subdued hurrah.

"So much for number one," he cried; "here goes for number two."

Number two was not half so refractory.

He had a new implement now to work with, in the shape of a ponderous bar; and he went to work with a will, now digging into the hard mortar, then using the bar as a lever to wrench its fellow away.

Finding resistance of no further avail, number two came out with a sudden jerk, that nearly sent our adventurous hero over on his back.

Dick did not mind the jerk at all.

Joyfully seizing the bar, he triumphantly placed it on the ledge, and turned his attention to number three.

Number three came out, so did number four; then number five, and lastly number six.

This was the remaining cross bar of the grating, and with something of the delight of a wild Indian, Dick took the six bars in his arms, and leaping from his perch, ran round his cell at least half-a-dozen times.

He was doing a sort of a triumphant war dance over the enemy, in the shape of the dislodged bars, which ended in his depositing them in one corner of the cell, and springing to the now open window.

Big drops of perspiration were by this time running down his face, and his shirt stuck to his skin.

It had been warm work, and he had not paused for rest.

He did not pause now, farther than to wipe his face with his sleeve.

He was too anxious to get a breath of what he fondly believed was the air of liberty.

The opening in the wall afforded just room enough for him to squeeze through, which he quickly did.

First one arm went outside, then his head and shoulders, another arm, he drew his body after it, and with one knee resting on the solid masonry, took his first look out.

The moonlight came full upon the prison wall, and showed him the dizzy height of his position, as its cold beams bathed his reeking temples; but the sensation of comparative liberty, of escape, if only for the time, from his close confinement, was so grateful and joyous, that it was with a delicious feeling of enthralment he gazed upon the outer scene.

It was a witching night.

The moon rode white and peaceful through the heavens, the air was cool and still.

Before him, its tall spire in dark relief against the sky, rose the church steeple.

Beneath him lay the sleeping town, with not a single light in any of the windows, far as his eye could scan.

It was some moments before he ceased taking in the balmy fascination of the scene, and then his reverie was only broken by the iron clamour of the church clock as it chimed again.

First the quarters—then the hours.

One, two.

He had been an hour then loosening the bars.

How much nearer was he now to liberty.

He looked down the steep wall.

The first sight his gaze encountered was a long sharp row of spikes, extending the whole breadth of the wall, about twelve feet below him.

This was not the roof, but merely the projecting ridge, sharply inclined, that even if a prisoner escaped the spikes in jumping which was a moral impossibility, there was no chance of holding on to save himself from the giddy descent.

Deeper down than this bristling *chevaux de frise*, the wall went straight and unbroken to its base.

No intervening roof—no projecting ledge or building, nothing to stop the headlong fall of anyone rash enough to attempt that frightful descent.

Dick drew a prolonged breath.

The reason of the gaoler's satisfaction was plain indeed.

The cell was the highest one in the building.

The prison roof was immediately over Dick's head.

In giving his prisoner an opportunity of passing out, he had done what he knew was best calculated to drive him to madness with the mocking impossibility of escape.

Very grave and thoughtful did our hero's face become, as he slowly drew in his head and body, and looked blankly round his prison.

He wanted something in the way of a rope, then he would not have feared the descent.

It is curious what a little circumstance sometimes influences the affairs of daring men.

Baffled in his first survey of the chance of freedom, it is hard to say whether our hero might not have been rash enough to attempt to clamber to the roof of his prison perhaps to be precipitated headlong to the basement.

But at that very moment he happened to lose his footing and stumble backwards.

The stool slipped from under his feet, and he rolled heavily into one corner of the cell.

Bruised and shaken by his unexpected descent, he was scrambling to his feet, when a remarkable circumstance connected with one of the flag-stones arrested his attention.

It was one of the small flag-stones, and fitted right into the corner of the cell.

His head had gone with a bump against the stone.

So had his elbow.

For the latter tap he was extremely

obliged, for he fancied that there was the least possible shake in the solid floor.

He could have sworn the stone moved.

Dick's nerves were strung to that excited tension which would have stopped at nothing, however marvellous.

He had heard of men who had been imprisoned for months, and had employed their time in fashioning tools from bits of stone and iron, wherewith to effect their release.

In one instance he had been told where a condemned prisoner had manufactured a rope out of his bedding, taking a few strands at a time, till at last the cord was long enough for him to reach the ground safely.

What if some such aids were hidden here.

He sprang on the oaken bench to get the broken link, and hurriedly inserted the end between the stone and the wall.

Joys of joys.

The stone was loose.

It came upon one end suddenly, and Dick tore it out with eager hands, while with bated breath he gazed into the hole underneath.

The dirt had been scooped out, perhaps a handful at a time, to be thrown out of the loophole window, and in the cavity, partly covered with loose earth, lay coiled what Dick was more rejoiced to see than a heap of shining emeralds.

The Open Sesame to liberty, a rope!

Of very rude construction it was, and had been fashioned from the roughest materials, shreds of cloth, strippings of mats, and in some places human hair formed its strands, but so well woven that it did not stretch in the least, when Dick, with a scarcely suppressed cry of triumph, dragged it forth and tried its strength.

Yards and yards of it.

He flung the coils far, and with his eyes blazing with daring pleasure, as he measured its length.

Hurriedly he coiled it over his arm, and stooping down again examined the hole.

There was a bit of rusty tin bent up at one end, and the broken blade of a knife, also very rusty, having apparently lain long in their concealment.

And scratched on one side of the gap in which the stone fitted, Dick read by the light of the moon these few words—

"Nearly long enough to reach the ground; one more night's work, and then if I can baffle their vigilance, the grating shall no longer bar my flight to liberty and life."

Nothing more—no signature or name.

Poor prisoner.

That one more night had never come—he had failed for a few more hours—failed after all his many nights of toil—failed when freedom appeared within his reach.

Dick sighed, and putting back the knife and bit of tin, replaced the stone.

He did not want those articles, nor could he conceive what use they could have been to the former and unfortunate tenant of the cell.

He wanted only the rope.

He hugged it to his breast—he could have kissed its coils.

Dame Fortune had indeed been kind, and removed every obstacle in the way of his exit from that prison.

"See what it is to have good heart in trouble," Dick cried; "had I yielded to my fate, I should have been lost. Now the path is open that leads to safety."

He started suddenly as he was stepping towards the window.

A heavy tread resounded in the corridor.

It advanced towards his cell.

Dick stood for the moment paralysed, as the truth flashed upon him.

The gaoler was coming to pay him a visit.

At the very instant when he was contemplating his flight.

The steps came nearer.

Another moment, and the door might be flung open, discovering him, as he stood with the rope coiled round his arm, the broken links at his feet, and the displaced bars flung at one end of the cell.

Wild thoughts flashed through Dick's brain.

Should he allow the gaoler to enter, and spring at his throat to choke the cry of alarm?

Or should he conceal the rope, replace the bars, and affect to be asleep?

Had he time?

It was worth the risk.

Like lightning he sprang up with the bars in his arms, and hastily fitted them in the gaps whence he had torn them.

There was a chance the gaoler might see them.

The footsteps stopped outside the door.

Dick thrust the rope inside his shirt, and rapidly slipped on his coat.

The bolts were noisily drawn

He gathered the links up, and laying them on the bench, flung himself full length upon them, as the key grated in the lock, and the door swung slowly on its hinges.

He was not mistaken.

The gaoler had come to pay him a last visit.

Dick closed his eyes as his lamp lighted up the cell.

His pulses were throbbing violently, and big drops of sweat beaded his brow.

But it was necessary he should seem asleep.

His right hand grasped the heavy iron links, ready to brain the gaoler if he should make the dreaded discovery.

Mark Napper looked as if he had just roused himself out of a cozy snooze.

His eyes were gummed up, and his aspect was otherwise sleepy.

He had brought a jug of water and part of a loaf, and setting both down on the stone floor, he turned his light on the boy highwayman's face.

"Asleep, eh!" he growled surlily; "aha, my fine young devilskin, you won't have many more nights' sleep, I'll warrant. I'll be 'squared,' and Jack Ketch will settle your hash for good. 'Taint my will you've got them irons off, but they'll be on again tomorrow, that's one comfort, and I'll see if I can't find a heavier set. Hi! wake up, you young vagabone, will you!"

He bellowed this out gruffly, and took a step nearer our hero.

It required all Dick's nerve to prevent him springing at the gaoler's throat.

He thought he was betrayed.

Starting up, with the assumed surprise of one disturbed in a deep sleep, he looked drowsily in the gaoler's face.

"Wake up, and be d—d to you," bawled that functionary, "and don't keep me bawling at you all night. There's your allowance—bread and water—I forgot it before. You can make up for lost time now—you won't want much more of anything, that's one comfort, you young gallows bird."

Scowling upon the youthful highwayman, he backed out of the cell, pulling the door to after him.

Once more bolts and locks shot home.

Then the gaoler's footsteps died away along the stone passage.

CHAPTER XI.

TYBURN DICK PEEPS OUT AGAIN—THE WATCHER ON HIS ROUNDS—"ALL'S WELL, THREE O'CLOCK AND A CLOUDY MORN"—THROWING A LINE FOR LIFE AND FREEDOM.

NOT quite sure but that the gaoler or some one of his myrmidons might yet be watching him, our hero made a pretence of rubbing his eyes, and although his heart was beating wildly with excitement, lay down and stretched himself out as if for sleep.

His precautions were not uncalled for.

In a minute or two he heard a stealthy step creep on tiptoe away.

One of the warders had accompanied the gaoler and had stayed outside to listen.

Satisfied that all was safe, he now retired, and Dick was again left to himself.

He still lay quietly on the bench.

He had two reasons for not making his hazardous venture yet.

The first was that some of the warders might still be going their rounds.

The second was that the moon was on the wane, and in less than another hour comparative darkness would reign over the sleeping city.

It would be a more perilous descent in the dark, but to be seen would be certain death.

The moonlight cast its last white gleam on a gap in the wall.

A deep shadow hid every part of his cell.

Now was his time.

He rose, and creeping quietly to the door, listened at the key-hole.

Not a sound, not the faintest echo or whisper, as lightly he stepped back again and went to the window.

Very softly he took down the bars one by one, and laid them in the corner of the cell.

Then he sprang to the window, and took a brief survey.

A second's thought, and he leapt softly down again.

Taking two of the iron bars, he tied them cross-wise with one end of the rope, so that they would go across the loophole inside.

There was nothing else he could secure the rope to, and having seen that the knot was fast, he again mounted to the window.

The iron bars fixed themselves, as was anticipated, and with the rope over his shoulder, and the coil under his arm, he clambered out.

A change had taken place since he went out one hour ago.

The moon had waned; black clouds hid the light of the stars; a chill wind had begun to blow.

Clinging fast to the rope with both hands, he slid quietly down to the stone ridge, and planted a foot each side of the bristling spikes.

With a rapid twist he coiled the rope round the spikes, drawing it tight against the wall.

This formed a support for him to hold on to by the left hand, while he peered out to see what should next be done.

It had evidently been the intention of the prisoner whose untiring perseverance fashioned the rope, to descend by it to the prison's base.

Our hero did not relish the idea of dropping so close to the gaol precincts.

He had formed another purpose, which was to throw the rope across to the houses, and make it fast somewhere on the roof.

It was a daring enterprise; the very thought in having to cross to the tower suspended by a single thread-like rope, which might snap with his weight, or slip at either end, was enough to make the hair stand on end.

Life seemed to hang on so slender a chance.

But to our hero, to conceive was to dare.

He knew that if he could accomplish that perilous passage, the rest would be comparatively easy; and nerving himself for the hazard, he balanced himself against the wall, whilst his glances moved to the houses beneath him, in quest of a fitting place for the rope to catch.

Hitherto, no sound had come upon the still night air; but at this juncture, there rose audibly from below the echoes of a heavy tread, tramping along the silent street.

Dick listened—every nerve strained to agonising tension.

It was the watchman going his round.

Almost underneath the prison wall he paused.

Dick's heart throbbed quicker.

Was he to be discovered—was he to be driven to take that headlong descent and trust the fortunes of that thrilling venture ?

Hark !

Deep, sonorous tones.

The watchman's drawling voice—

"All's well ! Three o'clock and a cloudy morn. Three, and a cloudy morn—all's well ! "

The sleepy echoes died away.

Tramp, tramp, tramp.

The watchman went on his round.

One—two—three !

The slow chimes rang out from the clock-tower of the ancient church.

All was still again.

The watchman's tread had gone out of hearing.

" *Now !*" cried Dick, in a deeply-thrilling tone of voice.

Daring resolve !

His nimble fingers quickly knotted the end of the rope.

Balanced well on his dangerous resting-place, he strained every nerve.

He had often cast a line out to sea—often when the sea-tossed barque had threatened to founder in the raging surf—often had his athletic skill and unerring eye availed, when life seemed lost.

Now it was to be tried for his own life.

Whizz !

A swift hurl ; the rope shot through the air ; coil after coil went out with frightful velocity ; and then came a jerking snap that made Dick's brain for the first time dizzy.

He had thrown the rope lasso fashion, that is to say, with the end curled so that it would whirl round the first obstacle with which it came in contact.

The mark was the chimney stack of a large mansion opposite.

If it sped true to its aim, all would be well so far.

The dangers he risked were, that the jerk of throwing the rope would hurl him from where he stood, that some of the coils would entangle in his limbs, and whirl him to destruction, and cause the cord to fall short, and snap like a thread.

All the muscular powers of his body were thrown into play as the rope sped from his hold.

Then, pale and haggard, with head swimming and heart benumbed, he leaned against the wall, clinging to the short length of rope tied from the window to the spikes.

A moment, and he rocked reeling on his treacherous foothold.

Is he falling ?

Is he to go headlong down that fearful abyss ?

No !

Hurrah !

He is safe.

The rope has gone true as an arrow to its mark and has hitched itself.

A slack line hangs between him and the opposite side of the tower, bridging the chasm beneath.

CHAPTER XII.

CROSSING THE LINE AND WHERE IT LEADS.

A SUBDUED exclamation of gratefulness escaped our hero's lips.

His eyes were moist.

That crisis was happily passed.

Now to try the rope, and see if it has caught well enough to bear his weight on his perilous venture.

Sliding down, he got his body between the wall and the line of spikes, and lying at full length, pulled the rope to the utmost of his strength.

It held firmly, and setting his lips together with unquailing determination, he got over the spikes and trusted himself on the slender line.

As soon as it felt his clinging weight, the rope began to slacken, so much so, that Dick began to apprehend it would part suddenly, and slip from his hold.

A frightful fate menaced him if that catastrophe occurred.

Either he must fall mangled to the ground, or swing back against the prison wall, and be dashed therefrom, bruised and mangled, to the stones beneath.

He would not trust himself to look down the gloomy chasm over which he hung ; but keeping his eyes fixed on the other end of the rope, began the thrilling passage.

His progress was horrifyingly slow.

One hand had to be shifted at a time, and during each interval his whole weight dragged heavily on the one hand that clutched the rope.

Slowly, laboriously, he made his way along.

To all intents and purposes he might have closed his eyes.

It was useless looking upon the rope.

He was too far out now to save himself should the slender cord part asunder, or slip from its hitch.

On, on—inch by inch—grip by grip.

A cold, clammy perspiration oozed out at every pore.

His finger ends were becoming slippery, but with terrible tenacity he clutched the thread of life.

His teeth were hard set.

His eyes fixed in a cold fierce stare.

Come what might, he was committed to his fate.

The tension of the rope was not yet at an end.

It grew slacker with each movement, and now began to swing ominously to and fro, threatening with its vibration to shake off his fierce grasp.

He had accomplished half the passage.

Midway between the prison and the houses, he rocked to and fro above an awful gulf, gloomy, horrible, and deep.

The black sky lowered overhead; the dull flag-stones of the city gleamed beneath.

The strains on his limbs appeared to force his arms from their sockets.

His grasp was getting treacherous—unsafe.

It seemed he must fall, if once he loosened either hold, yet he dared not rest.

On, slowly, tortuously slow; hand over hand.

His veins swelled to bursting; his muscles strained to exhaustion; his chest drawn up; his breath coming in short suffocating gasps; a chilly tremour at his heart.

The church clock chimed the quarter.

Fifteen weary minutes had he clung to that swaying rope—to cling another quarter of an hour was beyond his powers.

A desperate effort must be made.

Resting for one moment, with both arms crossed round the rope, he drew a deep inspiration.

Then, swiftly passing hand over hand, he clambered along the other end of the rope.

That sudden impulse got him over the worst part of his perilous journey.

The line had stretched so, that it hung below the level of the houses, and now he could use his knees and ankles to help him in the ascent.

Joy, joy—delicious, delicious joy.

The stonework of the houses came nearer, nearer—almost within his eager grasp.

Hark!

A sudden cry of alarm.

Dick paused to hear.

It came from the opposite side, and his heart thrilled as he realised its meaning.

He was betrayed.

No mistaking the tones or the words.

"Help, help! Ho there! Open the prison. Quick, your prisoner has escaped!"

Like lightning, the idea flashed to Dick's mind that the rope would be cut, in the hopes of precipitating him to the ground.

He gathered his nigh-spent strength, and, with new-found energy, literally flew up the remaining lengths of rope.

A swift furious bound, and he stood eager and panting on the roof of the house.

Safe!

For he feared no enemies now.

With almost ecstatic wildness he unhitched the cord and flung it back towards the prison.

As it whirled across, a tumultuous uproar arose on the air.

"That's him—he'll escape. Bring him down. Fire!"

A pistol flashed.

The report rang startlingly on the night air

The bullet whizzed among the house tops.

Dick stood erect and fearless for his foes to take a look at him.

"Ha, ha! he cried. "Free, free! TAKE ME WHO DARE!"

His voice rang clear above the hubbub beneath the prison walls.

It was too dark for him to see how near his pursuers were, or to judge if they saw him.

He was equally heedless of both.

All the rich blood of his body was tingling in his veins—the result of the reaction from the tension of his nerves during that hazardous feat of rope climbing.

Flinging back upon them a cry of defiance, he bounded along the roof, and taking a terrific leap through the air, alighted on the top of another house, as the cries and noise from the prison told him the alarm was given to rouse the whole town and effect his capture.

Critical as his position was, our hero paused on this second roof to deliberate.

The baying of the human bloodhounds fell distinctly on his ear.

He had safely passed through such frightful peril that he felt disposed to defy their power to take him now.

"No," he cried, "they'll not take me now. Were I to fall into their hands, after an escape like *this*, I should indeed lose faith in that kind fortune which has carried me successfully through every evil. I must not, however, be seen here. How these fellows howl —aha! my escape must tickle their nerves a bit. Let me see—where is the best hiding-place to be found?"

He leant forward and peeped over the other side of the roof.

The house he was now on had a large garden in rear, and less than half-way down at the back was a small balcony before one of the windows.

" A piece of that rope would be my friend now," Dick mused. "No matter, I must contrive without it. It is fortunate I have had some practice in climbing."

Slipping over the roof, he clung by both hands to the ledge.

His feet almost rested on the side of one of the upper windows.

The blind was drawn back; the window was unfastened; no one dreaming that any attempt at entry would be made at that height.

Still holding by one hand above, Dick with the other clutched the brickwork at the side, and let himself softly down.

He had leaned against the sash to keep himself from falling or going through the panes of glass.

Avoiding either mischance, he softly opened the window and peered in.

There was a bed in the room, and two night-capped heads appeared half smothered by the bed clothes.

One was unmistakably a female's—the other looked more suspiciously masculine — but our hero had no reason to concern himself about the matter.

The object of his entrance there was to find something in the way of a rope by which he could slip to the balcony beneath.

The only thing likely to serve his purpose and lying within his reach was a quilt, thrown over a chair under the window, as if removed from the bed by a pair of turtle doves lying there in each other's arms.

Not deeming it prudent to venture in and search for articles more suitable to his purpose, Dick, taking the goods the gods, or Dame Fortune provided, put in his arm and pulled out the quilt.

Then noiselessly he drew the window close

The precious pair in the bed stirred at that moment—doubtless disturbed by the slight noise he made.

Dick heard a muffled voice, then a sounding kiss, succeeded by words that left no doubt on his mind that one of the gorgeous man-servants had stolen amorously to the chamber of Mary, Jane, or Susan, and being willingly received by the frail fair one, was solacing himself with the soft delights of love.

Outside the window were wooden shutters —old fashioned, but strongly secured.

Taking the counterpane cornerwise, Dick drew it through the lower bars of the shutter, and holding both ends firmly, slid adroitly down.

He was now a few feet from the balcony, and letting go one end of the quilt, he dropped lightly on his feet, at the same time drawing it from beneath the shutters.

The windows he now stood in front of, opened like folding doors ; unlike those above, they were fastened inside, and our hero was wondering who was the occupant of the chamber, when the spring of a rattle in front of the house sent an electric shock through his frame.

Was he seen?

No time then for thought.

He must dare the worst.

Putting his shoulder against the glass doors, he forced them apart, and sprang within the chamber.

As he did so, a sharp frightened scream from a female's lips rose from inside.

Then again the watchman's rattle sprung.

It was answered by an another, and a loud voice cried—

"This way. We're sure to take him. He can't escape. Remember, the reward's the whether we take him dead or alive!"

CHAPTER XIII.

IN A LADY'S CHAMBER.— SEARCH FOR A HIGHWAYMAN.

PRETTY Ruth May, after witnessing our hero led away to prison, and as she supposed, an ignominious death, retired sadly to her chamber, and dispensing with the attendance of her maid, locked herself in to her own reflections.

The youthful highwayman had made a deep impression on her mind.

His gallant bearing, and graceful, handsome figure, charmed her romantic imagination, and when she thought of the fearful death to which he was doomed, she gave way to tears.

It was late before she sought the solace of her couch, and even after she had thrown her beautiful form on her soft bed of down, it was many hours ere she fell asleep.

Then her dreams were troubled.

She was with the boyish highwayman.

His mask was off and she had fallen deeply in love with his handsome countenance.

They were at a grand assembly, and he was more richly dressed than any of the gallants who sought to pay her their attentions.

Suddenly she found herself with him on a balcony overlooking a moonlit cliff.

While listening to his dreamy words of love, she lost her footing, and fell down the giddy steep.

But in the terrific descent she was caught his arms and saved.

Then she stood beside him on the heath.

It was night.

Inky blackness hid the view.

black steed, with fire leaving its was impatiently pawing the ground.

she was wondering if she were the youthful adventurer lifted her s, and sprang to his horse's back.

tant after they were speeding air on the phantom horse at such eed that her senses reeled, and to be put down.

The boy highwayman smiled upon her, but as he smiled his face took the looks of a demon; his eyes flashed fire upon her—his lips wreathed in a sardonic smile of triumph, and as he was pressing her in his embrace she awoke.

Awoke with a slight start and looked around.

Her dream had been so vivid that she could scarcely believe she was alone.

Her heart beat wildly, and raising herself on one arm, she looked about the chamber.

A small gilded lamp was gleaming on a little table by the bedside.

Her various articles of dress lay undisturbed.

She peered behind the rich hangings of velvet and gold to see that no one was hidden there.

It was at this moment that, without any previous warning, the casement windows were dashed open, and our hero sprang into the room.

Then that swift shriek left her lips, and she put out her fair arms to keep off the apparition of her dream.

Dick stood mute with surprise at finding himself in the chamber of the judge's ward.

He recognised her at the first glance, and the recognition sent a strange thrill through his heated veins. She looked, if possible, more lovely than when he saw her in the coach.

Perhaps the interesting position in which he beheld her heightened her charms.

She was half raised from the pillows; her rich purple black hair floated about her fair shoulders; her soft throat showed its dazzling whiteness, relieved by the lace of her night robe; her beautifully rounded arms were bare, as she held them supplicatingly towards him; her face was pale with alarm, but her eyes—those black eyes by which he had first recognised her—fascinated him with their startled gaze of wildness.

On her part, Ruth gave herself no time for thinking.

She knew our hero as soon as she saw him; for in the tussle at the carriage door his mask had got displaced.

Remembering his open countenance, she realized, too truly, why he was there; but

TYBURN DICK IN THE LADY'S BEDROOM.

the one idea that pervaded her mind was that a highwayman was alone with her in her chamber.

So, without giving a thought to his danger, she uttered another loud cry of fear, and exclaimed—

"Who are you—why come you here? Help! help!"

With our hero, action was an instinct.

He never stayed long to consider the consequences.

Perhaps he would rather have burst into any other chamber than pretty Ruth's; but being there, and with his safety depending on

her silence, he determined to make the best of the case.

His first act was to close the window of her casement, and draw the thick curtains.

Then he faced the trembling girl.

"Lady," he said, "I am that unfortunate and guilty being whom your guardian handed over to justice some few hours ago. They loaded me with manacles, but I am here, as you see—escaped."

"Escaped from prison? Poor fellow, what sufferings he must have undergone."

So thought fair Ruth, but modesty prevailed

over her womanly tenderness, and in a voice half hushed with horror, she cried—

" Sir, sir! you cannot stay here. Fly! Do not dishonour me by your presence in my chamber."

Dick folded his arms.

" Lady," he said, and his rich tones went direct to Ruth's sensitive heart, " when they placed heavy manacles on my wrists and limbs, and caged me in a cell so high, that from my grated windows I could just see the top of the church steeple, I thought my position perilous enough. I have managed to break from my prison, but here in a lady's chamber, I stand in greater peril, aye, greater than when I looked down upon the sleeping town from the hole I made in my prison wall— looked down with only a slender rope between me and a horrible death."

" Alas, alas," Ruth moaned, sobbing, and in tears, " why did you venture here?"

" On my sacred word, I knew not this was your chamber. By accident, not by design, I reached the roof above, thence I slid down to your balcony, and now I am here, for you to save, or give to death."

" Oh, sir," Ruth cried, " be generous, be merciful. Do not ask me to shield you. I cannot. Hark! The house is alarmed. Fly, or you must be taken."

" I hear them," Dick answered, " the house is alarmed—alarmed by your cries. Well lady, either I must be taken, or I must find a hiding-place. Will you give me refuge here?"

" I cannot, I dare not," gasped Ruth, " oh do not urge it. It is unmanly. Hark! they come nearer. You are wasting precious moments. I beseech you to begone. If you are seen here, I am lost for ever."

" Fear not. I'll not compromise you. There's time enough for me to spring outside your window when they knock at your door. Do you bid me do so?"

" Alas, what can I do, unhappy youth?"

" You can save or doom me. My life is in your hands. Listen. You hear those yelling hounds outside. They are my pursuers, ready to bring me down like a riddled squirrel the instant I show myself on your balcony."

A clamour of voices rose on the air—the cries and oaths of the prison officials and officers of justice.

Ruth shuddered

" What have you done," she cried, " to be hunted to death like this?"

" Enough to justify my doom in the law's sight, and call my murder a legal death."

Hasty footsteps were heard on the stairs as Dick spoke.

Ruth uttered an agonised cry.

" Oh, fly," she cried, " they will enter here, for the love of heaven go! If I dared——"

" Enough," Dick answered, " I have begged my life, you shall see how I can yield it without fear, for I'll not be taken alive; no, on your balcony they shall find me, a mark for their bullets. Listen, lady, when you hear them fire, and if I give so much as a sigh when the leaden missiles stretch me low, believe me to have been as I have seemed, a worthless coward!

He sprang towards the window.

His hands were on the casement, when a faint whispered cry from Ruth bade him pause.

" Hold," she cried, in an anguished whisper, " I cannot give you to death, I will shield you, even with my honour."

" Not so," Dick replied, " I thank you for your generous offer, but I'll not accept life as the price of your fair name. No, by this act, in which I give myself to my yelling foes, I will leave you to think better of me. Farewell!"

He wrenched open the casement and sprang to the balcony.

A moment more, with defiant scorn, he would have been facing his pursuers, but ere he stood erect, a small soft hand clutched him by the shoulder and dragged him back.

Scarcely believing his senses, he turned and beheld Ruth, pale as death and shivering from head to foot, standing beside him, in her *robe de nuit.*

Horror and fright at the thought of being the instrument of his fate had deprived her of the power of speech, and, as the only means of saving him, she sprang from her bed and plucked him from the balcony.

Now she stood in her virgin purity at his mercy, but thinking nothing of herself, only thinking of the life she could not see sacrificed.

As Dick gazed silently in her blanched

agonised face, some one knocked loudly at her door.

Dick started, and Ruth reeled as if stricken.

"Too late—too late," she murmured hoarsely, "we are lost—lost!"

The voice of the judge was heard from the outside bidding her to open the door.

Then came a loud cry from below.

"Ready, men; watch the balcony. Shoot him down when he appears. Open there, let us into your house. Dead or alive we're to take the highwayman!"

CHAPTER XIV.

AN ADVENTURE ON THE ROAD—HOW DEVIL DUKE MAKES A BARGAIN—A STRANGE SCENE—INTERRUPTION AT THE BALL—A WOMAN'S DEVOTION, AND ARREST OF A DARING HIGHWAYMAN.

THE night was peaceful and quiet.

The moonbeams lit up the peaceful highway, and revealed the form of a dashing, reckless fellow, mounted on a sleek, graceful animal, proudly cantering along beneath the branches of the overhanging trees.

"Now, Rosebud, my beauty, what do you say to go a little faster?" said the rider, patting the noble creature on the neck.

As though it understood what its master said, she threw up her head and commenced to trot.

"That's right, my beauty, we must have some fun to-night. The road is very quiet down this part; it may be more lively ere long—what do you say, eh, Rosebud?"

Rosebud neighed, as though she was of her master's opinion.

The rattling of wheels indicated the approach of a coach, or some other such vehicle, as was used in those days for the conveyance of lonely travellers with plenty of hard cash.

Rosebud and her rider disappeared behind a high hedge, where they waited quietly for the four-wheeled rumbler.

The sound grew nearer, and the horses' heads were the first to appear, as they lumbered up a steep slope, pulling a very quaint old brougham behind them.

A drowsy, red-faced, bloated coachman sat on the box, with the reins held firmly, while behind, asleep wrapped closely in a

thick rug, was a pampered groom, with his arms folded across his breast, and his head bobbing up and down as though it did not belong to him.

The jaded horses came to a sudden halt, when Rosebud and her rider bounded from the hedge like a phantom, and stood before them.

The coach stopped with a jerk, and the pampered nose of the flunkey came in contact with the back of the coach.

The force of the blow made his head rebound, and he went rolling backwards out of his seat, and laid in the road, yelling.

During this time, the coachman had sidled off his perch, and got inside his box, out of the way of the shining pistol tube, that was held in a straight line with his nose.

"Why the deuce, coachman, don't you go on?" said a conceited coxcomb, putting his head out of the carriage window.

"My dear sir, the coachman is nervous, and wisely got out of the way," said the highwayman, riding round to the coach window; "be kind enough to put your head in."

The head went in with a howl.

A timid scream followed the howl, as the trembling fop spluttered out—

"It—is—a—hi—high—way—man, my de—dear——"

"Yes, sir, I am a highwayman of his majesty's highway, and would trouble you for your toll fare."

"But—but, my good fellow, I never pay toll."

"Do you not?"

"No."

"Then you will pay now to make a beginning."

"My good fellow, be kind enough to let me proceed. I may see you again some other night, then you shall have anything you require."

"Probably."

"But you will let us proceed now. We are going to a ball, and the lady will be greatly disappointed if we are late. Meet me as we return."

"Thank you," said the reckless fellow, "the lady shall not be late, and you may meet us as we return."

The coxcomb howled despairingly at the

.n taking his lady to the ball.

"Shall I assist you to alight?" asked the highwayman coolly, as he opened the door.

"No," said the fop, trembling, while the lady was laughing merrily at the fear her beau exhibited, and in her heart she wished the handsome highwayman would take her to the ball, and roll the fear-stricken cur in the ditch.

The highwayman quickly went round to the other side of the coach, and letting down the window, he dismounted and presented a pistol at the young lordling's head.

"I will trouble you to alight without my aid since you refused my offer," he said.

The sight of the gleaming tube made the young lordling shriek, and rolling down the steps he laid in the gutter.

Bowing gracefully to the lady, who smiled in a most amiable manner as the roving highwayman approached her, Devil Duke (such was the name of the daring knight of the road) said—

"May I, dear lady, have the delightful pleasure of dancing with you before yon valiant chevalier escorts you to the ball?"

"I fear, sir, we should get on badly without my music," she answered, in a sweet encouraging voice.

"Then, sweet lady, we will defer it."

A light of disappointment shone in her soft blue eyes as he kissed her hand and closed the carriage door.

Devil Duke then lifted the trembling coxcomb up by the collar and stood him on his feet, but he doubled up and fell to the earth again with a groan, as though suddenly attacked with the cholera.

"My lord is not well," said the highwayman, to the lady, "I will escort you to the ball."

My lord soon recovered when he heard Devil Duke's proposition, and sprang to his feet.

"By Jove, I never saw a fellow recover quicker in my life," said Devil Duke, stepping into the carriage.

The young lord rushed at the highwayman, and tugged at his coat-tail.

The next instant Devil Duke was sitting on the ground.

"That was kind," he said, getting up, "and clever. Oblige me with that diamond pin."

The lord did not see it, and sneaked into the carriage.

Devil Duke lifted him out, and placed the cold barrel of a pistol in his ear.

"That diamond pin, as I before said, also those brilliant rings that adorn those mongrel fingers; the watch with that superb chain, and lastly, your heavy purse."

The young lord howled when the highwayman concluded his demands; the idea of parting with his treasured jewels was something awful; the jewels that he only wore when with his lady love.

"You are nervous my lord, and my finger is on the trigger of my pistol, and if you tremble much more I can't be answerable for the bullet leaving the barrel of my pistol, which is in your ear. I only tell you in case of an accident."

The trembling cur turned a ghastly hue, and big drops of perspiration rolled down his face.

"You had better give me those things which I asked for; I shan't be able to keep my finger steady much longer."

The terror-stricken lord took the hint and dropped the valuables into the highwayman's hand, groaning miserably as he parted with each article.

"Thank you, my lord," said Devil Duke, eyeing the purse of gold. "I will now trouble you for the order for the ball, then I may say my demands are at an end for this evening."

Plainly seeing by the look in the highwayman's eye that resistance would be useless, he produced it with a heavy sigh.

"That will be all, thank you," said the highwayman, "and to keep you from being plundered, I will put you out of harm's way, and call for you as I return. You need not look so scared. It is all right."

Dragging the pampered flunkey, who had left off yawning, and was now rubbing his bruised swelling member, to where his master laid groaning, he tied them back to back, drawing the young lordling's hands over the shoulders of the gorgeous, he bound their wrists together under the flunkey's chin,

Serving the other in the same way, he twisted a long cord round them, from their necks to their feet, and then rolled them into a ditch, where he left them.

The wicked young lady had witnessed the whole of the amusing scene, and had laughed until her sides ached, and the water streamed down her eyes.

Devil Duke lugged the sneaking coachman out of his box by his hair, and made him drive on.

The gallant highwayman would have sat with the lady inside the brougham, but he was deprived of that luxury by having Rosebud with him, so he had to be contented with riding beside the window, where they held a very interesting conversation, which made his heart melt, and the lady's beat much quicker than lady's hearts beat in general, not that we wish to say anything about what was said.

But when the brougham drew up in front of a large mansion, that was brilliantly lighted up, and the low rich strains of music floated through the air, the lady's face flushed with excitement, and she looked wickedly at her companion as she alighted, and squeezed his arm.

The highwayman squeezed her's in return, stooped and kissed her.

He whispered in her ear as they entered, looking very happy—

"You will keep your promise."

He received another squeeze on the arm in the affirmative.

Many merry looking guests cordially greeted the young lady, and looked curiously at her dashing companion.

Many a fair bosom heaved, and many pretty faces flushed beneath the thick layer of powder as their eyes fell upon the handsome features and well-proportioned form of the stranger ; envious looks, and many whispered words passed between the fair group, as Devil Duke strode through the long hall with his fair companion clinging fondly on his arm.

Suddenly the band struck up a lively dance, and in a minute the gay revellers were whirling past each other in couples. A shriek rang through the long hall that made every one stop on the instant.

Devil Duke drew his trembling companion

closely to his breast with his left hand, and drawing his majestic figure to its full height, his broad chest expanded, and his brow knitted. With a determined look on his face, he unsheathed his sword and waited for the officers as they rushed yelling, with the victimised dandy and muddy footman at their head.

Devil Duke had not proceeded far, when the clatter of approaching horses broke upon the discomfitted dandy's ear. Howling miserably to attract the attention of the horsemen, he tried to raise himself up, but failed, and in his endeavour, he drove the face of the pampered flunkey deep into the slimy mud.

The officers, for they were officers, and at least a dozen in number, heard the cry for help, and dismounting, they assisted the miserable wretches out, and unbound them.

The young lordling related the whole of the adventure to the officers, who went immediately in the track of the highwayman.

Devil Duke was not at all surprised when he saw the young lordling enter with the officers at his back.

"You can keep off," he said coolly, as the officers clustered round him.

"You are our prisoner," said a stalwart officer, with a huge horse pistol in his hand, assuming more authority than was his.

"Indeed."

"Seize him men."

"The men had better keep off if they know what is good for their health."

They knew what was good for their health, and kept off.

The leader grew exasperated, and threatened to shoot his eleven comrades with two pistols.

The men were frightened at the threat, and fearing the consequence, they closed round their prisoner.

A desperate struggle took place between them.

The highwayman had very little chance of getting away from his assailants while his fair companion clung despairingly around his neck, but in the struggle two of the officers came rather close to his sword, and they fell to the floor howling.

The young dandy tried to take his lady love from the highwayman's arms, but she did not like the idea of leaving the dashing fellow and clung more tightly to him, Devil Duke put his foot in the young lordling's chest, and sent him sprawling amongst the group of astonished guests.

"We've had enough of your pranks lately, my cheerful kiddy," said the commanding officer, "you had better come quietly, or it'll be worse for yer."

"Stand aside," the highwayman said angrily. Then turning to the lady in a softer voice said—"Come, Cecily, you must leave me now. I must go with these bloodhounds. Fear not, they won't keep me long."

"Won't we," said the officer, looking incredulously at the daring speaker.

"Silence, hound."

The officer winced and stepped back.

"No, no," said the lady pouting, "I won't leave you, if they take you they shall take me."

"Yes, men, take her," shouted the young lordling, almost beside himself at seeing the worthlessness of his intended bride.

"Now, my kiddy, we'll have the bracelets on yer," remarked the officer, producing the handcuffs.

"Will we?" said Devil Duke, between his teeth.

"Yes."

"Try it."

"Put out yer paws."

He did.

The officer went reeling over as the paws lodged between his eyes.

Devil Duke was seized from behind, borne to the ground, and the lady was torn from him.

His hands were secured behind him with the handcuffs; then he was led away between the gang of grinning officers.

The fair Cecily struggled with her captors to break away as the officers reached the door with their prisoner. A glad cry escaped her lips, and she bounded forward and threw her arms round the highwayman's neck with a determined resolve to be taken with him.

"It will be madness for you to suffer with me," said Devil Duke.

"It may be, but what you have to suffer, I suffer also."

Finding that his persuasions were of no avail, he said no more.

He was then triumphantly led away by his captors, the faithful girl following by his side.

CHAPTER XV.

SWIG AND BIG BULLSKIN OVERHEAR AN INTERESTING CONVERSATION, AND SCARE THE OFFICERS—THE KEYS OF THE ROUNDHOUSE—THE PRISONER'S SURPRISE AND JOLLIFICATION.

INFORMATION of the highwayman's capture was soon conveyed to the highwaymen's haunt.

Swig and Big Bullskin being the only two there, besides those on sentry, when the sad news was brought, they resolved to discover where their comrade had been taken.

Being boon companions, the dwarf and giant sallied forth together on their expedition of discovery, disguised.

"I'll smash the first officer I see," remarked Swig emphatically.

"If you do that you'll make a mess," laughed Big Bullskin, looking down on his little companion.

"What are you laughing at, eh?"

"Your rash remark."

"Well, don't laugh at me, you ugly helephant."

"Ha, ha, ha."

"I'll—I'll," said Swig foaming with rage, "I'll smash you too."

"Ha, ha, ha—ha, ha, ha!" laughed the other, amused at his little companion's wrath and indignation, "why, you little sprat, I could swallow you without boiling."

"Could yer, take that, and bolt me afterwards."

He got it.

A smack in the eye, and a vicious dig in the wind, and Bullskin rolled over.

Swig rushed upon him with a torrent of abuse.

"Hush, Swig," said his companion.

Swig was subdued on the instant, and listened attentively.

"Some one comes," said Big Bullskin, "let us hide."

They were now in a forest, and hiding themselves in a cluster of trees waited for the approaching persons.

"Are you going to see 'em scragged, Joe?"

"Who?" asked the worthy Joe.

"Why them cussed highwaymen, to be sure."

"I didn't know we had got any."

"Why yes, I should say we had, we cotched one to-night when he was playing his pranks at a ball."

"Did yer?" asked Joe, getting interested.

"I should say so. Some of our blokes has gone after some more, we means to have 'em all soon."

"Do yer," said Swig, nudging his companion, "I thinks they is wrong."

"Yes, so do I," answered Bullskin, in a whisper, "and they'll soon find it out."

Swig sniggered with delight; he knew his companion meant to play them a trick.

"I say, Bill, what's the name of the coon you cotched to-night?"

"Devil Duke they call him."

"Oh, I know him."

"Do yer?"

"I ought to."

"Why?"

"Why," said Joe, vehemently, at the recollection, "I had a chase after him one night, for more 'un ten miles, and just as I thought I had got him he turns round in his saddle and catches me such a clout on the nose, it knocked me off my horse, and away he bolts."

"Who, the horse or the highwayman?"

"The highwayman, in course."

"I spose yer didn't forget him then."

"No, I should say I ain't, and the first time I sees him, I'll pay him for that clump he give me."

"That's right, Joe, you should never be in debt. You can pay him to-night."

"How?"

"Why, by coming along with me. I have got the keys of the Roundhouse."

"Have yer? What are yer going there for?"

"To take charge of all prisoners that is brought there."

"Then I'll settle accounts with Devil Duke."

"Won't we have a lark with him, eh? I'll give him what for; they won't be able to help themselves."

"You infernal sneaks," said Big Bullskin, "you'll find your mistake out, that they will be able to help themselves."

"I say, Big Bull."

"Well, Swig."

"Can't we get those keys?"

"I should say so. I tell you what, Swig, suppose I mount on your shoulders, and frighten them."

"All right," said Swig, readily.

The two fat officers pursued their way in blissful ignorance of the plan being laid to scare them.

They only thought of the way they meant to torture the prisoners.

Their interesting conversation was cut short, and they fell back with a yell of fright.

The awful-looking apparition that slowly strode from the trees and stood in their path, made them cower back horror-stricken.

The worthy Joe, who held a blunderbuss, seemed rooted to the spot, his visage dropped, and his eyes almost startled from their sockets, while his brother officer, who at first had little more courage than he, drew pistol, but his nerves failed him and his arm dropped to his side.

He fell back awfully scared, and would have yelled, but his tongue seemed clove to his mouth, as the gigantic phantom put out its long arm, and in a sepulchral voice, said—

"Ye wicked men, turn thy footsteps the other way, or ye shall die on the spot."

The wicked men could not move either way.

They were perfectly paralysed.

Swig and Big Bullskin's plan to scare the officers was a capital make up.

It took wonderful effect.

Big Bullskin mounted on his companion shoulders, with a long black coat that hung from his neck to the top of Swig's boots, his long hair pulled straight round his head in shaggy ends, the black crape mask drawn over his face. The glimmering new moon's rays threw a peculiar shade on him, and altogether he presented a most horrible object.

"Ye have not moved—the time has come, ye must die."

"I wish you would make haste and kill them, then," said Swig, perspiring beneath the weight of his companion, "I shall drop you in a minute."

"Hold tight a little longer, Swig," said Bullskin.

Swig did his best, and tottered backwards towards the terror stricken officers.

"Prepare, ye wicked men, for thy doom," said the giant, in a deep, hollow voice.

The officers rolled over on their faces, yelling and kicking furiously.

Shooting Bullskin over his head, Swig pounced on them.

Bullskin got up, ruefully rubbing his head, while Swigg, who had gagged the officers, was actively stripping them of their coats, etc.

Having robbed them of everything but shirts and breeches, and taken the keys of the lock-up away from them, they were bound back to back, and laid in a ditch.

The scheming highwaymen then attired themselves in the officers' clothes.

Bullskin found it a more difficult task than his companion did.

"He, he, he, he, he!" laughed Swig, to see his friend struggling to get into the tight things.

"What are you laughing at?" asked Big Bullskin, drawing a long breath of relief, as he got his long arms through the sleeves of the coat.

"He, he, he—there's a sight."

"He, he, he!" answered Bullskin, savagely, "what have you got to laugh at, you little humbug?"

"Has yer mamme just let yer out?" asked Swig, still laughing at the ludicrous sight his companion looked.

"I shall have my laugh at you, presently."

"Will yer?" said Swig, slipping into the big coat, and pulling the officer's boots over his own.

"Ha, ha, ha," bellowed Big Bullskin in retort; "there's a rasher in a blanket. He, he, he!"

"I don't look so bad as you."

"Ho, ho, ho!"

"Ho, ho, ho—more I don't."

"Ha, ha, ha!"

"Take off your little brother's things."

"Take off your grandfather's."

"What's the good of laughing at me?" asked Swig, crestfallen.

"I can't help it," replied Bullskin, holding his long sides that commenced to ache through laughing, "you do look a sight."

"So do you."

"Oh lor, my jaws aches through laughing."

"I'll chuck 'em at yer if you don't leave off."

"My jaws?"

"No, the things."

"But you do look a sight, Swig."

"If I look as bad as you, I must look hereful."

They did both look ludicrous.

Big Bullskin looked like an uncouth overgrown boy, and felt very uncomfortable in his new character of dress.

The coat was small and fitted him like a vice everywhere.

The sleeves were obstinate, and would not reach his spiky elbow, despite all his desperate tugging to stretch them the fronts of the coat stuck fast on his shoulders, the buttons grinning at the button-holes, and would not reach across his broad breast by a few yards.

Every time he stooped, the tails glided up and down, a rough seam taking a piece of skin off his spine.

Making a frantic clutch at the grinning Swig, Bullskin felt with horror the coat split from collar to tail, and hang in two on his arm.

That was miserable. What was he to do, he could not walk about with a coat in two halfs hanging on his arms. The belt, that would not reach round his waist, he buckled round his neck. The hat too, he had tied on the back of his head, and lastly, the boots he wore on his hands as a pair of gloves.

Altogether the big fellow looked like an escaped lunatic.

Swig was polite enough to tell him so.

For which Swig received a kick that sent him rolling.

He rolled himself out of his coat.

Rolling back, he rolled in it again.

Swig's new costume was as large and loose for him as the other's was small and tight.

Swig comfortably wrapped his coat round himself three times, and then left plenty of room for any one to crawl up the back.

The sleeves flapped about a half yard over his hands, and the tails dragged along the ground like a lady's dress.

The hat fitted like an extinguisher, and only kept from smothering him by resting on his nose.

The boots he could have swam in, they came to the tops of his thighs.

On the whole, the two disguised highwaymen looked a comical pair of objects.

"Well I am blowed," said Swig, pulling the skirts of his coat off the ground, "you do look a miserable wretch."

"You don't?"

"You do."

"Give us your coat, Swig."

"I'll see you blowed fust."

"It is too big for you."

"And too little for you."

"You would give it to me if you could see yourself," continued Bullskin, persuasively.

"Would I; I look like a real hofficer."

"You look like a monkey in a officer's coat."

"If you had it you would look like a ugly gorilla with a monkey's coat on; so to save you from that affliction I'll keep it."

"Have you got the keys?"

"Yes," said Swig, significantly, "and mean to keep 'em."

"All right, but you might let me have the coat."

"Might I?"

"Yes."

"Then I shan't."

"You are greedy."

"You ain't?"

"No."

"Oh no, you ain't, when you split your own coat in two, and then want mine, which you won't get."

Big Bullskin, finding his persuasions would not go down with his little companion, pursued his way in silence towards the Round-house.

Swig strutted along with all the consequence imaginable, jingling the bunch of keys by his side, and assuming an air of supreme authority over his big companion.

Big Bullskin regarded the little strut with an air of disdain, quietly waiting for an opportunity to avail himself of the keys.

Swig, thinking that his comrade was deeply absorbed in thought, or otherwise would not notice his irritating way, inwardly got exasperated, and violently struck him on the knee with the heavy bunch of keys.

Bullskin had been quietly watching him with a side glance, and put out his leg as the little strut stepped forward and struck at him.

With a shout, Swig went sprawling over the big foot of his companion, and the keys flew from his hand.

Bullskin picked them up quietly, put them in his pocket, and then assisted his fallen companion to his feet, innocently inquiring why he was lying there.

"Didn't yer put out yer hugly great hoof," said Swig, passionately.

"Of course I did," said Bullskin, looking surprised, "if I didn't I should stand still. Don't you put out your feet to walk with?"

"What did yer want to put it in my way for, yer hugly great thief?"

"You had no business to get in the way of my foot."

"Don't do it again."

"I don't intend to. You trod on a big corn, and big corns are painful."

"Ugh," exclaimed Swig in disgust, looking about.

Big Bullskin walked on, grinning, leaving his little friend behind, looking for the keys.

"You're very clever, aint yer?" shouted Swig, running up to his companion, as an idea struck him that Bullskin had taken the keys.

"I am sorry I can't return the compliment."

"Are yer?"

"Very."

"You can return the keys though."

"The what?"

"You're very innocent, I dare say."

"What are you talking about?"

"Yer don't know."

"I don't."

"Why the keys, yer big thief."

"Where are they?"

"You've got 'em."

"Nonsense, I saw them in your hand not a minute ago."

"And since that minute you put them in your pocket."

"Since you so cleverly come to that truthful conclusion, I own it. But hush, Swig, we are near the lock-up, and I hear some one coming."

Swig was quiet, and getting behind Bullskin, he dexterously inserted his hand into his comrade's pocket, and therefrom extracted the keys.

The giant highwayman was unconscious of what had taken place, and attentively listened for the approaching footsteps that every moment grew more distinct, as the clamour of wrangling voices broke upon his ear.

"Move yer cussed carcass," he heard some one say in a coarse, brutal voice. "It aint any good of yer trying to get away. We've got you now, my pippin, and we'll make sure of yer till you'll be made a scarecrow of."

"I don't wish to resist, but you may let the lady go—she has done nothing."

"Ho, ho! I daresay not. Let her go eh? of course we will."

"You may. She is guiltless, and if you detain her, you will stand the consequences."

"All right, my tulip, yer parley won't go down here."

"You would, though, had I but my hands free."

"Come, none of yer cheek, or I'll choke yer."

"Take your knuckles out of my throat."

"Hallo, mates," said Big Bullskin, confronting the party, and addressing the officers, "have you got some more night hawks?"

"Yes," replied one, who held a fearless looking fellow firmly by the collar, "wants to pitch us a yarn to say his missus is hinnocent."

"It won't do here," exclaimed Swig, throwing his head up, and assuming a superior command; "hand the prisoners over to my man."

The other officer, who held a young and pretty girl, looked curiously at the form enveloped in a large coat.

"Who are you?" he said.

"I'll let you know if you don't do as I tell yer."

"I am blessed if I think they belong to us, mates," remarked officer number one suspiciously, who securely held the highwayman.

"Just my opinion, mate," replied officer number two, who held the pretty girl.

"You don't, you impertinent hounds," said Swig.

"No, we don't," replied officer number two; "who made yer coat?"

Swig foamed with rage at the outrageous insult, and could not think of words sufficient to express his indignation.

Big Bullskin, seeing his companion's difficulty, released him by saying—

"Look here, my men, Judge Gripp shall hear of your impertinence to-morrow. By his orders I and my friend have the charge of all the prisoners taken to the Roundhouse. Here are the keys if you have any mistrust. It is quite right of you to be careful, but at the same time you should be civil."

He stopped short as he drew his hand from his pocket, and glanced around.

"I have the keys," said Swig, coming forward with them in his hand, trying to look serious, though he could not repress sniggering at the ludicrous expression on his companion's countenance.

"I thought I had them," said Bullskin, not able to smother his feelings.

"So you did," remarked Swig, pausing to invent a lie, "only you dropped them in the fight to capture them desperate highwaymen that tore your coat."

"Oh, yes, I remember something jingling when they threw me down," Big Bullskin said, carrying out the lie that the other had begun, and thinking it a very good idea to elude the suspicions of the officers.

"Did they escape?" inquired officer number one, eagerly.

"Yes, cuss 'em, but I gave one of them a bullet in his neck. I don't think they have got far."

"Which way did they go?" asked officer number two, looking valiant.

"Through the common to the right," said Bullskin.

"Hand your prisoners over to my friend, then go after them hawks. We shall soon have a nest full if you catch 'em," said Swig, thinking he had said something clever.

Big Bullskin felt awfully disgusted at the horrible attempt at a joke, and pulled his dwarf friend aside by the collar, then stepped forward, and addressed the officers—

"Look here, my men, there is a grand reward and promotion for every highwayman you catch," he began, "so I should advise you to follow in their track. I should go after them myself, but I and my friend have the responsibility of taking care of all prisoners taken to the Roundhouse by the judge's wish."

Bribed by the temptation of a large reward, and the honour of promotion, the suspicions they at first entertained as to the character of the disguised highwaymen were lulled; they gave up their captives like lambs, and started in pursuit of the imaginary daring knights.

Bullskin had taken the lady under his own especial care, and held the other prisoner for Swig to secure.

Swig took him reluctantly, and, cast a spiteful look at his companion. He had anticipated the pleasure of escorting the lady to the Roundhouse with all the gallantry he could assume, and that was a considerable amount, for his size.

Never had he been so disappointed before. He would have throttled his captive for revenge, but fortunately he belonged to their band and Swig knew him, or it would have been a certain case of choking.

Big Bullskin fell back, and Swig, with his prisoner, walked on in sulky silence, while Bullskin talked to his fair prisoner in quite a winning manner.

"I really think, miss, those foolish men have made a mistake," he said, in his softest tones, while leading her gently along by the hand.

"They have, I assure you, sir, made an unpardonable mistake by taking me," she replied tearfully.

"I am very sorry, but I am compelled to take you to the lock-up," he said, "though I daresay I can manage to let you off."

"How can I thank you for the kindness you have shown me?"

"One kiss from those sweet lips of yours will be sufficient thanks," he said, persuasively bending his long back and smiling at her pretty face.

He had sufficiently won her favour to get the kiss, for the smack as their lips met made Swig start and clench his fist.

"There is no occasion to take the lady in here," said the highwayman to Swig, as they reached the Roundhouse.

"Ain't there?" said Swig, spitefully; "anyhow, she is going in, and so are you."

He had not forgotten the sound of the kiss, which he thought he had more right to than

his companion, and the thought of it made him spiteful.

"Now then, long shanks, are you going to stop behind?" he shouted to Bullskin.

Big Bullskin made no reply, but quietly walked up to the Roundhouse as Swig thrust his prisoner in, and rewarded his companion with a kick for his contempt.

"What ho, gallant Tom!" shouted Devil Duke, as the new prisoner entered, "they have nabbed you at last."

"Yes,' answered the highwayman, stopping an expression that would have been more expressive than polite, as the little hand of Bullskin's prisoner was laid on his arm.

"Hush," she said, "the men only did their duty."

"Cuss their duty!"

"Ha, ha, ha!" laughed Bullskin, "a nice lot of birds. Ah, but you have got your wings clipped now, and you won't fly far."

"No," said Swig, forgetting his indignation and wrath, as he slapped his companion on the back, approvingly for what he said; "their next fly will be to Tyburn."

"To hell and furies with you for tormenting hounds!" exclaimed Devil Duke, in a terrible passion.

The dwarf and giant highwaymen were neither recognised by any of their comrades, though there were several there. So they meant to have a lark with them before they threw off their disguises.

Devil Duke was in a fearful passion at being captured while Cecily was with him. His broad chest expanded and every muscle in his large massive frame worked convulsively as he desperately struggled to break his manacles.

"Vampires, devils," he shouted, at the supposed officers, "could I but break these accursed irons, I would crush your miserable lives out."

His disguised companions grinned in an aggravating manner at his furious gesticulation.

Gallant Tom, as Devil Duke called him, was a more quiet and passive nature, and took trouble much easier than his comrade.

"All right, my chickens, it won't be long before you have yours crushed out," said Swig

Devil Duke made a dash at him with his

'd hands, as he tickled him in the side with the point of his sword.

"You'll exhaust yourselves," said Bullskin, laughing, "it ain't good for your health to make such a hallo bollew about nothing."

"Confound you all, but I'll remember you when I get free again."

"You talk, my pippin, as though you expected some one was going to let you free. When you are, I have no doubt but what you will remember me."

"Perhaps they'd like us to let them all free," said Swig, taking his companion's hand and dancing round the prisoners. "We will, of course—decidedly—sure to—just so—anything else—also—likewise. Ha, ha, ha! Oh dear me, no, not for these coons—I should think not—what do you say, mate?"

"No," gasped Big Bullskin, for he was nearly out of breath through dancing round his enraged companions like a maniac.

"Hounds!" exclaimed Devil Duke, as they finished their war-like dance.

"Who are?" asked Swig."

"You, cursed miserable curs."

"We ain't hounds," said Bullskin, "but we have got some barkers, and they can bite."

"Blood-hunting wretches," hissed the enraged highwayman.

"You ain't," said Swig.

"Ugh," and the gallant fellow turned his head aside in disgust.

"This ain't the place for ladys," said Swig.

"Of course it ain't," said Big Bullskin, "what do you propose to do with them?"

"Take them away from these gallows, birds."

"Do you?" Devil Duke said, turning round with a dangerous look in his eyes.

"Of course we do."

"Lay your hand on them, and by heavens I will crush you where you stand."

"Very strong words from a very helpless person," said Big Bullskin, advancing towards the lady he had kissed, while Swig went to Cecily, and laid his hand on her shoulder.

The girls clung despairingly around the necks of their helpless lovers.

The disguised highwaymen tore them from the prisoners.

A loud kicking at the door made the supposed officers release their hold.

Swig unfastened the door, and ere he had time to move, he was knocked down half stunned.

It swung back, and a struggling prisoner was thrust in by two officers.

"Here's another one for you, mates," said one of the officers.

"All right, my men," said Big Bullskin, "you'll make a fortune. There is two more escaped, an extra reward for those who catch them."

The avaricious men stood grinning at each other at the idea.

It was something grand.

And they started off in time to prevent an awful calamity.

Had they stayed a minute longer they would have grinned each other's head off.

Big Bullskin picked his little companion up, and asked if he was hurt.

Swig gave him a kick for his kind interference.

"Mind yer own business," he said, rubbing his bruised nose.

"The ladies," said the giant, laughing at the ludicrous look of his comrade.

"All right, I had forgot them."

"Enough to make you, such a clout as that."

"You can hold yer mag, or I'll give you a clout," was Swig's ungrateful reply.

"Take your cursed paws off the ladies," said the new prisoner, who had so unceremoniously entered, as the supposed officers took the trembling girls away from the highwaymen.

"Of course we will for you," said Swig, as they closed the door of the roundhouse behind them.

"Listen, ladies," said the giant highwayman, "we are not officers, as we appear to be, but faithful companions of your gallant lovers."

"Every word what he says is true," Swig remarked, emphatically, "aint it, Bull, old boy."

"I suppose it is, if you say so. And, ladies," said the good-tempered giant, "we have come to rescue all those men that you saw inside."

"That's true," said Swig, "only of course we was obliged to have a little lark with 'em

CAPTAIN CLAUDE SEES TYBURN DICK'S STEED, FAIRY, CHASED BY THE OFFICERS.

first, just to make 'em savage, then the surprise will come more sweet, almost as sweet as that kiss I heard."

The lady blushed at the unexpected reproach, and Bullskin licked his mouth, and looked as though he would like another.

He did not get it.

Swig saw his head lowering, and pulled him away by the ear.

As they again entered, they had a torrent of abuse showered upon them by all the prisoners.

"What are yer all making a noise about?" shouted Swig, at the top of his voice. "We are your friends."

"Of course we are," said Bullskin ; "com to save you."

"Come to save us," sneered Devil Duke "you mean fiends, to drive us mad."

"Ha, ha, ha—ho, ho, ho !" laughed Bull skin.

"He, he, he—oh, oh, oh !" sniggered Swi

"Well, well, you are a fine lot of coon don't you know your old companions ?" sai Big Bullskin, throwing off his disguise.

"Well, well, you is a fine lot o' fellows, t swear at yer own chums," exclaimed Swi who could not let the opportunity pass with out saying something.

Every voice hushed on the instant as the

comrades threw off their disguises, and revealed themselves in their true character.

All stood as though paralysed, with their gaze fixed upon the daring adventurers.

Devil Duke was the first to recover from the surprise, and he exclaimed, in a short breath—

"It is!"

"Is it?" said Swig.

"Swig."

"And Big Bullskin," said another.

"Dear me."

"Then you did."

"No we didn't."

"Saved, saved!" shouted the whole of the prisoners.

"Who said so?" asked Bullskin.

"We know it."

"You know more than I do."

"You will free us from these manacles?" asked Gallant Tom.

"I don't know that I shall. You swore at me, and I don't like people who swear. I ain't got the keys."

"I have," said Swig.

"Then release them."

He did so, and as soon as they were all released, Swig and Bullskin's hands were grasped by their faithful companions.

The ladies were admitted. Then the two heroes of the adventure went in search of something to drink.

In a cellar underground, they found a hamper of wine, carefully packed away.

This they quickly had out of its hiding-place.

"I'll taste it, to try if it will suit our palates."

"After I have had a swig," said his companion, taking a bottle out, and draining it to the very bottom, dregs and all.

"Swig by name and Swig by nature," remarked Bullskin, thrusting the neck of a bottle in his mouth.

"Do you mean me," said Swig, digging his companion in the wind with the bottle he had drained.

"Yes," said Bullskin, squirting a mouthful of thick in his face.

Swig felt awfully sick, and left his companion to bring up the hamper.

"Gentlemen," he said, entering, putting the basket down, and sprawling head first over it.

"This is wine?" asked Devil Duke, picking him up.

"Ask Swig."

He asked, and Swig replied in the affirmative.

A bottle was handed to each person—the second and the third, until they were all emptied.

"Swig, old boy—hic—your brother is calling—hic—yer," said Big Bullskin, as the braying of a donkey sounded upon their ears.

"Hic—then I'll—hic—bring him in—hic."

Swig staggered, and in a minute he returned, leading a pair of asses in by the ears.

"Gem—hic—men—does you—hic—think they is like—hic—him—hic—Bullskin?"

A roar of drunken laughter rang through the place at the sight of the shaggy beasts.

"Swig—hic—I'll tell you what to do—hic—" said Bullskin, lugging one in by the nose.

"Go on—oh—hic," said Swig, as the hind legs of one of the animals were lodged in his stomach, and he was thrown over its head.

While he laid on the ground gasping, Bullskin fastened the two animals against the wall, and put the officers' coats over them.

Amidst the roars of laughter could be heard Swig's groans, as he got up and staggered.

The whole party then set out arm in arm with the females, and all raised a terrific shout.

"Bullskin, you blag—hic—hard, sing us a song," said Devil Duke, reeling from side to side of the road.

"Sing us a—hic——"

"No, a song," said Gallant Tom.

"All right—I'll—hic—sing you one of my own—hic—invention—hic."

After a great deal of spitting, coughing, and clearing his throat, he began—

"The lock-up is not far behind us,
Therefrom I have just let you free,
We are all now both happy and jolly,
And out for a kind of a spree.
The lasses are merry and smiling,
Their gallant knights' heart beat with glee,
The moon is above us all shining,
And on the road soon we must be.
Then hurrah for the gallant highwaymen,
And down with the Runners say we,
On the road is the place to be happy
Rollicking merry and free."

" Bravo ! Bravo !"

" Bravo, old boy ; didn't think you could do it. Stunning—hurrah !"

Such were the exclamations, amid "thunders of applause," at the conclusion of his song.

"I can sing a better one than—hic—that," said Swig, who saw no reason why he should not receive the same amount of approbation, "hold yer—hic—noises, and I'll—hic—sing."

"Thank you just the same, but you may reserve yours for another time," said Devil Duke.

"Why?" asked Swig, indignantly.

" Because the last was so good, that a little goes a great way."

" Oh—h——mine's better 'en that."

" Is it ?"

" Yes."

" Then yours will go farther than his."

Swig did not see it, and was about to break out, when the whole party struck up one of their favourite ditties, and merrily staggered along by the assistance of one another."

CHAPTER XVI.

THE ENTRY OF THE OFFICERS—RED MATTHIAS ON THE TRACK.

THE summons of her guardian and the officers at the door, seemed to deprive Ruth of all power.

She shivered, and our hero, closing the casement, and drawing the curtains with one hand, supported her with the other arm, drawing her fragile supple form to his broad chest.

For an instant or two her soft lithe body reposed in his arms, her pale face nestling to his bosom.

He could feel the timid beating of her heart—every pulsation of her throbbing frame.

Such a contact might have awakened in some hearts impulses of the most evil nature, but our hero's was free from impure guile, and thinking how dastardly it would be to wrong one who so nobly risked her honour for his safety, he raised her tearful face, and kissing her wan lips, said in a low tone—

"Fly to your couch, I will hide behind these hangings."

Ruth gave him a timid glance.

"They will find you there. I know my guardian will have every place searched."

"Not in your chamber, surely ?"

"Oh yes. His excuse will be that he you are concealed unknown to me."

Dick looked round the luxurious room.

" Is there never a hole or corner into which I can squeeze—no panel in the wall— eh, little trembler ?"

"Alas, no——"

"Well, it's not very romantic, but when life's at stake one must not be particular. So I will crawl beneath your bedstead, and await their search."

"You will be seen ; they will search there."

"The rascals. Then all I can say is, that much as the act might jeopardise my safety, I should feel a very strong impulse to knock their lubberly skulls in for daring such a thing."

Ruth looked gratefully into his handsome face.

"Well, little one, as your chamber does not seem constructed to shelter highwaymen, I will get behind the door, ready to pop out when they come in."

"They will shoot you on the stairs. No, no, you cannot risk that. You are weak now, and tremble, and they are strong, wicked men."

Poor Ruth !

It was her own gentle body that quaked and shivered so.

Our hero did not like to tell her this, but gently pressing her in his arms, he asked—

"Where then, little gaoler, am I to hide my ungainly body ?"

"There is only one place," Ruth said, hiding her tell tale face.

" And that ?" Dick asked.

" Is *inside* my bed."

Her voice was scarcely audible.

A modest blush deepened from her beautiful neck to her temples.

Dick started.

" Ruth, do you know what you dare? have you no fear of the unholy passions even of a hunted highwayman ?"

Ruth sobbed, as she replied brokenly—

" It is the only way—they will not dare seek you there, and surely you cannot look so noble, and be so base, as to take advantage of my helplessness."

"Not quite so base as that," he answered proudly. "No, no, Ruth, your innocence is a sure safeguard. I'll not pollute your angel goodness even by a thought of harm. Look up, dear girl, don't hide your face from me. Look into my eyes, you will see nothing there that even modesty's sweet self might shrink from."

She did look up, her face brimming with blushes, her eyes swimming in tears—looked into Dick's open countenance, and felt no fear at what she read there, for nature had stamped its true nobility on our hero's lineaments, and all the tenderness of his soul beamed from its expressive eye.

"I see you trust me," Dick said, "I thank you for that trust as well as for the pure devotion you have shown me in offering your honour as my safeguard; but lest I might prove the dastard which the devil can make of a man, and sully the purity of such an angel, I'll not accept—no, I'll stand my chance of fight and flight."

"Oh, sir," said Ruth, in shivering tones, "do not torture me—you must not face these men."

She clung to him with all the strength of her slender frame.

"Let me go, Ruth, I cannot stay to hide like a coward behind a woman's helpless innocence, to shiver like some mean craven wretch, trusting for life to the base chance that some sacrilegious hand may not tear aside the drapery of your bed, and discover me, palsied in my fear. No, no, rather death. I thank you, Ruth, and I'll give them a tough struggle ere they bring me down, but go I must."

Ruth burst into a flood of tears.

Her warm supple arms still entwined his body.

"You think so mean of me," she sobbed, "you will not let me shield you from these fearful men. I am debased in your eyes. Oh, sir, God knows my heart was pure when I offered my innocence to shield your life. Let me beseech you to relent—think of the act as that of a sister defending a fugitive brother from pursuit. You can depart when all is safe. Let my tears plead. Oh, sir, listen. They will fear some harm has happened to me if I do not answer. Hide yourself. Your

own nobleness will teach you how to share my couch, and yet not outrage my helplessness."

There was no resisting those pleading tones Our hero was touched to his heart's core.

He yielded, and while Ruth was standing by the door, he sprang to the bedside.

It was disarranged, just as she had left it.

The downy pillows were cast aside, and on the soft bed was the impress of her gentle form.

And into that sanctuary of purity and maidenhood, he was about to sneak like a thief.

It was a hard dose for one so generously brave, as the youthful highwayman, to swallow.

But Ruth was tearfully awaiting his disappearance in the bed, so giving a rueful glance at his heavy boots, he gulped down his compunction, and got in.

Ruth glided timidly to the couch, as soon as he had entered.

He had, with true delicacy, got under the clothes in such a manner, that they would be between his form and that of his gentle preserver.

The young girl, inwardly grateful for his modest forethought, arranged the curtains to fall over him, and put a pillow over his head.

Old Judge Gripp had by this time become more impatient.

He tapped louder at the door, and called nervously—

"Ruth, Ruth."

One of the officers, hearing no answer, proposed bursting in the door.

"The highwayman's been and cut her throat," was his coarse suggestion.

Ruth thought fit this time to answer.

"Thank God, you are well, child," mumbled the judge.

To which the arch little deceiver thought fit to answer by asking innocently what was the matter.

"A highwayman, dear child," gasped the judge. "We think he's come into your chamber—open the door that we may search."

Ruth placed the pillows over our half-suffocated hero's face, and stepped softly to the door.

"Do not enter till I retire," she said, as she turned the key to unlock it

The judge kept back the officers, who were eager to make a rush, and Ruth glided back to the bed.

The concealed highwayman could feel how she trembled as she got beside him, and he edged himself as far away as possible.

But Ruth, with womanly instinct, divined his motives, and, much to his dismay, nestled closer to him.

This she did, the better to conceal him from the prying eyes of the officers.

The door opened softly, and the judge crept in on tiptoe, and looked nervously round, as if he feared being confronted by the daring boy highwayman.

Then, one by one, marched in three officers.

Of course they were only anxious to capture the highwayman, and of course it was only in a natural way of looking after him that they all turned their glances towards the fair occupant of the bed.

If they expected any gratification from that stolen peep, they were taken in.

Pretty Ruth had covered herself up to the eyes with the bedclothes, and even the shape of her graceful form was hidden by the luxurious coverlet.

Our youthful hero's heart throbbed a trifle quicker, when he knew that his would-be captors had entered.

The old judge was the first to speak.

"Don't be alarmed, my dear child; we are certain to find him, if he is here—the highwayman, you know—that daring thief, that audacious villain, who stopped us on the road."

"Has he escaped?" Ruth asked, in a faint voice.

"Yes, my darling girl — escaped from prison. But we will have him—we've come to catch him. All the place is up in arms, and if he is not taken alive, he will be shot the instant he shows himself."

Ruth felt very glad she had not allowed Dick to have his own way.

Somehow her interest in his fate deepened the more his life was threatened, and she listened with breathless attention to one of the officers, who explained how the Boy Highwayman had got out of prison, and made his daring passage across the rope.

It made her shudder to think of his danger when at that dizzy height above the sleeping town, and almost unconsciously she moved closer to where he was concealed.

"Yes, miss," the man explained, "that's how the hardened young gallows bird got away, and if he didn't get in at this window, why, he must have flown away, that's all."

"Tell me, child," the judge asked, "were you awakened by any noise?"

"I fancied I heard some slight sound at the window before you came," Ruth answered, "and I fancied I saw someone there, but I must have been dreaming."

"No, no," mumbled the judge, "you didn'. dream. What was he like?—was he like the scoundrel who robbed us on the road?"

"He had big boots and a scarlet coat."

"The very fellow—that's him. Look about you men, he may have hidden behind those curtains, the villain."

The officers made a dart at the curtains and shook them aside, but no highwayman dropped out of them.

One of the officers was a big, savage-looking man, with thick red whiskers, and a red crop of hair.

His name was Matthias Grabbe — Red Matthias he was generally called.

He was a noted hand at thief catching, and had such an antipathy against highwaymen, that he enjoyed hunting them down above all other malefactors.

When the hue and cry of Dick's escape was raised, he chuckled with grim satisfaction, and made up his mind for a keen hunt.

It was his brag that he could scent his man, if a highwayman only looked in at a window.

So, when the curtains were shaken, he went sniffing about, poking his thick snub nose into all corners, and snuffing as if he could smell a highwayman in the air.

He had just laid his hand on the window frame, when the casement blew in with sudden bang, and knocked him back on of the assistant officer, who went rolling of the way in anything but a courageous manner.

"Hallo!—shoot him!" bawled the old judge, thinking it was the highwayman, and hiding behind the hangings of Ruth's bed.

The officer grasped at an imaginary malefactor, but looked exceedingly sheepish when they saw the cause of their alarm.

Red Matthias clutched a big pistol savagely, and peered out of the window, sniffing sagaciously the cool night air.

He did not see anything of the highwayman, so he pulled in his ugly head again, but looked wise, though baffled.

"He's been here," he said, "and he's somewhere here about; and if so be he is, the young lady won't be frightened—we'll soon have him out."

The judge put his shrivelled face close to Ruth's, and said—

"You won't be frightened, my child? we won't let him touch you."

"Now, you rascally highwayman," said Red Matthias, in an overawing tone, "it ain't a bit of use your skulking here; we knows your game, and means to have you; so you'd better show yourself, and not give us the trouble to hunt you out."

Matthias looked big. He coughed significantly as he concluded, but the "rascally highwayman" gave no signs of being overcome by his logic.

"Oh," said Matthias, speaking in the determined tone of a man who had made up his mind, and knew what he was about; "so you won't show yourself—you means to give us the job of finding you. Very well, very well, I will look for you then, that's all; only when we do catch you, perhaps yer'll be sorry you didn't come out when we asked you."

This impressive speech meeting with not the shadow of a reply from the rascally highwayman, who evidently preferred being scotched in his lair to creeping forth and showing himself, the three officers began their search in real earnest.

They looked behind the hangings, inside Ruth's wardrobe, on the top of the bedstead, under chairs, and in every corner of the room.

They pushed their inquisitive noses under her bed, and there they found, as Byron relates in a like instance—"No matter what, it was not what they sought."

They took up her dresses and shook them—rather awkwardly, it must be confessed, and as if ashamed of themselves; they even peeped into the china ewer, but no sign of the highwayman could they find.

Matthias still sniffed and snuffed; he was not easily put off the scent.

Tired at last of rummaging, he would have withdrawn from the search, but in an evil moment his eye alighted upon a suspicious sign—the prints of a highwayman's boots on the carpet near the window.

The prints of the savage's foot on the sands, on Robinson Crusoe's island, did not have such an effect on that shipwrecked adventurer as did this upon the red-headed officer of justice.

He stooped over it, walked round it, scanned its length and breadth, examined which way the toe pointed, and smiled with a satisfied air.

His brother officers, envying him his penetration, tried to look wise too.

"Ho, ho!" cried Matthias, "now we've got him."

Our hero, who suspected the truth, devoutly longed for an opportunity to plant on the skull of the officer the heavy boot which had made that tell-tale mark.

But he lay close and quiet, while the throbbing of Ruth's breast told him how she feared the consequences of the intelligent officer's discovery.

"I knowed I smelt him," Red Matthias cried; "he's been here—here's his footmark, and now I'll tell you where he is—he's up that chimbley."

No sooner had their brother officer spoken than the zealous pair of thieftakers sprang to the fireplace, and tore down the board in front of the grate.

The sagacious Matthias knelt down on the earth, and put his head and arm up the chimney.

"Aha!" cried Matthias, who thought he had his man.

"Aha!" echoed as before.

"'Taint no use your hiding any more."

"Any more," echoed solemnly in the flue. Matthias got rather savage.

"Come down, will yer, or I'll shoot up the chimbley."

"Shoot up the chimbley," was echoed in mocking tones.

"D—— you!" muttered Matthias, "here goes to bring you down."

As the echoing voice mimicked again he fired.

Such a bang!

The explosion echoed a dozen times as it went up the narrow flue.

Matthias had fired at a venture, on the supposition that if there was any one wedged up the chimney, the ball must hit him.

To his satisfaction he heard a cry of pain from above, and amidst a heavy fall of soot that showered all over him, a collapsed body came tumbling down.

The other officers heard the sound.

They saw their comrade's arms go up the flue, and make a clutch at something, and believing that he must have seized hold of the wounded highwayman, they assisted in dragging him and his prisoner forth.

A curious scene was then enacted.

First the head and shoulders of Red Matthias covered in soot, came to view.

Then the big arms; the sprawling hands holding on like grim death to a monstrous black Tom cat.

The feline tile wanderer had been hit by the officer's bullets, but though wounded and bleeding, it had not lost all its native ferocity, and on finding itself hauled from the chimney, it set up a succession of fearful howls, and extending its big paws, clawed the thieftaker's hair up by the roots, and struggled fiercely out of his grasp.

Giving a scared howl at its new foes, the cat sprang at the other officers, covering their faces with soot.

They dodged aside, and Tom, running round the chamber for a way of escape, bounded out by the open window.

There were beneath the casement two energetic officers, waiting with pistols primed to shoot the boy highwayman.

They heard the hubbub above, and seeing a dark object at the window, fired instanter.

Poor Tom, mad with fury, rolled headlong over.

He fell with a heavy thud on their heads.

They thought it was their man, and each grasped the other.

The soot had half blinded them, and each finding the cold muzzle of a pistol against his ear, set up a howl of fright, and dropped on his knees to beg mercy of the fancied highwayman.

By this time they were able to see a little better.

The slaughtered Tom explained the business, and getting valorously on their feet, they tried not to look foolish at the mistake they had made.

Matthias and his two brother officers were in as uncomfortable a plight.

Even the arrogant conceit of the red-headed thieftaker left him.

The game was up as far as searching that chamber was concerned.

He wiped the soot out of his eyes, and off his perspiring face, and with his two satellites, marched in discomfiture from the chamber.

But just before crossing the threshold, he glanced again towards the bed, and his eyes met those of Ruth's with a look that made the young girl shiver to the soul, for she saw that, though baffled, he was still unconvinced.

She was right.

Red Matthias scented his man, and meant to have him.

The old judge lingered beside Ruth.

"You will need some protection, dear child," he mumbled, "I will close the casement, and stay with you while they search the other part of the house. This bold highwayman might come again, you know."

He closed the window.

Ruth's heart beat quicker.

The rascally old judge was leaning over her.

Sinister impulses were at his shrivelled old heart.

The opportunity he had longed for was now before him.

Often had his sensual yearnings prompted him to steal to the chamber of his beautiful ward, and there was an unmistakable look in his eyes, as with bated breath and bounding heart, he got closer to the young girl.

"You must let me stay," he said; "I can sit by your bedside, and watch while you go to sleep. You know, my dear girl, you are only as a child to me. Indeed, it is quite proper I should remain to protect you."

Ruth did not think so.

She told him she was not frightened—that she would rather be alone; but the old libertine, mumbling in excitement, put his shrivelled hands on her forehead, making pretence of smoothing the hair from her brow, but in reality enabling him to shift one hand to her cheek, which he patted in a fatherly (?) manner, to her neck.

"There, be calm, my child," the old hypocrite mumbled, "I am sure you're very frightened. Your heart is beating quite fast. I can feel it beating in your natural fear."

It was beating fast, but from a different cause.

The sensual old villain sneaked his hand lower on her bosom, outside her night robe; however, he had not as yet dared to intrude within.

His other hand, outside the bedclothes, caressed, as he thought, one beautiful limb belonging to his ward.

He made a mistake.

It was the heavily booted leg of our youthful highwayman he was squeezing so lovingly.

"I should like very much," thought Dick, as he felt the old villain's caress on his leg, " to plant the sole of my heavy boot with a hearty kick in his stomach, the shocking old sinner. I shall do it, too, if he attempts to paw her about any longer."

Our indignant hero was saved committing himself by pretty Ruth herself, who with a grieved cry of anger, sat up in the bed, pushing her rascally old guardian away.

The hoary scoundrel had dared to lay his shrivelled hand on her bare bosom.

"Shame on you," Ruth cried, her face crimson at the insult. " Is this your protection of my innocence? Leave the room, sir, or I will call the servants, and disclose your dastard conduct!"

Sensual as the hardened old villain was, he was cowed by Ruth's outraged looks.

The contact of her pure soft bosom had sent a thrill through his withered old frame, and if he had dared, would have clung to her defenceless form, but the dread of being exposed, shame-faced before his servants, drove any further libertine thoughts out of his head, and dropping on his knees by her bedside, he implored her forgiveness in the most craven accents.

The justly indignant girl bade him quit her chamber forthwith, and darting furtive glances at the charms whose purity he would have sullied without remorse, Judge Gripp sneaked from the apartment.

Ruth lay very still after he had gone

Our youthful adventurer could detect the palpable beating of her heart, as she lay like a panting lovebird at his side.

While the rascally judge lingered, he longed very much to quicken his departure by a well merited kicking, but reserving that pleasure for a future opportunity, he waited till the sound of footsteps had died away before he attempted to move.

The care which his pretty protector had taken to hide him from his enemies had resulted in nearly suffocating him, and now he disengaged his head from the pillows and blankets, and raised himself for the purpose of slipping out.

He had meant to spring from the bed without daring a look at his fair friend, but she lay so quiet that he could not help stealing a glance.

Besides, he fancied he heard her sob.

He was not mistaken.

Poor little Ruth was lying with her face half buried in the pillow, sobbing and steeped in tears.

Dick guessed the reason, and clenched his hands; he thought of the old judge, and soliloquised aloud—

"The shrivelled old scoundrel! If I don't make him suffer for this may I never again escape! Don't cry, pretty one," he said, smoothing the rich tresses from the young girl's forehead; "you'll know his vile nature, and can be on your guard; besides, there will be a day of reckoning, and if I am his judge, rely upon it, I'll make him feel his punishment."

"Hush, sir," Ruth said, in a faint whisper, "they may be listening."

"No, I think they are all quiet; suffer me to tender you my dearest thanks; not so much for the life you have saved, as the noble way in which you saved it."

Ruth raised her tearful face.

"You will never think ill of me for what I have done?" she asked, faintly.

The youthful highwayman pressed her hand tenderly to his lips.

"I would as soon think ill of an angel sent from heaven! No, dear Ruth, this night will live in my memory while I have life; and when I wish to think of a dear, devoted, true generous-hearted woman, I shall remember you !"

The young girl attempted a faint smile, but did not reply.

"And now," Dick said, still holding her soft palm, "before I incur fresh danger here I will make my escape."

"Not yet," Ruth cried, alarm depicted in her entrancing eyes. "The danger is not yet passed ; they are watching the house. Hark, you can hear them."

"You are tenderly anxious for my safety, little one. Such sincere care would make me a coward. No, I have lingered long enough, ... your fair name; besides, sooner or later, I must take the desperate leap for life !"

"You must not leave till they have gone. Oh, sir, do not risk again the life I have saved. They are desperate men—eager for your blood ! I should hear you slain, and then what would it avail that I had jeopardised my honour to screen you from them ? Stay a little longer, please—at least, till all is safe !"

Poor little Ruth ; she hardly knew how to get the request out.

She was deeply solicitous for his safety— as anxious as if he were a brother or a lover.

She would have entreated in more pleading tones, but she feared lest he should put some misconstruction on her desire to keep him still longer in her chamber.

So, trembling and in tears, she put her lily hand on his arm to keep him there.

Dick gazed very tenderly in her ingenuous face.

"I am unworthy such gentle care !" he exclaimed, his voice subdued to unwonted softness. "Dear girl, the hour may come when it may be my pleasing chance to give this life as freely for you as now I take it. Such timid pleading would make me hide here till the hairs of my pursuers' heads turned grey— tears, too, and for me, ah—what devotion can equal a woman's ?"

"Then you will stay—till all is safe."

"Aye, till I were taken, did I not too dearly respect your honour."

Ruth's fair features wore a more satisfied look.

There was wisdom in her request, for it was unlikely that the human bloodhounds on his track would retire from the vicinity of that

house until their suspicions were fully dispelled.

This conviction dawned on our hero's mind, and though he did not see his chance of escape would be much bettered by remaining till the morning's light, he could not be so ungrateful as to thrust his head into direct danger against the wish of his kind-hearted maiden preserver.

So he stayed, and Ruth, half ashamed, half pleased, got him to tell her something of his life, why he was hunted by the law's officer —what was his name—and what crime he had done.

Her interest deepened as Dick told her the simple narrative.

She was even moved to tears at the relation of his interview with his unnatural mother, but her senses thrilled strangely as he explained his daring escape from prison.

Her heart throbbed wildly.

She could picture him so vividly making his desperate way along the slender rope above the frightful abyss yawning beneath

She shivered at the thought of how one slip —the slackening of the rope—might have hurled him a misshapen mass to the flagstones of the street.

In her awakened sympathy, she was scarcely conscious that the hand she had laid on his arm had grasped him by the wrist with fervid grasp and that her face had drawn closer to his as she looked pityingly into his daring countenance.

She was glad she had made him stay. In his weak state of exhaustion he would have fallen an easy prey.

If she could get him to snatch an hour's repose he would rise refreshed, and in an encounter would stand a treble chance of victory.

She saw that his face was pale and weary.

The excitement was leaving him, and the fatigues and reactions of his perilous escape began to tell.

When she hinted he had better sleep, Dick smiled proudly but winningly.

He patted her cheeks, but gracefully scouted such an idea.

He consented, however, to lie down again lest any one should see him.

Of course he did not mean to go to sleep

He would merely lie quietly awake.

So he did for some little time, watching the flickering light of a lamp as it burned dimmer and dimmer, thinking of his curious and romantic position, and blaming himself for staying so long in the sanctity of Ruth's chamber.

Fatigue of mind and body; the intense quiet of the room, his silent breathing lest he should disturb his fair bedfellow, told at last on his exhausted energies; the shadow of the expiring light fell upon his eyes, the lids closed, and Dick was asleep.

Yes, fast asleep. Ruth listened to his regular breathing, for she was wide awake.

The wicked world would have had a good deal to say against the young girl's actions if it could have peeped into her chamber then, for she raised herself on her arms, and scarcely conscious that the soft coverlid had fallen from her ivory shoulders, was guilty of the terrible impropriety of gazing long and earnestly in our hero's youthful features.

Poor, tender-hearted girl.

The naughty god of love had sent his winged shaft deep into her breast, and she was, for all her innocence, on the brink of a destiny that might lure her past all hope.

But there was no guile or impure emotions in her heart now.

She only thought how cruel it was that one so young and generous as the Boy Highwayman should be hunted by the world to such a career.

Thought how his heart must have been stricken when, seeking a mother's love, he was driven forth with insult and contumely.

His face took a more weary look of pallor in his sleep.

Ruth nestled closer to him.

He could not know.

There was no one to see, and so, with her heart beating as guiltily as if she were doing some heinous thing, she drew his head towards her, till it rested on her rounded arms, his damp brow lying on her maiden bosom and thus, with an angel's purity in her sinless soul, she lay listening for the slightest sound ominous of danger to the youthful adventurer, whom she pillowed so tenderly on a resting-place hallowed as the sheltering breast given to an infant by its mother.

Dick awoke suddenly.

He had been dreaming he was in Paradise, among the soft-bosomed houris who are to be found there in the pleasing but rather bare garb of nature by the faithful.

He had, indeed, some confused notion that his cheek had reposed on as soft a pillow, and his breast thrilled as he sat bolt upright and looked around.

The lamp had gone out, but the faint glimmer of daybreak shone in at the casement.

He realised his position in an instant, and gazed round for his maiden preserver.

Her cheeks were dyed with red blushes, and the snowy lids half closed her two tell-tale eyes.

Our hero felt awkwardly embarrassed—in the stillness of night his position had not seemed so shamefaced, but the morning's light rather discomposed his thoughts.

" I have slept—and here—forgive me."

Ruth pressed his hand.

" You will be stronger now, if they meet you," she murmured, hiding her glance.

Dick slid from the bed, and was about to reply with respectful gallantry, when both were startled by hearing a slight tap at the door.

Ruth gave a little shiver of a cry, and Dick grasping instinctively at his vest for a pistol, looked angrily around.

" In again, quickly," Ruth whispered, hoarsely.

And Dick, albeit extremely loth, tumbled in amongst the bedclothes once more.

" Who is there ?" Ruth asked, when she had placed the hangings so as to hide our hero's form.

The voice of her maid answered her, and a young sprightly-looking girl, softly opening the door, entered on tiptoe.

Looking archly at her blushing mistress, she noiselessly closed the door.

" They're all gone, miss," she said, in a low tone.

" All who, Kitty ?"

" The officers, miss—and such a fright as they might have given me, rummaging all about. They came into my room, and would you believe it, they had the impudence to say I had a highwayman in my bed.

"You're a nice little girl, I daresay," thought Dick, while the blush deepened on Ruth's face, "but I wish you'd take your prattle to the devil."

"Tell me," Ruth asked, anxiously, "are they all gone?"

"Laws, yes, miss. All but one, leastways."

"*One!* There is one, then?"

"Yes, miss, that red-headed Matthias, which perhaps you noticed his ill-looks when that fool of an old judge allowed him in here, and he was so impudent and so suspicious. Why, I declare, he actually hunted between my mattrasses."

"I wish I had been there when his head was between them," was the concealed highwayman's reflections.

"Yes, miss, and he wasn't even satisfied with coming to your chamber the first time."

"How?" Ruth asked, turning pale, "he has not been here again?"

"Not inside, but outside he has, miss."

"*Outside?*"

"Yes, listening at the keyhole, and trying to peep through."

Ruth's heart sank like lead.

"I caught him at it, miss. He'd got his big ugly ear stuck against the keyhole."

"I wish I had been behind him," mused Dick, "I'd have made his ugly skull ache all over."

Ruth's heart was beating timorously.

Listening and peeping.

What might he not have seen?

"You should have seen him jump up, though, the sneaking thief," continued the maid, "when I dropped a piece of lighted stuff in his other big ugly donkey's ear. I pretended it was an accident, and he was too ashamed to make a noise. He sneaked off, and then, miss, I peeped through."

"Kitty, how dare you!"

"Well, miss, I thought I had better come in, and I'm sure it's better for me than him to be here, and see that highway gentleman's boot sticking out from under the bedclothes."

"The devil!"

That unpolite expression came from Dick's unguarded lips.

He fell into the snare set by the simple serving maid.

Of course there was no bit of his boot show-ing, but the girl suspected or knew the truth and her ruse had the effect of bringing from under the bedclothes, not only his boot, but very confused and guilty looking face, neither of which seemed to scare the spruce waiting girl, who laughed archly at his dismayed expression of countenance.

Ruth would have felt extremely grateful if the bed had sunk with her to the foundation at that moment.

She could not look her maid in the face but averted her glance, while Dick sat on the edge of the bed, ruefully nursing one knee.

But his thrilling voice broke the awkward silence.

"My pretty little girl, you have discovered what the cunning sagacity of those keen-nosed officers could not detect—my presence here. I presume, by your silence, you are not going to betray me?"

"What, betray such a handsome young gentleman—highwayman, I mean! Betray my dear young mistress that I love so dearly! I have not come for any such purpose. No, miss. I am afraid that red-headed officer will come here again, and I thought that till he was gone, you, sir, could hide in my room. He has just gone sneaking down stairs; if you make haste we can miss him."

"You are worth your weight in jewels for getting us out of a dilemma," our hero began, but Ruth stopped him by saying—

"No fine speeches. I know what you highwaymen are—you have no time to lose, so come along."

Dick lifted Ruth's hand gallantly to his lips.

Even now he might have lingered to try his hand at tender speech-making, but the sprightly maid was in a hurry to get him away, and she pulled him away with a jerk that made Ruth smile, and the boy highway-man feel inclined to swear.

"If you stand there an hour you'll be be-trayed before another minute," she exclaimed, and pulling him by the sleeve she dragged him to the door

"There—across the passage—first door to the left—make haste! Oh, those big heavy boots of yours, they'd wake the dead!"

Staying to kiss his hand respectfully

Ruth, Dick stepped lightly across the landing ; so noiselessly, indeed, that Kitty's adjuration of his boots was scarcely called for.

Springing lightly to her mistress, she put her arms about her neck, and said, in a half-crying tone—

" Forgive me, dear miss Ruth, but you've been so noble to save his life, and if that red-headed brute thought you had concealed him here, he would never leave you any character —the thief."

Ruth returned the young girl's embrace.

" Then you do not think harshly of your mistress for what she has done ? " she asked, softly.

" Bless you, miss, no."

"Not even for concealing a highwayman in my bed ?"

" That's where you've done such a noble deed, for only that could save him, and I know how good you are, if the world even knew it I should never believe harm of you, besides, he looks as brave and noble as he is handsome."

A trace of Ruth's former colour stole back to her cheeks.

" Yes, he is brave and noble. The innocent would never suffer harm from him. God forgive those who make him less guileless than he is now."

" Aye, so say I, miss. But now let me arrange your bed. There—now I'll run and see after him. I know you won't be jealous at I've got him in my chamber."

Thus speaking, the light-hearted girl, who had seen the delicacy of Dick's concealment amongst the clothes, ran nimbly from the chamber, leaving her gentle mistress to think of what the world would say if it were known that her breast had that night been the pillow of a highwayman.

CHAPTER XVII.

HOW SWIG AND BIG BULLSKIN GET OUT OF WAY OF THE OFFICERS, AND FALL INTO A MESS—DEVIL DUKE AND CECILY LISLE—TEMPTATION OF LOVE—AN INTERRUPTION TO A SCENE OF JOY—FRIENDS ON THE WATCH, AND A SPY ON THE ALERT.

THE merry party had not proceeded far from the Roundhouse when an abrupt termination was brought to their caroling song, that seemed to sober them on the instant.

A ringing clatter of horses' hoofs, and frantic shouting of enraged officers galloping down upon them, plainly told their escape had been discovered.

Without a word they parted.

Devil Duke and Gallant Tom took different routes with their fair companions. The remainder of the party, except Swig and Big Bullskin, who scrambled through a hedge and tumbled into a dirty ditch, coolly strolled off in a group, ready to meet any adventure that happened to come in their way.

" Don't shove a fellow's head into the mud," said Bullskin.

" Keep yer hugly great knees out of my belly, then," replied Swig, who was lying on his companion ; " do you want to knock all the wind out of me ? "

" Why the devil don't you, boo——"

Before he had time to give utterance to the remainder of his words, something slimy hopped across his face, and rolled down his throat.

Swig looked surprised.

Ere he had time to inquire the cause of the sudden climax of his companion's speech, he received a terrific kick, that sent him flying several yards.

A wailing cry and a heavy splash followed his flight.

Then Swig disappeared, head and shoulders under the slimy mud, his two legs sticking up like sign-posts.

It was not long before he extracted himself from that critical position, and running furiously to where his companion lay, uttering a torrent of the most ill-natured threats of vengeance, looking an awful sight with the greasy mud dripping from his enraged features, he was about to put his barbarous threats into execution, but the sight of Bullskin with his head resting on his hand, looking awfully white and sick, brought pity from the little highwayman, and in a sympathising tone he said—

" What's the matter, Bull ? "

" Boo-oo-ugh."

" Anything turned yer up ? "

" Boo," was the only answer he got, and Big Bullskin opened his mouth to a dangerous extent, as though trying to force something from his throat.

ONE FOR HIS NOB.

"What is it?"

"I can feel it kicking," whined the giant, in a dismal tone.

"What?" asked Swig, looking scared at the pitable object of his companion.

"Why—boo—it's a frog jumped down my throat, ugh," and he gave an involuntary ·udder.

"Yer shouldn't keep yer mouth so wide open," said Swig, laughing.

"Can't you help a fellow, instead of grinning there like a monkey?"

"What can I do?"

"Hit me in the back and knock it out."

Swig did hit him in the back with such terrible force, that it sent the unfortunate Bullskin sprawling on his face.

He got up, and in a weak, but much clearer voice, said—

"Thank you."

Swig expected to get a clout, so he got at a respectful distance.

"Is it all right?" he asked, when he saw that his companion had no such intention of clouting him.

"Yes, there he goes.

Swig laughed when he saw the little reptile hopping away.

"Why didn't yer swallow him?" he said,

"What for?"

" Why they are good for worms."

" I ain't got worm."

" Oh, I thought yer had ; anyhow you are reglar rasher, and——"

" Yes. all right," said Big Bullskin, wishing to turn the subject. "Is them cussed officers passed yet ?"

" Of course they have, an 'our ago."

" Then we'll go."

" Where ?"

" Anywhere."

" Which road do yer take to go there ?"

"Come on, I'll show you."

" Do you think I am going to walk about covered with stinking mud."

There is nothing else for you to do, without you lick it off with your tongue."

" Ain't there ? it shows what a dirty devil you are," said Swig, disgusted with the other's remark, "there ain't any water, is there ?"

" I don't know that there is about here."

" It shows how much you know, because there is a brook not five minutes' walk off."

" I am very glad to hear it, because we can clean ourselves."

" Yer had better lick the mud off yerself, with yer long tongue."

" All right, old boy, when I have no other resource I'll turn cat."

Swig gave a grunt and led the way to the brook, where they cleaned themselves with the aid of a tuft of grass.

Then they started off as friendly as ever.

" Hallo," said Swig, in a whisper to his companion, "who's that in front ?"

" That's Devil Duke, and his lady, I'll swear."

" We'll follow him."

" We will."

So they did. In silence and in shade they followed the daring highwayman.

Unconscious of his two friends, who like shadows kept in his track, Devil Duke went on in silence, thinking or noticing nothing but the fair beauty by his side, and the extraordinary way by which they had been thrown together. But knowing such strange adventures were not uncommon to the handsome knights of the road, he did not trouble his head about it, but paid the whole of his attention to his companion.

" You have not told me your story," he said, drawing her lithe form closer to his side

" It is so sad," she said sorrowfully, "I fear it would make you unhappy, were you to hear it."

" It will make me more unhappy if not hear it," he said, gently.

" Why ?" she asked, prettily looking up him.

" Because you will have all your grief to yourself," he replied, earnestly, " and no one to sympathise with you."

" But my story is sad. very sad," she said, with a sigh.

" Just the reason, dearest, I should learn it, and share half your troubles."

" Since you are so anxious I will tell you."

He stooped and kissed her fair brow.

Then she commenced to relate her sad story ; her sweet voice seemed to give a sort of charm to its troubles as she continued.

The beauty of the hour was upon them both ; the soft subduing rays of the shining moon lighted up their path, and gave a thrilling influence to the quietness that prevailed.

The careless, reckless expression had left the gallant highwayman's face, and a look of deep, sorrowful regret suffused his features as he listened, in a kind of trance, to the sweet melody of her plaintive voice.

" Are you compelled to marry that despicable cur ?" he said, with a flush, as she finished her story ; " that conceited hound who laid in the road, shivering ? he who had not courage to protect you, his future bride, when I stopped the coach ?"

" It is against my inclination that the alliance should take place."

" By whose wish is it, then ?"

" My aunt's, the Duchess of Glenmore."

Devil Duke inwardly swore vengeance against the Duchess of Glenmore, and her choice for fair Cecily.

The fair Cecily neither swore inwardly nor outwardly, but walked on in silence, thinking of her helpless position.

She had been left an orphan at an early age, with an immense fortune.

Her aunt, the duchess, who had been chosen guardian by her dying sister, Cecily's mother, had been particularly careful to keep the fair Cecily, as she grew up, in very close confine-nent, away from the dashing cavaliers, who in those days would challenge one another to mortal combat for a pretty girl.

The bloated, red-nosed duchess, not wishing to have any such horrible encounters enacted about her fair charge, kindly kept her out of sight, for one of her own choosing.

The one of her own choice, the Hon. Augustus Toolittle, was then at college, where he had been the greater part of his life.

At twenty-two years of age he left college to go and live with the duchess, who gave her darling nephew the kindest reception, and introduced him to Cecily, who looked upon him with the greatest disgust and contempt.

She had anticipated seeing some handsome, noble, dashing gentleman, by what her aunt had said about her nephew.

Instead of which, however, she was presented to a diminutive, thin, sickly-looking fop, with a head like a huge pumpkin.

Cecily confined herself to her chamber, and cried over her disappointment for several days; and it was not without a great deal of persuasion that she would have an interview with her aunt.

When she did, to her surprise, the duchess told her that the Hon. Augustus Toolittle was her betrothed husband.

Cecily remonstrated against the proposition with all the indignation of her gentle nature, but to no avail.

The duchess told her that everything was being prepared for the coming wedding, which would take place a month hence.

The same evening as this was announced to her she was compelled to go to a grand ball with her hated intended husband.

The Hon. Augustus Toolittle was in ecstacies at the very idea of escorting such a beauty amongst the gay throng that would be assembled there.

He fancied that he would be admired by the ladies and envied of his fair companion by the dashing gentlemen.

But his conceited pleasant contemplations were obliterated by the appearance of Devil Duke, who, as the reader already knows, met him on the road, and before leaving lodged him in a ditch.

A shrill whoop made the lovers start, and broke the stillness that prevailed.

Cecily trembled, and clung to her companion, as a shadowy form bounded past them like a gust of wind.

A look of recognition came over Devil Duke's face as the form passed him.

Swig nudged his companion, and, in a whisper, said—

"Do you know who that was?"

"Yes," replied Bullskin, in an under tone "the Rusher. I wonder what he is up to to night?"

"Don't you know what he meant by cry?"

"Of course I do—to be on the look-out."

"He is a artful devil, ain't he? I never knowed such a fellow in all my life! Why, I've seed him get through a keyhole before now."

"So have I, and if there has been anyone in the room, he runs between their legs, throws 'em over his back, then escapes through the crack of the boards."

"Oh, that is nothing to what I've seen him do," said Swig, who always tried to tell a larger lie than his companion. "I've seen him jump clean over a 'ouse, fall down a waterspout head fust, then crawl out at the bottom unhurt."

"God forgive you," thought Big Bullskin. Having respect for his shins he did not say so. His companion wore heavy boots with thick toes, and had he breathed his disbelief he well knew he would have had the before-mentioned thick toes administered unmercifully to the before-mentioned long shanks.

Such being the case he said nothing, but inwardly called Swig a liar.

"Devil Duke is pitching a fine yarn to that gal," said Swig.

"I don't half like it," said Bullskin; "she ought to be my gal, I saved her."

"Your gal," sneered Swig, with much contempt in his tone, "just as if she'd have such a hugly clown as you."

"She would have you without the least hesitation."

"She 'ud rather have me than she would you," remarked Swig, with an air of self-confidence. "I am a better looking fellow than you are."

Little people generally have a tolerable amount of self-conceit.

Swig had a very great amount, enough for six ordinary persons.

Bullskin, knowing this, let him enjoy his own opinion, and, as before, walked on in silence.

By this time Devil Duke, with his companion, came in sight of a huge mansion, the residence of the Duchess of Glenmore.

"Must I leave you so soon?" asked Devil Duke, for his companion had intimated that would be best to part before they got too nr to her respectful aunt's domain, for fear being seen together. "And under such painful circumstances. Tell me, Cecily was it by your parents' wish, that you are forced against your will to marry a man you do not like, that is to say, this one in particular? I can't call him a man who hasn't sufficient animal courage to defend himself."

"No," she said, "not that I am aware of."

"Then, by heaven, you shall never marry anyone but one of your own choice, not while I have strength to use my sword."

They had now reached the large gates of the mansion, and Devil Duke felt the trembling form of his companion timidly clinging to him.

"Cecily, dearest," he said, "let me take you in and warn your loving aunt and the valiant gentleman against their base persecutions towards you."

"No, no," she said, nestling closer to the highwayman, "the servants would see you; we can get in at the back unseen."

Devil Duke drew her passionately to his breast and then followed her.

Traversing through a long gravel path, they came to a small door, which his fair guide noiselessly opened by a spring; then they entered a long narrow passage, and wended their way up a much longer and darker staircase, at the top of which was another small door which opened by the same means as the last; then they stood upon a magnificent broad-carpeted and well-lighted landing.

Cecily put her finger on her lip for caution, while she carefully looked about to see if there were any sneaking menials on the watch.

Appearing perfectly satisfied with the result of her search, she led the way up a second light of stairs, stopping oor

with her hand on the handle, her heart beating wildly, and her cheeks in a glow, she looked at her companion with swimming eyes and entered a luxurious apartment.

The highwayman glanced round the chamber with a bewildered look at the costly furniture. As his eyes fell upon a beautiful spring couch, a thrill ran through his frame that touched his heart, and sent the blood tingling through his veins.

He stood for some minutes vacantly staring, first at the couch, then at his companion.

His mind seemed as though wandering.

Probably there were some very strange thoughts wandering through his mind, but what they were we will not venture to say, but leave the reader to imagine what thoughts are most likely to wander through an impulsive fellow's mind at such a time, and in such an inviting place, and with such an irresistible beauty. Her charms would have tempted an anchorite, and set his soul dreaming to a dangerous extent.

Cecily laid her tiny hand on her lover's arm, and recalled him to his senses.

Devil Duke started at the touch, and his face flushed with a look of self-reproach.

Cecily Lisle fastened the room door inside, then disappeared into an adjoining room.

The highwayman carelessly threw himself on the couch, and waited anxiously for the lady to return.

She did not return in an exceedingly becoming costume, as her lover thought.

She had changed her dress, and had put on a long white robe that trailed behind, and showed every line and dimple in her smooth, round, and finely moulded limbs, as she advanced towards the couch.

Devil Duke took her in his arms, and clasped her to his breast, she going unresistingly to him, her eyes glancing with an impassioned light, and her heart palpitating wildly, as their lips met in a lingering kiss.

The highwayman felt the danger the time and impassioned kisses were drawing him and his guileless innocent companion into, so gently sat her by his side.

Thus they sat in silence, with each other's hand locked in their own.

The soft subduing influence of night, seemed

to have a charm in accordance with the gusts of passion at their hearts.

The highwayman was in an awkward situation, alone in the solitude of a dimly-lighted chamber, with that peerless creature by his side, heart throbbing against heart, lip clinging to lip, her glowing cheek resting on his breast, her soft white arm twined around his neck, and their voices hushed to a whisper.

No tongue could have told the eloquence glowing in their humid eyes, their love story would be only told by deep drawn sighs, and the passionless caresses following quickly one upon the other.

The place, the time, the mute drowsy influence that every moment came over them, and made them more helpless, this only added to the bewildering sense, the dreamy daze of mind, the helpless passionate caresses, the wild thrill of love that ran through their veins like liquid fire.

Devil Duke felt that he could not abstain from his over-coming senses any longer.

He also felt the warm pliant form of his companion throbbing beneath his arm.

He saw her helplessness, and his own perilous position.

His whole frame worked convulsively.

A struggling contest was going on within him, between his two morals, the one to satisfy his own sensual capricious desire, and thus destroy the maiden's purity and honour, or cast the thought aside with contempt and shame at his own vileness, for having wronged her by a thought.

For a moment or two he seemed to waver. "No, no," he said, springing up, his noble nature deciding the contest, "I would not sully her by such a base thought, sooner would I chop my right hand off."

He looked down upon her with an earnest, grave expression on his handsome countenance, then taking her trembling hand, he led her to the open casement, and stood out upon the balcony.

There she stood, with her gallant lover by her side.

The silvery moon, pouring forth its soft mellow rays, floating round the fair girl who stood beneath the light of heaven undefiled, looking like a descendant from the regions above.

Her long white robe, hanging loosely about her bewitching form.

Her long streaming bright gold-coloured hair hanging around her swan-like throat, swelling out into a high magnificent bust.

Her arms and shoulders were bare, and tiny white hand rested on the highwaym arm.

He, too, looked noble and grand, as stood by Cecily's side, beneath the shining moonbeams, a frank honest look on his handsome countenance.

Many a man of a less passionate nature than Devil Duke, would have delighted in the idea of taking a mean advantage of her helpless, yielding, innocent virtue, and would have sullied her for ever and thought it bliss.

The highwayman thought it sacrilege to harm her even by a thought.

Not that we wish to say that his morality and virtue were all perfection.

No, decidedly not.

Devil Duke was as great a sinner as anyone, and always sinned when he saw a favourable opportunity, but on this particular occasion a chord of his nobler nature was touched by the simple pure innocence of his fair companion.

She was an untutored child of nature, knowing nothing of the outward world and its subtle wickedness.

Her utter simplicity and confiding manner touched his deepest sense of honour.

He was in her chamber, in secrecy, at night, and at the peril of her reputation.

On any other occasion it would have been dangerous.

His mind would have been overpowered by carnal thoughts and base suggestions.

He looked on the peerless girl who stood by his side as a being only to be worshipped.

A being who could gladden the sad by a look from those diamond blue eyes, and bring pleasure to the unhappy by a smile from those cherry lips.

Devil Duke looked at his companion quite with a half mournful and half pleased expression.

"Cecily, dearest," he said, in a gentle tone that made her start and look up, "are you angry with me?"

"Angry," she repeated, while tears glisten

in her soft blue eyes, " no, Philip, dear. Why should I be angry with you?"

"I feared, dearest, I had stayed too long," replied Duke, taking her little hand and looking tenderly into her face, "I have jeopardised both you and myself in staying so long. I fear not for myself, but for you. Were I discovered leaving this room, your name would suffer by the base suggestions and comdemuations."

Cecily blushed to her temples and shyly faltered—

"No one need see you go. I possess a little secret which no one knows of but myself, and you can ever elude suspicion of your entry or exit."

"Such a secret is valuable in our transactions, dearest."

"It is, indeed; but for such a purpose it has not been used as yet."

The highwayman caressed her, and for a few minutes he was again lost in deep thought.

"Of what are you thinking, Philip?" asked Cecily, gently; calling him Philip by his wish, because he thought the name sounded much prettier than Devil, especially when articulated by her sweet voice.

"You, dearest," he answered.

"And why of me?"

"Of whom else should I think?"

Cecily glided her arms gently round his neck, and drew his face to hers.

Their lips met in a long affectionate caress; then she nestled closer to his breast, as though she found consolation and protection beneath his manly form.

"Philip, dear Philip," she suddenly broke out looking into his frank open countencnce, "I should have suffered so much had you been taken by those wretched men."

"So confiding," he said sadly, "and I so unworthy."

"Why, unworthy?"

"A felon," he said bitterly, " with a price t upon my head."

She started, and clung to him with a cry.

"Philip."

"Even now there are bloodhounds on my track."

"Do not talk so fearful, Philip, dear."

"'Tis true, dearest. Even to-night, when I leave you, I may be captured, and to-morrow morning be dangling at the end of a gibbet."

Cecily gave a faint cry, and trembled.

The idea of ever seeing his handsome form ------ging from a gibbet, was horrible.

"Do you love me?" he asked.

"Dearest Philip," she answered earnestly, "do I love in vain?"

"I am grieved to say you do——"

She recoiled as though bitten by a serpent at the words.

Devil Duke put his arm round her lithsome waist, and drew her towards him, and continued—

"Were I leading any other life but the reckless adventurous career, I should be proud and happy to call you mine, but at present I am not worthy of a love so pure and good."

"But, Philip dear, if I love you just the same," she said tearfully.

"Then I should not——"

Bang!

Crash!

Then the door of the lady's chamber flew back.

"I have been betrayed," hissed Devil Duke between his firmly set teeth, " some cursed spy has been on the alert."

Cecily Lisle trembled fearfully, when she saw the terrible danger of her lover.

The highwayman drew himself erect, supported the trembling girl on his left arm, with his right hand drew his sword, and defiantly waited for his foes, who swarmed in the room like wolves.

"Secure the villain, robber and highwayman," shouted the Honourable Augustus outside the door.

"Back, men, back, I say, if you respect your lives," said the excited highwayman.

The men respected their lives, but did not see the force of retreating, knowing they were twenty to one, and all were armed.

Devil Duke saw that he had no chance against the determined sturdy retainers, and thought his best plan was to fly.

Leading his fair companion to a couch, he laid her half fainting form down.

"Farewell for the present, Cecily, we shall meet again."

Then dashing down the chamber, he threw open the casement and sprang out.

A loud shout of defiance and triumph rang through the air.

The highwayman had fallen in the midst a group of officers.

ust then could have been seen Swig, Bull- and the Lusher gliding about like ws.

Lusher was not idle.

CHAPTER XVIII.

MATTHIAS GRABBE PEERS AFTER A HIGHWAY- MAN AND GETS " ONE FOR HIS NOB."

RUTH's lively waiting maid, found our hero, when she tripped into the room, performing a hasty toilet before her mirror.

She opened her eyes wide at this unlooked- for spectacle, and exclaimed—

" Well, I'm sure. That's how you make use of your time, is it ? There, that will do. You're quite handsome enough. Just like you highwaymen, though, that I've read about. Making themselves good-looking when they're going to the scaffold."

" Saucy pert, I am not going that journey just yet, I trust, but forty-eight hours of strife and flight render soap and water very refreshing."

" Well, you're very romantic, I must say, and you haven't been *all* your time at ' strife and flight.' I wish you had, and never have come here to disgrace my dear seduced young mistress, for I've no doubt you'll laugh in your sleeve at what you've done, if you break her heart."

" Little girl," the highway boy said gravely, " what is your name ?"

" Kitty Dove, sir, is my name, England is my nation, Cornwall is my dwelling place, and——"

" That will do, Kitty, I know the rest. You're a very nice young girl, Kitty, and some of these days I may find you a good- looking highwayman for a husband."

" Just like you, I suppose. Thank you. When I want one, I'll pick him out for my- self, but that won't be yet."

> Oh, I'll never marry, not I,
>   For men are such rogues and deceivers,
> Love or marriage is all my eye,
>   And fools are the would-be believers."

" A very complimentary song, but not so loud, saucy Kitty ; that red-headed officer has long ears."

" They were not long enough to hear when you were at your base tricks with my dear young mistress in making her your victim, poor darling lady."

" Hush, Kitty. As I said before, you are a very good girl, and for all you have done or are likely to do in my behalf, I thank you and will repay you. But mention that dear angel's name only with the respect I feel for her."

Kitty Dove tossed her head.

" I daresay. You highwaymen always do respect the name or honour of any lady who allows you in her house."

" Kitty, do not wrong your mistress."

" Ah, well. If you didn't, it was her good- ness, not yours. I've no doubt you're as fine a lover as ever stepped in two boots."

" I never thought to compromise that gentle lady, believe me, Kitty, there are blacker hearted men than me beneath this roof."

" There's one wicked old rascal certainly, and he'll get a bit of my mind in the shape of a pail of suds some of these days. The sanctified sinner that sentences people for crimes, not half so bad as himself. But never mind now. You come this way. Have you quite done your toilet ?"

This was asked so archly that our hero could not repress a smile.

" I thought you might want a little cos- matique for your eyebrows, or to show off your moustauche, or a little scent for your hair. But there, I daresay you've as good an opinion of yourself without."

" I daresay I have, Kitty, but as I fancy I hear some one coming up stairs, perhaps we had better finish our conversation another time."

Kitty listened.

Then softly closing the door, went on tiptoe to a wardrobe, which she opened.

" You'd think the solid wall was behind them," she asked.

" I should indeed."

" Well that shows what a dunce you are for it isn't. There's a place that runs along the wall, and that's where you'll have to hide."

" Be kind enough to lead the way."

Kitty slid open the back of the wardrobe and partly led, and partly pushed the youthful highwayman into a narrow cell-like place at the back, entering with him.

There was just room enough for him to avoid knocking his shoulders against either side, but small as the place was some attempt made to give it a comfortable look.

A small table was placed at one end, on which stood a lighted lamp, some wine, and some refreshments.

A bedroom chair was the other side of the table.

"There," Kitty exclaimed, "there's some wine for you to swallow and a chair to stick your great carcase in. There's a light for you to see your face by. You can have a looking-glass if you wish for one, and there's plenty of air, so you won't choke before your time."

"Thank you. I see you've had all prepared. You expected to hide me here."

"Of course I did, when l knew where you were."

"Which reminds me, miss. How did you find out where I was?"

Kitty laughed.

"If people will tell other people all their history, and forget that walls have ears——"

Dick coloured.

"It was as well the walls had such gentle ears," he said, patting Kitty's saucy cheeks.

"Hands off," the pert maid cried, "you don't come your tricks with me. I'll leave you now to you own reflections, and I hope to repentance."

"Stay," he caught her hand as she was about to leave, "how long am I to be cooped up here?"

"Till night, of course. You don't think we'll let you out before, for every one to know where you've been hiding. For shame! You ought to have more respect for my mistress, and if I *should* bring her to see you before you go, I'll make you go down on your knees, I can tell you."

"I shall be willing to expiate my crime, and before so fair a judge——"

"Now, no speech-making——"

"No, but something more telling—there."

He drew her towards him, and kissed her gallantly.

"Just what I thought you'd do," she said, struggling from his embrace.

"Say rather just what you were waiting for."

"Impudence. There—that's for you."

She gave him a sounding smack on the cheek.

It was given good-numoredly, but it made his eyes water.

Kitty, with a merry laugh, closed the secret door.

"A girl of the right sort," the youthful highwayman mused when he was alone. "So this is my new hiding-place. Humph! Twelve feet by two. Looks suspiciously like a condemned cell or a tomb. That's a thoughtful lass, though. A draught of wine will be refreshing. I see she's placed the chair so that I must vault over the table to get to it. Here goes then, for standing upright gives me the idea of being entombed alive."

He sprang over the table, and seating himself in the chair, uncorked the bottle of wine and prepared to defiantly pass the long lingering twelve hours from daylight to the coming night-fall.

Kitty Dove encountered at her door the red-haired officer of justice, Mattnias Grabbe, prowling like a sullen beast of prey in search of whom he might devour.

The comic visage of the brutal thieftaker lowered when his sinister glance fell on Kitty's saucy face, and grasping her rudely by the arm, he said gruffly—

"Here, girl—would you like to earn a guinea?"

"I must know first how I am to earn it. People get guineas for all sorts of things, you know."

The ruffian looked at her comely form with a smile.

"Oh, 'taint nothing of that sort. I'm not in the humour, I can tell you. I'd a sight sooner ketch sight of that 'ere highwayman's boot than see the crummiest gal as is here."

"You ought to have your ears boxed, you silly red head," Kitty said, colouring angrily.

"Don't be a fool, and mind me. Look here. I wants to take that highwayman, an I take him I mean to."

"But suppose he isn't to be found, Mister Grabbe."

"Oh, he's to be found right enough, and I think I know where to drop on for the right place."

"How clever you must be!

"Clever enough for that, as they'll find as is hiding him. Where's your young mistress?"

"In her bed. Where do you think she is?"

"I'll give you a guinea to let me hide here till she comes out of her room."

"Why? You don't think the highwayman's there."

The fellow looked wise.

"We'll see," he answered gruffly.

Kitty burst out in a violent fit of laughter.

The thieftaker did not like the idea of standing to be laughed at. He got as red in the face as he was at beard, and finding Kitty did not desist, he pulled her rudely by the arm to quiet her.

"You make me laugh so," the girl said, "but where's the guinea, you can stay here and welcome."

The thieftaker took out a shining guinea and placed it ostentatiously in her palm.

"There it is, but mind, no blabbing to your misses. I'll sit here and watch the door, an' when she comes out I goes in."

Kitty seemed inclined to indulge in another outburst of laughter, but controling herself, she tripped lightly away.

Left to himself, the thieftaker took the opportunity of making a further examination of Kitty's room.

Her wardrobe underwent a good deal of inspection at his hands, and he tapped repeatedly at the back, but without scenting the secret of the hiding place.

In an hour or so, Ruth's door, on which he kept close watch during all his movements, opened, and the fair young girl left her apartment and descended the stairs.

Matthias Grabbe, lynx-eyed and dangerous, his teeth set, his hand clutching the butt of a pistol, crept stealthily from his concealment, as soon as Ruth's footsteps were out of hearing.

Her chamber was in partial darkness, owing to the curtains being drawn in front of the casement.

The thieftaker closed and locked the door behind him.

He had made up his mind to prompt and decided action.

Bestowing no attention on any other part of the room, he walked direct to the bedstead.

The hangings were down, and he felt sure he saw them shake.

His man was there.

Grasping the curtains with one hand, and holding his pistol ready with the other, he thrust his malignant head in and cried—

"Aha, highwayman, I have you. Yield, or die."

The thieftaker's voice was hoarse with suppressed excitement.

His burly form shook with agitation.

There was a handsome reward for Dick's capture, which he was sure to get.

He was, but in a different way.

The curtains he had torn slightly open.

His bloated visage, ashy with malignant triumph, was peering in.

The pistol was clutched in his right hand ready for action.

Not a sound had come from the bed.

But now, swift and sudden, a highwayman's heavy boot was thrust out.

No more was seen, but sharp and sure, it struck the thieftaker full in his distorted face.

Full and with deadly force, as if a foot of steel had propelled it with lightning power.

There was a sickening crash, and Matthias fell.

Then the booted leg went in again.

The curtains closed.

And in the faintly struggling morning light, the thieftaker lay at the foot of the bed, senseless and still.

CHAPTER XIX.

BETRAYED.

DICK was getting weary of his cramped hiding-place, when to his relief the secret door slid back, and Kitty, putting her saucy face in, beckoned him forth.

He came gladly enough, and gratefully pressed Kitty's hand.

A second form stood awaiting his coming.

A lady—his fair preserver—Ruth.

Bashful and timid, she hid her face from his glance, but did not resist when he took her little form in his arm and held her to his breast.

"You must say farewell," she murmured. her eyes brimful of tears, "I may never see you again—if not, you will think of me sometimes."

"I shall never forget," Dick answered, brokenly, "lady, we shall meet again. My destiny will link me to many of those I meet. I feel that you are one—farewell. For the safe guard of your precious innocence, how shall I thank you. Words will never speak the fervent gratitude of my heart."

"I shall be well repaid if you sometimes think of me," Ruth replied, sadly, "we must part now, there is danger in this moment's interview—farewell, wear this for my sake, and let no hand remove it till you have ceased to remember me."

He felt her trembling hand slide on to one of his fingers a slender ring.

He kissed the token on which her tears had dropped, and then he kissed the pure soft lips, that seemed to long for his kissing and yet grew cold at his caress, that clung so wistfully and fondly to his lips, yet quivered with shivering dread beneath the burning impress of his love; a hurried tremulous good-bye; a fervent pressure of form to form, of heart to heart, then Dick was torn from Ruth's embrace, and dragged he knew not whether, till he felt the cool evening air on his brow, and knew that he was outside the threshold of Ruth's dwelling.

"Haste," Kitty said, as she too wrung her hands and sobbed out, "farewell. Friends are awaiting you at the house where you will see a light showing through the red blind in the window of a house in the next street to the right—good-bye."

"Good-bye."

A pair of arms suddenly encircled his neck; his head was pulled down and thrice Kitty put her lips to his with a hearty smack before she suffered him to go.

Then she pushed him off the step and shut the door.

Evening had just set in; the glare of the solitary oil lamps with which our towns were lighted a century ago, contrasted dimly with the clear starlight and the dying day.

Our hero looked up at the frowning walls of the prison, and saw the broken loophole through which he had made his escape.

He gave a glance at the tall church spire, the first object he had discovered from his prison, and almost smiled when he noticed the height above which he must have swung.

They had not yet repaired the grated window, perhaps they were waiting first to get him in there again.

Musing on the varied incidents of his night adventure, Dick made his way unchallenged to the street on the right of the judge's house, and sought out the window with the red blind.

He found it half way up the street.

"What friends of mine, I wonder," he soliloquised, "has that young girl summoned to ensure my escape. I shall find out I suppose by entering."

A shadow at that moment came between the light inside, and the red blind.

Dick started.

He could have sworn the figure was that of the thieftaker Jonathan Wild.

For an instant a suspicion of treachery flashed to his mind.

Dismissing it he entered the house.

It was a small kind of beer tavern. A rough brutish-looking man, the landlord, was the only person Dick saw in the outer parlour.

There was not much to recommend him in the fellow's face, but he put on his best looks when he saw our hero.

"If your expecting friends," he said, "they're in that parlour there."

He pointed to a heavy open door.

Dick bowed, and stepping towards it pushed it open, and stepped in.

One step.

The door closed behind him.

An instinct of danger had flashed to his brain before he heard the click of the lock.

That instinct was realised in the scene he beheld.

Six armed men stood in the room awaiting his coming.

Five officers of justice and their leader, Jonathan Wild.

"Betrayed, and by Kitty Dove!"

The coarse laugh of the king of thieftakers was the first sound to salute our hero's ear as he reeled with the sudden vision of treachery and capture.

"Aha, Dick, sorry to see you here, but there is a big reward, and nab you we must."

Dick's eyes flashed angrily on the officers.

A fierce exclamation broke from his lips.

He made a backward bound, gleaming

round for means of escape or defence, then in dauntless rage confronted his foes.

The thieftaker's dry chuckle of triumph.

Six pistols were levelled at his brain.

CHAPTER XX.

DEVIL DUKE'S MISTAKE AND FIGHT WITH THE OFFICERS—THE LUSHER TAKES A NEW CHARACTER, AND DOES GREAT SERVICE—HOW THE DUCHESS GETS UPSET, AND HOW THE CAPTURED HIGHWAYMAN TAKES HER PLACE.

DEVIL DUKE was never more astonished in his life than he was when he took that fatal leap, and landed in the midst of a group of officers.

Twenty huge rough hands grabbed him by the collar, while others grabbed at his legs, arms, and other parts of his person.

He was covered from head to toe with huge, ugly, and dangerous pistols.

His numerous captors looked big, and told him to get up.

He said he would if they moved their hands.

They did not believe in it, and held him down.

"How the devil can I get up," he said, "if you hold me down ?"

"Oh, we know," said a chorus of voices in accordance.

"Yes, so do I know."

"What ?"

"That you are a set of fools."

The knuckles of the hands which held him were dug spitefully into his flesh, and numerous thick boots were administered on his shins and back bone.

The highwayman got furious, and could not think of words sufficient to express his wrath, but coming to a sensible conclusion by thinking that useless threats and vile oaths would not avail him much, he thought it would be better to act.

He did so.

Suddenly twisting over, he broke from the men's grasps, then springing to his feet, he darted through the astonished group, flew like an antelope through a long field, and bounded over a hedge.

His astonished pursuers, after looking at one another with open mouth, as though they expected he had vanished down their throats, started after him.

The foremost of the enraged officers were suddenly confronted by Big Bullskin rising up in front of them, looking like a huge giant.

One of the officers, rather more energetic than his companions, struck Bullskin rather furiously in the wind with his head, then scampered off.

Bullskin staggered and fell backwards, almost crushing Swig, who stood behind h'm grinning.

"Hallo, hallo !" shouted the Lusher, "what the devil are you lying down there for, fighting, too. Well, well, you are a pretty pair of chaps, always fighting. Come, get up."

"Hallo, old boy," said Bullskin, pulling his long leg away from the grasp of his little comrade ; "why, what have you got on ?"

"Oh, just a suit my Mary Jane lent me," said the Lusher, looking at himself, "what are you two always fighting about ?"

"I don't know," said Bullskin, ruefully. "Swig's always getting in the way, and then slips into me."

"I should think so," said Swig, coming forward, "you're always throwing yer ugly carcase on me."

"Never mind, make it up," said the Lusher, "this aint the sort of thing when there is a comrade in trouble. If you want to fight, go and fight his enemies."

"What have you got that disguise on for?" asked Swig, who, like his companion, was curious.

"Oh, my Mary Jane gave it me. Fine suit, aint it ? Mary Jane smuggled it. It belongs to one of the keepers. Fits fine, don't it ?"

"Yes," said Swig, "like a sack, and touches you nowhere."

"Never mind what it looks like, I wear it for its use."

"What is the use of dressing up like that ?"

"Come and help Duke, then you shall see its use."

Without another word the trio started off in the direction taken by their comrade.

Before they had time to scramble through the hedge, the officers had overtaken Devil Duke in a group, forming a circle which gradually narrowed round the gallant highwayman.

Devil Duke took a quick but comprehensive survey of his position, and seeing that an attempt to fight for an escape would only result in useless bloodshed, he gave up the hopeless idea, and allowed himself to be taken with the gratifying knowledge that friends were near.

"Keep back, some of you," said Devil Duke, trying to speak cooly, "you can't all have the pleasure of taking me."

The officers made no answer, but crowded round him like a pack of wolves, each eager to make a grab at his collar.

"Two will be quite enough to hold me," he said spitefully. "I am your prisoner, but I don't want fifty dirty great knuckles stuck in my neck."

"Ho, ho, I daresay not. Perhaps you would like us to let you walk on in front," exclaimed one of his captors.

"Hallo, here," said the Lusher, coming up, "you have got him at last."

"Yes," said one of the officers, "we've got him safe enough, and it'll be a sure case of gibbet with him."

"Ugly spiteful brute, I should like to run my sword through that great carcase," the Lusher said significantly, meaning the officer who had spoken.

The officer thought he meant the highwayman.

The Lusher and Devil Duke exchanged glances.

Jack Evans, for such was the real name of the Lusher, had suddenly vanished.

Swig and Bullskin looked at each other in surprise, wondering where their companion had so mysteriously vanished, while Devil Duke was being led away by the officers.

In another instant the illustrious Lusher could be seen dodging amongst the officers, pretending to be very jolly, at the same time, by accident of course, nudging the group of Bow Street runners, and dexterously jerking the pistols from their belts.

Too much excited by the success of their capture to notice the peculiar frolics of the supposed keeper, they were innocent of their and proceeded on their journe~ each

man thinking he had the greatest right to the largest share of the reward.

They were each welcome to all they could get.

The officers came to a sudden halt, to make room for a sedan chair to pass, carried by two short stout men, who perspired beneath the weight that sat inside.

"Oh, goodness me, what is the meaning of this?" said a choked sort of voice, from a huge head covered with sausage curls, from the window of the sedan chair.

"Highwayman, your grace, caught him in the lady's chamber," said an officer coming forward, and making an awkward bow to the bloated red face.

"The villian. Goodness me—the wretch. I am shocked—the scamp, blackguard, highwayman, too. Take him away. Hang—hang—hang him," and the bloated head vanished forthwith.

Jack Evans, alias the Lusher, had again mysteriously disappeared.

He had put his head between the two short legs of the two fat carriers, and thrown them on their backs, then crawled under the sedan chair.

A sudden crash, and a succession of stifled screams.

Then the Duchess of Glenmore scrambled through the broken window.

In the excitement of the moment, the officers left their prisoner to aid the old duchess from her critical position.

In her hurry to scramble out, she had fallen.

It suddenly occurred to some of the officers that their prisoner was alone.

Some went to keep him company, while others assisted the old lady back to her sedan chair.

Devil Duke was gone.

He did not care too much for their company; besides, they were incautious—gave very unpleasant insinuations about strong walls, and so on.

When the officers found their prisoner had escaped, they called each other cursed fools and blockheads, and swore in a most unofficial manner, and started in pursuit of the runaway.

But Devil Duke had not run away.

secreted in a bush; he had seen

DEVIL DUKE RECEIVES AN ASSASSIN'S BLOW.

and overheard what they said, and when they had gone out of sight he crept forth.

His companions had crept out before him.

Taking leave of his companions, he started off on a new adventure, calling at an inn for a horse.

After riding through a great distance of the lonely country at a rapid speed, the animal fell into a slow canter, and Devil Duke for a few minutes fell into a deep reverie.

He thought of the strange scene from which he had just escaped; of the beautiful girl he had left behind in the hands of her base persecutors, and of his own wild life.

The gentleness of his late companion had made an impression on his fearless nature.

Suddenly his reverie was interrupted.

He was confronted by a coarse, brutal-looking fellow, who pointed a huge pistol point blank at his nose.

"What would you like?" asked Duke.

"Your money or your life!" answered the intruder.

"You shall have it," remarked Devil Duke, fumbling about in the breast of his coat.

"Now then, look alive!" said the brutal-looking stranger.

Devil Duke told him to have patience and he would deliver.

Drawing a pistol he fired at his opponent, without the shot taking effect.

"That's your game, is it," said the other, with an oath, returning the shot with wonderful rapidity.

Devil Duke saw the shot coming, and lowered his head just in time.

The bullet whizzed past him and sunk in the trunk of a tree.

Devil Duke smiled, and told the stranger he could extract the shot and save it for some one else.

The stranger glared at the fearless fellow, and drew his sword.

In an instant, Devil Duke's sword flew from its sheath, and the two men confronted each other with a determined look.

Devil Duke guarded the heavy furious blows of his adversary with his own weapon, with the cool quietness of an expert swordsman, which he was.

The other grew exasperated.

He cut and thrust madly at his opponent, and made a desperate lunge at Duke's neck.

But to no avail.

Suddenly he turned his wrist, raised his blade, and brought it down in a straight line for the highwayman's head.

Quick as the feint was to throw him off his guard, Duke was as quick, and caught the descending weapon on the flat part of his own blade.

The sword flew from his adversary's hand, and fell to the earth in two, while the pain caused by the concussion was intense.

Devil Duke felt as though a sudden blow had deadened the power of his arm from finger tip to shoulder joint.

The benumbing sensation had rendered his arm useless for a time, or he would have quickly brought his antagonist to the earth.

Devil Duke put his left hand in the holster; the stranger saw a gleaming pistol come forth, guessing the intent of his adversary, he plunged his heels in the sides of his horse, and galloped away furiously.

Devil Duke fired at the retreating coward; the shot took effect, it lodged under the man's coat tails.

With a yell, he sprang up in the stirrups, and groaned awfully.

"Serve him right," muttered Duke, rubbing his arm, "he won't be able to sit down for a month, I know."

Rubbing his right arm until he made the other fairly ache with continual motion, and tender blisters slowly rise on the tips of his fingers through the friction, the sense of feeling came back to his arm.

Regaining his sword, he started off, feeling particularly inclined to plunder some one. His late encounter had ripened him for an adventure.

It was a little out of his line to be stopped on his own beat, by any such merciless murderer. He felt it an outrage on his professional occupation, and meant to have revenge.

A sound on the road broke his reverie.

The comer was a young handsome cavalier, dressed in a princely style, with a princely figure.

Devil Duke looked at the gallant with admiration, and anticipated a good haul. Presenting his pistol in the almost feminine fair face of the young rider, he said—

"Stand and deliver!"

The other gave a musical laugh, and said he would if the highwayman would show him the way.

Devil Duke admired the young noble for his cool carelessness, and looked with surprise at his costly dress, the jewelled hilt of the rapier that hung at his side, and the beautiful steed upon which he sat like a statue.

"Come, my lord," said Devil Duke, "hand over."

"By jove, you are polite," remarked the other, drily, "what would you require?"

"Your money."

"I have none," replied the young noble, "you can have my sword."

"The hilt is valuable."

"The point dangerous."

Duke started at the cool defiant

The young stranger presented finely chased pistols at the head of Duke.

The act was so quick and quiet, that the highwayman was quite bewildered for a moment; he lost all self-possession; he was not certain that the world had not suddenly turned upside down, and so changed the gentlemen of the land into highwaymen, and highwaymen into mummies.

"By jove, not a bad idea. Stand and deliver," said the young noble, pressing a pistol tube to Duke's ear.

"I thank you," said Devil Duke, slowly and cautiously, for fear of moving his head, "that is the very thing I want you to do."

"Being our mutual want, we had better settle it as soon as possible."

"We will, when you move those pistols," was the reply.

"They are hair triggers."

"The very reason I want them further away."

"Pistols are not nice things to use, they are apt to make a mess, but I object to be stopped for nothing."

"I do not, as a rule, stop people for nothing," Devil Duke said.

"What would you like, a bullet or an inch or two of cold steel."

"I prefer the steel."

"Come," said the young stranger, "I have not had a fight lately. You are a highwayman, ain't you?"

"I am."

"With pockets full of plunder, I suppose."

"A little."

"That's a good thing, I'll have some of it."

"The deuce you will."

"Yes, I am quite cleaned out, and you are a gentlemanly kind of scamp."

"Thank you."

"Then suppose we make a bargain and have a fight."

"Fight by all means, but what about the bargain."

"How much is the hilt of my sword worth," asked the stranger.

The highwayman looked at it.

It was richly jewelled.

"About two hundred pounds," he said, reflectively.

"And what money might you have in your pockets."

"Just about that amount."

"Come on then, my sword against your two hundred. A fair fight and no pistol shooting. That two hundred pounds will be mine."

"Will it," said Duke.

It was certainly the coolest proposition he had ever heard, and he entered into the spirit of the adventure.

He felt a brave man's liking for the gallant fellow who with such careless grace had met him on his own ground.

The stranger replaced his pistols.

Duke did the same, and they both dismounted.

The stranger slung his reins over his left arm.

Duke followed his example, and the fight began.

The difference between the two was striking.

Duke, with his powerful figure and stately height, towered above his opponent by a head.

He was reckoned one of the best swordsmen in Captain Claude's band.

But the stranger, with a slender form, fair frank face, and quick daring eye, a wrist of steel, and could use his weapon well.

The highwayman thought to have an easy conquest, in which he was mistaken.

The stranger's finely-tempered blade clung to his like a serpent, and Duke had to be very keenly on his guard.

He tried one of his famous lunges, and the stranger laughed at him.

"An old trick," he said; "try it again, and see what you will get for it."

"This then," said Duke, and he tried another—a straight, terrible thrust, which few men could have parried.

His young opponent turned it aside easily.

Hitherto he had acted on the defensive; now he thought it was his turn to try a feint.

"I shall have the top button off your coat," he said, quietly.

"I shall take the feather out of your cap first," said Duke, regarding his opponent doubtfully.

The highwayman struck the weapon aside, as the point of the young stranger's sword grated on the edge of his top button.

"The next time I shall take it off," said the young noble.

"Try it."

As he spoke, the sword point of his assailant split the front seam of his coat open.

Devil Duke grew angry, and less careful. He made a terrible down cut at his oppo-t's head.

His sword was caught by the stranger's.

A shower of sparks flew from the ringing weapons.

"I shall wager my horse against yours that have that button off in another three inutes," said the stranger, guarding another ff his head.

turning the blow, the point of his slim er cut the button from the shank, and the ton flew from Duke's coat.

" I have won your horse."

'Have you," replied Duke, "I mean to cut the feather from your cap."

"You will take a piece of my head with it if you go on at this rate."

"That will be your fault."

"You are growing spiteful, my friend."

Duke laughed sarcastically, and made some furious thrusts at his fearless young opponent.

Devil Duke got enraged and violent.

His every stroke was turned aside by the lithe blade of his young adversary.

The stranger had gained his point, and now only guarded the impetuous strokes of the highwayman.

Every pass and thurst Duke knew in the art of fencing.

He tried to take the feather out of his opponent's cap, but to no avail.

His blade was guarded off by the cool steady hand of the stranger, and not once did the point of his sword touch his intended mark.

The fight had lasted some time when by instinct they both drew back, lowered their weapons, and looked at each other in surprise.

"It's nearly time this combat was over," said Devil Duke.

"Just what I was about to say," remarked the young stranger, "you have nearly scraped the blade of my sword away."

"You have a wrist like iron. Never have I fought with one with such cool skill as you."

The young stranger bowed.

"May I know the name of the gallant knight with whom I have been fighting," he asked.

"Duke," replied the highwayman.

"The Devil," said the other, surprised at the name.

"No, Devil Duke."

"Then I may say I have beaten the very devil himself."

The highwayman laughed and sheathed his sword.

His opponent smiled and did the same.

"May I know by whom I have been vanquished," asked the highwayman.

"Victor St. James."

"I am proud at having crossed swords with one so brave and gallant."

"And I am delighted at having met so gallant a gentleman of your profession. By Jove! it was a luxury to cross swords with you. I quite enjoyed that set-to."

"I wish I could say the same."

"Why?"

"Because you have won my two hundred."

"And your horse, too."

"The devil! You don't want to take a fellow's horse; you can't ride on two."

"You can keep your animal, but hand over the coin."

He handed over the coin very reluctantly The young noble put it in his pocket with much satisfaction.

"I hope I shall have the pleasure of meeting your lordship again," said Devil Duke.

"I hope you will," replied the young stranger. "By Jove! you are a stunning sort of fellow. Are you going so soon?"

"Yes. I am going to elope with a mercer's pretty little wife."

"By Jove! a capital idea. I must find a mercer's pretty little wife to elope with."

"I am going to London. We shall meet again before long."

He put out his hand as he spoke, which the other took in a warm, friendly grasp.

"Adieu."

"Adieu."

They raised their hats to each other as they parted, and went in different directions.

Victor St. James fell into a meditative sort of reverie as the sound of his late opponent's retreating animal's feet grew more indistinct.

"I feel myself again," said St. James, meditatively, as his horse fell into a slow trot. "By Jove! I had the blues awfully before. What a difference a little money makes in a fellow!"

He turned sharply round in his saddle, and looked inquiringly about.

"I could have sworn I heard some one," he said; "but it must have been my fancy. If I do catch any sneaking brute following me, I shall give him a bullet in his ugly skull. Perhaps somebody wants my two hundred."

"I do," said a deep, savage voice, and a rough, heavy hand griped the young horseman by the shoulder.

St. James turned sharply, and came face to face with a brutal-looking man, mounted on a huge, powerful steed. A deadly intent shone in his villainous eyes as he pointed a pistol in the young noble's face, and held him firmly by the shoulder.

"You want my two hundred, do you?" asked St. James.

"Yes; and mean to have it," replied his assailant.

"That's imagination on your part, you ill-looking brute."

"Is it?"

"Without a doubt."

"Well, I tell you, if yer don't hand over the coin, I'll pop one of these slugs into yer skull, my young cur.

"By Jove! what an ugly looking brute," said Victor St. James, covering the other with his pistols. "You see two can play at that game, and, as I have had to observe before, that the trigger of my weapons have hair springs, and are apt to go off suddenly."

Without a word the man fired in a line for his opponent's head.

St. James had been watching him closely, and lowered his head as the other fired.

The bullet whizzed past within an inch of his forehead, and took the feather out of his cap; the very feather that he had had such a fight to keep.

The intruder drew a long, heavy sword, and made a furious cut at the dauntless youth.

"The deuce! You are in a hurry to change weapons. It's my turn now to have a shot," replied Victor St. James, guarding a thrust off his chest with a pistol-barrel. "I never miss."

He did not want to kill the man, so he fired at his arm.

The man dropped his sword with a howl, and rolled off his horse.

St. James dismounted, and lifting the wounded man in the slender but powerful arms, he threw him over a hedge.

"Lie there and howl, you spiteful brute," said St. James.

He laid there and howled in a most awful strain.

St. James mounted and rode away to get out of hearing of the melancholy discord. He rode rapidly in the direction taken by the highwayman.

Devil Duke had had a good start, and lessened the distance towards London by a considerable number of acres.

A traveller, richly dressed and wearily costly jewels, came in sight, but Devil Duke allowed him to pass unmolested. He was so utterly disgusted with the thought of his last two adventures and losing two hundred pounds in the bargain, that he swore he would not stay anyone else on the road for the next three months.

It must have been a momentary impulse that caused the gallant highwayman to come to that fabulous resolution, for the next minute he drew in rein and waited for two young lordlings, who came along singing and rolling from one side of the road to the other.

Devil Duke liked to hear merry people; it was a sign their pockets were in a healthy state.

"In such a case as this," he moralized, "do a good action. Evidently these gentlemen have more than is good for their nerves, and are incapable of taking care of what they have got."

So, drawing his pistol, he confronted the gentlemen as they approached.

"Stand!"

"Hallo!" shouted one of the gentleman, "what's the matter now?"

"Oh! nothing," Duke said, pointedly, "only that I should like to make acquaintance with such merry company, and take care of what you have in your pockets."

"A highwayman, by St. George!" said one of the young nobles, leaning on his companion for support, "and a pistol in his hand."

"And several more in his pocket," said Duke. "What a splendid diamond pin that is in your scarf! That watch chain is superb."

He finished his brief speech of admiration by putting a pistol quite close to the end of the gentleman's nose. The gentleman was by no means a coward, but the cold tube coming in such close contact, it made him blink, and, stepping back, he trod on his friend's toe, for which his friend gave him a kick that sent him rolling into the highwayman's arms.

"If I had not caught you," said Duke, "your lordship would have fallen and disfigured your nose."

"I thank you for your aid, but at the same time you may return my jewels."

The highwayman looked at the watch and pin, which by some peculiar means had slipped into his hand.

"They must have fallen from your coat," he said, "so I will keep them in remembrance of you."

"No, my good fellow, I don't see it. I'll tell you what I will do."

"That's the idea," said his companion; "make an arrangement."

"I will fight you for them back," he said to Duke.

"Very well," said Duke; "nothing pleases me better than a passage of arms with a gallant man."

They drew their swords and stood in a fencing attitude.

"The one that gets the first three points will be victor," remarked Duke.

"Agreed," said the young noble. Guard!"

He guarded a straight lunge, and nearly dislocated his opponent's wrist.

"First and last point to me," said Duke, as he wrenched the sword from the grasp of the young combatant.

"By St. George! I never was served like that before," said the gentleman, ruefully; "but you have won fairly."

"And should be obliged for your purse and those brilliant rings."

"We only fought for what we had."

"Try another pass for the other," suggested Duke.

"I shan't be able to use my sword for another week, you have given my wrist such wrench."

"Then oblige me with the requested articles."

The young gentleman dropped them reluctantly into the highwayman's hand.

"Yours," said Dick, turning to the other.

"They are quite safe, thank you."

"They will be much safer in my care."

"Confound your impertinence; would you rob me of them?"

"I should prefer fighting for them."

"Come on, then; I shall win all the lot back."

Duke doubted it very much, and they commenced the combat.

The young noble fought well. They were evidently young bloods of the fast school, and had learned the gallant art of self-defence within a hair's point. On any other occasion the highwayman would have found it a tough job with them, but in their present state of half stupidity with drink, they were easily vanquished.

Duke got the three points in succession to his opponent's, won the wager, wished the young nobles a very good day, with the hope to meet them on some future occasion.

A few minutes' ride found the highwayman in London. Making his way to the city, he went to a well-known mercer's shop, passing round the back way through a beautiful garden, and saw, hanging from a window, a silk ladder.

Devil Duke got curious and meditative, and standing under the window, he muttered—

"Now I wonder who the devil that ladder is put there for."

He looked carefully round, then up at the open window.

"Some blackguard," he continued; "evidently bent on some sinful engagement with the mercer's pretty little wife. Now, suppose I get up there, and put a stop to their wicked intentions, and—exactly so."

Again looking round to see that there was no one near, he clambered up the silk rope like a monkey, and fell head over heels into the room.

Devil Duke had not seen a silent figure who lurked beneath the shadow of the trees beneath the garden wall.

A sinister look of hate and deadly revenge in his cold cruel eyes.

A young fair creature with bright brown eyes ran to the highwayman's assistance, and twined her soft, bare white arms round his neck, and tried to raise him from his undignified position.

"Are you hurt, Frederick, dear?" she asked, when the highwayman got up, nestling herself closely to his breast. "I have been waiting for you so long, I feared you would not come."

"Oh, lor, here's a lark! She takes me for some other fellow," soliloquised Duke, and kissing her enticing, cherry lips, he said—"You won't be angry with me, Jessie dear. I have been detained."

"I knew it was not your fault," she replied.

"Sinful little woman," he thought; "she wants to lead me astray, but she won't—oh, no."

"You are not Frederick!" she suddenly exclaimed, noticing him for the first time.

"No," he said, "but I shall do as well. Don't get frightened. Now, never scream—you will alarm the house. Have you forgotten the Duke of Deverell?"

"Are you Duke Deverell?" she said, quieting on the instant. She had heard his name before.

"Yes."

"You were very wicked to come into my chamber like this."

"It is much more wicked of you to have strangers in your chamber whom your husband does not know."

She blushed and hid her face on his shoulder.

The clumping of a thick stick, and weary footsteps coming up the stairs, made them both start.

"For heaven's sake, fly!" exclaimed the mercer's pretty wife, excitedly. "'Tis my husband. Were he to find you here, he would kill you on the instant."

"That would be sudden murder without notice," said he. "Must I depart so soon? 'tis a very short visit."

"Yes," she said, "but you may return, and then——"

"Of course."

"Depart at once, if you value your life and have any love for me."

"Of course I have love for you," he said,

raising her in his arms, and kissing her. "What about this other fellow?"

"You have nothing to fear, he shall not be your rival."

"If he does," said Duke, making for the open window, as the stealthy footsteps stopped outside the door, "why—why, the consequences will be bloodshed."

"Don't talk so terrible, Duke, dear; I swear he shall never come near me again—do you believe me?"

"While I am with you,"

"You are very cruel."

"I am jealous—that makes me so."

"Go, go!"

The highwayman leapt from the room on to the balcony, as a loud knocking was heard at the door, and the old mercer, in a feeble voice called for his young frail companion to let him in.

The young wife heeded not the summons, but ran to the balcony, as an exclamation of surprise left the highwayman's lips.

The silken ladder had been taken away.

Devil Duke heeded the matter lightly, and saw no difficulty in jumping from where he stood, it being no more than ten feet from the ground.

He could not resist the temptation of once more clasping to his breast the seductive form of the mercer's wife, and taking a parting kiss.

The old mercer had grown impatient at not being answered, and kicked violently at the door for admittance, swearing in a very unbecoming manner, considering his age.

Releasing himself from his trembling companion, Devil Duke dropped from the stone balcony. His feet had hardly touched the ground, when the sinister watcher sprang upon him, and buried a dagger in his side.

"Frederick! oh, Frederick! what have you done?" shrieked the alarmed young wife, leaning over the gallery; "you have murdered Duke Deverell!"

Devil Duke reeled backwards beneath the cowardly assassin's blade, with his hand to his side, the crimson gore streaming from the gaping wound.

The dastardly assailant sped on, like the guilty wretch he was, with the dripping dagger held out in his bloodstained hand, and a look of triumphant hate on his pallid countenance.

CHAPTER XXI.

THE LUSHER AND MARY JANE.—A COOL TERMINATION TO A WARM LOVE SCENE. —THE HIGHWAYMEN GO TO AN INN, WHEREIN THEY OVERHEAR A PLOT.

WE will return to the three illustrious individuals who had rendered Devil Duke so much assistance in his escape, and carry the attention of the reader to a private scene between the Lusher and his Mary Jane.

"What are you going to do with yourselves?" asked Jack Evans of his companions.

"Do with ourselves?" said Swig; "anything we can."

"I'll tell you the best thing to do with yourself," remarked Bullskin.

"What?" asked Swig.

"Why, hang yourself."

"I will," replied his companion, taking the joke in good part; "round the first girl's neck I come across."

"Fine, ain't it?" said Jack Evans. "I am going to hang round a girl's neck to-night."

"Are you?" remarked Swig, curiously. "Who is it?"

"Wouldn't you like to know?"

"Shouldn't mind."

"Well round Mary Jane. Good night. I am off."

"Hi! Stop!" shouted Big Bullskin.

The Lusher stopped and looked round.

"What's up?"

"Going to change my suit."

"Where does Mary Jane sleep?"

"Second floor, at the back."

"All right. Good night. See you tomorrow."

"Yes. Good night."

And away ran the Lusher like the wind.

His companions watched him enter the venue of the Glenmore estate, and then went to the Red Lion inn close by, where they satisfied the pangs of hunger and washed their rusty throats with some very bad wine, and again set out to watch the performances of their late companion.

The Lusher made his way to the servants' hall, where he found his Mary Jane.

A pretty, rosy-faced damsel, of about nineteen, with a round, supple form, and a pair of large black eyes, that seemed to penetrate to the very soul and read a person's inmost thoughts.

They were not sharp enough to pierce the veil that hid the base thoughts of her lover, though they had pierced his heart.

"Oh! Mary Jane," said the Lusher, throwing his arms round her neck and kissing her passionately, "how I love you!"

"Don't be stupid, Jack," she said, pushing him away. "Suppose any of the servants should see you."

"See me? What should I care. I could die on the spot with you by my side."

"How foolish you talk."

"Mary," he said, slowly, and looking into her face, "you don't love me. Those words went to my heart like a cannon-ball, and will cause my destruction. This instant will I go and drown myself—*with some beer in the kitchen*," he said, aside.

"Nonsense, Jack. You know I love you."

"Oh! angel of light, I could die and think it bliss for you."

Mary put her soft arms round his neck and kissed him.

Jack drew her too him, and hugged her with a leer of gratification.

"Mary," he said, "I will change these things for my own, and if you can get a fellow anything to eat and drink, why, of course I shan't refuse it."

"My own precious darling, my—my— There, I can't think of words enough to express my love."

"Stay here while I fetch you something."

"Give me a kiss before you go."

She gave him a kiss, and went.

In the meantime the highwayman changed his dress.

In a few minutes the bright-eyed young damsel returned with a meal sufficient for a giant, and before Jack had time to finish it, he was disturbed by the sound of approaching footsteps.

"Hide, for goodness sake," said the frightened maid. "If any one sees you here, it will ruin my character for ever and ever, and perhaps longer than that."

To prevent such an endless ruination, the Lusher flew without a word, knowing not whither, but by instinct made his way to the second floor back, and concealed himself beneath the bed.

The maid met the intruder with a bold, but lushing face.

" Well, Mary," said a tall flunkey, in white se, with green knee breeches, " didn't I hear mebody here ?"

" Yes."

" Who was it ?"

" Why, me."

The pampered flunkey shook his powdered head doubtfully, and walked on, looking about carefully as he went.

Mary made her way to the kitchen, trembling for fear that her lover should be discovered hidden in some cupboard or recess by the tall flunkey.

The flunkey, whose name was Charles, was very sweet on the pretty housemaid, and swore terrible vengeance against any other fellow who should attempt to rival him.

Mary Jane waited with tearful eyes and alpitating heart until the whole of her fellow-ervants had retired to rest, then she made a search for her lover, but searching in vain, she retired to her chamber, much disappointed.

With glistening tears chasing each other down her rosy cheeks, and muttering the name of the highwayman, she commenced to prepare for her night's rest.

Jack, who had watched her, caught hold of her tiny foot as she raised it to get into bed, and she gave a frightened scream.

" Don't be frightened, darling Mary, it's only me," said the Lusher, crawling from his hiding-place.

The girl smacked his face.

Jack did not mind that; he looked at it as an encouragement, and glided his arm round her neck.

" For shame, Jack; go out of my room, or I'll scream."

" Don't scream, there's a darling," he said, drawing her to him and kissing her. " I know you wouldn't like to see me killed, and if you make a noise I know I should be."

" It is too bad of you, really you ought to know better than to have come in my room."

" Oh! Mary—Mary! you will drive me mad! If you only knew how I loved you, you would not say that."

" I've a good mind never to speak to you again."

" Don't say that, there's a darling," said the highwayman persuasively. " Come, give me a kiss, and forget all about it."

The girl yielded to his impassioned words, gave him a kiss, and forgave him for his daring intrusion.

Jack took advantage of her gentle forgiving nature, and sitting on the bed by her side with one arm clasped tightly round her neck he kissed her passionately.

" Jack," said Mary, tearfully, and clinging to him affectionately, " will you be true to me ?"

" Of course I will."

" Will you marry me ?"

" On the spot if you like."

The young maid smiled sorrowfully, and hid her face in the pillow.

" Mary, dear," he said, soothingly, " don't fret, darling; I will never love anyone but you."

" Ah! if I could but think so," she said, looking at him reproachfully, " I might be happy."

" You may," he said ; you will ever find me true and constant."

" Can I believe you, Jack ?"

" No !" said a sepulchral voice outside the door.

Jack sprang to his feet, and his mistress like an eel dived under the bed covering.

The Lusher had barely time to gain his hat before the door was burst open, and in rushed the tall flunkey.

Jack, like a shot, made for the window the pampered individual dashed after him the highwayman being the quickest, reached the sill just as Charles clutched at his coat tail.

Loud, confused shouting, heavy splashes of water, savage barking of dogs, and miserable groans followed the Lusher's flight

To clear the mist from the reader's imagination, we will explain the cause of these sudden casualties.

Swig and his big companion had conjectured that their active friend would make his way where he had no business, so accordingly they walked round to the back of the mansion and sat beneath the window.

The light came

Swig mounted on Bullskin's shoulders, and Bullskin mounted on the top of a shed, by that means elevating the small person to the sill of the second floor.

Swig, with his grinning physiognomy close, had an excellent view of the whole proceedings that took place within the silent chamber; not knowing the meaning of the sudden leap the Lusher took from his fair companion's side, Swig awaited in breathless anxiety to see the next act of the interesting drama.

It came.

The curtain was drawn up. Then the comedy that had hitherto been performed suddenly turned into an exciting tragedy. The back scene flew open (the room door), and in rushed a tall person in knee breeches, with a look of deadly revenge and hate on his exasperated countenance.

Swig became so excited by the unexpected change that he fairly danced on his companion's shoulders, his heart beat quickly against his side, his cheeks were in a glow, and his eyes stared wildly.

Then a cloud seemed to come before his gaze, and he saw but dimly the scuffle that ensued.

A shadow approached the window, the tall person following close behind; the casement was dashed open, and the Lusher jumped out. He fell over Swig's head, dragging him off the giant's shoulder.

The three uttered a yell. Swig and the Lusher fell into a large water-butt that stood beside the wall.

Bigg Bullskin rolled off the shed, grazed his long nose, and howled dismally. Three huge bandy-legged bull-dogs pounced upon him, and inserted their teeth in the bulk of his person gratis.

The highwayman kicked and plunged furiously to extract their gnawing fangs, but, despite all his struggles, the canine tribe dragged him to their kennels and commenced a meal.

The howling of Bullskin and the yells and cries of the other two unfortunate men brought the body of retainers upon them, who had returned after an unsuccessful search for Devil Duke.

The Lusher and Swig were pulled out of the dirty water by the heels and dragged across the yard; the dogs were driven from Bullskin's prostrate form. Ere the men had time to secure him, the highwayman sprang to his feet, and sent them reeling in all directions.

His two companions came to his aid; the retainers closed around the trio, anticipating an easy capture; the highwaymen broke their circle; the men scattered from their furious attack, but in an instant were upon them again.

Then a general *mêlée* took place.

The highwaymen did not intend to be captured, and fought desperately for their liberty.

The retainers meant to capture them, and fought savagely to overpower the brave knights.

The brave knights were not so easily overpowered, and laid their opponents *hors de combat*.

A loud shout of defiance arrested the highwaymen as they were about to make their escape. Looking in the direction from where the shouting proceeded, they saw a second detachment of men standing at the large gates that enclosed the grounds, waiting for them.

CHAPTER XXII.

CAPTAIN CLAUDE LEARNS THAT TYBURN DICK IS CAPTURED, AND RESOLVES UPON A RESCUE.

A MOMENT'S pause succeeded the firing of the cowardly shot which had stricken Lucy Wayne in her devoted effort to save the life of Captain Claude.

A moment's ominous, appalling pause. Old Peter Wayne sat benumbed with terror as his fair young wife fell back bleeding and ghastly, while the ruffianly face of the coward assassin peered maliciously in at the window.

The shot had been so sudden, its effect so startling, that for the instant Captain Claude was paralyzed. The exultant laugh of the officer roused him.

Never had such a gleam of fearful passion flashed from his dark eyes. The craven murderer cowered from the withering glance, his speech deserted him, his jaw fell.

"Hound!" Captain Claude cried, "he'll

shall not be kept waiting longer. Had you twenty lives I would scatter them as I do now."

His fierce tones thrilled the heart of the dastard officer. The fellow shook like a leaf. One frantic convulsed shriek for mercy left his pallid lips, as Claude thrust the muzzle of a pistol between his teeth—one spasmodic, stifled call for help from his comrades.

Nothing more.

The unsparing finger pressed the trigger.

A sickening crash.

A horrid, gasping cry.

He rolled from the coach, and fell collapsed to the ground, his head literally blown to pieces.

The swift, deadly vengeance which had fallen on their comrade deprived the remaining officers of what little sense they had. The sight of his shattered face sickened them, and when Claude's scathing glance and his second pistol were turned towards them, they ignominiously fled to save their lives.

When their trembling legs had taken them out of sight, Captain Claude replaced his pistols in his belt, and lifted Lucy in his strong arms.

He tried to staunch the blood from the gaping wound in her devoted bosom, but the stream of life poured out too quickly, and with a sad sigh he laid her gently back in the carriage.

The brave-hearted fellow knew it was all over with her.

" Can you hear me, Lucy?" he said gently

Lucy's pale lips moved.

"Take—care—of—the—boy;—your—boy—Dick," she whispered faintly.

" Ay, with my life."

The dim eyes beamed gratefully.

Her pallid fingers clasped tightly on his hand; then Old Peter Wayne, who was shedding tears like a child, took her other hand.

There was a faint effort to speak again—a sigh—Lucy's eyes closed for ever.

Dick's gentle foster-mother lay back sleeping her last sleep, with a leaden bullet in her brave heart.

It was some time before Captain Claude could rouse himself. Hot blistering tears stood in his eyes.

His heart was heavy.

Poor old Peter was on his knees in the coach, moaning and clasping the cold arms of his dead wife, refusing to believe that the murderous ball had done its fearful work. anxiously calling her to come back to him.

Claude was roused by Selim giving a peculiar neigh.

Stepping down from the coach, spurning the body of the slain officer as he trod over him, he looked in the direction in which Selim's fine head was pointed.

His heart thrilled deeply at what he saw.

A horse riderless, galloping across the country with the fleetness of the wind.

In its track two horsemen urged their lumbering animals after it.

It was Fairy pursued by the officers.

" Fairy, and riderless !" Claude cried. " Then the brave boy is taken in his first night's ride; curses seize them if they have injured a hair of his head. By the living God, I will have revenge !"

Selim arching his graceful neck, began pawing the ground, and presently laid her nose on the highway chieftain's shoulder.

She was impatient to be off.

Claude stroked her glossy neck.

" We will go their way presently," he said. " No fear of their overtaking Fairy. How beautifully she leads the race ! Ha! they have taken out pistols. Dastards, would they shoot her ? Back Selim. Aha! they shall have a touch at long range."

Putting Selim's magnificent head aside, Claude took out a pistol.

One of the officers had just taken aim at the graceful steed.

Claude covered him and fired.

Almost simultaneously with the report the foremost of the two horses staggered and rolled with its rider to the ground.

The highwayman's bullet had gone through its brain.

" Turn back," Claude cried to the other horseman, " or you ride to your death."

The fellow heard the warning voice, and saw the highwayman's cocked pistol.

He had a keen idea that if Claude fired, the bullet might lodge in his brain instead of his horse's.

So giving a longing look at the rich prize, with the judge's valuables in its holsters—

prize he and his comrade had made certain of getting—he turned tail and fled, leaving his overturned companion to get out of harm's way as best he could.

It was singular to mark the effect of Claude's voice on Fairy.

At the report of the pistol she merely pricked up her ears, and flew faster over the ground.

But when Claude's well-known voice rang loud and clear, she stopped as suddenly as if she had been changed into stone.

For scarcely a second she stood with arched neck, mane erect, and ears laid flat.

Then giving a whinny of delight, she sprang clear over the sprawling horse and rider, and galloped madly to Claude's side, evincing her joy by every manifestation in her power.

Selim, too, got a share of her caressess, and the two faithful steeds rubbed noses together with all the affection of two newly united friends.

"Now, Fairy," Claude said, stroking the beautiful creature's neck, "if you could tell me where they have put Dick, we should not be long before we were riding to his rescue."

Fairy drooped her head at the mention of Dick's name. Selim, too, seemed to understand that her rider was taken, for he gave a mournful neigh.

Claude was busily cleaning Fairy's accoutrements.

"Ah!" he exclaimed, thrusting his hand into the holsters, where the judge's valuables were crammed, "the lad has been at work, I see. If the road is to be his destiny, he will not be the least amongst us."

A sad, thoughtful expression settled on Claude's face. Very gloomily he fastened Fairy's bridle, and shut up the holsters.

He was thinking of the stern fate which had shut our hero out from title and name, and given his rank and wealth to another, driving him to the fatal hazard of a highway life.

The overthrown officer had in the meanwhile scrambled to his feet. When Fairy made her nimble leap over him, he expected to get her hoofs in his chest or skull, and it was with a sigh of relief that he found he was not battered in at rib or brain.

The sudden fall had bruised and shaken him all over, and, cursing his cowardly comrade for leaving him there, he crawled away; but had not gone far before two of Claude's band, who were riding that way, pounced upon him, and put a climax to his troubles by well dousing him in a dirty pond.

Captain Claude heard the faithful fellows Putting a whistle to his lips, he blew a shrill call, and the highwaymen galloped to his side.

The brave fellows were grieved to the heart when they saw the catastrophe that had happened. Very tenderly they assisted him to lay Lucy on the cushions of the coach, and to soothe Old Peter Wayne, who was almost senseless and muttered brokenly his sorrow.

"My lads," Claude said, "you see what a foul tragedy has occurred. This was Dick's foster-mother. She gave her life to save me. There lies the hound whose hand fired the murderous shot. I slew him, but his death will not bring life to her brave heart. We must convey her to our haunt. Dick is taken; here is his riderless steed. We shall have to find out where they have placed him, and then rescue him. He is too young to be left in their hands, besides, he will like to look upon his foster-mother before we give her to her grave."

CHAPTER XXIII.
CAPTAIN CLAUDE VISITS JONATHAN WILD.

THE story of Dick's capture and daring escape from prison reached the highwaymen's ears, and many brave fellows' hearts throbbed with admiration at the fearless exploits of the new and youthful member of their band.

They heard, too, of the search that was made for him in Ruth's chamber, and of his subsequent capture by Jonathan Wild.

Claude set his teeth hard together when he heard that Dick had been betrayed into the thieftaker's hands.

He knew Wild must have had a deeper motive in taking him than the present reward, and he resolved to visit the ruffian in his lair, and learn why he had entrapped Dick.

"I will tear the secret from his heart," he muttered, as he went forth cloaked and disguised. "He has a price on my head; well, he shall have me in his presence—a brace of loaded pistols may bring us to a better understanding."

TYBURN DICK LISTENS FOR THE PROMISED RESCUE.

Arrived at the low, ill-looking house where Wild was usually to be found, Captain Claude fearlessly opened the door and stepped in.

A peculiar smile played upon his handsome features as he did so.

The man he sought, Jonathan Wild, had arrived before him.

The thief-taker gave a slightly perceptible start as his eyes and those of Claude's met. But he was too well versed in cunning and deceit to allow his actions to give the least betrayal to his thoughts.

It was a house of no very good repute, and one less bold and daring than Claude would not have ventured to enter into the society of those who frequented it; but firm in his resolution, and confident in his disguise, he seated himself beside the very man who would not have hesitated to place the halter round his neck, had he the chance.

Captain Claude was not ignorant of this.

He knew the danger to which he was exposing himself, but he was rendered daring and reckless with the knowledge that it was for the good of his friend.

9

Throwing himself carelessly back in his seat, he ordered the landlord, who was eyeing him rather curiously, to bring him refreshments.

The landlord obeyed, not forgetting to make the remark to his wife that a customer of a higher stamp than his usual visitors had dropped in, and entered into conversation with the man whose name was an abhorrence, not only to those who walked in fear of him, but those who heard of him, and whose company was shunned by all, even the servile, cringing wretches who hung upon his heels and crouched at his feet like so many curs.

The landlord placed the flowing tankard on the table (for he had things to suit all customers, and this was a silver one), then sauntered towards the fireplace, where he appeared to trouble his head with nothing but his own concerns, but in truth to listen to what passed.

"Rather cold this evening," remarked Captain Claude, as he poured out the sparkling ale into the goblet. "Do you mind drinking with a stranger? But there, perhaps you prefer wine?"

"No; I am not particular on that point," replied the thief-taker. "I drink with many in the course of a day. Are you strange about here?"

"Well—yes."

"Not been here before, I suppose?"

"Once, I think."

"When might that have been?"

"Well, really, it is so far back, I cannot recollect."

"Too long for you to recognise any faces you might have seen at that time."

"Yes, but you are not drinking."

Jonathan gave one of his peculiar, low, cutting laughs, and tried to assume an air of gaiety.

"'Tis you," he said, "who are not drinking. Taking into consideration that you paid for it, you ought to drink the most."

"No, my friend," said Captain Claude, placing his small gloved hand on his companion's shoulder, and causing Jonathan to start a little, "that is not my maxim; we have met here as strangers and I hope we may part as friends."

Jonathan Wild did not notice the slight curl of his lips as he uttered this last word, but muttered to himself, "We may."

Then aloud he said—

"Do you mean to say my face is not familiar to you? have we not met before, either friendly or otherwise?"

Captain Claude looked him full in the face, and after regarding him for a few moments answered—

"No."

"Have you no recollection at all of me?"

"Not the slightest."

"That is strange," said Wild. "I could have sworn I had seen you, but where I cannot at present bring to mind."

"Have you travelled far, sir?" he asked, determined not to let the matter drop.

"Yes, some distance."

"From what part?"

"Really, you grow inquisitive."

"No, no, not at all; I merely asked."

"And you merely want me to answer."

"I leave that to your own option," replied Wild; "it is of little import."

He spoke this rather carelessly, and Captain Claude, believing he had not seen through his disguise, became more bold.

"What may be your name?" he asked.

The thief-taker eyed him for a moment in silence.

"Cursed impudent," he thought, "but I will answer him nevertheless."

"I am Jonathan Wild, the thief-taker. You have, perhaps, heard of me before?"

He spoke this in such a sneering manner that Capt. Claude could scarcely refrain from grasping him by the throat.

"Then it was you," he said, concealing his rage, "that captured the daring highwayman?"

"Tyburn Dick, I suppose you mean?"

"The same."

"Yes, 'twas I that put a stop to his gallop, and before long more of his daring band will see the inside of Newgate."

"Ah, say you so?"

"I do, and I shall get the rewards."

Captain Claude could scarcely contain himself.

The cool manner in which Wild spoke to him, hit him to the quick.

"And by whose authority did you take him?" he asked.

Jonathan hesitated.

After a moment's thought he replied—

"The Lady Aldervale's; but why do you ask—what matters it to you?"

"Not much certainly, but I asked merely out of curiosity. What could be her motive for doing this?"

"It concerns me little—; so little, in fact, that I don't trouble my head about it. He is safe enough now, and that is all I want."

"Inhuman wretch," thought Claude, eyeing him loathingly.

"So you hunt this daring youth and drag him to jail to suit the fancies of a vile, capricious woman."

"Not that alone— I look at the reward."

"True, it was a goodly sum, but it will not last for ever."

"I am well aware of that," replied Wild smiling as he spoke, and glancing anxiously towards the door; "there are others on whose head hangs a heavy reward. They will not escape me long."

The entrance of the landlord put an end to their conversation for a time, and then Claude noticed a sign pass between them.

"Some treachery," he thought, "but I must be wary. He has not recognised me, or he would not have remained quite so long."

He was deceived.

Jonathan was only waiting the arrival of his men.

The sign passed between him and the landlord was, that on their arrival they were to be ushered into a private room, where Claude and the thief-taker were doing ample justice to the wine.

The landlord understood well his part, and, without hesitating, left the room.

"By Jove, you are a brave fellow," said Claude, as the landlord's fat carcase disappeared, "to attempt the capture of that daring boy; but were you not afraid his comrades would be revenged?"

"Aha! there is little fear of that; they will not knowingly come within my reach."

"Be not too sure of that," cried Captain Claude, his dark eyes flashing fiercely through the holes of his mask. "There are brave hearts ready to avenge his wrongs; he may yet escape; it will not be the first time, remember.'

Jonathan gave a grim smile.

"There is little fear of him escaping this time, or you either."

He hissed rather than spoke these last words, and seized Captain Claude with both hands by the neck.

"I know you, Captain Claude," he vociferated, fiercely; "you have walked into the lion's den, and you will find it no easy matter to get out again. Your disguise this time has failed you; you are my prisoner, and I shall lay claim to the reward."

This movement had been so sudden and unexpected on the part of Wild that he allowed the thief-taker to hold him down on his seat without offering any resistance, and he listened patiently to all he said. Releasing his hold with one hand, Jonathan tried to unmask him with the other; but Captain Claude recovering his self-possession, now spoke—

"Thief-taker Wild!" he cried, indignantly "take your accursed hands from off me."

"Never!" hissed Jonathan, "at least, not till I have seen you safely lodged, and pocketed the coin."

"That will never be!" cried Captain Claude, quickly starting to his feet and dealing Jonathan a tremendous blow in the chest that sent him reeling.

A half-muttered "Oh!" burst from his lips, as he released his hold of Captain Claude.

It was such a blow as in pugilistic circles would have been called a winder; but Jonathan Wild's rough-hewn carcase sustained no injury from it, though it made him pant for breath.

"That se—seals your fate!" he gasped. "H—o th—ere men!"

The truth flashed instantly to Captain Claude's mind.

That he had recognised him from the first, and that his bullying myrmidons were lying somewhere in wait for him, and listening for the signal from their dastardly leader.

The least alarm, would bring them upon him like a pack of wolves, and to prevent this he must silence him at once.

He could hear the ruffianly-looking landlord talking loudly to some one in the bar, so he was not afraid that he had overheard them.

But he might return soon, and then he would have two to contend with.

These thoughts flashed vividly through his mind, and he formed his plans at once.

Jonathan Wild had recovered his balance, but not his wind sufficient to raise an alarm, for the thick, heavy doors deadened the sound, but that would not avail him.

Quick as thought, and prompt to act, Captain Claude sprang upon him, and tried to seize him by the throat.

Wild, like a rat when pressed in a corner, and unable to run, turned fiercely upon him.

"Help! help!" he shouted, as loud as his breath would permit him.

"Aha! you may shout," said Captain Claude, ironically; "but I'll soon stop your infernal noise."

Suiting the action to the word, he fixed his hand so firmly on Jonathan's throat, that he became almost black in the face.

"M—e—r—c—y! mer—mercy!" he gasped. "O—h! don't choke me!"

"I'll wring the cursed life out of you!" replied Claude, "if you don't keep silent."

"O—h! oh! don't!"

"I will, d—n you! if you make the least noise."

"Oh! I'll be quiet—do anything you wish if you release me!"

Captain Claude, not wishing to kill him, though he might have done so at once if he felt inclined, relaxed his hold.

Jonathan Wild took advantage of this, and fearing to cry out, he leaped back a pace, and drew a pistol from his pocket.

Levelling it at Captain Claude's head, he said, with a determined air—

"Surrender, or die!"

Claude eyed his devilish-looking features with disdain.

"Think you I care for those paltry toys," he said. "I have one here that never by any chance misses fire; and the one you hold is very likely to, unless you have very recently primed it."

Captain Claude drew a small rapier from beneath his cloak.

"This," he said, flourishing it, "is worth twenty such as yours."

Jonathan Wild gave a low mocking laugh, as he cocked his pistol.

The next moment a startling cry of terror burst from him.

The captain had dashed the pistol from his hand with his sword, and now held him firmly with one hand, and the sword to the throat with the other.

"Mur—der! murder!" cried the terrified wretch, faintly. "He—lp! he—lp!"

"Silence!" muttered Captain Claude "another word and I let out your cursed breath!"

"Oh—oh! don't talk like that! I—I——"

"Yes, I know all about you," muttered Claude, fiercely, ; "you captured Tyburn Dick—you lured him into a snare, and now, curse you, if I don't reward you for it. You have had one from your worthy employers, but you have not yet had one from me."

Claude was greatly excited, and he felt a strong inclination to plunge the point of his rapier into the thieftaker's throat.

But his better nature prevailed.

He could not take the life of an unarmed man, though that man was more subtle, and far more dangerous than the poisonous serpent.

"Jonathan Wild," he hissed, while his whole frame shook with the efforts he made to repress his rage, "you are unarmed, and I am too much of a gentleman to take advantage of it; I will meet you on equal terms."

Captain Claude relaxed his hold of the thieftaker, and replaced his sword.

On finding himself free, Wild gave one of half-cunning, half-fiendish smiles.

With a growl like that of a half-baffled tiger, he dashed upon Claude, and fixed his hands upon his throat.

Then came a fearful struggle, deadly and fierce.

Over chairs, tables, or anything that stood in their way they rolled.

Oaths and fearful imprecations came from both.

Both were powerful men, and they held each other in a grasp of iron, and being equally desperate and determined, it was hard to decide who would be the victor.

The sound of heavy footsteps approaching warned Claude of his danger.

The ruffianly landlord had been alarmed by the noise of the scuffle.

Against two such low-bred and powerful

fellows Claude would have but a very poor chance.

This he well knew.

He had already found it tight work to master one.

But he did not despair.

Drawing his tall manly form erect, he called together all his energies, tightened his grasp on his opponent, and, with a powerful effort whirled him round, and hurled him from him.

The thieftaker gave a cry of baffled rage, as he went staggering backwards, and seated himself on the grate, bringing the after part of his person in unpleasant contact with the the fierce blazing embers.

At that moment the landlord's bullet-head appeared at the door.

On seeing Jonathan's precarious position, he commenced shouting at the top of his voice.

"This way, men. Quick! Make haste, or this highwayman will murder our blessed friend!"

The gallant captain had paused a moment to get breath after the desperate struggle, but the clattering of heavy-booted feet and the clamouring of voices soon aroused him again to action.

With one bound he reached the door, seized the landlord, who was more than half in, gave him one terrific jerk that sent him reeling to his knees, then closed the door and placed his back against it.

All this was done so momentarily that when the officers arrived they were astonished.

Loudly they clamoured at the stout oaken door, tried to beat in the panels with their pistol-butts and sword-hilts, and endeavoured to force it open with their brawny shoulders.

But all their efforts proved futile.

Captain Claude had spied a bolt on the inside of the door, and had taken the liberty to shoot it into its socket.

He now stood, sword in hand, regarding his crestfallen foes with a smile of satisfaction, giving the panel an occasional rap with his sword-hilt in answer to the heavy hammering without.

Both Jonathan and the landlord were almost foaming with rage—the former to think that he should be thus defeated, and set at defiance within only a few feet of his men, the latter to think that his dignity should be lowered, and his proud spirit humiliated under his own roof, in his private parlour, and that by a man whom, to all appearance, he could have eaten for breakfast, and then looked round for a dozen more.

This was too much for his proud spirit to brook, and scrambling to his feet, he possessed himself of a stout iron bar, that served as a poker, and flourishing it above his head in a threatening manner, cried in a bullying tone—

"Now, then, my fine fellow, you'd better give in at once. You've played your capers long enough, I should think. Come on, Wild," he added to that worthy personage, who stood trembling, and looking like the Knight with the Rueful Countenance.

Wild felt certainly more comfortable at having such a big, burly companion, though, it must be confessed, he was greatly chapfallen. Suddenly a bright smile lights up his brutish features, a deadly gleam of satisfaction darts from his eye, and he stoops and picks up the pistol.

Carefully he examines it.

It is none the worse for its fall, and he raises it on a level with Captain Claude's head.

The gallant captain would have sprung forward and tried to avert his deadly purpose, but he felt the door giving way, and if he left it he feared it must yield.

This was a trying moment to the daring fellow, and one of imminent peril.

Defiant and unquailing he stood waiting his exultant foe.

Not a muscle does he move as the sharp click strikes his ear.

Then follows a sharp report, a horrible death-wailing cry, followed by a howl of disappointed rage and mad despair.

The bullet passed within an inch of Captain Claude's cheek, pierced the door, and went crashing through the brain of one of the officers without.

"Cursed fiend!" cried Wild, making a desperate rush at Claude with the pistol.

The captain met the blow on the edge of his sword, but before he could return it the landlord made a swift and deadly blow at his head with the iron bar.

Claude's quick eye detected his movement, and he caught the bar in his left hand, wrenched it from the landlord's grasp, dealt him a blow on the head with it that stretched him senseless and bleeding on the floor, then turned and seized Jonathan by the throat.

In the struggle, Captain Claude's light rapier not broken, shivered off at the hilt; and now he had nought but his bare hands to defend himself.

Jonathan Wild still had his heavy pistol clasped in his hand, and was endeavouring to use it with effect.

Worse than all, the door was giving way.

Its rusty fastenings and time-worn hinges could not resist much longer.

This was horrible.

Captain Claude, though driven to the verge of desperation, did not suffer his temper to overcome him, nor his cool, determined courage to forsake him in the least.

The hammering grew louder.

The door was moving.

The thirsty bloodhounds of the law would in another moment be upon him.

He looked around for some means of escape.

He saw none but by a window, and that would take him some time to undo the fastenings.

Besides, the thief-taker was hanging on to him with the tenacity of a ferocious bull-dog, his flashing eyes fixed on the gradually yielding door in eager expectation of seeing it burst in.

This was a moment of bitter agony to the gallant captain, but though in the midst of all this, though beset and menaced on every side with danger, he did not despair.

Nerving himself for one final effort, he grasped Wild fiercely by the throat, held him from him at arm's length, and hurled him with terrific force to the other end of the room, where he tumbled over an upturned table, and rolled all of a heap into a corner.

One glance Captain Claude cast around.

The door was rocking to and fro.

Wrapping his cloak around him, he stepped up to the window, dashed out the frame with one blow of his booted heel, and disappeared through the opening as the door gave way with a crash, and a dozen officers, all armed, rushed into the room.

CHAPTER XXIV.

THE HIGHWAYMEN OVERHEAR A PLOT AND FOLLOW THE PLOTTERS.—BIG BULLSKIN ARRIVES IN TIME TO SAVE AN ASSASSINATED FRIEND.

THE highwaymen were astounded at the unfavourable turn in affairs; they had anticipated, after vanquishing their first gang of assailants, an easy retreat.

In which they were disappointed.

The sudden appearance of the men taking possession of the gates quite bewildered them, and for a few moments they were undecided how to act.

It was a clever manœuvre on the part of the retainers; they had skilfully cut short the flight of the highwaymen, and held them prisoners within the grounds of the estate.

But how long would they detain the highwaymen?

That we shall see.

Swig looked frightfully scared at his companions, the Lusher looked greatly disappointed, and Bullskin looked awfully miserable.

"Do you think they are going to keep us here?" asked Jack.

"It seems so by their appearance," replied Bullskin.

"They won't keep me here, I can assure them."

Making a run at the closed gates, the Lusher clambered up them like a monkey, and sprang over the men's heads.

Swig followed his example. On reaching the top of the iron barricade, his foot slipped and he fell with a heavy thud on a man's head, knocking him to the ground, nearly dislocating his neck, but breaking his own fall.

The man crawled away vomiting, his neck hanging on one side as though disjointed.

A dozen of his companions pounced upon Swig and belaboured him most unmercifully. Bullskin would have gone to his small friend's assistance, but the others kept him at bay by holding the gate against him.

This exasperated the gigantic fellow, and throwing the whole strength of his powerful form into his large muscular arms, he wrenched the gates open. The men, who held on like grim death, came sprawling in on their faces.

Big Bullskin gave a satisfactory grin, and stepping over their prostrate forms went to the aid of Swig, who shrieked madly for his comrade to help him.

Stepping in the midst of the enraged men, Bullskin sent them flying on either side by a pank from his hands, and then raised Swig to his feet.

The men in a body rushed after the high-ymen, who were walking away, as though hing had occurred.

" Don't let him escape," said one.

Knock him over," kindly voted another.

Hit him in the wind," said a third.

'Give him a topper," suggested a fourth.

Big Bullsk thought their suggestions had been plenty, and gave a fellow a topper in time to save a very feeling proposition he was about to propose.

" Down with him !" yelled a man who had first spoken.

" I shall down with you," said the high-wayman, spitefully.

The fellow went down with a bound.

The Lusher, who hated people to make a noise in the distance, quietly sneaked behind him and gave him an unmerciful kick in the back that sent him reeling several yards off.

The retainers had followed the highwaymen and got them against a wall.

Bullskin had not noticed this.

The men pressed upon him step by step, until his head come in contact with the wall; then he discovered the trap he had incautiously fallen into.

He seldom got out of temper, but the crafty advantage they had taken exasperated him beyond bounds.

He was dangerous when angry.

This the foremost of the retainers saw by a savage light kindling in his eyes.

They would have got further away from him, but their companions pressed forward and kept them within reach of the giant's powerful arm.

They had walked into a dangerous, critical position. They could not expect any mercy from their opponent whom they had driven into a corner.

Big drops of perspiration rolled down their cheeks as they thought of the consequences.

" Back !" thundered Bullskin, his eyes looking terrible in their expression. " Back ! I say."

The men shrank back, quailing beneath his eyes, and would gladly have got out of his way, but they could not.

Their companions who were behind and out of the highwayman's reach were brave ; they called the others cowards, pressing them close into langer.

" Back ! I say, again, you miserable curs," exclaimed the highwayman, in a terrible pas-sion.

To be called cowards by their own com panions was too much for their constitutions. They stood irresolute and tried to look defiant, but failed miserably.

Drawing a ponderous broad-sword, that he only used when in the greatest difficulty, he wielded it above his head and said—

" Curse you for a lot of obstinate fools. I will make a hole through some of you if you ain't all cleared away in another minute and he brought the sword down with terrible force.

He did not want to kill the men, so brought the blade flat across their faces, with a smack that made their teeth chatter.

Two men rolled to the ground with their jaws aching awfully

Those behind thought their companions were killed, and, inspired with a thought to avenge their death, they dashed at the high-wayman like so many fiends, with drawn swords.

Bullskin waited for them.

He stood in an attitude, with his sword drawn over his left shoulder, that would have done credit to the statue of Julius Cæsar.

Swig got a very nasty dig in the seat of honour from the point of one of the retainers swords, and, not wishing to receive a second one, he clambered up his companion's back and sat on his shoulders.

The Lusher was dodging about, inserting his sword in the soft parts of the men.

A general scrimmage took place. The men in the excitement got in one another's way and fought, each taking the other for some one else.

Big Bullskin was knocking him wn like so many reeds, while the Lusher was skipping about like a grasshopper, doing fearful damage to the comfort of the men, and Swig, who had filled his pockets with large stones, was so tively engaged trying to crack all the nuts that came within his reach.

At last the melée was ended.

The men retreated, howling and groaning miserably.

The highwaymen followed them as far as was safe, giving them a parting kick, then sallied forth victorious.

The trio made their way to a public-house, a place where they were well known by the worthy host.

As they entered, two suspicious-looking men of a villainous stamp came up to the door, but fell back as they saw the trio enter.

"I wonder what the devil they did that for?" remarked Swig.

"They are up to something," said Big Bullskin, knowingly.

"We'll watch their little game," proposed the Lusher.

"We will," chimed his companions,

So they did.

They told mine host they wanted to watch two men.

"What men?" asked the worthy landlord.

"Oh, two friends of mine," said Bullskin.

Seeing they had some hidden motive, the landlord put them in his private parlour.

They had a bottle of wine, and sat by a roaring fire to dry their wet clothes.

The landlord soon after entered.

"Well, Long Tom," said the Lusher, stretching his legs out, and pulling his wet breeches away from his flesh, "what news?"

"They have come in."

"Where are they?" asked Bullskin.

"They have taken a room."

"What number?" inquired the Lusher.

"Five."

"Have you got Six empty?"

The landlord said he had, so they engaged No. 6, and ordered wine and cigars, and made themselves comfortable.

They paused suddenly in their conversation.

They heard a voice.

Big Bullskin put his ear to the wall.

"Listen," said he.

"Mind, no violence," they heard a voice say.

"No, captain," interrupted another; "that we'll leave to you."

"Silence, Howard."

"Certainly, captain."

"Now listen," said the first voice again "there must be no violence, as I before mentioned, and if you go cautious and quietly you will be able to manage it all right."

"Never fear, captain, we'll do that all right."

"Will you?" thought Swig.

"I will show you the window, so that you won't make any mistake. I know the lady's chamber well," said the captain.

"The devil you do!" thought the Lusher, uneasily.

"You know the reward Lord ——," said the captain, mentioning the name in a whisper so low that the listeners could not catch a syllable, "has promised us if we abduct the Lady Edith safely."

"All right, captain; we'll do the job clean enough for his lordship. When do we start?"

"As soon as they are all gone to bed in this crib."

"How are we to get out?"

"By the window, fool."

"We will get out of the window also," muttered Jack, nudging Swig.

"You perfectly understand the arrangements?" said the captain.

"We do," said Bullskin.

The subtle plotters had settled a plan by which they could carry out their fell work, and were then silent.

The worthy landlord inquired of the scheming ruffians whether they intended to remain all night.

They said they did.

The landlord asked for the money for the apartment, which the men looked very blue about, and paid.

Then Long Tom paid a visit to the highwaymen, and asked them whether they intended to remain.

The highwaymen replied in the affirmative, and paid without looking blue.

Mr. Long Tom then closed the house and retired to rest.

The highwaymen heard their villanous neighbours moving about rather busily

"There they go," said Swig. "one's dropped out of the window."

"Let the other drop out," the Lusher said.

The other dropped out, and fell on his companion.

The highwaymen then opened their window and dropped out one after the other, and followed in the track of the two plotters.

"I wonder when the devil they are coming to the end of their destination," exclaimed Jack.

"Don't hurt yourself," said Swig

"In what way?"

"By using them big words; it's a wonder it didn't cause a lockjaw."

"He has got a large mouth, and finds no difficulty in pronouncing big words."

"People with large mouths never do," said Swig. "That's the reason you have such an easy pronunciation."

"There ain't enough of you to hold many big words," said Big Bullskin, "so you can shut up."

Swig shut up, feeling very much hurt at the remark.

"Returning to the subject," the Lusher said, "how much further are they going? We have followed at least seven miles."

"We'll follow seven miles more to spoil their nicely-arranged plan," replied Bullskin.

They had not to go seven more, for just then the men stopped in front of a splendid large mansion.

The highwaymen lay full length on the sward, so that they could watch the men's movements without being seen.

The two villains then commenced work. They had carefully examined the building, and throwing a rope ladder on a large hook beside a window, the captain was about to ascend it, when a heavy hand grasped his shoulder, and he was hurled back.

In an instant he was upon his feet and, like his companion, was dumbfounded by what he saw.

Standing round were at least a score of officers.

So suddenly had they appeared that the baffled men thought they must have come through the earth.

The perfidious brutes had not anticipated so fatal an interruption to their foul work.

Their plan for the abduction of the lady had been cleverly laid out, but a plan it had been constructed more clever.

The result of which we have seen.

The baffled men uttered fierce oaths, tried to break away from their captors.

But that was an absurd idea.

In an instant they were powerless, gagged, and bound.

The highwaymen were satisfied with the result of the adventure, and started off again.

It was late the following day when they reached the city, and while going along a lane at the back of one of the principal thoroughfares, their attention was arrested by hearing a faint groan, followed by a shrill scream.

Rushing through the bushes of the lane, they found themselves in a beautiful garden.

An exclamation of horror broke from Bullskin's lips, and he darted forward in time to catch the form of an assassinated friend.

Devil Duke!

He was falling from the deadly stroke of his dastardly assailant, who now fled for his life.

The Lusher took in the whole scene at a glance, and darted after the assassin.

CHAPTER XXV.

THE ESCAPE OF THE ASSASSIN—HOW JACK EVANS BORROWS A HORSE — THE LONE HOUSE IN THE MEADOW—THE HAUNT OF THE BLACK BRETHREN — DEATH TO THE TRAITOR—DEATH TO THE SPY.

THE giant caught his gallant comrade just in time; the dastard blow that sent the blood spurting out had been dealt by a sure and savage hand.

The pallor on Duke's handsome face told that the work was nearly done.

He closed his eyes, sick with inward pain and loss of the life-tide so swiftly ebbing out.

Joseph Munroe—or, as we have hitherto called him, Big Bullskin—glared like a tiger after the miscreant.

He was a true-hearted, faithful fellow, in spite of his uncouth aspect, his rough speech, and dogged bearing.

Devil Duke was a favourite with all.

The Lusher and Swig would have died for him.

"After the assassin!" thundered Munroe "Bring him down! Kill him! Curse him!

I would give much to have my hand upon his throat."

Swig and the Lusher waited no second bidding; they were on the track in an instant.

They saw the dark form gliding away towards a cluster of trees. Rapid as it was, they were not far behind it.

Swig drew a pistol.

"I don't often miss," he said, "so here goes!"

And he fired.

The smoke cleared away. A defiant laugh answered the report, and they saw the miscreant leap into the saddle of Devil Duke's steed.

A moment more, and he was careering away.

Strong as was their wish to follow and capture him, they saw it would be useless to give chase on foot.

Jack Evans ground his teeth as the daring rider turned and shook his clenched fist at them.

His hoarse voice was full of mocking malice as he cried—

"Now I have stricken one, it will not be the last."

"It will," Jack Evans thought, "if I catch you."

"Keep back," he said, to Swig, quietly. "Here is a chance for a horse, and a ride for a man who strikes with a dagger."

Just then a sturdy grazier trotted up the lane. He was thinking of his last day's market and the money he had made out of his cattle. He was thinking also of his comfortable home, and several other pleasant things; he was certainly not thinking of what was about to happen to him.

Swig had shrunk out of sight, and was watching from behind a hedge.

The Lusher stepped in front of the grazier's horse.

"Good evening," he said, civilly.

"Good evening," said the grazier.

"That's a fine horse you ride."

"Yes. He can get along."

"Is he tired?"

"Tired! No, he has got to go thirty miles yet."

"Then he will just do for me."

The grazier began to feel for one of his pistols. He thought it was well to be on his guard.

"Well, I want to borrow him," said Jack.

"Do you?" said the grazier, and out came a pistol.

The Lusher dealt him a smart blow over the knuckles, and the pistol went flying. The grazier went flying, too.

Jack had pushed him out of the saddle by the leg.

"Don't be in a hurry to get up," said Jack, as he mounted without the delay of a second, and away he went on the track of the fugitive.

Swig crept from the hedge.

The grazier was groaning and swearing violently as he gazed after his retreating steed.

"What has occurred?" inquired Swig, sympathizingly.

"Occurred! I've been robbed of my horse by a highwayman."

"Sad affair! Can't you give chase after the robber?"

"How can I give chase without a horse?"

"You can get one at an inn."

"Then I will."

"Do get two and I will accompany you."

"You are very kind."

"Don't mention it. Nothing would give me greater pleasure than a hunt after a highwayman."

The grazier thought it very kind of his new friend to offer to chase and capture the daring robber.

He had grazed his shins in rolling off his horse, and took Swig's arm to assist him to the inn.

In the meantime we will return to Big Bullskin, who had taken his gallant comrade into the mercer's house.

The mercer met them at the door.

"Whose work is this?" he asked.

"Just what I should like to find out," replied Bullskin.

"A sorry affair, and a friend of mine!" exclaimed the mercer in surprise; "Duke Deverell."

"Yes, sir," said Monroe, not at all surprised at hearing the strange name.

"Lay him on the couch, and let some one attend to his hurt."

"I fear it is much worse than it looks," said Bullskin."

"I fear so too."

Here they were interrupted by the entry of the mercer's wife, looking pale and sorrowful.

"Poor gentleman!" she said, approaching the couch where the handsome form of the highwayman lay.

She took his hand in her own as she spoke, and a tear dropped on his pallid brow.

Her husband saw this, and, like all old men who have pretty young wives, he felt jealous of the handsome fellow.

"Humph," he grunted, "I don't know what to do about it. Can't we send him home?"

"Oh! husband dear, we can't send him away to die."

"Humph, I suppose not. Pretty thing indeed. Suppose he dies here, or if he recovers you will fall in love with him, or something of the sort."

"Oh! husband, you are very cruel and unjust. You know I could never love any one but you."

The mercer looked at her incredulously.

"Do you doubt me?" she said, pouting, and her large brown eyes filling with tears.

But at that instant her tears subdued him, and he would have believed anything. He twined his arm round her neck, kissed her pretty pouting lips, and told her he did not mean it.

"It was very cruel of you," she said.

"Yes, my darling, it was, but there—dry these pretty eyes, and give me a kiss."

She put her face to his, and he took the kiss.

The lady had gained her point, and knew she could have her own way to any extent.

"Don't you think, dear, it would be better if the poor gentleman was removed from here?"

"Yes, my darling; 'tis a friend of mine. Carry him to my chamber," he said, turning to Bullskin.

He took the inanimate form of his comrade in his arms as though he was a child, and carried him to the mercer's chamber.

"A friend of yours!" repeated the mercer's wicked little wife, assuming the greatest surprise.

"Yes, my darling—Duke Deverell. Don't you remember him?"

"Is this Duke Deverell?"

The mercer repeated he was, and again began to feel uneasy at the interest she entertained for the wounded knight.

Joseph Munroe, seeing his comrade was in very safe hands and would soon recover, as the pretty young wife took the especial responsibility of nursing him, left, muttering—

"I have left them a dangerous sort of guest; he's a devil among pretty women. I shouldn't mind being Devil Duke for a month."

He made his way to the inn, feeling very curious about Swig and his new friend, whom he had seen pass him.

"Landlord," he heard the grazier say, "I want two horses, for myself and this friend here."

The landlord looked at his new customers inquiringly. Swig he recognised, and a very solemn wink passed between them. The grazier had not beautified himself by his recent acquaintance with the mud.

"Two horses," thought the host, who was perfectly acquainted with the nature of the profession followed by Swig and his companion; "I wonder if they have left him money enough to pay for a donkey."

"Post horses!" he inquired.

"Post horses be ——! No; good, rattling, swift saddlers that can run a highwayman down."

Their host rubbed his head.

"You have been robbed, sir?"

"Yes, of my horse; it was worth twenty pounds a leg."

"Not of your money then?"

"It was worth it of anybody's money—one of the best bits of horse-flesh in the country."

"But I mean to say you have not been robbed of your money."

"Oh! I should think not," and the sound that came when the grazier slapped his huge pocket, set Swig's fingers itching. "I've got the worth of a hundred and ten head of cattle here—and cattle are cattle now."

"Well, you can have two horses, but you

must leave a hundred pounds on them. We don't let our cattle go for nothing. Horses are horses now."

The grazier pulled out a big leather bag. It was heavy with gold.

"Saddle them quickly," he said, "or the robber will escape, and, having one, I'd ride a hundred miles to hang him. This gentleman is going with me."

"There's a thousand pounds reward for that identical fellow," said Swig, looking big. "I mean to have half of it."

"A thousand pounds for who?" said Bullskin, entering. "Then get a horse for me; we will all ride after him."

The landlord looked at Bullskin.

A glance satisfied him that they had some purpose in view, so he had the animal prepared and led to the door. The grazier left one hundred and fifty pounds as security for them, in case, as the proprietor suggested, anything should happen to them.

The grazier was emphatically grateful to his new friends. He swore they were the best fellows he had met, and when the high wayman was captured they should dine with him.

"I never like to ride about alone," said Bullskin. "The road ain't safe."

"There's a terrible wretch about these parts," said Swig. "He stops everybody, but no one takes him at first for what he is."

The grazier grew interested.

"No," said Swig, "for instance, he might meet you."

"He'd better not," laughed the grazier. "I carry two good pistols; besides, there are three of us."

"This man would not mind how many," said Swig; "he always has companions at hand, and he is so infernally that artful you never know what he is going to do till he does it."

"Like the thief who stole my horse," said the grazier; "he spoke friendly enough, but I was jerked out, and on my back in a moment."

"The one I mean would not do that; he does things in a different way."

gets the other; each puts a pistol to your —takes the reins of your horse and 'Stand and deliver!'"

Swig suited the action to the word, so did Bullskin. The grazier tried to laugh as though he enjoyed it, but it looked so real that he felt uneasy.

"He—he!" said Bullskin, "the worth of a hundred and ten head of cattle—out with it, my Trojan."

My Trojan began to tremble. There was a cold iron ring in the words, and fancy pictured two bullets meeting half way in the middle of his head. It was pictured by his fancy, but not to his liking.

"Gentlemen," he began, "this is carrying a joke too far, and I can't stand a joke."

"Then we won't joke, my Trojan."

"Thank you."

"We will be in earnest instead. Swig, find the swag while I keep guard. Steady, my Trojan. Don't move your hand, nor your foot, nor your head, nor anything else."

"Help! he——"

"Hold your row. You'll frighten the ball out of my pistol, and it will go through your skull. What's that, Swig?"

"A bagful of guineas," said Swig, giving the grazier a playful pat on the head with his own money; "t'other's pocket-book full of bank notes."

"Flimsies! all right. What else?"

"A watch, a whopper—silver."

"Let him keep it, Swig. No gentleman would carry such a bit of tin about with him. What does it weigh?"

"Pound and a half."

"They've put the family clock in the warming pan, and he thinks it's a watch. Anything else?"

"Only his pistols."

"Worth keeping?"

"No—big as young cannons. Knock the flints out and give them back. Has he got any wipes?"

"Two round his back and one in his pocket."

"Tie his hands behind him. Put your hands behind you, my Trojan, or this little engine is sure to go off. That's it, Swig; now his feet."

PROCLAIMED KING OF THE HIGHWAYMEN.

Swig followed his instructions faithfully. He tied the grazier hand and foot.

Bullskin was kind enough to turn the grazier's horse round.

"Good-bye, my Trojan," he said, giving the animal a smart kick. "Think of an old saying the next time you get into mischief—a pint less is always best. Go along, and find some more cattle."

Away went the horse at a tremendous pace. The grazier did not seem so miserable as might have been expected. He kept his seat well, and worked his hands free after a time, and released his feet.

Then he felt his boots with much satisfaction, and then gave an expressive whistle.

"Yorkshire," he said, with a grin. "They thought they had me, but they haven't. I was served out on this road once before, and this time they are rather taken in. They've got a pocket-book full of imitation bank-notes, and a bag full of bad money."

Our friend, the Yorkshireman, saved the good money in his boots. The highwaymen had not thought of looking there.

Quite ignorant of the clever trick played upon them, Swig and his companion rode rapidly after the Lusher.

Their horses were fresh and willing. They put them to their utmost speed. A dark object—a horseman—was just visible in the distance.

CHAPTER XXVI.

TYBURN DICK IN PRISON.—THE ATTACK ON THE GATES BY CAPTAIN CLAUDE AND HIS DARING BAND.—THE PRISON ON FIRE.— TYBURN DICK CHAINED AMIDST THE FLAMES.

FOR the second time during his short career our hero was a manacled prisoner, securely lodged in a narrow cell.

It was not the one from which he had made his daring escape. They were determined to have him safe now they had got him again. Loaded with the heaviest links, he was thrust into a deep underground dungeon, the walls reeking with slimy moisture, the floor in the filthiest state, and affording refuge to the most noisome crawling reptiles.

Dick bore his captivity bravely. He would not have been taken, betrayed as he was, but at the moment of finding himself confronted by Jonathan Wild and his associates, a heavy blow had been dealt him from behind, which brought him to the floor stunned and helpless.

In that state he was triumphantly bound and carried to prison.

The jailer, who had scarcely left his bed since Dick's escape, hurried to receive his prisoner. He felt no pity when he saw him pale and senseless on the stone bench where they had laid him.

He was too glad to have him again in his clutches.

His brutal visage beamed with joy, and swearing to keep him safe enough that time, he had him placed in the deepest cell.

"I'll make him bear all I can put on him," he muttered, as he locked the ponderous door on his youthful prisoner. "Escape, will he? I'll choke him myself first."

He crept down once or twice to see our hero. The last time Dick was sitting on the bench, taking a view of his situation."

When he saw the jailer's ill-looking face he quite understood how matters fared with him.

"So they have me here again," he mused, "ah! my old friend looks savagely pleased—it is to be hoped he won't have the disappointment of enduring my absence a second time."

"Well, my young gallows bird, we've got you here again, you see—clipped your wings this time, I fancy, eh?"

He brought his brutish features close to our hero's, who longed very much to get him a little closer, just within reach of his ironed hands.

But the jailer was too cunning for that.

Stepping back, he closed the iron-bound door, and tapped it significantly with his keys.

"Won't break through that in a hurry, I'll take my oath. The walls are thick, this cell is deep, no sound can reach outside. Look, here's the key, when you can get that and take them things off your hands and legs as I've put on, I'll give you leave to slip through my fingers a second time."

He flourished the key in Dick's face.

A sudden light shot from the young highwayman's eyes.

A sudden inspiration floated through his brain.

The hot blood shot swiftly through his heart.

The jailer had closed the door, and was alone with him in the cell.

If he could get the keys!

He glanced quickly up.

Swiftly as the inspiration occurred to him, he put the idea in practice.

One sudden, unexpected spring put him in the position he desired.

Between the jailer and the door.

A step towards liberty!

The jailer, appalled at the unexpected act, gazed dumbfounded on the youthful stripling who had taken such speedy advantage of his incautious act.

His heart sank with a deadened, sickening fear, as the boy highwayman's words thrilled him.

"Now we are more equal—you hold the keys, I am at the door. *The walls are thick—the dungeon is deep—no sound can reach outside!* So, my fine friend, either we go forth together, or we stay here till our bones rot together on the floor of this accursed cell."

Our hero looked as if he meant all he said and the jailer knew he was in a trap from which he had no means of escape, unless he made terms with his youthful prisoner.

He had taken such precautions to have Dick safe that he had not told any one which cell he had placed him in, for fear any of the highwaymen should get scent of it and then attempt a release.

By a fatality which he now cursed deeply, he was totally unarmed. Had he been a braver man he might have hazarded a struggle with Dick, but our hero's menacing attitude as he stood with his manacled wrists ready to strike the fellow down if he attempted to pass cowed him, though he slunk back crouching like a baffled beast of prey, preparing for a spring when he might take his enemy unawares.

"Well, friend," Dick said, laughing lightly at the chapfallen looks of the jailer, " are we to come to terms?"

The fellow tried to dodge by.

"Let me out, and I will promise to put you in a better cell."

"Thank you. When I leave this, I want to be out altogether. Am I to have those keys?"

"Never!"

"Very well; then here we stay."

"Beware! I am armed. I have a pistol."

"Psha!" Dick laughed again. "I am up to your tricks, friend."

"Dick," the jailer cried, huskily, "this is madness. You cannot keep me here long. They are sure to come to find me, and then it will be worse for you. Let me pass, and then I can make your captivity less irksome."

He tried again to sneak to the door.

"Back!" Dick cried. "I will brain you with these chains if you come a step nearer."

Big drops of sweat stood upon the jailer's brow. He ground his teeth savagely.

If he could have got near enough, he would have throttled his exultant prisoner.

To be trapped like that, when he had come to crow over Dick's bondage, was too galling Besides, he might be kept there till both perished.

The thought was terrible. In his deadly fear he begged of Dick to let him pass, but was only answered by the youthful highwayman's mocking laugh.

"Hark!" Dick said, presently "Sounds of rescue! My friends have come. If they find us here, it will be your death."

Seating himself gracefully beside the door, he listened intently, while the jailer shook in dread.

But soon Dick's handsome face clouded.

"My fancy has deceived me," he mused. "Even if they came, I could not hear them, and they would never know where I am confined. No! I must make up my mind to remain till my grim jailer relents, or my gallant comrades batter down these stone walls.

We will leave them for the present. The captive and his entrapped jailer—the one listening for the welcome sounds of rescue— the other waiting in palsied rage for his young prisoner's strength to give way, that he might leap upon him in his sleep and drag him from the massive door.

We must follow the adventures of those who were already prepared to attack the prison gates, and rescue their boyish comrade.

Captain Claude, after he had baffled the pursuit of Jonathan Wild and his myrmidons, drew his cloak tightly round about his symmetrical chest, and repaired to the Aldervale Manor.

His brow was pale, and his lips were strongly compressed as he trod the domains from which his youthful protegé was wrongfully driven, and a deep, fervid light shone in his dark eyes.

There was high revelry at the hall that evening. The countess had given a farewell party, and, with her evil-minded son, was doing the honours to the numerous guests, when a message was brought to inform her that a stranger desired to see her.

Both the mother and her vicious boy turned pale, and glanced significantly at each other. The simple news seemed to cause them equal uneasiness.

"A stranger!" Edward said. "Mother, I had better see him first."

Lady Aldervale's lips compressed tightly before she answered.

"No, Edward; remain here with our guests. I will go alone."

She shivered as she left the brilliant saloon.

She was thinking of the night when her own son—poor discarded Dick—had visited her there.

By a strange chance Captain Claude had been ushered into the very room in which Dick had been shown.

He was standing calmly erect, awaiting her when she entered.

He had assumed his mask, but his lips were pallid, and those who knew him could have told, by the restless gleam in his eyes, that the gallant Claude was affected beyond his wont.

When the Countess entered, and recognised her visitor, she started, but seemed relieved.

Assuming her most bewitching grace, she bowed, and looked at the highway chief, as if asking the meaning his visit.

Captain Claude bowed quietly. A nervous twitching of his features told of some deep emotion he endured at that moment, but his mask concealed it.

"Sir," Lady Aldervale said, in her sweetest tone, "you have called me from my guests, but I shall ask of you no apology until I hear what has induced the gallant Captain Claude to risk his life by visiting a lady whose secrets are too well known to him."

"Madam," Claude replied, in a strangely broken voice, "the reason of my calling you from your guests will not be pleasant when you hear it; but such as it is, you will have to bear it; and lest its disagreeable bitterness should unnerve you, I will take the liberty of securing your attention to all I have to say."

He walked quietly to the door, and locking it, put the key out of her reach; as quietly he tied a knot in the bell-rope.

Then, outwardly calm, but with his brave heart throbbing quickly, he stood before her.

The countess started in surprise.

"Sir, these are strange actions. Have I mistaken the honour of the man in whom I have put my trust?"

"Hold, madam!" Claude staggered as if shot. "Speak not of trust. I know those lips of yours can forge a lie, black enough to shame hell's minions! I know, too, that fair as your white bosom is, the heart beneath it shares the subtle perfidy and shameless cruelty of a devil! I can bear the bitterness of your acts, madam, but in my presence let not your perjured lips frame themselves to words of trust."

The countess uttered a faint cry of alarm, and stepped back, her lovely countenance ghastly with an unknown dread.

Claude followed her with quick, excited steps.

"Be not alarmed!" he cried; "I am not come to taunt you with the wrongs you have done me, though they have scared my brain. I am come, unnatural and adulterous mother, to warn you of your persecution of that poor boy, against whom you have steeled your bosom—forgetting that he first drew his sustenance from it. You have hurled him from these halls, which are rightfully his, and have driven him to a life of roadside robbery, and even now have hounded him to a prison, whose walls he may only quit to go forth to a felon's doom. We shall free him this time, but I warn you, fair-faced devil!—cold, callous, unwomanly demon!—I warn you, that if the bitter death you desire befals him —if a hangman's accursed hand crushes out his young life, you shall pay the penalty— and the penalty shall be death, though I myself tear your infamous heart from your unnatural breast!"

A subdued, shivering scream escaped Lady Aldervale's lips; she fell back step by step, as he followed her—fell back from his gleaming eyes, which scathed to her heart—fell back from his withering words, and stood ashy and speechless when he paused, with his sentence of doom yet ringing in her ears.

"Speak!" she faintly cried. "Who are you, who dare menace me with the doom of death? Speak—your name! A mystic warning in in my breast tells me that you are more than you have seemed.

"I am," Claude sternly cried, "I am the protector of that boy whom your hateful infamy has banished from a mother's love. I am more, murderess." His voice, deep and husky, rang like a knell of fate. "I am an AVENGER FROM THE GRAVE!"

Lady Aldervale shrieked. She was looking into his fascinating eyes, and seemed to read a terrible secret there.

"Answer, madam," Claude cried, " and tell me how many days of peace you have had since your pernicious infamy began. Recall that horrible night when a husband came in faith and love to meet his bride and bless his babe. Picture that horrible scene when his gurgling cry rose from the dark waters into which *your* hand hurled him. Conjure his ghastly face when your hired assassin's bullet sent him, stricken and bleeding, down beneath those inky waves you hoped would hide him for ever. Picture all this, and look upon these features—hidden, not by the mask of death, but by this silken one—the features of that boy's father and of your *husband!*"

He tore the mask from his face—such a handsome, noble face, though pallid and excited now, and with the unearthly light in his watchful eye.

The guilty woman gazed, speechless and appalled.

The grave had given up its dead. The husband whom her murderous hand had thrust into the yawning waters stood before her—the father whose caresses had given Dick life stood there, the accuser and avenger.

No wonder that she shook in every limb— no wonder that her tongue clove to her mouth—that her eyes started wildly from their sockets—that her breast rose with the throbbing of her guilty heart—that her brain reeled.

One hand passed before her eyes, to shut out the terrible vision.

The other clutched above her heart, where his words had shot like arrows of flame.

Captain Claude clenched the silken mask in his nervous grip. A half-suppressed cry of sharp anguish, which seemed wrung from his iron soul, escaped him.

He had loved that woman, and even in her guilty hour he could not forget she was the mother of his child.

A sudden and furious knocking at the door aroused them.

It was Edward. He had knocked before, but neither had heeded him.

Claude's hands clenched as he heard his voice

"Your boy!" he hissed, " whose life I will scathe as the lightning withers a tree, if he comes in my path. Heed my warning. I spare you now in your infamy ; but seek Dick's life again, and the sworn vengeance of my attached band shall be your death, and the death you shall die shall be the most pitiless and unnaturally horrible !"

The sound of Edward's voice aroused the stricken woman.

Leaping to the door as Claude retreated to the window, she dashed her white arms against it.

"Help! help !" she cried. " Close the gates —fly to the garden! Seize him ! oh, help!"

Claude was at the casement. His noble face, awful in its sternness, was turned towards her.

"Remember," he cried, huskily, "I have warned, and my warning is of DEATH !"

He leapt out.

The Countess sprang from the door.

She threw her arms in the air, and, with a wild shriek of anguish, fell senseless to the floor, as Edward, followed by a party of guests, burst into the apartment.

.   .   .   .   .

Night had closed around the sombre walls of the prison.

The officials, after a futile search for the missing jailer, went their rounds to see that all was safe, and retired, some to watch, others to sleep.

It was a clear, calm night, and the warders on duty were dozing on their posts, when the sudden clamour of the alarm bell, loudly rung by a more watchful one of their party, echoed with a startling clang on the still air

And then there was a hurried rush of feet to and fro, and a loud voice awakened the sleeping guardians of the prison with the cry—

"To arms ! the prison is attacked ; the band of highwaymen are at the gates !"

Men sprang from their beds, and hurriedly dressing themselves, seized swords and pistols and soon all were congregated near the window overlooking the entry.

And there, outside the strongly-barred ponderous wooden gates, were the band of daring men who had come under the leadership of Captain Claude to rescue their imprisoned comrade.

A band of hardy desperate men, all masked and armed to the teeth.

They battered at the strong doors with massive beams, and when a warder's voice challenged them, Captain Claude's stern tones replied—

"Release your prisoner. We are sworn to effect an entry if he is not given up. Save useless bloodshed by opening the gates."

The sudden and audacious attack on the gates took the warders by surprise. They did not like the looks either of the desperate highwaymen, but so long as the stone walls defied them they could afford to be brave.

The answer to Claude's speech came in the shape of a bullet, which one of the prison officials aimed at his head.

He missed him; but it whizzed close enough to his temples to put a tinge of sterner resolution in his tones, as he cried—

"We have made our demands; we will now make our attack. We are armed. If any one shows himself at that window again he will get a bullet in his skull. Now lads, the gates! Batter them, and let's show them how we can set a comrade free."

There arose a sudden crash! it lasted but for a few moments, and then, amid the uproar of many voices, the barriers gave way, and the highwaymen poured into the passage.

They were met by the body of warders, and the two armed parties of determined men were instantly engaged in deadly conflict.

Their long bright swords gleamed in the half-lighted corridor, and now and then the red flash of a pistol gleamed from their midst.

In the *mêlée* rose the voice of Captain Claude.

"Strike, lads, but not deeply. We seek no lives. Disable, but do not slay."

The brave fellows obeyed his commands.

They outnumbered the warders, but even if they had not, the resistance of the latter would have been of no avail.

A sharp, short, conflict—the warders gave way, were disarmed, and thrust into a room, and the highwaymen rushed from corridor to corridor in quest of Dick.

Our hero heard the noise of the battering in of the gates, and a pleased smile rested upon his calm face.

he could hear the sharp echo of firearms, and his eyes flashed in triumph upon the discomfited jailer, who was crouched in the farthest corner of the cell.

"They come," Dick cried. "I knew they would rescue me. Hark! They will be here presently, and once more I shall be free!"

Our youthful hero had scarcely spoken when a loud explosive report shook the whole building.

The jailer leapt to his feet as it shot.

"God's help now would not set you free," he exclaimed, in a terrified tone. "We are doomed! They have sprung the secret mine, and the prison will be in flames before another five minutes are over."

"The keys, then," Dick cried, angrily, "unless you will stay and perish here."

Dick's proposal, seemed the only possible means of delivering both, but the man appeared seized with a strange stupor.

He clutched the keys in his hand, and leapt away from Dick as he approached.

"Murder! Help! No, I'll save the keys!" he shrieked, bounding back with every distortion of terror on his brutish countenance.

"Are you mad?" Dick asked, his cheeks glowing with excitement. "The place is growing too hot to breathe. We are surrounded with this devilish fire. The keys, man! Unlock the door, that we may escape."

"No, no! Fire is all above us. We should be roasted alive. No help. Murder! Keep away! I'll never leave the keys!"

If Dick could have got one of his hands free, he would have grappled with the jailer; but, fetter-bound as he was, he was almost powerless.

And now the crackling and heat outside told too plainly that the plan for burning the prison, if attacked, and blocking up the passages with flame, so that the prisoners could not escape, had been well laid.

The air grew hot and suffocating.

No time was to be lost if they would not perish there.

Dick saw that the man was either too powerless from abject terror, or too doggedly obstinate to give up the keys.

His only chance was in, at all risks, getting them from him.

Following the fellow quickly round the

walls were not so thick either, but that

ell, he cornered him suddenly, and throwing the long links attached to his wrists high above his head, sprang upon him and hurled him to the floor of the cell.

The jailer's terrified glance had watched Dick's threatening movements, and now he fell with his knees doubled under him, and his heart quaking in the acutest terror.

"Mercy! mercy!" he gasped. "Don't murder me!"

"The keys," Dick cried, striking his hands sharply with his irons.

The jailer's hand unclasped.

The keys lay on the slimy stones.

Dick lost no time in grasping them.

Spurning the prostrate body of the jailer as he made a frantic snatch at them, he hurried to the door.

Kneeling down, he got the key in the lower lock.

In the act of turning it, he felt something pull at his manacles.

There was a sudden click, as of a spring and the jailer's triumphant laugh sounded in his ears.

With the instinct of treachery in his mind, he struggled to rise.

But a grip like steel held him down.

He turned, and saw the cause.

He was fastened by his chains to the wall!

There was a spring staple in the solid masonry near the floor, and into this the crafty jailer had jerked one of his links, thus pinning him effectually.

It was of no use jerking at the chains.

The links held fast—the wall itself seemed as likely to give way.

"Ha! ha!" the jailer laughed. "Got you now. Good-bye. You'll be better alone— ha! ha!"

He bent forward to take the keys.

Dick was exasperated to madness.

Putting his two hands together, he grasped the long links, and poising them straight and firm, dashed them into the jailer's exultant face.

The iron ring joining them struck him between the temples, the two long links dashed into his eyes.

He uttered a fearful groan, and fell blind, stunned, and bleeding.

"No, no, my fine friend," Dick said. "One good trick deserves another. No help for you unless I go too. We share this danger together."

"It grows frightfully hot," he muttered as the hot beads of sweat rolled down his face. "The cell is like an oven. There must be a furnace outside. Am I doomed to perish here? Confusion! why don't they batter down the walls? Ho, there! Help help! I am here chained to a wall amidst the flames!"

CHAPTER XXVII.

THE HAUNT OF THE BLACK BROTHERHOOD— A DISPUTE ABOUT A SPY—AN ATTEMPTED MURDER OF THE CAPTAIN AND CAPTURE OF THE ASSASSIN—EXAMINATION OF THE LISTENER—THE CHOICE OF DEATH OR BETRAYAL—JACK EVANS'S SUBTERFUGE.

THE distant rider seen by Swig and Big Bullskin was Jack Evans on the track of the assassin.

He had made good way, and never lost sight of the man he was hunting down.

"I'll follow him," the Lusher said, resolutely, "if he rides to the jaws of death."

The fugitive struck across a range of meadows. Jack kept to his word. He did not wish it to be seen that he was in pursuit

But he watched his man.

In one of the meadows stood a deserted house.

It was surrounded by a high, stone wall.

Through this the fugitive disappeared as if by magic.

He was lost to sight in a moment. Jack could hardly believe his own eyes.

"Horse and all," he muttered; "that's queer. However, if he got through, there must be a way for me."

Jack went to the wall, dismounted, and tied his horse to a tree.

Then he carefully searched the stonework In vain at first.

He tried the crevices with his dagger. It touched a hidden spring. A solid block of masonry began to revolve, disclosing an aperture.

Jack slid through. The stone went back to its place.

The Lusher knew where he was now. He had heard of the place before. It was a house of mystery and death that none had ever been able to penetrate and live to tell the tale.

The brave fellow did not fear. There were no cowards in Captain Claude's band.

"In the haunt of the Black Brethren," he said. "Well, I am in for it. Hand and sword must defend my heart. If I die, it will not be till I have avenged Duke, and slain the miscreant who stabbed him.

He looked round him. He was in a wide garden—a piece of waste ground, now full of weeds. The house stood before him.

Every window was barred, the doors were of iron. They did not seem to have been opened for a century, so thickly were they covered with rust.

The dark figure did not seek entry by door or window. The house was built of grey stone. The fugitive went through one of its walls as he had through the garden.

Jack followed him like a phantom. He had not been seen yet. He tried the crevices as before, and with the same success. The piece of masonry revolved—he entered.

The stone closed behind him, and he was left in darkness. He heard the retreating footsteps of the assassin, and followed his track like a shadow.

Through long, winding, subterranean passages, where they could not see a hand before them; the smell was strong and loathsome, the walls and ground slimy and damp.

Jack was not sorry when he saw the fugitive pass through an aperture in the wall, through which streamed a few rays of light; but to his disappointment the light was shut out as the aperture closed, and again left him in total darkness.

"He might have waited for a fellow," he muttered; "can't I make the wall go round by putting my hand on it as he did?"

He put his hand on it.

The stone was immoveable. It looked like a sold piece of masonry.

"Cuss it," he said, while rubbing his hand over the surface to find some means of moving it, "it won't move for me."

Just then he heard a click, his hand had touched a button, and the wall swung round.

Jack stuck to it as it went, and went with it.

The stone stopped, he slid off, and again the hole in the wall was well filled by the revolving stone.

He was now in a dark chamber. He heard the low hum of voices, and saw a faint streak of red light struggling through the top of the heavy black hangings that hung at the end of the chamber he stood in alone.

The Lusher felt anxious to know from where the light and the sound of low voices came, and made a search for something he could stand on.

His fist came in contact with a solid block.

He mounted on this, but it was not high enough for him to see through the opening.

"Suppose I make an opening," he muttered.

He drew his sword and cut a slit through the curtains, then he pulled them aside and peeped through.

His surprise was so great at what he saw that he nearly tumbled off his perch.

He took the whole scene in at a glance, and a strange scene it was too.

Sitting round a table that stood in the middle of a splendid large hall, luxuriously furnished, and decorated in the most costly style, were about twenty stalwart, handsome, but somewhat cynical and repulsive men.

Each wore a mask, and every other article of attire was of a raven black.

At the end of the table, raised on a high chair, sat one of the number, a tall, handsome, powerful fellow, of a majestic and commanding aspect.

Making a slight bow to the assembly, he said, in a deep voice—

"Gentlemen of the Black Brotherhood, we have assembled here this evening to carry out a resolution for the destruction of a rival band, namely, that of Captain Claude."

The Black Brotherhood were waving their plumed hats, and shouting in a most discordant manner.

"Hurrah for Captain Bertrand! Down with Captain Claude!"

Such were the mixed shouts of the Black Band.

Jack Evans got so excited, that, forgetting himself, he yelled out—

"Down with the Black Brethren! and hurrah for Captain Claude!"

"Who spoke that?" thundered a voice.

"I did!" he said, tearing the curtains open, and leaping down in their midst; "I, who, in the name of Captain Claude, defy you all!"

His sudden advent startled all. The Black Band gathered round the daring intruder, who, sword in hand, faced them fearlessly.

"Death to him!" they cried. "Death to him!"

"Death to the traitor—death to the spy!"

And twenty swords gleamed ready to drink his blood.

"Death to the first who moves to touch me!" said Jack. "I am in a den of wolves, but I shall fight like a tiger for my life!"

He was answered by the cry—

"Death to him! Death to him!"

The fearless defiance of the Lusher kept his score of ruthless enemies off him with astonishment.

Jack Evans had ventured into a haunt of men who were about as merciful to a spy as a tiger would be to a thing of prey when almost mad with hunger.

He knew this, and still was bold, and feared them not, though he could see the deadly look of their gleaming orbs through the holes in their masks.

The man whom he had been observing advanced towards him with an exultant laugh of savage joy.

"One gone," he said with a sardonic smile, "and another in the toils. You have done well, my friend, by following me. I should not have forgotten you, but since you are so kind as to save me the trouble of looking for you, I will settle the debt."

He drew a dagger as he spoke, and placed it at the Lusher's throat.

"Fiend of hell!" exclaimed Jack, striking his opponent to the ground with the butt-end of a pistol, "thus do I pay for that cowardly blow!"

The brutal assassin reeled, and fell.

His masked companions growled just like so many savage beasts, and closed round the daring intruder; but at that moment, when their long glistening weapons were raised menacingly above their heads, the man whom Jack had put *hors de combat* sprang to his feet with a savage oath, and breaking through his companions, dashed at the Lusher with a dagger in his impetuous grasp.

The Lusher saw his danger, and stepped aside. His assailant fell forward, and ere he had time to stay his arm, the dagger was buried in the heart of a companion who stood behind his intended victim.

A guttural cry came from the assassinated man, and they both rolled to the earth.

Again the Black Brethren dashed upon their solitary opponent; this time his life was in imminent peril : he was thrown down, and the points of his assailants' swords were at his throat when their chief interposed.

"Hold!" he thundered.

The men drew their swords away, and looked at the speaker in blank astonishment.

Jack Evans got up and looked as much surprised as the others; he had given himself up to his would-be murderers without a murmur, knowing that he had served his comrades devotedly to the last. He was willing to sacrifice himself to the appalling doom that threatened him.

"Why this interruption?" demanded the assassin, savagely, contracting his shaggy eyebrows over his cruel, cynical eyes. "Is every spy and traitor to escape the death you allotted them?"

"Silence!" exclaimed Captain Bertrand, his handsome face growing angry.

"Silence! why should I be silent?" fairly shrieked the other, with baffled rage; "nay, I will not be silent. If all our enemies are to escape and betray us, which will be the case ere long, *I* will take the command, and—and you shall die the death of a traitor! What say you, comrades?"

His comrades stood irresolute, uneasily glancing from one to the other.

Their chief for an instant was dumfounded, and then coolly looked the reckless wretch from head to foot.

"Stephen Rogers, or as you are more commonly called, Savage Steve," said Captain Bertrand, sternly and with deep emphasis on each word, "were our laws made for every such despicable, worthless villain as yourself, to turn round and threaten their chief who first established a league of men who can defy the very nation?"

Savage Steve's swarthy cheeks blanched with terror. He knew the cool, quiet manner of his captain was dangerous, so he got out of the way.

"Gentlemen of the league," continued the captain, turning to the twenty black individuals, "I observe that you are not very willing to serve under that gentleman who is so anxious to avail himself of my position. Say, are you content to still have me as your captain?"

"Yes! yes!" shouted the masked men.

"Since you have made your choice," remarked the captain, "name the punishment for members of the band who break the law of our league and revolt against their chief."

"Death! death!" responded the twenty masked men, in one voice, each striking his dagger in the table.

"You hear the decision of your comrades," said the captain to Savage Steve, who crouched back like a tiger at bay. "What have you to say in your defence?"

He had nothing to say, but a pitiless light gleamed from his cruel eyes that spoke his intentions, and warned the speaker.

"I give you but three minutes more to make apology for your conduct," said the chief.

"Fool!" said Savage Steve, with a laugh like a fiend; "this is my apology."

He fired a pistol full at the captain's face.

The shot whistled past within an inch of its mark, and flattened against the wall.

Captain Bertrand leapt forward like a leopard, but before he could reach his assailant, Jack Evans, who had been standing quietly, felled Savage Steve to the earth as he fired.

"Bear him to the judgment-room," exclaimed Bertrand, with a grim smile.

The daring villain who had endangered the life of his captain was seized by his comrades and carried to the judgment-hall, where he was bound to a rack to await his trial.

"Now," said the captain, quite cool and collected, as though nothing had occurred, "we have got rid of one troublesome customer, we will attend to this young man."

Meaning the Lusher.

"Bring him forward," continued the captain.

Jack was taken forward, and stood in a sort of dock

The twenty masked men sat round the table, and their chief, attiring himself in a long black robe, that hung from head to foot, and looked very ominous to the Lusher's imagination, seated himself in a high chair that was elevated three or four feet above the rest.

Jack watched the proceedings with a dauntless and almost defiant air.

The chief of the Black Brethren looked at the brave fellow with a grave smile, and, in a deep, solemn voice, said—

"Are you aware where you are?"

"In the haunt of the Black Brethren," replied the Lusher.

"Do you know the penalty for a spy or a traitor seeking an entry to our haunt?"

"I am no spy or traitor, nor do I fear the consequences."

"Our laws are death to a spy."

"I am not a spy."

"Then why did you seek to enter?"

"For revenge on him who struck a comrade of mine with a dagger."

"Who is your comrade, and who was his assailant?"

"My comrade," answered Jack, proudly "is a member of Captain Claude's noble band."

"Ah!" said the chief, with a start.

"You start as though surprised," said Jack.

"Captain Claude and his brethren are our most deadly enemies."

"I am an enemy, too, then," said the Lusher, coolly.

"For your sake, I am sorry you are. It is a pity that one so brave as you will have to die."

"Why should I die?"

"Because we have sworn a terrible oath to slay every member of your band."

"Then," said Jack, "your oath was sworn in vain."

The twenty masked men looked at the speaker doubtfully.

"Your name," asked Captain Bertrand, "is——"

"Jack Evans."

"Then, Jack Evans," said the chief, "your doom is sealed, unless you consent to one condition."

"Name it."

"That you are sworn in our band as a

member, and betray your old companions to——"

"Hold!" thundered Jack, leaping from his box on to the table.

The Black Brethren in an instant had surrounded their prisoner, and covered him with twenty long-barrelled pistols.

Jack looked wild and terrible in their midst.

Captain Bertrand waved his hand, and the masked men returned to their seats as noiseless as shadows.

"Do you consent?" asked the captain, leaving Jack where he had leapt, covered on either side with a line of glistening pistol tubes.

"No, I will not consent."

"Then you will die."

"I can die," replied their captive, solemnly, "knowing that I have proved faithful to my comrades to the last. But listen," he continued, his voice growing husky; "I am one of a league terrible and untiring when wronged, and as surely as I am killed, not a stone or a spade of dirt will remain untouched until my remains are discovered, and my death avenged in a manner that would leave but little or any of you to tell the tale."

"Your companions may be brave, terrible, and untiring, but an opponent thinks not of that when on the track of an enemy—they only seek for revenge."

"Why have you such bitter enmity against my brethren?" asked the Lusher.

"You shall hear a story now, and then think whether we have cause for our deadly hate."

Jack looked at the speaker, and waited anxiously to hear the story.

"The story is not mine," said Captain Bertrand, replying to Jack's inquiring look.

"I am anxious to hear it," said the Lusher.

"So you shall," replied the captain. "Bring Savage Steve here," he said, turning to two of his band.

Two of the masked men rose and brought their savage companion in, looking wild and haggard.

"Steven Rogers," said his chief, "you will tell our prisoner the cause you have for revenge against his comrades."

Steve made a crouching bow, and looking round at his companions, he wiped the clammy perspiration from his brow, and commenced,

"There was a time," he began, "when I was not what I am now—a time when I was happy—a time when I had a brother, whom I loved better than anything on earth—a fair, gentle, kind youth, whom I would have died for. His very touch—a look from his generous, noble eye would subdue my lion-like nature, when nothing or anyone dared come near me."

Here he paused, and, covering his face with his hands, heaved a deep, heavy sigh.

Not a breath was heard besides his own coarse voice.

"It seems strange that I should ever have had a heart, does it not?" he said, looking round wildly; "but I had a heart, that is now turned into stone, and thirsts for the blood of my enemies. And why am I the fiend I am? Ha! ha! ha! You shall hear. Picture to yourselves two children, left parentless, at a tender age, when they knew no care but the care of each other.

"Such was the case with me and my brother. We were left parentless, friendless, and without a relation to look after us, save an old servant.

"Week followed week, months rolled by, and so years wore on, until we grew to manhood. Still loving each other the same, never knowing a care save for each other, never did two brothers love each other more than we did, until at last the cursed hand of a fiend broke the charmed link and left me desolate."

His frame shook with emotion, and his voice grew thick.

Jack's eyes began to blink, and the cuff of his coat wandered to his face to wipe away a stray tear that rolled down his cheek.

"I had a sister, a dear, angel-like creature," he continued, "who had been abroad from infancy. One evening we received a letter to say she was coming home. My brother started out with a coach to meet her, and anxiously I awaited his return, but, alas! he did not return. The hours wore on, and yet he did not come. A strange foreboding took possession of me, and I was about to start out in search of him, when a fearful storm burst through the elements—a storm that I shall never forget. The thunder rattled round the house in terrible fury, peal following peal, till it shook the very foundation; lightning flashed in massive sheets, that lighted up the whole country, and the rain poured in torrents.

"Suddenly the storm ceased. My window was open, the black clouds swept away from the face of the heavens—the moon, bright and clear, shone forth. I strained my eyes across the open country in hopes of seeing him returning, when I heard a rustling in my room. I turned, and there I beheld——"

His voice sank to a whisper, and big tears rolled down his face.

The Lusher had a lump sticking in his throat, and made several gulps to swallow it, but it would not move.

"I wish he would not tell his story so affectingly; it makes me feel as though I had been smelling strong onions," he muttered to himself.

"My brother," Steve went on. "I fancy I can see him now, standing motionless, his handsome face whiter than the purest marble. I rushed towards him, but he waved his hand, and I stopped. He glided towards me with a sad, sorrowful look, and laying his hand on mine, which made me start, he said, in a low, plaintive voice, 'Steve, behold!' I looked where he pointed, and on his left side there was a stain of blood running from a gaping wound. I asked him who did it, and he said, 'A highwayman belonging to Captain Claude's band. I was returning with Ethel, our sister, when the coach was stopped by a masked man. He asked me to deliver; I resisted, when he deliberately fired at my breast. I saw him tear Ethel from the coach, and I expired as he began to search my body for plunder. The ball had entered my heart.'"

"'No, no, brother; you are not dead,' I shrieked," said Savage Steve.

"My brother said, 'Steve, I am dead. Avenge my death—avenge our sister's wrongs! Farewell—farewell! We shall meet again in the other world!'

"I was speechless, and before I had time to recover my senses, he floated to the end of the room, smiling sweetly, but oh! how sorrowfully! I dashed after him as he sank, as it were, through the boards.

"'My brother!'" I shrieked; but he was gone.

"'My senses left me, and I lay in that spot till the morning. When I recovered the morn was just breaking and the sun peeping forth. Then did I make that terrible vow to avenge his death; then did I swear by the breaking morn, with my hands clasped to heaven, for a just retribution for that bloody deed. Can you wonder at me being such a monster? Can you wonder at me having such deadly hate against your brethren?'" he said, turning to Jack Evans, whose hair had gradually stiffened with fright, and who vacantly glanced about, expecting to see the reappearance of the phantom.

"Did you speak to me?" asked the Lusher, vacantly.

"I spoke to you," shrieked the other, madly "Did you hear?"

"Oh, yes. I heard. It was a very sad story."

"'Tis not finished yet."

"Then I will listen to the rest," said Jack. "I think I remember something about it."

"Indeed."

"Yes."

"What was it?"

"The man that perpetrated that brutal, blood-thirsty deed was a new member of our band, the captain heard of what he had done and had him punished. He was taken to the torture-vault chamber, as it's called, his hands and feet were nailed to the wall, and then an awful, oh! most awful proceedings took place.'

"What was it?"

"I don't like to tell you; it gives me the backache to think of it."

"Beware how you play with us," said Savage Steve.

"Don't frighten a fellow," Jack said, "in course, if you want to know, why I'll tell yer.'

Steve ground his teeth.

"Well," said Jack, commencing to relate the fearful spectacle he had witnessed, "when he was nailed, of course I mean nailed to the wall, he began to shout—of course every fellow would shout if he was hurt—and he had something to shout for. Fancy having long spikes coming through the wall, and about fifty sticking into a fellow's back half an inch deep. That's the sort of thing to make you tell the truth the first time. That's what he had; they worked by machinery, jobbing

THE WARNING OF DOOM.

backwards and forwards in the same holes. He lived three days like that without any grub, at last he died through starvation and concussion in the back. There he is, hanging to the wall now, and every night the rats go and have a good feed! I don't know any more.'

'That was a just death,' said Savage Steve, laughing like a fiend

"Just so," I thought.

"A death I should like you to die."

"Thank you," replied Jack, with a shudder,

"I was going to say that you ain't told us the second part of your story."

"Listen then."

"I am all attention."

Savage Steve threw a pistol at him.

"Stop that," said Captain Bertrand, angrily, "finish your story."

The savage wretch looked daggers at Jack, and, could looks have killed a person, the look the Lusher encountered would have killed a dozen.

"I went in search of my wounded brother,

began Steve, " and I found him huddled in a pool of blood in the coach. He was buried, and again I repeated the oath of vengeance over his grave. Then for months I was in search of my sister, whom I had never seen and did not know only by a mark that we all bore on the neck. By accident, I fell into a den of desperadoes. I overheard what they were saying. I heard that the hound who assassinated my brother, and abducted my sister, was riding away with her, when a nobleman who heard her cries rescued her from the villain, and put her in the care of an old aunt of his.

"He was watched by the highwayman. This same fiend had been offered a thousand pounds by a profligate lord if he could procure him a young maiden for his toy.

"The highwayman had watched my sister's preserver to his house, and not having courage enough to enter, he informed his employer how she had been taken from him by a brave young cavalier, and where the victim was. The profligate lord's heart was fired by the description of my sister, and he thought of possessing himself of her. A week passed, when the villainous profligate, with his cursed ally, went to the lone house where my sister was staying, and in the middle of the night forced an entry and carried her off.

"The young lord went to his aunt's the following day, and learned the sad news. He took a fearful oath to track the daring abductors, and started forth. Week followed week without success, and, still untiring, he kept on his mission, until at last he fell into the right trail, and found them."

The narrator paused, and, looking around at the interested but sad faces of his listeners, he said—

"This story, as I have told you, I heard in a den of desperadoes who were friends of your companion," he said, turning to the Lusher with a bitter look; "but this part, the last and most terrible, I witnessed."

"One evening, when weary and tired after long fruitless search for my sister, I sat down beneath a cluster of trees in a garden. Ten minutes had barely passed when I heard a scream that caused a thrill of pain to run to my heart. By instinct I thought that voice was my sister's; it sounded like the very echo of my dead brother's. Again I heard the same voice in sorrowing, pleading accents. My head seemed in a whirl, and like a tiger I leapt through a window, regardless of danger. As I sprang into the room, the door was burst open, and in rushed a handsome youth. He dashed upon the ruthless villain, who was struggling with a female—my sister. At last !' shrieked the young noble, drawing his rapier, ' have I discovered you, despicable cur, and this shall end your villainous career.' He made a thrust at his breast as he spoke, but the profligate lord guarded it off, and ran his young opponent through the heart. I ran forward to catch him, but he fell lifeless at my feet."

His voice became almost gentle as he went on, and wiping the tears away from his blanched cheeks, he continued his sad story—

"I then dealt the murderer a blow that knocked him down. I clasped my sister in my arms, and in a voice almost choked with joy, I said, 'Ethel, my darling sister !' She looked at me for a moment almost distractedly, and with quivering lips said, ' Are you my brother ?' ' Yes,' I replied, ' your only brother. I know you by this mark,' for at that moment I caught sight of it on her shoulder —a mark exactly the same as I have here."

And he bared his neck.

"Her face brightened up with hope, and she clung to me affectionately. ' I am so happy you have come in time to save me from this wicked man, dear brother,' she said.

"' Ah, ah, ah ! you are glad, are you, and he is your brother ?' said the profligate springing to his feet with a savage laugh. I turned sharply, but before I was aware of his intentions he tore my sister from my arms, and, forcing her to the ground, he held a dagger at her bare white breast, when I dashed at him with my sword. A shriek of savage terror left his lips as my blade was sheathed in his black soul; then a faint cry came from my sister. In his last death-throes he had plunged the dagger to her heart. She uttered ' Brother,' in a whisper, and fell beside her slayer with a sweet pitying smile at me.

"At that moment my senses seemed to have left me, and I felt as though mad. I caught my dead sister in my arms, and dashed with her through the window. From that moment

I have been an outcast, a despicable thing, for men to torment—a brute who only thirsts for blood, and blood with retribution I mean to have. My story is ended. Now, can you wonder at me wanting revenge? Can you wonder at me having no heart, only that of a stone? Can you wonder at me gloating over my victims and drinking their warm blood? If you can, speak. Ah, ah, ah! I see you don't wonder. No, no, no; wouldn't any of you have been the same as I am had you been deprived of your only brother and sister whom you loved as I loved them? I know you would. My oath of vengeance shall be fulfilled, and my dead brother and sister shall be avenged!"

He threw up his arms and fell to the ground insensible.

CHAPTER XXVIII.

JACK EVANS BECOMES A MEMBER OF THE BLACK BRETHREN, AND GOES IN SEARCH OF GALLANT JEM.

HE had grown to such a frantic pitch of excitement while telling the last part of his story that every one looked at him uneasily, and even the Lusher shrank away trembling from his furious gaze.

"Take him back to his cell," said Captain Bertrand in a voice touched with pity. "His story is a sad one, but he has offended our laws, and must be punished accordingly."

The chief was a kind fellow, and would gladly have pardoned him, but he was obliged to make his word his law, and be severe with his bretheren, to keep any control over them.

"Now," he said, turning to Jack Evans, "you have heard one reason why we should have such an enmity against your comrades, and unless you consent to my proposition, you 'll never leave this place alive. Do you consent to become one of us?"

"No."

"You do not?"

"I do not."

"Then your fate is sealed!"

"So be it."

"Think before you sacrifice yourself," said Captain Bertrand, persuasively, looking on him with pride.

"I have thought," replied Jack, "and would die a dozen deaths sooner than betray one of my comrades!"

"You talk rashly. I do not wish to harm you, but unless you become one of our band you will never see daylight again."

"No! nor night-light, candle-light, fire-light, or any other light!" said Jack.

"Come, consider; you are young, strong and a brave life is a dear thing to part with. Your comrades may be dear in your own imagination, but when it comes to the contest you would find it a hard struggle to part with your own life for some one else."

The captain looked hard at the Lusher, who returned the look with an unquailing, truthful eye.

"Come, what do you think?" asked Bertrand.

"Nothing different to what I have told you."

"Listen!"

"I listen to no more!" interrupted the Lusher.

"Let me reason with you," persisted the captain. "By joining our band you will save your own life and"——

"Betray my comrades! No!"

"Nothing of the sort! You will simply show us where to find them. You say they are all brave, and surely would defend themselves were they attacked?"

The captain's words set Jack thinking, and he thought of a very feasible plan by which he might lure the Black Brethren to destruction through joining their band.

"Have you made up your mind?" asked Bertrand.

"Yes," answered the Lusher.

"And what decision have you made?"

"To die," answered the other, coolly.

"I am sorry that you think so lightly of death," said Captain Bertrand, gravely. "Come, drink some wine; you will think different presently. You have an easy way of purchasing your life and freedom."

The Lusher drank the proffered draught, and pretended to be drinking. He did not want them to see that he had so readily consented to become one of them, in case they should get scent of his treacherous design.

"Give me some more wine," he said, "and I will think of your proposition."

A couple of bottles were pushed towards him, which he soon drained to the very dregs

The captain of the Black Brethren, seeing that the strong liquor had taken effect on ir captive, said—

Of course you will join our brotherhood. the money we make, every farthing of is equally divided amongst every er."

don't half like the idea of compromising .d chums to your lot of black devils," Jack, swaying from side to side

The captain laughed at the remark, and, thinking he had made sure of his man, said—

"Come, take the oath, and let's have no more parley."

"I don't mind joining, but I'll not take any oath."

"But our rules are that every new member shall take an oath over a cup of blood."

"Is it?" said Jack. "You don't get any oath ou of me, so if you do not like me to join you can do the other thing."

"Put you to death?"

"Just so. "

"We won't do that, but should you attempt any treachery you will die on the instant."

"If you think I shall turn traitor, don't have me."

"That we shall have to chance," remarked Captain Bertrand, producing a huge book.

"Sign your name and follow my dictation in this."

"All right," replied Jack, quite off-hand, writing the following under the directions of Captain Bertrand:—

"I, John Evans, having with my own hand signed this document in good faith to Captain Bertrand and the Black Brethren, swear to keep every rule and secret written therein and do pledge my life in guarantee of faith.

"That I a member of the Black Brethren, join in every enterprise and common interest with my comrades, and promise to share with one and all any property that may come into my hands.

"That I swear by my life to link myself to my brethren through life until death, making their cause my cause, and in every way sharing the dangers with my companions, even to the shedding of my blood in their defence.

"Should I in any way compromise my trust or fail in any of those things, then as a traitor let me die such death as is allotted by the chief of the Black Brethren.

(Signed)   JOHN EVANS.

Jack gave a sigh of relief when he had finished. His hand was shaken by his twenty new comrades, and after receiving congratulations from every one, success was drunk to his first adventure.

The Lusher felt as though he would like to dash the glasses from their hands and run them all through with his sword at once.

But it not being practicable, he was forced to drink greatly against his will to the successful capture of his late companions.

"Hurrah for our new member!" shouted Captain Bertrand.

The solid masonry walls regularly rang with the echoes of the merry, boisterous voices that gave a hearty three times three.

"We shall soon have the road to ourselves," said the captain, smacking Jack Evans on the back; "it won't take long to clear it of our enemies."

"No," muttered the Lusher, "it won't take long to clear it of our enemies. It was the worst hour's work you could have done for yourselves when you took me into your accursed gang."

"Come," said Bertrand, "we are losing valuable time. Now, take what men you think will be necessary."

"Four," said Jack, "will be quite enough.

"How many do you intend to go after?"

"One at the time," replied Jack, "will be the best and surest way of capturing them."

"A capital idea," remarked the captain, enthusiastically, "do you know where to drop upon one?"

"Yes, one of the most gallant and daring in our band."

"His name?"

"Gallant Tom."

"A noble fellow?"

"Too noble to be sacrificed through you," muttered Jack.

The Lusher had got his four picked men armed to the teeth, and they started forth.

"Adieu for the present," said the captain, "I suppose we shall have two less in our way?"

"You shall," said Jack, with a look that spoke the meaning of his words.

"Hallo!" shouted the highwaymen, as two men, apparently farmers, approached them, "they are the sort of fellows that carry the swag."

"Are they?" remarked Jack, exchanging a wink between the two men. "I should have thought they carried very little."

"What do you say?" said the biggest of the two, coming up to the highwaymen.

"Hand over your coin, if you have got any."

"I'll hand you over a dig in the nose, if that'll do as well."

The Lusher had stepped aside, and was busy scribbling a note. He recognised the two farmers as his companions Swig and Bullskin.

The faithful fellows saw their comrade's form follow that of the assassin through the revolving wall, and, knowing the nature of the place he had gone in they were determined to wait until he or some one else came out, so that they could learn the secret of the entrance and make their way in to rescue their companion.

While they were anxiously waiting, two farmers came jolting down the road with a couple of clumsy plough-horses.

Bullskin, stepping from his hiding place, walked between the two horses, and jerked the farmers out of the saddles by their collars. As soon as they were lying on the ground, Swig having actively pounced upon them, he soon striped them of their smocks, which he and his companions put on over their coats.

Then tying the discomfited farmers on the backs of their jaded steeds, the highwaymen started them off with some smart cuts round their flanks.

Bullskin had put two of the Black Brethren *hors de combat*, while Swig was dodging round the other two.

"Hallo! what's the meaning of this?" said the Lusher, rushing at Munroe; "two of my comrades beaten by one of these country louts! Stand aside, mates, let's have a go in."

He made a furious cut at his comrade, but took particular care to prevent his sword touching him.

The other two had risen to their feet, and the four attacked Swig, who fought gallantly until he was disarmed, then he shrieked for his companion.

Bullskin made a thrust at his opponent, but his sword went within a foot of its mark, and the combatants rolled over together.

While in that position Jack slipped the note into his companion's hand, and whispered—

"Return to the haunt at once, and apprise the captain of what you have seen. The note will explain all. I am going on the track of the Gallant Tom. Meet me with friends. All you see or hear I do it for the best. Trust in me and all will be well."

"I understood it all when I saw you come out," said Bullskin, grasping the other's hand affectionately. "Leave it to me; these black devils are caught in their own trap this time. *Au revoir*, we shall meet soon; Swig is squealing for me; he is in a mess."

Big Bullskin was inspired with deadly hate against the Black Brethren, and firmly grasping his ponderous sword as he sprang to his feet, he dashed at his comrade's opponents.

His sword, like a flash of lightning, swept through a man's body who held Swig by the throat, then, like an enraged tiger, he sent the others scattering in all directions.

The Lusher, to prevent suspicion, dashed at the gigantic fellow, and in a minute they were engaged in a desperate encounter.

Their swords clashed loudly as they guarded off each other's blows, causing showers of sparks to fly from their ringing steel.

The Lusher wound his thin blade round the broad sword of his opponent, and with a sudden jerk, wrenched it from Bullskin's hand.

The disarmed highwayman ran at his assailant, and driving him in the chest with his head, sent him rolling over his Black Brethren like a ball, then, catching Swig up under his arm and regaining his sword, he darted out of sight like a shadow, in the direction of Captain Claude's haunt, little dreaming of the fearful enterprise his faithful comrades had gone on for the capture of gallant Tom.

The Lusher then took another direction with two men, leaving the others to convey their slain companion back to the haunt, while he led their comrades to a certain doom

CHAPTER XXIX.

THE PRICE OF LOVE, AND HOW A KING'S OFFICER TRIED TO WIN THE COUNTESS AND LOST HIS LIFE—ATTACK UPON THE PRISON —A DESPERATE ENCOUNTER WITH HIGHWAYMEN—RESCUE OF TYBURN DICK—REMORSE—JONATHAN WILD'S WARNING.

The sudden excitement that prevailed at the Aldervale Manor on the night of Captain Claude's strange interview with the countess, brought a heavy cloud over the gay scene of revelry, and caused many happy beaming faces to turn sad and sorrowful as they flocked into the room where the countess lay insensible.

Every one was anxious to learn the cause of the peculiar disaster; but, receiving no no answer to their many inquiries or eager expressions, the party broke up, and retired one by one until they were all gone but a dashing young officer of the King's Guards whose handsome face and gallant bearing had been the admiration of all the fair ladies and envy of all the gentlemen.

"I should like to know whose infernal work is this," said the young officer, with clouded brow and a determined look burning in his handsome eyes. "I would make the perpetrator answer me at the point of my sword."

"I expect it is the work of my old enemy; curse him!" replied the dastardly son of the countess.

"His name," eagerly inquired the young soldier.

"Tyburn Dick," was the other's brief rejoinder.

The countess had been conveyed to a couch, and restoratives were administered to her. A thrill ran through her frame as the name of her wronged son left the lips of her illegitimate heir.

The gallant captain of the King's Guards pressed her tiny fingers to his lips and breathed more freely when she moved. He had been her honoured companion for the evening, and was greatly smitten with her superb beauty—a beauty that had cost such a price of blood, and lured so many to destruction —beauty such as that possessed by a serpent, which by its fascinating charms would draw you towards it, and, when within reach, twine itself round you, and crush out your very life in its subtle

Such was the beauty of the Countess Aldervale, whose incomparable loveliness was luring the gallant young soldier by her side to a certain doom.

Little did he think of the snare he was being drawn into as he knelt by her side, patiently waiting for her consciousness to return, when he hoped and almost prayed to receive a kiss from those coral lips

Again she moved her beautiful white breast, having with inward agitation. She stared vacantly round the apartment, her wild eyes wandering from Lord Edward to the handsome face of the young captain who held her delicate little hand in his own.

"Is he gone?" she faintly inquired.

"Who, mother?" asked Edward.

"Who came to me, he who returned from the grave, from the ocean's depths, to threaten me with death?"

"Speak! In heaven's name explain, mother exclaimed her bastard son excitedly.

The young officer sprang to his feet. With flushed cheek and flashing eye he cried—

"Who dares threaten one so fair and gentle with death?"

"Oh! oh! who dares?" she laughed sarcastically; "many do; but who has the right to do so?"

Lord Edward, going to his mother's side, bade their young guest repair to a chamber for the night that had been prepared for his reception.

The young officer, with lingering look at the countess, retired, and left her alone with her unlawful son.

Then she told the young earl all that had transpired during the interview between her and Captain Claude, carefully selecting a little bit at intervals for her own especial benefit.

"What right of claim have these notorious ruffians to demand an interview with you whenever they please," sternly inquired Lord Edward, fixing his flashing eyes on the countenance of his wanton mother.

"None!" she answered, without changing a muscle of her devilish fair face. "Its s a scheme by which they think to extort money"

"Have you not sufficient influence to put a stop to it?"

"I have tried every means," she said, "and yet they evade and defy the law in every manner."

"Why trust to the law? Is there no other way by which they can be stopped?"

"I have tried other ways," answered the countess, "even hired the lowest ruffians."

"Who would sell your bribe for a larger one from their victims."

"Such has not been the case; the men have been found murdered in the road."

"By some means it must be put a stop to."

"You have said that before," she said, clutching him by the arm, and putting her lips to his ear, whispered—"Have you courage enough to try your hand at it?"

He sprang round as though a dagger had been driven in him, and confronted the temptress.

"I!" he exclaimed. "The Earl of Aldervale turn common assassin? No!"

"I thought not," was the taunting reply.

Lord Edward gave his mother a warning look, and turned to go.

"Edward, my dear boy," she cried pulling him back, "I did not mean it as an offence. Stay! hear me."

He turned his head, casting a disdainful look at his mother, with one hand on the door handle.

She then threw her arm around his neck, and kissed his haggard cheek.

"What is it you have to say?" he asked, softened by the fond caress.

"Listen, my dear son," she said, keeping one arm around his neck, and holding his hand in her own delicate little palm, "our lives are in imminent danger through these two outlaws, and unless they are silenced, we shall never have an hour's peace. They must be silenced—you understand?"

"I perfectly understand the meaning of your words," he replied. "But who is to do it?"

"Have you not eyes?"

"I believe I have. It is possible they are not so penetrating as yours."

"I should say so, too, if you have not noticed anything this evening."

"Nothing in particular. I am so used to those strange scenes between strangers and yourself that I take no notice of them."

The countess's face flushed crimson at the other's words, and the expression of her large blue eyes, as they were fixed upon her son's face, meant more than could be read in the expression.

"Did you not observe anything particular in the manner of the young officer toward me?" she asked quietly.

"Nothing more so than many others of your numerous admirers."

The countess bit her lips.

"You are a keen observer sometimes," she said, sarcastically.

The young earl bowed mockingly.

"Come," said the countess, with a strange laugh, "this is not the way for mother and son to respond to each other."

"What would you require?" asked Lord Edward.

"Listen, and answer as best you think. The young captain of the King's Guards, like many other fools, is desperately in love with me."

"That I already know."

"He would do anything to gain his suit."

"As he insinuated, like many more," remarked the earl.

"He is young, strong, and a matchless swordsman."

"Well?"

"Do you not think he would be the best person for our purpose? He has a steady hand, and could easily rid us of our troublesome friends."

"He would prove an invaluable friend did he do so; but suppose he fell, as others have done?"

"What matters that to me," was her cold reply, "if we are freed of our enemies?"

"Just so," Lord Edward said. "I will leave you now, mother; it is getting late, and I require rest. Good night: you will see him in the morning."

"Good night, Edward," said the countess, repairing to her boudoir. "My proud boy will not retain the earldom long unless the rightful heir is put out of the way," she muttered to herself, watching Lord Edward's retreating form.

The Countess of Aldervale had little sleep that night. The many scheming, treacherous plans that passed through her troubled brain made her very restless.

She thought of her wronged husband, of her disowned child, and then of the young officer whom she meant to draw into a snare.

In the morning the countess rose, and saw Wild waiting for her.

The thief-taker, with his usual sullen manner, stood quietly waiting for the countess to speak first.

She began without delay.

"I have sought you, Mr. Wild."

The thief-taker bowed.

"Have you heard anything of that daring boy whom I charged you to capture?"

"I have, my lady," answered Wild, with a brutal cunning leer; "I don't think he will trouble your ladyship any more."

"Is he captured?" asked the countess eagerly.

Wild grinned grimly, and said coolly—

"He is."

"How did you manage this?" she asked, with a pang of half-remorse and half-joy throbbing her fair bosom.

"Oh! very easily, my lady," answered the thief-taker. "We laid a trap which he fell into, and he was conveyed to a prison which he won't break through in a hurry."

"One stumbling-block removed from my path," she muttered.

Wild heard the words, and chuckled to himself. He meant in course of time to get the proud lady of Aldervale in his power.

"Since you have so cleverly and effectually captured one, perhaps you will be able to move another from the public road."

"Any, madam. There are few who can evade the skill of Jonathan Wild."

"So I've heard, and now strongly believe," replied the countess.

"Who is this other person," asked Wild, "whom you wish me to capture?"

"The renowned Captain Claude, chief of the highwaymen."

"It shall be done, my lady. But the price?",

"The same as the other."

"That was small, and this is a much greater person," said the thief-taker.

"It shall be doubled if he is moved as carefully as the other," the countess said, her eyes glimmering with triumph.

"A man when once marked out by me," said the thief-taker, "can never elude the vigilance I take for his capture. He is doomed and the career of Captain Claude will be, from now, but short."

"The shorter the better," remarked the countess. "Are you sure this boy you captured has no way of escape?"

"I am sure he has not," answered Wild, thrusting his huge hands in his pockets, and sticking his legs out.

His heel went to the countess's toe. She drew her foot up with a start.

The swarthy cheeks of the thief-taker flushed with a brutal passion, as he caught a glimpse of her beautifully moulded ankle.

"If his companions should learn, will they not try to rescue him?" asked the countess, blushing, dropping her dress, and hiding her limb from the other's fixed gaze.

"They may try; but they won't be able to to save him," was Wild's answer.

"The captain of his band," continued his fair employer, "you think will be captured?"

"I do, madam."

"Stay," said the countess, as Wild rose to go; "I have a captain of the King's Guard here, who perhaps could assist you."

Wild followed her retreating form with a cunning leer.

The young captain was in the next apartment, and as he entered his handsome face flushed with excitement.

The countess extended her hand with a sweet smile, that made the heart of her admirer beat unusually quick; he passionately kissed her fingers, gazing with swimming head at her white heaving bust.

"I trust, madam," he began, "you are not angry with me for encroaching upon your kindness, but I felt anxious to know how your ladyship would be after your fright last night."

"Thank you," she said, "I am now quite well. I am delighted that you stayed; indeed I hardly know how to express my gratitude."

The officer of the King's Guard had been praying for an interview with the countess; he worshipped the very ground she trod and longed to tell her his love, but could not summon courage enough now they were alone.

She noticed his agitation and guessed the ruse.

" I ought really to apologize to so gallant a gentleman for your brave conduct "

" My fair lady," he interrupted, " I was ungallant and not worthy of your sweet praise. I should have sought and followed the villain who dared to intrude upon so beautful a lady's privacy."

" Sir!" she exclaimed, looking full into his face.

" Madam!" he answered, bowing his head, " have I angered you?"

" Nay, but you flatter me."

" I am sorry if I offend," he said; "but believe me, dear lady, there is no one who could find words sufficient to flatter a lady who possessed such matchless charms as yours."

The countess patted his cheek.

" I have a good mind not to forgive you," she said; " you are very wicked to persist in your flattery."

" You are cruel," he said, unconsciously gliding his arm round her lissom waist. " If you do not forgive me, the King will have no more of my services."

" What do you mean?" asked the countess, looking anxiously at his earnest face.

" I could not bear the idea of having an angry word from your sweet lips," he said, drawing his sword; " and this should tell how desperately I love you by going through my heart."

" Oh! Frederick, do not talk so terribly; you frighten me."

He took both her little hands in his own, and looking her full in the face, he said, solemnly—

" Listen, dear lady, and drive me forth afterwards if you like, but I must ease my heart of its heavy burden. I speak boldly, but I cannot avoid it—my brain is distracted —my heart on fire. I am driven desperate; forgive me, my—my dear countess."

The Countess Aldervale was awed by the sudden outbreak of so gallant and handsome a fellow.

Scalding tears stood in the young officer's eyes. He trembled in every limb, and strangely watched his fair companion.

" May I hope," suddenly he exclaimed, "that I do not love in vain? the first time I beheld you a str ran through my frame—at the to dear little hand my heart was fire and since then it as grown into voted affection. Speak, dear lady you love, or discard me if you lik are another's, or do not love me, sa this shall end my life."

He placed the point of his weapon breast.

The countess turned pale, and dashing sword from his hand, said, with quiveri lips—

" Really, sir, this is strange conduct for a stranger."

" No, no, madam!" he cried, " I am no stranger—say not so."

" But "——

" You do not love me," interrupted the excited young soldier. " In heaven's name, tell me—release my heart of this terrible tor- ture, or I shall go mad!"

" Be more quiet," she said, " then I will tell you."

He clasped her to his breast, and pas sionately kissed her fair brow.

She did not resist, and he held her there, saying, in a much calmer voice than he had spoken hitherto—

" Blessed angel of light, my only idol and every thought, give me a little encouragement and I shall be happy."

" Silence, then," she said; " if you wish to gain your suit you must do something I am going to ask you."

" Anything," he almost shrieked.

" You have heard of the daring boy high wayman ?"

" A boy named Dick? Yes."

" And Captain Claude, the chief of high waymen ?"

" A gallant, noble fellow; I know him,

" I want them both killed," she said.

The captain of the Guards started

" My life," continued the countess, " perpetual misery through those wretched men. They have threatened the life of my son, and are continually extorting money. Last night I should have been assassinated had it not been for such timely aid coming to my assistance."

The King's officer stared aghast at the fair, subtle speaker.

" Your life in danger, and threatened by these despicable hounds," he exclaimed, clutching his sword; "curses on their base heads; my sword shall receive retribution for the wrongs you have suffered by drinking their vile blood."

" Will you capture the young one, and kill the captain at the first opportunity?"

" Will I?" he repeated. "I would face hell's demons were you to demand me to."

" I do not wish such a horrible thing as that," she said, with a bright silvery laugh.

If she did it would have been all the same.

"Mr. Wild," she said, "tells me he has captured the boy highwayman, and put him in prison, but he has escaped so many times I think it is possible he will do so again."

" There are not many prisons built that can hold him," remarked the officer. " Have you Mr. Wild here?"

" I came to ask you if you would like to accompany him."

" Yes, I am delighted at the idea of having a highwayman's hunt, and more happy to know that it will please you at the same time."

" If you rid me of those two men," she said, "your wish shall be fulfilled, and my hand shall be yours."

Her words struck his heart like a Cupid's dart, and sat his brain on fire with hope in his ecstacies of joy. He showered a dozen caresses on her coral lips.

The countess broke away from his embrace, beckoning him to follow her.

He did so readily.

They entered the room where Jonathan Wild sat patiently smoking a short pipe.

The Countess of Aldervale was about to introduce them to each other, when the thief-taker sprang up and clasped the hand of the young captain.

They knew each other was evident, but now she wondered.

The King's officer told her how.

The thief-taker had often wanted the services of the guard when he had any troublesome business, such as the capture of a half-dozen highwaymen, or the breaking up of a haunt.

Thus it was how they had got known to each other.

" Just the gentleman I want to see," said Wild, "got some more business on hand?"

" So I heard," replied the young officer, "highwayman hunt, and that sort of thing; capital ain't it?"

" Yes," replied the thief-taker, drily; " we had better have a body of guards; the more we catch the better it is for the———"

" Lining of your pockets," broke in the other; "it makes them strong."

" Exactly so," said Wild, with a grim smile. "Also for the benefit of the public."

" What, your pockets?"

Wild chuckled, and put his hand in his pocket, to make sure of what he had there.

" Will you send for your men?" he asked

" Yes," replied the young officer. " Will you send for yours?"

" They are already waiting for me outside."

" You are fortunate."

" Why?"

" It is dangerous, I presume."

" In what way?" asked the thief-taker.

" Because you have so many affectionate friends always ready to drop upon you if you are out alone. Nothing like being well guarded, eh, Mr. Wild?"

Mr. Wild took the insinuation, and glared at the jester spitefully. To speak about his *friends* always touched a sensitive chord of his brutal nature, that made him feel wild by instinct besides being *wild* by name.

The captain of the Guards had written a despatch for some of his men to attend immediately, and sent by one of the countess's servants, who shortly afterwards returned with a body of stalwart, handsome men, well-armed, and ready to fight to the death for their young commander.

The young officer, inspired with hope of gaining the countess's love, and eager to capture a highwayman, bade her good-bye and started forth with Wild.

There was a marked difference between the two class of men, Wild's rude and repulsive myrmidons, and the captain's handsome guards.

The party had not proceeded far when one of Wild's officers came rushing up to the thief-taker, breathless.

" What's the news ?" asked Wild, with an oath.

" The prison's attacked by highwaymen !" exclaimed the man, quickly. " They will pull the walls down, if they don't get Dick, they say ; and they mean it too."

" Curses ! hell's flames ! furies !" shouted the thief-taker. " These men are very devils."

" They are," remarked the young captain.

" Away with you at once ! Never mind about winding," said Wild, to the man who brought the news. " Pass the word that we are on the road."

" All right, guv'nor," cried the man, as he scampered off.

" On, then ; we shall have these men," said another.

" Of course we shall," replied the captain, turning to his guards. " Forward men, make ready. Make ready !"

" Now livelys, move them —— stumps of yours !" shouted Wild, addressing his ruffianly gang.

The party set off at a quick pace, preparing for the coming combat. The gallant officer of the King's Guard, little dreaming that he was taking his last walk on this earth, awaited him.

But he was—a death sure and terrible—as will be seen in the following chapter.

CHAPTER XXX

THE COUNTESS ALDERVALE AND JONATHAN WILD—ON THE TRACK OF HIGHWAYMEN —UNEXPECTED NEWS AND ITS RESULTS.

IT was a terrible time for Dick.

The fierce flames leaped and roared through the long corridor, and each moment brought them nearer to his cell.

He could feel the heat increasing, and fury pictured a sight his soul shrank from—a vision of himself chained there to the wall, and battling in hopeless desperation with the

he said, and, as if defying death, ...ot upon the fallen jailer's body.

Dick—there is a better fate in this; we will fight for it at all

He tore and twisted savagely at his manacles, but they would have held a maniac, and never a link started.

Dick wiped streams of sweat from his forehead.

" There might be a less brilliant end to my career," he said, with a curious laugh, " but I would rather take the choice of it. Accursed traitor !"

And his eye lit fiercely upon the jailer at his foot. Dick spurned him away.

" If I am to die," he said, " I shall not die alone; although it is but poor consolation to be made a burnt-offering with such carrion as this."

At that moment he heard a cry—it thrilled him with hope.

" Dick ! Dick ! where are you ?"

" Here," he said in reply, and away went despair, for the young highwayman had recognised the voice of Captain Claude.

" Oh, for a lion's strength," Dick muttered, as he wrestled madly with his fetters, " to break these killing links, and be free to fight for liberty."

" I am here, my champion—here is a boring rill."

As though the words had set his reason to attempt a superhuman effort, Dick heard a mighty crash, as of a falling wall.

" They are at work," he said, " and fire nor water will keep them out. The gallant Captain Claude and my brave comrades. By heaven ! I feel stronger as they come."

Again he wrenched at his chains.

He felt a link give—another twist—the chain was broken.

One hand was free—he was still fastened by the other and both ankles, and the red flames was beginning to cast a dusky glare in at the open door.

The stones grew hot.

He did not hear the voice of Captain Claude again.

All was silent after the crash.

Dick waited in deep suspense—he was weakened for a moment by the efforts made to liberate himself, and he leaned against the wall.

That, too, was hot.

There was fire everywhere around him.

..t his back, casting its fierce light on the

floor, irradiating the vaulted roof above his head.

It must suffocate him now; unless assistance came he was lost, for he heard no sound.

The mortar began to crumble—a huge black cloud of smoke rolled heavily down the corridor—a tongue of fire shot through it now and then.

Still no sign from without.

How intently he listened!

No sound—nothing but the fire's hoarse, angry roar.

"Was it a delusion?" he said lowly. "Did fancy bring the voice to us as I have heard it will conjure to the dying what they most wish to hear? Oh, bitter mockery!"

Suddenly a thought struck him like an inspiration.

He marvelled it had not occurred to him before, but the conflict of hope and fear had rendered it impossible for him to act collectedly.

"The keys! the jailer's keys!"

He sprang forward—hope died once more.

The man in falling had gone beyond his reach. Dick had the torture of seeing the means of freedom lying just where he could not reach them.

The man did not stir. Dick had struck him heavily.

"I'll break this chain or tear my arm from the socket," he said, and roused with desperation, as danger became more imminent, he deliberately wound the fetters round his arm.

The chain did not break—the steel was too firmly tempered, but the staple to which was fastened in the wall, snapped like a worm-eaten screw.

And now our hero's hands were free.

The fire had received a check; black smoke rolled sullenly where red light had been.

"Crash!"

The noise without commenced again.

"Crash!"

Strong, willing men were battering down masonry.

welcome voice rang out once more—
if you are still alive speak to me?"

e—I am here!"

a most herculean effort he

literally tore the chains at his feet from their staples.

"Liberty!" he said; "liberty!"

Though encumbered by his fetters' weight he dashed from the cell, and made his way into the corridor. He could see nothing, for the hot smoke filled his eyes, and made them close in pain.

He felt his way blindly.

His comrades battered at the solid stone The welcome noise cheered him on.

But Dick was weak.

Captivity, though but for a brief time, had scathed his wild spirit, the strength exerted in the breaking of his manacles left him almost powerless.

The fire, with its suffocating density, seemed to choke him.

He reeled.

"Help! help! help!"

He staggered a pace or two, groped sightlessly at the heated wall, it scorched his finger, and he staggered away.

Then dropped to his hands and knees.

He crawled away, and spoke faintly.

"Help! help! I can crawl no further; help!"

"Here!" and down with a crash fell the entire wall that divided the burning cells from the outer prison. A broad sheet of flame—a very sea of fire—swept over the scene, and through its midst came the noble form of Captain Claude.

Fearless, caring nothing for peril, daring all to save his hero boy, the chief of the band pressed to where he lay, and seized him in his arms, and bounded back again.

Back throught the broken wall, through the outer prison, and to the exterior, where the brave Knights of the Road were gathered waiting for their chief and Tyburn Dick.

When Captain Claude appeared with the youth in his arms, the highwaymen gave a ringing cheer.

"Hurrah for Captain Claude! Hurrah for Tyburn Dick!"

"Silence, my friends!" said Claude, casting a cautious glance at our hero's form; "he is not out of danger yet; and hark! what sound is that?"

It was a cavalry bugle.

The knights of the highway clustered

THE LUSHER MAKES A STARTLING DISCOVERY IN THE WINE VAULTS.

round their chief; they knew their foes were coming.

Captain Frederick, of the King's Guard—the young soldier whom the Countess of Alvervale had tempted—rode up with a company of his men.

Jonathan Wild and a party of Bow-street officers followed in the rear.

"We are too late, captain," cried the thief-taker, as he looked at the burning prison, "as the work is done for us."

"How?"

The soldier spoke haughtily; it chafed his military pride to be acting in concert with fellow whese character he detested.

"Hot fire. When we cannot keep our prisoners we burn them."

Captain Frederick recoiled in horror.

"What! purposely?"

"Ay—to be sure; as well the fire as the gallows, so that they are exterminated."

The soldier struck Wild with the flat of his sword.

"Hark," he said, sternly, "keep with your gallows crew."

The thief-taker retired; a look of hate was on his swarthy face, but he said nothing.

"Then Tyburn Dick is dead," the captain exclaimed, for as yet he had not seen the group who were outside the wall.

"Not yet," a voice responded; and as the smoke cleared away, it revealed Captain Claude and his men drawn up in a line. "Tyburn Dick is here—living, and able to fight for himself."

Captain Claude, who was prepared for every emergency, had unlocked our hero's manacles—the cool air had revived him—the sight of faithful friends gave him strength.

"A sword," he said, smiling faintly. "I am myself again."

"I have brought one for you."

The boy took it, tried it, and stood ready.

"Tyburn Dick," shouted Wild from behind the soldiers, "surrender!"

Captain Claude laughed grimly in scorn. Dick said—

"Come and take me."

Wild beckoned to his men. They did not move willingly; previous acquaintance with various members of the band had made them cautious.

"A brave fellow," thought Captain Frederick, "but I must kill him."

At any other time the dashing officer of the guard would rather have favoured the escape of the young highwayman, but now he was tempted by the beautiful countess, who had given him hope.

"Surrender at discretion," he said, "or bloodshed will ensue. Surrender at once, or I commence to attack you."

"Remember," yelled Wild from behind, "I take by the sword."

"You shall take it all," said Captain Claude, most significantly; and, turning to his men, he said—

"Six of you settle that rascally crew; slay Jonathan Wild and any of his men who oppose you. We can fight with gentlemen, not with bloodsellers."

Jonathan heard the order and saw the men advance; they rode past the soldiers and went at the thief-taker.

The latter gentry did not stay to fight. There was a chance of getting a stray bullet, and they thought they might get a better chance of capturing their prize some other time, when stray bullets would not be so plentiful.

Jonathan, though a man of brutal courage, had a deal of wisdom, and a keen regard for his own welfare. He knew the highwaymen would not spare him, and Captain Frederick did not seem inclined to act in concert with him, so he took to flight.

His men followed his example; the knights of the road did not go after them; they were wanted to assist their comrades against the soldiers.

Wild hovered about like a vulture a little distance away, waiting the issue of the impending battle; the same reward was offered for Dick alive or dead.

"If he gets killed," Wild thought, "I can take his body.

The fight commenced. Captain Frederick, eager to fulfil his promise, and enraged at being defied, rode forward, singling out Dick, who met him hand to hand.

Had none interfered between them, Dick would have acted on the defensive only; he felt his own superiority as a swordsman, and did not wish to kill his opponent.

But several of the Guard were at him on either side, and it wanted all his skill as a horseman and a swordsman to ward off their blows.

"One at a time," he said, "and after I have done with you I will take the troop, but five to one is not fair fighting."

The officer was stung into shame.

"Keep back, my men," he said. "I can fight for myself; you capture the others, there is a reward for each."

He was obeyed.

The odds were not more than two to one against the highwaymen; they did not mind that trifling difference; it was just enough to be a resistance and warm them for the work.

Captain Claude was opposed by a couple of big Guardsmen, whom he kept easily at bay; they had no chance of coping with him had he chosen to put forth his masterly arm.

It was not his purpose to slay them; they were but doing their duty; he wished to save our hero.

So that he did that, he cared not who

lived; but any who sought to harm Dick were doomed.

The fight was at its height, and the soldiery by mere force of numbers were hemming our hero and his opponent in, when a young cavalier, well mounted and superbly dressed, dashed into the midst of the fray.

He was tall, slender, and singularly handsome, and his face wore a charming look of reckless devilry.

"By all I can see," he said, as the Guard divided, " this seems a hot fight, two to one and a few to spare. I have not long to stay, but I can do a little. Ho, you hulking rascal! Stab a man behind, would you? Never try to hurt a fellow-creature's dignity."

And a man who had slipped round to run Dick through the back, fell heavily from his horse, run through the arm.

The stranger knocked a second over with his fist, wheeled among the rest, and caused a scattering that was of material assistance to Captain Claude, our hero, and the band.

"Who are you?" said Dick, "to fight like this for a stranger."

"A stranger! Egad, I may be unknown yet, but if my name does not ring through the world it will not be my fault. Ha! here come my own personal friends. They want to honour me with their company, and be dashed to them. Good-bye! we are sure to meet again."

He sprang away as two men rode out of the distance and went rapidly on his track.

"That's him; we've got him at last—that's him!"

"Who are you?" shouted Dick, for he wanted to know the name of his friend.

"Who am I? TOM TURPIN! Hurrah for the road! This is my first night on it, and I like it. Adieu!"

He had the unparalleled audacity to wave his hat in the faces of his pursuers as he rode on like lightning.

"Captain," said our hero, " there are two caitiffs after a gentleman who just did me the honour to knock over two of your men for my sake."

The captain parried a playful lunge as he said—" Well?"

"I want to go and knock over a few for his sake."

"Your career is over, Tyburn Captain Frederick, with inflexible "I must kill you."

"Why one would think you hate and Dick held his adversary's sword qu moment with his own.

"I must kill you."

"Very well; if we are to fight pitiless the fault is yours. I only want to escape. Enough of human life has been sacrificed already. The jailers of the prison have perished in the flames."

"Had you perished there too," said the officer, " I should have been spared the annoyance of killing you."

"Nay, do not be sorry on my account; and so we fight to the death. Nor will I now kill if I can help it."

"Guard!"

Dick let a fearful thrust pass harmlessly, and struck the captain's sword from his hand.

The young Guardsman, mortified at the defeat, and mad with passion for the temptress, forgot for the instant his honourable manhood. Dick did not strike, but waited, expecting him to ask for quarter.

But the captain backed his horse, called for a sword, and said—

"I am not his match at this. Take or slay him."

"Take me who dare," laughed Dick, " slay me who can. Captain, you have disgraced yourself as a gentleman and soldier. I spared you—I shall not again."

He dashed at the men, who, in obedience to the officer, essayed to cut him down. He put them to flight, then attacked the captain.

This time the fight was not of long duration. Our hero could not forgive the other's want of chivalry. He left him no choice other than his sword gave him, and to all appearance they were fairly matched.

Dick, however, could guard magnificently not with mere mechanical skill. His soul was in his sword when he commenced to fight in earnest, and he fought in earnest now.

Captain Frederick saw the change immediately. His heart misgave him; he looked into his adversary's resolute face, and a cold presentiment crept through him.

His nerves were strung, his eye watching the steady, kindling light in Dick's; and he threw all his strength into a well-delivered, lightning-like lunge at the Boy Highwayman's breast.

Our hero's countenance did not change a muscle till a pitying look stole over it. He held his weapon straight, and set his wrist like iron.

Captain Frederick's weapon had but pierced his coat. Captain Frederick himself sat his horse like a statue, and his form erect like marble.

He dropped his sword. Both hands went to his breast; then, stricken with the pain of coming death, he collapsed over the blade, which had gone through his chest and pierced a vital part.

"I am very sorry," said Dick as he drew the red steel out, "but your blood is on your own head."

He sheathed his sword in time to catch his falling foe, and bear him gently to the ground. Dick felt a great sorrow. It seemed hard that he should have had to kill the handsome young fellow who was now expiring.

With the fall of the captain the fight ended. The men lost spirit, and paused irresolutely, as if they knew not what to do. Captain Claude ordered his men to lower their weapons.

"Take away your wounded," he said to the non-commissioned officer in command, "and tell the King that Captain Claude entreats him to let us alone, or even his throne may not shelter him."

The men listened in fear. The chief of the highway spoke like a man who possessed a terrible frown.

"How fares it with your foe?" Claude asked of Dick.

"He is dying," was the sad reply.

Our hero was kneeling by the captain's side.

"Why did you seek my life so bitterly," he said; "were you set on?"

Captain Frederick clasped his hand.

"I forgive you," he whispered, "and forgive me. It was for her sake."

"Her sake—whose?"

"The countess's."

"The Countess Aldervale—beautiful temptress—she who is my mother," said the boy mentally. "My mother—a tigress would be kinder to a mongrel cub than she can be to me."

"The Countess Aldervale," said Captain Frederick. "Tell her I die for her sake. Forgive me."

"I do," said Dick, solemnly, "and may this red deed I have done be forgiven thee; it is my mother's work—I wish I had not killed you."

The young officer smiled on him and died.

"And so," our hero said, profoundly affected, "there is another tragedy done because of her bitter hate. When will it cease—why was I born?"

He unlocked the dead fingers from his hand. A dark figure rode up as he rose, and beckoned two soldiers to carry their officer away.

They lifted their burden—Dick turned away—the dark figure spoke—

"That will bring you to the gallows, Tyburn Dick," it said. "Think of him, and remember—the gallows."

Dick shuddered, but turned sternly; he recognised the ill-looking speaker.

"Keep from my path, Jonathan Wild, or I shall save the gallows your weight, at least."

"You threaten?"

"Ay, and not idly. Beware of me. Whatever my fate may be, my foes are not destined to live long."

"Jonathan Wild," said the solemn voice of Captain Claude, "go in peace, or you will fall as he has fallen. Remember, the men I mark are destined—the eagle does not fall by the carrion crow. Beware of Tyburn Dick, or he will be your fate."

The thieftaker bowed humbly. He was cowed. Captain Claude beckoned Dick to his side. The band fell in order and followed. The last red embers of the burning prison were smouldering duskily, and the highwaymen followed their chief through the night gloom.

CHAPTER XXXI.

DEVIL-DUKE LEAVES THE MERCER'S HOUSE.—
THE DRUGGED WINE.—THE LOCK.—THE

PARTING.—THE STRANGER AT THE TAVERN.
—SAVAGE STEVE ON THE WATCH.

DUKE was getting better.

The careful nursing of the mercer's pretty wife, and the attention of the kind old gentleman himself, helped to improve their guest wonderfully.

Devil Duke felt almost sorry he was getting better so soon.

He sighed when he thought of going away.

The mercer thought he had stayed long enough. He began to feel jealous at the attention paid to Duke by his wife.

He often missed his wife and found her in the highwayman's chamber; but as Duke always looked particularly ill when the mercer entered, the old gentleman retired with a grunt.

At last Devil Duke got well enough to be about. The mercer took the opportunity of quietly insinuating that Duke had better go that evening.

"I am more than grateful for the kindness I have received," said Duke; "had it not been for your generous hospitality I must have died. I am still rather weak, but having encroached so long, I cannot think of staying over to-day."

"I am sorry that I have spoken," said the mercer. "I did not mean that you were to go this evening, not by any means, if you are not well enough."

"I thank you sincerely," replied the highwayman. "I am sufficiently well to get to my quarters."

The mercer was glad to hear it, and anxiously awaited to see the back of his guest.

Night wore on again, and supper being prepared, Duke carefully drew the mercer into conversation.

"I shall never forget your kindness," said Dick.

"Or my wife's either," thought the mercer.

"My gratitude towards one," he proceeded, "I shall always remember."

"I hope I shan't have cause to remember you," thought the mercer, filling his mouth.

"And you, fair lady," continued Duke, sipping a glass of wine, "I shall always remember with the tenderest thoughts."

"The devil you will," muttered the old fellow half aloud. "I wonder what he means."

"I owe my life to your brave wife's tender nursing," said Devil Duke. "The heavy debt of gratitude can never be effaced."

"Humph!" grunted the mercer, "I suppose not. I don't wish to hurry you, but it is getting very late."

"By Jove! I had forgotten the coach will not wait for me."

"The coach never waits for anyone; it will pass in a few minutes."

"Then another glass of wine," said Duke, "and I will say adieu."

The mercer got up and went to the window to watch for the coach.

The highwayman took the opportunity to kiss his wife.

"I go," he whispered, "but return again —to-night."

The mercer's wife looked at him reproachfully.

Duke took a vial from his pocket and emptied the contents into the mercer's glass.

She caught his hand.

"Only a drug," he whispered; "it will make him sleep; he won't interrupt us."

"Here comes the coach," said the mercer.

"We drain our glasses and I go."

The mercer was very glad to hear it.

He swallowed his wine with apparent relish.

The coach guard's bugle sounded; the coach stopped.

Duke dropped his sash on the floor.

"Good-bye," he said, shaking hands with the mercer; "I shall come again soon and see you."

The mercer devoutly hoped he would do nothing of the sort.

Duke pressed the lady's hand, and went down stairs. He was hardly down the passage when the mercer saw the sash lying upon the floor.

"Here, Jessie," he said, "take this after him, for goodness sake, or he will be coming back for it. We shall never get rid of him!"

Jessie ran gladly on her errand.

Duke dropped his sash on purpose, expecting some such result.

He took the opportunity of speaking to her.

"I shall return in about two hours," he

said; "be prepared. You will know when I return by a low whistle."

Jessie squeezed his hand, looking tearfully into his face.

"You will return?" she asked.

"Yes, darling," he said, embracing her. "Bye-bye for the present."

He kissed his hand to her as he clambered up the coach.

The lady stood watching the coach as it rolled out of sight.

The mercer was nodding over the table when she returned.

The drug had taken effect.

The mercer's wife watched her old dotard husband fall into a deep snoring sleep; then she stole quietly from the apartment to prepare for the return of her gallant lover.

Devil Duke did not ride far; he got down at an ancient tavern by the roadside, where he stayed to pass an hour away.

He was smoking a long cigar, and thinking of the lady he had just left, when his reverie was broken by the entry of a man.

The stranger threw off his long cloak, took a seat beside the fire, lighted a short pipe, and ordered a tankard of strong beer.

Duke thought he was exceedingly cool.

The stranger looked at the highwayman with a savage stare of recognition.

Duke returned the look with a nod.

"Do you think you would know me again if we met?" he asked.

"Perhaps I might," returned the other.

"That's all right," said Duke; "you might look at somebody uglier—I could not."

The stranger glared at him.

"Don't look spiteful, my friend," said Duke.

"Keep your insinuations to yourself."

"All right. I didn't mean any offence—any fellow's allowed to speak the truth. Have a drop of wine?"

"No—keep your wine."

"Very well," replied Duke; "I can do that."

Duke looked up at the clock.

"I must be off soon," he said. "Have a cigar before I go?"

"Don't mind."

"That's the thing; always be jolly."

"Are you going far?" inquired the stranger, putting the wrong end of the cigar in his mouth, and burning the tip of his nose instead of the cigar.

"No," replied Duke. "Only to London."

"Rather late."

"Yes, it is; but not too late for me—got a friend waiting."

"A lady?" asked the stranger.

Duke looked at him surprised.

"Anyone would think you knew," he said.

"Merely a guess."

"Good night," he said.

"Good night."

He got up and followed as Duke went out.

"Then he has escaped—he lives!" he muttered. "He shall not see the night out. I suspect where he is going, and will follow."

Duke made haste to the mercer's house, little thinking the man he had just spoken to was his most deadly enemy, and was following stealthily in his footsteps.

The night was peaceful and quiet; the silvery rays of the moon lighted the country with its soft bright rays, and revealed the forms of the two men muffled and masked hurrying along the road.

Devil Duke only thought of the mercer's pretty wife and her beautiful form; the other black soul was throbbing with hate and deadly revenge against the gallant highwayman.

"You have escaped the first blow," muttered the stranger; "the next will kill."

He drew a keen stiletto from his belt and felt the sharp edge.

The cold glitter in the stranger's cynical eyes plainly showed his brutal intent as he followed the highwayman like an evil shadow.

He seemed to toy with pleasure with the dagger he held, and muttered—

"The point of this trusty weapon shall drink your cursed heart's blood to-night. You have recovered from the first blow, but the second the point shall go true to its work."

He chuckled triumphantly.

Duke thought he heard something, and turned sharply round.

"It won't be good for any one that follows me," he said, clutching the hilt of his sword.

The guilty wretch hid beneath the shadow of a wall just in time.

His swarthy cheeks turned ashy pale as he ught the other's words.

"It must have been my fancy," muttered uke, as he went on.

"Must it?" hissed the other, following at a eful distance.

The hour of twelve pealed from the many gloomy church spires, each following the dying echo of the other in dismal, solemn sounds as Duke reached London.

He glanced round carefully as he entered ine mercer's garden.

A silken ladder hung from the window.

He was about to give the signal, when he saw the pale face and fluttering dress of the mercer's wife, anxiously waiting for him.

Devil Duke liked to be certain.

He did not know whether it was somebody else waiting for him, so he said, in a low voice—

"Jessie, is that you?"

He received an affirmative answer in a trembling voice.

"Heard you that?" she asked in a whisper, as Duke began to ascend.

"What?"

"A footstep—a rustling among the leaves."

"Nothing," he said, drawing his sword, and clinging with one hand to the balcony. "Any listener or spy who comes will meet a sudden death."

Listening attentively for a moment, he heard no further sound.

The mercer's wife stood still, her breast heaving with excitement, the blood eddying to her fair cheek as the daring fellow scrambled into the room.

"My darling!" he said, passionately. "Jessie, my own."

He took her in his arms, clasped her to his breast, she going to him gladly, her eyes gleaming with fire, as she felt his kisses on her lips.

His passion for her had grown with their first meeting, strengthened since, and quickened, so that she was now his sole desire.

Their affection was mutual.

By instinct her old dotard husband faded into oblivion from the time she first beheld the handsome highwayman.

"I feared you would not return," she said, after a long silence.

"Not return?" he said gently. "Could I stay from you?"

"I feared, too, that you would think lightly of me for slighting my husband."

"I love you the better for it," said Duke, with a caress. "Your beauty is too good to be wasted on such an old brute. Does he still sleep?"

"Soundly," she repeated, with a shudder at her own treacherousness.

"Then we will go while safe. Come, dearest."

"There are a few things I should like to take with me," said the mercer's wife.

Duke thought there might be a few things he would fancy, and followed the mercer's false wife to her chamber.

They had barely left the room where they had held their conversation, when a stealthy figure entered the garden, and clambered up the silken ladder.

The intruder rolled over the balcony, and put his foot through a window.

The noise startled the guilty pair; and Jessie, thinking her husband had recovered, was looking for him.

A huge pair of arms encircled her waist as she entered the room she had not long since quitted.

"Jessie," said a hoarse voice in her ear, "don't make a noise."

The terrified young wife would have shrieked for help, but the warning look of her brutal captor held her speechless.

"You here?" she said, gaining a little self-possession.

"I am here," he said. "Ain't you glad?"

"Release me, wretch, before I call for aid!" said the mercer's wife, struggling to break away.

"Not yet, my pretty bird; you are coming with me."

"Unhand me, villain!"

"I couldn't think of such a thing," replied the ruffian, in a brutal tone. "If you knew how I love you, Jessie——"

"Brute, I despise you!"

"Listen, woman," commanded her captor, ferociously. "I love you to madness. I came here for you, and mean to take you with me Utter a word, and I will kill you!"

He dragged her to the window.

Struggling desperately, she got one hand free, and struck him a blow in the face that made him reel.

"Help! help!" she screamed, despairingly. "Philip! Philip!"

"Ha! ha!" laughed the man, savagely, "you call for your paramour—but too late."

His face was devilish and full of brutal revenge. His laugh was wild and satanic, as he grasped her wrist and threw her to the floor, and stripped her of her jewels.

Piteously, cruelly he tore the bracelets from her wrists and the diamond necklace that encircled her fair throat, and with a celerity which showed the practised thief, he crammed them into his pocket.

A savage oath from him, and then a shriek from her, as he tore open her dress.

Then came the glitter of a dagger against her white bosom, and a fierce, muttered oath, as he thrust his hand over her mouth to stop her cries.

There was murder in his eye and in his hand.

Another instant more, and her life-tide would have leaped from her throbbing breast.

But the door flew open with a crash, and like a tiger leaping on his prey, Devil Duke sprang upon the would-be murderer, and dashed him with terrible force against the wall.

The mercer's wife ran to her rescuer's arms with a glad cry.

Before either had time to say a word, the savage brute was upon his feet, and dashed at the highwayman with the gleaming dagger.

"My rival and enemy," he yelled, mad with baffled rage. "Die, hound!"

"Not yet, my impetuous friend," said Duke, striking the dagger from his hand with his sword. "I know you. Take that; it will pay you for the dig you gave me."

The cowardly wretch fell back stunned and bleeding, with a deep gash across his forehead.

"I shall know you again," said Duke, taking him in his arms and throwing him out of the window.

A dull, heavy thud followed his quick descent, then there came a low, dismal howl.

The fall had awoke him.

"Lie there and howl," said Duke. "I shall have the pleasure of meeting you some day, then I shall pay you for the dagger thrust. You will take that mark to the grave with you."

A low, savage curse arose in reply, then there came a sound of hurried feet.

"That's our man," shouted one of a group of officers.

"Serve him right; he's got pitched out of window," said another.

"That's broke his back, I know," remarked a third.

Savage Steve, for it was he who followed Devil Duke from the tavern to the mercer's house, after breaking out of his cell, and then set a lot of officers on his track.

He began to feel uncomfortable when the officers eagerly approached him.

He would gladly have got up and run away.

But he could not.

Serve him right, too; he had fallen into a trap he had laid for another.

"Hallo, my pippin!" said an officer, securing his wrists with a pair of manacles. "There ain't no bolting now."

"You have made a mistake," muttered the miserable wretch.

"Yes. We know all about that. We have got you right enough now."

"I ain't your man," persisted Savage Steve.

"Ain't yer? We'll take yer in case yer is," said one of the valiant officers.

"We ain't at all pertickler, is we, Jim?"

"No, Jerry, we ain't," responded the valiant gentleman. "It don't matter a cuss, as long as we get hold of some one."

"Curse you, for a lot fools. Don't you know a man when you see him?" said Steve, savagely.

"Oh, yes, we know a devil when we ever sees him and we ain't forgot you," said the worthy Jim.

Savage Steve broke out in a cold perspiration; he knew he was a marked man, and thought perhaps he had been recognised. He was a bold, ruthless villain. He had ventured to the station with a mask on, and ordered a body of officers out to capture Devil Duke.

knowing, had he been recognised, he would have been secured himself.

His mask had fallen off in his flight from the window, leaving his face bare.

"You shall all pay dearly for this," he said. "Again I tell you I am not the man. I am the one who put you on the scent of the highwayman."

"Who sent yer?" asked Jerry, with a broad grin, thinking he had said something clever.

"The right one is in that room," Savage Steve said, pointing to the window he had been thrown out of.

"We know all about that—we'll take care of you till he comes out."

"Bring him along, mates," said another; "he'll do for us."

Savage Steve was dragged away, regardless of all his furious threats.

Duke, with his fair companion, had been watching the scene much amused.

They were about to depart, when the mercer came swaying into the room, very dreamy and unsteady.

"You villain—you monster!" shrieked the mercer, clutching Duke by the coat tails; "bring back my wife! Stop!—help!—murder!—thief!"

Duke swung round and sent the old fellow reeling against the door, then clasping Jessie round the waist with one arm, he slid down the silken ladder, and made good his escape.

The mercer ran to the window in time to see the shadow of his wife leaning on the arm of the highwayman.

"Help! help! help!" he bellowed. "Stop him—stop thief! Help!—help! stole my wife! Help!—will no one help?"

"What is it?" asked a voice beneath the window. The mercer leaned over the balcony.

A body of Bow-street officers stood beneath with a man manacled in their midst.

"Quick!" shouted the old fellow. "A thief—a robber stole my wife! after him! A hundred pounds reward for the man who brings her back!"

"I said you had made a mistake," Savage Steve said, with an oath. "Curse you, for a set of block-headed fools!"

"Stop your blab!" shouted an officer; "an' help us to catch the right 'un."

"Take these infernal irons off my wrists," said Steve.

An officer took them off, then they started after Duke and the mercer's wife.

The party had been some two or three hours in search of the runaways.

The morning had far advanced; the scorching sun poured down upon them with the full powerful heat parching their tongues and drying up their very blood.

They were exhausted, tired, and weary, and were about to take refuge in a small inn on the roadside, when Savage Steve caught sight of two forms, turning the corner of a triangle road.

He gave a shout, and darted off; the officers took up the shout and followed him, inspired with fresh energy, with the idea of capturing the highwayman, restoring the mercer's wife to the rightful owner, and receiving the hundred pounds.

Devil Duke heard the shouting, and turned to see his pursuers close upon his heels.

No time was to be lost. His lady had grown fatigued. She could not go any farther.

Duke was in rather an awkward dilemma. He was used to difficulty. He caught up the mercer's wife under his arm as though she were a child, and darted off at a rapid pace.

The officers shouted for him to surrender, but Duke only laughed in derision at their threatening demonstrations.

He soon left his pursuers far behind. His pace again slackened. His companion was heavy, and he could not carry her much farther.

The officers, like a lot of bloodhounds, gained upon him every minute.

Duke saw it was utterly useless to continue his flight. Drawing his sword, he waited for his enemies.

A young cavalier, richly dressed, and mounted on a superb chestnut steed, came galloping up as the officers closed round the highwayman.

"Hallo! what's the meaning of all this?" said the handsome youth, "somebody in a nice mess. A friend of mine, by Jove!"

Duke looked at the new-comer.

"St. James!" he said.

"Duke, old boy, how are you? In a devilish fix, I see. And a lady with you."

"And a lady with me," replied Duke, "which these ugly devils want."

"And you wish to keep?"

"Just so."

"All right; you stick to the lady. I'll fight these scarecrows."

"Thank you," said Duke. "I shall return soon and help you."

"No occasion; I shall have them all secured in a very short time."

He dismounted, put the reins over his left arm, drew his sword, threw himself into a magnificent fencing attitude, and invited the officers to "come on."

They were in no hurry to accept his invitation, nor did they feel inclined to "come on." His defensive position was superb, and he could have delivered a splendid lunge to the first-comer.

The men kept at a respectful distance from his sword. They seemed to have a better liking for Duke, whom they eagerly clustered round.

Duke would have rather been without their company. He tried to edge out, but they were so fond of him they would not let him pass.

The fair handsome face grew angry, and he darted at the stubborn men who crowded the highwayman.

"Keep back, curse you," said Savage Steve, pushing him aside by the throat.

"The devil take you," said St. James, rather surprised, "just come on and defend yourself."

He struck the brutal ruffian across the cheek with the flat of his sword.

He darted at the fearless youth with a savage oath.

"That's the thing, by Jove! I know you," said St. James, striking the dagger from his hand; "you are the fellow that wanted my two hundred."

Savage Steve clutched a weapon from one of the officer's hands and made a furious cut at his young opponent.

St James turned it aside easily.

"Curse you." hissed the enraged highway-man, making a straight terrible thrust at his opponent.

"You are polite," said Victor St. James, twining his finely-tempered blade round the other's sword and wrenching it from his hand. "Take that?"

Savage Steve reeled round and fell to the earth, the red gore streaming from a gash in his breast.

"That'll do for you," said St. James, spurning his fallen foe with his foot.

The officers had gathered round the combatants, for the minute forgetting their prisoners.

"Come on, you scarecrows," said Victor St. James.

"Shoot him," shouted one of the officers "Kill him—shoot him down."

"Try it on," said the young noble, knocking the fellow sprawling amongst his companions.

His companions swarmed round the young cavalier, forming a circle.

Devil Duke had made good his escape, and regretted he could not return to help the brave youth.

"Sorry I can't help you," he shouted, "you see my difficulty!"

"All right," shouted St. James, with the greatest possible coolness, "don't worry yourself, I can settle the ugly brutes.

He broke through their midet as he spoke, then confronted the astonished party fearlessly.

"Stash this game," said another, "I suppose you are a new bird on the road?"

"You may suppose what you like," said St. James, planting his fist on the man's nose.

"Give him a topper, mates," exclaimed Jim.

St. James gave him a kick, then the others rushed upon him with drawn swords. The young noble held his weapon at arm's length, and looked round to see where Duke was.

That worthy gentleman was out of sight.

He was hurrying on to find a tavern where he could leave his fair charge, but taverns in those days were few and far between, and Duke saw no signs of one.

He began to almost regret that he had been in such a hurry to elope with the mercer's wife, when a dashing-looking horseman came trotting towards him.

The highwayman recognised the comer as a comrade.

"Hallo, Duke, old boy," said the handsome knight riding up ; "what, another one?"

"No," replied Duke, with a smirk, "the same—the only lady of my love."

"Oh! I beg the lady's pardon," said the graceful gallant Tom, raising his hat to Jessie.

"Friend of mine in trouble down the road."

"What's the game—runners?"

"Yes."

"Onward," said gallant Tom, raising his hat again to the lady ; "I shall see you at the Leopard inn."

Duke nodded assent, and away the gallant highwayman galloped to rescue his comrade's friend, while Duke made his way to the Leopard inn, a house of no very good repute.

Gallant Tom rode up in time to see Victor St. James's sword sink into the body of an officer.

He had been fighting like a young tiger, several slain and bleeding forms lying about him, their life-tide flowing from their writhing bodies showed the work he had done.

He cast a welcome glance at the highwayman as he slid off his steed, drew his sword, and dashed into the midst of the officers.

The Bow-street runners fell back. They saw the danger in his glittering eye. His sword was raised above his head ready to strike the first to the earth who attempted to take a step towards him.

"By Jove! what a capital fellow," said St. James. "It was growing warm and dangerous, and the fellows were getting hurt."

"So it appears," said Tom, pointing with his sword to the fallen men.

"That was their own fault, they got in my way. But how the deuce did you know I was not in the wrong?"

"Gentlemen never are," replied Tom; "and I knew you were not."

"The du—"

"Don't, my lad, you said that before; it sounds bad to use the same words twice."

St. James smiled, and took the other's hand.

"You are a jolly sort of fellow," he said. "By Jove! how the fellows cleared off when they saw you."

The officers had picked off their fallen companions, and retreated

"The ill-mannered scamps wanted to stop a friend of mine, and take a lady from him whom he had already to fight for," said St James.

"And you helped him?" remarked Tom. "He is a great sinner with ladies."

"Are you acquainted with the gentleman?"

"With Devil Duke you allude?"

"The same."

"A comrade of mine."

"A noble fellow he is," said Victor St. James ; "and I may say as much of his comrade."

"Allow me to return the compliment," said gallant Tom, bowing, "we will seek Duke at the Leopard inn."

"We will."

They vaulted into their saddles and rode in the direction taken by Devil Duke.

They had not proceeded far when a clatter of many horses' feet and frantic shouting of men caused them to look behind them.

Coming down the road at a furious gallop were a dozen officers mounted on better animals than were generally provided for the active ones of Bow-street.

"A ride for liberty and a fight to the death if we are stopped!" shouted gallant Tom, waving his sword above his head.

"A ride for liberty and a fight to the death if we are stopped!" echoed Victor St. James shaking his fist at the officers.

"That's my motto," said Tom.

"And mine, too," said St. James.

And away they thundered.

CHAPTER XXXII.

JONATHAN'S PRISONER TURNS TRAITOR TO CAPTAIN CLAUDE — INTERVIEW BETWEEN WILD AND JUDGE GRIPP—KITTY DOVE OVERHEARS A PLOT, AND WARNS DICK OF DANGER —THE HAUNT OF THE HIGHWAYMEN ATTACKED BY THE SOLDIERY—DESPAIR OF CAPTAIN CLAUDE.

WILD soon recovered the slight hurts he received in the terrible combat at the rescue of Tyburn Dick.

His ruffianly gang were reduced greatly in number after the fearful contest, and the thief taker's brutal nature burned with humiliation at having then been baffled.

He had been foiled in his attempt to capture our hero when, as he thought, at the very pinnacle of success.

His savage instinct was aroused to insubduable fury.

He swore to have a quick and terrible revenge while making his way to the Aldervale Manor.

The countess received him with a cool, haughty air.

Wild made a low, cringing bow as he entered.

The lady had heard the news of Dick's rescue, and the death of the young captain.

She felt barely able to conceal her passion.

She inwardly blamed the man who stood before her for letting the youthful highwayman escape.

"Well, Mr. Wild," she began, "I have learned the highwayman has again escaped."

"He has, madam," replied the thief-taker; "but this is the last time."

The countess gave a low, sardonic laugh.

"I shall believe that," she said, "when I hear he is hanged."

Wild knitted his brows, bit his lip, and said—

"You are at liberty to believe what you like, my lady."

"Thank you," she replied, sarcastically.

"He has foiled me this time," remarked the thief-taker. "He would have foiled the very devil with the band of demons he had to aid him. But I shall be prepared the next time."

"And Captain Claude?" she asked.

"I'll hang the whole lot," said Wild, vehemently.

The countess doubted it.

The thief-taker saw as much in the cynical look of her brilliant eyes.

"I have means," he said, "by which I can secure the whole band helpless in their den."

The lady's doubtful look changed to one of surprise.

The sullen, brutal visage of the thief-taker puckered up in a broad, triumphant grin.

"Trust me, madam," he said. "They shall both be removed from your path before long."

"I do not care how soon," she said; "for while they live, my life is in perpetual misery."

"You have no occasion for any fear, madam," replied the inveterate Jonathan. "Your bidding shall be done."

"When it is, you shall receive the reward I promised."

"Would it be convenient for your ladyship to let me have a little now?"

"It is here when the work is done," she answered, determinedly.

She produced a heavy purse.

Wild's eyes gleamed with a longing look.

"The work can't be done without some of it," said the thief-taker, quietly.

The countess started, and looked him hard in the face.

"How much do you want, and what for?" she asked.

"I want it for a bribe, and I require five hundred pounds," replied Jonathan Wild.

She hesitated for a moment, then gave him the required sum.

"Mind," she said, "if you do not fulfil your promise, Mr. Wild, beware!"

The thief-taker pocketed the money, bowed to his fair employer, and retired chuckling.

"I shall require as many thousands as you gave me pounds," he muttered, when on the threshold of the house, "before I have done with your ladyship. Jonathan does not work for nothing—oh no!"

The inscrutable wretch then made his way to a small, half-decayed old house, where he kept a few prisoners for his own purpose. He entered by an iron door, that appeared half-buried in the earth.

Wild had captured one of Captain Claude's band, and instead of sending him to the gallows, he kept him for his own use.

He entered a small loathsome cell. A man haggard and wild-looking, was chained hand and feet to the wall.

His eyes flashed fire as the thief-taker entered.

"Well," said Wild, leaning against the door, crossing his legs in the most easy, indolent manner, "how do you like your quarters? Had much company?"

His prisoner glared at him.

"Rats and those sort of things. Y as though you didn't understand."

CAPTAIN CLAUDE'S GALLANT BAND TO THE RESCUE.

"For God's sake, take me out of here!" shrieked the poor miserable wretch. "Hang me! kill me!—do something to put me out of misery; I can't stand this torture!"

Wild laughed tormentingly.

"Free my hands!" the man implored, piteously, "and I will squeeze out my own wretched existence. Shoot me in the head—do anything—I can't bear this."

He dropped his head on his breast and sobbed aloud.

Still the inveterate fiend in human shape remained untouched.

The suffering of his fellow-men gave him joy—he gloated in torturing them, and it pleased him to see his almost frantic prisoner imploring for mercy.

"Why torture me in this way?" broke out the man suddenly.

"Because it's good for your health," replied Wild.

"Cursed dog! would to God I had my liberty, I would crush you where you stand."

"Don't talk rash, or I might hurt you," said the thief-taker, maliciously.

"Cursed tormenting wretch, you shall suffer for this yet."

Wild laughed a hollow, brutal laugh.

"Will you release me?" implored the poor wretch again.

13

"Kill me, Wild, out of pity sake, kill me! The torture is driving me mad—the irons have eaten into my flesh! I am frantic with thirst—my life is being gnawed away with hunger! Will you free me?—release me—kill me! If you have any pity, take me from here! Let me go!—let me go!—let me go! I am mad—mad! I am mad!"

"Bravo!" said Wild, with a coarse laugh, "quite a tragic scene, you ought to get an engagement at the Theatre Royal."

"Why torture me? Why not kill me at once."

"Nonsense, I didn't come here to be a butcher, I come to know if you have altered your mind—but perhaps you prefer staying here?"

"No—no, I don't! anything but this!"

"That's business," remarked Wild. "Will you betray the secret?"

"I don't like to betray my comrades."

"Say the word, and you shall be released at once."

"Then I am yours."

"That's all I want," said Jonathan, unfastening the manacles.

The clinking irons, as they fell at his feet, sounded like delicious strains of melodious music on the ear of the miserable wretch.

He was free.

He rubbed his hand over his arms and legs to reassure himself that the irons were off. He looked at Wild, and would have hugged him, but his hate kept him back.

Wild put his hand on a pistol in case of emergency.

"Now," he said, "Simon Judas, you know what you've got to do."

"Scarcely," said the man.

"Then I'll tell you," said Wild, with a look that made the man shrink back. "You are to betray the secret of your haunt."

"And betray my comrades?"

"No," said Wild, "Tyburn Dick."

"I'll do that, curse him! I hate the young ptile!"

"Ho! ho! ho!" laughed the thief-taker. "So—so, the young highwayman is not loved by all his men?"

"Loved!" sneered the traitor, savagely; "I hated him from the first time he came to our band—I hate him worse since."

He did hate him with all the venom of his malicious nature. He hated the handsome youth because he had been chastised by him for being insolent.

He wanted revenge, and meant to have it.

He could now betray, capture, and hang his young chief.

That was revenge—real, true, deep, revenge, where he could go and watch the dying pangs of the gallant boy's agony. Sit beneath the gibbet, and gloat with triumph and pleasure over his victim's last death-throes.

He longed for the time to come when he would see the noble form of the gallant fellow hanging from the gibbet.

He knew how dangerous it was to take part in the betrayal of any of the band. That danger was greater and still more terrible when it was for the betrayal of one who was idolised by every one of his brethren.

Yet he risked all danger and accompanied the thief-taker on his treacherous work.

It will be as well to give our readers an idea of the traitor Simon Judas, who had taken such deadly hate against our hero.

He was a coarse, brutal, repulsive man, of middle height, an oxen-like chest, with limbs muscular and as powerful as a lion's.

His face was a study worthy of the pencil of Hogarth.

His cheekbones were high and ugly; his eyes were large, bordering on to goggles; his mouth reached almost from ear to ear; and his nose, the greatest ornament on his visage, resembled a diseased carrot smashed flat on his face.

He was a perfect Judas from head to foot—in every lineament and in every action.

Jonathan Wild, with his revengeful coadjutor, made their way to the residence of Judge Gripp.

The old sinner was at home waiting for him.

"Come in, Mr. Wild—come in, Mr. Wild!" he shouted.

Mr. Wild went in, took a seat by the table, and helped himself to a tumbler of wine.

The judge wished it might choke him.

But it did not.

There was something in reserve not quite so relishing as wine waiting to do that cheerful bit of work.

"I have received a despatch from his Majesty King George," the judge broke out.

"Indeed!" replied Wild, with a grim smile. "What might be the nature of it?"

"I will read it."

"Do."

The judge read the Royal document aloud, as follows:—

"Royal Palace,

"August 10, 17—

"Judge Gripp,—I conjure you without delay to hunt down and secure the malefactor or malefactors who slew the captain of my Guard.

"Spare not one of the desperate outlaws. Kill them all. And when you have found the right one, convey him to the rocky peak overhanging the sea, and shoot him.

"My Guards are at you service. When this is accomplished, let me know.

"KING GEORGE."

"Short and sweet," said Wild. "A very kingly note; it does his Majesty credit."

"It is to the purpose, anyhow," said the judge, sharply.

"Rather."

The judge looked hard at the thief-taker.

The thieftaker looked hard at the judge.

They were a pair of matchless villains.

Each knew the other's depravity.

"Jonathan Wild," said the judge, sternly.

"Judge Gripp," said the thieftaker, quite as sternly.

"What do you think of the King's message?"

"I am of your opinion."

"That it must be attended to?" said the judge.

"Exactly so," replied Wild.

"Will you take the affair in your own hands, and carry it out without delay?"

"To oblige you, I will."

"Have you the slightest idea where to drop upon the boy Dick?"

"I have a very slight idea."

"It might be strengthened by perseverance."

"It might be, but it won't," said the inveterate thieftaker.

"That is your business."

"Then why should it trouble you?"

"I am anxious for the capture, Dick."

"Then go and catch him."

"Don' let us quarrel about it," said the judge.

"Then don't let us quarrel," replied Wild with a bitter sneer.

A flash—a dangerous gleam—shot from the judge's eyes, and he clenched his hand.

"I should like to squeeze your cursed life out," he thought; "but I musn't."

Wild was thinking the same thing, but like his colleague, could not carry out his desire.

They again looked hard at each other, each reading the inward thoughts of the other.

Judge Gripp broke out into a cold, sardonic laugh.

Wild took it as an offence, reckoning it as a debt to be paid off at a more favourable opportunity.

He would not forget he owed the judge one.

"Come," said Judge Gripp, "if we are not quarrelling with words, we are nearly doing so by looks."

"I thought, perhaps, you were studying my face for a picture," remarked Wild, with a hateful smile.

"I should study a face better looking than yours."

"Then you wouldn't study the reflection of your own."

"Let us alter the subject, and talk about the capture of the highwayman."

"Nothing like business," said Wild. "Personal conversation is not pleasant."

"In some respects it is not."

"Then in ours it ought to be avoided."

"Most assuredly so."

"You proposed that we should proceed with the business."

"Yes."

"Listen, and I will carry your proposition out."

"Proceed," said the judge, drawing the cork of a bottle of wine.

"His Majesty," said Wild, "sent you a message, sealed and signed with his own hand."

"Exactly so."

"Demanding you to effect the capture of

the highwayman that killed the young captain of the Guard," resumed Jonathan. "I saw the one who ran him through."

"And who is the perpetrator?"

"The cursed young cub—the young viper who has slipped through my fingers so often —the Boy Highwayman—Tyburn Dick. He has had his last slip but one, and that one shall be at the end of a gibbet."

"Don't make too sure, brother Wild."

"Oh! but I can, brother Gripp."

"In what way?"

"A true and sure way."

"Explain."

"I will."

"I listen."

"I have got hold of one of Captain Claude's men," said Wild, his eyes gleaming with savage triumph; "a spy—a traitor. He hates his new leader. He will convey me to their haunt, and betray the secret entrance."

"Then you can say you have got them."

"No I can't."

"But they can't escape if you go about it carefully."

"Trust Jonathan for being careful," said Wild, with a peculiar grin.

"Lose no time," said the judge. "Every moment is valuable now. They might get scent, and then the game would be up."

Wild rose to go, leaving the judge to his own reflections.

"Good day, Gripp," said the thieftaker.

"Good day," said the other, shaking his fist after the retreating form of his coad-jutor.

A female form flitted across Wild's path when on the landing.

He was about to turn, when his foot slipped and he fell to the bottom of the stairs, taking the skin off his backbone, and bumping his head on the edge of each hard stair in his flight.

Kitty Dove, the faithful servant maid, had been an attentive listener to the villainous plotting for Dick's capture.

She hated her master, but still hated the thieftaker worse.

She meant to have revenge.

It was not long before she thought of a plan by which she could serve Wild a trick.

She soaped the edge of the top stair; the consequence was, as we have already seen, that the thieftaker fell from top to bottom.

He got up, swearing awfully, vowing vengeance against the perpetrator of his sudden downfall.

An hour later, Wild, with the King's Guard, was making his way to the highwaymen's haunt.

Simon Judas—traitor—stealthy and savage as a panther, led them on in silence.

Kitty Dove, faithful to the memory of the brave fellow she had defended from the clutches of the law, wrote a short note to Dick, and sent it to the haunt by pretty Ruth's page.

A boy whom our hero had taken into confidence taught him the passwords for entry to the rendezvous.

The brave little fellow hastened with all speed to the haunt, and delivered to our hero the warning epistle.

A strange commotion caused Dick to start and a flush of excitement spread over his handsome features while perusing the few faithful lines.

"Betrayed, by heavens!" he exclaimed.

Captain Claude, who sat by Milly, sprang to his feet, and clutched Dick by the arm.

"Stay, Dick," he said, "stay with Milly, and I will go."

Dick obeyed involuntarily.

"Oh, Claude! Claude!" sobbed Milly, her pretty eyes brimming with tears, her white breast heaving high, "when will there be an end to this terrible danger? I know there will something awful happen soon."

"Fear not, Milly dear," said Claude, with an affectionate look.

She hid her face on Dick's shoulder as the highwayman chief went out.

A terrible scene met his view as he entered the large hall.

The place was crowded with soldiers.

Each of his gallant men was covered by two or more of the deadly musket-barrels held in well-practised hands.

A huge-bearded soldier, captain of the Guard, stepped forward, and laid his hand on Claude's shoulder.

"Bring forth Tyburn Dick, or we fire," he said.

The highwayman stepped back, appalled.

The truth flashed to his mind, and he saw the fearful meaning of the other's words.

Tyburn Dick must be given up to save his comrades, or all his brave men would be sacrificed for him.

A fearful bond bound Captain Claude and his noble boy-hero together.

He could not sacrifice him.

He could not see all his men fall for one.

What was he to do?

His frame shook with emotion.

"One or all must be sacrificed," he mused, with a shudder, as he cast an eager look round the company.

His men stood resolute, but helpless.

The soldiers were determined, and waited for their leader to speak to decide the contest.

His gaze rested on the brutal, exultant visage of the inveterate thieftaker.

"Oh—oh! captain," exclaimed the malignant wretch, with something like a thrill of uneasiness, as he encountered the piercing gaze of the other's fiery look; "the game's up at last. I told you it would be."

The highwayman replied with a grim smile, that made the thieftaker shrink back, bold as he was.

With a savage laugh of triumph the treacherous Simon Judas said, "I did this, cap'n."

"I shan't forget you for it," replied Claude bitterly.

He would have sprung upon the miserable wretch and squeezed his despicable life out, but the vision of all his men falling, riddled to the heart, as he moved, kept him rooted to the spot.

"Oh! oh! I like that!" said the traitor sardonically; "why to-morrow I shall have the pleasure of seeing you and your cussed young cub swinging."

"Surrender Tyburn Dick, or we fire!" shouted the officer in command.

"Never!" exclaimed Claude.

"Give up the boy, or you die with your men!" the officer said.

"I can die," said Captain Claude, "a hundred deaths sooner than *my* boy shall be given up!"

By a sign from the officer, two men bound the highwayman's hands behind him, and he was stood in a line with his *doomed* comrades.

The last words Milly had spoken rung in his ears like a death-knell—"Something fearful will happen."

And now he had cause to believe something fearful would happen. His men, like himself, were covered with the deadly weapons.

A word from the officer, and the leaden missiles would enter their hearts.

CHAPTER XXXIII.

TYBURN DICK OR NOT TYBURN DICK—THE SOLDIERS' TRIUMPH—THE FATAL VOLLEY AND THE LAST OF CAPTAIN CLAUDE—TYBURN DICK TAKES AN OATH OF VENGEANCE.

IT was a fearful time for Captain Claude.

The fatal word "Fire!" lingered on the officer's lips; he would have pronounced the doom of the brave knights, but a nervous twitching of the highwayman's haggard face kept him silent.

Claude's sad look touched the sturdy old soldier's heart.

"Come, captain," he said, rather huskily, "I am only doing my duty, but I can spare all these men and yourself for the boy. Come, bring him forth.

Claude looked round at his noble followers with pity. He saw in each face an earnest look of self-resignation.

They would have died without a murmur to save their beloved young leader.

"No, no," muttered Claude, huskily, "I cannot sacrifice so many gallant lives for one. *He must be given up.*"

"That's right, captain," said the officer, his quick ear catching the other's low muttering; "it would be a pity to destroy so many for one."

"It would," said Claude.

"It would," repeated the old soldier. "Let's unfasten the cords from your hands then you can fetch the one we want."

Claude wiped the clammy sweat from his broad white brow with his freed hand, then turning to his men said—

"Comrades all," said the highway chief, "you cannot be sacrificed for one—Dick *must be given up.*"

This was received with ominous silence.

They devotedly loved their youthful leader,

and could not bear the idea of seeing him taken from their midst without resistance.

"Forgive me, comrades," said their captain, in sorrowful accents, "but it must be. Resistance, you all see, is useless—*your young thief must be sacrificed!*"

The men were still silent and gloomy.

"I do not covet my own life," continued Claude, "'tis yours; what I do will be for the best. It is better for one to die than all! Pardon me for what you see."

"We would rather die than Dick should," said one of the band.

"Yes, captain," said the rest earnestly "we can die for Dick."

"It would be useless," said the soldier. "The boy highwayman would be sure to die afterwards."

This was followed by a low murmur from the faithful fellows.

"You see it would be useless were we all sacrificed to save him," remarked Claude. "Have I your pardon for sending him forth?"

"Yes, captain, there is nothing else to be done," answered a highwayman.

"Bring him forth," shouted Simon Judas, "d— him, I long to see the rope round his neck."

One of Claude's men drew his sword, and would have dashed it through the speaker's heart, but the cold barrel of a musket being pressed against his forehead kept him back.

Captain Claude went back to send our hero forth, as the soldiers thought.

Dick looked eagerly at the noble preserver as he entered, expecting to hear something, but Claude was silent.

He cast a sorrowful look at the brave youth, then took the trembling form of Milly in his arms.

"Quiet, pretty one," he said, trying to sooth her fears.

But her quick instinct told her the danger of her keeper.

She read the meaning in his expressive, large eyes, as plainly as though she had been witness at the scene he had just left.

"Come, come, Milly," he said, "you must give way like this, you ought to be used to these scenes by this time. Come, dry these pretty eyes, and give your Claude a kiss."

She looked sorrowfully in his sombre face,

and twining her arms round his neck, passionately kissed him.

The gallant highwayman felt a huge lump rise in his throat, and turning his head aside, wiped the moisture from his eyes.

"Oh Claude! oh, Claude!" she implored tearfully, "don't leave me again! Oh, dear Claude, don't go from me! I know if you do I shan't see you any more."

"Nonsense, Milly, dear, you are getting quite silly."

"I know there is some fearful danger threatens you," she said, embracing him in her soft white arms, as though never to part with him again.

"I shall be very angry with you," he said, kissing her, "if you don't banish these stupid fears."

"But Claude, dear, you don't know the strange presentiment I have of danger coming to you."

"You must think, Milly, my life is one of dangerous adventure."

"I know, I know, Claude! but why not give it up?"

"I will, dearest; come, compose yourself, I have to go a little way."

The gentle girl tried to dry her tears, but they were irrepressible, and she buried her face in the soft cushion of a luxurious couch

Then the highwayman hastily wrote a letter, sealed, and put it on the table.

Then he went to Milly again, held her to his heart for a few moments, gave her a long, lingering kiss, placed her gently down, and clutched Dick's hand.

He would have spoken, but he could not; he was choked with emotion.

He looked at our hero sorrowfully, stroked his long wavy hair from his fair, noble brow, and squeezing his hand affectionately, left without a word.

He turned when he reached the door, cast a lingering look back, and said, in a broken voice—

"Dick, my noble boy, look after Mil' while I am away—be kind to her. Goo bye, my son."

Dick was spell-bound and amazed; could he have heard aright?

"His son." He muttered the words to himself several times.

He tried to shriek after the retreating form, but his voice died away in a whisper.

He glared around the apartment as though expecting to see the gallant Captain Claude there.

But he was gone.

Dick was about to rush down the corridor after his self-proclaimed sire, when his excited gaze fell upon the insensible form of Milly (for she had fainted). He stopped suddenly, summoned a female attendant to attend upon the fair girl, broke the seal of the letter, ran his eyes over the hastily written lines, and dropped the note with a cry of pain.

"'Tis my father," he exclaimed, madly. "And he to sacrifice himself for me! Never." "It shall not be, by Heavens! I cannot bear the maddening thought. My father to sacrifice himself for me; no, no!"

And away Dick dashed like a maniac.

He went for his coat and hat, but they were gone.

The noble Captain Claude, who intended to personate the character of our hero, and give up his own life to save the daring boy's, assumed Dick's coat, hat, mask, and silver star on the breast.

This completed, he stepped boldly forth.

Wild, with the soldiers, dashed forward, and eagerly seized the supposed Tyburn Dick before he had time to enter.

The highwaymen, forgetting their own danger, and thinking their disguised chief their beloved young leader, so great was the resemblance, they were about to rush to his rescue, but the prisoner waved his hand for them to keep back.

They obeyed with a murmur of disapproval.

Wild then sneaked forward, with an exultant grin on his sallow visage, and clapped a gag over the captive's mouth.

For which Mr. Wild was floored like a shot by one of the highwaymen.

Another took the gag from his chief's mouth, and smacked it across the grinning face of the exulting Simon Judas.

The gag stuck there.

It was very soft and sticky, made solely by the thieftaker for special people.

The soldiers drew up in file on either side of their prisoner, then hurried off triumph- antly, with the personated Tyburn Dick in their midst.

Simon Judas and the thieftaker not having any particular wish to stay in the haunt alone, scrambled out while they were safe.

The highwaymen could hardly restrain an eager impulse to rush after the guards and attempt to rescue their chief.

But they were held back by obedience.

Many a handsome face blanched with sorrow, and many a brave heart was touched to the core by the fearful thought of losing their gallant *young* leader.

With a last look at his faithful comrades, Captain Claude was led away.

Barely had the party with their prisoner died away in the gloom of the closing day, when Dick frantically dashed into the hall.

With a glad cry the men gathered round him.

"Claude! where is your captain?" exclaimed our hero.

The men were silent; none could answer his question.

"Your captain, where is he?"

"Can't make it out," said one, regaining his self-possession, "we saw you taken away not five minutes ago, and now you are here in a different dress."

"No, it was not me you saw taken away," Dick said; "it was your captain. He assumed my costume, and surrendered himself to save me."

In accordance, every man drew his sword, and eagerly looked at their young chief for command.

Dick read a resolute determination in every face ready to fight to the death for their noble leader.

"Prepare for a fight," he said; "I will save my father; or, by Heaven, I will have a terrible revenge!"

He raised the point of his sword toward Heaven as he spoke.

The highwaymen took the same silent oath of vengeance.

"Haste, my men," said Dick, throwing long cloak over his shoulders; "there is time to be lost."

The gallant men were ready, armed to the teeth, and prepared to meet any number of the enemy.

Dick was ready, too.

"Men," said our hero, "we go to save the life of our captain, or avenge his death—haste, comrades; forward!"

The devoted men readily obeyed, and followed their young leader from the haunt.

Dick peered through the rising mist; he caught sight of the retreating red-coats, waved his sword, and shouted for his men to follow.

A minute after, a flash of lightning revealed the soldiers drawn in a double line at the top of the rocky peak, with their victim standing on the verge of the precipice.

Then came another flash, suceeded by the report of the fatal volley, that rang ominously through the still night air.

The highwaymen, speechless and horror-stricken saw a cloaked form fall from the rocky peak, down a fearful, dark abyss, heard the body fall into the surging water. Then all was quiet.

The white smoke from the muskets coiled in fantastic shapes around the rocks, and hid the soldiers from view.

Tyburn Dick's face was ashy pale and haggard.

"Forward, men!" he shrieked madly, wiping big drops of clammy perspiration from his pallid brow. "I'll avenge my father's death, if we all die in the attempt."

He dashed forward as he spoke, with the fleetness of an antelope and the anger of an enraged tiger.

The gallant band followed close behind their young leader with drawn swords, a look a deadly revenge and set determination on their excited features.

"Death or victory!" shouted Dick.

"Death or victory!" echoed his men, dashing onward.

CHAPTER XXXIV.

THE CHASE.—A FIGHT AT THE LEOPARD INN. A STRUGGLE ON THE ROOF AND ESCAPE OF THE HIGHWAYMEN.—JACK EVANS CHASED BY THE BLACK BRETHREN.—REFUGE, AND WHAT HE SAW IN A WINE VAULT.—WHAT CAPTAIN RODERIC DID WITH A RIVAL, AND WHAT DICK DID FOR HIM.

VICTOR ST. JAMES and gallant Tom spurred away, and away after them thundered the officers.

The exciting chase suited the reckless nature of the young noble.

"It's a ride for life," remarked Tom, surprised at the other's fearless manner.

"It's all the sweeter for that," said the daring youth. "How many are there?"

Tom turned in his saddle, and counted the pursuers.

"Ten," he said.

"That's five to one. I can soon polish off mine. Is your horse tired?"

"I fear so, he has had a hard ride to-day."

"So has mine. Shall we wait for them?"

"It will only waste valuable time. Let us make for the inn. The landlord is a brave old fellow, and will help us out as far as he can."

St. James looked back. The King's officers were gaining so rapidly that a well-aimed shot from the foremost rider grazed the tip of the young noble's nose.

"Not a bad shot," he said, blinking.

"Those fellows could not hit a haystack by intention," said Tom.

"We are not haystacks, and I object to be made a target of."

"Surrender, or we fire!" shouted a voice in the rear.

"Fire, only take care of our noses," said Tom.

The man suited the action to the word, and fired; the bullet passed very close to Tom's ear. He reeled round.

The officers were not far behind.

The chase was getting warm, and the highwaymen thought it prudent to wait for his Majesty's servants.

Victor St. James thought so, too, so they waited accordingly.

"Random shots are not pleasant," he remarked, and these brutes have no respect for a fellow's head."

"They have not," answered his companion, "nor we for theirs, if they want to fight."

They wheeled round and confronted the advancing officers.

One man, more daring than the others, rode upon them with his sword.

"That's the man that hit me on the nose," said Victor St. James. "I am going to pay him for it."

Gallant Tom was about to do the same

thing, but his friend having a prior claim, he singled out a man for himself.

There was a clash of steel, and Victor's foe rolled from his horse wounded.

Gallant Tom's foe followed him stunned.

"If you will have it," said the daring youth, "why come on, that's all."

"The fault is theirs, not ours," said Tom; "there is two down."

"And by Jove! the rest will follow if they don't clear off."

The officers were so astonished by the way their companions went down, they did not hear the remark.

"Leave them now," whispered the highwayman to his friend.

St. James sheathed his sword, and before the active gentlemen of Bow-street could recover from their consternation, the daring fellows were thundering away again.

On flying speed, and urging their fatigued steeds forward, staying not to look behind, they went till nearing the Leopard Inn.

They rode into the yard.

Hearing the clatter of iron hoofs, the ostler came out and held the horses, as the daring fellows entered.

"Close the gates," said gallant Tom, "we are pursued."

"All right, cap'in, I knows that," answered the ostler.

"The devil you do?"

"Yes, cap'n. A cap'n inside told me yer was coming, so I got ready."

"That's a good fellow," said the highwayman, slipping a guinea into his hand; "take care of the horses."

"No fear, cap'n, Ben always looks after the hanimals."

"And the money, too, eh! Ben," said Victor St. James, slipping another guinea into his hand.

Ben touched his cap, and led the steaming steeds into the stable, grinning from ear to ear.

The worthy host of the Leopard Inn came out and led Tom and his friend to the hostelry by the back way.

Devil Duke, with the mercer's pretty wife, were doing justice to a sumptuous meal, that plainly showed the state of their appetites.

The savoury smell made his comrades' mouths water. They ordered a like repast, which they had hardly begun to partake off, when a clattering of horses' hoofs running down the road interrupted them.

Victor St. James went to the window; the officers were coming at a furious rate towards the inn.

"Don't choke yourself." he said, turning to Gallant Tom, "you will have indigestion, and won't be able to fight; you should never be in a hurry, they must wait."

"Here, old boy, wash it down with this," and he handed him a glass of wine.

Some stringy greens had stuck in the gallant highwayman's throat; he was nearly black in the face; the wine washed it down.

"Take the lady," said Duke, to the worthy host, and keep her safely till we have fought our way out."

Duke kissed her, and gave her to the landlord.

"We shall have a siege presently," said St. James.

A shout came from without.

Then a heavy crash, and the officers came rushing into the yard.

They had forced the gates down.

"Surrender, in the King's name!" shouted one.

"See the King d—d first," said Duke.

"Open the door, landlord!" shouted another, "or we'll pull down your house and take you."

"Try it," muttered the landlord grimly, handing Jessie to his wife.

"Down with the doors," shouted a third enraged officer; "remember, a thousand pounds for each, dead or alive'"

"A good price," said Tom; "but I don't think they will get it."

"One of them will get this," said Victor St. James, dropping a bullet down the long barrel of his pistol.

"He won't want anything more if he does,' remarked Duke, "by the Lord Harry!"

"They will certainly get in," said young St. James, while proceeding to load his pistols.

"And as certainly go out again."

The door gave way.

The three friends leaped to their feet.

There was danger in their look that awed the officers as they rushed in

"We have them now," said one.

"Don't you make any mistake," said Duke.

A shot struck the pistol from his hand.

It was a cowardly shot, and Duke hated cowardly shots.

He dashed amongst them, dealing death herever his gleaming sword fell.

"By Jove, that's a topper," said Victor, knocking a man over.

"That's a stopper," said Tom, drawing his sword from an officer's quivering body; 'he won't sneak behind a comrade of mine again."

The man Gallant Tom had given a *coup de grace* had got his sword at Duke's back, and Tom was only in time to save his comrade's life.

"I will come and help you in a minute, Tom," said Victor. "I have got a fellow here with a skull that won't break."

"Then crack it," suggested Tom, knocking over one out of two assailants.

"That's already done."

"Release Duke of one of his; three to one's not fair."

St. James went to work; he knocked over his own assailant, and then rushed at two of Duke's. He enjoyed the excitement of the fray, and did not hurt more than he could help.

A cry of disgust from Gallant Tom made him pause just in the act of driving his sword through a man's throat.

"What's the matter," asked the fearless youth, kicking the man across the room.

"Some spiteful wretch," said Tom, "has shot my favourite curl off."

The spiteful wretch alluded to uttered a yell and fell to the floor with his hands clasped over the lower part of his person.

Devil Duke had seen the act, and inserted his sword in a tender part.

The fight had grown to an exciting pitch. The officers fought bravely, and dashed at the highwaymen.

Duke thought he had done enough already, and beckoned for his comrades to follow.

Duke leaped through the window on to a balcony without, the other two followed him, and the trio clambered to the roof.

"They can't resist!" shouted the leader of the officers, "we have them now."

The officers followed their leader. They did not think that the brave knights of the road were flying to avoid further bloodshed, and not in fear.

Five already were laid *hors de combat*, two dead and three wounded. It is not unlikely that the others would meet the same fate if they persisted in pursuing the highwaymen.

"Don't forget, men, a thousand pounds offered for each; they can't resist."

"A thousand pounds is not bad, if you can get it," said Tom.

"Can't escape, can't we?" mused Duke, taking aim.

The foremost officer took aim too. His shot missed its mark, Duke's did not; his took effect; the man fell reeling, stricken through the brain.

"The odds are wonderfully lessened," said St. James, knocking an officer off the parapet. "A short time ago they were ten to two, now there is only five to three.

One of the two hurled his empty pistol at Duke's head. Duke's head got it; and Duke himself, stunned with the force of the blow, lost his footing and slid down the roof. He would have rolled over and broke his neck, but Tom only just in time secured him by running his sword through the tail of his comrade's coat, and held him in the gutter.

Duke's body was heavy, and Tom's sword was slipping, and so were the two highwaymen.

St. James saw the jeopardy of his friends, and ran to their rescue. He wound one arm around a chimney pot, and clutched Tom's hand.

Fearful knowledge! the chimney pot was loose, and coming out.

Each pictured an awful vision of the other as he fell crashing in a shapeless heap to the earth.

Another minute, and the three brave cavaliers would have met their doom, but that minute saved them.

Duke recovered from the blow, sprang to his feet, and then scrambled to the other side of the roof, dragging his comrade with him.

At the same instant Victor St. James rolled over with the chimney-pot in his arms.

He was soon on his feet again, and with

the chimney-pot he extinguished one of the officers.

Being something out of his style to see a solitary foe prowling about, he gave him a dig in a part that made him think of his latter end.

The man, with a yell of pain, grasped his coat-tails, and leaped over the parapet.

The last but one gone.

The last of all was lying in the gutter, groaning with the chimney-pot over his head.

"I hate to hear a fellow making a noise," said gallant Tom, taking the fellow up in his arms and dropping him over.

The crashing thud with which the bleeding body reached the ground made the highwayman shudder, and he turned to his comrades, looking very white.

"By Jove! I never saw ten fellows cleared off so quick in all my life," said Victor St. James. "What a splendid mill we have had!"

"I wish they had not gone quite so quick," remarked Tom, in a tone of pity; "they were brave fellows, and only did their duty."

"And we only did ours," said Duke. "If they had not sought us we should not have sought them."

"True. How many are there killed?"

"Only two; and the rest are wounded more or less."

"Then they will recover," said gallant Tom. "Let us make for the haunt; we have done sufficient for one day."

"We have; but it ain't all we shall do," said Duke; "for by the Lord Harry, here comes a troop of infantry."

His information was unmistakeably true— a troop of infantry coming towards the inn as fast as their thoroughbred feet could bring them.

They had been fetched by an idler—men who were always hounding about with the officers, ready to help to capture any malefactor to share the reward.

The troop raised a shout as they caught sight of the highwaymen leaning over the parapet looking down upon them reflectively.

A line of muskets being levelled in a line with Duke and his companion's heads, made them move with wonderful velocity.

"I can see the prospect of another cheerful fight," remarked Gallant Tom.

"I can see the prospects or a very rueful capture," said Duke. "I intend to slope."

"By Jove, I'll slope with you," said St. James, "there's twenty-one of these fellows waiting for us; that's just seven bullets for each of us; rather too many."

So his companions thought.

And beat a retreat by sliding down th waterspout into the yard, one after the other.

Ben was waiting for them with the horses fresh and ready; the highwaymen had vaulted into their saddles in an instant, and rode round to the yard gate.

The soldiers were waiting for them with fixed bayonets.

"Be kind enough to lower your bayonets," said Tom. "Thank you."

"Surrender in the King's name or we fire,' shouted the officer in command.

"See you blowed first," said Duke.

"Surrender or we fire," said the officer again. "We must take you dead or alive."

"Go to the deuce," said Victor St. James, drawing his charger back, ready for a leap.

The highwayman saw his movements, and did the same.

The trio sat motionless, their horses' heads drawn back ready to take the daring leap for life or death.

The officer guessed their intent; his face flushed angrily, and a cruel glitter shone in his dark eye.

"Ready!" he shouted, "present—fire!"

Like a flash of lightning the three noble steeds in a breast sprang over the soldier's heads just in time to save their fearless riders from the volley of deadly missiles that followed and flattened against the wall.

So quick and so daring had been the act, that for a moment the soldiers were unable to realise the fact that the highwaymen had escaped their deadly shot.

"Hurrah, hurrah for the road!" yelled the three as they thundered down the road.

The officer sprang to his feet as the echo of the defiant cheer rang through the air. In a wild shout he dashed after the three riders, his men reloading their muskets as they followed him.

Duke and his comrades waved their hats in defiant scorn at the pursuing party, and dashed onwards, leaving their pursuers far behind.

A distant shout of welcome echoed their cheer, and looking in the direction from whence the sound came, the highwaymen saw two horsemen riding towards them; one a tall, gigantic fellow, and the other nearly a dwarf, his legs barely reaching across the horse's back.

"By the Lord Harry!" exclaimed Duke, in surprise, "here comes Bullskin and Swig."

"Something wrong!" remarked Gallant Tom.

"By Jove, what a huge fellow!" remarked St. James, at the sight of Bullskin; "shouldn't like to be in the little one's place when the other's hungry."

"How do you do, gentlemen?" said Big Bullskin, riding up to his comrades. "Just the gentlemen we want."

"Couldn't have fallen in with better," said Swig, pressing his horse forward to make himself seen. "One of our brethren is in a devil of a mess."

"Who?" asked Devil Duke.

"Jack Evans," interrupted Bullskin, "joined the——"

"Black Brethren's band," interrupted Swig in his turn, "to betray ours."

"No, he didn't," said Bullskin, looking spitefully at his companion.

"You are very clever."

"That will do," broke in Devil Duke, to stop further argument. "If your comrade is in trouble tell me, Joseph."

Joseph felt honoured by the preference. Swig felt disgusted, and gave his companion a dig.

"By Jove! what a cheerful pair of wranglers," said St. James, laughing; "worse than two washerwomen rowing about the last word."

Bullskin handed Gallant Tom the note Jack given him.

"Looking after me, are they?" said Tom, with a laugh. "That's kind of a comrade."

"We have seen him since then," said Munroe, "he is in a devilish mess; the black varmints have suspected his game, and threatened to kill him."

Duke's handsome face darkened, and became sad on the instant.

"How long is it since you left him?" he demanded.

"About half an hour," answered Bullskin.

"No time must be lost, or our band will lose a faithful comrade."

"Another fight in view—that's the thing!" shouted Victor St. James, darting off with his friends. "What a glorious life! all excitement, plenty of pretty ladies. That's the thing, by Jove! I think I shall turn highwayman."

"Do," suggested Gallant Tom; "you would make——"

"Hallo!" shouted Devil Duke. "There he goes, tearing away on a black horse, like a phantom, and at least a score of phantoms on black horses tearing after him."

There was no mistaking the Lusher; his comrades knew him at the first glance.

The unfortunate Jack had been betrayed, and was now pursued by the whole band of Black Brethren.

"To the rescue!" shouted Gallant Tom.

"To the rescue!" echoed St. James.

The rest took up the words, and the whole party thundered after the Lusher's pursuers.

We will leave our friends following in the track, and follow Jack in his hazardous ride for life.

Away he went on his maddened steed, clearing all before him, each minute leaving his savage pursuers further behind.

Through the country he flew, leaping hedges, ditches, fences, and everything that stood before him; his steed foaming, with nostrils expanded and ears laid flat on its neck, still kept onwards regardless of any obstacles, like the Wild Horse of Tartary.

Jack ventured to look back once. His pursuers were still in sight, bearing down upon him. He dug his spurs furiously into the panting sides of his charger, and with a dart like an arrow the noble animal cleared a high gate, and fell dead the other side.

In an instant Jack had extricated his legs from beneath the horse's heavy body, and tore away for dear life.

No time was to be lost; he could hear the angry voices of his foes. Jack still ran towards; he knew not whether. Perspiration ran down his excited face in streams, as he

TYBURN DICK RESCUES GRACE FROM LORD EDWARD AND HIS MYRMIDONS.

thought of being overtaken and hacked to pieces by his brutal pursuers.

Leaping a broad ditch, he broke through a thick hedge, and found himself in an open road. He looked up, and his heart bounded with hope.

Not a quarter of a mile in front of him stood a large building, the Glenmorris estate.

With a glad cry, he darted forward; he still had hope of saving his life.

His pursuers had reached the gate where his horse had fallen, and dismounted, swearing terrible oaths of vengeance, while looking about for the spy who had entered their haunt, and betrayed some of their watchwords.

They had not seen him escape, after falling with the horse. With this refreshing idea, the Lusher made his way through the grounds of the estate.

On he kept like a madman, passing many retainers in his flight, who made a clutch at him.

At one of the back entrances he encountered Mary Jane, and his rival, Charles, in deep conversation.

Mary Jane uttered a scream at the sudden

appearance of her faithless lover, and before the tall flunky had time to ascertain the cause of her outcry, Jack had knocked him breathless on his back, and darted past the alarmed pair like a shadow, making his way to the underground cellars, where he began to breathe more freely.

He was in total darkness, but he felt safe, and the strong smell of the malt revived his shaken nerves.

"S'help me!" he muttered. "I thought they had catched me then, but they didn't arter all."

He began to sniff.

"Oh, cricky! what a fine smell; it smells like lush, an' if I don't diskiver where it is, an' 'ave a swig, why, my name ain't Lusher."

So saying he groped about, and struck his thick nose against a thick door. The thick door apparently did not suit his smelling powers, so he turned to another door that was seasoned with a stronger odour.

This he opened, and entered a large vault filled with huge barrels marked from E to X, and were stocked to the ceiling. The place was dimly lighted through a small grating.

The Lusher's mouth began to water, and his huge eyes looked greedily round the well-stocked vault.

"S'help me!" he mused, while glancing from the bottles to the barrels, not knowing which to make the first attack upon. "I's fell into stunning luck; won't I do a lush now, that's all; won't I—oh, no!"

By the way, he drew a bung from a small cask, and commenced sucking away at the hole. We should rather say he would.

Smacking his lips, after the first large draught, and rubbing his long stomach with much satisfaction, he said—

"S'help me! that is fine. I ain't tasted a drop o' lush like that since I don't know when."

Taking the cask up in his two hands, he turned it rather too sharply round, and the malt well shaken, spurted out all over his face, and nearly smothered him.

"Boo—oo!" he whined. "I don't want so much as that."

After shaking himself, and kicking the cask cross the vault, he selected a dozen bottles of different wines, and seated himself behind some large barrels.

"Now, I'll do the dainty!" he said, drawing a cork, and draining a bottle without taking it away from his mouth.

"That—hic! is—hic! stunning—hic!" he hiccuped, nodding forward, and bringing his head back with fearful force against an iron hasp. The force of the blow made him blink and he saw at least a thousand sparkling bottles dancing mockingly before his aching eyes.

Jack only rubbed the injured member, and muttered, reflectively, that he had a lump added to his cranium that he was deficient of.

He soon drained a few more bottles. He had got the ninth in his hand, and had loosened the cork, when he heard approaching footsteps.

His face lengthened, his mouth dropped, and turning his eyes towards the door, forgetting he held the bottles between his legs, in a dangerous position.

It was a sudden cry Jack uttered; a yell of pain, turned a somersault in the air, and finally settled in a former position, still clutching the neck of the bottle.

Jack thought he had been shot, and began to hollow.

But he made a mistake, it was only the cork that flew from the bottle struck him under the nose, and was the cause of his sudden exclamation.

The matter did not trouble him much; he finished the remainder of the dozen wines, and began to sing—

"This wine's sublime,
So rich and fine,
So juicy and so nice,
It makes me feel so—a'br, boo-oo'—

This sudden termination to the Lush caroling song, was caused by the door be swung open and a tall, powerful-looking handsome but cynical and cruel man entering with a slim youth thrown helpless over his shoulder.

The intruder glared round savagely, a murderous look in his small piercing eyes.

The Lusher's limbs began to shake.

"Oh, lor!" he muttered, his teeth chattering; "dont he look horful? S'help me! I wish I could get out of here."

"Whew!" laughed the individual with murderous eyes, "my small dandy friend won't stnad in my way any longer—no, no!"

Jack had to thrust the neck of a bottle in his mouth to keep him from uttering a frightened shriek.

The man with his lifeless burden cast a searching glance round the vault, then with hurried stride strode into an adjoining cellar.

By some irresistible power, Jack was drawn off the ground and before he could exactly realise his elevated position, his legs ran after the retreating form of the intruder.

"There, my venerable friend," said the individual, throwing the small individual into a dark corner and covering him with old sacks, "Captain Roderick never stands for trifles when a rival stands before a pretty girl. That will do for you!" he said, administering a blow.

"And that 'ill do for you," said Jack, striking him fearfully on the back of his head with a bottle.

Captain Roderick, as he called himself, fell stunned across the inanimate body of his victim.

The same power that took the Lusher there took him back again with wonderful velocity.

The way his legs scampered across the vault was a caution to crawling insects.

At that moment he heard a cry; it thrilled him with horror; he sprang round in bewilderment, fell over a barrel, and gave utterance to some most fearful screams.

A bottle came whizzing through the air, shattered against the wall, and sent its thousand fragments flying in all directions.

The Lusher thought he was suddenly beset by a legion of unchained demons.

His bewildered imagination pictured a sight that made him quake with fear—a vision of himself attacked by the whole troop of his Satanic Majesty's stokers dancing around him with glee at his helpless position.

He could not bear it any longer. Dashing at the imaginary imps, he flew with lightning speed from the wine vault.

Blindly tearing onward, he thought only of leaving his tormentors behind. But his flight was brought to a climax. With terrible force he came in concussion with a retreating form, the retreating form fell forward, and Jack turned a summersault backwards.

In an instant the Lusher was upon his feet, and pursuing the retreating form that was upon his feet also, and flying upstairs four at a stride.

Jack vowed vengeance against Captain Roderick, the retreating person, and made a desperate clutch at his coat-tail just as he entered a room and slammed the door.

The highwayman was not to be done, though the door had caught him a fearful blow on the nose, and knocked him over. He sprang up, dashed open the door and caught the captain by the throat just as he was in the act of clutching the insensible form of Cecily in his arms, and about to spring through the open window.

"No, you won't," said Jack, struggling desperately with his powerful adversary. "You can't frighten me with those ugly looks. You struck me on the nose, and I'm going to strike you on the nose, too."

"Fool!" hissed the captain, savagely, "leave go, or I'll choke you."

"Oh no, you don't."

Captain Roderick caught his almost helpless assailant round the waist, raised him in his powerful arms, and, with brutal force, dashed him to the ground.

The poor fellow lay stunned and bleeding at his feet.

He looked with apparent satisfaction at the huddled form of his victim, then, with a triumphant air, stepped to the couch where the beautiful Cecily lay, awakening from her troubled trance.

He bent over her with flashing eyes, put his lips to hers, and took a passionate kiss.

Cecily gave a start, darted up, looked wildly at her persecutor, uttered a frightful scream, and covering her pretty face with her hands, buried her head in the pillow and sobbed convulsively.

A dark scowl flitted across Captain Roderick's cruel, handsome face. His rude nature was fired with her matchless beauty.

"You are mine now," he said, clutching her delicate white arms. "There is no gallant lover to save you now. You shall learn to love me alone; and, by Heaven, you shall be mine. Ha! ha! ha!"

A crash from without made him start.

Then there was a heavy tramp of feet, a

shout of many voices, and a hurried rush upstairs.

Captain Roderick threw open the window, snatched the trembling girl up in his arms, but before he had time to reach the window, the room door flew open, and in rushed Devil Duke and his companions.

"Hound!" shouted the infuriated highwayman, leaping upon the baffled libertine.

With one blow he struck him to the floor, and took the lady from his arms.

"Only in time," muttered Duke.

Cecily gave a glad cry, and nestled to her lover's breast confidingly.

"You were in danger, Cecily, dear," said Duke with a fond caress.

"You are very wicked for staying away so long," she said.

"That's consoling to a fellow," thought Victor St. James.

"But I came at last," said Duke, "and in time to save you from that cur!—villain!"

"My life and——" She hesitated.

"Just so," Duke said. "Who is he who would have committed such a daring outrage upon you, darling?"

Her fair face blushed crimson, as she answered—

"A guest of my aunt's, Captain Roderick. My life has been in perpetual misery through his persecutions, and more than once he has threatened that if I did not elope with him, he would carry me off; and to-night he came to carry his base design out."

"And would have succeeded, had I not so fortunately come in time to stop him."

"I vote we chuck him out of the window," suggested St. James.

The rest agreed to his idea, and were about to carry it unanimously out, when Duke spoke—

"Let him be placed upon the window sill, and if he does not jump for life, you, Bullskin, fire."

Big Bullskin said he would, and, amid cuffs and kicks from all sides, the miserable wretch stood upon the window sill.

Bullskin counted—

"One—two—three."

The man uttered a shriek—Bullskin fired, then the discomfited captain turned a somersault in the air, and fell heavily to the ground.

"Serves him right," said Gallant Tom.

"He has received a just punishment," said Swig.

"Just my opinion," remarked St. James.

A loud clamour of voices made the party start; even the Lusher groaned and turned over.

Then a stentorian voice sang out—

"Forward, men; we have tracked him at last—the spy, traitor, and enemy!"

Duke sprang to the window and looked out.

Bullskin clutched his double-handed broadsword, and stood with knitted brow, awaiting the coming contest. The rest prepared, and, like their gigantic companion, awaited the fearful combat.

"The house is surrounded by the whole band of our enemy, the Black Brethren," said Duke.

"Let them come," said Bullskin, quietly.

They came with a fearful crash, like a pack of savage wolves.

CHAPTER XXXV.

CAPTAIN CLAUDE'S LAST LETTER—THE CORONATION OF DICK—THE OATH OF FIDELITY—THE WARNING OF DOOM—THE VISION OF THE DEAD.

The tragedy was over.

Darkness came and hid the soldiers from their foes, and in the gloom the men saw nothing; they only heard the sullen murmur of the sea and the distant tramp of feet as the guard marched away.

There was a hush of silence.

Then Dick spoke.

"A light," he said, sadly, "let us seek for him, there may be hope yet."

Torches were kindled, and a search made for their missing chief.

Every inch of the place where the fearful tragedy had been enacted was carefully scrutinized, but nothing could they see that gave the slightest clue to their noble commander.

The night was peaceful and quiet, and save for the splashing of the sea as it rolled up the beach in rude billows, and broke against the rocks, the stillness that prevailed would have been painful.

The search was over, and the highwaymen returned to the haunt.

As they left the fatal spot, the sombre clouds cleared away, the mist rose from the earth, and the moon shone forth with its radiant rays, and cast a gladdening light over the lonely country.

Dick had changed wonderfully. His handsome, fair face, haggard and sorrowful, showed the bitter grief he felt at heart.

A sad, but strange light, shone from his large eyes as he looked round at his faithful followers.

"Comrades," he said, slowly, his voice quivering with emotion, "I will solve the contents of my father's letter as he directed."

The highwaymen bowed.

Dick opened Captain Claude's last letter, and read as follows :—

"Comrades, repair to Hounslow Heath—to the haunt beneath Tyburn Tree. Make Dick your King. Call him Tyburn Dick, and serve him as you all have served me, devotedly and faithfully to the last.

"Make his cause your cause, be always ready in the time of need, and let your motto be one for all, all for one.

CAPTAIN CLAUDE."

"We start for Hounslow Heath to-morrow," said our hero, in conclusion.

"We proclaim you our King now," said one of the highwaymen.

"Hear! hear! hear! Hurrah for Tyburn Dick!" shouted the whole band, their loud, clear voices ringing through the haunt.

"No, no!" said Dick, trying to make himself heard; "not now."

"Yes, yes!" shouted the men again.

"Hurrah for Tyburn Dick! Hurrah for our King!

"Gentlemen," said Dick.

Again his men broke out in a ringing cheer.

So eager were they to make our hero their King, they could not wait until they reached Hounslow Heath.

They loved the daring, handsome boy.

Beautifully embellished silver goblets were brought out, and filled with a delicious, sparkling wine.

The highwaymen each grasped a brimming cup and held it high above their heads. Then they clustered round their young chief, and all drew their bright swords forth with one accord, then there was a ringing clash as they met and crossed above the head of their idolized leader.

Dick, for the time, seemed in a trance.

He stood in their midst, his stately form drawn erect, his noble head thrown well back, and his right hand resting on the jewelled hilt of his rapier.

A grateful smile of acknowledgment suffused his pale, handsome face, then it died away, and a sad look clouded his broad white brow.

A gallant, handsome fellow on Dick's left, with his long cloak hanging carelessly from his shoulders, spoke—

"We swear by the memory of our beloved Captain Claude." he began, "to serve you devotedly as we have served him ; to protect you from all danger from your enemies, and to die in your cause."

"We swear!" shouted his gallant comrades.

"By the memory of our noble captain," said a highwayman in a long cloak on Dick's right, "we swear to serve his son, Tyburn Dick, faithfully."

"We pledge our faith to Tyburn Dick, our King," shouted the highwaymen, solemnly one and all sipping the wine.

"Then, comrades," said the highwayman on our hero's left, "clear your throats, and give a hearty cheer for our King."

The goblets were drained and again refilled.

Dick spoke in time to be heard.

"Gentlemen," he said, "bring me a goblet, and let me drink fidelity to my faithful comrades."

"Hear! hear! hear!" shouted the men, enthusiastically.

Dick raised the jewelled cup to his lips and said—

"Here, over this cup of sacred wine, do I pledge an oath of devotion to my gallant comrades, as you have all sworn to serve me, to join you all in every enterprise, and share your every danger!"

Here he paused, again sipped the ruby wine, and kissed the point of his sword ; then raised his eyes to heaven, and said—

"I swear solemnly by the light of heaven to avenge the death of my father!"

"And solemnly we swear," said the highwaymen, "to have a quick and bloody retribution for the fearful wrong."

Again the cups were drained, and again refilled.

"Then, comrades," said the tall highwayman, with the long cloak hanging from his shoulders, "as I before suggested, we will give a hearty cheer for our King."

"Bravo! Hear! hear!"

Then their loud, ringing voices broke the stillness of the night.

"Hip, hip, hurrah! Hurrah for Tyburn Dick! Long life to our King!"

For a minute they paused to wash their throats with the delicious wine that flowed about like water.

Then they renewed the cheering.

And amidst the clamour and excitement the door flew open, and in dashed a tall, dauntless, fearless fellow, with his hat stuck jauntily on the side of his head, and bunches of gay ribbons flying from the tops of his boots.

He made a polite bow to the astonished revellers, took a brimming goblet from the table, raised it above his head, and in a clear, musical voice, sang out—

"Hurrah for Tyburn Dick! Long life to the King of the Highwaymen! May he be successful—vanquish his enemies, and send the Bow-street runners to the devil!"

He drained the cup, bowed to the highwaymen, and retired with the greatest coolness imaginable.

He turned when on the threshold of the haunt.

"Don't forget Tom Turpin," he said "Dick, old boy, we shall meet again soon. Adieu! hurrah for the road!"

The next instant he was gone.

Tyburn Dick put on his gold-laced hat, and dashed after the daring highwayman.

"Stop, stop!" he shouted; "if you are my friend, stay."

The intruder had vanished, Dick looked bewildered, he gazed to his right and left, but nothing could he see of Tom Turpin.

The moon at that moment shot from behind a cloud, and brought out in strong relief the

shadow of a horse and rider tearing along with the swiftness of an antelope.

Dick uttered a slight cry, and darted after the retreating shadow, but it vanished again, yet he kept onward.

A croaking cry made him start; he stared around; the cry was hollow and unearthly.

Again the cry was repeated.

"Tyburn Dick, beware!"

"Who and what art thou?" said Dick rather surprised. "He turned, but could no see the speaker.

"Behold the Death Witch."

Dick fell back, as his eyes encountered a most hideous spectral object, seated on a hill.

"Art thou of this world?" asked the boy king, with a slight shudder.

"I am of both, and know the fate of all," answered the miserable being.

Our hero rather doubted the assertion, though, from the strange appearance of the speaker, anyone of a more superstitious nature than Tyburn Dick would have imagined she was from the other world.

But the Boy King of the highwaymen was better used to the trickery of the Cornwall witches than the Cornwall population were, generally speaking.

We must confess that the object that confronted our hero was not at all a cheerful person to meet on a lonely heath, at a lonely hour, beneath the soft, subdued rays of the moon, that give everything a phantom-like appearance.

It was a sight that would have made many a lonely traveller recoil with terror.

Picture to yourselves at a midnight hour, in a lonely country, perched on a high, rugged hill, a horrid-looking form, enveloped in a long, dark robe, with an awful ghastly countenance, and a pair of small satanic eyes, gleaming spitefully from almost fleshless sockets.

Dick for a few moments stood staring at the awful-looking spectre sitting before him.

"Why are you here?" he said. "Have you no home to which you can go and rest?"

"I have," was the explicit reply, in a croaked, mocking voice. "I come to warn you of your doom."

"   with you," said Dick, rather impetuously, drawing his sword, and stepping towards the huddled-up form.

"Back, back, rash boy. Beware of my warning!" shrieked the Death Witch. "Thou art just proclaimed king of the highwaymen; your career will be short, your days are numbered, and you are doomed to die on Tyburn Tree. Remember my warning."

"Infamous old wretch! what think you I care for your cursed witchery? My sword shall discover of which world you belong, despicable juggler!"

He dashed up the hill furiously, as he spoke.

The Death Witch slid down the other side and vanished into the shadows of night, as our hero reached the top.

"Remember my warning, Tyburn Dick! Your life is short! You are doomed for the gibbet! There is a fearful danger threatening you!"

The warning was spoken in a whisper, close to his ear.

He turned sharply round, with upraised sword, ready to strike.

"I could have sworn I heard her voice again," he said, drawing his hand across his brow.

"Yes, yes, Tyburn Dick," said the whispered voice again in his ear, "you heard aright. Take heed of the warning—it was no idle babble."

"Fiend of hell! or whoever thou art," shouted the excited boy, with blanched cheeks, "show yourself again, and I swear my sword shall prove thy identity!"

A mocking laugh rang through the still night air in reply.

Then he saw a flickering shadow dart amongst the trees and die away in an instant.

He would have sprung from where he stood and followed the strange shadow, but when, in the act of taking the leap he saw another and a more fearful vision, that kept him spellbound and helpless.

A vision of a more supernatural nature than the other, though not so hideous.

A tall, graceful figure sat like a statue on a splendid, graceful steed.

Horse and rider were of the purest white.

They seemed as though carried along by the wind, so swift and graceful did they move.

There was a sad, troubled expression on the rider's handsome face, as he turned and looked in the direction where Dick stood.

A shriek of pained horror escaped the young chief's lips, as the shadowless horse and rider faded from his view.

"A vision of the dead," he screamed, madly, his face haggard and wild.

One frantic shout, and he sprang through the air, and dashed in the direction of the faded phantom.

"I follow," he said, mentally, "if it takes me to my doom."

A distant voice rang through the air, in a sad tone.

"Return to the haunt, Dick, if you love the memory of your father! Follow no further a vision of the past!"

Dick took the advice of the sepulchral voice, and returned to the haunt, depressed and sorrowful.

As he entered, a dashing, reckless horseman rode up.

"What, ho! within!" he shouted.

The young monarch came out.

"What's amiss, Ralph?" he asked.

"Friends, captain, in danger," answered the other; "attacked by the Brethren of the Black Band."

Dick's handsome face clouded on the instant.

"What, ho! within!" he shouted. "To horse!"

In a few minutes the whole of Captain Claude's gallant band appeared, mounted on beautiful steeds, and armed to the teeth.

Our hero's faithful animal, Fairy, was led to him.

He fondly patted her white, sleek neck, and sprang into the saddle. Then he drew his sword, rode before his comrades, with dashing Ralph by his side, and cried out—

"Away, gentlemen! Away to the rescue of our comrades!"

And away they thundered.

CHAPTER XXXVI.

TYBURN DICK TO THE RESCUE.—GALLANT TOM'S REVELATION.—VICTOR ST. JAMES'S STORY OF LOVE AND WRONG.—A RIDE, AND MEETING WITH AN ENEMY.

THE Black Brethren had forced their way in, and would have made short work of their four enemies.

But Big Bullskin stood in their path, and kept them back by his angry, determined look.

His powerful, majestic form, drawn to its full towering height, his terrible weapon raised above his head, he stood ready to strike his first foe to ground, who dared to move a step forward.

They saw it, and kept back.

He was quiet and docile as a child when not angered, but then he was dangerous, and savage as a tiger.

He was dangerous and savage now. His comrades were almost helpless—he meant to defend them.

"Back!" he thundered, "or I scatter a few of you."

The men stood resolute, they moved neither one way nor the other.

Bullskin stood resolute too, nor did he move.

"Are you all such cowards as to be frightened of one man?" exclaimed Captain Bertrand, urging his lawless band to the attack. "Forward, every one of you."

"Come on," said the giant highwayman, grimly.

Their inclination was good, but the vision of a shattered head kept them back.

The highwayman's threatening attitude added greatly to their discomforture.

Captain Bertrand grew furious.

"Cursed lot of cowards," he yelled. "Follow me!"

He sprang before them, and dashed at Bullskin.

Bullskin saw him coming, and waited.

His sword fell with crashing force. It missed the captain, and cleft the heads of two of his men.

The rest, at seeing their comrades fall so suddenly, dashed at the gigantic fellow like unchained devils, regardless of danger.

Bullskin swept all before him.

His comrades were fighting terribly.

Victor St. James's graceful figure was in fearful danger, but his finely-tempered rapier went to work, and kept off the furious thrusts that were delivered at him.

The conflict had reached to a fearful pitch.

The superior number of the Black Band were fast overpowering our friends.

Bullskin's strength was giving way. Gallant Tom and the Lusher were disarmed.

Swig, who, while his huge companion kept fighting like a gladiator, looked very valiant, now looked crestfallen and frightened.

Duke, St. James, Bullskin, and Swig fought bravely, and kept the Black Brethren from attacking their helpless comrades by standing before them, knocking down all who came within their reach.

Another minute, and it would have ended the career of our brave comrades.

The Black Band had made a desperate effort, and dashed upon their opponents in a body, knocking Bullskin off his feet, and sending the rest scattering.

Swig thought his time had come.

Bullskin thought his was very near.

Captain Bertrand had got him down, weaponless, with his foot on his chest, and a sword at his throat.

The big fellow did not despair; he thought his life was worth a struggle.

Captain Bertrand looked at him with deadly hate. He pressed the point of his sword against Bullskin's throat.

The highwayman moved his head aside, and the weapon slipped off his neck.

Ere his assailant had time to raise his sword again, Bullskin threw himself up like an eel, struck him violently in the chest with his head, and sent him flying breathless across the room.

Again, the gigantic fellow regained his weapon, and dashed at his opponents.

But again he was overpowered.

With his comrades he was driven in a corner, a score of glittering blood-stained weapons levelled at their breasts.

The gallant fellows would again have resisted, but they saw it was useless.

The line of deadly weapons were steadily advancing, and they bravely gave themselves up to the pending death that threatened them.

They saw no hope by which they could escape the fearful doom.

Slowly and steadily the weapons were pressed forward by the pitiless crew; the sharp points penetrated the thick clothing of their defenceless victims; the cold steel touched their breasts and entered their flesh.

Not a cry, not a murmur left the lip of any.

Deeper and deeper the deadly weapons were driven, yet none moved a muscle. They offered up a silent prayer, and were prepared to die a martyr's death.

I may say there was one who yelled awfully —the redoubtable Swig; but he had not got a weapon levelled at his breast.

He had crawled on his face to get out of the way.

One of the hawk-eyed, black individuals observed his movements, and secured him, by inserting his sword in a more prominent part than his breast.

Swig yelled to be released; that amused his assailant, and the sword went deeper.

So did the sword in his comrades' breasts.

The blood slowly trickled down their coats; their life-tide ebbing out as the thirsty weapons sank deeper into their flesh.

Crash.

The men started; the weapons were drawn back.

The doomed knights started, too, and drew a long breath.

A second crash, and the casement flew open.

Hanging by his hands from the bough of a tree was a handsome youth.

A shriek of terror left his lips as his gaze encountered the fearful tragedy that was taking place.

With the agility of a wild Indian he sprang from the tree, bounded across the room, and struck the captain of the Black Band to the floor by a fearful blow.

"Tyburn Dick!" shouted the baffled brutes.

"Tyburn Dick!" echoed our hero. "To the rescue of his gallant comrades!"

He dashed madly amongst the Black Brethren, striking down all who stood before him.

"By Jove!" exclaimed Victor St. James, pale from loss of blood, "what an unexpected deliverance!"

"By the the Lord, Harry!" said Duke, drawing his hand across his brow to wipe away the clammy sweat, "give me a sword, captain."

Dick gave him a sword he took from the foe.

Big Bullskin's grasped his young chief's hand affectionately, picked up his terrible weapon, and went to work again more furious than he had done before.

The rest of his comrades regained their weapons, and following their big companion's example, went to work furiously.

They were revived with fresh vigour; the sight of their daring, youthful, and beloved leader inspired them with life and energy.

They gave no quarter to their would-be murderers.

A bloody combat ensued.

The Black Brethren were falling like reeds.

The change in affairs was so sudden and unexpected that the black individuals began to cry for quarter.

Though in number they were five to one, they saw it would be useless to continue the fight.

The captain saw his men falling.

His face was diabolical and savage with baffled rage. He plainly saw his companions had no chance against the fighting Titans.

He sprang to his feet, swung back the door, and called his men to follow his retreat.

They did.

So did their opponents.

As they reached the hall, the door flew open, and in dashed Captain Claude's gallant band.

The Black Brethren had fallen in a fine snare.

They crouched back like a lot of beaten cubs.

They had no chance of flight now the enemy were in front and behind.

"What ho! comrades!" shouted Tyburn Dick, leaping down the stairs into their midst.

"Hurrah for Tyburn Dick, Prince of the Highwaymen!" shouted his faithful comrades.

"Give them no quarter," said the boy prince, sternly. "Slay every one. They would have slain our comrades in cold blood."

A clash of steel, and the highwaymen's swords gleamed in the air above the heads of their foes.

The beaten, miserable wretches cried for mercy.

They got it.

But not the sort they wanted.

Those who did get it never wanted anything else; and those who didn't get it, thought they were as well without it, and made a desperate effort to get out of the way.

Like a pack of savages, which they were, they dashed past their opponents, uttering exultant yells, and made good their escape.

The highwaymen were about to pursue them, but Dick's voice stayed them.

"Let them go," he said, "we shall meet them at a more fitting time and place than this."

His men obeyed.

"Move this carrion!" he said, meaning the dead and wounded of their enemies.

It was moved quickly, with very little ceremony, though with proper respect shown to the dead.

"Now, my comrades," said the Boy King, kindly, "are your hurts dangerous?"

"Mine," said Duke, answering for himself, "mine is a mere scratch; I have had many worse."

The others, who shared the danger, made similar remarks.

"But you have lost blood?" remarked the young chief.

"We had it to spare, that's a consolation," said Gallant Tom.

Dick smiled.

"Whom may I have the pleasure of knowing," he said, meaning Victor St. James, "in this gallant gentleman who fought so bravely and shared your danger?"

"A friend of mine," said Duke introducing the brave youth.

Our hero extended his hand.

The young noble took it warmly, and they exchanged a friendly grip.

Dick admired the slim, careless, handsome youth.

The slim, handsome youth admired the graceful, noble bearing of the young chief.

Their admiration was mutual.

"I give you my sincerest gratitude for taking part so nobly in the defence of my comrades," said Dick, "you will always find a friend in me or any of these gentlemen."

"I am happy that I have had the pleasure of rendering my humble services, and you may always rely upon Victor St. James to fight in your or any of your comrades' cause.'

"I should not wish you to endanger your life."

"Danger be blowed. It's as fair for me as it is for you."

A stifled shriek stopped all further conversation.

"Cecily!" shouted Duke, excitedly, "is danger!"

He sprang up the stairs, his sword drawn, he dashed into the chamber where he had left her, while engaged with his companions in the war against the Black Band. The window closed as he entered, and he saw the form of a man with his lady-love spring from the window-sill.

Duke threw open the casement, and sprang after them.

He had barely gone, when Tyburn Dick and his companions rushed into the room.

"Where the devil's he vanished?" exclaimed St. James. "By Jove! he went like a shot."

Gallant Tom looked out of the window; he saw nothing of his comrade.

"What a lunatic he must be to go like that," he said.

"The cause of love," remarked St. James reflectively.

"That reminds me," said Tom. "I have a little work on hand concerning a love affair."

"What is the nature of it?"

"Forced marriage, and that sort of thing, which I intend to stop."

"May I accompany you?"

"With pleasure."

They mounted, wished their comrades adieu, and rode away. The others disappeared in different directions.

"The lady," said Gallant Tom, to his companion, "whom I shall try to save, from the plotters I overheard, is the most beautiful creature, I think, it has ever been my good fortune to rescue."

"Where does she reside?" asked St. James.

"At Graystone Chase."

St. James started.

"By Jove!" do you know her name?"

"Edith Berville."

"She!" exclaimed the youth, his handsome face undergoing a convulsive change.

"Do you know her?" asked Gallant Tom.

"Do I know her!" said St. James, his frame quivering with emotion. "I will tell you; but first tell me how you became acquainted with her.

"I know but little of her, but heard something that may be useful to you, if you have any interest in the lady."

"I have. Tell me what you know."

"It is some considerable time ago," began the highwayman, "I was riding past Graystone Chase. I heard a scream of a female. I dashed in the direction from whence the cry came, forgetting that I had a pack of the law blood-hounds at my back. I saw on the ground a female struggling desperately with a man.

"I rode after them, but before I could dismount, her cowardly captor caught the lady round the waist and ran away. I pursued him, drew my sword, and challenged him to fight. His brutal courage failed him, and he fled.

"I was about to take the lady back to her home, when I heard a shout I knew too well—my pursuers were close upon me. I sprang into my saddle, with the lady and tore away."

"I had not got far, when the officers captured, and took me, with the lady, to the round-house."

"I was not there long before some of my comrades rescued me, and I took the lady to her home."

"The lady expressed her gratitude, and I left. I had not got far from the mansion, when my attention was drawn towards two men conversing in a low tone. I recognised the younger one as the persecutor of the lady, and, as you may guess, I felt anxious to hear the nature of their conversation."

He paused, and looked at his companion.

St. James looked wild and excited.

"What did you hear?" he asked, quickly·

"Give a fellow time to breathe."

"Excuse me, old boy."

Tom took the proffered, delicate hand.

"Well, I sneaked behind a tree, where they stood, and listened," continued the highwayman, "and, to make a long story very short, the old fellow, her father, I presume, consented, Lord Berville wanted an exorbitant dowry in exchange for his peerless daughter. After a great deal of wrangling Reuben Frampton, I think, was his name, consented to the agreement, and they are to get married next week. That's the end."

"To be married next week, are they?" said Victor St. James, bitterly, grasping the jewelled hilt of his sword. "By heaven, we shall see."

"Tell me your story now," said Gallant Tom.

"This lady, whom you so nobly protected," began the youth, his fair boyish face clouded and sorrowful, "was the idol of my dreams, the light of my life. I loved her as few know how to love, and she loved me in return, with all the passion of her innocent, confiding nature. We lived on, caring nothing for the outward world, knowing no care but the love of each other.

"But alas! my dream was broken, and so was my heart."

He spoke this in such a sweet tone of deep earnestness, that it touched his companion to the heart, and caused a tear to run down his handsome face.

Gallant Tom looked at him with pity.

The youth had buried his face in his hands, to hide his tears.

"Come, old fellow!" said Tom, kindly, his voice husky and choked.

"Forgive me," said the youth faintly, grasping his friend's hand. "Oh, Tom! if you have ever loved, you will pity me!"

"I do pity you—I have loved, said the other, sadly.

"Then you can sympathise with me."

"I do; and will avenge the wrongs you have suffered."

"You have not heard all yet."

"Don't tell me the rest. It only pains you to bring up the memory of the past."

"No," said St. James, trying to assume a carelessness he did not feel.

"Then continue."

"My dream was broken," resumed the youth, "when a cousin of mine—the one you once heard—a cruel, subtle wretch—came like a serpent in my path, drew me to the gambling table, disgraced me, and caused my sire to thrust me from his house an outcast.

"It was then I discovered my cousin's treachery. But too late; the mischief was done. I was disinherited, and he took my place.

"I sought Edith, to take a farewell, for I intended to depart for the Continent. Her father refused to let me see her.

"I did not despair. I waited, and met her; but she spurned me from her, called me a profligate—gambler—spendthrift.

"I left her, and from that time I have been roaming about as I am now."

"'Tis a sad story," said Tom. "The lady may have been excited when you met her, and sorry for what she said afterwards.

"She was," said St. James. "Now we are here, I must see her or *him*."

"You can't get admittance! You would be recognised!"

"What! when I am disguised?"

"You have no means for a disguise."

"I am always prepared," remarked the youth.

Tom wondered how.

Victor St. James slipped off his beautiful blue and silver coat, and turned it. The inside was a brown silk. He took the long plume from his cap, and put it in his pocket, and then put a false moustache on his beardless lip. His toilet was complete.

"One of the quickest make-ups I have seen," said Tom. "I should not have known you had we met."

The young noble smiled.

"That will do." he said. "Now to see one or both!"

"I shall be at hand if I am wanted," said the highwayman.

"Adieu!" said St. James, dismounting.

"I would see Lord Berville," he said to a tall flunkey who admitted him.

"My lord's not within," answered the tall flunkey.

"Sir Frampton?"

"Yes, my lord."

The lackey stood aside. St. James entered.

"Whom have I the pleasure of knowing?" asked his treacherous cousin.

"My name is of no consequence, Reuben Frampton," replied the youth, who felt ready to choke him.

Sir Frampton sprang to his feet, and looked at his guest confounded.

"Pray be seated, my dear sir," said St. James, sarcastically.

"State your business quickly," said the other, angrily.

St. James bowed.

"There is a rumour afloat," he began, "that you have purchased Lord Berville's daughter for a certain ransom——"

"Sir!" exclaimed the other, with a start.

"A little deaf?" said St. James, with biting sarcasm. "I will repeat the sentence."

"Begone!" shouted Sir Frampton, "before I summon the servants to thrust you out."

He clutched the bell-rope.

"Don't be in a hurry, Reuben Frampton," said the youth, quietly. "Be kind enough to drop that bell-rope."

He drew his rapier, and confronted his alarmed cousin.

"Thank you," he said, as quietly as before, as the other dropped the bell-rope, "you can again be seated, and listen quietly."

Sir Reuben stared in blank astonishment at the daring youth.

"State you business," he exclaimed, foaming with baffled rage.

"I was about to do so," replied his guest. "I said that you had bought Edith for a ransom, and are about to be married next week."

"Well," said the other, frowning.

"I learnt this much by rumour."

"Rumour speaks the truth; but what has it to do with you?"

"You shall hear," St. James said, between his teeth, his eyes flashing dangerously. "You shall not marry her!"

Sir Reuben nearly fell off his chair; then he sprang at the intruder with intent to choke him, but his hands fell at his side, and he glared at him savagely.

"Who are you that you should threaten me?" he demanded.

"You asked me that before," said St. James, calmly. "I again say that you shall not wed the fair Edith."

Sir Reuben drew his sword impetuously.

"Guard, for your base life, fool and braggart!"

"Wait a minute, my friend."

He drew back.

"You!" he exclaimed, staggering.

"I," said St. James, sternly.

His cousin sprang at the bell-rope again.

"Stay, Reuben; attempt to raise an alarm.

AS THE FLOOR GAVE WAY THEY CLUNG TO THE SASHES.

or raise you voice above a whisper, and this blade shall answer for your treachery."

Again his arm dropped helplessly, and he looked around the room for some way of escape.

St. James stood by the door, and kept him from the window.

For at least two minutes they looked at each other breathlessly.

"You see, cousin Reuben," said St. James, bitterly, "I don't intend you to have it all your own way. Your subtlety cannot last long;

you have turned up your best cunning card to-night—your game's played out—I have come for revenge!"

The black-souled villain saw the determined look on the boyish face, and plainly understood the meaning of his words; his cunning features turned ashy pale, and his lips quivered

"Have you come to murder me in cold blood, cousin?" he faltered.

"Cousin," sneered the youth, mockingly, "I am no cousin of yours, white-livered cur—base poltroon. Treacherous villain, I have

cold blood—I have retribution for the caused me. Guard, despicable

Despicable hound didn't see it. He stepped aside as a splendid lunge was delivered at his breast.

He was well aware of the matchless skill of the graceful youth who stood before him.

"Guard!" repeated St. James, raising his sword.

The other saw he had no alternative, and guarded. He was a head taller than his adversary, of a powerful build, and brutal by instinct to the very core; yet he lost courage, and could not cope in any way with the youth he had so fearfully wronged, and who now stood before him.

Their swords clashed as they met.

Victor St. James cut and thrust furiously at his treacherous cousin, and it took all his courage and his whole skill to keep off the furious blows.

"Curse you!" hissed the youth; "I shall now pay you for all."

He made a feint at his adversary's head as he spoke, drew his sword back, and, with lightning swiftness, made a terrible thrust forward.

Sir Reuben gave a piercing shriek, and fell to the floor bleeding—the sword had gone through him.

His youthful opponent was mad for revenge. He put his sword at his chest, and in a voice fierce and passionate, said to his fallen foe—

"Die, dog, die!"

The beaten wretch gave a gurgling cry for help.

His opponent laughed grimly.

Again he cried for help. His life-tide was flowing out from the gaping wound back and front—he looked into his wronged cousin's eyes imploringly, and met with a steady, deadly look of hate.

His heart sank within him like a piece of lead—he saw no hope; the deadly weapon gleamed before his eyes; the point entered his neck; he gave a gurgling cry; his frame shook convulsively; he saw his time had come, and closed his eyes, a deathly pallor coming over his distorted features.

St. James was pressing the sword through

his neck, when the door flew open, and a group of retainers dashed upon him. At the same moment the window was thrown up, and Gallant Tom sprang into their midst.

CHAPTER XXXVII.

A DARK CHAMBER AND ITS FAIR PRISONER—A FAITHFUL SPY DOES SERVICE — TYBURN DICK RESCUES GRACE MERTON FROM LORD EDWARD.

WE return as far back as where we left the beautiful girl, Grace Merton, in the custody of Lord Edward.

The sinister, cruel boy was smitten with her matchless beauty. He determined to make her live with him by fair or foul means, and, like his mother, he cared not what his victims suffered so that he gained his own point.

The fair girl hated him as much as she loved our hero—who, it will be remembered, so gallantly saved her from a wreck.

She loathed his presence, and spurned him from her.

He tried in every way to win her, but failed miserably.

Baffled in every attempt, he grew exasperated, and confined her in a dark, lonely chamber, thus thinking to break her resolution and make her his.

But she remained as firm as ever, true to her lover.

Very sadly the poor girl endured her confinement, and each day she grew more pale and delicate.

She bore her sufferings bravely.

A week had elapsed since her cruel persecutor paid her a visit. When he entered her prison one evening he saw his devillish work was telling.

Her graceful form had wasted away, her face was pale and haggard—she looked but a poor specimen of what she had been.

A gleam of satisfaction shot from Lord Edward's sinister blue eyes as he gazed upon her.

She was lost in deep reverie; her eyes red with weeping, and glistening tears still clinging to her aching eyelids.

She sprang from her couch as his hateful voice sounded upon her ears, and confronted him with a wild look.

He laughed sternly.

"Well, pretty one," he said.

Grace shuddered.

"Have you come here again to taunt me?" she said, faintly.

"No, my pretty Grace; I come to see you," he said, trying to take her hand. "I have given you a week to consider—have you decided?"

She pulled her hand away from his, and confronted him; her form erect, and her pretty eyes flashing dangerously.

"I have decided," she answered, bitterly.

"What conclusion have you arrived at?"

"None for your benefit or triumph, mean-spirited wretch?" said the enraged girl, hotly.

"Indeed," said the other, with a scoffing laugh.

Grace regarded him with calm quietude.

"Listen, madam," he exclaimed, his face tingling with the hot mounting blood; "I have been fooled by you long enough."

Grace still confronted him with an unquailing look.

"You shall be mine *now*," he hissed; "take your choice, I am not in a humour to be played with; consent willingly, and become my wife, or refuse, and you shall be *mine*."

She made no reply; her face flushed, her bosom heaved high with excitement, and she cast an indignant look at her persecutor.

A look that meant more than he read in his madness.

"Will you consent?" he added.

"No," she answered, boldly.

"Do you defy me?"

"I do," was her steady answer.

"Fool!" he exclaimed, rushing upon her.

"Back, despicable thing," she said; and her tiny hand struck him with fearful force between the eyes.

He reeled, staggered backwards, and rested against the door for a minute, half stunned and mad with rage.

The whole venom of his cowardly nature rose to a fearful pitch of anger.

"That rash blow has cost you dearly, woman," he said, grasping her delicate arms cruelly: "you shall be mine now."

"Release me, worthless villain, release, or I call for aid."

"You would get none," he answered, tormentingly; "I will release you when I have done with you—when I have made you thing no longer holding the name of woman.

"I warn you," said Grace—her eyes sparkling like burning coals—"release me, or the fault will be your ruin."

"You threaten," he said, with a satanic laugh.

"I warn YOU," she repeated.

Lord Edward released her arms, awed by the determination of her tone.

"Do you think I am to be kept from my purpose by the idle threats of a weak girl," he said, though suddenly conscious of dropping her hands.

"You will find, coward," she exclaimed, drawing her beautiful form erect, "that a girl can sometimes defend herself, and protect her honour against such degraded wretches as you."

He gave vent to a cold triumphant laugh

Grace stood ready for an attack.

She looked magnificent as she stood defying her cowardly assailant.

Her handsome form, drawn to its height; her fair face, flushed with excitement; her bright golden tresses, hanging about her white round shoulders in wild disorder, and her dress, torn open, exposing to the gaze of her persecutor her beautifully moulded palpitating bust.

Lord Edward thought he had never seen so lovely a creature before.

His nature fired as he gazed at her enrapturing charms, and, before the poor girl was aware of his intent, he sprang upon her with a base design.

For some minutes they had a most desperate struggle.

Grace contended against her brutal assailant with almost superhuman strength.

She was a gentle-hearted creature except when she was roused, then, like her lover, she was dangerous.

She was dangerous now.

Her dastardly assailant had forced her to the ground.

She gave a cry like an enraged tigress, sprang to her feet, and dashed her clenched nend with such force in her opponent's mouth as to loosen several teeth, and cut his lips in deep gashes.

This aroused him to such a fearful pitch of madness that he almost forgot his purpose.

He fiercely clutched her ankles, and pulled her down with terrible force.

He would have brutally struck her, but again she leaped to her feet, and dealt him another fearful blow that knocked him prone on the floor.

Lord Edward Aldervale had not imagined the beautiful girl whom he had so long kept in captivity possessed so dangerous a nature, or he would have tried other means.

Her last act had rendered him perfectly powerless, and he fairly groaned with pain and baffled rage.

The brave girl was not done yet: she had been in danger, her passion was aroused, and she meant to have revenge.

She clutched the beaten hound by the hair, and dragged him across the room, opened the door, laid his head upon the threshold, and then slammed the door to, crushing his neck.

He gave a fearful groan, and sprang to his feet, with a murderous look at the fair excited girl.

He drew a dagger from his breast.

Grace gave a shriek.

He leaped upon her, clutched her by the throat, raised the gleaming weapon before her eyes, and, with a fierce curse, brought the deadly blade swiftly down in a line with her fair palpitating bosom.

Grace closed her eyes. She expected no mercy; she had shown him none.

But ere his hand delivered the fatal thrust he received a blow in the neck that sent him spinning across the room, the stiletto flying from his grasp.

"Take that," said a manly voice; "I've watched your little game lately, my lord; mind you don't find yourself in gaol very shortly. You'd 'ave murdered this pretty critter if I 'adn't come just in time; I've had my hie on you. Come, my lady," he said, turning to Grace, "I'll take you safe out of this cussed ole."

Grace looked at him with bewilderment.

His frank, open, though not handsome countenance, assured her she was safe in his company; she ran gladly to his side with a look of deep gratitude beaming from her large brown eyes.

"Oh, how can I thank you for this noble act?" said Grace, tearfully.

"No thanks, me lady," said her rescuer 'I only done me dooty, though perhaps it wasn't a servant's dooty to hit his master; but I ain't his servant no longer—no, cu' him, I ain't."

Making that gratifying speech, he shook his fist at his discomfited master and led his fair charge away.

The baffled young lord sprang to his feet, swearing in a most ungentlemanly manner, summoned his retainers, and dashed after the man who so bravely rescued the poor girl from his murderous hands.

He arrived in the grounds with the pack of hirelings at his back, just as the man with Grace, faint and weak, leaning on his arm, emerged from the secret passage.

"Seize him," shouted the infuriated young lord.

"Keep back," said the faithful fellow, "keep back all of yer; I've got a sword and can use it; keep back, I tell yer—keep back —keep back."

The retainers were advancing towards him quickly.

"Keep back—keep back, I tell yer. Men, men, keep back," he urged—quickly drawing his rudely made weapon, and assuming a defensive attitude. "Men, men, keep—ah— back, I tell yer, or some of yer'll get a hawful dig."

"Secure him," shouted Lord Edward, frantically, "and bring the lady to me."

"No yer don't," said Grace's preserver; "keep off."

He made a flourish in the air with his rusty sword, and the retainers kept off.

But their young master's voice made them walk forward, and despite all the poor fellow's furious gesticulations and comical antics, he was made a prisoner by his fellow-servants.

"Now, dog," said Lord Edward, giving vent to his spleen, "you shall repent that outrageous act."

"Shall I, murderer?" said the other, spitefully.

"Silence, hound!"

"Shan't, cur."

"Remove him, men," said their young master; "let him be confined in a cell."

"I warn yer," shouted the poor fellow, while being skull-dragged away. "I warn yer. Lord Edward, Jacob Martin ain't the boy to let things pass. I've seen enough of you a-late to bring yer to the gallus, and I'll do it."

The villainous young lord's disfigured face turned a deathly hue, and a thrill of dread ran through his veins.

The man had been a long time in his service, was a good, faithful servant to his employers, but he had seen enough to arouse his suspicion.

He determined to watch the Countess and Lord Edward very closely.

Which he did, and learnt many secrets.

He had also been a faithful spy over Grace Merton, and waited for the opportunity to get her away.

The exultant young reprobate had got the fair girl again in his grasp; he would have run his sword pitilessly through her trembling form had they been alone; but his hirelings were gathered around him in a group, and thus saved him from one crime by their presence.

He glanced at her savagely.

Grace shrank from his brutal grasp.

"Ha, ha, ha!" he laughed sardonically. "Who's triumphant now?"

"Not you, hound," thundered a voice.

Lord Aldervale turned sharply.

A graceful white steed cleared a hedge of high bushes and landed by his side.

The rider, a young, handsome fellow, slipped from the saddle and confronted him with drawn sword.

Lord Edward fell back.

"Tyburn Dick!" he gasped.

"Tyburn Dick," repeated our hero.

"He still lives, then," mused the terror-stricken Earl, shaking in every limb as though he had got the palsy.

"Still lives, and at your service to any amount," said Dick.

"Ho, men!" shouted Dick's half-brother, "secure this highway robber."

The men advanced in a body.

Grace shrank away and covered her face.

"Highwayman, is he?" she murmured.

Lord Edward's face brightened up with triumph, as he caught the trembling girl's words—

"Yes," he said; "your lover's a highwayman, murderer, footpad, robber, and—"

Grace gave a sharp shriek; the words struck her heart like a dagger.

"Liar," exclaimed Tyburn Dick, dashing at his dastardly brother. "I will ram those infamous words down your lying throat at the point of my sword."

He made a terrible down-cut as he spoke.

The other stepped aside only in time to save the gleaming weapon from splitting his head in twain.

Dick rushed upon him with a deadly thrust; his sword would have gone home, but the retainers saw their master's danger and stood before him.

"Grace," said the Boy Prince, "come to me."

She broke away from her brutal captor, and ran gladly to her lover's side.

Dick put his left arm round her lissom waist, and confronted his foaming enemy—

"Now, dastardly wretch,' said Dick; "fight for your worthless life."

Lord Edward's face went as white as marble; he saw the dangerous look in his opponent's angry eyes.

"I would not stain my blade with a murderer's blood," he said.

"Then, by heaven, I will stain mine with yours, since you are too craven-hearted to cross swords fairly," said our hero.

The brave boy's words stung the other to the quick; still he was too cowardly to chance a passage of arms with the young highwayman.

A cruel sneer curled his thin lips, and stepping away from his opponent's advancing blade, he got nearer his hirelings.

"Down with him, men, a thousand pounds offered for him."

"Come and take me," said Dick; "don't send your cut-throats to do what you are afraid to do."

The men were inspired with the idea of a thousand pounds.

They were five, and only one stood between them and the thousand pounds.

They anticipated an easy capture, and dashed upon the brave boy.

Dick waited for them. One fell pierced to the core; another rolled over his companion with an ugly dig through the shoulder.

"Two," said Dick, quietly. "I shall put the others with them, and then you shall follow."

Lord Edward bit his lip; he saw the tiger-like spirit of his enemy was roused.

"Come on," said Dick.

The men stood terror-stricken; the loss of their two companions blighted their hopes, and they began to despair about the reward.

"Take or slay him," shouted the exasperated young noble. "Are you frightened of one—a boy?"

The words rather shamed them, and they immediately attacked the boy highwayman.

Dick laughed at the idea, and swung his sword round playfully.

A miserable howl made him look round; he saw a man running away, the others following him awfully scared.

"If you are not wholly the dastardly coward I take you for, draw and defend yourself," said Dick.

Stung into shame by the boy highwayman's taunting words, he drew his sword and attacked the fearless youth.

Dick was a matchless swordsman, but it took all his skill to parry the cowardly thrusts aimed at his fair charge.

He saw the devilish look in his adversary's cruel glistening eyes; he watched closely his base design, and guarded his every lunge.

Dick was growing warm. The fight had been a long one, and our hero wanted to end it.

Lord Edward saw the change immediately come over his opponent's handsome face. He looked into the boy highwayman's resolute eyes, and threw all his strength into a well-delivered straight lunge for his adversary's breast.

Dick saw his danger and stepped aside; the weapon passed him harmlessly. He raised his sword, and with terrible force struck the combatant's grasp.

With a yell like a beaten tiger he leaped back and would have fled.

Dick was as quick to move as he was to act, and again raising his sword, he sprang forward with Grace leaning on his arm, and struck his foe to the earth.

"You see," said the boy highwayman, angrily, "Tyburn Dick still lives to avenge his wrongs. Your time, Lord Edward, has come. Die, wretch!"

He stamped his foot on his conquered foe's chest.

Lord Edward saw the pitiless look in his opponent's eyes, and called for help.

It was some moments before his cry was answered, then a huge sturdy man rushed out.

"Go back," said Dick, striking him across the face with the flat of his sword.

The man went back yelling with a mark across his cheek.

Lord Edward groaned miserably. He saw the truth of his foe's words—his time had come.

He closed his eyes with a bitter look of hate, and gave himself up for lost.

Dick's sword was at his heart.

Grace shuddered, and turned her head away to shut out the terrible tragedy.

Our hero shuddered himself at the idea of killing a man in cold blood, but he had no remorse for the one at his feet. He knew he was his bitterest enemy, and had tried more than once to sacrifice his life.

"Tyburn Dick never strikes a fallen foe," said the boy king, "nor would I raise my hand against a brave man. You are a coward—you would mercilessly have taken my life—the game has changed, and now I take yours."

His weapon was making its way to the other's black heart, when a deep coarse voice said in his ear.

"Not yet, Tyburn Dick," and his arms were pinioned behind.

Dick turned to meet the vulture-like face of the *Thief Taker, Jonathan Wild.*

CHAPTER XXXVIII.

THE STRANGE CHAMBER.—THE DEA
A STRUGGLE FOR LIFE—VICTOR
AND GALLANT TOM SAVED FROM AN
DOOM—"STAY, YOU ARE DOOMED

THE sudden appearance of G

awed the servants who rushed to Sir Frampton's assistance, and they fell back.

But only for a minute.

They saw the danger of their young master, and rushed forward, knocking the highwayman off his feet in their flight, and dragged Victor St. James to the floor by his hair.

Not before his sword had gone through his villainous cousin's throat.

The young nobleman was rather astonished to find himself on the floor so suddenly; so was Tom, and in their astonishment they rolled over and over, and came face to face.

"Tom," said St. James, in surprise.

"Victor," said Tom, springing to his feet.

Victor St. James jumped to his feet.

They were awfully astonished to find themselves alone, the wounded man gone, and the window closed.

"This is strange," said St. James, with a comical look on his features.

"I don't like the look of it," said Gallant Tom.

"They vanished like a lot of phantoms—so noiseless, too."

"They did."

"Perhaps you fought a phantom," suggested the highwayman.

The young nobleman's brow clouded.

"Phantom or not," he said, "I killed him."

"Sooner we get out of here the better," said Tom. "It's too cheerful for me, it seems like being buried in a tomb; hallo, the light's going out, too!"

St. James went to the door, Tom went to the window.

They were both securely fastened.

The lights had gone mysteriously out—they were in total darkness.

"This is still more cheerful," said Tom, with a shudder.

"It's enough to give a fellow the blue devils," remarked St. James, in a tone of awe.

"I vote we burst the door open."

They made a rush together; the door was immovable.

Another rush—and another. Still it did not move.

"This is what I call falling into a trap," said Tom.

"Falling into a trap," said a mocking voice.

St. James felt a chill of dread creep through him. There were strange tales afloat about the old house and Lord Berville.

Again the mocking laugh was heard in some part of the room.

Gallant Tom had a momentary cold shiver.

"Things are getting stranger," he said.

"Stranger," echoed the sepulchral voice.

"I should like to find the fellow who is mocking me," said the gallant fellow, feeling anything but comfortable; "I would stop his mocking."

A strange unearthly laugh sounded close behind.

The highwayman sprang round and made a fearful sweep with his sword.

"Victor, old boy," he said, big beads of perspiration rolling down his face. "we are in a den of demons."

"We are," said the handsome youth. "I don't care how soon we get out of it again."

"Let's have another try for the door," said Tom.

They had another try. St. James's hand was on the handle when the wall suddenly flew back, and left him standing on the verge of a hideous chasm.

He gave a cry. Tom grasped his arm and pulled him back, only in time to save him from falling down the fearful pit.

"Thank you," said the reckless youth, gratefully. "That's a cheerful place down there."

The highwayman peered down—the wall slipped back to its former position.

Tom had seen enough in that instant to chill his blood.

Beneath the floor on which they stood was a spacious stone vault, the sides decorated with grisly grinning skulls and decayed bones of victims who had fallen into the trap. The floor was covered with thick clotted blood, and in the middle stood a long wooden table with several human bodies upon it.

The sight made the highwayman sick and giddy.

The bodies on the table were of both sexes; long daggers were driven through them, and the limbs were still quivering.

They had not long been killed

Click !

Tom jumped aside dragging his companion with him.

The floor slowly slipped from under their feet.

" Come," said Gallant Tom, springing across the room.

He dashed at the window, where the pale blue streaks of the moon shone through faintly.

The glass shivered in atoms as his arms went through the panes, and he hung to the framework for dear life.

Victor St. James was at his side in an instant, and they were both clinging desperately to the creaking sashes.

The whole floor had gone down.

Their position was one of fearful danger—both clinging desperately to the thin giving wood—both holding their breath in horrible suspense.

The highwaymen ventured to look down ; floor had vanished altogether, leaving ing but the terrible vault beneath them, a score of masked men, holding long ering daggers, waiting for their victims fall.

Gallant Tom closed his eyes, and turned his dizzy head away ; his strength was deserting him—the frame to which he hung was giving way—another minute and he must fall a victim to the murderers below.

Each moment seemed like a dreary hour of fearful suspense ; with awful racking brain he saw his companion struggling desperately to retain a fresh hold.

The frame to which St. James clung had broken in the middle ; the ends were loosening and coming from their sockets.

The young nobleman's face was almost demoniac in its expression ; his eyes wild and bloodshot, his cheeks haggard and sunken ; never had he experienced such horrible torture as he did during those few minutes he was in that position.

Gallant Tom had been through some strange, wild adventures, but never had he been in such a predicament as now ; every drop of blood in his veins seemed to turn to ice ; his hair stood upright on his head, and cold sweat poured down him in pools.

He could not hold on much longer ; his grasp had relaxed, and he hung by the tips of his fingers.

" It's for life or death," he said, in a faint husky voice. " If we fall we shall be sacrificed ; if we succeed we shall live."

" What would you do ?" asked his companion, in a whisper.

" Make an attempt for life."

As he spoke, he threw the whole of his strength into his arms, and with wonderful velocity he drew himself up, and grasped a beam above his head.

A shriek from St. James made his heart leap into his mouth.

The jerk he gave in that daring leap had shaken his companion's hold.

With terrible strained eyes, he saw the youth falling. Forgetting the danger of his own position, he grasped at the handsome boy.

He shrieked with agony, his hand reached within an inch of the falling youth.

" Clutch, clutch, clutch," he shouted frantically, swinging about one leg.

The youth clutched at the swinging member, and grasped the toe of the highwayman's boot.

" Come on," raved Tom, scalding tears rolling down his cheeks with joy, " clamber up my leg."

St. James, with the activity of an ape, clambered up his leg.

Tom grasped him by the collar, and drew him up to the beam where they were both suspended by their hands.

Their position was almost as dangerous as their former one.

If either let go they must fall.

Gallant Tom did not mean to let go. He held on like grim death.

" Can't hang here all night," he said.

" I can't hang here five minutes longer," said St. James.

Tom's legs were again put in use. Swinging them back, he brought them forward with terrible force, and smashed the top panes of glass.

" Can you hang by one hand," he asked, " and hold me with the other ?"

" If I let you fall, I shall follow," replied his companion.

"All right, go a-head; give me your hand."

St. James gave him his right hand, and hung by the other. The highwayman let go his hold and gently let himself down.

"Hold tight," he said.

St. James held his breath and said nothing.

Tom drew his sword, and put his arm through the broken window, and commenced to cut round the beading of the window.

"That will do," he muttered, battering the framework down with the pommel of his sword.

This had been but the work of a few moments.

Windows in those days were very different to what they are now; the frames were made of thick ash, and held twelve squares of glass.

Gallant Tom had broken enough away to admit his body through.

"Draw me up, Vic.," he said, "and we shall be safe."

"We are safer as we are."

"The devil."

"'Tis the fact."

"Explain."

"If I draw you up, I shall pull myself down," said St. James.

"This is a cheerful position for a fellow," said Tom.

"Hang on my coat."

He hung on to his coat.

St. James held on to the beam with both hands.

"How long have I got to hang here?" asked the highwayman.

"Until you choose to turn monkey, and clamber up as I did."

In an instant he had clambered up his companion, and scrambled through the hole in the window.

Safely outside, he put his arm through, clasped St. James round the waist, and drew him outside.

Barely had they got a safe footing when a terrible shouting of angry voices arrested them.

Again the voices rent the still night air.

Tom and his companion stood spell-bound, their eyes riveted on the room they had just left.

The lights were rekindled by the same mysterious means as they had been put out, and the floor suddenly shot up with the twenty masked men standing in a line still holding their long glittering daggers.

"Be wise, and away," said Tom.

"Stay," said a deep stern voice; "you are doomed men."

The highwaymen were terror-stricken.

They were surrounded, back and front by the same fearful-looking beings.

The masked men closed round them like shadows, and in an instant the two brave fellows were menaced with the long deadly weapons.

CHAPTER XXXIX.

HOW FAIRY SERVES WILD AND SAVES HER MASTER—BIG BULLSKIN ARRIVES IN TIME TO PREVENT A COWARDLY THRUST—DEVIL DUKE OVERTAKES HIS ENEMY AND HAS A DUEL TO THE DEATH—VICTOR ST. JAMES AND GALLANT TOM SAVED FROM AN APPALING DOOM.

DICK was rather surprised at being baulked when at the point of having revenge.

He cast the thief-taker a look, such a look as a caged tiger would cast his captor, then he glanced longingly at his sword that had been jerked from his hand and lay at his feet

Grace without a word broke from his embrace and ran like an angel of light to get him his weapon.

Lord Edward, who thought himself dead, but not feeling the cold steel penetrating his cowardly body, opened his eyes and with a glad cry saw the position of his enemy and sprang to his feet.

Grace had just regained Dick's sword, when the cowardly young ruffian clutched her by the shoulders with an exultant laugh, and held her back.

"Not so quick, my beauty," he said; "that is a dangerous toy for your lover to play with."

He tried to take it from her hand, but the brave girl struck him with the pommel, and caused him to reel, blinded with the blood that ran from the wound she inflicted on his forehead.

He hissed a savage curse and struck her brutally in the neck.

Dick's look spoke the meaning he could not

find words to express, so intense was his rage. He struggled madly with his captor to get at the dastardly wretch, but Wild held him securely by the elbows from behind.

The brave girl did not murmur, though the cowardly blow nearly caused her to faint. She thought only of her lover's danger, and held the weapon out at arm's length towards Dick. He struggled forward, caught the point between the tips of his fingers, slid the blade throught his hand, and grasped the hilt.

He breathed with fresh hope, he felt comparatively safe—his life was in his sword.

When he lost his weapon, his courage went with it.

The noble boy's face flushed a dark crimson, and he made a spring towards his dastardly brother.

Wild had to exert all his brute strength to keep him back, or he would have spit the other on the point of his trembling blade.

It hurt the thief-taker's dignity to be pulled forward.

He grinned spitefully, his thin lips curling up, displaying a row of broken decayed teeth.

"Curse you!" said Dick, meaning his half-brother; "were I at liberty your life should answer for that cowardly blow."

He received a look of cunning malice in reply.

Lord Edward's hirelings crept forward now they saw him safe, and looked very valiant at one another.

"I am going to take care of your dear Grace again," said the spiteful boy, with a sneer.

"Are you, by heaven!" exclaimed our hero excitedly. "Release me, Wild, or you will suffer for it. Have you forgotten the warning you received?"

He had until Tyburn Dick mentioned it; en he remembered it with something like a shudder.

"Have you forgotten so soon the warning f Captain Claude?"

"Beware of Tyburn Dick, or he will be your fate."

Dick watched the effects the words had on the thief-taker with a gleam of satisfaction.

As bold and brutal as Wild was, of the young highwayman struck and he felt a sensation of dread cre him.

"Come along with me, Grace, dear s Lord Edward to his trembling captive am going to take care of you again."

Dick gave a cry of pain.

"Good-bye, Tyburn Dick, highwayma and murderer," said the young lord, with laugh of triumph.

He dragged Grace along by her hair.

Dick was maddened to exasperation: writhed and twisted, but could not break away from his captor.

"It's no good, my pippin," said Wild, gleefully.

Dick unhappily was of the same opinion without some friend suddenly turned up and came to his aid.

"Is there no one to help me," he said, "o stop that cowardly wretch?"

A man running answered him.

Wild called the retainers to hold his prisoner while he secured him with the hand cuffs.

The men rushed upon Dick and surrounded him.

Wild had got his hand in his pocket to bring out the before mentioned articles, when he gave vent to a dismal howl.

Fairy, who had been a quiet spectator of the scene, thought it quite time to make a move when she saw her master surrounded and by a peculiar instinct only known in a faithful dog or horse, she bounded forward and seized the thief-taker as the most dangerous enemy.

She sent her heels out and scattered the retainers; then fastening her teeth securely in Wild's shaggy hair, she playfully galloped round the ground, occasionally giving her captive a quiet kick to stop his groans.

Dick in an instant made a passage through the crowd who surrouneed him, and dashed after the cowardly young brute who so roughly treated the fair Grace.

The poor girl had fainted through the brutal treatment of her base persecutor.

Fortunately for his lordship that he dropped the fair girl in time, or Dick's sword would have found a resting-place.

The young chief did not pursue the cowardly cur; he turned his attention to his lady-love.

"Cursed hound!" muttered our hero, raising the insensible girl up and holding her to his breast; "the most degraded wretch would treat so gentle a child of nature with more honour and manhood than *he*."

The noble boy's face was clouded and sorrowful as he gently pressed his lips to her pallid cheek.

For a time he had forgotten where he was, and the danger that surrounded him; the angry look that clouded his brow had cleared away, and his handsome face became gentle and almost child-like, while he gazed with wandering thoughts at the beautiful creature he held to his breast.

He did not see the crouching figure sneak behind him—he had not noticed his bitter enemy crawl out again—his cynical features lighted up by a deadly gleam, and his sword drawn back, ready to lunge it through his and his fair charge's heart.

No, he had not noticed this; another minute and he would have never noticed anything else.

There was murder in Lord Edward's cruel eyes as he crouched behind our hero, and, undoubtedly, murder in his heart as he grasped the hilt of his sword and drew it back for a deadly thrust.

Dick was unconscious of his danger.

The young Earl muttered some inaudible threat and would have assassinated the young lovers in cold blood.

He had risen to his feet, taken a line from Dick's back to make sure that his sword would through his heart; and was in the act of aling the cowardly thrust when a bullet fired some unseen person, struck the weapon om his hand, and sent a stinging sensation hi- arm that made him howl.

Mad at thus being baffled, he was in the act of sneaking away, when the sudden report of fire-arms awoke Dick into fresh action. He turned sharply, and seeing the baffled knave crouching away on all fours, pounced upon him like a panther.

Grace had also aroused and stood trembling for her lover's safety.

The retainers seeing their master's danger, rushed upon the boy highwayman, tled him about brutally.

Dick had more opponents than very well contend against. He fought ingly, and many fell never to rise again.

Again the Boy King was being overpowered.

A well-known voice rang out for Dick t stick to his foes. The next instant a hug powerful steed cleared the hedge, and land in the midst of our hero's enemies.

Big Bullskin slid from the saddle and w to work like a gladiator.

The men saw the terrible weapon raised, and knew the consequence should it descend amongst them, and awed by the angry determined look in the gigantic fellow's face, they fled while they were safe, leaving their master to his foes and their mercy.

A dismal groan could be heard at intervals from the exhausted thief-taker, and a dead thud as Fairy lodged her heels in his chest to stop his music while she continued her playful amusement.

A loud shout and a prolonged groan made Bullskin turn.

The big fellow broke out in a hearty laugh at the deplorable sight of his little companion, who lay huddled in a heap on the ground.

Swig had seen the graceful way his comrade cleared the hedge, and thinking he could clear it as gracefully, came to grief in the attempt, by losing his balance and flying over his horse's head.

"Why, Swig," said Bullskin, lifting the little fellow up in his powerful arms; "what the deuce are you lying there for?"

"Why, my cussed horse chucked me over his head," said Swig, ruefully. "I shan't ride on him any more."

"No, don't, Swig; ride on a donkey in future."

"I'll ride on you, then."

"So you shall, if you can get the bit in my mouth."

Swig turned away in disgust, and pommelled into his horse by way of giving vent his spleen.

Dick called his faithful animal by a low whistle.

"Come, my beauty," said the Boy King, as the sagacious creature stopped and looked at her young master.

She gave a low whinney to his call, bumped Wild's head against a tree, and finally sent him flying by a good kick, then trotted gracefully to her side.

The boy vaulted into the saddle, and setting Grace in front of him, rode towards the haunt, leaving his enemy stunned and bleeding.

"Cowardly brutes," said Bullskin, as he rode along with his companions; "they might have had a set-to."

"You're very brave, I dare say," remarked Swig, contemptuously.

"Any way, I mean to have a go in to-night. I haven't had a good mill since I don't know when."

"Hallo, there's a mill," broke out Swig.

"Where?"

"Yonder."

Bullskin looked yonder.

"Ain't they going at it," he said.

"I'm blowed if it aint——"

"Yes, it is."

"Who, clever?"

"Duke."

"You are right—a lady with him, too."

"A lady with him, too!" repeated Bullskin.

"Not that it's anything extraordinary for him to have a lady with him."

"No, he is an awful sinner—there's a clout."

"Who got that?" asked Swig, straining his eyes.

"The other fellow."

While they had been conversing, they were urging their steeds forward to the scene of action.

"Hallo, that's a hot 'un for Duke," shouted Swig.

Duke had got a hot 'un, using the little fellow's expressive term, that knocked him over. He would have got a hotter one, had not his comrades ridden up in time to stay his combatant from taking a mean advantage by striking a fallen foe.

"Wait a minute," said Big Bullskin, pulling Duke's assailant back by his hair as he rode up.

"Who the devil are you?" asked the fellow as Bullskin put him out of reach, "that you should interfere?"

"Stay there, and don't make a noise," replied the gigantic fellow, coolly.

Then he turned to Devil Duke, who had received a very ugly cut across the forehead.

"Come, Duke, old boy," he said, "you are not dead yet."

"Not yet," said Duke, faintly, "Why, Bullskin! By the Lord Harry, who the deuce expected to see you?"

"Can't imagine; but now I am here, I be of any service to you?"

"You have been. Why, Swig!" he claimed, extending his hand to the little highwayman; "you here too?"

"Of course I am. Don't you see me?"

Just then Duke received a challenge from his opponent. He turned upon him instantly, and again the combatants were foot to foot, with steady eye watching each other's movements.

"Stay," said Bullskin, interposing between them. "You, Duke, are not fit to continue this fight."

"Stand aside, or I'll run you through!" said the other.

"My friend," said Bullskin, turning upon him, "is not well enough to continue this fight, but if you have no objection I will fight for him."

"I have an objection. He received the wound in a fair fight, and I mean to finish it with him; I have no cause to fight with you."

"Only on the principle that my friend is wounded, and I fight for him."

"A very feasible tale," remarked the other, sarcastically; "that I, in a fair combat, wound my combatant, and then have to fight his friends. No, I fight with him to the DEATH!"

"You will have to kill me first!"

"No, no," said Devil Duke. "It is not fair that he should have to fight more than one. I can defend myself, and will fight Captain Roderick."

"But you are faint and weak from loss of blood," persisted Bullskin.

"It's merely a graze."

"But surely you will postpone it. You have a lady with you now!"

"Whom I shall leave in your care whilst I polish off this gentleman, which, by the Lord Harry, won't take me long to do! He

TYBURN DICK ASTONISHES THE THIEFTAKERS.

has insulted me, and outraged the lady by carrying her off from her home."

"Well, if you insist, why go on," said Bull-skin, despairingly.

"Duke, dear, I implore you not to endanger your life by fighting with that fearful man," said Cecily, tearfully.

"Take care of her," said Duke aside to his comrade; "you can draw her attention from me."

"A duel to the death?" asked Duke.

"A duel to the death," answered the other sternly.

The highwayman threw himself into a splendid fencing attitude; the other was a beautiful swordsman, and was on his guard in an instant.

They were fairly matched—were both strong, powerful men, and knew every guard and thrust.

Almost breathless they stood watching the changes in each other's eyes, and guarding off the blows as they fell.

The thin tempered blades of their rapiers glided and twisted about and around each other like linked snakes, each trying to get the first point, and aiming for the other's heart.

Two swordsmen were never better matched in the old days of chivalry then were they. Each had a wrist like iron, and a nerve cool and collected.

Feints and points were tried by each, and carefully guarded off by the other.

Devil Duke was getting warm, and his opponent was getting warm too.

Duke's sword was raised for the other's head, and at the same moment he raised his sword too.

They fell, and met with a ringing clash; a shower of sparks flew from the trembling steel.

Captain Roderick's weapon made a circle round Duke's head like a flash of lightning, and fell with terrible swiftness for his left side.

The act was so quick that the highwayman was thrown off his guard, and only brought his weapon round in time to catch the other's descending blade.

The edge of Captain Roderick's sword caught Devil Duke's blade flat and split it exactly in half.

The captain stepped back, then dealt a furious blow at his opponent's head.

Duke was on his guard, and quickly turned his enemy's sword aside with his own half weapon.

Another and another—terrible cuts—he aimed at Duke with wonderful rapidity, but they were caught and turned aside harmlessly.

"Here you are," said Swig, running to his comrade's side. "Have my sword."

"No, thanks," said Duke, without moving his eyes away from his opponent. "I began with my own, and will finish with what remains."

The combatants had grown less careful and more furious. Heavy blows were exchanged on either side, and carefully turned aside from their intended destination.

Captain Roderick drew back his sword quickly, and with a satanic light glaring from his small grey eyes, he delivered a terrible straight thrust for his opponent's heart, and stepped forward to send his weapon home to its mark.

Duke moved aside, but not in time.

Swig, who stood by his side, turned white, uttered a shriek, and fell over.

He saw the weapon go through his comrade's side, and come out of his back.

It had gone through the *side* of his coat.

Captain Roderick gave an exultant yell of triumph. He thought he had made sure of his enemy, but ere he had time to withdraw his weapon Duke sprang upon him, and buried his broken sword in his body.

A low moan came from his lips, his hand relaxed from the hilt of his sword he imagined was through his foe, his face became a deathly pallor, his eyes rolled about wildly, his frame shook convulsively, and, grasping his hands till the nails penetrated his flesh, he reeled round with a last death-gasp lingering on his lips, and fell to the earth stiff and prone.

Devil Duke turned away with a sad look at his bloody work, and accompanied his comrade and his lady.

Bullskin saw by his looks what had taken place, but made no comment.

Cecily ran to her lover's arms gladly.

Duke recoiled with a shudder.

He could not clasp that innocent, unsullied child to his heart with the hands that had just committed murder.

He was sorry for what he had done, and for the instant unjustly looked on the beautiful creature who stood tearful and trembling before him, as the cause.

"Why are you so stern and cruel?" she asked, sweetly.

Duke made no answer. He stepped back as she came towards him with outstretched hands.

"Tell me, Duke dear, what have I done to make you so cold towards me?" she sobbed.

Her gentle voice struck to his heart.

He looked at his own hands regretfully, then at her.

Cicily implored him to notice her, but he turned his head away.

"Oh! Duke—Duke, dear, do tell me what I have done!"

"Away he said, roughly pushing her from him.

"No!" she said, "I will not leave you Tell me what has happened?"

"Tell you what has happened?—No!" he said.

"Why not?—Do!"

"No! I say away from *me !*"

"Why away from you?"

He glanced at her almost sternly; then his face changed, and he became radiant. He extended his arms towards her, then drew them back, and again his handsome face became clouded and sorrowful.

Cecily could bear the torturing suspense no longer. She rushed upon him, and twined her arms round his neck; her pretty pouting lips touched his, and, unknowingly, he took a long lingering caress.

His arms twined round her supple form, and he held her tightly to his breast.

"I am unjust and cruel, as she said," he muttered.

"The fault was not hers; it was my own impetuous temper that caused the work to be done."

He looked gently at her, caressed her again, and continued his musing.

"It is better, perhaps, as it is; had I not killed him he might have killed me. I don't like the idea of killing any one, but the thing is done, and can't be undone."

"What route are you going?" he asked Big Bullskin, who had strolled out of earshot.

He caught the echo of his comrade's voice, and turned.

"Did you speak?" he inquired.

"What road are you going? I asked."

"I have no particular destination—any road will do for me.—Why?"

"I will accompany you when I have taken this lady home."

"Do."

"Will you wait?" asked Duke.

"Yes; here."

"Adieu for the present."

"Adieu."

And Duke was gone.

In few minutes he returned, mounted on a beautiful steed from the duchess's stables.

"Where do you propose to go, comrades?" he said, riding up to Swig and Bullskin.

"Anywhere that will take us to adventure," said the giant highwayman.

"Suppose we go anywhere, then?" said Duke.

"Agreed? My horse has keen scent for smelling out game; he shall be our guide."

Big Bullskin dropped the reins on his horse's neck, and said something in a whisper to her, which she seemed to comprehend

The noble animal threw up her head proudly, as though in answer to her master, and putting her nose to the ground, she began to sniff as a bloodhound would for the trail of any runaway. Suddenly she pricked up her ears, and darted off at a rapid pace.

"By the Lord Harry!" exclaimed Devil Duke; "she seems to think there is something in the wind."

"There is, too," said Bullskin, as his comrades followed by his side; "she seldom makes a mistake."

"She is going a peculiar roundabout road," said Duke.

"She's right enough," said the huge fellow, with the greatest confidence.

The noble animal kept onward, suddenly turning down lanes, then scampering across fields, and cutting across corners to save time, as though in a hurry to get to her destination.

Devil Duke watched her every action with pride, and Bullskin patted her sleek, glossy neck with an affection of more love and truth than he would have shown a woman.

"She apparently has some idea of where she is going," remarked Duke.

"Undoubtedly she has."

Has she ever proved a faithful guide?"

"I have never known her once to fail."

"'Tis very strange," mused Devil Duke.

"She is on no ordinary mission now," said Bullskin; "there is danger where she is going."

"How do you know that?"

"By her hurry,"

"By the Lord Harry! it puzzles me to imagine how you taught her."

"I did not teach her; it is a natural instinct."

"How did you discover it?"

"We were going down a road one night, very quietly," said Big Bullskin, "when she made a sudden stop, put her nose to the ground, galloped off in quite a different direction to the one I intended to take. My curiosity was aroused by her strange move, and I let her go her own way."

' And then ?" said Duke, curiously.

" She started off, after taking me about five miles out of my way, into a thicket, and concealed herself beneath a clump of trees. She listened intently, with her ears bent forward; I listened too, but her hearing was more acute than mine. I knew she heard something before I did by her uneasy movements; then presently I heard the distinct rumble of a coach, and, as it came in sight, she suddenly sprang from where she stood and confronted the front horses of the coach. She put me in for a nice little job of three thousand pounds."

"By the Lord Harry! what an extraordinary creature!" exclaimed Duke, surprised.

" No more strange than true."

The extraordinary creature, as Duke called her, came to a sudden halt, then she trotted forward and back again.

Bullskin sat bewildered. He had not yet learned the meaning of her strange movements.

She turned her head, and tugged at his sleeve.

"What am I to understand? Am I to dismount ?

She nodded her head.

Bullskin dismounted.

He was in as thick a fog now as before.

Again the steed trotted forward, and then went back.

" Am I to go this way ?" he said, pointing to the left.

She shook her head.

" This way, in front ?"

This time she nodded assent.

Bullskin and his comrades went on in the direction indicated by the strange animal.

A cry of distress caused the trio to stop irresolutely.

" I told you we were going to danger," said the giant highwayman.

Again the cry was repeated, this time of two voices.

The night was intensely dark, and hid from view anything or any one who might be near, and they were obliged to listen for the cry once more.

It came, again with a piercing shriek, that seemed to rend the air with its agonizing distress.

The trio rushed in the direction from whence it came, and each shrieked with horror, and stood rooted to the spot.

Before them were two handsome dashing cavaliers in fearful danger; they stood upon a windowsil, and were surrounded by a group of horrible masked and black-cloaked figures.

Each figure held a long glistening dagger in his hand.

Bullskin's ponderous weapon leapt from its scabbard; a look of terrible determination was on his handsome swarthy features.

"Our comrades," said Duke, in a whisper, putting his sword between his teeth, and drawing bothhis pistols.

Swig drew his pistols, but left his sword alone.

He could fire at a respectful distance, and then retreat; he always looked after his personal welfare.

Not that we wish to say that Swig was deficient in courage, but he might have had more.

He always said himself he had plenty, but liked to keep out of other people's way.

Big Bullskin's ponderous weapon swerved round his head, and he made a scatter amongst the black individuals.

Duke discharged his pistols, then fought by his gigantic comrade's side.

They fought as only two brave men can fight.

Bullskin's terrible weapon did fearful slaughter each time it fell. Duke was busily engaged by actively guarding off long dagger thrusts from himself and companions.

Bullskin soon made a passage through the cloaked figures, Duke was at his side, lashing Swig's sword about on all sides to knock people down and strike the daggers from their hands.

"By Jove !" remarked Victor St. James, cheerfully to his companion, Gallant Tom. " we are not beat yet ! Friends are near !

"Yes," said a stentorian voice, "friends are near." Duke and Bullskin stepped forward to greet their gallant friends, when the lights were suddenly extinguished, and the cloaked figures vanished like so many shadows.

Bullskin knew treachery was at hand.

In an instant he had sheathed his sword, and had sprung forward with his companions in his arms.

They had scarcely got twenty yards from the accursed place when a shower of bullets fell about them.

A shrill cry of pain made Bullskin run forward.

He knew who it was had got hit by the pitiful tone.

"What an unfortunate little devil Swig is," said Munroe. "Where are you, Swig?"

"Here," answered the little fellow, miserably, I be; I know I've got killed."

His companion soon acertained the truth of his assertion.

"Got killed," laughed Bullskin. "You are a fine fellow to make a noise about nothing."

"Is it about nothing?" answered Swig; "if you had a bullet where I have got one, you wouldn't say it was nothing."

"Where have you got it?"

"I can't sit down."

Big Bullskin could imagine where it was, and suggested that he had better get it extracted.

Swig didn't see it.

"Where the deuce is my horse gone?" said Victor St. James.

"Here," said Duke. "All our horses are taught to know what this means."

He made a low peculiar whistle.

There was a neighing, and five faithful steeds came scampering to the spot.

"Come, comrades," said the giant highwayman, vaulting into his saddle.

The rest were mounted in an instant, and the party thundered away—Swig had forgotten the bullet.

CHAPTER XL.

THE INTRODUCTION BETWEEN GRACE AND MILLY—SWIG'S HEROISM—THE APPALLING DOOM OF SIMON JUDAS.

"Adieu, gentlemen!" said Devil Duke, raising his hat, as he rode away.

"Adieu, old boy!" said Bullskin.

"I say!" shouted St. James.

"Hallo!"

"Don't forget to remember

Duke laughed.

"Mind what you are at!" said Munroe, "you know the proverb—angels when in love, devils when angered."

"She is always an angel, and never gets angered," said Duke.

"Don't tempt her, then,"

"I don't intend to."

"Stick to that and you will do!"

"Adieu!" said the gallant fellow, again, and he dashed away.

"Now," he muttered as he went along, "I wonder how mine host of the Leopard Inn has taken care of the mercer's wife!"

He fell into a reverie.

He grew sentimental, and looked back upon his own wickedness.

"I always was a sinner," he mused. "I don't know who could help it when a fellow has such a lot. There is the mercer's wife, whom I am going to see, if she has not eloped with some one else; then there's the inukeeper's daughter, a most ravishing little beauty; then there's——'

He stopped there, his face grew grave.

"I am a bigger sinner than I thought I was," he continued. "I love her; it would be sacrilege to wrong her by a thought."

He tapped the sides of his mare with his heel, the graceful animal took one spring forward and seemed to sweep over the earth barely touching the ground.

"That's the style, my beauty!" he said, stroking her sleek neck. "We have a long ride before us, but we must stop before we reach London."

"Duke's an awful sinner with the ladies," said Gallant Tom, as his comrade rode out of sight.

"By Jove! he is a sinner," said St. James. "He elopes with an old gent's wife, and and leaves her at an inn while he goes to see another, and so on."

"We are all sinners, more or less," said Bullskin.

No more was said on the subject, and a few minutes' ride brought them to the haunt.

"Is the captain within?" asked Munroe of a comrade, who held his horse while he dismounted.

"Yes," answered the highwayman; "he just brought a lady with him."

"Thanks," said the gigantic fellow as he passed in.

Our hero had reached the haunt in safety with his lady-love.

The fair girl was faint and exhausted. The excitement and peril she had gone through was too much for her frail constitution.

Tyburn Dick kissed her pallid brow, as he gently laid her on the couch in Milly's chamber.

Milly looked sorrowfully, first at the handsome youth, then at the fair unconscious girl.

Dick knelt by the side of the couch, and took the delicate little hand of Grace in his own.

Milly watched him tenderly. Poor girl, she had received a heavy blow when she learned the sad news of Captain Claude's devoted self-sacrifice.

The blow had struck her heavily, crushed her young life, and left her a shattered wreck of what she was.

Gradually she drooped and pined, like some delicate flowers that wither with the biting frost, and fall in their young blossom.

So it was with her. The idol of her daily dreams had been suddenly, cruelly, pitilessly snatched from her.

Her song, that once made music and charmed the ear of the listener, had now ceased, and she felt a dull, heavy pain at her heart.

Dick suddenly started to his feet, as though a wandering thought had flashed in his mind. He advanced towards Milly, then stopped as his eyes met hers, a look of awe overspreading his handsome features.

"What a change!" he mused, his brow grown sad and sorrowful.

There was a change. The once queenly girl was now but a skeleton of what she had been—her soft blue loving eyes sparkled with a fitful lustre, an excited flush mocked the 'ily whiteness of her sunken cheeks, as Dick moved towards her and took her thin little hands.

"Milly, dear," he said, sadly—"Milly—" emotion choked his utterance, and he buried his face on her shoulder.

"Dick," she said, in a sweet plaintive voice, "who is that lady?"

The gallant boy looked earnestly into her face.

"A companion for you, Milly, dear," he replied, wiping the moisture from his eyes.

"A companion," she repeated, with a heavy-drawn sigh.

"Are you not pleased?" he asked.

"Selfish, ungenerous girl I was to have spoken it," she said, yielding to her tears; "of course I am glad. I want a companion."

"Be firm, Milly dear, for my sake, for her sake, and for your own sake."

"I will, I will," she said, in such a distressing way that it sent a pang of remorse to the Boy Highwayman's heart.

"Come, Milly, you must not give way like this," said the young highway chief. A painful choking sensation in his throat stifled the words that rose to his lips, as he fondly pressed the faded beauty in his arms.

"You will try and be firm," he said, after an almost painful pause; "that friendless, homeless creature will want a sister's care— a sister's love."

Grace shifted uneasily on her couch, and stared vacantly round the apartment.

"Where am I?" she faintly murmured.

Milly broke from Dick's arms, and threw herself beside her new companion.

A very touching scene took place between the two fair friendless and beautiful girls. By instinct each clasped the other affectionately to her breast; then there was a mutual weeping with them.

During which cheerful time Dick felt as though he had been smelling strong onions, and could not keep the water from running down his cheeks.

He felt much more comfortable when their gush of passion was over. He approached the couch. Grace twined her arms affectionately around his neck, and nestled her head on his shoulder.

"Tell me, Dick, dear," said Grace, suddenly starting up and looking at her lover steadily; "are you that fearful being you were called by those men? Tell me, can it be?"

Tyburn Dick hesitated.

"If I were?" he asked.

Grace looked at him with swimming eyes, and with quivering voice she said—

"The blow would kill me."

"Not if you heard his character truthfully."

"But say that you are not," persisted the

poor girl, with a slight suspicion arising in her fair bosom.

That was a difficult thing to do. He knew she must know it some time, yet he did not like to divulge the terrible truth; it would blight her young dream, or, perhaps as she had said, kill her.

Milly saw the agitation of the handsome fellow. She called him aside.

"Leave us, Dick," she said, in a low whisper; "I shall be able to break it to her better than you will."

"Dear girl," said the Boy Prince, fondly pressing her to his breast. "Be cautious, Milly."

"Trust me," said the faithful girl. "You had better not see her any more to-day."

Dick kissed them both and went out.

The two delicate children—they were but children—untutored, confiding, innocent, and loving children of nature—without an unholy thought.

"Where is he gone?" asked Grace, as Dick closed the door.

"He will return soon," said Milly, twining her arm around her companion's neck.

"He did not answer my question," said Grace, with a slight flush.

"If you are very good," said Milly, "and compose yourself, I will tell you all about him."

"Tell me he is not the wretched outlaw, with a price upon his head," Grace implored, tearfully.

"I will not tell you anything until you are quiet and composed," fair Milly said, a little severely.

She tried hard to smother her emotion; she conquered, and, in the attempt, fell asleep in Milly's arms, and, like a babe reposing on its mother's breast, she slumbered, nestling close to her companion.

Milly, like an angel of light watching the innocent, pressed her frail companion to her bosom, as though she feared there was some hideous monster crouching near, who would suddenly spring forth, snatch the delicate girl from her, and again leave her desolate.

Thus Milly sat in dread, a thousand strange thoughts streaming upon her. Anxiously she awaited the awakening of her delicate companion.

"Dear girl!" she murmured, as Grace opened her eyes, and cast a grateful, loving look at her young guardian.

"Milly," said Grace, faintly.

"Yes, darling," Milly said, with an affectionate caress.

"Has he been back?"

"Not yet."

"I had such an awful dream," said Grace, with a shudder.

"Don't think of it, dear," said Milly, persuasively; "dreams are stupid things, and only trouble you with strange fancies."

"But," persisted the queenly girl, "mine was a warning dream."

"Nonsense, nonsense."

"I dreamt that Dick was captured," Grace continued, not heeding the interruption, "and taken to prison. Tell me, Milly dear, is he what he is represented."

"Promise me that you will be quiet," said Milly.

"Yes."

"And not think any more of your dream."

"I promise you I will try and forget it."

And as a token of good faith she kissed her companion's little raised hand.

Milly related her own sad story, thinking by so doing she could the easier break the truth of Dick's position. Grace listened with much interest; the plaintive simpleness in which it was told touched her tenderest heart's chords, and she pitied the fair narrator the more for her loneliness.

Slowly and cautiously Milly commenced to talk about our hero, and it was not until she had finished that Grace knew the pretty romantic story she had paid so much attention to was of her lover.

Milly had so cleverly constructed every word, and made the young highway chief the dashing adventurous hero of her little narrative, that it quite enraptured Grace. Her pale cheeks flushed with excitement.

But only for a moment.

The truth flashed through her mind. The danger he was exposed to—the terrible name he bore—the fearful price upon his head—and, lastly, the way he was hunted by the law.

She shrieked, and fell into Milly's arms.

It took Milly some time to heal the wound

that had been so tenderly yet deeply inflicted. But the poor girl grew more calm. She clung to her companion in her solitude, and found comfort in the gentle loving nature of her lonely sister.

A shrill, wailing cry rang through the haunt.

The poor girls started, and looked at each other in awe.

Again the cry broke the stillness, and sent a chill to the hearts of the two unprotected girls.

Then there was a scuffle—a clamour of many voices—but above all could be heard the angry, commanding voice of the Boy Prince.

"No mercy for spies!" said Dick. "Bring him out, comrades."

"Me! no, no, captain," shrieked the miserable wretch.

He was dragged from under the table, where he had crouched.

"Mercy! mercy!" he shrieked.

"Silence, hound!" said the Boy Prince, with flashing eyes.

The low, cunning brute trembled beneath the steady gaze of his young chieftain.

He knew the laws of their band: he had broken those laws, and now feared the death he richly deserved.

"Simon Judas," said Tyburn Dick, "you were a penniless beggar, a footpad, an outcast, and were being hunted by the bloodhounds of the law, when Gallant Tom saved you from their clutches and brought you amongst his comrades. You hardly knew how to express your gratitude at the time."

The treacherous brute's heart sunk within him—he knew the force of the noble boy's words.

"They took compassion on you," continued Dick. "You were sworn in as one of them —as a brother—in every way you were treated as they were; they fought in your cause. You have shown your gratitude in return."

The blood curdled in the traitor's veins as the Boy King hissed the last words.

"You know our laws," Dick went on; "you swore by your life to abide by them in every way. You broke the laws, and have forfeited your life!"

"No, no, no!" shrieked the crafty villain.

Dick waved his hand, and turned a deaf ear to him.

"What else but death should a spy and traitor expect?" he said.

"Mercy! mercy, captain! I am not a traitor," whined Simon Judas.

His late comrades regarded him with a look of contemptuous disgust.

Swig strutted forward, assuming all the consequence imaginable.

"Why, yer lying sneak!" he broke out, not able to restrain his wrath; "didn't I collar yer just now, when you was trying to sneak in? Didn't I, yer liar? In course I did; and didn't yer begin to holler?"

He certainly did, but would not confess it,

Swig was looked on as a hero by his comrades. He felt like one.

He had decidedly proved one. The courage he showed was enormous for his size. Alone and unaided he had captured Simon Judas when in the act of secreting himself in the haunt for some wicked purpose.

Swig, after administering a few kicks for the benefit of the spy, strutted back again.

Big Bullskin, who had watched his conceited little friend, thought to take the dignity out of him, and as the unsuspecting Swig marched after his huge companion, he was clutched in his powerful arms, and thrown up like a ball.

Swig commenced to threaten in a desperate manner.

The whole of the highwaymen broke out in a hearty laugh at the ludicrous sight of their little comrade.

Swig soon found that threats only added to his discomfiture, and commenced to be persuasive.

Bullskin took compassion on him, and stood him on his feet.

The first thing Swig did was to rush at his companion, strike him furiously in the wind with his head, and ran into an adjoining apartment.

His comrades all raised a shout as he retreated.

Dick spoke.

The men were quiet on the instant.

"Comrades, what should be the punishment for a spy and traitor?" he asked.

"Death!" they all shouted in a breath.

"Death!" repeated Tyburn Dick.

"Death!"

And Simon Judas sprang round savagely.

He struggled desperately with his captors, got an arm free, drew a pistol from his belt, and took aim at the president.

The pistol was struck from his hand, and his arms pinioned behind him.

His brutal nature was aroused, and savagely he struggled to break away; he knew he had forfeited his life by attempting such a dastardly act.

Dick regarded him with a scornful look.

"Bring him here," he said.

The miserable wretch was dragged to where the angered boy stood.

Dick beckoned Bullskin to his side.

Then he spoke.

"Simon Judas," said Dick, "you are a cruel, pitiless wretch—you are not worthy the name of man; and, after committing such an act, can you think of mercy? No; there is none for you—your life shall be spared."

The boy paused.

The cruel monster thought he was mocking his fears, and glanced at the handsome youth with a look of bitter hatred.

"You would have shot me in cold blood, with your right hand," said Dick; "your right hand shall be cut off."

The terror-stricken brute shrieked for mercy.

"As much mercy as you would have shown me. Joseph Munroe," Dick said, turning to Bullskin, "amputate his right hand from his wrist, mark him with a crimson stain on the brow, and send him forth an outcast."

Piteously he implored for mercy, miserably he howled; and, in his wild despair, he threw himself at the feet of the young chieftain.

The boy's heart was impenetrable to the entreaties of such merciless villains, he spurned the wretch from him with his foot.

Maddened and wild with despair, he turned upon the boy highwayman like a savage tiger.

Big Bullskin caught him by the throat, and hurled him aside, as he sprang towards Tyburn Dick with a savage intent.

"Bring him here," said Munroe.

He was dragged to the block where Bullskin stood, his arm was bared, and, despite his fearful struggles, his hand was forced open and held down.

Bullskin raised a gleaming axe in the air; the doomed wretch groaned, and closed his eyes.

The axe fell like a flash of lightning, and cleft the trembling hand from the traitor's arm.

One convulsive throb of his body, and he sprang from his captors with a howl of pain.

His severed limb was a terrible sight, the warm thick blood spurting from the living flesh.

Frantic with pain he dashed about like a savage, knocking everything and everyone over who came near him.

Three of the highwaymen rushed upon him; one he sent sprawling by dashing his handless wrist in his face.

Sick and faint by the terrible act, the highwayman reeled, his face besmeared with the warm blood of the wretched man.

Bullskin seized Simon Judas by the waist, and, laying him full length on the table, as though he were but a mere child in his grasp, he drew a small silver stiletto and cut a star on his brow with the point; then he poured some liquid from a phial into the palm of his hand and rubbed it in the traitor's forehead

His cries and shrieks were heartrending.

Bullskin felt no pity for him. He rubbed the liquid in until there appeared a brilliant star on the man's brow that would not leave him while he lived.

He was marked like Cain, and discarded from the band.

Driven reckless and daring by the just cruelty he had received, he turned upon his late companions with a look of deadly hate.

He sprang towards Tyburn Dick with a terrible oath.

The brave boy held out his sword.

Simon Judas stopped—the sharp point looked dangerous. He did not like the idea of getting in too close proximity.

"Curse you all," he hissed, shaking his severed arm at the highwaymen, and casting a malicious look at Dick, "you shall suffer for this. One by one will I hunt you down, and bring you to the gallows. And you, curse you!" he exclaimed, turning to the Boy Highwayman, "may your soul wither! you shall suffer treble what you have caused me to suffer."

And shaking his left hand threateningly, he went out.

Dick sprang forward and darted after him, but he was gone.

Tyburn Dick felt anything but comfortable —the words of the traitor grated harshly on his ears.

A rustling among the foliage made him start. He turned sharply with a dangerous look.

"If I do catch him sneaking about he won't leave this place again," he muttered.

A low, mocking laugh rang through the air.

"Tyburn Dick—that's him! Forward men. A thousand pounds' reward for his capture!"

Dick looked in the direction from whence the voice came. He saw a body of men advancing towards him.

In another instant he was surrounded by Wild's officers.

CHAPTER XLI.

DEVIL DUKE MEETS THE MERCER—TWO CUN-NING OFFICERS MAKE THEIR ACQUAINTANCE, AND CAPTURE THE HIGHWAYMAN.

"Now, my bonny lass," said Devil Duke, patting the sleek neck of his steed, "we will see what way we can make to London."

The faithful creature pawed the ground anxiously.

She was quite ready to start at her master's bidding.

A good night's rest, and a good ostler to look after her, had refreshed her for a long run.

The highwayman was soon in the saddle, and going up the road in a style that would have done credit to Dick Turpin and his famous Black Bess in his ride to York.

The inn where he had spent a very comfortable night was soon left far behind, and he had to put up at many more inns, and spend many more comfortable nights, before he reached the "Leopard Inn."

A ride from Cornwall to London in those days, before locomotives were thought of, was of long duration and tiring, the distance being something like two hundred and fifty miles.

The faithful ostler must have known the sound of different horses' feet, for, as Duke rode up to the gate, he came out, and readily caught the horse's bridle.

"I am glad to see you come back safe again, cap'n," he said.

"Are you, Ben?" said Devil Duke, dropping a shiner in his hand. "How is the lady?"

"The lady, cap'n?" echoed Ben, in a dismal tone, drawing a long face; "the one you left?"

"Yes," said Duke, with a vague suspicion that something had occurred. "Is she well?"

"I can't tell you, cap'n."

"What the devil do you mean?"

"It ain't my fault," said the ostler, still drawing a longer face, and speaking in a more dismal tone.

"What is not your fault?" asked the highwayman, hurriedly

"The lady, cap'n."

"What do you mean? Explain."

"Well, cap'n, if yer had left her in my care, she'd been all safe now."

"What do you mean? Is she gone?"

"Yes, cap'n; she's gone."

"Gone, you scamp!" exclaimed Duke, his handsome face livid with excitement.

"Yes, cap'n; it warn't my fault," exclaimed Ben, dodging out of the way of a kick.

"Not your fault, hang you?"

"No, cap'n."

"Haven't you got any eyes?"

"In course I have, cap'n."

"Then why did you not look after her?"

"Why, cap'n, when I had to go away for two days some one came and took her."

"That's your tale?"

"It's the truth, cap'n."

Devil Duke regarded the poor trembling fellow scornfully. His handsome face had grown stern and cruel in its expression.

"Well, cap'n, you needn't look as though you could eat me, as it wasn't my fault."

"Well, Ben," said Duke, touched by the other's earnestness; "if you were away, it is not your fault."

"No, cap'n," said the honest fellow, grasping the highwayman's hand; "cuss 'im, if I ever catches hold of the sneaking skulk that collared her, I'll break his ugly skull."

"Never mind, Ben; look after the horse. I shall start in the morning."

He dropped the ostler another shiner, and strode into the inn. Mine host met him with a very sheepish look.

"You are a nice fellow, certainly," said Duke.

"Well, cap'n, it wasn't my fault."

"I heard that before."

"Can't help it, cap'n," replied mine host; "you hear it again, and it's the truth."

"That may be; but how the devil did you manage to let her go?"

"I didn't know nothing about it."

"Explain. Tell me how it occurred."

"Well," began the worthy landlord of the Leopard Inn, "a traveller, as he says, comes here, and wants to put up for two or three days. You know, cap'n, I didn't like the look of the cove, but I thought of an old saying you musn't take people by their looks, so I lets him stay, and in the night he bolts with the lady!"

"What sort of a fellow was he?" asked Duke.

"Why, a spiteful, ugly brute, dressed in black."

"Tall, and powerfully built?"

"Yes, cap'n, with a chest as big as a bullock's, and a wild look in his eye."

"My old enemy!" muttered the highwayman.

"You know him, cap'n?"

"I have had the pleasure of meeting him more than once."

"Oh!" drawled out the landlord, with gaping mouth.

"Let me have some supper," said Devil Duke.

"All right, cap'n."

And the landlord trotted off.

. . . .

The young sun shone forth with all its splendour. The night vapours were chased away by the morning rays, and the little feathered songsters gave a charm to the quietude of the breaking morn.

Devil Duke had risen early, and was cantering along the road in deep reverie. His handsome face wore a placid calm expression, but his brow was clouded, and a look of set resolution kindled in his large bright eyes.

A huge bird fluttered from a cluster of trees, and went shrieking past the highwayman.

"Being or devil?" said Duke, with a start that put to flight his pondering.

The bird flew back, and kept up a continual shrieking while whirling itself round his head.

Duke made several cuts at it with his whip, the bird shrieked and howled the louder in wild scorn at his vain attempts to knock it down.

The horse pricked up her ears in a timid manner and flew along at a furious rate, as though anxious to leave their ominous escort far behind; but the bird was not to be shaken off or left behind.

"I can't stand this," exclaimed Devil Duke.

He drew a pistol from his holster, took deliberate aim, and fired.

The bird, as though in mockery, uttered a terrible scream, and fluttered in his face.

The highwayman was not superstitious, but the strange ways of his assailant awed him, and a cold chill ran through him.

What could it mean? Was it something unnatural sent to warn him of danger? Could it be an omen of evil, or was it some hideous thing in disguise sent to torture him?

These thoughts rushed through his mind, and with a strange foreboding of impending evil, he urged his frightened steed onward.

Away it dashed like the wind, yet the feathered monster kept flying in a circle around the highwayman.

"Curse the thing!" exclaimed Duke, his handsome face white, and showing signs of fear, "I can't bear this fearful torture."

He drew another pistol, and fired as the bird flew round. The bullet went through its wing. It did not fall, but gave one piercing scream, and fluttered away.

Duke gave a sigh of relief as it disappeared, drew in the speed of his horse, and stroked her glossy neck.

"Wo, woa, my beauty," he said, drawing in the reins; "steady, Rosebud."

Rosebud pranced about uneasily, and snorted loudly.

"Steady, old girl," said Duke, "it's gone now."

Rosebud was quiet, and turned her head round, as though to satisfy herself.

"I am not superstitious," muttered the highwayman, as they went up the road at a more moderate rate, "but I don't like the look of that cussed bird flying about me; it has some evil omen with its presence."

He revived his scattered thoughts with a little brandy he kept in a flask.

"That's better," he mused. "I have no occasion for fear now; no one knows me down here. What care I if they do? I have got a sword and a good strong arm, and while I can use it I shall not be taken."

That was satisfaction, certainly; he seemed to find satisfaction in the force of his own thoughts.

"But now to business," he began, after a lapse of several minutes—"to hunt down my kind friend. Confound the fellow; I shall have to kill him. I hate killing people; but if I did not they will kill me—and, besides, the charms of that little damsel are worth risking your neck for. By the Lord Harry! I could not lose her for twenty fellows. Now, my beauty, what is it?"

Rosebud had come to a sudden standstill, and put her head to the ground as though listening; her bold rider bent over in the saddle and listened too.

"Some one coming, eh, Rosa?" he said to her in a whisper.

The sagacious animal pawed the ground, and sprang from the road into a meadow.

"Very well," said Duke, good humouredly, "you know better than I do, so I will wait."

He did not wait long.

A portly old gentleman came trotting round the bend of a road, mounted on a powerful grey mare.

The highwayman recognised the new comer at a glance, and covered his face.

By a slight pressure from her master, Rosebud sprang lightly from the meadow, and went down the road to meet the lonely comer.

"Good morning," said Duke, raising his hat.

"Good morning," responded the other, somewhat more timidly.

"Enjoying the morning air, I presume," continued the highwayman.

"Morning air? no sir, I am not," said the portly old gentleman, snappishly.

"Oh, indeed; I have a particular liking for early roving."

"I have not."

"I may suggest that it is important business that calls you out so early," said Duke, with a mischievous smile.

"You may suggest what you like, sir," said the old fellow sharply; but I don't intend to satisfy your curiosity, though it is important business that calls me out so early—very important, sir. Yes, sir, confound it! it is important—looking for my wife that some scoundrel ran away with; and if I catch him, why, damme, sir! I—I—I would—yes, I would!"

"I am out on a similar errand," remarked Devil Duke; "but I have time to do a little business."

The old fellow looked hard at the highwayman, and suddenly seemed in a hurry to part from his new acquaintance.

He urged his grey mare forward.

Duke drew Rosebud across his path, and presented a long-barrelled pistol point-blank in the astonished old gentleman's face.

"Oblige me, my dear mercer," he said, politely bending forward, "with that bulky purse you have in your breast-pocket."

The old mercer gave a yell, and shrank back.

Devil Duke bent still more forward, in a careless attitude, with one hand resting on his horse's neck, and with the other he altered the line of his pistol, and put the bright tube in very close contact with the chattering teeth of the mercer.

"Be kind enough to hand out the rhino," he said. Quick, my pistols are hair-triggers, and I can't be answerable for their suddenly going off."

The pistol had been discharged at the bird, but the mercer was innocent of this. He broke out in a cold perspiration, and trembled as though he had got the palsy.

"B—be ki—nd enough to move the pistol as—a—aside," he gasped.

"There are two beautiful bullets in it; they would be very indigestible pills should it suddenly go off," said the highwayman putting the muzzle within an inch of his

DEVIL DUKE MEETS THE MERCER.

mouth. "To save such a calamity fork out the purse, or by the Lord Harry you are a dead man."

With trembling hands and groaning miserably, the mercer forked out the purse, as Duke suggested.

The highwayman weighed it and put it in his pocket.

"Your watch," said Duke.

The watch was dropped into his hand, and it followed the purse.

"That locket, you old sinner, or that little girl you wear round your neck."

The old sinner gave a groan.

The locket he kept sacred; he would have refused to part with it, but the cold barrel of Duke's pistol touched his teeth, and the locket was produced with wonderful celerity.

"Thank you," said Duke, as he put that with the others. "That gold mounted riding-whip."

A clatter of horses' feet at that moment made the highwayman turn his head. He thought it was police officers, but apparently they were two countrymen.

In that instant, while Duke's head was turned, the mercer took a cowardly advantage. He raised the whip above his head, with a savage look of revenge, moved aside in case the pistol should explode, and dealt the highwayman a fearful blow.

Duke reeled in his saddle, and fell to the ground stunned, a deep wound cut across his brow.

The mercer dismounted, and commenced to rifle the pockets of his helpless opponent. He had just got the purse and other property belonging to him, when he gave a dismal howl, and fell on his face.

Rosebud, who whined like a child for her master's safety, rushed at the mercer, and grabbed spitefully at his hair.

Fortunately for him, he wore a wig, or otherwise he would have been scalped. As it was, he got a kick that sent him flying.

Having thus disposed of her master's assailant, she stood over Duke in a threatening attitude. Her posture was decisively defensive, and the way she showed her large white teeth meant danger to any one who interfered with her master.

Duke opened his eyes as the two countrymen rode up.

"Moi oyes," exclaimed one, "there 'ave been some foine work here."

"That there be," said the other.

They both dismounted in a clumsy way.

"Why, mon, how did thee coom like this?" asked one, at a respectful distance.

"I have been plundered, and almost murdered."

The countryman looked knowingly at Duke's face, and exchanged a cunning wink with his companion.

"Be thee much hurt?" asked countryman mber one.

"Rather," answered Duke.

"Oh!" exclaimed the mercer, recognising Duke, as his mask had fallen off. "It is at highwayman, Duke Deverill."

"That's me," said Duke, as he confronted e mercer, "but you are the highwayman."

"Liar!" yelled the mercer. "Robber, you an away with my wife."

"You robbed me of a purse," said Duke.

"You robbed me of it first."

"I say Bill," said countryman number two, "this be a rummy case."

"Eh, eh, eh," laughed the other, "we dunno which can be the robber, but we know which one is hurt."

"He is the robber," said Duke, meaning the mercer.

Knowing winks were exchanged between the countrymen and the mercer, which Duke did not observe.

"I say, guvner," said one of the men, addressing himself to Devil Duke, "don't thee think thee had better coom to yonder inn, and du a little summat before thee goes thee journey?"

"I suppose you want a little something, eh?" said Duke, smiling.

The countrymen had no objection, and the trio started off for "yonder inn." The mercer followed in the rear.

Devil Duke was startled by a horrible shriek as he dismounted at the inn-door, and a strange suspicion of dread came over him. The bird he had winged suddenly flew from some part, and, screaming as it flew around him, vanished as it came.

The highwayman thought there was something decidedly ominous in the appearance of that bird. He felt uneasy, he knew not why; but a strange foreboding of evil crept through him.

He turned sharply, and looked suspiciously at his companions. He saw them conversing in a low tone with the mercer.

The countrymen ceased on the instant when they saw they were being watched, and swaggered into the inn.

Duke called for some ale.

The countrymen stood particularly close to him. They were fumbling about their pockets under their smocks.

Presently one carefully draws a pair of handcuffs out, and passes them to his companion behind the highwayman.

Duke hears a clink of iron; he turns sharply—the men are standing as demurely as possible; he glares from one to the other —neither changes a muscle of his face, but there is a strange twinkling in their eyes.

A suspicion creeps over Duke that these men are not what they represent.

watches them closely, and sees a cunning leer pass between them—they are fidgety. His suspicions are confirmed that he is in danger; his hand wanders to his breast.

Why does he not fly?—danger surrounds m.

The low whining of his faithful horse makes him turn towards the door—she is pawing the ground uneasily.

He is in the act of dashing out; a low mocking laugh rings in his ear, and his arms are caught in a vice-like grip.

He struggles desperately to free himself.

The men have thrown him to the floor.

"A clever trap," exclaimed Duke. "It does you credit, but it won't catch me."

He dashed his fist in the face of one of the men, and sprang over the counter

"Come on, Bill," said one of the men; "we have got a devil to deal with, but he don't slip through my fingers."

The worthy Bill was on his feet in an instant. The blow Duke had dealt him had not hurt him much. His head was thick, and would stand any amount of punching.

"Let's take these cussed smocks off," said Bill.

"We ain't got no time to lose," said Jerry.

Like magic they slipped off their smocks, and were after the highwayman.

They were two daring thief-takers; they always worked together, constructed the most cunning plans for capturing highwaymen, and seldom lost a man when on his track.

The mercer had put them on the scent of Devil Duke, and they were determined to capture him.

We shall see.

Duke had sent jugs, bottles, and everything scattering as he sprang over the counter.

He dashed towards the parlour; mine host stood in the doorway; Duke had no time to lose. He struck the landlord a fearful blow in the face that sent him sprawling, sprang into the room, and barricaded the door.

"It's no good, captain, the game's up," shouted Jerry, while battering away at the door.

"You had better give in; we means to take you," said the other.

Crash.

The door swayed to and fro.

Duke stood like a rock, with his back against it. There was a dangerous gleam in his eyes.

Crash—bang!

The pannels began to splinter; the door being battered in with some heavy implement.

The landlord had got a huge hammer, and was working away with all his strength.

"Surrender!"

"Give him a bullet, Jerry," said Bill.

Jerry drew a pistol, and fired.

A shriek of pain followed the report, as the bullet went crashing through the door.

The bullet entered Duke's shoulder. One painful cry and he fell to the floor. The door was burst open, the barricade came crashing down and the thief-takers rushed upon their prey.

Faint and bleeding as he was, the highwayman made another desperate effort for his life. The hands of the thief-takers were upon him, when he sprang to his feet, dashed them aside and leaped through the window.

A shout—a wild frantic shout, that rent the air—came from the enraged throats of the thief-takers as they bounded after the highwayman.

They had not far to go, for Duke had fallen exhausted.

Like savage bloodhounds they pounced upon the helpless fellow, handcuffed him, and dragged him away in triumph.

"I told yer the game was up, captain," said Jerry. "We are going to take you to Newgate now."

"I shall come and see you swing at Tyburn," broke in the mercer, spitefully. "You won't run away with any more men's wives."

"Yes cap'n, the gentleman speaks the truth," said Bill. "You'll swing at Tyburn before long."

"The rope is not woven that will ever go round my neck," said Duke.

Rosebud came trotting up to him as his captors led him away.

Thief-taker Jerry made a clutch at her bridle, and got his hand bitten through in the attempt.

"Cuss the horse, shoot her," he yelled, foaming with rage, and almost mad with pain.

The other thief-taker fired. Rosebud had sprung aside by a sign from her master.

She took the lace carvat from Duke's neck with her teeth, and by another sign and a word she galloped off like wind.

Duke was bound on a horse, and led away by his captors to Newgate.

"You're sure to swing, cap'n," said one of the captors. "We shall have a few more soon, and they'll keep you company."

"There is not a wall in Newgate that will hold me a week," said Duke.

"Oh, oh, oh, !" laughed the worthy pair; "we shall see."

CHAPTER XLII.

TYBURN DICK TAKES REFUGE, AND ASTONISHES THE TWO CUNNING OFFICERS.

"Hi, hi, hi—stop him—a thousand pounds for the first that stops him. Surrender, Tyburn Dick—surrender, I say! Stop him—stop him—close the gates—shut the gates—bring him down—Fire!"

Another moment and the whole scene was lighted up by a vivid flash from a line of pistols that were levelled and fired at a youthful rider.

"Over my beauty," he said, in a musical voice, to his cream-coloured steed.

A podgy old toll-keeper rushes from his box, closes the gates, and cringes down as the daring outrider comes dashing along.

He gently strokes the sleek neck of his faithful steed, and again dashes along the road.

The pursuing party raise a shout; there is another flash, a ringing report, and a shower of bullets fell close to the daring rider.

Defiantly he turns in his saddle raises his gold-laced hat, and in a clear boyish voice calls out—

"Come, Wild, there is a thousand pounds reward for me—you have had a run for it, you shall have a longer one yet. Tyburn Dick is not to be caught until his name has echoed through the country."

"Surrender, or I fire," shouted the thief-taker.

A taunting laugh answered him.

"Away, away, Fairy; 'tis a hard run, but you shall have a rest presently," said our hero to his faithful steed. "'Tis a ride for life and liberty."

Away she went like wind, through field and common, leaving her pursuers further behind. At each graceful stride the trees the fences, the gates, the hedges, she leaped seemed to pass her like lightning.

On, on, she kept tearing along, not once slackening her pace, never stopping for any obstacle, but flying past everything, while her rider sat as motionless as a statue.

His handsome face was flushed with excitement, his bright eyes looked more brilliant than ever, and his long brown hair fluttered in the breeze, and hung around his boyish face in wild profusion.

Lighthearted and comparatively happy to what he had been since the disappearance of Captain Claude, our hero enjoyed the danger of the ride with reckless daring.

Had he been aware of the fearful storm that was gathering over head—of the chaos of danger and peril he was running into—he would have stopped and confronted his pursuers.

But, no, he was innocent of all, and each moment took him nearer to the terrible fate that awaited him.

On he kept, his pursuers following in his track like a pack of bloodhounds. The noise and the clatter as they thundered after the daring Boy Prince disturbed the peaceful little rabbits in their lair, and caused them to rush about in wild disorder.

The loud angry shouts rang through the lofty trees with a strange weary sound, and at intervals were echoed by a wild shriek from a startled bird.

Peasants, officers, and Wild's bloodhounds, as he termed the men, formed a large body, and all were anxiously pursuing a guiltless youth, whose only fault was his daring nature and chivalric spirit.

Had his pursuers been treble in number Dick would have defied them while his bonny mare held on her legs, he himself had strength to use a weapon.

On he kept—nothing appeared an obstacle in his daring course. The angry voices of his pursuers sounded upon his ears, but that did not deter him. His handsome face was a defiant smile, and pushing strait ahead

"Stop, stop,—surrender, Tyburn Dick—the game's up—you can't go much further."

Dick knew the voice to be that of Jonathan Wild, and laughing outright he turned his head, and sang out in a clear musical voice—"No, no, Wild; the game is not up yet. Tyburn Dick will never surrender. When you can catch me I shall be yours. That won't be yet. Keep the game up—I am fresh for another thirty miles.

Then bending over, he said in Fairy's ear—

"Away, my beauty—away for another thirty miles. We will give our friends a run for us."

Fairy threw up her head, snorted loudly, and started off at a terrific rate.

There was never a horse that ran on a course could have matched her in the rapid strides she took, and the graceful way she swept over the ground.

Though a calm night, our hero was obliged to hold his head down to keep the cutting wind, caused by the motion of the speed, from stopping his breath.

Again his pursuers are left far behind and out of hearing.

Dick now is within ten miles of London; a short ride will take him to the great city of noise and bustle.

He starts, listens attentively; he clutches desperately at the reins, and tries to pull up Fairy.

But, no. She heeds not the pressure on her mouth. On, on she dashes, as though maddened by excitement. Her ears are laid flat on her sleek white neck, her eyes stare wildly, and on she goes, leaping everything before her, her master knows not whither.

The boy's handsome face is changed to an expression of awe; his brow is clouded; he gasps for breath; he trembles in every limb, and struggles despairingly with the reins.

His steed stumbles over a fallen tree. In an instant she is upon her feet again, and about to dart off.

"Woa, woa! Fairy," said Dick, in broken accents.

The noble creature starts at the sound of her master's voice, then she prances about uneasily.

"Woa, my beauty," the boy said, patting her neck.

Fairy neighed, turned her head to look at her master, and then stood as quiet as a lamb.

"Woa, woa! Fairy, lass—quiet. Had you forgotten that I was on your back, eh?"

The pleasure she exhibited while Dick spoke to her plainly showed that she had forgotten him in the heat of the excitement.

"I thought so," he said. "You would have ridden me to eternity had you not fallen. Ah! do you hear something?—so did I."

Fairy pricked up her ears, stretched her head forward, and stood in listening attitude. Dick leaned over her head, with his hands on her mouth, and listened too.

A clatter of horses' feet sounded plainly on the still night air.

Dick drew Fairy under the shade of some lofty trees in a hedge, took a pistol from a holster, and strained his eyes in the direction of the approaching sound.

"Enemies front and rear," muttered the Boy Highwayman. "The first that crosses my path will not cross a second."

He put his pistol on full cock, and sat in readiness to pick the first rider off his perch, should they be riders that were coming towards him.

"Can I see aright?" he exclaimed, putting the pistol in its case. "A horse without a rider."

He rubbed his eyes with his hand and looked again.

By the faint glimmer of the twinkling stars he saw a shadow that appeared to be a horse—harnessed, but without a rider, as he said—and something white fluttering from its mouth.

His blood ran cold through his veins, and a look of dread came over his features.

He gave a low, peculiar whistle.

The riderless horse neighed loudly, and hastened her speed—she knew the signal.

"As I suspected, when I saw the cravat in her mouth," he said, with a troubled look "one of my comrades in danger, and that is his horse with the sign."

He touched Fairy gently and she sprang into the road.

She looked knowingly at her companion; they exchanged a familiar neigh, and rubbed their noses together, by way of a friendly greeting.

Dick took the cravat from the horse's mouth, and patted her neck affectionately.

In the middle of the cravat, worked in silk, were these words—"Captain Duke."

The handsome boy reeled in his saddle, and nearly fell.

"He!" exclaimed Dick, "one of my bravest comrades; by heavens, not a stone of a prison shall stand until we have found him!"

He folded the cravat, and put it in the breast of his coat, and looked inquiringly at Devil Duke's horse. The faithful animal had been the bearer of a signal, but she had not the power of giving information of her master's whereabouts.

Dick felt sorry she had not.

He had no time for reflection; the voices of his pursuers could be heard at no great distance.

He must escape—to delay another minute would be sacrificing himself.

The boy looked in the direction of his advancing foes.

"To continue a straight course will not avail me much," he muttered, "the beggars are sure to keep on the track; I must try a manœuvre."

Watching the officers closely, he took a triangular route on their left, leaving Wild and his myrmidons behind, while he scudded along in the direction they had just come.

Rosebud trotted beside Fairy without the least attention from Dick.

Half an hour later the Boy Prince of the Highwaymen was at the Leopard Inn.

Ben, as usual, was ready to welcome "the cap'n."

"You've had a hard run, cap'n," he said.

"Yes, Ben; I have been at this at least a week now," replied Dick.

"As yer, cap'n; are the hofficers after you now?"

"Yes; look after Fairy, and keep her ready; I may want her suddenly."

"All right, cap'n; but I say, I forgot to ask where Cap'n Duke is?"

"He has been captured, I expect," replied Dick, sorrowfully; "I met his horse on the road."

"Oh, sir!" exclaimed the ostler, "does yer think they'll scragg him?"

"I don't *think* they will."

"I say," shouted Ben, catching Dick by the arm, as he was in the act of entering, "be on the alert, cap'n, there's two on 'em inside."

"Ah! waiting for me?"

"I don't know, cap'n, but I don't like the look on 'em."

"Officers?" asked Dick.

"Not exactly. cap'n, but in that line."

"Thanks, Ben, you are a good fellow."

"Cap'n, where did you start from?"

"Cornwall."

"What for?"

"You seem interested," said Tyburn Dick, smiling.

"Yes, cap'n, I should like to hear."

"I will tell you, then."

Ben seated himself on a corn-bin in the stable, leaning on the fork he had just been turning over the straw with, and Dick leant against Fairy, with one arm twined round her neck.

"We had a traitor in our band," began the Prince Highwayman, "there is sure to be one or more black-legs amongst a number of men——"

Bang.

Dick leaped round, and drew his sword.

Ben fell backwards, and vanished amongst the beans.

"What's that?" asked Dick, looking in the bin after the ostler.

Ben was some time before he could recover his breath.

Bang.

"What is it?" demanded Dick.

The ostler broke out in a loud laugh.

"He, he, he! Didn't it give me a turn?" he said; "but it's only a horse in the next stable—a kicker."

Dick was satisfied.

He sheathed his sword, and they both took their former positions.

Dick continued—

"The traitor in our haunt," he said, "is a most brutal wretch; several times he has tried to betray me, and the last time he was caught in the act."

"What did you do to him?" he asked.

The boy laughed grimly.

" Tortured him; cleft his right hand from his wrist."

Ben dropped the fork, and put his hand in his pocket.

" Then he was marked and cast forth. He ished a terrible curse against me. I dashed 'ter him, and would have finished him, but e was gone."

" Where ?" asked the ostler.

" To fetch the men he had brought to capture me. But at that time I did not know it, and while I was looking about for him I was surrounded by Jonathan Wild and his officers."

Ben shuddered at the name of the thief-taker.

" My comrades did not know of my danger," continued Tyburn Dick. " I whistled for my faithful horse, and in a minute she was at my side; in an instant I was in the saddle and away, and they followed me."

" They have followed you pretty well," exclaimed the ostler.

" Yes. I have not had much resting time; at every place I put up they ferreted me out, and so I have kept on. I think, though, I have done them this time."

" I shudn't like any of 'em to come here and try to nab yer, else I should show 'em what I could do."

Ben flourished the fork above his head, and fiercely brought it round with terrific force, and stuck it in the door, giving a satisfactory grunt as he left go of the handle, it stuck out quite straight.

" There, cap'n; that's how I shud send it into a few," he said.

" That's the thing, Ben; keep your eyes open and be ready, you may be useful," said Dick.

" No fear, cap'n."

Dick left the ostler grinning over a handful of money, while he sought the worthy host.

" Well, Davey," said Dick, pulling his fingers apart after shaking hands with the landlord, " how is the world treating you by this time ?"

" Pretty fair, pretty fair, captain. My boy, I am glad to see you—almost a stranger down this part."

" What an awful brick-bat hand he has

got !" thought our hero, wincing under the pressure of the other's huge hand; "he squeezes a fellow's finger's like a vice."

" Yes, landlord, almost a stranger down here," replied Dick, in answer to mine host " I am coming to Hounslow shortly, with my comrades."

" That's right, my boy, that's right; Hounslow is the place for *business*, and you will always find a friend in me."

" That's the thing, Davey; we can be useful to each other. But let's have a bottle of burgundy now, and a quiet weed."

" Yes, yes, my boy, you shall; I will get you one of my best. You know the sort— eh, captain ?"

The landlord trotted away gleefully.

Dick was left alone in the parlour.

Presently the door gently opened, and a very pretty blushing face peeped in.

" Lizzie !" exclaimed the Boy Prince, jumping up, and running towards the timid intruder.

The girl, with a glad cry, ran into his arms.

" What's the matter, pretty one ?" he asked, caressing her.

" I am so delighted to see you," she sobbed, overcome with joy; " I feared I should never see you again."

" Why, eh ?"

She looked tearfully into his face.

" Ah ! Dick, why do you ask me so painful a question ?" she said.

" Painful question !" said the boy, kissing her pouting lips.

" Yes; you know why I am always so anxious to see you."

" Is it because you never know when I am safe ?"

The pair of soft arms that were round his neck tightened, and a pair of pretty enticing lips met his.

" You are glad to see me, eh, Lizzie ! Dick remarked, looking wickedly into her eyes.

" You know I am, you naughty fellow," replied the girl, playfully smacking his face.

Our hero, like all the gentlemen of the road, was of a very sinful disposition, and when in the presence of a pretty girl, everything else was forgotten.

So it was with Dick.

Mine host had been a long time selecting the favourite bottle, and in his absence Dick forgot everything in the world but Lizzie—even his queenly Grace and the landlord.

"Captain, captain, this is not right," exclaimed Davey Jarvis.

Dick looked confused.

Lizzie was lying on his breast sobbing.

The landlord entered rather abruptly. He looked anything but pleased with the conduct of his young guest.

He was not like the generality of innkeepers. He loved his child with a pure, fatherly affection, and would have crushed anyone who wronged her.

His brow clouded angrily.

He placed the bottles down, and looked straight at our hero.

Dick returned the look unquailingly.

"What have you done to my daughter?" demanded the landlord in a husky voice.

"What do you mean?" said the boy, springing up and confronting his accuser.

Davey Jarvis stepped back. There was a looked in the highwayman's eye he did not like.

"Look you here "—Dick's face flushed as he spoke—"I do not take an insult from any one, Mr. Davey Jarvis, and, if you don't apologise, I and you shall fall out."

The landlord was taken aback by the determined tone of the Highway Prince; he felt that he had wrongly accused the boy, but his suspicions were strong.

They would have been stronger, had he known all.

Tyburn Dick felt ashamed of himself but thought it best to brave it out, which he did, and came off best.

The landlord meekly asked the boy's pardon, which he got, and again they were as friendly as before.

"Come, Lizzie, my dear, you must leave us now," he said to his daughter.

Lizzie would rather have remained where she was; very reluctantly she left Dick, and cast a lingering look at the handsome boy before she left.

"Go, Lizzie, there's a dear, when your father speaks," said mine host.

"The devil!" shouted Dick; "Mr. Jarvis, let your daughter stay—Lizzie, come here."

The girl looked longingly at the youth.

"Go, Lizzie," said her father.

Lizzie was going, her pretty eyes overflowing, when Dick sprang up and took her hand.

"Mr. Jarvis," he said.

Mr. Jarvis cast an angry frown upon the youth.

"I intend her to stay," Dick said.

"Very well, captain, you must have your way, I suppose, but it is very wrong," the landlord said.

"Why? she will learn no harm."

"No, no, my boy, I know."

"Then why should she not stay when she wants to?"

"Because you make a fool of her when you are with her, while all the time you know you do not think anything of her."

"How do you know?" Dick remarked.

"I am sure you don't, and when you are not here she is continually fretting. I know it is all through you. You should be more careful, my boy; you have got such captivating ways, I should not wonder if you are not the cause of more than one broken heart."

"I hope not," said the boy. "You, Lizzie, should not fret about me."

"I can't help it when I think perhaps you are in danger."

Dick drew her towards him and kissed her.

"Try and not think of my danger. I shall be here more often soon, and then you will have no occasion to fear."

The boy's kind delicate ways to the landlord's daughter quite reconciled him again.

"Upon my soul, my boy, you are the best fellow I know," he exclaimed. grasping the Boy Prince's delicate hand. "I am sorry, very sorry, for what I said."

"That's the thing; let's be jolly, and banish melancholy," the boy said.

In a few minutes they were very jolly.

Coarse boisterous laughter from another apartment made Dick grow inquisitive.

"What neighbours have you here?" he asked.

"Oh!" Davey Jarvis exclaimed. "I forgot to tell you before, captain, they are two enemies of yours. Would you like to see them ?"

"Delighted I should be, were it possible, without them seeing me."

"We can manage that, captain."

Mine host slid a panel aside in the wall; a heavy pair of curtains then only divided the two rooms.

Tyburn Dick put the landlord back, and pulling the curtains slightly apart, he peeped through, and listened attentively to their interesting conversation.

Our hero had thrown a loose wrapper over his right shoulder to hide the jewelled star on his breast, but a part of it showed that he did not notice. He was too absorbed watching the two thief-takers.

They were seated at either end of a table —a bag of coin and a lot of loose money lay on the table between them.

"We nabbed him to rights, did'nt we, Jerry ?" said one, leaning half-way over the table, with his hand ready to sweep off the money in case his companion should attempt to touch it.

The officers rushed upon the audacious boy ; Dick was upon his feet in an instant ; his jeopardy made him desperate ; mercilessly he struck at all who opposed him.

"We did so, Billy. Fifteen hundred pounds ain't a bad day's work, is it ?" remarked the other, watching the movements of his companion stretching his hand over the glittering metal.

"He, he ! We've got him safe enough in the jug ; he'll be hung soon."

"He, he !" grinned the other; "an' I'll go and see him swing."

"So'll I. We'll share the swag now."

"We will."

Thief-taker Mr. Billy commenced to count.

"Ten for you, Jerry, an' ten for Billy—that's me."

"And the rest for Tyburn Dick—that's me !"

The two cunning thief-takers uttered a frantic yell, and clutched at their ill-gotten gains.

"Don't be in a hurry," said Dick, stepping forward, and grasping each by the shoulder.

They had never been so surprised in their lives as they were at the sudden appearance of the famous Boy Highwayman, whom they had been so long hunting after.

The change that came over their visages was a study, and the miserable way they howled after their money was a horrible discord which Dick did not appreciate.

He shook them violently by the shoulde

"Miserable, cunning wretches, blood-hun ing brutes !" he said.

By a sudden jerk he drew them forwar and then sent them flying over the backs the chairs.

In their flight they overturned the table and scattered the money, and were actively engaged in putting what they could in their pockets.

Tyburn Dick placed a finely polished pistol in the ear of each.

"Take that money out of your pockets, pick up all off the floor, and put it in the bag,' said the boy, pushing the cold tube in their ears.

The cold steel had a wonderful effect on their nerves.

The way their pockets were turned inside out, and the money went into the bag, was a caution.

"Fly, fly, my boy," shouted the landlord, putting his head between the curtains ; "fly for your life ! The house is surrounded, you haven't a minute to spare."

Shouts and yells of hundreds of voices rent the air, the gates were battered down, the doors were burst open, and flocks of people and officers surrounded the house outside, while Wild and his men made a search inside.

Unfortunately for our hero, the inveterate thief-taker happened to stop outside the room door where Dick was.

"Surrender, Tyburn Dick ! Surrender quietly, or it will be the worse for you,' shouted Wild.

The Boy Prince laughed grimly.

"I am sure to surrender," he shouted, fiantly.

The th ef-takers he kept down would have tried to capture the daring boy now, but he cautioned them that his pistols might go off and make a mess with their brains.

The idea was horrible—it kept them quiet

Jonathan Wild had heard Dick's defiant reply.

He swore terribly, and threatened to take his life.

Bang!

Crash!

The door fell in, shattered to atoms.

One prolonged shout of triumph, and the officers dashed into the room.

Wild was the first to spring upon his victim, and clutched his arms. The pistols Dick held went off; the ball had gone into some one by the painful groans that arose above the clamour.

In an instant the boy was surrounded.

"Ha! ha! ha! your race is run, Tyburn Dick!" laughed Wild exultantly.

CHAPTER XLIII.

A CHASE FOR A BOY HIGHWAYMAN—TYBURN DICK MEETS HIS DARING COMRADE, TOM TURPIN — WILD SHOT — APPEARANCE OF RED MATTHIAS—A PHANTOM TO THE RESCUE.

HAD a tiger been suddenly entrapped in its lair, it could not have been more furious than was our hero.

Savagely he glared at the thief-taker who held his arms.

Dick still clutched the pistols, and waited for an opportunity to use them again.

He had done a little mischief.

In his hurry he had not taken a sure aim, but one of the balls had taken off Jerry's ear, and left him stunned and bleeding; the other, that had missed its mark, went through the heart of one of Wild's myrmidons, leaving him stricken amidst his companions.

"They are the last two you will kill, Tyburn Dick," said Wild, pointing to the prone men; "It is my turn now."

"I shall rid the world of you next, Jonathan Wild," said Dick.

The thief-taker laughed scoffingly.

He stood behind Dick, and held his wrists tightly.

"I never break my word," the boy answered, grimly.

There was a mischievous glance in our hero's eyes as he spoke.

The words had barely left his lips when he threw himself on his face, drew his arms forward, and pitched Wild over his back.

The officers fell back awed. The Boy Prince meant mischief, and they had no wish to get in his way.

The sudden jerk had rather shaken the thief-taker; but he soon recovered. He was in the act of clutching his opponent's leg, to pull him down, when Dick struck him a fearful blow on the temple with the pistol barrel.

Wild fell with a groan. Dick leaped off the ground and sprang at the window. A crash followed his flight as he disappeared through a square of glass, like a harlequin would through a tissue paper window.

There was no blanket held to catch him. The eager hands of his enemies, who were waiting for him, broke his fall, and spifflicated their arms.

His face and hands were slightly cut with the glass, but no further injuries deterred his daring spirit.

The exultant yells and shouts of triumph that welcomed the appearance of the Boy Prince were deafening.

A regular siege by the group of people was made upon our hero as he fell.

A hundred hands were stretched out to clutch the defenceless boy, and, in their eagerness, they fell one upon the other.

Dick was nearly smothered; he struggled to extricate himself from beneath them.

He got his head out; his collar was clutched by a rude hand.

Ostler Ben had watched the proceedings. He thought it quite time now to interfere. Leaving Fairy ready in the stable, he made his way to the scene of action, and brought the fork down on the hand that held our hero.

The hand relaxed, and the owner of the hand yelled miserably.

Ben went to work with the fork.

He picked the people off Dick, one at a time, with the prongs.

The last was off; Dick sprang to his feet.

Ben used the fork as a very formidable weapon, and kept the eager blood-hunters from attacking the daring Boy Prince.

Our hero was making the best of his freedom, his slim sword was going to work, doing fearful damage.

He did not want to spill more blood than was necessary. He called Fairy! The faithful steed answered him by a glad whinny, and with one graceful bound she sprang to his side, scattering her master's opponents in ll directions.

Dick vaulted in the saddle.

There was a crash—a loud shout.

The window through which he had sprung was battered down, and Wild, with his myrmidons, scrambled through.

"A thousand pounds for the one that captures Tyburn Dick!" yelled the infuriated thief-taker.

"Two for the one that can hold me!" shouted the boy, defiantly, and away he went.

A volley was fired after him by the officers as Fairy cleared the high gates.

It was now broad daylight, and many more stragglers who had just turned out joined in the pursuit.

Tyburn Dick had got the start. While his enemies were mounting, Fairy had traversed over many miles of foliage ground, and left their pursuers a great distance behind.

The chase was kept up the whole day.

The fleetness of our hero's milky-white steed kept him out of shot range.

His enemy untiringly kept up the pursuit. The excitement was too animating, and the idea of a thousand pounds made them vigorous, and eager to capture him.

Jonathan Wild, like a bloodhound, when once on the track, never gave up the hunt until he had overtaken his victim.

The day was drawing to a close, the night shadows were creeping over the heath, and the Boy Highwayman was fading from their view in the distance.

Their horses began to flag, and show signs of distress.

Fairy kept on at the same pace. The faithful ostler had rubbed a lotion into her joints that gave her power to outstrip any horse that ever ran, but she would not be able to keep at the speed she was going much longer.

Several of Wild's men had fallen back, and the horses were, one by one, dropping to the ground dead or exhausted.

The thief-taker swore terribly, but that did not avail him much. All who could kept up with him.

"Ho, there! within!" he shouted, halting at the gates of a livery stables.

His party drew up.

An ostler or stable-boy rushed out and threw open the gates.

Jonathan Wild entered; the others followed him.

"What now, governor?" said a man, coming up to him.

"All the horses you have got in the stables, and quick about it,' the thief-taker replied.

The man stared at him vacantly.

"Can't you understand, fool?" said Wild, viciously. "Saddle all the horses you have got in the stables. I want them."

"Do you?" said the man, shoving his head in Wild's face; "then I'm blowed if you'll get 'em."

"Fool! do you know who I am?"

"I don't care who you are."

And away he went.

In a minute he returned with several of his sturdy companions, each looking very valiant, and armed with a huge blunderbuss.

"Now, my joker," said the man who had before spoken, putting the blunderbuss to his shoulder and presenting it point blank at the thief-taker; "if you ain't cleared out of here in half a jiffey, why, damme, if I don't show you what I can do."

Wild laughed grimly.

The man did not like the sound of the laugh, it was so grating.

"Do you know you are speaking to Jonathan Wild?" said the thief-taker.

The man dropped the blunderbuss, and scampered off yelling.

The name of the inveterate wretch struck terror to the hearts of all who heard it, and many would have preferred the presence of his satanic majesty to that of Jonathan Wild.

The thief-taker gloated over the power he had, and delighted in torturing any one he saw was the least timid.

"Now, blockheads, can't you help yourselves to the horses?" he shouted.

"'Spose we can," answered a man who had no particular love for his master.

"Look sharp about it, then," growled Wild.

The fatigued horses were stripped of their harness, and as many steeds were brought out of the stables.

Again the party were in pursuit of the Highwayman.

Our hero had made good headway during this time. Fairy began to show signs of fatigue, and Dick, thinking that he was now safe, slackened the speed of his faithful animal, and went along at a steady trot.

The horses the thief-taker and his party had procured were brisk, and carried their riders along at a rattling rate.

Wild knew he must soon overtake Tyburn Dick if he kept in the right track.

The same idea inspired his companions, and they kept up a continual shouting.

It was not long before their wild yells reached the ears of our hero. His face flushed angrily. He prepared his pistols for action, and kept as much in the shade as possible.

Fairy was nearly done up. Dick did not despair—he trusted to his usual good fortune.

The moon, that threw down her bright rays and lighted up the whole scenery, was suddenly hidden by a huge black cloud that drifted slowly along and shut out the light from the earth.

Dick fell into a reverie, and covered his face with one hand.

A horseman—a dashing, handsome fellow—mounted on a coal-black steed, noiselessly, and with the swiftness of lightning, sprang from some secret hiding-place, and rode beside our hero.

There was a reckless, dare-devil look on his handsome features. He watched Dick closely.

The sudden apparition made Fairy start.

"Dick, old boy!" said the strange horseman, bringing his hand down smartly on our hero's back.

Dick turned quickly.

"Tom!" he exclaimed, gleefully—"Tom Turpin!"

"That's me," remarked the daring highwayman.

Dick grasped his comrade's hand warmly.

"The very fellow I want," he said.

"What's in the wind?" asked Turpin.

"I can hear very noisy shouts," said Dick.

"Hawks on the trail?" quoth Tom Turpin.

"They have been on me several times," Dick remarked.

"Is there a fight in prospective? that's the thing."

"There will soon be one in reality."

"That's the thing; I'll have a go in at them," said Turpin. "But, old boy, your mare seems tired."

"So would yours if the had had the devilish run mine has."

"My dear boy, I have been dodging about for this last week, and even more. I have got some friends coming after me. You would not believe how fond they are of me but I don't like their company; and the further I go they are sure to follow me."

"I am troubled in the same way," said Dick; "they are an awful bore to a fellow. Hallo, Tom!"

"What's the matter, Dick?" asked Turpin.

"Get ready, old boy!" exclaimed Dick, excitedly. "My friends are not fifty yards off, they will be upon us in a minute."

"There is plenty of time," said the other, coolly. "Don't upset your equilibrium; you should never be in a hurry; take things quietly. Get the barkers ready; that's the thing."

Dick's pursuers were now groping about for him amongst the clusters of trees. Many passed so close to him that it was as much as he could do to refrain from sending a bullet through their heads. He thought discretion the best policy, and let them pass uninjured.

Wild then made his way to where the two daring knights were hidden, and passed within a yard of Fairy's head.

At that moment the moon struggled through the clouds, and threw its brilliant rays upon the two highwaymen.

An exclamation broke from the lips of Tyburn Dick.

Wild turned.

He saw our hero

"So, so, my daring boy; we meet again," he said, exultantly. "Forward, men! here is our man. Tyburn Dick, you can't resist."

"Liar," yelled the impetuous youth, dashing forward.

"Liar, Jonathan Wild," echoed Tom Turpin, following his comrade.

"Oh, oh, oh," laughed the thief-taker "Turpin the highwayman, too?"

VICTOR ST. JAMES DEFENDING TYBURN DICK.

"That's me," said the daring fellow; "you want my comrade?"

"And you, too."

"Take us."

"I am going to."

"Try it on."

He made a cut at Wild, and fired at a man who caught the bridle of his faithful Bess.

The man rolled over with a bullet in his head, and Wild dodged out of the way of the cut.

Dick was going to work furiously; his sword flashed like a meteor, and dealt destruction wherever it fell.

Shower after shower of bullets were fired at him, but they only flattened as they came against him.

He was impenetrable. A suit of chain-mail, that fitted him like a skin, protected him from all destructive weapons or shots.

He dashed into the thickest of his enemies, and cut them down on all sides.

Wild sprang to his side, clutched him by the throat, and hurled him from his saddle.

Dick did not lose his presence of mind through his unexpected downfall; he still held a pistol, and, taking deliberate aim as he lay, he fired at the thief-taker.

Wild reeled in his saddle, and fell to the earth with a cry.

"I am shot," he gasped; "kill him! shoot him!"

His voice was faint, and died away in a whisper. His men did not hear what he said; they saw him fall, and ran to his aid.

A deathly pallor spread over his distorted visage, his eyes were closed, and he lay as though dead.

Driven to desperation by the loss of their leader, the men dashed savagely upon our hero, and bound him hand and foot.

Tom Turpin saw the peril of his comrade, and cut his way through his opponents to get at him.

"Back! back! The fault will be your own if you get in the way of my sword."

There was a dangerous light in his eyes that showed his determination, and as he spoke his bright weapon flashed before the eyes of his assailants.

The men fell back.

Tom severed the cords that bound his comrade, and raised him from the ground.

"You are not done yet," he said.

"Done—no!" shouted Dick, rushing at the nearest man.

The man saw him coming and got out of the way; so did many more.

"Don't let him go," whined a voice; "he's got my money."

"No, don't let him go; he's got my money, too," whined another voice, and the two thief-takers, Bill and Jerry, appeared.

"How much is it?" asked a bold-looking officer.

"Fifteen hundred," whined Jerry.

"We'll have a struggle for that," said the man.

"All right," said our hero; "come on!"

The man looked steadily at the youth for a moment, and, when Dick least expected it, he sprang forward, caught him by the throat, and bore him to the ground.

Tom Turpin struck the man on the head and knocked him over. Some one behind struck Turpin; then there was a general melée.

The men suddenly broke out in a ringing cheer.

Dick and his comrade, who were fast overpowering their opponents, were surprised, and looked for the cause.

The appearance of Red Matthias, a clever well-known thief-catcher, whom our hero had cause to remember and Turpin did not forget

"Tyburn Dick!" he shouted."

"I am here," was the daring reply.

The officers Matthias had with him were more active than Wild's men. By a sign from their master they rushed upon the highwaymen, and before either of our heroes had time to realize their positions they were secured, and being led away prisoners.

There was a sudden halt; the men shrieked, released their captives, and shrank away terror-stricken.

Bold as Matthias was, the fearful apparition that confronted them made him quake with fear.

A spotless white steed with a majestic rider who sat like a centaur, grim and motionless.

Horse and rider were white; a strange light appeared to surround the pair.

Noiselessly they approached the thief-catcher without disturbing a leaf.

The horse was a strange weird-looking animal, the rider was handsome in every feature. An awfully troubled, sad expression was on his marble-like face, and his large eyes glared wildly at Red Matthias.

The thief-catcher tried to shriek, but his tongue refused utterance, and clave to the roof of his mouth. His eyes were as though riveted on the strange being; he could not move them. He would have fled from the awful, fascinating scene, but his legs refused to move.

With fearful racking brain, he watched the phantom glide nearer to him. He saw a light flash before his eyes, felt a stinging pain across his temples—the next instant he lay huddled in a heap on the sward.

He was stricken by the phantom.

With a pain at his heart, Dick watched the strange being. He would have run forward, but his comrade held him back.

What thousands of strange thoughts rushed through his young brain at the moment.

The phantom turned towards him. Dick held out his arms eagerly, while his comrade shrank away.

The spectre clutched the two round the waist, and, before either could realize the truth of their position, they were borne away by the phantom. Fairy and Bess followed.

" Oh, lor," groaned Jerry, who had hidden himself up a tree. " A phantom to the rescue, and carried off Tyburn Dick, with all my money."

" *A phantom to the rescue!*" repeated the spectre, in a hollow voice, and it vanished in the gloom.

CHAPTER XLIV.

THE MASQUERADE.—THE COUNTESS AND THE YOUNG GREEK UNMASKED.—A COWARDLY BLOW.—VICTOR ST. JAMES DEFENDS TYBURN DICK.

THE night of horror and danger has passed away.

Our hero awakes, as though from a dream, to find himself in Cornwall with his bonny white mare—a thousand strange thoughts course through his excited brain.

How did he get there?

He knows not.

Rescued from the very clutches of the thief-takers, and carried off by a phantom.

The strange incidents rush to his mind.

He tries to think of it as a dream.

But no—the scene rises visibly before his eyes, he plainly pictures to himself the whole of the mysterious occurrence.

He distinctly sees the majestic being that saved him—the pale sad face haunts him.

The vision is gone.

Dick reels. His brain is distracted, and he clutches the mane of his faithful steed for support.

For several minutes he is lost in deep thought.

"My comrade," he exclaimed, starting. " Where is he—Tom Turpin? Alas! gone."

Again his head is buried on the neck of his steed, and he is for the time lost to the world.

He is thinking of his daring comrade, who shared his danger—he wonders how he got back to his native place, for he knows not.

He remembers but little after being carried off with his comrade by the phantom, for he fainted when he beheld the mysterious being.

He glances wonderingly at Fairy.

It puzzles him more than all the rest to know how she escaped the danger that threatened her, and how she reached Cornwall.

He had been in a trance.

When he awoke he found himself lying in a pretty remote spot, his faithful steed standing over him.

With Fairy he had walked away from the place.

A strange impulse caused him to go back.

" I know not why I have come back here," he said to his steed.

Fairy, as was her usual custom when her master mentioned her name, pawed the ground and commenced a loud whining.

Dick cast his eyes to the ground—his attention drawn there more by the pawing of his horse than anything else.

A cry escaped his lips, and he sprang forward. Eagerly he clutched at something that lay on the ground.

There was a strange light in his eyes as he examined it.

What was this little trophy that caused the handsome boy so much agitation, mingled with joy and sadness?

A trophy that gave him a clue to a horrible mystery—a trophy he recognised, and valued more than his own life.

" Ha—ha—ha! I know it—I recognise it —ha—ha!" he almost wildly exclaimed, while gazing with fixed eyes on a handsome scarlet cloak, lined and trimmed with blue silk. " 'Tis something in remembrance of *him.* Does he still live? No, no, he cannot. I saw him fall into the surging waters, riddled through and through. Oh, wretched thought!" he murmured, and covered his face with his hands.

Fairy looked grave, and, as though understanding her master's grief, she approached him, and laid her head on his shoulder, sympathisingly.

The mark of affection roused our hero.

" Ah, lass," he said, sadly; " thou would pity thy master, but alas, my beauty, thou hast not comprehension enough to know of my troubles. I see," he added, "thou art anxious to leave this place; we will away."

In an instant he was in the saddle, and cantering towards the haunt, his young spirit depressed and sad.

"Surely, this cloak," he broke out, "must have been over my legs while I slept, or was it placed there by Providence for a purpose—a purpose that has a mystery attached to it, and which mystery I must seek out? I will; I swear it, by the light of heaven."

And he vanished in the gloom, for the morn had not yet broken.

.   .   .   .

A fortnight elapsed, and nothing more was heard or seen of our hero.

A continual search was kept up by the law for the gallant Boy Prince of the Highwaymen, but to no purpose; the search was fruitless, at at last it was given up, thinking that the boy had made his way to France or some other part.

The fair summer months have passed away. A dull December day changes the aspect of Cornwall, and leaves it a dreary-looking place, stripped of its beauty.

The snow in huge flakes fell, covering the earth with its spotless white pall, and in crystal masses clung to the leafless arms of the gigantic trees, that swayed to and fro with a gust of wind and shook themselves of the chilling burden.

As the night wore on the fleecy clouds cleared away, leaving the sky blue and speckless, the young moon sheds its silver splendour down upon the white crystalled earth, and revealed a scene of joy and gladness at the Aldervale Manor.

The magnificent mansion was brilliantly illuminated by numerous lamps and wax candles, and decorated with the most choice of rare fragrant plants that filled the air with a delicious odour.

Such lovely faces and forms of grace as might people fairy-land were there with their chosen lover or companion of the night.

The time was all for gladness.

The stately old manor was represented in all its splendour, and on this night there was a masquerade—a grand gathering of fashion and beauty such as thrilled the heart to gaze upon, and wrapped the senses in a whirl of delight.

The revelry was at its height when there entered a gentleman on whom much attention was bestowed—a gentleman young and handsome, moving with the grace and dignity of a prince, dressed in the rich costume of a Greek, stately of head, and altogether of noble aspect.

As he passed down the spacious hall the fair masqueraders could not but look with admiration upon him, and many a gentle breast quickened with a thrill as he cast a look around at the gay gathering.

He seemed difficult to please, though there were many whose beauty would have charmed an anchorite.

He heeded none, but strolled through until he met a richly-dressed cavalier, whom he quietly greeted and passed on.

"Ah, ah," muttered the young cavalier, as he leant against a pillar, "the fellow must have as many lives as a cat; he is here after my sword passing through his neck. Sir Reuben Frampton," he added between his teeth, "there will be a row here, by Jove. I see it brewing, and you will get the worst of it."

His eyes were following a tall powerfully-built cavalier, and a queenly girl, who seemed to loath the presence of her partner, as they whirled through the many couples.

"Ah!" exclaimed the young cavalier. "So my Greek friend has make a compact with the countess. What an angel she looks, but what a devil she is in reality! By Jove! there will be another row. That's the thing—plenty of excitement. I am here."

And he tapped the jewelled hilt of his rapier and strode away.

Sir Reuben Frampton, when the cavalier cast such spiteful looks, had just broken down miserably in the midst of a splendid dance, and beat a retreat to another apartment with his fair companion.

"By Jove, there's a wretched muff," thought the young cavalier, "to spoil a dance like that. He shan't have the lady's hand for the next, if I have to fight for it. Hallo, young gentleman, what the deuce are you after?"

The latter part of his speech was addressed loudly to a rather graceful but small individual, who dodged round the pillars with a silk handkerchief between his fingers, which in an instant vanished up his sleeve, and the small person was lost amongst the crowd.

The young cavalier felt for his handkerchief.

"Gone," he said, " and that sneaking little brute has taken my only handkerchief, by Jove—there, gone."

He made a grab at the small person.

The small person was active ; he dodged round the pillars, ran between a fat old gentleman's legs, and disappeared amongst the revellers.

He would have followed, but his young Greek friend came whirling past with the countess, and he lost sight of the little pickpocket.

"Never mind," he muttered. "By Jove, there's that brute with my lady. How I long to sheath my sword in his body ! I will, too."

He walked to where Reuben Frampton sat, and as the young cavalier approached him, he got up and led the lady away to an ante-room.

The young Greek mask who at that moment passed with the countess, cast an inquiring look after his friend.

The countess's eyes sparkled brilliantly through the holes in her mask, her fair face flushed bewitchingly. her beautiful bosom heaved and fell at each word from her youthful companion.

Her whole soul seemed enamoured by the beauty and refinement of her companion, and many were the envious looks and scandalous whispers exchanged by the fair groups about their lovely hostess and her fair companion as they passed up and down.

Little did the proud lady of Aldervale dream with whom she was walking—little did she imagine that the princely masquerader was her own *son*—the wronged heir of the splendid domain in which she held the grandest gatherings of festivity !

No, she did not think that ; her thoughts were drawn in a halo. She thought of him by her side with the tenderest of thoughts—a being whom she could worship as an idol to share her future life, and drown the bitter remembrance of the past.

Happy ignorance.

How soon the heart is led away, but how soon will it change !

The countess is dreaming. Never, during the whole of her wicked career, did any one make such an impression on her heart as does the young Greek.

Her companion is telling her a strange story about a bad woman, who murdered her husband, wronged her only son of his inheritance. and drove him to crime.

The deep pathos of his voice and some words that he puts a particular strain on touch deeply to her heart.

She winces and seems uneasy. The story strikes her to be very personal, yet she banishes the idea thinking there are more than herself of the same nature.

Her companion's voice grew plaintive as he neared the end of the narrative, and, taking her little hands in his own, he looked fixedly into her large luminous eyes.

"No, no," she cried excitedly, " I will not listen to any more ; the story is too sad."

"Too sad ?" he repeated. "Suppose I be the outcast ?"

"No, no—you are too good, too gentle," she said, and, hanging tightly to his arm, she glanced with swimming eyes into his, as they walked away from the inquisitive crowd who were watching them. "You must not say any more about it. No one could be so cruel to you. Yes, yes—you are too gentle. I—I—no, I cannot, but if I wait for him to discover," she murmured to herself, "I may lose him altogether. I may not see him after tonight. Yes, yes—I will tell him. I will be bold and tell that I love him."

Her lips quivered as though she would have said something, but her voice failed her, and she could not utter a word. Her head drooped, and half fainting, her companion led her to a settee and procured some refreshments for her.

Greatfully she pressed his small hand, and in her impulse she put it to her lips.

She barely knew what she did ; her brain was in a whirl. Her heart beat much quicker than was its usual wont.

How she trembled to pronounce that word of love !

Had looks ever spoken what the heart felt, her companion must have read the words she longed to speak to him in those sweet smiles and large expressive eyes of hers.

He saw and knew all, but his motive was not to take the slightest notice.

He played his part well. He brought pangs from her heart he so long thought had turned hardened and insensible to any sense of feeling.

That was all he desired.

His story was one of touching interest. It had taken the desired effect on his infamous mother. In shame she listened to her own shame and his sufferings, but she knew not of whom he spoke.

Like an aspen leaf she trembled from head to foot. Her lips formed to ask him his name, but again she failed to articulate a word.

She smiled sweetly into his face, as though she would have had him to understand the meaning.

But the young mask pretended not to understand her meaning, and turned his head aside.

A sharp cry, as though through pain, made her companion turn, but only in time. The countess fainted, and fell into his arms.

In an instant there was a great commotion amongst the revellers, and they came crowding round their beautiful hostess.

There was another cry, and the crowd stood irresolute, not knowing what to do.

The second cry issued from an antechamber, and then there arose angry voices.

The young cavalier who had followed Reuben Frampton confronted his foe with one hand on his collar.

"Selfish hound! Miserable wretch! By Jove, I could shake the despicable life out of you," exclaimed the young cavalier, angrily. "You have no claim to the lady's hand."

"Eh—what?" said a portly old fellow, coming forward, dressed in costume that little became him. "What's that eh—? No right to the lady, my daughter Edith, eh? What the deuce do you mean, young sir? Release my son's throat directly."

"I will, my Lord Berville, to take hold of yours."

"Eh—what the deuce—now, now, keep off—eh—ha—don't—take your hands away."

The young cavalier kept his word. He released his rival's throat, and shook the portly old gentleman.

"Then, my Lord, attempt to oppose me and I will stop your jacobitism—you understand?"

It apeared so; Lord Berville turned extremely white and shrank back.

The band at that moment struck up a beautiful dance that set every one in motion.

The countess had recovered, and was whirling through the delighted masqueraders with her youthful companion.

"May I have the honour of your hand, Lady Edith, in this charming dance?" asked the cavalier.

Lady Edith consented, no less delighted with her companion than surprised to hear him call her by her name, and to the discomfiture of her bloated old "pa" and her spiteful-looking betrothed husband, the dashing young fellow led her away and they went through the dance in a splendid style.

"Who the devil can he be," said Lord Berville to Reuben Frampton.

"I can't imagine! He appears to know us very familiarly by name," answered the other, with a change of countenance that belied his words.

"Yes, very familiarly indeed. I wonder who the deuce he can be, eh? It strikes me I have heard his voice before somewhere."

"So I fancy. Here he comes! I will make him answer for his insolence."

"Eh, yes; do my boy—kill him. I know he is an enemy—perhaps he knows too much, more than is good for him. Kill him, my boy, and you shall have my daughter without the ransom. Kill him! that's the thing to do—there is not another girl here like my daughter—she is incomparable. Kill him you know!"

The young cavalier brought the young lady back, bowed to the pair of plotters, and handed Edith to her father.

"Stay, sir," demanded Reuben Frampton loudly.

The cavalier turned.

"With pleasure," he said. "What may be your wants—a few inches of cold steel?"

The braggart did not answer—he trembled visibly.

Lord Berville dug him in the ribs with his knuckles.

"Go on," he whispered? "Egad man!

hast thou lost thy courage ? my daughter shall not have a coward! *Kill him!*

"Come, Reuben Frampton, what do you want of me ?" said the cavalier.

"Your life, hound," exclaimed the other suddenly, prompted by his tempter.

The young cavalier laughed scornfully.

"By Jove, you speak boldy!" he said. Try and take it! I want yours, but I shall have to kill you eight times more before I can have it."

Reuben Framptom drew his sword and made a frantic thrust at his opponent.

The cavalier's rapier leaped from its sheath.

There was a clash and a shower of sparks as the weapons met.

"I don't want to make a mess here," said the young cavalier, making a pass to disable his asailant, "so I shan't kill you. I have had my sword through your throat once— it shall go through your heart next time."

"Egad, Reuben, the fellow braggeth!" shouted Lord Berville. "Ah, ah, ah, you nearly got that—kill him!"

"Wicked old sinner, I am no braggart," the cavalier said, "but by Jove, I know something about the secret vaults, where you murder people, and the floor that goes from under your feet, that were I to disclose what I know, you, Lord, Berville, would have your bragging stopped! No, you don't try again."

The last part of his speech was addressed to his opponent.

"Hallo, I am wanted," exclaimed the young fellow. "I have no time to spare now, a friend of mine is in trouble. I will settle you another time—by the altar, on the wedding day!"

Lord Berville had fallen back on a lounge speechless. The disclosure of his villany by a stranger had so astounded him that for a few moments he lay gasping for breath.

Rhuben Framptom was so astonished by the coolness of his young opponent, that he lost all power, and his sword, which the young cavalier wrenched from his hand.

"Don't forget, Reuben Framptom," said his assailant, "we meet again at the church and at the altar! I shall kill you, and claim Lady Edith Berville as my bride. Farewell, my lord; the next one you try to catch in your trap, mind it is not Victor St James."

Edith, my own, I have not forgotten our early love; farewell, my darling."

Edith gave a cry and ran after him.

Victor St. James held her to his heart, raised his mask, and kissed her gently.

The fair, beautiful girl, clung to him affectionately.

"You do not still spurn me from your side," said the handsome youth. "Edith, my adored! you cannot imagine the torture I have endured since we parted. And to-night," he said, with a strange look, "I felt half mad —I can't explain to you how I felt, when I saw you with that villainous cousin of mine. But there, dearest, we must part for the present, but not for ever, as you told me when we last met."

Again he kissed her.

"You reproach me," she said, tearfully.

"No, no, dearest, I do not; the fault was not yours; you were driven to it." St. James held her to him as though reluctant to part with her again. "You have been made a victim of base villainy, Edith. Do not despair; they shall not carry their infernal plot out. Adieu, darling, for the present. We must part now, for see, we are being observed. Do you believe me innocent?"

"I do! I did!" she cried.

One lingering caress, and, holding her tightly to his breast for a moment, he led her back to her father, and was gone.

Victor St. James was right. His friend was in danger, but not when he spoke.

Every minute that passed the countess became more fond of her companion. In every way she tried to make him understand her feelings towards him.

But no; he took no notice of her, or he was dull of comprehension.

At length the suspense grew torturing; the proud beauty could bear it no longer.

She felt as anxious to see his face as she was to tell him her love, and at last they made a compact to unmask.

"Behold, my mother," said the handsome young Greek, removing his mask; "behold your son, Countess, Lady of Aldervale."

The countess gave a piercing shriek of disappointment, and fell cowering back.

Tyburn Dick stepped towards her, and took her hand.

She recoiled as he touched her, and called for help.

How soon those bewitching smiles turned into bitter looks of hate—how soon those large blue eyes, that not five minutes before looked languid and spoke volumes of love, flashed fiercely—how soon her sweet melodious voice turned into a harsh, cruel shriek, and her soft words of love changed to pitiless words of condemnation!

"Help! help! help!" she shrieked; "help, everyone. I am robbed. Help, for mercy's sake! I shall be killed by a highwayman."

"No, no, mother of mine—cruel, unnatural mother that you are to me. You need not fear," said our hero, his voice choked by emotion; "I, your lawful son, have not come here to harm you, though I am an outcast, a robber, with a price upon my head. And whose fault is it?" His eyes flashed dangerously, and his voice rang out long and clear as he continued. "Your fault. I am the rightful heir to this domain and the surrounding estates. The cur whom you call son should be the outcast, and I the lord of Aldervale Manor. And so it shall be. Beware, beautiful demon, of me, your son."

The music ceased; the masqueraders broke up in wild confusion, and rushed eagerly forward to catch a glimpse of the gallant Boy Highwayman.

The fair ladies crowded in front, and kept back those of their companions who were eager to capture the handsome youth.

More than one pretty eye was dimmed with a tear at seeing their hero's danger, many beautiful breasts heaved with excitement, and many a gentle heart fluttered with fear.

The fair masqueraders shrieked and fell back, as Lord Edward suddenly broke through them.

"What's the meaning of this?" he demanded of his mother.

"Ah!" he exclaimed, meeting the fierce gaze of his enemy.

He drew his sword, cast a withering look at Dick, and struck the defenceless boy cruelly to the ground.

"Wretch!" exclaimed St. James, rushing to our hero's rescue; "you shall pay dearly for striking that cowardly blow."

He drew a pair of beautifully silver-chased pistols from under his cloak, and standing over Dick in a splendid attitude that brought murmurs of applaude from the cherry lips of the pretty bystanders, he extended them at arm's length, confronting the guilty mother and son.

The countess cowered back, and clung to her son for protection.

The crowd fell back, thus giving the Boy Prince room in case of need.

"Move one step forward—raise your voice to call for aid—or if I find you have hurt my comrade, I will blow your currish brains out, my Lord Edward. Put your sword back in its sheath," said Victor St. James, in a tone of resolution that showed he meant what he said. "Dick, old boy, get up if you are not hurt; but if you are, don't move until I can help you. Now, my lord," he said, turning to the young earl, "unless you—ah! coward, not yet."

Victor St. James caught the descending weapon as Lord Edward made a furious down cut at his head.

Our hero was not hurt by the cowardly blow he had received from his dastardly half-brother, though it had been aimed with savage intent.

"Stand back, Vic.," cried Dick.

St. James stepped back; but did not alter the line of pistols.

Dick sprang to his feet, and dashing at Lord Edward, he grasped him by the throat, and, with the strength of an angry tiger, swung him to the floor.

The countess shrieked the revellers fell back, then there was a rush made towards the daring boy.

"Stop him, Tyburn Dick; a thousand pounds for his capture; block up the doors and windows; don't let him escape."

Such were the cries raised by the gentlemen masqueraders as they gathered round the defenceless boy.

Dick glanced round savagely.

"Here, here," said St. James, breaking through the crowd to get at his companion's side; "take my pistols."

Dick took one.

"This will do," he said.

Eagerly he grasped the jewelled weapon,

and glancing round at his enemies, he defiantly cried, in a clear, musical voice—

"Stop me who can—take me who dare!"

One bound—a bound such as a wild Indian would take—he took through his opposers, scattering them on all sides, and he dashed down the hall.

There was a yell of defiance from many ough throats—a crash, and more yells of triumph. The casement flew open, and, as our hero reached the end of the hall, a body of servitors sprang through the window and confronted him.

"So, so, my daring highwayman, we have got you now; there is no escape for Tyburn Dick."

"Liar!" shouted the enraged boy.

"Stop, stop," shouted the men.

"Stop who can."

Then there came a report that rang through the hall, and struck terror to the hearts of all who heard it.

A cry of agony—the man rolled over—and Tyburn Dick sprang through the casement.

In a moment the gay assemblage flocked down the hall.

They saw the cause of the cry—one of the servitors lay dead at his companions' feet.

Then there was an angry shout, and a rush was made after the daring Boy King of the Highwaymen.

Many people tried to stop Victor St. James, as an accomplice of the highwayman, but he was too quick for them, and, breaking from his would-be captors, he leaped through the open casement into the garden, and followed in the track of Tyburn Dick.

"Ah!" he exclaimed, suddenly stopping and catching up something off the ground; "this is Dick's costume; he has thrown it off, then."

The young cavalier's suggestion was right; our hero had thrown off his disguise, for underneath he wore his own true dress.

St. James rolled up the dress, and again darted off to the rescue of his comrade. He could hear the angry voices of the pursuers in front. He well knew that the daring boy could not hold out long; but above all the angry voices rang through the clear night air that of Tyburn Dick, in bold defiance:

"TAKE ME WHO DARE!"

CHAPTER XLV.

TRACKED BY THE FOOTPRINTS IN THE SNOW—TYBURN DICK SEEKS REFUGE, AND IS WARNED BY THE DEATH WITCH.

THE dull chilly morn had now made its first appearance; the grey streaks broke through the fleecy clouds, and spread its glimmering light over the whitened earth.

The earth was carpeted with a thick layer of snow, that glistened as though it had bee sprinkled with diamond dust.

The country was wrapped in sombre quietude—not a soul was astir, and even the feathered little songsters appeared as though they had deserted the cheerless place.

Not a mark, save for one straight track, had broken the surface of the crystal carpet.

A track that lengthened as a handsome youth, flushed and excited, hurried through the lone country.

Anxiously he turned as he continued his course, and appeared as though listening for sounds of pursuit.

Yes, there is a sound—a clamour of voices that breaks the stillness of the waking morn.

The boy hears them—his handsome face grows clouded.

The clamour of voices grew louder.

A body of armed men are following the track of the footprints in the snow.

"I thought as much," exclaimed the youth; "they are following in my track. All will be lost unless I can throw them off the trail. But how? At every step I leave a mark. It must be done some how. Madness! I cannot sweep the snow in front of me, nor can I fill up the mark I leave behind. I would confront them, but I am weaponless—unarmed, and should be their prisoner. No, no, that would not do. Tyburn Dick, you must not give way to despair."

On he kept, his brain in a whirl of perplexity.

"No, no, it would not do for me to be taken," he said. "They are not far behind, but I don't think they will take me just yet."

His pursuers were not far behind.

He could see them from where he stood.

But they could not see him—our hero concealed himself behind the trunk of a huge tree.

Fatigue overcame him, and he sank to the earth exhausted.

Every moment brought his pursuers nearer—ere five minutes they must come up to where he lay helpless, and make him their prisoner.

With distracting brain our hero thought of his perilous position.

He knew he could not resist, should his enemies surround him before he gained sufficient strength to try to escape.

His strength was not likely to increase—it was fast deserting him.

A deep, heavy drawn sigh of anguish escaped his lips; the slightest hopes he had before entertained now vanished.

All possible idea of escape had now gone.

He lay half embedded in the bitter chilling snow, his thoughts now wandering to that beautiful demon-like woman from whom he had just escaped.

His mother.

He thought of the bitter wrongs he had endured at her hands—how she had bribed people to hunt him down—ah, and even kill him.

But he had escaped all her villany—all her plotting, and defied her hirelings.

His heart revolted at the remembrance of her baseness, and he tried to banish the thought.

His head drooped on his breast, his handsome face turned a deathful pale, and his lips quivered nervously.

Emotion had taken possession of his manly frame.

The loud hooting voices of his pursuers rang in shrill, grating, vibrating sounds, through the clear frosty air.

Dick raised his pale, haggard face—his benumbed hands wandered over his pallid brow.

His gaze he fixed on the tree beneath which he sat.

A thought, an idea, to break the track and escape rushed through his excited brain.

The suggestion gave him strength.

Another instant he had sprung to his feet, and climbed up the tree with the agility of a monkey.

From branch to branch he springs to each precedent tree.

Suddenly he stopped at the end of a huge branch.

"No, no," he murmured, "I cannot reach the next. I must try; if I fall I must stand my chance."

For a moment he crouched back, then breathlessly he took a daring leap.

His fingers clutch the next branch

For a minute he is swinging in the air, undecided whether to drop or try another effort.

He tries another effort.

He obtains a firmer hold of a branch above his head, then he continues his perilous flight.

Again he stops and looks behind him.

Distinctly he sees his pursuers.

They had halted beneath the tree where he had fallen. Terrible oaths and threats escape their polluted lips.

"I think I have outwitted my worthy friends this time," muttered our hero, a bright smile playing about his lips. "It won't do to stay here though. I think the other branch is a little out of my reach—I wish it would come nearer, but it won't."

He took a careful survey of his position

To reach the next tree was impossible.

Dick knew it. There was but one thing for him to do.

And that was to drop, and make good his escape.

Another moment he had dropped from the tree, and was flying over the earth with the swiftness of an antelope.

On—on he kept, never daring to look back until he reached the top of a hill, that gave him a very elevated position, and would probably reveal him to his pursuers, should they look in that direction.

For an instant he stood to recover breath, then he dived down the declivity, and dashed into the thickest of a cluster of brushwood.

Again he paused.

His pursuers were in hearing.

Day had by this time quite made its appearance, but the morning had come over thick and murky, and the light was barely strong enough to penetrate the thicket in which our hero was concealed.

Dick began to breathe more freely.

Hope gave him energy, and his strength seemed to return.

He began to beat about for a nook where he could lie in ambush without being seen should his pursuers suspect he was hiding there and make a search.

Dick stopped; he fancied he heard a croaking voice close by.

Yes; he was not mistaken, the same voice came distinctly upon his ears.

"Strange," he thought; "surely no human being can be living hereabouts."

He listened; the voice was repeated.

"The owner of that voice must be hidden in some secure spot," he muttered. "Surely could I discover his or her hiding-place they would give me shelter. Perhaps not; probably give me over to my bloodthirsty hunters. I must chance it—here goes,"

He groped his way in the direction from whence the sounds came.

Suddenly he stopped.

He found himself at the mouth of a cave.

A cave of solid stone, constructed solely by the hand of nature.

For a moment he stood enthralled, gazing on the interior.

It was a strange place.

A bright wood fire burned in one corner; from the roof hung, in fantastical shapes, congealed water; while the wall in some parts, where more exposed to the damp, was green with slime; and in other parts the solid stone was dry and crumbling with decay.

A strange place, indeed, it was.

No one knew its age.

Few persons ever sought the place, through a superstitious fear of it being haunted.

It had achieved the name of the Hermit's Cave, through the simple fact that the skeleton of a man had been discovered in it, who it was supposed had been the only occupant of the solitary place, and in his old age, in his solitude and desolation, he had died, and thus been left to decay in his lone habitation.

No one found courage to move the poor remains, until some men, who by chance passed that way, and seeing the decaying bones, dug a hole in the earth, and, with a tender reverence, put them in a place of rest.

They were not there long.

The spot was sought, and some officious hands removed them, and put them in the place where first discovered.

Our hero's eyes rested on the horrible object, and a cold shiver ran through his frame.

A skeleton! Yes, the skeleton that had been removed from the earth was stood in a corner of the cave, with its bony arms outstretched, and its grisly skull, with eyeless sockets and open mouth, grinning as though in mockery at Dick's fears.

"Horrible," muttered our hero, and he stepped into the cave.

A low mocking laugh rang from the further end.

"That's cheerful," said Dick, repressing a shudder.

He glanced round the cave in search of the owner of that mocking laugh.

Seeing no one, he seated himself on a stone at the entrance, and fell into a reverie.

"So, so, Tyburn Dick, you are here," said a voice.

Dick looked up.

"I am," he said; "I hope I am not intruding."

"Ha, ha, ha!" laughed the spectre-like form that confronted him. "No, no, Tyburn Dick, you can't intrude. Wherever you fly, danger will follow you."

"Nay, nay," remarked Dick, his cheeks paling, "don't talk so awfully vicious—say something more cheerful."

The Death Witch laughed again.

A low, deep growl came from a huge mastiff at her feet.

"No, no, Tyburn Dick; I can't say anything more cheerful to one that is doomed to the gallows. You are—your enemies are now on your track. They have discovered the footprints in the snow. Can you hear them? I can."

"I can't," said Dick.

"The dog raised its huge head, rolled its gleaming eyes at Dick, and growled viciously,

"Hist, hist!" croaked the old witch; "lie down, Demon."

The demon dog obeyed with a growl, and laid its huge head on its paws, close to Dick's feet.

Dick did not like the idea of having it so close to him, but not wishing to show any fear, he sat in a careless attitude, with his gold trimmed hat in his hand.

"List, Tyburn Dick," exclaimed the Death Witch.

Dick raised his head, and looked at her with a careless smile playing over his handsome face.

"I am all attention," he said.

The Death Witch raised the wand-like stick she held, and pointing to our hero with her long bony fingers, said—

"You are doomed! Doomed to death!"

"We all are."

"Mock me not! You know not the power I possess!"

"Indeed! Who are you?"

"I am the Death Witch. Listen."

"Go on"

"The lady you love, rash boy, will be your fate."

"I wish for no other. What better fate could a fellow have than the lady of his heart?"

"She will be your doom—your death—the torture of your life. You will endure nothing but misery by——"

"Say no more—say not so—no! no!" exclaimed Dick, springing from his seat. "No! no! it will not—cannot be so. The very idol of my heart—the only being for whom I live."

"Heed what I say. She will be your fate."

"Wretch! incarnate fiend!"

Dick sprang towards her.

For a moment he glared into her horrible eyes.

"Back!" she said.

Dick fell back.

"Say no more. Aid me to escape—my pursuers are close here."

The horrible creature took his small white hand in her own, and looked steadily at him.

Dick shrank at her touch.

"Do not shrink, Tyburn Dick," she said, "I do not wish to harm you. Where do you want to go?"

"Anywhere—I care not whither."

"Come, come then, I will aid you."

"Oh, thanks, a thousand thanks."

"Thank me not, I shall lead you to danger. Don't shrink from me, danger surrounds you whichever way you turn."

Dick felt bewildered.

"Will you aid me to escape from them?" he asked.

"I will, I will. They shall not take you— no, no! I had a son—I loved him. I love you, and will defend you with my life. Come!"

She led him to the further end of the cave. They were in total darkness.

Dick raised her thin wasted hand to his lips.

"Go, go!" she exclaimed, pushing him through a small opening in the stone wall.

Before he had time to say a word even to thank her, she closed the aperture with a huge stone that he found immoveable.

He was shut up alone, entombed alive.

Was he to stay there to linger out his life in close captivity, shut up from the world— to die, to rot, and his bones to be devoured by the horrible reptiles he heard scampering around his feet?

Had he been led into a snare—had the gush of affection been a scheme of treachery by the witch?

Such fearful thoughts rushed through his mind.

He heard a clamour of angry voices, a scream from the witch, a barking of the dog, and cries of pain from his pursuers.

Then he heard a terrible conflict.

He knew the witch and her dog, Demon, were battling with his pursuers.

His brain seemed in a whirl. A vision floated before his eyes—a vision of himself dangling from a gibbet.

A shriek escaped his lips, his hands clasped his side, and reeling round, he fell prone to the slimy earth.

His brow pallid, and a deathly clamminess oozing out of his handsome face, he lay stiff and quiet as in death.

CHAPTER LXVI.

THE ATTACK UPON THE HIGHWAY HAUNT— BULLSKIN'S PRESIDENCY—THE SCOUT'S INFORMATION—LORD EDWARD'S BRIBE FOR THE CAPTURE OF GRACE, AND HIS TRIUMPH.

WE will now take a glimpse into a dark cell of Newgate, where we see one of our favourite friends seated on a low wooden stool, with heavy manacles fastened round his hands and legs.

TYBURN DICK SEEKS REFUGE, AND IS WARNED OF HIS DANGER BY THE DEATH WITCH.

Devil Duke it is, who was captured by the two cunning thieftakers, and conveyed thither.

The highwayman was particularly quiet in captivity.

He knew it was no use to make a noise.

To escape he saw was entirely impossible, and, like all clever philosophers, he waited quietly for the turn of events.

Which turn, to all appearance at present, would condemn him to the gibbet.

The idea was not pleasant, and Duke tried to think of something else.

"I am in a pretty situation, certainly," he mused. "I wish these infernal irons were off me."

He made a jerk at the manacles.

The solid irons clashed together; the sound rang ominously on his ears.

"What a beastly sound!" he said. "I wonder where my comrades are now? Scattered about in different parts, no doubt; forgotten all about me. I wish I could see them."

The heavy tread of the gaoler made Duke start.

The gaoler put his bloated head into the highwayman's cell.

"Well, my pippin, how are you getting on?" he bawled out.

"Pretty well, thanks—how are you?" said Duke.

"Do you like your quarters?"

"Can't grumble. Will you come and share with me?"

"Ho, ho, ho,! I like that."

"Don't laugh," said Duke; "your voice is not at all musical. But, I say, old boy."

"What now?" growled the gaoler.

"Just unfasten these irons, there's a good fellow."

"He, he, he,! ain't that a likely tale? Do you see any green?"

"You won't do it?"

"'Taint likely. Do yer see any green?"

"Yes, blow you; you are as green as the very devil."

The gaoler vanished, and slammed the huge iron door.

"There's a spiteful devil," muttered the highwayman.

The door opened, and again the gaoler put in his burly head.

"I forgot to tell you something," he shouted.

"Don't shout," said Duke. "Is it anything good?"

"Yes. You are going to be tried the day after to-morrow, and two days after that you'll swing."

The burly head disappeared.

Duke was left to his own reflections.

"Tried in two days," he mused, "condemned if found innocent, and swing two days after the trial—mockery I mean. That's the way to do business. A cheerful prospect for me, certainly."

He swung his heavily-ironed legs about uneasily.

"I should like to know how my horse is. Ah, poor Rosebud, she is a faithful steed," he murmured; "shall I ever have the pleasure of another ride on her sleek back down a moonlight road? Perhaps not; the poor creature may have been shot before she could reach the haunt with the signal, and I am left to die alone."

He drew a heavy sigh, and looked round his dismal cell.

"None of my comrades can know of my danger," he continued; "if I thought they did, I might have hope; but no, they cannot. I must die without ever seeing any of them more, but not without a thought and a prayer. Farewell, friends—farewell, my bonny mare —we shall never meet again. Four days will soon expire, and then I shall die."

His head dropped on his breast, his thoughts wandered to his companions.

He had borne his captivity bravely, but now he began to despair—he saw no hope.

He knew not all—there *was* hope.

Gallant Tom had called at the Leopard Inn and learned the news of his comrade's danger.

He lost no time in riding back to the haunt.

Big Bullskin met him with a troubled look on his colossal features.

"Hawks in the wood," he said.

"Confound it, no!" exclaimed Gallant Tom.

"What's the matter?" asked the gigantic fellow. "You look troubled."

"Troubled! I am troubled, comrade. Duke is in prison, and unless we make all possible speed to London it will be too late."

The other understood his comrade's words —his brow clouded.

"The captain, where is he?" he asked.

"I know not," replied Gallant Tom.

"In danger, too, I suppose."

"Danger has come upon and surrounded us all at once. You say hawks are about?"

"Scouts are on the look-out; reinforcements will soon arrive."

"Then, comrade, we must fight for liberty."

"To the death," said Big Bullskin, and his hand wandered to the hilt of his double-handed broadsword.

"To the death!" echoed Tom.

They entered the large hall.

Big Bullskin took the principal seat at the head of the table, Swig sat on his right, the Lusher on his left.

Gallant Tom and Dashing Ralph sat at the end of the table facing them.

Bullskin was the first to speak.

"We will summon the scouts."

His comrades bowed assent.

Bullskin touched a silver bell.

The bell was answered—a masked man entered.

"North Scout Scott!" the giant highwayman said.

The man bowed and retired.

The bell tingled twice.

Bullskin answered the same number of times.

Another masked man appeared.

"North Scout Scott," he said.

"Right; what have you seen and heard?"

"A body of runners have just arrived, and Red Matthias is their leader. I heard nothing."

"That will do."

The man retired.

Again Big Bullskin sounded the bell.

Again it was answered, and the man who first entered now made his appearance.

"East Scout Jones."

The man bowed and retired.

Another entered.

"East Scout Jones," he said.

"What have you heard and seen?"

"Jonathan Wild and his bloodhounds are searching in every corner. I heard the thief-taker offer his men ten pounds each if Tyburn Dick, our captain, was captured."

He retired.

South Scout Montague was summoned, and entered.

"South Scout Montague," said the man.

Bullskin put the same question to him as he did to the others.

"A body of the King's Guard have been sent for; they are expected to arrive every minute. They are to scour the whole woods through until they ferret us out."

He retired to his respective post to watch the proceedings. His comrade West Scout was sent for examination.

"West Scout Brown," the man said.

"What have you heard and seen?"

"A body of footguards have arrived, and are making a search in earnest. The Lord of Aldervale Manor is here; he has offered a hundred pounds to any of his hirelings who capture our King's lady. He has a carriage and four with postilions waiting on the heath ready to carry her off."

"Go back to your post; watch carefully.

If you see anything particular come back and acquaint me."

"I will."

And the man went back to his post.

"Gentlemen," said Big Bullskin, "you have all heard the statements of the scouts, and, no doubt, can fully understand the perilous position in which we are placed. Our brethren must be summoned, a plan arranged for the defence of the haunt and the rescue of Duke—our comrade must be saved."

A low clapping of hands, and "Hear, hear!" in an undertone followed this speech.

"Caution, gentlemen," said the noble fellow, putting his hand up for silence; "the slightest noise might betray us."

A dead silence prevailed in an instant.

The highwayman touched a different bell to the one he had before used.

The chimes were repeated in the distance.

The same stillness prevailed until the sounds died away; then a heavy pair of hangings were drawn aside, and a score of handsome stalwart fellows entered.

Each wore the same kind of dress—gold and scarlet.

Each had a pair of pistols in his belt, and a long bright sword dangling at his side.

They were dressed and armed for a conflict.

One by one they passed round Bullskin in silence, and as they did so, each laid a strip of paper before him with his name and number written thereon.

So they passed round and took their seats.

Bullskin, the president of the proceedings, rose when they had all taken their places round the table.

"Gentlemen," he began, "our King being absent, I thought it fitting I should preside on such an emergency as the present, and arrange plans for the welfare of my comrades."

The highwaymen all raised their hands by way of silent approval.

Bullskin bowed and continued—

"The woods, as I daresay you already know, are crowded with our enemies; a siege will be made on the different entrances of the haunt, and an attempt will be made to capture us all. This must be obstructed. But, firstly, comrades, I have very bad news to tell you."

All eyes were directed anxiously towards the speaker.

"Devil Duke has been captured and taken to prison," he said, "and unless a speedy rescue is made, we shall lose a gallant comrade. I also fear that our young chief is in danger."

Just then there was a tingle of a bell.

"What the deuce do you mean, fellow?" said a voice.

"You can't enter just yet, my lord, till the bell is answered.

"Go to the deuce."

Bullskin answered the bell.

The next moment Victor St. James dashed into the hall.

He came to a sudden stand-still as his gaze met the strange scene, then he saluted the assemblage and approached Bullskin.

The highwayman grasped the young noble's hand warmly.

"You are excited, my lord," he said.

"Excited! by Jove, yes," said St. James. "I have had a devilish scrimmage, and a hard run. Have you seen anything of Tyburn Dick?"

"No," exclaimed Munroe, looking at the youth inquiringly. "Have you seen him?"

"I was with him at a masquerade."

"Yes,"

"He was discovered, and had to escape—a whole troop was after him.'

"Did they capture him?"

"I don't know; I was captured and prevented from following. I fear he is in danger."

Each and every one of the highwaymen's faces clouded on the instant.

They loved their young chief, and the very thought of him being exposed to danger sent a pang to their hearts.

"I feared as much," said the giant highwayman. "Let them look to it who harm a hair of his head."

The tone in which he spoke these few words and the angry brilliancy of his large orbs were sufficient meaning of his terrible anger.

"He shall be the first consideration," he said, "as soon as we can get rid of our enemies. Tom, you, with ten of your comrades, get to the north entrance, and you, Ralph, go to the south entrance."

The two captains rose, and each calling together his own division, marched to the place allotted.

"Swig," said Bullskin, "you keep a close look-out at the east entrance, and you, Jack Evans, do the same at the west entrance."

They, like their companions, went to their respective posts.

"Now," said the highwayman, turning to St. James, "you keep with me."

"I will," said the youth gladly, "and fight while I have strength."

"You are a brave fellow—Hallo! what the deuce is that? The fighting has commenced, you can now show your skill."

Bullskin drew forth his ponderous weapon as he spoke.

St. James had got his already.

Loud clamorous voices now rang through the air.

A volley of musketry was fired—another volley; then arose shrieks and groans mingled with cries of pain.

The highwaymen are fighting desperately against their overwhelming foes.

They cannot stand against them long—they are thrice their number.

The scouts are driven from their hiding-places at the point of the bayonet.

From all directions they dash madly into the hall.

"It's all up—we can't stand against them—we are all lost," shrieked the men.

Then there is a terrible yelling—a rush of feet—the highwaymen dash into the hall.

"The game is up," said Gallant Tom, despairingly; "we are all lost."

"No, no!" yelled Bullskin.

He took one leap and dashed in the midst of the invaders. His ponderous sword went to work and did fearful slaughter, but it could not last.

His giant strength was being fast overpowered

Dashing down all who stood before him, he sprung to the side of his comrades.

"Follow me!" he cried.

"Fire, fire! shoot him down!" yelled Wild.

A deadly volley was fired by the soldiers, but too late—the gallant band of highwaymen had vanished as though through the solid stone wall.

The bullets fell harmlessly against the revolving stone.

"Jonathan Wild, we will unearth the place; they shall not escape," said Red Matthias, the thief-taker.

"Yes, unearth the place. Set to work, men," said Wild.

The men set to work, and huge stones were being removed from different parts of the haunt.

A shriek—a piteous shriek for mercy—rang from a female throat.

Then a brutal-looking ruffian dashes through the haunt, with a beautiful girl swung over his shoulder.

"You are worth a hundred pounds to me," he said.

The man is met by Lord Edward, the girl is thrust into a carriage, and away they dash.

"You are mine again, dear Grace!" said the hateful boy.

CHAPTER LXVII.

THE SMUGGLER'S CAVE—THE TWO LISTENERS —TYBURN DICK FOLLOWS A FOE, AND OVERHEARS A PLOT.

WHEN Dick recovered from his insensibility his limbs were stiff and cold.

He knew not how long he had been lying in that loathsome place.

Quietness prevailed inside and out of his horrible tomb.

Everything had the stillness of the grave.

With difficulty he dragged himself to his feet, and leant against the slimy wall for support.

All the horrors of his last remembrance returned to his mind.

A thrill ran through his frame, and his blood in hot streams gushed through his veins.

The circulation of his blood roused the lethargy of his body, and put fresh energy into him.

"I cannot stay here to die—to rot—hidden from the world—shut away from the one I love. No, no! I cannot—I will not."

With this determined resolution our hero began to grope about.

He soon discovered that he was in a subterranean passage.

A sharp, bleak air gushed from some unseen opening, and bathed his heated temples.

How thankful he felt for those refreshing gushes. How his heart leaped with new life—with hope of escape, and once more standing on the pure heath with the clear blue heaven above him.

It was now he knew that the Death Witch had not proved treacherous.

He has come to a wider part of the underground passage, where a glimmer of light comes from three different directions.

There is a passage on either side of him, and one in front.

For a moment he stands undecided which direction to pursue.

A purer air blows down the passage before him.

He will continue the straight course.

On he goes. His legs are weak, but his heart is joyful with the hope of once more beholding the heavens, light, and liberty.

The further he goes the light grows more distinct.

It is the light from a glimmering lamp.

He hears boisterous voices and coarse laughter.

Dick pursues his way carefully.

His heart beats quicker than is its custom to do. He remembers the words of the witch—

"Wherever you turn danger awaits you."

Cautiously he crawls along on his hands and knees.

He is at the end of the subterranean passage.

Stealthily as a cat he crawls still further on. Then he stops, and gazes breathlessly upon a strange scene.

He is at the mouth of a cave.

A smuggler's cave, embedded far back in the bowels of the solid rocks of the Cornwall coast.

A gang of ill-looking seafaring men are lounging about in various attitudes.

Some seated on bales, others on casks, and any such rude furniture as the place afforded.

Amongst the rough-looking crew was an old grey-headed man, of a sorrowful cast of features.

"Cheer up, my hearty!" exclaimed a young burly fellow, smacking the old man rudely on the back. "Now, yer ain't going to show the white feather. What's the use of being down when yer are on yer beam-ends? It only once in a way. Come, cheer up, dad. We shall have a fine haul in soon."

"Oh, dear!" said the old man, sadly; "it is but little I shall want of it."

"No, no, mate, don't say that. Now yer know very well yer ain't agoing to kick the bucket just yet, Father Wayne."

"Wayne!" exclaimed our hero. And he sprang to his feet.

He tried to catch a glimpse of the old man's face.

He did. The grey-headed old fisherman raised his head to his sturdy young companion.

Then Dick caught sight of the pale, wan face.

"Yes, yes, it is he!" muttered Dick; "he has escaped from the murderous clutches of the law, and is now living with these men. Perhaps it is best that he should live here; they will look after him while he lives. No, no, he shall not stay with them—a man whom I respected and loved as my father to be living a life of crime and degradation. No, no, I say it, and it shall not be; he shall be removed to a place where he can live the remainder of his days in peace and quietness."

Dick's cogitations were disturbed by the entry of another gang of the seafaring gentlemen.

A loud clamour arose from the dirty-looking crew, and shouts of welcome were raised for their captain.

A huge fellow, encased in a tiger's skin, and very formidable-looking weapon dangling at his side.

"Glad to see yer back, cap'n," said one.

"We is—we are glad yer is back," shouted others.

"Did yer have a fair run?" asked another.

"A fair run," laughed the captain; "cuss it, no! I ran foul of two sharks."

"Ho, ho, ho!" laughed his companions; "you got it hot."

"No I didn't, lads."

"Showed 'em yer teeth, didn't yer, cap'n?" said one.

"No, I didn't shew 'em my teeth."

"Then what the blazes did you do?" said another.

"Why, turned my little craft round, and showed them her stern; then scudded away."

"And did you get clear off?" was the anxious query put to him.

"Clean as a shot," he answered.

The man who had accosted Dick's foster-father shouted at the top of his voice—

"Shiver my timbers! why, is it the cap'n?"

"Yes, lad, I am that individual."

A mutual greeting was passed between them; then the young smuggler put a number of questions to his captain.

"You say you ran across old monsieur?"

"Yes, I met the old lubber," answered the captain.

"Has he heard anything more about the pirate barque?"

"Well, yes; seeing as how he does a little business with 'em, and seeing as how he's an old sneak, why it don't take him long to find out anything he wants to know."

"Well," broke in the young smuggler, "if the sneaking old shark does business with 'em, does yer mean to say he'll betray 'em to us?"

"I should rather say he would," replied the captain: "'cos if he didn't, why he knows it wouldn't be good for him."

"Why?"

"Why!" repeated the captain. "Yer don't remember, does yer, there's a thousand pounds offered for him?"

"Yes, we knows that."

"And ain't we the only kiddies that knows he's the one that's wanted, seeing that when the revenue cutters were after him for overhauling that little craft that there's been so much row about——"

"What o' that?" asked a man who had just awoke from a drunken sleep."

"What of that! ho, ho, ho!" laughed the smuggler captain. "I guess if yer ain't all got heads as thick as a lot of blocks. Can't none of you remember when he run on to these here rocks?"

"Yes, yes," shouted the smugglers; "we remember the time, cap'n."

"Well, didn't we save him from the sharks, an' keep him here till the revenue officers had cleared out, an' left him a clear run?"

"Yes, yes, we remember that too."

"Well, that gives us a pull on him, 'cos

hey don't know who it was that overhauled their craft."

"How the devil can they offer a thousand pounds for his apprehension if they don't know who it was?" said one of the smugglers.

"I'll tell you," the captain said.

The smugglers were interested, and gathered in a group round their leader.

"Seeing as how I can't remember exactly what it says on them big bills as is stuck all over the place, I can't tell yer every word," the captain said; "but," continued he, "I know it is something about navigators, savage-haters, or something like that,"

The men burst out in a roar of laughter.

Dick did a quiet titter, and put his hands over his mouth.

The smuggler captain for a few minutes was lost in deep thought.

"Oh!" he exclaimed, with a start, "I re-member."

"Let's have it, then, cap'n."

The captain began.

"I can't remember all, but it ran somehow like this—whosumever shall give such infor-mation as will lead to the conviction of the perpetrators of an unlawful and bloodthirsty deed, committed on the high seas between the 15th and 16th of August will receive the above reward, which is a thousand pounds," said the captain in conclusion.

"Hear, hear, hear! bravo, cap'n, that's fine," shouted the lawless band.

"Ain't there no more?" asked the young smuggler. "I'm blowed, cap'n if yer aint a good spokesman."

The captain felt flattered and laughed.

"There is a lot more, but I forget it," he said. "It tells yer what ship it was, and whereabouts, and all the rest."

"Which we know," broke in one of the men.

"Exactly so," replied the captain. "Now don't yer see, mates, how it is we have the pull on him?"

"Yes, in course we does. Shiver my top-lights, I see how the lubber stands."

"Douse my top-lights if I can understand how he's going to betray the pirate to us, if he does a little trading with him."

"You don't?" said the captain; "well you must be a lot of blockheads."

"Cuss me if I understand yet," said the young smuggler. "Perhaps, cap'n, you'll tell us."

"Well, lads, I'll do that. The Frenchman and Felix—that's the pirate chief—has had a fall out, and old monsieur has sworn to have revenge, and so is going to betray him to us, and share half the cargo."

The speaker put his finger aside of his nose, and made a peculiar grimace.

"The cargo the pirate carries is a valuable one," the captain continued; "and finding the other side of the Channel getting too full of sharks who follow him, he is coming over here."

"We'll receive him," said one of the smugglers.

"We will—his cargo," put in another.

"When is he expected to arrive?" asked the young smuggler.

"In three days from this," replied the captain.

"*Three days!*" said a low voice.

The captain turned sharply.

The men grasped their weapons—they also heard the voice.

"A spy!" said the captain.

"Death to him—death to a spy!" exclaimed the men.

Another moment the weather-beaten crew were searching in every corner for the spy.

Our hero felt anything but comfortable in his critical position. He heard their angry exclamations, and retreated in a dark recess as they sprang up and searched for the listener.

More than one passed uncomfortably close to where he stood, but the darkness was im-penetrable, and Dick remained unseen.

The smugglers gave up the search, and re-sumed their former positions.

"Ha, ha! cap'n, what a stir about nothing," exclaimed one. "Why, arter all, it must a-been the heco of yer own sweet voice."

"I suppose it must have been," the cap-tain said.

"You suppose wrong, my friend," mut-tered our hero, creeping from his hiding-place; "the echo was not of your own voice."

Dick's eyes wandered across the cav and rested on a motionless form crouched down low between two large stones.

The echo had come from there.

Dick watched the crouched form with a look of the bitterest hate.

The smuggler chief spoke again.

"If the weather continues as rough as it is now," he said, "our work will be easy. The beacon must be put on the east side of the Wreckers' Gully to make sure of our prize. The captain of the pirate barque is an artful cove."

"Right, right, cap'n; we know. Yes, yes."

"The Wreckers' Gully!" said the young smuggler.

"The Wreckers' Gully, Dan; that's the place to make sure of a prize. What's the matter with you?"

Dan had turned pale, and a strong light kindled in his eyes.

"The Wreckers' Gully. I remember the place," he said, shivering palpably.

"Well, what of it?" asked the captain.

"It ain't been used lately."

"We all know that. What the devil are you driving at?"

"The last time it was used I remember having a struggle with a brave little fellow for the light."

"Well, what of it?"

"I was very fond of that little fellow, only at the time he made me wild, and I chucked him into the water."

His voice grew thick and husky, and his eyes were dimmed by a moisture rarely seen on any of his companions' cheeks.

"Tarnation furies!" shouted the captain; "what the devil is the matter with the lubber?"

"Nothing, cap'n," said Dan, brushing the tears away; "only, when I thinks of him, I can't help——"

A dirty kerchief was put to his eyes.

"Can't help! A pretty lubber you are! Who was he?"

"I haven't seen him since that night; he was one of the prettiest and bravest little fellows I ever knowed."

"Who was he?" asked the captain again.

"Dick Wayne."

"Dick Wayne, my foster son!" cried the old man, who had been sitting apart from his companions, but now jumped up excitedly.

"Young Dick Wayne?" echoed the rest.

"Yes," replied Dan; "I wish my cussed hand had fell off before it pushed him over the rocks!"

"No, no, don't say that," cried the old man; "he is not dead."

"Not dead!" exclaimed the young fellow, springing up, and grasping the old man by the arm; "how know you this? Have you seen him? Does he still live? Tell me—do tell me!"

"He lives," replied the old man.

"You say so—he still lives! What has become of him?" Why has he left us?"

The old smuggler covered his face, and groaned aloud.

The swarthy gang were startled by a stone falling in their midst.

Dan sprang forward, and picked it off the ground.

None saw from what direction it came. It fell as though from the rugged roof.

"Here, here! Look mates!" shouted the young smuggler, excitedly.

All eyes were turned towards him.

Dan held a piece of paper between his fingers.

"This—this," he cried, "was wrapped round the stone."

"Well, what of it?" inquired the captain.

"Read it, read it!"

The captain put his hand out to take it, but Dan snatched it from him.

"No, no!" he cried, "no one shall have it —it is mine."

"Keep it," the captain said.

"Read it out, mate," yelled the smugglers.

"There, there,"—he held the paper out— "read for yourselves."

The men read a few words hurriedly written in pencil. They ran thus:—

"Dick Wayne still lives. He is not far off. You will see him soon, not as Dick Wayne, but "TYBURN DICK."

When these were read out the crouching figure that our hero was watching moved about uneasily.

The smugglers were so bewildered by this sudden appearance of the strange epistle, that for a few minutes they all stood in profound quietness, gazing vacantly at one another.

The crouching figure cast a glance around the cave: in another moment it stealthily crept out, and passed our hero like a flash of lightning.

The loud ringing voice of the smuggler captain broke the death-like silence and startled his followers.

"If you stand there gaping," he said, "you'll fall down one another's throats. Rouse yourselves, you lubbers, and look for the spy."

"No, no, captain, he is no spy. I implore you not to hurt him," entreated old Wayne; "take pity on an old man's grey hairs—as my son, my foster son, pray don't hurt him, captain."

"Peace, old man; no one's going to hurt him," said the captain.

The old man threw himself on his knees before the captain and clasped his hands.

"Oh, thanks, thanks! I know—I know you are a kind, generous fellow. Take the gratitude of an old man; a thousand thanks —ay, more than a thousand times thanks— for your kindness.

The supplicating entreates of the old man went to the smuggler captain's heart; and, taking Wayne's hand, he raised him from the ground.

"There, there, Father Wayne—peace, peace. No one shall hurt him. We only want to look at the young land-lubber."

"Where is he?" asked Dan.

"Lying to somewhere about the cave. Get torches, my lads, and make a good search for the young lubber. Highwayman, indeed, I think h   better been a smuggler!"

In another minute torches were kindled and the rough crew were searching for Tyburn Dick.

But he had gone.

The boy had followed the flying figure that passed him—an enemy—an enemy indeed, being no less a person than the captain of the Black Band.

Dick recognised him at once, and, with the quiet stealth of a cat, he followed to discover the object his enemy had for being at the smugglers' cave.

Captain Bertrand never once turned to look behind. On he kept, flying like the guilty wretch he was through the long dingy passages until he came to a door.

Then, and only then, did he venture to look behind, but he saw not the stealthy follower.

Dick had hidden in a dark recess.

Captain Bertrand passed out into the cool sweet air.

Dick crept forth and followed him.

"If I have to follow you to your accursed den of tigers, I will discover the motive you had for being at the smugglers' cave," muttered our hero, keeping within fifty yards of his foe through grove and field.

The noble boy had a kindred feeling for the people with whom he had been brought up, and resolved to defend them against any danger to his last comrade.

Presently Captain Bertrand stopped before an old ruined chapel.

Dick came to a sudden halt, and watched every movement of his enemy.

Captain Bertrand entered the ruined edifice.

His stealthy follower crept along beneath the shade of the huge trees that grew in abundance in that part of the country in which they were, and, crawling along on his hands and knees, he watched the chief of the Black Brethren raise a large flagstone from the floor of the chapel and descend.

Then Dick crept in.

The stone was replaced.

"Another entrance," mused Tyburn Dick. "My friend should be more careful to see before he enters that there are no eyes watching him. I think my presence will rather surprise him."

He laid his ear to the floor and held his breath, while he listened to the dying footsteps beneath.

"Here goes," said our hero, "to enter the tiger's den unarmed."

He carefully raised the stone and descended as the captain of the Black Band had done.

The dull sound of the heavy piece of masonry, as it fell into its place, sent an involuntary chill through our hero.

He had descended into a kind of vault by a few slimy stone steps, but in doing so fell, and grazed the skin off his spine-bone.

He was now in intense darkness: the air was thick and murky. Not a breath—not a sound could he hear.

Again it seemed as though he was buried alive.

He escaped from one danger to fall into another more terrible.

The warning of the Death Witch rang plainly on his ears, and he began to fancy there was some truth in it.

"Tyburn Dick—Tyburn Dick!" he muttered, with a shrug of his shoulders, "you must not ponder over the perfidious croaking of an old woman. No, no; there must be some way of exit from this cheerless place, and you must find it."

He brushed his long curly hair from his temples, and then groped his way in the direction he fancied had been taken by his mortal enemy.

He was not mistaken.

A bright flood of light broke through the darkness.

Dick paused. He heard voices. He recognised one as the captain's, and listened.

"In three days from this," said the voice. "The cargo is one of immense value, and if we succeed in taking it from the smugglers, it will afford us to live in luxury. I shall require the whole of our band, well armed, for I fancy we shall have an interruption."

"What do yer mean, captain?" asked another voice.

"While I stood there listening," resumed the captain, "a piece of paper was thrown in the midst of the men, and one of the smugglers read the following words written in pencil—'Dick Wayne is near; you will see him again, not as Dick Wayne, but Tyburn Dick.'"

"Was he there?" exclaimed a chorus of voices.

"Yes, and he is here!" thundered a voice, and our hero sprang into their midst.

In an instant there was a tremendous uproar, and Tyburn Dick was surrounded by a band of deadly foes.

CHAPTER XLVIII.

RESCUED FROM THE GALLOWS—A FIGHT AT TYBURN TREE—DEVIL DUKE'S STRANGE ADVENTURE.

THE law was again baffled by the highwaymen.

Jonathan Wild gazed round the hall with the look of a fiend.

At every attempt—at every point he was defeated.

Soldiers and police officers had worked with an untiring will to discover the secret retreat of the gallant knights of the road.

Huge stones were raised from the floor, and the earth removed, but no signs of any underground passage was discovered.

Then they worked away at the solid masonry walls. Not twenty times their power could have moved the revolving stone through which the highwaymen beat a retreat.

At last their attempts were given up as fruitless, and the invaders dispersed.

The haunt in itself was not a very secure place; but the vaults beneath were strong holds, and defied the strongest power to discover them.

Victor St. James was awfully astonished at being so suddenly dragged from the terrible battle in which he was an active member, and being shut up in total darkness.

The others were not astonished; they were well acquainted with the vicinity in which they were, and felt quite at ease.

They told him so.

Victor St. James said he did not, and wanted an explanation, which Swig gave him.

Truly it was a strange place in which they stood—a place such as may yet exist in some undiscovered part of the world—a place that caused the mind to wonder how even the hand of Nature could construct it.

St. James gazed around him, enraptured by its strange, picturesque beauty.

"Strange and beautiful," he mused; "such a place as a fellow very seldoms dreams of, though fellows have strange dreams sometimes. By Jove! I remember a strange dream one night. Ugh! I shudder to think of the horrible two-headed brutes that hunted me through the most fairy-like land into the very depths of Hades, and then, when I was getting warm, the scene changed into a splendid silvery lake, in which I found myself swimming in a most indelicate state of nature, surrounded by a group of beautiful mermaids.

The voice of Big Bullskin broke his reverie, and he joined his companions.

To enlighten the reader's mind, we will give

an outline description of the highwaymen's underground secret haunt.

When they disappeared through the revolving stone, they were in a dark, narrow passage, t the end of which was a kind of spiral descent ! rugged rock, which led to the cave in which iey were now gathered.

The cave was of tremendous dimensions, and embedded a fearful depth in the bowels of the earth.

A clear, silvery stream flowed through the rocks on one side, and, making its way through the rugged flooring, sank into a well or kind of reservoir that never seemed to fill above one certain height; and in other parts of the cave a wild herbage grew, that was infested with a varied descripiton of horrible little reptiles.

It is evident they thought they had more right to the place than the highwaymen, for, as soon as any of our friends made their appearance, the little creatures crept forth, and began to hiss in a most dissatisfactory manner.

"I think," said Bullskin, "our enemies have wisely retired; and, such being the case, we will make a move."

"What do you propose to do first?" asked Gallant Tom.

"That we divide into two companies," replied the gigantic fellow; "you, Ralph, and Evans, with ten of our brethren, had better start for London and rescue Duke."

Joseph Munroe then turned to St. James.

"You," he said, "will accompany me."

"With pleasure," answered the young nobleman.

"And you, Swig, with ten more of our brethren, will accompany me to go in search of our young chief."

The idea was readily agreed to by one and all.

Then the party emerged from the cave into another strange recess, where the horses were kept, and in a few minutes the whole band were mounted, and, dividing into two companies, rode away in different directions.

.   .   .   .   .   .

It was now Monday morning! A day that had been dreaded as it grew nearer—a day that would see the last of many a poor fellow who had been cruelly sentenced to death for a petty crime by the stern old judge.

Devil Duke was amongst the condemned.

The morning was wet, and a bleak wind whistled through the narrow streets of London, blowing roofs and numerous chimney-pots off the dilapidated old houses, and dealing destruction to the decaying city.

Thousands of miserably clad poor people were gathered round the dingy building of Newgate, shivering with the bitter cold.

Shouts and yells rent the air at intervals from the living mass as any official passed to or from the ponderous gates.

What a terrible pang of horror each shout sent to the hearts of the poor fellows within those huge walls! To know, to think that thousands of their fellow-creatures were anxiously waiting to see them dragged forth like so many dogs, and led to execution.

Had they not human hearts? Could they not feel the least remorse for the sufferings of others? Why were they allowed to collect there to hoot, to shout, and join in dissipated revelry, as though mocking the coming fate of the doomed?

Such were the *laws* of the time.

Devil Duke felt his situation keenly.

Bravely he had borne his troubles to the last, and even now, when brought from his dingy cell with three other prisoners, heavily manacled, and put in a cart to be conveyed to Tyburn Tree, he did not despair.

No, not then; although the cart was guarded by a body of soldiers and police officers.

There was no hope of escape—no, none.

The multitude of people that followed the cart to Tyburn increased treble in number as the prisoners neared the fatal spot.

The uproar was terrible when the cart stopped beneath the dreaded tree. Madly the mass pressed forward, and more than once it was thought a rescue would be made.

The dragoons were forced to charge amongst the people to keep them from the prisoners.

Then the scene rose to a fearful pitch of excitement.

To be driven and scoured about by the red-coats aroused the anger of the rough populace. Suddenly and with conformity the whole multitude attacked their opponents.

There were terrible shouts of pain, mingled with screams of fear, and an awful battle was being enacted.

Suddenly there came a fearful shrieking as a fresh detachment of soldiers came to the rescue of their comrades, who were being beaten from their ground.

The came only in time.

A few minutes later the people would have had their way, and the prisoners would have been rescued.

Then the officers charged, the populace were driven back, the soldiers guarded Tyburn Tree, the execution was to take place without a moment's delay.

The executioner appeared.

A savage brutal-looking man, with a shaggy bull-dog head, and a face of such satanic malignity that many people shrank back in terror at the very sight of him.

He seemed to gloat with pleasure over the job he had to do. Brutally he pulled the caps over the men's faces, and, slipping the nooses over their heads, he clutched hold of Duke by the shoulder, and drew him nearer.

His hand was raised above the highwayman's head, with the noose ready to drop over him, when a loud thrilling voice rang through the air, and made every one start.

"Hold!" thundered the voice, in its clear ringing tones.

Every one looked in the direction from whence the voice came.

Mounted on a powerful black steed was a majestic figure.

The malignant face of the hangman looked demoniac and horrible.

He turned to a man who stood by his side.

"I know'd there'd be something of this," he said; "don't you think we had better settle him at once?"

"Ah, ah, to be sure," answered the other; "bid Robinson withdraw the cart directly. Move quickly."

"Hold!" shouted the advancing horseman. "Put your hand near the reins, and I will blow your brains out!"

There was a pause for a few minutes, then the people broke out in a ringing cheer, welcoming the new comer.

"Cuss me if I am going to be cheated," exclaimed the hangman, and with a sudden twitch that nearly strangled Devil Duke, he tightened the noose round his neck.

"There was a report of a pistol, a puff of smoke, and the hangman fell to the earth with a shattered skull.

"He won't scrag another," said one of the bystanders, quaintly.

The remark caused a general laugh.

The horseman dashed through the crowd. He blew a shrill note on a whistle.

It was answered in the distance; then he fought his way to the gallows, and, clasping Duke round the waist, he cut him down.

At that moment the cart was pulled away, and three other men were left dangling in the air; then the soldiers, who were so astonished by the appearance of the daring intruder, made a dash forward to secure their prisoner.

"Back! Back!" thundered the highwayman, who held Devil Duke under his left arm. "Back! The first that dares to bar my path will fall!"

There was a terrible look in his burning orbs as he spoke. His sword made a circle in the air, then came down with terrible force on the heads of those who opposed him.

"Save the others! Yes, yes; save the others!" shouted the people.

"They shall be saved," said the highwayman, in answer to the appeal of the populace.

As he spoke a dozen more handsome looking fellows dashed up to the scene.

"Ralph, Ralph, old boy, is that Duke you have got?" shouted a handsome fellow, with form slim and elegant.

"Yes," said the highwayman, in a faint voice under the cap.

"Tom! Tom!" shouted Ralph, "our comrade speaks."

"Take this cap off my head," said Duke.

In an instant Dashing Ralph tore the ominous black cap from his comrade's head, and looked affectionately into his handsome but haggard face.

While this was being done, the three men were rescued from an awful death of strangulation by the highwaymen.

Another fight broke out.

Devil Duke was not much hurt, and a draught of brandy revived his shaken nerves.

"HOLD! COWARD!" THUNDERED A VOICE AS THE CASEMENT DASHED OPEN.

His gallant comrades brought with them his faithful steed, Rosebud.

Duke soon bestrode her glossy back, and arming himself with a pair of finely finished pistols and a trusty sword, he felt safe.

Gallant Tom administered a draught of brandy to each of the poor fellows his comrades saved from the gallows, and escorted them out of danger.

"Now, Duke, old boy," he said, turning to his comrade, "having the pleasure of once more seeing you free, we will off and away while we are safe."

As though in answer to his words there was a shout, and a regiment of the King's Light Guards came thundering towards them.

"Come, come, comrades," shouted Gallant Tom; "we have no chance against these fellows. Our only chance for liberty is flight."

Another moment, a defiant cheer rang from the merry throats of the dashing knights of the road, as they galloped away as the King's

20

Light Guards came thundering towards them.

The soldiers did not halt; on they kept, after the daring fellows.

The chase was getting warm.

"We had better disperse," suggested Gallant Tom; "it will be the only way to throw our pursuers off the scent."

"We will meet again at the haunt," said Dashing Ralph, lifting his hat to his brethren. "*Au revoir*, comrades."

"Bye, bye!"

"Farewell!"

"We meet again at the haunt. *Au revoir!*"

And with such friendly partings to one another they dispersed singly, and took different routes.

This manœuvre brought the Light Guards to a standstill. It was some time before the officer in command knew what course to pursue, but finally he broke up his company, and sent them after the highwaymen.

One of the fellows stuck to Duke like a leech, and never lost sight of him for miles.

Duke did not want his company.

"By the lord Harry, how the fellow sticks to me!" muttered the highwayman. "If I stop he's sure to come bang against me, and then we shall get entangled, and perhaps I shouldn't be able to untangle myself. I won't stop. Away, Rosie—away, my lass!"

Away she went, soon leaving the Light Guard far behind.

"Hi—hi—you highwayman fellow! Stay, or I fire!" shouted the soldier.

"You may fire, and be blowed," laughed Duke.

He dived round a narrow turning.

The soldier dived after him.

That's what Duke wanted. He was waiting for him. He clutched the soldier by the throat as he whirled round the corner, and swung him from his saddle; then the highman galloped away again.

He turned several times while flying down the Kensington Road, but saw nothing of his pursuer.

"I think," mused Duke, going along at a more moderate pace, "that fall has stopped that gentleman's gallop—ah!"

Duke halted beneath the window of a pretty villa.

A female voice rang out from the window above in piteous tones.

"A lady in trouble! by the Lord Harry. Duke, old boy," said the highwayman to himself, "there is a lady in that house in danger, and a true knight of the road never passes a place where he knows or fancies a lady is in danger. You must not."

The voice in supplicating accents sounded more plainly in the still night air to the highwayman's attentive listening ear.

"If I haven't heard that voice before," he said, "I haven't been in the dirty cells of Newgate. I must discover what's the matter. Quite a romantic adventure for my first night's sport, after so long an absence from the road. But to reach that window. Come here, Rosie."

Duke had dismounted. Rosie went and stood beneath the window.

There came another cry—one more painful than the others. A coarse brutal laugh answered it.

Duke's handsome face flushed angrily. Another moment he was standing erect in the saddle. He saw such a scene being enacted in the chamber that made his blood course through his veins like liquid fire, and his hand wandered to the hilt of his sword.

A savage, ruffianly fellow, whom Duke recognised at a glance as an old enemy—Savage Steve—was struggling desperately with a pretty little dark-eyed lady, whom Duke also recognised as the mercer's wife.

The dark-eyed little lady fought bravely to protect her honour against her low ruffianly assailant.

Her delicate strength was no match for the brute power of her persecutor. He forced her back.

She fell upon her knees, and again tried to rise to her feet, but the brutal villain held her firmly.

There was a glow of lustful fire gleaming in his savage eyes; he looked at her gloatingly.

Another moment and he would have triumphed.

His brutal hand grasped her rudely. He was forcing her to the floor. The base purpose he intended to carry out could be seen by the glow on his swarthy features.

The mercer's wife gave herself up for lost. Her assailant exclaimed with savage glee—

" You are mine."

" Hold, coward!" thundered a voice as the window was dashed open.

Savage Steve sprang to his feet as though suddenly struck by a thunderbolt. The mercer's wife fell senseless to the floor, and Duke, with the strength of a young lion, grasped his enemy round the waist, and hurled him out of the window; then turning to the lady, he took her up in his powerful arms, and descending from the window to the back of Rosie, he galloped away with his fair charge.

CHAPTER XLIX.

TYBURN DICK STOPS THE CORNWALL MAIL—
APPEARANCE OF A SECOND TYBURN DICK.

THE night was peaceful and quiet.

The bright silvery moon and the pale glimmer of the twinkling stars threw down their radiant glare over the whitened country, and revealed a body of masked horsemen riding along the hard frosty road.

A majestic-looking personage rode in advance of the others, mounted on a splendid black charger.

His noble brow was clouded. Some heavy trouble was upon his mind that touched him deeply.

He had fallen into a deep reverie. His colossal features wore a sombre expression. The reins fell from his hand, and he noticed not the conversation of his companions.

His horse sniffed and snorted as it went along. The faithful creature had got the responsibility of discovering a trail of which her master's followers wanted to reach the end.

" Mr. Munroe," said a musical, boyish voice," do you hear the sound of an approaching horse?"

" I do not," said the leader of the party, starting from his reverie. " Ay, now I do; halt!"

The party came to a halt.

Distinctly the clatter of horses' feet came upon the air.

A horseman flying along at a maddening pace came dashing up.

He drew in rein on beholding the party in the road.

" Godfrey," exclaimed Big Bullskin, for it was he who was the leader of our other friends.

" Yes, sir," gasped the man, completely out of breath through the hard ride.

He was one of the spies belonging to the highway band of Tyburn Dick.

" What news?" asked Munroe.

" There's bad, I fear."

" Tell me, have you seen anything of our young chief?"

" Yes, yes, I have."

" Explain quickly."

" I saw our prince on foot, following the captain of the Black Band!"

" Well, yes. Did you see where he went?"

" Yes, yes, I did. He followed him into the ruined chapel; and if ever he gets out alive, why, he'll be able to do anything."

Munroe's face darkened.

" Should they have injured a hair of his head," he said, " not one of their cursed band shall live another hour."

He turned to the spy.

" Do you know anything of this ruined chapel?"

" Yes; I watched the captain follow Bertrand down a stone trap, which I fancy leads to their haunt."

" That will do. Lead the way to the ruined chapel."

Godfrey led the way.

A half an hour's ride brought them to the ruined chapel.

" You," said Bullskin, turning to the man, " will look after our horses."

The man bowed.

The party dismounted.

The huge stone was raised from the sacred floor, and the little band descended the same way as our hero.

Angry voices were heard.

" We are only in time," said Bullskin.

" By Jove! what a noisy lot of brutes! This is a cheerful den for a fellow to fall into, certainly."

" Hush."

" Won't I give the first fellow an awful dig that comes within reach of my sword, that's all!"

" Thank you," said Munroe. " Listen!"

They listened, and heard the following words—

"No mercy for our enemies."

"No, no! no mercy for Tyburn Dick! Kill him! kill him!"

"Try it, my friends," Bullskin heard his young chief say.

There was a rush, a cry from our hero, a report of a pistol, and a yell of agony from some rusty throat.

Big Bullskin drew his ponderous weapon, and waving his hand for his comrades to follow, he dashed forward.

The gigantic fellow swept one searching glance round for his beloved young chief.

He saw him struggling with two masked men. He held a pistol in his hand; the coiling smoke still hung about the tube, that denoted it had not long since been fired. A few paces from him lay one of his enemies, dead.

Dick had sent a bullet crashing through his skull.

"Stop your foul work!"

The angry voice of the speaker sent a quiver through every one of the guilty wretches.

Dick looked up.

A cry of hope and joy escaped his lips.

Suddenly endowed with a strength he did not before possess, he dashed his opponents aside and ran to the side of his huge comrade.

For a moment Bullskin pressed the youth in his arms.

"There, there," he said, kindly, "we must now make these gentlemen apologise for their rash conduct."

"What!" shouted Captain Bertrand, "would you defy my power?"

"Ay, twenty times the power of such worthless curs."

"At the point of the sword you shall answer for the insult."

"Readily," replied Bullskin, with an angry flash of his eyes.

"Guard!" shouted the other, and he made a straight lunge for the highwayman's breast.

"Nay, I would not soil my blade with such carrion blood as yours. This is how I serve such foes as you."

The powerful fellow clutched Captain Bertrand by the throat, and lifting him from the ground, hurled him amongst his followers.

The fall did not hurt him—he was insensible to any feeling.

In an instant he was upon his feet.

"Forward, comrades," he shouted, frantic with rage. "Secure every one of the enemy Hack them to pieces, pommel their bones to dust, scatter it to the wind, and leave not a trace to show that such scum ever existed."

Bullskin stood quiet, but not calm; he felt as though he would like to throttle his foe where he stood.

Dick was so amazed that he was rendered quite powerless.

St. James was not idle; he felt the necessity of getting as many as possible out of the way, so, singling out a man, he picked a quarrel with him, and commenced a duel.

"Forward!" shrieked the captain. "Again would you see this place invaded, and your brethren killed by our enemies, and then let them escape? No, I say it shall not be so and if you are all such cowards to be frightened of less than half the number of yourselves, I will blow the place up, with you in it."

"Including yourself, eh?" inquired Swig.

Captain Bertrand ground his teeth.

"For what purpose was our brotherhood organised, if this is the way our enemies are allowed to come and go?" said the Black Band captain.

"None of us said we intended that they should go," exclaimed one of the men, "only give us time, captain, to get our arms."

Tyburn Dick and Big Bullskin waited patiently. They expected a sudden outbreak.

They had it.

Not more than two minutes elapsed after the man spoke to his captain, than shoals of men crept forth from secret doors and crevices in the wall, and commenced a fearful attack upon our hero's small band.

"That's the game, is it?" exclaimed the angry boy. "Cowardly, sneaking wretches, we fight now to the last man."

Captain Bertrand laughed to scorn his words.

"Have you counted your men?" said Bullskin, wielding his ponderous weapon above his head.

"That is needless. You'll have none to count soon."

"We shall see," exclaimed our hero, dashing two to the floor who stood near him. "There's two to commence with."

This roused the Black Brethren.

The struggle commenced in earnest.

It was one of blood and excitement while it lasted.

Big Bullskin went to work. The men fell like so many sticks beneath the heavy blows he dealt.

St. James was actively engaged. He rendered invaluable services.

Our hero was attacked by the greatest number of the enemies. He wrenched a sword away from one of his opponents, and then fought nobly.

The Black Band were losing men fast. The captain cast such a look around as a beaten tiger would, and then crept away.

He blew a shrill whistle. The men ceased fighting on the instant, and disappeared.

Tyburn Dick and his band were left alone.

"Come, captain," said Bullskin, "we will leave here now they have retreated. We have conquered. There is some devilish treachery at work, I feel sure."

"Lead the way," said Dick. "How many men have we lost?"

"Two, and Swig's wounded."

"They have lost enough, anyhow," said Dick, looking at the dead and wounded bodies of his foes. "Comrades, bring our brethren with you."

The men obeyed.

Bullskin took charge of his brave little companion, who had been wounded while defending our hero from a cowardly thrust.

They emerged safely into the open air.

Dick mounted Swig's horse.

"I shall be at the haunt soon," he said, turning to Bullskin. "Look well after Swig's hurt, and keep your comrades together. Adieu!"

He rode away. Munroe was left in bewilderment.

"By Jove!" exclaimed St. James. "A fellow ain't got time to say a word to him before he's off."

"He," said Bullskin, with a sombre smile —"he don't say much when he's got anything on hand, as I suspect he has at present,

but he will return to the haunt shortly, and then we shall have an opportunity to speak with him."

With the pleasant anticipation of seeing their beloved young leader, they returned to the haunt.

Both the beautiful girls were gone. A thorough search was made to discover their whereabouts, but to no avail.

Whither was our hero going at such a rapid rate, at such a time of night, and in such a place?

Riding through an open expanse of country, with nothing but huge leafless trees standing erect, and towering one above the other.

"I even now hear it approaching," muttered Dick. "I must reach Graystone Common before it passes, or I shall lose the booty I have so long been waiting for."

Digging his heels into the sides of his horse, he reached the common as the clear shrill notes of a bugle rang through the still night air. It was the guard's signal that the coach was nearing the town.

"If that be not the Cornwall Mail I am much mistaken," mused our hero. "Yes, yes; I am right. It comes! It comes!"

At that moment the mail emerged from a triangular into a cross road that cut through the common.

Dick touched the neck of his horse gently; the sagacious animal bounded forward, and stood beneath the shadow of a cluster of trees.

The coach came dashing onwards. The horses were almost hidden by the steam from their reeking hides.

Dick emerged from the hedge right into the centre of the road, and in a voice clear and musical he cried out—

"Stand! Stand! Pull up for your life, or you will roll off your box a bullet heavier than you are now."

By an impulse the coachman drew rein, and saved Tyburn Dick the trouble of pitching him off his perch by rolling off and lying passively in a ditch.

Dick then grasped the bridle of the two foremost horses, that were madly plunging about, and turned their heads to the left of the road.

"Hi! What's the meaning of this?"

houted the guard from behind the coach. "Coachy, coachy! Why the blazes—oh! hi! mur—no, please, I—oh lor! What shall—now don't—murder! I'm dead!"

The guard finally rolled off the roof of the coach, and fell prostrate in the road.

The sudden appearance of Tyburn Dick's shining pistol-tube put between his eyes was the cause of his spluttering.

"Mary, Mary, my dear!" said an old croaking voice from inside the coach—"Mary, give me my pistol from under the seat. I really believe we are stopped by—eh—oh dear me! What's that?"

The window was let down with a slam that shook the coach and its occupants.

"There, there you old scoundrel!" shrieked a female voice. "There, you murderous old brute! This is all through you—I know you will get us all murdered—I know you will. Ugh, you beastly old wretch!"

"Eh! Mary, Mary, what are you—oh dear! my nose!" bawled the old fellow when that storm of spleen was showered by his better half, who had a liking for the gallant highwayman—"Mary, what the deuce—oh, my nose!"

The old gentleman's better half had spitefully clutched his nasal organ, and was knocking his head against the back of the coach.

"Pray, good Mr. Highwayman, do spare my life," whined a man from one corner. "I am a wicked sinner. Oh, lor!"

The gentleman finally subsided by giving utterance to a long yell at the sight of a bright pistol-barrel, and rolled under a seat.

"Take that, you villain," screamed the old lady.

She gave her husband a final tug, and inflicted a scratch down the side of his nose.

"There," she said, "you will attempt to use fire-arms again."

"Not in your presence, if I know it," mumbled the old fellow.

Dick had ridden to the window, and sat quietly watching the amusing pantomime.

The barrel of his pistol lodged on the edge of the window.

A gentleman who sat in one corner of the coach could see into the bright tube.

His position was not a comfortable one.

"Be kind enough to move your pistol aside," he said, uneasily.

Dick laughed at his fears and put the trigger on full cock.

The gentleman broke out in a cold perspiration—

"Don't be a fool! You fool!" he exclaimed, "suppose the pistol should go off."

"It is more than probable it will," responded our hero, "if your money and other articles of value don't quickly change owners."

The gentleman indulged in a low peculiar whistle, and fumbled about in an inner pocket of his coat.

Dick watched him closely. He saw a mischievous smile of treachery playing about the other's features.

"You can give that pistol to me," remarked Dick.

"Here you have it, then," said the other, quickly.

At that moment our hero was pulled aside by some one behind.

Then there was a loud report, and a bullet came whistling from the coach window.

The friendly hand that saved our hero was only in time.

The shot was fired with deadly intent, and had it hit its intended mark it would have proved fatal.

The warlike gentleman who had fired it gave vent to an exclamation of triumph. He thought he had settled the career of the highwayman.

So quick was the assault, and so unexpectedly was he saved from the deadly shot, that for a few moments the handsome boy sat bewildered.

Then he turned his head to thank his kindly person for saving his life, but there was no one behind him.

He pressed forward—his hand was on the handle of the coach door. An angry look burned in his bright dark eyes—his purpose was plain.

"Are you ready?" said Dick, putting a pistol in at the window, and in a straight line for the man's head who had fired.

"Eh! Oh, dear me. Don't be a fool!" bawled the gentleman in the corner. "Don't be a fool. You fool! Mr. Highwayman, I knew the bullet wouldn't hit you. I only fired to frighten you."

"Oh," said Dick, "then I will only fire to frighten you."

"Hold!" said a sweet feminine voice. "Shed no blood, Tyburn Dick."

Our hero turned quickly. The voice sounded familiar in his ears.

"Good heavens!" he exclaimed, and the pistol fell from his hand.

Is it a vision of himself, or is it an impostor that confronts him?

Tyburn Dick sat motionless, bewildered, and almost terror-stricken to be confronted by a perfect representation of himself. It made him feel sick at heart.

A mass of black clouds at that moment was swept from the face of the moon. A stream of brilliant light poured down upon the strange horseman, and revealed to Dick his, second, sitting mute as a statue upon a splendid black steed.

In every way the rider represented our hero, even to the jewelled star on the breast and save for the beautiful golden tresses that hung round the other's shoulders in wild profusion, it would be difficult to know which was the original Tyburn Dick.

Dick was almost fascinated by the steady gaze of the other's soft blue eyes.

"Am I dreaming?" he muttered.

"No," said the other, musically.

"Then why am I mocked by having a second following me?"

His representative laughed loudly.

"For a reason," he said. "Be careful what you do—we shall meet again. Farewell!"

"No, no," shouted Tyburn Dick. "Stay, stay, I know you."

"Away, Selim," said the other. In a minute horse and rider vanished.

"Selim, Selim," repeated our hero. "Yes, yes; it is. I remember the horse—it is my father's—Captain Claude's. What terrible mystery is this?"

"Coachman, coachman!" shouted a voice from the other side of the mail, "why don't you go on? The highwayman's gone."

"Is he?" said Dick. "I want that ten thousand pounds."

"Which you won't get," remarked the warlike gentleman, presenting another pistol at the boy highwayman's head.

"Oh, indeed!" said Dick.

In another moment he had dismounted, and was inside the coach.

Then there was a report of a pistol, a cry of pain, and our hero rolled out of the coach; a stream of blood flowing from a gaping wound on his temples.

He held firmly in his agonised grasp a square box of solid rosewood, secured by many silver clasps.

One of the travellers sprang from the coach and pouncing upon his helpless victim, he tried to wrench the box from him.

"Wretch!" exclaimed a voice, and the next instant the warlike gentleman fell to the earth stunned by a blow on the head.

Then our hero was raised from the ground and borne away by the second Tyburn Dick.

CHAPTER L.
DEVIL DUKE'S LOVE SCENE—THE CRY FOR HELP—A HIGHWAYMAN TO THE RESCUE—DISCOVERY OF MORE VILLANY.

OUR gallant friend, Devil Duke, did not proceed far with his fair mistress, whom he rescued from Savage Steve, before he wandered in the path of some old enemies, one being the mercer himself, in search of the fair damsel whom the highwayman claimed, and the others very diligent gentlemen in the service of His Most Gracious Majesty King George, Defender of the Faith, and ruler of several countries.

The diligent gentlemen in the service of His Most Gracious Majesty, &c., unfortunately remembered Duke, and seeing him with another man's wife, they gave him a pressing invitation to go with them quietly.

Devil Duke thanked them kindly for their courtesy, but declined their invitation, and knowing how desirous they were for his company, he put spurs to his horse and soon left them nowhere behind.

An attempt was made to follow, but the idea of catching him was quite absurd.

So the diligent gentlemen discovered after a fruitless ride of two hours for the highwayman.

When Duke found he was not being followed, he fell into a canter and made for the nearest inn.

The mercer's faithless wife lay passively in his arms, and seemed to enjoy the excitement of the ride.

Duke looked in her face inquiringly, and held her tightly to his breast.

"Oh, me!" sighed the wayward little beauty.

"What's the matter, love?" inquired the highwayman, drawing her face to his so that their lips came in contact.

"You are a very wicked fellow, Duke."

"That's what I call grateful," muttered Duke to himself. Then he said to her, "Why am I such a wicked fellow?"

"Because I don't believe you love me the least."

"Why do you think that?"

"I know you love some one better."

"That I certainly do, but it won't do to let you know it," he mused.

"Nonsense, my darling. I adore you to distraction. You certainly must be under the influence of jealousy, my love, or I am sure would not wrong me by thinking I am true to you."

"I am sorry I have offended, but——"

"You have not offended, but you have wronged me by such an unjust thought."

"Still, I can't think you do love me as much as you profess to."

"It is very cruel of you to say so, and—and——"

"Never mind, Duke, dear, time will show," she said.

"Yes, darling, time will show," echoed Devil Duke; and they had an affectionate hug.

"Now," thought the highwayman, "it is my turn to pretend I am an injured party.

He put the dark-eyed young beauty away from im coolly, and returning her look of surprise with a haughty air, he said—

"I have a little bone to pick with you, my celestial beauty."

"Well," she said, with a petulant smile, and a toss of the head.

"I think I have more cause to think that you have not been true to me, than you have to think I do not love you."

"Duke!" exclaimed Jessie, with a start that nearly upset them both.

"My dear."

"Don't 'my dear' me!"

"No, darling."

"You are a brute. Let me down—I won't go another yard with you."

"Don't love; return to your infernal old husband."

Jessie did not see it, and commenced to weep.

"There, there, don't cry," said Duke, wiping her pretty eyes. "Strange," he murmured to himself, "a woman's tears are sure to soften me."

"This—this—is—is—all—the—th—e—," she sobbed.

"There, there, that will do," said Duke, wiping his own eyes, and squeezing her tightly to his breast.

"Let me down," she said, clinging to him tightly; "you shan't accuse me of what I've never done. I can swear, by the memory of everything I hold sacred, I am innocent."

"Are you, though?"

"Yes, I am. I won't go with you."

"No, don't."

"Let me down. I will return to my husband, and—and ask forgiveness."

"You are sure to get in."

"Let me down. I will—I will return to my dear husband."

"Shall I take you back to him?"

"Oh, Duke! You are an awful brute. I never thought, when I deserted my home, and trusted to you all I held dear, that you would prove so false!" Again she burst out in a flood of tears.

By degrees her soft warm arms glided round Duke's neck, and she laid her head on his breast.

"Why have you changed so?" she murmured, sobbing convulsively.

"I have not changed, Jessie, love," Duke said, tenderly, in spite of his wont to be severe. "You are so impetuous. Come, dry those pretty eyes, and listen to what I have to say."

The pretty eyes were quickly dried. A smile half sad and half happy met his eyes, and a pretty pair of pouting lips were held up to him enticingly.

The highwayman availed himself to kiss them, and again the loving pair were reconciled.

"What would you say?" asked the mercer's wife.

"You mustn't be angry with me if I put a few questions to you."

"What is the nature of them?" she inquired.

"You remember the time when I left you at the Leopard Inn?"

"Yes," she answered, meekly.

"Of course you perfectly understand that it was under very pressing circumstances that I was compelled to leave you?"

"I suppose so, if you say it."

"Well, some days elapsed before I could get rid of some very troublesome friends who were following me, and when I did slip them, I returned to the inn for you."

Here he stopped, and looked fixedly into her blushing face.

"You need not look at me like that," she said. "I know what you think, but I can assure you, Duke, I am quite innocent of your wicked thoughts."

"I am happy to hear you are," replied Duke, "but when I returned to the inn, expecting to see you, I found that you had eloped with another."

"Duke!" she exclaimed, sharply, her pretty face flushing indignantly.

"Jessie!" responded Duke.

"Do you wish to make me angry?"

"Not by any means."

"Then you will, if you dare say such a thing."

"What thing?" inquired Duke, trying to assume an innocent aspect.

"You know very well."

"I do not; pray enlighten my mind."

"You said that I eloped with another."

"Did you not?"

"Certainly I did not; you ought to know that."

"Then you will forgive me, I pray," was the highwayman's response. "Will you inform me how it was you left, or by what means?"

"I was carried off in the night by that fearful man from whom you rescued me."

"I did not know anything about it until I found myself in that house at Kensington."

"I don't yet understand how that could have been."

"You will when I tell you," she answered, pertly.

Duke shut up.

"The brutal great ruffian," she continued, "must have entered my bedroom while I slept, and drugged me to accomplish his base design."

"Oh!" shouted Duke, "drugged you to accomplish his base design."

"No, no; don't put an evil meaning to the words."

"My dear, I do not want to put any evil meaning to what you said, but what should he drug you if he did not have a purpose?"

"His purpose was," said the mercer's wife, "to carry me off."

"Which he accomplished without your knowledge."

The wayward little lady was silent.

Duke waited for an answer.

"Was it not so?" he inquired.

He received a nod in the affirmative.

"Very well," he continued. "He having done so much without your knowledge, how do you know that he did not do more?"

"I know he did not, and if you persist to talk in that way, I shall certainly leave you and find my home as best I can."

"But Jessie, my love, it is only right that I should know."

"Well, when I tell you he did not, is that not sufficient."

"How do you know he did not?"

"I know, and that is enough."

"Very well, but——"

The highwayman suddenly drew in his rein and leant forward.

"What have you stopped for?" asked his companion.

"Why, my dear," replied Duke, "as you have asked me, I am bound to acquaint you with the painful fact that I haven't a brad in my pocket."

"Brad—brad?" repeated Jessie, wonderingly.

"Yes, dear; brad means rhino—coin."

"I don't yet understand the meaning of those absurd names. What on earth do you mean?"

"Money—money, my dear," responded Duke; "and hearing a coach coming along at a very quick pace, it is a sure sign that the owner or occupant has got more money with him than he knows how to use, and when that is the case, you must know, love, that they have a little to spare, which of course, I am never above taking."

"Surely, Duke, you are not a highwayman?"

"Now, Jessie, do you wish to hurt my feelings?"

"No, no. Hark! a female in distress."

"They always are. Females are an awful trouble."

"Well, I am sure!" pouted Jessie.

"What is it, my dear? I said nothing gave me greater pleasure than to rescue the little angels—such as yourself—from any danger. Hullo! hi, stop!"

Without waiting to put the mercer's wife down, the highwayman sprang into the road, as a coach and four splendid spirited horses flew down the road and passed Duke in an instant.

"Hi! stop, or I fire!" he shouted.

The postilions slashed the foaming steeds, and away they went at a maddening rate, the coach swayed from side to side, first going along on the two off-side wheels, and then on the others in a perpendicular position, still not having time to fall on either side.

A shriek, wrung from the very bottom of some poor female captive's heart, rent the air, and sent a thrill of pity to the hearts of Duke and his companion.

Again and again these piteous cries for help rang out, and as the carriage went further off the supplications for aid died away into melancholy sounds.

Jessie shuddered and clung to Devil Duke.

"There is certainly some poor creature in terrible distress," she said.

"Yes, there is, and I must follow," answered Duke, excitedly. "I never let any one suffer if I can prevent it."

"Will you follow and rescue the lady in that carriage?"

"Yes, Jessie, I must follow; there is a strange impulse urging me to follow. I must—I will save her!"

"But, Duke, they are out of sight."

"That does not matter; my Rosie will soon overtake them. Won't you, eh, Rosie?" he said, addressing his steed.

Rosie implied by a nod of the head that she would.

"Why are you so excited?" inquired Jessie.

"I know not, my dear, but something seems to tell me that I know the lady—her voice, I swear, I have heard before!"

"I shall be a burden, if you intend to follow. Let me stay here until you return."

"No, no, Jess. Your weight will not make much difference to my steed. Away, Rosie, away my beauty; you must catch that coach—off!"

The noble animal took one long, sweeping bound, and then went off at a pace terrific.

It was not long before Rosebud overtook the coach.

"Hi! pull up, pull up," yelled Duke, "or I fire!"

The first postilion was so terrified at the sight of a long-barrelled pistol confronting him that he pulled up so suddenly that the jerk sent him flying over the horses' heads, while the other postilion on the wheelers, not by any means an active individual, urged his horses forward, and the consequence was that the four came in concussion, and the man joined his companion under the feet of the plunging steeds.

The coach stopped; the occupants rolled into one another's laps, and knocked their heads together.

Duke heard them, and could not help laughing.

Then he heard an oath or two exchanged.

"Sniggers," shouted an angry voice within the carriage.

"Yes, me lord," responded a pitiful voice.

"See why the coach has stopped."

"Becose the horses won't go, I expect, me lord."

"Idiot."

"Yes, me lord."

"Look directly, or I will throw you out of the window."

"Yes, me lord; which window?"

My lord jumped up, and Sniggers got a punch in the head.

"Now look, you clown."

"I can't, me lord, that clout in the 'ed's bunged up me hies."

"Uh! you jackass."

"Thank yer, me lord," replied Sniggers, slowly.

"Don't answer me."

"No, me lord," answered the lacquey quickly.

There was a thud. Sniggers got another "clout" in the head that knocked him half out of the carriage window, where he lay until suddenly startled.

"Oh, hi, pray don't shoot! Oh dear me, me lord!" bawled Sniggers, and his head went in again.

Devil Duke had been watching the pantomime quite amused, a climax being brought to the scene by the appearance of the lacquey's head. The highwayman laid the cold rim of his pistol on the tip of his nose.

The effect was magical.

His eyes were clear, and in a moment he took in the whole scene, and gave vent to the exclamation as above.

"Now, fool," said his master sternly.

"Oh! me lord, we shall be murdered."

"What do you mean? Explain."

"Oh, lor! the horses are smashed, and the coach is run away, and there is about five hundred highwaymen with great big pistols. Ugh! twenty was shoved in each of my ears, and ten up each side of my nose; I——"

"Stop your infernal, lying tongue," said his master, administering a kick that lodged the shivering lacquey doubled up like a hedgehog in a corner.

The young libertine put his head out of the window to ascertain the cause of the stoppage.

Duke met him half way with the pistol.

"Confound it—a highwayman!" exclaimed the young lord.

The lacquey groaned.

"Sniggers, you shivering swipe, here's a highwayman."

"Boo—oo! yes, me lord; I knew it, and we 'ave left the pistols behind."

"Never mind pistols; take my sword and kill him."

"Yes, me-e—I, me—no, me lord, I can't use a sword. You go kill him; I'll stop here."

"Damn your impertinence! Get up, or I will kill you."

"Oh, lor! I'll get up, me lord. Please

don't hurt me. Take the sword away a little further."

"Get up."

Sniggers got up, and put his head out of the contrary window.

"He, he, he!" he sniggered; "I—I don't see any highwayman, me lord."

"Look the other side."

"He, he! Oh, lor! ain't it funny?" he said, with chattering teeth. "Really, the highwayman's got a lady with him."

"Yes," thundered the highwayman, in a voice so loud and stern that man and master started and fell into each other's arms, "and I intend to have another—the one you have got in there."

"The devil you do," said the young lord.

"Stand down a minute," said Duke to Jessie.

"Be careful," Jessie said, as her lover put her gently down.

"Fear not," he said, dismounting, and drawing a pair of pistols from the holsters, he threw open the carriage-door, and held one at each of the shivering curs.

"What's the meaning of this, robber?" demanded the young lord.

"Ah!" exclaimed Devil Duke, stepping back a pace or two, "'tis you, my Lord Edward Aldervale. What villany are you at now?"

"You shall see, sirrah," replied Lord Edward, thrusting furiously at the highwayman.

Duke moved aside in time to save the sword going through him, and before his assailant had time to draw the weapon back, he clutched hold of the blade, regardless of cutting his hand.

"Now, my lord," Duke said furiously, "release the hilt of the sword, or by the lord Harry, I will scatter your brains with a bullet."

The daring young libertine was so astonished by the courageous act of the highwayman that he dropped the sword, and crouched back.

He saw the angry determined look in the highwayman's eyes, and knew it was dangerous to oppose him.

"Thus do I render you weaponless," and as he spoke, Duke snapped the sword in twain across his knee.

Lord Edward gave vent to a savage howl.

Sniggers had crawled under one of the seats, where he lay groaning.

"You will now give me what money and jewels you have about you."

"I have none," answered the baffled libertine.

"You will give me what money and jewels you have about you, or I shall give you a bullet, and then help myself."

Seeing he had no alternative, the Lord of Aldervale groaned, and produced money and jewels as demanded by the highwayman, even to his cravat-pin and the gold buckles off his shoes, besides the buttons off his clothes, which, to his chagrin, he had to cut off one at a time.

"I will now have that knife you so skilfully used to cut the buttons off—also those brilliant studs. Thanks."

"You shall suffer for this. I know you."

"Don't brag, my lord. I know you."

"I am the last person you shall stop on the king's highway, or any of your accursed band. Tyburn Dick too—your leader—his race is nearly run."

"Don't lie. Tyburn Dick will live to bring you to the gallows, my lord. You have kindly done, without a murmur, hitherto, every thing that I commanded you; please turn inside out every one of your pockets."

Lord Edward hesitated for a moment.

Devil Duke placed his finely polished pistols in a line with the young nobleman's eyes, so that he could see down the barrel of each, and knew exactly what they contained, and what he would get if he did not obey quickly.

"I never miss, my lord," said Duke insinuatingly.

My Lord Edward knew the meaning of his words, and in a moment the whole of his pockets were turned inside out, and a bundle of crisp notes fell to the ground.

Duke stepped into the carriage, put the notes in his pocket, and opened the other door of the carriage.

"You can go now, my lord," he said, coolly backing the young libertine out.

He went. Then Duke roused the lacquey from his hiding-place, and sent him after his

Duke then persuaded the postilions to mount their horses, and drive away as fast as the steeds would take them.

For their own personal welfare the men consented.

"That's right," remarked Duke, approvingly; "ten pounds for each of you is better than a bullet in your thick skulls."

So the postilions thought, and pocketing the money they mounted, and by the time Duke had bound Lord Edward and his lacquey back to back, and hurled them in a ditch, the men were ready to start.

Another minute and the coach was dashing along furiously.

Duke and his fair companion were suddenly startled by a timid scream that came from the opposite seat.

Duke jumped up.

"Jessie," he said, "I had forgotten through that young villain, what I stopped the coach for."

Again the cries were repeated.

"Hush, hush, dear lady!" said Duke, taking a tiny hand. "Hush, dear lady; you are quite safe now."

"No, no, you took me from those I love—I am not safe—I am in danger," said the lady, tearfully, and struggling to take her hand from Duke. "you are not my friend—you tried to kill Dick."

"Dick," repeated the highwayman.

"Yes, yes; they call him Tyburn Dick. You tried to kill him."

"No, no, lady, I am a friend. You speak of my captain," Duke said excitedly. "Tell me, dear lady, are you not the Queen of the Highwaymen? I remember your voice."

"Yes, yes; I am styled a such," and suddenly springing from her seat, she clutched Duke by the shoulder, and tried to penetrate his features through the darkness.

At that moment the coach gave a jerk, and stopped them. There arose a clamour of voices.

"What's the meaning of this?" muttered Duke.

"Nothing, my dear boy," said a voice that the highwayman too well remembered belonged to his mortal foe, Jonathan Wild, and a face of such cadaverous malignity was exhibited at the window, by the light from a

RE-APPEARANCE OF THE DEATH WITCH.

lantern that the thief-taker held, that the lady shrank back horrified.

"It is," shouted Duke, catching sight of the lady's face; "it is our queen, the captain's lady."

"Is it?" said a voice from the other side of the coach, and the malicious face of Lord Edward Aldervale appeared. "If that's the case, you and your queen shall be put in Newgate together."

Duke sprang at the young libertine, but too late; he received a blow that struck him senseless to the carriage floor.

CHAPTER LI.

VICTOR ST. JAMES MAKES A STARTLING DIS-
COVERY — THE FASHIONABLE GAMBLING-
HOUSE, AND THE EXIT OF A CHEAT.

OUR reckless young friend, Victor St. James, felt wretched without the companionship of our hero.

He went to the haunt, but that was deserted. The men were out in search of their beloved young leader.

"Can you give me any information as to which route they have taken?" inquired St. James of one of the sentries.

"No, my lord," answered the man; "Captain Munroe said he would not return without discovering the whereabouts of our king."

"Thanks," replied the young noble, and away he went.

"A very pleasant time, certainly," he mused, while riding towards his chambers. "Ah, never mind, I will fetch that disembodied shadow of a valet, Shanks—a good faithful fellow—he has stuck to me like a brick, when I was thrust from my father's house, through the villainy of that treacherous hound—Reuben. I have got my reckoning to have with him yet." Here the dashing young fellow fell into a reverie—his youthful brow clouded and sorrowful.

"Ah! here I am," he exclaimed, looking up, as his horse stopped in front of a large hotel.

A tall flunky dashed down a flight of steps, and, bending almost to the ground, he seized the bridle of the horse with one hand, and held the stirrup with the other, while St. James dismounted.

"Is the horse to go to the stable, sir?" inquired the functionary.

"Thanks, no; tell the groom to saddle my valet's horse, and bring it round."

"Yes sir."

"Shanks, you blackguard!" shouted St. James, entering a handsome suite of apartments, and looking round.

"Shanks!" repeated St. James, receiving no answer. "Where the devil are you?"

"Yes, my lord," responded a voice; the young noble knew not from whence it came.

"Where are you?"

"Here, my lord," and a tall ungainly but honest-looking fellow bounded into the room.

Victor St. James confronted his valet sternly.

Shanks looked shyly at his master, wiped his large mouth, and looked suspiciously at the door.

"You have been with the chambermaid again; have you?" said St. James.

"No, my lord, I ain't," whined Shanks.

"Don't lie, confound you!"

"No, my lord!"

"Have you the confounded impertinence to stand there, and tell me you have not been near the maid?"

"No, my lord, but I couldn't help it."

"You sneaking effigy, and if—there, never mind. Get yourself ready to accompany me to London."

The valet looked at his master aghast.

"Oh, my dear lord!" he said, taking young master's hand, "are you going to me with you?"

"Yes; did I not say so?"

"My dear, good, kind master; I'll never go near Susan again," said the faithful fellow, pressing the small white hand he held to his lips.

"That's a good fellow," said St. James; "and now, Shanks, make haste."

"Yes, my dear lord," and away went Shanks.

"A more faithful fellow never lived," mused the young cavalier, looking after the retreating form of his valet. "He has proved a true friend—the only one I have."

The young nobleman then walked to the window, and bent over the balcony.

"A strange life is mine," he continued. "Shunned by my kindred—cast alone on the world of sin and crime—the only tie for which I lived was sundered, and my life's idol torn from me."

The youth's handsome face became clouded.

"What is life to me without her?" he meditated. "What care I for the world, or any one in it? Why do I live? For revenge!" he hissed between his clenched teeth; "ay, revenge for the wrongs I have suffered—revenge such as few have ever heard of!"

Here Shanks came in.

St. James stared at him vacantly.

He had forgotten for the moment the arrangement he had made with his valet.

"Ah, yes; you are ready to accompany me to London," he said, suddenly remembering.

"Yes, my lord."

"What have you in that wallet, Shanks?"

"Why, my lord, I thought you would want something on the road, so I packed up a little wine and biscuits."

"Upon my word, Shanks, you are a good thoughtful fellow."

Shanks bowed for the compliment.

"We will now go, Shanks," said his young master.

Shanks was glad to hear it. He was anxious to be off.

A few minutes later they started for their long journey.

The rich sun of one afternoon was slowly sinking behind the fleecy clouds when St. James and his valet neared London.

Shanks looked a pitiable object.

The journey had been a long and weary one.

The cold bleak weather did not improve the beauty of the faithful fellow's long nose and thin face. It gave his features a purple tint, and make him feel extremely uncomfortable.

Neither did St. James look so bright as when he first started.

"Shanks," he said, turning to his worthy valet "your cheerful chump is a perfect resemblance of a hatchet."

"Is it, my lord?" whined Shanks, drawing his visage into peculiar distortions.

"Beyond question," replied St. James, laughingly. "What do you say, Shanks, if we turn in somewhere and have a freshener?"

"Yes, my lord; I wish you would. I feel horful."

"We will, then; but we must find a den first."

He looked at his follower inquiringly, as though expecting to be informed where they could find a "den."

As though reading his master's thoughts, Shanks said—

"I don't know where there is a place."

"You don't? Then we will look for one."

For some distance they rode along in silence—Shanks completely smothered in a huge cloak, and Victor St. James buried in a deep reverie.

Even the horses, like their masters, were weary, and jogged along lazily, every now and then coming in violent concussion with one another, and giving their riders a sudden shock that nearly precipitated them headforemost into the road.

But that did not disturb either. St. James was too absorbed in his own meditations to notice anything, and by the audible snoring that came from under the cloak, and the way the muffled form jerked about, it was evident the worthy Shanks had fallen fast asleep.

Presently there came a stifled shriek that startled St. James.

He looked round and saw the legs of his valet sticking up out of the ditch.

His horse suddenly fell on his knees. Shanks was precipitated over its back, and it was not until his head made a hole in the soft mud that he awoke with a shriek of horror.

His master indulged in a good laugh, then assisted the unfortunate fellow from his critical position, and pulling the cloak from off Shanks's head, he smacked him across the mouth with the dirty part.

Shanks began to splutter and blink quickly—stared at his master inquiringly—wiped his mouth on the sleeve of his coat—kicked his horse spitefully, and then finally gave vent to his feelings in blubbering.

"Well, certainly, you are a pretty effigy," said St. James. "What the deuce did you take that sudden leap for?"

"I didn't take a leap, my lord; it was the horse that chucked me over its head."

"Oh, oh, oh," laughed St. James; "come, mount quickly, and don't fall to sleep again."

Shanks mounted, and took particular care to keep awake.

"I don't see any signs of a den as yet," remarked his master.

"No, my lord; I wish we did."

"By Jove! here comes a coach. I tell you what, Shanks, suppose I pretend to be a highwayman, and stop the coach, eh? What do you think of the joke?"

"Capital, my lord; you've got a mask?"

"Yes, I have got a mask. Hide in the hedge, and when the coach comes along you spring out, stop the horses, and knock the coachman off his box, while I go to the window and frighten the inmates."

"Jolly, my lord; won't it be a lark? Ha, ha, ha," exclaimed the valet in ecstacy. "And won't I give the coachey a topper if he don't roll off his perch pretty quickly."

A chariot, drawn by four splendid chestnut-brown horses, just then came rolling down the road, and passed the spot where the two amateur highwaymen were concealed.

"Shanks," said St. James, in a whisper.

"You'll have to knock these postilions over."

"Yes, my lord, I can do that."

"Go on, then. Put on your mask."

Shanks covered his face with the black crape, and drawing a pistol from the holster with quite a professional air, he galloped along behind the bushes that divided the field from the road, and when in a line with the chariot, he sprang over the hedge and confronted the two foremost horses.

Without a word, he pulled the horses across the road and brought the carriage to a stop.

The postilions commenced to shout frantically.

Shanks put his pistol in the man's face, and quietly clutching him by the leg threw him over the horses' backs; the other just slid out of the saddle as Shanks rode to help him off.

St. James could not help laughing outright to see the neat way his valet stopped the chariot.

"Charles, what's the meaning of this stoppage? Have the horses fallen?" inquired a gentleman, putting his head out of the window.

"No, my lord," replied St. James, bowing politely.

"The deuce! who are you?"

"A gentleman, at your service."

"The deuce! you are a highwayman!"

"If you like to use the term."

"Insolent fellow! What is it you require?"

"Being a highwayman, I should have thought you were acquainted with my wants."

"Is it that you want to rob me?"

"No, my lord; I merely take what you give me of your own free will."

"You will get nothing from me," said the gentleman in the carriage; "but yet you are not like the general robbers. Take this ring. I see you are not used to this thing."

He drew a massive gold ring from his finger as he spoke.

"I shall wear it in remembrance of you, generous sir," said the cavalier, politely.

The gentleman retained his hand, as he took the brilliant diamond ring.

St. James had assumed a coarse voice hitherto, but, forgetting himself, he spoke in his own musical way.

The change startled the gentleman, and he trembled palpably while trying to penetrate the features of the gentleman highwayman through the mask he wore.

St. James tried to disengage his hand, but the other held it firmly.

"Good God!" exclaimed the gentleman.

St. James started, surprised.

"Your name, sir," the gentleman said, quickly.

"That little concerns you, sir."

"It does concern me. Tell me, for the love of memory."

"Nay, my lord; the love of my memory is bitterness."

"But your name?"

"I cannot, dare not oblige you with it."

The young nobleman withdrew from the coach.

The only occupant—the gentleman—leant forward and held his hand.

St. James turned angrily.

The moon at that moment threw down a brilliant flood of light, and revealed the features of the traveller to the young cavalier.

St. James fell back as though suddenly bitten. The mask fell from his face. The gentleman gave a cry of joy, and springing nimbly from the carriage, threw his arm around the young cavalier's neck.

"Victor, Victor, my son!" he exclaimed, "I repent. Speak to me—speak to me, my darling boy! Speak to your father!"

St. James shook his sire off.

"Repent!" he said. "Farewell, my lord!"

The gentleman fell to the earth, and sobbed aloud.

"Shanks," cried Victor St. James, "come!"

"No, no; don't leave me," cried the self-proclaimed sire of our young friend. "Victor, Victor!"

"That's my Lord St. James?" remarked the valet to his young master, wonderingly.

"Silence, Shanks!" demanded St. James "Never mention his name."

"No, my lord; only, why did you leave him like that?"

The handsome youth laughed satirically.

Shanks rode on in silence, wondering at

his master's strange conduct, and every now and then casting a curious side glance at him.

"They are coming after us," he exclaimed suddenly.

"They must not catch us. Come on," replied St. James. "Wake your animal up."

Shanks woke the animal up by plunging his spurs into its sides, and soon they left the chariot far behind.

Riding through Piccadilly they made their way to Jermyn-street, and giving their horses to a groom to look after, they entered a house—one of the most fashionable gambling dens in existence at the time of our story.

Shanks followed his master rather timidly while ascending a dark narrow staircase that led to the upper apartment, where the grandest of the gamblers where gathered.

On entering, Shanks gave utterance to an exclamation of surprise.

The elegance of the place awed him.

From the ceiling hung three massive glass chandeliers, each containing about fifty wax candles.

The walls were hung with dark crimson velvet, the floor was covered with rich carpet that the foot sank into at every step, and the whole place was one of magnificent splendour, decorated in the most tasteful style.

A long table, that ranged from one end of the apartment to the other, was laid out with the most delicate viands, and graced with elegant vases of choice flowers.

Many small tables were in different parts of the room, round which lounged the gamblers in an easy attitude, playing for thousands, and ever and anon laying a hundred or two on the turn up of a card.

At other tables were the more practised players.

The general confusion and uproar was exciting.

St. James took in the scene at a glance.

"Follow me, Shanks," said St. James, "I see two of my friends."

He walked to the further end of the apartment, where sat two of our adventurers—Gallant Tom and Dashing Ralph—watching closely two very quarrelsome gentlemen playing at cards.

"How do you do, gentlemen?" said St. James, shaking hands with the two handsome knights of the road.

"Now, who the deuce expected to see you here?"

The young cavalier laughed.

"Neither of you, I vouch," he replied.

"No, by Jupiter!" put in Dashing Ralph.

"We have two very interesting neighbours, trying like the devil to cheat one another."

Victor St. James seated himself, and, like his friends, listened to the two gamblers.

Shanks seated himself behind his master's chair.

"Three more will put me out," said one of the gamblers.

The other bit his lips, and glared spitefully at his opponent through the holes of his mask.

"Ten," he said, throwing down the jack of spades.

"Twenty," exclaimed the other, with an exultant laugh, putting down the jack of hearts; "two for a pair—one to go."

"Thirty," responded the next, triumphantly; "half-a-dozen for three jacks."

"You are fortunate, my friend."

"Is it a go?" he said, without heeding the other's words.

"Without you can make it."

"Play."

"Nine."

"And six are fifteen—two," the other said, pegging the two.

His opponent grinned maliciously; he had got his hand on his knees, and several more cards than belonged to him. He selected a six, and throwing it down, said—

"Twenty-one, and the game is mine."

"But not the money," the other thundered, and springing up he swept the heap of gold and notes off the table.

The cheat leapt over the table, and clutching his opponent by the throat forced him down to the floor.

Then commenced a terrible struggle.

Each holding the other in a deadly grip, and fighting to obtain the stakes that lay scattered over the carpet.

"Release my throat!" gasped the cheat.

"Curse you, I will strangle you!" responded the other, and throwing his assailant, he got one knee on his chest, and with the ferocity of a panther tried his best to slay his opponent.

The cheat foamed at the mouth like a mad dog, and driven desperate by agony, he with a sudden wrench freed his hands.

The struggle changed.

The cheat clutched his assailant round the neck, and with mighty strength pulled his head down, and dashed him to the other side of the room.

Then he sprang to his feet, and bounded upon his opponent.

There was murder burning in his savage-looking eyes. He seized the other by the throat with both hands, and squeezed it with all his might.

The man turned black in the face, his eyes protruded from their sockets, blood spirted from his nose and ears, and his tongue lolled out of his mouth.

It was a horrible sight to behold.

A few minutes more, and it would have been his last.

"No, by Jove!" said Victor St. James; "to see a fellow served like that ain't fair."

He sprang up as he spoke, dashed at the cheat, and hurled him off his victim.

The savage ruffian turned upon him madly.

"What business had you to interfere?" he said.

"I will answer you, blackleg and cheat," replied St. James, coolly.

The other drew his sword impetuously, and without a word dashed furiously at the daring intruder.

"Tom," said the young nobleman, turning to his friend, and guarding the other's thrust at the same time; "look after that gentleman while I settle this one."

Gallant Tom took the half-strangled gambler under his care, and soon brought back a little of the life the other had squeezed out.

"Now, sir, I am ready for you," said the aring youth, falling into a splendid attitude.

The other made no answer. His teeth were firmly set, and a terrible look shone in his eyes.

St. James took his blow playfully.

By this time a group of lookers-on had gathered round them, and heavy bets were being laid on and against our young friend.

One gentleman, who appeared to have more money than he knew what to do with, particularly attracted St. James's attention.

"Fifty to one that the young one loses the fight," he heard him say.

"I will bet you even odds for a hundred pounds that I get the first three points, and then disarm him," said St. James, turning to him.

"Done!" cried the other.

"Ralph," said St. James, turning to the dashing highwayman, "lend me a hundred, and hold the stake."

The cheat grew more furious than ever.

He did not like the idea of being made the subject of betting.

He delivered such a terrific lunge at St. James that those who had backed him began to quake with fear.

Not because the fearless boy might have lost his life, but because they thought of losing their money.

St. James turned the lunge aside easily, and gave his combatant a stripe across the face that dismasked him, and left a deep gash on his cheek.

"One to me," remarked St. James.

The man gave a howl, and furiously leapt upon the young cavalier.

"Two," said St. James, as he struck his opponent down.

So quick and with such perfect skill was this feat done that the lookers-on applauded the youth loudly.

The man in a moment was upon his feet.

His sword flashed about like forked lightning, and Victor had to use his rapier quickly to keep his foe's weapon from touching him.

"Three," he said, as he slit the sleeve of his opponent's sword arm, and wrenched the weapon from his grasp by putting the point of his own rapier in the hilt of the other's and giving it a twist.

"Bravo, bravo!" shouted the lookers-on, clapping their rough hands loudly.

"You have lost, my lord," said St. James, turning to the gentleman with whom he had betted.

"Aw—damme—ya—as," replied the aristocrat, and turning on his heels, he strode away.

The beaten cheat was like a demon. Burning with mortification, and smarting with pain, he sprang at his late opponent, and griping him by the throat, hurled him to the floor.

The lookers-on raised a shout of disgust.

"Coward! Coward!" they yelled.

Gallant Tom struck the cheat a fearful blow in the face that felled him senseless.

"Let's throw him out of the window now," suggested one.

"Kick him down stairs."

"Give him a ducking," proposed another.

And such with many others were the suggestions for the expulsion of the cheat and coward.

"Suppose, gentlemen," remarked Gallant Tom, "we carry out the first proposition, and throw him out of the window."

"Hear, hear, hear! Throw him out of the window! That's the thing!" shouted a chorus of voices.

The casement was opened, and the senseless cheat was clutched by as many hands as could get near him, and carried to the window.

"No, no!" yelled a voice, and the gentleman who had been half strangled ran to the window to save the blackleg from being thrown out.

But not in time.

He fell with a heavy thud.

"Why did you do that?" cried the man who tried to rescue the cheat. "It was my brother—I did not know it before; we were both masked, and knew not each other."

The poor fellow looked wild, and went on in a most lamentable way; then he ran to the window, and before any could save him he fell from the sill in a fit.

The company stood spell-bound.

The scene they had just witnessed was one of lamentable horror. Every one felt a pang of remorse for what they had done, and glared at one another speechless.

The prevailing silence was suddenly broken in a way that made them all start with such wonderful alacrity that many fell to the floor, through coming in violent contact with their neighbours.

Then there came a renewal of the terrific shouting that had so statled the fashionable gamblers.

Then there came a terrible banging of doors, and other obstacles that barred the way of the invaders went crashing down.

Another minute and the grand gambling hall was filled with Bow-street constables.

"Shut the doors and windows! Let nobody pass, in the King's name," shouted lustily the officer in command.

"Ah, ah, that's their game, is it?" laughed Gallant Tom. "Ralph, old boy, we are in a trap."

Ralph drew his sword, and said they must fight their way out of it.

Shanks crept behind his young master and tapped him on the shoulder.

"My lord," he said, "there's going to be a fight."

"So it appears," replied the young noble; "we shall require your aid, Shanks."

Shanks felt honoured.

One of the officious officers at that moment espied the highwaymen, and raised a shout.

Our four adventurers formed a square, and each holding in a firm grip a sharp gleaming sword, they waited for their foes.

"Surrender at discretion," shouted the commander.

"Go to —— with your discretion," replied St. James.

The officers rushed towards them.

"The windows," yelled Gallant Tom, seeing they had no chance against the overwhelming number of the officers.

He sprang out as he spoke.

Dashing Ralph, St. James, and Shanks made a run together.

The officers closed round them.

Another minute and the three were prisoners, securely manacled, and being led away to Newgate.

Poor Shanks bitterly regretted having come to London.

CHAPTER LII.

A RIDE—A FIGHT—AND A RESCUE.

RIDING carelessly through a lone country road was a gentleman of much grace and beauty. His figure was tall, slender, and of the most perfect sculpture; of fair complexion, his features finely chiselled, but now with the pale moonlight thrown on them they were pallid, and looked a little careworn or thoughtful.

A deep scar was visible on his white temple, from which the blood slowly ebbed and was trickling down his handsome face.

His small delicate hand—a hand that many a lady would be proud to possess—ever and anon wandered to the wound with a silk kerchief, and bathed the crimson stream away.

His dress was partially hidden by a loose cloak that hung carelessly over his shoulders. But a portion of a crimson coat, embroidered with gold, was visible.

His high, black, shining boots, his buckskin breeches, and the gay cap he wore over a mass of rich, brown curls, gave him a reckless air.

Altogether, he resembled a highwayman.

Presently, when his cloak blew open, he looked the very *beau ideal* of Tyburn Dick.

A jewelled star, too, glistened brightly on his breast—the facsimile of the star our hero wore to distinguish himself from any other knight of the road.

Which of the two is it?

Can it be the gallant Boy King of the Highwaymen, whom we left being carried off by his second? or is it the counterfeit of Tyburn Dick?

The traveller raised his head and looked around at the silent expanse of country.

"The change is wonderful," he cogitated. "The last I remember is rolling out of the Cornwall Mail. I had a narrow escape," and his hand wandered to the scar on his temple. "It is a very natty scratch," he continued, rubbing the place reflectively. "If I ever have the pleasure of meeting the gentleman again, why, I shall remember him; but——"

His hand wandered over his forehead, and he seemed as though pondering over thoughts that troubled him.

"There is a strange mystery," he broke out, "I cannot solve. How the deuce did I escape the deadly intent of the warlike gentleman who assailed me? Who saved me from his clutches? How did I get to the inn? Who dressed my wound? Who was my kind friend? It is all a mystery, and likely to remain so."

Again he was silent, lost in reflection.

"Had I not fainted, I should have known all," he commenced again; "but now it remains a mystery, as I before said."

"There is one thing that troubles me more than all the rest," he went on, after a pause, "who can my second be? I have heard the voice before; it sounded to my ear like melancholy music, and the face was sad; it resembled one that I knew so well, yet I cannot call to mind where I have seen it before. The form, the features, the hands were all too finely marked for a man, yet it could not be a woman, it wore a similar moustache to my own, but the hair was like so much golden thread, and hung around a face as beautiful as Eve's."

"This, too, is a mystery," he muttered, after waking up his horse by with a dig with his heels.

"Wake up, you brute," he said, administering another kick to the horse.

The horse woke up with a start that nearly upset its rider.

"I don't like the idea of any one else going about assuming my dress and title," the horseman said, aloud. "I am Tyburn Dick, and if ever I come across the other person who goes about representing himself as me, I shall certainly take the liberty of stopping him, or her, whichever it is, and inquire what motive he or she has for representing itself as me! and if I don't get satisfaction, why——"

He tapped the hilt of his jewelled sword, and resumed his cogitations.

"I wonder whether that fellow who knocked me out of the coach took the box back? It had ten thousand pounds in it, and now I haven't got any—I must have some. Ah! what's that?"

A shriek of a woman in great agony rang through the still night air.

Dick started.

He heard the clatter of a horse's feet thundering along the road.

"I am wanted," he muttered and drew rein.

He turned his head and looked in the direction from whence the sounds proceeded.

In the distance he could discern the shadow of a horseman with a female lying across the saddle. They were coming at a terrific pace.

Tyburn Dick drew his sword and waited for the coming rider.

He did not wait long.

The maddened steed carried its riders along like the wind.

Tyburn Dick sprang into the road and grasped the bridle of the other horse.

It reared and plunged furiously to break away.

Our hero held it firmly and quieted it with a crack on the nose with the pommel of his weapon.

The horseman clasped the lady tightly round the waist, and with difficulty kept his seat.

"What now?" he thundered.

His fair captive tore the cloak away he had put over her head, and looked up.

"Help—help me!" she cried, earnestly.

Dick gallantly raised his hat to her, and placed a pistol in the man's face.

"That lady wishes to be released," he said, coolly. "Put her gently on my saddle, or my pistol will go off."

"But, but," spluttered the man, "she is my wife."

"No, no—I am not! I pray you take me from him."

"Fear not, dear lady," Dick said, "you are perfectly safe while I am here."

He turned to the man.

"That lady—quickly," he said.

The man glared at him through his mask furiously, and removed his arm from around the lady's waist as though about to pass her to our hero, instead of which he drew forth his sword, and made a terrible cut at his assailant.

The lady shrieked and closed her eyes; she imagined the sword as it fell would cleave the daring highwayman in twain.

But it did not.

Our hero had faced too many dangers to be thrown off his guard.

His sword leaped from its sheath, and met the descending weapon of his opponent.

"Base coward," he hissed, "were it not for endangering the lady's life, I would strike you to the earth."

"Braggart!" exclaimed the other, madly, and he made another furious cut at the Boy Highwayman.

Dick saw the weapon coming; he waited, and as his opponent thrust out, he swung his blade round, and brought the pommel down on his sword-arm.

The man dropped his weapon, gave utterance to a long howl, and clasped his arm.

Dick caught the lady's hand in time to save her slipping from the saddle.

"Thanks—many thanks," she said, and gave him a look of tender gratitude.

"Allow me, fair lady," our hero said, twining his arms round her waist to lift her from the saddle.

"Not yet," said the man suddenly, and he grasped the lady rudely by the arm.

"Release your hold, hound!" said Tyburn Dick, his handsome boyish face flashing angrily.

"Not if I know it," replied the ruffian. "If I lose her, why I lose fifty pounds."

"So you are a hireling," Dick said, quietly, but in a tone that meant danger.

"If yer like to call me so, but anyhow, I ain't agoin' to lose the lady."

"Remove your hand from the lady's wrist!"

The man glared at Dick savagely.

"The lady's in my power," he said.

"That's the reason I want her under my protection, and if you are wise you will give her up quietly, and depart while you are safe."

"See yer d—— first!"

Dick struck the ruffian violently on the knuckles with a pistol-barrel.

The ruffian released the lady.

Dick drew her into his saddle.

The lady smiled at him confidingly; she felt quite safe under his care.

"Go!" Dick said to the baffled caitiff.

The man wheeled his horse round, and drawing a dagger from an inner pocket, made a sudden deadly plunge at his youthful opponent.

Dick was not aware of the brutal attack.

The lady shrieked; she saw the danger of her young protector, and put up her white delicate hand at the peril of her own danger to protect our hero.

The blow was aimed with savage, bloody intent.

The gleaming blade descended with violent force in a line for Dick's heart.

The boy turned, but too late.

The deed was done.

The lady fell into his arms with a gurgling cry.

The deadly blade sank into her hand, tore a long gash in her delicate flesh, slid down her white arm, ripping open the spotless skin in its course, leaving a red stream of her life-tide gushing forth, and then finally plunged into her palpitating bosom.

Dick took in the whole terrible scene at a glance.

His eyes blazed fiercely, the hot blood mounted to his cheeks, and in an instant he drew a pistol and fired at the coward's head.

The flint missed fire.

The man gave a defiant yell, and digging his spurs furiously into his horse's flanks, galloped away.

"Curse you," hissed Dick, and he hurled the pistol after him.

It struck him on the head.

He reeled and fell from the saddle.

The horse galloped on madly.

The ruffian's right foot got entangled in the stirrup, and he was dragged along, head downwards, his skull being battered into a shapeless mass by the iron hoofs of the maddened steed.

The gallant Boy Highwayman looked remorsefully at his fair charge, and with much tenderness he drew forth the murderous steel from her throbbing breast.

A stream of her life-tide flowed from the wound as he drew the dripping blade out.

"In defending my life," he murmured, "she has endangered her own to an extent, perhaps, beyond recovery."

He put his lips to hers, and kissed her tenderly.

She lay quite inanimate in his arms.

With much delicacy he opened her dress and bound the wound with his handkerchief, and then rode along as quietly as possible without jerking.

The lady suddenly awoke, and smiled faintly into his face.

"Dear madam," said Dick, rapturously; "generous, noble-hearted lady, this is all my fault."

"No, no," said the lady; "it was not your fault."

"Tell me, dear lady, is the wound deep?"

"No," she answered. "Thank Providence the thrust did not touch you, or it would have been fatal."

"I would rather it had been so than you should have the sufferings intended for me."

"No, no; you are ungrateful."

"Say not so, lady. I cannot express my gratitude and admiration for the noble and courageous act."

"I see," she remarked, looking up, "you have got a scar of a recent wound on your temple."

Dick told her how it occurred, and soon they got into a very pleasant and interesting conversation.

"But," Dick said, turning from the subject, "you have not yet told me who that man was."

"I do not know myself," she replied.

"Have you no idea of ever seeing him before?"

"None."

"May I be so bold as to ask your place of residence?"

"Stanhope Villa," was her answer.

"A pretty place—picturesque and romantic."

The lady laughed prettily.

"Where, I remember——" she broke out.

"You have seen that man before?"

"No; but I have noticed a gentleman for several days hovering near our villa, and whenever I went out he made it a point to follow me, but I always avoided his presence."

"To what conclusion does that bring you?" Dick inquired.

"Why, I think it very probable that, finding he could not get hold of me, he hired some one to carry me off."

"Very probable; but how the deuce did they manage to carry you off?"

The lady hesitated for a moment.

"I went out this evening to meet my husband, and——"

Our hero indulged in a low peculiar whistle.

"Married, by Jingo!" he muttered.

The lady looked at him curiously.

"What did you whistle for?" she asked.

"Did I whistle?" said Dick.

"Yes."

"I was not aware of it. Pray proceed."

"Somebody must have been watching me,

for I had not got more than a quarter of a mile from the villa when I was held by some one behind, and before I had time to resist or call for help, something was thrown over my head, and I was carried off."

"And now you are safe out of the clutches of these dastardly villains shall I take you back to your husband?"

"If you will."

During their conversation they had been oing along at a steady trot.

Presently a man sprang from a hedge, and confronted our hero in a menacing attitude, with a huge club held in his two hands above his head, ready to strike.

"Get out of my path," shouted Dick.

"Stand!" demanded the man.

"I will with a bullet."

He drew a pistol, and presented it point blank at the man's head.

"Knock him over, Bill. That's the lady we want," yelled a voice from the hedge.

"Do you?" said Dick; "then you will certainly have to knock me over to get her."

Bill didn't see it; he crept out of the road.

Tyburn Dick held the pistol in a very straight line with his head. It made him feel uncomfortable.

"Come on, Bill. We'll help you," said the voice again behind the hedge.

Dick looked in that direction.

A slight shudder ran through him as his gaze encountered the body of the lady's abductor lying in the road, with his head battered into an indistinguishable mass.

Dick urged his horse forward.

"Move another step, and I fire!" thundered a voice.

"Well," said Dick, "I can fire too."

And he did.

The bullet hit somebody, and somebody yelled with pain, but in another moment a gang of a dozen ruffians sprang from the hedge and surrounded him.

The Boy Prince drew his sword.

He slashed at those nearest to him, and some fell howling.

Fortunately for our hero none of the men had firearms, so he managed to keep them pretty well off him.

He received an awful blow on the head from behind, that rendered him helpless for a few moments.

His fair charge saw their danger, and taking the sword from his hand, she fought like a Tartar.

Dick took the weapon again, and soon made a passage through his opposers.

Then he made his way to Stanhope Villa.

They reached the house.

It was a pretty little villa, with a garden and ground tastefully laid out.

"I am very grateful for your kind protection," she said, and sighed.

Dick bowed.

"Believe me, I shall carry the remembrance of this meeting for years, and look back to the memory of a lady so kind, so brave, and so lovely as yourself."

"Our companionship was, I trust, at least a mutual pleasure," she said.

"A pleasure, lady, that I shall not soon forget."

Her lips parted in a smile, as with a thrilling glance at his handsome face she gave him her hand, for they had dismomnted.

The pressure of his hand, his rich deep voice, and the gaze of his brilliant eyes had a strange influence over her.

She longed to invite him in, but for fear of her own reputation and the fear of her husband suddenly returning deterred her from taking such a daring step.

"Good night!" she said, in a low tremulous voice.

"Must we part so soon?" said Dick, gazing steadily into her beaming eyes.

The lady sighed.

"I would invite you in," she said, "only my husband might return, and he would be sure to be jealous."

"I thank you, but on no account will I intrude where, though I am glad to know I should be welcome, my presence would be almost a sacrilege."

The lady blushed deeply, and her beautiful breast heaved high.

"You may come whenever you like," she said, with charming frankness, "and my husband will be happy to welcome one who so nobly saved me from such an ignominious fate as would have befallen me."

"To come, dear lady, would afford me much pleasure."

He raised her trembling hand to his lips, and thought what a delightful companion she would make to pass a few hours away.

She was really a superb creature, with limbs of such voluptuous symmetry that it is no wonder our hero—a youth of no ordinary passions—was enamoured by her bewitching beauty.

He was not yet possessed of that rare virtue—constantcy—neither was he inconstant with those he loved, but when placed in such a tempting position as the present, all else for the time was forgotten.

It is more than probable that the charming young wife in a very short time would have given way to the eloquence of her gallant cavalier, and even forgotten her husband, but suddenly there arose in the distance a tremendous clamour of angry voices, which banished such thoughts as their heads entertained at the moment.

Dick looked in the direction from whence the voices came, and by the faint glimmer of the stars, he saw a man tearing along with the swiftness of an antelope.

Close behind him came a crew of men armed with all conceivable kinds of weapons.

On kept the fugitive, never once turning his head to look back at his pursuers, but bounded forward, leaping high hedges, springing over ditches, and clearing everything that stood before him.

It was a race for life, and a minute might have lost it.

Panting like a panther, and looking wild, and almost ferocious through the terrible excitement, the man bounded across the road, leapt over the gates, where stood our hero with his fair companion, and dashed down the avenue of the villa.

"My husband!" exclaimed the lady, excitedly. "What is the meaning of this, Tom?"

"Quick, quick, Fanny! The bloodhounds are after me. Open the door, and follow me,"

The astonished young wife flew to the door, and in a moment swung it back.

Tyburn Dick was rather astounded at the sudden change in events, but he soon recovered, and was ready for action.

He drew his sword, and fugitive, said—

"Fear nothing, friend; two trusty blades and strong arms to wield them, can stand against twice the number of such a hireling crew as those coming."

The man did not stay to question him, but cast an inquiring look at the gallant youth, and said while following his wife—

"If you are a friend, follow me. It is safer inside than out."

Dick was exactly of the same opinion, and followed him.

"Bar the doors and windows," shouted the man.

Another minute huge bolts were shot into their sockets, ponderous iron bars were placed across the windows, the door was cased with a body of sheet-iron that made it utterly impenetrable.

The place was only secured in time.

Fortunately for the fugitive, our hero, and the fair lady.

Barely had the last bar fallen into its place when without there arose a tremendous clamour of voices holloaing one against the other, each trying to make the most noise.

Finding their noise did not bring out the man they wanted, they commenced battering away at the door with might and main.

"Keep at that," laughed our hero; "it don't hurt us, and it amuses you. Nothing like physical exercise, and I know that's good."

He meant hammering at the door.

So it was, too good for some, especially those who got in the way of a big fist, and were floored by a punch in the head.

Through the intense excitement, the fair lady, in her bewilderment, rushed into Dick's arms, instead of her husband's.

Our hero was not at all angered by the mistake. He rather liked the idea of having a pair of soft warm arms twined around his neck, and a pair of pretty lips meeting his occasionally.

Her husband looked quite contented; perhaps it was that he did not exactly realize the fact that his wife was locked in another man's arms.

The noise without was increasing in fury,

THE CORNWALL COACH STOPPED BY TWO TYBURN DICKS.

and the fury of the men was increasing to madness.

"Surrender in the King's name," shouted one of the men, lustily.

"You had better give in quietly, Tom Fox," shouted another.

Tom Fox laughed grimly. He beckoned Dick to follow him upstairs.

"I will show them how I surrender," he said to our hero, when they stood in an upper room, from the window of which they could look down upon their enemies.

"Do," replied Dick.

Tom Fox disappeared for a moment, but when he returned he brought with him two enormous blunderbusses.

"I think we shall be able to scatter a few," he said, handing one to his young frind.

"I think we shall," iterated Dick.

A horrible discord of shouts and yells rea the air as our hero made his appearance at the window.

"Tyburn Dick! Tyburn Dick!" were the cries.

Dick raised his hat to the yelling crew.

"Have I the honour of being in the presence

of the Highway Prince, Tyburn Dick," exclaimed Tom Fox, surprised.

"You have," said our hero; "and while there's danger I'll stand by."

"Many thanks," said the other, raising the noble youth's hand to his lips.

"Come," Dick said, "our friends outside are growing impatient. Ah! Red Matthias is their leader—a mortal enemy of mine."

"And mine too," responded Fox.

"It would be as well to rid ourselves of such a dangerous foe," Dick remarked.

"Yes," answered the other.

A dangerous light kindled in his eyes as he shouldered his huge weapon and went to the window.

"Fire," yelled Matthias, furiously, as Dick put his head out.

Tom Fox pulled the trigger of the blunderbuss as the thief-taker spoke; it exploded with a tremendous roar, scattering its destructive fragments amongst the party below. Barely had the sound of the report died away when it was answered by a dozen pistols from the officers.

Everything for the minute was hidden by the cloud of dense vapour that curled upwards from the weapons.

A cry of pain came from Tom Fox—a bullet had entered his shoulder. The blunderbuss fell from his hands, and staggering backwards he sank into the arms of Tyburn Dick.

"My husband, my husband! he is killed," cried Mrs. Tom Fox, rushing forward in great distress.

"No, I am not," said the loving husband, faintly; "but I have got a bullet in my shoulder which I don't care how soon comes out."

Dick led the wounded man to the couch, and then proceeded to extricate the leaden missile with a nerve cool and collected, regardless of the tearful tumult outside.

He had just finished the operation by binding up the wound, when there appeared at the window a burly head and a face of such malicious aspect that the lady, on turning suddenly, caught sight of the apparition and uttered a scream of alarm.

Dick turned and saw the face too.

He made a sudden rush to the window with his drawn sword. The man belonging to the malicious face yelled and fell to the ground.

"Tyburn Dick," said Red Matthias, persuasively, "you had better give in quietly; you can't escape, and in trying you may only get hurt."

"Thanks for your advice," said Dick. "When you catch me I will go quietly."

"Very well. I have a warrant to take you alive or dead."

"That's the thing; make sure of me, one way or the other, if you can."

"Will you surrender quietly?"

"Not if I know it."

"Fire at him," shouted the thief-taker.

The men had fired once, and consequently they had all got empty weapons when they received the second order.

Matthias roared and swore frantically.

"Get in at the window," he exclaimed. "Seize him—shoot him—kill him, if he resists; we must take him, dead or alive."

The men commenced like so many monkeys to climb up the front of the house, saying nothing of those who, when up half-way, fell down with a thud.

Dick saw it would be dangerous to tarry there any longer.

"Farewell!" he said, shaking the wounded man by the hand; "we may meet again."

"Oh, no!" cried the fair lady, tearfully, clinging to him, "you are not going to surrender."

"Me?" laughed our hero. "Let those take me who dare!"

"Where are you going?" inquired Tom Fox, looking admiringly at the gallant youth.

"By staying here," answered the Boy Prince, "I only endanger your life and my own, too."

"But you can't leave here without being taken," put in Mrs. Fox.

"They shall take me by my own free will, if I can't," said Dick, squeezing her tiny hand. "You watch me, and see the way I shall astonish the officers."

"No, no; don't go," persisted the lady. "I implore you not to venture out."

"If I stay, I shall be taken, and so will your husband; if I jump from this window, I shall escape. The officers will follow me, and forget your husband."

The lady saw it was no use to argue. She sighed sadly, and gave way.

"Adieu! I shall come soon," Dick said, "when your husband is out," he added, in a whisper.

The lady blushed deeply, whispered something in return that made his cheeks glow, and taking a parting kiss, he sprang to the window.

His sudden appearance brought a shout from his foes.

Dick was rather astonished to find himself surrounded on either side of the wall by the officers.

They looked like so many apes clinging to the ivy that grew up in front of the pretty little villa. Many of the valiant gentlemen, who secured a stout piece of the climbing plant, clung to it for dear life, fearing to move another inch either way; there they hung in fearful agony, perspiration oozing out of every pore in their bodies.

"Stand back!" shouted Tyburn Dick to the officers who were waiting for him beneath.

They stood back.

Dick was standing erect on the window-sill. His handsome figure was shown off to its full advantage. Many of the coarse law-hunters looked at him with a touch of pity, and in their own hearts wished he might escape their brother officers' greedy grasp.

Dick cast a disdainful look at the thirsty hounds, who waited eagerly to capture him for the sake of the blood-money offered by the King.

"I am coming," he said, with a dauntly air.

As he spoke he drew his bright jewelled sword, and, raising the point over his left shoulder, he sprang from the window-sill, bringing the gleaming weapon round in a circular cut to clear a path as he reached the ground.

For a moment he gazed steadily into Red Matthias's eye, then suddenly he darted forward, struck the thief-taker a violent blow in the chest with his head, that sent him spinning over, and taking the opportunity to knock down a few of the gaping officers, he scampered off to a meadow, where his horse was grazing.

In an instant he sprang into the saddle.

Red Matthias and his bloodhounds were soon upon him.

"Stand, Tyburn Dick, or I'll shoot you where you sit!" the thief-taker said.

He held the horse by the bridle with one hand, and pointed a pistol with the other at our hero's head.

Our hero did not see the force of it. He leant forward in the saddle, clutched the thief-taker by his shaggy hair with his left hand, at the same time seizing the pistol by the tube, taking especial care to turn the muzzle away from himself.

The thieftaker was so astonished at being so unexpectedly attacked that he lost his speech.

After the lapse of a few moments, he said—

"What are you going to do, Tyburn Dick?"

"You were going to shoot me with this pistol," Dick said.

Red Matthias was a brave, daring fellow, and would not tell a lie to save his own life.

"I should, if you did not give in quietly," he said.

"Oh!" said Dick, twisting the thief-taker's arm round, and pointing the pistol in his face; "I will try the experiment on you, and see if you like it."

Our hero did not intend to fire.

The thieftaker did not know that. He struggled desperately to regain the weapon in his own power, and the trigger was pulled in the wrestle.

There was a report, a flash, and a puff of smoke.

Matthias uttered a cry of pain, and fell to the earth stunned. The ball struck him on the temple.

His myrmidons made a rush at our hero.

Dick put spurs to his steed, and off he went.

"Stop him—stop him—shoot—take him, dead or alive!" yelled one of the men.

"TAKE ME WHO DARE!" shouted Tyburn Dick, defiantly.

And away he went.

. . . .

Tyburn Dick had ridden some distance in silence. He was passing a lonely spot when an aged woman stopped in his path and confronted him. She looked poor and miserable.

"What now, good mother," said Dick,

recognising the intruder as the Death Witch. "Why do you so often cross my ath?"

"Beware, Tyburn Dick," she said, "you are riding a race with the shadow of death hanging over you. Beware of the lady you have lost."

"What mean you?" asked Dick, wonderingly.

"The shadow of death hovers near you. Beware of the fair lady you love, she will be your fate. The one—the one you have lost—she is gone."

"Tell me why," he began, when she spoke again.

"On, on—go your way; the shadow of death will follow you. Beware of the lady you love."

And waving a long stick above her head, she pointed to a tree and disappeared, while Dick turned his head to look at the object she pointed to. A thrill of horror crept through his frame as his gaze rested on a man hanging from the arm of a huge tree.

The poor fellow presented an awful spectacle. He was bound securely by thick cords, his flesh was shrivelled up by the frost, his eyes had sunk back, leaving horrible fleshless sockets, that plainly showed the fearful agony he had endured through the agonising death.

Dick turned away with a shudder. He was not superstitious or easily influenced, but the weird warning of the Death Witch, and the terrible sight of the gibbeted man, sent a chill to his heart.

He gave his horse the reins, and went forward for the haunt.

He had curious misgivings; the strange warning of the witch about his lady-love set his brain in a whirl of wonderment.

He had yet to learn the worst, to receive a blow that would strike deeply to his innermost heart.

He did not know that Grace had been torn from the haunt.

He did not dream of the grief and sorrow he was to learn.

CHAPTER LIII.

A MISSION OF LIFE OR DEATH—A TERRIBLE CONFLICT WITH THE KING'S GUARD—THE DESPERATE ATTACK UPON NEWGATE.

of the gambling-house, Gallant Tom hastened to the stables where he had left his horse.

The ostler brought his horse to the gates, at the sound of the highwayman's voice.

In a moment Tom sprang into the saddle, and rode swiftly away.

"Off and away!" he said, patting the animal's sleek neck. "Every moment endangers my noble comrades' lives. If they once more get inside the cursed walls of Newgate, they will be lost."

While thus cogitating he passed Dashing Ralph, St. James, and his valet, being led away by a body of officers.

He pretended not to take any notice of them, but his manly breast throbbed with agitation and fear.

He saw how helpless their position was, and unless he could soon overtake his comrades, whom he had sent back to the haunt, he well knew that the dauntless fellows who were being led to Newgate would be sacrificed.

On—on he went, dashing through the streets at a maddening pace.

London was soon left behind.

More than one heavily-laden traveller passed him. He heeded them not. His only thought was for the rescue of his comrades, piercing the gloom as he went along.

Suddenly he started, brushed his eyes and leant forward.

He saw the shadow of a body of horsemen in advance.

"What ho, comrades!" he shouted.

The horsemen halted.

"What ho! What name?" came a voice in response.

"Captain Tom of the Silver Star!" replied the highwayman.

The horsemen turned, and rode towards him.

"What's the matter, captain?" asked one of the men, as they came up to the highwayman.

"Life or death!" exclaimed Gallant Tom, turning his horse's head to ride back with his comrades. "Captain Ralph and two of my friends are captured, and being led to Newgate. We must reach there within half an hour, or all will be lost."

The men asked no more questions.

by their side, and they kept the same swift pace, until a sudden turn in the road brought them face to face with a body of the King's Guards.

"Stand aside!" exclaimed Gallant Tom, as the soldiers ranged themselves in a line across the road. "By whose authority do you dare to intercept us?"

"The King's!" replied the captain, riding forward. "Back, gentlemen! You cannot pass!"

"Slave!" thundered the highwayman; "draw your men from our path, or we will make a way that shall be marked in blood!"

For reply the captain of the Guards drew his sword.

Like a thunderbolt Gallant Tom rode upon him, and dealt him a blow that made him reel in his saddle.

Roused by the sudden onset, the captain of the Guards dashed upon his opponent. His sword gleamed in the air, and then came down with terrible force.

Gallant Tom raised his weapon only in time. The blades clashed as they met, and a shower of sparks flew from the ringing steel.

It was as much as the highwayman could do to keep his combatant's sword from cleaving his skull in twain. Had he not possessed a wrist as strong as iron, the blow aimed at him would have been fatal.

They were both good swordsmen, and well-matched, but it required all Gallant Tom's skill to parry fearful blows of his opponent off.

Had his sword been made of anything but the finest flexible steel, it certainly would have been shattered to pieces by the huge weapon of the soldier.

Blows and thrusts were being made on both sides.

The highwayman wanted to end the conflict.

Suddenly wheeling round he threw all his strength into one terrible blow that he aimed at the captain of the Guards' head.

Again their weapons met.

The soldier's fell from his grasp, shivered to the hilt.

He was at his one's mercy.

Gallant Tom's sword was again raised, but he did not wish to slay the man who did but his duty, and altering his intention, he swung his sword round, caught the point, and dashed the pommel heavily on the soldier's forehead.

The captain reeled and fell.

The highwayman went to the assistance of his comrades, who were fighting fiercely with the Guards.

More than once had they been driven ba by their many foes, but now as their captain came to aid them they charged boldly, and broke through the close phalanx of those who tried to oppose them.

No blood had been shed on either side, but as Gallant Tom rode through the line of soldiers, one of the men lunged furiously at him, but missed his mark, and fell forward on the point of the highwayman's sword, that he drew to parry the thrust.

The next moment he gave a gurgling cry as the sword pierced his heart.

The jerk he gave as he fell startled his timid animal. It reared up, plunged forward, and in its flight struck another man from his saddle, who was whirled away by the onward motion of the maddened steed, and falling beneath the horses of his comrades, the unfortunate man was trampled to death by their iron hoofs.

The rest raised their two dead comrades from the ground, and thus with their wounded captain they sternly followed the highwaymen, whom they tried in vain to stay.

The bright silvery moon had just broken through the dense columns of grey fleecy clouds as Gallant Tom and his comrades neared the city.

"Ah!" ejaculated the highwayman, on perceiving a body of men going down the road. "Surely this cannot be our friends. Come, comrades; we must see."

He rode forward in advance of the rest as he spoke.

Surely it was a friend, but not the one he meant.

He nearly fell from his saddle on perceiving the captive's face.

Who was it, that he should start so?

"Duke," he muttered, "and captured by Jonathan Wild!"

Devil Duke it was, and in the grasp of the incarnate fiend, Jonathan Wild, the notorious thief-taker.

"We must rescue him first," mused Tom, riding back to his brethren.

Wild did not notice him, or he would have raised a cry to capture him—Gallant Tom.

"Another of our comrades in danger," said the highwayman to his companions.

The men looked surprised.

"Who is it?" asked one.

"Captain Duke," replied Tom.

"How many bloodhounds around him?"

"Five and Wild."

"We must have him."

"Wild or Duke?"

"Captain Duke," said the man.

"Yes, our comrade must be saved," said Gallant Tom. "They are five—we are eleven —that's just two to one, and a bit over."

"Don't you think, captain," said the man, "we had better go on them quietly?"

"Just so," answered Gallant Tom. "They will turn down the road on the left—we must ride across this field, and get in the road to the left before them, and wait for them; then, as they turn the corner we can meet them face to face."

"That will surprise them."

"Exactly my idea, and while they are re-covering from their surprise, we can make a sudden attack, and rescue our comrade."

"Suppose Wild should catch sight of us. He's got devilish hawk-eyes."

"That will make no difference; but to be on the safe side, suppose you all get your pistols well primed, and meet the thief-taker and his company point blank."

The eleven highwaymen rode across the field, and by the time they reached the road to the left their pistols were primed.

They waited for Wild and his crew, also vil Duke.

They did not wait long.

The party emerged from the open road, and turned into the road on the left, which was rather narrow, and excessively dark.

"Halt!" thundered Gallant Tom.

Wild fairly leapt from the ground.

"Who dares cry halt?" exclaimed Jonathan Wild, fiercely.

"I, Jonathan Wild," and dashing through he small body of officers, the highwayman seized the thief-taker by the collar, dug the spurs into his horse's sides, and dragged Wild

along for some distance, and then struck him down by a blow on the temples.

When Tom rode back to his comrades, he found them in terrible conflict with the four officers.

The highwayman let them fight on while he freed his comrade.

He took a peculiar instrument from his pocket, which he dexterously plied to the manacles that bound Duke's wrists, and with a little twisting and turning picked the lock.

Duke was free.

He warmly grasped his noble preserver's hand. They passed a few words of affection-ate friendship, and then aided their brethren to dispose of their enemies.

That was soon accomplished.

The four men were bound together with a rope, which was tied round their waists, the end thrown over a huge branch of a tree, and the four officers, being hauled about three feet from the ground, were left hanging.

It did not take the highwaymen long to accomplish that little piece of devilry.

In less than five minutes after Duke was freed, they were on their way to Newgate.

Devil Duke rode on his favourite steed— Rosebud—which one of the officers had been kind enough to take possession of when the highwayman was captured, and which Duke availed himself of when freed.

They would stop for nothing now.

They were on a mission of *life* or *death*.

They were twelve noble men. Each knew the peril of their adventure. They would have risked twenty times the danger that they were now riding into in defence of any of their brethren.

There was a look of set calm resolution on each of their faces, and a determined look in their eyes.

They reached the city.

None had spoken during the journey—still all remained silent.

"By heaven, Duke, we shall be too late!" exclaimed Gallant Tom. "See!"

They had now turned down Newgate street.

"Forward, comrade!" shouted Devil Duke, excitedly.

The men urged their steeds forward.

They were within fifty yards of the dingy

building, when the ponderous gates were swung open, and Dashing Ralph, Victor St. James, and his valet were led in triumphantly by their captors.

"Hold!" sung out Duke, in a voice that echoed like a peal of thunder.

The party at the gates halted.

Another moment the highwaymen dashed up to the gates, dismounted, and with drawn swords rushed upon the officers who surrounded the highwayman and his friends.

So sudden and terrible was the attack upon the officials of Newgate, that it took some moments before they could recover from their amazement.

Then they suddenly seemed inspired with energy. A rush was made towards the gates to close them and secure the intruders, but the highwaymen fought desperately, and kept them back. Alarm bells rang furiously. Men shouted loudly, and then a whole troop of about fifty warders, and other inmates of the huge prison, came rushing towards the scene of confusion, armed to the teeth.

The highwaymen were not unprepared to meet them. As the men bounded towards them Duke sang out—

"Fire!"

A flash—a terrible report—cries of agony—and then the volley was returned.

Everything was now hidden by the dense white smoke. The ponderous gates suddenly slammed to.

A shout of triumph rang through the air.

Are the highwaymen entrapped by some sneaking wretch, who, in the fog, has managed to close the gates?

There is another shout—a rush of feet—again the huge ponderous gates are opened, and a silent but terrible conflict seems to be going on.

CHAPTER LIV.

THE WRECKERS' PRIZE—A FIGHT FOR THE CARGO—HIGHWAYMEN TO THE RESCUE.

It was a terrible night of excitement!

The Cornwall coast shook and reverberated by the force of the fearful storm that raged.

The rain fell in torrents, the wind howled and shrieked in fitful gusts; but above all could be heard the roar of the angry sea, as it threw its huge billows mountains high.

It was a night in which few people could live, yet hurrying about the coast were a group of rough seafaring men, every now and then casting an anxious glance seaward.

The night was pitchy dark, and the seafaring gentlemen in hurrying about on the coast came in contact with one another, and then gave vent to fearful oaths, each calling the other a clumsy fool or a long-shore lubber.

Suddenly the storm abated; then came across the deep angry ocean voices of distress.

Then a rocket flew upward, as though from the bosom of the battling sea.

Then there was a prolonged shout from the seafaring men on shore.

Another moment, and a beacon was raised on the Wreckers' Gully.

Another rocket answered this signal from the ill-fated ship that was being tossed and buffeted about.

The ship was doomed!

Every minute the treacherous beacon lured it nearer to destruction.

Another minute, and it was dashed upon the breakers.

Then arose fearful shrieks of distress, cries for help, despairing yells, groans of agony and frantic screams, as some poor wretches hung desperately on to a raft to save their miserable existence, and were again washed into the sea.

It was now time for the smugglers to carry on their fiendish work.

The storm ceased to rage so furiously, the wind lulled, and even the rain fell more gently.

It seemed as though the tempest had risen to destroy the ship, and stay the wicked career of its bloodthirsty crew.

Boats were manned and pushed off, and soon returned, crammed with the costly cargo which the ill-fated bark was laden with.

The valuable booty was brought ashore.

The smugglers who crowded round it, with their swarthy faces brightened up by a look of pleasure at the idea of having such a haul, did not observe a pair of hawk-like eyes glaring at them through a crevice in th rocks

The hawk-like eyes suddenly disappeared the others did not.

The smugglers had just got their treasure

carefully stowed away in the cave, when a loud ringing voice made them start.

"Confound it, mates!" exclaimed the captain. "What the blazes is that?"

Another chorus of yells rang through the cave.

The smugglers sprang to their feet and prepared for an emergency.

They were prepared only in time. A third wild yell rang through the rocks; then there came a rush of feet, and a score of the Black Band brethren headed by Captain Bertrand, dashed into the cave.

"Back, every one of you," said Bertrand.

The smugglers fell back, awed by the sudden appearance of so many black individuals.

The Black Band gathered round the cargo.

The captain of the smugglers looked at the invaders in blank astonishment.

"Shiver my timbers, mates!" he exclaimed, "are we going to let them long-shore lubbers overhaul us in our own cabouse?"

"'Tain't likely," yelled one. I'll have the first shot at 'em."

Suiting the action to the word, he fired at the Black Brethren. One fell prone.

This inspired the rest of the smugglers, and in another moment the whole crew dashed upon the intruders with naked cutlass.

They were met by their savage assailants.

The Black Brethren took a mean advantage of their opponents by firing a cowardly volley into them.

This decreased the smugglers' number, but made the others more ferocious, and like savage tigers they attacked their combatants.

The Black Band were considerably too many in number for their assailants, and the war showed signs of being victorious on their side.

It would have been so.

But at the very critical moment a voice loud as thunder rang through the cave, and caused the combatants to pause.

"Is that some more land-lubbers here?"

"No," thundered the voice again, "It is friends."

"Into these lubbers, lads!" said the smuggler captain, inspired with the hope of friends coming to his rescue. "Into them—give 'em to quarter!"

"Ay, ay, captain," bawled the crew.

The vision of the costly treasure began to fade from the brethren of the Black Band.

They knew not who, nor how many of the new-comers there were. They heard the heavy tread of many feet, and began to look for a way of exit.

They saw it, but were kept back by their infuriated foes, who fought like Titans.

"Give them another volley of lead, comrades," yelled Captain Bertrand, beside himself with baffled rage.

"Fire another shot, and not one of you will leave this cave alive," responded a boyish voice from some unseen part of the cave.

Captain Bertrand laughed ironically.

"Do as I command, men," he said. "Let the braggart come forth, and I will answer him."

A heavy hand was laid on his shoulder, and held him in a firm grip.

"Answer, dispicable hound," hissed a voice in his ear—"answer me, sword to sword, Captain Bertrand—answer your enemy, Tyburn Dick."

The captain of the Black Band shrank down with a groan, more like the growl of an enraged lion than a human being.

For a few minutes he was deprived of speech by the sudden appearance of his foe, and he stood staring aghast at the dauntless boy who confronted him.

Our hero with his gallant band kept his word. Though having passed through so many fearful dangers of late, he was here to defend the people with whom he had been brought up.

He had taken his comrades through the hermit's cave, and thus led them to the smugglers' haunt, where they awaited quietly until the critical moment.

The band were not long in following their young leader.

The Black Brethren had driven the smugglers into corners of the cave, where they would have ended their career, had it not been for the timely aid of our hero and gallant friends.

"Forward, comrades," said Big Bullskin, making a furious cut with his ponderous weapon at the Black Brethren, who surrounded the cargo first landed from the wrecked pirate bark.

The cargo was left alone, and the Black Brethren rushed behind anything likely to afford them shelter from their angry foes.

Our friends were not so desirous for bloodshed as were their enemies.

The Black Band, seeing they were not met with the ferocity they expected from their rivals, made a sudden attack upon the highwaymen.

This cowardly assault aroused the terrible anger of Joseph Munroe's lion-like nature, and calling his comrades together, they went to war in real earnest.

"Give them no quarter, comrades," shouted Big Bullskin.

His comrades did not want that instruction —they were already fighting like so many demons.

"That's it, my kiddies," shouted the smuggler captain; "let the lubbers have it. Give 'em a broadside, mates. That's it— bravo!"

The Black Brethren were fastly retreating. They could not compete against their foes' superior strength.

"Come on, mates," yelled the smuggler captain! "follow the lubbers up."

Inspired by the energy of their leader, the rough crew fought bravely by the side of the highwaymen, and soon drove the invaders from their haunt without bloohshed on either side.

Captain Bertrand and our hero were left alone in the cave.

Firmly they stood, foot to foot, fighting with untiring skill, each trying to seek the other's life.

A deadly glitter burned in their eyes, and bitter hatred swelled their breasts.

"I shall kill you, Captain Bertrand," said Dick, coolly.

Captain Bertrand laughed bitterly.

"You will have to come to life again after my sword has gone through you to do that," he replied.

"We shall see," Dick answered, grimly. "One of us will fall."

"That will be you."

"I am agreeable, if you can kill me."

Dick delivered a furious blow at his antagonist's head as he spoke.

Captain Bertrand was on his guard. He caught the trembling blade on his own, and made a fearful plunge for his opponent's heart.

It went uncomfortably near to its mark.

A flush of anger mounted Dick's fair face. His sword made a circle in the air, it met his opponent's with a ringing clash, and dashed it from his hand.

Captain Bertrand gave vent to a groan.

For a moment he stood glaring at his assailant.

Could he spring forward and close with his opponent?

That would be dangerous he thought.

He saw the terrible resolution in Tyburn Dick's eyes. He knew there was no mercy for him.

His sword lay a few paces behind him.

He stepped back to regain it.

Tyburn Dick leaped forward. His sword swerved round his head. Down—down it came, with the swiftness of a lightning-flash, dealing terrible destruction, and struck Captain Bertrand prone to the ground.

Again the impetuous boy drew his weapon back, with deadly intent to finish his enemy.

A rush into the cave and a yell of many angry voices stayed the death-blow.

Dick turned.

A few of the Black Band, that had concealed themselves, now crept forth with an avaricious intent to carry off the booty, while the enemy were chasing their companions, but seeing the critical position of their captain, they rushed towards our hero.

With all the gallant boy's quiet docile nature, when roused he was as ferocious as a panther.

He was roused now, and quite as ferocious as that prowling beast of prey.

It was decidedly indiscreet of the black individuals to make such an unpremeditated attack upon so furious an enemy as Tyburn Dick, the Boy Prince of the Highwaymen.

The power of the youthful knight of the road, and the activity with which he moved, would have astonished a few of our modern gymnasts.

The Black Brethren surrounded our hero with murderous design.

Dick sprang round. His sword made a sweep like a gleaming meteorological serpent—if we may use the term—and two of the black individuals fell dreadfully injured.

The others cleared out, and before Dick had time to extricate his weapon from the body of one of the unfortunate men, he received a fearful blow from a thick cudgel on the back of his head.

He whirled round, glared spitefully at the perpetrator of so cowardly an act, and fell stunned to the earth.

The men, who a few moments before had rushed away from him, now clustered defiantly around the defenceless youth without the slightest fear, and loudly applauded their companion for his courageous act.

"Rejoice not when your enemy stumbleth," saith the proverb.

Probably the men who rejoiced over our hero's downfall had not learned that Christian doctrine.

Brutally they seized him in his unconscious state, and the barbarous design was apparent by their fiendish looks.

A pitiful shriek made the guilty wretches start.

An old grey-headed man rushed towards them with outstretched arms.

"No, no," he cried, "you shall not hurt my foster-son. Release him. Have mercy on him!"

"We will," growled one of the men, "and to you too, old man. The best thing you could have done would have been to have kept out of sight."

"No, no; you shall not hurt him!" exclaimed old Wayne. "I will defend him with my life."

"Oh, very well; a life don't make much difference to us, so you can go along with him."

The old man threw himself upon our hero, and with his feeble strength tried to wrench him from the grasp of his brutal captors.

"Away, old man," said one of the men, with an oath.

"I will not. Release my son!"

"Your son!" reiterated another of the men.

"Yes, my son.. Take pity on me, and release him."

"Away with you, hoary-headed old fool!" and the dastardly wretch struck the old fellow a blow that felled him to the earth.

Old smuggler Wayne did not leave go of his foster-son. He clung desperately to the Boy Highwayman's garments.

"Have none of you any feeling?" he implored. "Why do you wish to harm my son?"

"Why," thundered one of the men, "aint he nearly killed our captain?"

"It was in self-defence," persisted the old smuggler.

"Can't help that. "We're going to have revenge, and if you don't get out of the way, you will share his fate."

"No, no; you shall not kill him. Help! Help!"

"Curse the old fool! Take that." The man dealt the old man a fearful blow on the temples with the pommel of his sword.

"That's done for him," remarked another of the Black Brethren, as smuggler Wayne fell prone at their feet without a sigh or a groan.

"You shouldn't have killed the old man," said one of the Black Band, looking remorsefully at the lifeless body of the smuggler.

"It can't be helped now," remarked the perpetrator of the dastardly deed; "old men should look after their grey hairs, and keep out of danger."

"The body had better be removed," suggested the man who had before spoken.

"Yes," growled the other; "we had better hide the carrion, and then settle this young gentleman."

Meaning our hero, who was totally at their mercy.

Having removed old Wayne, the Black Brethren then dragged Tyburn Dick through the cave into a narrow recess of the rocks.

"Now, a light," yelled one of the men.

A light was shown by the aid of a glimmering oil-lamp, and the former speaker holding it over a gap in the earth, the faint light revealed a fearful depthless pit.

"We shan't have any more of his pranks when once he is down here," remarked the with the lantern.

"No," responded another, "and the sooner he is out of sight the better."

"Right—bring him here."

Dick was clutched by the rough hands of his enemies, and dragged to the verge of the yawning abyss.

A thrill ran through his frame, and at that moment he opened his eyes—at the very moment of his fearful danger—to look upon the cruel, pitiless faces of his foes.

"Ah!" exclaimed the most brutal of the gang; "he awakes! Come, comrades, let's get this job over before he recovers enough to resist. He may sleep an everlasting sleep at the bottom of this chasm."

Another moment and our hero was held over the yawning gap by his arms and legs.

His lips quivered. His handsome face was haggard, and worked convulsively, and by the terrible glare of his large dark eyes, it was evident he was conscious enough to realize the danger of his position.

His frame shook with a convulsive throb, and suddenly drawing up his legs, he struggled to free himself.

The jerk threw several of his enemies who held him, nearly down the terrible gulf, and by trying to save themselves, they pitched the gallant boy headlong down.

Then for a moment all was quietness, and the men stood breathless, staring at each other.

Then there was a dull splash, a gurgling of water, and a groan, loud and melancholy, issued from the depthless pit, and struck terror to the hearts of the guilty wretches.

Again all was silent and quiet as the tomb.

The deed was done.

The Black Brethren hurried from the cave, taking with them their wounded captain, and forgetting the booty.

Barely had they reached the threshold of the haunt, when Big Bullskin and his comrades from another entrance dashed into the cave.

"Gone!" he exclaimed, glancing around anxiously. "All gone! Come comrades!" he said, turning to the highwaymen; "our captain is either in danger, or he has returned to the haunt. He must be sought, and protected by our lives. Away, gentlemen!"

And away they went on a fruitless search for their beloved leader, Tyburn Dick, Boy Prince of the Highwaymen.

CHAPTER LV.

A DEN OF VILLAINS AND THE FAIR CAPTIVE.

"HURRAH, hurrah, hurrah!" rang out the clear voices of the highwaymen, in bold defiance.

They were outside Newgate.

The smoke of the firearms enabled them to creep out with Dashing Ralph, Victor St. James, and his valet unobserved.

But their retreat was soon discovered by the officials of Newgate, who rushed out to re-capture their prisoners.

The highwaymen did not run away. They waited for their foes with a cold determined air.

The two companies met. A quiet desperate conflict ensued, but no great loss on either side was sustained.

Gallant Tom brought the war to a climax by ordering his men to mount and away.

Some of the men were vicious, and gave their foes a parting dig.

Ten minutes later, Victor St. James and his valet had obtained their horses, and were riding along with the three captains.

"You have not yet told us your story, Duke," said Gallant Tom.

"Then I will."

His companions waited in breathless anxiety to hear him commence.

He began.

"I had the good fortune," he said, going right into it, "after my narrow escape from strangulation, to rescue a very interesting damsel from an old enemy, whom I pitched out of the window."

"To get him out of the way," interrupted Ralph.

"Just so."

"Two's company, three's—you know the rest. I hate repeating these old sayings," put in St. James.

"More especially when a fellow rescues an interesting damsel from another fellow, who is not so good as he ought to be," remarked Gallant Tom.

"Now, gentlemen, if you are all done I will continue my story," said Duke smiling.

Seeing they were all quiet, and anxious to hear his narrative, he continued—

"After pitching the fellow out of the window."

"You were in no hurry to go yourself," Tom said.

"It ain't fair to interrupt a fellow," said Duke, "but nevertheless I did not stay."

"I slid from the window with the lady, and while we were riding along, a carriage passed us with a lady inside, screaming most piteously for help.

"I soon put Rosie to her speed, and overtook the coach, and bringing it to a stand, made the occupant hand over all his coin, jewellery, and every little article of value.

"I and the gentleman of the coach had a row. I quietly pitched the gentleman in a ditch, got into the carriage with the lady, I had rescued, and persuaded the postilions to drive off.

"We had proceeded no great distance when my attention was drawn to the opposite seat."

"By the lady?" asked Ralph.

"By a lady, certainly," replied Duke "but firstly, by a faint cry that came from the lady's lips.

"I sprang up, and tried to discern the lady's features, but the night was so obscure, and I could not see a hand before me.

"The coach was suddenly brought to a halt. The lady held me by the shoulders. She knew my voice, and I knew hers.

"A light was brought to the window by Jonathan Wild, who had been kind enough to stop the carriage. I saw the lady's face—I knew it."

"That's nothing new for you," said Gallant Tom. "I believe you know half the ladies in the nation."

"That's complimentary, but not satisfactory to any of the fair sex, should they hear u," said Duke; "but, being serious, old fellow, you will be surprised to hear who the lady was. Can you imagine?"

"I cannot—can you?"

"I know for certainty."

"Let's hear it then."

Duke looked serious.

"I just had time to recognise her, and she me." he said, "when I was struck down stunned. I remember no more until five minutes before I met you, when I recovered to find myself in the hands of my ever-mortal foe, Wild."

"You have not yet told us who the lady was," said Ralph.

"Our chief's lady—Grace."

"The devil!" exclaimed Tom.

"No, a beautiful girl!"

"Who was the lady's abductor?"

"Lord Edward Aldervale."

"Curse him! He shall suffer for the outrage."

"Gentlemen," said Dashing Ralph, "we must lose no time in finding where the cowardly cub has taken her. We must defend her with our lives."

"We must," remarked Duke, "but we must discover where she is taken."

"As I said."

"To do that," put in St. James, "we had each better disperse, and make a thorough search."

"I propose," said Duke, "firstly, to put up at the Leopard Inn, and to-morrow morning we all go to Wild's house, and take him by storm, then if he won't tell us—for he knows—we will torture him like the brigands do, and so make him divulge the secret."

"Bravo, Duke!" said Ralph.

"A jolly good idea, by Jove!" seconded St. James.

"Duke, I shouldn't have thought you were capable of such an idea," remarked Tom.

Duke laughed, and the brave little party made their way to the Leopard Inn—their favourite haunt.

St. James's attention was attracted from his companions by a note fluttering from the window of a strange Gothic house, that lay back in a large piece of wilderness ground.

Lightly touching his steed, the young noble sprang forward, cleared the high decaying fence that surrounded the ground, and vanished from his companions' gaze.

"Where the deuce has he gone?" said Gallant Tom in surprise.

Shanks, with a wild cry, bounded forward, and like his master disappeared over the fence.

"Gone mad, I should imagine," said Ralph, in a whisper.

"THANK HEAVEN! I AM SAVED!" CRIED THE FAIR BRIDE, AS THE PRIEST THREW OFF HIS ROBE.

The highwaymen were bewildered. They could not understand the meaning of their young friend's abrupt departure.

"Where did he go?" asked Duke, looking all the surprise he felt.

"I know not," replied Tom.

"If they had been phantoms, they could not have vanished more quickly," remarked Ralph.

At that moment they heard a gay boyish laugh, and then St. James and his valet reappeared.

"An assignation?" asked Duke, curiously catching sight of the note held between the youth's fingers.

"Something of the sort," replied St. James.

"A clandestine meeting," Ralph said.

"Is the lady beautiful?" inquired Duke.

"That I have to find out."

"Come read, the note, old boy," said Gallant Tom.

St. James folded the note up, and put it in his pocket. He had not the slightest intention of making the contents known to his companions.

23

Gallant Tom dropped behind, and tapped Victor on the shoulder.

The young nobleman dropped behind too.

He could confide in the highwayman, Gallant Tom, that which he did not wish the others to know.

"Are the contents of that note a secret, Vic.?" asked Tom.

"To your comrades."

"And me?"

"You shall hear."

Tom waited.

"You never saw where I went to," said the handsome young cavalier.

"In faith, I did not," replied Gallant Tom.

"While we were passing that quaint old house that looked very much like a ruined abbey, I saw a note flutter from an upper window." St. James went on. "I knew its mission before I read it."

"Perhaps you were previously acquainted with its contents."

"Not so; but I have had many such before, and know the nature of their meaning."

"A lady in distress for a lover"

"No; a lady in want of a champion."

"There is little difference. Champions generally make lovers."

"In many cases."

"You will be no exception. I vouch the truth. of that," said Gallant Tom, with a laugh.

"I hope not, by Jove. It's a devilish bad case, if a fellow, after saving a lady, can't make love to her."

"You have nothing to fear on that point.'

"Why?" asked St. James.

"You are fishing for compliments."

"No, no; on my word."

"Truths are stubborn facts," said Tom; and, to tell the truth, you are such an irresistible fellow with the ladies, that any fellow who is with you can't get the slightest particle of a chance."

The youth laughed outright.

"Never mind, Tom," he said; "if I get the slightest particle of a chance, I will make love to the lady for you."

"Thank you, I prefer making love for myself."

"But you won't have the chance."

"I will keep the assignation for you—you don't want the lady."

"But I do the adventure."

"Adventures are dangerous, especially when a petticoat is at the bottom of them."

"Love-making is dangerous, too," St. James said. "Adieu, old boy."

"Mind what you are about, Vic, it may be a snare."

"I think not," answered the youth carelessly 'You and your comrades will be at the Leopard Inn."

"Yes, will you meet us there?"

"Within an hour."

"If we do not see you by then, we shall know that you have fallen into danger, and will come after you."

"If I do not join you within an hour, I shall have fallen into danger." His voice faltered as he spoke the last word. He warmly grasped the highwayman's hand, and rode away without another word.

For some distance he heard the patter of horses' feet behind him.

He suddenly turned his horse's head, and confronted his follower.

"Shanks, is that you?" he inquired of the horseman, who had pulled up.

"Yes, my lord," answered the faithful fellow.

"Who the deuce told you to follow me?"

"Nobody, my lord; only I thought you were going to danger, so I kept a look-out."

"There is no fear of my going into danger, Shanks. Return to the inn with my friends, and wait until I come."

The faithful fellow never disobeyed his young master. With much reluctance he turned his horse's head, and, with a tear rolling down his cheek, he sternly trotted back.

Victor St. James look reflectively at the strange, dreary old building.

"A nice-looking place," he cogitated. "The thing is, a lady is in there in danger —she must be saved. I hope she is young and beautiful. I like to rescue young and beautiful girls."

He touched his charger lightly with his heels; the noble animal with one bound vanished from the road.

St. James dismounted.

He stood beneath the decaying, crumbling

wall, up which the ivy crept in abundance, penetrating its fibres into every visible crevice to retain a hold and keep its massive body from falling with destruction to the earth.

"It it plainly evident I cannot get up by the wall," he muttered with dissatisfaction.

He looked up at the window.

He saw a white face watching him anxiously.

His breast throbbed with excitement.

The lady at the window put out her arm, and waved a handkerchief for him to hasten.

St. James waved his handkerchief in return.

"How the deuce am I to get up," he wondered.

A tall elm tree stood about six feet from the wall, towering high above the strange building.

"That is my only resource," he mused, looking at it despairingly, and inwardly wishing he possessed the power of a wizard to move it nearer to the window.

While he stood thus, the lady threw a coil of rope from where she stood.

It fell at his feet.

He clutched it eagerly—pulled it to try its strength.

The lady had fastened it securely above.

The gallant youth kissed his hand to the lady, and then commenced his ascent.

The fair captive, if she was a captive, took his hand, and drew him into the room as he reached the window.

Victor raised the trembling little hand that held his to his lips, then pulled in the rope to prevent any one else from making an ascent who felt particularly inquisitive.

He turned to the lady, and, in a sweet musical voice, said—

"You are in danger, dear lady."

The lady released his hand, and stepped back.

St James felt wonderfully surprised.

"You are not my lover," the lady said, in a faint timid voice.

"By Jove! she has taken me for some one else," he thought.

"I am a friend," he said, turning to her, after a pause of several moments that was only broken by the deep loud sighs of the lady.

"I understood by a note I picked up under the window, that you were in captivity against your will."

His soft eloquence reassured her that he was a friend, and timidly she advanced towards him.

"My lover brought me here," she suddenly broke out in a low sweet voice. "He told me to wait until he returned."

"Is your lover a true cavalier?" asked St. James, taking her hand. She did not resist.

"I always thought him true," she answered; but since he took me from my home, I have strange misgivings of his affection."

The youth's handsome face clouded.

The lady was young and very beautiful; innocent, and at an age easily led astray by the false flattery of some adventurous libertine.

Probably that was her case. We shall see as we proceed.

"Did your lover give you any reason for bringing you here?" asked the youth.

"He said that he knew my papa would not consent to our union," she replied, confiding wonderfully in her young champion; "and he said we could get married in secrecy here."

"Do your parents know your lover?"

"No;" and the lady sighed sadly as she answered. "He courted me at school."

"Ha!" exclaimed St. James, his fair boyish face flushing indignantly; "your lover is a villain! He has deceived you, dear lady. Come, trust to me. I will take you home while you're safe. Every moment's delay brings the impending danger nearer. Will you confide in me?"

"Will you prove true?" she queried, looking innocently into his face.

"By the light of the stars," he replied, solemnly; "this shall seal the compact."

He kissed her brow as he spoke.

The betrayed fair lady clung to him with all the confidence of her pure childish nature.

"Come, then, lady," he said, taking her hand.

He had cast the rope out of the window, fastened one end to a huge nail on the wall.

They were standing at the casement—St. James was in the act of getting out—when there came a loud shouting—a rush of many feet, and, ere either could recover from their surprise, a gang of handsomely dressed men dashed into the room.

"Ha!" exclaimed the youth, turning like a young lion.

He twined his left arm round his companion's slender waist, and drawing his rapier, he waited quietly for the intruders.

The lady trembled violently. She suddenly appeared to realize her perilous position. She saw now the snare she had been drawn into.

She bitterly regretted having trusted the perjured villain who had won her young affections and thus betrayed her.

Her girlish love turned into loathing hatred as her gaze fell upon the wretch who had deceived her.

Victor St. James saw her terrible agitation, and fearing she might faint, he tried to soothe her by his kind consoling words.

"Fear nothing, dear lady!" he said, in a loud voice, so that all in the room should hear him; "we are in a den of villains, but no harm shall befall you while I have power to use my weapon."

The daring youth had great belief in his own skill in swordsmanhip. He knew that few could stand against him.

The young lady felt comparatively safe under his protection.

"I know you are brave and noble," she said, confidently, "quite different to *him*"

"Dear little angel!" murmured the youth, holding her tightly to his side.

The party raised a shout, and rushed towards the young nobleman.

"Ah!" exclaimed St. James, preparing for a thrust at the new comer, whom he recognised, "I know you, my Lord Edward Aldervale."

The libertine young lord laughed satirically.

"And I know you," said another of the party. "Whose turn is it now, cousin Victor, to triumph?"

"Not yours, hound!" thundered the youth, and he aimed a fearful blow for his villanous cousin, Reuben Frampton's head.

"Prick him, prick him!" said the cynical-looking roué.

The rest closed round the youth with their drawn swords, and slowly forced him against the wall.

He stood undaunted, fearless, and defiant,

with twenty gleaming weapons levelled at his breast.

Slowly the weapons were pressed forward—slowly the sharp points penetrated his coat and scratched his flesh

Yet he did not move.

He kept his gaze fixed steadily upon merciless foes. His face looked demon and a dangerous light kindled in his flashing orbs.

"Strike!" he shouted, suddenly, "cowardly hounds."

His assailants started involuntarily, and the weapons moved from his breast.

That was what he wanted.

He did not lose the opportunity.

In an instant he had drawn a brace of pistols, and put his hand through the hilt of his sword, so that it hung from his wrist

"Curses!" hissed the fellow who had proposed the pricking operation; "kill him, gentlemen."

St. James laughed.

The fashionable libertines dashed forward.

"Back," exclaimed Victor, in a tone that spoke his intention if they did not comply with his command.

They did not.

And as they dashed upon him with murderous intent he fired.

There was a flash—a sudden report of pistols, followed by a shriek.

One of the bullets had entered Reuben Frampton's shoulder; the other went crashing through the door.

The wounded man staggered back, and then fell amongst his companions.

Like a pack of savage wolves pouncing upon their helpless victim, so the rest of the libertines dashed upon St. James.

His pistols in an instant were replaced in his pockets, and his rapier was darting about like a gleaming snake.

Regardless of his savage opponents, the youth turned to see why his companion was clinging so desperately to him.

The man who had proposed to prick him was trying to pull her from him—St. James.

The young cavalier's sword swung round, and came down for the other's head.

But the other moved aside, and the weapon came down wide of its mark.

The lady gave another shriek as she felt herself violently torn away from her gallant protector.

Victor St. James leaped forward, thinking nothing of his own danger, and tried to regain his fair companion

The gang of *roués* stood in his path, and kept him back.

They might just as well have tried to keep a mad lion at bay.

He dashed furiously into their midst, striking right and left.

He soon broke through them, but the lady was gone.

"Don't let him escape," cried one of the men.

Then there was a rush, and the whole crew closed round him. He had wounded another of their companions, and now they attacked him more savagely than before.

"Revenge, revenge!" they yelled.

St. James stood no chance with the number of foemen he had to contend against.

Could he escape?

He looked round. He was near the door. The angry foemen surrounded him, thrusting and cutting at him madly. It took him all his time to guard the blows, aimed as they were with such power and rapidity.

His strength is deserting him; he must escape, or he will never leave that accursed den alive.

Has he any chance of escape?

None.

It would be better to die in the attempt to escape, than to stand and be butchered by his cowardly opponents.

He must escape.

Desperation lent him strength.

With renewed vigour he beat down his assailants' weapons—suddenly dashed at those nearest the door, scattering them from his path, and with a bound he crashed through the panel, and disappeared.

The fashionable *roués* stood for a moment awed—it was only for a moment. Recovering from their surprise, they pursued the daring youth.

Victor St. James had no time to spare. He was now in a kind of corridor. The yells of his pursuers rang loudly through the long stone passage.

They were close upon him.

He heard the rush of their feet.

"Shoot him where he is!" yelled one, catching sight of the youth tearing along before them.

Crash!

Victor burst open a door and bounded in.

A lady sprang from a couch, where she had been reclining. Her eyes were wet with tears that rolled down her sad beautiful face.

She ran gladly towards the intruder.

"Milly! Milly!" exclaimed the youth.

"Yes, yes! Save me! Save me!" she implored.

"I don't understand," said St. James, bewildered. "Explain; how the deuce did you get here?"

"I was carried off when the haunt was attacked by the soldiers. You were there—you remember."

"Yes; but Grace, where is she?"

"I know not. It was her they wanted. I was taken away by mistake."

"Who was your abductor?"

"Lord Edward Aldervale, and ever since he discovered his mistake he has kept me in close captivity, and swears to have Grace."

"By heaven he shan't, or you either any longer!"

"Liar!" thundered the young libertine, and bounding into the room, he levelled a pistol at the cavalier's head. "Ho, ho! Die, interfering fool!"

Then came a report—a puff of smoke—and St. James fell to the floor collapsed.

CHAPTER LVI.

THE TWIN BROTHERS AND THE MORNING PHANTOM.

A FEARFUL gloom seemed to fill the smugglers' cave.

All within was still and quiet.

No traces of the fearful tragedy that had been enacted there were left to tell the tale of horror.

Not a voice—not a step broke the sombre stillness. Even the angry sea that a few hours before had been raging to a fearful pitch of fury, had now subsided into a strange silent calm, barely disturbing a pebble as it gently rolled up the beach, as though in shame of the awful destruction it had caused.

Not a living person was to be seen in or near the smugglers' haunt.

All had gone.

The morn was slowly breaking.

A flood of blue metallic light poured through the mouth of the cave, and mingled with the dull ghostly flickering glare from an oil-lamp that hung from the ceiling.

Presently there came the sound of low aces, then two men, alike in every respect, wly and cautiously entered the cave.

They were tall, powerfully built, and not unhandsome, though with a sinister look in their eyes and cruel expressive mouths.

Both were dark, with faultless colossal features. Both were of the same height, of the same stature, and both had massive heads of black curly hair.

Doubtless they were of the same age, and the same parents.

It would have been a difficult task to tell one from the other, so exactly were they alike

They each took a careful survey of the place, to see that they were alone, and then seated themselves before a still smouldering fire

Villany was plainly stamped upon their dissipated countenances.

One of them cast his eyes to the further end of the cave, where was heaped the costly cargo that had been taken from the wreck.

"A wealthy heap that," he said, turning to his companion.

"Wealth we no longer require, Reginald," responded the other.

"No, though we did our share to get it."

"Yes, yes; but why should we take what a do not want?"

"It is as well to prepare for a rainy day."

"That be ——. Two years have now elapsed since we took possession of the deeds that will make us masters of Merton Grange when we like to go forward."

"Then by all means we will go forward at oe, Percy," replied Reginald.

"What's that?" said Percy, turning sharply.

"What?" asked the other.

"Did you not hear it?"

"I did not."

"I swear I heard somebody cough."

"Fancy," remarked Reginald, turning over the burning embers with his feet, and looking contemptuously at his companion.

"Percy," he said, lighting a huge peculiar-shaped pipe, and speaking between every long puff—"Percy, I think you are haunted. Why the devil can't you forget the past, and only think of the future—bright glorious future—twin brothers, Reginald and Percy Merton, masters of Merton Grange? Think of that, my boy—think of that, and then give way to fear."

"I think of it, brother Reginald; aye, I think of it, but not as I should wish to think of it."

"Why? What the devil's the matter?" asked Reginald, troubled by the sad expression of his brother's face.

"It was two years ago last night," said Percy slowly and sadly, "when the craft that contained our uncle, aunt, and niece was wrecked."

"Well," the other responded, half fiercely.

"We helped to cause their destruction."

"So we have many others."

"We might have saved our uncle and aunt."

"As we might many others, and afterwards had our necks stretched for the trouble"

"George Merton was our father's brother, our uncle and our kinsman."

"So much the better for us."

"Yes, yes; so I thought."

"I have strange apprehensions that we shall never take possession of Merton Grange."

"Bosh! you are worse than a fanciful girl," said Reginald, severely. "Look here, Percy, I intend to take possession of the Grange. If you fear the after consequences, remain here; be a smuggler, a cut-throat, a common outlaw to be hunted about, while I live in luxury and bid defiance to the world. When once I am in the Merton estate, I will defy the nation and her power to put me out again."

"I fear nothing," replied the other, animated by the determination of his brother.

"Then why are you making a noise? There is nothing to fear. You remember walking along the beach with me two days after the wreck?"

"It will be two years age to-morrow."

"Exactly. Do you remember what we saw—what we found on the rocks?"

Percy turned white, and glared suspiciously round the cave.

He did not see a feeble old man, with a pallid, haggard countenance smeared with blood, lean eagerly forward from a kind of hole in the cave.

No, the guilty men did not see; they were not aware that a spy, a listener, was so near—a listener who knew so much of their villany, and who would hereafter prove so dangerous a foe.

"Do you remember what we found?" inquired Reginald, eagerly.

"I do. In the name of heaven bury the remembrance."

"Ah, ah," the other laughed, "so my brother laments. Does the remembrance pain him? Picture to yourself, Percy, the two forms we found lashed to a spar—our aunt and uncle Merton. We thought they were dead, but they were not. No, no, we revived them, did we not, Percy? They did not know us; they asked for their daughter, our cousin Grace. Do you remember that?"

"Yes, I remember," exclaimed the other, springing to his feet. "Reginald, our cousin, Grace Merton, was saved by Dick Wayne, the old fisherman's son."

"I remember," replied the other, his brow growing dark. "What became of the girl?"

"I know not. The boy, Dick, a few days after the wreck, was taken up for robbery, and the girl disappeared."

"Have they not been heard of since?"

"The girl has not."

"And Dick Wayne?"

"Some say he is a highwayman, the handsomest fellow on the road, causing great excitement, especially among the ladies. It is said that he assumes the title of Tyburn Dick, and has got the cheek of the very devil."

"How's that?"

"Why, I have heard that he wears a splendid star on his breast to distinguish himself."

"I don't believe it," growled Reginald. "The boy has plenty of good pluck, but I don't believe he's a highwayman."

"That matters not to us," remarked Percy. "Return to the subject we were talking of."

"You say the girl suddenly disappeared," remarked Reginald, a troubled look coming over his handsome face.

"Some say she was taken away," replied Percy Merton; "but, however, she has not been heard of or seen since, to my knowledge."

"She still lives, then, Percy?" he said, turning to his brother and looking steadily in his face. "We have a stumbling block in our way I was not aware of. *It must be removed.* You understand?"

He clutched his brother tightly by the shoulder as he spoke.

"You would not murder her—our cousin?" said Percy, with a shudder.

"Her life must not bar our way; we have done much, we must do more to gain our ambition. One nor twenty lives should not deter me. I would wade through a river of blood up to my chin sooner than release the power I now hold."

Percy did not answer.

He knew the desperate character of his brother, and feared to offend him.

"Does your chicken heart fail you?" said Reginald, in a sneering tone. "Would you lose it all, for the sake of her? What is she to us more than any other? Look you here Percy, you have hitherto done as much as I have, and rather than you should now give it up, I would kill you."

"As you say," remarked Percy, "I have hitherto aided you in your villany and crime; but you will not get my aid or consent to murder Grace Merton, should you find her."

He sprang to his feet, and, like an angry tiger, confronted his brother as he spoke.

"Sit down, Percy," said Reginald, quite calmly.

Percy sat down, but not without being prepared.

He kept his hand on the hilt of his sword, in case of emergency.

"This is child's play," Reginald began, keeping a steady look on his brother. "The girl has not been heard of for two years. We have nothing to fear. When once we have taken possession of Merton Grange, we must not stand for anything that should come in our path."

"Nothing," replied Percy; "are Mr. and Mrs. Merton dead?"

"You ought to know."

"I do not."

"They were bound together and flung into the sea—that was the last of them."

A terrified shriek rang horribly through the cave, and struck terror to the hearts of the two plotters.

Reginald Merton jumped to his feet.

The oil-lamp fell crashing to the ground, as though struck from the ceiling by some mighty weight.

The wood fire suddenly commenced to flicker and crack, sending showers of sparks flying over the cave, and then went out.

The twin brothers were in total darkness; each clutched to the other for support.

Neither could speak.

A dead silence prevailed.

Then there came a rustle.

The noise made them start.

Both stood in silent terror.

The blood in their veins seemed to freeze.

Percy tried to move forward, but could not; he felt as though held to the ground by some powerful hands; his tongue refused utterance, and clave burning to his mouth.

His brother, too, stood in torturing agony.

A guttural cry escaped the lips of one.

Then they both stood mute—breathless—their eyes glaring like balls of fire, and big drops of cold sweat rolling down their haggard faces.

They saw a figure robed in white slowly glide toward them.

Their terror grew fearful.

The female passed them with such a look on her fair pale face that ever after haunted them.

On passed the spectre-like form until it reached the further end of the cave, then it turned, raised a thin wasted arm, and pointed towards them with a threatening gesture.

The two men tried to keep their gaze from the awful vision, but their heads turned by some irresistible power.

At that moment, and as though something had been suddenly moved from the mouth of the cave, the rays of the morning's cold blue light burst through and fell upon the strange vision, making it appear terribly unearthly. The men were fascinated, yet terrified by the melancholy face and the steady gaze of the large blue, but wild-looking eyes that seemed to pierce their inmost soul.

Percy suddenly sprang from his brother's side with a horrible shriek, and bounded towards the phantom.

But it had gone—vanished—as though through the solid rock.

"My aunt!" he yelled, and throwing his arms wildly up, fell prostrate on the ground.

"Keep off! keep off!" yelled Reginald, madly, dashing about as though battling with some imaginary being. "Keep off! I did not murder Aunt Merton. Keep off, I say; you shall not take me."

"Percy, Percy! Help, help! they are dragging me away. Percy, save me! save me from the torturing flames."

Then for a moment he stood still, and glared around with such a look of wild excitement, that any one who could behold him at the time would have shrunk away in fear.

His gaze rested upon the inanimate form of his brother; he darted forward, raised him in his powerful arms, and rushed towards the entrance of the cave.

"Ah!" he exclaimed, dragging his brother; "they come back for me! I will not go! Keep off—keep off! Percy, Percy! why don't you help me? Ah, ah! he's gone—they have taken him away; they must not take me. Back, back fiends! I will not go with you!" he stepped backwards and put forth his hands as though pushing some one from him. "You say I must come!—no, no! Ha, ha! the devil laughs at me—he mocks me—he guards the gates—he points to the fire, the torturing flames, and waits for me—no, no! Come!—go! I can't come—release me; your fingers burn—help, help!"

And then he fell to the ground with a terrible wailing cry for help, tearing madly at his hair, and plunging frantically about.

Then again all was quiet.

The white-robed figure that had been the cause of the guilty man's terror, mysteriously appeared for a moment, stood over the two prostrate forms, and then vanished.

A low unearthly voice floated through the cave as she disappeared, and as the sound died out it echoed more than once—

"The Morning Phantom."

CHAPTER LVII.

THE PRISONER OF THE WELL.

HAD Tyburn Dick perished?

Had he sunk to the bottom of that fearful well never to rise again?

We shall see.

It was a moment of terrible agony for him when he recovered from the cowardly blow he had received to find himself in the hands of his foes.

He shuddered as he caught sight of the hideous-looking abyss above which he was held, and in another minute would be hurled down.

He was in a fearful dilemma.

Too faint to resist, he remained totally in their power.

Helpless as he was, he did not like to die without a struggle.

As the reader already knows, he gave one sudden plunge and fell.

Down—down—fathoms deep in the depth of the gulf he rapidly descended.

The atmosphere was bleak and murky.

Sparkling showers of clear crystal water spurted through numberless crevices in the shaft of the well.

The rushing tide below roared like so many angry beasts as it dashed up the side of the orifice, and in melancholy sounds echoed through the obscure shaft, adding a thousand terrors to the scene of horror.

He shrieked a last farewell to the world as, with a dull splash, he reached the surface of the surging waters.

How many more fathoms deep had he yet to descend?

Was that the depth of the limitless gulf?

He felt the soft sand beneath his feet, and the gushing water playing around his legs.

What was it that made him stand bewildered for the next few moments?

Was it that he had hope?

The water was not more than three feet deep!

Then came a gush of cool air.

His heart bounded with joy.

Saved—saved!

Uninjured and without a bruise, save for the blow he had received on the head.

Was he the first human being that dis-covered how harmless was that horrible-look-ing gulf?

He started.

A groan issued from no great distance.

Then he was *not* the only person that had discovered the problem of the well.

Another groan came, more loud and agonizing.

Dick looked troubled.

"Surely no living being can exist in such a place as this," he cogitated.

A living being did exist in such a place, and had done for a considerable time, as our hero will soon discover.

Now all was silent—even the gushing water seemed to have stopped its course.

Tyburn Dick stood in breathless anxiety listening for the sound, should it be again repeated.

A shriek, so wild and shrill, suddenly broke the stillness.

As though shot, Dick involuntarily sprang from the ground, and dashed forward.

His head came in contact with a project-ing crag; he reeled back half stunned, and fell.

Splash!

As he fell, he sank beneath the surface of the water; but only for a second, the cold stream revived him.

He was upon his feet in another moment.

The cries again and again rang out in piteous accents.

Dick felt a strange desire to discover the whereabouts of the prisoner.

Guided by the sound of the voice, Dick commenced to make a search for an outlet, determined to discover the person in distress, or perish in the attempt.

Warily groping his way round the bottom of the pit, and drawing his hand over the rugged surface of the rock.

Suddenly he stopped.

A cry of gladness left his lips.

He stood at an opening—an arch that ran through the side of the shaft of the well, through which gushed a current of bleak fresh air.

He was also nearer the prisoner, the cries sounded more distinct.

Dick went forward in the direction whence the voice proceeded.

"Who comes?" yelled a frantic voice.

The person had evidently caught the sound f proceeding footsteps.

Dick stopped.

The man repeated the query.

With a more cautious step our hero continued his course.

An exclamation of horror burst from his lips as he turned into another kind of passage, into which passed the bright rays of daylight from a hundred little crevices, and revealed a sight that curdled his blood.

Chained to the solid rock was a man, looking wild and haggard. He was tall, and had the fine-formed features of a gentleman, but which were wasted and worn.

His whole appearance was that of one of the superior class of persons.

Why was he chained to the wall, kept from the world, and all who were dear to him?

Had he been put there for some hideous crime, or was he kept there by some villain for a purpose?

He glared terribly at Dick.

The gallant boy was deeply touched by the awful sight, he could not keep back the scalding tears that started to his eyes and chased each other down his blanched cheeks.

Suddenly the man gave a fearful shriek, and sprang forward with his hands stretched out ready to clutch our hero.

Tyburn Dick fell back almost terrified; the attack was so unexpected and so desperate that it startled him, and he lost his balance and fell.

The length of the man's chain did not admit of him proceeding far from the wall, or Tyburn Dick would have suffered severely.

The maniac, for such he was, fought desperately to get at him.

"Come nearer, come nearer," he said.

"Thank you," said Dick, "I am quite contented to be where I am."

The maniac laughed spitefully, and showed two rows of white even teeth.

"Won't you come?" he said.

"Not if I know it."

"Come," persuaded the lunatic, "I have got something to tell you. Come near me."

He kept his glaring eyes fixed steadily upon the Boy Highwayman, and his long bony fingers twitched nervously.

He longed to get them on Dick's delicate white throat.

Dick had a very keen perception. He read the madman's brutal desire, and kept out of his reach.

"You know me!" exclaimed the lunatic, "I know you. Come nearer me. I will tell you something."

"We are alone. I can hear just as well where I am."

"Come nearer me. I want your life."

"Do you?" thought Dick.

"You put me down here," the maniac continued. "You are young—I forgive you. Come to me—pity me!"

He dropped his head on one of his wasted hands, and groaned aloud.

"I am mad, they say, but I ain't. Ha, ha! Do you think I am mad?' he asked, quietly.

"No; you are perfectly sane."

"Liar!" thundered the lunatic, sharply.

Dick leapt round surprised.

"I shall leave you if you are not more quiet," he said.

The poor fellow looked at Dick surprised, and then burst out in tears.

The gallant youth knew it would do him good to leave him alone while he wept.

It did.

He was quiet and subdued.

That horrible glare left his eyes—he was now more tame. Putting out his hand to our hero, he said—

"Listen to me, and I will tell you a story. I am not mad now. You are gentle and kind, you are a friend. Will you release me, so that I can leave this place when I have told you my story?"

"I will release you now if you wish it." Dick's voice was husky as he spoke.

He took the man's hand in his own trembling palm.

The poor fellow looked at him affectionately, and gently smoothed the long rich curls from his white noble brow.

"You believe I am not mad," he said, in a melancholy voice. "The cruelty and sufferings I have been forced to endure have distracted my mind, and I am often wildly deranged, but I am quite sane now—am I not?"

Dick inclined his head—he was too choked to speak.

"I will tell you my story now," the prisoner went on. "I was returning from India about two years ago, with my wife and child—God bless them!" he said, fervently. "They are happy, and at rest in heaven. My darling child, Grace was the image of her mother."

"Grace!" murmured Dick, with a start. The name struck him like a death knell.

"We had a splendid voyage," continued the man, heeding not the interruption; "but when within sight of the Cornwall coast, when every one on board crowded to the ship's side, their breasts throbbing with happiness at once more beholding the dear native land, there suddenly arose a fearful storm."

Here he paused, and drew his hand across his heated brow.

Dick shuddered visibly. The scene struck him to be familiar with his early career.

His companion went on—

"Within half an hour of the storm the ship was hurled upon the breakers and dashed to pieces.

"Some kindly person lashed my wife and me to a spar, but my child was gone; she sank beneath the surging waves, never to rise again.

"I remember nothing more of the fearful scene until I awoke to find myself and wife in some strange house, and each with a man bending over us. His face I knew well, but I could not call to mind where I had before seen him.

"We recovered, and made the house our home for a few days, until we preferred to start for Merton Grange, a splendid domain of my own.

"My wife and I were out on the evening previous to our departure. We were quietly walking over the peaky rocks overhanging the coast, with the beautiful moon shedding its glorious light over the rippling water beneath which my angel daughter lay, when suddenly we were attacked from behind by a band of ruffians, bound back to back, and hurled from the fearful precipice into the sea."

Again he paused.

Again our hero shuddered.

The man was growing excited. His eyes glared with a dangerous wild lustre.

"Again I was saved from the ocean," he broke out, in an altered voice; "my wife was taken from me."

"This time when I returned to consciousness I was in the hut of an old fisherman. I asked him how I got there, and he said he found me on the beach alone.

"From the hut he put me down here, where I have been ever since. My wife and child gone from me, and I left alone—kept in confinement, away from the world," he said, in conclusion.

It was a strange horrible revelation.

Dick stood bewildered. The story had unravelled a thread by which he could trace a mystery that greatly interested him, and will hereafter make a prominent part in this romance.

"Your daughter's name was Grace," queried Dick, his frame working convulsively with inward emotion.

"Lady Grace Merton," replied the man; "my wife was Lady Merton, and I am Lord Merton, of Merton Grange."

A cry escaped Dick's lips. He staggered, faint and weak, and leant against his companion for support.

Surely it must have been decreed that he should have been hurled down the well to discover the poor deranged prisoner, and learn the secret he had learned.

Why did he not disclose to the childless father the secret he possessed, concerning the daughter of Lord Merton.

He could not. He dared not.

To relate to the bereaved father the secret he held would only be to gladden his broken heart with forlorn hopes, and then to crush out what little life remained in that frail frame, when he should learn the terrible truth, that his only child, he so long thought had been taken from him by the mighty hand of Providence, was perhaps in worse hands than those of death.

Dick must still keep the secret, until he regained his lost bride.

Then, and not till then, would he part his lips to let pass a syllable.

"Why do you tremble?" asked Lord Mer

"Do you believe my story?"

"I do," answered Dick, faintly, "and with 'l my heart pity you. I have a strange cry too to tell. You shall hear it by-and-by."

"Will you not tell me now?"

"Let's leave this place, and I will convey you to a place of safety."

The man laughed horribly with joy.

"Unfasten these chains," he almost shrieked, lancing about in his excitement.

Our hero had nothing with him by which he could sever the manacles.

He moved away to find a stone that would serve as a hammer to break the chain.

"Stay!" yelled Lord Merton, clutching him by the hair.

"I am going to look for something, by which to free you."

"You are not."

Dick began to feel uncomfortable. The gentleman's senses were fast leaving him, and he glared at the youth in a most fearful manner.

"Come, come," said Dick, kindly; "you must be quiet, if you wish to leave this place."

"Silence! You are a fiend!"

By a sudden jerk he threw our hero to the ground, fell upon him, twined his large fingers round the boy's white throat, and with mighty strength tried to strangle him.

Dick struggled desperately to break away, but in vain. His assailant held him firmly down in a vice-like grip.

Tyburn Dick's handsome face turned blue, and horribly distorted. His eyes glared fearfully, and his tongue protruded from his mouth.

His life was being squeezed from his body.

The lunatic exulted over his brutal triumph.

A few more minutes and our hero would have terminated his career.

He cannot free himself. His assailant has got too firm a hold of him, and is kneeling on his chest.

A happy thought rushed to his mind—a resource by which he may be able to save his life.

His hands are free.

He drew his sword. In another moment he ripped open his assailant's arm.

The maniac shrieked, and released his hold.

Dick gasped for breath, and staggered as he sprang to his feet.

There is not a moment to spare. The lunatic, like a savage bloodhound, tried desperately to break away from the wall.

Dick slowly recovered the life the other squeezed out.

There is a crash, and a wild yell. The maniac has snapped the chain, and is free.

Dick sprang aside, as the other leapt at his throat.

Away speeds the gallant Boy Highwayman through the darkness, like a hunted deer with a savage bloodhound following in his track.

On, on he goes, with the madman close upon his heels, thirsting for his blood.

Joy, joy!

Dick knows not whither he has been running. His heart beats with joy. He has hope

He is in an open pit with the clear heavens above him.

Around is nothing but huge cragged rocks

He must reach the top of that fearful rocky acclivity. His pursuer is close upon him.

Dick sprang forward, and commenced a rapid ascent up the dangerous cragged wall, as the lunatic bounded into the rocky chasm.

He fairly howled with disappointment at the sight of his prey disappearing.

He raved and tore about in a terrible rage, then sprang forward, and with wonderful celerity clambered up the rock after his victim, drawing himself from each impending crag.

Perspiration rolled down Dick's face, through exertion and fear of being overtaken.

A cry of despair escaped his lips.

His pursuer grasped him by the leg, caught him round the waist, and with terrible force hurled him down again into the fearful rocky abyss.

The lunatic gave one piercing shriek of triumph as he looked down at the handsome boy lying senseless amongst the rocks, and then, like a rocket, he darted up the pit, and disappeared.

CHAPTER LVIII.

TYBURN DICK ESCAPES FROM THE RAVINE.

UNDAUNTED by the peril he had just gone through, Tyburn Dick made another attempt to escape.

' LOUD REPORT AND THE RIDER FELL.

"No giving way now," he thought; "there are no more lunatics to fight."

He commenced an ascent up the rocky crags, but not with the agility he showed when pursued by the madman.

He had now reached nearly the top of the acclivity.

He came to a stop.

The next projecting crag was some distance from his reach.

He stood in a dangerous position.

To descend again would be risking a fearful danger.

Yet he could not ascend.

Around him were but small crags, which it seemed an impossibility to maintain a hold on.

Dick surveyed his dangerous position with a look of astonishment.

"I can't hang here," he thought; "I must reach the top. If I stumble it won't be my first downfall."

His indomitable spirit blinded him to the awful peril he risked by venturing to ascend.

Nothing deterred his daring nature.

He knew not the meaning of danger. He feared nothing.

"I must reach the top," he mused mentally.

The fact was unquestionable by the determined look in his dark eyes that he meant to reach the top.

But how?

We shall see.

Fastening his toes tightly in the crevices of the rocks, he drew himself firmly together, and carefully gliding his hand over the rugged surface, he clutched two projections.

Thus he stood for a moment.

He had but frail hopes of a safe ascent.

His footing was so insecure that the slightest slip of the hand would hurl him headlong to the bottom of the fearful ravine.

His fate seemed inevitable.

One hand was raised to clutch the next crag—one foot was loosening to take another step, when he started at the sound of voices above, which he thought was the maniac battling with some one.

A cry of horror escaped his lips.

He was falling.

Down, down into the fearful precipice, to be dashed and mangled to a horrible mass.

Is the gallant boy to die thus?

No.

His end is not so fated.

He stops. His feet have caught against a ridge.

Then he is safe.

For a moment he stands and wipes the perspiration from his face, that had oozed out in the time of his perilous descent.

He smiled at his own fears, and again prepared for an ascent, dauntless as ever, and forgetful of the narrow escape he had just had.

Grasping crag after crag, he gradually drew himself up.

Again he stops.

He has reached that point from which he fell, and there is every possibility of him making another rapid descent.

A voice calls from the top of the ravine.

Dick looks up.

A cry of hope escaped his lips. He recognized the face looking down upon him as that of his faithful follower, Big Bullskin.

Tears ran down the faithful fellow's cheek's and his heart misgave him. He saw the perilous position of his beloved young leader, and knew unless some timely aid could reach him he would be lost.

It was an impossibility for him to descend. He was placed in a hazardous position, lying full length on his belly at the top of the ravine, with just his head peering over the fearful precipice.

His colossal features blanched with horror. The faithful fellow lay in fearful torture, every moment expecting to see his young chief stumble backwards, and fall crashing on the sharp-pointed rocks beneath.

"Cheer up, my faithful fellow," said Dick, in a voice choked by emotion; "there is life while there's hope. Have you any of your comrades with you?"

"Yes," faltered Bullskin, big scalding tears rolling from his eyes, and dropping on Dick's upturned face.

"Have you not got a rope, or anything you can lower to me?"

"Keep a firm hold, captain!" exclaimed Bullskin, excitedly. "I shan't be a minute."

Dick tried to smile an assent, but his heart misgave him. He was clutching desperately to keep a hold. His hand grew sweaty. He felt himself going.

He could not retain a hold another minute.

Bullskin had disappeared.

Dick gave a cry of despair. A dizziness seemed suddenly to take possession of him. His head seemed to whirl round as though on a swivel. A mist gathered before his eyes, and in another moment he felt himself falling down, down, fathoms deep, into some bottomless pit.

Had he fallen, or was it only an alienation of his mind.

He had not fallen. By a miraculous power he clung to two small ridges. His fingers seemed as though riveted to the rocks.

"Quick, quick!" cried a voice above.

The next moment Bullskin peered over with an expression of awe.

"Quick!" he shouted, "hand me the noose. One of you hold my legs, or I shall fall over.

A hand appeared over the precipice with a coil of leather, which was placed in Bullskin's hands.

"Keep a firm hold, but let me have more play in my legs," he said.

Then he wriggled his body until he hung half over the perpendicular rocks.

Big beads of perspiration rolled off his face. His blood coursed through his veins like liquid fire, and the torturing suspense he endured while preparing his comrades' belts, that were fastened together, into a noose to throw over his young leader's body was horrible.

The line was ready. He made a kind of slip-knot, which he opened to a large size circle. He let the whole drop, retaining the end of the line.

Our hero was insensible to the whole proceeding. His head hung back. His handsome face pale and distorted. His limbs hung loosely, but his hands kept their vice-like grip.

He gave a sudden jerk as the noose encircled his body. His hands slipped, and he fell.

Bullskin held the end of the line, so Dick did not fall far.

The jerk awoke him.

For a few seconds he looked around with a wild incredulous look.

"Saved! saved!" he exclaimed, drawing his hand over his brow.

His face beamed with a joyous flush. His eyes sparkled brightly, and animation returning with hope, he suddenly seemed endowed with energy and strength he had not known for some time.

"Come here, Swig," said Bullskin.

Swig went, but not too near to the edge of the precipice.

"If you are frightened," remarked Munroe, angrily "let some one else come. Don't stand there shivering."

"I ain't frightened," faltered Swig, with chattering teeth, "only I don't want to fall."

"You won t fall; hold tight to my coat, and when I throw the line, draw it in."

The poor little fellow was too terrified to answer. He clutched his gigantic comrade tightly by the collar, and wriggled his legs under Bullskin, waited in the most fearful agony for the line to be thrown to him.

"Now captain, dear," Bullskin said, addressing Dick, "keep your hands and feet against the rocks while I draw you up."

Dick smiled affectionately at the honest, tender-hearted fellow, kept his feet against the ragged surface of the ravine, and aided Bullskin to draw him up by grasping the crags.

Slowly and cautiously he was pulled up.

Bullskin held the line tightly. Dick was within reach; the gallant boy highwayman's heart bounded with joy, his adored young leader had nearly escaped from the fearful peril that threatened him.

Another moment he was griped by the arm.

Joseph Munroe called lustily for aid.

A pair of hands appeared over the precipice.

Dick was grasped—pulled from the fearful ravine.

Free and safe.

He once more stood on *terra firma*.

Bullskin sprang to his feet, he clasped the handsome youth in his powerful arms as though he were a child and hugged him to his breast.

Swig, Jack Evans the Lusher, and the other highwaymen clustered round their beloved chief and eagerly waited to kiss his hand.

Bullskin was so overcome with joy that he fairly shed tears like a woman, in his happiness at once beholding our hero free and unscathed.

He kissed the boy's white noble brow. Dick returned the caress warmly.

Then one by one he greeted his subjects.

"Oh, captain!" broke out Swig, smothering his face in his hands, "I thought we'd never see you again."

"Thanks to Providence, I am safe and sound," replied Dick, "and happy to again see my faithful comrades."

"You have had a fearful time of it," said the Lusher.

Dick smiled.

"Yes I have had a very hazardous time," he replied, "but what enjoyment is there in life without the excitement of danger? Come, Munroe, let your comrades return to the haunt."

The highwaymen raised their hats and departed. Bullskin went with Dick.

"You must be faint," he said; "take a draught of this brandy—I brought it with me for you."

He produced a horn flask.

"You are kind and generous," replied Dick; "a little will put some life into me."

And he drank.

"By-the-bye," he continued, "where did you get to when we were at the cave?"

Bullskin laughed loudly.

"Oh! we drove the Black Band Brethren before us like a lot of sheep."

"I should have thought they were more like a lot of wolves."

"Well, they were as savage, but they did not turn; they were wise, and went, knowing it was better for their health."

"I expected," continued Bullskin, "when I returned to see you standing over their captain with your sword through his heart, but you were gone."

"Yes," replied Dick. And he told him all that had occured.

The gigantic fellow's face grew sad and angry.

"Curse him!" he said, "he shall answer for that cowardly blow. The whole of that band shall be exterminated, and by me, one at a time."

"There is room for them if they do not molest us," interposed our hero.

"Curse them! they shall not live; one by one I will slay them. They shall know who the avenger is by a mark I will leave on their breasts. I can be terrible when I begin."

"Terrible indeed," said Dick; "you are terrible now, and I almost begin to be frightened of you. Come, change the subject. I will tell you of a strange mystery I heard."

"Do; but, my dear captain, you will never have occasion to be frightened of me."

"No, no; you are too faithful. But listen to my story; pay much attention to it, because I want your opinion."

Tyburn Dick then commenced to minutely relate his adventure with the maniac, and the strange, but true revelation he heard from the lips of that unfortunate gentleman.

"There is some terrible mystery hanging to the end of that revelation," said Bullskin, his colossal features calm and wearing a troubled expression.

"A mystery," iterated Dick, solemnly "that I will fathom."

"They must be cruel, pitiless wretches to torture a man as he has been tortured. Did the poor fellow mention having relations?"

"Two, his brother's twin sons—Percy and Reginald."

"Ha! then we have a clue."

"Whereby?"

"More than once I have seen two very suspicous-looking men that particularly attracted my attention."

"Well?" queried Dick, anxiously.

"I have followed them—I have listened and heard things that would now prove of great importance."

"Have you heard aught of what we speak?"

"You shall hear."

"I am anxious."

"Listen," said Joseph Munroe.

"Proceed."

"Hear me," and Bullskin commenced. "While we were in the smugglers' cave I saw the two men I have so often seen before; they are exactly alike, tall, powerfully built, dark, with massive black curly hair, and not unhandsome features.

"They are or were smugglers, but superior to their companions in appearance; they did not exert themselves in the struggle to protect the cargo.

"Suddenly they disappeared. I felt much disappointed, and had a strong desire to keep them in view. I should have followed them, but when I returned after hunting our enemies out, I found that you were missing.

"I felt that you had fallen into some treachery, but to make sure I returned to the haunt. Finding that you were not there, I set out with my comrades, and took an oath not to rest until I had discovered you dead or alive."

Here he paused to take breath—and a little brandy.

"After you with the flash," said Dick, smiling. "It is a great exertion to talk too long. It puzzles me to know how the ladies can keep at it so long; it's a wonder they can keep their mouths in shape."

"Their mouths would sooner lose their shape if they ever left off taking."

"It's a wonder they don't talk in their sleep," Dick said.

"They do!"

"The devil! How do you know?"

Bullskin winked knowingly.

"We must not talk about the ladies, or we shall forget our present business, which is more important," he said. "I will finish my narrative."

"Do," replied Dick, guzzling down some of the fiery liquor.

"We were tired, dusty, cold, and hungry," he went on; "having searched for you in every conceivable and inconceivable place, when night wore on, and we could not proceed any further until we had taken in a little provender.

"I and my comrades—your most obedient subjects—made for the nearest inn, for which we had to walk ten miles, but we were repaid for that by the jolly host, who made real welcome, and provided us with a sumptuous supper.

"We were washing the gorgeous meal down with a bottle or two of fine old crusted wine, when our feast was suddenly disturbed by the entry of two men, looking exhausted and horrified. I recognised them at a glance as the two *smugglers*, and as soon as they caught sight of me, one nudged the other, and they left our room."

"Did you follow them?" queried Dick.

"The landlord provided them with a room and supper. I dropped mine host an extra sovereign to put me into an apartment next to theirs, which he did. I made the best of my ears by putting them close to a crack in the partition, and caught cold in my head, but I did not mind that; I listened to their undertoned conversation."

"What did you hear?"

"Much."

"Concerning me?"

"No; Lord Merton."

"Well, it's all the same."

"Was the lunatic Lord Merton?"

"The same."

"Then how the deuce can it concern you?"

"Much; because I intend to discover the mystery of the poor gentleman, bring the perpetrators of his suffering to justice, and reunite Lord Merton with his daughter and wife, if she still lives."

Dick looked inquiringly at his comrade Bullskin, and seemed lost in deep abstraction.

"Of what are you thinking?"

"Of what I heard," replied Munroe.

"Let's have it. We have been a long time talking, and not yet arrived at any conclusion."

"This is what I heard," said Bullskin, and again he commenced his story. "'Do you think, Percy, it could have been her?' one said, addressing his companion. 'Impossible, Reginald,' answered the other."

Here Dick again interrupted.

"Then they are the same Percy and Reginald!" he exclaimed, surprised.

"Yes, the same; but don't interrupt again, or I shall never get through my story," said Bullskin. "'Then it must have been an apparition. We could not both have been deluded by fancy,' said Reginald, and then they went on talking. They said they were safe. Their aunt and uncle—Lord and Lady Merton—sleeping at the bottom of the ocean, they had nothing to prevent them taking possession of Merton Grange, but one thing, and that was their cousin Grace, whom they had lost. They swore to discover her whereabouts, and quiet her."

Dick's face flushed. His eyes sparkled with a terrible light, and every muscle in his body worked with emotion.

He did not speak.

Bullskin was silent.

"Is that all?" asked Dick, anxiously, after a few seconds' pause.

"All I heard," answered Munroe.

"You understand who the lady is they want to find?"

"Perfectly."

"If you ever see them again, capture them, and keep them in close confinement at the haunt. We have work to do that will require great precaution. These men must be stopped in their villany. Lord Merton must be found. He has escaped from his prison. Grace must be discovered, and if I find that they have got her in their murderous clutches, let them beware!"

The tone in which he spoke the last three words fully substantiated his meaning.

"Look!" he said, and pointed to a crouching form beneath the shadow of a cluster of huge trees.

"Ah!" exclaimed our hero; "one of the Black Brethren. We will watch his little game."

The next moment there was a clatter of a horse's feet on the road.

The form beneath the tree drew a pistol, as the horse came along at a furious speed. Its rider—a country peasant—was evidently on urgent business.

Little did the rider think that he would be stopped by the ruthless fellow that watched his coming with eager eyes.

"On, on, old boy," said the traveller to his steed, in a timid voice, and he crouched down in his saddle as though warned of some terrible danger that awaited him as he passed that fated spot.

The figure poised his pistol at the rider. There was a click as he pulled the trigger back.

Dick stepped forward, but too late.

A flash, a report, and the rider fell.

"Coward!" thundered our hero, bringing his clenched hand down heavily on the assassin's shoulder.

The man whirled round, felled Dick to the earth by a blow on the temples, sprang into the road, and pounced upon his victim before Bullskin could realize what had taken place.

The poor fellow groaned piteously as his ruffianly assailant fell upon him.

"Hell and furies!" exclaimed Joseph Munroe, stooping over Dick.

The blow had not stunned our hero, though it made him powerless for a few moments. He was soon, by the tender assistance of his companion, able to regain his footing.

"The fellow was devilish quick!" smiled our hero. "The blow took me off my feet."

"And laid you on your back."

"Surely; but the blow was only tit for tat."

"Curse him! It shall be his last tit for tat," said Bullskin, maliciously. "This is an unexpected pleasure. I did not think we should meet one of our enemies to-night. He will be my first victim, but not the last."

A fearful agonized shriek came from the fallen man. The murderous knife of his assailant was at his throat.

Dick and his companion sprang forward.

"Damnation!" fiercely hissed the man of the Black Band.

Tyburn Dick, beside Bullskin rushed through the hedge just in time to prevent the dastardly act of the assassin. The ruffian had plundered his victim of everything he laid his hand upon, and was in the act of completing his brutal work by cutting the man's throat, when the appearance of our hero arrested his cowardly hand.

He did not waste time by taking a second look at his enemies.

Foaming at the mouth like a mad dog with baffled rage, he dealt his victim a fearful blow with the swiftness of an antelope, and the savage ferocity of a panther. He cleared the hedge on the other side of the road with one bound, and tore away for dear life.

"Bring him down," shouted Dick.

Bullskin laughed a savage kind of laugh as he pursued the fugitive.

"Ha!" he said, "to shoot him would be a death too easy. He will not go far, let him have his run—'tis his last."

Dick shuddered; he knew his companion was terrible in his wrath when he once commenced.

Bullskin was on the track of his enemy.

Dick knelt by the side of the wounded man. The gallant boy was deeply touched by the agonized expression on the poor fellow's face.

"Where are you wounded?" inquired Dick, his voice quivering with emotion.

The man tried to smile, but pain and anxiety distorted his features, and his lips quivered as he tried to explain

Our hero put his ear close to his mouth, but the poor fellow's articulation was too inaudible for him to catch a word.

Fortunately Dick had forgotten to return Bullskin's brandy-flask; he drew it from his breast-pocket, and poured what little of the liquor remained down the peasant's throat.

With wonderful effect it seemed to revive the exhausted man. He raised his hand, clasped his left side, and in a feeble voice said—

"'Tis here—the ball is here."

Our hero's handsome face grew sombre; he well knew should the ball have gone deeply into the flesh, or touched any vital part, there remained but little hope of the man's recovery.

"Can you stand if I assist you to your feet?" he asked.

"I fear not—I feel too weak," replied the wounded man; and he sank back off Dick's arms as though talking was too much for his feeble strength.

"I wish Munroe was here," muttered Dick. "He is a capital doctor, and would perhaps be able to save this poor fellow."

Munroe was just then returning; he had overtaken his enemy, captured him after a little tussle, and was now dragging the assassin along by the collar.

The wounded man squeezed Dick's hand gratefully for his tender kindness; his own hands felt so cold and clammy, our hero had an awful misgiving that the poor fellow would expire before Bullskin arrived.

With his face buried in his hand, Dick was pondering over what was best to do, when a heavy hand was laid upon his shoulder.

He looked up.

Horror!

A chill ran through his body.

The cold iron of a huge pistol was placed against his forehead, and before him stood a tall powerfully built man robed from head to foot in spotless black.

"Ha, ha! Tyburn Dick, we meet again!" vociferated the strange person, in a hollow unearthly voice.

Dick knew the man.

"Captain Bertrand!" he exclaimed.

"The same."

"You are in time to see one of your accursed band die."

"You won't have that pleasure," said the chief of the Black Band mockingly. "Die, dog! your time has come!"

"Liar," thundered a powerful voice.

The next instant there was a report—a flash of light, and a bullet came whistling through the air from a field from behind a hedge.

Captain Bertrand gave a horrible laugh, clapped his left hand to his brow, from where a stream of blood poured; and ere the echo of the report died away he fired full into our hero's face.

Dick gave a cry, and fell forward over the prostrate form of the peasant.

Captain Bertrand turned and fled with an exultant yell of triumph.

There was a third report.

The chief of the Black Band gave a wild whoop, sprang into the air like a savage Indian, and fell to the earth bleeding from a wound in the back.

Our hero had managed a very clever little piece of stratagem. He knew his assailant's foul design, and closely watched his every move; he saw his finger on the trigger and as he pulled the hammer back, Dick fell forward, just in time to avoid the deadly missile that passed over him instead of going in his face.

Dick's was the third—the effectual shot that brought down the enemy.

He raised his head to see what effect his shot had taken when Bullskin came up to him with his captive.

"Hold this man," he said, "while I fetch his captain."

"No," said Dick, authoritatively, "if Bertrand is not dead, I will not have another hair of his head injured."

"No, no," replied Bullskin, quickly, and in a tone of anger, "I do not wish to kill him now; let him see his men die one by one and when they are all done for, then he shall die."

And without waiting for his young chief's consent, Big Bullskin fetched the maimed captain of the Black Band to witness the fate of one of his men.

"Look, Captain Bertrand," said Bullskin, calmly, but with fearful vehemence, "this is one of your men. I have sworn to exterminate your league, and this is how I shall do it."

Captain Bertrand closed his eyes to shut out the awful tragedy. His man called imploringly upon him for help, and he, Betrand, put his fingers in his ears to shut out the cries.

He was powerless, and unable to render him any assistance.

Joseph Munroe, the terrible avenger, had got the shivering wretch—the guilty assassin—by the throat in a firm grip. A dagger was in his hand, the bright blade gleamed in. the air ere it descended into the man's heart.

The man was forced back upon Bullskin's knee; his coat torn open, exposing his bare breast to the deadly knife that was about to be buried in his heart.

"Hold!" shouted Dick, as his companion's arm descended, and the weapon was within an inch of its mark.

"Hold," repeated our hero. "Before you stain your hands with such foul blood, attend to this poor fellow's wound."

Bullskin obeyed; the dagger was replaced in his belt, and the man bound and thrown to the ground to await his execution.

The highwayman went to the assistance of the wounded man.

"Attend to this poor fellow's hurt," commanded Dick.

Bullskin stripped the man of coat and vest, and baring his side, carefully examined his wound.

The ball had not entered any dangerous part; it lodged between two of his ribs, from where the highwayman was not long in extracting it with a pair of small instruments with which he was always provided.

The blood flowed copiously from the wound as soon as the leaden missile was removed.

"He bleeds freely," remarked Dick.

"It will do him good," Bullskin replied, administering a potion to his patient. "This will put life into him."

So it did.

Barely had Bullskin moved the phial from his lips when he raised himself up upon his arms.

"Be steady," said Munroe, "while I bind up the wound."

The man sat patiently while his kind preserver put a bandage over the wound.

"Do you feel strong enough to stand?" asked Bullskin.

"Quite," answered the man. "What draught was that you gave me? it has given me new life and strength."

"Yes, it is a powerful medicine. Have you far to go?"

The man's face grew clouded and sad; he appeared terribly agitated, as though something had suddenly occurred to him.

"Ten miles," he said. "Where is my horse? I have come twenty."

"Your horse is not far off."

"Thanks, thanks; I will fetch it, I have not a minute to spare; but how can I repay you for your kindness? I fear I shall never be able to efface the heavy debt I owe you. My gratitude is but a poor recompense."

"Your gratitude suffices. I did no more than one man should do for another if it lay in his power."

"Command me to do anything, and, even with my life you have saved, I will do it."

"Tush, tush; I see you are in trouble. Did that coward that shot you take anything?"

"Ten pounds," answered the man. "I went thirty miles to borrow it to buy nourishment for my wife to save her life."

Bullskin's spleen rose ten times in power against his enemy.

"Stay a moment," he said to the man.

Dick went to get the poor fellow's horse. A horrible guttural cry made him start as he returned, and, turning to ascertain the cause, he saw his companion at his bloody work.

Bullskin's anger was insuppressible. He had got his foe by the throat, and for the second time his dagger was raised to strike, when our hero's voice arrested him.

"Stay!" shouted Dick. "Why seek his life? Would you have his blood upon your head?"

"Ay," returned Bullskin determinedly; "and will the blood of all their accursed race."

The brave boy would willingly have prevented the horrible crime, but, ere he had time to interpose, it was done.

A faint cry escaped the man's lips as he fell to the earth, with the dagger driven into his heart's core.

"See, Captain Bertrand," said Bullskin; "this is my first—you will be my last; but there are more to come before it's your turn. You won't forget the Avenging Chief!"

Captain Bertrand closed his eyes to shut out the horrible sight. He was silent, but his aching brain was working with treacherous revenge.

Big Bullskin took the ten pounds from the

dered man that he had taken from the poor peasant, but he did not touch an extra in, though his pockets were well lined.

Our hero had captured the horse, and asked the poor fellow to re-mount.

"Take this money," said Joseph Munroe, adding ten to it from his own pocket. "Hasten with all speed to your home. Lose no time. The potion I gave you is to lend you strength, and energy in case of emergency, and soon loses his strength. You will require rest by the time you reach home."

The poor fellow was too agitated to express his gratitude. He raised the kind-hearted highwayman's hands to his lips, and, kissing Dick's hand fervently, galloped away.

"You have done one generous action, but the other——" Dick's voice faltered. He did not like to reproach his comrade.

"The other was a just retribution for the wrongs you have suffered. We did not seek them—they sought us."

"True," said Dick; "they have been terrible foes to us."

"They will not trouble us much longer," said Bullskin, with a savage kind of glee.

"They will avoid you in future as much as possible."

"I can wait. My vengeance is sure."

"And terrible," Dick said. "You will return to the haunt. I have something to do, but I shall be with you in a few days. You will keep a sharp look out for those two men. They must not be at liberty, or they will do more mischief than we shall be able to undo."

"My first mission shall be to hunt them down," replied Munroe. "Why not take some of my comrades with you?"

"Why?"

"It is not discreet for you to be alone. You know not what danger you're subject to."

"Fear not. I shall not get into any more wells or rocky ravines."

"But you are so fearless and defiant. Why not wear a disguise, if you are going anywhere likely to prove dangerous?"

"A disguise!" our hero said scornfully. "I, Tyburn Dick, wear a disguise? No; it shall never be said that I was afraid to wear my distinguished dress."

"But there is a thousand pounds set upon your head, and a full description given of you on the placards. Any one might know you by the star on your breast."

"So much the better. I have all the more to brave."

"As you will," said Bullskin, in despair. "Where go you?"

"First, to seek Grace,"—his face clouded as he answered—"and then to discover Lord Merton, her father."

"In what direction?!"

"I know not. Adieu!"

"Good-bye. Be careful!"

And they parted. Tyburn Dick made his way to an inn. He drew a small cloak he wore hanging from his left shoulder over his breast, to cover the conspicuous star.

Mine host of the Stag and Hounds was a long gaunt man, with a huge mallet-shaped head, a pair of small twinkling grey eyes, a short shock head of blazing red hair, a pair of ears that would comfortably meet at the back of his head. His mouth, without exaggeration, was as large as a moderate crocodile's, and his prognosticating nose —it was a nose! I hardly (k)nose how to describe it, but let it suffice to say that it was a full-blown one, and covered half his physiognomy.

Altogether he was a beauty.

Dick stood at the door staring at the man in surprise.

"A pretty image, certainly," muttered Dick, making bold to enter, though not certain that the form that stood behind the counter or bar was not a starved animated giant, waiting for the first person he could clutch to make a meal of.

Mine host bent like a cane over the counter

Dick stepped back.

"A bottle of canary—bring it to me," he said, making his way to the parlour.

The man nodded, and followed him with the bottle of wine.

All eyes were turned towards Dick as he entered.

There were many in the room besides himself. He paid for the wine, ordered some cigars, and got rid of mine host.

"What an object!" thought Dick. "But he don't keep bad stuff."

He poured out the third glass, put it by his elbow, and lit a cigar.

"Excellent wine that," said a voice.

"Very," replied Dick, feeling for his glass.

"Confound it !" he muttered, turning to see where his glass was.

Dick took the cigar from his mouth, and stared in blank astonishment at a smart little young fellow by his side, who had got the canary bottle's neck thrust in his mouth, and was gulping down the delicious wine with great gusto.

"Oh !" ejaculated Dick, " do you think I pay for wine for you to drink ?"

The smart young fellow took no notice, and went on drinking.

Dick got up quietly and hit the smart young fellow a smart blow between the shoulders.

The bottle flew from the smart young fellow's mouth, and his hands were clasped over his stomach.

He stood breathless; he was turning blue in the face—the wind had caught the wine in his throat.

Dick did not want him to choke, so by way of a winder he gave him another blow in the back, to make the wind leave go of the wine.

"You needn't have spoilt a cove's wet," remarked the smart little fellow, recovering.

"Confound it !' said Dick, "you might buy your wet."

"All right; I can stand another bottle."

"Do; that's the thing."

The smart little fellow did ; and in a very short time he and our hero became intimate friends.

"I don't believe it, do you ?" said Dick's companion.

"Believe what ?" asked Dick.

"That they've captured Tyburn Dick ?"

Our hero started.

"Captured Tyburn Dick ?" he said, wondering what the other meant.

"Why, yes ; captured Tyburn Dick."

"Who ? Jonathan Wild ?"

Dick laughed outright at the absurdity of the joke, as he thought.

"What are you laughing at ?" inquired Dick's active companion.

"Do you suppose Tyburn Dick is such fool as to be captured ?" replied our hero.

"I didn't think he was, but they say he is I don't believe it."

"Nor I," said Dick, with a peculiar smile

"I should say you knew him."

"I do," Dick said; "I am very familiar with him. We are great companions, and he always goes where I go. I am with him, and consult him on different things every day."

"Have you seen him to-day ?"

"I was with him not ten minutes ago, outside."

"Lor !" and the active youth looked at our hero incredulously ; "you was with him ten minutes ago ?"

"Since then."

"Then who am I to believe ?"

"Who told you he was captured ?"

"I was told so by Tom King. He saw him captured."

"Impossible," laughed Dick.

"Well, look there,"—the active youth pointed to a proclamation plastered against the dingy wall—" that bill was sent out by the King."

Dick felt amazed. There, surely enough, was a printed report of *Tyburn Dick's* capture.

It ran as follows:

CAPTURE OF TYBURN DICK.

THE
NOTORIOUS HIGHWAYMAN.

"Whosoever will give such information as will lead to the conviction of any of his lawless band shall receive £100 from His Most Gracious Majesty, King George, for the apprehension of each of the depredators.

"Should there be any person or persons discovered aiding the lawless men to escape, or in any way sheltering them from the vigilance of the law, they will be arrested as confederates, and suffer for their illegality by *death*.

"Should any one have anything of importance to communicate to Tyburn Dick before he takes his trial, they can visit him by an order from His Majesty, at Jonathan Wild's Keep, Newgate-street, London.

"By order of ——"

Our hero read it over and over, yet could

conceive the meaning of such a false report.

"Is this done for a blind to throw me off my guard?" he thought.

"What do you think of that?" asked his companion.

"I think it's a false report. I know it."

"You do?"

"Most certainly."

"Such knowledge might be dangerous."

"Why?"

"They might take you for him."

Dick looked at the active youth inquiringly.

"You ain't unlike him," said the youth, with a knowing wink.

"Thank you," replied our hero. "Ah! I know who it is."

"Who?" asked his companion, quickly.

"I was thinking of something else."

"Oh."

"Curse the fellow! How sharp he is," thought Dick. "Yes, it must be," he continued, cogitating to himself—"it must be my second I met at the Cornwall mail. There is a mystery about that person. Surely—no, it cannot be—yet an inward voice seems to say that it is *she*. I must discover, and should it be my Grace—my dear devoted girl—that cursed fellow, Wild, shall suffer for his meddling."

Here he brought his hand down heavily upon the table, scattering glasses, and upsetting numerous quantities of liquor, which he paid for.

Dick again looked up at the proclamation, and burst out laughing.

Two gentlemanly-looking fellows at the further end of the room stared hard at our hero.

"He don't believe Tyburn Dick's caught," remarked the youth to the two gentlemen.

"Don't he?" *sotto voce* in the distance.

"No, gentlemen; I do not, and can prove it," said Dick, boldly.

The company rose, and gathered round the table.

Two miserable-looking men, with battered faces, quizzed our hero closely. By the appearance of their attire, and a huge pair of horse-pistols, besides a tremendous cudgel they were rammed in their belts, it was evident they belonged to the vicinity of Bow street.

Dick knew them at a glance as the two thief-takers, Bill and Jerry.

"Did you say you could prove that the highwayman is not captured?" asked a dissipated-looking gentleman.

"I can," replied Dick.

Everyone looked at him in wonderment.

"I know better than that," said thief-taker Jerry.

"I saw him captured," remarked his confederate.

"I can prove to all here that Tyburn Dick is *not* captured."

"Don't believe it."

"Prove it."

"You can't prove it without you can bring him here," cried several voices.

"I will bet every gentleman in the room a hundred pounds each that I can prove that the real Tyburn Dick is not captured," said Dick, boldly, well knowing that he could afford to bet, though at the time he did not possess five pounds. "I can bring him here within ten minutes."

"You can," shouted several, eagerly.

"I can."

The thief-takers exchanged a doubtful look, and shook their heads.

"I'll bet you a hundred you don't bring him forward," said a gentleman.

"I'll bet a hundred," said another. "I don't mind if I lose—it's worth a hundred to look at him."

"I'll bet fifty you can't prove he is not captured."

"I'll bet a hundred."

"I fifty."

"I twenty."

"I twenty."

"I ten."

"I two hundred."

"I fifty."

Dick held up his hand to stop them, or they would have gone on for another five minutes.

"Very well, gentlemen," he said; "I am willing to take all your bets."

Heaps of gold and notes were put upon the table.

Dick had none to produce.

"I will hold the stakes," he proposed.

Gentlemen placed their hands over their money.

"You shall have them if you produce Tyburn Dick," said one.

"Very well, gentlemen, Tyburn Dick shall stand before you within five minutes," said our hero, " but I must hold the money; I shall not leave this room until you have seen the favourite highwayman."

"How can you bring him here without leaving?"

"You shall see," said Dick, drawing the money into one heap before him.

His frank handsome face banished the suspicion some entertained about his origin.

Every gaze in the room was turned towards him watching his slightest movement. Dick wanted to go through a transformation, but could not without their attention could be drawn away.

Happy thought; pretend to call his companion, Tyburn Dick. His face brightened up with a mischievous smile; the idea was not bad, and would answer his purpose admirably.

"Now, gentlemen," he said, " my friend is coming."

All turned their eyes from him, and followed his gaze to the door.

He blew a little warbling note like that of a nightingale.

It seemed to be immediately answered from without.

Everyone stood in awe.

"*Hi, hi, there within! clear the road, gentlemen, and get your purses ready for Tyburn Dick, King of the Highwaymen!*"

The gentlemen instantly fell back on either side, leaving a clear passage for the orator of these words that seemed as though spoken the other side of the door, but which in reality were spoken by our hero, who stood at the table pocketing the money. He had thoroughly achieved the art of ventriloquism, and could make his voice sound in any part of a room, or appear to issue from any person.

the door burst open, and the dashing Boy Highwayman dash into the room.

Dick made the best of his time while they were anxiously waiting for the supposed Tyburn Dick to enter, he silently slipped out of the window at one end of the apartment, threw off his valise, put on a mask, donned his cap jauntily on his head, and drawing his rapier, cried—

"All right, old fellow, we shall meet again! I shall do a little business with these gentlemen—*au revoir* for the present."

Then he shook the casement while entering as roughly as possible.

The gentlemen turned confounded.

"Why, not a moment ago he was at the door!" said one, awfully astonished.

"Yes, gentlemen," said Dick, leaning on the hilt of his sword in a easy attitude, his left hand resting on his hip, " and now I am here, TAKE ME WHO DARE!"

"Why, the fellow must be the very devil," remarked one.

"Rather a good-looking devil," said another.

"Devil or no devil," thief-taker Jerry said, "there's a thousand pounds offered for him, and I shall make one to catch the devil."

"And me another," said his colleague.

"Your friend's got my money," said a gentleman, despondingly.

"And mine too!" shouted another.

"And mine."

"And mine."

"All the better for me, gentlemen," Dick said, with a quiet laugh; "I and *my* friend always share what we get."

"You ain't the real Tyburn Dick," remarked one.

"Ain't I," replied our hero; "find another."

"Won't I?" shouted one of the party.

"In the King's name, gentlemen," said Jerry, "you will help us to capture this daring fellow."

"But is he the real Tyburn Dick?"

"Yes; I can answer for that," replied the thief-taker.

"Jonathan Wild has got a Tyburn Dick."

"That's a friend of his."

"I am going to see my fri

TYBURN DICK PREPARES TO DEFEND HIMSELF AND HIS FAIR COMPANION FROM THE OFFICERS.

bounding to the window; "good night, gentlemen."

A ringing shout came from the company as they rushed to the window after the daring Boy Highwayman. He had gone.

CHAPTER LIX.

THE HAUNTED OAK.

THE tidings gathered by Dick were in some measure true; some one resembling Tyburn Dick had been captured.

We will go back a little, and follow the adventures of our hero's second.

One fine morning after the adventure at the Cornwall Mail, the self-styled Tyburn Dick was riding leisurely through a very picturesque part of the country in profound abstraction.

Surely the place was one of fairy-like beauty. The loneliness of the hour, with the rich metallic rays of the early sun throwing its gladdening light over the verdant heath; the barren cliffs, and the silvery, rippling stream that flowed through the treacherous rocks, would have enraptured the soul of a less admirer of nature than our early wanderer.

So absorbed in his own reflections was he that he did not hear the rattling of wheels coming through the avenue of trees beneath the mossy acclivity upon which he stood.

His coal-black steed stopped in its nibbling at the sprouting shrubs, and turned its head disdainfully, as though not liking the idea of being disturbed so early.

"What is it, my pretty?" said the rider, waking from his reverie by the low, uneasy whining of his horse. "Come, come, Selim, you need not be uneasy, there is no one about."

Selim knew better; she tried to make her rider understand that there was a chariot coming towards them.

"Oh, you are right, my beauty!" said the denominated Tyburn Dick, patting the sleek neck of his steed with a tiny white hand, "some one comes, but we have no desire for interference; go your way, my pet."

The horse threw up its head with much dissatisfaction; it was evident that she did not like the opportunity of a chance to stand and deliver pass unnoticed.

"It is very naughty of you, Selim, to disobey; come, go along directly," said the handsome young horseman, tapping his prancer with a small silver-mounted riding-whip.

Selim felt injured by the sharp rebuke, and trotted off.

The chariot stopped at the bottom of the hill. A gentleman, young and handsome, stepped out, and mounting a servant's horse, made an ascent of the verdant hill.

"Ah, by Jove!" exclaimed the gentleman, catching sight of Tyburn Dick, "then I am not the only early visitor?"

The highwayman turned.

The gentleman rode forward, raised his hat politely, and said—

"Ah, by Jove! I am delighted to discover I have a companion visitor to this most charming place. Delightful, is it not?"

"It is indeed a perfect fairy land."

"Aw—yes—demme; you know, my dear fellow, I visit this place every morning." Sotto voce—"By Jove, very much like a girl! Jolly fellow, though! Are you a constant visitor?" he asked aloud.

"Well, no, I can't say I am."

"Aw—by Jove! a pity; you have not seen half its beauty!"

"Really," laughed Tyburn Dick, "I think I could show you something you have not seen."

"No, you don't mean that you have discovered a part more pretty?"

"If you are not too nervous to cross these rocks, I can show you the most splendid view in the world at the bottom of that grove."

"By Jove! I am willing to cross these rocks, certainly."

"Come, then,' said Tyburn Dick, "If you are fond of picturesque prospects you shall see one."

They rode together over the rocks through the grove, chatting friendly to each other, until they reached the bottom. Tyburn Dick halted.

"Where is the prospect of your search?" asked the gentleman, looking around.

"Here!" replied his companion, pointing a pistol at his forehead.

"A bright prospect, certainly!"

"One that never misses."

"But, my dear fellow, you would not commit a crime so outrageous in such a divine part of the earth as this?"

"No, certainly not; your money and other valuables—quick! Promptness often saves unpleasant——"

"Yes—yes, by Jove, I perfectly understand. My money, with the greatest pleasure."

"Your watch!"

"By all means, but I——"

"Your watch!"

"It don't go."

"It will go from you beyond doubt."

"Aw—my dear fellow, I should not like to give you one so common."

"I am not particular."

"It's only a Geneva."

"You will find in a minute that it will prove to you a lever."

"By Jove, it's very unfair! Damme, what can a fellow do without time? I tell you what I will do if I give you this——"

"Your watch!"

The cold rim of the pistol barrel lodged just on the tip of his nose between his eyes.

The close proximity of the chilling steel sent an electric shock through him, his watch—a splendid repeater—tumbled out of his pocket without further parley, and his rings followed with wonderful velocity.

The highwayman put the booty in a holster, and removed the pistol from the gentleman's sweaty brow.

"A very fine prospect, was it not?" he said.

"Yes," replied the gentleman; "but rather an expensive one."

"Come," said the highwayman, smiling at the gentleman's rueful face; "you seemed loath to part with your watch; you shall have it back on condition."

"Of what?"

"That you pay for it."

"Willingly."

"What is its value?"

"I would give treble its value to again possess it, for the sake of the giver."

"A love-gift, I presume?"

"I'faith, you are right; and I should say, were you a *lady*, you are not unlike the giver."

The highwayman started, and changed colour.

"What would you give to have it back?" he said.

"Five hundred pounds."

"But that is more than its value."

"It's value is a hundred."

"Bring a hundred with you this evening, at eight o'clock. I will meet you at the haunted oak on Hounslow Heath at that time."

"By Jove, I will be there! but may I be honoured with the name of so chivalrous a person as yourself?"

"It will be only fair to exchange names."

"With pleasure; but yours?"

"Tyburn Dick," said the highwayman.

"Tyburn Dick," repeated the gentleman.

"The same; and yours?"

"Bright Prospect. That will do for me fine, I have been so easily gulled."

They indulged in a hearty laugh, and parted to meet at Hounslow Heath.

.   .   .   .

Day waned, and a thousand flickering phantom shadows of night slowly crept over the earth, for a time keeping the gladdening sun and glorious light of day in another world.

The sombre clouds rolled along in all their grandeur from the face of the celestial canopy, leaving it spotless, save for the twinkling stars, and the silvery moon, that poured upon the earth, lighting up the world with its soft metallic rays.

Hounslow Heath, the renowned rendezvous for highwaymen, had that dreary aspect that makes the lonely traveller hurry past the dreary place in nervous anxiety, as the remembrance of some horrid story he heard in early youth rushes to his mind, and he fancies he hears the sound of footsteps following close behind him; yet he cannot summon courage enough to look behind to ascertain the truth of his imagination, but whistles the first tune that comes to his mind, to drive away the fearful thoughts and pictured visions of some bloody murder.

Suddenly he breaks down in his ditty that he don't know the name of, or has, perhaps, never heard, which, in such cases as the present, are generally original—and beautiful things they are. It is a pity there are not a few travelling music composers; they would make a splendid livelihood by following nervous people who whistle their own ditties and drive other people mad. Fancy a collection of fifty different pieces placed in rotation as they were found! Wouldn't it make a magnificent opera for an uproar in the back garden at midnight to scare the cats that sit so playfully on a fellow's window-sill, and sing a long tune, with plenty of variations, all in the highest pitch, just as a fellow has retired with a distracting headache, and is dozing on ;

But this, the reader will say, has nothing to do with the story, and we decidedly agree with him; and so, without using further space for the author's remarks, we will continue.

Suddenly he breaks down in his ditty (that is where we left off and begin again), his heart bumping furiously against his side; his mouth feels like a furnace; he puts motion in his legs, and runs until compelled, at last, to stop through exhaustion. He leans against the nearest thing likely to give support, keeping his eyes shut until he recovers sufficient breath to pursue his journey.

Few persons would venture out after dark to pass Hounslow Heath alone, so the huge wilderness was left pretty well to itself and its night birds of prey.

But on this night there was one person—a young, handsome, delicate horseman youth, seated like a statue on the back of a beautiful Arabian steed.

The only person that inhabited the dreaded heath.

Horse and rider stood motionless beneath the broad shadow of a huge towering tree—the "Haunted Oak."

There was a sad, weary look on the young horseman's face as he turned his head and looked around.

"Ten minutes more," he muttered, "and he comes perhaps to drag me to a felon's dock. Why did I make this appointment? I feel assured there is some ill omen attending it. There, there, I must take my chance as he has done, and if I get captured it will be no worse for me to bear than it was for *him*."

He paused, looked round to see that he was alone, and then drew a miniature from his breast.

By the moon's rays that fell upon it, it looked like a portrait of himself, but to a practised person it resembled our hero.

The young horseman's large blue eyes grew dim, as he gazed intently upon it.

It was strange that, were the young rider a man, he should be touched so deeply by the likeness of himself or a companion.

"Dear Dick," he muttered, pressing the miniature to his lips, while tears fell fast from his eyes. "Shall I never see you again? Are we to be parted to meet no more? Why did I not return, and tell you all that had happened? Why did I persist in following a fruitless pursuit? My sister is taken from me, and the only one whom I love is kept from me. Oh, what hours of weary bitterness I have brought on myself and on him Oh! Dick, Dick, Dick! if you only knew the unhappiness and sorrow I have endured, you would pity and forgive your poor Grace. Am I never more to see him? Am I never more to hear those words of sweet love he was wont to use? Oh! how I yearn once more to be leaning on his true manly breast. But alas! we—— Ah! some one comes. Bright

Prospect for his watch. I must be prepared, in case of treachery."

She primed her pistols, and waited for her visitor.

The clamour of several voices, and the clatter of approaching horses came distinctly through the stillness of the night.

"I say, Prospect," said one of the advancing party, "how the deuce do you know the fellow will come?"

"I have not the slightest doubt but what we shall find him waiting."

"I should like to have a look at the fellow," another. "I have heard that Tyburn Dick is the most gentlemanly scamp on the road."

"By Jove! I can vouch the truth of that," remarked Prospect; "he is an honourable and the most confounded cool fellow I ever saw."

"As you found out to your cost."

"I never knew anything like it before," said Bright Prospect. "He asked me if I was fond of picturesque views. Of course I answered in the affirmative. He then promised to show me a beautiful prospect if I would cross the rocks with him, which I did, and every moment expected to be precipitated headlong down the declivity; but we arrived safe the other side. I then asked him where the prospect was, when he deliberately put a pistol to my head, and said—'Here.'"

"You had a capital prospect of a bullet," said one of his companions.

"And a few were in perspective."

"I thought you said the highwayman was a girl."

"Ah, by Jove! I'll wager my life the highwayman is a female."

"I hope not," said another.

"Why?"

"Because I came down for the purpose of a highwayman hunt."

"You are a——"

"Hush, gentlemen," said Prospect, "I will ride forward, and make a sign when you are to come."

The party of young nobles stood back, while their companion went forward.

The hour of eight pealed forth from some distant spire as he rode across the heath.

" Bright Prospect," said a low voice, and the supposed Tyburn Dick met the gentleman.

"I am here at my time," said the gentleman.

"To the minute," replied the highwayman.

"Have you the watch?"

"For the money."

The gentleman produced a small roll of notes, and they made a mutual exchange.

They neither saw a crouching form at that moment creep from a cluster of brushwood, and hide behind the Haunted Oak.

They neither saw the malignant face that watched them with a savage gleam of triumph in his small twinkling eyes.

The young noblemen received the signal, and in an instant rode forward.

"Treachery!" said Tyburn Dick.

"No," said Prospect.

"Why this?"

The young sparks had gathered round the dashing highwayman.

"I want your horse."

"And I your sword."

"I advise you to get them," said Grace.

"I'll fight you for your horse."

"And I'll fight you for your sword."

"Very well, gentlemen," said the poor girl, in an awful state of fear.

Our hero had taught her the art of fencing, and she could use the sword with admirable skill, but her strength would give way beneath an antagonist she could not easily disarm; and then she trembled for the discovery of her sex.

"I will fight you for the horse first."

"My horse will fight for herself. If you can get in the saddle you are at liberty to keep the horse."

Grace dismounted, told Selim to look after herself, and called the gentleman who had such a particular wish to have her sword.

The beautiful girl fell into a splendid attitude to receive the furious onset of her fiery young opponent.

Grace did not move an inch; without flinching or shifting her steady gaze from the eyes of her combatant, she waited coolly for the attack, caught the heavily aimed blow of the young noble, and easily turned it aside.

"Furies!" exclaimed the infuriated young spark, "I want your sword."

Grace smiled. She did not answer. Her handsome face turned lily-white. She was sensible of the fearful risk she ran by duelling with a man strong as a young lion, and with an inscrutable nature as that of her opponent.

Yet sooner than own her sex to save her from the peril of the contest, she would rather face death.

The young noble suddenly leaped forward, making a terrible round cut at our heroine's head.

The fair girl was quick and skilful. Her finely tempered blade in an instant was brought round for the descending weapon.

There was a clash of steel as their blades met and clung together, then the young nobleman fell back howling. His sword had struck flat. The shock sent a benumbing pain running up his arm.

For a few seconds he was powerless.

His eyes glared with a vindictive light.

He meant mischief.

Grace stood on her guard. She had watched the kindling of his eyes, and knew he meant treachery.

"I shall kill you!" hissed the young noble.

He made a feint at her head, and drawing his weapon back, delivered a straight furious lunge for her breast.

Grace beat his sword aside, and angered by his cowardly impetus, she made a rapid stroke for his head.

Her sword made a deep gash across his cheek, and clipped a piece off his ear.

The vanquished young nobleman fell back, howling miserably. His companions rushed forward, uttering fearful threats, and clustered round the highwayman.

Poor girl! She was in a terrible dilemma. She could not resist against her many opponents that gathered angrily around her.

She was perfectly aware of the danger she incurred upon herself by assuming the dress of the celebrated highwayman, Tyburn Dick.

She knew her gallant lover never flinched from anything, and she must not stain his daring character by showing any signs of fear.

"Back, gentlemen!" she said; "back, if you value your lives!"

"Yours won't be of much value, if you have injured my friend," said one of the gentlemen.

"Don't let him go," shouted another; "we may as well have the thousand pounds for his capture."

"Certainly," laughed Grace; "but first you will have to hold me."

She made a cut at one of the gentlemen, who was sneaking behind her.

The sneaking gentleman rolled over with an ugly cut across the nose.

An angry shout arose from the party as a second of their companions fell.

The supposed Tyburn Dick was struck to the earth, and the whole of her opponents commenced a brutal attack upon her, but ere they could accomplish their intended capture, they were scared by a terrible vision.

THE WHITE PHANTOM.

The haunted oak shook with such terrible force, as though it would have shivered every bough to atoms.

Then there was a fearful roaring. It appeared to issue from the trunk.

The young nobles stopped in their cruel sport, and stood terror-stricken by what they saw.

The tree suddenly opened, and a white luminous form sprang out.

Cries of horror rose from the terrified nobles as the phantom dashed noiselessly amongst them.

Away they sped, shrieking frantically.

The malignant form crept from behind the tree, and bounded upon our heroine.

A fearful shriek rent the air as he raised her in his powerful arm, and he fell to the earth *stricken by the phantom*.

CHAPTER LX.
THE CAPTURE AND ESCAPE.

NIGHT wanes.

The grey streaks of morn fell upon the ghostly features of two forms lying beneath the haunted oak on Hounslow Heath.

Our heroine and the brutal thief-taker, Jonathan Wild, lying side by side in the spot where they fell the previous night.

The noble steed, Selim, stood over her handsome young rider, watchfully.

It would not have been good for any one to have touched her then.

As the morning wore on the brave girl awoke, faint, weak, and mystified.

Her little hand wandered over her pallid brow. Her gaze searched around the dreary heath. She shuddered, as her eyes rested upon the inhuman brute by her side, and turned her head away to encounter her faithful steed bending over her.

"You here, my beauty!" she exclaimed, gladly; "truly thou art a welcome friend."

She rose to her feet, and in a moment was in the saddle, and riding away.

"A welcome friend, truly," reiterated Wild, rising on his elbows, and he glared savagely after the gallant girl, "but methinks thy faithful steed will not carry thee far."

He sprang to his feet, cursing his ill-fortune, and followed our heroine.

With the stealthy tread of a panther he kept in her track through the green country until they reached Brompton.

Grace halted before a small inn, and giving her faithful steed to the ostler, she entered.

Jonathan Wild chuckled with savage delight.

"Ha, ha! I have you now, Tyburn Dick!" he said, exultantly.

He pulled his cap over his ill-looking face as far as to cover half his features, and entering the parlour seated himself opposite.

"Good morning," he said.

Grace did not recognise him, but his coarse, hollow voice made her shrink back.

An evil shadow seemed to hover about him, and our heroine felt his presence boded no good to her.

Wild bit his lips, and contracted his shaggy eyebrows over his cold, cynical-looking orbs, until they appeared to sink so far back in their sockets as to be lost from view.

"Have you heard of that terrible scene that took place on Hounslow Heath last night?" the thief-taker said.

Grace did not deign to answer him.

All Wild's vindictive spleen arose at the contempt of the highwayman.

"I want you," he said, tapping the fair girl on the shoulder.

Grace turned as though stung by a serpent.

"Do you?" she said, coolly.

" Do you know who I am ?"

" I haven't that pleasure,"

" I am Jonathan Wild."

" What's that to me ?"

" You are Tyburn Dick."

" I am supposed to be."

" I want you."

" I will talk with you after breakfast," said Grace, putting a cup of boiling coffee to her lips.

" You have no more of that," said Wild, pulling her arm down.

" Then you shall !" exclaimed Grace, fiercely, dashing the scalding liquid in his face.

Blinded and half mad he clutched at the heroic girl, and received a stunning blow from a heavy pistol that sent him reeling backwards.

Grace made for the door.

" Don't let him escape, landlord !" shouted the thief-taker.

The landlord leaped over the bar, and stood in the doorway, with his arms outstretched to bar the way.

Grace drew her sword.

Her soft, dreamy blue eyes were kindled with a dangerous light.

" Stand aside !" she said, determinedly.

Mine host stood irresolute, and gazed into her excited handsome face.

" Move !" she said again.

Her sword was upraised.

Mine host saw that it was dangerous to to oppose her ; he moved aside, and as she sprang for the inn door he hurled a huge tankard at her.

It struck her on the head, and felled her to the floor half-stunned and bleeding.

In a moment Wild was upon her ; he grasped her small delicate wrists in his iron fist, and while the poor girl was helpless he secured her hands behind her with a heavy pair of handcuffs.

" Now, landlord, let me have some sort of conveyance to take this young gentleman to Newgate."

" I ain't got any, only a small cart."

" Bring out what you have got, and be hanged to you," said Wild, fiercely.

" All right," said the worthy landlord ;

" don't people have a reward for catching a highwayman ?"

" You shall have a *reward* if you are not quick with the cart," replied the thief-catcher spitefully.

Mine host was an artful old soldier ; he suspected the character of his early ruffianly guest, and would not, if possible, be cheated out of the blood money he had earned.

" Look here," he said emphatically, " I mean to have my share of the reward ; I earned it, and I'll have it."

" Curse you for a fool !" exclaimed Wild. " You can't have the reward until the highwayman is safely in Newgate. Get the cart quickly."

" Your ill-looks won't frighten me ; if you want the cart, get it."

" Do you know who you are talking to ?" the thief-taker said, in a fierce whisper, his eyes glaring like those of a demon.

" I don't care a straw who you are."

" You don't see Jonathan Wild every day, do you ?"

" Would that make any difference to me ? I shouldn't be frightened of him."

" Oh !" ejaculated Wild, aghast at the inn keeper's boldness. " If you are wise, my friend, you will take twenty pounds for your trouble, and provide me with a conveyance."

" I dare say, and you stick to all the re—. No, I don't see it."

" You will if you are wise."

" Too wise for you, my friend."

" Get the cart ready, do you, or you shall suffer for your insolence," thundered the thief-taker, losing his temper.

" Oh, oh ! Suffer, and by whom ?"

" I, Jonathan Wild."

" Don't make any mistake, my arch fiend of Newgate, I am not even frightened of you."

" Don't make too bold," said Wild, grimly.

" I make bold enough to defy you."

" Beware."

" Of what ?"

" The gallows."

A momentary chill ran through the man.

" I can bring you there," continued Wild.

" But I have done nothing."

" It matters not ; I have sent people there for less than you have said.

" I don't doubt you, but I flatter myself I

am almost as wide awake as you, and it would be no easy matter to condemn me."

Wild laughed a fiendish laugh.

" I could have you arrested to-morrow."

" For what ?"

" Harbouring highwaymen here."

" But it would be a false assertion."

" That would not matter ; my word would send any man to the gibbet, despite all his evidence of innocence.

The innkeeper remained as firm and undaunted in his resolution, spite of the fiendish threats of the thief-taker.

Wild saw that persuasions or threats would not answer his purpose—he must use more forcible means for compelling the innkeeper to comply with his demands.

" Get that vehicle ready within five minutes," demanded he, producing a huge pistol and presenting it full in the innkeeper's face.

There was a mischievous glitter in mine host's eye as he turned away and entered the parlour.

Wild chuckled ; he thought he had forced him to submission this time.

But his thoughts took a different turn when mine host returned with a huge blunderbuss over his shoulder, and a long rusty sword hanging by his side.

Wild gave vent to a violent imprecation. Mine host looked defiant, and told his foe to keep his station ; his weapon to the muzzle with destructive shot was loaded. Wild heard the fatal tidings, his frame with fury goaded, and like a fiend unchained from hell commenced to rave and swear. Mine host again interposed to tell his foe profanation was not allowed there. Swift as a shaft from a famous bow Jonathan sent out his fist, caught mine host a stunning blow that made him writhe and twist. A flash—report—a fearful scream—then arose a savage shout ; a second flash lighted up the scene—from the inn Wild staggered out. The struggle over, the victory won, mine host had gained the day. A rush of feet—a clamour arose—men approached where Wild lay : in silent reverence they raised the form and bore their chief away.

And thus ended the battle between Jonathan Wild and the innkeeper.

But mine host had not yet done with the thief-taker. He wanted the reward for capturing Tyburn Dick, and he meant to have it.

He called down his worthy dame to take care of the shop, and then set in pursuit of Wild and his party.

They had got some distance in advance, when he emerged into the Brompton Road.

He saw their fading forms in the distance, and hastened onward.

" Halt !" he shouted, when in earshot.

They party halted.

The officers were surprised to see him rushing towards them. It was not often they had any one to run after them ; generally they had to run after other people.

Wild turned upon him a savage glare.

" I am coming with you to Newgate, for the reward for capturing the highwayman."

" You shall have it," replied the thief-taker, with a coarse triumphant laugh. " Secure him, men ; he is our prisoner !"

" What the devil do you mean ?" said the astonished innkeeper.

" You are our prisoner. It's plain enough, ain't it ?"

" Not for me. The first one that lays a hand on me will have to blame you for the consequences."

He drew his rusty sword, and stood ready for an attack.

" Put that file away," said Wild. " Men, do your duty !"

The word duty was out of place with these bloodhounds of the law, but they understood its meaning.

The whole troop rushed suddenly upon the innkeeper.

He was thrown upon his back, the rusty weapon wrenched from his grasp, and in a moment he was manacled, and being led away with our heroine.

The brave girl bore her horrid situation nobly, though she felt sorely the pang of shame that would ever after stain her character.

Her step was firm and steady, her graceful form drawn erect, and her handsome well-shaped head thrown back, she walked fearlessly through the busy streets, surrounded by her captors and gaping throngs of people, who gathered round them in groups as they proceeded on their way.

" Go," said Wild, turning to one of his mysidons; "get one of the chambers ready at my Kemp in Newgate-street for the reception of our *guest*."

The man started off without a word.

Wild smarted from the effects of the hot coffee.

"Curse you!" he said, shaking his huge fist in her face; "you shall suffer for throwing that coffee in my face."

Grace cast on him a disdainful look.

A thought rushed to her mind—a thought of escape.

The irons on her wrists were long and loose. By a little perseverance she could slip them off.

How her heart bounded with excitement as she got one tiny hand through the rough hard circle that bound her wrist.

Liberty was in her hands—she was free from her bonds.

She grasped the heavy irons firmly.

One bold stroke, and she might escape.

She cast her brutal captor a look of terrible revenge. Danger gleamed like fire from her eyes.

Quick as a lightning flash her arm came round, and the heavy irons went crashing down on his head.

The thief-taker, half stunned, staggered into the arms of his men.

His head was thick, and the blow did not take much effect, but ere he recovered his fair prisoner had escaped.

With the swiftness of a frightened deer that had suddenly broken from its savage bonds, she sped along.

"After him! bring him down!" yelled Wild, madly; "dead or alive, we must have him!"

Away went the men in pursuit.

The innkeeper was left in charge of two officers; then Wild, with his craft cunning-less, took a different route.

The chase was long and tiring. Many were the hairbreadth escapes the brave girl encountered in her flight.

Through Holborn, down St. Martin's Lane, in and out the courts and back streets, dodged our heroine, with her savage pursuers close upon her heels.

On—on she kept, panting and exhausted.

A shout was raised as she dived down a narrow alley of not sufficient width to admit of two persons to pass through in line.

She reached the bottom. The yelling of the officers told plainly they were not far behind.

"Take me who dare!" she said, defiantly.

"I dare!" said a gruff voice, and Wild stood before her.

CHAPTER LXI

MERTON GRANGE.

A FINE old ancestral pile was Merton Grange, standing in a secluded part of the country not twenty miles from London.

It had been the name of an honourable race of Saxons from generation to generation.

Lord Merton was the last that remained. He had but one brother who married at an early age, and soon followed his gentle wife from this world, leaving two sons—Reginald and Percy—who little supported the good name of their sire.

With the setting sun there arrived two closely muffled forms, like guilty beings whose deeds were of such darkness they could not face the holy light of day, and concealed themselves in a kind of hut that lay some distance in the rear of the grand old house.

As night wore on, and dancing shadows played o'er the earth, they glided forth—the most guilty-looking and dark shadows of all.

A shriek—a piercing fearful cry—broke the stillness of night!

The men started.

"What means that?" exclaimed one.

"I know not," replied the other. "Hark ye, didst thou hear that?"

A voice like thunder shook the Grange within.

The men stood petrified.

Bang! crash!

The massive hall door swung back. A man of wild aspect darted down the stone steps; he raised a shout as past the men he flew; another moment he was lost from view.

"Reginald," said one of the men in a terrified voice.

"Percy," the other said, in a tone quite as terrified.

"Am I dreaming?"

"I think not."

"Did you hear—did you see, Percy?"

" All, Reginald."

" His face—did you see?"

" I did."

" And was it——"

" The one we saw sink under the waters of the deep two years ago."

" Good heavens !"

" What think you of this strange affair ?"

" I know not.   This is a terrible reception for us."

" My head is in a whirl—my mouth parched with thirst—for heaven's sake, Reginald, give me water !"

His features were drawn up in convulsions ; his eyes glared demoniacally ; and his hands tore at his massive curly hair.

" Water, water !" he cried.

" Percy, Percy ! you unnerve me."

' Water !"

" Come to yonder brook ; I can't bring the brook to you," said Reginald, assisting his brother to his feet.

He tottered, with his brother's assistance, to the flowing stream, and, throwing himself upon the green sward, drank greedily of the crystal fluid.

" I hope your nerves are cooled," said Reginald.

His brother deigned not to answer, but cast him a look that spoke all the disgust he felt at the remark.

" Percy."

" Well."

" Superstitious fears must not deter us from our work."

" What would you think we saw ?"

" I know not, nor care."

" But should it be *he* ?"

" Bosh !   We saw him sink."

" He may have risen again."

" Impossible !"

" How so ?"

" Were they not bound back to back ? Did we not see them hurled into the sea ?   Did we not see them sink ?   Did we not wait, but they did not rise again ?"

" Yet we have seen them since."

" Seen them ?" echoed the other, scornfully.

" What, then, would you believe we have seen ?"

" Nothing."

" 'Tis a pity nothing should have frightened you so at the smugglers' cave."

Reginald changed colour, and glared at his brother fiercely.

" Do you believe in ghosts ?" he said, with a sneer.

" We are led to believe there are such things."

" I pity you."

" What was it we saw ?"

" No ghosts."

" Then it must have been the original."

" Damnation !   cease this !" exclaimed Reginald, warmly.

Just then a large black ominous bird flew shrieking over their heads.

Reginald drew a pistol and fired at the bird.   It fluttered for a moment as though winged, but the next instant it rose, flew back shrieking, skimmed through the air, then for the third time it sailed round their heads, flapped its wings in their faces, and with a piercing yell darted over the mansion top, and faded from view.

" This is a lively place," remarked Percy, with a shudder ; " what with yelling phantoms, shrieking falcons, and ghostly fights."

" Did the appearance of the bird scare you ?"

" It did you."

So it had.   Reginald, with all his devilish hardihood, did not feel quite at ease.   There seemed some foreboding of evil with the presence of that strange bird.

" It gave me a momentary turn, I own," he said.

" We are haunted night and day."

" If a whole legion of devil's imps stood before me, it would not deter me from my purpose."

His brother strongly doubted it, but ere he had time to say so there arose a cry that sent a chill through them.

Then there was a rustle amongst the trees.

The brothers turned.

Another yell made them start.

" I will discover the knave of this artifice," exclaimed Reginald, trying to conceal the terror he felt.

He saw a form—a shadowy kind of form —fluttering about amongst the trees.

Drawing his sword, he was in the act of

springing forward, when the form darted past him.

He made a pass at it.

His weapon seemed to sink in the body. The figure kept onward.

The same weird, wild-looking form they had before seen.

Reginald recoiled with horror.

" 'Tis no being of this earth," he gasped. "My sword went through it, yet it laughed in scorn at me."

"Gone!" exclaimed Percy, as the form vanished in the gloom.

"What means this mystery?"

"I know not, unless it is that we are to be tortured until the day of our death."

"Goblins, ghosts, or devils shall not keep me from my purpose! Come, Percy."

"Where would you go?"

"To discover the retreat of the phantom—phantom should it be."

" 'Tis gone."

"Then we will search to find it."

"Madness! Would you endanger your life?"

"Ay, sooner than be haunted hourly like this! Will you follow me?"

"If you wish it, but the search will be useless, and we have a better use for our time than ghost-hunting."

"To what other use would you put it to-night?"

"To see the lawyer. We cannot take possession without having the deeds drawn up."

"True; but London is a long way, 'tis late now, and we should not arrive there in time to see Mr. Brief to-night."

"By starting now we shall catch the last coach, be able to have a night in town, and see Brief the first thing to-morrow morning."

"The last coach starts at ten from the Leopard Inn. It is half-past eight now. I have time to reconnoitre our future home."

"Why not leave that?"

"How do we know it is safe?"

"It is as safe now as it has hitherto been."

"Your persuasions are no good, Percy. I mean to enter."

"Enter, and stand the consequences."

"I can defend myself against any danger I shall encounter there."

"You know not."

"I am certain."

"How will you enter?"

"By the window. Will you come?"

"No."

"Then go back," exclaimed Reginald, angrily.

Pushing his brother rudely aside, he made his way to the back of the Grange.

Percy slowly followed, abashed. His brother's reproachful words stung him keenly.

"Why be so headstrong? Do not enter, Reginald."

Reginald did not answer. He mounted a balcony, and with the point of his sword forced open the casement.

Percy shuddered. As he entered a chill of awe fell upon him. He felt that his brother would meet with some terrible danger.

For a moment he stood irresolute, undecided whether to follow or not.

He heard his brother's heavy tread as he strode across the room. The sound of each step echoed dismally, and died away.

"I will enter," he murmured; no harm shall fall upon my brother if I can help it."

He was in the act of ascending the balcony, when he heard a cry that held him petrified.

He could not move; his blood froze in his veins. He stood breathless and motionless as a statue.

The cry came from his brother in piercing accents, and then died away in a faint gurgling scream.

He heard a fall as of a body.

Then all was quiet—silent and gloomy as the tomb.

His hand wandered to his brow. He looked wild and haggard. A hollow unearthly cry escaped his lips.

Again he was about to mount the balcony, when again he suddenly stopped.

His eyes fixed on an advancing figure with a stony glare.

The figure came—glided towards him—the same wild being he had seen twice before. His hand was upraised, and from his bony long fingers dripped drops of steaming gore.

"Blood! my brother's life-blood!" exclaimed Percy, and he fell to the earth.

CHAPTER LXII

TYBURN DICK HAS A SERIES OF ADVENTURES AND NARROW ESCAPE OF HIS LIFE.

OUR gallant hero did not find much trouble in escaping from the Stag and Hounds.

He laughed heartily at the way he gulled the guests at the inn, and when out of danger smacked the money he won with much satisfaction.

He was passing through a small village one early morning, when his attention was attracted to a group of farm labourers standing round a small, thin, greedy, half-starved, cynical, crafty man.

Discontent and disconsolation was stamped upon every sturdy face.

"Hear me, mister; I beant agoin' to work for nothing," said one.

"Can't help it," said the weasel individual, sharply; "if you don't like to take the money, leave the farm."

"Well, guvner, I don't see neither why you should stop half our money cos we was five minutes late."

"You can leave the farm to-day, then, Brown."

"It's all very well for you," said another, "but we've got a wife and family to keep out of our earnings, an' if we are out o' work they have to starve."

"Take your money and be contented," replied the tight-fisted overseer.

"Contented," growled another of the labourers, "sixpence out o' two shillings a day, because we're late five minutes, makes a big hole in our wages. It ain't stopped by the squire's wish."

"You can leave to-day then, Jones."

"What am I to do if I leave—starve?"

"As you like."

"Can't do that," muttered the man, despondingly; "couldn't bear to see my wife and little ones crying for bread."

"Are you going to take the money and commence work again, or refuse and leave the farm?"

"We must take the money, I suppose," the men said, having no alternative but to refuse, be out of work, and starve."

The old money-grubber paid the poor, worn, hard-working fellows, and walked away.

Dick had concealed himself, and overheard all that was said; his noble nature revolted to see how the poor fellows were being robbed of their hard earnings, and by that miserable blood-sucking specimen of humanity.

The old worshipper of gold went on his way chuckling and fingering the sixpences he had robbed those hard-working men of.

He let each coin drop through his avaricious fingers—the sound seemed to be delicious music to his ears.

"Ha, ha!" he laughed, "money, money, beautiful money! why should I give thee to those clowns! No, no, thy bright glistening faces warm my poor old heart with pleasure when I toy with thee for hours."

"Miserly old scamp," muttered Dick, following the overseer.

"What good art thou to those poor fools who sell thee for their bellies? That is not right. No, no! they should keep thee—prize thee as I do."

"You don't give them much chance to save much," thought Dick.

"What do I live for?" commenced the old money-grubber again.

"Money, I should say," muttered our hero.

"Money—yes, bright, glorious, money," continued the grey-haired old scoundrel—"yes, I live for money—money, that gives you power—money, that makes you rich—money, that gives you glory and raises you high in the world. Money is my life—I love money better than anything in the world."

"Do you!" Dick said, loudly, tapping him on the shoulder.

The old fellow turned sharply.

His eyes lighted upon the bright barrel of a pistol, held in a very steady hand.

"I want a little of that bright, glorious, money," Dick said, coolly.

"Money?" echoed the overseer.

"Money," iterated Dick.

"Would you rob a poor fellow of his hard-earned money?"

"Sneaking old cuss — grey-headed old schemer!"

"Young sir!"

"Blood-sucking old scoundrel!"

"Verily, sir, and——"

THE MIDNIGHT DEED.

"Thieving money extractor — despicable old miser—spoiler of useful money!"

"Oh! thou wicked sin——"

"Despicable old wretch, hand out that money you have robbbed those poor working men of."

"I—I——"

"Yes, you."

"Oh, verily, and——"

"The money!"

Dick suddenly put the rim of his pistol on the shaking old fellow's nose.

The old money-grubber gave vent to one horrified yell and fell upon his knees.

He clasped his hands together, and in a withering voice cried—

"Oh! have mercy upon——"

"The money!" said Dick, sternly.

The old fellow seemed reluctant to part with his ill-gotten gains.

Dick clutched him roughly by the collar, stood him on his feet, and forcing him against a tree put the pistol to his forehead.

"The money you robbed those poor men of!"

"Oh, I never."

"Liar!"

"Dear me, what shall I do?"

"Give me that money if you value your life."

"Oh, lor! I wish some one would come."

"Am I to blow your brains out?" said Dick, sternly, though hardly able to repress a smile at the old fellow's woeful visage."

"Oh, dear me! no, no, no!"

"That money, then!"

"Yes, yes; you shall have all, and I, poor old man, will have to starve."

"Sneaking old thief!" exclaimed the proud boy, shaking the miserable old miser severely by the collar.

"I shan't ask you for the money again."

"No, no! don't! I know you wouldn't be so cruel as to take a poor old man's money."

"Curse you for a miserable old sneak," Dick said contemptuously, "you have tried to evade me in every way; I shall help myself now."

He threw the trembling old man on his back, and in a minute robbed him of every coin.

"Remember," he said, binding the old man hand and foot, "when next you go gleaning don't make your stacks from the poor man's crop, or Tyburn Dick won't show the same mercy next time."

The miserly old scamp groaned for the loss of his money.

Our hero returned to the labouring men.

"Come hither, good fellows," he cried.

The men dropped their tools and looked at the handsome youth in surprise.

"Come here," he said again.

The men timidly advanced towards him.

"Your master has cheated you of your money," he said.

"Not the master," said one.

"Then the foreman."

"Yes, yes!" responded several voices.

"How much did he keep back?"

"Sixpence out of two shillings, if we are only five minutes late of a morning."

"He won't stop any more."

The men wondered why not.

"I see you don't understand me. How many are there of you?"

"Twenty."

"Then he makes ten shillings from the sweat of other men's brows," muttered Dick. "Curse him, if it had not been for his age, I would have put a bullet through his skull. Here is the sixpence each he stopped from you this morning."

Each man took the small coin, and gratefully pressed the noble youth's small hand.

"Are you satisfied?" Dick asked.

"Quite, thank you," they replied, not knowing how to express their gratitude.

"Here are twenty sovereigns; divide them equally amongst you."

"But—but," spluttered one of the men, not knowing whether the youth was a prince in disguise or the old gentleman from the lower regions come to bribe them.

"Don't be frightened," said Dick, smiling, "my motto is to take from the rich to give to the poor; take the money with pleasure, and never think badly of Tyburn Dick, the highwayman."

"Tyburn Dick!"

"Tyburn Dick!"

Echoed from mouth to mouth.

"Tyburn Dick," replied our hero, raising his hat, politely; "good day, gentlemen."

Another moment he was gone.

The men stood in awe.

They swore by their lives to one another to prove his friend, and fight for him where and whenever they should meet him, did he require help.

The brave boy wended his way along, feeling proud of the generous act and help he had given to those true honest English workmen.

He did not proceed far without another adventure.

He heard a cry for help.

His hand wandered instinctively to his sword.

"Some one in trouble," he muttered.

He looked around, but saw no one.

He was now in a very dense part of the country, where huge trees grew in clusters, and furze bushes blocked up the gaps between the gigantic trees.

He stood wondering from when sound could have proceeded.

He did not wonder long.

A terrified cry from a female came distinctly from amidst the thicket.

Then he heard the supplication of an old man pleading for mercy.

He did not stay to think of his own danger, but darted forward and broke a path through the thick foliage.

"Cowards!" he thundered.

His eyes fell upon a fearful scene.

A gang of ill-looking, murderous ruffians and got a beautiful young girl down.

She was stripped of every article of dress, and lay totally helpless and in their power.

Had our hero been a moment latter the beautiful girl would have fallen a victim to their brutal lust.

With the ferocity of a savage panther he sprang upon the ruffian who knelt gloatingly over the fair girl.

Dick grasped him by the throat, hurled him aside so that his vile blood should not stain the immaculate skin of the fair girl, and ere any of his companions could interpose, the angered boy's bright blade swept through his heart, and came out of his quivering body reeking to the hilt with his black blood.

"One!" he said, with terrible calmness.

He sprang into the gang.

Two fell over their companion, dead.

Tyburn Dick did his work quick and sure.

The rest of the brutes fell back, awed, terror-stricken, and bewildered.

So sudden, and with such fearful vengeance did the daring boy come amongst them, they seemed to lose all power and brute courage.

"Come on, cowards!" exclaimed Dick.

He raised his dripping sword, and dashed at them.

The men turned to meet him with deadly vengeance, but ere a sword was raised to strike, another of their associates fell to the earth, with his skull completely split in twain.

The sight of their companions falling like so many sticks was too much for them, and they scampered off.

Dick followed them for some distance. They did not turn once, but kept on at terrified speed.

Our hero saw they had no intention of returning, so left them to their onward flight, and made his way back to the lady.

The poor lady lay half fainting from fear and exhaustion.

Her cheeks blushed deeply with shame, and she turned her head away as our hero's gaze rested upon her beautiful form.

He stood in a very delicate position.

The lady lay nude as Eve, her rich chestnut-brown tresses flowed in wild profusion over her heaving bosom, about her swan-like throat, and over her smooth, round, and finely-moulded shoulders.

Dick looked around for something to cover her, while he searched for her clothes.

Gladness! he saw her attire lying in a heap, and rushed forward.

"Come, dear lady!" he said, throwing her dress over her splendid limbs, "you are safe now. I will retire."

"My sire," said the lady, looking at her young preserver gratefully, through her tears. "is he safe?"

"Your sire?" responded Dick.

He suddenly remembered the piteous cries of an old man he had heard.

"Your father shall be found, lady," said Dick. He kissed his hand to her, and went in search of the missing gentleman.

He did not proceed far without success.

His gaze fell upon the form of a man, gagged, and bound to a tree.

It did not take him many moments to release the aged captive.

"Many thanks, my noble sir!" said the gentleman, grasping both Dick's hands.

"Thank Heaven, you are safe!" Dick said. "I did not expect to see such mercy shown by a band of those desperate ruffians."

"Mercy, sir! Mercy you call it!"

"They have spared your life."

"But they plundered me of everything else"—the gentleman stopped, glared at our hero, and suddenly said—"Where is my child?"

"Quite safe."

"How know you, sir?"

"I had the pleasure of saving her from a wretched fate."

"Then they did not——"

"They did not. I came in time to prevent it."

"You have saved her, sir, from a disgrace that would have blighted her young life."

"I feel proud to have saved one so young and beautiful."

"Had she been violated by those brutal outlaws, nothing would have washed the stain out. I know not how to express my gratitude, but you must return with me, and be my guest for a while."

"You honour me by the invitation, but at present I am placed in such circumstances as will not admit of me accepting your generous offer. Rely upon my word, sir; I will do myself the honour of——"

"Tush, tush; I hear of no excuses. You must accept my offer. Come, young sir; convey me to where you left my daughter."

"I would not return for a few moments. I left the lady to attire herself."

"Honourable youth!" muttered the old gentleman.

"Did you capture any of the ruffians?"

"I slew three," replied Dick, grimly; "the others escaped."

"You slew three!" the gentleman exclaimed, in surprise.

"The others would have shared the same fate, had they not fled when they did."

"Brave, noble youth!" and again the old fellow grasped Dick's hand.

"Papa," came in a faint timid voice.

"The lady is ready to receive us," remarked Dick.

"Come, sir; you shall be my daughter's cavalier while you stay."

"You honour me, but really——"

"That will do. You can't refuse. Oh, my child!" he said, as his fair daughter ran nimbly into his arms.

They had an affectionate embrace.

Dick almost wished the soft little arms were round his neck.

That luxury had got to come.

"Haven't you a word for your brave champion?" said the old gentleman to his daughter.

She timidly advanced towards the gallant boy. Her cheeks glowed as she extended her tiny hand.

Was it that the thought rushed to her mind that the handsome youth had seen her in the wild state of nature, or was it that she felt something stronger than gratitude towards her captivating preserver?

Her hand trembled as Dick took her taper fingers, her voice quivered with emotion as she addressed him in the following manner—

"Believe me, noble sir, if I say I cannot find language enough to assert my gratitude for your gallant conduct. My pa' I am sure will make you gladly welcome as his honoured guest, and I should be too happy to—to——"

Her head fell upon her heaving breast. Her voice grew faint, and she could not finish her sentence.

"Sweet lady," said Dick tenderly, "gladly will I avail myself of the honour conferred upon me since you are so anxious for me to become your guest, and dine with you this evening."

"This evening only?" she said, in a tone of disappointment.

"I should be most delighted could I stay longer, but matters of importance will not admit of my absence."

The lady sighed sadly.

Dick felt strangely agitated by the lady's beauty.

He thought of Grace. An unpleasant thought flashed through his mind.

"Why did she leave me if she loved me?" he thought. "Perhaps she has proved false. Let her go."

Then he reproached himself for thinking of her thus, and resolved to leave the lady and her sire to go instantly in quest of his own love.

But when he raised his head and encountered the lady's pleading face, her expressive eyes that spoke the language of her heart, his resolutions were banished, and with them the remembrance of Grace, for the time at least.

"Come," said the gentleman, "we will return home. We have the chariot waiting for us if the robbers have not run away with it."

He led the way through the thicket leaving his beautiful daughter for Dick to escort.

Our hero politely offered his arm. The fair girl slipped her own beautiful round soft limb through, and then followed the stately old gentleman.

A chariot and four splendid bay horses stood on the border of the forest.

"Good God!" exclaimed the old gentleman, perplexed. "What have the villains done with my servants?"

A melancholy groan came in reply, from whence none knew.

"Speak, in the name of Heaven, speak, my men!" cried the gentleman.

A groan more melancholy than the last came in reply.

Yet none could trace from whence it issued. It seemed as though floating in the air.

"The voice seemed to come from the forest," said Dick. "Stay, sir, while I make a search."

"Nay, brave sir; I must accompany you."

"Excuse me if I decline your company."

"Why decline my company?"

"By your leaving your daughter would be exposed to danger. These villains may yet be lurking about."

"True, true; but by going alone you may fall into their murderous hands."

"Fear nothing for my safety. I am too used to face danger to be scared by a few such wretches as they."

Away he went, without another word, leaving father and daughter standing in awe and admiration as their gaze followed the retreating form of the gallant boy.

Dick had more than one reason for going alone. He stood in a very uncomfortable position of being discovered in his own character, should the cape he had kept over his breast suddenly blow aside and reveal the conspicuous star he had been careful to keep hidden.

He knew too well should he be discovered as the daring boy knight of the road his hopes—hopes of infatuation that throbbed his soul for the beautiful girl—would be crushed, and himself be exposed to the taunts of sarcastic men.

He made his way into the thickest part of the forest, and looking round to see that no eyes were watching him, he tore off his cape, turned his coat, and hiding his pistols, reappeared.

The transformation was the work of a minute, but it made a wonderful difference in his appearance

The lady's face flushed with admiration. His graceful form and bearing were well set off by the blue silk and velvet coat trimmed with silver lace.

"You have seen nothing of them?" asked the gentleman.

"Nothing," replied Dick.

A groan for the third time, louder and more miserable than the rest.

Dick's acute ear detected its direction. He wheeled round on his heels, and looking up through the trees, an exclamation of horror broke from his lips.

The gentleman stood bewildered. Dick darted forward, clambered up a tree with the celerity of an ape, and scrambled along a huge bough, at the end of which hung two men, bound back to back.

Our hero dropped from that bough on to one below, clasped the men round the waist, cut the cord that suspended them in the air with his sword, and slowly lowered them to the ground.

When he reached the ground and began to unbind the men, he saw that one was quite insensible and blue in the face.

Strangulation had very nearly completed its work, though the other was not so bad as his companion.

"I think, my friend," said Dick, by way of consolation, "five minutes' longer hanging out would have seen the last of you."

The lacquey shuddered.

"However," continued Dick, "since you are safe, and don't feel disposed to take your reckoning from this jolly old lord, let's make the best of our time, and try if you can stand on those pampered feet."

"I am very grateful for your timely assistance," murmured the man."

"I dare say you are. Never mind about your gratitude; see if you can rouse your companion. Your master and your mistress are anxious to return."

"Do you think my mate is dead?"

"Dead! no. Come, rouse up, and see what can be done."

"I can't move."

"Why not?"

"I want some water.'

"Where the deuce do you think I can get water about here?"

"I saw a little stream while up——"
The man shuddered, and pointed to the tree.

"Oh!"

"I wish I could get some."

"Where from?"

"The stream."

"Where's the stream?"

"In the forest, just past——" The man pointed again to the fatal tree.

Dick made his exit, and vanished through the forest, and in the lapse of three minutes he returned, holding a huge piece of hollow bark filled to the rim with water.

"There, that will rouse you," he said, dousing the man.

"Give me some to drink."

Dick held the bark to his lips.

"Don't drink too much," he said. "Ah! what are you up to? If you bite the bark I shall growl at you."

"I've had enough," said the flunkey; "you can stalk off."

"Without your leaf," replied our hero, smiling at the horrible jokes.

He was not long in bringing the other poor fellow back to consciousness; then he returned with his two patients to where he had left the gentleman.

"You see," said our hero, "I have brought them to you quite safe, though they had a very narrow escape of being left for meat for the crows."

"God forbid!" said the old gentleman, fervently; "but where were they."

Dick told him. The gentleman expressed his admiration at our hero's conduct, ordered his servants to mount without further delay, and drive home.

The carriage rolled rapidly along.

Dick was seated beside the beautiful girl, and immediately opposite the old gentleman, who, through exhaustion, or perhaps thought it more convenient, went to sleep with his ears wide open.

Our hero felt his arm unconsciously gliding round his companion's slender waist, and in return her arm glided round his neck. Their heads came very close together, and their lips met.

Then their breasts began to beat; their cheeks glow, and they gave sigh for sigh.

Dick wanted to say a lot, but could think of nothing; the lady thought a lot, but dared not breathe a word; so they reached home in silence, and only exchanged the signals of love each felt for the other by a tender caress.

The carriage stopped at the door of a splendid mansion.

Dick stepped out, and aided the lady to alight.

The huge doors were thrown open, and the powdered lacqueys stood aside while they entered.

"We dine within half an hour," said the gentleman, addressing his gallant young guest; "my valet is at your disposal. He will conduct you to a chamber."

Dick bowed, and followed the valet, who was summoned for his assistance.

"You may retire," said Dick.

The valet bowed himself out of the room, and retired accordingly.

Our hero was alone in a splendid boudoir. For a few moments he stood admiring his own elegant figure in a large mirror.

"Not so bad," he cogitated, admiring the change in appearance his coat made. "How fortunate for me to save that delightful little creature from these ugly brutes. Ugh! the idea is horrible, to think that she should be sullied by their vile touch. But she isn't—I saved her. Ain't the old buffer awfully grateful? Very kind of him to go to sleep; I think he is fond of me already. Not a bad spec—a marquisate and a marquis's daughter; much better than risking a fellow's neck by running after—after—now, Dick, where the deuce are you rambling? You ought to be ashamed of yourself."

He gazed at himself in deep abstraction; his thoughts were flying about in every direction but the right. It is evident that the beautiful girl had made a deep impression on him.

He thought of Grace, the devoted girl, and their early love, but the image of his new companion would rise before his eyes and rack his brain with her gentle beauty.

"No, no!" he suddenly exclaimed, "I must not forsake my own true, brave girl for her."

Dinner was announced.

"Dinner," muttered Dick. "Who are the

gentlemen to be assembled. Wonder whether I shall be recognised? Dare say I shall—unfortunate devil—always get into some scrape or another. Have revenge if I do—won't lose a marquisate for nothing."

Thus saying, he went downstairs, and was introduced to the many guests as the hero of the day.

He was honoured by the next seat to the peerless girl.

Dinner went off quietly.

Every one looked wonderfully knowing at the other, and each seemed to have a personal animosity against our hero; for the fierce glances that were cast over him would have made any one of a less gallant nature feel very uncomfortable.

But Dick did not; he enjoyed his dinner, enjoyed the company of his fair partner, and greatly enjoyed the idea of making the rest of the company jealous by the attention he paid her, and the attention she paid him in return.

Dinner over, the gentlemen rose to adjourn to another apartment, and as each passed our hero they tapped their swords significantly.

Dick tapped his in return to each one.

Many a gallant gentleman had been won by the witching face of the fair Lady Bertha Grey, and whispered into her ear such words as a maiden loves to listen to; yet she took little heed of what they said. Gentle and guileless as she was, she was not to be easily won. She loved her father too well to be lured away by the charm of a flatterer's tongue.

She knew little of the outward world, and rarely spoke to strangers.

Yet when Dick said he must part, she clung to him despairingly, and it was with the greatest difficulty that he could tear himself away.

Marquis Grey made him promise faithfully that it would not be long before he would call again to see him.

Dick promised, and departed. A gentleman who had sat opposite our hero at dinner appeared in an awful hurry to leave, and went just before Dick.

The night was dark, and the park dreary, as Dick emerged from the large mansion; and before he had proceeded fifty yards, a cloaked figure sprang from a dark corner and lunged at him with a dagger.

The gallant youth was lost in deep reverie at the time. By instinct he sprang aside at hearing a rustle behind him, and so avoided the murderous weapon. He raised his sword, struck the dagger from the would-be assassin's grasp, and in a warning voice said, as he cut the back of the man's hand open—

"I shall know you when next we meet. That mark will never leave you!"

CHAPTER LXIII.
A RACE FOR LIFE.

"Stop thief! Stop him! Stop Tyburn Dick, the highwayman!"

Such were the cries raised by the rabble who joined in the chase after the supposed Tyburn Dick.

Our heroine's daring spirit was roused when confronted by Jonathan Wild at the end of the court.

He faced her fiercely.

Yelling and shouting madly were other pursuers coming down behind her.

She knew her danger.

Not a moment was to be lost.

Wild stretched his arms out to bar her way.

He spoke with exulting triumph.

"You're trapped now, my high toby flyer," he said.

The brave girl cast him a fierce dangerous look—a look that meant mischief.

But the thief-taker did not heed it; he thought his own brutal power exceeded that of Tyburn Dick.

"Give in quietly," he said; "the game's up."

"Is it?" hissed Grace, the hot blood mantling her handsome face with indignation, and her eyes looking demoniac in their expression.

There was a pause.

For a second they looked at one another, each wondering what the other was going to do.

Grace made a slight move.

Wild made a clutch at her.

As he moved, Grace rose from the ground, sprang forward, and hurling her antagonist aside, darted through the yelling crowd like an arrow.

On, on she went, traversing over miles of ground with the swift gracefulness of a race-horse, breaking through all human barriers formed across her path to stop her flight.

The chase now became one of terrible excitement.

Such a scene was rarely seen in London, and all who could join in the chase did so for the mere matter of sport.

Nothing gave the people greater pleasure than to hunt down one of their fellow-creatures; innocent or guilty, it was all the same to them, if the law offered a reward for their apprehension.

We doubt whether they would have found the same pleasure in the human hunt had they been made aware that the fugitive was a gentle girl of high birth.

It was not likely they would be made aware of their error until it was too late, so they continued the chase vigorously.

"There he goes," shouted one.

"There he goes."

The cry was taken up by hundreds, and lustily bawled forth.

Jonathan Wild sprang forward.

He was within a few feet of his prey.

Grace suddenly turned, struck him fiercely in the face with her tiny fist, and before he could recover from the effects of the blow, she darted up a ladder that stood against a dilapidated old house.

A rush was made towards the ladder.

The thief-taker was as ferocious as a maddened tiger.

"Back!" he thundered, and brutally beat his way through the crowd with a thick cudgel.

The mob fell back, yelling and shrieking, some with bleeding skulls, others holding a bruised arm, and many trying to rub the effects of a heavy blow off their backs.

"Bravo, Wild, bravo," yelled the people, as he ascended the ladder.

"Hurrah! hurrah! hurrah!"

This arose in a deafening shout, and a clapping of hands applauded him to keep up the chase.

He was now about half-way up the ladder.

Grace just then reached the top.

With a glad cry she sprang over the parapet.

Wild quickened his ascent.

Another deafening shout arose as our heroine reappeared over the parapet.

Her face looked wild and excited.

Wild stopped on the ladder, held by hand to the rail, and drew a pistol.

His finger was on the trigger, and large iron muzzle near the noble girl's fac

Another moment and her head would h been shattered to atoms.

But she saw his design, and ere he could pull the hammer she grasped the top of the ladder, and with the strength of a young lioness hurled it from the wall with its brutal burden.

Down, down it fell, trembling as it swayed to and fro with its own length and weight, and made more unsteady by the terror-stricken thief-taker, who fought desperately to save himself from being crushed as it reached the earth.

The confusion amongst the mob was fearful; screaming with fear, they fought and pushed one against the other to get away from the falling ladder.

Their struggles only tended to make the scene more horrible.

Battling on every side, and all wanting to rush away, they got wedged in like a square block.

The ladder came sweeping down.

The people stood terror-stricken—motion-less and in fearful agony, they saw that their fate was sealed.

Those who had not lost their senses offered up a silent prayer.

Down, down came the ladder.

Wild sprang off.

The ladder swung round, and with terrible force came crashing down on the terror-stricken mob.

Cries, screams, yells, and groans of agony, arose from the living mass as they were struck to the ground; some crushed to a shapeless mass, others with shattered skulls, some with limbs broken so fearfully that they would have to be amputated—more or less, the greater portion of them were maimed for life.

We will leave them now to be assisted by those who were not hurt, and follow Jonathan

Wild, who so miraculously escaped from being crushed.

He cast a brutal, unconcerned look at the horrible scene, and made his way after our heroine.

He burst open the nearest door he came to, dashed through the passage and up the stairs, when the occupiers rushed out in alarm, and inquired the meaning of his sudden entry.

He answered them by a brutal blow that felled them to the floor, and without a word made his way to the upper room, clambered through the trap-door, and got on to the roof.

For a moment he stood and gazed around to see which way his bird had flown.

"Ah!" exclaimed Wild, "he goes there; I think I can wing him from here."

He drew a pistol, and fired.

Grace had got some dozen roofs in advance.

She turned at the report.

The bullet struck a chimney-pot, and shattered it to atoms.

"Curses" hissed Wild, "everything seems in favour of the damned young cub."

He drew another pistol, took deliberate aim or her head, and again fired.

"That's done it, I think," he said.

But when the smoke cleared away, he saw to his chagrin the noble girl standing deliberately behind a stack of chimneys, with a bright gleaming pistol in her hand, levelled in a line for his head.

There was a report, a flash, and a shriek.

The shot was fired with a hand not so used to fire-arms as the thief-taker, but the shot hit its mark, and the thief-taker rolled down the tiles swearing awfully.

The shots and sword-cuts Wild had received would have killed a small nation, but nothing seemed to injure his brutal iron nature.

He got up, drew his hand across his bleeding head, and shook his fist at our heroine.

The shot she fired struck him on the forehead, and made its course across his head, tearing up skin and hair, leaving a deep gutter from which the thick black blood flowed freely.

"You shall pay dearly for this," he said spitefully.

Grace laughed at his threats.

Wild had no more pistols ready; he could not wait to reload, so darted after his foe.

Springing from roof to roof, crawling along gutters, and dodging round stacks of chimneys they kept the game up for at least half an hour, until at last fortune favoured our heroine.

Gliding down a sloping slate of roof, she slid over the gutter, and fell into a kind of stone terrace that ranged along in front of a row of dingy, paper-patched, and dirty windows.

She hastily ran along this for some distance, and seeing a window open, she sprang into a room that was evidently unoccupied by its being unfurnished.

Barely had she got in and secured the window, when Wild's legs appeared over the parapet.

She knew she could not contend against his brutal strength at close quarters; therefore she must fly from that room.

The other leg appeared over the parapet, then gradually lowered until half his body came in view.

Not another minute was to be lost.

Grace flew to the door.

Her heart bounded with joy—it was unlocked, and the key on the outside!

She made her exit from the small attic as her pursuer dropped on the terrace.

In another second she had locked the door.

Wild bounded into the room.

His first act was to try the door.

"Locked!" he fairly shrieked with baffled rage. "Curse him! he does me in every way; but I'll have him yet."

With that self-congratulatory remark he continued hammering away at the door; but it withstood his every effort.

Grace stood in the room beneath; she heard him swearing and tearing frantically about.

Then all was quiet.

The brave girl held her breath while she stood listening for the slightest sound of her enemy.

Suddenly she was startled by the fall of bricks and mortar.

She ran to the window.

Wild was making his way over the terrace;

CHAPTER LXII

TYBURN DICK HAS A SERIES OF ADVENTURES AND NARROW ESCAPE OF HIS LIFE.

OUR gallant hero did not find much trouble in escaping from the Stag and Hounds.

He laughed heartily at the way he gulled the guests at the inn, and when out of danger smacked the money he won with much satisfaction.

He was passing through a small village one early morning, when his attention was attracted to a group of farm labourers standing round a small, thin, greedy, half-starved, cynical, crafty man.

Discontent and disconsolation was stamped upon every sturdy face.

"Hear me, mister; I beant agoin' to work for nothing," said one.

"Can't help it," said the weasel individual, sharply; "if you don't like to take the money, leave the farm."

"Well, guvner, I don't see neither why you should stop half our money cos we was five minutes late."

"You can leave the farm to-day, then, Brown."

"It's all very well for you," said another, "but we've got a wife and family to keep out of our earnings, an' if we are out o' work they have to starve."

"Take your money and be contented," replied the tight-fisted overseer.

"Contented," growled another of the labourers, "sixpence out o' two shillings a day, because we're late five minutes, makes a big hole in our wages. It ain't stopped by the squire's wish."

"You can leave to-day then, Jones."

"What am I to do if I leave—starve?"

"As you like."

"Can't do that," muttered the man, despondingly; "couldn't bear to see my wife and little ones crying for bread."

"Are you going to take the money and commence work again, or refuse and leave the farm?"

"We must take the money, I suppose," the men said, having no alternative but to refuse, be out of work, and starve."

The old money-grubber paid the poor, worn, hard-working fellows, and walked away.

Dick had concealed himself, and overheard all that was said; his noble nature revolted to see how the poor fellows were being robbed of their hard earnings, and by that miserable blood-sucking specimen of humanity.

The old worshipper of gold went on his way chuckling and fingering the sixpences he had robbed those hard-working men of.

He let each coin drop through his avaricious fingers—the sound seemed to be delicious music to his ears.

"Ha, ha!" he laughed, "money, money, beautiful money! why should I give thee to those clowns! No, no, thy bright glistening faces warm my poor old heart with pleasure when I toy with thee for hours."

"Miserly old scamp," muttered Dick, following the overseer.

"What good art thou to those poor fools who sell thee for their bellies? That is not right. No, no! they should keep thee—prize thee as I do."

"You don't give them much chance to save much," thought Dick.

"What do I live for?" commenced the old money-grubber again.

"Money, I should say," muttered our hero.

"Money—yes, bright, glorious, money," continued the grey-haired old scoundrel—"yes, I live for money—money, that gives you power—money, that makes you rich—money, that gives you glory and raises you high in the world. Money is my life—I love money better than anything in the world."

"Do you!" Dick said, loudly, tapping him on the shoulder.

The old fellow turned sharply.

His eyes lighted upon the bright barrel of a pistol, held in a very steady hand.

"I want a little of that bright, glorious, money," Dick said, coolly.

"Money?" echoed the overseer.

"Money," iterated Dick.

"Would you rob a poor fellow of his hard-earned money?"

"Sneaking old cuss — grey-headed old schemer!"

"Young sir!"

"Blood-sucking old scoundrel!"

"Verily, sir, and——"

strength. The stone was large, and, judging by its size, it must have weighed over a hund-ed-weight; yet she held it out at arm's length without the least exertion.

"Help!" cried the thief-taker again, despairingly.

"Help! Yes—ha, ha, ha!—this will help you to *hell*."

She looked like a beautiful demon as she spoke.

Wild looked up.

"Mercy!" he implored.

"As much mercy as you showed me."

Wild saw the stone held above him. He saw the look of hate, revenge, and triumph burning in the gleaming orbs of the supposed Tyburn Dick. In despair and horror he closed his eyes, for he saw no mercy.

Grace gave an exulting yell. The stone fell from her hands.

Wild sank beneath the water in despair.

There was a crash.

The butt overturned, and with the gush of water the thief-taker was shot on to the flag-stones, where he lay insensible.

Grace clapped her hands gleefully at what she had done, and in her excitement she fell back into the room in a swoon.

How long she remained insensible she knew not.

She was faint and weak when she returned to consciousness. Her cheeks were pale and haggard. Her eyes still retained that wild glare.

After several efforts she raised herself, and staggered to the window.

A shudder shook her frame as she looked out.

In the yard beneath, where the above scene was enacted, the butt was set upright, but the stones were still wet and smeared with blood.

Grace covered her eyes with her hand, tottered backwards, and sank to the floor.

"Have I been dreaming?" she faintly murmured. "Yes, yes; it must have been a dream—a strange horrible dream, and yet—" she cast a hasty glance around the empty room, and scanned her own beautiful form—" why am I here alone, and in this dress? Where is *he*? What does it all mean? Can I be awake? Ah!"

She started.

A clamour of voices broke upon her ear.

"That voice," she exclaimed, with sudden energy. "It brings back the remembrance of the past. 'Tis his. I know all now. What evil power could have tempted me to do that evil work? I must have been mad—yes, yes, mad; but he lives. He comes for retribution. I cannot be taken by him. No, no."

Her face glowed with a hectic flush. Her eyes were dimmed with tears, yet a light burned within them like a living fire.

The voices grew louder.

Grace sprang to her feet.

There was rush up the stairs.

She knew they were her pursuers, and upon her track.

"I am weak," she muttered, "but I will not be taken. I cannot resist, yet I will not yield—no; I would rather kill myself."

"They come!" she exclaimed. "Let them come; they shall not take me alive. Heaven will forgive me for what I shall do. Dick, my only love, we shall never meet again. Farewell! I die for you. May God bless and protect you!"

She stood a moment with her face covered, and seemed to be offering up a silent prayer.

The voices of her pursuers came more distinct. They were outside the door.

Her face was calm when she removed her hands.

She ran to the window.

Crash!

The door was being battered in.

She cast a hurried—a last look around, and sprang out, as the door yielded, and fell crashing to the floor.

A body of Bow-street officers rushed into the room, headed by Wild. He looked bold and brutal, as though nothing had occurred.

"Gone!" he thundered. "Run to the window, and see if he has escaped that way. Quick!"

The men in a body rushed to the window.

Cries of horror escaped their lips.

Wild dashed forward, swung the officers aside, and leant out to see what occasioned those cries.

He recoiled at what he saw, then drew a pistol.

"Dead or alive," he said, "I have you now."

He pulled the trigger. The weapon hung fire.

"Curses!" he yelled, and hurled the pistol with brutal force at our heroine's fair head.

It missed.

He drew the second, but ere he fires let us explain to the readers where she was.

When she sprang from the window, her foot slipped on the edge of the sill, and she fell.

She had prepared bravely to meet her death, yet it was not destined that she should die by her own hands.

She had fallen about half way down, when her embroidered coat hitched on a hook in the wall, and there she hung almost by a thread.

Jonathan Wild levelled the other weapon point blank at her head.

Grace closed her eyes in horror.

"I triumph now!" said Wild, in mocking derision.

The brave girl did not flinch at meeting her death, but she would have preferred dying by any other means than by his hands.

There was a sudden report, a shriek, and the fair girl fell from the wall.

CHAPTER LXIV.

THE MYSTERY OF MERTON GRANGE.

PERCY MERTON was not superstitious or a coward, but the shadowy form that passed him with the bloody hand awed him for a time.

Recovering from his fright he remembered the agonised cries of his brother.

He was upon his feet in a moment. Putting his sword between his teeth, he clambered up the window, and bounded into the room.

The apartment was empty, save for some old dingy-looking furniture, and a few huge pictures, that had so faded with age and want of care that they were almost indistinct; but, strange to say, the eyes of each were bright, and seemed to fix an angry scowling gaze on the intruder.

Percy inwardly shuddered. Whichever way he moved they seemed to follow him.

The place wore a sombre aspect. Not a breath could be heard. The chamber was as quiet as the tomb.

"Not here!" cogitated Percy, wonderingly, "Where is my brother? How dreary seems this place! It is almost like being entombed alive."

"*Entombed alive.*"

Percy sprang round.

The phrase was repeated in a sepulchral voice. It sounded mockingly in his ear.

"Was that fancy?" he exclaimed, terrified. All was quiet.

"It must have been the echo of my own voice."

He turned to leave the chamber, when lo he stood transfixed, his gaze riveted on a pool of steaming gore.

"Blood!" he gasped; "my brother's blood!"

"*Blood!*"

The same unearthly voice that had been spoken repeated the word.

"Mock me!" shrieked Percy, frantically—"mock me as you like, but should I have to face the incarnate fiend himself, I will revenge my brother's death!"

He drew his sword. Again he turned to depart when a noise like a tempest of thunder shook the house and arrested him.

One of the large pictures that ranged from the ceiling to the floor suddenly vanished, and in the massive gold frame stood that weird-looking figure that he had so often seen before.

It stood motionless, with its eyes fixed upon the quailing man. One long arm was outstretched menacingly. The thin bony hand was still crimson with blood.

"Speak, in the name of Heaven, speak!" suddenly exclaimed Percy. "What art thou, of this world or the other?"

The figure remained silent.

The horrified man passed his hands to his burning temples, and when he again looked the figure was gone.

There stood the dirty oil painting, as though it had not been moved for more than a century.

"Gone!" yelled Percy.

For a moment he stood bewildered.

"What mystery is this? I will discover it. I cannot endure more than I have already gone through."

THE BLACK MARE ROSE LIKE A BIRD—THE LEAP WAS TAKEN.

His eyes were fixed upon the picture. His bright sword gleamed before him as he dashed towards that mysterious painting.

On he went, with intent to rip the picture open.

His weapon was within a foot of its mark, when again the picture vanished, and he fell headlong through the frame.

He shrieked with horror.

He stood alone in a chamber of horrors, with no way of exit. The aperture had closed.

Truly it was a chamber of horrors. His blood curdled as his gaze wandered over the treasured relics of departed men and women.

The chamber was decorated with bones of every part of the human form. In some parts lay whole legs and arms.

In the four corners of the chamber stood four gigantic skeletons, perfect to the smallest bone; from their mouths, eyes, and noses issued a blue flame, and in the right hand of each was grasped a torch that seemed of endless duration.

The most horrible of all were the skulls placed upon stands, at which incense burned.

The ghastly relics presented a fearful sight.

"Is there no way of exit from this horrid chamber?" said Percy, growing quite calm.

His gaze fell upon the floor.

He started back surprised at what he saw.

A pool of blood lay in the middle of the chamber.

"Strange," he muttered; "what's the meaning of this?"

He went forward, dipped the point of his sword in the blood, and was in the act of swearing an oath of revenge when he heard a—Click.

He felt himself whirled round. He knew he was being hurled down some terrible dark abyss, yet he had not sufficient power to save himself.

The floor which was stained with blood whirled round when he put his foot upon it, and before he had time to save himself he was hurled headlong down into some dark pit below by some unseen agency.

The floor righted itself as soon as he disappeared.

He was now in a dark loathsome cell in obscurity, and surrounded by rats.

"Help!" he cried, "I cannot stay here."

A tapping responded to his call.

"Help me!" he said again; "help me, whoever thou art, help me!"

No answer.

For a moment he stood in painful anxiety.

A massive door was suddenly thrown open, and the strange weird being stood on the threshold.

"Save me from here!"

The Mystery of Merton Grange—that is what we shall call him in future—beckoned the ex-smuggler to follow him.

Percy sprang forward with a glad cry; he wanted to ascertain whether his deliverer was of this world or the other.

His deliverer seemed to know exactly what the other wanted to discover, and kept a certain distance in front all the way.

Through corridors, down flights of stone steps they traversed on.

Every moment seemed like an hour of terrible torture to Percy Merton.

At last Percy's strange conductor halted in front of a large iron door.

He waved his hand as if desiring his follower to stop at a certain distance.

Percy stopped impulsively.

The door swung open with a grating sound.

The Mystery of Merton Grange beckoned Percy to come forward as he entered.

Percy hastened forward and entered, but the strange man had gone—vanished; it appeared as though through the solid stone walls.

While he stood wondering where the mysterious being could have gone, he was suddenly grasped by the nape of the neck in an iron-like grasp.

He struggled to free himself, but in vain; his unseen antagonist was powerful and silent.

"What is this that twines round my throat?" gasped Percy, in fearful agony. "Is it a serpent? No, I feel the very fingers— they tighten—they squeeze my life out. Release me ere I die! Oh?"

He was suddenly raised from the ground, and borne down another flight of steps into a vault.

His gaze fell upon his brother, in a sitting posture against the wall.

His face was lifeless and haggard, his arms hung loosely by his side, his head rested on his breast, and at his feet lay his sword From his side oozed a stream of blood.

"My brother!" shrieked Percy, still held by his unseen assailant. "Release me—let me go to him."

He was thrown down.

His assailant had gone.

The ponderous door closed with a bang, and a mocking laugh said—

"Entombed alive!"

CHAPTER LXV.

THE PRISONER OF THE IRON ROOM.

WHEN our heroine again returned to consciousness she found herself a prisoner chained to a wall—an iron wall, in a solid iron room, with nothing to give ventilation and light but a small grating.

She shuddered as she looked.

dreary musty walls, and closed her eyes, praying she may never wake again.

In her agony and despair she fell into a sound sleep, and dreamed many strange troubled dreams.

She was suddenly awoke by a gruff voice that called upon her to rouse up.

When she opened her eyes, her gaze fell upon the fierce countenance and muscular form of her brutal persecutor, Wild.

Her soul revolted at his sight.

Despair took possession of the poor girl.

"There, my bird; I think your wings are clipped for a time," grunted the thief-taker.

Grace shuddered.

"I have a proposal to make you," continued Wild.

Grace did not answer.

"Curse you! have you lost your tongue? Speak, or I'll settle you at once!"

"What would you have me say?" Grace stammered timidly.

"Answer the questions I put to you."

"All that I am able, I will."

"That's right; perhaps after all we might become good friends. You know, Dick, I don't want to hang you, because it'll pay me better to let you live."

"How can my being at liberty pay you better than the thousand pounds offered by the King for my apprehension?"

Wild laughed.

"You won't be at liberty."

"I don't understand."

"Oh, oh! then I'll tell you."

Wild had not yet discovered his error in taking her for our hero, so she meant to extract from him his villainous plot concerning her lover.

"Where am I?" she asked.

"Oh, you are in my house."

"What place is this?"

"This is the iron room; I keep it especially for such friends as you."

"I hope, if you intend to keep me, you will find a better place than this for me."

"I will; you shall have every comfort you wish for."

"Then I shan't mind staying a short time with you."

"Fifteen months will soon pass away."

"Fifteen months!" iterated Grace.

"Fifteen months," repeated Wild.

"Why that stated time?"

"You will be twenty in June; it is March now."

"Well!"

"By the expiration of fifteen months you will be twenty-one."

"What then?"

"You will see when the time comes."

"Does it concern me?"

"Much."

"And who else?"

"The Countess Aldervale."

"Oh!"

"You start," grinned Wild.

She did, with well-affected surprise.

"Since it concerns no others," said Grace, "it will only be fair to acquaint me with your intentions."

"Well," said Wild, "since you are in my power I need not be afraid to inform you."

"In your power?"

"In my power; but you have nothing to fear if you do as I advise."

"Go on."

"You are the rightful heir to Alverdale Manor."

"Well."

"The countess is your mother, and that pet boy of hers is a bastard."

"You seem well acquainted with the history."

Wild grinned.

"No one better."

"You know it almost as well as I do," said Grace.

"Perhaps better."

"Perhaps so."

"You are the lawful heir to Alverdale Manor and its surrounding estates," Wild went on; "the countess knows this and fears that when you come of age you will claim your rights."

Grace was silent and fearfully agitated.

Wild continued—

"She has bribed me with five thousand pounds to capture and hang you without any delay."

"Inhuman wretch!" exclaimed Grace.

"Yes," remarked Wild, "she likes to have all her own way, but she won't get it. I shall bring her to the scragging-post yet."

"Remember, Wild, whatever her faults are she is a mother; don't talk of her like that again in my presence."

Jonathan looked confounded.

"Oh!" he exclaimed, "so you would let her off, though she tries every way to get rid of you."

"She may repent," said Grace.

"As much as I shall," replied the thief-taker with a horrible demoniac laugh. "She can't cheat Jack Ketch."

"I am cheating you, though," thought our heroine. "Proceed, Wild."

Wild proceeded.

"Do you remember the time," he resumed, "when your haunt was attacked by the soldiers and you dragged forth, taken to the top of the cliffs and shot into the sea? That was a clever piece of stratagem of Captain Claude; he sacrificed his own life to save yours."

"Poor devoted fellow," murmured Grace.

"There was a little difference between mother and father, wasn't there?" put in Wild, "however, you are still alive, that's all I want."

"Come to the point." said Grace, anxiously.

"This is the point," the thief-taker said; "the countess has offered me five thousand pounds to hang you."

"Very kind of her," muttered the fair girl, bitterly.

"I have got you here, and intend to keep you for fifteen months," he went on, not heeding the interruption. "I shan't hang you; I shall hang some one else in your clothes."

"That's kind."

"The countess will think you dead, you will still be alive. I shall keep you until you are twenty-one; then you will go forward, surprise everyone, kick your bastard brother out a beggar, have revenge for what you have suffered, take possession of your own property, and give me half your income for saving your neck from the hempen cravat. Don't you think it a fine plan?"

"A worthy piece of scheming," replied Grace, *sotto voce*, "but I think my black-souled villain will be greatly disappointed."

"Do you agree?" asked Wild.

Grace hesitated.

"You have only one alternative,"

"And that is——"

"The gallows."

Grace was silent for a few seconds. Her cheeks were suddenly suffused by a crimson flush, and her eyes glistened with the brilliancy of diamonds.

Wild looked at her curiously.

Grace looked at him.

They looked at each other, and each tried to read the inward thoughts of the other; but, neither having the power to penetrate the other's soul, they shifted their gaze.

"Do you consent?" asked Wild.

"To what?" inquired Grace.

"To the proposition I made."

"I have no alternative."

"Only the gal——"

"It's ungenerous to talk like that," interrupted Grace.

"Then you consent?"

"I can do nothing else."

"Then it's settled you are my prisoner for fifteen months?"

"Your guest, Mr. Wild."

"Guest, then."

"It is not usual for a host to keep his guest chained to the wall."

"In such cases as the present it is."

"I should say no. It will only be courteous to let me have my liberty."

"You are perfectly safe there."

"But not contented. Will you release me? Surely you do not suppose I shall succumb to remain in this horrid place for fifteen months?"

"You will if I choose to keep you."

"But you will not," replied our heroine, in an altered tone.

"You can't prevent it," replied the thief-taker, in a tone of triumph.

"Unless I say I shall not agree to the arrangement you so cleverly made."

"What!" exclaimed Wild, stepping back, and a vindictive light gleaming in his ferret-like eyes; "if you do not, by —— I will drag you to Tyburn this very hour."

"You cannot."

"Aha!"

"I must first be tried, and, when tried will reveal your villainous scheming."

"Beware!" said the thief-taker impetuously. "Beware, Tyburn Dick, how you menace *me!* If you dare breathe another word like that, I will blow your brains out where you stand."

He drew a pistol, and presented it full in the fair dauntless girl's face.

Grace laughed carelessly.

"If I thought you meant treachery," said Wild, between his teeth, "your life would not be worth much."

"I mean no treachery; but I don't intend to remain here," answered Grace, determinedly.

"I don't want to keep you here."

"Then unfasten this iron girdle, and stop all further foolery."

Wild looked at the speaker in profound silence, and a sardonic leer appeared upon his countenance.

"Do you concur in the compact?" he inquired.

"If you let me have my liberty."

"In other apartments?"

"If they are more cheerful than this."

"They are fit for the reception of a prince."

"That's as it should be. Don't keep me here any longer."

Wild drew a bunch of keys from his pocket, and selecting one, inserted it in the lock of the manacles. He was in the act of turning the key, when his gaze rested on the excited face of his prisoner.

"Ah!" he exclaimed, and stepped back; "you mean treachery."

"Treachery!" said Grace.

She laughed, and a very unpleasant laugh it was.

She certainly meant to try to escape, but, being deprived of her defensive weapons, she waited an opportunity to take the thief-taker unawares.

Her hands, fortunately, were free from any bonds, and only an iron circlet kept her in captivity.

If she could possess herself of the keys, she would stand the risk of a battle with her powerful foe.

"If I thought you meant treachery," said Wild, with brutal calmness, putting a pistol close to her white forehead, "I would shoot you where you stand."

"Shoot me," said Grace, with a change of countenance that startled the thief-taker; "better were I dead tnan be in your power."

Wild's brow darkened as with a thunder cloud.

"Then you retract," he said, with a cyni expression.

"I do," replied the fair girl, growi desperate.

Wild's cheeks flushed hot with wrath, an he glared with fury at his captive.

"Die, then," he said, his voice hoarse with suppressed passion.

"Not by your cowardly hands," exclaimed our heroine.

Leaping forward as far as her chains would admit, she snatched the pistol from his hand.

There was a report, and the bullet went crashing through the iron wall.

Wild had pulled the trigger, but too late to accomplish his evil work—the deadly missile passed transversely over his intende victim's head.

So quick, so daring was the act, and with such adroitness was Wild disarmed, that for a moment he stood bewildered.

Grace confronted him fearlessly; she had a weapon at least to defend herself with, and the weapon had one shot left, the pistol was double-barrelled—only one varrel had exploded.

She placed the pistol quite close to his nose; the cold steel roused him instantly.

"I want you to unfasten these manacles Mr. Wild," Grace said, sarcastically.

"Do you?" said the thief-taker, bitterly

"I do," was the cool rejoinder.

"So I shall."

A cruel sneer wreathed his lips as he spoke Grace looked at him inquiringly.

He dived his hand into his huge pocket, as though for the keys, but in reality was putting a flint on the nipple of a pistol.

Grace watched the kindling of his eyes, she saw them change into a cold cynical expression of hate, and knew the meaning of that change.

She was on her guard.

Wild suddenly drew forth his hand.

He grasped a huge pistol.

Grace read his cowardly intent by the sardonic glare of his eyes, and waited for the attack.

She did not wait long.

The vindictive wretch thought to take her at a disadvantage.

He suddenly levelled the pistol at her breast and pulled the trigger.

The flint had fallen off, and the weapon only snapped.

An oath escaped his polluted lips, and with baffled fury he hurled the pistol at her head.

Grace saw it coming and ducked; it passed her with a whiz.

A flash—a dangerous deadly gleam shot from Grace's eyes.

"Well," she said, with perishing quietude, "have you any more pistols to throw away? I am going to have a shot now."

Wild ground his teeth with suppressed passion and deadly revenge as he leaped forward and tried to grasp our heroine by the throat.

Our heroine objected to being grasped by the throat, and dealt him a spiteful blow in the face with the butt of the pistol.

She was averse to bloodshed, and never killed anyone only under very painful circumstances, as the last resource for liberty, and then only her worst foes.

Wild was now mad with fury; he stepped back and again sprang forward, he drew a sort of cutlass and made a round sweep for his prisoner's head.

The dauntless girl met him fearlessly, and as he tried a deadly cut with his formidable weapon she brought the pistol barrel down heavily upon his knuckles.

He dropped the blade and fell back swearing awfully.

So cleverly had he been baulked by his lithe graceful adversary that for a few moments he stood motionless.

Self-possession seemed to entirely have deserted him.

The fact that he had been met and conquered at every attack by so slight an opponent so puzzled him that he appeared lost.

He did not stand inanimate long.

His countenance changed into a fiendish expression, his eyes were quite invisible beneath his shaggy curved eyebrows, and his fingers twitched nervously, as though he

longed to have them twined round the white throat of his captive.

Suddenly he sprang off the ground, and for the third time dashed upon his prisoner; he lowered his head as he went forward.

Grace stood ready—she was not thrown off her guard by the sudden onset. As he came towards her she caught him by the nape of the neck and held him down, then unmercifully she laid the blows on the back of his skull with a pistol-butt, thick and heavily.

The thief-taker groaned, and rolled over at her feet completely *beaten.*

By way of addenda she gave him a settling tap that made him wink.

He now lay totally helpless but not insensible, because he watched his gallant young adversary with a look of terrible hate.

Grace stooped over the prostrate form and searched for the keys.

How her heart bounded with excitement and hope of escape as she drew the keys from his pocket and inserted one in the lock of the manacle.

The key turns in the lock, her blood spins through her veins, gushes round her heart, mounts to her fair cheeks, hope gives her fresh energy, she is wild with joy, with hope of freedom, her thoughts take flight, rapid as the fleetness of her gallant steed that she again longs to be on the back of and coursing over the level road, the verdant heath, and the boundless country, with the silvery moon above her to give gladness to her heart and light her on her way.

She is exhilarated by the idea, her foe is forgotten, and she clapped her tiny hands together in wild ecstasies.

The iron girdle is unfastened from her waist, and falls to the ground; the ringing clash of the iron sounds on her ear like a low, sweet clash of music.

She hurries to the door, and is about to make her exit from the iron room, when a heavy hand grasps her by the shoulder and hurls her back.

She turned, and met the savage, exulting features of Jonathan Wild.

"It's my turn now," he said, speaking in a hoarse whisper.

Grace was electrified; she could scarcely

believe her own eyes, and looked upon the floor to see if it was really him.

She shuddered when she saw it was her foe who confronted her.

All her exhilarating joyful hopes fled; she saw that she had a tougher antagonist to contest against than she had anticipated, but the noble, brave girl did not despair.

"Come with me," the thief-taker said, clutching her round the waist.

"Wretch!" exclaimed Grace, indignantly.

Wild laughed, and carried her back to the wall.

The poor girl struggled desperately to break away from his grasp, but in vain.

His arm encircled her slender waist, and held her in a vice-like grip.

Grace found that her struggles did not avail her much, only exhausted her, and exerted her strength to no purpose.

She must try other means that would prove more effectual.

She did.

And it had the desired effect, but the act was cruel, and not pleasant.

Wild held his head close to her mouth.

In an instant she fastened her teeth in his ear and bit it through.

The thief-taker howled painfully, and the next instant dropped her.

Our heroine did not lose any time.

A pistol lay on the other side of the room, she bounded forward, and picked it eagerly off the floor.

The thief-taker, more furious than ever, mad with passion, and goaded at being baffled by his slight adversary, suddenly dashed upon our heroine while she stooped.

His iron fist caught her just under the left ear and sent her spinning round like a top.

She staggered for a moment, then turned and confronted her foe, furiously.

For a few seconds they stood face to face; then by one accord, each grasped the other by the throat in a deadly grip.

A desperate hand-to-hand struggle took place; each meant to do the other grievous bodily harm, as they say in the papers.

Wild fastened his hands on the collar of his opponent's coat and tried to throw her.

Grace was too active to be thrown; she slipped round her foe and dealt him heavy blows with such wonderful rapidity that Wild did not get an opportunity of returning any.

He grew desperate and shook the active girl as though she were but a child in his powerful grasp.

Our heroine suddenly swung herself round to wrench from his grasp; in doing so, her tunic came unfastened, and exposed to the fiery gaze of her brutal captor her beautiful white heaving breast.

Wild started back bewildered.

Grace recoiled with shame and horror. Now that she saw that her sex was revealed, all that courageous, fearless defiance, deserted her; she cowered back helpless and terrified at the sight of her advancing assailant.

Wild went towards her with a triumphant leer.

"You have played your part well for a woman," he said. "I admire your courage; you are a brave girl, but you will have to pay the penalty for your freak."

"What mean you?" said Grace piteously.

"You will have to hang," replied the thief-taker, with deliberate devilry.

Grace shuddered.

Wild watched her with a gleam of satisfaction.

Even her matchless beauty, exposed as it was to his gaze, did not make the slightest impression on his cold impassive nature.

He shook with suppressed fury; it suddenly flashed to his mind that he had been duped by her, and the secret of his villainous plot she knew.

That secret he did not wish any one to know but Tyburn Dick, and he only when entirely in his power and unable to resist.

For a moment he gazed abstractedly at the trembling girl; his brain was working more villany.

He had said to her he would hang some one in Tyburn Dick's place.

Now was his chance; his captive had played the part of the dashing young knight excellently.

Wild had captured her as the real Tyburn Dick, he would hang her as the real one.

The idea he thought sublime.

His next object was to capture our hero; he could not hang his present prisoner while the true Tyburn Dick was at large.

He would exact the secret of our hero's whereabouts from his captive by brute force if persuasion would not do.

When he had once got the gallant Boy Highwayman in his power, he would force him to submit to his plan, and then hang his beautiful mistress.

Wild clutched our heroine by the arm and glared into her pale haggard face.

"What think you of your situation?" he asked triumphantly.

Grace recoiled at his touch.

"You are in my power now," he said exultingly.

"For a time," replied the noble girl, not wishing to let him see that despair had taken possession of her.

"You think to escape;" and he laughed tauntingly.

"I shall not remain in your *power* long," she answered.

"You will, until you are conveyed to Tyburn Tree, like all felons are conveyed there in a cart, with a mob hooting after you and pelting you with stones."

"We shall see."

"We shall."

In her heart our heroine maintained an idea that she would escape, though her position had the more ominous appearance of the gallows than the bright glorious heath.

"You think my case a bad one?" she said, looking at him, inquiringly.

"I do," he replied; "yet I could save you."

"How?" inquired Grace, eagerly.

"By your answering a few questions I put to you."

"Of what nature?"

"Concerning your lover, Tyburn Dick."

"And what of him?"

"Tell me where I can find him."

"Betray him! No; I would suffer twenty deaths sooner than one word from me should lead to his apprehension."

"You won't?" said Wild, trying to smother his rage.

"No," answered the girl proudly. "Hang me—shoot me, if you like, but never shall a word of mine cause him a moment's misery if I know it."

"As you will," the thief-taker said, in an unconcerned tone, but in reality he hardly knew how to keep his hands from crushing out her life. "I shall find him, and you will be hung."

"Any way no word of mine shall betray him into your merciless hands."

Wild could no longer suppress his rage. It got the upper hand of him, and suddenly burst forth in a fearful storm.

"By furies!" he yelled, madly; "tell me where Tyburn Dick is, or I will shoot you without further ado!"

He pressed the cold muzzle of a pistol against her forehead.

Grace looked at him fearlessly.

"Shoot!" she said.

"I will by hell! without you tell me where Tyburn Dick——"

"Is here!" thundered a voice.

The iron door swung back with tremendous force, and our hero dashed into the room.

The panther bounding on his prey does not make a quicker or surer leap than did Tyburn Dick as he sprang upon Jonathan Wild.

The thieftaker was dashed away, and Grace clasped, clinging tremblingly to the noble boy's breast in an instant.

Wild was upon his feet in another moment, and confronting his young foe dangerously.

"You are nicely trapped, Tyburn Dick," he laughed, sarcastically.

"You think so," our hero said, with a look of terrible hate kindling in his dark eyes.

"You have saved me the trouble of coming after you," the thief-taker went on.

"And now I am here?"

"I intend to keep you."

Dick drew a pistol—a beautiful, slender, long-barrelled weapon.

"You will convey us safely from this house," he said, quietly, but in a tone Jonathan Wild knew the meaning of.

He looked at the graceful boy with a mischievous leer. A cruel sinister setting of the muscles round his mouth warned our hero of danger.

He poised his pistol in a direct line with the thief-taker's temples.

"Take us from this house," he said again. "Should you attempt to play me false, I will send a bullet through your skull without hesitation?"

Wild backed to the door.

Dick saw he meant treachery and fired.

The bullet flattened against the iron pannel as the door slammed to. A demoniac mocking laugh rang in our hero's ears. He was alone with his love in the IRON ROOM.

CHAPTER LXVI.

THE HIGHWAYMEN GO IN SEARCH OF VICTOR ST. JAMES.

WE will now take the opportunity to seek our gallant and adventurous friends, whom we left waiting at the Leopard Inn for the return of their dashing young companion, Victor St. James.

The hour passed. The time given for the nobleman's return expired, and every one waited anxiously for him to arrive.

But he came not.

The three captains grew uneasy.

"Let us wait another quarter of an hour," said Devil Duke, looking up at the clock.

"He promised faithfully to be back within an hour," said Gallant Tom; "now it is a quarter of an hour over his time. I feel assured that he has fallen into some danger."

"Comrades," remarked Dashing Ralph, "we had better wait until the half hour, and then if he does not come, we will go in search of him."

The gallant knights of the road agreed, and waited with much anxiety for the rusty hands of the dirty-faced, sombre clock that stood in a corner of the room and ticked dismally to travel round its course. They all seemed impressed with an ominous gloom.

The three captains rose as the hands of the clock marked the half hour.

Ben, the ostler, had had previous instructions to get the steeds ready. He had done it faithfully; and, as the highwaymen emerged into the yard, he stood with the reins of the three graceful creatures.

"You are a good fellow, Ben," said Devil Duke, dropping some money into his hand.

"I knows my dooty, cap'n," replied the faithful fellow, gratefully, "and allus likes to please sich gemman as yerself an' other cap'ns."

"I tell you what, Ben," said Gallant Tom, vaulting into the saddle, "you shall join our band, if you like—the life, I think, would suit you better than this."

"Thank yer all the same," replied the ostler, "but I is better where I am; besides, I ain't got nothin' to fear, and can allus serve you as I have done. Another thing," he went on, "if I was to leave here, perhaps there would be some sneaking curs get my place, an' blow on yer the first time the bull-dogs was after yer."

"There is philosophy in that remark," said Dashing Ralph, mounting, and dropping Ben some loose cash.

"Very cleverly said," remarked Duke, "Ben is a true, faithful friend to us, and he shall not be forgotten for his honesty. Good-bye, Ben."

"Good-bye," shouted Ben, in ecstasy, as the highwaymen rode away.

"I would die for e'm," he muttered, turning towards the stables, and a tear glistened in his eye; "I luves all the cap'ns, bless 'em! It won't be good for the fust one I catches peaching on any of 'em. Cuss me, if I wouldn't brain the fust sneak!"

Thus giving way to his feelings, he entered the stables, shut the gates, and curling himself up like a ball amongst some clean straw, he fell into a comfortable sleep.

The highwaymen proceeded on their way to the old priory in silence, each pondering over his own miserable thoughts.

Victor St. James was much respected by our gallant friends, and the thought that he might have fallen into danger grieved them greatly.

"I told him to be careful," remarked Gallant Tom, his handsome face clouded and sorrowful; "I knew it was a snare."

"He would go alone," said Duke; "I fear we have lost a brave companion. It is no ordinary danger that could have kept him; he can fight like a gladiator, and would conquer any half dozen common fellows."

"I fear, Duke, as you say," Gallant Tom said, "it is no ordinary danger that could have prevented him from returning, but should he be in that cursed old den not a stone shall remain unmoved until we have found him."

The priory was reached; the trio halted before the green decaying fence that surrounded the ground, with its wilderness of and wild herbage.

The dreary building loomed out in the

sombre darkness with an aspect that filled our friends with dread.

The priory was just such a place as would be selected by a band of fashionable adventurous libertines to carry on their foul, lawless work.

Not a light disturbed the darkness, not a sound broke the stillness; the place maintained that gloomy aspect which makes one shudder with an inward feeling that some impending calamity is about to occur.

"I see no other way of getting over but leaping it," said Ralph.

"That's easily done," Duke said, drawing back his steed ready for a leap.

"Come, Tom, old boy, what's the matter?" inquired Duke, turning to his comrade, who sat moodily with his hand to his brow.

"Duke," he said, impressively, "Duke"—his voice faltered.

"What ails thee, comrade?—what ails thee, Tom?" asked Duke, anxiously.

"I know not," answered the gallant fellow, querulously. "I have a presentiment that I shall not see to-morrow's rising sun."

"Nonsense, Tom. Come, cheer up; you must not give way. Remember, old fellow, what we have to do."

"I would I could shake this feeling off; but I can't.

"Come, cheer up, Tom; don't be down on your dumps," said Ralph, cheeringly.

"I can't help it, Ralph. I know something *will* happen; I shan't be with you long, I fear."

"Come, come, don't talk like that," Duke said, with an involuntary chill. "Return to the inn, comrade, and wait for us; you don't feel quite at ease."

"No, no," replied Tom. "The feeling may go off. Come, let us search for our friend."

They cleared the fence in an instant.

Gallant Tom trembled like an aspen-leaf. His handsome face was horribly white, and his eyes glistened with an unnatural brilliancy.

They dismounted, tied their three steeds to tree, and searched for an entrance.

The uneasy whinny of a horse made Duke start. On turning, he saw the young nobleman's horse and his valet's standing side by side.

Duke grew thoughtful. He patted the animal's sleek neck affectionately.

"Waiting for your master, eh, my beauty?" he said.

The horse, docile as a lamb, rubbed her head on the highwayman's shoulder.

Duke felt a tugging at his sleeve.

"Ah!" he said, patting the other horse; "you, too, waiting for your master. That reminds me of my friend's valet. He must be in danger, too. They shall be found."

"I have found a door," said Ralph, coming up; "but I think it will resist all our efforts."

"Then we will try the window."

They tried the window, the only one on the ground-floor, but that likewise defied them. It was strongly protected with iron bars, crossed and recrossed like network.

"It's no good wasting time here," Duke remarked, in a spiteful, disappointed tone, "we will try higher up."

"We shall have to get up there first," was Ralph's comforting suggestion. "Perhaps you can clamber up; I can't."

"I'll try." And Duke commenced an ascent up the ivy that clung to the decaying wall.

He had got about half way up when he was suddenly made aware of an unpleasant fact

The ivy commenced to give way.

With pained disappointment Duke discovered that he was giving way too, and would make a rapid descent. He called for his comrade.

"What's the matter?" shouted Ralph. "You are falling."

"Yes. Put your back under to catch me," Duke said, despairingly.

"Not if I know it, old boy. Fall—I'll catch you."

Duke fell, grasping in his hands a branch of the treacherous plant.

Ralph caught him round the waist, and landed him safely on the ground.

"Don't be valorous another time," he said.

"I won't," replied Duke. "Where's Tom?"

"Here." The voice came from aloft.

The highwaymen looked up.

Gallant Tom stood in a precarious position on a swinging bough of a tall elm.

"What are you going to do?" asked Duke, wonderingly.

"Jump it," answered Tom. "Come on."

"Don't fall.

"I don't intend to."

"If you don't we'll follow."

The highwayman, throwing his sword to his comrades to catch, took a graceful, flying leap, and grasping fast the edge of the crumbling window-sill.

For a moment he hung to recover breath, then hitching his feet in the ivy, he held on with one hand, and forced the window open.

Another moment he was inside the room, and while his comrades stood beneath wondering how they could follow him, he reappeared.

He threw a rope-ladder to them, the one Victor St. James had made his ascent by.

They did not wait to inquire how he got it, but quickly made their way up and joined him.

The room was darker than the night—so dark, in fact, had there been any one there besides themselves, they could have safely passed unseen.

"We cannot proceed any further without a light," said Dashing Ralph.

"A fact of which we are all aware," answered Duke. "The thing is, how are we to get a light?"

"That's consideration; but I think I have an idea."

"Hold it tight, old boy. What is it?"

"Have you a dry wipe?—mine are awfully wet."

"I have one dry," said Duke.

Ralph took a very fine cambric handkerchief from his comrade, and going to the window he struck his sword against the stone wall.

The effect caused a shower of sparks to fly from the ringing steel, and the cambric was ignited.

"Don't you call that a fine idea?" he said, with much satisfaction.

"Splendid! I'll make a note of it," replied Duke.

"Now, gentlemen, for a reconnoitre of this old place, and a search for our friend." He led the way from the apartment, puffing away at the cambric to throw a glare around him.

Gallant Tom followed, silent and gloomy.

"Hallo! here's luck," yelled Ralph, from another room.

"What?" inquired Duke, running forward.

"A tinder-box and two lanterns."

The lanterns were lighted by the aid of the tinder-box, and the highwaymen continued the search, inspired with fresh energy.

Every room was carefully examined; the corridor well searched to see if there were any secret panel or door, and anything that was large enough for a man to conceal himself in was examined, and parts they could not see into their swords examined.

So far they had gone without encountering any one or finding any trace of a sword conflict, until they entered the room where St. James had been shot by Lord Edward Aldervale, and there, on the floor, where the young noble had fallen, was a pool of blood.

The trio looked at it for a few moments. Each seemed engaged with his own conflicting thoughts.

Gallant Tom spoke.

"This, I think, is the last we shall ever see of our noble young friend," he said; "but he shall be avenged."

"He shall," said Duke, solemnly, and Ralph took up his words; "but come, let's hope we may find him."

They looked for a trail by which they could follow the assassin's track, but not one spot of the still warm blood lay apart from the pool.

They left the room gravely.

Many other rooms were searched, but nothing could they see by which they could gain a clue of his whereabouts.

They then made their way downwards, through long dark corridors, down spiral staircases, in and out traps, secret doors, and lastly into the vaults underground.

They began to despair, their search had been fruitless, though not a corner was overlooked, not an inch of ground passed unnoticed; yet they could not trace a mark of their friend throughout the large strange building.

With aching hearts they turned to go.

Gallant Tom, more downcast than eve.

lingered behind. He seemed suddenly to come over helpless and faint, and leant against the wall of the vault he was in for support.

Devil Duke and Ralph went on, thinking their comrade would follow.

They were ascending a flight of stone steps when the slam of a door suddenly startled them.

They turned, stood breathless for a moment, and listened; then came a shrill shriek—a faint cry—again all was silent.

Simultaneously they leaped down the steps together, and rushed to the vault where they had left their comrade.

The door was closed.

It yielded with a push. The highwaymen dashed into the vault.

Gallant Tom—where was he?

The vault was empty. On the slimy stone floor was a stream of blood—fresh blood.

The highwaymen looked at each other in silent horror.

Had their comrade been murdered and carried off by some unseen person?

Duke wiped the clammy beads of sweat from his brow.

Ralph gasped short with breath.

"Ah! what does this mean?" stammered Duke. "What unseen treachery is this at work?"

"Is he gone?" said Ralph, in a whisper hoarse with horror.

"Look!" exclaimed Duke, frantically, throwing the light of his lantern on the bloody stream as he clutched Ralph's arm. "Blood of our comrade."

"This is horrible. See, the assassin has left a trail behind."

Duke bent eagerly forward.

"Yes," he said. Look here, Ralph."

Ralph looked. A trail of blood ran across the vault to the further end, where the wall was of one huge piece of granite.

"Through there," he said, "our comrade must have been taken. Come Duke, let's see if we can move this stone."

They tried with all their power, but tried in vain: the solid piece of masonry remained immovable.

"We are foiled, and our comrade is lost," Duke said, despairingly. "I did not think

the poor fellow's words would come true. By the power of our Father he shall be avenged. Come, we can do nothing alone."

They departed with a heavy weight at their hearts.

"You, Ralph, take the horses to the inn, and with all speed hasten to the haunt. Tell them what has happened. Bring back with you the whole of our brethren. The place shall be unearthed. I will ride to London and gain what tidings I can. Farewell, till next we meet."

"Farewell!" said Ralph.

They grasped each other's hands affectionately, mounted, and rode away.

CHAPTER LXVII.

DEVIL DUKE MAKES A STRANGE DISCOVERY.

THE following day Duke was riding through Finchley. A thousand thoughts occupied his excited and troubled brain. He was thinking of the fate that befel his comrade—his brave young friend. He thought of his beloved leader. Tyburn Dick, whom he had not seen for so long, and wondered whether he was in danger too. He thought of the lovely Cecily, of the mercer's wife, and a hundred others.

His gaze rested on his gallant steed; his eyes filled with tears—tears of pure affectionate love.

"Thou, poor lass," he said, patting her glossy neck, "art my only true companion, art ever loving, obey thy master's slightest command, have no cares save for me, thou defends me from danger with thy own gentle life. Nothing seems to part us, Rosie, my beauty; I would not part with thee for all else in the world."

The faithful animal gave a low whinny and turned up her head at the sound of her master's voice.

Again he was lost in deep ponderings.

His horse made a sudden timid start.

He looked around, and from the hedge two closely-muffled men emerged. He watched them cross the common, then he turned his horse's head, and taking the road followed them at a distance behind until they stopped at a quaint little inn, lying back some fifty feet from the road.

"Stay, holy father; I shall return in

THE SHOT TOOK EFFECT.

minute. I had better see if they are prepared for you."

This was spoken in a low tone by one of the muffled men, but Duke's acute ear caught every word.

The speaker entered the inn with a key.

Duke was hidden behind a clump of trees that grew near the side of the inn.

He slipped silently from the saddle, and going as silently behind the man who stood waiting for his companion, pinioned his arms behind—at the same instant gliding his arm over his mouth to stop his cries.

The man stood dumbfounded, so sudden, so unexpectedly had been the attack. Had his mouth been free he could not have found breath enough to call for help.

Duke kept his hand firmly over his mouth, and with the other hand took a handkerchief from the shivering wretch's pocket.

He dexterously slipped it over the man's mouth, removed his hand, and then with his own handkerchief tied his hands behind him.

This done, he laid the man on his back, took a pistol from its holster, put the muzzle to his ear, then removed the gag from his mouth, and, in a stern voice, said—

"Raise your voice above a whisper, and I scatter your brains."

The man trembled palpably.

At that moment the cloak in which he was muffled came unfastened and fell from his shoulders. Duke then discovered that he was a priest in disguise.

His pistol went an inch further into his captive's ear, and seemed to take a firm bite.

The priest drew up his visage in hideous contortions, and began wincing.

Duke gave him a jerk; the wincing was stopped.

Duke spoke.

"Why are you here?" he asked. "Answer me truly."

"Truly, my dear brother, I was called upon to wed a happy pair in the holy bonds of wedlock."

"To wed whom?"

"Verily, and that I do not know."

Devil Duke replaced the gag, secured his legs, and laid him on his back.

He had barely accomplished this cautious task when the door opened.

Our highwayman sprang forward and secured the man firmly by the throat as he emerged from the inn.

Like his reverend accomplice he was surprised by the sudden attack, but soon recovered. At a glance he seemed to discover the motive of his assailant. His lip curled with scorn.

"Why this?" he asked, carelessly.

"You shall know anon," replied Duke, coldly.

"I'll know more, sirrah, or you will repent for this outrage."

The highwayman's eyes kindled dangerously.

"No threats, or I blow your brains out," he said.

The man laughed sardonically.

Duke put a pistol on full cock to his head. His fingers twitched nervously on the trigger.

The man shuddered, his cheeks blanched with fear. He plainly saw the highwayman meant what he said.

"Don't be a fool," he said. "Remove that pistol. Why do you hold me?"

"You are concerned in a plot to marry a girl against her will."

"Well, what's that to you?"

"Much. That you will quickly discover."

The highwayman's intention was conceivable by the tone of his voice.

The man saw to play with him any longer would be risking a fearful danger.

Duke's grip tightened on his captive.

The libertine grasped his assailant by the shoulders, and stood at arm's length confronting Duke with the look of a tiger.

"What are you going to do?" asked Duke sartirically.

"This," answered the other, throwing all his strength into his arms. With one mighty effort he forced Duke backwards, and then fell before him at the same time, thinking to hurl the highwayman over his back.

But Duke was not to be tricked; he was used to these kinds of feints. He bent forward—the man went on his face. Duke held him down.

"That's your game, is it?" he said, spitefully. "I think this will settle you, my pugilistic friend."

He dealt him some heavy blows on the head with the butt of a pistol, and so placed his assailant *hors de combat*.

"Two," muttered Duke, with satisfaction, looking at the helpless rascals. "I shant' mind if I can dispose of the rest as easy."

He tried the inn door. It was fastened.

"How the devil am I to get in?" he cogitated. "Wait till some one comes out. No; I have an idea—that window. Happy thought, by the Lord Harry. Rosie!"

The noble animal neighed, in answer to her master's voice, and came from her hiding-place with a bound.

"Good lass," he said, patting her; "you must not move, my beauty, or you will precipitate me over your head."

He drew her under the window, from which a rich flood of light streamed forth and the sound of many voices.

The window was not very high; when Duke stood in the saddle he had to stoop to look into the room.

Rosebud stood quiet as a lamb. She looked

reflectively upon the discomfited parson, whose head lay very close to her nose. He broke out in a cold perspiration. He had a fearful apprehension that his hair might be taken in mistake by the snorting animal for a mouthful of hay.

But it wasn't. Rosebud did not want to be made sick; the smell of his greasy head was unpleasant to her nostrils; so, to move him, she put her nose between his shoulders, and turned him over like a ball.

"Steady, lass," said Duke, nearly losing his equilibrium.

He had made a strange discovery.

The inn was small, but it contained one large room, and in this large room were gathered a fashionable gathering of libertine scoundrels.

Amongst the group Duke recognised Lord Edward Aldervale and Milly, the late Captain Claude's beautiful mistress. There were many others whom our adventurer did not recognise; but amongst them were Reuben Frampton, the villain who abducted that gentle girl St. James had tried to save at the priory. She was there, too, pale and trembling.

"As fine a selection as ever I saw," Duke muttered. "By the Lord Harry! I shall put an unexpected climax to their villany, and astonish them awfully. They are waiting for the priest—I suppose to marry our pretty queen to that ill-looking rascal."

"Curse him! why does he not return?" said Edward Aldervale, his malignant face scarlet with rage. "Are we never to have this job done?"

"Not if I know it," muttered Duke, and he tapped the hilt of his sword.

The ill-looking scoundrel, as Duke called him, was a young noble standing beside Milly.

"Hark you, my Lord Edward, I have waited patiently long enough for this fair lady to be my bride. I wait no longer. I can wed her elsewhere."

"That is against our rules," said the young Earl of Aldervale, who appeared to be the chief.

"Curse the rules!" said the other, fiercely; "I don't take the lady for gain; it is because she is beautiful, and I love her."

"Do you!" muttered Duke, still a quiet listener and spectator. "You love her for her beauty, do you, you sneaking thief; and want to rob us of our pretty bird!"

Duke saw by the movement of the young earl's mouth he was going to speak, so stopped his own cogitations to listen.

Edward Aldervale spoke sternly.

"Sniggers," he said, turning to his valet, "go you and see what has become of the messenger; hasten away, and return quickly."

"Yes, me lord," said Sniggers, bending himself like a cane as he retired.

He stepped outside the door and indulged in a few curious antics, firstly, by shaking his long leg, then kicking his cap about for an imaginary part of his master's person; again he changed the performance by putting the end of the thumb of his left hand on the tip of his nose, and joining the thumb of his right hand and the little finger of his left, he extended the little finger of the right and "took a sight."

A pretty sight he looked while taking it; his face was drawn into all manner of variable shapes. Feeling perfectly satisfied by his own idiotic performance, he made his way downstairs at snail's rate, muttering as he went all manner of unpleasant things against his master.

"Ain't agoin' to be kicked about by him," he went on. "Quite as good as he is; I'll tell him so when I go back, and expose him before all his gemmen friends. Thinks a lot o' himself, but I can take all o' that bounce out o' him. I ain't a fool, if he thinks I is, an' I knows summut about him an' his flash mother as'll be a hot'un for him some o' these times."

He reached the door, and when he emerged out into the cold night air he was so absorbed in his spiteful reflections that he passed the man Duke had settled unnoticed, and went across Finchley Common still muttering.

Another painful suspense was endured by the party, and Lord Edwards grew irritated by the absence of his valet.

"Confound the fellow! where is he gone?" he suddenly blustered out.

"I wait no longer," said the nobleman; taking Milly's trembling hand, he led her towards the door.

"Stay!" thundered Devil Duke.

Every one leaped round and glanced in bewilderment at one another.

None knew from whence the voice came, and while they stood half terrified, fearing to move, Duke dashed the window open and leaped into the room.

Milly rushed from her captor's grasp, and with a glad cry she ran into the highwayman's arms and fell sobbing upon his breast.

The sudden appearance of a handsome, daring, and reckless fellow dashing amongst them seemed to rob them for a time of speech and power.

Edward Aldervale was the first to recover from the surprise.

He spoke—his tone full of bitter sarcasm.

"You have done well," he began; "some men would be more careful of their necks."

"I fear nothing for the safety of mine, dastardly hound!" replied Duke, boldly, and a dangerous light kindled in his orbs beneath his broad angry brow. "You have much to fear for the safety of yours."

Lord Edward winced; the remark was sharp and stinging.

"Who is this fellow?" suddenly exclaimed the baffled libertine, realizing the fact that he had lost his affianced bride.

"A common cut-throat and robber!" replied the Earl of Aldervale.

Duke's handsome face flushed hot with anger at the base words.

"Liar!" he exclaimed, and his weapon flashed in the speaker's face. "I do not hire assassins to do my work. I do not take innocent girls from their home and insult them; neither am I a *common cut-throat*, but I could cut your throat remorselessly."

Lord Edward fell back white with terror, and away from the cold blade that darted about before his eyes like a lightning-flash.

"And you," said Duke, turning to the nobleman who asked who he was, "if you are not the base poltroon and coward I deem you to be you will answer me by the sword for the insults you offered this lady."

The young noble's cheek tingled with the hot blood; his eyes suddenly seemed to change into balls of fire, and without answering he drew his sword—he sprang forward, making a terrible cut at the challenger's head.

Duke met the descending blade on his own and turned it easily aside.

His adversary was maddened with fury; it took Duke all his time to guard the quick and heavy blows.

Burdened as he was with the trembling girl clinging to him he had no opportunity of making a cut or lunge, but kept his steady eyes on his opponent and watched carefully his every move, or very soon the darting blade would have been buried in the heart of himself or fair charge.

He did not flinch or move an inch either way; his foot was firm, his wrist strong as iron, his nerves cool, his eyes fixed upon the blazing orbs of his foe he stood motionless as a beautiful statue, with one arm unerring to guard his opponent.

The rest of the company gathered round and watched the combatants with admiration; none knew on which side victory would fall.

Duke had no chance of vanquishing his antagonist without his strength outlasted that of the nobleman; then, on the other hand, the nobleman had no chance of vanquishing Dick unless he could throw him off his guard and put in a thrust that would settle the contest.

The libertine noble grew more excited, and cut and lashed more furiously than before.

Devil Duke still retained the cool cautiousness with which he began; a smile played about his lips.

That was a sign of no good; it always meant danger to an opponent.

He knew his combatant could not last much longer; he gradually saw with satisfaction his opponent's arm was tiring, and knew the fight must soon end.

It did.

The nobleman suddenly became aware that he was losing strength, and his sword-arm was tiring.

"One of us shall die," he exclaimed.

"Very well; it will be you," answered Duke, grimly.

No more was said.

Duke watched his excited combatant carefully.

The lookers on held their breath in suspense; they saw the end of the battle was near even now—they could not decide which side it would be on.

While the two blades clung like snakes together, coiling and hissing round each other, the nobleman suddenly struck Duke's weapon aside, leaped off the floor, sprang at the highwayman, and made a terrible lunge for his breast.

Duke had too thoroughly achieved the art of fencing to be thrown off his guard; he brought his weapon round with terrific force, and stayed the deadly course of the blade levelled at his breast.

There was a ringing clash as their steel met—a shower sparks followed—a snap—and then was seen spinning across the room a half blade.

Devil Duke's terrific blade split his opponent's weapon, and ere he could stop the furious onward flight of his impetuous blade he felt with horror it sink into the nobleman's body, penetrating his heart, and coming out of his back reeking with his foe's life-blood.

Not a murmur, not a cry escaped his lips; his eyes fixed with a stony glare, his teeth clenched firmly together, one convulsive throe shook his body — shook the sword that impaled his body, and sent a chill of remorse through his slayer.

He reeled, staggered, fell stiff and prone at his feet by his shattered sword.

What a history that weapon could tell of many battles and many fights—battles of honour and disgrace. Alas! they both have run their race, and shattered lay side by side; when the sword gave way its owner died, and their deeds will no longer dwell. Let their memory rest with the peaceful night.

Duke drew his bloody weapon from the body of the stiffened corpse, and with a look kindling in his eye that kept the others back turned to go.

Like a tiger suddenly breaking through a jungle Lord Edward leaped forward, and with a drawn sword stood before the door.

"Back," said Duke, pressing forward.

"You don't leave here," said the Earl of Aldervale; "you have killed a valued friend of ours, your life shall pay for his."

"Blood for blood," shouted the rest; and like a pack of wolves they surrounded the highwayman.

Duke's weapon was upraised; he did not speak, but his look warned them, and they shrank from his path.

"Should any of you follow me I will not be so merciful as I was to him. I warn you," he said; and throwing the door wide back, he gently raised Milly in his arms, and left the inn.

"Stand a moment, lady," he said, with deep respect, putting her down to mount Rosebud.

The poor girl was faint and weak; she held the bridle for support.

When Duke had seated himself he raised her from the ground, seated her before him, and rode away.

He did not see the hateful face of his enemy, Lord Edward, watching him from the window, and as soon as he was out of sight the whole party of libertines rushed forth.

As if by magic, horses were brought to the inn door.

Edward Aldervale was the first to mount, the rest followed him.

The hateful young lord spoke—

"Gentlemen," he said, "that highwayman must not escape. That girl knows enough to hang us all; they must be overtaken and killed. They must not live an hour longer."

"By Heaven! he shall not," cried the others.

They raised their swords to heaven, and by the light swore to have retribution for their companion's life, and, dividing into two companies, thundered away on their mission of death.

CHAPTER LXVIII.

TYBURN DICK FOILS JONATHAN WILD.

THE iron room.

Our hero did not make himself unhappy about being kept. He wisely decided to wait for a chance to escape.

He was too happy at having found his lost bride to take much notice of where he was.

The sweet, plaintive melody of his love's voice as she related to him all that had taken place between her and Wild enthralled his every sense, and he listened to her as one in a dream.

"Grace, dear girl," he said, affectionately, "tell me, love, why you left, and endangered your life by assuming this dress that so unbecomes one so fair."

Grace looked tearfully into his face, and twining her arms round his neck, said—

"Are you angry with me?"

"I ought to be," replied our hero, imprinting a kiss on her blushing cheek.

"But are you angry with me?" she asked again, sadly.

"No, my darling. How could I be so cruel? Come, tell me, Grace, why you left me."

"I was unhappy about you," she began, "and feared you might be in danger, and when poor darling Milly was taken from me I was desolate, and in the excitement of the moment assumed this dress, and went out, arming myself as you are armed, with pistols and sword, and taking Selim, with the resolution of finding my dear companion, and ever being near to protect you."

"Devoted, dear girl!" exclaimed Dick, clasping her to his breast; "and so you were my second that saved me at the Cornwall mail?"

"Yes."

"Why did you wish to keep yourself unknown from me?"

"I knew you would not let me have done it had you been aware of it."

"I should not," said Dick, again kissing her. "You must change these things for the others that more become your sex, and you must never do it again."

"I will not," and she hid her face on his shoulder; "but it was fortunate, after all. I have suffered a little, but I could suffer anything for you. It has taught me to be brave; and should I again be in danger I shall be able to defend myself. I have also learned a secret from that terrible man that will guard you against his infamy."

"True, darling," said Dick; "the black-souled wretch will be hung with the rope he is weaving for others."

Just then they heard some one coming upstairs.

"He comes!" said Grace, and she clung to her gallant lover for protection.

"Let him come" said our hero.

The iron door swung open, and Wild, armed to the teeth entered.

He cast a triumphant look upon the lovers, and drew a huge pistol from his belt.

"Now, my chickens," he said, "attempt to move, and I'll put a stop to your love-making with a bullet through your skulls.

Dick sprang up, put Grace aside, and confronted Wild.

"Keep back," said the thief-taker, pointing a pistol in the handsome boy's face.

Dick did not move.

"Look to it Wild," he said.

"To what?"

"The villainy of your scheming. You will fall into the pit you are digging for me."

"Oh! so that lady has informed you of my intentions?"

"She has."

"And you know exactly what they are?"

"The world shall know them, Wild, and your villainy shall be made public, and by me."

"You threaten," said the thief-taker, dangerously.

"I do, and not idly."

"Such words might be your death-knell; but I know you boast."

"Not idly."

"Look here, Tyburn Dick, I hold your life in my hands, and at any moment can give you over to the hangman; be careful what you say."

"I fear not your power; I shall live to see you swing."

Wild's eyes completely blazed.

"Another word and I send a bullet through you. You shall be my prisoner for fifteen months; at the end of that time I put you into your own property, and all I require in return will be half your yearly income."

"I know your intentions, Wild."

"Do you. What are they?"

"To get me into Aldervale Manor, as you say; but how long should I be lord of my own domain? Not long. No, I can read your thoughts. You would see me enjoy the luxury of wealth for a time, until you had so worked your own plan that you would put me out of the way, and take possession of the estate yourself; is that not correct?"

It was, exactly.

Wild started with surprise.

"No, it is not," he said. "I shall be satisfied with half your fortune."

"I dare say; and how are you going to account for my sudden disappearance from the road?"

"Hang that girl as Tyburn Dick," said the thief-taker, and with deliberate calmness he pointed to Grace.

"Incarnate wretch!" thundered our hero, hotly; "that is your game, is it? I think you are foiled this time."

Ere Wild was aware of it the pistol was dashed from his hand, and our hero's hands clung to his throat with the tenacity of a young lion.

"Leave go! Curse you! you are choking me," gasped Wild, and a rattling in his throat plainly showed the truth of his words—he was choking.

Dick answered him with a fiendish laugh.

Wild struggled desperately to remove Dick's hands from his throat.

He swung round, they fell. Our hero lost his grasp.

Wild was upon him in a moment, his huge knee on the gallant boy's chest, and his hand grasping his throat.

Grace gave a cry of horror as she saw her lover was being strangled by that merciless murderous wretch.

She took one bound from where she stood, and fell upon the thief-taker, savage as a tigress.

Wild hurled her aside.

The next moment she was upon her feet, and again at her lover's assailant, struggling to pull him off.

Dick looked at her in his agony pitifully; he felt that his case was hopeless.

"You shall not die by him," cried the fair girl, painfully.

She threw herself upon her lover, and kissed his distorted cheek.

"Fly, Grace—save yourself," said the noble youth in a whisper.

"No, no! I cannot leave you to be murdered!" Then turning upon Wild with all the ferocity of a young tigress, she said—"Wretch! release him or you will repent it."

Wild cast her a dangerous look that plainly spoke his meaning, and that was, that he would attend to her as soon as he had settled her lover.

Grace read his thought—she felt distracted, half mad with terror—her eyes lighted upon the thief-taker's weapon—a demoniac expression rose to her face with a flush.

Her little arm darted forth—her hand grasped the hilt, and the sword leaped from its sheath like a flash of lightning.

Wild gave vent to an oath, and made a clutch at her, but too late; the blade flashed in the air, and ere he had time to stop its progress it swept through his shoulder.

With a groan like a dying wolf he rolled over on his side and lay bleeding.

Again the weapon was raised, dripping with gore, but ere it fell Dick spoke and stayed the deadly blow.

"Do not kill him, Grace," he said—"do not sully your hands with his blood; a death more terrible awaits him than we can inflict."

The bloody weapon fell from our heroine's hand, and with a joyous cry she threw her arms around her lover's neck.

Dick held her to his heart for a moment, imprinted a kiss upon her lips, and taking her hand led her from the iron room.

Wild lay helpless and bleeding, but his eyes followed them with a look of hate and revenge.

"Lock him in," said Grace.

Dick looked at his fair companion in surprise; the words were spoken with such vehemence our hero was quite startled.

Dick locked the door, put the key in his pocket and began to descend the dark narrow staircase.

Dick stopped suddenly, drew his bride aside, and stood with his sword ready to strike.

"What's the matter, Dick, dear?" asked the courageous girl in a whisper, and not in the least frightened.

"I fancied I heard some one breathing," replied Dick; "there might be some sneaking devil waiting for us."

"Come on," said Grace boldly, "I have got my sword; nobody will stop us if they are wise."

"My darling," Dick said, "this is not how you should talk."

"Why, Dick?"

"Methinks my gentle love has wonderfully changed."

Grace laughed.

"I am no longer the timid bird I was."

"By my faith I think so too."

Grace clutched her lover's arm.

A creaking noise as though some one was sneaking up the old stairs made them both start.

Had there been an assassin only a foot from them, the darkness would have prevented his discovery.

"This will find them, if there is any one in front of us," said Grace; and snatching a pistol from our hero's belt, she fired.

Simultaneous with the report there was a shriek, and some one rolled down stairs.

"I thought so," said Grace calmly, "if he hadn't been in the way he wouldn't have got hurt."

"A good shot," remarked our hero, "but I would rather have fired it than you."

"Why?"

"It is bad enough for me to do this sanguinary work, and you should never use a firearm."

"Would you have me be a coward?"

"I would have you what you were."

"So I am,"

"The deuce!"

"I love you the same."

"I know, my love, but I do not like to see you so sanguinary. It spoils your beauty."

"I can love the same, and be gentle too," replied the queenly girl; "but come, this is no place to talk."

"Come, then," said Dick.

He took her hand and led her through the darkness.

"I thought so," he suddenly exclaimed, as a rush of feet was heard, and a group of ill-looking men swarmed into the passage, armed with formidable weapons, which they flourished about in a way that was not at all pleasant to Dick and his companion, though they did not seem much concerned about it.

"Hallo! Here's one of our mates," cried one of the men, who carried a light. "Who did this?"

"He's dead," said another, "a bullet clean though his skull. Who did it?"

"I did."

The men all sprang round as the voice sounded behind them.

"Who the devil spoke?" said another of Wild's men.

"I did."

This time the voice sounded in their midst, and in their confusion they grabbed at one another.

"I've got him."

"So have I."

The men had got hold of each other.

"Don't be a fool," said one, "leave go of me."

"Why I thought I had hold of him," said the other in surprise, letting his companion go.

"So you did."

"Who is it speaking?"

"Me."

"He's somewhere about."

"He can't be far off," said another. "I wonder who the devil it is?"

"Tyburn Dick, Prince of the Highwaymen."

"The devil!" cried the men.

"No, Tyburn Dick."

"Tyburn Dick!" said a valiant-looking individual, with a long rusty sword, and a flaming torch held in his hand. "I say, mates, he's amongst us."

"That's certain," replied the one addressed.

"Is it?"

"Hallo, I've got him!" exclaimed the valiant individual, springing round and clutching a companion by the nose.

"Leave go of my nose! What the devil are you doing?"

"Is it you, Bill?"

"Of course it is. Don't collar my nose agin, or me and you'll fall out."

"All right, mate; quite a mistake, 'pon my sivvy. I could 'ave sworn he spoke just then in my ear."

"He's amongst us for a certainty," replied Bill, rubbing his nasal organ reflectively.

Perhaps it would be as well to let the reader know who was the instigator of the confusion. We have before mentioned that Tyburn Dick was a capital ventriloquist, and profiting by the clever device on one occasion when in very imminent danger, he thought it a feasible plan to adopt it in the present instance.

As the men rushed out with lights that would have probably revealed our hero and heroine, Dick drew back into a dark recess, determined to play them a game, which he did by throwing his voice amongst them at intervals, and causing great consternation.

" Can't see him," said one.

" No more can I," said another

" Because you don't look in the right place," said our hero, making his voice sound between two men.

" There !" exclaimed the men, in a breath.

" He's amongst us," said another coming up.

" You said that before."

This time the false voice was spoken behind the last speaker's left ear.

The last speaker turned sharply; sent out his fist with terrible force ; hit one of his companions in the eye; floored him flat as a flounder, and, without a word, fell upon him with savage fury.

" What the furies are yer up to ?   Get off of me, cuss yer !" cried the astonished man.

" I'll let yer know," replied the other, pummelling away at his companion with right good will, " Tyburn Dick, are yer ?"

" Cuss yer, no !   What are yer after ?"

" Oh, I dare say not," and he kept up his pugilistic science.

The other could bear it no longer ; he hurled his assailant off, and dealing him one on the nose—a straight heavy one from the shoulder—with an iron fist, he sprang to his feet.

" Now, yer wretch, come on if yer want anything," he said, sparring up to him like a prize-fighter.

The other, meaning the one that got the one on the nose, foamed at the mouth with rage, and half blinded with blood, which prevented him from seeing his companions, he went into it furiously.

They sparred up to each other manfully, took blow for blow, and had as many rounds as would have killed three or four prize-fighters.

" Bravo, Joe !" yelled some of the men: " give him one on the smeller !"

" Go it, Johnson, let the hound have it hot ?"—this arose from the seconds on the other side.   " Lift him under the listener. That's right.   Now then, give him one on the tater-trap !"

Sanguinary Johnson was about to carry the proposition into execution, when his furious foe rushed in, hit him in the belly with his head, and put him on his back.

Johnson was dragged up, gasping, by his seconds, and stood upon his feet.

" Hit him in the peepers !" cried one.

" Punch him in the bread-basket !" said another.

And so the cries continued, while the pugilistic gentlemen were dodging round each other like a pair of young fighting-cocks.

" Keep it up, my kiddies ; I am looking at you !" cried our hero.

The men were so astonished that they left off sparring, and looked at each other, speechless.

" Was that you ?" asked one of the pugnacious gentlemen.

" No," said the other ; " was it you ?"

" Why," exclaimed the first speaker, looking hard, and apparently bewildered, " you ain't Tyburn Dick ?"

" No.   Who said I was ?"

" Why, Billy, I thought you was Tyburn Dick."

" Did yer, Joey," said the injured Billy Johnson sulkily.   " I ain't agoin' to be punched about by you."

" Beg pardon ; quite a mistake—took yer for the highwayman."

" Did yer ?   Well, I ain't; and your pardon won't mend my nose.   We'll have it out."

" What's the good of us fighting ?   We ain't bad friends."

" Ain't we ?   We are now—so come on ;" and Billy commenced sparring round the other, greatly against the other's will.

" What's the good o' us fighting ?   we ain't got nothing to fight for," said Joey, dodging about to avoid the blows delivered at him.

" Ain't we ?   Yes, we have.   You've broken my nose, an' I'm going to break yours."

" You've blacked both my eyes ; so we are quits, an' we had better have some swipe to make it up."

"Well, Joe, if yer didn't know who yer was slippin' into, and is sorry for it now, why I don't mind making it up," said the pugnacious Bill, bought over by the other's offer; "so we'll have a glass and shake hands."

They shook hands, and went out to have their glass.

"I tell yer what it is, mates, Tyburn Dick is amongst us," said one of the men, seriously; "perhaps dressed up as one of us."

"No, he ain't. Tyburn Dick's here!"

The voice appeared to issue from the room on the left of the passage.

"Here he is!" and the men made a rush towards the door.

"Don't let him escape! Keep a sharp look-out!"

The whole of the men dashed into the room.

"Now, my darling," said our hero, with a smile, as they disappeared, "let us escape while they are looking for the imaginary Tyburn Dick."

"How clever of you," remarked Grace, as they hurried down stairs through the passage.

"It is a very useful gift," replied Dick, noiselessly opening the ponderous door.

"Who taught it you?"

"Nobody, love; it came to me one day when I was making some of those peculiar noises in my throat I was so fond of."

Grace felt mystified.

"Now, my dear," said Dick, "we shall have to make use of our feet, or we shall have those brutes upon us like a herd of wolves."

He had barely spoken the words and got twenty paces from the door, when a shouting arose, and the whole gang of men dashed into the street.

"Bring the lights! bring the lights! he can't be far off."

Lights were brought; but the fugitives were nowhere to be seen.

"I saw him go," said one.

"I saw him go, too," said another.

"So did I," put in a third, and twenty more took up his words.

"Where is he now?"

"*Here!*"

The word "here" seemed to issue from the bottom of the street in a faint voice, as though the speaker was far off.

The men set off at a run, and seeing two forms turning a corner, they raised a shout for the supposed highwaymen to surrender.

Highwaymen or not the two forms took to flight, and lustily bawled out in defiance—

"Hurra for the road!"

Our hero and heroine made their appearance from a dirty alley.

"I wonder who they are?" thought Dick; "none of my comrades, I hope."

"I think not," answered Grace. Dick thought loud—so loud, in fact, that his fair bride caught the words, and replied—"the voices were not like any of our comrades."

"'*Our* comrades!'" iterated the Boy King, looking hard at his companion.

"'Our comrades,'" reiterated Grace.

"But they are not comrades of yours, my love."

"They are of yours," replied Grace; "wherefore should they not be comrades of mine?"

"But," began Dick, when Grace interrupted.

"Come," she said, urging him to hurry off, "the men are returning."

They made their escape without another word as the red glare of the torches threw their fitful light upon them, and revealed their retreating forms flying down the street.

A loud shout arose from Wild's bloodhounds, and the men set off in pursuit.

The fugitives seemed to be carried along by the wind, and soon they were out of sight.

The officers returned, giving up the chase as hopeless.

Our hero and his companion did not stop until they were in the Strand, then they darted down one of the by-streets, thinking it unwise to be seen in the open thoroughfare.

"The very thing!" exclaimed Dick, stopping before a shop that supplied people with every article of dress for any occasion. "Come, Grace," he said, turning to her, "we will get a dress more fitting for your pretty figure than the one you wear now."

"Oh no," urged our heroine, not feeling disposed to part with the distinguished costume she wore; "why do you want me to change my dress?"

"Because it is not the dress fitting for you." Dick spoke rather sternly, and his handsome face flushed with anger.

"It is more fitting than any other for the time," Grace pursued. "We may not be together one hour longer."

"My dear,"—Dick was startled by the earnestness of her tone—"why do you speak thus?"

"We are pursued still," answered the noble girl. "It will be quite impossible for us to remain together should we be set upon by our enemies, and if I change my dress my courage will go with it."

Dick knew not how to answer. He stood reflecting.

Grace continued—

"Should I be taken," she went on, "it will depend upon the sex I represent how I act. If I still keep the costume I wear I shall imagine that I am the character I represent, and do as he would do; but if I change it for the dress of my sex, I shall fall a victim to my captors, let them be who they may."

"This is nonsense," said Dick, with a start. "You can as well defend yourself in one dress as another. I hope, my love, you will have to do nothing of the sort."

"No, Dick, dear, you are wrong. I am totally helpless when in my own dress; but if you wish it"—here she sighed and looked at her lover with tearful eyes—"I will change my dress."

"That's a dear good girl," our hero said. He could not resist kissing her, though under the lights of the windows. "I do wish you to change your dress—happy thought!"

"What?" inquired the fair girl, eagerly.

"You can put a dress or so on over your cherished suit."

"So I can," said Grace, gladly.

They entered the shop, purchased a dress which our heroine put over her highwayman's costume, threw a cloak over her shoulders, and altered her hat by trimming it with a feather and some ribbon.

Again they sallied forth. The well-known and unpleasant cries of "Stop thief!" "Look out for the highwayman!" and so on, rang upon their ears before they had proceeded far.

"Confusion!" muttered Dick. His hand-some face grew dark, and almost savage in its expression. He had had enough chasing for one night. "Let him come," he said, "I will not move another step."

He drew back with his fair companion under the shadow of a wall, drew his sword, and waited grimly for the coming of his foes.

Grace was in the act of drawing her sword from under her dress, when her lover stopped her.

"No, my dear," he said, "while I have a sword, and strength to use it, you shall not draw a weapon."

"He ain't far off," said a voice.

"Not far," muttered our hero, as two officers turned the corner of a street opposite where he stood. They both had drawn swords, and held a torch high above his head; the other shaded his eyes with his hand.

Duke put Grace behind him, and peered forth. His eyes glistened demoniacally; his mouth was compressed, his teeth biting his under lip, and his hand grasped the hilt of his sword, ready to strike the first who came near.

The light of the torch fell upon his form— the men raised a shout, and rushed forward.

"Surrender!" said the first, authoritatively.

"That's old," said Dick, with an unpleasant laugh, "and a thing I never do. Take me if you can, or dare."

"Oh, oh! that's it, is it?" said the second officer.

"Just it," replied the Boy Highwayman.

"Give in quietly," said the first officer; "it will only be the worse for you if you don't. We have got plenty more of our brethren at hand."

"Keep them there," said Dick, "and you join them."

"With you," replied the first officer."

Our hero was in no mood to parley with them. He was hungry and tired. When a fellow is hungry and tired he always feels spiteful.

Dick felt spiteful, and warned the officers to keep back; they were getting uncomfortably close to him.

"Back!" ejaculated the Boy Highwayman, furiously.

"Surrender! you are our prisoner!"

"Fools! keep back!" Dick raised his weapon as he spoke.

The officers put the points of their swords close to his breast.

Grace shuddered, and covered her face. She would have shot them down, but Dick commanded her not to use a weapon while he had strength to fight.

Dick had warned his assailants three times. They did not heed him. One pushed his sword forward—the point entered our hero's breast. He winced, his eyes gleamed like those of a demon, his weapon swung round his head, it flashed like a meteor through the air, and descended like a flash of lightning.

There was a crash, and one of his assailants fell to the earth, his skull split in twain.

The other fell back horrified. An agonized shriek of terror escaped his lips, and ere the cry died away a group of at least twenty officers rushed upon the scene.

Our heroine thought it time for action, and drew her sword.

" Put that back," Dick said.

Grace put it back reluctantly.

"Tyburn Dick," rang from mouth to mouth. The whole troop set upon him. The noble boy fought like a young lion for liberty, but the overwhelming number of officers soon made him a captive.

He struggled, though held by four strong brutal ruffians, and got one arm free.

His small white hand clenched, struck one, and put him *hors de combat* in an instant. Another he gave a quietus with a thrust through the heart.

Two held him now. The others were maddened by the loss of their companions. They were coming upon him with terrible vengeance.

There was a sudden report, a shot fired by some unseen person, and ere the advancing officers came upon our hero, another of their gang fell with a bullet between his shoulders.

Dick, finding himself now held by one only struck him to the earth, and darted like an arrow amongst the others, digging, thrusting, and cutting furiously at all near him.

Heavy blows were aimed at him with terrible vengeance. Empty pistols whizzed past his head, and the officers, savage as a lot of Indians, clutched at him, but missed, and in two instances out of three fell over, and hit somebody in the wind with their heads.

The combat was now drawing to a close. Dick had unfortunately got in the way of a big fist that hit him under the ear, and before he knew where he was, he was stretched full length on his back in the road, counting the stars as the fleeting clouds vanished in large masses from the horizon.

Dick was awfully tired. He thought by lying there it would give him a rest, and when the officers crowded round him, not to disturb himself, he imagined them to be shadows of the clouds cast around him.

His imaginary idea was quickly altered when one of the men fell upon him. He no longer thought of them as shadows. His fist went out, planted in a substance, and the substance rolled over with a groan.

Dick sprang to his feet.

The officers, like a lot of bees crowding round a sugar-cask, crowded round the daring youth ; not because he was so sweet, for at the time he felt awfully bitter towards them.

" You've had your game, Tyburn Dick," said one.

" You mean to insinuate that the game is up," replied our hero.

The man made a grab at him as he sprang aside ; that man missed him, but another caught him, held him tightly by the collar, and spitefully pressed his bony knuckles in his throat.

Another of the valiant officers produced a pair of handcuffs, but ere he could put them on the captive's wrist, they were suddenly clutched from him by a little hand that came from behind him.

He turned with an oath, and received a blow on the nose with the heavy irons that made him blink. He saw more stars at that moment dancing before his eyes than our hero had counted in the heavens.

Dick looked round to see who was his friend, and his gaze fell upon his fair, faithful, and devoted bride standing in a splendid attitude of defence. She looked like a beautiful tigress. Her lover's cheeks flushed with admiration. He thought he had never seen her look so beautiful as she did at that moment of excitement.

There was a rush made towards her by the officers. They did not respect the sex ; it

THE MYSTERY OF MERTON GRANGE.

mattered little to them who the defender was —man or woman, brother or sister, son or daughter, it was all the same to them. They got paid for the apprehension of disturbers of the peace of his Most Gracious Majesty George Rex, Defender of the Faith, his people of England, Ireland, Scotland, and several other anonymous countries.

The noble girl fought bravely, and resisted while her strength lasted, but that was not for long. Her powerful assailants soon conquered her, bore her to the ground, and secured the small wrists with the manacles intended for Tyburn Dick.

The captives were being led away when a party of fashionable nobles rode past. One, on catching sight of one of the prisoners' faces, gave utterance to an exclamation of surprise, wheeled round his horse, and confronted the officers.

His companions followed his example, and wheeled round too.

The officers were compelled to stop—the horsemen barred their way across the road.

Our hero's brow darkened as with a thunder cloud, as his gaze fell upon two of the horsemen.

The first gentleman spoke—

"What are you going to do with that lady?" he asked of the officers.

"Take her to prison for aiding Tyburn Dick to escape," was the prompt reply of the officers.

"Tyburn Dick," echoed the gentleman, and his face brightened with a smile of triumph.

"Tyburn Dick! impostor, dastardly villain," thundered our hero.

The gentleman laughed.

"So the highwayman remembers me," he said.

Grace looked up—she recognised his voice; it sent a chill through her blood, and she shuddered.

"Remember you!" he cried, "I do. You will have a cause to remember me ere long, cheat," replied Dick, in a terrible passion, his frame quivering with emotion.

The nobleman scowled at the gallant youth hatefully, and then turned to the officers.

"You cannot take that lady," he said.

"We must," he got in answer from one of the men.

"But I say you cannot—must not. She is my bride, taken from me by that lawless robber and murderer."

"Curse you!" our hero almost shrieked, hoarsely, "you shall repent saying these words, miserable bastard."

The gentleman turned savagely, drew his sword, and would have ridden upon our hero, but some of the officers caught his horse's bridle and kept him back.

"Back," some said; "he is our prisoner."

"Stop his mouth," exclaimed the young noble, foaming with rage, "and give me that lady."

"Lay a finger upon her," broke out the highwayman, "and as surely as you cheat me out of my title, Edward Aldervale, so surely will my sword make a passage through your churlish heart. Remember I do not brag idly."

Lord Edward Aldervale—for it was he, with Reuben Frampton, and the others whom we introduced the reader to at the little inn

on Finchley Common—turned a deathly pallor. He well knew his noble half-brother did not threaten idly; on more than one occasion he had had a specimen of his revenge, and a narrow escape of his own life.

His eyes first wandered to the beautiful trembling girl, and then to the stern handsome face of our hero; he saw the helpless position of his brother, and knew he could now triumph. Turning to the officers, he said—

"I must have that lady instantly."

"On your lives release not that lady into his hands, exclaimed Dick; I would rather see her die than she should be in the villain's power."

Lord Edward dismounted, and went between the officers who held Grace.

"That lady must be released instantly," he said.

"It can't be done," replied one of the men; "she is our prisoner, and we can't let her go unless we know who you are."

"I am lord of Aldervale Manor," replied the young earl.

"If you want to know more inquire of Judge Gripps; now let me have that lady." He took a tightly filled purse from his pocket, and slipped it in the officer's hand.

The runner gave his companions a wink; its intimation was predicted by those who saw it, and on the instant Grace was released of the heavy weight of iron that bound her wrists.

The poor girl shrank back as the hateful young earl advanced to take her hand.

Lord Edward, with a gleam of satanic triumph in his impassioned eyes, stretched forth his hand. Grace shrank further away.

"Really," he sneered "you do not appreciate my kindness."

"Back, base usurper! You dare not lay hands on me."

"Lord Aldervale," cried Dick, with a terrible calmness—

Terrible, because it meant death—

"Lay a hand upon her, and, by God! the tortures of hell shall not equal my revenge."

Lord Edward quailed.

One glance at that stern, rigid form—one glance at those cold glittering eyes told him the speaker would keep his word.

His cheek paled, and he wavered in his intention.

From the startled officers to his friends' faces his gaze wandered.

One of them cried—

"Faith, Ted, and are you scared by the words of a man who can only use his tongue?"

Dick gave the speaker one rapid glance of his brilliant eye that seemed to flame with the passion that was rising up in him.

"We shall meet again," he said between his set teeth; "then, sir, beware, for Tyburn Dick never forgets—nor forgives."

Lord Edward, emboldened by the words of his companion, leaped forward.

Grace was taken thoroughly off her guard, and before she could move a hand in defence, the ruffian nobleman caught her in his arms.

With a taunting laugh he bounded to his horse, and vaulted in the saddle with the struggling girl held firmly to his breast.

The more she endeavoured to get her arms free, the more his base, sordid passions were aroused.

He said in a hoarse, thick whisper—

"My beautiful little mistress, you are not so modest as you should be. I do not care for my friends seeing those beautiful limbs, and there is time enough for me."

Dick did not hear the words.

But a glance at Grace's lovely form, crimson to the very roots of her hair with shame and indignation, told him all; as Lord Edward, with a laugh of defiance spoke to his companions and rode away, Dick became in a terrible paroxysm of rage.

He was held firmly; the officers feared he would make the attempt, and rough hands were grasping him from his very heel to the collar of his coat.

To look at him it was hard to tell whether he was dreaming or mad. His lips were firmly locked—his form like one carved from marble—his frame began to tremble like one with the ague—he seemed to think—to compress all his muscles and sinews—his breast throbbed—one more convulsive shiver his frame gave—then—

The muscles relaxed—his sinews stood out like cords—his splendid lithe form became erect, as all his wonderful strength was thrown into the one effort he now made to escape.

One sudden and powerful wrench he gave and he had broken from his captors, who, with cries and yells of pain, were hurled from him, their finger-nails broken and their wrists nearly put out of joint.

A tiger-like spring he made at the foremost officer, wrested the sword from his grasp, then he cried, in a voice cold and pitiless—

"Come on! You gave up that dear girl—you have driven me to this—come on!"

As he spoke, his sword gleamed round; a cry—a gasping sob—an officer fell dead.

He strode on—no mercy for his enemies now; his face was set with a look of grim ferocity as he mowed them down.

Swords were bent or broken like reeds, and men fell like blades of grass.

Cries, screams, and yells, loud and appaling, rent the air.

But he was deaf to it all; his heart was closed against pity, as, wading through the pools of human gore, he cried—

"Ha, ha! I warned you—you wanted death—by heaven and earth, you shall have it!"

And so they did; his reeking sword, which ran from point to hilt, cut down all who opposed him. He laughed at his wounds, and slew those who gave them.

It was a fearful spectacle. Eight or ten men lay dead and dabbled in their own blood; the rest were horror-stricken. He seemed a perfect fiend; he was.

He could be a lamb when not aroused; but when aroused his fury was greater than the lion's.

The men turned, and, with yells of fear fled.

Fled in any direction from that terrible form, from the mighty arm that wielded the reeking blade.

The last remaining man had fallen, the others had fled in wild terror.

Even then he did not pause, but drawing his streaming sword from the body of his last assailant, he darted off in the direction taken by Lord Edward—sped along with the speed of a racehorse, his blood-covered weapon leaving a dark and terrible trail behind him.

CHAPTER LXIX.

FORESHADOWING OF COMING EVIL.

ENTOMBED alive!

Three days and nights the brothers had been shut away from the world; three days confined in an underground vault, without either light or food.

Left to a lingering death, with all the horrors of famine; driven frantic by an unappeasable thirst, they licked the humid floor, and sought to imbibe the nitrous drops from the loathsome walls to moisten their withered lips and inflamed tongues, but instead of allaying their thirst they increased it, and trebled their fearful agony.

Every hour brought fresh tortures, and added to their sufferings. In such a state were they brought to now they knew their fate was inevitable, yet the thought was too fearful to contemplate, and vainly they tried to banish it.

To linger out their wretched existence in such a place, hidden from the world, where no ray of light shone in upon them in their dreary dungeon, was horrible.

They could not give themselves up without another struggle—life was too dear to part with.

Percy awoke.

It was now morning, but they knew not the change; day and night were alike to them —a blank oblivion of obscurity.

Percy turned and stretched out his aching limbs. His brother's hand was locked tightly in his own; it felt cold and lifeless, but his own was quite as chill.

"Reginald, my brother," he said, despairingly.

His brother answered not; stiff and motionless as death, he lay where wearily he had thrown himself down.

"I cannot let him die—I cannot die self here," Percy murmured. "Cursed the hour when we sought this place, en——"

Reginald suddenly started.

"Percy," he frantically exclaimed—"Percy, I dreamt we were free!"

"I wish we were," replied Percy, with a sigh that shook his manly frame.

"Yes, Percy, I dreamt we were free."

"Did you dream how we got out of here?"

"I did."

"Ah!"

"My brother starts!" Reginald said, with a wild laugh. "I was foretold in my dream how to escape."

"Your dream was a mockery, a torture; banish it from your mind, and let us die in peace. Do not kindle a spark of hope; we shall never see the light of day again." The poor fellow's head dropped upon his breast.

"I tell you, Percy, we are to escape from here. In my dream I was shown how we could get out."

"Tell me." Percy had thoroughly abandoned himself to despair.

No earthly power could now save them, he thought.

Three days, without sup or bite, had they been prisoners in the dungeon, where neither light nor air was near. Twenty-four hours more of the fearful sufferings they had endured, and they must terminate their existence in the most wretched misery.

Percy saw not the slightest hope of recovering their freedom.

None knew of their retreat but the revengeful being who had shut them there; it was not very probable that he would come to free them.

Then what hope had they?

None!

Reginald, who had given way even before his brother, and resigned himself to the fate that seemed so inevitable, now arose with new life and sunny hopes.

He tottered to his brother's side, and leant upon his arm for support.

"Percy, we shall live," he said, emphatically. "In my dream I was shown the way to escape."

Percy shook his head.

Reginald was some minutes before he could recover sufficient breath to continue. He had suffered doubly what his brother had, though the time had wrought a wonderful change in both.

Their powerful muscular frames were shrunk, their once bold sturdy faces were pale and haggard, and their unquailing eyes looked wild, and sank far back in their sockets.

Reginald was far the weakest; the loss of blood he had sustained from his mysterious assailant, had decreased his physical strength and subdued his tigerish nature.

"You don't answer me," he went on.

"I am waiting to hear your dream," replied Percy. "Dreams do sometimes prove true; but still I should not like to put any faith in them."

"Nor I, Percy. At any other time I have regarded them as wanderings of the mind; but I am strongly impressed by this one. It appeared more like a vision than a dream. I fancied you for the last time were crawling round the wall, when a huge stone flew aside, through which the light poured joyously. We made our escape from here, and I also thought we found our uncle asleep and—and —never mind."

"What—what, Reginald? You are agitated—you tremble. Tell me what ails you."

"No matter, Percy," replied his brother, harshly; "go see. Try every inch of the wall; there may be a hidden spring."

"Tell me why you are so agitated."

"No, no; go."

"Why not tell me, Reginald? It may be the last favour I shall ask of you evermore. Did you see anything very horrible?"

"Horrible!" repeated the other, with a shudder. "Horrible!—too horrible to contemplate in such a place, or act as I dreamt I did after escaping from this fearful fate."

"What was it?"

Reginald drew his brother close to him and put his mouth to his ear, as though fearful of hearing the sullen echo of his own voice.

"I dreamt, Percy," he whispered, in a voice almost inaudible, and trembled as though with the ague as he spoke, "when we escaped from here we discovered our uncle—the being that has so haunted us, and caused us such fearful misery. He was asleep on a couch. A dagger lay by his side. The dagger he drove into my breast. I grasped the stained weapon. Thirsting for revenge, my arm was raised, and a moment more I should have driven the dagger into his heart; but he awoke with a cry that startled me. He sprang up, dashed from the room. We pursued him —caught him, and were about to strike the blow, when we were interrupted by a stranger." Here he paused to wipe the clammy sweat from his brow, and drew breath.

"Fearful!" said Percy, with a shudder. "I hope, if we are spared and escape from here, your dream will not be realised. The sin would be too great in the sight of God, should the crime be committed, for us to be spared another hour. I hope you, Reginald, will give up all ideas about taking possession of the Grange. I shall."

"I shall not," said the other, resolutely. "Though confined here, as we are, without any conceivable way of getting out again, yet, if we should, I will not give way an inch, but pursue the course I have taken with redoubled energy until I am master of Merton Grange."

"Yet, if your dream should be true, and uncle still lives?"

"He will *not* live long."

"To contemplate such a foul crime with death hovering around you is something fearful. Reginald, henceforth you pursue your course of crime alone. I'll have nothing further to do with it. Rather than steep my hands in deeper blood of our kindred I would take to the road for a livelihood."

"As you will," replied the black-souled wretch, coolly. "This is no fitting place to arrange plans. I will tell you the rest of my dream if you will lend a listening ear."

"I listen."

"I had got as far as where we were interrupted by a stranger, I think," Reginald said, and resumed his narrative. "My dream then became muddled. A lot of horsemen appeared upon the scene. One bore a beautiful girl in his arms. By what I can remember, I think he called her Grace. My antagonist started at the name. He caught sight of her face, gave a cry, and shrieked out, 'My daughter! my daughter!' The young stranger sprang at the man who held the girl —all became a scene of confusion, and then I awoke; but the girl was our cousin."

"A strange dream; very strange. I know not what to make of it," said Percy.

"Curious, rather; but let's get out of here, if possible, and then we shall see how much comes to pass."

"I would sooner that we should perish than escape, if you intend to continue your bloody work," Percy said, in a deep, troubled voice.

"Speak no more of it, but let's get from here." Reginald spoke in a hollow, unnatural voice—in a voice treacherous. "Who knows? Perhaps when I once more see the light of day the thoughts that now swell my breast may vanish as yours have done."

"I would they did," responded Percy, almost reverentially. "You would live more happy than you do if you give up this work that will bring you to an ignominious end."

"I may change, brother," replied the hypocrite, "but it will not be done in a minute. See, Percy, if, as I saw in my dream, there is a hidden spring, and, in the name of heaven, let us leave this place, or I shall go frantic."

Percy put his brother aside, and crawled along by the wall, reaching from ceiling to floor, rubbing his hands over the rough surface. He did not pass an inch unfelt. Every little piece that projected he carefully examined with his fingers.

He felt strongly agitated, as he continued the search for the hidden spring, not because he entertained the slightest hope of escape, nor did he put faith in his brother's fancies; but some inward power urged him on, and endowed him with a strength and energy not his own.

Could there be a spring hidden in that solid masonry?

Percy did not believe there was; but to satisfy his brother's whim he kept crawling round the wall. Every step he took he reckoned as one towards his fate.

"Ah!"

He stopped. The exclamation broke from his lips so sudden that it startled himself.

Hot blood mounts his sunken cheeks; his eyes glisten with a bright light, and his heart beats time to the working of his pulses.

What is the cause of his sudden excitement?

Can he have discovered the secret spring?

His hand rested on something round and smooth.

He pressed it.

Joy of joys!

The something beneath his hand sank back. There was a slight click.

He felt the wall going away from him.

His senses are enthralled with wild excitement. He tries to call upon his brother, but his tongue refuses utterance. His head seems in a whirl, and he totters back.

The wall comes with him.

Again he starts.

His hand seeks for the spring.

Too late.

There is a second click. The wall had gone back into its place, solid and immovable as ever.

Percy stood for a time lost. He hardly knew whether the scene had been a vision, or whether he had seen the way to fortune and life in reality.

He now became quite calm.

Could he but again find the spring he would not lose the chance of liberty again.

He knew the spring could not be far off, yet his hand had traced fifty times over the same part that it had before.

He did not now despair. He knew it could not be far off, and with great patience he sounded and felt evey part of the wall over again.

Click.

The wall moved.

Percy clung to it for dear life—clung to a small projecting iron knob, and pressed it harder as the solid masonry revolved.

Slowly, and with a grating sound that sent a chill through his blood, a massive stone moved from the wall, and left an aperture, through which the golden rays of the morning sun poured in all its splendour.

The joyous light fell upon Reginald, crouched up in one corner of his dreary cell, writhing with the agony of his fearful tortures.

A cool, refreshing gust of air came through the opening, sweeping the thick unwholesome atmosphere of the dungeon before it, and bathing the heated temples of the prisoners, striking anew the fire of life and energy of which but a spark remained.

Percy called upon his brother to hasten. The stone was coming back, and the power of the hidden machinery forced the knob out, despite all his exertions to try to keep it back.

There was something peculiar about that stone. It went back to a certain distance, remained stationary for about three seconds, gave a click, and began to gradually revolve into its former position.

Reginald rose to his feet, but his physical strength was not enough to support him, and again he sank to the earth with a cry of despair.

"Reginald, Reginald!" called his brother, "make one effort. We are safe if we can get out of here."

Nerved by his excitement he sprang to his feet. He saw unless he could make one sudden spring, and leap through the aperture before it closed, he would have to perish in misery and desolation.

His face took a horrible change. His eyes glared with a demoniac light, and his form quivered; every muscle, every nerve and sinew in his body was at work, through some powerful animation.

Crouching back, as a panther crouches back when it is about to spring upon its prey, he prepared for a desperate effort.

A last effort that would prove either liberty or death.

The aperture had closed to within a foot and a half.

A moment more and it would be too late.

"Reginald!" shrieked Percy, despairingly, "an instant more and it will be too late. Come, take the leap. I cannot keep the stone back, it quickens in its progress. Quick, quick!"

He put his foot against it, and threw all his strength into his arms. He stood against the moving masonry, and tried to keep it back.

Nothing stopped its progress. The poor devoted fellow placed himself in a dangerous position. Should he not move, the stone as it closed would crush him to a fearful mass.

He saw not his own danger. He thought only of his brother, and tried to save him at the peril of his own life.

The gap had decreased. There seemed not sufficient space to admit of a man to pass sideway between the revolving stone and the wall.

Reginald looked more like a wild beast at bay than a human being as he crouched down, his limbs and body drawn up in a heap.

Percy turned—gave a cry. A howl of a dog it resembled.

Reginald sprang from the ground like a dart and dashed forward.

There was a crash as of a human body being mangled between some fearful rollers.

A cry—a shriek rang through the dungeon in piercing accents.

Why?

The revolving stone suddenly went round with lightning rapidity, and a grating crushing noise.

A second cry rent the air.

Reginald fell to the earth a huddled heap.

CHAPTER LXX.

FORETOLD BY A DREAM.

FREE.

Free from the dungeon of horrors.

With such lightning rapidity did the stone revolve as Reginald took the frantic leap for liberty, that at the time it was impossible to say whether he had escaped or got crushed between the stones.

He flew through the air like an arrow. With a cry of horror he saw his peril and shut his eyes.

Clean as a shot he went through the aperture.

The stone, with a crushing grating sound, closed behind him, but not before he had dragged his brother with him.

The reiterating shock of the revolving stone closing hurled him to the earth.

For two hours they lay doubled up.

When they awoke it was with the greatest joy they had ever known, to find themselves free from their dark, loathsome prison, and once more lying beneath the glorious face of the heavens.

They awoke divested of all their tortures, all their sufferings; and their powerful frames, that had withered and shrunk with the sufferings they had endured, were grown strong.

But where were they?

In a kind of pit, with four stone walls around them of a height impossible to be reached from where they stood.

To ascend that wall would be the work of time and skill.

There may be another way of exit.

The brothers were of the same opinion. To ascertain the possibility of such a thing, they made a careful survey of their position.

Far back in a deep recess was a small grating; by its position they thought it likely to give ingress to the house.

They must have that grating out.

There was not room for both to pull at it at once, so they took a tug by turns.

At length they had the satisfaction of seeing a few small pieces of mortar tumble out.

That was a good sign.

So they thought, and renewed their efforts with inspired vigour.

More mortar fell.

There was a crash.

The iron was giving way.

Percy got behind his brother, and locking his hands, they jerked together with good will.

One, two, three jerks.

The grating became quite loose.

Another good tug and they would have mastered their enemy.

Leaning forward, they prepared for one mighty effort.

The effort was taken. The irom came from its sockets and both the brothers rolled over, Reginald grasping the grating triumphantly in his hands.

Another minute they were upon their feet, the iron was thrown aside, and one after the other they crawled through the hole in the wall.

They were now in a vault as dark as the one from which they had escaped.

They soon discovered where the door was, and made their exit; they traversed through a long stone passage.

They entered a large room on their left.

Dame Fortune certainly seemed to favour them.

On a large oaken table were the remnants of a meal.

This led them to make a further search for more of the same description.

In a capacious cupboard they found such eatables as supplied their hunger, and what was still more delightful, there was a stack of fine old wine.

With little ceremony they made a furious attack upon the eatables, and washed them down with a dozen of wine.

"I suppose," remarked Percy, "ghosts eat, or this would not be here."

"Such ghosts as infest this part," repli Reginald. "They have an idea, anyho what is a good diet."

Percy nodded; he had got the neck of a bottle in his mouth, and the juice he was imbibing was delicious and exhilarating.

So it proved by the unstady gait it caused upon the drinkers.

Their blood was fired, a dangerous gleam shone in their eyes; the slightest provocation would make them savage as tigers.

They left the kitchen together, and proceeded up-stairs.

It is needless to say they were in Merton Grange, as no doubt the reader has discovered.

Excited and maddened as they were by the fiery drink, they had sufficient sense to proceed with caution in case of discovery.

Had they been trained for the stage, to take some tragic part, they could not have proceeded more stealthily.

Doors were opened mercilessly, and two dark fierce heads peeped into the rooms.

"At last!" This seemed to come from Reginald's chest, in a hoarse, fierce whisper.

"What?" inquired Percy, clutching his brother by the arm and leaning his head forward.

"He sleeps."

"Ah!"

The two double-dyed villains stood for a few moments at the door of a splendid suite of rooms, furnished in the most elegant and costly style; a dagger was held firmly in the hand of each.

Reginald grasped his brother's arm nervously, but his soul of dark crime was firm,

"Percy, he sleeps," he said, not above his breath. "He sleeps; he must never wake again—you understand?"

Percy nodded. He was the weaker villain of the two—second villain, he might be called.

Slowly, cautiously, breathlessly, and on

tiptoes, they strode across the room towards a couch, whereon lay a tall, handsome gentleman. His face wore a troubled, wild expression.

Reginald leaned over the sleeper with a fiendish look of triumph

His arm was raised—a gleaming weapon grasped in his hand.

Twice he looked at the sleeper before he could strike.

" You, curse you! have been the cause of all my misery," he muttered. " You are the only obstacle in my way ; I remove it now."

The dagger went up, and then descended.

But ere it reached its mark the sleeper suddenly awoke, uttered a fearful shriek of terror that made the would-be assassins start, and springing from the couch, he dashed the murderer aside, and fled from the room.

" After him—he must not escape!" yelled Reginald, with baffled rage.

Percy dashed from the room.

Reginald was not far behind him.

Away they went, and away went the poor gentleman, flying before the wind for dear life.

The assassins were after him, pursuing him for his life.

They were now in the grounds. The fugitive dashed among the woods for refuge, but his pursuers were after him in an instant.

Away he went again, flying over the ground fleet as a hare.

" Go round there, Percy, and meet him," said the other.

Percy started off and vanished round a small wooden building.

There was a shriek.

The gentleman came face to face. A dagger gleamed before his eyes ; but ere the cowardly hand could strike, the poor fellow fled.

Fled to meet danger as bad.

On turning sharply round he fell into the arms of Reginald.

The villain gave a yell like the war-cry of the wild Indians, and he folded his arms tightly round his captive, pinioning his arms down.

Percy came forward.

" Strike!" said Reginald, looking into the gentleman's horrified face.

" The dagger was raised—the point poised in a line for the captive's back.

A clatter of horses' hoofs thundering down the road arrested his arm.

" Strike, villains, strike your uncle," cried the poor gentleman piteously ; I know you both. May my dying curse wither your souls as your torture withers me. Look to what you have brought me."

With a sudden twist he broke from his captor's grasp, and confronted the two quailing villains fearlessly.

" Look at me," he continued wildly—" look at me, pitiless wretches, and picture what I was. Where is my wife and child? Answer me ; tell me where they are?"

He took two steady steps towards Reginald.

He meant danger ; a fierce light burned in his eyes.

Reginald gradually went back.

" Keep off," he said.

His uncle laughed a demoniac laugh.

Percy went between them.

The gentleman turned upon him fiercely.

" You have escaped my vengeance once," shrieked he.

With a bound he leaped at Percy.

With a cry of terror the trembling wretch shrank back ; the dagger fell from his hand.

Reginald ran to pick it up ; as he stooped a hand twisted round his throat and hurled him back. His uncle snatched the weapon triumphantly, and turned upon his foes.

He did not make a sudden attack, so Reginald had time to prepare for an onset.

A cruel sneer wreathed his lips as he watched his uncle.

The gentleman sprang forward just as Reginald prepared for a leap ; the consequence was that they met half way, and closed with each other.

A desperate struggle then ensued for possession of the dagger.

Reginald's lion strength exceeded the feeble power of his assailant.

Reginald threw his opponent forward, and wresting the weapon from his grasp, was about to strike.

The dagger was at his throat, the point broke through his skin, and he recoiled with horror as the cold steel penetrated his flesh.

Helpless beneath his powerful assailant,

his hand pinioned behind him, and the huge knee of his foe pressing on his chest, he could not move an inch.

Was he to lie there, conscious of his fate, looking his murderer in the face, while he slowly robbed him of his life?

The thought was terrible. Piteously he pleaded for mercy, but the only answer he got was a brutal exultant laugh.

He had heard the clatter of approaching horses; he listened, and again heard them more distinct than before.

Surely, he thought, if they are gentlemen, and have any chivalry or pity in them, they would come to his assistance.

He turned his head; the cold steel went further into his throat, and ripped a gash along his flesh. A cry of pain escaped his lips.

The horsemen were at that moment passing, and by the light that fell upon them, he saw that they were a body of handsome young men.

Lustily he shrieked, in hopes of bringing them to his aid; but on they went in great confusion. One turned his head and said something to his companions, but they urged forward, and were followed with a last look of the fated gentleman.

The poor fellow saw no hope now, and, with a heavy drawn sigh, he closed his eyes and gave himself up to his murderer.

Reginald did not appear to be in any particular hurry to finish his victim; on the contrary, he took a fiendish delight in torturing him.

Percy stood watching his brother, bewildered. Once or twice he stepped forward with the intention of interposing on behalf of his uncle, and then he went back as his evil nature conquered his better feelings.

At length he grew impatient.

"Strike!" he suddenly exclaimed.

Lord Merton gave a gurgling cry as his assailant withdrew the dagger from his lacerated flesh.

The bloody weapon was raised on high, the point poised for his heart, but ere the slayer's arm fell, a youth, wild and excited, broke through the hedge, and bounded forward with a naked sword in his hand, crimsoned to the hilt with gore.

One terrific leap he took, and fell upon the murderous wretch, snatching the dagger from his grasp, and hurling him aside with terrible vehemence.

"Cowards!" thundered the bold youth, and he sprang forward; his sword swept through the air, and descended in a line for the astonished villain's head.

Astounded as was Reginald with the sudden appearance of the furious young stranger, it did not prevent him from seeing the danger of his own position, and he leaped backwards as the weapon fell with such terrible force, that had he not moved when he did it would have cleft his head from his shoulders.

Evidently the young stranger's blood was heated with some previous encounter in which he had failed. Probably he was in pursuit of some one, and having come so fortunately to the rescue of Lord Merton, he again turned savagely on Reginald.

That worthy gentleman, half frightened of his assailant's fury, prepared for a sudden onset.

The brave youth glared like a tiger upon the dastardly wretch.

"If you are not the cowardly assassin I deem you, defend yourself," exclaimed the handsome youth, throwing himself into a careless picturesque posture of defence.

"Who are you that you should thus challenge me?" inquired Reginald, wondering who the young fire-eater could be.

"Tyburn Dick," replied the youth, throwing back a valise from his shoulder, and disclosing the jewelled star.

"Ah!" exclaimed Reginald.

Percy went to his brother's side, whispered something in his ear that changed the colour of his cheeks, and while our hero turned to answer a feeble voice that called upon him, they took the opportunity to vanish.

"Base curs, despicable hounds!" muttered Dick, seeing that they had gone.

The poor gentleman rose to his feet, and tottered to the side of his gallant preserver, laying his arms upon his shoulder.

Dick turned.

The gentleman wanted to thank the youth for his brave conduct and timely interference, but his voice was gone.

Our hero was subdued in a moment, the

fearful condition of the poor gentleman touched his generous heart deeply, and with his own pocket-handkerchief he tenderly bound Lord Merton's lacerated throat.

With a sudden start, as his gaze fixed upon his patient's countenance, he stepped back, and ejaculated—

"Impossible!"

Then he went forward, took both the gentleman's hands, and stared steadily into his face.

"Can it really be my companion of the sea-well?" he said.

The gentleman nodded.

"Lord Merton?" Dick queried.

Lord Merton nodded again.

"Who could these villains be?" muttered Dick. "Very fortunate that I came in time to save him from the coward's knife. I shan't forget them when next we meet. I wonder who they were? Strange that they should have such deadly enmity against this poor gentleman. Now I have found him, I will keep him under my protection until I have again saved my dear girl. Ah!" He started as a thought occurred to him, and he continued his cogitations. "Perhaps they are the men Bullskin is after; they are very much like the description he gave me. If they should be the villains I suspect, I will hunt them down and slay them remorselessly."

He was startled by a clamour of voices and the neighing of horses.

He turned, and, to his utter astonishment, he came face to face with his old enemies, the party of horsemen who had ridden past the Grange when Lord Merton called upon him for assistance.

In a moment our hero's handsome face assumed a terrible demoniac expression.

He drew his sword from the earth where he had thrust it while he attended to Lord Merton, and was about to leap upon Edward Aldervale, who still held the beautiful girl before him, when his gaze fell upon Reginald, who, like the guilty wretch he was, kept behind the others, and waited for an opportunity to plunge the dagger he held in his hand into his uncle's heart.

Dick was undecided which to make the first attack upon.

Lord Edward Aldervale might escape if he attacked Reginald Merton, and if he attacked Edward Aldervale, Reginald Merton might take the opportunity of completing his bloody work.

Dick stood in an awkward position.

Lord Merton clutched Dick's arm and went forward. He looked strangely at our heroine held powerless by Edward Aldervale.

The fair girl returned the look, and both seemed strangely agitated.

"My daughter!" exclaimed Lord Merton, and he rushed from our hero with a bound.

Grace shrieked, and tried to break the bonds that bound her wrists.

Lord Edward tried to exert all his strength to keep her from throwing herself to the ground.

The scene now became one of strange excitement.

Every one appeared bewildered, and stared at one another in stupefication.

Suddenly there was a general move. Percy made his appearance, clutched his brother, whispered something in his ear; then they both fell upon Lord Merton, who was struggling with Edward Aldervale for the possession of his child.

Dick suddenly leapt between the two villains, and striking one to the earth with his sword, he clutched the other by the throat, and nearly squeezing his life out, hurled him powerless upon his brother.

At that moment Lord Merton gave a cry, and fell bleeding upon his two enemies.

Edward Aldervale gave a wild yell of triumph, made a slash at Dick, but missed, and then spurred away with his beautiful captive.

Dick was roused to a fearful pitch of fury. He drew a pistol and fired after his dastardly brother; the shot missed its intended mark, and carried Reuben Frampton from the saddle.

Reuben Frampton swore in a most ungentlemanly manner, and limped after his horse. The bullet had settled in a very uncomfortable part, and he thought with terror of the pain he would experience by sitting down.

Dick dashed past him like a savage Indian, and pursued his cowardly brother.

"Draw in your horse," yelled the Boy

Highwayman, " or, by Heaven, I will bring you to the earth with a bullet in your skull."

Lord Edward laughed tauntingly.

" Fire!" he cried, " your dear Grace will get the bullet."

Dick knew too well the truth of the coward's words; if he fired, the base wretch would guard himself with the beautiful form of his captive.

Dick was baffled again, and by the cowardly artifice of his dastardly half-brother.

" If you are not worse than a coward," shouted our hero, beside himself with rage, " face me like a man, and let one of us fall by the other's sword."

" I haven't time, mad boy," replied Edward, scoffingly; " besides, I do not want to kill you —it does me more good to see you live in torture. Good-bye, Dick, I am going to take this pretty girl home; you shall have her when I have done with her."

The noble Boy King could stand the taunts of his villanous brother no longer. He made one bound, leaped off the ground, and sprang upon Lord Edward like a panther.

Dick grasped his throat, the horse plunged up madly, there was a shriek from Grace, a cry of pain from one of the combatants. and a form fell from the horse.

CHAPTER LXXI.

A CHAPTER OF EVENTS.

TYBURN DICK lay on the earth panting for breath. The horse had thrown him, and its heavy iron hoofs struck him heavily on the chest.

He watched with a savage gleam in his eyes his assailant ride away with his fair bride.

It was some time before our gallant hero recovered sufficiently to follow, and when he did rise his breast swelled with mortal hatred and deadly revenge against his cowardly half-brother.

He concluded that the party had made their way to the Leopard Inn, and he followed— followed with the savage intensity of the bloodhound, his hand grasping the hilt of his sword.

While our hero is proceeding towards the Leopard Inn, let us follow the adventures of our heroine.

Lord Edward Aldervale bore her away triumphantly, and placed her in the care of mine host's pretty daughter, Lizzie, while he and his friends took refreshments.

Grace quickly dismissed her pretty handmaid, and cast the refreshment that had been placed for her disdainfully aside.

" So he thinks to get me in his power again," said the fair girl, bitterly; " fool! I fancy he will be rather surprised when he comes to fetch me."

She hastily scanned the room, and went to the window.

She was on the ground floor; the window was about six feet from the ground.

" That will do," she muttered.

She cautiously turned the key in the lock, listened attentively for a few moments, and lightly stepping back into the middle of the apartment, she divested herself of the gown, and tearing the trimming from her gold-trimmed vestments, she stood in the daring highwayman's costume, that so well became her magnificent form.

" He may come now," she said, unlocking the door.

She had barely stepped two paces back, and drawn the crape mask over her flushed features, when there arose a fearful skirmish in some other apartment.

Grace appeared to know from what it arose, she heard her lover's angry voice above the many others.

She stood ready, with her little hands resting on the butt of a pair of pistols.

Lord Edward bounded into the room like a madman, a cry of terror left his lips when his eyes came in contact with a pair of bright pistol-barrels, and a highwayman confronted him in place of his beautiful captive waiting helpless for his return.

For a few seconds he stood transfixed; he seemed powerless.

Battling with his friends outside was Tyburn Dick, yet a Tyburn Dick stood before him.

Was his brother a conjuror?

He turned to fly as he asked himself the question, but at that moment the room-door swung open, and Tyburn Dick sprang into the room: his combatants followed him like a pack of wolves, thirsty for his blood. So

CAPTAIN CLAUDE WATCHES THE PURSUIT.

veral of them looked faint, and bled profusely from deep gashes, and our hero's weapon dripped with their gore.

He glanced at his cowering enemy, and motioned to Grace to retreat.

Lord Aldvervale's cowardly heart sank within him like a heavy piece of lead as his glance met that of his angry brother, and he sprang at the window as Dick leaped towards him.

Grace struck the dastardly cur to the floor by a blow on the temples with a pistol.

Dick, savage as a tiger, was upon him in a moment, and in another moment Lo'
Edward's friends were upon Dick.

Grace went into them bravely, and defende
her lover from their thirsty blades.

The *mêlée* now reached its highest standard —men rolled over one another, digging at anybody, and the cries and oaths that arose were terrible.

Dick had gained his footing. He and Gr^cte stood back to back, and fought like gladiators, knocking down all who came near them.

Mine host stood at the door, terrified, and

called upon them to desist; but, of course, his cries were unheeded.

At the window, occasionally, could be seen the faithful ostler, with a huge three-pronged fork flourishing in his hands.

"Cut him down!" yelled the young Earl of Aldervale, furiously, who, after much struggling, had got to his feet. "Cut them down—they shall both die!"

"Come on!" said Dick, calmly holding his sword before him.

"Come on!" said Grace, trying to speak in the same tone as her lover.

The young noblemen gathered round the daring pair, forming a circle that gradually grew smaller, and their weapons' points went uncomfortably close to Dick and his companion.

Tyburn Dick suddenly swung his sword round, and half the circle of weapon-points were lowered immediately. Grace swerved her sturdy rapier round, and the other half were lowered.

But they were soon raised again, and went much closer than before.

Our hero's quick eye detected one of the party sneaking behind his companion. Dick knew the coward's intention. He drew a pistol with his left hand, and pointing it over his shoulder, he said—

"If you don't come from behind there with that pistol, I shall fire."

The sneak dodged out of the way with a howl of disappointment.

Dick replaced his pistol. He had enough to do to keep the points of his assailants' swords from perforating his body.

So close did the weapons' points go to him and his companion, and so rapid were the furious blows aimed at them, that Dick well knew he could not hold out much longer against the fearful odds.

His blade was darting about like a meteor amongst three of his foes, when Grace uttered a shriek that curdled his blood with terror. He turned, regardless of his own danger, to defend his darling idol. His gory weapon was raised, and as it descended, with terrible force, for Lord Edward's head, the cowardly young earl swung the beautiful girl round to receive the blow.

Dick recoiled with horror at the dastardly act, and, falling back a step, he managed to divert the blow as it fell.

His evil nature goaded with baffled fury, Edward Aldervale raised the girl in his arms and dashed her in her lover's face.

Our hero dropped his weapon, and caught the beautiful supple form of his devoted bride in his arms.

At the same moment one of Lord Edward's cowardly friends dashed a pistol at him. It caught the noble youth under the ear, and he fell heavily to the floor, the brave girl clinging to him for protection, for she had had her weapon wrested from her by a number of the young libertines, who dashed upon her in a group.

There was a peal of triumphant yells, and before either could get up the whole gang of nobles set upon the defenceless pair.

Ben gave a wild cry, and sprang in at the window to the rescue of his beloved young captain. His three-pronged fork went to work, and made very uncomfortable the most prominent seats of honour.

Mine host now ran into the room, and, falling amongst the thickest of the combatants, hurled them on either side of the room with his muscular arms.

Our hero and heroine once more rose upon their feet, but they stood weaponless.

Each made a dart for their own swords, and as they stooped to pick them up, the assailing party again attacked them.

Ben had suddenly vanished—a strange commotion in the yard aroused his curiosity.

Dick was now going into his enemies with redoubled energy; his blade was running with fresh blood, when he turned with a deadly intent to strike his dastardly brother to the floor, who, with three of his companions, was attacking our heroine in a corner.

"Cap'n, cap'n, cap'n, fly!" shouted Ben; "the hofficers is after yer."

The words had barely left his lips when the room was swarmed with Bow-street runners who poured in at the door and windows.

"Bravo!" shouted Lord Edward. "Come away, friends, let the officers pour a volley into the cut-throats."

Dick leapt round and thrust out, with intent to pin his brother, but his intent was frustrated by a big officer, who caught the impetuous youth in his arms, and stayed his wrist from dealing the deadly blow.

The big officer got a dig in the ribs from the point of our heroine's weapon, and the big officer, with a yell of terror, dropped Dick.

"Two of 'em!" exclaimed one of the runners, aghast.

"Two," said Dick; "which will you have first?"

"You," replied another, "as we knows you to be the old 'un."

"Very well," Dick said, with a quiet smile, and his lips writhed as he spoke; "take me."

"Give in quietly," said the big officer, rubbing his injured side.

"Don't be a fool," was our hero's cool rejoinder; "you know that's a thing Tyburn Dick never does."

"It'll be the worse for you if you don't."

"It'll be worse for me if I do."

The big officer drew a big pair of pistols from his belt, and put one in a straight line for our hero's head and the other in a line with that of our heroine's.

Our heroine objected to having a big pistol pointed at her head. Her hand suddenly came round, her sword gleamed like a flash of lightning before the big officer, and the big pistol was struck from his hand.

Simultaneously with striking the pistol from the officer's hand, Grace gave her lover a push just in time to save him from the bullet, which struck into one of the officer's thick heads.

"Shoot them down!" yelled the big officer, foaming with rage. "We must take them dead, if we can't get them alive."

"Fly, Grace! fly, while you have time!" said Dick, in the brave girl's ear.

She lingered, and looked wistfully into his face. He understood that look.

"Go," he said, "if you love me. I shall be quite safe."

She took his hand, pressed it to her lips, and with tears running down her pretty cheeks, she turned to go.

Several of her enemies and a group of officers stood in her way.

"Stand back!" demanded our hero, in a voice of thunder.

The men looked at him for a moment inquiringly, and then broke out in a laugh of derision.

Dick said no more. He sprang amongst them, his sword made a passage, and Grace, with the swiftness of an antelope, darted through the scattered throng and vanished.

A body of officers closed around Dick ere he had time to follow her.

"Fire!" yelled one of the men. "Fire! Bring him down."

"Hold," said Edward Aldervale; "put your weapons back. Leave him to me; you take care of the one you have got."

The pistols that were produced as the order to fire was given, were replaced when the Earl of Aldervale spoke.

And our hero saw, his breast heaving with inveterate fury, Lord Edward and his companions start off in pursuit of his queenly bride.

He looked round at his surrounding foes, and saw what little chance of escape he had; yet, were he opposed by twenty times the number, he would make an attempt for freedom.

As yet, not a hand was laid upon him. He did not want any more bloodshed; but should they oppose him he would fight to the last.

His quick eye rapidly surveyed his position.

The casement was wide open, but a barrier of men, three deep, armed and on the alert for the slightest movement on his part, kept him from it.

Why should they prevent him from escaping? Was it not a true chivalric mission for which he wanted to get away—to save a beautiful girl from the clutches of a base sordid wretch who would make her a thing without a name, should he get her within his power?

Dick argued the point in his own mind, and came to the conclusion that should they oppose him he was justified in seeking their lives.

The officers had gradually got so near to him that several hands were stretched out to clutch him on the first sign of a move.

Dick was awakened to the fact that he had fallen into a trap.

"What are you all standing around me for?" he asked, with an assumed carelessness.

"Just waiting to put the darbies on you," replied one of the men.

"What for?"

"It's dangerous to take you without 'em."

"You won't put them on, nor you won't take me."

"Oh, won't we?"

"Not if I know it."

"You're our prisoner."

"I am glad you told me, I was not aware of it before."

"Well, now yer knows; shove out yer fists, and 'ave the bracelets on."

Dick shot out his fists, hit the speaker heavily on the nose; the man staggered, and his companions moved aside to give him room to fall.

While he was falling and clutching at the air, Dick bounded through the opening, and sprang from the casement into the yard.

"Bring forth my Arab steed!" he cried wildly.

"Here yer is, cap'n," said a voice, and, before the sound had died away, there came forth and stood by the side of the daring Boy Highwaymen a man holding the bridle of a splendid Arabian steed.

"She's fresh and frisky, cap'n, worth fifty of the hofficers' hosses," remarked the ostler, as Dick mounted.

"Which way did my comrade go?" eagerly inquired Dick.

"The other, cap'n, like you?"

"Yes—yes."

"Oh, let me see."

Ben covered his face to consider.

The officers were coming through in groups. Dick knew that another attempt to take him would be made; he sat trembling with anxiety waiting for the ostler's information.

"Let me see," Ben soliloquised; "oh, he went across there, cap'n, and struck across Barnes Common, and all them gemmen tearing after him."

Dick sighed with relief.

"Was he on foot or horseback?" he asked.

"Well, he was on foot, but he pulled one of the gemmen off his horse and jumped into the saddle.

"Thanks! Good-bye, Ben; stand aside," said our hero, wheeling his horse round.

The Bow-street officers had nearly all gathered round him, and resolved that he should not leave that place alive unless it was with them.

Each man was determined, and held a huge pistol ready to send a bullet crashing through the daring young rider's head did he attempt to escape.

Dick saw their intention, still his daring spirit was not deterred, and at the peril of his life, though surrounded as he was with the deadly weapons, he resolved to break his way through the body of determined men who stood before the gates.

At a glance he took in his position—he saw how hopeless it was.

"The leap must be taken," he soliloquized, looking at the high closed gates. "I trust my life to you, my beauty; it depends entirely upon how you clear that infernal obstacle whether I fall or not."

He knew the matchless qualities of the steed on which he sat, and unhesitatingly trusted himself to her care.

The noble animal seemed to know the responsibility she had to guard against the many men who surrounded her. She was uneasy, and eager to be off.

"In a moment, Selim, my beauty," said Dick, patting her sleek neck.

The officers stood perfectly quiet—none moved—every man kept a keen watch on the highwayman's slightest movement, and every eye followed his gaze.

They knew he would not surrender while he had life, and so they waited until he should attempt to escape, when they would fire upon him, and so make sure to take him.

"Now!" exclaimed the daring boy.

He struck Selim slightly with his heels.

The noble creature rose with the swiftness of a dart from the ground, and like a fleeting shadow her dark form vanished over the high gates and the heads of her rider's foes.

Quick as the leap was taken the officers were as quick to fire upon the defiant highwayman.

As the black mare rose every deadly weapon was pointed towards our hero.

Then there was a flash, a broad sheet of

fire that spread along the line of pistols; a deafening report followed, and a shower of bullets fell like a storm of hailstones upon Tyburn Dick.

He staggered, and fell forward in the saddle, and Selim, giving vent to a wild, unearthly shriek, dashed away at a maddening speed.

CHAPTER LXXII.
OUR HEROINE FULFILS HER VOW.

WHEN our heroine escaped she put the steed she had taken from one of the young noblemen to its utmost speed, and soon left her pursuers far behind.

She did not care about the peril of another encounter with them, her only thought was for her lover.

She rode briskly to London, thinking that the most likely place to meet her champion if he escaped, of which she had not the slightest doubt, knowing his indomitable spirit.

It was past midnight when she reached the metropolis—a time when the busy streets are deserted, and everything has subsided into quietude, save for the night strollers, the vagrants, and the noisy fashionable men of London, who had just turned from their haunts, and were rolling towards their respective dens in small groups, bawling forth some vulgar ditty, waking the peaceful inhabitants, and defying the watchmen, who rushed forth and protested against their turbulence.

While Grace was riding through Pall Mall, lost to everything but her own thoughts, she was suddenly roused from her reverie by the piteous cries of a woman.

Her pretty cheeks turned a deathly pallor, and looking in the direction from whence the cries came, she saw a group of fashionable men.

Somebody was evidently struggling in their midst by their movements, Grace concluded; and turning her horse's head from the direction she was going, she rode towards the roisterers, to see the victim of their brutal sport, and render what assistance she could.

A cry of indignation and horror escaped her lips as her gaze fell upon a beautiful girl, struggling to get away from her tormentors.

Our heroine was out of the saddle in a moment, and drawing her sword from its sheath she dashed amongst the inhuman wretches.

Had a thunderbolt suddenly fallen in their midst they could not have been more scared than they were by the sudden appearance of the queenly girl that stood before their victim, like an angel of light.

"Cowards!" she said, confronting them angrily, her sweet voice hoarse with passion —"cowards! can you find no better sport than to torture a poor girl?"

The men looked at each other, abashed.

"Who the devil are you?" exclaimed a big, surly brute. "Do you know the laws for interfering with the Mohocks?"

Mohocks was a name given to a class of men who in the olden times infested London by night. After they had turned from their haunts of infamy, where vice, from the highest to the lowest degree, was pursued to a fearful extent, they would pitch upon the first person, male or female—it mattered not to them who their victims were—but if the latter, they were exposed to more horrid tortures than a man.

Grace, not knowing the meaning of the word "Mohocks," did not answer. She stood quietly watching them, with a deadly glitter in her eyes, and her tiny hand grasping firmly the hilt of her sword.

"Pink him, pink him!" suggested one of the brutes.

"Yes, yes—pink him!" shouted the rest.

Their swords were drawn, and in a body they rushed upon our heroine, to carry into execution their brutal purpose.

The noble girl did not move a step, but waited, and as they came upon her, her sword darted out, and ere any could stay the deadly thrust, the glistening blade swept through one of the brute's hearts, and with a gurgling cry he fell at her feet a doubled heap.

The others fell back stricken with horror.

Like a tigress who has tasted blood, and is eager for more, Grace leaped amongst the astonished Mohocks and sought to take their lives.

They retreated, and she followed them, striking down all within her reach.

Her sword, from point to hilt, was reeking

with blood, and her hands and face were spattered with their black gore.

More like a beautiful fiend than the lovely girl she was, she went fearlessly amongst them, and mercilessly mowed them down, until the pavement was strewed with writhing bodies, and blood flowed like water down the gutter.

Her wrist was aching, but she would not show signs of fatigue, and with supernatural strength she beat down the weapons of her combatants, and buried her own blade into the bodies of her foes.

She fought with an untiring energy until, at last, the inhuman wretches turned, and like the base cowards they were, fled, leaving their dead and wounded companions lying dabbled in their blood.

Grace laughed a fiendish triumphant laugh as they scampered off, and then she returned to the poor girl who had crouched back in a doorway, trembling and weeping with fear.

"Milly!" said our heroine, sheathing her sword.

The trembling girl started at the sound of the voice, and looked up inquiringly into the speaker's face.

"Is it you, Dick?" she said.

"No, darling, it is Grace."

"My dear Grace in these clothes?"

"Yes, Milly," the brave girl, overcome with emotion, answered in a sobbing, sad voice.

"Yes, yes, I see it is my dear companion, Grace," said Milly, and she fell upon her defender's breast.

Grace twined her arms round the affectionate girl, and for a few minutes they indulged in a mutual weeping undisturbed.

"Milly," said Grace, being the first to recover.

"Grace," sobbed Milly.

"Don't weep any more, love," our heroine said, kissing away her companion's tears.

"I am so happy, Grace, we have met," said Milly, hugging her affectionately.

"I made a vow, Milly," emphasized Grace, solemnly, "on the night you were taken away that I would not return to the haunt until I had discovered you, and from that night I have been out in search of you."

"But I was taken away by mistake," said Milly. "You were the one they wanted."

"Then when he discovered his error, why didn't he bring you back?"

"Because he was annoyed at being thus foiled through his own carelessness, and being of a mean, cowardly nature, swore to keep me in captivity."

"How did you manage to get away then?"

"You shall hear, anon. I was taken from the room where he had put me, and brought out before a lot of young noblemen; one of them took an immense fancy to me, and greatly against my will he was going to marry me." Here she shuddered as some terrible thought crossed her mind.

"And then?" put in Grace.

"Let us away from here," urged Milly

"You will have to share part of my horse."

"Gladly," replied Milly. "But where is it?"

"Stay a moment, Milly love. The brute has strayed down the street," and kissing the delicate girl, Grace nimbly ran down the street after the horse.

She brought it back; they both mounted, and Milly continued her story.

"We were at an inn on Finchley Common," she went on; "the priest was sent for, but, fortunately, Captain Duke was passing at the time; suspecting something was wrong, he waylaid the priest, and sprang into the room just as I was about to be carried off."

"A quarrel ensued, in which Duke killed the gentleman who wanted me, and saved me from the others; he had not gone far before he was set upon by a troop of soldiers who pursued him for many miles, but at last his horse outstripped those of his pursuers.

"He placed me at an hotel, where I remained for three days until to-night. I came to the door to inhale a little fresh air. I had not been there many minutes when one of those ruffians from whom you bravely saved me spoke to me under some pretext, and before I had time to answer he slipped one arm round my neck, put his hand over my mouth to stop my cries, and carried me away."

"What became of Duke?" asked Grace.

"He was discovered at the hotel, and had

to fly," answered fair Milly. "That is my story; now, dear, tell me yours."

"I have suffered much," said Grace.

"And all for me."

"Yes, darling; but I will tell you my story," and she began as they rode along, her voice sweet and plaintive.

Milly sighed many times, and kissed her fair companion during the time. Her childish nature was touched deeply by the story, and now that they were once more together she clung to our heroine with all the gentle love of her affectionate nature.

"Nothing shall ever part us again," she said.

"I hope not, love," replied Grace.

How little they knew of the terrible calamity that hung above their young heads by a mere thread—a thread that would soon give way, and as it broke sunder their re-united happiness, part them, and leave each desolate.

They thought not now of danger; they were happy with each other, and with the crescent moon shedding its luminous rays along their path to light them on their way, they, with buoyant hearts and brighter hopes than they had ever dared to think of since they were parted, continued their journey.

The rattle of wheels and the clatter of horses were heard in the distance coming down the road.

Grace heeded not the sound; she had almost forgotten the life she had been pursuing, but she was suddenly startled as the out-riders thundered past her.

Her horse, too, was startled, and pranced about in a frightened manner.

A shouting then arose, and a body of guards galloping down the road demanded her to draw her horse aside to let the royal carriage pass.

Grace exerted all her strength to do their bidding, but her steed was totally unmanage-able, and as the royal coach came dashing along the road the timid animal plunged madly amongst the royal horses, causing much confusion, and giving the royal personage a great shock.

The scene, in less than a minute, became one of terrible confusion.

The timid animals of the royal carriage were so startled by the sudden interruption that they all took fright; the postillions were thrown, and the spirited animals plunged madly to break from their bonds.

The carriage was overturned, and George, King of Great Britain, bawled lustily in bad English for assistance.

The guards came tearing back; our heroine was unceremoniously torn from her saddle, and her horse was run through the body by one of the soldier's swords, to stop its further pranks.

His majesty, after being assisted from his dilemma, sneaked like an old porpoise towards the bewildered girls, and after quizzing them, and muttering some incomprehensible German dialect, ejaculated—

"Eh! what a highwayman! Gad-zooks, sirrah, you shall be taught better manners than upsetting your king's guards. Guards, seize this highwayman."

The guards came swarming round our heroine.

"Sire," she said, in a tremulous voice, "the fault was not mine; the horse I ride was un-manageable, and I hope your majesty will pardon me for being an innocent disturber of your peace."

"Eh! what! pardon you!" exclaimed his majesty, casting sheepish eyes towards fair Milly. "Gad-zooks! pardon you, a highway-man—Tyburn Dick—the most daring robber on the road. No, sirrah, you'll get no pardon from me. Here, guards, seize him instantly."

"No, no!" implored Milly, clinging to her companion. "No, no, your majesty, he is not a highwayman. For my sake I beseech your pardon."

"Hush, Milly, dear, waste not your breath; his majesty's will be done," said the noble girl, and, kissing Milly, she put her aside, and fold-ing her arms across her heaving breast, she said, in a firm voice—

"Sire, I am at your disposal."

His majesty grinned gleefully, and motion-ing the guards to secure their prisoner, he turned to Milly, and said—

"For your sake, my pretty bird, you will have nothing to fear. I shall take care of you."

"Your majesty had better be careful," said Grace, with terrible calmness, as the soldiers bound her hands behind her, "even a king can get into trouble."

The German blood in the King's veins boiled with suppressed rage, and, without a word, he glared savagely at the daring speaker, and then advanced towards Milly, who shrank back from his touch as she would from the sting of a serpent.

The King, growing desperate, clutched the trembling girl, and thrust her into the carriage.

She struggled to break away from him, and in her desperation bit his hand.

"Egads, you bite," he said, with a slight oath; "your beauty saves your head from the gallows."

The postillions after a time succeeded in quieting the spirited horses, and the royal carriage, with its fair occupant, was rolling furiously towards St. James's Palace, while our noble heroine was being taken a prisoner to Newgate.

CHAPTER LXXIII.

TYBURN DICK TAKES A HAZARDOUS LEAP FOR LIBERTY.

OUR hero's fate seemed inevitable when the shower of bullets that followed his flight fell around him.

But he escaped safe, thanks to the swiftness of his steed, his own alacrity, and to the chain mail he wore next to his breast.

The officers dashed after the flying steed, thinking that their prey was hit for a certainty, and would fall from his horse's back.

But he did not, and Selim soon outstripped her pursuers, leaving them nowhere behind.

Dick laid full length forward on the noble animal's back, with his arms twined around her sleek neck.

The bullets that showered against his form with such terrible force gave him a severe shock, and rendered him powerless for a time, and in that condition clinging desperately to his steed, he was carried to London.

It was not until the maddened condition of the horse, and the helplessness of himself had attracted the attention of the wayfarers, and link-boys, watchmen, and a multitude of the lowest rabble were giving chase to stop the onward course of the spirited animal, that he recovered sufficiently to realize his precarious position, and when he did, and rose in the saddle, a tremendous shouting greeted him.

"You have brought me into a fine mess, certainly," he cogitated.

At that moment Selim reared up on her legs, and then plunged forward.

Two rough, brutal fellows stood in the road to stop her, but they got out of her way, seeing a likelihood of being trampled to the earth, but not before they had recognized our hero, and then they raised a shout of "Highwayman!"

"Tyburn Dick, Tyburn Dick!" was the cry.

"Stop him, stop him! A thousand pounds reward for Tyburn Dick!"

"Well, certainly," muttered Dick, "this is cheerful. Dash away, lass. Go, my beauty! Get out of this."

Selim, though going a terrific speed, pricked up her ears, and suddenly rising from the ground she went along with the swiftness of the wind, leaving the pursuing rabble yelling and shouting in the rear, and dashing through all who were brought out to bar her way by the others' cries.

On, on she went, dashing through the dark and narrow streets, passing everything in her course like a fleeting arrow.

Dick drew her in a bit when he had got a respectful distance from his pursuers, so that she should not excite the suspicion of any one else. He felt that he had had sufficient chasing for one night.

What is so exciting, so exhilarating, so delightful, and so inspiring as the life of a highwayman, when he is pursued, not only by his enemies, but by people who join in the hunt for its pleasure, for they ever find pleasure in hunting down one of their own fellow-creatures!

Then it is, when one is pursued like that—when, after you have been dodging about to elude them, and fancy that you are again safe, and cooling down from the excitement, you are turning a corner, and suddenly come face to face with the whole of your foes—then it is that you find the excitement—then, when the blood rises like fountains of liquid fire, gushes through your veins, and sets in rapid motion every nerve in your body, you feel energetic, defying, and endowed with the strength of a lion, and the ferocity of a tiger.

You turn, face your foes, and defiantly dare them to follow you. A burst of triumphant laughter, and a "Hurrah for the road!" breaks from your lips. Taking one sweeping bound you are free.

You seem as though carried through the air in a delicious delirium. Every sense is enthralled with wild joy and excitement.

There was not another knight of the road such a lover of the daring, adventurous, roving life as was our hero.

But for one night he had had enough.

Enough was as good as a feast, but he was compelled to feast on more than enough, and now that he had a few minutes' peace, he began to reflect upon the course he had best pursue.

"Firstly," he began,—throwing the reins on Selim's neck, and telling her to gallop at her own pace—"firstly, as I said before—Dick, old boy, before I begin, I may as well remind you that it will be no good of you to get out of temper with your own reflections, so go on."

Now he paused, rubbed his forehead reflectively, looked behind him, and then began his cogitation.

"Dick, my boy," he began, "you had a narrow escape from the Leopard Inn; but thanks to the impenetrable armour you wear, none of the leaden marbles entered your graceful body, or you would not be riding here now, and your disappearance would be a great loss to the ladies; therefore we cannot spare you for the hulks just yet. But what the devil am I jabbering about? Let me see. That hateful swine of a brother—cuss him! I should like to have my sword through his pampered carcase; I guess I would make short work of him, the infernal villain! I wonder whether he has captured my dear Grace. If he has—if he has—don't get out of temper, Dick—but if he has, may the curse of heaven and the blight of hell wither his soul!

"Should he have captured her and exposed her to any insults, nothing shall save him from my vengeance, that shall fall upon him sure and quick—a vengeance terrible, that will for ever exterminate every trace of his existence, leaving nothing that will recall his remembrance—nothing by which his fate can be traced—so sure shall be my work.

"Come, Dick—come, Dick"—he spoke out in an altered tone, his countenance changing from its fiendish expression, and leaving it half gay, half sad—"your best course will be to hasten to Aldervale Manor, that being the most likely place he would take her to. Aha! that has recalled something to my mind—Jonathan Wild's plot, cuss him! Wonder where the old thief is, he has not troubled me lately; perhaps he's had a bellyful of the 'iron room.' Perhaps he has, and perhaps he ain't got out of it since I left him. All the better if he ain't. Won't trouble me any more; but that's not what I was talking about. Let's go back to the topic of which we were conversing.

"Wild's plot; that's the thing. My unnatural, my fiendish mother, wants to get me out of the way. I'll go and see her—that's the idea—go and astonish her."

Dick here became thoughtful; his head dropped into his hand, and for a few moments he was abstracted in deep reverie.

"How I hate him!" Dick suddenly broke out, with bitter vehemence of voice. "The thought is maddening to think that I should be cheated out of my rights by a dastardly wretch like him, and the tenderness of a mother's love, that ought to be mine, is lavished on a bastard. By Heaven! I cannot stand it. They have had their sway long enough, and now I will stop it. No longer will I be kept out of my own by a wanton mother and a bastard brother. I will denounce them; the world shall know that I, Tyburn Dick, the notorious highwayman, am the lawful heir of Aldervale Manor and estates; let those who will deny my claims, and they shall see that even an outlaw has power; but," he added, in a grave tone, "there is one thing wanting—the certificate of my birth. I will have it!" he exclaimed with sudden energy. "Why should I stand at scruples? She has shown me no mercy; and, by Heaven! I will force her, mother as she is, to reveal the secret of my birth, or her death shall pay for her treachery!

"I will to Cornwall without further delay. Come, Selim, my beauty, you must bear your master some distance on the road before we think of rest. I shall not rest until I have accomplished my plans. Away, lass, I think we have a clear road now; we have nothing more to fear from our foes—we shall hear no more of them until we return. Away, lass!"

He gathered up the reins, sat firmly in the saddle, and prepared for his journey.

His faithful steed, always obedient and untiring, swept gracefully over the ground; but they were destined not to proceed far without fresh danger.

He was just turning out of Fleet-street when a horseman came dashing down Holborn, and as he passed our hero, he ejaculated—

"The captain!"

Dick recognised the voice.

"Duke!" he said.

"Turn," shouted the other, still dashing onwards, "or you will run into the lion's jaws."

Dick pulled up Selim, and stood irresolute; but seeing a troop of cavalry thundering towards him, he turned, and followed his comrade.

"Your horse seems fatigued," he remarked, keeping pace with the highwayman fugitive.

"She musn't give in just yet."

"How long have you been at this? You seem worn."

"Three hours."

"Your horse had a stiff run."

"Yes; and I feel pretty stiff, too; the brutes are a mark on me."

"Why is that?"

"Can't imagine; but they have been at this sort of thing for more than a week."

"They imagine you to be one of the enemy's scouts."

"Do they? I wish they would imagine somebody else to be a scout, now; I have had enough of it."

"They find it capital exercise."

"No doubt; I don't."

"It keeps them in practice."

"So it does me."

"You don't seem to like it."

"Try it, and see how you like it."

"I have just had a run."

"Have another to keep me company," suggested Devil Duke.

"I see every prospect of doing so," replied Dick.

"That's the thing."

"Is it?"

"Yes. It ain't right that one fellow should be hunted alone. The devils are gaining upon us."

A shouting from a cracked-voiced old sergeant for them to surrender fully substantiated Duke's remark, and putting their horses to speed, they got a safe distance from their dangerous companions.

"I had just started," said Dick, "for Cornwall."

"I had started for Cornwall, too, but had to turn on suddenly coming in contact with some of my old friends."

"I wish you had taken another route."

"Why?"

"I shouldn't then have met you."

"That's kind; you can go back."

"Thank you; you need not be spiteful."

"I ain't."

"Give me your hand."

Duke grasped his young leader's hand affectionately.

"I am tired and sore," he said, "and when a fellow's tired, without being sore, he always has a tendency more or less to be savage."

"I felt savage a little time ago, but I found on reflection that the idea was absurd, so I banished my savage ferocity for a *time when it will be useful.*"

Dick spoke the last few words in such a strange tone, that it caused Duke to look at him bewildered.

"Our pursuers," said Tyburn Dick, "are rather quiet."

"All the more dangerous for that."

"I had a narrow escape this evening."

"So had I."

"What was your escape?"

"Something miraculous."

"Let's hear it."

"As I before said," began Duke, "the brutes have followed me about for more than a week, but every night up to to-night I have either outstripped them or they have given up the chase, and so I have had an opportunity of putting up for a rest.

"Last night I put up at a little inn, and early this morning I was awoke by a tremendous hammering at the door. I got up, looked out of the window, and to my amazement was greeted by a shout of recognition from my pursuers. I drew my head in just in time to save it from being perforated by a shower of bullets that came crashing through the window.

"The greeting was rather warm, so I thought the quicker I made my exit from the little den the better. I scrambled on my clothes, and going to the back of the house jumped out of the window, which was ten feet from the ground. I had barely landed when four soldiers rushed upon me; I quickly disposed of them by throwing two, and nearly strangling the others. I then broke into the stable, jumped into the saddle of Rosebud, who was ready for me, and dashed away. My flight was followed by a shower of bullets, some of which carried away the feathers from my cap, and two of my favourite curls. My head, fortunately was left untouched, but my cap, as you see, was made a perfect sieve of."

He took off his cap, and held it up. The grey streaks of morn was just peeping forth, and our hero was enabled to see perhaps about a dozen bullet-holes in his comrade's cap.

"Your head must be infernally thick," said Dick.

"Why?" asked Duke.

"For the bullets to hit it and bound away without you feeling it."

Duke laughed.

"Tell me your escape," he said.

"I escaped from the Leopard Inn. Selim leaped over the gates, and, as she took the leap, about fifty bullets came showering around and against me like hailstones."

"Did any hit you?"

"They flattened against me like a lot of boiled peas."

"Didn't it hurt you?"

"No."

"Your head must be infernally soft."

"Why?"

"For the bullets to stick in without you feeling it."

Duke laughed good humouredly.

"Not bad, Duke," he said.

"I thought so," exclaimed Duke, as a detachment of the Guards met them in Cheapside.

"Surrender!" demanded the officer in command.

"Never!" answered Duke, boldly. "Adieu, captain; we shall meet at Cornwall."

"Adieu!" said Dick.

They hastily exchanged a grip of the hand and parted.

Devil Duke struck off towards Holloway, with the soldiers after him, and Dick turned towards London Bridge.

He had got to about the middle when suddenly there appeared at either end a group of watchmen and officers.

"I have fallen into another delightful trap," muttered our hero, between his teeth, and his hand clasped the hilt of his sword. "Shall I fight my way through? No, I can't afford to hazard my life like that; I must jump it. Now, Selim, my beauty."

He drew her back and plunged his heels into her flanks.

The black mare rose like a bird—the leap was taken.

The men rushed forward, pistols in hand, as they saw the daring act.

They fired as horse and rider disappeared over the parapet. The hazardous leap for liberty was taken, and as the men crowded to the side of the bridge to see the effect of their firing, our hero and the beautiful Arabian steed sank beneath the filthy surging water of the Thames.

CHAPTER LXXIV.

OUR HEROINE HAS AN OFFER OF ESCAPE.

ALONE with her saddening thoughts.

Alone in sorrow and solitude sat our heroine in a gloomy cell of Newgate.

Heavy iron manacles bound her delicate limbs.

The officials had secured her in such a way as to baffle any attempt of escape that she might make. An iron girdle encircled her slender waist, to which was fastened five chains; at the end of each of four was an iron circlet—two secured her wrists, and the others clasped her ankles—the fifth chain was fastened to a ring in the stone floor, and kept her stationary.

At her side was a wooden bench, on which stood a jug of cold water and a loaf of dry bread.

It remained untouched just where the gaoler had put it.

Grace sat on a low stool, her pretty face downcast and sorrowful. Her brow was resting in her tiny white hand; she was in a deep, sad reverie. Her thoughts wandered back to earlier scenes and happy days of her childhood, when she knew no grief, when her heart was free, and she knew no care.

She could have borne anything, no matter how perilous, while free; but to be confined in that gloomy cell, shut from the world, from those most dear to her, crushed her daring spirit and left her desolate.

Her humid blue eyes were dimmed with tears as she raised her head and cast a desparing look around her dreary prison. The gloomy walls seemed to loom out in sombre shadows of some terrible impending calamity.

She shuddered as she thought of the danger she had got herself into by personating the character of Tyburn Dick, still, if her identity was not discovered she would not own it; and she nobly resigned herself to die on the scaffold instead of her lover.

Her daring, defiant nature was quelled by her present helpless position, and without a murmur she gave herself up to the fate that seemed so inevitable.

"I could die happy," she sighed, "if I knew that he was safe; it would be hard to sacrifice myself if he is in danger and suffers too."

A thrill shook her frame at the thought, and putting the brown stone jug to her lips, she took a draught of water.

"I should like to have seen Milly before I died," she murmured. "Fate seems terribly against me. It was very hard that she should have been taken from me so soon after I saved her from those brutes. Poor dear girl," she continued, in a sweet sad voice; "she has endured bitter trials. I would that I could save her from her royal persecutor; but no, I suppose my destiny is so fated that we are not to meet again."

A mist gathered before her eyes, and two tears like glistening gems trickled down her pale cheeks, and then she sang a sweet sad song, her voice low and plaintive.

Her song ceased, and her head once more sank into her hand.

She had not seen the bricks that were taken out of the wall, and left an aperture large enough for a man to get through, so noiselessly did the prisoner of the cell adjoining her accomplish his work.

A head appeared half way through the aperture, and the owner of the head was about to say something when our heroine's cell-door was opened, and the gaoler entered.

Grace looked up, her pretty eyes swimming in tears.

The man advanced towards her respectfully; he was wiping his eyes with his handkerchief.

He looked steadily at our heroine in silence for a few moments, and then, in a husky voice, said—

"Are you Tyburn Dick?"

"Why do you ask?" inquired our heroine, with a sad smile.

"Because I don't think you are. At least, if you are, you ain't a man."

"What makes you think that?"

"The song I heard you sing."

"Was there anything particular in the song that should make you think that I am not a man?"

"Well, yes."

"What was it?"

"Why, you sang about your noble lover, and so on."

"Don't men sing about noble lovers?"

"Not like you did; besides, your voice was so pretty, and sounded so beautiful. I very well know no man has a voice like that. Why, it was so sweet, and the words of your song were so delightful, that it brought tears in my eyes."

"Do you think my voice is too sweet and pretty to be a man's?"

"Yes, I do; and you are altogether different to the person I have before had in my charge for Tyburn Dick."

"If you talk in that way," she said, "you will make me vain."

"Look here," said the gaoler, impressively "I have taken a liking to you; it don't matter a button to me whether you are a man or woman, but you are too good to be here; so if you like I will set you free."

DEVIL DUKE ARRESTED BY THE SLEEP-WALKER.

"What!" exclaimed Grace, with a start; "set me free?"

"At the peril of my life," replied the man, earnestly.

"No," answered the noble girl. "It shall never be said that I, to save my own neck, risked the life of a true, honest man. I thank you, from the bottom of my heart, for your generous offer, but I will not flee from danger."

"You won't!" said the man, in astonishment. "You will be hung, as sure as fate, if you don't accept of my offer."

Grace was silent. Her head bowed low, and her bosom heaved with emotion.

"Come, consider," the man said, kindly; "think what a fearful thing it would be for one so young, so beautiful as you are, to be dragged out with more brutality than would be shown to a mad dog—dragged forth to an ignominious death—a death shameful to the lowest extremity. Accept of my offer, you must be freed from here. It is my duty to assist you in every way to escape, at the peril of my life."

Grace looked up, surprised.

The speaker met her steady gaze with a frank, thoughtful look.

He was a young man, with an open, handsome countenance. His form was lithe, muscular, and graceful.

Grace kept her eyes fixed upon him, as though trying to recall to her mind where she had before seen that face.

"Why are you so interested in my fate?" she inquired.

"Because it is my duty."

"I presume your duty is to guard the prisoners against escaping."

"I am here, my lady——"

Grace leaped from the ground with astonishment at the words "my lady." She looked confounded, and her pretty cheeks changed as many colours as there are hues in the rainbow.

She was not the only one the words of the gaoler astonished; the face at the aperture in the wall wore an expression of bewilderment.

"I am here," he continued, with a quiet smile of satisfaction at the effect his words had upon his prisoner, "to guard against danger, and set at liberty those to whom I am leagued by an oath."

"Who are you, then?"

"That I am not at liberty to say. But you must escape from this accursed den."

"No, no," said Grace; "let me at least face my danger."

"Why do you wish to peril your life? If you are here by the time another sun rises your fate will be inevitable."

"I have my trial."

"A mere mockery."

"However, the prisoner is allowed to speak, and I may prove that I am not guilty."

"Your evidence would not be listened to, especially as you are in that costume, and represent the most celebrated highwayman on the road, for whose apprehension there is offered a thousand pounds. Why, the very fact that you wear Tyburn Dick's dress is enough to condemn you, without anything else. The only path open to you for life and liberty is to accept the offer I made, and escape without further delay."

"Never!" answered Grace, firmly.

"You cannot be aware of your danger."

"Perfectly aware of it."

"You will receive no mercy at your trial."

"I must take my chance."

"You had better take your liberty while you have a chance."

"No. Leave me; your persuasions are useless."

The man turned away with a sigh.

"You may change your mind by the time I return," he said, standing at the door of the cell. "Think over what I said, my lady; you will never have another chance like it. Consider the imminent danger you stand in, and the risk you incur to your life by refusing."

"Go—leave me," said the fair prisoner, waving her hand impatiently.

The man retired with a last, long, sorrowful look at that beautiful form, sitting there alone in solitude and sadness.

The door closed with a grating sound. Grace sprang up with a start. She felt that the only ray of hope that did exist was now gone from her, and she inwardly wished that her visitor had stayed.

"Well, may I be stuck in a rack to be laughed at!" said a voice that proceeded from the hole in the wall.

Our heroine looked round rather astonished at the sound.

"Well, if ever I saw such a thing as a fellow to refuse to go from prison!" By the Lord Harry, I wish he would give me an offer!"

"Who and where are you?" exclaimed Grace, a little startled by the voice that sounded so near to her. She looked round again, but she saw no one.

"Here, captain."

Grace this time looked in the right direction, and saw the face at the aperture.

"How do you do?" and the head nodded in recognition.

A sad smile passed over the fair girl's face at the comic effect of the other's face.

"Duke!" said Grace, recognising the frank, handsome face.

"Yes, my lady."

"What were you brought here for?"

"Nothing, my lady. A lot of selfish

soldiers who had been chasing me for more than a week, brought me here, because they said I looked tired and wanted a rest. I did, but not here."

"Did you see anything of your captain in your week's ride?"

"Yes, my lady; he was with me on the night of my capture."

"Was he pursued?"

"No, my lady; I was."

"Then he is safe?"

"He was when he left me."

"Thank Heaven! that is one burden off my mind," murmured the beautiful girl. "Do you know where he intended to go when he left?"

"He said he would see me at the haunt. At present I don't see much possibility of it."

"Then he has returned to Cornwall?"

"I believe so, my lady. I wish I had too."

"Surely, Duke, you do not despair?"

"My nature is void of the cowardly malady," replied the daring highwayman. "I know no fear, but I certainly don't like the idea of being shut up here. The open heath would be more welcome. I only wish I had the offer of liberty you had. Are you tired of your life, my lady, or are you fond of the gloomy desolation of a prison?"

Grace was startled by the question. It was put so direct and in such a tone of bitter reproachfulness.

"Why do you ask such a question?" she inquired.

"I heard you refuse an offer of freedom, so I instantly inferred that you must be tired of existence and the outward world."

"I am tired of neither," replied the proud girl, rather sternly, "but I do not wish for freedom."

"Why not?"

"Were I to escape, it would only cause a fresh pursuit, and perhaps your chieftain might be captured. Sooner than he should suffer, I would suffer twenty deaths, were it possible!"

"If he thought your resolutions were so formed he would instantly give himself up."

As Duke finished his sentence the cell-door was opened and the gaoler entered; he looked curiously around, but he saw nothing of the highwayman. Duke's head had disappeared, and the aperture was filled up with bricks.

"I have come to set you free, my lady," said the young man respectfully.

"But I told you my resolutions were made. I will not leave this cell."

The gaoler produced a bunch of keys, evidently taking no heed of what our heroine said.

"Allow me," he said, "to unfasten these manacles."

"Who are you?" asked Grace. "I remember your face."

"You will know," he said, throwing off a wig, and letting his own rich brown curls fall in clusters around his white broad brow. "Do you recognise me? Ralph—Dashing Ralph, I am called by my comrades—your devoted servant."

"Ralph, my dear boy!" shouted a voice. The bricks tumbled out of the wall, and Duke's head appeared through the hole. "Ralph, comrade, is that you?"

"Hush! Duke," said the disguised highwayman.

"By the Lord Harry, here's a delightful surprise! Come and set me free, old boy. I can't get further than this; my feet are chained to the floor."

"Presently, comrade; and in the meantime keep quiet, while we set our queen free. You will escape now," he said, turning to Grace.

"Was it your chief's wish that I was to escape?"

"It was, my lady."

"Then hasten to unfasten these irons."

Ralph undid four. Her arms and legs were free, and the highwayman gaoler was upon his knees trying to unfasten the chain that held his young queen to the prison-floor, when he heard a shout that made him recoil with horror.

"Treachery, by Heaven!" shouted one of the gaolers, who dashed into the cell.

"Shoot him!" yelled another.

The faithful fellow turned with a horrified look of despair on his face—turned in time to meet the line of deadly weapons that were presented at his head.

CHAPTER LXXV.

THE COUNTESS ALDERVALE FRUSTRATED BY THE SUDDEN INTERVENTION OF CAPTAIN CLAUDE — TYBURN DICK SAVED FROM A TERRIBLE FATE.

THE moon was shining out pale and clear, like a silver crescent in the drifting clouds, and its brilliant light fell full upon the figure of a young and singularly handsome man.

He stood at the door of a little wayside inn on the road to Cornwall. He was tapping his foot impatiently on the step, and his gaze now and then wandered to the stable gates.

"How long is the confounded fellow going to be?" he muttered.

Just then the stable gates were thrown open, and a sleepy ostler came shuffling out, leading by the bridle a splendid black mare.

"Come, Selim, my beauty!" cried the impatient young gentleman.

The horse answered him by a whinny, and leaped towards him, leaving the ostler on his face shouting for help.

The pitiful cries of the ostler rather amused the young horseman. He laughed merrily, and vaulting into the saddle, he gave the fellow a smart cut with his whip and rode away.

His form had barely faded in the distance, when a tall, fair, and not unhandsome youth crept from the inn, more like a thief than a gentleman, which he was by the costly dress he wore.

"So," he muttered between his teeth, "the Boy Highwayman escaped after all, and is now making his way to Aldervale Manor. Fool!" he hissed, with concentrated rage. "Does he think his lying tale will be heard? Ha, ha, ha! Why, my mother will put him out of the way. She has been waiting for this chance some time. Ha! he returns."

The speaker, Lord Edward Aldervale, crouched back, and hid beneath the shadow of a clump of trees.

He had said rightly. The young horseman was returning, speeding back to the inn with the utmost fleetness of the steed.

"Landlord!" he shouted, pulling up at the door. "Landlord! What ho, there! Within!"

The landlord made his appearance.

"What is it?" he asked, gruffly.

"I have left my pistols in the parlour."

The worthy landlord grunted, and went in.

The young horseman thought he heard a slight noise. He turned sharply. There was a rustle amongst some leaves. He drew a pistol, and pointed in the direction.

"I don't think I am mistaken," he muttered. "It isn't very often Tyburn Dick is deceived."

A ray of light that just then fell upon his features showed that the speaker was our hero.

"However, before I fire," he continued, "let me listen. I don't want to waste shot."

At that moment my host of the wayside inn made his appearance with Dick's sword.

Our hero was again on his way to Aldervale Manor. He had not proceeded far before the cowardly young earl crept from his hiding place. He looked after the retreating form of his wronged brother with a cruel cynical expression in his eyes — a pistol was in his murderous hand.

"I think now I have a favourable opportunity of ridding the world of one thief, at least, and myself of a bitter enemy."

While speaking he was following our hero with the noiseless glide of a serpent.

Dick suddenly drew up, and cast a suspicious look behind him. The evil-minded young earl took advantage of the darkness, and bounded up a tree.

Dick thought he saw a dark form in the distance.

"I don't like people who sneak about in the dark," he muttered; "I should like to see his face."

He rode back rapidly, but the dark form was gone — gone like the shadow of evil that it was.

But Dick was not satisfied; he felt that danger was near. He was passing along under the drooping branches of a large oak tree when he heard a click.

A click of a pistol, as if being cocked.

He was on the alert, and giving Selim a dig with his heels, she bounded forward, but not before the treacherous young villain had fired.

The sudden report in so lonely a place and at such a time frightened our hero's steed she made a fearful plunge, and darted off.

Fortunately the ball did not strike Tyburn Dick; it hit the saddle, and glided off.

The maddened plunging of the frightened steed threw Dick as he moved to avoid the shot.

His feet got entangled in the stirrups, and for some distance he was dragged along the ground.

Lord Edward Aldervale chuckled with triumph when he saw the effect the shot had taken, and going back to the inn, he ordered his horse to be got ready for him to start for Aldervale Manor.

Our hero was dragged along totally at the mercy of his steed; all he could do could not stop her.

On, on she went, totally unmanageable, heeding not the cries that at any other time would have brought her to him through the thickest of danger.

Dick's only fear was that her iron hoofs might strike his head. He could bear the pain caused by being dragged over the stubble fields, but the thought of her hoof coming against his head gave him more pain than he had ever endured.

At last she stopped.

A tall majestic form—a form beautiful because of its statuesque symmetry, stood motionless and with outstretched arms before her.

The horse did not attempt to pass him; she came to a sudden standstill, and looked at him as though she knew she had done wrong.

"Why, Selim," said the stranger, in a deep mellow voice, "what have you been doing?"

She whinnied, and turned her head to see how fared her gallant young rider.

Dick had extricated his feet, but had not strength to rise. The shaking he had received had weakened him.

The stranger went to him and raised him in his muscular arm. He held the brave boy to his breast, and looking tenderly into his haggard face, tried to speak, but emotion choked his utterance.

"Bullskin!" said Dick, faintly, recognising his kind preserver.

"Dick, my dear boy!" exclaimed the faithful fellow, in a voice choked with glad emotion—"Dick, tell me are you hurt? How did this happen? What has arrived?"

"Some treacherous brute fired at me from a tree," he answered.

"Did the bullet hit you?" eagerly inquired Joseph Munroe.

"No; the report startled Selim, and I was thrown."

"Then you were not hit?"

"I had a narrow escape; the shot struck the saddle."

"Thank Providence it is no worse. How far have you been brought along the ground?"

"Goodness knows. It seemed an endless distance; the brute has given me an awful shaking."

"We had better return to an inn. I have much to tell you."

"I want to go to Aldervale Manor."

"You can't go like this."

"When once we're in the saddle I shall be all right."

"Surely you do not wish to part so soon? There is time enough to go to the manor."

"I must not delay a moment."

"Why, is your commission so urgent?"

"It is, or I would not part with you just yet."

"May I ask the nature of it?"

"That cursed villain, my dastardly brother, has taken Grace from me, and I think he has carried her to the manor."

"And that is the only reason for your visit?"

"Is not that enough?"

"Truly; but I think I can enlighten your mind upon that subject."

"How?" queried Dick, eagerly.

"I have seen the Earl of Aldervale about here."

"About here?"

"Even so."

"Alone?"

"He appeared to be."

"Can you give me any idea as to which way he went?"

"I watched him, for I thought his presence boded no good."

"Yes," broke in our
you see where he went

"To an inn down the road."

"The very inn from where I set out to-night."

Bullskin looked surprised.

"Then," said Dick, "his was the hand that fired that cowardly shot."

"Probably; but did you see him?"

"No; but he might have seen me."

"If you are able we will proceed to the inn; it is likely we may see him there."

"If we should we'll pay him for that cowardly shot."

He mounted the saddle with the assistance of his faithful follower, and returned to the inn. Big Bullskin walked by the side of the horse's head.

The part in which the little inn was situated was very lonely, and had a bad repute for being infested with highwaymen; so he had but few customers of a night, as people were frightened to venture out after dark. He made our friends welcome, and showed them into a snug little parlour.

"What have you got in the larder, mine host?" asked Dick.

"Well, your honour," replied the man, rubbing his hands together, "you see, as we don't have many customers, we don't keep much in stock, but I have got some very nice venison, some game, and some ham."

"Bring up the venison and some good old wine," Dick said.

"Yes, your honour;" and away the landlord trotted.

"Hi!" shouted Dick.

The landlord returned.

"You had a gentleman staying here. He was here this evening."

The man looked curiously at the interrogator.

"Which room does he occupy?" Dick thought by putting the question direct that it would throw him off his guard, if he had any intention of playing false.

"He was here, and he occupied the room next to yours," replied the man, truthfully; "but he left soon after you went the first time, and I didn't see any more of him until half an hour after you returned for your sword, and then he paid his score and rode away."

"Thanks," said Dick. "Bring up something to eat."

"Then you may depend upon it," Dick said, turning to Bullskin as the man left the room, "the infernal cur has gone home."

"Undoubtedly; and since you learned that he was alone, you have nothing to fear for the safety of Grace."

"From him I have not, but I don't know who else may have taken her."

"You have little to fear for her safety. She is a brave girl, and well capable of defending herself."

"True," answered Dick, his face flushing with admiration as he thought of her bravery.

Here mine host entered with a substantial meal.

Our hero and his gigantic companion soon made a decrease in the bulk of venison, and while discussing the crusted old wine, they discussed a few matters concerning their comrades.

"You have not seen any of the captains?" inquired Dick, awfully surprised.

"None," replied Bullskin, sadly; "even our gallant young friend—Victor St. James—I have not seen or heard anything of him. He departed with Duke and Ralph to go to London. There is some evil work going on, or they would not have deserted us in this manner."

"It must be seen into," said Dick, very much troubled. "I would not lose one of those brave fellows for the wealth of the world. I am glad we have met, and now I am here we must inquire into their disappearance."

"I have inquired, and searched Cornwall through, but not a trace of them could I find. My only fears are that they have been entrapped by some hidden agency, and secretly disposed of."

"If such is the case." said Dick, his cheeks blanching at the very idea of such a thing, "there shall be a terrible disturbance through the land."

His words spoke a fearful meaning.

He was calm, and his calmness was always dangerous.

"The earth shall be ransacked!" he continued, speaking steadily. "The ravages of pirates and brigands of old, when they us'd to invade and take colonies, shall be nothing to equal my vengeance! At an hour's notice, Munroe, I can demand thousands of sturdy resolute men who would gladly join us in such an enterprise, and while we have such a stronghold of wealth as we have, we need not fear about succeeding in the undertaking. We have enough to bring half the nation did we want it, and as surely as there is a God above, if our comrades are not found within three days from this, my resolve shall be carried into execution!"

"And now," put in Big Bullskin, seeing that his young chief was getting terribly excited, "the best thing to do before we proceed any further will be for you to retire to rest for the night."

"No, Munroe," answered the boy, firmly; "there is no rest for me while our comrades are missing. How know we that they may not be, even now, suffering torture too fearful to contemplate? You, I am sure, would not wish for rest at such a time."

"I do not," replied the faithful fellow. "I speak for you; you require rest."

"I could not sleep in peace. The thought of these noble fellows being in danger would torture me worse than the tortures of hell."

"It is too late to go anywhere to-night," urged Bullskin.

"It is not."

"Where would you go at such an hour?"

"To Aldervale Manor, to claim the certificate of my birth. It is ten o'clock now," he said, looking up at an old-fashioned clock. "I can reach there in an hour and a half."

"The inhabitants may have retired to rest."

"Then they will have to get up."

He rose and called for his horse. Bullskin paid the reckoning, and as Dick mounted, he said—

"I will accompany you."

"With pleasure; but I am in haste, and you have no steed."

"I can get one from here."

Mine host heard the remark, and without a word he went to the stable, and brought a horse round, to the surprise but gratification of Bullskin.

He was in the saddle in a moment, and dropping a few sovereigns into the landlord's hands, rode away with his young chief.

"You will return to the haunt," said Dick; "don't let one of the band leave until I return."

"I will not," replied Bullskin. "Be careful. You know not the treachery of the woman you are going to see."

Dick laughed a sardonic fiendish laugh.

"Don't I?" he said, bitterly. "If I don't know, who should? But fear not; her devilish witchery won't keep me from my purpose."

"Be not too rash, or you may repent afterwards," said Bullskin.

"Repent?" repeated Dick; "what think you I should repent?"

"You know not. With all her faults, she is your mother."

"True," Dick said, sobering down. "Let's change the subject. You have not heard of my last adventure, have you?"

"I have not."

"I suppose you have discovered how dirty my clothes are?"

"Well, I thought they looked strangely dirty for you."

"I haven't much time to relate how it occurred, as you see we are near my destination; but I will tell you the most extraordinary part. I had just escaped from one fearful danger, where I had a perfect storm of bullets showered upon me, and I was riding through London, when I was attacked on London Bridge. I had no way of escape, both ends of the bridge being perfectly blocked up. I knew if I attempted to pass them it would be running into a certain death.

"For a moment I was undecided what to do. The men, seeing that I did not know how to act, made a rush towards me. I then saw I had no chance but one, and that was to make a leap for life. I drew Selim back, and in a moment she had disappeared over the parapet of the bridge.

"A shower of bullets followed me as I sank beneath the surging waters. The sudden shock rendered me half senseless. We were under the water several moments; but, in my delirious state, it appeared like several hours, and when we rose to the surface I saw that the current had carried us some distance from the bridge."

"Selim kept in the middle of the stream until after we passed Blackfriars, and then I took her to the bank, where she made her way as far as Lambeth. Having got clear of my enemies, I made my way to some strange old place of not much account, but it served my purpose. I dried my clothes, had Selim thoroughly attended to, and then set out again; and here I am, after several hard days' journey."

"And delighted I am to see you," said Joseph Munroe. "I think you have gone through the strangest perils and most extraordinary adventures that have ever been heard of. Many people would not credit the truth of them."

Dick laughed.

"The more extraordinary, the more true," he said. "Truth is always more strange than fiction.

His companion assented to the remark.

"You remember the time when I swore to exterminate the Black Band?" asked Bullskin, his colossal face clouded with some sudden thought.

"I do," answered Dick; "the night, you mean, when you commenced your work—the night when the poor farmer was stopped by one of them."

"Yes.

"Well?"

"Well, since then I had been too busy to think any more about it, until one night we found one of our men lying dead at the entrance of the haunt, with a dagger driven into his heart. To the dagger was fastened a piece of parchment, on it was written these words—'the vengeance of the Black Band.'"

"What!" exclaimed the Boy King of the Highwaymen, "one of my faithful band murdered by these wretches?"

"One, only," said Bullskin, quietly. "On that discovery my smothered wrath rose to a fearful pitch. Then and there I set out on a mission of death, leaving the poor fellow's comrades to perform the burial ceremony. I took an oath to have a terrible retribution for his death, and kept my word. Four of our foes I caught, in four succeeding days,

and the four, as I captured them, I laid each at the entrance of their haunt, as they did with the poor fellow with a dagger in his heart."

"It's a fearful thing," said our hero, "that two bands, of the same vocation, should be so terribly at variance; but it is their fault."

He drew Selim up before the large gates of Aldervale Manor

"You won't forget," he said to Munroe; "don't let any of the band leave the haunt before I return."

"They shall not," answered the gigantic fellow, taking his young chief's small white proffered hand.

"Adieu! you will wait, then, until I return?" Dick said.

"Adieu! be careful. I shall be anxious until you return,' he raised his hat, and rode briskly away.

Dick watched him out of sight, and then sat in a moody kind of reverie.

The merry peals of laughter and the low rich strains of music that broke upon his ears roused him from his thoughtful mood.

He looked up with a vacant kind of stare, as though he had forgotten where he was, or the errand he had come on.

A grand festival was being held there in honour of the countess's birthday; and even while our hero sat there on his steed, carriages drove up to the grand entrance, with their fair lovely occupants, and fat old dowagers and dukes who were on their way to join the gay festive gathering.

Dick watched them. As the persons of each carriage alighted at the splendid hall his breast throbbed with the fearful confli that was going on within him.

He was not yet lost to all feeling, though he had endured wrongs enough to turn the heart of any one to stone.

He had gone there resolved to see his inhuman mother, under any circumstances, and demand from her the rights of his birth.

But now he sat undecided; by asking an interview with her he would cause a disturbance, and upset the pleasure of every one for the evening.

He did not wish to do that; and yet why should he turn away from his own domain as though he was a thief, and frightened to enter because people were about?

"No!" he ejaculated, "why should I study the comforts of others? I should not get pity from any who are gathered there, although I am the rightful master of this domain. But that," he continued, "none would believe; and why should they, without I could produce proofs of my claims? The proofs I must and will have."

"But you must get them," said a croaking voice close behind him.

The sound of the voice grated horribly upon his ears. Startled by the sudden interruptions to his cogitations, he turned sharply and his gaze fell upon the crouching form of the Death Witch.

She stood back from the rich flood of light that poured through the casements of the mansion.

The fearful aspect of her form loomed out from the shade like a shadow of evil. Dick thought her presence like an omen of evil, and boded no good to him.

"Why are you here, you unearthly old hag?" said Dick, angrily.

"To warn you, rash boy," replied the fearful being.

"I want not your warning or presence."

"Ha, ha, ha!" she laughed, in such a way that our hero could not repress a cold chill that ran through him. "So you begin to fear me, Tyburn Dick?"

"Fear you? No, you evil old crone, I don't."

"Listen! I have not come to harm you; I come to warn you."

"Of what?"

"Danger."

"Away with you, or, by my sword, I will send you to the devil!"

The old hag waved her wand.

"List!" she said. "You want to see the Countess Aldervale. You will see her. Be on your guard. She will be treacherous, and unless you are careful you will lose your life by her small white hands."

"How know you this?" asked Dick, surprised by the serious tone of the witch.

"Never mind how I know, but heed what I say. Do not be thrown off your guard by any artifice she may try, or you will never

leave there again. Be warned. You will be surprised by a visit from one you long since thought dead. Farewell, Tyburn Dick! What I have told you is no idle fable."

"Hi, stay!" shouted Dick.

But she was gone like a passing shadow, and our hero sat bewildered. He was fearfully impressed by her words.

"A visit from one I long since thought dead!" he muttered. "What the deuce does she mean? I never saw such a strange old being in my life before. Wonder how she knew all this—perhaps it's only fudge. However, as she said, I want to see the countess, and must see her, but how can I do that without disturbing the company? Let me consider."

He cast his gaze upon the ground, as though he thought to see the impress of an idea stamped there.

"I have it!" he exclaimed. "Give a false name, and say I must see the countess privately on an urgent matter."

We cannot say whether he did find the idea on the ground, but it suited his purpose capitally.

He dismounted, put Selim out of the way—that is to say, he put her where she could not be easily found by any one but himself—and altering the aspect of his coat, he boldly walked up to the entrance, where two powdered flunkeys stood like automatons.

Dick looked at the powdered individuals for a few moments, as neither spoke.

He made a step forward.

A padded leg of each of the lacqueys was put out to stop his way.

"Your card of invitation, sir?" said one, putting out his hand.

"I wish to see the countess privately," said our hero.

"Impossible, sir! My lady won't see anybody separately from her guests."

"She will see me."

"I shouldn't like to ask her," said the flunkey.

"Yes, you would," said Dick, at the same time slipping a piece of gold sideways into the man's hand.

"However, I can but see," said the man slipping the piece of gold up his sleeve, so that his companion should not see it.

But his pampered companion did see it, and as he stepped forward to ask the countess to see the strange gentleman, the other stepped after him, and in a whisper said—"Halves."

"Where are you going?" asked our hero of the man who had got the gold piece.

"Going to ask her ladyship to see you, my lord," replied the lacquey.

"Without my name?"

"Beg your pardon, my lord, I didn't think that."

"Tell her Count de Adrian would have an audience with her on urgent business."

"Yes, my lord,"

Away the man went, again trying to avoid his companion.

But his companion was not to be avoided.

"Halves," he said, wishing to impress upon the other's mind that he had seen the quiet tip.

The " other " went on without noticing his companion's remark. Dick's messenger's companion took his post again at the door with a savage frown, and was not over polite to the guests of the Countess of Aldervale who arrived.

Dick's intention was to give him the same amount as he had given the other, but when he saw the greediness of the fellow by following his companion and asking for " halves," he altered his mind, and gave it to the other.

"Her ladyship will see you, my lord, in a few moments," said the messenger, returning. "Come this way, if you please."

Dick followed the flunkey, who conducted him to an ante-room, the window of which looked out into the splendid grounds at the back of the manor.

Our hero availed himself of that little bit of information by surveying the position of the apartment while alone in case of emergency. Then he sat down, and waited for the presence of his cruel mother.

He did not wait long.

He heard her stately tread. The hot blood mounted to his cheeks, and mantled them with a crimson glow, and his breast throbbed with excitement.

The door gently opened, and the beautiful woman entered.

Dick rose, fearfully agitated, and bowed his stately head.

The countess, not at first recognising him, returned the salute by a slight inclination of her proud head and a winning smile, thinking, perhaps, he was a handsome young nobleman whom she could make a toy of.

Dick felt the tears start to his eyes as his gaze wandered over the magnificent form of the woman who stood before him.

With all her cruelty and faults, he felt a yearning towards her, and would have given much had she then taken him to her breast with a truly motherly affection he had never known.

He felt it hard that he should have a mother so beautiful—the only parent living, and the only relative he knew—and yet dared not go near her with anything like affection.

He watched her closely, and saw her start. She turned hastily to leave the room or call for assistance, but he spoke, his voice tremulous and sad.

"Mother," he said, with a sorrowful look upon his handsome face; "excuse the term, but I must call you mother. You are my mother, and mine only. Gladly would I forgive and forget the past I have suffered, if I could but hear you call me son."

He paused—his head dropped into his hand, and a tear glistened between his fingers.

The countess was moved to pity by the grief of the gallant youth. Her soft blue eyes filled with a moisture, and she went slowly towards him. Her tiny hand rested on his shoulder.

Dick started, and looked inquiringly into her face.

For a moment her gaze met his. Then her head drooped. She could not look into that handsome honest face, so full of grief and sorrow, knowing that she was the cause of all.

"Mother!" exclaimed Dick, with a sudden energy—"mother, speak to me! Mother call me son! Oh, that I could hear those words from your lips! I would sacrifice all —everything I hold most dear—could I but know I had a mother's love."

The countess looked into his pleading face, and her hands sought and locked firmly in his.

"Tell me, mother," Dick went on; "speak but one word. Am I not your son?"

She could not speak, but she assented by a nod.

Dick, in ecstasies, drew her palpitating heart, kissed her velvet cheek, and held her to him as though never to part with her again.

And she, overcome by the elegant youth's sad, pleading face, and his sweet, musical, plaintive voice, sank upon his heaving breast, and sobbed bitterly.

Our hero's joy was unbounded. He had never known such a boon of gladness in his whole life. He was acknowledged by the proud, lovely Countess of Aldervale as her son, and in her he had found a mother, and with her a mother's love—a thing he had never known from his earliest childhood— and now he was happy.

The countess, too, was happy—happy because she held to her breast her rightful child, and she felt the natural love for him she had never known for the other.

She kissed our hero in the tenderest manner, and her beautiful arms clung affectionately round his neck.

They stood locked in each other's arms, forgetting everything for the time, and caring only for the love of each other.

The picture was perfect.

Never could there have been a scene of more happiness than there was there. Mother and son, after years of bitter variance, united. The long pent-up love of each flowed now in one rich deep vale, blending the hearts to harmonize with each other.

The countess kept Dick's head resting on her soft white shoulder, and her tiny hand was laid upon his noble brow.

She pictured to herself the two youths, the one she had hitherto cherished and nestled to her breast, and the one she held now. She pictured them as they were, and she could see them as she had seen them when in strife, and she drew the contrast.

The bold, fearless disposition of our hero, his elegant form, his generous nature, and his frank, handsome face.

Then she drew the other in her mind's eye —his tall slender figure, the treacherous, livid, lurking countenance, and his base, cowardly disposition; and as she thought of it

she severely reproached herself for the wrongs and sufferings she had caused her own true noble boy.

"My darling boy," she murmured, and she drew his face to hers; "you have suffered fearfully, but not wholly through me. I have been tempted to do what I did, and never any happiness I knew but now. Now that I have once more got you to my heart, nothing on earth shall take you from me again."

She broke into tears, and held our hero so firmly in her arms that he had to draw hard for breath.

"Let the past be forgotten" said Dick.

"Forgotten?" the countess repeated. "Can you, my dear boy, forget the cruelty you have suffered, and through me?"

"I do forget," said Dick. "It is enough for me to know that I have got a mother and a mother's love; that alone would pay for doubly what I have suffered.

"And can you forgive me?"

"Willingly, mother. Never mention the subject again."

"My brave, generous boy, I know now what a mother can feel for her *own!*"

She looked at Dick with that devoted fondness of a mother when she unexpectedly sees one of her children who, perhaps, has been abroad for many years.

The countess, while gazing at Dick, thought there was not another like him in the world.

How long was she to maintain that thought?

How long were they thus to be happy?

Alas! their happiness was but a dream—a dream from which they would soon awake, and find themselves sundered as far apart as ever.

But why should it be so?

The presence of the charming countess was missed from among the revellers, and one of them was raising a storm—a storm which would soon break over the heads of the countess and our hero with mighty power.

"You will leave that terrible life you lead?" said the countess.

"If you wish it," said Dick.

"I do, and you must never more be seen with these men.'

Dick started, and as the door was suddenly thrown open Lord Edward Aldervale hastily entered, but he stopped in the middle of the room, and stood staring in dumb amazement at the scene that met his gaze.

"What means this?" demanded Edward, his face turning an ashy paleness.

"The meaning is exactly what you see," said our hero. "I am restored to a mother."

"The Countess Aldervale the mother of a highwayman! Liar, I will ram these words down your throat at the point of my sword."

"Base slave, draw and defend thyself!" thundered Dick. Putting the countess aside, he leaped forward, and drew his sword.

Lord Edward made a furious cut for his head. Dick's weapon was raised and caught the blow, and he returned a lunge with deadly fury. His mother stepped back as the gleaming weapon darted forward like a meteor.

"One of us shall fall," said Dick.

"No, no! Why do you fight? Can't two brothers live without so much quarrelling?" the countess said.

"Brother!" Dick reiterated. "Do you think, mother, I could call him brother of mine? No; if I fall by his hand, he may then claim my title, but while I live he shall not."

"Your title, madman!" shrieked Lord Edward. "Do you think, cut-throat and robber, that any one but a fool would believe your lying statement?"

"One of us shall claim the title," Dick said; "it remains entirely with the best swordsman, who shall be Lord of Aldervale Manor."

Blind with maddened fury, the young libertine lord stood his ground bravely, and fought with a firmness that bespoke his determination to conquer or die.

Dick watched him with a glow in his large black eyes of admiration for the courage and skill with which he fought, though he stood face to face with his rival brother, his soul burning with inveterate hate, and his hand aiming each blow to kill.

"My combatant fights well," said Dick, as he turned aside a lunge that went exceedingly close to his seventh rib.

The young reprobate did not make any reply. His teeth gleamed like the fangs of a tiger between his thin bloodless teeth, and his deep blue eyes glistened with a light of deadly revenge.

"There's one almost as close as yours," said Dick, ripping up the side-seam of his foe's coat with the point of his sword.

"A little closer would have given you the title of Lord Aldervale," Edward remarked, with a sardonic sneer.

They fought, blow for blow—stood foot to foot, and watched each other's slightest movement.

Dick had had many a passage of arms with his companion, but he had never seen him display the skill he did now.

Neither spoke, but threw such force and beauty into their fencing skill that each had to do his best. Dick was feeling his way warily to accomplish a disarm done by a trick known only to himself, taught to him by Captain Claude.

It was a point without precedent or parallel, and only to be achieved by incessant, tireless application.

Dick quickened the time of his play. His weapon twined and flashed like an electric serpent round his opponent's blade, gliding, clinging, clashing, and dazzling by its meteor twirling, while all the time he sustained a powerful pressure on the other's wrist.

Then a rapid dash, and cling, and glide together, and the sword of Dick's antagonist went ringing from his hand.

The countess, who had been watching, gave an irresistible cry of horror.

Lord Edward sprang back as Dick leaped towards him, with a merciless look, his hand raised to strike the last and deadly blow.

But ere he could carry out his revengeful purpose, the countess glided noiselessly behind him and pinioned his arms as the gleaming blade was raised in the unerring hand of the Boy Highwayman.

Edward Aldervale gave a yell of triumph, and springing forward with a long dagger in his hand, he was about to leap upon our hero and drive the blade into his heart.

But Dick, not quite seeing the force of being held while the baffled libertine drove the blade into his heart, suddenly broke away from the countess, and closed with his dastardly foe half-way.

TURNING SHARPLY ON THE NARROW PLANK, HE BOLDLY FACED HIS PURSUER.

Then a fearful struggle took place for the possession of the dagger. The countess seeing the danger that threatened her favourite son, went between them, and snatched the dagger from Edward's grasp.

The two boys looked at her, wondering which she was going to help, and then as her gaze wavered between the two, they both thought she meant treachery. They, in accordance, made a clutch for the possession of the weapon.

The fair, beautiful woman stepped back with an angry cry as they advanced.

In hastily drawing her hand back, the weapon with a thud sank into Dick's side, as the treacherous young earl pushed the noble boy for that purpose.

The countess stood petrified with horror; and as Dick staggered back, faint, she was left with the dagger in her hand, dripping with the proud, noble blood of Tyburn Dick, the Boy Highwayman.

" Ha, ha, ha!" laughed Lord Edward, fiendishly. " At last I triumph."

" For a time," said our hero as he sank to

the ground, his life's blood flowing from the wound.

"For a time! Ha, ha!" Lord Edward said, "you won't trouble me again, Tyburn Dick."

He picked up the sword that our hero had dropped, and with a devilish purpose gleaming from his eyes he went towards the helpless youth, and putting one foot on his neck he pitilessly put the point of the weapon in the already made wound.

The cold steel, tantalizing the live flesh, sent a thrill of fearful pain through our hero. A groan, coming from the bottom of his soul, by the inhuman cruelty of the pitiless brute, escaped his lips, and the proud boy, giving his assailant one last look of bitter hate, closed his eyes to die.

The Lady Aldervale turned in time to see the murderous hand of her dastard son raised to strike the fatal blow.

"No, no!" she shrieked. "Don't kill him."

"Would you be pestered with him longer, when one stroke would rid us of him for ever?"

"No, no! In Heaven's name, don't strike!"

"You would have him live?"

"I would."

"I wouldn't," replied the hateful youth, savagely.

"Should your hand strike the blow to kill that noble boy, your death would be one of a quick and bloody nature."

"So, you seem interested in this cut throat's fate," he said, with a brutal sneer.

"I am."

"Indeed! and why, pray?"

"Because he is my son."

"Your son. Then who am I?"

"My son, too; but not a lawful one."

"What! after all these years I have been the Lord of Aldervale, would you disgrace me now?"

"I would, should you injure him," replied the countess, firmly.

"What!" thundered the young earl, leaping from our hero's prostrate form to the proud lady, and clutching her by her soft white throat.

"Release me instantly," she said, "or you shall be thrust from the grounds like a disgraced beggar."

"Look you, beautiful demon," he said, with terrible calmness, still retaining her throat despite her struggles; "I could as mercilessly run this sword through your beautiful figure as I could through his."

"Do it," replied the lady.

He forced her against the wall, and put the point of the cold blade between her lovely breasts.

"He is your son," said the earl.

"He is," replied the lady, without changing colour.

"And you would take him from the road to your breast?"

"I would."

"And would proclaim him the rightful heir to this domain?"

"He is the heir, and would proclaim his rights."

The excited youth glared at her savagely, and eventually throwing her aside, he said—

"Think you I would let such a dangerous rival as he live? No, by Heaven, he shall not, and now while he is in my power—ha, ha!—shall he die!"

He walked slowly to where the insensible youth lay. The sword was raised above his heart, but ere his foul hand dealt the murderous thrust the casement at the end of the apartment was dashed open with a tremendous crash, and a white figure—a figure more like a spectre than anything human—sprang noiselessly into the chamber, and glided like a shadow to the murderous young earl, and clutched him by the throat with a hand cold and marvellously white.

The cowardly young villain dropped the sword, trembling like an aspen leaf, and shrieked for mercy.

The mysterious being raised him in his arms, and hurled him with tremendous force through the window.

The countess ran to the casement, as her boy went crashing through the glass.

"Stay, pitiless woman," said the mysterious being, in a voice deep and musical.

The lady immediately turned.

The intruder clutched her arm.

She shrieked with terror.

"Do you not know me?" asked the

mysterious person, "Look, fair devil, well into this face, and see if you have no remembrance of the past."

The lady shrieked as he removed a kind of thin white mask from his face, and left uncovered a frank, handsome countenance, marked with timeworn lines of bitter sorrow.

"You know me," he said.

The lady shrank back, and covered her face.

While she stood thus the strange being was going through a peculiar process. He divested himself of a thin white gauze, and then stood out in the beautiful picturesque costume of a highwayman.

The countess suddenly turning, and not seeing the transformation, uttered a cry.

"Captain Claude!" she exclaimed.

"Captain Claude, or rather——"

"No, no—not that name," shrieked the lady.

"This, then, is your work?" he said, raising the prostrate form. "Look to it, Lady Aldervale; this foul play will cost you dearly."

He drew the helpless boy tenderly to his breast, and vanished like a shadow as he left the chamber.

CHAPTER LXXVI.
DEVIL DUKE TELLS A STORY.

THE poor faithful Dashing Ralph being caught in the act of letting our heroine free, was dragged away by the warders, and confined in a dark loathsome cell beneath the prison.

Grace then gave up the hopes of escape that she had entertained.

When all was quiet Duke removed the bricks from the wall.

Grace looked up with a sad sweet smile.

"You are lonely, my lady," said Duke.

"How can one be otherwise in such a place as this?" she replied. "Come, you have had many strange adventures; try if you can't think of a pretty one that you can relate to beguile away the time."

"I know one," he said—"a strange old legend, romantic and interesting."

"A legend! Something horrible, I dare say."

"You shall hear, and judge for yourself," said Duke, as he began :—

A massive and magnificent structure was Winchester Castle. Heavy masses of rough hewn stone formed the basis of the walls, and the time-worn crests of the towering turrets reared upward in majestic grandeur.

The castle stood in the midst of a spacious courtyard, around which arose a lofty wall of impregnable strength; a myriad of retainers were grouped in various parts, each armed and dressed after the suggestion of his own uncouth fancy.

With their armour or weapons clanging at every step of the heavy, soldierly tread, the rough jest and the wild laughter, their fine stalwart forms, and rugged, reckless bearing, they formed a scene at once suggestive of the times in which they lived, as it was full of savage, picturesque beauty.

A deep moat surrounded the castle wall on either side, and the ponderous drawbridge was guarded well by a watchful and heavily armed sentinel.

Altogether it was a fit home for the strong hands and daring hearts of its indomitable possessors. More than once had the red king cast a longing eye on the stately home of the Saxon chief.

But the grim, terrible ferocity with which Cedric had repelled every attempt of the Norman invaders to dislodge him from his ancestral home, the number of his stalwart retainers, all and each of whom would fight like an inspired demon at their chieftain' bidding.

Leaving the retainers to their rough jest and rude, though not inharmonious merriment, we will proceed at once to the interior.

Passing through a long corridor, and an ante-chamber of no inconsiderable dimensions, we enter a large and lofty hall, furnished with a reckless disregard as to cost, and where luxurious ease was evidently studied, rather than elegance or taste. Heavy hangings of rich tapestry covered the unpolished walls, and the huge couches, and various lounges, though of antique make, and uncouth appearance, were luxuriant, and comfortable to a degree. Trophies of many a wild foray adorned the tapestried wall—a lion's—a panther's hide—the antlers of a stag—some glittering weapon, wrought of costly metal—a blood-stained gauntlet, and a tattered banner, were ranged, or rather thrown together in strange disorder.

Seated near the centre of the apartment was a man, whose appearance was at once patriarchal and imposing; his hair, of snowy whiteness, fell in thick tresses on his shoulders, and a beard of the same colour rested on his broad and still powerful chest. His massive features were finely carved, and the dark blue eyes flashed from beneath his heavy brows in all the quenchless fire of an unconquered soul. The calm set of the mouth indicated his iron will, and the lofty brow betokened the possession of a powerful intellect and a great capacity of thought. His limbs were as those of a giant, and even now had lost none of the immense muscular power for which he had in youth been noted, and which made his name so terrible to the foe.

Such was Cedric the Saxon, Earl of Winchester.

Seated by his side, and with her fair head resting confidingly on his shoulder, was a maiden of strange, and almost marvellous beauty. Her skin was as white and pure as the leaf of the lily's flower, and her rich, luxuriant tresses, of a soft golden brown, fell over her shoulders, and veiled a bosom whose whiteness and beautiful moulding Diana's self might have envied. Her features were finely chiselled, yet gentle in expression; her eyes soft and earnest as those of the wild gazelle. Her form was tall and perfectly developed; her bearing at once proud and full of quiet grace. The rounded arm, and the soft white hand were of matchless beauty, and her whole mien was such as well became the high lineage and noble blood of the house of Westmoreland.

This was the Lady Edith, the daughter of Cedric's kinsman, and who had been the friend of his earliest boyhood.

On the death-bed of her father had Cedric registered a vow to cherish and protect her; and the old man had died in peace, well knowing that his friend would keep faithful trust.

For Cedric was a man of pride and honour, and his word once given was held as a sacred one.

A little apart were a group of four persons, whom we have now to describe.

One was a fair maiden, of soft winning beauty, who sat listening, with a pleased smile, to the gay conversation of a graceful youth who knelt at her feet.

The remaining two were cavaliers of chivalrous aspect and gallant bearing. Both were tall, of slender yet powerful build, and evidently of nearly the same age.

The one, whose rich attire and golden spurs proclaimed him a knight, was the brave and only son of Cedric, the gallant Percy.

The other, who wore the dress of a royal huntsman, was Master Albert Tyrrell, a captain in the king's guard and the monarch's chief huntsman; and what gave him more proud delight than the honours he had already gained, the favoured suitor of the sister to his chosen friend—Cedric's daughter, the fair Lilian, who was now laughing gaily at the discourse of Roland, her favourite page, the youth who knelt at her feet, and who was beloved by all for his winning speech and his boyish daring.

"Thou art merry, my daughter," said Cedric, as he looked fondly at his gentle child. "What is the young scapegrace telling thee, thus to arouse thy mirth?

"I was relating to the Lady Lilian of how I led the Norman soldier into the morass and beat him with the huge staff with which he threatened my life, please you, my lord," replied the page, speaking with the respectful assurance of a petted favourite.

"Thou wert ever a graceless imp, but a gallant one nevertheless," exclaimed Cedric, smiling at the recollection of the event to which the boy alluded; "and if thou dost continue as thou hast given promise, thou wilt wear the golden spur yet."

"I trust so," said Roland, springing to his feet, while his slight frame dilated, and his eye flashed in the ardour of his fiery spirit; and, even as he spoke, the boy's slender hand instinctively clutched the hilt of his sword.

"When thine arm is as strong as thine heart daring thou wilt do so," and Cedric laid his hand affectionately on the brave boy's glossy head as he

time, Roland, do not rush heedlessly into danger; for, though I cherish thee for thy gallant spirit, it would grieve me much should thy indiscretion lead thee into peril. How now!" he exclaimed, as a retainer entered.

"A messenger from the king, my lord, seeks instant audience," replied the henchman.

"Admit him."

The retainer bowed, and withdrew.

Then the heavy door swung back, and the king's messenger—a Norman knight, by his dress and bearing—entered the apartment, and bowed with a cool soldierly grace to the assembled company.

"Your mission?" exclaimed Cedric, briefly.

"This will inform you," replied the Norman, as he drew a roll of parchment from his breast, and placed it in the hand of Cedric.

He perused the missive in silence, and placing it in his girdle, said, "May I ask your name, sir knight?"

"Brian le Noir," replied the Norman tersely.

"The name of a brave soldier, and a gallant gentleman," said Cedric, stretching forth his hand, which the other grasped heartily. "Know you the contents of this missive?"

"Enough to give me some surprise that you have thus calmly read it," replied Sir Brian.

"Why so?" returned Cedric, with a half smile. Then turning to his son, he said, "What think it doth contain?"

"I know not, father," he replied, somewhat wonderingly.

"Simply a request that we take your affianced bride, my beauteous Edith, to the palace, there to be given in marriage to a Norman knight—one Sir Halbert Gardonel."

A cry of rage broke from Percy's lips, and his sword flashed from its sheath. "I would tear the king from his throne, and trample beneath my heel the insolent hound who would dare assert his right to stand in my path."

The Lady Edith clung to Cedric's arm, while Tyrrell stood with Lilian and Roland, each looking an indignant protest against the royal mandate.

"Is that the answer I am to take to my royal master?" said the Norman, with a quiet smile on his bronzed face.

"Tell my liege monarch we will in person give our answer," exclaimed Winchester, calmly.

You will not take me, then?" said Edith, pleadingly.

"Fear not, my child," said the old warrior, as he smoothed the fair tresses caressingly from the white brow. "I will obey the mandate so far as that; but there will be strong arms and bright swords to shield thee from danger or harm. Monarch as he is," he added, "he would pause ere he raised the wrath of old Winchester; and though he promised thee to an honest Norman, the fulfilment of the same is a matter somewhat different."

"By my halidame!" quoth Sir Brian, "but thou art right, and if the hopes of my countryman rests upon no surer footing than the king's bare word, I give him scant joy of his prospect. Adieu, fair ladies!" he said, raising his plumed casque gracefully "Farewell, my lord; and you, sir knight, be of good heart," he said, turning to Percy, "for while there is a sword in the grasp of an honest hand there is hope for a soldier's love." And so saying the gallant Norman bowed courteously around, then turned and strode away.

"Despair not, my son," said Winchester, as he noted the knit brow and gloomy looks which overspread Percy's handsome features; "let no shadow cling as yet around thy heart, for even should the worst come to the issue, my castle walls are thick, and our followers have strong hands and faithful hearts; and now for the palace of the king."

.   .   .   .   .

While the inmates of Winchester Castle are preparing to answer the king's summons, we will follow Sir Brian to the royal palace.

The monarch was one whose nature blended a strange chaos of good and evil; for though he was at times arbitrary to a degree, and harsh to the verge of tyranny, he was generous to a fault and brave to rashness.

Perhaps his worst quality was a startling and dangerous impulsiveness, which would

surprise, a gang of handsomely dressed men dashed into the room.

" Ha !" exclaimed the youth, turning like a young lion.

He twined his left arm round his companion's slender waist, and drawing his rapier, he waited quietly for the intruders.

The lady trembled violently. She suddenly appeared to realize her perilous position. She saw now the snare she had been drawn into.

She bitterly regretted having trusted the perjured villain who had won her young affections and thus betrayed her.

Her girlish love turned into loathing hatred as her gaze fell upon the wretch who had deceived her.

Victor St. James saw her terrible agitation, and fearing she might faint, he tried to soothe her by his kind consoling words.

" Fear nothing, dear lady !" he said, in a loud voice, so that all in the room should hear him ; " we are in a den of villains, but no harm shall befall you while I have power to use my weapon."

The daring youth had great belief in his own skill in swordsmanhip. He knew that few could stand against him.

The young lady felt comparatively safe under his protection.

" I know you are brave and noble," she said, confidently, " quite different to *him*."

" Dear little angel !" murmured the youth, holding her tightly to his side.

The party raised a shout, and rushed towards the young nobleman.

" Ah !" exclaimed St. James, preparing for a thrust at the new comer, whom he recognised, " I know you, my Lord Edward Aldervale."

The libertine young lord laughed satirically.

" And I know you," said another of the party. " Whose turn is it now, cousin Victor, to triumph ?"

" Not yours, hound !" thundered the youth, and he aimed a fearful blow for his villanous cousin, Reuben Frampton's head.

" Prick him, prick him !" said the cynical-looking roue.

The rest closed round the youth with their drawn swords, and slowly forced him against the wall.

He stood undaunted, fearless, and defiant,

with twenty gleaming weapons levelled at his breast.

Slowly the weapons were pressed forward —slowly the sharp points penetrated his coat and scratched his flesh

Yet he did not move.

He kept his gaze fixed steadily upon merciless foes. His face looked demon and a dangerous light kindled in his flashing orbs.

" Strike !" he shouted, suddenly, " cowardly hounds."

His assailants started involuntarily, and the weapons moved from his breast.

That was what he wanted.

He did not lose the opportunity.

In an instant he had drawn a brace of pistols, and put his hand through the hilt of his sword, so that it hung from his wrist

" Curses !" hissed the fellow who had proposed the pricking operation ; " kill him, gentlemen."

St. James laughed.

The fashionable libertines dashed forward.

" Back," exclaimed Victor, in a tone that spoke his intention if they did not comply with his command.

They did not.

And as they dashed upon him with murderous intent he fired.

There was a flash—a sudden report of pistols, followed by a shriek.

One of the bullets had entered Reuben Frampton's shoulder ; the other went crashing through the door.

The wounded man staggered back, and then fell amongst his companions.

Like a pack of savage wolves pouncing upon their helpless victim, so the rest of the libertines dashed upon St. James.

His pistols in an instant were replaced in his pockets, and his rapier was darting about like a gleaming snake.

Regardless of his savage opponents, the youth turned to see why his companion was clinging so desperately to him.

The man who had proposed to prick him was trying to pull her from him—St. James.

The young cavalier's sword swung round, and came down for the other's head.

But the other moved aside, and the weapon came down wide of its mark.

Sir Halbert questioned somewhat nervously.

"How?—the manner?" repeated Le Noir, as he broke into a loud laugh at the recollection of Percy's impetuous speech. "I will tell thee, Sir Halbert." And while the other waited impatiently a reply, Le Noir dismounted calmly from his steed, and giving the reins to his esquire, Cressy, turned, with a smile on his dark face, to Sir Halbert, who was chafing inwardly at the torturing delay.

"The Lady Edith clung to her guardian's arm as for protection, and her affianced husband swore to trample thee beneath his heel," exclaimed Le Noir, smiling at the look of blank dismay which gradually overspread the other's face.

A wild oath broke from Sir Halbert's lips as Le Noir concluded, and he said fiercely—

"By the rood, Sir Brian, but thou seemest to exult in the insolence of the haughty Saxon."

"I have given thee the tidings thou didst ask," replied Le Noir, his bronzed cheek flushing at the other's tone. "It is for thee to receive message and messenger as thou thinkest fit."

"A challenge!" exclaimed Sir Halbert, as he grasped his sword-hilt.

"Ay!" replied the other, with stern haughtiness. "Thinkest thou I care to brook thy mongrel insolence? By Heaven and St. Denis! I had rather rot beneath the palace wall, or gnaw my sword in want and very hunger, than creep, as thou hast done, to grovel in the sunshine of royal favour."

An approving murmur arose from those who had gathered round at the first signal of a quarrel, and Sir Halbert, foaming with rage, dashed forward, and ere an arm could interpose he was engaged in desperate conflict with Le Noir.

"Beat down their weapons, gentlemen!" exclaimed Cressy, rushing forward. "Thou knowest that a weapon drawn in the king's palace is death to the drawer."

In spite of his remonstrance the duel would have undoubtedly ended in bloodshed had not an old knight, of reverential aspect,

come forward and sternly ordered them to desist.

"For shame, gentlemen!" said he, "have ye so little regard for the duty ye owe yourselves and country that ye strive thus in mortal strife?"

And thus speaking, he drew his weapon and with a single blow struck Sir Halbert's sword from his hand, and crossed Sir Brian's blade with his own.

Le Noir lowered the point of his weapon instantly.

"I cry you mercy, my lord of Weston!" exclaimed Sir Brian. "I was the first to begin the quarrel, and," he added, turning sternly to Sir Halbert, "I will be the last to finish it!"

Gardonel picked up his weapon, and with a countenance livid with fury said, "I may yet find means to repay thee for this. Meantime, Sir Brian, look to it."

Sir Brian's lip curled with scorn as he answered, "I fear not thy sword, Sir Halbert, nor do I fear the influence of thy smooth tongue, albeit," he added, with a laugh, "it is the more dangerous weapon."

A quiet smile stole over the face of many a grim-looking warrior present, as they heard the biting sarcasm, for it was more to the possession of a flattering speech than to any knightly achievement that Sir Halbert owed his present favour with the king. Not daring to trust himself to speak, Gardonel shook his fist in impotent wrath at his late antagonist, and strode into the palace.

"Thou wert wrong to chafe him thus, Sir Brian," said the old Earl of Weston, "for his voice hath potent power in the royal ear, and he may do thee harm yet."

"Let him do his worst," said Le Noir. "I fear him not; I have a good sword and a strong right arm, and if the king knows not their value, there be other monarchs who may. Meantime, my lord, I thank thee for thy kind thought." And exchanging a warm shake of the hand with the brave old noble, Le Noir crossed the courtyard and entered the palace to announce the result of his mission to the king.

*   *   *   *   *   *

The Earl of Winchester was essentially a man of action. With him to think was to art, and he had no sooner received the royal mandate than with his usual promptitude he resolved what to do.

He knew that to follow out the line of conduct he had determined upon would place him in a position of some peril, but he also knew the weight of his own power and influence; and though he fully appreciated the danger of arousing the king's impulsive and fiery nature, he felt no fear as to the issue. With a due regard, however, to the safety of his own person, and the welfare of those dear to him, he gave instructions to the chief of his retainers to advance with a strong guard within bugle-sound of the palace, and should it be necessary they were, upon hearing a certain note, to dash at once to the rescue.

Leaving his gentle daughter to the care of his trusty warders, and to the more especial trust of the boy Roland, he had, accompanied by his son and the Lady Edith, together with Master Albert Tyrrell, whose temporary leave had expired, prepared at once to journey to the monarch's residence, and following closely on the heels of the king's messenger, he arrived almost as soon as the king received word of his intention.

No sooner had the monarch heard of their arrival than he prepared at once to receive them in all the splendours of royal state he could command, and gave orders for their immediate admission to the presence-chamber.

He knew that his request would be exceedingly distasteful to the Saxon chief, and in spite of himself, felt some hesitation and sundry misgivings as to the result of their meeting.

But he summoned his kingly pride to his aid, and by the time the herald announced the approach of Cedric, he was strong in the resolution to carry his point at whatever cost.

The chamber in which the royal monarch sat was one of most spacious dimensions; the furniture was rich and heavy, the hangings of the most costly description; the chair of state was placed at the extremity of the apartment; the large folding doors, which, save for an outer hall, led direct to the court-yard, being on his right hand.

Sir Halbert and the most favoured courtiers hovered near the royal chair

The general retinue being ranged in lines around.

As the door swung back to admit Cedric and his party William descended from his lofty seat, and gave him courteous greeting.

The old Saxon returned the salutation somewhat coldly, and after bowing in recognition to such among the royal train as he knew, he gave the maiden to his son's charge, and stood immediately opposite the monarch, and slightly inclining his stately head, said—

"Sire, I have attended you in person to give answer to your royal request."

"My lord of Winchester," said the king, "we have ever respected and loved thee as a true and loyal subject, and for the proof of thy fealty we give thee thanks."

The king strove to speak with an air of royal condescension, but his voice somewhat faltered, and his eye quailed beneath the calm, searching gaze of the proud Saxon.

Cedric bowed as the king concluded, then regarded the king in silence as though waiting to hear further.

"Thou hast received the scroll penned by my royal hand," said the king, chafing inwardly at the stern composure and erect bearing of the old Saxon. "We would now hear thy reply."

"Sire," exclaimed Winchester, as he confronted the king in all the majestic grace of his fine presence, and spoke in slow measured accents, "thou would have mine answer—listen. Thou mayest remember that some years since thou didst, in person, lead the attack against the arms of thy rebellious subject, the Lord of Brendon; thou mayest remember, too, that I was with thee, side by side with my brave companion in arms—the cherished friend of my boyhood—the noble father of this fair maiden—the Earl of Westmoreland. Sire, thou must remember that in the fierce heat of the conflict, when thou wast surrounded by thy foes, and inevitable death seemed to threaten thee, that the brave Westmoreland, assisted by mine own good sword, bore the brunt of the yeoman's rage. Well and nobly did he fight in thy behalf, sire, until, overpowered by numbers, he fell; the mortal wound in his brave breast, given by the death shaft that had been strung for thine own heart, sire," continued Cedric, each word pealing from his lips clear and sonorous as the note of a cathedral bell. " When the fray was done, and thou wert safe from the scene of carnage, thou didst give thy royal word to my noble friend to cherish and protect his loved and only child, even when the loyal heart was growing cold for thy sake, didst thou promise this—and now, here amid thy trusted followers, here in thy royal palace, and beneath the attesting eye of heaven, do I, in the name of my friend, now dead, and as the chosen protector of his child, do I reclaim thy royal promise."

He ceased, and with his stately form drawn to its full height, his head thrown proudly back, and his eyes glowing with fire, he stood calm, silent, and imposing.

The King glanced round somewhat uneasily.

His impulsive majesty felt rather at a loss as to the manner of proceeding. After a pause, however, he said—

"My lord of Winchester, our memory is not so shallow as to need the recalling to it of a service we have not, or ever shall, forget; but touching the last part of your speech, in what manner dost thou intend to redeem our royal promise?"

"Inasmuch as this," replied Cedric, with the same unmoved firmness. "The maiden, as thou knowest, was by her father's wish betrothed to mine own son; therefore, my liege, I urge it is impossible that she can accede to thy veriest wish."

"We will see to that anon," said the monarch, sternly. "The maiden we would have speak unsupported, therefore we would have thee retain thy present place until our interview is ended."

Cedric led the maiden to the King, and then strode to where his son stood with Tyrrell.

Even in his rising wrath the King could not repress a thrill of admiration as he viewed the noble form of the maiden standing before him, so calm in her statuesque beauty.

"Maiden," he said, trying to throw some gentleness into his voice, "we would have thee listen to us with attention, and weigh well our words, ere thou shouldst decline the honour it is our intention to do thee."

"Sire," said Edith, her low, melodious voice falling in rich music on her lover's ear, "I have no answer to give thee, save that which from my adopted father thou hast already heard; for the honour thou didst intend I give thee grateful thanks, but I cannot bestow my hand on a strange knight for whom I have no heart."

An angry flush mounted to Sir Halbert's forehead as he heard this exceedingly terse and decided objection.

"Thy speech is prompted, maiden," said the monarch, sternly, " but beware how thou dost presume too far on my forbearance."

"Doth it need prompting for a Saxon maiden to despise the hand of a mercenary, whose love is for the rich dowry I inherit?" and the rich blood mounted warmly to her fair cheek, while her soft eyes flashed fire as she answered him.

"By the bones of my father!" cried the King, as he sprang to his feet, "we will no longer brook this defiance! I have given my royal word that thou shalt wed Sir Halbert, and it is my will that thou shalt do so! My lord of Winchester," he added, turning towards Cedric, " thou wilt leave the maiden in our custody; we will brook no denial— our interview is ended——"

"No, by the grace of Heaven, it is not!" thundered Cedric, as his sword swept like a meteor from its sheath; " take thy bride, Percy, and away!—slay the base hireling who dares oppose thee!" and Cedric glared around like an enraged lion.

"Close the gates!" shouted the King, furiously. " Slay all who attempt to pass! Why stand ye thus inactive?" he said to his followers. " Arrest and disarm yon daring traitors!"

Simultaneously with his father, Percy had drawn his weapon, and throwing an arm around Edith, he strode towards the door.

The guards sprang instinctively from the fiery eye and glittering weapon of the young knight, and he would have passed out un-supposed, had not Sir Halbert rushed forward suddenly, and stood in his path.

With a rapid sweep of his arm Percy struck him senseless to the earth, and then pressed through the throng at the gate with Lady Edith moving fearlessly by his side.

"Close the gates!" again shouted the King, his brown cheek white with baffled rage. "Take you old traitor alive, or slay him if he resists."

A cry of rage broke from Cedric's lips as he heard the order, and with his face full of deadly purpose he sprang towards the King.

The knights shrank in terror from the terrible fury of the old Saxon, and the next moment would have assuredly seen the King a corpse had not Tyrrell, who had watched the entire proceedings in silent agony, sprung forward and interposed his form between the King and his enraged foe.

Even as he did so the blow was aimed.

It was too late to stay the avenging arm, the hot blood gushed from Tyrrell's breast e Saxon's weapon smote deeply in.

ithout a cry he fell at the feet of his ued King.

With his fury redoubled at having thus wounded a youth whom he really loved, Cedric turned on his Norman foes.

A phalanx of armed knights had formed around the King, while a body of the royal guard kept the door.

Cedric paused not an instant.

A powerful blast from his bugle told his retainers without of his peril, and with his white hair streaming over his shoulders, and a deadly gleam in his eye, he dashed like an old Titan amid the foe.

His blood was up, and with his excitement had returned all the powerful strength of his youth.

In vain did the guard oppose him.

With his powerful weapon grasped in both hands he dashed among them in fearful wrath.

He cut his way through as though with a scythe hewing down all who stood in his path.

Many times did the foe surround and enclose him in their midst.

The protracted conflict was fast telling upon him, and his giant strength was failing.

But with a last desperate effort he rushed through their ranks, as his retainers, headed by his son, battered down the gates and rushed to his rescue; then he turned fiercely upon his foemen and did fearful slaughter.

"Upon him!" shouted the King from behind the sheltering phalanx of his knights, "cut him down, or make him prisoner."

But even as he gave utterance to the words, the Saxon band, headed by Percy, rushed with resistless force into the scene of the conflict.

After a brief resistance the royal guard were overpowered, and the King stood there in his own palace at the mercy of his incensed enemy.

"Is that all?" asked Grace, who had listened with much interest.

"No," replied Duke; "the best part is to come, where there are several fearful tragedies——What's that?"

Grace started and turned pale.

Duke's head vanished into his own compartment, and the bricks were being quickly replaced.

The noise that had startled both—a sepulchral kind of tapping beneath the cell floor—continued with redoubled energy.

Duke felt assured that it was no official of Newgate coming to inquire after his health, so making himself happy on that point he again removed the bricks.

The noise ceased.

"Glad of that," said Duke. "Don't like strange noises; always make a fellow feel uncomfortable."

Grace smiled amicably.

"You may as well finish that legend."

"Yes, my lady."

Duke cleared his throat, and was about to commence, when the knocking was repeated.

"They might let a fellow alone here," he said, and then shouted at the top of his voice—"What do you want? Who are you?"

Some one from beneath answered him; but the voice was too indistinct for Duke to catch the words.

"For gracious sake, Duke," said our heroine, "don't make that noise, or we shall have the warders upon us, thinking we are trying to escape."

"Escape! I wouldn't escape if I had the chance. I like this place too much."

"You don't mean that, surely, Duke?"

"If I had the chance of escape, and any one stood in my way, you should see how soon I would dispose of them."

"Doubtless."

"That fellow won't leave off knocking."

"Probably it is some one trying to make their way into here."

"Don't care if it is; but they need not make all that row. By the lord Harry, if I was standing behind him wouldn't I exert my toe."

"How do you mean?" inquired Grace innocently.

"Lift him through."

She didn't see it, so gave it up.

Duke looked at her and wondered, and then he thought he had made use of an expression very coarse for her ears, and he blushed with shame at his own want of thought.

"It must be some poor fellow trying very hard to escape," remarked Grace.

"He works perseveringly, and deserves to escape."

The tapping then stopped, and scraping and digging took place. That continued for half an hour.

Chip, chip, chip!

This process, as though chipping away at a stone, kept up for another half hour.

Then again all was silent.

"Given it up in despair," thought Dick.

He was about to say so to his fair companion, when Grace gave a scream, as the stone on which she stood was suddenly jerked, and she thought she was going through into some dark abyss.

Duke was so surprised that he went into his own dingy cell, and sat upon the cold floor muttering something about stupid women who frighten a fellow when he is about to say something good.

Grace dexterously jumped aside as far as her irons would admit, as the stone was again jerked, and she saw it move.

The clanking of the iron ring on the stone attracted Duke's attention, and he again made his appearance at the aperture of the wall.

"By the lord Harry, if he goes on like that he will have the floor up," said Duke. "Keep it up, old boy; you will succeed presently."

As he spoke the stone was raised two feet from the level, and threw them aside

It fell with a loud crash.

Duke uttered an exclamation of glad surprise as his comrade, Dashing Ralph, gradually drew himself up through the opening, and Grace extended her tiny hand to greet the brave fellow.

He took it and kissed her fingers.

"They didn't keep me there long," he laughed.

"You are as bad off now," Duke said.

"Oh no, I am not."

"How's that?"

"You shall see."

"How the deuce can I see when I am chained to this infernal wall?"

"Did you hear me working? It was a warm job, I can tell you."

"I can imagine so; and didn't I bless you for making the noise, that's all."

"Quite enough, I have no doubt; but come, you don't want to stay here."

"Not if we can get away," put in Grace.

"And I don't see any likelihood of such a thing," said Duke.

"I don't suppose you do; but I do."

"Where?"

"Here," said Ralph, taking a key from his pocket.

"What's the good of that?"

"It fits all these manacles and locks."

"Does it? Then come and set me free. But how did you get it?"

"Which am I to do first? Set you free or answer your question?"

"Answer the question; it will ease my inquisitive mind."

"Well, when these inquisitive brutes nailed me in the act of setting you at liberty, I slipped this useful article into my pocket, where I have treasured it with tender care ever since."

Certainly it will be a release when our limbs are divested of these irons," said Grace; "but I don't see any chance of escaping from here."

"No, nor I!" shouted Duke.

"Well, don't be in a hurry," Ralph said: "I have a way of escape, my lady, through the dungeon in which I was confined. You may be sure I was not idle when I found myself there unmanacled, and it was not long before I discovered that the wall was crumbling to dust with age and mildew, so I made a hole in it large enough for any one to crawl through, and that hole leads into one of the back slums through which we can make our escape with safety."

"Then, by the lord Harry, I don't care how soon I am out of here!" said Duke. "But I have another question to ask you, which puzzles me awfully: how was it you became warder?"

Ralph's brow darkened and his face grew grave.

"I heard you both were captured and brought here," he began, "so I resolved, under any perilous circumstances, to get in somehow to see you. There was one man a gaoler here, who had always been an inveterate enemy to me, and it chanced one evening while I was waiting about, I met him.

"I owed him a long score, which I paid him, and flung him into the Thames with a bullet in his infernal skull, after stripping him of his clothes, which I put on, and came here instead of him.

"No particular notice was taken of me, as I had pretty well disguised myself to look as much like him as possible; and had I not been detected in the act of letting you free, the difference, perhaps, would never have been known, that is, if I had stayed—which I should not."

"You deserve more praise for your clever and daring trick than I can express, old boy. Ah! what's that?"

"The gaoler's tread," said Grace with a palpable shiver.

Ralph was by her side in a minute, his heart beating wildly with fear of discovery.

The chains fell from her beautiful limbs, and in her joy at being free, she hugged the daring fellow round the neck, and imprinted kiss upon his glowing cheek.

He gracefully returned the caress, and then sprang to Duke

There was a second clanking of irons, and the highwayman was free from his bonds.

They exchanged an affectionate pressure of hands, and then Ralph said—

"Go down there, Duke, quickly."

"No; you go down, you know the place better than I do."

Ralph vanished down the hole in a moment.

"Let the lady down gently," he said, softly.

Grace was carefully lowered into the dark underground vault, and then Duke let himself down half way; he had got the stone in a perpendicular position over the hole, when the cell door was suddenly swung open, and a gaoler dashed in; he drew a pistol from his belt and fired.

Duke gave a shriek of pain; the stone fell with crushing force upon his head and closed over the hole.

CHAPTER LXXVII.

CAPTAIN CLAUDE'S STORY.

THE sable veil of night sank beneath the peaceful light of a glorious spring morn.

Beneath the shadow of a clump of sprouting trees, where the little feathered songsters gathered to welcome the breaking day, and carol forth their morning song, stood Joseph Munroe.

His colossal features were clouded with some sad reflecting thought as he stood there anxiously watching, waiting for the return of his beloved young chief.

He knew the danger of the brave boy's visit, and the thought troubled him—troubled him the more because many hours had gone since he ought to have returned.

The faithful fellow had neither slept nor eaten since the absence of our hero.

Each moment seemed a dreary hour of suspense, bringing with it fresh thoughts that racked his brain.

He started as the echo of some distant clock, tolling forth the hour of six, broke upon his ear.

"I can bear this no longer," he muttered, and was about to steer off in search of Tyburn Dick, when a figure passed him bearing the inanimate form of our hero, and without a word entered the haunt.

AT BAY.

Bullskin recognised the stranger as the gallant Captain Claude, and was startled by his sudden appearance; for his loss had been lamented by all since the time of his surrender and supposed death on the Rocky Peak.

Bullskin followed; his worse fears were realised, and his head bowed with sorrow when he stood by the side of the couch whereon the youth was laid by the gallant captain.

They stood gazing mutely at the stricken youth, and their souls swelled with bitter rage against the coward traitor, whom they adjudged as the assassin.

Captain Claude stood by the side of the couch and laid his hand on the boy's heart.

He inwardly breathed a silent and stern determination to seek atonement for the dastard blow.

"He is not dead," he said, with a sigh of deep relief, "There is something of life yet in his gallant heart; bring some bandages to dress the wound."

Bullskin spoke but little, he turned away with a look of pitying interest at the senseless form.

And, in truth, it was such a spectacle as might cause ruder hearts to shudder and recoil.

Our hero's fair, handsome face, so still, so ghastly, and so strangely quiet; the white lids drawn closely over his frank, genial, eyes ; and the soft brown hair, which clustered so thickly over his pale brow, stained and wet with the purple flow that welled from his breast ; his fine powerful mien, so listless and inert, and ill ; his magnificent strength crushed out by the cruel blow which had smote him down.

Joseph Munroe returned, and with the assistance of Captain Claude, he dressed the wound—a deep, dangerous wound, made by a dagger being driven in his breast, but no vital part had been touched, and when the liniment and bandages had been applied, they watched intently for the first token of returning life.

He spoke at last, and Captain Claude bent down to catch the whispered words.

"My mother!"

It had been his last thought when he fell by her hand—it was now the first that came to his dull senses, and he forgave her for her treachery, as he thought.

"What would you, my boy?" asked Claude.

Dick unclosed his eyes, and gazed at the speaker in astonishment.

"Where am I?" he asked faintly, looking round the apartment.

Captain Claude saw the agitated expression of the boy's face, and knew its cause. He wished now he had kept out of sight until he had quite recovered, for he knew that his presence would cause him much amazement, and feared that the surprise, in his present state, would give him a shock from which he might not recover.

He took Dick's hand in his own, and in a gentle voice said—

"Be calm. You must not excite yourself. You shall learn why it was that I have been so long absent when you are better."

"But," began Dick, marvelling much, "I thought you were———"

"Hush! You mustn't trouble yourself now," interrupted Captain Claude. "You must rest, and when you are better you shall know all."

The gallant boy pressed his hand, and sank back exhausted, and slept a troubled restless sleep.

Captain Claude and Big Bullskin watched in silence by his side, and when he awoke his face was flushed and his eyes sparkled with a wild excited brilliancy.

His first act, on opening his eyes, was to scan the grave faces of his watchers, and then, with a start that astonished them, he sprang up, and threw his arms around Captain Claude's neck.

"Father! father!" he cried; "this is happiness I did not expect."

"Quiet, Dick, or I shall go away from you again," said Claude, trying to keep back the hot scalding tears that gushed to his eyes.

Bullskin turned his head, and wiped his eyes with the cuff of his coat.

The scene was one of touching sympathy, and it raised a fountain he could not stop.

He was suddenly clutched hold of by a pair of arms that twined themselves around his neck from behind, and he was astonished when Dick laid his head upon his shoulder.

The boy loved the gigantic fellow for his fidelity, and now, in his enjoyment at the union with his long-lost sire, he did not forget his faithful follower, who had watched and cared for him with the love of a parent.

"Dear, good fellow," said the youth, enthusiastically, "I don't know what I should have done in all my troubles had it not been for your kindness."

"I should have been worse than a brute had I been otherwise than kind to one so young and exposed to such danger as you are, without a friend to watch over you."

"And you," Dick said, "have watched over me in my bitterest hour with all the tender care of a parent."

"For which I am grateful," Captain Claude said, taking the generous fellow's hand, and pressing it warmly; "had anything happened to my brave boy in my absence, I should have had nothing to live for."

"And now that I am still living?" Dick said, looking anxiously at the captain.

"I have you to live and care for," replied Claude, putting his arm round the boy's waist, and holding him fondly to his breast; "and it was by a peculiar occurrence that I have you left me."

"I was in danger," Dick said, with a troubled expression on his face.

"You were in terrible danger," replied Claude.

"Yes, I now remember all that had taken place. How did I escape from his sword, that was at my breast?"

"Whose sword?" asked Bullskin, his colossal features excited.

"Edward Aldervale's."

"Did he strike the blow that left you stricken and at his mercy?" inquired Claude.

"No," Dick answered; "his was not the hand that did that."

"Then it was *she*—that fair, treacherous demon!"

Dick was silent. The tenderness with which his fair, beautiful mother had received him softened the inscrutable feeling of hate and revenge at his heart, and now he did not want to blame her, though he believed the blow had been struck by her tiny hand, with treacherous, deadly intent.

"How did it occur?" asked Claude. "Tell me, Dick. Did she not win you with her perfidious face and gentle words, and then, when you least expected it, strike you?"

"She did," replied our hero, gloomily.

"Incarnate wretch! she shall suffer doubly for what she has made us suffer," said Claude, with terrible fierceness in his tone.

"Don't speak of her in that way," said Dick; "she is my mother, and therefore her faults should be buried in oblivion."

"Poor boy!" said Captain Claude, tenderly, "she must be a heartless being to cause one so young and forgiving so much sorrow!"

"Let her faults be forgotten with her name," Dick said. "Tell me: did you bring me from the manor?"

"I did," replied the captain.

"'Tis very strange," murmured Dick to himself.

"What?" asked his sire.

"It puzzles me much to know how you were there at such a time."

"I was passing, when I heard a scream. I knew that some foul work was going on, so I dashed open the casement and sprang into the room, in time to prevent that cowardly villain from thrusting his sword into your breast."

Dick shuddered.

"Providence protects the brave," remarked Munroe.

"My father's hands protected me," laughed our hero. "Tell me, father, your story, and why you have been from us so long."

"You thought me dead," he said, with a sad smile.

"We did," said Bullskin, "and mourned your loss."

"Exceedingly kind of you," smiled Claude. "I will to my story, for I see that you are anxious to know how I escaped the shower of shots fired at me on the Rocky Peak."

"When I surrendered myself as you," thus he began, addressing our hero, "I was at the very pinnacle of the rocks overhanging the sea.

"I was placed at the very verge. A line of carbines were levelled at my breast. I watched them closely, and when the soldiers placed their fingers on the triggers, I turned and sprang into the sea as they fired. They, of course, thought I was hit, but I was not, and I sank beneath the boiling surf.

"The next thing I remember was to find myself upon a reef. I did not feel much the worse for my rapid flight, so I quickly made my way to the shore."

"And why did you not return to the haunt?" asked Dick.

"I knew that if I made my appearance too soon that it would only cause a fresh disturbance."

"But," Dick said again, "you having been taken for me, and I still going about in my real character, the mistake was sure to be soon discovered, which it was; and I, therefore, think it would have been much better for us all if you had returned."

"That could not be, or I should have gladly returned," Captain Claude answered.

"Why not?" queried our hero.

"My person was required as much to adorn the gibbet as yours, my brave boy, and the inscrutable Government were on my track for leading a conspiracy against the King, for which I was innocent, and so had to hide away, shunning the light of day for fear of being seen, and only creeping forth with the owl at night, when all was quiet.

"This solitary, miserable life I endured

until last night, when I crept forth from my hiding-place, and longing to see you and my faithful comrades, I grew bold, and resolved under any hazard to return.

"And so it happened, when I was passing Aldervale Manor, I saved you from a death that would have been inevitable, had I not so fortunately heard that cry that sent a thrill of horror to my heart, which caused me to break into the house."

"You won't leave us again?" Dick said, clinging to the noble captain.

"Never more," Dick, while I have strength to use a sword against my enemies."

"And a band of devoted men to stand by you," put in Bullskin.

"I am quite well now," said Dick, "and before the sun sets we must be out in search of our comrades."

"Of whom do you speak?" inquired Claude.

"Ralph, Duke, Gallant Tom, and St. James."

"Where are they?"

"We know not. They have been missing for some time, now, and I fear to think of what have befallen them. I have resolved to find them, dead or alive."

"By what means?" inquired Captain Claude.

"This," replied our hero, and drawing a long scroll from his breast, he gave it to his sire. "Those men, whose names you see there, I have befriended, and they, in return, would serve me with their lives."

"What is your plan?" asked Captain Claude, rolling up the scroll.

"To arm these thousand men, whose names you see there, defy the King, and ransack the country."

Captain Claude's brow darkened at the boy's resolution.

"It is a dangerous undertaking, and I would not advise it."

Dick laughed.

"Dangerous?" he repeated. "I see it not, with a thousand such men at our backs, and our own brave followers."

"Rush not rashly into heedless bloodshed, but let's see what can be done quietly."

"We have been quiet long enough. We have worked day and night, and tried strata-gem, but no trace of my noble comrades could be found. It wants force, and force I will have! Every nook shall be ransacked, and the very bowels of the earth upturned, but what they shall be found!"

"The enterprise is great, my brave boy," Captain Claude said, stroking our hero's glossy hair, "and perilous, for should his Majesty get scent of the design, he would order out his whole military force to meet us."

"And we," said Dick, "would stand against them while we had one arm left to wield a sword."

"When do you propose to set out?"

"We have not a minute to waste. The men have to be called together, armed, and attired."

"That cannot be done here," said Claude.

"Not here? I don't understand you," said Dick.

"This haunt is not secure enough."

"Where else have we?"

"The haunt on Hounslow Heath."

"Then," said our hero, "we will proceed to there without delay," and turning to Bull-skin, he said—"go at once; tell the men to prepare to leave this haunt."

Bullskin retired.

Captain Claude's gaze wandered round the chamber. He missed something, and his brow grew sorrowful. He missed the sweet childish face and the rich, musical tones of his fair mistress Milly.

The place had a gloomy, desolate aspect without her presence. His gaze wandered round the apartment, and then rested pleadingly on our hero.

The brave boy felt the bitterness of the noble captain's disappointment as though it had been his own.

"Milly—where is she?" he asked, his voice trembling with emotion, for he dreaded the reply that he knew would confirm his worst fears.

Dick knew not how to answer. He feared the sad truth would tell severely upon the noble man whose very soul had been garnered with the sweet memory of his true and gentle love—the only solace he had had in his long dreary hours of desolation to look back upon.

"Tell me, Dick," said Claude, taking the boy's hand, while a moisture gathered in his proud eyes, "tell me the worst. Torture me not by this suspense."

Dick turned his head aside to hide a tear that rolled down his cheek; the sad, sorrowful face of his father, so pleading, and with such a look of utter despair upon it, touched his heart's tenderest chord.

"She is gone," Claude said, in a tremulous voice. "Did she leave by her own consent, or was she taken?"

"She was torn from here on the night we were attacked," replied Dick, with a desperate effort to speak distinctly.

"By whom."

"I know not."

"Heaven protect her!" murmured Claude, as his head drooped in anguish.

"Don't give way," said Dick, sympathetically. "Milly may be out of danger. Grace has been taken from me, but I do not despair. I trust to her womanly resolution to protect herself when I am not near."

Claude looked at the speaker in surprise through his tears.

"Of what avail is a delicate, weak woman's dignity for protection," he said, "against the ruffians whose hands they may fall into?"

"Much," Dick replied. "For instance, take this as an idea. The day following Milly's abduction I missed Grace, and it was not until some considerable time afterwards, when I had given up all hopes of ever seeing her again, that I found her under very peculiar circumstances."

"Large bills were posted throughout the country, stating that Tyburn Dick had been captured—meaning me—and could be seen by any one who could obtain an order from the King, before his execution. I felt curious to know who it was had been representing me, so I started for Jonathan Wild's lock-up, and resolved to get admittance to see his prisoner.

"However, I got in undiscerned, crept upstairs, and burst into a room from which proceeded loud quarrelsome voices. It was then I discovered who was my second."

Captain Claude listened with much attention and interest.

"Who was it?" he asked, as Dick paused.

"Grace."

"Grace!" that fair, beautiful girl!"

"Even so," replied our hero, promptly, "she it was who had been captured for me, and, in spite of the danger that threatened her, she would not own that she was not the rightful Tyburn Dick, because she feared by so doing she might peril my life."

"Noble, devoted girl!" Claude exclaimed. "But how did she get your dress?"

"She took my second suit from my wardrobe."

"With what intention did she assume your character?"

"One reason was that she would ever be near me, in case of danger, and twice she saved my life. The other reason why she assumed my character was to discover her fair companion, Milly."

"Which the brave girl has not succeeded in doing, I fear. How long is it since you saw her?"

"Several weeks, but I fear not for her safety; she fights like a Tartar, and could vanquish any three fellows. The last time we met I, of course, got into one of my peculiar scrapes. We were attacked at the Leopard Inn by a regular regiment of officers and a swarm of infernal young libertines, who fought against us. Grace put several to their last accounts, and I sent a few home before their time; but, of course, that was like knocking down one of a swarm of bees, the rest turned upon us the more savagely, and we had to make a desperate effort to escape. Grace made a dash, and cut her way through the phalanx that had closed around us. I followed her.

"We were no sooner outside than we were once again set upon. Grace rode away unmolested, but the beggars stuck to me like a lot of infuriated devils, and I had to make a leap through a volley of bullets to escape."

Bullskin entered.

"My comrades are ready," he said; "everything is prepared for the departure."

"Let Selim and Fairy be saddled," Dick said.

Joseph Munroe bowed low and departed.

"How do you propose to leave here?" asked Captain Claude.

"In what way do you mean?" inquired Dick.

"Would you proceed with all our comrades in a body, or divide them into parts and take different routes, so as it should not rouse suspicion."

"Proceed in a body, decidedly."

"And when do we start?"

"Within two hours from now."

"It is now ten—we start at midnight."

"Yes," replied Dick, "so we had better take in a little provender, and get what rest we can before we start; the journey is a long and tiring one."

So saying, they left the apartment together.

The door had scarcely closed upon them when a crouching form crept from behind a pair of heavy hangings, and taking a careful survey of the chamber, the branded traitor, Simon Judas, cried in a wild, exultant tone—

"So, so, my noble captain has come to life again; better had he stayed away. You start at midnight—ha! ha!—for Hounslow Heath—two hours hence. I have that two in advance of you to apprise the King of your intentions. I think you will be mighty astonished to find Hounslow Heath surrounded with soldiers waiting for you by the time you arrive. Ha! ha! ha! Revenge! revenge!" and with those hateful words he opened the window and sprang out to fulfil his fell purpose.

CHAPTER LXXVIII.
THE HAUNT ON HOUNSLOW HEATH.

THE crescent moon shone down brightly on the rich cavalcade of gallant men who were gathered round the entrance of the haunt, waiting for their young leader.

The men drew back in double line as Dick and Captain Claude emerged from the haunt, and every hat was respectfully raised to salute their beloved young chieftain.

Little Swig stood by Fairy's head, holding the bridle; and the Lusher held Selim. Bullskin had already mounted his gallant charger, and took his place as first lieutenant.

A distant clock struck the midnight hour, and as the last toll died away in a dismal echo, the cavalcade started on their journey. Tyburn Dick and Captain Claude rode in front of the party.

To give a minute description of the procession is unnecessary, as they had no particular adventure during their journey worth recording, and when they rode on to Hounslow Heath, they were pretty well exhausted with the fatigue of their long tiring ride.

Captain Claude rode forward into a thicket.

The men halted as he pulled up before a gigantic old oak surrounded with impenetrable bushes.

Dick went forward.

"Where are we?" he asked.

"This is Tyburn Tree, so called in honour of your title," replied Claude. "Beneath the earth we now stand on is the haunt; do you see any way to get to it?"

Dick dismounted and made a careful search, but to no avail; the secret entrance was not to be found, only by those who knew of it.

"I think this will be a little more secure than the other," said Claude, with a quiet smile.

"Secure! By my faith, it would defy the very devil himself to discover the entrance," Dick said, as Claude kicked aside a huge trunk of a fallen tree, that appeared immovable with the moist and wild herbage growing about it.

"This is not the only entrance; there is one leading from yonder."

"From yonder—where?"

"The old priory."

"By what means does it communicate with the haunt?"

"There is a kind of subterranean passage that extends from here to the priory. Come, we will enter, and you shall see for yourself."

At that moment Jack Evans dashed up to Captain Claude, and clutched him by the arm as he was in the act of entering.

"What now?" he asked, startled by expression of the Lusher's face.

"We are betrayed, captain."

"Betrayed?" exclaimed Captain Claude and his son simultaneously with each other and by instinct each clutched the jewelled hilt of his sword.

"Look, Captain; look. Do you not see the soldiers coming down upon us?"

Captain Claude broke from his arms and peered through the trees.

"They are indeed soldiers," he said. "We cannot fight them, I fear."

"I see no chance," said Dick. "They number, at least, ten to one of us."

"We must stand our ground," replied Claude, fiercely. "We will not sneak off like a set of curs. Ah, they are loading their muskets ready to fire upon us."

"The deuce they are," muttered Dick, sternly. "Let us muster all our strength and give them the first volley."

Captain Claude motioned to the highwaymen, and a volley was poured into the ranks of the red coats.

Barely had the report died away, when it was followed by one from the red-coats, and the leaden missiles that went amongst the men like a storm of hailstones—but with more destruction—laid many low, and the green sward was strewn with the highwaymen.

Every one of our friends had fallen, but not with the enemy's shot; they all dropped to the earth in accordance as they fired, and so escaped the volley from the soldiers that scattered amongst their own comrades.

The volumes of white smoke that curled from the carbines seemed to have a tendency to adhere to the ground.

Captain Claude thought it a favourable opportunity to make a quiet move, so he gave a silent order for that purpose.

"Quick, men," he said in a whisper; "follow me on your hands and knees."

The ground was suddenly alive with the highwaymen, who were crawling away like a lot of crabs when the smoke cleared away, and revealed them to the astonished gaze of the soldiers.

The men stood petrified, and the officers' hair was erect; they thought their foes must be supernatural, or they would not have escaped the volley poured into them, and to test the truth of their suspicions they were making ready to charge with fixed bayonets.

But before they were quite prepared the highwaymen sped to their feet, took the bodyguard by surprise who were keeping them from their horses, and, hurling them aside, vaulted into their saddles.

"Shoot them down! fire at their heads!" yelled somebody from the background.

"Simon Judas, the traitor!" exclaimed the Lusher.

He it was, indeed; the cruel, bloodthirsty wretch, who had overheard our hero's intention to leave Cornwall, and take up his quarters on Hounslow Heath, and with his black soul burning for revenge for the just punishment he had received, he gave information to the King of the highwayman's plan, and triumphantly led the soldiers to take or slay the gallant men.

"Simon Judas, is it," quietly said Dick, taking a beautifully-mounted pistol from his holster. "I think this will settle his hash."

He took deliberate aim, and fired.

The incarnate wretch gave a horrible cry, and rolled to the earth.

"Now," said Big Bullskin, "we must prepare for the decisive battle."

"This will be the concluding struggle, one way or the other." Our hero spoke in a tone that prepared his men to conquer or die.

They were only prepared in time. The soldiers dashed upon them furiously. A quick and bloody contest took place.

The highwaymen stood their ground firmly, and fought with an unerring determination to conquer or die, while their comrades fell around them, stricken down by the soldiers' thirsty blades.

The gallant knights of the road could not stand much longer against the overwhelming number of the enemy, and our hero saw with sorrowful regret the decrease of his noble band.

"We must retreat, or we shan't have a man left," said Captain Claude to our hero.

"No," replied Dick, with calm determination. "We conquer or die."

"We have no chance to conquer, and why should we cause the death of all these noble men? Look around, and see the many we have already lost.

"It can't be avoided; you know my resolution," said Dick, riding forward to meet two stalwart horsemen who were dashing onwards.

They met, there was a quick passage of arms, blows were dealt heavily on both sides, but Dick was proof against anything, and he soon disposed of his assailants.

Maddened by the loss of his men, he rode

into the thickest of the foes, and did fearful slaughter. But even that could not last long, impenetrable as he was; he could not retain strength enough against such fearful odds.

Big Bullskin rode round the lines of the enemy, and with his ponderous weapon mowed them down as with a scythe.

But with all that the numbers of the soldiers were too much for our friends, who were falling fastly, and in a very short time the last one would have been stricken to the earth, but at that moment the highwaymen formed in a square block, and made a dash at the advancing body of soldiers.

The manœuvre had been so tactically arranged, with such skilful adroitness, by Captain Claude, and so suddenly carried out by the desperate energy of the men, that they scattered the soldiers on either side, and broke through the strongest companies before a weapon could be raised against them.

The next moment the commanding voice of an officer brought the soldiers together, and they were once more advancing towards the gallant knights.

A quick and bloody battle took place, and men on both sides fell like reeds beneath the scythe.

Step by step the highwaymen were forced back by the soldiers, and at last, despite all their resistance, they were repulsed, and had to fly, to save what lives there were left, to the mortification of Tyburn Dick, who stood in the midst of the enemy, watching the quick retreat of his comrades with a lowering brow.

Dick made a dash forward to follow. The officer of the guards sprang in his path, and exclaimed—

" Stay. You are our prisoner !

Dick was in no mood to be stopped, so without a word he raised his bloodstained weapon to strike.

The officer saw his danger, and got from the excited youth's path.

Dick did not seek the fellow's life, and, to prevent further strife, he darted off before anyone could interfere.

Captain Claude was heading his men, and tried to make them turn and face the enemy. The men were willing to do so, but Claude and Bullskin urged them forward.

A hot chase was kept up until they reached the old priory. Claude rode into the garden, and drew up before a ponderous iron door let in the solid masonry.

He dismounted, and by some hidden means opened it, and then led Selim in.

Tyburn Dick, Bullskin, and the rest dismounted and entered also, but before the door was closed the soldiers dashed upon the scene, and endeavoured to force their way in.

Dick drew his men round the door and ordered them to fire.

The order was quickly obeyed. A volley was poured into the soldiers and felled many to the earth.

The door was then closed, and as the party proceeded through a long dark corridor, they could hear the dying groans of their victims.

CHAPTER LXXIX.

DASHING RALPH RESCUES LADY FLORENCE WINTERMEARL.

WE will leave Tyburn Dick and his companions proceeding through the subterranean passage from the priory to the haunt on Hounslow Heath, and visit Duke, who, it will be remembered, was knocked down by a blow on the head from the huge stone that fell on him.

The weight of the stone raised a lump on Duke's head considerably larger than was comfortable.

He sat on the earth where he had been floored for at least five minutes, making a peculiar noise, between crying and laughing.

When he arose, he felt unsteady, and staggered about; had he not fallen into Ralph's arms, he would have fallen on to a large sharp piece of iron that projected from the wall, but its utility there none could ever conjecture.

" We had better leave here," said Ralph.

" We had," replied Duke. " Perhaps you will lead the way."

" Mind the lady," the other said, in a whisper.

Duke held Grace's little hand, and Ralph disappeared. The others could not see where he had gone.

" All serene," cried a voice from the other side of the dark vault.

"Is it?" Duke said, in a whisper. "Show us a glim."

A glim was shown by Ralph removing the bricks from the decaying wall, and a flood of murky, dreary kind of light passed through.

For a minute the light was kept out by Ralph passing through the hole.

Devil Duke led his fair companion across the vault, and stopped before the hole.

"How can you, my lady, get through there?" he asked.

A light, silvery kind of laugh answered him, and the brave girl in an instant was upon her hands and knees crawling through the aperture.

The dashing highwayman assisted her to the ground as she got to the other side. Duke then went through, and the trio made a move, but in what direction they knew not.

They soon discovered, though. Slowly they were proceeding along in deep conversation, when Duke looked up, and to his unutterable horror he found that they had walked round to the gates of Newgate, and what was worse a body of the officials were just then coming out armed to the teeth, and under the command of the man who had rushed into the cell when our friends were about to escape, and was the cause of Duke's misfortunes.

Ralph and Grace had stopped by instinct when Duke stopped.

As yet they had not been seen.

It was night, and very dark. Nothing more favourable for our friends than that. It gave them a capital opportunity to make their escape unobserved, which they did.

"If those brutes ain't going after us, may I be swallowed by a crocodile!" said Duke, as the body of Newgate officials passed within two yards of him.

"Let them go; they won't find us," that was Ralph's reply.

"But where are we going?" asked Grace.

"Well, my lady, we had better go to the Leopard Inn for our horses," Ralph said.

"How know you they are there?"

"They are trained, my lady, to go there whenever any of us are taken.'"

"I shall want you, Duke, to accompany me to the royal palace," said Grace.

"With much pleasure," said the highwayman, gallantly.

"You would like to know the nature of our visit, no doubt."

"I am not inquisitive, but still I should like to know for what we are going."

"Then you shall. I saved Milly one night from a gang of ruffians, and while we were riding away together my horse ran against the horses of the royal carriage, and caused terrible confusion. His Majesty jumped out, had me taken to Newgate, and took Milly with him to the palace."

"Come, my lady," said Duke, "let's hasten on; we may be too late. His Majesty won't wait too long, especially when he thinks there is a chance of losing his prize."

"Would you go on foot?"

"Yes, my lady; I think it would be a surer way of getting admittance."

"For a change, I think I will proceed on foot," said Ralph. "Adieu, my lady! I shall see you soon, Duke, old boy."

"Probably. Adieu!" answered Duke, and they parted.

We will follow Dashing Ralph, and leave Duke and his fair companion to reach St. James's Palace.

Ralph watched his comrade with the beautiful girl leaning on his (Duke's) arm out of sight, then he turned, and slowly wended his way towards the City.

He was deeply abstracted in meditative thought when a half-stifled scream caused him to stop and look around.

Seeing nobody near, he resumed his walk, but the cry again broke upon his ears in a sad plaintive voice, and he stopped and listened, determined, if the cries should be again repeated, to discover and rescue those who might be in danger.

The cry came again.

It issued from one of those old-fashioned wooden houses, of which there are but few left standing now.

Ralph could barely detect from whence it came, and he anxiously waited for a repetition.

He was in Farringdon Street, and near the Fleet Ditch, that has long since been done away with.

Again he heard the same sweet sad voice

that he had heard before, and this time he detected from whence it proceeded.

"This, then, is the den," he muttered. "A very nice place for disposing of any one."

He stood beneath the house from where the lamentations came—a strange dilapidated old place, with the front above the door projecting forward, and stretching over the murky pool.

How was he to enter?

That was a difficult question to answer.

For nearly five minutes he stood surveying the place, when the cries rent his heart.

The door.

He tried that, but it resisted his every effort, skilful as he was.

The window.

He tried several, and these, too, proved obstinate.

At last.

The casement shivered beneath the pressure of his dagger-point that he had driven n the crevice, and with one steady wrench the window-frame parted noiselessly.

He entered the room, a small, dark, and badly furnished apartment, and silently closing the window after him, he crept round the wall for a way of exit.

The rattling noise of the crumbling mortar and torn pieces of paper that fell from the wall beneath the pressure of his hand on to the bare boards stopped the wild beating of his heart, and caused him to stand breathlessly.

He heard a buzzing of voices, but the cries had ceased, and a cold perspiration trickled down his back as the thought came vividly to his mind that some poor girl might have fallen a victim to the occupants of the strange old house he now stood in.

He continued his search for some means of quitting the den he had got into.

Joy !

His heart gave one bound, and commenced a rapid pulsation ; his hand fell upon a cold iron knob in the door.

He looked through the keyhole and caught cold in his eye. All within and without appeared to be perpetual darkness.

The door he quietly opened, and emerged into a narrow dark passage.

He ascertained that it was a passage by the fact that he fell over a barrier of rickety old banisters, and after a rapid flight of some hundred feet descent he alighted, greatly to his surprise, perfectly safe.

He fell upon a soft substance which he discovered to be sawdust, and there he lay, not daring to breathe, for he heard people about.

His fall made a tremendous noise, and disturbed the buzzers he had heard, and now he heard them swearing vengeance against any daring intruder who may, as they supposed, have entered.

After a vigilant search he heard, with a feeling of delight, the men retire. Then he arose, and felt inquisitive to know where he was—that he soon learnt.

"A vault," he muttered.

A vault it was.

"The sooner I get out of here the sooner I shall feel comfortable."

So saying he made for the stairs, and ascended them four at the time. He was once more in the passage ; he was very careful in avoiding the rickety banisters.

"There's another flight of stairs here," he thought. While walking down the passage his foot came in contact with the bottom one, and almost dislocated his big toe.

He could have sworn, but he thought he had better not. He knew that it would not ease the pain, and so he commenced to mount the stairs.

At each step he took the stair would give a prolonged creak beneath the pressure of his foot, and as he raised it.

It was with great difficulty and after the lapse of some time that he reached the top.

He heard voices issuing from a room, and he knew by the manner of their talk that plotting was going on, so he stooped and put his ear to the keyhole.

"Is the child to be kept or put out of the way ?" he heard a gruff voice say.

"The child must be kept—kept in secrecy, you understand," said another voice, that of a Frenchman.

"Perfectly."

"That will do, then. This you may take in advance ; when next you see me you shall have double what you have got there."

Ralph put his eye to the keyhole and saw the Frenchman give the other a bag of gold.

The highwayman's fingers itched, and while one hand wandered to the butt of a pistol, the other fastened on the handle of the door.

He was in the act of entering when a scream made him leap round.

That voice!

Was the same that he had before heard.

From whence did it proceed?

A room up a few more stairs.

Ralph made his way up the few more stairs, and went into a room where he could hear some one sobbing.

He did not see any one on first entering, but some one saw him, and he heard a glad cry.

He turned and looked in the direction from where it issued.

He saw the fair prisoner, a pretty little girl between seven and eight years of age, with languishing black eyes and a profusion of rich chesnut brown hair, that fell over a form marvellously moulded and beautifully white.

The little thing looked up tearfully into the highwayman's handsome face. She scanned his features as would a person of four times her age, then she asked in a pretty childish voice—

" Have you come to take me to mamma?"

"I have come to save you from the wicked men who brought you here," replied Ralph, kindly, his reckless nature quite subdued by the sad, sorrowful aspect of that little innocent face.

" These wicked men promised to take me home if I was a good girl," the child said, rising from the floor and leaning confidingly on her protector's arm. " I have been a good girl, but they have never come, and I have been here such a long time now."

" Dear little girl, they shan't keep you here any longer," said Ralph, caressively stroking her rich hair from her white broad forehead. " What is your name, little one?"

" Lady Florence Wintermearl."

" Do you remember where you live, little Flo?"

" No, I don't; it is so far."

" Then you shall stay with me until I can find your mamma."

The child nestled to him confidingly.

" Come along, Florie; let us leave here."

He took the little creature in his arms and descended the stairs. Stopping outside the door where he heard the men still in conversation, he muttered—

" I shall want some money."

He took a pistol from his belt, looked to see that the priming was all right, and with a sudden push he sent the door flying open and entered the room.

Two men who were seated at a table immediately sprang up.

The French nobleman uttered an angry exclamation, and made a dash at Ralph for the child.

Little Florence screamed as he approached.

The highwayman put the tube of his pistol in the foreigner's face and forced him back.

" I want your money," he said. " Make the least resistance, and I'll put a bullet in your infernal skull."

" What are you going to do with my child?" asked the Frenchman, his teeth chattering, and his face livid with fear.

" I am going to take care of her," replied Ralph, " and of course I shall want paying for it, so out with the coin, or, by Jupiter! you are a dead man."

The Frenchman would have made some comment, but the dangerous look of the pistol so close to his forehead held him dumb, and after several efforts to get to his pocket, he drew forth a long purse filled at both ends, and held secure in the middle by a ring that went round it.

Ralph put out his hand.

The purse was dropped into it, and the Frenchman drew back his hand as though afraid of being stung by the touch of the highwayman.

Ralph weighed the purse in the palm of his hand. It was well stocked and rather heavy. He put it in his pocket with an air of pride, and then turned to his victim, whose fingers were playing nervously on the hilt of a huge sword.

" Look here, my friend," he said, " if you don't want to go to the devil just yet, you will put your hands behind you and lie in the corner. Take my advice as a friend."

The Frenchman looked curiously at the

cool speaker, and thinking, perhaps, that it would be as well to comply with the other's commands, for his own safety, he locked his hands behind his crooked back, and slid down on his heels into a corner.

" That's right," said the highwayman, and then he turned to the other, a big, burly bully.

" I want your money, also the money you just had given you," he said.

" Do you ?" said the man, doggedly.

" I do. Will you give it to me ?"

" I'll see you —— first!"

" I never ask more than three times. I have asked twice already; once more, and if you don't out with the coin, you deliver up the ghost."

The man surveyed the daring highwayman with a dangerous look. He was very suspiciously fumbling about in the breast of his coat.

Ralph kept a sharp look upon his every movement; but, before he was aware of it, the man sprang upon him with a long, rusty dagger.

Ralph caught his arms and tried to keep the weapon off, but that he could not do, being burdened as he was with the weight of his timid little charge.

The Frenchman, seeing the noble fellow's difficulty, thought it a favourable opportunity to seek atonement for the loss of his money.

He drew his ponderous weapon as he sprang to his feet, and made a fierce cut at Ralph, who, at that moment, dashed his assailant from him by throwing all his lion-like strength in his powerful arm for one thrust.

The man reeled round, rolled against the Frenchman, and they both fell together.

Ralph dashed open the window and sprang out, his little protege twined her arms around his neck, and clung to him tremblingly as he ran along a plank of about two feet wide that extended across the Fleet Ditch, to the window of an opposite house.

The vibration of the board beneath his feet, and the loud shouting of the Frenchman close to his ear warned him of danger.

Turning sharply on the narrow plank he faced his angry pursuer.

" Back !" thundered Ralph; " another step and I scatter your brains."

The Frenchman's hand was locked firmly round the hilt of his large sword, that was raised with murderous intent to cut the bold highwayman down.

Rapid as the thought rushed to his mind, the dashing Ralph drew a pistol and presented it full cock at his pursuer's head.

The act was only in time to save him, for the other's weapon glistened brilliantly as it rapidly descended through the moon's silent rays, but it stopped half way, and the Frenchman went back a step or two as the cold iron of the pistol touched his forehead.

" Give me back that child, or I'll cut you down," he said.

" Fool ! Do you think I would leave her to be murdered by you?"

" She is my daughter."

" Oh, I am not !" cried the child.

" No, no, my dear, I know very well you are not," said Ralph.

The Frenchman glared at him furiously.

" You must give her up," he exclaimed.

" Not if I know it," answered Ralph.

The Frenchman sprang nimbly forward and made a vicious dig at his adversary.

Ralph did not want to kill the man; but his own, and the life of his little charge were at the villain's mercy, so he fired, thinking it better to rid the world of a heartless wretch, and so prevent further misery he might cause.

The Frenchman bounded like a stricken tiger, and fell from the plank.

There was a loud splash as his body sank beneath the murky water; then it rose, and the highwayman watched it out of sight, borne down on the breast of the rapid current, the white blood-stained face turned upwards, and the eyes fixed with a stony glare on his slayer.

" That's settled him, I think," muttered Ralph, as he crossed the plank and entered the window of the house opposite the one he had just left.

He was not long in making his way through the old place; he passed through several rooms, but nobody did he meet, so he made his way out with very little trouble.

He thought the child very quiet, and looking at her uneasily, he found that she had fainted; the excitement and the fearful

THE HIGHWAYMAN PLEADING FORGIVENESS.

...gedy she had witnessed were too much for her.

"Poor little thing," he said, imprinting a ...ss upon her pale cheek; "I could almost ...ish that she might not be owned, for already ...feel a sort of paternal affection. I could ...eep her and be happy, she would be some-...ing to live and care for; but," he mused, "I ...ust not keep her in this state—I must seek ...r some place where I can get her refresh-...ents, and bring her back to conscious-...ss."

So saying, he drew her closely to his ...east, wended his way along the side of the ...ch, the water washed up the bank with a ...llen splash.

The silvery light played on the ripples, and while he watched one recede from the other, he was startled by seeing a dark form float past him—the form of his late opponent, the Frenchman.

He shuddered, and turned his head away to shut out the steady gaze of his victim's eyes, and when he ventured to look again the form had passed.

He seemed fearfully oppressed, and hastened his steps to pass the dreaded flood.

He suddenly stopped, and a cry of terror left his lips.

Before him stood the ghastly form of the Frenchman, that but a few seconds before he had seen floating down the stream.

"Can it be?" he gasped.

"The dead returned to life for retribution," replied the other in a sepulchral voice.

CHAPTER LXXX.
PAUL CLIFFORD AND TOM KING.

SEATED round a long oaken table that ranged from one end to the other of a grand, spacious hall, were Tyburn Dick, Captain Claude, and the remainder of their brethren.

The hall in which they were gathered was a magnificent building of solid stone, and in several parts of it stood huge granite pillars that supported the roof, which was likewise stone.

It was a strange place to be buried in the earth on Hounslow Heath, and how it got there we cannot say, without it had been built by some of the ancient Britons for refuge in the time of the Romish invasions, which probably was the case; but, however, our friends now took possession of it as their haunt and stronghold against all enemies.

The Boy King of the Highwaymen arose to address his comrades.

"Gentlemen," he began, "three of my most noble men have been absent for some time now.

He paused, and looked around at the many anxious faces.

Every one waited breathlessly to hear the rest of his address.

Dick continued—

"I have determined upon a plan to bring them amongst us again, if they are still living. A thousand men I have got who will gladly join us to search for them; but before we take such a step as that, we will try what we can do by making a vigilant search by ourselves.

"I propose that every one of you start in a different direction, and return here in three days hence, with or without what tidings you may have gathered."

The men were silent until he had done, then they rose and clapped their hands in approval.

"Let's drink success to the undertaking, and then set out without delay," said the brave boy.

Splendid goblets were produced upon the table, and filled with a delicious wine.

Every man raised a cup, drank success to the enterprise, and departed in silence.

Tyburn Dick and Captain Claude were the last to leave, and they rode away together.

They rode on in silence. Captain Claude was in a sad kind of reverie. They had turned their horses' heads towards London, and that is where they were going to make their first search.

The ride from Hounslow to London was not a short one, nor was it too safe or pleasant for travellers.

At night time especially, when the watchmen and patrols were few and far between, and the wayfarer knew not whether a masked highwayman might ride out from behind the next bush or tree and demand his money or his life.

But Captain Claude and his son were well armed, and had no thought of fear.

They were magnificently mounted, and each carried a sword of fine Damascus steel, keen-edged and sharp-pointed, and each had a pair of heavy steel-barrelled, silver-hilted pistols.

The night—or early morning rather, for it was past midnight—was beautiful and bright, gemmed with stars that twinkled out through white transparent clouds, and high in heaven rode the summer moon.

A distant church clock tolled the hour of one.

"I heard that same clock chime at midnight," said Tyburn Dick, "when I saw the White Phantom on Hounslow Heath."

"Never mind the phantom," said Claude.

"Here are some living people; perhaps that will be better," said Dick. "By the way, I was just wishing for an adventure to rouse you up."

"I am ready without rousing," said the captain, with his hand on the jewelled hilt of his weapon. "How many and what are they?"

"Two, and highwaymen, I think. Here they come, however, to speak for themselves."

The faint trampling of horses' hoofs, which for some few minutes had been heard behind them, now came more rapidly and more distinct.

"You are right," said Claude; "there are two, and they are highwaymen."

"They are masked," Dick added, "which I take it is a conclusive sign."

The night was so clear that the shadows of the trees were like photographs on the moonlit roadway and the sward.

So it could be seen distinctly that the coming riders were masked.

On they came, each mounted on a noble steed, each dressed like a high class gentleman of the period, each full of gallant, graceful bearing, and each well provided with weapons.

On they came past the two friends, then wheeled round and suddenly confronted them.

"I thought so," said Dick, as he drew his sword, "but they are gentlemanly rascals. They did not attack us behind, but came face to face."

Captain Claude drew his sword, and waited for the masked men to speak.

"What is it?" asked Dick. "Why do you come in the way of gentlemen? Don't come too close, or you will get hurt."

The two masked men laughed like men who find pleasure in being gallantly defied.

One of them answered with prompt decision—

"Stand and deliver!"

"These are two things we never do," said Captain Claude, "but we will see you damned first."

"We don't see the point of it," said Dick, "but you may feel both the point and edge."

One of the masked men clapped his hands in applause, and said—

"Good! Bravo!"

"That fellow *must* be a gentleman," thought Dick, "for he can appreciate a joke."

"If you will not deliver," said one of the two masked men, who drew their swords, "we must make you."

"If you can," said Dick, "but you will find the task difficult."

Each singled out his man, and the contest began.

"If all the gentlemen of the road were like you," said Tyburn Dick, forgetting that he was one, "it would be a pleasure to meet with them occasionally."

The man in the mask accepted the compliment with a graceful bow, and parried a skilful thrust with incomparable ease.

"I was about to say the same thing to my antagonist," said Captain Claude, who had tried some of his best points, and found that his opponent knew as much as he did, "but you always anticipate me. I never think of a good thing without your putting it out, just when it's on the tip of my tongue."

"That shows congeniality of mind," said Claude's antagonist, trying his seventh lunge, and finding his weapon held safely aside, instead of seeing it in Claude's breast. "And you fence remarkably well."

"You know a little," said the captain, "and I shall teach you a lesson before we part."

The masked man laughed at the threat.

"You fence like a man," he said, "but boast like a boy."

"Do I?" said the captain, quietly, "but I keep my temper like a veteran. Don't I, Mr. Artful? Did you think to get me out and make me impetuous?"

Mr. Artful evidently had that intention, for he laughed on finding it discovered.

Amid all this banter there had been continuing, perhaps the most marvellous display of sword science ever witnessed since the days of chivalry; it would have been impossible to decide for superiority in either of the four men fighting—each was such a combination of incomparable qualities.

The perfect mastery of the equestrian art, so necessary to a duel on horseback, must not be forgotten.

And this entire mastery each combatant had.

Horse and rider moved by instinct, rein hand and sword hand, eye and foot, were never for a moment out of unison.

Captain Claude's opponent had an iron wrist, but so had Captain Claude, and the latter's wrist was the more supple of the two—he was more lithe and agile altogether.

"Dick," he said.

"Well."

"How many passes have you made?"

"Ten."

Captain Claude made another pass, it went

so close that when parried the sword point picked a button off the masked man's coat.

"So have I," said Captain Claude; "that was the tenth I just made. How many have you parried?"

"Ten."

"So have I."

"Are you wounded?"

"No."

"Neither am I."

"Is your opponent?" asked Dick.

"No."

"Neither is mine."

"So," said Captain Claude, "it seems that all we have done has been to make and parry ten passes, except that I have picked a button off my fellow's coat."

"Then you have done more than I have by a button," said Dick, watching his adversary's eye, which seemed to promise something more than our hero had received as yet.

"I can't pink my fellow," said Claude, "and am equally certain he can't pink me; so I want to wager a supper for four that I disarm him before you disarm yours."

"Done," said Dick.

And no more was said for a while.

The two highwaymen with whom our friends were fighting seemed considerably astonished by the coolness of the wager.

Their sublime skill was completely ignored by Dick and Claude, who were treating them simply as feinting men upon whom to practise a disarm for a wager.

The idea seemed to make them slightly angry. They fought with more energy.

They did not speak, but threw such force and beauty into their fencing skill, that Captain Claude and Dick had to do their best. Dick was feeling his way warily to accomplish a disarm done by a trick known only to himself and the captain.

It was a point without precedent or parallel, and only to be achieved by incessant tireless application.

Dick quickened the time of his play; his weapon twined and flashed like an electric serpent round his opponent's blade, gliding, clinging, clashing, and dazzling by its meteoric twirling, while all the time he sustained a powerful pressure on the other's wrist.

At last his arm.

A flash of Dick's eye, and in the instant an imperceptible touch upon the rein raised the fore-legs of his obedient steed, Fairy, so that he obtained greater height, and with it greater power, without altering his distance.

Then a rapid dash, and cling, and glide together, and the sword of Dick's antagonist went ringing from his hand.

At the self-same instant Captain Claude did the self-same thing.

The sword torn from his adversary's hand went flying upward and caught the sword of Dick's antagonist, both weapons descending to the earth together.

Captain Claude and Dick lowered their own blades immediately.

"Come," said the two masked men, grasping our hero and his sire's hands by a spontaneous impulse, "we are beaten—fairly, wondrously."

"Forgive me," added Captain Claude's antagonist, "for saying that you boasted like a boy."

"We have not disgraced our teaching," said Claude.

"Come, gentlemen, we are fellow pupils, and should be friends—you would do us honour, and we no shame to you."

"With all my heart," said Dick; "and the supper for four, though neither lost nor won, shall be a banquet for the four who are here. Let us know each other."

"I," said Dick's late antagonist, removing his mask, and showing a noble face and princely head, "am proud to introduce my comrade. Come, old fellow, unmask, and bow uncovered to these gentlemen."

The other rode up, unmasked, and lifted his hat.

"Paul Clifford!" exclaimed Tyburn Dick, "and Tom King!"

CHAPTER LXXXI.

THE HEARSE THAT CONTAINED TWO GLASS COFFINS, IN WHICH THE MISSING HIGH-WAYMEN WERE DISCOVERED BY THE FOUR KNIGHTS OF THE ROAD.

"THEN I have fought with Captain Clifford," said Tyburn Dick.

The gallant highwayman bowed as he said—

"And beaten him."

"Nay, it was but a trick of fence."

"A trick that has won the supper."

"Let me say, gentlemen," put in Captain Claude, "that we are glad and proud to meet you."

The highwaymen bowed.

"Had we known you when we met," said Tom King, with his princely grace, "we should never have stopped you on such terms."

"Thanks for the grace," said Dick, bowing in turn with Captain Claude; "but we should have been sorry, for then we should not have fenced with two such swordsmen as Captain Paul Clifford and Tom King."

"And we, too, would have been sorry, for we should not have known two such famous gentlemen as——"

"Tyburn Dick, King of the Highwaymen, and Captain Claude," added Tom King, before Clifford had time to finish.

"And now, gentlemen, I vote for the supper," said Clifford.

"By the way, I know a capital place where we can get a splendid supper, at a *café* in the Haymarket," Tom King said.

"Then I vote we go," said Dick.

"So do I. Ugh! Here's a lively thing!" exclaimed Claude, and he shuddered.

The others followed the direction of his gaze, and shuddered too at what they saw.

A ponderous hearse, drawn by four spotless black horses, and driven by a solitary individual perched upon the top of the coach, robed in black velvet, the whole glided like a sombre shadow along the road.

The highwaymen, awed by its horribly gloomy appearance, fell back in silence to let it pass.

"See you that light?" asked Dick, not above his breath.

He pointed to the back of the hearse; through the crevice of the door streamed a flood of mellow light.

Paul Clifford's handsome dark face was awfully grave as he looked in direction of our hero's indication and saw the light.

"This is very strange," he said.

"Very," echoed Tom King.

"It strikes me there is some mystery about it," remarked Claude.

"I suggest that we stop it, and have a look inside," said Dick.

The rest agreed, and the four highwaymen rode forward.

The ominous-looking hearse, with its four noiseless horses, and the silent driver, went on at its same steady pace.

The highwaymen divided, King and Clifford went one side, and Claude and Dick went the other.

"Halt!" cried Dick.

They received no answer—the driver sat motionless.

"Halt!" cried Clifford.

Still no answer.

"Stop, or I'll shoot you down!" exclaimed Dick.

As before, there was no answer.

The highwaymen looked at one another in silent terror.

"I don't believe in supernatural visions," said Dick; "but this is something more than human."

"Try," said Claude; "test him by a shot."

Dick presented a pistol and fired.

The muffled form vanished, and the horses came to a sudden stop as the shot went whizzing over the hearse.

The knights of the road were terrified by the sudden disappearance of the man, and for some moments stood bewildered.

"Well," said Paul Clifford, "this is something terribly strange."

"It is," said King.

"I feel anxious to know why these lights are there," said Captain Claude.

"That we will quickly discover." Dick rode round to the back of the hearse as he spoke.

The rest followed him.

The door was forced open, and the gallant men were greatly surprised by what they saw.

The hearse contained two glass coffins. At the head and foot of each stood a large bright-oil burning lamp.

The thing that was most strange, and caused the highwaymen to wonder much, was two young and lovely women who sat between the coffins, and looked sadly upon the lifeless forms of the gallant men who were confined in them.

Dick gave a cry, and recoiled with alarm.

His companions looked anxiously for the cause of his alarm.

"See you, father, these men in these coffins?" exclaimed Dick.

"I do, and see no reason for your agitation. The men are dead."

"They are not. I saw one move."

"Pull the coffins out, and let us see," added Paul Clifford.

The two women in the hearse raised their heads and looked at the highwaymen. There was a strange, wild look in their eyes, that rather startled our friends.

"Out with the coffins," said Captain Claude.

The two strange women sprang up, and glared savagely at the highwaymen, who caught hold of the glass cases.

The women screamed as the coffins were pulled from them, and then threw themselves full length upon them.

There was a crashing of glass, and the two beautiful forms disappeared, and fell upon the men interred.

The lamps flickered and went out by some mysterious means.

The highwaymen began to get frightened, and while stood undecided how to act they were startled by the apparition of the man who had vanished from the box suddenly springing from the hearse.

He fell at Dick's feet.

"Give me a pistol," said Dick. "I will see, anyhow, whether he is supernatural or not."

Captain Claude handed him a weapon.

The boy fired.

The flash lighted up the scene for a moment, but no form was at his feet where it had fallen.

Dick was awfully mystified.

So were all the others.

Everything seemed so strange and mysterious; they were used to curious adventures, but this one out marvelled all.

The highwaymen, bold and daring as they were, were kept at bay by the seeming unnatural events.

What with the sudden disappearance of the coachman, the two beautiful women

sitting beside the coffins, and the lights going unexpectedly out was too much for them.

A death-like silence reigned for some minutes; the highwaymen stood fearful to speak, afraid of breaking the ominous spell by the sound of their own voice.

Dick clutched his sire's arm for companionship, and in almost a whisper asked if any one had a flint and steel.

Tom King said he had, in the same silent voice.

He took a small flint, a steel, and tinderbox from his pocket, and soon kindled a light.

Then by the light from the brimstoned stick he lighted the wick of the oil lamp.

The highwaymen then indulged in a general laugh at one another for their temerity.

"Never mind, old boy," said Dick. "This is anything but a cheerful kind of adventure."

"Anything," said Tom King. "Show us a light, Paul, old boy, and let's see what these lively coffins contain."

Paul showed the light.

Dick looked to see what the coffins contained. Each contained two persons.

The women sprang up simultaneously with each other as they were touched.

Dick was leaning over the coffin, and when the fair occupant of his sprang up, he was sent flying over Captain Claude's back, who stood behind him.

He did not lie long on the ground; he had caught sight of a face he knew, and in an instant he was upon his feet.

The women had gone—fled like passing shadows.

Captain Claude looked anxiously at Dick, who, without saying a word, after regaining his feet (not that he had lost them), commenced quickly, but carefully, to pick the pieces of glass out of the coffin and off the form he was so anxious to get at.

The last piece of glass Dick had thrown aside; he was in the act of lifting the form out of the coffin, when the person sprang up and clasped the boy round the neck.

"By Jove! here's a delightful sort of position to be found in," he said.

"Victor, my brave sir," exclaimed Dick "this is what I never dreamed of."

"I don't suppose you did. By Jove! I

had it in reality. Where's Gallant Tom?" asked Dick.

"Gallant Tom. Here! said the handsome highwayman, leaping from the coffin.

Captain Claude reeled round on his heels with astonishment at the sudden apparition of the daring fellow.

"Why, captain, have you, too, returned to returned to life?" said Gallant Tom, grasping Claude's two hands.

"After a long absence, yes. You must tell me where you have been, and how you came to be in this gloomy affair."

"Right, captain, we will tell story for story."

A mutual greeting was exchanged between the long-parted friends, in which Tom King and Paul Clifford joined, after going through the ceremony of introduction.

The party were gathered together for a start, when they were startled by the reappearance of two women.

One flew towards Victor St. James, and fell upon his breast, while the other was struggling with Gallant Tom.

"Dick," cried St. James, "get this she-devil away from me, or I shall be choked."

Dick sprang angrily at the lovely woman.

"Come away," said our hero, trying to pull her off the young nobleman; "come off, or I'll kill you."

The woman laughed fiendishly, and with a sudden wrench sent St. James reeling back into the coffin.

At that self-same instant there was a crash and Gallant Tom was swung into his coffin by his fair beautiful assailant.

Clifford and King instantly dismounted, and went to the rescue of their newly-found comrades.

They sprang upon the women and remorselessly hurled them with terrible wrath to the earth.

Gallant Tom and Victor St. James were assisted from their critical positions.

They were weak and very much altered, but the young nobleman's gaiety had not left him. He was as bold and daring as ever, but with all that he carefully got out of the woman's way as she rose to her feet.

There was a terrible scream as the women

dashed past the highwaymen and leaped into the hearse.

The door closed with a bang, and shut the two beautiful but strange women in the sombre-looking vehicle.

The coachman was seen upon his box, silent and motionless, and the four Arabian horses, that had hitherto stood stationary started off at a pace terrific.

The highwaymen stood bewildered.

"Follow!" exclaimed Gallant Tom, with sudden energy, "save the women."

"Save the women," added Victor St. James.

The highwaymen were upon their steeds in an instant, and galloping after the hearse with its two fair prisoners.

St. James and Gallant Tom had to share a part of their friend's saddle.

CHAPTER LXXXII.
THE REVEL—THE KING'S PALACE—THE FIGHT
WITH THE PALACE GUARD.

"GONE!" exclaimed Dick.

The party drew up.

They had ridden partly in the track of the hearse, but it had outstripped them by its stealthy glide.

"Well, this beats all I have ever seen," said Tom King.

"This is nothing. You should have been where I was," said St. James.

"Come, tell us your story," said Dick.

"So I will, but not here."

"The supper!" shouted King. "Come along; we will hold a revel to-night. Come, gentlemen."

"Supper and a revel," seconded Paul Clifford. "We'll hold the revel at your house, eh, Tom?"

"And the supper too, so come, gentlemen."

The gentlemen went, and after half an hour's riding they drew up as Tom King halted before a splendid mansion.

The door was opened by a livered flunkey, and as our friends were ushered into a spacious hall, their steeds were led away by several grooms to the stables.

A banquet was laid in a magnificent room brilliantly lighted up by the massive chandeliers that hung from the ceiling.

Dick and his companions were astonished a

the tasteful splendour of the place, and wondered much that a single man should keep such a place.

A delicious odour arose from the fragrant plants and rich bouquets that decorated the room, and gave it more the appearance of a fairy land.

The highwaymen were seated round the table. Powdered lacqueys waited upon them until our friends were fired with wine, and fearing lest these men should hear too much, they were ordered to retire.

The lacqueys retired.

The highwaymen were alone.

Our hero had lost all dignity. He was leaning back in a state of happy ignorance; hanging half-way over the back of his chair, with his arms swinging about as though they didn't belong to him.

One or two of the party had subsided into quietude underneath the table, and others had got their feet over the back of some one else's chair.

Captain Claude was the only one that could see at all straight, and he spoke—

"Gen—hic—gemmen, this is—hic—really too bad."

Somebody grunted.

"Too ba—bad—weally," said Tom King, looking through his small white tapering fingers. "I—I ob—hic—object to such proceedings. Demme!"

"Hear, hear, hear," exclaimed Paul Clifford, hammering a decanter that he had drained on the table.

"Ye—s, hear, hear!"

The voice proceeded very faintly from under the table.

Victor St. James, who had rolled off his chair, sat under the table.

He could not get up without some support, so he clutched the table-cloth, and tried to make his ascent.

He fancied he was rising.

So he was; but unfortunately the cloth slipped, he fell, and a plate of rich preserves, very sticky, fell into his face, and stuck there.

"Coffee!" groaned Dick.

"Ah! Coffee; that's the thing," said Clifford.

"Yes, I say coffee," shouted Tom King.

"Fred—Fred, you blackguard! Where the devil's the bell-rope? Dick, old fellow wake that sneaking cuss up—we want coffee."

Dick crawled along on his hands and knees to the fire-place, and clutched the bell rope.

Victor St. James, Paul Clifford, and Tom King all crawled after him, and clutched the bell-rope too.

The continued tinkling of the bell brought several lacqueys dashing into the room.

They looked in astonishment at the four gallant men swinging on the bell-rope, and they were not at all surprised when the rope gave way, and the four gallant men went rolling over one another.

"Coffee!" yelled Tom King, spying the grinning face of Fred.

"Coffee!" echoed Dick.

"Yes, my lord—yes, my lord. Coffee! yes, my lord, directly," shouted the fellow, frantically, and away he went.

Coffee was brought in. The highwaymen were soon refreshed by a little of the beverage, and after a quiet game at cards, Victor St. James related the story of his adventure.

It ran as follows :—

"Some considerable time ago, when I left Cornwall, I was passing the old priory, near the Leopard Inn, and saw a note flutter from the window. I picked it up, and read it, but the words exactly I have forgotten now, but they ran to the effect that a lady had been taken there by a gang of ruffians, and she wanted to get away. This lady was your fair mistress, Milly."

He addressed Captain Claude.

The noble highwayman was awfully agitated.

"Did you save her ?" he asked.

"You will hear as I go on," replied the youth. "I went back to the old priory, and ascended to the window by a ladder that was lowered for some one else. When I got in at the window I was surprised to see, instead of Milly, another fair captive. I was about to escape with her, when a party of young reprobates dashed into the room, and set upon me furiously.

"The young lady was torn from me, and I had to fly for dear life. I ran along a long corridor, and by a miracle burst open the chamber in which Milly was confined.

"She had only time enough to tell me she had been taken there in mistake for her companion, Grace, by the libertine young lord, the Earl of Aldervale.

"I was determined to defend her with my own life against her persecutors, and did so. With great presence of mind I put Milly behind me, as Edward Aldervale rushed into the room and fired.

"I was shot, and from that time I remember no more until I awoke in fearful pain, and found myself in a dungeon. There I remained in solitary confinement, never seeing any one but the man who came masked to bring me my food, and there I was when Gallant Tom was trapped and put with me. I was glad he came, for I wanted a companion."

"I was for your sake," said the highwayman, "but for mine own I was not."

"I'll continue," said St. James.

"Do."

He did.

This is what he said.

"I had most of the dungeon."

"I had enough of it," said Gallant Tom.

"Don't interrupt."

"Go ahead."

"Where was the dungeon?" asked Dick.

"Beneath the priory," said the youth.

"The priory," mused Claude. "Why, we pass it to go to the haunt."

"What haunt?" inquired Gallant Tom.

Dick told him.

Victor St. James continued his story.

"As I said, Tom was not with me long in the dungeon. We were visited by these two strange women, who had an extraordinary wish to throw us back into the coffins. They offered us freedom if we would consent to marry them. We refused. They had us taken from the dungeon, and conveyed blindfolded to a splendid apartment in the priory. They visited us again, and again asked us to marry them, but we didn't see it.

"They said if we refused they would kill us. We asked them why they had such a desire to tie us to them, but they refused to give us any satisfaction beyond that they were the owners of the priory. We told them we did not care if they owned twenty priories, they would not get us to marry them.

"They left us then, and some days expired before we saw them again. Then, more urgently than before, they pressed their suit, but we remained firm to our resolution. They then suddenly became gentle, and lived with us for some time, and we pretty well enjoyed ourselves. But they again began to entice us to marry them. I was quite contented with her unmarried, and told her so; so did Tom. They then turned upon us like demons, and told us blankly we should not have had the enjoyment we had at their expense if they thought we were after all determined to refuse. We told them we didn't ask them for it. They grew more savage still, and left us.

"But they returned again and lived with us.

"One afternoon, while at tea, we were drugged, weren't we, Tom?"

"I believe so; I didn't remember anything from then."

"I suppose they then put us in the glass coffins, but for what purpose I don't know; but I shall try and find out. That's my story, gentlemen."

"Were you unconscious while in the coffin?" asked Dick.

"To a degree I was. I could see all that went on, though I could not comprehend where I was. One thing rather astonished me was the man who came through the top of the coach."

"Then he must have been the coachman?" said Dick.

"Probably," remarked Captain Claude; "you mean the man you shot at?"

"Yes, the supernatural individual; he must have gone through a sort of trap-door."

"Which is most likely," said Tom King. "I propose, gentlemen, that we wind up the evening by going to the ball at the royal palace."

"Have you cards?" asked St. James.

Tom King said—

"I have."

Dick said—

"The deuce!"

Tom King drew from his pocket a book, and took therefrom four cards of invitation.

"May I ask," said Captain Claude, "without being inquisitive, where you got them from?"

"I borrowed them of four horrible old brutes."

"On the highway."

"Just so."

"Then we want two more?"

"I have got four, too," said Paul Clifford.

"May I ask if you borrowed yours, too?" said our hero, with a smile.

"I did."

"And from whom?"

"From four horrible old brutes, too."

"Then you met eight?"

"Exactly."

"Were they feminines or masculines?"

"Both."

"All in one carriage?"

"No."

"There were four fusseys and their old rogeys," said Tom, "two of each in each carriage."

"Then you robbed them?" said Dick.

"No, we did not; we only borrowed their tickets, because they were such shocking old fogeys, and I knew they would not be able to enjoy themselves."

"After that we will start out," said Paul Clifford.

Tom King touched a small silver bell.

A groom entered.

"Get the horses ready," said the highwayman.

The man retired.

"We can't proceed on horseback," remarked Captain Claude.

"Why not?"

"We should arouse suspicion to halt at the palace."

"We can halt before we get to the palace, and put the horses up at the livery stables."

The groom announced that the horses were ready.

"How many?" inquired Clifford.

"Six," replied the man.

The highwaymen rose and departed.

.   .   .   .   .   .

The palace was reached while the ball was at its height.

It might have been that the six handsome men would not have passed unchallenged,

even after tendering the tickets, but for the presence of Captain Claude, who was known to the usher.

The captain did not keep the company the others with a closeness sufficiently defi to compromise himself in the ▒▒▒▒ ▒ ▒ covery, but still closely ▒▒▒▒ ▒ ▒▒yserfy stately lacqueys, who ▒ ▒▒▒▒ ▒ them doubt as they passed.

But their noble bearing awed them. They might have expressed something of the confusion occasioned in their mind at reading the name of an old marquis on Tom King's card, and seeing a graceful young gentleman instead; but King, seeing one of their mouths about to open, turned to bow to a high and mighty nobleman, as though he knew him, and, in turning, set his heel on the man's foot.

The highwaymen had prepared their toilet by a very simple process.

At a court ball, when not a state occasion, boots were allowed.

They had only to turn their coats, therefore, which, being made for this purpose, were a very dashing general style on one side, and full court dress on the other.

On they went, following not too closely on the heels of Captain Claude and St. James, and attracting much observation by their distinguished grace and noble carriage.

When fairly in the rooms they separated, each had his own particular game to follow.

King was making love to a duchess, as was his custom. His taste was rather high, and nothing less than a duchess suited him.

Paul Clifford was making love to a lady-in-waiting.

A lady of title and fashion—rich and lovely.

Tyburn Dick had nothing particular to do, except to study women's nature, and make the accquaintance of such people as he might find it to his advantage to meet on the road at some future time.

"I should like to dine with my duchess," thought Tom King, looking wistfully towards a lady who leaned on the arm of an elderly don. "I wonder who the old buffer is?"

While he was wondering Paul Clifford was engaged with his lovely lady-in-waiting.

Our two gentlemen of the road had met these ladies before, during an adventure,

...en the coach in which they were was stopped by some of the Black Brethren band.

Not having the heart to terrify or rob such beauty, the two rode up, dispersed the band, and were mistaken by the ladies for brave deliverers.

Hence the favour with which they were received on the present occasion.

While King was praying for an opportunity to speak to his duchess, a gentleman of the household stepped towards her, and bowed to the elderly don by her side.

He was well received, and remained with her some time.

Tom felt uneasy, and wanted to get her away.

Probably the gentleman was a suitor to the lovely duchess; if he was, King hoped he might break his neck.

The gentleman suddenly left the duchess, while Tom King was wishing these evil things against him, then he stepped up himself and bowed to the lady, who was leaning on her father's arm.

The duchess recognised him.

"Dear papa," she said, "this is the gentleman who so kindly rescued us from the dreadful robbers."

"So you rescued my Beatrice, brave sir," exclaimed the old duke.

The music of a waltz began.

"May I have the honour of your daughter's hand for this?" asked Tom King.

"Certainly, sir, certainly; nice fellow, very," he added.

Tom glided away with his arm round the waist of Beatrice, so close that her arm and swelling breast pressed his.

The gentleman returned at this moment.

"Who is that person?" he asked of the duke.

"That person, sir, said the duke, with dignity, "is Sir Thomas Wintermearl—great family—very old—splendid castle—rich—
...e—rescued Beatrice from robbers."

"Curse him."

"Eh?"

"Curse him—I see it already, Duke of Clevedon—he has ruined my hopes—destroyed me in the sight of Beatrice. I do not think he is what he says. Let him beware of my revenge."

He turned away scowling, and ran against another gentleman who was scowling very hard at the lady-in-waiting and Paul Clifford.

The second scowler was the captain of the Black Band.

"Are you leaving the saloon?" he asked of the other.

"Perdition! yes; that meddling fool, for whom I shall wait with my sword, has done too much."

"That man—he with the duchess?"

"He."

"Leave him to me," said the captain, with a peculiar smile. "I have been watching him with several others. You will see an interruption to the festival presently."

He went out.

A few minutes after his departure a page entered and approached our hero.

A young and singularly handsome youth, with fair clustering hair and soft blue eyes, that shifted from the penetrating gaze of Dick.

"I have a message for you," said the boy.

"For me?" inquired Dick.

"For Earl Richard Aldervale."

"From whence has it come?"

"Read, and you will see," said the boy, with a smile.

He took the missive, and let the messenger's hand rest in his own while he perused the note.

The page's frame thrilled, and his eyes lit with a strange fire as he watched the young highwayman's form, while Dick read the message.

The thrill of emotion and the looks were evidence of more than boyish love.

"It shall be done," said our hero, whose face had grown graver while he read, "at once."

The page kissed the youth's hand, then withdrew.

"The lad seems fond of you," observed St. James, stalking up to his friend: "and what a handsome lad he is, one might fancy him a lady in disguise."

Our hero did not reply to this.

"Warn our friends that they are in danger," he said, in a low tone; "they have been betrayed."

"Betrayed!"

"I have just received this note from Milly, and it is here she overheard the plot for our arrest."

"The deuce!"

There was a flourish of trumpets.

"Way for the King," cried the chamberlain, loudly, "way for his Majesty."

The throng fell back to make a path for his Majesty, King George the Third, Defender of Faith, &c.

He came in leaning on the arm of the Queen Regent, and while the guests were bowing, there came a startling outcry at the door.

Everybody looked to see what was the matter, and in came two old fogies out of breath, and in an awful state of indignation.

The duchess and the lady-in-waiting had just returned.

Tom King was looking like a lounging lover at the door through which his body had disappeared, when, unfortunately for him, he was seen by one of the fogies.

King was thinking of no evil and no danger, scarcely heeding the outcry at the door; he was giving all his mind to the memory of a few words he had whispered in the ear of the beautiful duchess, and the few words she had whispered back, when he was startled by the words—

"That's the man—the wretch of a highwayman, who stole my watch and rings."

King turned, and found himself the centre of observation.

He was not at all disconcerted.

He walked quietly up to the duke, and took his arm in the most familiar manner.

"Can you tell me the meaning of the uproar?"

"Deuce take it! no."

"Beware of the highwayman!" cried the suitor, suddenly. "Ho, there, for the guard —seize that man—Tom King, the highwayman."

"Dear me," said Tom, still with his hand in the duke's arm, and looked round with his jewelled eyeglass to his eye; "is it possible that the notorious fellow is here?"

"Possible, egad, they are looking for him."

The lady's suitor, who was an officer, came up with his sword drawn.

"My dear duke," he said, hotly, "the scoundrel on your arm is the highwayman."

The duke jumped away.

"Egad—no—a mistake—sir, Sir Thomas Wintermearl—great family—very old—rich —saved my daughter, egad."

"Seize him!" cried the officer, and the guard entered. "Let not his companions escape."

"His companions?"

"Tyburn Dick—Paul Clifford—and Captain Claude."

These three were together now.

The game was up.

They were betrayed, and each had his hand upon his sword.

The guard advanced.

"Seize them!" exclaimed the King. "Cut them down if they resist!"

"Very well, your Royal Highness," said Dick to himself, and when he said very well, this princely highwayman resolved to sacrifice himself in an heroic attempt to save his friends.

Looking round, his eye fell upon the captain of the Black Band.

Dick made a secret sign, unseen by all but Bertram, and he seeing it, trembled.

Without a word, but with lips white as ashes, he quitted the palace.

Then Dick approached the Prince Regent.

"Your Royal Highness," he said.

The prince took a step back

"What would you, sir?"

"This."

He spoke, and with the word he had caught the prince in an iron grip, and the po   o his sword was at the prince's throat.

"Now, your Majesty," said Dick, fixing the King with his glittering eye, "say the word, order the guard away, let my comrades go, or I will kill his Royal Highness."

The King was in a dilemma.

The act was so astounding that a motionless pause and a breathless silence fell upon the whole assembly.

Before any one had time to recover from the surprise Tom King and Clifford had slipped through the throng and disappeared.

Captain Claude might have gone the same way, but he preferred to stay and share Dick's danger.

THE ASSASSINATION.

It was a rule with them that when four got into danger, two should try to escape, and save the others afterwards.

The officer, with a part of the saloon guard, stood at the door, waiting for the King's commands.

Our hero kept in attitude like a statue.

The pause was broken by the Prince Regent himself.

He wrenched himself suddenly from Dick, and drawing his sword, shouted—

"Follow the two who have fled, bring them back dead or alive!"

And he himself attacked Tyburn Dick.

James was keeping a party of the at bay.

"The countess's suitor thought this sweet revenge, so he went forward, and attacked Dick.

When he came the prince retired.

He had had enough of it.

So the matter stood.

The guests dispersed.

The saloon doors were shut.

The King and the Prince retired, giving orders to the officer to capture the four highwaymen at any risk.

Tom King and Clifford, when they escaped from the banquet-hall, ran into another chamber.

The tramp of feet behind them told that they were pursued.

Clifford shut the door and barred it.

King ran to the window.

No way of escape there.

A row of glittering pikes told them that the garden was filled with soldiery.

"We must fight for it, that is all," said Paul, "and here they come."

A thundering crash at the door was heard.

The panels yielded.

The soldiers, headed by the officer, burst against it, and in another instant they would have been in the room.

The two gentlemen of the road set their teeth, and grasped their swords.

"Somebody will die if they come in," said Tom King. "Ha!"

He gave an exclamation.

One of the enamelled panels, partly covered with Gobelin tapestry, slid back in the wall.

The beautiful eyes and face of the page appeared.

"This way," she said, "follow quickly."

It was a place of refuge, and they leaped in.

The panel closed just as the door broke in, and the soldiers found the room empty.

The two highwaymen found themselves in a secret chamber with fair Milly and Duke, who was seated beside her to protect her.

He had been there since the night he had set out with Grace.

Both of whom got in the royal palace through the assistance of one of the royal servants, whom they bribed to let them pass.

Once in, they soon became friends with the household.

Our heroine assumed the dress of a page, and looked very beautiful in the pretty costume.

As we have before said, for she was the page who took the message to our hero.

Devil Duke from the time he got admittance sought for Milly, and seated himself by her side. He looked like a ferocious lion.

The King wondered much that he could not entice her to leave her apartment.

But he could not.

So he wisely decided to wait until she would come round.

We think he will have to wait a long time.

But, however, while he is waiting we will return to our friends whom we left with Duke.

The highwaymen knew the two celebrated knights of the road; they had met before, and had an adventure together.

"You here, old boy," said Tom King.

"Yes—hush," said Duke, "I sent for you. Where are the others?"

"Here," said Grace, the lovely page.

A panel slid aside, and she stepped through the aperture, leading her lover by the hand.

Captain Claude followed.

He leaped forward, and clasped his fair mistress to his breast, and she laid her head on his shoulder, and sobbed with joy.

She told him all that she had gone through, how she was taken to the palace, and how nobly Duke and Grace had perilled their own lives to save her.

Grace, in her page's dress, and unknown by our hero, leaned upon his shoulder, and looked saucily into his grave face, and then she broke out into a light laugh.

Dick looked at her curiously.

"Forgotten me already?" she said.

"Grace, my darling, is it you?" exclaimed Dick, and he caught her in his arms.

The brave girl fervently kissed her lover, and greeted Captain Claude and the rest.

"I wonder what dress next you will assume," said Dick.

"Any that is useful," replied Grace. "Cautious, I hear footsteps."

Footsteps were distinctly heard.

The highwaymen clutched the hilts of their swords, and waited for the soldiers they heard approaching.

There was a sudden crash.

The door was battered down, and in rushed the guard, headed by the revengeful officer.

The highwaymen were entrapped.

They had no means of escape.

They had no alternative but to fight. This they meant to do at any rate.

They were six, the soldiers numbered over a hundred.

Dick said—

"We must fight our way through them."

The officer laughed, and said—

"Surrender while you are safe."

"See you blowed first," said Tom King.

"Forward, men; take them dead or alive!" said the officer.

The soldiers advanced with fixed bayonets towards our friends.

Dick was the first to raise a weapon to strike. Drawing his lithe form erect, he prepared for the fight.

He struck the bayonets down and dashed through the men.

Captain Claude followed him.

"Have no fear, Milly," he said; "I shall return for you soon."

"Will you?" said one of the soilders, making a thrust at him with his bayonet.

The thrust was deadly, but Captain Claude parried it. With the skill of an expert swordsman, he turned aside the sharp point of a bayonet that was about to enter his chest. Turning, he found himself face to face with the officer.

"Surrender!" cried the officer, making a slash at Captain Claude's sword arm.

He missed. Captain Claude passed on unhurt.

The rest of our friends made a rush to get through, but they were opposed by the resolute soldiers, and brought to a stand before the glittering bayonets.

Paul Clifford went into it furiously; his finely-tempered blade clashed against the bayonets. Showers of sparks flew from the clanging steel.

A skilful battle then ensued. The highwaymen got together, and fought with swords against the soldiers' fixed bayonets.

In a moment, as it were, the room was changed to a mimic field of battle.

The highwaymen formed a square, and with their pistols laid many of their enemies in the dust.

The sharp pistol volley caused the soldiers to draw back, and in this momentary pause the gallant few had time to recover breath.

The cessation was not of long duration, for the soldiers, aroused from their trance-like stupor by the voice of their officer, renewed the fight with right good will.

Back to back the gallant fellows fought.

Right well did they repulse the desperate charge made to break through their little square.

The soldiers, enraged at being defeated by a handful of men, drew back the hammers of their firelocks, and would have poured a deadly volley into them had not the officer heard the click, and shouted—

"Hold! Do not fire, take them alive. A thousand pounds is on the head of each. Wound them, but do not kill."

The soldiers obeyed the officer's orders reluctantly.

One, more impetuous than the rest, and who was bleeding from a cut on the cheek caused by Captain Claude's sword, let fly his piece, and the bullet made a hole in Paul Clifford's hat.

Captain Clifford, seeing his party getting weaker, and fearing that another stray bullet like the last might thin their number, whispered to his companions to make good their retreat.

This at first seemed impossible, but an opportunity soon offered itself.

The gallant knights beat their way through phalanx of fierce warriors, and then darted down a long corridor.

"Fire!" shouted the officer, raging like a baffled tiger.

The highwaymen sped along swiftly, but in fearful terror, for they at least expected a shower of bullets to penetrate their backs.

They were breathless; at the thought their blood seemed to turn into ice.

They heard a click as the hammers fell, and by that sound they knew the flints had got knocked off the nipples.

Then they raised a shout of defiance, and scampered past the sentries on guard like madmen.

The soldiers kept up a hot pursuit, but they were outstripped by the highwaymen, who went along fleet as the wind.

Victor St. James was at the stables when they got there, and the horses were ready for instant use.

His friends cheered him for his thoughtfulness, and in a second they were in the saddles, and away they went as the soldier dashed up.

"To the Leopard Inn!" said Dick.

The rest waved their swords, and rode away furiously for the Leopard Inn. The soldiers were still behind, and an exciting chase was kept up.

At last the soldiers lost sight of the flying knights, but they kept up the pursuit, and loaded, to pour a volley into the men at the first opportunity.

CHAPTER LXXXIII.

MIDNIGHT ATTACK UPON THE LEOPARD INN—SURRENDER OF THE HIGHWAYMEN.

THE highwaymen reached the Leopard Inn in safety. The soldiers they did not trouble their heads about; they knew when they were under the roof of the Leopard Inn, they could defy any number.

So they made haste and got in.

Ben was at hand in a moment; the sound of horses' feet worked upon him like a magnet, and be it friend or foe he could not stay away.

But if the latter, he would do everything he could think of to put them to inconvenience.

"Look well after the horses," said Dick; "keep them ready, in case of an emergency, and if any of our old friends do come, you know, Ben."

"Yes, cap'n," added the ostler, with a broad grin. "Take care of their horses too, eh, captain?"

Dick nodded, and followed his comrades into the parlour, where their host waited to receive them.

"Well, Samson," said Dick, "how's the world been using you of late?"

"'Tain't the world, captain, it's the people in it," replied Samson. "I am glad to see you all, gentlemen, and hope you are all well."

"Pretty jolly, thanks," said Gallant Tom.

"By Jove, you don't look very jolly, like me," remarked Victor St. James.

"He speaks on congeniality," said Captain Claude.

"I am jolly," said the highwayman,—"jolly, because I am amongst my comrades again."

"Where have you been? You don't look very bright," said mine host.

"Bring up some old wine, and we will have a quiet chat," said Gallant Tom.

Samson Leopard, of the Leopard Inn, went down to the cellar where he kept his rare old stuff, and brought up several bottles of the oldest brand.

The highwaymen gathered round the fire, and each in his turn had to relate the adventures they had gone through since they had last met.

Their adventures were told, and they had retired to rest.

The silent hour of two had dolefully tolled by a distant village church clock, when our hero, after restlessly turning from side to side, finally settled down and dozed off.

The night, or rather early morn, was dark and heavy; clouds seemed to hover round the Inn; the stillness of the hour was almost painful for those of our friends who still lay awake.

Three o'clock.

The first grey streaks of light began to burst over the earth.

The cock rose on his perch, flapped his wings, and crowing lustily, settled down to wait for an answer from one of his feathered neighbours.

It was answered by a distant faint crow.

Then all again was quiet.

And amidst the peaceful hush of this silent hour, the inhabitants of the inn were suddenly aroused from their heavy sleep by a tremendous hammering at the door, as though the place was suddenly besieged by a legion of giants, who were using their ponderous clubs in trying to batter down every piece of woodwork connected with the inn.

Dick sprang out of bed, and slipping on his clothes, ran into the further apartment.

"Did you hear that?" he asked.

"I was awakened by something, but what I cannot tell," replied the captain.

"The soldiers have tracked us out," said Dick.

Bang! bang! bang!

Came at the door, and they could hear the wood splitting beneath the heavy strokes.

"In the King's name, open!" came a voice from beneath.

The worthy landlord stalked like a huge giant into the room.

"They have come," he said grimly.

"Confound them, yes," said Tom King, coming in to his comrades; "they might have waited until the morning."

"Cowardly idea," said Clifford, "for them to wake a fellow out of his sleep; they know he don't feel in the humour to fight."

"Ho, there, within! open the door in the King's name!"

Samson Leopard went quietly to the window and looked out; the house was surrounded with soldiers, and a myriad of bayonets formed an impassible barrier.

"There's no way for you to get out there," he said, turning to the highwaymen.

"We don't wan't to get out," said Dick, "if we can keep them where they are."

"That is impossible; if they keep up this hammering much longer we shall have the house tumble down about our ears."

"Then we must fight," said Gallant Tom, resolutely. "Hullo, there goes the door."

There was a tremendous crash, as if some huge timber were falling.

"It's not the door?" said Samson.

"What is it then?" asked Dick.

"The shutters; the door is of solid iron."

"Then they will get in at the window?"

"They will have to pass a double row of crossed bars before they can do that."

"Then we are safe."

"While the house stands," replied the genial landlord.

The thundering now ceased, the men below were silent; that was a bad sign, for it showed that surer means for the capture of the highwaymen were being taken.

The officer had concocted a plan—a cruel, treacherous plan—to bring out his intended prisoners.

Mine host had a suspicion that the quietness boded no good. He went quietly to the window and looked out. He was horrified by what he saw.

Piled up under the window and around the door were heaps of sticks and timber, the soldiers were collecting together all the dry herbage they could find, and the officer stood with a light in his hand ready to fire it.

Then they meant to burn down the inn and consume the noble highwaymen in the fierce flames.

"Hi! what are you going to do?" shouted Samson, excitedly.

The officer looked up.

"Burn the highwaymen out," he answered, "unless you open the door directly."

"Do you mean it?"

"You will see."

The highwaymen were in a painful dilemma. They had heard the threat, and knew full well it was not an idle one.

It was astonishing the change that came over every handsome face.

"Let them in," said Dick, gravely.

Mine host looked at the boy in surprise.

"While there are six such men as we it would be a hard struggle for them to take us," continued our hero.

"I think not," said the landlord.

"Let them come," said Paul Clifford. "I think with Dick, while we six remain together, many of them will fall before they take us."

"That may be, but in the end you would be sure to be overpowered."

"That we will chance," added Tom King.

"It is evident, for us to stay here," said Captain Claude, "will be for us to be baked."

"Let them in by all means," shouted Victor St. James, flourishing his sword. "By Jove! if we don't beat them we deserve to be beaten."

"The thing is this," said the landlord of the Leopard Inn. "Are you gentlemen aware of the number you will have to stand against?"

"I think so," said Claude; "we had a set-to at the palace with them."

"Look, and satisfy yourself."

Tyburn Dick went to the window. He was cautious not to be seen, but not cautious enough though he peeped round by the side of the casement, not allowing more of his head to project than was necessary for him to take a survey. The quick eye of the officer caught sight of him, and a shout directly was raised for him to surrender.

Dick went in quickly.

"They have trebled their number," he said, with emotion.

The captains looked at one another perplexed.

"What can we do?" asked Gallant Tom.

"Take our chance," replied Clifford "We cannot stay here to be burnt."

Dick left his comrades; his boyish face was fearfully pale and clouded; he was going to let the soldiers in.

Mine host took two strides to the door, and stood before him.

"Stay a moment," he said.

"What would you do?"

The officer's voice was heard.

"Open the door in the King's name, or I burn you down!" he cried. "I ask no more."

Samson Leopard took a pistol from our hero's belt, and went to the window.

"Let us in," cried the soldier. Again he held the light near the foliage as he spoke, and waited for an answer, looking up triumphantly into the landlord's stern face.

He got the answer.

Mine host fired.

The officer gave a death cry, and fell forwark. The torch he held fell amongst the litter, and in an instant there arose a fierce roaring fire. The tongued flames leaped upwards, licking the dry wood, and becoming a burning mass wherever it touched.

Samson staggered back with horror.

Dick ran forward, caught him in his arms, and was about to ask him the cause of his change, when the roaring elements burst in one gush into the room.

For a moment everyone was petrified.

Captain Claude broke the spell.

"Save the house, save the house!" he said.

"My child—save her!" frantically yelled mine host.

Dick sprang from his side, and bounded down the stairs. Room after room he entered, but with no success.

At last!

He stood in the room.

The innkeeper's pretty daughter, Lizzie, lay in a peaceful quiet sleep, quite unconscious of the fearful danger that surrounded and threatened her with a torturing death.

Dick had almost forgotten his mission, so earnestly did he gaze upon the innocent display of the sleeper's beauty.

The clothes were thrown carelessly aside, displaying a form and limbs of beautiful mould and perfect symmetry.

Dick approached her, and kissed her pouting cherry lips. She started, and with maiden modesty drew the covering over her. She was not quite awake, and would have gone to sleep again, but she caught sight of the youth standing by her bedside.

She gazed at him in drowsy terror.

Dick, seeing her about to shriek, said gently—

"Don't be frightened, Lizzie, dear."

She knew his voice, and smiled at him favourably; but her pretty face crimsoned deeply as the thought came to her mind that he had seen her lying in a state void of covering as Eve.

"Why have you come?" she said reproachfully. "You are very wicked to come in so silently. Suppose father should find you here, what would he say?"

"He told me to come."

The little beauty looked at him doubtfully.

"Oh, Dick, dear! how can you say such a thing?" she said.

"It's the truth, I assure you. Come, darling."

"Come where?"

"With me, or you will be burnt to death. The place is on fire."

As he spoke the word "fire" the thick choking smoke burst through the boards, and forked flames leaped up between the crevices.

All the passionate colour vanished from the maiden's pretty face, and she turned a deathly pallor with terror. Regardless of the daring boy's presence, she sprung up in bed and tried to shriek, but fright clove her tongue burning to the roof of her mouth.

Dick threw a blanket around her supple form, and clasping her to his breast rushed from the room. He was met on the stairs by her father.

"Is she safe?" he inquired, excitedly.

"Quite," returned Dick, as he passed on.

The innkeeper returned to the highwaymen, whom he had left with the soldiers quenching the fire, while he came to look after his only child.

When Dick left his comrade to save Lizzy, Captain Claude fully realized the danger of their situation.

"Gentlemen," he said, turning to the others, "we have not many moments to decide what to do. There are but two ways; one is to remain here and be consumed by this fearful fire, and the other is to fight our way out and risk the chance of life. Which shall it be?"

"Fight our way out!" they all spoke of one accord.

"These men below are Englishmen, I believe," said Tom King.

"Well?" said Claude.

"They are Christians, and have hearts, and in such a time of peril as this they would not be too exacting. Make a compact with them."

"Come," said Claude, "I understand your meaning perfectly. Draw not a weapon; if they rush upon us face them quietly. It would be better for us all to surrender than to be burnt alive here, or be beaten by them and then taken."

"Hear, hear!" shouted his comrades, approvingly.

They descended the stairs; the door was no sooner opened by Captain Claude than the soldiers made a dash forward with stern determination to avenge their fallen leader and take the highwaymen dead or alive.

"Stand!" demanded one, a corporal, "or we fire."

The gallant knights of the road were gathered in a group in the passage, near the door.

"Gentlemen," said Captain Claude, addressing the soldiers, "we surrender."

The corporal was surprised at the earnestness of the captain's voice and the grave expression of his face.

"Give up your arms, gentlemen," he said, respectfully.

"It is on these conditions that we surrender," Captain Claude went on, "that you and your comrades help us to put out this fire; I have said that we have surrendered, and when we have quenched the fire we are your prisoners. You need not doubt my word."

"I do not," replied the man, frankly.

He ordered the soldiers to put down their arms and help to put out the raging fire. Their carbines in a minute were stood up in clusters, and the men, that not a minute before were deadly enemies, were now working friendly together.

That showed the true honour of the English disposition.

The highwaymen worked gallantly, so did the soldiers. Every vessel that would hold water was clutched by an eager hand.

The fire had taken a firm hold, the inn being mostly built of wood; there appeared little chance of quelling the destructive elements.

No modern firemen could have gone into the dangerous work with more vigour and daring hardihood than did the soldiers. who even had been eager to fire the inn they were now working laboriously to quench.

The water had to be drawn from a well, there being nothing more convenient near at hand.

A dozen soldiers stood around it, and worked in turns to draw the water, while others of the gallant warriors, who had formed a double line from the well to the fire, passed the buckets and other vessels to one another, and so kept up a continual supply for their comrades and highwaymen, who risked their lives in the thickest of the flames to lull the conflagration.

Dick could scarcely believe his own eyes when he saw his friends working in a friendly manner with their enemies. Claude saw his perplexity, and explained to him the compact they had made. Our hero uttered an inward "very well," and putting Lizzie safely out of the way, went to share the dangers of the fire.

In a few seconds he was seen dashing about from one room to the other, surrounded by sheets of fire and volumes of suffocating smoke.

He lowered pails from the windows by ropes, and pulled them up by the same means.

The gallant youth worked vigorously; huge beams and pieces of timber were cut away in one mass of flames with his sword, and sent flying through the air like bars of fire.

The fire fought desperately to keep up its fierce roar and destructive raging in spite of the water, but it was beaten back by the torrents dashed upon it, and soon it was extinguished.

A lusty cheering then arose from every throat, in which the sufferer of the devastation, Samson Leopard, joined, and then tapped several casks of malt liquor, and made everyone drink.

The inn was not so far destroyed as to be

uninhabitable. The front had suffered the most, the inside suffered quite enough.

"I am sorry 'tis so bad," said Captain Claude.

"Can't be helped, captain," said the staunch old fellow; "it might have been worse."

"It might have been better," said Dick. "If we had surrendered at once, it would not have occurred."

"It is no good repining over what can't be helped," said the landlord.

"Just my opinion," remarked the corporal, giving Captain Claude a significant glance. "I am sorry, gentlemen, but duty compels me to desire your company."

"The devil it does!" said St. James. "By Jove! what an unfriendly kind of idea."

"A soldier is not his own master," answered the corporal; "and were you my own brothers, I should be compelled to take you just the same."

"You want us?" said Captain Claude.

"You promised to surrender, and I did not doubt your word."

"Neither have you occasion to do so. Have you a warrant for our apprehension?"

The soldier took from his breast pocket a roll of parchment, and held it open.

"Here is the warrant," he said, "signed by the King."

"Tyburn Dick, Paul Clifford, and Tom King," said Captain Claude, reading the names down.

The three went forward.

"Then we may reckon ourselves your prisoners," remarked Dick.

"For a time, until we reach the palace."

"And then?"

"You will await the King's pleasure."

"Lead the way," said Dick, proudly. He took a tender parting of his father, and whispering something to him, waited for King and Clifford, who were parting with their comrades.

The soldiers formed a double line on either side of them, and the three gallant men were led on in single file.

Captain Claude and the rest returned to the haunt.

CHAPTER LXXXIV.

THE KING MAKES A MIDNIGHT VISIT TO A LADY'S CHAMBER, AND MEETS WITH AN UNPLEASANT INTERRUPTION.

THE disturbance caused in the royal saloon by the appearance of the highwaymen upset the equanimity of his Majesty, and that night he retired to his chamber very ill at ease.

Several things disturbed the peace of his kingly mind, the daring highwaymen having escaped and defiled all his power, and the disappointment occasioned to him thereby. But he had signed a warrant for their immediate arrest. He chuckled as he thought of it, and rubbed his big red hands together in glee, for he knew the man he had sent after them would not return without his prize.

It is very evident he would not return with them, as the reader knows Samson Leopard disposed of him.

His Majesty was disappointed, more because the fair beauties he had particularly admired on entering the saloon had departed immediately on the outbreak of the uproar; that he didn't wish, for he had anticipated a glorious coquetry with them.

He swore most vulgarly, then he was quiet.

He started, took three steps across his chamber, stopped, looked up, bit his lips and said—"I won't wait any longer."

What he meant we are at a loss to say; but by watching him closely and paying particular attention to his cogitations we shall probably discover.

"I won't wait any longer."

He said that before.

He walked slowly round the apartment, carefully examined the thick hanging tapestry to see that no one was listening, and then sat down.

For several moments he was perfectly motionless

"Why should I wait?" he broke out, making himself start by the gruffness of his own loud voice.

King George that night was bent upon some evil disposed design, and his guilty conscience was started by the slightest noise.

"Two weeks," muttered the king; "two weeks she has confined herself in her chamber, and forbidden my presence. I wait no longer."

So his most kingly majesty was desperately in love, and fair Milly was his idol.

Having resolved not to wait any longer, he took off his rich dress boots, and put on a pair of noiseless slippers.

He then quietly opened the door, and sneaked along a long corridor like a thief. At the door of Milly's chamber he stopped. His heart was beating wildly with excitement, and his cheeks glowed with triumphant imaginations.

He tapped lightly with his knuckles, but receiving no answer, he silently entered.

He paused with one foot in the sacred chamber, and the other on the threshold of the door.

He fancied he heard a slight creaking, as if some one was opening another door, then he grew bold, and laughed at his foolish suspicions, arriving at the likely conclusion that the noise was occasioned by the restless turning of his intended victim.

He approached the bedside where the fair girl lay peaceful and quiet, and taking the taper that burned on a small table, he leaned over her, his brain in a delirious whirl as he gazed upon her pale lily cheeks; his lips clung to hers in a passionate kiss.

She did not stir. He placed the light down, and for a time stood contemplating how next to proceed.

He looked around the chamber, and examined under the bedstead. He and the unconscious sleeper were the only occupants.

Devil Duke, her watchful guardian, had left her when she retired to rest, but he was not far off. His beloved fair charge would bring him upon the base insulter like an infuriated panther.

The King knew not of that; even if he had, we doubt whether it would have made much impression upon his sated mind at such a time.

His hand trembling with agitation, clutched the clothes that covered the beautiful form, and pulled them aside.

The act displayed a limb magnificent; the King gazed upon it, almost stupified, his every sense enthralled with libidinous passions.

Again he was startled by a slight noise.

Making sure that no one was near, he blew out the light, and with an infernal intent began cautiously to sidle into the bed.

A stifled shriek of terror left his lips, as an iron hand grasped his throat and pulled him back.

"This is the King of England," said a voice in his ear, hoarse with terrible passion.

The King struggled and tried to break away from his fierce captor.

"Raise your voice even in a whisper, and your vile blood shall tell the tale of England's king's base treachery."

The King trembled violently, he was in a fearful position.

"Guar——"

He stopped himself, for he knew to call the guard would be to bring the whole household to his assistance and that would expose him; to be found in a lady's chamber at such a time, his intentions there could not be mistaken.

The King was in an awkward dilemna.

And he knew not how to get out of it.

"Who art thou that dares stay me?" he demanded, thinking by assuming such a voice to quail his assailant.

"A highwayman known as Devil Duke. Your Majesty has offered a thousand pounds for my apprehension. I am here, and now I have you in my power."

The King foamed with suppressed rage.

"Your most gracious Majesty, night renegade, will give me that thousand pounds, and grant me a free pardon; refuse, and the echo of this pistol report shall bring your myrmidons to this chamber, to find you a corpse, your brains scattered with a bullet."

"Release me instantly, or you shall be taken to instant execution. Eh—ah—oh!"

Devil Duke put the muzzle of a pistol in his royal captive's ear.

"Don't brag, my liege," he said; the slightest pressure of my finger would send a bullet through your brain."

His Majesty shook with a cold thrill

"Write me out a free pardon."

"Remove that pistol," the King stammered.

"The document," said Duke.

"I can't do it here, answered the King.

"Come with me," said Duke.

The king was obliged to obey, greatly to his chagrin, through the highwayman keeping the pistol in his ear—the discomfited King was compelled to follow.

Duke procured a light, writing materials, and brought him back to Milly's chamber.

Strange to say, the fair girl had not awoke during this time; exhaustion, for want of sleep, had locked her eyelids, and took her to another world.

Duke placed a chair for the King at the table, and stood behind him with the pistol not an inch from his head, while he wrote the free pardon.

When it was completed and sealed with the royal crest, Duke bowed, took the scroll, folded it carefully, and placed it in an inner pocket of his coat.

"I have to trouble you, my liege, for the thousand pounds."

The King looked in his face, and meeting the shining pistol-barrel, produced the money in notes.

He beat a quick retreat from the room as the highwayman pocketed the money; but Duke stayed him at the door by laying his hand on his shoulder.

"Should your majesty make a second attempt of such base dishonour, I shall shoot you down without warning," he said.

The King slunk away like a beaten cur, cursing his ill-luck, and inwardly vowing to have revenge.

He did not go to bed then as a peaceful king would have done, but sat brooding over his misfortunes, and trying to concoct a plan to quietly dispose of the highwaymen.

He was roused from his miserable thoughts by the entry of a soldier who came to report the capture of the highwaymen.

The King sprang up on hearing the welcome tidings.

"Captured Tyburn Dick!" he exclaimed.

"Yes, my liege," replied the corporal; Paul Clifford and Tom King."

"Capital! You shall be promoted," said King George, rubbing his hands together with glee, and grinning like a chimpanzee in a fit. "The captain, where is he?"

"He was shot, my liege, in the fray"

The kingly brow darkened.

"Hang the highwaymen the first thing in the morning. No, shoot them! Revenge!" he muttered, gleefully.

"Yes, your Majesty." The man bowed himself to the door.

"Stay!" yelled the King.

The man stopped.

"There is a highwayman in the palace here. Capture him, shoot him when you see him, and you shall be promoted to be captain of the guard."

The soldier saluted his royal master, and retired from the royal chamber.

The corporal was a skilful soldier. He understood strategy, and rarely lost any one when he was sent after them, and then he made some careful arrangements with his men, and resolved to capture Devil Duke within an hour of the King's order.

CHAPTER LXXXV.

THE ROYAL TEMPTER—THE KING'S PAGE'S STRATAGEM—MILLY IN DANGER—THE KING OUTWITTED.

WHEN the door closed after the exit of the soldier from the King's presence, his majesty sat down to ruminate over his unsuccessful adventure, and the loss he had sustained by the audacious highwayman.

"I, frustrated by a common highwayman," he cogitated; "he shall be hanged. No, shot. Ha, ha!" he murmured. "I shall have nothing to keep me from that beauty." I only wait for the tidings of his disposal, before I make my second visit."

With these thoughts he contented himself to wait for the return of the soldier, and the issue of the highwayman's death, before he made another dishonourable visit to the fair girl's chamber.

In spite of the King's vigilant search to see that there were no listeners, the fair page, Grace, had thwarted him, and concealed herself behind the hanging tapestry he had been so careful to examine.

She had overheard his conference with the soldier, his self-cogitations, and how she parted the hangings, shook her fist at the royal head, and went to inform Devil Duke of his danger.

The gallant fellow had left his charge and returned to his own chamber, a small anteroom he had taken possession of. He was reclining on the outside of the bed to snatch a few minutes' repose.

He sprang up as Grace entered.

"Come, Duke, instantly," said Grace, lowly.

"Whither?" queried Duke.

"To a place of safety."

"Wherefore?"

"The King has set the guards upon your track, and, unless you are in a place of concealment, you will be lost."

"But I have the King's pardon."

"I know, but that is of no good; the King has given orders for the men to shoot you without warning.

"Murderous wretch!" muttered Duke.

"Come, we have no time to lose; I even now hear them approaching."

"But Milly?" said the highwayman perplexed.

"She is safe!"

"Nay; the King has been in her chamber."

"I know."

Duke wondered how.

Grace read his thoughts by the expression of surprise on his face.

"I have followed the King about as a cat would a mouse," she said, "and stood not two yards behind him when he was in Milly's chamber. Had you not been there to interfere he would never have left there again, for I should have driven this to his heart."

She plucked a long stiletto from its sheath beneath her tunic. The blade was long, thin, and keen-edged, and her small white hand tightened on the jewelled hilt as she spoke, and her humid blue orbs glistened like stars shining through a dark cloud.

Duke was about to express his astonishment and admiration at her remark, when she clutched him by the coat sleeve, and tried to pull him after her, as she said—

"Come, or it will be too late."

Duke stood firm, though he heard his enemies outside.

"I cannot leave Milly to the King's baseness," he said.

"You will be instantly killed if found," urged the noble girl, in great distress for the brave fellow's safety.

"Then I shall die for a good cause," he said, calmly.

"And so sacrifice both Milly and me, as well as your own life."

He looked sadly upon the imploring beauty before him. He knew not how to act. To comply with her desire for him to escape would, he thought, be to leave Milly a victim for the King, and he had taken an oath to Heaven to protect the fair girl with his own life; yet it was hard to refuse the entreaties of the one before him.

How could he act? What was he to do? There were three lives at stake, and it depended upon the step he should take whether they all fell to eternity or not.

He beat his forehead with his clenched hand in perplexity.

The soldiers could be heard outside the door.

He had but a moment to decide how to proceed.

Grace spoke hastily.

"The King is waiting for the tidings of your death before he makes a second visit to Milly's chamber, so come."

Duke took her hand, his own trembling like a leaf fluttered by the wind.

"And if I am not discovered?" he asked.

"The King will stay away."

The door-handle was tied from without.

Grace had taken the precaution to turn the key, so that the door was perfectly secure.

The corporal demanded admittance; then waited for an answer; but hearing none, he tried what force would do.

Bang, bang, bang!

The door shivered and cracked. Some instruments much heavier than muskets were being used as battering-rams to force an entrance.

"We have no way now," said Duke.

Grace motioned him to her side, as she stepped lightly across the room.

"Follow me quietly," she said.

Duke was about to ask her which way, when she opened a panel in the wall.

They both sprang through as the door yielded with a crash, and the soldiers—at least twenty, besides the corporal—rushed into the room.

Duke and his fair preserver were in another chamber, very similar to the one they had just left. They could distinctly hear the soldiers making a search.

" I am confident he was here," Duke heard one say.

" Why, here is a piece of a cigarette he has been smoking," said another.

" How could he have escaped?" asked a third.

" Don't know," replied the corporal. " Perhaps he has gone through the wall. I believe this palace is full of secret panels. However, I'll try."

With the pommel of his sword he tapped every inch of the wall as he slowly walked round the chamber.

He stopped—stopped at the panel through which Duke had made his exit. Just there sounded extremely hollow to what any other part did, and it aroused the soldier's suspicion.

" I thought so," he said, tapping again ; " this is how he escaped, through here."

" There must be a spring for the means of opening it," said a man.

" If there aint," replied the corporal, " we will soon have it down."

Duke heard him say so ; so did Grace.

The latter thought it advisable to go a little further.

She said so.

" Before they have it down," she remarked to Duke," we will make another move.

" Most willingly," answered the highwayman.

They made a move only in time. They had barely got out of the chamber, when the panel slid aside, and the corporal leaped through.

He called upon his men to follow,

They did, and two of them got fixed in the aperture in their hurry; but the others who were behind bounded upon them, and the lot fell to the floor.

This delay gave our heroine and her companion an opportunity to get a little further.

Duke was dragged by the fair girl into another room, through another secret opening, and through a narrow opening between two walls.

At the end of this long dark passage Grace again stopped and opened another door; they were now in a small chamber—a very small one indeed, there being barely

room for them to turn. Duke had to remain in a position extremely uncomfortable, the place not being lofty enough to stand erect.

The place was so intensely dark neither could see the other. They heard his pursuers still hunting about, and stood breathless until the sound had died away in the distance.

" I will return and see how his majesty is getting on," she said.

" Do," replied Dick. " How long am I to remain here?"

" Until I return. Be cautious. Adieu!"

She pressed Dick's hand and was gone.

" It's all very fine," he muttered; " but if she's long, I am blow'd if I shall stay here. I have already got a stiff neck."

By the time Grace reached the royal chamber the King began to get impatient. Sitting there alone as he was, he pictured to himself the fair beauty as he had seen her lying like an angel of purity, and his heated imagination aroused his brute passions. He could wait no longer; under any hazard he resolved to return to his fair captive's chamber and satisfy his sensual desire.

Our heroine had concealed herself behind the tapestry; she saw him go to the drawer of a bureau, and take therefrom a small phial.

He placed it in his pocket, and sneaked like a guilty wretch from his chamber. Grace crept from her place of concealment, and followed him to Milly's bedroom.

The light was still burning by her bedside.

A scream startled the King as he entered, and he jumped round with astonishment.

The fair girl was awake; she saw him enter and was terrified.

The King bit his lips with anger.

" Eh, pretty one," he said in his most winning tone, and sneaking to the bedside, " did my presence startle you?"

" Why have you come?" asked Milly, thinking it better not to show her terror.

" Why have I come?" he repeated. " To see you; for what else should I come?"

" This is not a night to come."

" It will do for me."

" I pray your majesty will go instantly."

" Nay, don't be angry. I have dared to come now because you would not give me audience."

THE VILLAIN DEFEATED.

"Your majesty might have chosen a better time than this to come."

"I think not," he said. "When is the time more beautiful than the silent hour of midnight, in such a place as this?"

"Your majesty has no right here."

"I was lonely; your beauty impressed my mind, and I dared to come."

"For what?"

The King looked at her slyly, squeezed her hand, and putting his head close to her, said something that made the fair girl recoil with shame.

Starting up in bed, her pretty face crimsoned to the temples, she exclaimed—

"Begone! or my voice shall bring people to my aid, and your majesty will repent the daring liberty you have taken of coming here."

The King was stung deeply by these words. His first impulse was to force her to submission, but on second thoughts he would try what he could do with persuasion.

Without a word he left the chamber.

Milly jumped out of bed to lock the door; but before she had time to do so the King returned, and she had to hasten back to prevent being seen.

"You have returned," said Milly.

"I could not stay away," replied he. "I hope you have thought over what I said."

"I have."

"And will you submit to my desire?"

"No."

The King was startled by the depth of the voice.

"Very well," he said, trying to assume an unconcerned voice, though all the time he knew not how to contain himself. "To-morrow you will, perhaps, think different."

"Never!" retorted fair Milly.

"Then I will leave you till you do."

He had no intention of so doing, though he said he would.

"Wear this little gift for my sake, and forget what has passed." He took from a gold casket a splendid ruby and diamond necklace. "The Queen has not such a jewel in her keeping. It was purchased for her; but I would sacrifice all for you."

"I pity you much," returned Milly, scornfully.

"I pity myself, but it's a weakness I can't master; accept of this," he said, handing her the necklace.

She dashed it from his hand.

"Tempter!" she exclaimed; "not all the jewels of the royal palace would buy me for your base desire."

The King was greatly astonished by the liberty she had taken, to knock from his royal hand that costly treasure; his eyes wandered from the necklace on the ground to her, and his face turned purple with anger.

"Had anyone else done that," he said, with suppressed fury, "they would have lost their head."

"Had anyone dared what you have dared," retorted Milly, "they would have instantly died for the insult."

The King laughed hoarsely.

"What I have dared will be nothing to what I shall do," he said. "I have fooled with you long enough, I shall try other means of conquering you of that obstinate temper of yours."

He took the phial from his pocket, and poured some of its contents into a cambric handkerchief.

Milly watched him, wondering what he was going to do; she did not suspect his base design.

Replacing the bottle in his pocket, and gathering the handkerchief in his hand, he suddenly seized the fair girl by the arm and held her down, while he covered her face with the cambric.

Almost instantly he felt her relax beneath the pressure of his hand.

He removed the drugged handkerchief from her face, and stood gloating over his lovely prize, insensible and totally in his power as he thought.

He was not thinking of evil befalling himself; his sated mind was too engrossed with his own plans to give a thought to anything else, and while he stood triumphantly contemplating the fair beauty, our heroine was slowly creeping behind him, to stop him before it was too late.

She had heard and seen all, and now thought it time to interfere.

The King was stretching over his victim, his lips glued passionately to hers, when he uttered a terrible howl on feeling himself unexpectedly seized from behind.

The drugged handkerchief was torn from his hand; he was pulled back and the cambric held to his nostrils.

He struggled with his unseen assailant to tear it away, but the powerful odour he inhaled soon rendered him powerless, and he fell senseless at the feet of our heroine.

The brave girl stooped over the prostrate regal form and took from his pocket the bottle containing the drug.

"This may be useful," she mused, contemplating the small phial; "his highness did not think he would fall by his own invention."

She regarded him contemptuously, and then went to Milly; the fair girl still lay in the same unconscious state.

Grace shook her and tried every way to arouse her, but life for a time appeared perfectly extinct.

She turned almost savagely upon the senseless form of the King and appeared as though about to strike him, when the sound of the soldiers returning made her hasten from the chamber.

She knew it would not do to be found there with the King lying at her feet.

Entering the corridor that led to Duke's secret confinement, she had to crouch back to avoid being seen by the soldiers, who were then returning after their search for the highwayman.

As they passed she thought she saw a man being led away between them.

Her fear was that Duke had been discovered, and to ascertain that she hurried away, her heart beating wildly as she neared the place where she left him.

Duke was gone.

She reeled with fear as she opened the door and saw the place empty.

"Had he been taken," she thought, "Could he have been discovered by the soldiers in that out-of-the-way place?"

She left the place with a heavy heart, and made her way back to Milly's chamber.

She, too, was gone, as was the King.

This seemed terribly strange.

"Duke captured," she muttered, "by the soldiers; the King, I suppose, has returned to life and taken Milly."

"Dick and his companions," she went on, "have been captured, too, and are confined in the guard-room. They shall escape, if I fall; the King shall bitterly rue his base undertaking."

With this resolution she repaired to her own chamber, changed the dress of page for that of the highwayman, and made her way to the guard-room, risking her own gentle life for that of her companions.

CHAPTER LXXXVI.

A STRANGE CHAPTER.

THE guard-room, though pleasant enough to the weary sentry, especially when half frozen, or in want of a cheerful smoke, was no desirable spot for our knights of the road.

So thought Tyburn Dick, and evidently his companions thought the same, for they seemed about as easy as caged eagles.

Paul Clifford once ventured a song, but failed most miserably.

Tom King could not raise his spirits anyhow, and as to Tyburn Dick, though ready for any emergency (in the way of fighting), he could devise no means of raising his companions' dormant spirits.

Paul Clifford was ever ripe for a game, and he kept hammering and moving until the sentry, who had strict orders to listen for any unusual noise, was quite on the *qui vive.*

Opening the door with a huge rusty key that hung to his belt, he thrust his head in and demanded, in a voice that seemed to come more from a sepulchre than from the breast of a man—

"Keep quiet, you gentlemen."

"Keep quiet?" iterated Paul. "A fine place to keep quiet in."

"Well, then, hold your noise."

This speech raised Paul Clifford's ire and before the sentry could make an apology or a retreat, which he would most likely have done, Paul clutched him by the hair of the head.

With the strength of a lion he dragged him, and swore he would throttle him if he made the least noise.

This threat, coupled with the fierce gesture, was enough to silence any man.

At least the sentry stood as mute as a mouse.

"Well, my man, "said Paul, "I can see by the cut of your physiognomy that you have not spent all your life here."

He paused for an answer.

"No, sir," replied the terrified soldier.

"Well, let's hear where you have been."

The man screwed his face into horrible contortions, and seeing there was no chance of escape, especially as Tyburn Dick had promised to cut him as small as mincemeat if he refused, he complied.

"Well, sir," he began, "I have been a marine in my time, and served many a long year on the ocean, both in the naval and mercantile employ, so I'll just give you a rub down as we call it."

"What?" cried Tom King, "springing to his feet; "give me a rub down?"

"No, no," said Paul, interposing, "don't be hasty, my friend; you misunderstood him."

A few words of explanation from Paul set them to rights, and then the old soldier began—

" ' What say you, boys, a caulk, or a yarn?' says one of the 'quarter gunners,' addressing indiscriminately the watch one night, as soon as they were mustered.

" ' Oh, let's have a yarn, as we've eight hours in,' replied one of the top men. 'Bob Bowers will spin us a twist.' "

" And away to the galley a group of eight or ten instantly repaired.

" ' Well, boys!' says Bowers, ' let's see, what'll you have?—one of the Lee Virginney's, or the saucy Gee's?—Come, I'll give you a saucy Gee.' "

" ' Well, you see, when I sarved in the Go-a-long Gee—Captain D——(he as was killed at Trafflygar), aboard the Mars, seventy-four—ay, and as fine a fellow as ever shipped a swab, or fell on a deck.'

" There warn't a better man aboard from stem to starn. He knew a seaman's duty, and more he never ax'd; and not like half your capering skippers what expect unpossibilities.

" It went against his grain to seize a grating-up, and he never flocked a man he didn't wince as if he felt the lash himself!—and, as for starting,—blow me if he didn't break the boatswain by a court-martial for rope's-ending Tom Cox, the captain o' the fore-top in Plymouth Sound.

" And yet he wasn't a man what courted, as they call it, cocularity; for once desarve it, you were sure to buy it; but do your duty like a man, and hang it, he'd sink or swim with you!

" He never could abide to hear a man abused—let's see, was't to the first or second leeftenant he says—no, 'twas the second—and blow me, too, if I doesn't think 'twas the third, 'kase I remember, now, he'd never a civil word for no one.

" ' Well, howsomdever, you see,' says the skipper, mocking the leeftenant in a sneering manner one morn, who'd just sung out, 'You, sir,' you know, to one o' the top men — ' You, sir, I mean,' says the skipper, looking straight in the leeftenant's face—' Pray, sir,' says he, ' how do you like to be you sir'd yourself?'

" Well, the leeftenant shams deafness, you know; but I'm blowed but he bard every word on't—for never a dolphin a-dying tarned more colours nor he did at the time.

" But avast there a bit—I'm yawning about in my course. Howsomdever, you know, 'tis but due to the dead, and no more nor his memory desarves; so here's try again —small helm bo—steady—ey-a.

" Well, you know, the Go-along Gee was one of your flash Irish cruisers—the first of your fir-built frigates—and a hell of a clipper she was !

" Give her a foot o' the sheet, and she would go like a witch—but somehow o'nother, she'd dag on a bowline to leeward.

" Well, there was a crack set o' ships at the time on the station. Let's see, there was the Le Revolushneer (the flyer, you know), then there was the fighting Feeby, the dashing Dry'd, and one or two more o' your flash-uns; but the Gee took the shine on 'em all in reefing and furling.

" Well, there was always a cruiser or two from the station, as went with the West Ingy convoy, as far as Madery or so to protect 'em, you know, from the French privateers, and bring back a pipe of the stuff for the admiral.

" Ay, and I take it the old boy must have bowsed up his jib stay pretty often, for many's the pipe we shipped in the Gee for him."

" Howsomdever, you see, we was ordered to sail with one of those thund'ring convoys, the largest that ever was gathered together in Cove—nigh-hand a hundred and eighty or ninety sail.

" Let's see, there was the Polly-infamous; sixty-four, was our commodore, you know; and 'sides we in the Gee, there was a ship Cravatte, and an eighteen gun brig.

" Well, we sailed with the convoy from Cove on St. Patrick's Day, with a stagg'ring breeze, at east-north-east. We was stationed astarn, to jog up the dull-uns, and to ' touch 'em up in the bunt' with the buntin.

" Well, a'ter we runs out of one o' your reg'lar easterly gales, what has more lives not a cat, and going for ever like a blacksmith's bellows, till it blows itself out, we meets with the tail of a westerly hurricane (one o' your sneezers, you know).

" Four of five of our headmost and leeward-most ships, what tasted the thick on it first, was taken aback; two was dismasted clean by the board; but the Ge-along Gee was as snug as a duck in a ditch, never straining as much as a rope-yarn aloft, and as tight as a bottle below.

"Well, howsomdever, we weathers out like a 'Mudian; though we lost, to be sure, the corporal of marines overboard, as was consulting his ease in the lee-mizen-chains.

"Well, a'ter the wind and sea get down, the commodore closes the convoy, and sends shipwrights aboard of such of the ships as needed 'em most.

"Well, at last we gets into your regular trades, with wind just enough for a gentleman's yacht, or to ruffle the frill of a lady's flounce; and on one of those nights, as the convoy, you know, was cracking on everything low and aloft, looking just a forest afloat—we keeping our station astern on 'em all—the top-sails lowered on the cap—the sea as smooth as Poll Paterson's tongue, and the moon as bright as her eye—shoals of beneties playing under her bows; what should I hear but a voice as was hailing the ship!

"Well, I never sees nothing till I looks well around (for you see I had the starboard cat-head at the time); so I waits till I hears it again—when sky-larking Dick, who'd the larboard look-out, sneaks over and says—

"'Bob, I say, Bob-bo, did you never hear nothing just now?'"

"Well, he scarcely axes the question, when we hears hailing again—

"'Aboard the G—e, ahoy—a—'"

"Well, there was nothing, you know, in sight, within hail (for the starnmost ships of the convoy were more than two miles ahead)—so I'm blow'd if Dick and myself wasn't puzzled a bit, for we weren't just then in old Badgerbag's track.

"Well, we looks broad on the bows, and under the bows, and over the bows, and everywhere round we could look, and the voice now nearing us fast, and hailing again, we sees something as white as a sheet on the water.

"Well, I looks at Dick, and Dick looks at me—neither of us never saying nothing, you know, at the time—when looking again by the light of the moon."—

"'I'm d—d,' says I, 'if it isn't the corporal's ghost!'

"'I'm d—d if it isn't!' says Dick, and aft he flies to make the report.

"Well, I felt summat so queerish—though I says nothing to no one, you know, for 'twas only a fortnight afore the corporal and I had a bit of a breeze 'bout taking my pot off the fire.

"'Well,' says the voice, 'will you heave us a rope? I don't want a boat?' was the cry.

"'D—n it! ghost or no ghost,' says I, 'I'll give you a rope, if it's even to hang you.'

"So flying, you see, to the chains, I takes up a coil in my fist, and heaves it handsomely into his hands.

"Well, I was as mum as a monk, till he fixes himself in the bight of a bowling knot, when, looking down on his phiz, says I, just quietly over my breath—

"'Is that Corporal Craigh?' says I.

"'Corporal Hell!' says he. 'Why don't you haul up?'

"Well, I sings out for someun to lend us a fist (for Dick was afeared to come forward again—and I'm blowed but the leeftenant himself was as shy as the rest of the watch).

"So I sings out again for assistance; for there was the unfortunate fellow towing alongside like a hide what was soft'ning in a soak.

"'Will no one lend us a hand?' says I, 'or shall I turn the jolly adrift, and be d—d to you?'

"Well, this puts two of the topmen, you see, on their pluck, for both on 'em claps on the ropes, and rouses clean into the chains. Now what do you think?

"'Why, the corporal's ghost, to be sure,' said one of the group.

"No, nor the sign of a ghost—nor a ghost's mate's minister's mate—nor nothing that looked like a lubberly lobster, dead or alive; but as fine a young fellow as ever I seed in my days.

"For, you see, the whole on it is this: 'Twas no more than a chap of an apprentice, whose master had started him that morn; and rather nor stand it again, he takes to his fins and swims like a fish to the Gee—mind!

the *stanmost* ship of the convoy! though his own was one of the headmost; ay, and running to risk not to fetch us, you know, nor another chance to look to for his life.

"'And why?'

"Why—bekase the ship had a name.

"A sure! she *was* the Gee!!!

"That's all;" said the man, in conclusion.

"Sorry for that," said Dick.

The strange little narrative had amused them very much, and beguiled away the monotonous time of the highwaymen's confinement. They were sorry when it ended.

"Being an old tar," said Paul Clifford, "you have got more than one yarn down in your log, so come, pitch us a story of another."

"All right, yer honours; I am willing."

He drew the stool on which he sat closer to his companions, and was about to begin another when the creaking of a door being quietly opened made him turn.

"Don't disturb yourself," said the person, who was no other than our heroine.

"You are a highwayman!" said the man, astonished at the coolness of the visitor.

"Just so   There are highwaymen here."

"Yes, but what have you come for?"

"To keep them company." With that she walked in.

Dick knew her at a glance.

The others did not, and wondered who it was. The face they had a faint recollection of, but could not imagine where before they had seen the person.

"What were you talking about?" asked Grace, throwing herself back carelessly and crossing her legs.

"I was just going to spin a yarn," replied the soldier, eyeing the daring girl curiously. In his own mind he thought she was remarkably fair and feminine looking for a man, though he did not say anything.

"Go on," said Grace; "I should like to hear it—I am very fond of the sea."

"So am I," said the man. "Give me the wide ocean to live on; you can learn something there. I'll give ye a yarn, only first tell me as the corporal ain't coming round, because it wouldn't do for him to find me here."

He rose and went to the door.

He did not go any further. Grace rose when he did and stopped him there; for, had he gone outside, her skilful arrangements would have been frustrated.

The man did not have time to call for assistance, so stealthily did she glide behind and secure him; the drugged handkerchief she held to his nostrils, and like many other of her victims, he fell prone to the earth without a murmur.

"What have you done?" inquired Dick, alarmed

"Quieted him for a time," was the cool rejoinder.

Paul beckoned Dick to his side and whispered in his ear—

"Who's that?"

Dick slightly coloured. It was a thing he greatly objected to—for his love to assume the dress of a highwayman.

"Come, gentlemen," urged our heroine.

"Where?" queried Dick.

"To see Milly and Duke before it's too late."

"Are they in danger, then?"

"Can you ask such a thing when you know how you left them!"

The answer Dick thought severe, yet he felt that he deserved it for asking a question so regardless.

"You have not answered my question," said Paul.

No, nor Dick did not want to; but he could not avoid it without offering an insult to his friend.

"It is Lady Grace," he replied. "She has done this to save us, gentlemen."

"Bravo," shouted both Clifford and King "What a capital joke."

The noble girl bowed gracefully.

"Come, gentleman," she said, "the way is perfectly clear now."

The three highwaymen followed her from the guard-room. On their way to the interior of the palace they passed four soldiers lying apparently lifeless.

"Whose work's this?" inquired Dick.

"Mine!" replied Grace. "You have nothing to fear: they are not dead, and will wake quite soon enough for us."

CHAPTER LXXXVII.

HOW FAIR MILLY WAS HELPED TO ESCAPE FROM THE PALACE—RED MAT? WAS AGAIN ON THE TRACK OF TYBURN DICK.

MINUTES seemed to lengthen into hours, while Duke remained in his pent-up position; his neck grew stiff, and his back ached fearfully; he could bear it no longer. Grace's absence appeared an age to him in his close, obscure confinement, and listening to the last retreating tramp of his pursuers' feet, he crept forth.

His sole thought was for the safety of Milly. Grace not having returned, he feared she too might have fallen into danger, and her disguise discovered. His noble breast swelling with anxiety, he wended his way to Milly's chamber.

The taper had either burned out or been extinguished, and the darkness was so intense, not a thing was discernible.

He stopped at the door and listened, but not a breath broke the sombre stillness.

He feared some treachery had been at work, and his charge was gone.

To ascertain the truth of his suspicions, he went forward towards the bed where Milly slept to see if she was there. The first step he took, his foot came in contact with a soft substance, and he fell forward over a prostrate form.

This accident gave him a severe fright, and he lay for several moments, not daring to move; he knew, should his pursuers, who were still searching for him, have heard the noise, they would be upon him like a pack of wolves, so he lay perfectly quiet, holding his breath, and trying to stop the wild beating of his heart.

Not hearing the approach of any one, he dared to rise and examine, as well as he could, the body he had fallen over. He discovered it was that of a man, but of whom he was at a loss to conjecture.

Wishing to inquire further into this strange mystery, as it appeared, he dragged the lifeless form into his own apartment, and, kindling a light to his lantern, surveyed the person.

Imagine his surprise when he found it was the King.

"Wonder whose work this is?" he mused. "Grace, I shouldn't wonder ⁓ ⁓ ⁓

found him sneaking there again, and gave him an unlucky crack—wonder if she's settled him—bad job if she has—hope she hasn't—no mercy from her when her ire's aroused—examine his body and see."

He turned the King's person over with very little ceremony, in search of a wound he expected to find.

"Don't see how it was done," he went on, throwing the royal person in a corner, and covering it over with a blanket. "Shouldn't go where he had no right, then he wouldn't have got this. Hope he ain't dead—seems like it—very foolish of Grace—hope she ain't got in trouble—go and see if Milly's there. Wonder when I shall get out of this? Had enough of it by the Lord Harry. I won't come here when I do get out. Grace disappeared now; find Milly, look for Grace, and leave the palace."

He adjusted his mask, and providing himself with his lantern for light, returned to the sanctuary of Captain Claude's fair mistress.

Duke was awfully astonished by the apparition of the beautiful girl walking slowly towards him.

The rays from his lantern fell upon her form, drawn erect, and robed in spotless white. She stood out in strong relief from the surrounding darkness.

Her eyes were wide open, and fixed with a strange glare. She did not appear to take any notice of the highwayman's appearance.

Duke thought this very strange; he knew not whether he was looking upon the original or the shadow; if the latter, it was not pleasant company for a fellow to be in, all alone, and at such a time.

He was prompted by a bold feeling that mastered his fears, to discover which he took three steps forward, stood before her, and threw the light full upon her pallid countenance.

She stopped, one cold hand was laid upon his wrist, and the other pointed to the ruby necklace the King had tried to tempt her with.

The idea of visions instantly left his head; the hand laid upon his wrist was a substance, and he came to the quick conclusion that he was arrested by a sleep-walker.

Such was the case.

Duke was very careful not to startle her; he knew in such a state that would be fatal.

He looked upon the floor, and his eyes glistened as bright as did the jewel his gaze rested upon.

Disengaging her hand from his arm, he secured the ruby necklace, and thrust it in an inner pocket of his coat.

The somnambulist turned then and got into bed.

Duke turned to watch her, when the rays from his lantern fell upon something glittering upon a marble stand.

"A gold casket!' he exclaimed on examining it, "I wonder how it came here. I did not see it before—perhaps the King brought it—dare say he did—wonder if he tried to tempt this pretty sleep-walker—s'pose he did— didn't succeed, though—awfully disappointed, no doubt—lost the casket and necklace, and his life, for all I know—what an unfortunate King!"

"You here?" said a sweet, faint voice.

Duke twisted round on his heels.

"Eh? ha! yes; by the Lord Harry!" he exclaimed. "Who was it spoke?"

"I—Milly."

"Oh!" he said. "Yes, I am here."

"What for?"

He thought it best not to tell her that she had been walking in her sleep. And she did not like to tell him that she had been drugged.

So they both remained in happy ignorance.

"I came to see if you were safe," he replied, answering her query.

Yes, thank you; though rather faint. Will you kindly give me a glass of water from that bottle."

She pointed out the one vessel—there were several there. Duke immediately complied with her wish.

"If you are strong enough, we will leave here?" he said, receiving the empty glass. "We only endanger our lives by remaining. I shall feel an awful amount safer when I am a mile or two from here."

"Oh, yes!" replied Milly. "Quite strong enough, and only too willing to go. I shall be ready in a few minutes."

Devil Duke took the hint and retired.

He was humming a lively, pretty air while waiting for Milly. A heavy tramp of feet brought his tune to an abrupt termination. He clutched his sword hilt, and waited while they passed.

A second tramp of feet at no great distance, but in a different direction, made him wonder much.

One of the party that were passing through a passage spoke; he heard distinctly the words, and recognised the voice as that of the corporal.

"Our comrades, like me, are unsuccessful,' said the soldier.

"If they are our comrades who are returning," replied another.

"It can't be anyone else," said the corporal. "But, however, we will see."

Duke heard them retreat with a feeling of joy.

"By this time," he muttered, "Milly is ready. I'll go and see."

Before he could take two steps the fair girl came to him and laid her hand on his arm.

"It is not yet safe for us to leave," she said, timidly. "I saw the soldiers."

"I heard them," answered Duke; "that was quite enough. If we are quick we may get out while they are going round."

Milly allowed herself to be led away by the highwayman; but they had not got far before they were compelled to draw back to avoid being seen by some approaching persons.

Duke could faintly see many faces in the distance through the gloom; he kept one arm round Milly's waist to keep her back, while he waited the coming of his enemies, as he thought, his hand closed firmly over the hilt of his sword; he was determined not to lose his fair charge again.

Milly trembled palpably, as the sound of feet grew louder, and the approaching forms became more distinct.

The party stopped and held a low consultation just where he was concealed Duke could not distinguish the dress or features of any, but he knew the voices of several.

He sprang out gladly from where he stood, his unexpected appearance startled the men, and they fell aside in awe. Another moment, as Duke spoke, they collected round him and his fair charge.

The party were our friends whom Grace had rescued from the guard-room.

The noble girl spoke.

"Milly, are you safe?" she said.

The fair maid understood the meaning of her words, and clung round her neck.

"Quite," she faltered.

"These fellows have the scent of blood-hounds," said Dick. "If we don't make a move we shall be removed to where we just came from.

"You must be brave, Milly," said Grace. "We may have more danger to face yet."

Nothing seemed more possible. The soldiers Duke had heard talking meant, as they said, to see if the second tramp of feet Duke had heard belonged to their comrades, but when they got to where the sound came from the tramp had proceeded farther on in advance. They had followed it up, and were now exceedingly close to our friends.

Dick thought a move advisable.

Grace had undertaken the management of the proceedings, being more acquainted with the secrets of the palace than any of the others.

"Caution, gentlemen," she said in a whisper. "Follow me."

She led the way with Milly through one of the long corridors, to which our readers have been before introduced.

Barely had they got to the end when they were brought to an unpleasant stand by the soldiers, who suddenly came upon them like a group of shadows, and surrounded them without the slightest noise.

The corporal had worked with good strata-gem in ordering the men to proceed without their boots.

The highwaymen were awfully astonished by the unfortunate advent, and, worst of all, held resistless through the double row of bayonets that surrounded them, and kept them prisoners within the centre of the glittering dangerous pointed weapons.

This was a bit of triumph the soldier did not anticipate.

"Hallo!" he exclaimed, on perceiving his three former captives by the light from a lantern one of his men carried. "How the ——did you get from the guard-room?"

"By the same means as we shall get from here," replied Tyburn Dick.

"No, we shan't," said Grace.

"No, I don't think you will," said the soldier.

"You can't stop us," said Grace.

"O! can't I? Try it on.

"You had better not prevent us."

"It will be your own fault if you resist."

"You have no authority to detain us."

"Indeed!"

"Exactly," the brave girl answered, knowingly; "you can only arrest one of us."

"I should say you know."

"I do, and he is Devil Duke."

The soldier looked at her, puzzled; he wondered how she, or as he thought he, knew so much.

"Pick out your man and you may have him," she said.

Duke thought that very kind of her.

The soldier was puzzled again; he scanned their features, but he knew not one from the other.

"You have got me," he said, "this time; but I don't let you go until I have seen the King."

Duke thought now he was perfectly safe, so said defiantly—

"You will have to find him first."

The corporal looked at him inquiringly.

Just then there was a miserable kind of groan that made Devil Duke feel awfully uncomfortable.

"Help, help!" shouted a voice, the owner of the miserable groan; "guards, help, help."

"The King in danger!" exclaimed the corporal, and he dashed off in the direction from whence the voice proceeded.

The soldiers, all in fearful excitement, shouldered their muskets and dashed after him, leaving the highwaymen unprotected.

The highwaymen were very thankful for the timely deliverance, and made a quick re-treat by following our heroine, who led them through a secret panel, and down a long, nar-now, and fearfully dark staircase; three or four minutes' careful traversing took them once more into fresh air.

They breathed freely when they were outside the palace.

They were now in the court-yard.

"Stop a minute," said Grace, holding up her tiny hand for them to halt; "Duke, you take care of Milly, while I see if all is quite safe."

"No, no, my dear," said Dick; "I'll see; it is too dangerous for you."

"Stay where you are, there's a dear fellow," said the graceful girl.

She was gone before her lover could stay her. While he stood amazed by her audacious daring she returned.

"Come quietly; there are only two on guard," she said, "and they are in conversation at the further end."

The highwaymen moved noiselessly forward, nor did any of them speak until the palace was left some distance behind.

Then Dick ventured a remark.

"I am glad we are out of there," he said; "I hope we shall have a little rest before we are made sport for any one else to run after."

He had no sooner spoken the words than a shout in the rear made him aware that there was some one behind him.

He turned like a tiger with rising anger.

A shout from his old adversary, Red Matthias, greeted his ears.

"Cursed, infernal wretch!" hissed the boy between his clenched teeth. He knew he was the only one wanted.

Grace watched him. She was troubled by the expression of his face.

"What is it, Dick?" she asked.

He took her hand tenderly.

He could not speak for a few seconds. He felt a dread of the thief-catcher he had never known before. His handsome face was wild, and he was awfully agitated.

"That man," he said, squeezing the tiny hand he held, while Grace looked sadly up into his face, "swore, when I first took to the road, to hunt me down."

"Those six men he has with him won't take you while we are here," replied the noble girl, her eyes lighting up with a dangerous fire, and her cheeks crimsoned deeply with the hot rising blood.

"I am not frightened of fifty such," answered Dick; "but he alone it is of whom I am now frightened.

"Don't talk like that, old fellow," said Tom King, kindly; "there's not a man in existence you are frightened of, I know, and why talk so now? We are four, and can stand against fourteen such fellows, I know, so we have nothing to fear about the handful coming down the road; I alone would dispose of them."

"Ah! Tom," he said, "there are times when a fellow can lose his courage, and be oppressed with strange presentiments."

"There are times, true; but they should never exist with such men as we. Look here, Dick, you are not going to be taken?"

"No," said Dick, "I don't intend to be; but for my sake, comrades, don't raise a weapon against these men."

"Won't we though?" said Paul Clifford. "We are not going to stand inactive while you are taken. Are we, Tom?"

"Not if we can help it, Paul," said the other.

The thief-catcher had ridden to them within shot range, and he bawled lustily for Dick to surrender while he was safe, at the same time pointing a pistol in the direction of the boy's head.

Our hero glanced at him maliciously; he thought there was very little chance for him to escape his savage enemy.

Red Matthias drew up in front of Tyburn Dick, and his myrmidons ranged round the rest.

"We have met again, friend Dick," said the thief-catcher, gleefully. "I told you I would hunt you down; and it won't be long now before you adorn the tree you were christened after—*Tyburn*."

"Don't make too sure of that."

"No, my bird, I don't; but you are already fledged, so I can make sure of you."

"Even now I might fly away."

"You wouldn't go far; I never miss."

As he spoke, his fingers played nervously about his pistol, and Dick could see by the murderous look in his eye his treacherous intent. The noble boy stood in a very dangerous position. At his slightest movement to escape, a bullet would be sent crashing through his brain.

The clattering of a horse's iron feet coming rapidly down the dry road drew the inquisitive attention of the thief-catcher from his intended prize, and in that moment he lost him.

Dick, seeing the rider, a butcher, thought it a favourable opportunity to obtain a horse.

He dashed into the road, clutched the man by the leg, and, without any ceremony, pitched him head first from the saddle.

The thief-catcher made a bound forward to stop the daring boy, but Dick was in the saddle before he could interfere, and tearing madly away.

The highwaymen stood bewildered, so sudden had the transformation acted.

Red Matthias and his men thundered hotly in pursuit of Tyburn Dick, and when the pursued and pursuers had faded from the gaze of our astonished friends, they wended their steps to Hounslow Heath to get horses to ride out in search, and rescue the daring Boy King of the Highwaymen.

CHAPTER LXXXVIII.
HOUNSLOW HEATH.

It was night—dark, tempestuous, and bitterly cold—when a solitary horseman urged his jaded steed along the road that skirted Hounslow Heath.

He was a man who had seen much care in his day, at least if we might judge by his appearance.

A slouched hat almost concealed his features, and an old grey cloak protected him from the pelting rain and bitter cutting winds.

Of the horse we can say but little.

A lumbersome old hack that had been driven almost to death's door it seemed to be, and at every step it stumbled, and almost threw its rider.

"Woa! Hold up, Nell!"

Thundered the gruff voice of the rider, as he jerked at the reins, and dug his heels into the horse's flank.

But Nell either did not hear him, or took little heed of him, for before they had gone many paces she fell.

Her rider was of course pitched head-foremost to the ground, and lay there some considerable time after Nell had scrambled to her feet.

"A pretty fine mess for a feller to be in," growled the prostrate man.

"I'm afraid my arm's broken this time."

He rose up in a sitting posture, and began to examine the wounded limb, but to his joy he discovered that the only injury it had received was a slight bruise.

"Thank Heaven for that," he murmured.

"But," he added, "I don't know whether I'm safe or not yet, nor my little darling either."

The little darling he was so anxious about was an old canvas bag; but by the peculiar chink it gave it was evident it contained something precious.

"Ah, ah!" he laughed, half maniacally. "This is the fruit of my evening's work; what a fool he must have been to lay so rashly."

"Ah, what was that?" he ejaculated mentally; "a footfall, I could swear."

He cast his eyes anxiously over the heath, then fixed his gaze on a clump of trees that bordered the road.

There he could see nothing to enhance his fears, but his mind was mistrustful, and he tried hard to pierce the darkness.

"A man," he muttered. "Yes, by heavens, methinks I see in him a robber come to ease me of my gold."

The idea so startled him that he leapt to his feet and sprang into his saddle.

"Ah, now I see him," he vociferated, as his eye rested on the stump of a fallen tree, "but let him come too near, and I'll soon tell him who I am."

Clutching the butt of a huge horse pistol, he gave a defiant glance at the supposed robber, and pointed the barrel towards the fallen tree.

"By Jove! come out now, if you're not afraid," he shouted, though not too loud; "come out, and I'll blow out your brains."

With this desperate resolve he turned his horse's head, and once more tried to pursue his journey.

But the horse was too lame.

The poor thing hobbled along at a pace that would have taken at least two days to convey him to the next inn.

With many a bitter curse he belaboured the weary steed, but to no avail, and finding all his endeavours to make her go useless, he dismounted. Scarcely had he done so when the report of a pistol startled him.

Another, and then another followed.

The clatter of horses' hoofs broke on his

voices and shouts became plainly audible.

And then, before he could become fully aware of his danger, he was surrounded by a body of officers.

"Surrender!" shouted the foremost.

The astonished traveller made no reply, but stood still and silent.

Still we say, that is with the exception of his knees and teeth, the former of which knocked violently together, and the latter chattered pretty freely.

"Surrender!" repeated the officer.

Still no answer.

This raised his ire.

"Do you hear me?" he shouted indignantly.

Still no reply.

"Seize him," cried the officer, turning sharply to his men, "but be careful—he has a loaded pistol."

One of the bull-dog looking fellows instantly dismounted, and this aroused the stupified traveller to his senses.

"Stand off!" he cried, "or your blood be upon your own heads. How dare you insult me on the King's highway?"

A coarse brutal laugh was the only reply.

"Seize him," cried the officer, petulantly; "don't listen to his palaver, cut him down if he resists."

"Villains!" thundered the traveller, "stand off, or by heavens I'll——"

"Well, do, my cockolorum," retorted the officer, whose duty it was to make him prisoner; "you hear I have to take you, and if you shoot or make any resistance, why a brace of bullets through your ugly skull will make up for the difference."

The determined tone in which this was uttered was sufficient proof of the man's words.

So thought the traveller, and, seeing the odds so much against him, he trembled a little.

But still for this he was a brave man, and as up to this time he had no idea of the real character of the men who had thus surrounded him, it is no wonder his nerve should fail him.

Owing to the darkness they were unable to distinguish each other's faces, or even dress.

"Now, then, don't stand parleying there, Jem," thundered the leader, angrily. "Seize him; remember the reward that attends his capture."

The traveller started.

"Reward!" he muttered. "What do they suppose me to be, I wonder?"

This last was unconsciously uttered sufficiently loud for the blustering myrmidon of the law to hear, and he replied—

"What do we take you for, eh? Why, a very respectable gen'leman, in course, or we should not have rode all this way after you; and now we've taken all this trouble, I hope you will accompany us quietly."

"In course he will," chimed in another who by this time had left his seat and joined his companions. "Come, I will lend him my horse, as I see his is lame."

The jeering tone of this speech went to the traveller's very heart, and he chafed inwardly.

Nevertheless, he grasped his pistol firmly, and stood ready to resist the first attempt to capture him.

"Stand off, cowards!" he vociferated, fiercely, "or by all that's holy I'll send a bullet through your villanous hearts!"

"Oh, oh; strong talk, Mr. Tyburn, but it's no use; you don't do us this time!" said the thieftaker, with a cunning leer.

The officers were a party who had been sent to apprehend two highwaymen for stopping the mail coach on the previous night, and happening to come across the famous Tyburn Dick in their journey, they gave him chase.

As the chance of coming up with him by fair means appeared hopeless, they fired a pistol volley after him, which he returned with warmth, but, owing to the darkness, no shots took effect.

On turning a point in the road, the daring highwayman saw his chance of escape.

Wheeling his horse sharply round, he leaped the hedge, and made for a small copse.

THE ENCOUNTER.

The officers were astounded at his sudden disappearance, and were about to pull up and search the spot, when a shadow in the distance attracted their attention.

"Curse him! The very devil seems to aid him!" cried the leader. "One would think that horse of his had wings. Fire, my lads, fire!"

Another random volley was fired.

Fortunately for the traveller, he was further from them than they anticipated.

Had he not been so he would have fared badly.

When the officers came up with him, they had little doubt that one of the bullets had wounded either him or his horse, and they were in hopes it was the latter, that they might make a prisoner of him easy.

They knew the desperate character of the daring highwayman too well to go too rashly to work.

In fact, the leader, though anxious for the praise and a share in the reward, would not have laid a hand on him for all the world.

This accounts for his ordering Blustering Jem to dismount.

Jem was a famous bully, and being a big fellow, with a bullet head and short scrubby whiskers, he often terrified his prisoners into submission.

Upon the traveller, however, it had the opposite effect.

There was something hidden between his shirt and his skin that was worth standing all the bullying for, and, if needed, a fight.

There was a nervous twitching of his lips as the second officer approached him, and raised his hand to draw aside his cloak.

"Back! touch me not. Lay your hand upon me and it will be your death!"

"Do you hear that, Jem?"

"Certainly, and I dare say you can hear that."

Jem cocked his pistol as he spoke.

The ominous click went to the traveller's heart, but he quailed not.

The pistol was loaded with slugs and an extra charge of powder.

To shoot one of the officers and dash out the brains of the other was the thought uppermost in his mind.

Then, in the confusion, to leap on the back of one of the riderless horses and gallop off as fast as possible.

Jem seemed to anticipate his intentions, for, holding a pistol in each hand level with the traveller's head, he approached him cautiously.

"Back, fool!" yelled the traveller, and drew the trigger of his pistol.

Jem went all of an icy coldness as the click struck on his ear.

He made sure that his time was come, and it so unnerved him that he dropped both arms powerless by his side.

Fortunately for him, in the fall from the horse, the flint of the traveller's pistol had become dislodged so that it missed fire.

"Lucky escape, Jem," cried his companion, springing foward and grasping the stranger by the throat. "Now for it; I've got him!"

"Hold him fast," cried Jem, as soon as he could recover breath.

By this time the others had dismounted, leaving one in charge of the horses.

In a moment all was confusion.

The cloak of the supposed highwayman was torn from his shoulders.

His arms were held by three or four stout fellows.

Then the leader of the party approached him.

An execration of mingled rage and disappointment came from his lips as he did so.

He had anticipated seeing the form of Tyburn Dick upon the prisoner's cloak being removed, but was disappointed.

"Some trickery," he hissed; "but, by ——, I'll find it out."

The traveller, now things began to assume a dangerous aspect, began to be alarmed; the more so as one of his enraged captors had placed his hand on the spot where his gold was concealed.

Almost breathless with terror, he stood trembling in every limb.

As the pale moon broke through the straggling clouds and illuminated the traveller's features, they looked perfectly ghastly.

Not so the avaricious officer, who soon lightened him of his precious treasure.

The chink of the yellow dross was music to the ears of his captors.

"A highwayman, by Jove!" exclaimed the gratified leader, who, now the table of fortune had turned, screwed up his features into a ghastly smile.

"Yes, but not Tyburn Dick, though," growled one.

"Never mind, it's just as good," argued another; "there's enough swag here to line all our pockets."

"Oh, you wretches—you villains!" groaned the horrified man.

"It's all very fine," growled Jem.

"You've helped yourself nicely to some poor devil's purse."

So saying he slapped his hand on the bag, making the contents ring again.

For a moment the trembling man seemed ready to sink into the earth, and then he underwent a sudden change.

On seeing his treasure in the hands of his exulting captors, he seemed suddenly inspired with new life.

Clutching eagerly at the bag, he strove to get it into his possession.

For this he was rewarded by a smart blow from Jem's fist.

Fire flashed from the stranger's eyes, and, dazed and bewildered, he staggered backwards and fell.

For a moment he lay as dead, and then the gluttonous villains commenced dividing the spoil.

This was the signal for a row.

The leader laid claim to the largest share, which was disputed by the fellow who made the discovery.

Big Jem then declared himself the only one entitled to any privilege, urging as his reason that had it not been for him they would all have been shot.

In this manner they spent nearly an hour.

The leader then warned them that it would soon be light, and that if discovered in their present position the result would prove very unsatisfactory to him.

These words had a great effect upon the rest, and they ultimately agreed to share all alike.

The next difficulty was as to how they were to dispose of the plundered man, for blind as they were to all reason, they could not hoodwink at the fact that the stranger was a man other than what they had at first supposed him to be.

CHAPTER LXXXIX.

It was the morning following the recovery of Victor St. James and Gallant Tom, when they awoke after their strange night's adventure, they found themselves in a weak state of mental debility and unable to rise from their beds.

Joseph Munroe proved a watchful guardian and careful nurse, he humoured their appetites with every little delicacy, and when they were lonely he read to them.

At the expiration of three days they were much stronger and able to leave their beds, for which they were not sorry.

"You are not in a fit state, gentlemen," said Munroe to his patients, "to venture out just yet."

"I feel sadly," said St. James, "not that I ant to leave you just yet; but I am anxious about several things in Cornwall. My poor valet, I should like to see him again, he was a faithful fellow. You will excuse me for taking my departure, and allow me to tender my gratitude in this."

He took from his finger a splendid emerald ring and placed it on Bullskin's little finger.

The highwayman received it as a token of friendship more than a recompense for his kindness.

The young nobleman took his farewell of the highwaymen and left for Cornwall.

Captain Claude, who had been out seeking what information he could about the position of his son, soon after returned; he gained information as to where Dick was lodged, but he did not know where next he would be removed to.

A private council of three was being held between Captain Claude, Joseph Munroe, and Gallant Tom; they were plotting for the rescue of their new comrades and Tyburn Dick, when our heroine and the others she had saved entered. Captain Claude was the first to spring up and welcome their return. Milly's innocent gladness broke forth as her handsome lover caught her buoyant form in his arms, and held her gently to his breast.

Grace soon imparted the cause of Dick's non-appearance, and made known her intentions of following to his rescue.

"Let me entreat of you, my dear girl," said Captain Claude, "to remain here with Milly. Dick shall be saved; I with Duke and Tom will save him."

"I could not rest," replied Grace, "while he is in such danger."

"But as his father," said Claude, "I must claim the right of preceding you in the claim."

"Not in this instance."

The highwayman saw she was fully bent upon carrying out her resolution, and he said, laughingly—

"If you persist in going, I shall have you put under arrest until I return with Dick."

"That would be very cruel of you," said the girl, gravely. "To keep me back while he is out in such danger would be to inflict the most torturing punishment upon me."

"Yet in the end it would be the best for both of you."

"In what way?"

"This; if you go out, Dick may return, and, of course, expect to see you here. Upon being absent he would immediately set out in search of you, and so this unhappiness would be kept up until one of you got into such danger that it would be beyond our power to save you."

Grace remained silent and resolute.

Claude saw that his argument had only tended to make her more firm. He whispered something to Milly, and the fair girl said—

"Grace, dear, let me entreat of you to

remain with me. I have a presentiment that if you leave me, I shall be taken away from you again."

"Nonsense, Milly, you are so stupidly timid; besides, Claude will be here to look after you."

"I shall not," put in the highwayman. "Whether you go or not I am in duty bound to look after him."

"Then I am very sorry," said Grace.

She kissed Milly in silence, and bowing to the rest left the haunt.

"Her daring hardihood will lead her into danger some of these days," said Bullskin. "I will follow her, or we shall lose her."

"Do," said Captain Claude.

"I must keep out of her sight, or from perverseness she would run further risk. Adieu, comrades; rely upon me for keeping her from danger."

All was peace.

Captain Claude drew Milly to his side, with his arm around her waist, and spoke to Devil Duke.

"We must not let any harm befall Dick if it is in our power to prevent it," he said. "I, as his father, naturally feel anxious about his safety, and intend to go out in search of him. I leave in the care, and look to you and gallant Tom for the presence of Milly, your charge, when I return."

"You surely, dear Claude, are not going to desert me?" said the poor girl, pleadingly, for the thought of again parting with her gallant lover grieved her greatly.

"Only for a short time, Milly."

"But why go at all?"

"Milly, dear, you must not let your love make you selfish. Think what I should feel if Dick was taken, when, perhaps, my aid might save him."

The girl was quiet.

"Good bye, Milly; I shan't be away long," said the highwayman, kissing her gently. "If cannot learn any tidings of him I shall return immediately."

"Keep out of danger for my sake, Claude, dear."

"I will, darling. Adieu."

The captain went to the vaults beneath the old priory, which had been converted into capital stables for their horses.

The Lusher had prepared Active for his chieftain's departure.

"That's a good fellow," said Claude, vaulting upon the saddle of his gallant steed. "I have no time to lose."

"No, cap'n," replied The Lusher. "Does yer think yer 'ill want me for anything, cap'n?"

"Not if you have any desire to make an excursion for yourself"

"Thank yer, cap'n. Well, yer see, it is this. I wants to go to Cornwall."

"There is a lady in the case, then?"

"Well, cap'n, there is, an' I ain't 'shamed of saying it, for she is one o' the prettiest black-eyed lasses you ever seed; and I is anxious to see how she is, for yer must know, cap'n, when I com'd away from Cornwall, there was another fellah trying after her, an' this other fellah, being a lackey in the same 'ouse, with big white legs, which he stuffs with hay, to make 'em stick out, I think he's a villain; for he said if she wouldn't have him, which I know'd she never would, he would kill her. Yer honner knows what it is to love, an' in course can imagine how I feel."

"Very uneasy for her safety, no doubt," replied Claude, trying to keep a serious face.

"Yes, cap'n, I does; and as yer honner is kind enough to say yer doesn't want me, why, I'll go by the next coach, and make what I can on the way."

"By all means go; but be careful in making out the way, or perhaps you will not have the pleasure of seeing your pretty, black-eyed lassie any more."

"Oh! don't say that, cap'n."

"*Au revoir!* Evans. I wish you success."

"Thank'e, cap'n," said the Lusher, making off, without any preparations, to catch the next coach that started for Cornwall from the Leopard Inn.

Captain Claude had not gone far from the Priory when he saw, or fancied he saw, the shadows of several horsemen. He drew Active beneath the shade of a huge tree, and watched.

Presently the moon broke out through a mass of dark clouds, and, by its bright radiance, the captain was able to ascertain whether his fancy was imagination or reality.

He strained his eyes to scan the expanse of earth, and in the distance he distinctly saw beneath the silvery rays of the moon several horsemen, tearing madly across the heath.

He discovered the foremost rider to be Tyburn Dick by the glittering star upon his breast.

He put spurs to his steed, and went off in pursuit; but ere he got half-way across the heath, the whole party faded from his gaze.

Our hero found a difference in the speed of the horse he was riding and the one he was used to bestride.

The brute was broken-winded, and Dick had to treat it in a most brutal manner to get it to go along, greatly against his nature; even then, with all the whipping and spurring, he had the greatest trouble to keep it ahead of his pursuers.

Red Matthias stuck to him like a leech. Our hero was very nearly under his clutches several times. He knew unless he could stop him, he would be quite lost; then, turning savagely in the saddle, he drew a pistol and fired.

The ball struck the thief-catcher in the shoulder, and, with a fierce curse, he fell from his horse.

Dick urged his animal onwards, knowing if he could get a start, he would be able to escape while the officers crowded round their fallen leader.

Red Matthias swore awfully at his men, and ordered them to pursue Tyburn Dick. He was rendered more fierce and mad by the vision of the Boy Highwayman escaping them.

Dick saw, with a feeling of disgust, the men thundering down behind him, his horse began to tire, and trembled fearfully; the boy knew he would not go much further, but while he did last he meant to have all he could out of him.

He beat the poor brute unmercifully. It made several attempts to quicken its pace, but failed, and, with a piteous, wild cry, staggered and fell.

Barely had Dick time to extricate his feet from the stirrups, when it fell over on its side dead, bleeding fearfully from the nostrils and mouth.

Dick had broken its heart through riding it so hard. He cast a sorrowful look upon it, and without waiting to take any survey of his pursuers, he trusted to the speed of his own legs, and went off before the wind in a manner that astonished the officers.

The earth was sufficiently lighted by the brilliant rays from the meteor in the heavens to enable the officers to see the stumble of our hero's horse, and they, thinking he was being half crushed beneath it, urged their sweating steeds onward, thinking, for a moral certainty, that they were going to make sure of their prize.

But when they came up to the dead animal and turned it over, in hopes of finding the Boy Highwayman helpless, and discovered that he was not there, they swore most awfully.

Red Matthias's wrath knew no bounds at the disappointment. He heaped curses upon his followers' heads, and called them everything he could think of but beauties.

"Move yourselves!" he yelled frantically. "Again he has slipped through my fingers."

"You should have held him tighter," said one of the men, energetically.

"Say that again, and I'll "——

The thieftaker was about to say shoot you, when another of the lively myrmidons bawled out—

"Hallo! there he goes!" meaning, of course, Tyburn Dick.

And so it was. The youth was making his way to the Leopard Inn as fast as his legs would carry him, but on hearing the officer's denunciation he turned his steps another way.

He had not proceeded far in the new direction, when, unexpectedly, he was brought to a stand by the officers who had robbed the traveller wheeling round before him.

"I must get through them," thought Dick.

But ere he could carry out his intentions by breaking through their rank, the men slipped from their saddles, and stood firm before him.

Dick was certainly in an unpleasant trap.

He thought to retrace his steps would be the safest way, but too late. Red Matthias and his band had gained wonderfully upon him in that direction. He saw no chance of escape.

The voice of the thief-catcher was ringing out loudly for his brother officers, who now opposed Dick, to capture the daring boy.

They appeared in no particular hurry to do so; they rather appeared to enjoy his perplexity.

He had left it now to the last moment, and the only chance that remained for him was in a desperate effort.

"Shoot him!" yelled Red Matthias.

"Oh, no," said one of the officers before him, "we won't do that. Let's take him all at once."

Dick stood perfectly still, and looked the speaker steadily in his swarthy face.

"Well, my chickabiddy, what are you thinking of?" asked the man.

"Thinking that you won't take me tonight."

The officer whistled incredulously.

"Won't take you! Why, we've got you, man!" he said.

"Make sure of me," he cried, and sprang forward between two men.

Then he was wedged for a moment or so.

The men squeezed together, and pressed around him.

Using an old proverb, Dick had "jumped out of the pan into the fire," and he felt that it was more than he could stand; and how to get out of it before it grew hotter, he was some moments deciding. But finally, he clenched his hand, dealt one of his captors a blow in the face that felled him senseless to the earth, and dashing away from the others before any more could interfere, he sprang at one of the horses.

His hands barely caught the ends of the mane—the animal, startled by the sudden shock, started off quicker than it had ever gone before.

Dick held on for dear life.

He was being carried along in a perilous position, but he did not fear the danger he incurred.

It was enough for him to escape his enemies; and while the horse kept on he was perfectly content to be taken away with his legs hanging down, risking the consequence of a kick from the animal's hoof that might dislodge his knee-cap, or take a little more than the bark off his shins.

The officers watched him in mute astonishment, every moment expecting to see him fall, maimed and crushed.

Even Red Matthias drew up his steed and stared breathless, his mouth wide open, and his gaze following the horse retreating with his prize.

"Fire after him!" he suddenly yelled.

His voice fell like a thunderbolt amongst the men, and the alarm caused thereby rendered them more helpless than before, for a time.

"Fools, to let him go!" exclaimed Red Matthias, in a deep, disgusted tone of voice; and, ordering his men to follow him, he again pressed on in pursuit of Tyburn Dick.

The daring young highwayman had now drawn himself up, and with a little difficulty, got into the saddle.

He waved his handkerchief in triumph at the thief-catcher.

The act exasperated Matthias. It was bad enough for him to bear the humiliation of losing his prize, but to be defied, in a manner so daring, was more than his fiery nature could bear; drawing a pistol from the holster, he fired at the fugitive.

Dick smiled quietly to himself, and returned the fire.

His shot, likewise, fell far of its mark, but it intimidated the thief-catcher, and caused him to slacken the pace of his charger.

He was smarting from the effects of the one shot from the boy, that had laid him in the dust, and he had no wish for another.

Hounslow Heath was long since left far behind, and the end of the main road, along which the chase for the last ten minutes had been continued, was now reached by our hero.

He sharply turned the corner, and leaped a high hedge that would take him a near way to the back of the Leopard Inn.

His horse cleared the hedge, but fell heavily on the bank of a wide ditch on the other side.

Dick, sitting in the saddle firmly to retain his seat, was unable to disengage his feet from the stirrups, fell with the animal, and got his leg severely jammed.

The horse, too, was fearfully injured by the fall, but the noise the officers made on turning the corner, and seeing the catastrophe that had occurred to the boy highwayman, frightened the horse, which, in a state of madness, scrambled from the ditch, and tore away with its young rider.

It did not go far, excitement lent it artificial strength, but that could not last.

Dick felt it stagger ever and anon, and its whole body quiver. He knew it was all over with the poor creature, and he prepared himself for the critical moment when it should fall.

He was now within a quarter of a mile of the inn. His gallant steed made a dead stop, and whined piteously, fell to its knees, sprang up, and took a leap forward that surprised its rider, then it fell, as Dick drew his legs over the saddle, and slid from its back.

He knelt for a few seconds by the horse, raised its head on his arm, and affectionately patted its sleek neck.

The sagacious animal licked the boy's hand, and fixed his eyes upon his sad, troubled face, and in that gaze Dick saw a look of love and regret.

"Poor beast," he said, kindly; "you deserve a better fate than this. You have served me well, and I, in return, should protect you."

He drew a pair of long-barrelled pistols from his belt, and stood over the body of the steed, with the determination to save it from their cruel hands, for he knew they would wreak their vengeance upon the poor dumb animal for cheating them of their prize; but, on seeing the number of men that were coming towards him with all speed, he left the steed with a revengeful look; but with the intention, should the officers not hurt it, to return, should he escape, and render it what assistance he could.

It was with difficulty that he could manage to get along at all, so badly was his leg hurt.

He saw very little hope of reaching the inn before he was beset by the officers.

The pain he suffered was excruciating, but he did reach the inn yard by quickening his limping steps and adding to his tortures.

True, he reached it, but he had scarcely got the other side of the gate when he fell to the earth exhausted.

He looked around in agony for a friend, but no one was in sight but his enemies who then rode up dismounted, and crowded round him.

"Ho, there! within!" yelled Tyburn Dick as a last resource, "to the rescue of Tyburn Dick!" And he sank back helpless, and at the mercy of his enemies.

CHAPTER XC.

THE HUT BY THE BLACK QUARRY.

"What ho! Within, there!"

This summons was given at the dead of midnight, and the man who gave it stood at the door of the hut.

A desolate dwelling that, and built on a bleak and barren ridge of broken land, where gaunt, bare trees made ghastly shadows, and the winter wind sung weirdly.

A hermit or a savage human thing, hating the world and his fellow-men, might have chosen such a home.

It was formed of roughly hewn trees, sunk deeply into the hard clay, and its rudely thatched roof was black with the work of time and tempest.

"What ho! Within, there!"

This time he who summoned knocked with a pistol butt, but no reply came, and he called again.

"Bertram must sleep soundly, or the devil has claimed his own, and I have come too late. What ho!"

He dropped his voice, for the echoes took up his sentence, and sent it back with horrible mockery.

"Had the devil claimed his own, Sir Gabriel Carnwood would not be here," said a deep tone at his side, and starting at the sound, he turned, and saw a dark colossal figure.

"Ha, Bertram! You heard me?"

"The echoes told their story. I am here!"

"Where were you?"

"Out with my midnight company—things that would scare your sight, and make you speak less loud, Sir Gabriel—the phantoms—the Phantoms of the Black Quarry!"

"Hush! man. That mad talk makes my blood creep. I shiver. Let us enter."

Bertram unfastened the door, and entered the hut, followed by his visitor, whom he called Sir Gabriel.

The interior was profoundly dark, and Carnwood felt his teeth chatter at the icy chill.

"Have you no fire—no light?"

"Wait."

The inhabitant of the hut did not treat his titled guest with much courtesy.

He knelt, and struck with flint and steel till a red shower of sparks fell into the tinder-box.

He fanned the glow into a flame, then kindled a torch, which he stuck upright in a hole in the clay.

"Now," he said, turning his dusky face towards the baronet, "what brings Sir Gabriel here? Did the silent dwellers in the quarry tell their story truly? and is there some more unholy work to be done?"

The baronet—a young and handsome man, whose beauty was marred by five hard, sinister lines—bent his keen grey eye upon the poacher—for such was the keeper of the hut.

"I do."

The Lord of Kingston Chase comes here at dawn."

"Returns? I thought he died in battle."

"So did I. But you remember the stranger who came here a month since—he whom an accident befel?"

"He who sleeps in the quarry's pool. Driven to sorry death by you, and buried by me. That crime has made us slave and master—master and slave."

"I do remember."

"His purpose here was to tell me that my cousin was not dead. He had been taken captive, but was ransomed. So he sent his comrade with a loving message to his wife and me, and said he should stand once more beneath his old ancestral roof, to grasp my hand, to kiss his wife and child."

The poacher's brow was hidden in his hands.

"Go on, Sir Gabriel."

"Lord Kingston's bride was fair, good Bertram, she loved her husband, and she mourned for him when thinking he was dead."

"But she is beautiful, and—I—I have a heart."

Bertram laughed grimly.

"I did not think it."

"And Bertram," the baronet said, under his breath, "because of the burning passion in this heart of mine, I never let her see her husband's messenger, lest the love I was beginning to win should return to him we had thought dead."

"And so you killed him. It was a ruthless deed, Sir Gabriel. You gave him treacherous death when he thought to drink with you as a friend."

"I would have given him a hundred deaths, for passion knows no mercy."

"I know the Carnwoods have it in their veins—a tigerish ferocity. But proceed."

"Is not the rest clear? That which she does not know must still remain unknown. I have prepared the way."

"How?"

"A letter sent last week by me tells him that his wife was faithless with his friend, and that to avenge his honour I slew his friend, and his wife fled.

"The demon must have whispered in your ear," said Bertram, with a strange change in his swarthy face, "for the plot were worthy Satan. And you would kill this cousin, he who trusted you to keep his home, and wife, and child?"

"My foot is on the red track, Bertram, and though Kingston were my twin brother I would not let his life stand in my way. Here—here is gold, but the black quarry claims its prey to-night, and you shall have a purse ten times the weight of this."

The Poacher took the purse Sir Gabriel gave him, and weighed it in his hand.

The gold glittered through the silken web

"Like eyes of devils," Bertram said, moodily, "tempting me on the way in which lies miserable crime."

The tempter watched him narrowly.

A doubt seemed to steal into his mind.

His white hand played upon a pistol in his belt.

"I can trust you, Bertram?"

"Are we not linked in sin?"

"The hireling should not speak so to his master."

Wild Bertram rose to his herculean height

"Master!" he echoed, with a laugh, "be

cause your hand is white and mine is swarth. Because your ancestors were of delicate birth and noble lineage, and mine were gipsy vagabonds Because the red stain on your palm covered by your proud rank, while the red sin on mine is redder from my poverty. Do ose make you my master?"

The baronet drew a pistol.

"Peace!" he said, fiercely, "or I scatter your brains. Dare to answer me, Sir Gabriel Carnwood, in such terms, and you shall die."

"Ha, ha! No threats, Sir Gabriel. My hand is on a weapon, too, and I am quick of eye, as sure of aim. I could twist your neck with a single grip, and, standing on the threshhold of my dwelling, hurl you into the quarry's depths. So keep your menaces for those who dread them."

"Peace!"

"As it may please me What if you were to fire? There are many chances that I might be wounded only, and then your fate would be sealed. For, with a tittle of my strength I could crush out your feeble life, and leave a mangled carcase for the ravens to pick Speak with more respect, or you may find a heirling otherwise."

The baronet let his passion cool, and put the pistol back.

"Why should we quarrel?" he said, holding out his hand. "There, you are a faithful fellow, and I was wrong."

"You were. But I want not your hand— there is no true fellowship in sin."

"But I can trust you."

"Have I not proved it?"

"Freely. So, put that purse in your pocket, and do not foil me. It is done the easier as he comes alone, and none knows his purposed destination."

"Is not that strange?"

"The Kingstons, like the Carnwoods, are friends," said the baronet; "and Lord Arthur would keep his friend I know unknown. He would not return at all, if it were not to see his child."

"And love for him, the little one who calls him sire, will bring him to his doom," said Bertram, with some sorrow in his tone.

"See you," said Sir Gabriel, "how the end of this places the broad acres in my posses-

sion; with Arthur gone, nothing but the boy stands between the inheritance and me."

"I see. It is not all passion that tempts the crime. The boy, I cannot harm him, Sir Gabriel. Yet he must die."

"The child—young Tom—he, too, sacrificed? I could not do it—though ambition is a pitiless fiend that has no thought of mercy. But the urchin has smiled in my face, nestled in these arms, and slept upon my breast."

"Why destroy him, then?"

"He were better dead, out of misery, than kept captive in a lonely dungeon till his young heart broke. I will bring him here."

"Hem! well, a life is not much to me. My career has been a wild and dark one, and the house-dwellers showed little mercy to me or mine. Had I not sought mercy in this desolation—had you not been generous to me, I should have been shot like a dog, or left to starve to death ere this."

"Think of that, and let it steel your soul."

"That turned to iron long ago, Sir Gabriel, and I can sleep without a thought of all the bitter past—all that has been done to me— all that I have done."

"So much the better. I bring the boy here before the dawn breaks, and then let me look upon him then. But let me see his grave in the Black Quarry."

"He shall sleep by the side of his sire."

"Then, Bertram — then there is more gold for you. And you must go to some foreign land, away—far away—that these scenes may not haunt you."

"When the work is done, Sir Gabriel, let me have the gold, and I will go. The soil of England is accursed; the wrongs—the bitter oppression—that made me what I am, sprung from it."

"Forget them!"

"Would that I could!"

"Will you want help with the Lord of Kingston Chase?" asked Gabriel, and the crimson torch-glow in his working face showed how he shrank from mention of the deed.

"To make sure, you had best drag him here, lest if I intercept him, my hand should fail."

"So be it. I will lead him here to look upon him whom he thinks his wronger —to look upon his grave."

"To look upon his own. So the compact is made, Sir Gabriel, and I have the first wages in my pocket."

"You will not betray me?"

"Dare I?"

"No! that awful oath, sworn over the dead body of him who sleeps beneath the quarry pool, will lock our lips in eternal silence; and so farewell until my rival comes, and we meet here again."

"Farewell! Be careful that the lady does not wake."

"I have taken care of that. The wine she took was drugged, and she slumbers heavily; and when she wakes, my triumph will be complete, for I shall be by her side."

"Oh, devil! devil!" said Wild Bertram, as his tempter strode back to Kingston Chase; "but for the oath that binds my tongue—but for the power that makes me your slave—I would denounce you to the world, save the innocent lady, and tell her husband the whole hideous lie."

"Slay him!" he said, lifting his brow to the midnight stars. "Kill the pretty lad, who smiles on me, fearing not, though my fellow men shun me as though I were a tiger. Never! my noble benefactor shall be warned. The child shall not die. I have sworn it—I have sworn it!"

He went into his hut; the torchlight died, and left him in darkness.

PROLOGUE.—SECOND PART.

THE MURDER AT THE QUARRY.

THE mighty bell of a distant church chimed out to tell that the solemn midnight hour was gone, when a solitary horseman rode through the gloom.

He was in sombre thought. He had ridden far, ridden slowly, for the sorrow upon him would not let him ride rapidly.

It was not as he had thought to return.

Arthur, Lord of Kingston Chase, the gallant soldier who had fought his country's battles, and endured captivity, had longed for the time that should see him spurring swiftly on his way to meet his lovely bride and fair-browed boy whom he had not seen since babyhood.

Now all was changed. His house was his home no longer. His bride was faithless,

and his friend had betrayed him. It was a bitter thing to think.

"But Gabriel, my good and faithful cousin, did avenge me well," he muttered. "It was bravely done to slay the traitor within sight of the house he had dishonoured. And she, my false and perjured wife, 'tis well she fled on thinking of her hideous treachery. I might have forgotten her sex—forgotten our sweet hours of love, and, remembering only her falsity, slain her in my outraged wrath."

"Lord Arthur Kingston."

The traveller reined in, and instinctively placed his hand upon his sword.

He stood before Wild Bertram's hut.

"Who speaks?"

"A friend."

"Then would that I could see his face," said the soldier, bitterly, "for friends are few."

"Your name?"

"Bertram."

"I remember the voice. What would you say?"

"Go not to Kingston Chase."

"Ha!"

"The shadow of death is there—be warned, more I dare not tell; but be warned."

"What should I fear? The shadow of death has gone before me many a time, and yet I live—live. Would that I were dead!"

"Lord Arthur Kingston, take a solemn warning, turn back; ride fast, and each stride will take you from inevitable doom."

It was dark—the soldier could not see the face of him who spoke, but he felt his hand upon the rein.

A suspicion of treachery crossed his mind.

"Out of my path!" he said.

"Turn back, my lord, turn back—back, I adjure you!"

"Out of my path! What's he who bids a soldier fear to reach his home? Away!"

His sword left its sheath with a dull gleam, and, heedless of the warning voice, he rode on.

The cry went after him.

"Turn back, my lord, turn back! Beware of him who smiles upon you—turn back. Beware!"

"A madman," thought Lord Kingston, "who should harm me?"

"Lost—lost!" said Bertram, despondingly. "Lost—lost!"

The soldier sheathed his sword again, and his brow relapsed into its previous sadness, as the towers of Kingston Chase loomed out in the murky light.

Suddenly, as he neared its doors, there came a gleam of light—a torch was waved—and Gabriel Carnwood stood before him.

"Ah, Gabriel!" he said, with a sad smile, "I did not think to find such a mournful welcome."

"Nor I to give it, Arthur; but who can trust his friend? But that I saw with my own eyes, I would not have believed your comrade could be such a traitor."

"But you slew him, Gabriel?"

"Gave him poison—stabbed him to the heart!"

"That was well—you knew his guilt."

"I saw him leave his chamber in the night —followed him, and said nothing. I waited till I could wreak my revenge."

"Curse them both!—traitor and traitress! Curse him in his grave—curse her living or dead! This wrings my heart, Gabriel. Let me see his grave that I may utter my male-dictions."

"Now?"

"Now—even now—before I enter the accursed house."

"But your child!"

"He shall come with us, that he may see it done, and give more bitterness to him who wronged me. Bring him forth, Gabriel. I feel that I cannot enter until I have seen where sleeps the traitor."

Gabriel wrung his hand—then disappeared in the house.

Even, as Lord Arthur waited alone, he thought he heard the echo of the warning.

"Turn back—beware! Turn back—beware!"

Sir Gabriel Carnwood re-appeared, leading a child by the hand.

"My boy! my own fair child! so like her!" the soldier said, as he pressed the little one to his aching breast, "the only pledge of her love while it was true! come to me!"

"My father!—dear father!"—and the child's hand caressed the bronzed cheek of his sire, "will you not come and see mother?"

"See her? Never—never more! Speak not her name, child! It tortures me!"

"Not see my mother! Poor mamma!"

"Hush! hush!"

The wondering child nestled to his father's heart. It seemed very strange that he must not mention his mother's name.

"Now, Gabriel, lead the way," said Lord Arthur, keeping the little one's hand locked fast in his own, as though clinging to the last link of love he was to be sundered from so soon. "Lead on; and when I have gazed upon the fatal spot, to say a long farewell to my native land, I shall never see it again."

"Never!" thought Gabriel. "If Bertram's arm fail him, mine will not fail me!"

The distance was not great from Kingston House to the hut. Behind the hut lay the black quarry.

"I'll call upon a faithful servant," Gabriel said—"he who digged the grave of your treacherous friend and debtor. Bertram! what ho!"

Bertram appeared. He, too, bore a torch, and its glare threw sombre shadows over his swarthy face.

"The man who warned me!" said Lord Arthur. "What did you mean, good fellow?"

"Warned you?" said Gabriel.

"The night is dark," said Bertram, and his deep tone had singular power. "I feared Lord Kingston would lose his way."

"Nay, I could count every tree and stone. But I thank you, nevertheless. Take this purse of mine. It is not heavy, but you are welcome."

Bertram shrank from the proffered gift.

"What! poor and proud?"

"I earn my bread, my lord, and I have few wants."

"Well, have your way. Gabriel shall reward you anon. And now, good cousin, let your torchlight shine upon a traitor's unhallowed resting-place."

"It lies deep in the black quarry," said Bertram. "Shall we descend, or will you see it from the brink? The way is steep, and to the unaccustomed foot may not be safe to tread."

"From the brink be it, then."

They were in the hut.

Lord Arthur paused. A strange presentiment had come over him. He drew his hand dreamily across his brow.

"I have a curious fancy, Gabriel," he said. "The night is weird, and voices seem to whisper to me."

"It is the sorrow, Arthur."

The soldier did not heed him.

"Come hither," he said, taking the child in his arms. "Kiss me again!—yet again! Heaven bless you, boy! I had not thought to hold you to a sorrowful heart!"

"My father, why are we here?"

"To see a sight I would not have your innocent eyes blighted with, poor little one. So stay you here with Bertram. I will come back presently."

"With Bertram!"

The swarthy poacher took the child's hand. His countenance was touched with emotion.

"Even he can feel for me," said Lord Arthur to his cousin. "But come!"

Gabriel went first.

The soldier followed, but paused at the door, and looked back, with a lingering, wistful look.

"Poor child!" he said; "poor child!"

He turned his face towards the sky; the moon peeped like a pale spectral face from behind a drifting mass of cloud, a rush of wintry wind went slinking past.

"A fitting spot for such a grave," Lord Arthur said, when the door was closed, and Gabriel was with him.

"A fitting spot for such a deed," thought Gabriel, and he felt the stealthy dagger in his breast.

He led his unsuspecting cousin and victim along the broken height, and to the brink that overhung the quarry.

They looked down from a terrible height, a withered branch touched by Arthur's foot fell over the precipice, it was a long time ere it reached the bottom, and struck the bosom of the stagnant pool with a dull splash.

Gabriel threw the torchlight glare into the thick darkness; the red glow and the falling sparks of fire shaped fitful shadows.

"I cannot see so far," said Lord Arthur; "shall we descend?"

"We will. I can recall the scene vividly, Arthur, when we carried him here and cast him into the gulf."

"Traitor! yet I did love him. We fought

side by side, Gabriel; slept in the same tent, and were like brothers."

"That thought nerved me to slay him. We stood face to face. as you and I stand now, and just as now I speak, I said—

"Say your last prayer, for your time is come."

"Ay! that was brave. Go on," said the soldier, exulting in the supposed vengeance done for him; "that savage frenzy in your eyes must have struck terror to his soul."

Sir Gabriel's voice sounded harsh and hoarse as he plucked his dagger out.

"I took him by the throat like this; ha, ha, ha! laughed at him as now I laugh, and tightening my grip thus—said, 'Die, die!'"

"Gabriel!—Gabriel!"

The assassin blow was dealt, the keen dagger quivering through Lord Arthur's breast, came out reeking.

The truth broke upon him then. He had not fallen yet, but with the sudden energy of coming death, clung to his murderer's arm.

"Gabriel! my cousin, Gabriel! What means this? Gabriel, mercy! let me live, Gabriel, my wife! my child!"

A savage laugh, a savage blow, and his hold began to relax.

He tottered on the verge of the abyss, and the murderer slashed his fingers with the blade.

"Down! down to death! Ha! ha! die and know this dying!"

"Gabriel, what have I done?"

"Stood between me and Kingston Chase —been my rival with the Lady Margaret. She is mine now! Mine!"

"Gabriel! Gabriel!"

Still he clung, but voice and grasp were growing fainter. There was a mist before him. His head swam; his feet were strengthless.

"Gabriel, strike no more. I am dying. Tell me, is she innocent? Ah, I see it all. My child! my poor child!"

"She is innocent. Die with that consolation and so—so——"

The gallant soldier, the betrayed master of Kingston Chase, the husband of Lady Margaret, was dead. The stiletto of his fell kinsman went twice into his heart.

Gabriel held the helpless, swaying body for a moment; the blood gushed over his hands, he pushed it from him, and it went down.

TYBURN DICK KEEPS THE OFFICERS AT BAY.

Down, with a heavy plash, into the pool. The black quarry had another victim—the dabbled corse by whom it fell. And Gabriel said—

"Bertram shall dig its grave."

He wiped his bloody hands on a tuft of grass, then went to his accomplice.

"It is done!" he said; "he struggled, but it is done."

He then wiped the sweat from his forehead. The child leaped away.

"Uncle Gabriel," he said, "your hands are red. Where is my father?"

The question struck the assassin now like the charge of an accusing angel. He put an arm before his face, that the boy might not see him

"No more," he said, sheathing his dagger. "I can do no more. Strike, Bertram, strike, and let this one night's treason compass all. The sky is red. The air is the hot breath of blood. Away! away! I did not think to feel like this."

"Away!" thundered Bertram, forcing in Gabriel, who seemed mad with momentary remorse. "Leave the rest with me. Away, lest the dead rise and haunt you from the earth!"

A shriek, like that of a lost soul going to the pit of hell, broke from Gabriel, and he dashed out into the darkness. He ran like a maniac. Conscience was at work, and peopled the road behind him with a thousand phantoms giving chase.

CHAPTER XCII.

THE shriek that would have left her lips was stifled, and Lady Margaret lay panting, dumbly, in terror. Gabriel Carnwood was there, with the purpose of a Tarquin in his face.

"Margaret," he said. "Margaret! awake to hear my prayer—to forgive my madness—to listen to my love."

"Gabriel—ah!—my dream—what does this intrusion mean? How dare you steal at night into my chamber? I will summon help."

"On your life," he said firmly. "Not a word—there is a raging demon in my soul, that you, sweet love, alone can quench. Will you listen?"

"Some other time, Cousin Gabriel; but not here, and like this. How wrong of you to frighten me."

And she smiled through tears that made her more beautiful—smiled to hide her fear.

The evil passions of his nature were aroused, the lady saw her helplessness and his fell intent, for he had locked the door.

The key lay on the table.

He had severed the bell ropes, they were in his hand, so was the dagger—the dagger she had seen in her dream.

The stains were wet upon it yet, thin red streaks in the creviced hilt.

"My dream," she said, shuddering. "My dream; or am I dreaming still? Gabriel Carnwood, where is my husband?"

He started.

"Here!"

"Here?"

"Look upon me, I am your husband now. Oh Margaret, I have done much for you, burdened my soul with heavy crime, and you must be mine."

"No, no! a thousand times no!"

"I have sworn it. Have some pity, Margaret, think how beautiful you are, how fondly I loved you before you were his; how tenderly I guarded you while he was away. Do you hate me?"

"Gabriel! Leave me, or I'll shriek till madness comes. Oh, my husband! The dream was truth. The black quarry! The grave in the pool! The red stain on your dagger! Help! help! Carnwood has killed—"

His ruthless hand choked back her cry, but she struggled from her couch, and in the maddening disorder of her night robe, battled with him. Shriek after shriek rang out, but no help came.

"I have dared perdition for you," he said, his fierce eyes flashing fire; "and the last crime of this night's horror shall reward me. Silence, silence! or this dagger shall be red from point to haft again."

"Kill me, Gabriel! kill me! better death than infamy! Kill me!"

"Not yet, sweet Margaret; you are too beautiful to die."

"Kill me, or I shall go mad!"

"And even in your madness you are beautiful. Silence! Was that a footstep? No. Hush! So, quiet at last!"

Her cries were stifled; her struggles ceased.

.   .   .   .

When the cold, grey morning dawned, the last and most pitiful tragedy of the horrid night was done. The destroyer, white and more pallid than his haggard victim, watched the rising sun, with guilty, remorseful eye.

The lady never knew her shame—never knew the black cloud of dishonour which had wrecked the purity of her hitherto unsullied life, for when the cold, grey morning dawned she was mad.

.   .   .   .

"What ho! within there!"

Wild Bertram came out to the haggard man who summoned him.

"Is it done?"

Without a word the poacher led Sir Gabriel to the depths of the black quarry, and pointed silently to two graves newly dug in the shallow, stagnant pool.

"It is done," Sir Gabriel said.

"It is done," said Bertram. Sire and son, Lord Arthur and his child—the last of the Kingstons—sleep side by side in the black quarry.

END OF THE PROLOGUE TO BOOK TWO.

TOM KING.*

*This celebrated character having been brought into this work without any introduction, it is our intention to give the startling history of his early life, which will commence Book the Second, and will be a separate story from the daring adventures of Tyburn Dick. The two will be combined in this work.

CHAPTER XCIII.

THE LUSHER MAKES A STROKE OF BUSINESS IN THE CORNWALL MAIL—A CRY FOR THE THIEF—THE LUSHER'S EXIT.

It so happened that the Lusher took the same coach for Cornwall as did Victor St. James, but neither was aware of the other's presence.

Though the night was fine, and the ride outside beside the driver would be very pleasant, the young nobleman was compelled to take his seat inside on account of not feeling very well.

The Lusher looked longingly at the box-seat disengaged, but his profession required his presence inside, where he thought to make a stroke of business during the journey that would defray his expenses, and enable him to make a present to his beloved Mary Jane.

So he got inside, and sat between two very dashing-looking men, an old and a young man.

He did not wish to commence operations too soon, but his fingers had a desire to wander into other people's pockets, and handle even other people's property.

It was with the greatest difficulty that he could keep his pilfering fingers quiet until the coach started.

They then had an idea that business ought to be commenced, and so slipped into the younger gentleman's coat-tail pocket, and turned over its contents, until the fingers stuck to a pocket-book, which was carefully drawn forth.

The Lusher was noted for a clever filcher, and certainly he was. He had a knack of taking things even out of people's hands with whom he was talking, examining them before their curious eyes, and if he did not think them worth taking, he would put them back, as he did with the pocket-book, which he contrived to convey into his own pocket, unseen by any other occupant of the coach.

Then with the greatest *nonchalance* imaginable, he took it out, held it under the light, close to the owner's eyes, and carelessly turned the contents as though looking for something; but, seeing nothing of much value, he closed it with contempt, even while the gentleman watched him curiously, and thought how strikingly alike it was to his own, and

Jack Evans returned it to its original receptacle with an air of disgust.

Only just in time, though, for no sooner was it replaced than a suspicion caused the gentleman to feel for it.

The Lusher was fumbling about in another of the gentleman's pockets, even while the gentleman was feeling for his pocket-book.

Master Jack caught hold of something bulky and rather heavy. It felt like a well-stocked purse or a bag of money.

Slowly, and with more caution than he had hitherto used, he tried to extract it.

He worked it to the top of the pockets, but could not get it any further.

This was a moment of trying suspense.

He felt that all eyes were upon him, yet he durst not glance around to see if such was the case.

He began to get in a fever-heat.

The gentleman shifted uneasily several times.

The Lusher got nervous, as he generally did, when in any difficulty.

He certainly worked with much patience, and presently was rewarded by getting out at the top of the pocket the mouth of the bag.

He perspired freely, with increased emotion; his heart beat rapidly, and every pulse in his body throbbed vigorously.

A quick tug.

The money bag was half way out.

One more trial, and he would succeed.

He had nerved himself for the final effort, and had almost accomplished his task in gaining his prize, when a hand closed on his wrist like a vice of iron.

Imagine the state of the Lusher in such a position, pent up as he was, surrounded with men who would have set upon him like a lot of wolves, even had they suspected his little game.

He could fairly have shrieked with agony; but he knew to do that would be resigning himself to their mercy, and that would not be much in such a case.

Here he prayed for the coach to break down that he might make his escape.

His captor appeared as though he did not wish to let any of his fellow-travellers know what had occurred, and while Jack Evans sat slowly melting away with terror, his captor released his hand, when he had regained his gold, and touched the Lusher quietly on the arm.

Trembling like an aspen leaf, he turned to face his conqueror with painful despair.

On recognising the gentleman, he indiscreetly gave vent to an exclamation of joy that startled every one in the coach.

Victor St. James being the daring thief's captor, warned him to be more careful in future.

"You made a very fortunate mistake, my friend," he said, quietly.

"And yer ain't a-goin' to do nothing to me?" returned the Lusher.

"I must pardon you for the cleverness you used."

Getting over his fright, the Lusher thought he would try on the other side of him, having got off safely this time.

"I must have coin," he thought, "so here goes."

There it went, too.

His hand, like a dart, went into an old fogey's pocket.

Horror!

The Lusher's hand was fixed.

The pocket was lined with short pins.

This was a snare laid by the artful old fogey for the reception of gentlemen who could not find occupation enough to keep their hands employed, without visiting other people's pockets.

The contortions the Lusher drew his visage into, caused by the pain, were a caution to physiognomists.

How he was to get his hand out without tearing the flesh in deep gashes was more than he could conceive.

He tried several ways to extricate the pins and draw out his hand, but the slightest movement drove the pointed instruments further into his hands.

Once he thought of telling the old fogey he had put his hand into the wrong pocket by mistake, through sitting too close together.

But, on second thoughts, he thought he would be making a mistake if he said so; so he held his tongue, and suffered the most tormenting pain in trying to extricate his hand.

At last he succeeded, and when he got his hand out, it was in a fearful condition, torn in deep gashes, and bleeding profusely.

Fortunately for him, the old fogey, before starting on the journey, had largely imbibed some crusted port, and, in consequence was rather drowsy, or otherwise the Lusher would have been detected there.

"I'll serve him a trick," thought Jack Evans, spitefully, "and see if Jack ain't as good as his master."

Thus cogitating, he took a small knife from his pocket, and, in less than a minute, had ripped the pocket from the old gent's breeches.

The old gent, by this time, had partially fallen into a delicious sleep.

The Lusher took the pocket out, fully bent upon a revengeful intent, and rent the seam open.

"Now," he thought, "I'll give the d——d old buffer a stinger."

And such was his purpose.

Sliding the pocket down the leg of the old fogey's breeches, with the spikes towards his flesh, the Lusher thought it a good opportunity to make a little while most of the passengers were asleep.

He firstly commenced upon his associate, the old fogey with the spiked pocket, by cutting off the gold buckles from his shoes, filching the diamond pin from his cravat, and converting a splendid gold watch from his pocket to his own.

His next victim was a podgey old fogey who snored loudly, and had a knack of nodding his head, as though he was bowing at court, and grinned all over his face like a Chinese image.

His hands were red and big, and rested upon his knees, much bigger. On three fingers of each hand he wore the most brilliant rings, costly and rare, the Lusher had ever seen.

Their brilliancy was so great that they dazzled the Lusher, and he imagined that they were on his own fingers.

The fact of it was, the Lusher wanted them.

And he meant to have them.

But how?

That was a consideration.

Taking rings from a man's fingers, in a coach, too, where there were a lot more men who were pretending to be asleep, and, probably, watching all the time!

Jack thought of all this.

But the rings?

He meant to have them.

Their beauty had infatuated him. So have them he must, and risk the consequences.

The peril he would incur by such a daring act.

Yet the rings were worth a little risk.

The Lusher studied for a few moments, meditating a plan how to get these precious jewels.

"I have it," he almost exclaimed aloud with joy at the cleverness of his communication.

A dig in the ribs from Victor St. James's sharp elbow deprived him of wind, and like a fish out of water for a few moments he was gasping, his eyes almost starting from their sockets,

"What did yer honour do that for?" he asked, when he had recovered sufficient breath to speak.

"Be more cautious," returned St. James, in a whisper, "without you want to be dragged off to the gallows."

The Lusher shuddered at the word gallows, it always seemed ominous to his ears, and for several moments he contemplated the rings he so much coveted, as though hesitating whether to carry out the clever device.

"Blow the gallows!" he ejaculated with a shiver, to himself; "I ain't a-going' to lose them ere rings, no, not if fifty gallows stood afore me, and a hundred hangmen were going to drag me to 'em."

He had now fully made up his mind to obtain these dazzling rings, and the mode he used for that purpose was certainly worthy the Lusher.

In the further end of the coach, where it was conveniently dark, sat Mr. and Mrs. Fogey, suspiciously close together.

A rather sweet voice saying to Mr. Fogey—

"Don't, dear! For shame!"

Aroused the Lusher's curiosity; and to see what cause the lady, who was young and very pretty, who was with Mr. Fogey, who was old and ugly, had for such a strange remonstrance caused him to defer his filching process.

Master Jack did not look all at once, he hadn't the nerve, but, firstly, took a side glance with the corner of one eye.

It happened at that instant sinful Old Fogey was taking a side glance with the his eye, and so their corners met.

The Lusher felt bashful, and looked another way.

So did Mr. Fogey, upon the charms of his fair companion.

His fair companion was a merry-minded little beauty, that could be ascertained by the wicked look of her large dark eyes.

"Don't dear, or I shall go away from your side," said the lady again; "consider how bad it would appear were anyone looking."

The Lusher ventured another glance with the corner of his eye, and gradually turned his head until both fell full upon the wicked old Fogey and his wayward companion.

This time, the wicked old Fogey was not aware of the Lusher's observance. He was otherwise engaged, and in a quiet tussle that ensued between the lady and her fair companion, a most superb limb was displayed to the Lusher's gaze, from the ankle to far above a crimson band and gold clasp that kept the silk hose from slipping down.

Such a display of so beautifully moulded a limb set the Lusher dreaming of his Mary Jane, and he longed to be in Cornwall.

The remembrance of his own true love, and how he had liked her in his company brought a hot flush to his cheeks and a strange kindling fire to his eye.

In the happy remembrance of his past amours, Jack had completely forgotten the rings, but a loud snore from his neighbour rung in his ears as though calling upon him to fulfil his purpose.

Sinful old Fogey's lady had compelled him to desist in his purpose. Mr. Fogey did not like it, though he was obliged to abide by his fair companion's wish for the benefit of his future desires, and by way of revenge for his disappointment he fixed the corner of his eye upon the Lusher's movements.

But our friend the Lusher was too clever for him.

Master Jack was aware of the watchful glance fixed upon him, so he proceeded to execute his pilfering with more caution than otherwise he thought would be necessary.

He rubbed his eyes with his knuckles, as though overcome with a heavy, fatiguing sleep, after several false attempts to keep awake, he fell forward, and snored loudly.

His knees touched the knees of the old fellow, his hands slid along his thighs, until they came in contact with the hands that wore the rings, and then his fingers twined round the fingers of the sleeping fogey, and one by one he drew the jewels off without disturbing his victim.

Of course the Lusher then suddenly awoke, and looked out of the coach window into the dark night, as though he had slept a week, and passed his place of destination.

Ah! what is that he espies lying on a seat besides a lordly-dressed young fop?

The redoubtable Lusher's eyes were extended and looked more like greengages than gooseberries, when his gaze fell upon a beautiful casket.

"I must have that, too," he muttered.

Dropping a handkerchief upon the floor, he stooped to pick it up, and, in doing so, extended his hand to the seat where the casket lay.

He put his thumb and forefinger on the edge, top and bottom, and slowly drew it from under the hand of the fop, who, in his sleep, guarded it with treasured care.

He started, and gave a cry as it vanished from his side.

But of course the Lusher was sitting quietly, and looked quite unconcernedly upon the astonished visages of the awakened travellers, who were feeling for their jewels.

Master Jack Evans had made a fine stroke of business, and he knew it would not be beneficial to his health should he be discovered as the culprit of the casket, with the other things not belonging to him he had got carefully stowed away about his person.

I have lost my watch," cried old fogey.

"I owe you summut," thought the Lusher, remembering how he had placed the spiky pocket; "yer shall 'ave it now, yer spiteful old brute."

He squeezed closely to the old fellow, and drove the thousand sharp points into his thigh.

The old fogey cried loudly with pain.

"Murder—murder! Hi, hi! young man, don't push so hard against me. What is that you are sticking into me?"

"That's the thief," yelled the spiteful old fogey, from the corner.

"Oh, lor'!" thought Jack Evans, "the game's up with me."

He prepared for a row.

"My rings have been taken from my fingers," cried fat old fogey, in despair.

"And my watch from my pocket, a pin from my scarf, and even the buckles from my shoes," seconded another.

"And I a casket, that I would give a thousand pounds to get back," yelled a fop miserably.

"Then, I'll it," thought the Lusher, "for it's worth more."

"Guard! guard!" bawled lustly fat old fogey. "Guard! keep the door closed, we have got a thief here; don't let anyone escape. Five hundred pounds for the recovery of my rings."

"A threepenny watch and pin."

"A thousand penny casket."

"And I will give five hundred for the discovery of the thief," put in a disinterested party, who had nothing to lose, and knew there was not one there who wanted five hundred, had he had it to give, which he had not.

"He's the thief," yelled the fat old fogey, clutching the Lusher by the collar.

"He's the thief."

"Hold him tight."

"Search him."

"Secure his hands first."

"Get a pistol ready in case he resists."

Such were the cries, with numerous others, that rang through the coach, and made it reiterate and reverberate with the stunning echoes.

But none of them were enforced.

The Lusher thought it high time now to make his exit; so, disposing of his podgy assailant, with a blow that felled him flat on the floor, he dashed amongst the rest, scattered them right and left, and sprang through the open window of the coach door.

In his rapid flight he knocked the guard off his perch into the road.

"Fire!" shouted one of the passengers, frantically.

One did fire, and the Lusher got the bullet just underneath the coat tails.

The horses took fright, and the coach rattled along at a furious pace on its course to Cornwall.

The passengers crowded to the door window, and saw the thief with their property lying helpless in the road, yet none could leave the coach to capture the culprit.

CHAPTER XCIV.

VERY NEAR A CAPTURE—DISPOSAL OF THE OFFICERS—DICK KEEPS HIS PURSUERS AT BAY.

"Ho, there! within! To the rescue of Tyburn Dick!"

The cries were raised by our hero, who lay totally at the mercy of his pursuers, where he had fallen in the yard of the Leopard Inn.

Red Matthias laughed grimly as he dismounted.

"Your time's come now, my pippin, as sure as eggs is eggs," he said.

Turning to his officers he growled—

"Lend a hand here, Big Jem. Let's tie the cub on one of the horses. He can't show his teeth now."

Big Jem, a fellow of the size of a moderate giant, and with the strength of several oxen, approached the helpless boy, cautiously. He had seen him on previous occasions, and had good cause to remember him.

"You big—" exclaimed the thief-catcher, "are yer frightened of a boy, helpless too?"

"I should say not," replied the officer, summoning his brute courage.

"Collar hold of his feet," said Matthias, going to the head of our hero.

The big officer stooped to grasp Dick's legs, when, with the uninjured member, he gave the fellow a kick under the chin that sent him staggering backwards.

"Do that agin," thundered the officer, foaming with rage, and stooping savagely over Dick; "do it again and I'll smash yer."

"Do you want to humbug about the time till someone comes to his rescue?" said Red Matthias, spitefully. "Lend a hand and hoist him up on one of the horses."

Dick gave one more cry for help; it was his last.

His mortal foes bent over him. His legs and arms were held down by at least a dozen, while Red Matthias slipped a gag over his mouth.

The dimmest ray of hope fled.

Could Samson Leopard have heard his cries for help? If so, had he turned treacherous, and left the noble boy to his fate?

Dick did not think when he sank helpless to the earth within the bounds of his most secure place of protection, where he had so often fled from the savage bloodhounds of the law, for shelter, and always found a staunch, brave champion in mine host, who would, at any time, have died in his defence.

He did not think, after the struggle he had fought, to get there, to be taken from such a place, without a friend near to give him a helping hand to save his life.

He knew, should he be taken now, nothing would save him from a speedy, terrible death.

So often had he escaped the vengeance of the law, and laughed in the face of death, each time making his enemies pause—they were now merciless.

Until at last the King issued a warrant for his capture, dead or alive, with a reward of a thousand pounds for the apprehender.

It was further stated, by the King's command, that the daring boy should only have three hours' grace after his capture, before he died upon Tyburn Tree.

These were terrible things to think of.

The thought of dying, his ignominious fate witnessed by thousands of the lowest rabble, tortured him more than all else on earth.

He could have died without a murmur, with a shot in his head, or a sword pierced through his heart, such a fate would have been an honourable one to the gallows tree.

Such thoughts, with gentle thoughts of his devoted bride, rushed like lightning through his mind, rent his soul with bitter agony and despair.

It seemed terrible that he should be torn from all he loved, at such a gentle age, by one cruel blow that would sunder him from the world, and cast him, just at the prime of life, into eternity.

He cast one lingering look around as his enemies raised him from the ground; but seeing no friend near, he closed his eyes in utter despair, to shut out the evil, triumphant faces of his captors.

Certainly, all did seem lost.

The noble boy who had so often defied, fought, and conquered so many men lay helpless in the power of these brutal men of an unjust law.

He was tied securely upon the back of one of the officer's steeds, and the officers, mounting guard around him, began slowly to move away with their long-coveted prize.

Had he fought with them, and been overpowered, his capture would not have been so shameful. But to be taken while unable to defend himself wounded the boy's proud feelings.

He heard a cry that inspired him with new life.

He struggled to rise, but the bonds held him down fast.

The officers drew up.

Had friends come to his rescue at the very last moment?

He opened his eyes.

A mist gathered before his sight, and prevented him from seeing.

His head seemed to swim, and his limbs lost all power.

He heard horses approaching his captors.

He gave one glad cry, and fainted.

Friends had come to his rescue.

Captain Claude had followed his track, and arrived at the Leopard Inn just as the officers were marching away with his noble son.

The captain knew he could not contend against so many.

Without delay he informed Samson Leopard what had occurred.

The honest fellow provided himself with a huge club, and told Ben to get some defensive weapon and follow him.

Ben secured a long three-pronged fork, and shouldering it, hastened after his master to the rescue of Tyburn Dick, with the air of an old conquering veteran.

The trio mounted, thinking to have more scope with their old enemies, who were also mounted.

They were not long in overtaking the officers.

The officers stopped when they came in sight.

Captain Claude rode forward.

"What name?" demanded Red Matthias, as the highwayman confronted him.

"I want your prisoner!"

"Stand aside!" yelled Matthias. "Men, shoot him down!"

"It will be worse for the men if they attempt it," said Claude, coolly; "and much worse for you if you don't have that youth released very shortly."

"You threaten, then?"

"I do."

The thief-catcher drew a horse-pistol.

"Don't attempt to stay us in the execution of our duty," he said, "or I'll put a slug in your skull. Go your way, and be content for being at large. I hold a warrant now signed by the King for your apprehension; and your head is worth a thousand pounds at any moment.

"That shows how they value me; for yours they would not give twenty farthings; and, to show you of what little consequence I think it, I shall put the contents of this in it unless you obey my command."

Captain Claude put the rim of a bright pistol close to the thief-catcher's head.

"I am but doing my duty," stammered the thief-catcher.

"And I but mine," replied Claude, resolutely.

"If I didn't do it, somebody else would."

"It is exactly the same case with me."

"I was commanded by the King to apprehend him."

"And I by a strong devotion to rescue him."

"So you mean to try?"

"Most assuredly."

"Then from now we are bitter enemies, Captain Claude. Hitherto I have left you unmolested."

"Because," broke in Claude, "you were frightened to do otherwise. What do you care about sacrificing a life if it will bring you a few pounds? Little."

"However, from now I shall do my best to bring you to the gallows!"

"You have done your best since I first knew you," replied Claude, firmly. "Come, Matthias, give up the boy quietly. Resistance will only cause useless bloodshed."

"It will be upon your own head, then."

"I don't care whose head it's upon. I want the boy. Do you intend to give him up?"

"No, and defy you to take him."

The highwayman replaced his pistol. Rising anger brought the hot blood to his cheeks, and his eyes burned with a dangerous fire.

"Do you intend to give up your captive?"

"No; death sooner," replied the thief-catcher, resolutely.

"So be it."

Their horses stood side by side. The men were within arms' length of each other.

Captain Claude made a tiger-like spring in his saddle and closed with the thief-catcher.

The two men in physical strength were an equal match, but in statue they differed greatly. Red Matthias was big, brawny, with shoulders and chest like an ox. Captain Claude was tall, slim, very graceful, sinewy, and with the strength of a tiger.

They swayed to and fro in a deadly grip, and intent on a deadly purpose.

Claude made a slip in trying to jerk his antagonist from his seat. The thief-catcher took advantage of the mishap, and with a sudden powerful wrench hurled the Captain from the saddle.

Claude clung to his assailant while falling, and dragged him after him.

They struggled and fought on the earth, each trying his best to take the other's life.

Captain Claude finally got Matthias beneath him. He put his knees upon his chest, and grasped his throat with intent to strangle him.

The officers seeing the peril of their leader, dismounted and rushed to his rescue, and Captain Claude was thrown aside, but, ere any of the assailing party could carry out their brutal intent of finishing him, Red Matthias was upon his feet and again battling with the highwayman.

The officers seeing very little chance for their leader against his skilful assailant, who was thrashing him about like a foot-ball, suddenly set upon him furiously.

Mine host thought it was time to interfere. Dismounting he stalked amongst the combatants like a giant, with his ponderous club raised on high, swinging it round his head,

and brought it down on the head of the fellow nearest to him.

He quickly disposed of a few.

They fell one after the other beneath the heavy strokes of the huge club-like reeds.

The thief-catcher grew mad with rage and the loss of his men, who fell stunned an bleeding.

"Fire upon them!" he yelled.

"The first that draws a weapon dies," said Claude. "I have avoided bloodshed as yet, and, should you begin it, I will have a pint for every drop."

"Fire!" cried Matthias; "are you frightened of two men? Fire!"

"Fire!" said Samson Leopard, quietly; "I can stand a few shots."

The men stood irresolute, the quiet determination of Captain Claude, and the firmness of the innkeeper, awed them.

While the strife was at its height, Ben bravely availed himself of the opportunity to trot off with the steed that held our hero.

He got off undiscovered, nor would the loss have been discovered but for the pause that now ensued. Red Matthias glared round.

A wild cry left his lips. He sprang past Captain Claude and his companions, and darted off in pursuit of the fugitive, who had eloped with his hard-fought-for prize.

Captain Claude was rather astonished by the occurrence, and looked after his retreating foe to ascertain the cause of his sudden flight. In the distance he saw Ben making his way with all speed to the Leopard Inn.

"Come," said the highwayman, "or we shall be too late. That scoundrel means mischief."

At that instant the officers, who had silently mounted, sped furiously in the direction of their leader.

Captain Claude and mine host had to follow on foot, for their steeds had strayed away.

———

BOOK THE SECOND.—PART ONE.
CHAPTER XCV.
THE STORY.
THE EXILE—A REVERIE—THE FIGHT—THREE TO ONE
—THE MEETING UNDER TYBURN TREE—THE BALL
—THE RIVALS—THE QUARREL—LORD ERNEST
D   THE RESCUE—A NOBLE FRIEND—

In the quiet of as fair a night as ever lent beauty to the earth a cavalier rode slowly out of Edgware. He had suffered the rein to drop idly on his horse's neck; it suited him to go slowly. He could meditate thus; indulge in bitter, sorrowful reverie.

He had the charm of beauty in a rare degree. A lithe and slender figure, full of powerful grace; a splendid chest; a fair, full throat and limbs, like sculpture. His hair was black, and curled round his noble head in clustering tresses. He wore a slight moustache, but for that his countenance was bare.

Many a warm heart beat the quicker, and many a bright eye lit up with admiration at the sight of his handsome face, but warm heart throbbed and dark eye kindled for him in vain. His brow was lowered, shadowed deeply in sombre thought.

"The dear old land—the dear old place," he soliloquised, sadly. "And I have come back to it at last—an exile, a stranger, an outlaw—uncared for by those who were my friends—forgotten by those who loved me. I am here at home, and I am here alone."

"Alone!" he repeated mournfully; "unrecognised even by my foes, so changed that I wonder if Marion would know me? They say the memory of love is faithful, and she did love me."

He rode on thinking of the past—the old times that were sweet in recollection still, when a sudden cry, followed by the quick clash of steel, sent the blood to his cheek, and his hand to his sword.

Out it flashed like lightning. He looked round to see who wanted succour.

About three hundred yards behind him stood a coach, and outside this a group of men were fighting desperately; there were three to one, and the one was an old man with grey hair.

But the winter of age had not withered his courage. He had evidently leaped out of the coach, when it was stopped by his three assailants, and now he kept them at bay like a lion.

"What would you?" the cavalier heard him say, and a deep, stern voice replied—

"Your life, or the lady?"

"My daughter? Mercies!—my child! Never! while this old hand can hold its weapon, and it is no stranger to it. Lord Sydney does not yield what is more dear to him than life."

"Nor while this arm can help you," said the cavalier, who had spurred swiftly to the spot. "Back, dastards! Attack an old man three to one. My sword and I shall equalise the odds."

"A friend," said Sydney, eagerly.

"A friend! By St. George, a man needs 'em in such a time as this. Here's at you, ruffian!"

And he singled out a powerful fellow, who seemed bent on reaching the gallant nobleman.

He caught sight of a lovely, wistful face in the carriage, and a pair of beautiful eyes beamed on him gratefully.

Lord Sydney's assailants were not common robbers.

They were richly dressed, and each wore a mask. Their purpose was made known. It was to take the lady, or kill her sire.

"That lady is my wife!" said the cavalier, who was opposed to one stranger. "I claim her by the strongest right, and it is at your peril you interfere."

"My peril!" laughed the stranger, "well, that is my look out. Peril and I are old acquaintances."

He put his horse across the coach so as to effectually defend its occupants, and fight the three leisurely.

Lord Sydney tried to aid him, but the stranger said—

"Stay with your child, my lord. You are on foot, and cannot cope with mounted men. A few, more or less, make little difference to me."

So indeed it seemed, for he fought like a man used to dealing with heavy odds.

He was a splendid rider, too, and that helped him through the battle. His horse obeyed the slightest touch or pressure, as though it knew its master wanted aid.

The old man did not like to see his gallant champion fighting alone, and would have gone to his side, but the fair girl clung to him, and he could not get away.

The groom, a brave honest lad, who had been on the box by the coachman's side, took the long whip, and coiling the thong round his arm, attacked one of the masked men, leaving only two for the stranger to deal with. His courage was of material assistance.

"Don't be afraid of hurting him, good lad," the stranger said.

"Never fear, sir."

Round swung the whip, and, dexterously avoiding a thrust, the groom brought the heavy butt end with terrific force on his antagonist's wrist. He dropped his sword with a cry of pain.

"That's one," said the groom, quietly; and with a second blow he struck the masked man from the saddle.

At the same instant the stranger disarmed his foe, who turned and fled, leaving his comrade to do the best he could.

His comrade thought the best he could do would be to follow his example, which he did, and then the fight was over.

"A battle, and no bloodshed!" said the stranger. And so, my lord, you are safe."

He sheathed his sword, and lifted his hat. Lord Sydney caught his hand.

"Words cannot thank you," he said; "but for your gallant aid my daughter might have have been fatherless. Surely we have met before?"

The stranger started slightly.

"If I speak to Lord Richard Sydney," he said, "we have met before. I was a soldier in your lordship's regiment some few years ago."

The nobleman scanned his countenance leisurely.

"I do not remember you as a soldier," he said, after a pause; "yet your face is familiar."

"I have been absent long from England," said the stranger, with a sigh, "and if you have forgotten me, no wonder."

Then he changed his tone abruptly.

"I am glad I was able to render you and your fair daughter some service," he said, "and suffer me to say adieu."

"Stay," said Lord Sydney, as the cavalier was about to depart. "I cannot part like this with the noble gentleman who saved me. I may make you some return—call you friend, give you welcome by the fireside that would have been desolate but for you."

"Pardon me if I say it cannot be. The way of life is wide, and we may meet again; our paths lie far from each other now, and I must go mine alone. Adieu! sweet lady. Farewell! and may Heaven guard you always."

An irrepressible burst of sadness in his musical voice touched fair Agnes Sydney.

"Do not refuse me, noble sir," she said. And her lovely countenance at the window caused him to stay the hand upon his rein. "Tell me your name, that I may think of you —pray for you."

"Name!" he repeated, sadly. "I have no name; pray for me, I may have need of prayers. Think of me; for there is salve in a pure heart's grateful thought, and, if you knew my name, I should not have thought of prayer."

"My house stands there," said Lord Sydney, pointing to the brow of a distant hill, on which the moonlight fell; "and whether you come nameless, or bearing a title that must belong to one so generous and brave, there is welcome for you always. You have an old soldier's word and an old soldier's hand upon it."

The stranger returned his grip heartily.

"I shall not forget," he said; "and I may need a friend."

He stooped low in the saddle to raise the little hand Agnes extended to him, pressed a kiss upon it, and rode away.

They watched him out of sight, and the maiden sighed, in sympathy for his sadness.

Lord Sydney muttered—

"A soldier in my regiment? He would not speak a falsehood; but I think I should recognise so princely a fellow."

The groom was still standing over the masked man he had felled, and was waiting quietly to see whether he would revive, and require another touch of the whip handle.

"Take off his mask," said Sydney.

The groom obeyed.

Whatever was the thought that came when the noble saw the face, it wrought a change in his purpose.

"Is he dead, or stunned?"

"Stunned, my lord. I let him have it on the head."

"Let him lie there, Sam."

"What, my lord; and he escape?"

"Let him lie there. Get to your seat, and drive on."

The groom touched his cap. Lord Sydney was used to command, and he obeyed.

"Why were we stopped, papa, dear?" asked Agnes. "Why should people seek to injure us? We never injured anyone."

"There are evil spirits in the world, my child," he replied; "men who return sinister malice for good. Do not question further. This night has left more sorrow on me than I ever thought to bear."

Agnes said no more.

She saw there was a mystery which he did not wish her to penetrate.

The stranger went up the Edgware-road, a lonely place then, with a house here and there, and on either side green hedgerows, and fields of corn, waving like drooping flowers of gold in the soft autumn night.

"At evening, on the last day of September," he said, "when the moon rides over Tyburn Tree, be there, and we shall meet."

So said that strange, inscrutable man, Bertram—Bertram the mystery.

"And the moon is rising now," he went on, "like a silver globe through the one dark cloud that breaks the beauty of the autumn sky, and overhangs the ominous spot of dreadful death. Is it emblematic of my destiny? the cloud, my past; the majestic moon a light of future promise? and that single, solitary star—a radiant gem magnificent amid a coruscation where all is beautiful? It seems to shine upon me, a beacon to drive despair away, and say, Live on! fight bravely in the war of life."

Even as he meditated with his dark eyes fixed upon the star, it left its lofty throne and shot downward, athwart the heavens; and the black cloud rising higher, became dark, and obscured the moon.

The stranger's head then drooped almost to his breast.

"All over!" he muttered, "all over! my star has fallen."

A moment passed, and the cloud had rolled away. The moon shone out more brilliantly than before.

Two stars, as radiant as the fallen, were in the place where it had been.

"A mystic world of wonder!" he said, lifting a reverent brow. "Do I read aright what seems a prophecy? Darkness has gone; twin stars twinkle, and the resplendent vault of heaven is cloudless! There is gladness in the exile's heart. Hope—sweet strength giver— is with me, and I am prepared to meet the worst—and meet it like a man!"

And now he stood before the leafless tree, on whose bare, accursed branches a human body swung and creaked in chains.

He shuddered at the sight.

"A fellow-being, who has lived and loved, and hoped as I have," he said; "and now see to what he has come—a piece of common clay, that chills one's blood to touch it! What if such a fate were to be mine?"

"It is not so written," said a deep, thrilling voice, and a horseman advanced from the shadow of the tree. "Your destiny is inscribed on the scroll of Fate. The page is a strange one, and there is a red line in it, but the end is spotless."

"Bertram!"

"Ay! I am here."

And the stranger saw before him a man whose fine, impressive features wore the aspect of a monarch.

A sable beard descended to his chest, and in bold, colossal majesty he sat like a grand old statue, a demigod rather than a mortal.

"Here to save me," said the stranger; "here to tell me what course I shall pursue, here to cleanse the dark stain from my name, and prove that I am not the wretched, sinful criminal the world has branded me."

"An exile," said the horseman.

"An outlaw, with a price upon your head, and the wolves of the law upon your track, a murderer! a bastard!"

"I am not these," said the stranger, proudly, "I did but slay the man who dared insult my mother's memory, brand me with injury, and my father with dishonour!"

"But you were hunted out of England."

"Shame upon the bitter iniquitous laws that denied me justice! Let them drive me to desperation, and they shall find the outlaw

THE RESCUE.

can defend his head, and wrest his rights from those who keep it wrongly!"

"Poor boy!" said the man of mystery, and his deep melodious voice rolled on the stranger's ear with the solemn, tender cadence of cathedral music. "You will have much to bear, but be brave and patient—trust in Heaven, and despair not!"

"I have borne much, and have been patient."

"Be patient still, and endure much more; but see! the moon is waning, and a storm threatens! Your destiny begins! Listen!"

The stranger bowed his head.

"Go to the house of her you love—seek your foe, and demand your own."

"My foe!"

"Archibald Carnwood!"

"Is he my foe?"

"Your bitterest enemy."

"Bertram! you who read the souls of men as though they were books laid open to the eye—you from whom the human heart keeps no mystery—tell me why?"

"Is Marian beautiful?"

"As the stars are bright and pure."

"And beauty tempts men's passion, and passion is the abyss of Heaven—the blight of friendship—he loves her."

"Torture! Torture!" the stranger said; "my friend a traitor!"

"Listen, and believe, as you shall prove

At Kingston Chase to-night there is a ball in honour of a betrothal—the betrothal of Archibald Carnwood and Marian Sydney?"

"She faithless, too?"

"Lord Sydney and his daughter—Marian's uncle and cousin—have gone thither. Lord Sydney's brother, the stern Judge Carnwood, is on his way, and with him his two sons."

"Ha! it was Lord Sydney whom I rescued from three masked men."

"I know, said Bertram, calmly, "and you saved him. It was destined."

The stranger wondered more and more.

"It was Judge Carnwood who decreed against you," Bertram continued. "It is Judge Carnwood who gives your bride away —it was Judge Carnwood who made you an outlaw, and set a felon's price upon your head, should you return."

"It was. He hates me bitterly, and I never gave him cause."

"Ask him to-night to remove from your brow the stigma of shame. Tell him he knows the truth. Ask him to give your bride to you, and take away the ban of outlawry. Tell him to proclaim your innocence. *Ask him who killed your father?*"

"My father!" said the exile; "was he murdered?"

"He fell by as foul a deed as ever branded a Cain; and now no more. I have said enough. Go to Carnwood House; this card will admit you. Act as occasion may direct, and make your claim at the fitting time. Fear not whatever may ensue. You wear a sword, and whenever danger threatens, Bertram will be there."

With the last word he spurred from the exile's side. A sullen peal of thunder rolled over head; huge drops of rain began to fall; a gleam of lightning, quivering through the gloom, revealed the form of Bertram in the far distance.

"My father murdered!" said the stranger. "My bride given to another! By the destiny that is marked out for me, I swear to have full avengement, to wring justice from the oppressor, and save Marian, or the outlaw's name shall be a death-knell to the outlaw's foes!"

The exile rode to the ancient place.

"There is no welcome for me here," he said,

as he alighted. "I enter with my hand upon my sword. I enter at the peril of my life. Let come what may, I am strong in right, though I may be uncared for and forgotten."

A servant, standing in waiting, thought him an expected guest, and took his horse. The stranger crossed the threshold when he was challenged by the groom.

"Your name!"

He presented the card given to him by Bertram the mystery.

The attendant bowed low, and let him pass. Strains of soft music were floating softly through the house. The revellers were dancing an old-fashioned minuet.

The stranger passed through the line of retainers drawn up before the entrance of the grand saloon. The wide door opened at his approach. He entered.

There was a hush. The music ceased. Every eye was turned upon the stranger, whose travel-stained costume, heavy riding-boots, and long, plain sword, seemed singularly out of place in the midst of the glittering, silken throng.

He, proudly self-possessed, bore the scrutiny calmly. His gaze singled out a familiar face —the face of Marian Sydney, who stood by the side of her betrothed, Archibald Carnwood.

A thrill went to the stranger's heart. Time was when he had stood by her side, as stood his rival now. Her smile had been for him.

Yet, as with the rest, her glance rested on him, no glance of recognition moved her. He was forgotten—quite forgotten.

Looking at a group near to his rival and the fair Marian, he saw the old soldier and the lady whom he rescued from the three masked men. With Lord Sydney and Agnes was a young, richly-dressed gentleman, who advanced towards the stranger at once.

"Be your name what it may," he said, with a smile, "and your errand here what it will, Lord Ernest Dallas is your friend."

They shook hands. The exile was glad to find that, in a place where he seemed a stranger, he had some friend.

"I thank you, Lord Ernest Dallas, from my heart," he said. "I may want your friendship soon; but how have I deserved it?"

"Agnes Sydney is to be my bride!"

There was a stir at the other end of the saloon. Judge Carnwood—a stern, dignified man—led forward Marion.

"Listen!" he said, "my kindred and my friends. In the name of my fair ward's parent, and in the presence of Lord Richard Sydney, I solemnly betroth her to my eldest son, Archibald Carnwood."

"No! no!"

It was the stranger's voice.

"Who speaks?" said the judge, angrily. "Who dares say this should not be?"

The stranger stood forward, his dark eyes flashing, and his fine form drawn to its full height.

"I, by the strongest right of manhood—the right of faith and love! Marion! Marion! speak with me. Come to me—here to my breast—and say the unhallowed betrothal shall not be."

She gave a cry, broke from her guardian's grasp, and, after one long, wistful look at the speaker's face, threw herself into his arms.

Archibald Carnwood sprang towards them, his brow was black with passion, as he said—

"Who is this stranger? Who is he that dares to come between me and my bride?"

"One who should be remembered," said the stranger, sadly, while a resolute, tender arm still encircled Marion's waist; "but Richard is a traitor like the rest, and the exile comes back alone, with none to help him in his peril."

"Ha!" said Judge Carnwood, "it is the outlaw."

"The outlaw!"

"Ay, Marion!" the outlaw said, and his hand was on his sword, for threatening faces were gathering round him; "you, whom I knew so beautiful, and thought so fair, say that this betrothal is not of your choice."

Her white breast rose and fell, heedless of her guardian's angry look of menace; heedless of Archibald's savage rage, she turned and clung to her outlawed lover.

"It is not my choice, but I dared not say nay."

"My own, true, faithful girl! then cling to me, and by my father's death, my own bitter wrongs, and the retribution I have sworn, we will not part while we have life."

Out flashed his sword

"Make way!" and his face was turned towards his foes, for at a signal from the judge a crowd of Carnwood's kinsmen hemmed the daring outlaw in. "Make way, or there will be some red work done!"

"Seize him! Cut him down! Drag her from him!"

"Down with the outlaw!"

Half a dozen swords were drawn against the stranger's one, and he, in gentle care for Marion, put her from him, that no hurt might befall her.

"Fear not," he whispered, kissing her trembling lips; "be true to me, I shall come again."

He waved his weapon, and the crowd of enemies made way while he led Marian to her cousin Agnes.

The poor girl gave a despairing cry.

"I love him," she said, "oh, I love him."

"Sweet saint," he murmured, "I could die happy with that knowledge; but there are brighter days in store, when the exile will have claimed his own. Hear me, Judge Carnwood, and listen all."

Upon his countenance there was an expression that warned his foes to keep back while he spoke.

"Two weary years have rolled away since I left my native land. I went forth innocent of crime, yet proscribed by him. He knows my innocence. Look in his guilty face, and see how the truth pierces to his soul."

"Strike him down."

"Back!"

And they recoiled before the glittering weapon held so fearlessly.

"Who moves to touch me, dies. Wait till I have done, and then strike me, or take me if you can. Judge Carnwood, I came for justice. Proclaim my innocence, remove the ban of outlawry, give me my bride, and tell me—Who killed my father."

The judge went white.

"I'll hear no more," he said, hoarsely "Upon him now, there is a price upon his head. A thousand pounds for him, dead or alive, should he return from exile. Seize him there. Capture or kill him!"

Alone and dauntless, the outlaw kept his ground.

The judge's retainers advanced to the

attack, when Lord Ernest Dallas leaped before them.

"Touch him if you dare!" he said. "Outlaw or not, were he the devil's brother he has done me a service, and my sword is here to help him. Back ruffians! Keep your distance. His cause is mine. I fight for my companion to the death."

There was a pause.

"My lord," said Carnwood, "this is dangerous—rashness. You implicate yourself by defending a felon."

"To perdition with you! I support his claims—assert his innocence, and I, Lord Ernest Dallas, am his friend. So, now, if you attack him, I am here."

Lord Sydney spoke—

"Carnwood," he said, "for my sake, be at peace. Call your men away; he claims my gratitude, he saved me from death, my child from worse."

"Silence, Lord Sydney. I am master here; he has insulted me, and let the consequence be on his own head."

"Carnwood, I am an old man, but I am not weak, and the arm that never failed my King will not desert my friend. Must we of kindred blood be foes?"

"To eternity, if you brave me. Once more I say, down with the outlaw. Let all who champion him share his fate—the fault is theirs, not mine."

"Carnwood—"

"I answer with my sword."

"And I," said Lord Sydney, "with mine."

They met. The two old men with deadly purpose, and blood would have been shed had not the outlaw interposed.

"The justice you deny me I will claim another time," he said, "and let my foes beware—the wronged will have retribution—the dead shall be avenged! Now, let me go, or my path to liberty shall be a red one."

But his antagonists only hemmed him in the closer.

Archibald and Ralph were the foremost.

The outlaw could not reach the door, but he fought, and retreated to the window.

Lord Ernest gave him gallant aid. The young nobleman's blood was up, and he used his weapon with matchless skill.

The cries of frightened women mingled with the clash of steel.

The outlaw's foes were many.

Like a lion worried by a pack of wolves, he held them at bay, till a treacherous blow from behind brought him down.

The sword of Archibald was raised to deal his death blow.

The exile was disarmed and helpless.

Lord Ernest, struggling desperately, was borne away in the conflict, and the assassin's weapon would have done its work, but for a startling interruption that came.

The windows were dashed open, and the colossal form of a majestic man stood in the broad moonlight glare.

His mighty voice rolled through the place like thunder—

"Away, false kinsman!—treacherous wretch!—away! Beware!—beware of me! —and tremble at the outlaw's name! Judge Carnwood, repent while there is time, or a red doom will be yours! I have said it—I, Bertram!"

Archibald Carnwood, stricken by the man of mystery, fell, stunned and bleeding, at his father's feet.

The outlaw, helped up by Bertram, faced his foes once more, but they shrank back appalled.

The figure of the man in black struck them to their souls.

They cowered away, like frightened dogs.

Judge Carnwood fell upon his knees.

"That voice," he shrieked, "that voice! Do I dream, or can the grave give up its dead? Say, who are you?"

A terrible peal of laughter answered him. The window closed.

The outlaw and his champion disappeared.

When the startled group looked out to see him, the outlaw and the man in black were gone!

CHAPTER XCVI.

CARNWOOD AND SYDNEY.

BEFORE a plan of pursuit could be organized, the outlaw and his rescuer were safely away.

Archibald and his brother Ralph were mad with rage; both had cause to hate and fear the daring exile.

And Archibald hated him the more for

having appeared at so untimely a moment, and interrupted the betrothal.

Judge Carnwood, for a reason known to himself, did not make effort to have the outlaw captured.

The appearance of Bertram seemed to have strangely terrified him.

Lord Richard Sydney was the first to speak.

His voice roused the guests from their stupor of consternation.

"My friends," said the titled veteran, confronting them with dignity, "you have witnessed a scene which my kinsman, Sir Gabriel Carnwood, Lord of Kingston Chase, might well have spared."

"Lord Sydney," broke in the judge.

"A moment's courtesy, please. I am a rough old soldier, and I like fair play. That youth who went but now has not had much of it. I remember him a gallant soldier in my company—Lieutenant Montrose.

"Who killed a comrade in a duel, and was outlawed for the act."

"You were his judge, and sentenced him," said Sydney, fixing the other with his keen grey eye; "had he been tried by court-martial, there is not a man in the regiment that would not have given him a verdict of honourable acquittal."

He was fairly tried, Lord Sydney."

"I do not accuse you of injustice. You were severe upon him, and why you were so is a matter between yourself and your own conscience. I only know this, I believe he had great provocation before he drew upon and killed his foe, and my best endeavours will be made to procure a pardon for him."

"Permit me to say you might spend your time and influence to better purpose."

"That is for me to judge," said the soldier, haughtily.

"Not altogether, since to do so would be to charge me with false judgment."

Lord Sydney waved his hand.

"We are kinsmen, Sir Gabriel, though in a distant degree, and I could not willingly have ill blood between us, but after what has taken place to-night, we must be strangers henceforth."

"As you will. The tie cannot be strong that can be broken with so slight a pretext."

"Slight!" The veteran's lip curled. "The tie would have been broken altogether, had not that same brave fellow fought for me this evening. I was set upon by three ruffians—three brutal villains, who had no regard for an old man's life, or a fair girl's happiness."

Judge Carnwood's sons changed colour; the veteran's gaze penetrated their dark souls.

"Indeed," Sir Gabriel said.

"In truth. But I do not appeal to you for justice.

"I know the malefactors."

His gaze was still fixed steadily upon the Carnwood brothers—they quailed before it.

"Why not have them arrested?" inquired the judge, uneasily.

"They were not common ruffians. The charge against them would be difficult to prove, and I prefer to keep watch over them. This, however, is not the purpose I have in view at present."

"What, then?"

"We are joint guardians of my niece, Marian, my younger brother's child?"

"We are."

"I have reasons—which, at the fitting time and place, I may state—for saying that in future I shall take sole charge of her, if she wish it."

"My lord!"

"I use plain terms. Marian shall speak for herself. Come, my child. Say, would you rather be with Judge Carnwood than with me?"

"My lord," said Carnwood, making a fierce gesture to confirm Marian's silence; "this is unlawful—audacious—to tamper with my ward. The lady whom her father left in my care."

"Because I was absent at the time, and he could not leave her in mine," said the veteran, bluntly; "but I am here now, and she shall take her choice. Say, my child."

"With you, dear uncle," said Marian, clinging to his arm; "with you."

Judge Carnwood's brow grew black as night.

"I do not so easily relinquish my trust," he said. "Marian must stay with me."

"No," said Marian, "no; I am afraid

"Of whom?" asked the old soldier, and his hand went to his sword.

The fair girl pointed at Archibald, and she said—

"Him."

Archibald Carnwood—he was a handsome fellow, but with his father's beauty he had his father's sinister darkness of expression—approached her with a deprecating air.

"Of me, my gentle love?" he said. "Surely I never gave you cause?"

"Keep your distance," said Lord Ernest Dallas, who had recovered, and rejoined his lady love. "Let her speak for herself."

"Lord Ernest Dallas, do not interfere."

"To the devil with you. Knit your black brows lower, and then I shall care nothing. I wear a sword, Archibald Carnwood, and you can try its merit if you like."

"Peace," said the judge, sternly to his son. "Let the wayward girl have her way."

"I intend she shall," said Archibald, "when she is my wife."

"That will never be," said Lord Sydney. "The betrothal was against my wish. I came reluctantly to see it ratified, and was glad of the interruption to it. I am a blunt old soldier, and I picked up plain words when I picked up hard knocks and glory. That was on the battle field."

"No one doubts Lord Sydney's plainness nor his valour," sneered Archibald; "but may I ask a few plain words that will explain your meaning in saying my betrothed shall never be my wife?"

"That she does not love you is one reason," said the veteran, unruffled by the sneer. "There are several others, but the one is good enough."

"What are the others?"

"You are not good enough!" and the old man's grey moustache curled with an angry laugh. "Shall I whisper in your ear and tell you why?"

"Ay, if you have aught to say, and dare to say it."

He approached. Lord Sydney bent to him, placed one hand like iron on his shoulder, and whispered a few words.

Their effect was startling. Young Carnwood looked and glanced at the old man like a wolf.

"That is sufficient reason, I think," said the veteran, smiling again.

"And now, good night, my friends and gallant kinsmen! Come Marian, Agnes, and you Lord Dallas—the rest are excellent company for each other, and we will leave them so."

He gave Sir Gabriel an abrupt salute, and, without noticing the others, took the hand of Marian and placed it on his arm and left the saloon.

Dallas followed with Agnes; when going, he exchanged a significant glance with Archibald. It was made more significant by his gesture—he touched the hilt of his sword.

Young Carnwood did the same. No words were spoken—the challenge to a duel was given and accepted silently.

"There shall be hot revenge for this," said Archibald, when the guests were gone and he was alone with his father and his brother. "We are not safe while that old man lives!"

"My son," said Judge Carnwood, impressively, "cherish no thoughts of blood. One deed—a blow struck in premeditated malice, or in sudden anger—cannot be recalled—cannot be forgotten."

"Do you speak from experience?"

The father felt the sting.

Crime had brought its punishment to him. He had thankless children.

Judge Carnwood retired.

He was terribly agitated, and, in the loneliness of his chamber, he meditated bitterly.

"Bertram," he said, "Bertram! the same in form and voice, the same in face; but how changed in bearing! He has come like an avenger from the grave!"

He mused again.

"Who is the outlaw?—this Montrose! I have a haunting dread of him. My suspicion is stronger because of his acquaintance with Bertram. He will not betray me His oath locks eternal silence on his tongue. But he swore another oath as terrible, and it was that he would make my life a curse—blight my career, and send me to a wretched grave! I must beware of him—I must beware of him!"

He paced the floor.

"But the boy—the outlaw! In him Lord Arthur lives again; and if he be, as I suspect, the boy I thought buried in the quarry,

I have much to fear. Let me prove it. The dark secret must be kept, even if I have to seal his doom!"

CHAPTER XCVII.

THE OUTLAW AND THE MYSTERY.

WHEN Bertram and the outlaw went from Carnwood House they rode in silence till they reached a dwelling, at the door of which the stranger drew rein.

Montrose had accompanied him so far without questioning, now he asked—

"Why are we here?"

"It is my house—enter without fear."

"I do not fear one who has proved himself a friend."

"A friend?" said Bertram, bitterly. "Well so I seemed, and so I shall be; but you do not know all."

Though he had made no summons at the door, it was opened, and a servant came out.

He led the horse away.

Bertram conducted the outlaw to a chamber.

It was richly furnished.

A king's palace could not have shown such abundance of wealth in costly fittings and rare works of art.

The house, so far as Montrose had noticed the exterior, was an old-fashioned building, chiefly of stone.

The interior walls were panelled with oak, quaintly carved, and covered with rich tapestry.

Montrose sunk into a luxurious seat; he was tired with fighting and excitement.

Yet at his heart there was a glow of ineffable joy—his love.

The beautiful Marian was true—true to him—the proscribed exile—the outlaw.

Bertram sat facing him, watching him keenly.

He seemed to take a sad, grim kind of pleasure in watching the emotional workings of the outlaw's noble face.

"Well," he said, "what has the night proved?"

Montrose started from his momentary reverie.

"That woman's heart is true."

"And that, at your age, is the first thought, the all-sufficient dream. While the tender-ness of love is with you, there is no place for hate."

"Why should there be? If I have foes I have friends, and I have hope, the strength of youth, the courage to dare and do; the name that is denied me here I may win elsewhere."

"So hopeful, yet so poor!"

"Not poor! True I have an empty pocket," and he laughed lightly; "but it may be full to-morrow."

"Have you no sorrow?"

The firm face clouded.

"I have—the mystery of my father's fate."

"And your mother?"

"I sometimes dream of her, Bertram. I sometimes dream of him. You know the secret of my birth!"

"I say not yes or no. Tell me what you remember—what has happened to you—what you know."

"I can recal the days of childhood," said Montrose, dreamily; "but I do not remember my parents distinctly. My first definite remembrance is of you."

"Go on."

"This was my home. I have called you father. You taught me not, but you were kind to me."

"Yet we are not related to each other?"

"In no degree. But proceed."

"At the age of sixteen, you told me to choose my career, and I found Lord Sydney's regiment. I went to battle, fought, and won fame. I had a brilliant path before me, but my comrades were jealous of my rapid promotion; they knew, for I was truthful, and saw no reason to disguise it, that I was parentless, and had never known my parents."

"Then?"

"One—a man whose tongue was keener than his sword—taunted me, fastened a quarrel on me, reproached my mother's name I slew him."

"And were tried for murder," said Bertram. "The man you killed was Carnwood's friend, and Carnwood was your judge."

"He did me bitter wrong. Our native land is always dear to us, and to be exiled from Marian was more than I could bear."

"So you returned at peril of your life."

"I had often put my life in peril for my

king; why should I not venture as much for myself? Besides, it was at your request as well that I returned."

"To meet me under Tyburn tree—to take the first step in your new career.'

"My new career?"

"Listen. My lips are sealed, or I could tell you all—the mystery of your father's fate—the secret of your birth—but until the time shall come, I may not speak of them. I can say but this."

Montrose listened eagerly.

"Your father was an honourable man—your mother a pure and beautiful woman—your name is noble."

"By heavens! I swear to seek out all!—my father's fate—my name—the dark and hideous mystery that seems to beset me. Tell me, Bertram, I implore you!"

"I cannot yet," said Bertram, moodily. "Be patient, boy; it will be told in time. Do you care for me?"

"Almost as much as though you were my father."

"Then if I tell you that the day when I reveal that secret will be the day of my death, will you still say tell me all?"

"No," said Montrose, promptly. "Deeply as it troubles me I would not sacrifice a noble friend. Rather would I die in ignorance."

"Say not that, boy, say not that," said Bertram, visibly affected. "The last act of my life will be one of expiation, and the expiation is due to you."

"I wonder more and more."

"I may not speak the truth, but I may help you to fathom the mystery, help you to avengement."

"How?"

Bertram went to a black cabinet, and opening a bureau, took from it a curious old bracelet, worked in slender threads of gold.

"Keep that," he said, "and when you find its fellow on the left wrist of a lady that lady will be your mother."

"My mother!" and Montrose leaped to his feet. "Does she live?"

"Poor lady, yes."

"Lives!" repeated the exile, reeling with the intoxication of conflicting feeling. "Then the darkest corner in the wide earth shall not hide her from me. Oh Bertram, direct my footsteps, lest they stray, and I grow sick with wandering."

The man of mystery shook his head.

"Fulfil your destiny," he said. "Seek out what you would learn. Avenge your father—sparing none!"

He spoke the last word moodily.

"Spare those who did not spare him!" said Montrose, with flashing eyes. "Would the tiger spare the hunter? Set me face to face with my sire's murderer, and my sword shall find a red passage through his heart!"

CHAPTER XCVIII.

TOM KING.

TINKLE, tinkle.

The tongue of the little silver bell ceased to vibrate, and there was silence again.

Silence in the City, for the hour was late. There were few astir—silence in the quaint, old-fashioned house, on the outskirts of London.

It was the house of Captain Walter Montrose, the handsome, petted favourite of fashion, who had set many a fair lady dreaming.

Montrose, whose slender, graceful form reclined on a massive couch of velvet, touched the bell with his delicate hand.

Tinkle, tinkle.

"Jacob," he said, languidly; "Jacob, you lazy rascal."

"Here, captain."

Jacob Dingle, an odd, misshapen fellow, with the stature of a dwarf, the strength of a giant and the fidelity of a dog, stood before his master.

"I rung twice."

"Yes, captain."

"You heard me?"

"Yes, captain."

"Then why the deuce did you not come?"

"I have come."

Captain Montrose did not care to argue against the stolid assertion. He closed his eyes as if in reverie.

"Is there any money in my purse, Jacob?"

Jacob took it out of his pocket, and counted the contents.

"Six guineas."

"Six——"

"Guineas, three d'mond rings, and a ruby necklace."

"In my purse?"

Jacob nodded.

"The deuce!"

"I said so, captain, and that isn't all, here's five bracelets, seventeen gold snuff-boxes, a lace handkerchief."

"A what?"

"A lace handkerchief."

"A lace handkerchief—the deuce!"

"So I said, captain."

"Anything else?"

"Two pair of silver buckles, a jewelled fan, and a ticket for Ranelagh."

"The Devil!"

"So I said, captain."

"I must have been dreaming?"

"So I——"

"Silence! you scamp. Let me think, eh! I remember."

"Also several cravats, one toothpick, and a love-letter."

"The—the——"

"Queer, captain."

"Jacob!" said Montrose, gravely.

"Captain."

"I can speak for myself."

"As the cove said when he was had up afore the judge and scragged for saying too much."

The captain looked at his man—Jacob's face was wonderfully solemn.

"My riding-whip is on that chair, Jacob."

"A werry good place for it."

"Give it me."

"Not for Jacob! You might give it me."

Captain Montrose laughed.

"Bad practices brings some wicked things, as little boys may roo."

"Silence, rascal!"

"For whips they have wings, and backs they stings."

Montrose clutched a boot—Jacob watched him, ready to dodge, and finished—

"Which ain't nice, though it's true. That's poetry, captain. I was taught by my——"

"Be quiet, you infernal rascal, and listen to me. I will have no more of your——"

"Grandmother! a poor old lady as took snuff out of a tortoiseshell box, in a large white nightcap, sitting afore the fire."

Montrose sent his boot at Jacob's head, and missed him.

"What a thing it is to have a bad temper," said Jacob, in an audible whisper, "and not be able to see straight."

"Hold your tongue!"

Jacob took his tongue between his two fingers, and waited with mock solemnity.

Montrose closed his eyes languidly, and did not see him.

"I remember," said Montrose, "I remember now. Yet it seems strange. I will tell you all about it, Jacob, and you will think it strange."

Jacob nodded twice at his master's closed eyes.

"I was at Lady Sydney's ball last night," the captain went on, "and I made acquaintance with a young nobleman, the Viscount Barry. We left together."

Jacob nodded twice more, as though he quite believed it.

"We left together, Jacob," said Montrose, wondering at the fellow's silence, "and on the road home several fellows came after us. We—the Viscount and I—were coming the same way, so I gave him a seat in my sedan-chair.

Here he paused, and waited for Jacob to speak.

"Sedan-chairs are not comfortable sitting, Jacob. You nod at each other, and if the carriers don't keep step you jolt. When the men behind put the right foot first, and the men in front put their left foot first, you seem to be going forward and backwards."

Another pause. Jacob was still mute; his master looked at him.

"You image!"

Dingle nodded, quite agreeing with him.

"You idiot!"

Jacob held up two fingers, pointing one at the captain and the other at himself.

"Put your tongue in. What the devil did you put it out for?"

"You told me to hold it, captain. So I did."

"And if I told you to swallow a bootjack, you would do it, I suppose?"

"There's no accounting for supposition," said Jacob, drily.

"Where did I leave off?"

"You image."

"What?"

" You idiot."

" Impertinent scoundrel !"

" Put your tongue in.   What the devil did you put it out for ?"

" Now, by Jupiter, this too much, to be called an image, and an idiot; and asked what the devil I put my tongue out for ?"

" That's where you left off, captain. I was getting interested."

The captain sat down again.

" I shall thrash you some day, Jacob. However, I gave him a seat in my sedan-chair, and we were coming home, when half-a-dozen wretches—foot-pads—thieves—or Bow-street runners——"

" Which they're werry much alike."

" That's a sensible remark, Jacob. You may keep one of the guineas. They are not mine—but no matter."

Jacob took it like a philosopher, and said it did not make a bit of difference.

" Runners," he said, like a stage prompter giving the cue.

" Stopped our sedan-chair."

" Got out and knocked 'em down ?" suggested Dingle.

" Not just then. The Viscount drew the blinds down, and said, politely—

" We are about a size, I think, and I have a dim idea that I may be mistaken for some-one else. Now, if you would kindly change seats with me for the occasion, it would save me a great deal of trouble."

" And——"

" I assented. We changed seats. The Viscount got out—said we should meet to-night at Ranelagh—thanked me for doing him an inestimable service, and walked away."

" Then ?"

" Then the half-dozen fellows—thieves or runners—dragged me from the chair, and said they had me at last. I wanted to know what for. They said I was a celebrated pickpocket. I said they were not gentlemen. They would not let me go. I ran one through the body."

" Killed him much ?"

" No !—only a little ! After that I began fight. When I began to fight they saw their mistake—made an apology. I got into the chair—came home."

" Looks very like it, captain !"

" That I came home ?"

" Pickpockets. Viscounts don't take snuff out of seventeen boxes !"

" Nor wear fine bracelets, Jacob."

" Nor a rooby necklace."

" Nor three diamond rings—tiny things that would only fit a lady's finger."

" To say nothing of two pins, a silver buckle, a fan, stuck with jims all over."

" Jims !"

" Red di'monds !"

" Ah, the rubies !"

" That's it—roobies. I've got a cousin Roobies, and he's got a rooby nose."

" The cravats look suspicious. How many cravats, Jacob ?"

" Five. Worth a guinea each, p'raps two."

" My friend the viscount must have eccentric taste. He evidently goes about collecting articles of *vertù*."

" A wery good-looking kind of virtoo. I never saw any with seventeen snuffboxes. One of them di'mond rings would buy enough to last a week !"

" Enough what ?"

" Virtoo—giniwin wirgin innocence."

" Silence ! you immoral scamp. It does look suspicious."

" Immoral scamps does generally."

" Tush ! I mean the contents of the viscount's pockets. Did you read the love-letter ?"

" Bits of it, sir—one or two words put the curb on."

" Try again, Jacob."

" Ahem !"

Jacob cleared his throat, produced the epistle—three-cornered, pink and perfumed—and read—

" My beautiful—my own—sweet fairy-adored one——"

" Bravo !"

" Nice, ain't it ? He must have been in for it bad."

" Go on."

" Give me but ass-mile——"

" Ass mile ? Why the fellow must have been thinking of himself. Spell it."

" A double s—m—i—l—e."

" A smile, you image."

" Werry well. Give me but a smile, you image."

"Is that in the letter ?"

"No; but it's right if you say so."

"Do go on."

"Give me but a smile—a look—such rapture will then be mine. If I am not—not—not. Here's a fellow to write a love letter! He spells damned with two o's."

"Nonsense. It is doomed ?"

"That it. Why don't you be honest, and write damned in plain English ?"

"If I am not dammed, with two o's, to despair, meet me to-morrow night at Ranelagh."

"At Ranelagh ?"

"I will say it again, if you like."

"I don't like. Read the letter."

"Yours, queen of my soul,
        "Orlando, Earl Shipmarsh."

"Orlando, Earl Shipmarsh is very much in love. Who is the lady ?"

"Lady Elizabeth Hamilton !"

"A very beautiful girl. Orlando is a youth—a man of taste. But it's odd !"

"His taste ?"

"No! that a letter written by Orlando should be found in Viscount Bury's pocket."

"It's a strange world, captain—we never know each other. I never knew my own father. I thought I did, but my mother knew best."

"It is a strange world, Jacob, and we never know each other."

He said this sorrowfully.

Looking keenly at Jacob while he spoke.

The faithful serving man changed countenance.

His glance rested with a strange uncouth sort of affection on his master's face.

"Knowing isn't much," he said. "Caring's all."

"And what cares the world, if I were a poor outcast wretch, homeless and penniless to-morrow? Who would care for me ?"

"Jacob Dingle !"

"If I were a disgraced felon ?"

"Jacob Dingle !"

The words — the mere names, oddly, abruptly spoken, were uttered in a tone and with a manner that expressed a rich wealth of rugged, undying devotion.

"I believe you, Jacob," said Montrose, looking up with a smile, "and here's my hand

upon it. Give me that boot, and fetch my whip ; get my horse ready. I'll go to Ranelagh !"

"Captain ?"

"Well ?"

"May I follow ?"

"May you follow ? What the deuce for ?"

"I like to be with you, captain. I never left your side when we were out in battle, and a poor rough soldier ; you, my captain—you were not ashamed of me then."

"Why, Jacob—brave old friend—ashamed of you ? I would ram the idea down the throat of any man who dared say it. Ashamed ? Not of an honest heart, no matter what the shape that carries it."

"But you always bid me stay at home !"

Montrose buckled on a light dress sword.

A shade of pained regret was on his brow.

"I would gladly let you share my danger, Jacob. But the rest—no."

"Master "—

"Hush ! Some day, perhaps—in other times—you may know more. Then away !—my horse !

Jacob went, without another word. Montrose paced the floor.

"Good, faithful fellow ! If he but knew if—why doubt him ?—if he knew all, and saw the worst, his honest heart might break ; but each atom would beat love for me."

He laughed—not in mirth—he stamped his foot, as though impatient at himself.

"Montrose ! Montrose ! There must be no weakness now. The career is begun, the end lies in the future."

"The mystery ! the mystery !" he went on, still pacing restlessly, "my birth, my home, my father's fate ! When these are known, then—then "—

"Your horse is at the door."

"Ha ! ha !" He assumed a gaiety that was not in him. "Put two of these snuff-boxes in my—the viscount's coat, the ruby and emerald and the one set with opals, the bracelet, too, and the rings."

Jacob obeyed him.

"I shall return at dawn, Jacob. Truth to say, these late nights weary me."

He patted the arched, glossy neck of his splendid steed. The docile creature knew him well, and whinnied with delight at his touch.

They formed a fine picture—steed and rider. Never a more gallant figure sat a saddle—never a more proudly perfect horse trod road or war plain.

Montrose, in his coat of crimson velvet, fitting tightly, defined every curve from wide sloping shoulders and statuesque chest to narrow waist—his hips, though slender, were graceful and full of nervous grace—the soft, oven coloured buckskins and boots of polished leather, became them well.

It was just the dress that suited his dashing chivalric style; and his beaver, shaped like a Spanish sombrero, laced with gold, and surmounted by a drooping plume, shadowed a fine face of classic beauty.

A touch to his barb, and he was on his way. No sooner was he in motion than a change came over him. Every trace of pain and sadness went—a charming recklessness, blended with a gleam of frank mischievous devilry, took its place.

"Let me see," he said. "My purse is empty. I must fill it."

He rode slowly, and was on the alert.

He heard the distant sound of a horse's feet behind him. He reined-in, and waited.

Waited with his hand upon a pistol—a very richly mounted, slender-barrelled weapon, fit for a monarch's use.

The traveller came on.

He was a cavalier about the same age as Montrose—as handsome, and as brave.

Montrose put his mask on, and barred the traveller's way.

"My friend," he said, disguising his voice with wonderful facility, "I must have a word with you."

"Must!" said the traveller. "By St. George, here's an adventure at last. A man with a mask on, who must have a word with me."

"Are you rich?"

"What the deuce is that to do with you?"

"Lend me ten guineas."

"What?"

"Ten guineas."

"Not a bad idea to go about lending ten guineas to every fellow you don't know."

"Come."

"Come. "Well, we had better come to terms. And so you only want ten guineas?"

"A modest need; and if you lend them freely you shall have them back."

"That sounds likely."

"My friend, I am a man of honour."

The traveller laughed ironically.

"An honourable highwayman; though, by the way, there is one gentlemanly fellow—Tom King."

"Tom King," said Montrose, lifting his hat gracefully. "In the name of a comrade, let me thank you."

"Thank away. Can you fight?"

"Try."

"You will have to, if you want the ten," said the traveller, drawing his sword. "See."

He produced his purse, counted out ten guineas, and threw them on the ground.

"There, now for a fair bargain. I haven't had a fence lately, except with Valentine. So, if you get the best out of three points, the money is yours."

"As a loan only," said Montrose. "Shall we fight on foot?"

"Yes."

He showed he had a fearless spirit by dismounting first, and so placing himself at a disadvantage.

A moment more, and they were foot to foot.

Two gallant, skilful swordsmen, fighting without malice.

The very singularity of the proposition had a chivalrous fire in it that won Montrose's sympathy.

Clash!

Their swords met.

Clang! Glided—met again.

"One."

"Was it?" said the traveller.

"Yes; I felt it fairly. See, here is the mark on my button."

Montrose turned his sword to let his adversary approach and look. He, struck by the knightly frankness of the act, said—

"I am glad it went no further."

They resumed position.

Clash—cling and glide—a thrust—parried—a lunge—touched.

This time Montrose spoke.

"One to me!"

THE DUEL.

"By St. George, you have touched my button exactly where I touched yours!"

"I made the point with that intention."

Clash and cling—cling and glide—a touch—another—simultaneous.

Each had the point of his weapon at the other's breast.

"Touched!" said Montrose. "You are not hurt, I hope."

"How were you to thrust? I found my ord was a little longer than yours."

"Now it was point and point. You have made a little hole in my friend's coat, and it really is a very handsome coat."

"It is displayed to advantage."

"Thank you."

Clash and cling—cling and glide.

"A touch!"

"A touch!"

"It is!"

"It is!'

"Then it is a drawn contest,' said Montrose, sheathing his blade; "and I must ride to Ranelagh with an empty purse."

"To Ranelagh—no, deuce take it—take the money. You are a soldier and a gentleman, I could swear, in spite of whatever may have driven you to the road. Here!'

He picked the money from the ground, advanced, and placed it in Montrose's hand.

"Meet me here to-morrow night," said

Montrose, "or let me know where I may bring it, and it shall be returned."

"Come to my house   I am Lord Ernest Dallas."

"A nobleman of noble nature. I will come."

"And be welcome. I shall tell Valentine, and he will meet you; and so, with a lady or two, we shall have an originality—a supper with a real highwayman.   Now your name."

"I can trust you with a secret?"

Ernest Dallas put his hand on his heart.

"On my honour."

"I am Captain Walter Montrose, to some."

"Walter Montrose! surely, you jest? Show me your face?"

Montrose unmasked.

"It is, by George. Oh! it is a trick. You saw me coming, and played this trick."

I will not act a lie to a noble friend," said Montrose, gravely. "Despise me, Dallas— turn from me if you will. I am Montrose; but I have another identity—another name."

Dallas clasped the other's hand.

"Shall I swear it Montrose, that, hear what I may, I will not despise or turn from you? Now, tell me, what other name?"

Lifting his hat, and bowing his head low, Montrose said—

"Tom King!"

CHAPTER XCIX.

THE OFFICERS' JEOPARDY—DICK'S ESCAPE— THE WAGER—THE APPOINTED HOUR OF TWELVE, AND THE APPEARANCE OF TWO TYBURN DICKS.

BEN had rescued Dick bravely.

When Captain Claude and mine host reached the inn, they had to cut their way through the officers who surrounded the door, and who were hammering to get in.

"What, ho! within!" shouted Samson.

"What, ho! without! responded a voice from above.

The swarthy landlord looked up.

Ben was hanging half out of the window.

"Oh, it's you, is it?"

"Yes, open the door."

"Can't."

"Can't? Why not?"

"If I let you in, them ill-looking devils will want to come in."

"They must get in, though."

"No."

"How's the captain?"

"Pretty well, thank'ee. How are you?"

Mine host tried to keep down a smile that rose to his face.

"You impertinent scoundrel."

"Yes, your honour."

"Open the door."

"Yes, your honour."

Ben disappeared.

A moment or two more heavy bolts could be heard flying back from their sockets.

The officers pressed forward with intent to make a rush in as soon as the door was opened; but the big form of Samson Leopard, standing like an immovable rock before them, kept them back.

The door opened.

The officers made a dash forward.

Samson took a step into the passage, turned, with a heavy scowl darkening his face, and his ponderous club raised on high.

The men fell back.

"Keep there," said the landlord.

His deep-toned voice made the men quail as it fell upon their ears.

"Keep there, or you will find yourselves in a lion's den!"

He passed in with Captain Claude.

"Where's the captain?" he asked.

"All right, yer honour," replied Ben.

"Where is he?" demanded the landlord

"Where is he?   Oh, I'll show yer."

"Lead the way."

Ben trotted on in front, up two flights of dark stairs, and stopped before a green-baized door.

He tapped with his knuckles, and glanced suspiciously at his master.

"Who's there?" inquired a voice from within.

"I," said Captain Claude.

He entered with mine host.

Dick was reclining upon a couch, and the innkeeper's daughter Lizzie sat by his side. She blushed deeply, and hung down her head upon meeting the fixed, angry gaze of her father.

Mine host had a suspicion that all was not right between his daughter and the boy; he could not say anything, for he had no foundation beyond suspicion; but could he have confirmed that suspicion, he would have shown little mercy to the betrayer of his child.

"Father," exclaimed Dick, extending his hand to Claude, "how came you here?"

"I came to look after you," replied the captain, "and fortunately came in time. Had I been two minutes later, they would have got you away safely."

"How's that?" inquired our hero, as though forgetting what had occurred.

"Do you not know how they took you?"

"Yes; in leaping a hedge, the horse fell, and before I had time to extricate my feet from the stirrup, my leg got jammed. I managed to limp to the yard, where I fell exhausted. I called loudly for help, but no one came to me. The officers took advantage of my helplessness, and bound me to the back of a horse. I then fainted, though before then I have a dim recollection of hearing a cry, and the officers' steps. I remember no more."

"Did you call," inquired mine host, "for help, when in the yard below?"

"I did, and lustily, too; but hearing no reply, I thought you had deserted me, so I sadly gave myself up in despair."

"You thought I had deserted you, then, captain? That is not in me."

"No, my friend, I never thought so," said Dick; "but at such moments as these a fellow can't be answerable for what he thinks."

"How is your leg, now?" asked Claude, anxiously.

"Much better, thanks to this sweet little angel," and Dick slid his arm round Lizzie's waist, and drew her blushing face to his.

"I believe Ben nobly saved me, while you were engaged in the terrific strife with my captors; and when I awoke, found myself lying here, and Lizzie, like a kind goddess, quietly administering to my wants."

It was plainly evident, by the dark gathering of his brows, that mine host did not relish the fondness Dick used to his daughter.

"Lizzie!" he said, sternly.

"Yes, father," faltered the little one, timidly; for she knew the strictness of her sire.

"You can go down stairs."

The girl clung to her lover.

"Mr. Samson," said the boy, gravely.

"Well?" was the laconic reply.

"Why do you wish her to go down stairs?"

"You have done with her services."

"Well?" returned Dick, in the same tone as the landlord had used.

"This is no place for her—alone with a gentleman."

"She has done no harm."

"Then, to keep her from it, I wish her to go."

"Mr. Leopard, we have once before quarrelled anent the same thing."

"I have no wish to quarrel the second time."

"Then mind your own business; Lizzie's going to stay with me."

Mr. Leopard turned aside to scowl.

"Have your own way; only don't anony the girl," he said, menacingly, "or you will find a savage enemy in me."

"Speak like that again, and I and you will have a row."

"She is my only child—the only remembrance I have of her mother. Big and rough as I am, my love for her is deeply rooted. Should she fall a victim to anyone, the Lord have mercy upon her betrayer, for I should have none."

"You have nothing to fear for her safety with me."

"If I have offended, you must forgive me. You do not, perhaps, know my feelings as a father."

"All right, friend; bring up some wine, and let it pass. Lizzy can answer truthfully I dare say."

This remark seemed to pacify the landlord. He was about to go for the wine when a rush of feet coming up the stairs alarmed him that the officers had got in.

He stood aside and let them come.

Dick sprang up, and took a pair of long-barrelled pistols from his belt.

He confronted the officers at the room door.

Lizzie ran timidly into her father's arms, Captain Claude drew his sword.

"Down with him!" shouted Red Matthias,

from behind his myrmidons. " Down with him! Mind we go not away without him."

" You won't go with him," said the innkeeper.

" Then we'll leave him dead for you."

Dick laughed at the threat.

Pointing a pistol in a line with the thief-tcher's head, he said—

"I shall stop your noise presently."

Matthias yelled frantically, and pushed his men in. Dick did not budge an inch; he stood firm, and kept his pursuers at bay.

" Don't come any nearer," he said to the men, coolly, " or some of you will fall. I am an unerring shot."

" So am I," said some one in the rear. As he spoke, a thick cudgel came whizzing through the air, struck Dick aside of the head, and felled him to the floor.

" Upon him, men—secure him—shoot all who interfere."

" That's Red Matthias," said Dick, jumping to his feet.

The officers had advanced into the room, and confronted the boy highwayman determinedly; each and every one had prepared their pistols, and twenty deadly weapons were aimed at our hero's breast.

" Yield quietly?" said the thief-catcher, " or this will be your last moment, Tyburn Dick."

" Never!" replied Dick, firmly.

" Fire, men!—let every shot go into his accursed carcase!"

" No—no!" cried Lizzie, and, bounding from her father's side, she threw herself before the brave boy.

" Shoot them both!" shouted Matthias, foaming with rage. " Spare none who interfere in his behalf—shoot all!"

He placed the muzzle of a big pistol against the fair girl's breast, his finger was on the trigger—another moment, and the deadly missile would have penetrated both their young hearts.

But at that moment Captain Claude sprang forward, knocked the thief-catcher's murderous arm aside, and grasping him by the neck, hurled him amongst his followers.

" Keep back, Dick!" he said.

The boy put his arm round Lizzie's waist, and led her to the further end of the room.

Mine host went to the door, and forced the men on to the landing.

" Ben," he called.

" Yes, yer honour," responded the ostler, from the bottom of the stairs.

" Put the cannons down there."

" That's already done."

" That's well—"

" Yes."

" If these bloodhounds try to pass you——"

" Fire into 'em. All right, never fear, won't I give 'em a nice dose of grape and canister, as I likes 'em so well."

The landlord turned to Dick—

" Make your exit, quickly——

" Which way?"

" The window. You will find a coil of rope in the next room."

Lizzie went to get it.

" You shall pay for this!" exclaimed Matthias, dismayed by the peril of his position.

Samson laughed hoarsely.

His daughter returned with the rope.

Dick securely fastened one end to an iron ring in the wall, and dropped the rest out of window.

" Adieu!" said Dick, mounting outside the window to make his descent. " Adieu! we shall meet again soon."

" Yes, in hell," thundered Red Matthias, his concentrated rage bursting out like a sudden clap of thunder.

" Silence! blackguard!" said Claude, " or I will send you there first."

" Pass that man at the bottom my men, or we shall lose the thousand pounds," said the thief-catcher, despairingly. " You are not all frightened of one?"

" The men ain't frightened," answered one of the officers. " You lead the way, we'll follow you."

" Yes, come on," said Ben.

Matthias looked savagely down upon the ostler, who stood between two cannons placed at the bottom of the stairs, with a torch in his hand, ready, at the least sign, to send the destructive contents of these fearful weapons amongst them.

The officers had never been in such a position before; and the worst of it was they had to stand patiently while their intended victim made his escape.

When he had gone completely out of sight on the back of Selim, they were allowed to go, and glad they were to get away safe.

CHAPTER C.

A GAME AT DICE.—THE INTERRUPTION.—THE STORY OF A NOBLEMAN, HOW HE GOT ROBBED.—FOUR TO ONE.—THE TWO TYBURN DICKS.—CAPTURE OF THE PURSUERS.

SELIM bore the daring boy highwayman along before the wind with unsurpassable fleetness, and in one short hour they had traversed many leagues.

Dick drew rein before an hotel in the Hammersmith-road.

"You need not unharness her," he said to a stable-boy who came out and took the bridle, while our hero dismounted. "Look well after her. I shall want her again in less than half an hour."

The boy respectfully touched his hat, and led Selim away.

Dick entered the inn. The host advanced, bowing almost to the ground, thinking, in a traveller of such noble bearing, he had a grand customer.

"What may I have the honour of providing your honour with?" he asked.

"I want a little supper, quickly," said Dick.

"Yes, your lordship, but we have nothing hot; but we can soon prepare something for you."

"Never mind about anything hot. Have you anything cold?"

"Yes, your lordship, we have cold ham and 'owl, and some——"

"Ham and fowl will do for me."

"Yes, my lord—wine with it?"

"A bottle of your best."

"Yes, my lord. Would you prefer a room to yourself, or would you like to go into the supper-room where there are other gentlemen?"

"Well, they appear to be pretty merry. I think I should prefer their company."

Mine host swung open the door of a large hall, Dick entered; every one was silent on the instant, and all eyes were upon him, as he took a seat.

The company consisted of many gay gentle-men, seated round various tables playing at cards, dominoes, and dice.

A party of four gay young noblemen who played at dice, and lost or won thousands with the same cheerful mirth, particularly attracted our hero's attention.

"By Jove!" exclaimed one of the players, "you have completely skinned me out."

"Never mind that, old boy, I'll lend you a thousand to go on again," said another. "You may have a change of luck."

"No; I don't see it. I shan't play any more. Perhaps this gentleman will take my place."

"With much pleasure," said Dick, as the young nobleman indicated to him.

He finished his repast, and took the loser's seat.

"What shall we play for—a thousand a throw?" asked his opponent.

"The half that will do."

"Five hundred, so be it."

Dick rattled the dice, and threw.

"Fifteen!" he said, "a good throw."

His companion threw seventeen, and won.

Dick paid, and doubled the stakes.

His next throw turned up nine.

The other turned up ten.

"Go on again!" said Dick. "I have yet seven hundred and thirty pounds more, the odd money I'd better keep."

He threw again and lost.

"You have beaten me shamefully," he said.

"Not through science!" replied the other. "Come, drink with me, you may have better fortune next time."

"I have nothing more to play."

"That ring on your finger."

"This!" cried Dick, in astonishment, holding up his hand. "Why, it is worth two thousand."

"I will put two thousand against it."

"No! I should not care to part with it."

"Do! It may bring back all you have lost."

"Very well!"

"Don't let me persuade you, my dear fellow, to part with it, if it's a family relic."

"Don't you believe it," said Dick, "if I had not the mind, no one could persuade me to part with it."

"Will you throw?"

"Yes; but not for the ring all at once."

"No! Four throws, at five hundred eac will be the thing."

Dick threw, and each time lost.

His ring changed owners.

He played for his horse, and equipments, that he had left in the stable boy's care.

That, too, went from him.

Luck was certainly against him that night.

He had gone so far now, he grew careless.

And, had he possessed a million, he would have played for it.

But only having his sword left, he determined to see, as a last resource, what that would bring him.

"The jewelled hilt of my sword," he said, tapping it with much pride, "is worth five hundred, you will stake five against it."

"A thousand, if you wish it."

"No! Five hundred is its value. Throw!"

Their play had created some excitement amongst the company.

And now they gathered round the table, where Dick and his opponent sat.

Things now took a sudden change, our hero won the five hundred laid against his sword.

The next throw he won back his horse.

And so he kept on, until he had regained all his property, besides two thousand from the gentleman with whom he played.

"Fortune's turned its back upon me," said the gay young nobleman, pleasantly. "You will have a run of luck now."

And so he did; for he reduced the gentleman, as he had been himself, down to his sword.

"You have won over ten thousand pounds from me," said the young nobleman.

"I shall think of you as I spend it," replied Dick.

"Besides those splendid rings."

"Which I shall wear in remembrance of so honourable a gentleman."

"My watch, too."

"Which keeps excellent time, and will add to your remembrance every twenty-four hours."

"Even my horse you have won."

"Which shall receive particular attention from me, and which will be the cause of often bringing us in contact with each other."

"And now, as my last chance, here goes my sword, as went yours."

"Should I win it, I shall be able at any time to use it in your defence."

"Well, if it fences as faithful as yours, I shall be able to use it in my own defence."

He threw fourteen.

Dick threw twelve.

The young noble kept his weapon, and won back his rings.

So they kept on winning and losing.

The party were suddenly startled by the rapid entry of a young noble, who looked terribly heated and excited through great exertion.

He cast a rapid glance round the players, and exclaimed—

"Frank, I have been robbed!"

"The devil you have!" said Dick's opponent. Where?" and pocketing a heap of money he had just won, he threw the dice aside, and, turning to our hero, said, "How do we now stand?"

"Coming from Hounslow," replied the new comer, answering the query of "Where?"

"We have each got our own," said Dick.

"Then we leave off as we began," laughed his adversary. "And I keep my ten thousand and over, which, when I spend it, will remind me of you; the rings I shall wear with kind remembrance of you; the watch still keeps capital time; the horse, since it had no inclination to change owners, shall receive the most indulging attention; and my sword I shall be most happy to use in your behalf at any requiring opportunity."

At this reproach the whole company roared out laughing.

Dick keenly felt the sting of the words, though they were spoken inoffensively.

Seeing this, he took it good-temperedly, and joined in the laugh.

"What the deuce are you all laughing at?" asked the new-comer, greatly perplexed.

"Oh! you were robbed, weren't you?" inquired one of his companions.

"Robbed! confound it, yes; the very horse I was riding was taken from me."

"By whom?"

"That audacious fellow, Tyburn Dick."

"The deuce," exclaimed another. "Where

did you see him?—what sort of fellow is he?"

"A very capital fellow in his way, no doubt; too good for me by far. He might have been contented with taking my purse, without robbing me of my horse."

"Tyburn Dick you met?" queried our hero, with marked curiosity.

"Yes," answered the other, "and I should say that you were he, for I never saw two fellows so much alike in my life, save that your hair is brown, and his is a beautiful flaxen, which I thought rather uncommon for a male."

"Very unfortunate for me," said Dick, with a smile, "that there is that difference between us, as it might make it unpleasant for me."

"Perhaps that hair was a disguise," suggested another.

"If so," said the pillaged nobleman, "I should say, without meaning any offence, that this gentleman was my late assailant."

"I thank you for the compliment," said Dick.

"This gentleman," put in our hero's late opponent at dice, "has been in our company for the last three hours."

"Then it could not have been he, for I was robbed not two hours ago."

"How did it occur?" inquired Dick.

He had no doubt as to the person of the perpetrator whom he surmised to be his devoted love—our noble heroine.

"This, gentlemen, is how it occurred," said the young noble. "I was riding from Hounslow, and while passing the heath my notice was drawn to a most elegant form walking leisurely along the road.

"I had no sooner got abreast with him, when he turned his head languidly round, as any one would do.

"I fancied at first that he might have taken me for a highwayman, being all alone and at such a time, and thought that perhaps he was timid.

"I was about to draw in rein, and ask him for where he was destined, when, with three steps from where he stood, he confronted my horse, brought it to a stand, and in the most gentlemanly manner raised his hand and said—

"'My dear sir, I must trouble you to dismount!'

"I hesitated a moment, wondering at such a request.

"He drew a delicate pistol, and coolly presented it in a line with my head.

"'Dismount, if you please,' he said.

"I did so.

"My ideas of his being a timid gentleman took a very different turn, you may guess.

"'Why do you wish me to dismount?' I asked.

"'Because,' returned he, 'I want your horse, my one having been shot from under me.'

"I heartily wished he had been shot with it, but I did not say so.

"'Who are you?' I asked.

"'This will explain,' he replied, throwing open a cape, and displaying a beautiful jewelled star on his breast.

"'Tyburn Dick!' I exclaimed, in astonishment.

"'The same,' said he, raising his plumed hat. 'I must trouble you for your purse.'

"I again hesitated, but his pistol was again produced, and so my purse went from my pocket into his.

"'Is there anything more you want?' asked I, keeping my hand on the butt of a pistol, ready at the first opportunity to send a bullet through his skull.

"'Yes,' he said, 'those pistols you are playing with.'

"He pressed his own weapon against my forehead, and kept it there until my pistols were safely in his possession. Then, he turned to me sharply, and said—

"'Now, run for your life, nor don't stop for anything. Unless you're out of sight in less than five minutes—don't hide behind any hedge or tree—you will get a bullet where you won't like it.'

"I instantly set off at the pace of a racehorse, nor did I stop more than once to draw breath during the journey here."

"Why did you not fight him?" asked one.

"I did not think of it."

"By Jove! it was a capital adventure. I wish it had been I instead of you," remarked another.

"Come with me, then. I am going back for my horse."

"How do you mean going back for it?"

"Why, I am going to look for him, and have revenge."

"I'll go with you."

"So will I."

And so shouted a dozen.

"I should advise you, gentlemen, for your own safety," said Dick, "not to do anything of the sort."

Everyone looked at him surprisingly.

"What do you mean to insinuate? asked one.

"Why, for so many of you to go, you would all fall into danger. He would not mind coping with two, three, or four, but did more than that go to attack him, he would bring fifty of his band to make you all captives."

"How the deuce do you know all this?"

"I have heard it from people who know him."

"Then four of us had better go. Will you be one of us?"

"I thank you, but I must decline, having to keep another appointment by twelve," Dick said.

"We are sorry for that, because we shall lose your company," said Dick's companion at dice.

"You don't regret more than I do," replied our hero. "Tyburn Dick won't be on Hounslow Heath before twelve. Probably we shall meet again there. Good evening, gentlemen." And rising, he took his hat and departed.

The gentleman sat in silence some minutes after he was gone.

"He appears a strange fellow," said one.

"Knows a deuced lot about that highwayman fellow," said another.

"Perhaps he's the very one, and none of us know him," suggested a third.

"How the deuce can that be?" cried the young nobleman, angrily, "when Tyburn Dick stopped me on Hounslow Heath, and you acknowledge that the gentleman who has just left had been in your company two hours previous to my being robbed."

"If you were not mistaken in the time, I am positive that such was the case."

"Mistaken! Confound it! Haven't I got a watch, and can't I tell the time? I tell you, Frank, it was nine when I was robbed, and you say that the fellow who just went out was here before seven. All I know is that we are wasting time while that confounded fellow's walking off with my property."

"Did you not hear what that gentleman said when he went out, that Tyburn Dick would not be on the heath before twelve."

"Confound the gentleman! Do you suppose that I am such a fool as to believe what he says?—a confederate, who, probably has gone to let his companions into the secret of our intentions."

"Well, and if such is the case, what then?"

"The fellow will make a clean breast of it, and I shall lose my horse."

"Look here, Heric," interposed one, "there are twelve of us, and staunch old friends whom, I know, will stick to each other in any difficulty."

"Well," said Heric, wondering what was coming next.

"Well," repeated the other, "if what you surmise is right about that other fellow, it would not be safe for one or two to go alone."

"I don't fear him," said Heric, boldly.

"No. I did not for an instant think you did, nor do any of us here; but discretion is the better part of valour, to use an old saying."

"Well," Heric said again, "what are your ideas?"

"I simply propose that we all go, but in three different companies, and deposit ourselves in different parts, in case of a row."

"That's all very well, but how the devil can I go without a horse!"

"The landlord will lend you one, and I should think by the time our steeds are ready, and we have prepared our warlike weapons for an encounter, we shall be none too early to reach the heath by the appointed hour."

The horses were prepared, and brought round in front of the inn. The young noblemen looked carefully to the priming of their firearms, tried the keenness of the edges of their swords by trying to cut off the legs of chairs and tables, and then set out

They were indeed a handsome group: young, and with that dare-devil carelessness that took them to war with the same gaiety as they would have gone to a court revel.

They divided into three companies of four each, when they had got a short distance from the inn.

Heric, with three others, took the shortest route to Hounslow, while their friends went in quite different directions.

Our hero, when he left the company, proceeded to the heath, went straight to the haunt, and acquainting his men of what he expected, put them under the command of Joseph Munroe, and left with instructions for them to be on the alert for the slightest signal.

One thing he particularly noticed was that Grace had not returned. He feared now that she might fall in with these young noblemen. This thought greatly distressed him, and he urged Selim onwards in the direction he knew they would come.

"Ah!" he exclaimed, with a start, "that's the game, is it?"

Two groups of men rode cautiously from behind a neighbouring hedge, and entered the heath.

Dick secreted himself behind a huge, sheltering, grand old tree, and watched them.

They passed very close to him, but he remained silent and indiscernable—hidden in the sombre shadows, while he could see and recognise the face of every man who passed.

"Eight," he muttered, when the last had concealed himself in some secure spot.

"There's four men to come. They would not take the same way. They must come, then, by the Hammersmith road."

He rode on in that direction.

A clashing of steel and the prancing of horses made him urge his own faithful steed forward at a more rapid pace than they were going. The soft light that the moon shed over the earth revealed to his gaze a group of four or five persons in angry strife, not a quarter of a mile in advance of him.

"Four to one! Cowards!" he thundered, riding up, and with an angry stroke he struck the foremost of the assailants from the saddle.

The others fell back.

"Which is Tyburn Dick?" exclaimed one half, in terror at seeing two beings so much alike.

"Judge for yourselves," said Dick. "You, my friend, take a rest, while I have a set-to with these gentlemen."

He extended his hand to the fair girl.

Grace could not express the sudden joy at being again brought into contact with her gallant lover, which brought tears of happiness to her eyes. Raising the proferred hand to her lips, she fervently pressed a kiss upon returning the affectionate grip, she turned aside to hide the tears of happiness that trickled down her pretty cheeks.

"Now, gentlemen, do you wish to know which is Tyburn Dick," said our hero, turning to the astonished noblemen. "See if you can't find out by the sword."

Two instantly rode upon him.

One drew back as the highwayman crossed swords with the other.

"Don't kill him all at once. I want to have a dig at him," he said.

"Oh," said Dick, with a laugh, "you have nothing to fear on that score. I shall be quite sound when you come on, and just as sound when I have done with you."

"You boast, methinks," said Dick's opponent.

"I'll stake my purse against yours, and my sword against yours, that I disarm you before you get one pass."

"Done!" cried the other, readily.

He could use the sword moderately well.

Dick used his much better; and before his opponent even got the shade of a pass, he made three splendid points, and at the third wrenched the sword from the noble's hand.

"Won!" cried the boy.

He took the money and sword from his antagonist, put the money in his pocket, swung the sword at his side by passing one end of his belt through the hilt, and then turned to the other.

"I am ready for you now," he said.

"With the same terms?"

"Yes, and with the purse and sword I have just won."

Dick was not long in disposing of him. His weapon, at the first clash, split in the middle, and the two halves, spinning through the air, glittered in the moon's rays like forked lightning.

The young lordling groaned as he delivered up the money.

Dick said—

"You may keep your sword. Is there anyone else that would like to learn a trick in fencing?"

"I tell you what it is, old fellow," said Heric, "you have vanquished my two friends; but I don't mind having a set-to with you, on these conditions, that if I conquer, your friend gives up my horse."

"And your money, too," put in Dick.

"Done!" cried the young nobleman, drawing his weapon and facing our hero.

"And if I conquer," said Dick, "what am I to have?"

"You can't have my purse, because your companion has already got that."

"Then I must be content with the honour of beating you."

"Just so, as you can't have anything else; so, come on!"

Dick drew his blade. The weapons met —missed—a dash. Heric was a much better swordsman than his companions. He fenced with remarkable skill—easy and graceful. Dick admired his play, and favoured him as much as possible by letting him get a few passes, though he could have disarmed him at the first onset, by a trick only known to himself and Captain Claude.

"You fence very prettily," said Dick.

His adversary did not reply, he inclined his head for the compliment, watching very closely, at the same time, for an opportunity to disarm his opponent.

A shadow, as Dick fancied, flickered twice across the road. An irresistible impulse caused him to turn his head. Down the road he saw flying the man he had knocked from his saddle. He laughed contemptuously at the fellow's cowardice.

His adversary at that moment took the advantage to fix the point of his own sword in the hilt of the boy highwayman's, and wrench it from his grasp.

Dick turned as it left his hand, and caught it as it descended. The young gentleman made a furious down-cut, to strike it from him again, but Dick held it too firmly, and,

angered by the other's impetus, he made three rapid strokes, that so perplexed the young nobleman, that he held the blade perfectly helpless.

"Regain your weapon if you can," exclaimed Dick, suddenly twisting the sword from his combatant's hand.

The young noble reeled in his saddle, with the pain caused by the twist Dick had given him.

"I wish you a fair adieu," said Dick, raising his hat, "and better success when you next go in search of Tyburn Dick."

He rode to his fair companion's side, and they were about to ride off together when a voice yelled out—

"You highwayman, Tyburn Dick, stay."

"Certainly," laughed the boy.

And looking round to see from whence the voice came, he beheld the eight noblemen he had seen waiting in ambush come thundering towards him, preceded by the gentleman he had thrown from his saddle.

"There will be a row," said Dick, "and they will get the worst of it."

Grace smiled at her fearless lover, her tiny hand was firmly locked over the jewelled hilt of her beautiful rapier, and she sat undaunted, waiting for the assailants.

A shout of welcome echoed through the lofty trees as the noblemen joined them.

The twelve then rode towards our hero and heroine, each with his sword drawn and held up against his right shoulder in quite a military style.

"Gentlemen of the highwaymen fraternity," said one, riding from the company and confronting Dick and his fair companion, "it is my duty as a gentleman of this land of freedom to take upon myself, in the name of my friends, to demand from you and your associate the property that you and your associate have taken from my before-mentioned friends."

"To the devil with you!" Dick said.

"Gentlemen, this is unwarrantable," continued the spokesman. "I asked you in a most civil manner for what belongs to my friends, and you tell me in a most pert manner to go to the fire-king; it is disgraceful on your part. For the last time, and before you compel me to use physical power to return the property, I ask you to give it up.

"No," Dick said. "I certainly shall not give it up. The property I now hold was won from your friends by a fair and friendly passage of arms."

"Confound it! So you call it fair to be forced from your horse, and then be compelled to give up your money to keep a bullet out of your head?"

"Now, down with the highwaymen!" shouted all the rest.

"Oh, that's it, is it?" said Dick; "come on," and he whistled a sort of cuckoo's note.

It was instantly answered in the same tone.

Grace and Dick were the only ones that heard it, so faintly audible did it come in reply.

The noblemen all crowded round the highwaymen.

"It will be useless for you two to resist," said one, "so give in quietly."

"The first that comes too near," exclaimed the boy, "will fall."

"Attempt it, and you shall be riddled with a score of bullets."

Dick laughed at the threat.

The twelve horsemen dashed suddenly upon the two highwaymen.

Tyburn Dick fired two pistols.

Both shots passed the noblemen harmlessly,

Grace drew two pistols from her belt, but before she could fire the young noblemen threw her from her horse. Dick dashed upon them furiously with his drawn sword.

His arms were caught, and he was dragged from the saddle.

"Bind their hands and feet," suggested one of the party.

Dick struggled with the strength of a maddened tiger to break away from his six captors.

Grace lay more quietly with her six assailants.

She was frightened to resist, for fear of displaying her sex; so she was soon overpowered, and her arms and legs tightly secured with several handkerchiefs of her captors.

She was then left, being full length upon the sward, while her assailants went to assist their friends to secure her lover.

Even with the twelve they found it a difficult task to overpower the daring boy, and while they were struggling, one falling over the other, seven men rode upon the scene.

Dick recognised the foremost one as his dangerous enemy, Red Matthias, the thief-catcher.

The noblemen thought the new comers were friends of the highwaymen, but looking up into the malignant faces, they saw they were officers of the law.

"Bravo!" shouted the thief-catcher.

"What's the matter?" inquired one of Dick's assailants.

"You have captured the very fellow I have been looking for so long."

"Indeed; we have captured two."

"Two!"

"There is one lying there, bound and helpless," the noble pointed to Grace.

"Two Tyburn Dicks! Ha, ha! we shall make sure of the right one this time."

"Will you?"

"Yes; tie that one on his horse," cried Matthias, giving orders to his men. "Allow me, gentlemen, I will manage this daring fellow."

"To the devil with you! Who wants your interference?"

"But I have a warrant for their apprehension."

"Keep it, then."

Matthias looked at the young nobleman in blank astonishment.

"What do you want?" inquired Horace.

"The highwaymen you have captured."

"What for?"

"To give them over to justice."

"What then?"

"They will be hanged, and these gentlemen will be able to travel in safety."

"Look here, you blood-hunting thief, if you and your ugly company don't go your way we shall have a row."

"What do you mean, sir?" asked Matthias, amazed.

"Do you suppose for an instant that we should give such brave men as these into your murderous clutches," said Horace; "they are an ornament to the country."

"Then why are you using them like this?"

"We are settling a little affair among us."

"And when you have done, I'll settle my little affair," said thief-catcher."

"Oh, you will, will you?" Horace remarked, quietly. "Gentlemen, this ugly-oking scoundrel wants this highwayman—he to have him?"

"Certainly not!" was the general cry.

"I must, gentlemen," Red Matthias exclaimed. "I am but doing my duty—the King's mission."

"Blow the King, we will fight for Tyburn Dick, one and all."

"To the death!" cried the rest.

"This is treason!" Matthias said. "Gentlemen, you will get yourselves into trouble."

"Away with you, or we will make a pepper-box of your ugly carcase."

Red Matthias stood resolute, and called his myrmidons around him.

"I took a fearful oath," he began, addressing the company in general, "the last time I had an encounter with Tyburn Dick, to take him, or die in the attempt when we next met. These men are determined to fight for him. Men do your duty."

The officers drew their clumsy weapons, Matthias drew his, a long and dangerous instrument.

"Let's come face to face with Tyburn Dick and one of us shall fall," he spoke with a determined resolution—his eyes gleamed with a demoniac glare.

"Oh, that's your game, is it!" said Horace. "Gentleman, unbind the captives!"

The fair Grace and her lover was released instantly.

Dick sprang to his feet, drew his sword, and set furiously at the thief-catcher.

"We fight to the death!" he said, "It is time one of us was out of the way, you will fall."

The thief-catcher made no reply; they fought with a resolution to slay each other.

The officers dashed into the noblemen. Grace went into them like a tartar.

A bloody, deadly combat then ensued, not a word was spoken, only the ringing clash of steel was heard.

Dick and his enemy stood foot to foot, neither budged an inch, both were bleeding from several wounds.

Our hero had received many ugly cuts from his opponent; not that the thief-catcher was so scientific, but because he fought with maddened fury.

Dick played to kill, not to guard off the other's blows; so he got digs that he could otherwise have turned aside easily, but the thief-catcher's cuts numbered many more than did our hero's.

A gurgling cry arose from one of the officers as he fell to the earth with one of the combatants' sword through his body.

Matthias saw the fate of his man.

With the look of a fiend, he made a stop, and plunged forward to end the battle and the career of Tyburn Dick.

Tyburn Dick was on the alert.

He dashed his opponent's weapon aside by heavy stroke, and fixed the thief-catcher on his (Dick's) own blade.

Red Matthias roared like a dying tiger after a fierce encounter, and fell forward.

Dick's sword pierced his opponent's heart, and the boy turned sick with horror as his sword hilt went with a dull thud against his enemy's throbbing breast.

He reeled backwards, with his hand to his head. The sight of his own fearful tragedy rendered him powerless.

Grace, seeing her lover stagger, thought he was hit. A lamentable cry that struck pity to every heart escaped her lips.

With one bounding leap she sprang to his side and caught him in her arms.

"It is done," he said faintly.

"No, no, Dick, dear, say not so," she cried in distress, misconstruing the meaning of his words, and seeing blood trickling down his clothes.

"Yes, yes, 'tis done, look," and he pointed to Red Matthias, who then sank lifeless to the earth, his hand locked in a death struggle over the sword that still quivered in his heart—the sword that had robbed him of life, and sent him to an untimely fate.

Grace shuddered at the sorrowful sight.

"You, Dick, dear; you are not hurt. Say that you are not," she murmured, almost deprived of speech, terrified with fear, and at the sight of her gallant lover's blood-besmeared garments.

THE SCENE IN THE CELL

"No, no, I am not hit," said Dick; "but he—he—I—I have killed him."

"So much the better," exclaimed the fair girl; "but you are hit, I am sure. What is all this blood?"

"Merely a scratch, my darling," he said.

"Thank Heaven 'tis no worse," murmured the devoted girl.

A third shriek then rent the air in piercing accents, and a second officer fell dabbled in the gore of his companion, mortally wounded.

"Stop this bloody work," exclaimed Dick with sudden energy.

Every sword was lowered.

At that moment there was a clatter of approaching horses.

A few seconds more, and a large body of highwaymen came thundering upon the fearful scene, surrounded by Big Bullskin.

"Sad work this," said the gigantic fellow.

"Of their own seeking," said Dick. "Munroe, I put these gentlemen under arrest."

"Blindfold every one and take them to the haunt."

The noblemen looked at the boy in speechless surprise.

"This is confounded ingratitude," exclaimed one.

"No, it's not," said Dick.

Despite all their remonstrance, they were blindfolded, and led away to the haunt.

Dick turned away with Grace, and followed his comrades as the remaining officers raised the dabbled corses of their leader and companions, and bore them away from the tragic scene.

CHAPTER CI.

OUR young friend, Victor St. James, on arriving at Cornwall, formed a resolution to see his father, from whom he had been sundered so long, through the treachery of his cousin Reuben; but each time he neared his childhood's home a strange feeling took possession of him, and caused him to return to the little inn where he had taken up his quarters.

The third day now dawned, the young noble growing uneasy through the hideous presentiments that racked his brain with the torture of their terrible nature, started out with the firm determination to learn the worst, for he feared that some terrible impending calamity awaited him.

Again, on nearing his grand old ancestral home he became fearfully depressed and melancholy sad.

He stood and gazed at the window, where often in bygone days when returning from a ramble he saw the proud, glaring face of his sire watching him.

He saw no kindly face there, nothing to recall the happy days gone by; all was wonderfully changed and sombre.

He heaved a deep, desponding sigh, and with a longing, troubled look at his old homestead he was turning to go, for he could not find courage enough to inquire after his sire, when he caught sight of a sad, beautiful face looking from an upper window anxiously at him.

The apparition of that fair, white face sent a pang to his utmost soul that bewildered him.

"What means this terrible mystery?" he murmured; "*she* here? and with all the appearance of a captive! Heaven! What can it mean?"

The young noble drew his hand across his throbbing brow, and then clasping his hands together he looked up imploringly at the face at the window.

"Edith, my own! I pray you tell me what this means," he murmured.

His wail floated up in melancholy accents, and brought tears to the pretty eyes of the captive.

She put a finger upon her lip to demand silence, and then vanished from the window.

He stood—his fancies taking a thousand different shapes—waiting with expectant joy for her to come to him; but he kept his gaze fixed upon the window where he had first seen her, and there she appeared again.

Her little hand, trembling, was put between the iron bars that guarded against any ingress, and a little note floated to his feet.

He picked it up, and anxiously scanned the contents, which ran thus:—

"Victor,—If you love me still, disguise yourself, and make your way to my assistance. I am kept here a prisoner by my unnatural father. To-morrow he forces me to marry one whose presence I detest. Come soon to rescue   "Yours still devoted,
"EDITH."

St. James read it over several times, as though hardly understanding it.

"Her father keeps her here!" he cogitated. "I barely understand. If I fall in the attempt she shall be saved."

And kissing his sword-point to heaven and his hand to her, he departed.

On arriving at his lodgings he sat down, meditating how next to proceed.

A knocking at his chamber-door startled him.

"Who's there?" he asked.

The door opened.

Mine host put his head timidly into the room.

"If you please, sir," he said, "a young man, who says his name is Shanks, wants to see your lordship."

"Shanks!" exclaimed St. James, with gladdened surprise. "Shanks, my valet."

"Yes, my lord," shouted the faithful fellow.

Before the landlord had time to make a retreat, Shanks bounded like a ball over his head, and fell upon his young master's breast.

"Oh! my dear master!" cried Shanks. "Oh! my dear master! I—I—"

Ere he felt the apple core, of which he was supplied with, a moderate-sized piece rise in his swallow, and stop his utterance, he fell upon his knees, and pressed his master's hands to his lips, while big tears rolled down his sunken cheeks.

Even St. James had recourse to his white cambric.

"Come, there's a good fellow," he said, in a choked voice, now and then applying the handkerchief to his eyes. "Get up Shanks."

Shanks sprang to his feet; then master and man clung in grief and happiness around each other's neck.

"My kind, good master, I am so happy to see you again," said Shanks.

"And I, Shanks, am quite as happy to see you; but tell me—"

After several moments of affectionate embrace, Victor St. James sat down, and told his valet to do likewise.

He did so by his master's side.

The poor fellow had wonderfully wasted away, his long face, with sunken cheeks and hollow eyes, wore a horrified expression of pitiful misery.

His master noticed the alteration.

"By Jove, Shanks!" he remarked, "you would make a capital Don Quixote."

"What for?" inquired the valet, innocently.

"I never saw a more perfect resemblance to the adventurous knight before. What the deuce have you been doing with yourself?"

"Nothing, my lord—nothing."

"Why, you look as though you had not tasted food for the last six months."

"More I ain't, not since that time when you took me up to London and lost yourself."

"Shanks, you respectable liar, you unmanageable lacquey."

Shanks looked at his master with his hungry mouth wide open, staring at his master in blank astonishment.

"You disembodied shadow, can you sit there?"

Shanks got up to see if there was anything under him, and then sat down again.

"Yes, my lord, quite comfortable, thank you," he said.

"Can you sit there?" continued St. James, severely.

Shanks nodded.

"And tell me those confounded lies?"

"What lies?" asked the valet, surprised.

"Have you the confounded impertinence to tell me you have not eaten anything since we parted?"

"More I ain't, my lord."

"Then how did you live?"

"Why, I had to force it down my throat, else I should have been dead long ago."

"And why was it you lost your appetite?"

"Because I've been very much worried," simpered Shanks.

"Worried! in what way?"

"Through your absence," said Shanks, meekly, blinking to keep back the scalding tears that ran down his careworn cheeks. "I never slept night or day since you've been away, and—and—now I've found you, you are cross with me—boo—oo."

No longer could he keep back the emotion that swelled his breast. Giving vent to his pent-up grief, he fell upon his knees at his master's feet.

St. James was deeply touched by this mark of true devotion; taking the poor fellow's hand, he faltered in a broken voice—

"I did not mean to be cross, Shanks; get up, there's a good fellow, and let's hear what's been going on since I have been away."

Shanks looked the picture of sorrowful despair as he raised his head and gazed imploringly into his master's face.

"Come, jump up," St. James said, "I have some very important matters on hand that must be seen to this evening."

"And I," said Shanks, getting up, "have something very important to say to you."

"Well, let's have dinner. We can talk over what matters we want settled. I feel awfully peckish; and to judge by a hungry man's look, I should say you felt almost wolfish."

"No, my lord," Shanks said, faintly, "I ain't hungry."

"Nonsense; drink that glass of wine, it will give you an appetite."

The valet drank the beverage with an apparent relish, and held out the glass for a second supply.

St. James filled it again, and told him to order dinner for both.

The wine produced a wonderful effect upon Shanks. It brought a cheerful flush to his cheeks, and invigorated him with new life, and, in fact, entirely altered his miserable appearance.

"Shanks himself again," exclaimed St. James, with a smile, as his valet marched out of the room with a stealthy step to command the innkeeper to prepare their banquet.

Mine host sent a waiter up to prepare the table. Shanks followed him, and stood, leaning over the back of a chair, watching with an air of inspired dignity until he spread the cloth and laid the things.

The man was leaving the room, when Shanks took two strides after him, clutched hold of his collar, pulled him back, and twisted him round.

They stood face to face, glaring at each other like a pair of demons.

"What's that for?" asked the waiter, a good mind to floor his assailant; but a better mind told him he had better not.

Shanks pointed to the table.

"Do you call that laid fit for two gentlemen?" he said.

"Yes. Don't you?"

"No."

"Then lay it better," was the pert answer.

"What!" thundered Shanks, crimson to the roots of his air with rage. "You shadow of a washer, lay it better, or I'll—I'll smash you, you animated lath!"

The man laughed at him mockingly.

"What are you?" he said.

The man was lost for a simile, or he would not have asked.

"What am I?" shouted Shanks. "I'll show you, if you don't alter that cloth."

"Look here," said the waiter in his turn, growing furious, "I don't want any of yer sauce, or I'll soon put you on yer back."

"You?" said Shanks, shaking his head in the other's face.

"Yes, me," said the man, clutching Shanks by the nose, and pushing him backwards.

This was more than the vain-glorious Shanks could possibly stand.

To be degraded by such an outrage.

Struck before the eyes of his master.

For several seconds he stood contemplating how to seek revenge.

But before entering upon any deadly encounter, he wished to ascertain—by drawing

the back of his hand under the end of his squeezed nasal organ—if the other fellow had drawn the ruby.

Finding he had not, he muttered—

"He pulled my nose."

"And I'll do it again," said the other, overhearing his enemy.

Shanks had cooled down a little, and reflected upon the danger which he might incur by any rashness; but when his opponent spoke to add a fresh insult to those already simmering in the hero valet's breast, the whole boiled over, and caused a fearful explosion.

Before the waiter was aware of the contemplated attack, his assailant made one bound across the room, and fell upon him like a thunderbolt.

The sudden, unexpected shock brought him heavily to the floor.

He clutched as he fell, caught hold of Shanks's long, untrained hair, to which he held on like grim death, and pulled the lacquey down.

Then a fierce encounter took place.

Clutching at each other's legs, sending out the fists like sledge-hammers, with intent to bung up a optic, or disfigure their thoroughbred Roman nasal organs, which often got in the way, and received a heavy blow for being too forward.

They closed.

Had a fierce struggle.

Rolled over.

Parted.

Rolled from each other.

Rolled forward again.

Met.

Another fierce struggle.

Shanks got a black eye.

Other fellow gory nose.

Other fellow had enough.

Cried quarter.

Shanks, not envious of black eye, gave the other fellow one.

Other fellow, not envious of gory nose, gave Shanks one.

The odds they had fairly squared up.

Shanks felt immediately confused.

A blackened optic and gory nose was more than his dignity could bear.

The other fellow was getting up, when he

hit him a fearful blow in the wind, that knocked him down again gasping, and entirely at the mercy of his enemy.

Mercy, is there such a thing in war, when everyone fights for life and glory?

Shanks argued the point in his own mind, and mentally ejaculated—

"Revenge! Ha! ha!"

Springing nimbly to his feet, he clutched the pepper-box with trembling hand—a dark, cruel purpose kindling in his blinking eyes.

Stooping over his helpless foe, his face gleaming with fiendish triumph, he deliberately shook the torturing dust over his nose.

It worked with magic effect. His features were drawn up into horrible contortions. He sneezed, the shock shook the room, everything rattled and vibrated.

Shanks was terribly startled. He thought he had thrown gunpowder over the lacquey, and he had exploded.

While standing, fear-stricken, through the cruelty of his own act, the waiter bounded up, and darted upon him with the fury of a maddened tiger.

They fell. Another battle took place. Shanks soon overpowered his assailant, raised him from the floor by the collar, dragged him out of the room, stood him on the edge of the top stair, and placing his foot in the other's extremity, hoisted him over the banisters.

When he returned, with all the consequence of a conquering hero, he found his master rolling over the floor in a fit of convulsive laughter.

Fearing that there was something serious the matter with his young master, he clutched the nearest vessel at hand that contained water, and dashed the content's over St. James's face.

He recovered on the instant.

"Confound the fellow! What are you doing?" he exclaimed, jumping up.

"I, oh dear!" spluttered Shanks. "I thought my dear master——"

"You idiot!" interrupted Sir James.

"No I didn't."

"Didn't what, you effigy?"

"Think you idiot—effigy."

"By Jove! now, this is too bad to be called an idiot and an effigy by one's own lacquey. I shall certainly have to teach you better manners."

"Why, my lord?—what for? You misunderstood me."

"How, sir? Explain."

"Yes, sir, I will."

"Make haste."

"Oh dear, yes, sir; well it was this."

"What?"

"Why, when I came into the room, I thought you were in a fit, so I dashed the water over you to bring you to again."

"And how dare you take such an unwarrantable liberty?"

"I did it for the best."

"Did it for the best, did you?"

"Yes."

"Don't do it again."

"No."

The young nobleman tried to keep a serious face, but the deplorable object Shanks looked caused him to burst out laughing again.

"A pretty beauty you look, certainly," he said.

Shanks did not think so.

"Do you think I can take you out, looking that sight? Your face was never too handsome!"

"No," said Shanks," hurt by the sharp rebuke, "it ain't the face that makes the man, my heart was always in the right place, and though——"

"There, there!" interrupted St. James, touched by the sad earnestness of the other's voice. "You are a very stupid fellow. I did not mean what I said. Go and see if we are to have any dinner to-day."

Shanks forgave his master, and went to obey his command, but just as he got to the door mine host entered.

He glared spitefully at Shanks as he put the repast on the table, and left the room in a sullen, dogged manner.

"Now, Shanks," said Victor St. James, as they sat down to dinner, "I should like to know how you found me out here."

"It is some months since you went to London; that was where I last saw you," began Shanks; "I think, as well I can remember, that you and several other gentlemen, to serve some lady who had been decoyed from her home to the Old Priory, near Hounslow, where you went. I wanted to accompany you but you would not let me. However, I followed you in the distance. Saw you enter, and waited for you to come out again; but none of you made your appearance. Three days and nights I kept a careful watch over the place. At length I became uneasy and frightened at your absence; for I felt that you had fallen into danger.

"Still, I had a little hope, thinking, perhaps, that you may have got out another way; so, with that hope, I went out day after day in search of you at least a fortnight, going all over London, and calling at every place where I knew you frequented; but everywhere I went I met with the same answer. No one had seen or heard anything of you.

"As a last resource, to find you I returned here to Cornwall, and when I arrived I met with a terrible adventure."

He paused to look at his master with a troubled expression that plainly showed his mind was burdened with a fearful remembrance.

"What was the nature of your terrible adventure?" inquired St. James.

His brow clouded, as though he feared to hear the evidence.

Shanks hesitated. His mouth was opened several times to speak, but emotion shook his frame and choked his utterance.

"Speak! Why this apparent horror?" demanded St. James.

"Ah! my master," the valet began, "it is horror, I know. If I tell you, the shock will be fatal news."

The young nobleman looked dismally at his man.

His suspicions now took a torturing turn.

All the misgivings he had felt—all the strangeness of his childhood's home—and the fair captive—now rose before his eyes in a terrible vision.

"Don't tell me, Shanks," he said faintly.

He drew his trembling hand across his sweaty brow, and fell back in his chair, powerless—his handsome face fearfully white,

and his eyes exhibiting the torture of the fears he felt at heart.

The faithful Shanks sprang up in an awful fright, ran to his master's side with a glass of whine, and endeavoured, by forcing St. James's clenched teeth open, to pour the contents down his throat.

He succeeded.

The stimulant had the required effect upon the young nobleman.

"I am better," he said, kindly grasping his valet's hand.

"I am very glad. Do you think you will go off again like that?!' Shanks asked, anxiously.

"No, it is merely weakness brought on through close captivity."

"Captivity?" queried the valet.

"Yes; you have not heard where I was. Sit down, I will tell you."

Shanks drew his chair to his master's side.

"Well," began St. James, "the night I went to the Old Priory, near Hounslow. it was, as you say, to save a young lady, who had been decoyed there by some rascally villians. I did my best to save her, was treacherously shot in the attempt, and conveyed to a dungeon without light or air. Of course such treatment played upon my constitution."

Shanks assented to the truth of that.

Victor St. James then entered into the long rigmarole of his confinement, relating the offer he had had made to him by the two strange women.

The unexpected but welcome appearance of gallant Tom.

And finally their gloomy journey in the house, and the curious way they escaped.

Shanks expressed his astonishment at the revelation.

"But I should like to know how you discovered me here?" said the nobleman.

"Well, my lord, since I've been in Cornwall I've been on the watch for you," replied the young man, that I was stayin here."

"I knew that you would return some day."

"Well, but that's not telling me how you learnt."

"Well, this is how it was. I had been on

the look out in the morning, as I am every morning (but I shan't say for what), and when returning I saw you enter here. Only seeing your back I thought, perhaps, I might have been mistaken, so I inquired of the host if you resided here, and he said yes; so that's how I came to find it out."

"It was fortunate, Shanks, that you should be passing at the very time I was entering.

"Yes, my dear master, it was; and you don't know the joy I felt when I found it was you."

Shanks shook his head, as though he knew what his master was about to say.

Our young friend evinced some surprise at the coolness of the action.

"How the deuce do you know what I was going to say?"

"Pretty well guess."

"The devil you can?"

Shanks nodded.

"On what point?" inquired his master.

"Concerning your home?"

St. James started.

"How know you this?"

"I think so."

"Well, listen."

Shanks was all attention.

Victor went on—

"Three days since, I was in Cornwall."

"And me not to find you before."

"Don't interrupt."

Shanks was silent.

"Three days I have been in Cornwall."

"Yes," said Shanks, as though he fairly understood his master the first time, and did not care for repetition.

"Silence !"

Shanks sank back in his chair.

"Three days since I have been in Cornwall, as I before said."

"The third time," groaned Shanks.

"The third time what, image?" asked St. James, angrily, annoyed at being so often interrupted.

"Nothing," said Shanks.

"Then don't speak again."

"No."

Victor looked at him sternly.

"For the fourth time I repeat," he began again.

Shanks knew what was to follow, so put his fingers in his ears not to hear.

"I have been in Cornwall for three days," Sir James went on.

Shanks now removed his fingers, his master having got over Cornwall.

"This morning," the nobleman continued "I went out with the intention of seeing my father."

Shanks changed countenance.

He was the keeper of a fearful mystery—a tragedy of foul darkness.

St. James did not perceive the change, so he went on—

"I reached my home, but some strange feeling of dread kept me from entering, and I fancied that it seemed wonderfully changed since I last saw it. For some moments I stood transfixed in a kind of stupor, and when, with a last look at the old house before I departed, I was startled by the white beautiful face of Lady Edith at an upper window; this apparition bewildered me alarmingly. I endeavoured to make her hear me. I asked her why she was there. She remained in silence, and dropped a note to me."

He took the missive from his pocket and read it.

"This," he said, "troubles me more than anything else. How her brutal parent can keep her a captive in my sire's house entirely puzzles me. Where can be my father? Shanks, do you know anything?"

He asked this in a strange tone of voice.

"I do," answered Shanks, gloomily; "but you had better not hear it until after we have saved the lady, because it would unnerve you, and make you unfit for the adventure."

"You are right, Shanks. What you know keep to yourself until we have safely got the lady out of her captor's power. She must be saved, and if I fall in the attempt I shall not have to hear that which I dread to think it is."

"You said you would take me with you, said Shanks.

"Yes; I shall require you, but how can we get admittance to the house, if strangers?"

CHAPTER CII.

THE MYSTERIOUS TRAVELLERS.

It was morning, and the first grey streaks of dawn began to light the sky when two travellers, weary and lame, left the shelter of a deep wood and pursued their dreary way.

The one was hale and strong, and his cheek flushed with youthful health; the other was bowed with age, and leant heavily on his taff.

"It's no use, lad," said the elder of the two, "my leg's too bad to walk; that cursed bullet has nearly broken the bone."

"Oh, come on, don't give way like that; we shall be caught if we linger here."

"I cannot help it, lad; but you need not stay."

"What! leave you to your fate! No—no! if they scent us out, let them."

"And you will have to share my sufferings."

"Certainly! and fight for you with the last drop of my blood, if needed."

The old man groaned with the agony of his wound; but the words of his companion seemed to cheer him a little.

"Your arm?" he said, "I feel weak."

The arm was extended, and by its aid he managed to reach the hollow of the old oak tree.

The trunk was sufficiently large to hold the pair, and the young man having assisted his weak companion to enter, followed after.

"I feel better now," said the old man; "thanks to your help."

"No thanks, father. I have my health and strength!" Would you had the same!"

"Ah! well, boy, it is no use wishing. Come, tell me, how it comes that I see you here. You are many miles from your home?"

"Yes. I am," replied the youth; "a great many."

"You must know, I was bound apprentice to a tailor in Huntly, a little crooked wretch, who, whenever anybody offended him, always wreaked out his ill nature on me.

"I bore with him long, not daring to break my apprenticeship for fear of the fine that would fall on my poor father, although many a thrashed skin I got, and every time my knuckles itched to be at this tailor's ugly face. I was always obliged to sir and master him, and if by chance I called him any other name, I got the length of the needle in my flesh instantly.

"This was not long to be borne by a lad of any spirit.

"One time we were sewing on a board together at the manse of Auchindoir, and the minister and his wife were sitting by the fire in the same apartment.

"It was Saturday evening, and my master was anxious to have the job done that night, and kept urging me to ply and make long stitches.

"This last injunction he durst not give openly, but there was an understood term which conveyed his meaning.

"This was, 'Sit yond, boy, sit yond.'

"This he kept repeating and repeating that evening, and at every hint gave me a prod with his needle, until, in a fit of impatience, I returned—

"'The deil's i' the bodie, for I can sit na farther yond unless I baiss.'

"He gave me such a look. I regarded it not, but laughed, and joked, and crooned—

"'Cauld kail in Aberdeen, an' sowins in Strathbogie,' and 'The Tailor fell o'er the bed, needles an' a'.'

"But the minister said, 'Aha, William, so the secret is out regarding the order to your lad always to _sit yond_, therefore give up, and go your ways home, and come back on Monday morning, for I will not have my clothes, or my boy's clothes, spoiled by your long stitches.'

"'But tell me this, sir,' said my master, who wanted to put the matter off as a joke, 'whether do you think long stitches or short sermons are the worst?'

"'William, I want none of your profane and homely jests,' said the parson, 'therefore keep them to yourself, and give up my work; I can have another tradesman to finish it.'

"'Yes, you can, sir,' said my master, 'and so can I go and hear another minister.'

"'I have the advantage of you there, for you cannot have a tradesman like me in Aberdeenshire, whereas I can have a far better minister.

"'For I maintain, that in short sermons often repeated, there is greater blame than in long stitches on new ground.'

"Thus parted the parson of Auchindoir

and my master in high chagrin, the consequences of which I was doomed to abide.

"No sooner were we beyond the glebe lands than he said with ill-feigned civility—

"'Well, you have behaved yourself like a sensible young man and a young gentleman to-night.'

"I was going to say that I had spoken rashly and unadvisedly, and was sorry for it, but that it was the severe prick with the needle that caused it."

"Before I got my answer arranged he struck me such a blow above the right eye that made the blood stream.

"I chanced to have the lapboard carrying in my right hand, a substantial plane-tree deal more than two feet long, with which I gave him such a rap over the head that I made his skull ring again, and his eyes to stand in back water.

"'How dare you for your soul, sirrah, lift your hand against your master?' said he.

"'I'll not be struck like a dog in that manner by the King, or the Duke of Gordon,' said I, 'and far less by a bowed tailor.'

"This answer put the creature perfectly mad, for he valued himself greatly on his personal appearance, and he flew on me like a tiger.

"My spirit of resistance was fairly up.

"I returned blow for blow, and then as desperate a battle ensued as ever was fought.

"In a few minutes he began to quail, and though his lips quivered with rage, he was rather frightened, and wanted to call a parley.

"'Come, come, this will never do,' he said, 'down on your knees, and beg my pardon.'

"'I'll be —— if I will,' said I.

"'You, sirrah, you'll be —— if you will!'

"'Do you say so to me?' said he in a loud, majestic tone, for two masons appeared coming before us.

"'Then, sir, know that your life is in my hand, and I will chastise you till you be no more.'

"He threw off his coat and waistcoat, and fell to me like a day's work.

"I held down my head, and took a tempest of blows on my shoulders and neck.

"I then ran with my head full drive on the pit of his stomach, which made him stagger and fall backward.

"I gave him just one fundamental kick, and then turned and laughed aloud.

"He flew after me in desperate fury, striking with both feet and hands, fighting in glorious style, for the two masons were now close at hand.

"I could fight none, save as a bullock or ram, but having frequently seen these fight desperately, I followed their example instinctively, and ran always against my dumpy, mis-shapen master with my head full drive.

"He tore out my hair, and cursed and swore most manfully, but I regarded not these, giving him always the other punch, and whenever I hit him fairly, whether on the face or breast, I knocked him down.

"The two mason lads rolled on the green with laughter, for, to make the thing the more ludicrous, whenever I knocked him down with my head, I turned round and flung at him with my heels like a horse, thus in my warfare imitating the beasts only.

"I soon mauled him so that he could not rise, but there he lay, threatening future vengeance, and cursing me most emphatically.

"He threw first the goose, and then the lapboard at my head, which I eschewed, and then ran up and flung at him like an incensed or vicious horse, giving him some good hard kicks, and then went off and left him.

"Instead of going home, I went straight to Aberdeen, where I could have procured employment as a journeyman, but durst not remain for my late incensed master; so I went on board a Hull coasting vessel, and continued in her five years as a cabin-boy and sailor, and by that time had become quite attached to a nautical life.

"I went one voyage to New York and another to Lisbon; but the description of these voyages would only tire you.

"After sailing about for some time, I got acquainted with a gang of smug——"

"Ah, what's that?"

CHAPTER CIII.

"THERE is only one way."

"And that is?"

"By going in disguise."

"And then?"

"It will be all right if we can get it."

"That's the thing; but how are we to get in?"

"Well, I'll tell you."

"Go on, there's a good fellow. I am anxious to hear your plans."

"Will you dress up as a lady?"

"A lady!"

"Yes, you don't know what a pretty one you would make. Lord Ecclestone, the gentleman you will have to ask for, will be quite enamoured with you."

"Don't be stupid, Shanks, who's Lord Ecclestone?"

"Oh, you know him."

"Nonsense, my good fellow, I never heard the name before."

"Well, having it your own way, how am I to get the disguise, and how am I to proceed even if I do get it?"

"I can get the disguise; at least Susan can. You'll wear it. Go to your own house and ask to see Lord Ecclestone. The flunkey will take you for some mighty fine lady—give yourself a grand name—and he'll want to usher you into the drawing-room. But don't go; object on the ground that you wish to see his lordship immediately. The lacquey will then retire to announce your presence.

"Directly he's turned his back quietly open the door to let me in.

"We must then make for the closet at the top of the kitchen stairs, and wait till all is quiet before we do any more.

"We shan't be found there, because they think the closet is haunted, and no one will go near it; but in case we are discovered in the attempt to get there, we must be provided with a pair of pistols each and a sword."

St. James listened to his valet's instructive device without once interrupting.

He thought it more easily arranged than carried into execution.

The idea was as good as any other they then thought of, and the young nobleman resolved to put it into execution.

"What do you think of it? asked Shanks."

"Very capital indeed! Go and get the disguise, we have no time to lose, the hour is getting late."

Shanks went out quite elated.

Half-an-hour later he returned with a complete beautiful attire of a female.

Our young friend donned the things; admired himself in a mirror, and thought he made a capital lady.

Which he did.

"Look to the priming of the pistols," he said, "and try the temper of the swords."

Two pairs of chased barrelled pistols were laid on the table, primed, and two swords polished to a dazzling brilliancy laid by their side.

Victor hid his weapons in such a position as to have them ready to hand at any moment.

Shanks did likewise.

Then they both set out.

To prevent suspicion, Shanks was attired as a thorough-bred lacquey and followed at a respectful distance behind his young master.

When Victor came in sight of his old home he was filled, as on previous occasions, with those fearful misgivings that made him awfully faint and nervous.

He knew to give way now, or retract from his purpose, would be forfeiting his own honour and the life of the gentle girl he loved.

He pictured her pleading, tearful face at the window, remembered the silent oath he had taken to heaven to protect her, and with these thoughts he made a desperate attempt to shake off the lethargy that oppressed his spirits.

Motioning to Shanks to keep back, he dashed up the steps, and with trembling hand he knocked loudly at the door.

The door was opened by a powdered flunkey, and all the ceremony the valet had predicted was gone through.

Shanks sneaked away under the wall while his master entered, and stood by the side of the steps, his heart beating at an unusual rate, and his mouth parched with the fire of suspense.

The door opened quietly.

Shanks from where he stood bounded into the hall with the elasticity of a cat.

The door shut with a bang.

"Quick!" said the young noble. "The man is returning."

He clasped his valet's hand, and both flew towards the haunted closet.

At the very moment when they were about to enter, two of the house menials came out from an adjoining room.

Seeing our two adventurers enter that dreaded place, they were terrified, and sank down, shrieking with horror.

The piercing cries that rang through the house brought the whole household to the scene of excitement.

Victor St. James fastened the door on the inside.

"We are discovered," he said, "and must fight to the death!"

"To the death!" repeated Shanks, with chattering teeth.

CHAPTER CIV.

THE BANQUET—THE INTERRUPTION—DICK'S RIDE FOR LIBERTY—MEETING WITH AN OLD FRIEND—HOW THE OFFICERS WERE THROWN OFF THE TRACK OF TYBURN DICK AND CAPTURED OUR HEROINE.

THE twelve noblemen who fought in Dick's defence were taken to the haunt, blindfolded, assisted from their horses in the same state, and conducted into the large hall.

The bandages were removed from their eyes, and the elegant display that met their gaze banished the fear of treachery on the highwaymen's side they entertained.

A splendid banquet was spread upon the table—a glorious feast.

Every description of viands, choice and rare delicious wines, and every species of fruit was there—handsomely decorated with elegant vases of fragrant flowers, that filled the air with a delicious odour.

The head of the table was occupied entirely by our hero, Captain Claude, fair Milly, and the beautiful Grace, who was now attired as her sex should be.

Dick's face flushed with proud admiration each time his gaze fell upon her, so queenly did she look on that evening.

His was not the only admiring gaze.

Many of his noble guests almost envied him of the lovely girl.

Bullskin and Swig sat at the end of the table, where all the others—the highwaymen fraternity and the twelve noblemen—were seated.

Dick rose to speak.

There was a hush on the instant.

"Gentlemen," he said, "I wish to sh my gratitude for your gallant behaviour me you see the gentleman at dice."

"By jove! how capital!" exclaimed of the twelve.

Dick continued—

"When I left you at the inn, I said we should meet at twelve. Near Hounslow we met."

"By Jove!" said another of the twelve, "and to think we did not know you."

"We met," he went on, "but as I was overpowered, and remained at your mercy and disposal, when the officers came up to capture me, you saw my danger, severed the bonds that held me powerless, and fought nobly in my defence. Gentlemen, accept my grateful thanks."

The gentlemen received this with a hearty cheer.

"Hurrah! hurrah! hurrah for Tyburn Dick?"

When this last deafening shout died away, and the guests were again seated—

"We hold a grand revel here to-night," Dick said. "Gentlemen, you will do us the honour of staying?"

The highwaymen received their delighted assent.

The repast was then began.

But, suddenly, there came a startling interruption.

A pistol was fired by some unseen person.

The ball whizzed past, within an inch of Dick's face, flew over the table, dashed a splendid decanter into a thousand atoms, and finally passed under a highwayman's arm, as he was in the act of raising a glass to his lips.

He dropped the glass in horror, thinking for a certainty he was hit.

But he was not, the shot passed without touching him.

Alarmed by this startling event, every one sprang up, swords leaped from their sheaths, and pistols gleamed in their hands.

Bullskin took his ponderous double-handed

'ord and went in the direction from whence the shot came.

"Brethren," he said, "there is a spy about. What shall be his doom, if found?"

"Death!" answered every voice.

"Follow me, and let's seek for the traitor."

He went forward, and after him a body of resolute men.

The gigantic fellow pulled aside a heavy pair of curtains that led to one of the entrances of the haunt.

A group of twenty officers were there concealed, with Simon Judas crouching down like a panther before them.

"I've done this," he said.

"Wretch! and this shall do for you," thundered Dick. He leaped forward, and made a furious cut at the traitor with his sword.

Bullskin caught the impetuous boy by the arm, and put him aside.

"Nay, my chief," he said, "such a death for him would be too good."

"What do you want?" he asked of the ing's officers.

"Tyburn Dick, for the murder of Matthias; give him up and the rest of you will be safe. Resist, and a bloody scene shall tell your fate!"

The man's lip curled in scorn.

"We could crash the life out of you all," "and not a mark should be left to tell that you ever existed."

"Do you mean us?" asked one of the officers.

"We do."

They dashed out; Munroe seized the traitor.

Dick went forward as his comrades prepared to meet the invaders.

"I am yours if you can catch me," the aring boy said. "Claude, detain the gentlemen till I return. Now, follow me!"

Out he dashed, with the officers after him.

The gallant boy made his way to the stable, mounted Fairy, and away he went.

No sooner had he gone than Grace appeared in her highwayman's costume, vaulted into the saddle of a white horse her lover had given her, and rode off too.

Away thundered the gallant steed with Dick on her back, and though the excited officers lashed and spurred their horses after him, still he kept far ahead.

The King's officers were going at their greatest speed.

But the boy was not making the least exertions to keep the start he had gained.

"They will have a cheerful ride," said Dick, caressing Fairy's neck; "but that is all they will get, I think."

Fairy thought so too, for ever as they fled, and their noise grew louder, she threw up her graceful head, as though in disdain at their attempt to overtake her.

Past Brompton and the adjacent neighbourhoods, sweeping like a whirlwind across the waste of land where the parks now bloom in verdant beauty.

And right on, using neither whip or spur, but riding on recklessly—joyously—gallantly —fearing nothing, daring all, and revelling gladly in the wild excitement of the chase!

The country, though open, was thorny, rough, and even, rising into hills, sloping into valleys, and here and there being shut off by great belts of trees.

With the last the boy was glad to meet.

Fairy had scampered away in the direction of the road to Edgware.

And had just reached the withered oak, known as Tyburn Tree, when three or four mounted men, who had been riding in another direction, turned at the sound of the horse's feet, and joined in the pursuit.

"The devil!" muttered Dick, "this is too bad; they are not fifty yards behind!"

Which was true, though disagreeable.

"I'll stop for a moment," thought the boy again, "the ill-mounted rascals! they are actually swearing at me!"

He drew rein suddenly.

Wheeled round.

And came to a dead halt.

Greatly puzzled by the sudden manoeuvre, the two foremost officers drew rein too.

The other six were still a long way behind.

Dick surveyed the astonished group with a cool glance of curiosity.

"What the deuce do you mean by clattering after me?" he asked, "you confounded impertinent scoundrels!—damme! you don't rob me, you rascally highwaymen! so you'd better keep back."

THE ENCOUNTER.

"Ha!" yelled one of the men, "here's a go! he thinks as how we're the high toby blokes, and he's a-going to shoot!—murder! —oh!

He turned round.

And cautiously got out of range of the long shining weapons held by the daring boy.

"I know you; but you don't plunder me. My pistols carry a long distance, and I aim uncommonly well; so now, gentlemen, right about! turn your ugly faces the other way. I shall shoot the last man."

The officers turned simultaneously, and were about to retrace their way, when a shout from the others caused them to pause.

"Hoy! hoy!"

"Stop him!"

"It's Tyburn Dick, the Boy Highwayman!"

With a cry they wheeled round again, and forward.

At that moment the form of a second rider, mounted on a beautiful white horse, and habited so like our hero that at a distance it was impossible to tell one from the other, made from a clump of trees about a hundred yards in advance of the hindmost pursuing party, and with a shout rode past those who were about to follow Dick.

"That's him!" shouted one. "That's the highwayman!—stop him!"

"If you can," said the rider.

And his heavy whip went against the speaker's head with a suddenness that raised an astonishing bump, and sent him head first to the ground.

Then the rider went on.

Passing Dick, and saying as he did so—

"Back to Hounslow as soon as these bloodhounds are off the scent."

Then away he went.

"Grace!" muttered Dick.

By this time the daring girl was nearly out of sight, with the three first officers riding after her.

"The highwayman!" they shouted, "we shall catch him!"

"Bang!"

"Oh!—murder!—I'm hit!"

A second officer rolled out of his saddle, and putting his hand underneath his coat tail, performed some extraordinary gymnastic gyrations on the ground.

"Hit him!" said the boy, replacing his weapon, "two down! they can help each other up."

But the man with the bump on his head, and the man with the bullet in his extremity, seemed to prefer lying down and uttering idiotic yells to anything else.

The other six on coming up were in doubt as to which one to follow.

Our heroine's sudden appearance on a white horse had mystified the whole affair.

The officers were in a difficulty.

One man hit upon a thought so brilliant that when he spoke it the effort made him fall over.

"We'll follow both," he said, "two more of you after the first rider; four of us will stick to this one."

"Quite an idea!" shouted Dick, who had not yet taken to flight again, "that's worth recollecting."

Drawing a second pistol, he shot the man in the leg.

"Now you won't forget?" he said, "good bye."

Touching Fairy's neck, he bounded away.

Fairly enraged, the officers kept up a spirited chase after both.

The second horseman dashed away towards Kilburn, hotly pursued by his pursuers. The boy went towards Harrow.

It was all open country there, right away from the spot where Tyburn Tree once stood, to the distant meadows of Kilburn, and the hill of Harrow looming up miles ahead.

A few houses intercepted the view here and there, a gentleman's mansion, perhaps; a roadside inn, or a block of smaller dwellings, converted to the use of the noble peasantry.

The circumstances of both the escaping horsemen being dressed nearly alike, and each riding a white horse, caused some doubts in the officers' minds as to which was Tyburn Dick, the Boy King of the Highwaymen, and which wasn't, they being both very young and so strikingly alike.

So, as we have stated once or twice before, they followed both.

But did not catch either.

The second rider on passing Dick, had said—

"If you escape, come back to me at Hounslow."

Then the boy knew her.

And some time afterwards the officers made her acquaintance.

Grace thought she had led the officers far enough out of her lover's track, so having gone a mile or two beyond Kilburn, she slackened her pace, that is to say the horse did, and dropping into an easy canter she let the officers draw near.

"He's winded," said one of the men.

"You be blowed," said another; "it's his way, then directly you goes to touch him he's off like a shot, and gets out of sight like a—"

He paused for a simile, and not finding one, said, "You be blowed," again.

But, contrary to their expectations, the horseman did not go off like a shot.

He seemed suddenly to discover that he had no cause to hurry.

It was a lovely day; calm, serene, and beautiful; rich with the song of birds, bright with the sun's glow, and fragrant with the perfume of flowers.

Our heroine seemed lost in admiration at the beauty of the scene; her gaze wandered from the verdant meadows, bright with daisies, and fertile with foliage.

"What do you want?" she asked, coming down suddenly from the sublimity of her meditation to the prosaic knowledge that two or three men were surrounding her.

"You," said the man. "We're up to these tricks; won't you come with us?"

"Ruffian!"

"I dare say. I know you."

"Indeed!"

"Yes, indeed. You're the Boy Highwayman, or I'm a Dutchman."

The fair girl laughed.

"Of course," said the officer, "you ain't a boy any longer; but the name sticks to you, though you have grown older."

"Take your hand from my bridle, or something may stick to you."

Grace drew her hand suggestively.

The officer drew back.

"Keep close, mates," he said. "Shoot him if he shows fight."

"You dare not."

"Dare not?"

"No."

"Why?"

"Because it is so decreed by the King."

"Aha!" said the first officer.

"Aha!" said the second. "Now we've got him."

"We know it's him now," observed the third.

"Who?"

"Why Tyburn Dick. That's the very order we've got."

"Then you still intend to molest me?"

"We intend to take you now we've got you."

"You will repent this."

"Shall we?"

"I am not the one you take me for."

"No," said the officer, with a grin, "of course not."

Grace sheathed her sword."

"You think yourselves right," said she, "therefore, do but your duty; but I tell you over again, you are again in error."

"No use, captain, you're such an old soldier that there is no knowing how to take you. You never look twice alike, so we'll take you now and chance it. If we are wrong, we'll ax your pardon afterwards. Any how, we're only doing our duty."

"You persist, then?"

"We do."

"Very well, then, I will accompany you."

"That's the sort—saves trouble."

The whole party turned their horses' heads and rode back.

Our heroine did not seem greatly angered or terrified at the fact of her capture. A smile of satisfaction curled her lip, and she rode on in silence.

Meanwhile the others still stuck to Dick.

He was well in advance of them yet, riding down the road meditating on various things, and thinking of his fair one, when the sight of a single horseman coming towards him set his thoughts to work in a professional train, and, covering his face with a mask, he drew a pistol, and brought Fairy to a stand and waited.

The horseman saw him do this, and, with a shout, quickened his pace, drew his sword, and came down in gallant style.

"By Jove!" he said, "the real Boy Highwayman at last."

"The devil!" muttered Dick, "the very gentleman I saved from three ruffians the other night."

This was an adventure the readers have not heard of—in a few words we will relate it.

One evening, when our hero was returning to the haunt, his attention was called to a dark lonely spot in a field, from whence cries for help and loud fierce oaths proceeded, he jumped a ditch and hurried to the scene of action, where he found three brutal ruffians molesting the gentleman who now came towards him and his wife, a very beautiful woman.

The lady was snatched from her husband's side while they were walking along and carried into the field by the caitiffs.

The gentleman dashed after them, very much alarmed, to save his wife, and received a heavy blow on the head that felled him to the earth powerless.

Dick arrived in time to spoil the brute intent the men were going to carry out on their fair captive, and saved the gentleman from being murdered, and his lady hidden in a filthy bog, as was the intention of the footpads.

The brave boy slew two, the gentleman ran his sword through the other.

The lady was safe, and her husband was saved, and all through the intervention.

The two left the tragic scene, the wretched

496 TYBURN DICK.

corpses of the three ruffians remained food for birds of prey.

Dick received the tender gratitude of the lady for his warlike defence, and the eternal friendship of Lord Temple Grey, her husband, with a pressing invitation to make their home his whenever he chose.

"Stand!" said Dick, as the gentleman rode forward.

"By force!—the impertinent scoundrel! Why don't you do it in the old style—say your money or your life?"

"That's exactly what I mean."

"The devil!"

Temple Grey wheeled round, and raised his sword.

"Stand back, or I fire!" said the boy.

"Fire, you scamp! Draw your sword, and fight like a man!"

"Your money!"

Dick put his finger on the trigger.

"See you hanged first!" said Lord Temple. "If you won't fight, like a coward shoot me, and rob me!"

"Very well; I shall"—

"What?"

"Fight."

Dick replaced his pistol, and drew his sword.

"By Jove! that's the thing. I like that. By the way, I know a fellow exactly like you."

"Can he fight?"

"By Jove! you should see him."

"He don't fight as well as I do."

"Don't he? By Jove! you should see him."

"Did he ever fight with you?"

"No, he fought for me; and, by Jove, he soon polished off two fellows."

"And you killed the third."

"Ah!"

"Lord Temple Grey very nearly lost his life, and a very beautiful wife, in that affray."

"Why, now the devil"——began the noble.

Dick sheathed his sword, and removed his mask.

"So you really did not know me?" Dick said, coolly. "Why, my dear lord, if you

did not recognise me, no wonder the officers take me for the real knight of the road."

"I don't wonder, either," said Temple Grey. "I took you for him, and was going to pitch into you."

"I am glad I spoke in time," said Dick. "Hallo, who have we here?"

At that moment Devil Duke swept past like a whirlwind, with nearly two dozen officers in full pursuit.

Bill and Jerry, the two thief-catchers, were amongst the number.

No sooner did they see our hero than, detaching themselves, they called several of their companions towards them.

"Temple," said the boy, putting spurs to his horse; "those stupid fellows still take me for that desperate character, Tyburn Dick. Shall we humour the idea, and give them a ride?"

"We will," replied Grey, "by Jove! Hurrah!"

And away they went.

Temple Grey was well mounted, and he could keep in advance of the officers with but little effort.

Fairy went at an easy pace, or both officers and Temple would have been left far behind.

"I like this," said Lord Grey. "By Jove, it must be jolly to be a real highwayman."

"Do you think so?"

"Rather."

Dick shook his head.

"Such parts of it as this are all very well," he said; "but there are darker scenes in the dull reality."

"Never mind the dark scenes," exclaimed Grey. "Keep ahead! We'll ride to the deuce, and let them follow us."

"If they will."

They tried.

The pursuers followed bravely on, keeping the daring boy and his companion in sight until London was reached, and even then it required all the skill the boy possessed to elude them.

"I have an idea," said Lord Temple Grey, suddenly.

"What is it?"

"We'll go to my friend's house, he'd like to join in the fun. These fellows seem quite satisfied that you are the man they want."

"Let's have the idea," said Dick.

"It's coming."

"I am listening."

"Why, you lend Horace Clare your coat and your horse, and let the officers follow him."

"Capital," said Dick.

"We will keep close to them, and after Clare has led them about half round London, let them catch him."

"Excellent."

"It will be great fun to see how savage they will be to think that they have followed the wrong fellow."

"A glorious idea."

"It is," said Temple, "it's wonderful how I came to think of it."

So Dick thought, but he was too polite to say so.

They rode at a pace exceedingly tantalising to their intended capturers.

Temple Grey's horse was a thorough-bred —an animal of great speed and power; it was not like the beautiful Arabian, but it had a noble style of action, and great power of endurance.

So having, by going rapidly at first, and seeing what was the utmost speed at which the officers could follow, got some little distance in advance, our hero and his friend measured their pace, and kept it.

The officers were exasperated.

They were growing quite hot, and their horses were beginning to blow, but they were as far from catching the daring highwayman as ever.

"Temple," he said, "we shall want a little time for Horace Clare to change his coat, and say a few words, so we may as well leave those fellows behind."

"All right," said Lord Grey, "shall we tell them so?"

"We will let them see it; that will, I think, be sufficient."

"By Jove, yes; save a fellow's breath. I wonder how long a fellow could ride at this pace, without wanting a good Samaritan to bring oil and balm."

His horse was going at a pace rather unusual, and his master was therefore accustomed to his style of action.

The consequence was, to some extent, unpleasant.

But the gallant gentleman cared little for personal discomfort, when engaged in the excitement of such a chase.

Obedient to his companion's wish, he spurred onward, and soon left the officers out of capturing distance.

"We have done them now," he said, as they turned into the street where Horace Clare lived; "they are quite out of sight."

"But they will follow closely," said the boy; "they seem to possess some peculiar faculty of finding people out."

"Not very strange," said Temple.

"Why?"

He pointed to the ground.

"Our hoof-marks," he said. "We wust be quick, or they will follow us by them, and spoil the rest of our fun."

"Confound the hoof-marks," said Dick. "Why do they not put stones in the road?"

They drew up at Clare's house.

"Hallo," said Horace, appearing at the drawing-room window; "what's afoot?"

His friends dismounted, and entered the house.

"Come here," said Grey, "here's such fun, there's a lot of officers after Mr. Henry Winter (a name Dick had given) they think he's the real Boy Highwayman."

"What an idea."

"Yes, by Jove; so we have led them such a distance; and then I had an idea. Mr. Winter said it was brilliant."

"Glorious," said Dick."

"Glorious, was it?—just the same."

"But the idea," interrupted Clare.

"Is that you should put on Mr. Winter's crimson coat, mount his horse, and give the fellows a devilish run."

"So they take him for the real Boy Highwayman then?" asked Clare.

"Yes, confound their impertinence," said Dick.

"Can't wonder at it, though, considerin I made the same mistake," Temple Grey said.

"What a capital idea."

"Though not pleasant," said Dick.

"Especially when a fellow has a herd of

these brutes shouting after him," Lord Grey remarked.

" It's not comfortable," said Dick.

" By Jove! I should like it," said Horace Clare.

" Try it, old fellow," the friend said.

" Willingly. What is the idea? I am to put on Mr. Winter s coat?"

" Hat, boots, and ride my horse," put in Dick.

" Do you think I shall look like the Boy Highwayman then?"

" As much like him as I do, don't you think?" asked our hero.

" I hope so."

" You would not if you were hunted after like I am.

" It will be capital fun if the stupid asses do take me for Tyburn Dick, won't it? By Jove! won't they be wild when they discover their mistake!"

" By Jove! I do hate those fellows!" said Temple Grey. " You must lead them a devilish good run."

" Won't I, that's all."

" They have got the scent of bloodhounds,' said Dick, " and if you are not out pretty sharp they will storm the place."

" They had better not," said Clare, pointing to a huge blunderbuss that hung over the fireplace.

At that moment they heard the clatter of horses feet coming down the road.

Lord Grey went to the window.

" They come!" he exclaimed.

" Let them come," replied his friend.

A few seconds more they came thundering past the house, in full pursuit of some unfortunate traveller they saw riding peacefully along, and whom they took for their intended prisoner.

" These idiots!" said Temple Grey; " they are after some other fellow now—for the Boy Highwayman."

" The deuce take them, why did they not wait till I had got out! How the devil shall I make them see me?"

" Ride round the other way, and meet them," said Dick.

" Bravo!" exclaimed the young noble enthusiastically.

He had during this time exchanged costumes with our hero.

" Will you follow me?" he asked.

" We," said Dick, " we will meet you near Hounslow.

" By Jove! now for excitement! Adieu, old fellow!"

On he went.

Dick and Lord Temple Grey watched him from the window as he rode away on the back of the boy's steed Fairy.

" They have found out their mistake," said Lord Temple, " and are returning."

So they were. Horace Clare waved his handkerchief and shouted—

" Follow, if you dare!"

This exasperated the King's officers, and turning their horses' head in the direction he had taken, they thundered after him.

" Do you think they will overtake him?" asked Lord Grey, anxiously.

" Not while the steed he rides has got a leg," replied the boy. " We shan't have much time; he will be at Hounslow as soon as we."

" Then we will now depart."

They went out, rode away, and reached the appointed place.

Half an hour they waited, every moment expecting to see their friend.

An hour passed.

Still he came not.

Temple Grey grew weary.

" He must have met with danger," he said, sadly, for he loved his friend as a brother. " He is very rash, and would face the greatest peril when excited. I wish I had gone instead of him."

" Fear not," said Dick, " he may have mistaken his road."

The remark eased the mind of the nobleman.

Another hour passed, but still no Horace came.

Lord Temple's brow grew sad and thoughtful, his cheeks turned pale, and his eye restless, scanning the distant plain with an anxious look.

Dick, too, was sad. He blamed himself for his noble friend's unhappiness.

" The fault is mine," he said.

" No, do not reproach yourself," the other

said, kindly. " Evil often comes of practical jokes: and if my friend has come to any danger, it is his own seeking."

" Let's tarry no longer, and save him from his captor's keeping."

" And save him from," the other said, " a dungeon sleeping."

" Where," continued Dick, in the same poetical strain, " walls and floor with damp are reeking."

" What say you, follow, or turn back."

" Follow! at such a time would you give him the sack?"

" Nay! a thousand times sooner I would die in his cause."

" Then away to his rescue, not another minute pause."

" While he's in danger it's too bad to be joking,"

" It will do us no good to look blue or be weeping."

Then they turned their horses' heads to seek their absent friend, their gaiety fled, and both depressed in gloomy thoughts, rode on in silence.

They were suddenly startled by the appearance of a white horse that came madly towards them.

They drew aside to leave a clear space for the fiery steed as it came onward.

It passed them like a dart.

Lord Temple Grey uttered a cry that came from his very soul.

Upon the horse's back hung a listless form, bleeding from a deep gash.

The crimson stream dyed the steed's milky hide, and left a bloody trail on the earth, as the horse tore madly onwards.

" 'Tis he!" gasped Temple Grey, terribly white, " he—my friend!"

Dick shuddered as his gaze for a moment rested on the fearful spectacle.

He beckoned to his companion, plunged his spurs into his charger's flanks, and dashed off in pursuit of the white horse with its lifeless burden.

CHAPTER CV.

THE LUSHER IN DIFFICULTY.—THE STRANGE LANDLORD.—A STRANGER BEDSTEAD.—A NARROW ESCAPE FROM A DARK PIT AND A BLOODY DEATH.—CORNWALL AT LAST.

WHEN the Lusher escaped from

mail, he fell into the road, and sat upon the bullet that had gone underneath his coat-tail; nor did he feel inclined to get up when the coach had rolled out of sight.

He made several attempts to rise; but when he moved, the shot moved too, and the pain was so great that he sat down again. and howled.

Night wore on; heavy black clouds passed over the earth, and in their fleeting shadows Jack Evans pictured beings of an unearthly, horrible description.

Crime will bring its own judgment.

To judge by the terrified face of the Lusher, it had brought it to him.

He fancied the gigantic trees, with their swaying branches, were monsters of an unknown world, come to torture him.

He gazed upon the grim and silent sentries that stood statues for years, flourishing in their green and verdant mantle at each early spring, and declining through the chilly blasts of coming winter, that stripped them of their cheerful robe.

The Lusher strained his eyes in silent terror; a mist gathered before his sight, and through that mist he fancied the giant limbs were stretched towards him.

He shrieked in frenzied horror, and shrank to the earth to avoid their touch.

He shuddered as the wind blew past him, and started at the falling of a leaf.

He could endure this torture no longer. Springing from the ground, as a startled hare would spring from its lair, he made one bound, leaped a high hedge, and fell into a dirty ditch on the other side.

Terror deprived him of speech, but horrible thoughts flowed freely.

Had he been struck dumb by some mighty unseen one?

He thought he had.

To avoid another such collision, he scrambled out o. the thick mire, and scampered off for dear life, miserably wet and awfully dirty.

Was there anyone in sight?

He looked, but to his misery could not see one.

On he went, going over the earth swift as an antelope.

A light in the distance, glimmering through

the clustering trees, struck a cry of hope in his heart.

He stopped, and drew a deep sigh of relief.

A rustling at his feet, made by some species of the reptile community, made him start.

And off he went again, kindling afresh the fears that had lulled.

Nor did he pause until he reached the inn from whence the light shone.

The worthy host, a tall, gaunt fellow, with a face cadaverous, and anything but interesting, ran out of the parlour, and went straight to the Lusher, with intent to seize him for some desperate robber.

The Lusher put up his hand.

The innkeeper went back.

"Beg pardon," he said; "thought you some one else."

"But I ain't," said Jack, spitefully. "Got a room?"

"What sort?"

"One to sleep in."

"Yes."

"Show me the way."

"Five shillings."

Jack dived his hand into his pocket, and brought out a heap of gold and silver.

The innkeeper's eyes glistened greedily.

The Lushed threw the required sum contemptuously upon the counter, and returned the rest to his pocket.

"Had a good haul?" said the landlord.

"Don't know what you mean," replied Jack.

Mine host laughed; his voice had an unpleasant, grating sound.

"Had a fall?" he said, looking at Jack's dirty clothes.

"Yes," said Evans, sharply. "Show me the room."

"Want anything to drink?"

"Show me the room!" shouted Jack, getting out of temper.

"Follow me."

Jack followed the gaunt form up a dark, narrow, spiral staircase.

"That's the room," the landlord said, stopping on a narrow landing, from which it would have been easy to precipitate his guest down the stairs.

Some such thought entered his head, but another more powerful expelled it, and took its place.

Jack felt a chill creep through his veins.

"Ugh!" he shuddered.

"Which room?" he asked, his hand seeking the butt of a pistol, ready for use, for he expected treachery.

"This," said the landlord, trying the handle of a door. "Locked?"

"Well, ain't yer got another?"

"Five shillings more."

"Look here," said Jack, impressively, "don't ye go getting at me; ye ain't got a fool to play with."

"Yer won't have the room without paying for it."

"I paid yer five shillings, that's enough for any room."

"Well, yer won't get one for five shillings here; so, if yer don't like that, go!"

"Not without my money back," said the Lusher, determinedly.

"What!" exclaimed the host, as though astonished at the assurance of the Lusher asking for the return of his money.

"I ain't a goin' without my money."

"You ain't going without your money?"

"No."

"Oh!"

They looked at each other.

Jack knew did he go or get expelled he would not find another place for miles, and he did not feel in the condition for a journey in such a state.

Reflecting upon these thoughts, he thought it better to comply with the swindler's desire, and pay the extra five "shiners," than be turned out, cold, hungry, tired, wet, and at the loss of five shillings. So he paid, took possession of a small, meanly-furnished room for the night, and ordered a supper.

Had it been at another time, when he was more at ease, he would have noticed a look on the innkeeper's face, as he went out of the room, that would have warned him of danger.

The supper was brought up steaming, and the savoury odour that rose from it soon brought the Lusher to a fresh attack upon it.

"Anything to drink?" inquired mine host.

"Wine," said Jack, proudly throwing

himself back in the chair, and trying to swallow a very hot mouthful that brought tears to his eyes.

"Yes, sir," said the landlord, with mock courtesy, and bowing, he left the room.

Jack thought he was a long time gone for the wine, but he said nothing when he returned.

The landlord wished him good night, and a long sleep.

A sardonic, triumphant smile played about his lips as he went out.

The Lusher locked the door when he went out. To tell the truth, the Lusher did not not feel comfortable in his new quarters, and yet he knew not of any foundation he had for fear; but he thought it best to be on the safe side, and barricaded his door with most of the furniture in the room, as a guard against danger.

He then took the precaution to examine under the bed, and every conceivable place likely to shelter a spy from observation.

Being perfectly satisfied that he was alone, he divested himself of his wet clothes, drew a chair up to the fire, finished the bottle of wine, which he drank with much relish, and then began to scrape the mud off his coat with a rusty old knife he found in a corner of the room.

With every flake of mud that came off, a piece of the coat went with it.

The Lusher felt particularly dreamy after finishing the wine—so much so, that he could not keep his eyes open.

"Time for me to get to bed," he muttered.

Rising, he staggered; but not having sufficient strength to walk across the room, he fell powerless into the chair, where he slept in a dead unbroken sleep.

The light went out.

A steady step then ascended the stairs, and stopped outside the door.

"He sleeps," muttered a suppressed voice, "his sleep of death."

A very cheerful consolation for a fellow to go to sleep with.

"Ha, ha!"

That was the landlord's voice.

"Fool that he was," the same voice continued, "he signed his own fate when he displayed that money."

"Yes!" said the landlord, "I fairly do his wine, and, as dead men tell no tales, are safe enough to get his money."

The voices gradually died away as pair descended the stairs.

So that cold-blooded wretch the innkeeper drugged the poor fellow's wine, in order to obtain the paltry sum displayed to his avaricious eyes.

Jack slept on undisturbed.

A strange noise aroused him.

The drug was working off.

In a half drowsy sleep he jumped up suddenly, startled by a peculiar screeching, as if some heavy piece of furniture was being drawn across the room.

He looked around, and to his unutterable horror he saw a large gap in the wall, through which the bedstead was steadily moving.

Transfixed with terror he stood and watched it disappear.

When the foot was even with the wall the bottom of the bedstead tilted the pillows and the clothes into a fearful dark pit.

The Lusher would have gone too. had he been there.

He shuddered at the thought, and breathed a silent prayer for his providential escape.

But was he now safe?

He asked himself this question.

Loud cries and angry voices arose from the dark fearful pit.

Jack summoned courage, drew a pair of pistols, and with trembling steps approached the hideous gap.

He looked down into that horrible abyss.

And there he saw two men, by the rays from a glimmering lantern that threw its sickly light on their fiendish features.

In one, he recognised the landlord.

The other was a wretch only fit to die.

Jack pointed a pistol at his head, as he began to ascend, by some unseen means, to the room, in quest of Jack.

Jack had no desire for his company.

As a warning, he said—

"Keep back!"

The man looked terror-struck when he felt the rim of a pistol pressing its cold circle against his forehead.

He gave a startled cry.

Then dropped.

Jack fired.

The report startled him.

A groan—a death-groan of agony issued from the death-vault, where many an innocent, who had gone to that accursed inn for shelter, and to avoid the midnight prowlers, had lost their lives—as our friend would have lost his, had he gone to bed.

The Lusher looked down to see what damage he had done.

The man lay at his companion's feet, a bloody corpse, with his head shattered to atoms.

The host stood over the body looking like an unchained fiend.

Murder gleamed rom his eyes.

Jack spoke the man's doom.

"As you would have served me, pitiless wretch," he said, "and served many others, so I deal with you."

The second pistol was fired.

A second corpse lay in that secret vault of death, dabbled in its own black blood.

Jack moved aside, sick at heart.

His hand slid along the wall.

He felt something give beneath its pressure.

Click!

He had touched the spring of the devilish machinery.

The gloomy bedstead went back into its former position—the aperture in the wall closed.

The Lusher then listened for any sound.

Not a breath save his own broke the stillness of the silent hour.

Were those two hearts whom he had just sent before their Maker to answer for the bloody sins of the early occupants of the house?

He listened again, but heard no sound.

The hour being early, Jack pulled off a bed, threw it before the fire, and laid his weary self down to rest.

He slept soundly as though nothing had occurred to disturb the peace of his mind, and when he awoke, the gladdening sun shone cheerfully through the window.

He got up washed himself, loaded his pistols in case of an emergency, and removing the barricade from the door, descended the stairs.

He went through the bar—the place was quite deserted—the doors were still bolted—he let himself out, and breathed more freely when in the fresh air.

That day he journeyed on towards his destination, carefully avoiding everyone he saw in sight, for his guilty conscience still haunted him for so heartlessly robbing his fellow passengers.

As night wore on, as it generally does, Jack began to feel tired and weary.

A natural cause for walking all day.

Jack came in sight of another inn—he looked at it longingly, but the remembrance of the scene he had gone through at the last deterred him from entering.

So his journey he pursued with the determination not to take refuge in any such place as the one he had last entered during his journey.

The midnight hour tolled out from a distant spire in long and measured strokes.

Jack stopped instantly.

As Whittington did when he ran away from home.

He looked back in the direction of the inn he had just passed, a voice, as he stood, he fancied told him to return—Jack, not Whittington.

But Jack did not like to break his resolutions.

Again he walked on, but not with so much vigour as when he first started.

He took the road, it being more open than the fields, and there he had less fear of being stopped; but he had not proceeded far when two weary looking men passed him with a suspicious side glance that made poor Jack fear.

He ventured to look behind him.

It so happened at that moment they looked behind them too.

Jack stopped.

They stopped.

Jack moved on slowly.

They stood stationary, watching his retreating form.

Jack, by degrees, quickened his pace, and whistled to keep away his fears as well as to appear bold and defiant.

Jack set off at a run.

They, thinking he had gone far enough, set off after him.

A very interesting chase was then kept up for little over half an hour, dodging round trees, jumping over ditches, and scrambling through ditches, and so on.

Little boys, who take a delight in tying strings to knockers, pulling bells out of sockets, and various other delightful sports, would call it " follow my leader."

Jack wished they had broken their necks before they had followed him.

But such evil thoughts did not avail him much; he was captured and thrown roughly on the ground.

A desperate struggle ensued, in which the Lusher got the worst of it, and lost his money.

His assailants left him there as they thought half dead, but Jack only shammed.

He sat on the ground, took deliberate aim at the man who had taken his money and fired.

The shot took wonderful effect, the man went on his back like a rocket.

His companions suddenly missed him, and turned round to look for him.

To his astonishment, he saw him lying on his back counting the stars overhead.

"Get up," the other said, " what are you lying there for ?"

The one down swore.

His companion mentally muttered something about " ungrateful people, when other coves looks arter their welfare," and went on alone.

" Hoy ! where are you going ?" shouted the one down.

" To blazes," the other answered in deep disgust.

" Go, and be——"

We will leave out the rest; it will rest with the reader to discover it.

He went.

This gave the Lusher an opportunity he otherwise would not have had, of firing the other bullet.

Jack walked leisurely up to the man on the ground.

The man was too much absorbed in his own fierce mutterings at his companion's desertion to observe the approach of his enemy, nor was he made aware of his dangerous situation until suddenly finding himself upon his back and a pistol gleaming very pointedly at his nose.

Jack stood over him triumphantly.

He saw it would be useless to resist in his weak state.

The bullet had made an opening for the egress of the blood, through which it flowed freely.

Jack spoke.

" Not long ago you robbed me," he said. " You took all my money. I'm going to Cornwall; I can't get there without money, so must have that back."

" You won't."

" I will."

"If my mate's got it, you can't."

" I'll have yours, then."

Without further parley, Jack put his knee on the other's chest, and so held him at his mercy while he searched in every pocket.

He drew out a long, well-stocked purse, containing more than thrice the amount he had taken from him.

" Don't take that," pleaded the man.

" You didn't take mine," the Lusher said, ramming the money in his pocket.

" I've got a wife and six children at home starving," continued the wounded man, despairingly.

" I was driven to this. I have been out of work more than three months, I couldn't bear to see them want, and cry for bread any longer."

Jack heartlessly turned a deaf ear to his enemy's sad story, and turning upon his heels walked away with his treasure.

He had not proceeded far when a well-directed shot from his adversary struck him on the heel. He leaped off the ground like a wild Indian, and then started off at a run in the direction of the inn he had passed previously to meeting with the two robbers.

He found it a more comely hostelry than the one he had spent his last night of horror in.

He ordered coffee and brandy, a sumptuous supper, bespoke a room for the night, but before retiring to rest he drew a chair in front of a blazing fire in the parlour where many more travellers were gathered.

A pompous old gent was relating to the company how he and many more of his fellow travellers had been robbed while on their way to Cornwall.

"Yes," continued the old gent, "the scoundrel even had the audaciousness to take rings from my fingers while I was asleep."

Jack began to tremble.

This narrative was very much like that of his late adventure in the coach, and what was more to increase the uneasiness of his mind was that the narrator had a very familiar similitude to the gent he sat opposite.

"I was destined for Cornwall," the old fogey went on, "but after that daring robbery, I stopped here in hopes of catching the thief. The villain can't be far off."

Jack wished very much that he had been a little further off.

"I will give anyone a hundred pounds to catch him," the old gent said.

Every one listened attentively, and wished they only had the culprit in arms' reach.

Jack devoutly wished he had been many more arms' lengths out of their reach.

"If we only had him here," the old gent said.

"Oh!" ejaculated everyone in a breath.

"Why," suddenly exclaimed the old fellow, his gaze fixed on the Lusher's guilty countenance, "speak of the Devil and he's sure to appear."

"Where?" exclaimed all in the room, jumping up, except the Lusher, who tried very hard to drink his coffee in an unconcerned manner, but every mouthful he swallowed nearly choked him.

"Lor' bless me, how like!" said the old fogey, with a sly twinkling in his eye. "Excuse me, sir, but—but I am under a mistake."

The apology being addressed to the Lusher he ceased trembling palpably, and in so doing upset the cup of scalding coffee into his lap, he sprang up, and exclaimed—

"Confound it!"

Every eye in the room was turned suspiciously towards him.

The old gent again apologised for being the cause of the Lusher's misfortune, he had a hidden meaning for not wishing to recognise him.

Jack sat down again to finish his supper not in the least degree eased through the old gent's apparent recognition of him. He saw in his eyes a comical glitter that belied his words, and this made the Lusher uneasy.

The old fellow now bade Jack a very good night with a cunning look, and repaired to his chamber.

The rest of the company then soon dispersed, save one man—a brutal-looking ruffian; a man with cruel features, a forehead low, and projecting forward his thick dark brows met over his nose, and partly hid a pair of small, pitiless grey eyes sunk far back in their sockets; his mouth, too, added greatly to his ungainly appearance, with lips thin, bloodless, and tightly compressed, like two streaks of shrivelled parchment.

When Jack had retired the landlord rather timidly approached the ruffian, for he felt a strange dread of the man.

"I wish to close," he said.

"Close, then," was the laconic reply.

"But——"

"I'm going to stay."

"I haven't any beds."

"No, I s'pose not," the ill-looking brute said, in a sarcastic strain.

"No, I really have not," replied the host greatly embarrassed through the sullen dogged manner of the other.

"Then I'll stay here. Will that do for yer?"

"No; I don't allow that."

"Then turn me out."

The man drew himself up to his herculean height as he spoke in a defiant tone, and cast a fierce look upon the landlord, who retreated several steps back for safety.

The ruffian followed him with his iron hand closed firmly.

Backing mine host out of the parlour, said—

"Disturb me until the morning, and I'll cut your throat!"

Mine host felt that if he did not cut his throat, he was there for the purpose of cutting someone else's before the morning; and to prevent such diabolical work from taking place, he locked the door on the outer side.

THE OATH.

keep the ruffian caged, and then went to bed trembling with fear.

The landlord was right in his suspicion as to the ruffian's purpose for staying there.

The pompous old gent had incautiously displayed a leathern pouch that contained a goodly sum while in the parlour before the whole company.

As soon as the glittering dross caught the eye of the villain who now took possession of the room, his evil brain was immediately set to work for the purpose of possessing that magnetic charm.

The poor old fellow, when he retired to rest, little thought what danger he had brought upon himself through the simple act of displaying his gold.

Nay, he gave it not a thought.

He went to bed elate with the imagined success of his own concocted plan of revenge he meant to carry out early in the morning, and he laid on his back, chuckling with delight.

He recognised the Lmsher at the first glance, but kept it to himself, for he intended to get up while all others were asleep, and fetch the officers of justice to capture the daring robber while he slept a peaceful sleep.

Would he carry out his plan successfully?

He imagined so, anyhow, and fell off asleep, in ecstasies at the stratagem of his own plan.

The Lusher laid wide awake, restlessly turning from side to side of the bed, picturing the most horrid phantoms hovering about his chamber a delirious brain could imagine.

He listened with beating heart to the measured tick of the clock below, he listened with throbbing pulse to every sound, every breath that disturbed the stillness, and shuddered when the deep snoring of the old gent who slept in the next chamber broke through the partition.

More than once he fancied he heard the stairs creak, as though angry at being disturbed by the stealthy steps that ascended them.

Three o'clock struck.

Jack started.

Barely had the doleful echoes died away, when a piercing shriek rang through the whole house.

The Lusher was out of bed in an instant. He stood bewildered when a second cry, more heart-rending than the first, told him that someone in the next chamber to his was in danger.

He made a dash at the wall thinking to find a door. The partition came crashing down, as he fell against it with fearful force.

A few seconds more he had recovered his feet and scattered senses.

At a glance he took in the scene before him.

On the bed lay the fat old gent, struggling for his life with the powerful ruffian of the parlour, who slashed at him with a long, gleaming dagger, held with murderous intent in his murderous iron fist.

"I ain't going to see the poor old fellow murdered," thought the Lusher. "I'll save him even if he blabs on me to-morrow."

He made a sudden spring on to the would-be assassin's back, and tightly locked both his arms around his bull-like throat.

The ruffian, taken off his guard by this unexpected attack, dropped the bloody blade.

It was instantly and eagerly clutched by the old gent who would ere now have been no more had it not been for the sudden and providential intervention of the Lusher, for the poor old fellow's strength was fast failing him, and he could not have held out much longer against the brutal treatment of his vicious assailant, but he had vigour enough left now that he was free, to deal that brutal ruffian a fearful blow with the reeking blade.

The point grated against the ruffian's breast-bone, as it broke through his skin.

The old gent turned sick with horror, and left the weapon quivering in his foe's iron frame.

The man gasped.

The steel had touched a vital part.

His hand closed convulsively over the hilt.

He reeled, and, as he fell, drew the weapon forth.

His life-tide gushed from the deep, dangerous wound, and there he lay helpless, weltering in his own thick, vile gore.

This scene had been but the work of a few minutes.

The whole household by this time aroused, and came rushing, terror-stricken, into the chamber of horrors.

"I thought he would do something of this," exclaimed the landlord, looking with dilated eyes at the stricken ruffian.

When aroused from his peaceful slumber by the terror-stricken cries for help, he jumped out of bed, and in his fearful hurry shoved his legs through his coat-sleeves in mistake for his trousers.

The Lusher, on perceiving the mistake, could not refrain from exclaiming—

"Oh, crikey, there's a guy!"

The landlord wondered at his mirth, but his contemptible disgust at such heartlessness before such a scene kept him from speaking.

He had not discovered his error, though he thought the wind blew unusually stiff and cold about his legs.

The stricken wretch tried to rise, but his lion strength had deserted him, his swarthy cheeks grew haggard, his eyes protruded with horror from their sockets.

He knew his fate was sealed.

"No, you don't," ejaculated the Lusher, bounding to his side, and standing over him with a drawn pistol; "lay quiet, or I'll finish you off with a bullet in your skull!"

The man glared at him viciously, and hissing a withering curse upon them all, fell back powerless.

He had not breath enough to speak.

"To the window!" shouted the landlord; "I hear the clatter of horses! See if it is the officers approaching."

Jack devoutly hoped it was not; but when he went to the window he saw at least a score. This, as may be imagined, added greatly to his uncomfortable feelings.

He would have fain made his exit, but such an act might arouse suspicion, and probably he would be captured as an accomplice of the would-be assassin, through the mere fact of his guilty appearance, by sneaking out of the way at the time when all evidence that could be got would be wanted.

He weighed this over in his mind. He wondered if the old gent, after the invaluable protection he had received, would hand him over to the officers for the robbery he had committed.

He very timidly approached the bed where the old gent lay exhausted, with the determination to ask pardon for his late audacious sins.

The old fellow gave him a grateful look as he neared the bedside.

That was encouraging.

"Did the villain hurt you much, sir, before I came?" inquired Jack, by way of a wheedling commencement, to bring the bluff old fellow round a bit before he entered further into the subject.

"Hurt me!" blurted the old fellow; "it's a wonder I've got a sound limb."

"Dear me!" said Jack, gravely, "how shocking."

"Shocking! why, it was cruelly murderous —yes, murderous!"

"Very!" Jack said, sympthetically.

"Fairly monstrous, to be attacked like that while in one's sleep."

"I think I've settled him, though."

"Yes, yes, you have settled him. There's my hand."

He put out his hand to the Lusher, forgetting he himself had settled the ruffian.

Jack took the proffered member gladly.

"You are a brave, noble fellow," continued the old fellow. "I shan't forget your noble bravery, my life I owe to your daring courage."

"No, you don't," said Jack.

The old fogey looked at him in surprise.

"How's that?" he asked.

"Cos I owed you mine."

Old Fogey looked at him again, perfectly at a loss to understand his meaning.

"Well," said Jack, his limbs beginning again to tremble.

"Well," he said again, feeling nervous at having to come to the point.

"Well!"

For the third time he paused.

He looked steadily at his interlocutor.

"Well! well!" suddenly blustered the old man. "Out with it."

"Do you know me?" exclaimed Jack.

The words were frightened out of him.

"Know you, you dog! yes."

Jack heartily wished he had not.

"You are," the fat old gent said, severely, "you are a thief."

"Oh, no, I'm not," said Jack, shaking his head.

"Did you not take my diamond"—

"Don't speak so loud," broke in the Lusher, nervously.

"From my fingers," the old fellow continued. "Did you not steal someone else's money, someone else's watch, and someone else's jewel case?"

"Yes," answered the Lusher.

"If you can do that, are you not a thief, a villanous thief?"

"No," said Jack.

"Well, then, why did you take the things?"

"Only to take care of them."

"Very thoughtful of you," said the pompous old fellow. "I am now able to take care of my own rings."

Jack thought he was just as well able to take care of them for him.

The old gent said—

"Perhaps you will now be kind enough to return them."

Not if Jack could help it.

"Ain't got 'em," said the Lusher.

"You have not got them?"

"No."

"Where are they?"

"Left them in London."

"Go and fetch them."

"If you'll come with me."

Jack knew he was perfectly safe by making this arrangement.

If the old gent consented, and desired to start off immediately, he could soon give him the slip.

Besides, there was another thing to Jack's advantage.

The old fellow could not run, and he could.

But he was determined to keep a sharp eye upon the Lusher until they started for London, which they arranged to do on the third day from the one of the tragedy.

The officers had dismounted, and were now being admitted by one of the servants.

Jack knew there was no time to be lost.

The heavy tramp of the officers grew louder as they ascended the stairs.

Jack broke out in a violent perspiration.

"And now." said Jack, stammering, "will you pardon me for what I did?"

"Pardon you, you scoundrel! Why, you deserve to be hanged with that ruffian there."

And he pointed to the man, still writhing in a pool of blood on the floor.

"But——"

"You'll forgive me this time?"

"I don't know that I shall."

"Didn't I save your life?" pleaded Jack.

"True; and that is a heavy debt I owe you. There's my hand, you blackguard. I will forgive you this time."

Jack kissed the hand in gratitude—the hand that not many days previous had been raised, with many more, to drag him to the gallows, could the many hands at the time have got a hold upon him.

The officers entered.

They looked closely at the horrible spectacle before them.

Not a fibre or muscle of their faces moved.

They were used to such sights.

Their hearts were steeled against scenes that would have made anyone less brutalized than they recoil at a mere glance.

One of the King's officers stepped forward —the leader, evidently, by his assumed air of consequence.

"What's the meaning of this?" he asked.

"The meaning is," said the worthy host, "that this ruffian attempted to assassinate this gentleman."

He pointed to the fat old fogey.

"Humph!" ejaculated the officer. "How long since is it that the tragedy was attempted?"

"About three," put in the Lusher.

"Are you sure of that?"

"Quite."

"Explain."

"I was lying awake when the clock struck: and not a minute afterwards I heard a cry."

The authoritative officer fixed upon him a penetrating glance.

Jack shifted his gaze.

He always felt uncomfortable under penetrating glances.

Especially from an officer.

"Well," said Jack's interrogator, "then what followed?"

"I did," said the Lusher, with a grin.

The officer frowned.

"This is no time for jesting," he said.

"Quite true," said Jack. "I did follow."

"Well, as soon as I heard the cry I sprang out of bed, and dashed through the wall to the rescue."

He pointed to the shattered partition.

The officers raised his eyebrows when he saw the proof of the Lusher's bravery.

Mine host saw it, too, but groaned at the destruction of his dwelling.

"Did this man," said the officer, meaning the ruffian on the floor, "use any weapon?"

"The one you see in his hand," said Jack, "and the gentleman, to keep him from murdering all the lot of us, stuck it into him while I held him."

"How did he enter?"

"Can't tell yer," said Jack.

The leading officer then referred to the old gent.

From him he received the same reply.

"Strange," muttered the officer.

Then aloud, he added—

"Where did he sleep?"

"Greatly against my will," said the landlord, speaking in his turn; "he took possession of the parlour, and defied me to turn him out."

"Ah!" ejaculated the general interrogator;

"then all through he appears to have been a desperate ruffian."

"Until me and the gentleman settled him," said Jack

"And the sooner you get him out of here the better I shall like it," said mine host.

"'Tis hardly my duty," said the officer.

"Hardly your duty, sir!" exclaimed the old gent, jumping up. "Do you mean to say that your duty is not to put under arrest an assassin?"

"Well, you see, sir, we were sent out on a different affair.

"Indeed."

"Yes, sir. We were sent out to find the murderer of the landlord of the Peacock Inn, some thirty miles from here."

"Oh, lor'!" trembled the Lusher, thinking for certain that he was in a trap, now calling to his mind the adventure of the previous night at the inn mentioned.

"This same man may be the perpetrator of both deeds," suggested the old fogey.

"Very likely, sir," said the officer. "But I don't think he will do another."

Jack felt very glad to hear it; yet he could not bear the idea of a dying man being accused for the crime he had committed; so, to take the weight off his mind, he was determined to reveal all truthfully, and so make a clean breast of it.

"No," he said, bravely, "this man did not do the deed at the Peacock."

"Oh!" exclaimed the officer. "Perhaps you know who did."

"I did."

Everyone started back.

"You!" said the old gent. "You, who were the first to come to my assistance?"

"Yes, me; and I tell you for why."

"Tell us quickly, or you will find yourself in the wrong box," said the officer.

Jack then related all that had occurred.

His narrative was received with much approval, and he received great praise for his whole courage.

"And," he said, in conclusion, "I should not wonder, if you were to look in the vault, you would find a few of their victims, who have fallen into their accursed trap the same way as I should, had I slept."

"This shall be looked into," said the officer.

"You have acted most bravely—the King shall hear of your noble conduct."

"No," said Jack. "I don't want nothing of that. I did what I did to save other people."

"You acted bravely." The officer turned to his companions, and said—

"Take this man out—let him hang in chains from the bough of the nearest tree!"

The poor wretch, half dead, was conscious of his fate.

He murmured not; his hardened nature would not let him ask for mercy.

The officers bore him from the inn, and in less than half an hour he was swinging in chains, suspended from the arm of a peaceful old oak—suspended in the air, there to remain to linger out the rest of his life in torturing agony, and afterwards to rot in those iron bonds, as a warning to those of his class.

The Lusher then, accompanied by the officers on horseback, made their way to the inn, where he had disposed of the landlord and his accomplice.

They searched in the vault, and there, hidden in dark crevices, they found besides the two bodies of the murderers twelve corpses of men and women, whom, as the Lusher had said, had fallen victims to the landlord's devilish work.

The bodies were interred in the surrounding ground. The accursed inn was then fired, and, in less than an hour, it was burned to the ground with the two bodies of the men.

The whole then remained one heap of dust, from which it all originally arose, to be scattered by the wind.

Thus ended the redoubtable Lusher's startling adventure, and, with a lighter heart but saddened spirit, he continued his way to Cornwall.

CHAPTER CVI.

HOW FAIRY REVEALED HENRY WINTER AS THE BOY HIGHWAYMAN—MEETING OF FRIENDS AT THE HAUNT—THE REVEL—GRACE MISSING—THE EXECUTION OF SIMON JUDAS —TYBURN DICK AGAIN GOES OUT IN SEARCH OF HIS LOVE.

THE maddened steed with its lifeless burden kept on at a headlong speed, flying hedges, ditches, and everything in its path.

Dick, and his companion, Lord Temple Grey, followed at the utmost speed of their steeds, but every minute Fairy left them further behind.

Dick saw the direction she was taking, and knew that she was making for the haunt.

He felt sorry for it, because that would be the means of revealing him in his true character to his new friends.

"By Jove!" said Temple, "anyone would think you knew where she was going."

Dick laughed.

"She knows her way," he said.

"Let's keep her in view in case Clare should fall," Temple said.

"It's astonishing how he has kept on so long without falling," Dick said.

"He can't be as badly hurt as I thought when he passed us," said Temple Grey.

"Let us hope that he is not."

"He must be conscious of his position, as it would have been impossible for him to have remained on the steed's back so long."

"Doubtless."

"Hallo! where the deuce has your horse gone?"

"Home," said Dick.

They were now near the heath. They saw Fairy make her way through the clustering trees, and spring over a high hedge that surrounded the old priory.

Then she stopped before a curious old gate, and snorted.

A score of the gallant band suddenly appeared in great alarm. The snort of the horse's was always a signal of their young chief's danger.

Every face grew dark and sorrowful as they lifted the bleeding form from the steed's back, whom they supposed to be their gallant young leader.

But when they laid it on the grass, their alarm was increased to find a stranger in their chief's dress and riding his horse.

"What's the meaning of this?" inquired Big Bullskin, who then stalked out, his majestic form towering high above his comrades, and his colossal features wearing a troubled expression.

"This is some foolish trick of your captain's," said Claude, who was more accustomed to our hero's pranks than any of the others.

"Surely," said Munroe, "he would not get trifling at such a time as when he left us."

"I doubt not but he has, and this noble has perhaps sacrificed his life to save him."

"Do you think the captain is taken?" inquired several anxious voices.

"Without a doubt," said Claude. "Let us try if we can bring any life into this gentleman. Perhaps he may be able to give us some information."

Three or four of the highwaymen started off for water and other stimulants.

The young noble laid perfectly inanimate.

Captain Claude bathed his temples, and poured an invigorating draught down his throat, but no signs of life returned.

"Bear him gently in," he said, "and lay him on a couch. We will leave him in your care, Munroe, you being the best doctor."

The bleeding form was carefully raised by four of the gallant knights, and being carried into the haunt when Tyburn Dick and Lord Temple Grey appeared upon the scene.

In a moment they slid from their saddles.

Lord Temple, in great distress, made a dash at the highwaymen who were carrying away his friend.

Bullskin respectfully stopped him.

"I presume the nobleman is your friend?" he said.

"Yes, yes; don't stop me," cried Temple Grey, frantically. "Let me see him."

"By-and-by. He is not now well enough."

"Would you keep me from him?" exclaimed Grey, impatiently.

"I cannot allow you to see him just now."

The nobleman's hand wandered to his sword.

Dick came forward to intercede.

"Then, if he is in safe custody, why keep me from seeing him?" Temple said.

"This gentleman," said Dick, meaning Munroe, "will bring him round safely presently. My comrades get many ugly cuts, but I have never known one to die under his treatment."

"May I see him as soon as he is conscious?"

"With great pleasure."

Grey was satisfied.

Dick then took him into the haunt, and produced a very agreeable meal, and several bottles of luscious wine, which was very acceptable after their fatiguing ride.

Temple Grey, looking straight at Dick, over a glass he held to his lips, said—

"You are?"—

"Tyburn Dick," concluded our hero.

"The devil!"

"I hope not."

"Well, really, by Jove, finely I have been sucked in!"

"In what manner?" inquired Dick.

"How the deuce can you ask, after swindling a fellow?"

"Swindle you?"

"By Jove, yes. Did you not stop me as the Boy Highwayman?"

"Well?"

"Then, did you not raise your mask, and reveal yourself as Henry Winter."

"Just so."

"And after all ain't you Tyburn Dick?"
Dick assented.

"The very fellow I have so long wanted to meet."

"And are you now content?" said Dick.

"Proud!" said Temple Grey. "You are a capital fellow, and by Jove, if I ever hear anyone say anything about you, won't I give them the length of my steel?"

"You are generous," said Dick.

"I am sorry we did not meet before I knew you, on the road."

"Why?" asked Dick.

"Because I have heard what a devil you are to fight, and I have always longed to have a set-to with you."

"Can you fight?"

"There are not many who can beat me."

"Then suppose we have a trial."

"But we are friends!"

"Then we will have a friendly passage of arms."

"By Jove! Yes, capital! What shall we fight for?"

"To see who can get the first six points."

"Done!" exclaimed Temple Grey; "I shall disarm you before three points."

"Very well," said Dick; "however,

before we fight, perhaps you would like to see "——

"Your friend," said Bullskin, coming in, "is now recovered sufficiently to see you."

Lord Grey and our hero immediately rose, and went to the chamber of the wounded nobleman.

"Ah! old fellow;" he said, putting out his hand to Grey, as he lay on a couch, still looking very pale and weak.

"By Jove!" said his friend, a tear starting to his eye; "you don't look like the same fellow. What has happened?"

"Why, when I got up to these cowardly brutes, of course they took me for the Boy Highwayman. I did not tell them different. We had a glorious fight. I had put two *hors de combat*, and was just polishing off the third with a splendid stroke, when one from behind gave me a dig in the back."

"Curse them," said Dick.

"On the instant I lost all power," continued Horace Clare. "I knew that I should faint from loss of blood, for the fellow's sword went in rather deeply; and, knowing I should be taken unless I made some attempt to get off, I gave my faithful steed the rein, touched her slightly with my heels, and off she went with the whole troop of officers after her. I then fell forward and fainted. When I recovered I found myself here, with some very attentive fellow giving me all the attention of a nurse. I can tell you it was a welcome surprise, for I at least expected to be overtaken and lodged in some dreary cell."

"Do you know where you are?" asked Dick.

"No; it all seems a mystery how I got here, where I am, and how the deuce you found me."

"Well," said Dick, "I will clear the mystery."

"Do," the other said, eagerly.

"Well, you are now in the haunt, on Hounslow Heath, of the Silver Star band of highwaymen."

"No!" exclaimed the young noble, in surprise.

"The fact."

"Then I am off; but how did you get here?"

" By the right of free entry," said Dick.

" By the right of free entry! How the deuce do you mean ?"

" Being master here, the chief of a band of brave men, with faithful hearts."

" But you are not a highwayman ?"

" I am king here," said Dick.

" Surely, you are jesting ?"

" Never more serious in my life."

" You are not the famous Boy Highwayman ?"

" No; I used to be, but time, you know, brings its changes."

" And you are no longer a boy," put in Lord Temple.

" No," said our hero; " but still the name clings to me."

" You are, then, Tyburn Dick ?" said Horace Clare, greatly perplexed.

" The original."

Horace Clare raised himself from the couch by supporting himself on his arms, and looked straight into the boy's face, as though bewildered by the assertion of his noble young friend.

" Are you trying to hoax me ?" he said.

" No," said Dick, seriously.

" Highwayman though you be," said the young noble, " you will always find a friend in me; there's my hand upon it. By Jove! I have never known a fellow I like more than I do you. Tell me how it was you became a knight."

" Some other time," said Dick, with a shade of regret on his handsome face; " when you are able to get up I will introduce you to twelve gentlemen whom we have here."

" You never spoke to me of that," said Lord Grey.

" I had forgotten it," said the boy.

" I am quite ready now to join you," said Horace, rising from the couch with much difficulty.

Dick saw it pained him to move.

" Nay," he said, " you are not well enough just yet, don't disturb yourself, I pray."

The young noble fell back.

" I think I will take your advice," he said, " and remain a little longer before I move. Don't leave me, it's awfully dull for a fellow to be here alone with nothing to do."

Dick introduced cards.

The three friends played until the wounded nobleman had recovered a little of his former strength, they then left the sick chamber, to join the twelve noblemen who were gathered with the highwaymen in the grand hall.

Temple Grey and his friend knew several of the company.

Another banquet was laid.

This passed off without any disturbance.

When they arose everyone was excited and fired through the wine they had drunk.

A noisy scene then took place, a wild kind of revel, in which they all got awfully drunk.

Suddenly there was a startling interruption, that made many wonderfully sober on the instant.

Especially the highwaymen.

Swig was crying murder.

Big Bullskin went to see the cause of his companion's distress.

He found the miniature highwayman engaged in a desperate encounter with the traitor Simon Judas, who had escaped from his cell.

He grasped the howling wretch in a grip like iron, and hurled him mercilessly against the wall.

The murderous traitor staggered to his feet, and tried to crawl away, but Munroe secured him again, and stood him in the middle of the hall.

" Gentlemen," he said, " this despicable wretch was once one of our brethren; he turned traitor to sell his comrades to the hangman for the blood money. Twice before we have caught him in some villanous act, and each time gave him his liberty, he knew not the meaning of gratitude. This is the third time: now I have got him, he won't have liberty again. He tried in a foul manner to betray us all and shoot the president. His life must pay the penalty of the crime."

" Mercy !" shrieked the miserable wretch.

" The mercy you would have shown the captain—death !"

" Death to the traitor !—death !" shouted the rest.

" No, no !" yelled Judas; " I will not die !"

" Won't you?" said Bullskin. " We shall see. If you don't, after what you will go through, why you may live."

" No, no ! mercy, mercy !"

A deaf ear was turned upon him.

Munroe raised the struggling brute in his arms, and bore him to the torture chamber.

Most of the others followed.

To witness a scene of torture, but one of just punishment.

The beseeching wretch sank to the earth in speechless horror when he saw the torture that awaited him.

"Kill me!" he gasped.

Bullskin laughed grimly.

Every one looked on in dread silence, while the gigantic fellow prepared the machine for his victim.

A peculiar piece of ingenious, devilish construction.

A rack, formed like a cross, with a socket at each end.

Bullskin touched a spring. A wheel at the back of the cross immediately revolved at a measured pace, and the four sockets were slowly drawn out on powerful springs.

He looked at the trembling wretch with a sort of satisfaction.

For the first time the heartless brute's face showed some signs of fear.

"Prepare yourself to die," said Munroe, eventually. "Ask forgiveness of your Maker before you are sent before HIM to answer for your past career."

A vile oath left his lips.

He sprang up, ferocious as a maddened tiger, and made a dash to break through the barrier that stood before the entrance of the vault.

Dick caught him by the throat, and hurled him back.

His head went with fearful force against the cross. He reeled as though stunned for a moment, glared fiercely at the boy, and made a second attempt.

But not at Dick.

He leaped as for the young chieftain's throat, but, when within three or four yards of him, he altered his direction, to throw the others off their guard, and dashed amongst the noblemen.

The collision was so unexpected that several fell, and while the rest were trying to seize the traitor, he fell upon those already down, and drew a sword from one of their scabbards.

He then went along on his hands and knees, intending as he went to make a path.

But, ere his weapon drew a drop of innocent blood, the powerful arm of Bullskin drew the desperate wretch back.

The sword was taken from him, and a heavy blow, dealt on his temple, felled him to the floor.

He was then certainly quiet for a few seconds.

He groaned, glared viciously on all around, drew his wounded hand across his bleeding brow, and once more sprang to his feet.

Big Bullskin's hands fell upon his shoulder ere he had time to move.

"Mercy!" shrieked Simon Judas.

"'Tis mercy you will receive, wretch," was the stern answer that made the traitor recoil.

Again and again he implored for mercy, while desperately struggling to break away from his powerful captor.

His pitiable cries and shrieks would have touched many of the lookers on deeply, but he was such a cold-blooded wretch, their hearts were shut against his cries.

Bullskin held him down while he touched a bell to summon some of his brethren.

Three times the iron-tonged bell tolled dolefully, and as its last ring echoed through the death-like silence that reigned, a door opened, and six stalwart men, robed from head to feet in spotless black, approached the doomed man.

They knew their work.

Munroe left the traitor, and took his place by his young chieftain's side, to watch the execution.

A gag was placed over the quailing wretch's mouth to stop his cries.

He fought to tear it away, but all in vain.

He struggled to free his limbs, but they were held as though in vices by his captors, and he was carried helpless to the torture rack.

The sockets, or rather clasps, were put round his wrists and ankles, his head was drawn back by a sort of staple that went round his neck and held it firmly.

The six men now stood aside.

Their work was complete.

Simon Judas, the heartless traitor—the

branded outcast, was now held a victim in the iron grasp of death.

For a few seconds his features worked hurriedly, his eyes glared and protruded from their sockets.

Then his features relaxed.

His eyes became calm.

He looked from face to face.

He saw no hope.

His heart smote him.

His head dropped on his chest.

Then again he raised his head, and looked imploringly at Big Bullskin as though he wished to say something.

Had he relented?

Did he wish to offer up a prayer to his Maker, to save his crime-stained soul from perdition?

Munroe approached him, and removed the gag from his mouth.

"For the love of God," he said, calmly, and he turned his eyes up beseechingly, "if I am to die, let me hear a sermon. I cannot be cast from this world with all my sins upon me."

He paused, and looked round at all.

"I have been bad," he said, "I deserve my fate. Forgive me, brethren, if you can, and pray for me!"

These few words came from his very soul.

He felt now the crisis of death, and the torturing weight of his own sins.

He was penitent, and many men whose ears were deaf to his cries felt pity for him from their hearts.

Bullskin read the most touching parts from the Bible, and when he had concluded, he knelt with the six robed men around the doomed man and prayed, as did Simon Judas —prayed forgiveness—prayed to cleanse his dark-stained blood.

And so did all who were there, with heads bare and reverential brow, they breathed a silent prayer to save his soul from the everlasting torture we are supposed to believe sinners are cast into, when departed from this life.

"I am prepared to die now," said the poor wretch, in an altered, subdued tone. "I can die in peace. Do not torture me; let my death be sudden."

Bullskin said—

"It shall be."

He drew a pistol, and held it in a line with his victim's head.

Simon Judas fixed his eyes upon our hero.

"May I hope to be forgiven," he asked, "for all the wrongs I have done you?"

"With all my heart," said the noble boy, and he went forward with extended hand.

Bullskin released one of his victim's arms.

Simon Judas grasped his young chieftain's hands, and pressed a reverential kiss upon it.

Tears started to Dick's eyes, and he turned away, feeling that he ought to intercede for the traitor's life.

"Let him live," he said, his voice choked with emotion.

"As you will," said Bullskin; "I am agreeable. He has repented, and may be hereafter a different man."

"No, no," said Simon; "I must die some time, let it be now, while I feel repentant."

"Would you not rather have liberty and life?" asked Munroe.

"No; if I am forgiven I can die happy."

"Let it be so, then," said Dick; "you are forgiven by one and all."

"Brethren, I am grateful." He could not say any more, his iron frame shook, and big tears rolled down his cheeks.

"Release him from the rack," said Bullskin.

The six black-robed men took him from the rack.

He was again free.

He stood perfectly quiet there, and an altered man in every way.

"Had you suffered on that rack," said Munroe, "every joint in your body would have been pulled apart."

The doomed wretch shuddered as his gaze wandered over the hellish machine, with its long piercing needles and torturing springs.

"Comrades," he said, "kill me; I am suffering more now through the remembrance of my own sin than all the tortures of a dozen racks could do."

Bullskin whispered something to the men.

A few minutes later they could be seen digging a grave near Tyburn Tree, on Hounslow Heath, and when the culprit was led out into the open air, his blood ran like ice through his veins, as his gaze fell upon the pit that a few minutes later would hold his lifeless form, and for ever shut him out from the world.

He stood over his own grave calmly, with his arms folded across his breast.

Bullskin, the executioner, took his place at twenty paces.

The noblemen and highwaymen stood on either side in line.

Bullskin took deliberate aim with a long-barrelled pistol, and counted slowly ten.

He paused ere he fired.

Simeon Judas closed his eyes.

A few seconds later, when all held their breath in dreadful suspense, there was a livid flash, a deafening report, a slight cry, and the traitor fell lifeless into his grave.

The earth was thrown in upon him.

They all returned to the haunt.

The guests slowly departed, and when the last had gone, Dick looked around.

There was *one* absent.

"Where is Grace?" he asked of Captain Claude.

"We have not seen her since you left the last time," returned the captain.

The boy's brows gradually grew dark.

"Is this, then, the way you look after her?" he said sternly.

"I missed her the moment you had gone, and made a search for her, but to no purpose."

"Then," said Dick, deeply pained, "she has again assumed that accursed dress of mine, and been taken."

He prepared himself as though for a long journey.

"Where would you go?" asked Claude.

"In search of her," replied the boy.

"It is useless, I have sent out ten of our brethren, and they will soon return with her, or intelligence of her whereabouts."

Dick laughed scarcastically.

"Do you think I would trust to such a chance," he said, "should she return while I am away, detain her, even should it be in a dungeon."

"But my dear boy"——

"'Tis no use, father, to raise any objections, farewell, I shall not return without her.

Claude watched the noble boy out.

He sighed sadly, and went for solace to his devoted mistress, Fair Milly.

CHAPTER CVII.
THE COTTAGE ON THE HEATH.

IT was on one of those dreary and cheerless nights which makes us draw near the warm fireside, and thank Providence that we have not to venture out, that a poor pedlar boy trudged his way over the dreary heath of Hounslow.

He was hurrying onward, when, on suddenly raising his head, he beheld the blackened beams of a gibbet.

This sight filled his very soul with horror, and he thrust his fingers in his ears to keep out the sound of the rusty chains as they swung to and fro in the night air.

A thousand frightful traditions connected with this dread scene darted across his mind.

Every blast, as it swept its hollow gusts over the heath, seemed to teem with the sighs of departed spirits; and the birds, as they winged their way above his head, appeared, with loud and shrill cries, to warn him of approaching danger.

The whistle, with which he usually beguiled his weary pilgrimage, died away into silence, and he groped along with trembling and uncertain steps.

A light now glimmered in the distance, which would lead him, he conjectured, to the cottage of the woman; and towards that he eagerly bent his way.

His first call for admission obtained no visible marks of attention, but instantly the greatest noise and confusion prevailed within the cottage.

They think it is one of the supernatural visitants of whom the old lady talks so much, thought the boy approaching the window, where light within showed him all the inhabitants at their several occupations.

The old woman was hastily scrubbing the stone floor, and strewing it thickly over with sand, while her two sons seemed with equal haste to be thrusting something large and heavy into an immense chest, which they carefully locked.

The boy, in a frolicsome mood, thoughtlessly tapped at the window, when they all instantly started up, with consternation strongly depicted upon their countenances.

He shrunk back involuntarily, with an un-defined feeling of apprehension.

But, before he had time to reflect a moment longer, one of the men suddenly darted out at the door, and seizing the boy roughly by the shoulder, dragged him violently into the cottage.

"I am not what you take me for," said the boy, attempting to laugh, "but only a poor pedlar, who visited you last year."

"Are you alone?" inquired the old woman, in a harsh, deep tone, which made his heart thrill with apprehension.

"Yes," said the boy. "I am alone here; and alas!" he added, with a burst of uncon-trollable feeling, "I am alone in the wide world also. Not a person exists who would assist me in distress, or shed a single tear if I died this very night."

"Then you are welcome," said one of the men with a sneer, whilst he cast a peculiar expression at the other inhabitants of the cottage.

It was with a shiver of apprehension, rather than of cold, that the boy drew towards the fire, and the looks which the old woman and her son exchanged made him wish that he had preferred the shelter of any one of the roofless cottages which were scattered near, rather than thrust himself among persons of such dubious aspect.

Dreadful surmises flitted across his brain, and terrors which he could neither combat nor examine imperceptibly stole into his mind.

But alone, and beyond the reach of assis-tance, he resolved to smother his suspicions, or at least not increase the danger by reveal-ing them.

The room to which he had retired for the night had a confused and desolate aspect.

The curtains seemed to have been violently torn from the bed, and still hung in tatters around it.

The table seemed to have been broken by some violent concussion, and the fragments of various pieces of furniture lay scattered upon the floor.

The boy begged that a light might burn in his apartment till he was asleep, and anxiously examined the fastenings of the door, but they seemed to have been wrenched asunder on some former occasion, and were still left rusty and broken.

It was long ere the pedlar attempted to compose his agitated nerves to rest, but at length his senses began to "steep themselves in forgetfulness," though his imagination remained painfully active, and presented new scenes of terror to his mind with all the vividness of reality.

Suddenly the boy was startled from these agitated slumbers by what sounded to him like a cry of distress.

But the noise was not repeated, and he endeavoured to persuade himself it had only been a continuation of the fearful images which had disturbed his rest, when, on glancing at the door, he observed underneath it a broad red stream of blood silently stealing its course along the floor.

Frantic with alarm, it was but the work of a moment to spring from his bed and rush to the door, through the chink of which, his eye nearly dimned with affright, he could watch, unsuspected, whatever might be done in the adjoining room.

His fear vanished instantly when he per-ceived that it was only a *goat* that they had been slaughtering; and he was about to steal into his bed again, ashamed of his ground-less apprehensions, when his ear was arrested by a conversation which transfixed him aghast with terror to the spot.

"This is an easier job than you had yes-terday," said the man who held the goat.

"I wish all the throats we've cut were as easily and quietly done."

"Did you ever hear such a noise as the old gentleman made last night?"

"It was well we had no neighbour within a dozen of miles, or they must have heard his cries for help and mercy."

"Don't speak of it," replied the other; "I was never fond of bloodshed."

"Ha! ha!" said the other, with a sneer, "you say so, do you?"

"I do," answered the first, gloomily; "the well is the thing for me. *That* tells no tales —a single scuffle—a single plunge—and the fellow's dead and buried to your hand in a moment. I would defy all the officers in Christendam to discover any mischief *there*."

"Ay, nature did us a good turn when she

THE ABDUCTION.

contrived such a place as that. Who that saw a hole on the heath, filled with clear water, and so small that the long grass meets over the top of it, would suppose that the depth was unfathomable, and that it conceals more than forty people who have met their death there. It sucks them in like a leech!"

"How do you mean to dispatch the lad in the next room?" asked the old woman, in an under tone.

The elder son made her a sign to be silent, and pointed towards the door where their trembling auditor was concealed, while the other, with an expression of brutal ferocity, passed his bloody knife across his throat.

The pedlar boy possessed a bold and dar-

ing spirit, which was now roused to desperation.

But in any open resistance the odds were so completely against him, that flight seemed his best resource.

He gently stole to the window, and having by one desperate effort broke the rusty bolt by which the casement had been fastened, he let himself down without noise or difficulty.

This betokens good, thought he, pausing an instant in dreadful hesitation what direction to take.

This momentary deliberation was fearfully interrupted by the hoarse voice of the men calling aloud, "*The boy has fled—let loose the blood-hound !*"

These words sunk like a death-knell on his heart, for escape appeared now impossible, and his nerves seemed to melt away like wax in a furnace.

Shall I perish without a struggle? thought he, rousing himself to exertion, and, helpless and terrified as a hare pursued by its ruthless hunters, he fled across the heath.

Soon the baying of the blood-hound broke the stillness of the night, and the voice of its master sounded through the moor, as they endeavoured to accelerate its speed.

Panting and breathless, the boy pursued his hopeless career, but every moment his pursuers seemed to gain upon his failing steps.

The hound was unimpeded by the darkness which was to him so impenetrable, and its noise rung louder and deeper on his ear—while the lanterns which were carried by the men gleamed near and distinct upon his vision.

At his fullest speed the terrified boy fell with violence over a heap of stones, and having nothing on but his shirt, he was severely cut in every limb.

With one wild cry to Heaven for assistance, he continued prostrate upon the earth, bleeding, and nearly insensible.

The hoarse voices of the men, and still louder baying of the dog, were now so near that instant destruction was inevitable.

Already he felt himself in their fangs, and the bloody knife of the assassin appeared to gleam before his eyes.

Despair renewed his energy, and once more, in an agony of affright that seemed verging towards madness, he rushed forward so rapidly that terror seemed to have given wings to his feet.

A loud cry near the spot he had left arose on his ears, suspending his flight.

Then came the report of a pistol, a cry of agony, and the hoarse baying of the hound redoubled.

"Fools!" yelled a voice. "What is your object in setting your hound upon me?"

A fearful malediction was the only response.

A second report startled the affrighted boy, who wandered unconsciously to the spot.

He was surprised to see one of his pursuers laying bleeding on the ground, and the hound rolling over and over in the agonies of death.

A horseman, muffled in a large black cloak, appeared to be his deliverer, and as he turned, the cloak drew aside, and the boy beheld a blazing star upon his breast.

Unconsciously he exclaimed—

"Tyburn Dick, the highwayman, has saved my life!"

CHAPTER CVIII.

DETERMINATION OF VICTOR ST. JAMES AND HIS VALET TO CONQUER OR DIE—REUBEN FRAMPTON IN A NEW CHARACTER—A CLEVER TRAP AND ITS VICTIMS.

VICTOR ST. JAMES had only secured the closet door in time.

Shanks began to use courage as the clamouring voices increased outside.

The young nobleman divested himself of his female attire, and now stood in his own cavalier's costume.

He drew his sword, and stood in a splendid fearless attitude, should the door break in.

Shanks drew his sword, too, and with great difficulty held it still. He tried very hard to stand in a similar attitude as his master, but his legs would not keep still to support his gaunt form in the same graceful ease as the young noble.

"Shanks," said St. James.

"My dear master," replied the valet.

"The door will give way presently."

In all probability it would, did the ruffians on the outside continue their furious attack.

"I fear so," replied Shanks.

"Shanks, you should have no such thoughts as fear at such a time as this."

"I ain't,—that is to say, I don't fear fighting.

"Well, stand still."

"I am willing to, but my legs won't."

"I believe you are frightened."

"Oh, no, I aint."

Bang!

The door shivered.

Splinters flew in all directions.

St. James sudddenly put the blade of his sword through the crack.

There was heard a prolonged howl and a heavy fall.

St. James drew his sword in.

By the glimmer of light that now peered through the shattered panels, he saw that the point answered.

"There is one of them down," he said in a low voice.

"That will be one the less to knock down when we get out," said Shanks.

"That's a brave remark. Stand by me Shanks, the door won't last much longer."

Shanks hoped it would, but he said—

"I don't suppose it will."

Bang! bang! bang!

Crash.

A thick club went through.

The young nobleman and his lacquey had to get aside or they would have gone down with bruised skulls.

The thick club disappeared.

Victor's sword followed it.

There was another yell.

But no fall.

Vile oaths and ungentlemanly curse was a capital substitute.

The attack grew more furious than ever.

The men must have made their arms ache awfully by the way they kept up a continual battering at the door.

Some heavy instrument than as yet had been used was now introduced.

A fearful crash followed its first blow, and shook the whole mansion like the shock of an earthquake.

A second crash.

The door fell in splinters.

Victor St. James and his valet made a dash out.

The first who met the young nobleman's gaze was his treacherous cousin, Reuben Frampton.

His appearance rather staggered our young friend.

"That's Lord Ecclestone," said Shanks.

Reuben glared at him viciously.

"Reuben Frampton," Shanks said again; "the assassin of Lord—"

The vindictive nobleman made a dash at him with his drawn sword.

Shanks jumped aside just in time to keep his body from being perforated.

"No, you don't," he said, dodging behind the retainers.

The warning glitter in Victor's eyes kept the hirelings at bay.

He stood in a fearless, graceful attitude; his gaze wandered from face to face of his opponents.

All were strange.

His sire's house was filled with a gang of hired ruffians and a treacherous foe.

"We have met again, cousin Reuben," said the young noble, "and in a strange way. Perhaps you will give me an explanation of how you became possessor of my property. Where's my father?"

Reuben shrank back, his face livid, betraying the fear the pointed question produced upon him.

St. James watched him closely.

"Where's my sire?" he said again.

His cousin started suddenly, a deep flush effaced the terror from his cheeks, and, looking round at his servants, whose faces showed signs of great astonishment, at what had been said, he exclaimed, in a deep commanding voice—

"Thrust this impostor his and hreling from the house!"

"What!" thundered our young friend, with terrible anger.

He leaped round and confronted his cousin.

"Not while an inch of this steel remains in my hand does anyone attempt to thrust me from my own home!" he said.

Reuben got for protection behind his retainers.

"Do your duty at once," he said, "if you value your place."

"Not until Shanks has got a sword to fight with," said the faithful valet.

He stood, back to back, with his young master, and looked quite a hero.

The men hesitated, they could not easily get at either; one protected the other. Their swords were long, and looked suggestive of going into their ugly carcasses rather farther than would have been comfortable.

"Do your duty!" thundered Reuben, foaming at the mouth like a mad dog. "Am I, your master, to be thus insulted by two prowling vagabonds, who choose to come and lay an infernal claim upon my property?"

"Prowling vagabonds!" echoed St. James,

in a voice of anger. "Reuben Frampton, impostor!"

"And assassin!" put in Shanks.

"Cut them down!" yelled the infuriated villian.

St. James and his faithful follower expected a sudden attack, and stood prepared. They watched every movement on the part of their assailants, and kept a careful glance upon their treacherous master, whose hands were steeped in foul crime, and whose brain was then working a dark plan for their destruction.

We say their destruction—because he meant to wreck his vengeance upon both.

And yet, why upon the poor servant if upon St. James, his kinsman and rightful heir to the title and estates he held possession of.

He had a reason for ridding himself of St. James, if he wished to save his neck from the gallows.

And that reason was because he knew the rightful claim the young nobleman had upon the property.

If Shanks lived, his life would be one of perpetual misery, of torturing suspense, fearing each hour that passed over his head to be denounced by the valet.

Shanks knew too much; he had seen and heard too much; for that reason he must die.

So thought the black-souled wretch, and during the pause, the men hesitated to fulfil his orders. He had formed a plan for their quiet disposal.

"You may retire," he said to his hirelings, waving his hand contemptuously for them to go. "I would speak with you," he said, turning to our young friend.

"No doubt," thought St. James; "but you don't if I know it."

"O dear me, no!" muttered Shanks, "it ain't good enough for me."

"Come," said the false villain, "you may sheathe your swords."

"I should like to," thought Victor, "but in your body."

"There is no occasion for fear now," Reuben continued. "It was necessary to take such a rash step, but the sudden alarm excited me to go farther than I should have done."

He looked stedfastly at his cousin, and extending his hand, tried to smile a welcome to his noble relative; but the devil had branded his own, and Reuben Frampton showed the mark plainly that warned the young noble of treachery.

"Victor, my dear cousin," said the hypocrite, trying to show signs of emotion that was not real, "can it really be you?"

"And no other," replied St. James, coldly refusing the proffered hand.

"Welcome, welcome,' said the other. "This is happiness I did not expect."

"What mean you?"

"I heard that you were dead, that is, I heard that you had been lured into a trap, and nothing more was seen of you. But come, we will discuss things in a place more *secure* than this, and where walls have *not* ears."

"He means mischief," thought our young friend, as he sheathed his sword, "but I shall be prepared for it, whenever it should come."

Shanks sheathed his sword too, and they followed the plotting wretch into an ante-room.

"Be seated, cousin," said Reuben, pointing to an ottoman, "I will call for wine."

He watched his two guests with a gleam of satisfaction, as they sat down, and he went to the door.

In that moment his whole aspect changed, his countenance wore the expression of a fiend.

He turned, holding the outer handle of the door in his hand, and burst out, his voice full of ireful triumph—

"Cousin, you have escaped the death I meant for you," he exclaimed, "you won't escape now. Farewell, we shall meet *below.*"

Victor sprang up, and made a dash at the trapper. The door was shut as his hand touched the panel.

"We are caught," he said, as he staggered back to the seat, "but it won't be good for anyone who should try to get in here."

"No," said Shanks. "If we are in a trap, we will hold it against all comers."

The poor fellow was very faint-hearted at their failure, but he did not like to show it for fear of dispiriting his noble young master.

The apparent courage of Shanks delighted St. James, and under their painful situation they made themselves pretty comfortable.

"By Jove!" said Victor, looking up for the first time since his capture, for during the two hours of their imprisonment he had remained wrapped in deep sombre thought, and Shanks had watched him with the discretion of a faithful, uncultivated nature. "By Jove, Shanks, there's a cupboard! Just look and see if they have left us any provender. I don't see why we should stay here without they feed us."

Shanks got up, and, to his surprise, found several bottles of wine, besides a very acceptable supply of food, which they both sat down to with appetites of hungry men, and when they rose, there remained but a scanty remnant to show the destruction of their attack.

St. James opened the fourth bottle of wine.

"A few cigars now," he said, "and I should be quite satisfied to make a night of it."

Shanks paused.

Victor jestingly moved from his side to keep a safe distance from the gap, and on turning his head, he beheld on a small marble table a box full of choice cigars.

"The devil!" he exclaimed, looking suspiciously at the new prize.

"Where?" ejaculated Shanks, with a start.

Victor pointed to the box."

"Bo, oo, oh lor," said Shanks; "don't touch 'em in case."

"Devils or cigars, if smokeable, I shall try their flavour. Give me the box."

Shanks approached it very timidly, and looked at it for some moments before he could make up his mind to touch it; when he did, he almost threw it at his master.

The daring young noble took up one of the fragrant weeds, and lit it.

Shanks watched him curiously, and imagined all manner of things in the blue, curling smoke as he blew it from his mouth.

"Try one," suggested St. James.

"Are they nice?" inquired the valet.

"Capital!"

Shanks tried one.

Another soon followed it into smoke.

The cork of the sixth bottle of wine was now drawn.

Whether this wine was any stronger than the other we cannot say, but it took a very strange effect upon both the drinkers, and soon afterwards they both fell back asleep.

They slept soundly, and their loud snoring told the density of their slumbers.

An hour passed, and still they slept.

All now was hushed and still.

The candles in the chandelier burned low, and threw a dusky, flickering gleam about the room.

An expression of horror passed over the handsome, boyish face of the young nobleman, and starting suddenly in his sleep, as though struggling, he groaned, as with agony, and again lay quiet.

Shanks slept on undisturbed, and unconscious of the danger that even at that fearful moment was slowly creeping towards them.

The room door was silently opened, and six masked men approached the sleepers.

Murder gleamed from their blazing orbs, and it certainly gleamed also from the bright daggers each were provided with for their dark work.

Black bandages were put over the heads of our two adventurers.

The intruders then raised the inanimate forms, and bore them carefully and quietly from the chamber.

CHAPTER CIX.

TYBURN DICK MEETS THE TWO STRANGE TRAVELLERS.

THE noise that startled the elder of the two travellers, and interrupted the younger at the colloquy, was the sound of horses approaching.

They secreted themselves in the deep shadows of the surrounding trees, and waited in breathless anxiety for the coming of their foes, as they thought, with whom a very short time before they had had a rather stiff encounter, in which the aged man got wounded in the leg by a bullet from one of the ruffian assailants.

The clatter gradually became more distinct, then died away in the distance as the riders turned their horses' heads in another direction.

The old man breathed freely when again the solitude of the hour remained undisturbed by any noise he so much dreaded.

"It was not them," the young man said, as they crept fearfully from their hiding place.

"Thanks be to the Lord!" feebly ejaculated the old man, "but tell me, Tom, your story. You were saying something about smugglers. I know a little of that life."

"Yes, yes, I am aware of it," replied the other. "Let me see, I got acquainted with a gang of smugglers after sailing about for some time."

"Yes, that is where you left off. Let us be walking on; but go on, give us your story."

"Yes, true; we may as well be going on somewhere, the Lord only knows where. I know of one place where we can rest our weary limbs for the night."

The old man sighed sorrowfully.

"It's very little rest I shall require before I rest in the grave for good," he said.

"I would that I were there now. You know not how weary I am of my wretched life," the young man said, sadly, his dark eyes filling with tears from his heart as he spoke, "but come, father, we must not be ungrateful for the life we have enjoyed. Let us trust in Providence, things may take a different change ere long."

"Spoken nobly, my lad; we must not abuse the life we have enjoyed, as you say. There is one whose watchful eye protects the weak, and guides them to the right path."

"Let us hope for the best," the other said, "and to pass away the time I will tell you a little of what I have gone through."

His companion inclined his head and waited.

"During my last cruise," began the young fellow, "we had on board an overbearing lieutenant, with whom none of the men could bear. His chief aim was to pick a quarrel with me, but, to my best, I always tried to avoid it, for I well knew the temper of the skipper, and had I in any way insulted the lieutenant, he would immediately have had me put under arrest.

"Time flew on, and I, leading a torturing life of misery through his continual bickering, managed, by readily doing my duty, to keep from his clutches, until one day, when he struck me for crossing his path while he was walking forwards.

"The slumbering tiger I had kept chained in its cell—my breast—was suddenly let loose in all its ferocity. I sprang like an incensed devil at the lieutenant's throat, and bore him to the deck, where I fully wreaked my unfolded vengeance upon him, caring little for his loud threats, and thinking nothing of the after consequences.

"Finding in me a determined foe, and knowing he had but little hope for his life in my hands, he bawled loudly for help. The men stood around us with folded arms, none raised a hand in his defence or against me save the skipper and two other officers, who made a run at me, armed with cutlasses and pistols.

"I saw my danger, but did not flinch, not even when the captain put the muzzle of his pistol against my forehead, and swore to blow my brains out. This threat made me the more desperate, and tightening my grasp upon the lieutenant's throat I was determined that he should die with me.

"The skipper saw how things stood, and knew if he carried out his threat he would lose his officer, and that I knew he did not want, for they were a pair of sworn friendly villains.

"'Release your superior officer immediately, and your life shall be saved,' he said; but I laughed. I dared him to the worst. He struck me heavily on the temple with the butt of the pistol, and I fell half stunned, but still with an iron grasp on my foe.

"The skipper striking me was the signal for my messmates to interfere on one side or the other. They turned upon their officers, and had them secured, with their captain, before I had recovered my senses sufficiently to understand what had taken place. I was raised from the deck by old Ben, the boatswain, a man who had always treated me with almost fatherly affection from the first hour I went aboard. Even as he lifted me in his arms I retained my hold upon the lieutenant's throat, whose life I had nearly squeezed out.

"Old Ben bade me release the miserable wretch. I did so, and he fell stiff as a marling spike to the deck, a fearful sight, his face a dark purple, his eyes protruding from their sockets, expressive of the most horrible ture, and his tongue lolling out of his mouth, covered with blood and foam, like that of a mad dog.

"I thought I had sent him to his last account, but my shipmates knew more of his hardened nature than I, and secured him, in case of recovery, to keep him quiet. The captain watched the proceedings, his brow gathering black as a thundercloud, and indicative of a threatening storm, which, had he had his liberty, would have broken out and done fearful destruction to the ship's company.

"The men were aware of this, so to prevent such a catastrophe they detained him as their prisoner. During this time the duty of the ship had not been neglected, and, with a fair wind, she was making good headway towards England, where, had we gone into port with our commanding officers under arrest, would have been signing our own death-warrant, for we should all have been shot for mutiny.

"We were aware of this unpleasant fact, so to arrange a place for our mutual benefit we had the ship's course stopped, and held a consultation. Captain and officers were brought on deck, and old Ben, the coxswain, was selected for spokesman. Confronting the skipper he hoisted his slacks, pulled his forelock, and turning his quid several times from side to side of his mouth, cleared his throat ere he commenced his impressive address.

"'Cap'n,' he began.

"Then there was a pause, a look of despair and astonishment overspread his weather-beaten, honest face.

"Of course we were all wonderfully surprised at this change, and one of the men, thinking he had lost all courage, sang out—

"'Spit it out, Ben!'

"'Can't,' replied the old salt, in a tone of grief, 'it's clean gone.'

"'What?' inquired another.

"'My last piece of bacca, m'cud,' said Ben, and tears trickled down his brown cheeks.

"M'quid I've chewed ev' since we set sail on this unfort'nate cruise."

"Have mine, Ben?" said the boatswain, taking an immense quid from his mouth.

"'Rather had m'own, 'cos I got used to it,' Ben said, refusing several pieces of greasy twist held towards him. 'No, thank'ee, messmates, might git m'own agin to-morrow.'

"This caused a roar of laughter from stem to stern of the ship, for men of such a class are always ready to misconstrue the meaning of another's words when there's the slightest opportunity, as they did with old Ben, greatly to the salt's disgust.

"'Heave it up!' shouted one of the men.

"'Clap a stopper on your jawing tackle,' retorted the old fellow, sharply.

"Getting over his loss, he again faced the captain and officers, and then began something after this style, to the best of my remembrance—

"'Captain Bernard,' he said, speaking steadily, and pulling his forelock at every word, until his head must have felt quite sore, 'let me speak on behalf of my messmates and myself. As yer honour knows, I've been in yer honour's service for more'n nine years, an' never in all that time has yer had to speak a angry word to me, and in course, as a old salt as I'm in yer honour's service, it goes greatly agin my grain to 'ave to speak on such a thing as the one I now speaks of, which I owns looks very much like a mutiny, but it ain't. No, yer honour, it ain't, every one aboard is true to their skipper, an' they surely lent a helpin' hand to their shipmate 'as always done his dooty while he's been aboard, an' why the lufftenant was always agin' him I can't say; but as yer honour might 'ave seen, he always was on the poor young feller; had a very bad time of it; so, axin' yer honour's pardon for being so bold to speak, I hopes as how yer will forgive him for strikin' his superior hofficer.'

"He looked straight at the skipper as he concluded, but the stern gaze of the captain made him shift about uneasily, and poor old Ben thought that he had put his foot into it. The captain said, in a determined voice—

"I'll make no terms, nor listen to any complaints, whatever their nature, while this mutiny lasts. My commands are, that you at once liberate your officers, every man of you get to your duty, and put that rebellious scoundrel in irons.'

"He looked face to face, and saw that my messmates were determined not to move a step until he granted a pardon for me. He smiled to conceal his anger, and said—

"'Come, my lads, to your duty, and no more of this child's play. This is the first time that a disturbance has ever been created amongst you while I have been commander, and I hope it will be the last.'

"'Yes, yer honour, remarked Ben, 'if yer promises to forgive Tom. The lad was driven to it. I've watched the lieutenant ever since he comed on board, and knowed by the first look at his figger'd that there'd be no fair sailing while he was among us.'

"'Silence!' thundered the captain.

"The coxswain fell back several feet, and it took him some time to recover his scattered courage before he could speak again, but he did, and bravely in my defence.

"'Cap'n, I axes pardon for making bold agin, but my feelings makes me. Young Tom has allus been a good lad aboard, and done his dooty, and I've allus respected him for it. So if yer honour ses you'll pardon him, why, we'll set yer free, and all go to our duty.'

"'What!' exclaimed Captain Bernard, 'you, too, rising against me?'

"'No, no, yer hon——'

"'Silence! you, too, shall swing from the yardarm!'

"The old boatswain turned a dirty white at this threat, and walked aft.

"I could plainly see the captain, though helpless as he was, was determined not to give in.

"Nor would the men.

"A look of set determination was upon every face.

"I knew this would not do to last long, and what was more, in the distance we could see a sail bearing down upon us.

"So, to end further delay, I said to the skipper, 'Captain, think of the assault I have committed as you like, and punish me us far as lays in your power, but first think if I had not provocation enough to drive me to it.

"'The lieutenant, as no doubt you have observed from my first day on board, has had an unknown spite against me, trying by taunts, threats, and giving me the hardest the ship's work, and doing all that laid in h power.

"'This he did to make me commit myse in some way, that I might give him a cau to punish me.

"'He found that I treated all this wi contempt, and to-day he struck me for i cause.

"'I could bear with him no longer, ar retaliated. Do as you like with me, captair I now give you your liberty."

"No sooner had I severed his bonds tha he sprang at me.

"I stepped aside, and he fell forward int the arms of his crew.

"An excitable commotion then ensued.

"The officers got free, and arming them selves, dashed amongst the men to the rescu of the captain.

"This outrage incensed the crew to des peration, and they rose in mutiny.

"A fierce conflict took place, in which finished my enemy—the cause of the whol disturbance—by running my sword throug! his breast.

"The captain was stricken to the deck and the other officers fled, and secured them selves in the cabin for safety.

"Ten minutes later, the ship I had seer bearing down towards us was now alongside and it did not take me more than one glauce to see that they were either pirates o smugglers.

"They were the latter, and soon they let us know their business by boarding us with about fifty murderous-looking ruffians.

"Raised in mutiny as they were agains! their captain, the men were true to the! colours, and strongly objected to having their ship overhauled by the unwelcome comer.

"The conflict they had had ripened them for a fresh encounter, and soon they showe! the smugglers the metal they were made o by pitching them headfirst over the ship' side into the surging waves, and many wen to a watery grave.

"I stood by unmoved, nor could I raise a hand on either side. I remember receiving blow from a heavy musket on the head from some ungentlemanly brute behind, that de prived me of my senses.

"When next I awoke, I found myself in the cabin of the smuggler craft, attended by a rather pretty girl, whose tender kindness had brought me round, and saved my life from the murderous clutches of the smuggler chief, whose intent, as she informed me, was to hang me in sight of my ship.

"I soon recovered sufficiently to go on deck, mixed with the villanous crew, as the only source of retaining life, and soon became a favourite with the captain, a most gentlemanly fellow for his profession, I must confess.

"The time passed quickly, as it generally does when a fellow's happy.

"I was happy, although on board a smuggler craft. You look astonished, father."

"Astonished! egads, lad, I am!" said the old fellow, for the first time speaking dering the long colloquy of his companion, "you, who was brought up by the tenderest of parents, talking about being happy, with a gang of brutal men, whose hands were steeped deeply in innocent blood! No, no, lad you must have been dreaming. I know what the life of a smuggler is."

"No doubt," replied the young man. "But while I was abroad I never mixed with that fraternity.

"No, no—not for Tommy! Whenever they were engaged in their slaughtering profession, or blowing other ships out of the water, I remained below, quite content to be with my pretty Greek girl.

"A beauty she was, too—the best out of three the captain took from a harem, and had to kill the Pacha to keep him quiet.

"The captain of the smugglers was exceedingly kind to me.

"The girls he had only got on board the day he fell in with our ship.

"He told me, when we became friends, to choose which I liked.

"I did so.

"She was the best of the three, as you may imagine, as I had my own pick.

"From childhood I always had an admirable taste for pretty girls.

"But this one outdid all I ever before or since saw.

"The captain kept the other two for his own especial use.

"But I was quite content with mine, and spent nine months of very blissful happiness with her—the time I remained with the smugglers.

"We had on board one besides, a very beautiful English lady.

"A curious being she appeared to me.

"I fancied that she was a little deranged, and my curiosity grew so strong at last, that I was tempted to inquire about her of the captain.

"He never would answer a question I put to him concerning her.

"He maintained the most profound silence, besides warning me to keep from her presence.

"I thought this very strange, too, and consulted my pretty Greek about her, knowing women generally learn other people's secrets quicker than anyone else.

"But she declared she knew nothing about her, and appeared quite jealous when I mentioned the strange lady.

"So I had to remain in ignorance.

"She had a splendid cabin to herself, and an English waiting-maid.

"The captain treated the lady with the most marked respect, as though she was a superior being—which she was, but an awfully melancholy one.

"Another thing appeared particularly strange to me.

"She always wore on the same white wrist a splendid bracelet of a costly description.

"I became more and more concerned about this strange, sad lady.

"Her pale beautiful face haunted me, and I could not rest.

"I resolved, while on our way to England, to discover something concerning the lady; and as the only means of doing so, I sought an audience with her English maid.

"The girl was very cautious, and I had to try for some time, and very hard before she would let me into her confidence.

"But as I told her I should leave the ship as soon as we reached our dear native shore, she appeared gladdened, and immediately told me all she knew, which she had learned from the lady herself

"The lady's husband, a young officer, being called away shortly after their marriage on account of a threatened war, left his young wife in the charge of her cousin—a man with a handsome face and a silvery tongue, but a soul darker than the pits of eternity.

"He loved the gentle lady, and in her husband's absence urged upon her his base suit.

"She, of course, rejected him with stern dignity, for she loved her noble soldier-husband.

"The treacherous villain found his persecutions did not avail him much.

"His brute passions gradually grew stronger, and he at last became desperate.

"He went out one day in a very strange manner, took the lady's only child with him—a gallant boy, who bore the proud lineaments of his sire; and when the cousin returned in the night he came alone, and made his way into the lady's chamber.

"She awoke with a sudden start as his burning lips clung to hers in a passionate kiss.

"She shrank from his fiendish look, then started up in bed with a cry of terror, wrung from her gentle soul through his appearance, which recalled the vision of a horrible dream.

"'My husband!' she shrieked in terror; 'my husband! You have murdered him! I saw it in my dream. I saw you strike the assassin's blow that has robbed me of all I loved. See—see! your hands are dyed in his blood!'

"The maid said the lady remembered no more.

"The wretch struck her a blow that rendered her helpless, and made her his victim.

"When she awoke in the morning, lying by the betrayer's side, she was mad.

"Deranged as she was, she remembered all that took place.

"The assassin the same evening had her conveyed by some means to some seaport, and given into the hands of the smuggler for him to dispose of her as he chose, so that the wretch should never see her face again. He paid the smuggler liberally for his work, and that is all I could learn; but you know I may find a clue some day in which my knowledge may be useful."

"Well, lad," said the old fellow, "you have seen some strange scenes in your young life, but what you have said corresponds greatly with a rumour I heard about Lord and Lady Kingstone being suddenly missed, and the estate falling into strange hands in a most mysterious way. Tom, boy, be advised by an old man who knows a little more of the world's wickedness than you. Don't mention what you know to any one without you think they are personally interested in the affair; your knowledge may prove useful to you some time or another, murder will out—let it be committed ever so secretly, it will bring its own retribution."

"You are right," replied the young man, "but now I will tell you the remainder of my adventure when the ship was run into the smugglers' haunt off the Cornwall coast."

"Ah!" ejaculated the old man, "was that their haunt?"

"Yes."

"Many a ship have I watched from these towering crags driven to destruction by the wild waves, and when the storm had abated, helped to collect the spoil of the wreck."

"Yes, yes, and when I came ashore I looked for your pleasant hut, and found but the remains of a once happy home."

The old man sighed.

"True, lad, it was once a happy home when I dwelt there with my gentle wife, when the blood-thirsty dogs of the law shot her one day soon after Dick, my foster-son, left us."

"You must have missed your wife greatly."

"Missed her! Alas! I did," replied the old man with tears in his eyes.

"By-the-bye, I have not told you how I parted from my pretty Greek girl."

The young fellow suddenly changed the conversation in order to banish the cloud of sorrow that overspread his companion's brow.

"No, Tom, you have not. I should like to hear; but how did you manage to understand her?"

"Oh," said Tom, "that I managed easily enough. You must understand that ships' crews are in general a mixture of all nations—we had two Greek sailors on board my last ship, and I soon learned sufficient of their dialect to be able to understand the sweet words of my pretty mistress.

"You seem very fond of her, boy."

"I was," said Tom, sighing heavily, "and though I may never see her again I cherish her memory with the tenderest thoughts. When the ship was in harbour," he continued, "and I was leaving to come ashore, she threw herself upon my breast, and burst out in a flood of bitter grief. She wanted to come ashore with me or remain aboard. She was quite willing to be with me anywhere, but I told her it was utterly impossible. And so, after a very touching scene, that almost reconciled me to remain aboard with her, I managed to tear myself from her, and took my departure with a promise to see her again when next they returned."

"And do you intend to keep your promise?" inquired his companion.

"I see no reason why I should not. I love her as I never loved a woman before, and I know I should live happy hereafter with her as my wife."

"Spoken honestly, and if every one were guided as you are by their passions there would not be so many unhappy marriages."

"True. But what is that cloud I see rising yonder?"

"Eh? Why it is the men coming down upon us."

"Let them come; I know not why they should beset us more than other travellers."

"Nor I, lad," replied the old man, tremblingly. "I can't move, my strength is already overtaxed."

"Seat yourself down there," and the young man assisted him to the foot of a tree; "if they want you they will have to take me first, and that will be no easy matter. I am prepared for them."

And so he was, rather warmly, too.

He stood in a splendid resolute position, with his right hand resting on the hilt of a naked sword, and a pair of huge pistols, more useful than ornamental, secured in his waistband, loaded to the muzzle, and primed for immediate action.

The horsemen came thundering down towards him, the old man exhibiting some signs of fear as they drew nearer.

"If they could have escaped us," said one of the mounted hirelings, as they came dashing along the road, "they must be possessed of more than human powers."

"Hallo!" there's one," said another, pointing to the road side where Tom stood.

"Do you want me?" said the young man boldly, as he stepped into their path.

The horsemen immediately gathered around him.

"Well, not exactly," said one, "but by making sure of you we shall find the one we do want."

"And is he the poor old man I rescued from you, cowards that you are?"

"Silence!" demanded another, in an authoritative voice; "'tis the old man we want."

"May I ask why you want him?"

There was a pause, in which the men seemed to hesitate, and looked rather uneasily from one to the other.

The leader dismounted. The others did likewise.

Tom stood resulutely before them.

He knew their intention was to make a search for the old man, and the young fellow was determined to oppose them while he had strength, and protect his aged companion.

"Stand aside, young shaver," said a big, burly fellow.

Tom stood his ground, and looked steadily into the other's fierce eyes.

"Stand aside!" exclaimed the man, with an oath, and laid his hand on his opposer's shoulders, with intent to hurl him from his path.

At that instant, when the ruffian's grip was tightened like a vice, the young man dealt him a blow with his clenched hand between his eyes, which caused him to stagger backwards several yards.

Several of the others saw the act, and rushed fiercely at the offender.

Tom drew his sword, and pointed a pistol.

He stood undaunted, without a thought for his own safety, even as his many ruffianly-looking foes dashed towards him in no degree deterred by his threatening.

Pistols were presented at him, and swords glittered like lightning in the darkness as his enemies rushed upon him.

He fired.

One man fell to the earth with a bullet in his thigh.

The loss of one of their companions incited them to a more furious attack.

Every sword was raised in menacing fury to seek his life.

It was a moment of life and death, and it depended upon the issue of his own caution how the battle should terminate, though to an observer there appeared very little hope for him to entertain, yet he met them calmly ; his sword was raised above his head, and descended with a clash among the cluster of deadly weapons levelled at his breast.

A stream of sparks flew from the trembling steel, and fell to the earth like a shower of golden rain.

Several of the men dropped their weapons through the tremendous pain that ran like an electric shock up their arms, but those who still retained their swords slashed at their young opponent with maddened fury.

Again the young man's sword clashed with theirs, but unfortunately shivered to the hilt. The blade shattered to fragments, and he was left defenceless. Nay, not altogether, he yet had a pistol undischarged.

This he drew, and stood unflinchingly; he meant death to the first who dared lay a hand upon him.

"Back," he said, as one of his assailants approached, "back! or I scatter your brains."

The man came to a stand, suddenly swung his sword round, and knocked the pistol from his opponent's hand; his companions dashed upon the young man, and soon he was bound hand and foot.

Helpless, and totally at their mercy, he expected nothing but death.

Though their will was good for that purpose, they were restrained from the bloody work through duty.

"Say where the old man is, and your life shall be saved," said one.

"Never!" replied the young man resolutely.

"Never mind about him," said another of the party; "the old man can't be far off."

A groan from the poor old fellow just then —who heard this remark, and fearful of discovery—betrayed to his ferocious pursuers his whereabouts, and immediately the whole gang set off in the direction.

The old man was discovered lying at the foot of a tree perfectly helpless, his long silvery hair of many summers hanging about his wan face expressive of the most abject agonised misery.

Yet this deplorable scene did not touch any of the brutal ruffians with pity, in a most savage manner they dragged their feeble victim to his feet, and was roughly pulling him along when an interruption occurred they did not expect.

A gallant looking youth suddenly leaped amongst them like an angel of deliverance sent to save the grey-haired old man from his inhuman captors.

The ruffians stood rooted to the earth, where they came to an irresolute stand, and looked in awe at the daunted young stranger.

The youth put his arm around the feeble old man's waist, and confronted the brutal gang with terrible vehemence.

"Cowards !" he thundered.

His fair boyish face flushed deeply with indignation.

"Base slaves! Is this the only sport you have, to illtreat an old man ?"

He lunged furiously at the astonished group, and one of the ruffians who then stepped forward to speak, got a dig that brought him to the ground.

"Away !" exclaimed the youth, following step by step the baffled villains. "Away! ere I slay you all."

A second of the caitiffs fell.

The rest fled in terror, and mounting their steeds galloped away for dear life.

The old man looked up into the face of his young preserver.

"What !" he exclaimed joyously. "Can it be you, Dick, my dear foster son ?"

"Yes," replied the youth (our hero). "I am your foster son, Father Wayne. Tell me what these men wanted with you ?"

"I know not; but I will tell you all I know when we see if young Tom is quite safe."

"Young Tom," said Dick.

"Yes—yes. Come, let's seek for him."

Dick was very willing to do so, and moved along, but old Wayne had not strength to accompany him.

Dick sat him down by the roadside, and

HE UTTERED A CRY AS HIS STEED CLEARED THE GATE.

then went off in search of the gallant young man.

"Young Tom!" shouted Dick at the very top of his voice, "where the devil are you?"

"Here," came a voice in answer from the eastward.

Dick followed the direction, and found the young fellow a captive to the bonds that bound his limbs.

"Why, Tom," said our hero in astonishment when he had released him, and he was upon his feet, "why, old fellow, this is something I never anticipated."

The young fellow looked at the youth with a puzzled air.

"Surely," he said, "I remember that voice, and have a slight remembrance of your face."

"Of course you have," said Dick, relieving the other of his embarrassment, "have you forgotten your playmate, young Dick Wayne?"

"Yes, yes, of course, I now remember. But Dick, old fellow, how wonderfully you have changed."

Dick sighed sadly.

"Time brings changes and strange scenes too."

"Aye, replied the other, "so I have learned, but what do you in these clothes ?"

"You shall know all anon, but come to old Wayne, who I have left alone."

The boyhood companions walked hand in hand to where the old smuggler passively awaited their return.

"You see, father," said Dick, "we have returned safe."

"Thank God," the old fellow said fervently. Come lads, help me to some place where I may die in peace. I cannot live much longer."

"Say not so," replied Dick, wiping a tear from his eye. "Come, cheer up, you will feel better by-and-by."

"Nay, lad, 'tis too late. My time has come. I hear now my wife's sweet voice. She calls me to her celestial home, where all is bright and glorious. Assist me from here. I would reveal something to you, Dick."

The two young men sorrowfully raised the poor old fellow from the earth, and gently bore him away to an inn, some half-mile distant.

They were kindly received by the hostess, and conducted to a neat, comfortable chamber.

Old Wayne was laid upon a couch, and Dick sent a maid for a physician.

"Come hither," he said, his voice growing almost inaudible.

Dick knelt by his side, and took his withered hand in his own.

The old man made several efforts to speak, and then fell back exhausted.

He squeened the boy's hand, and drew his head to his; and putting his mouth to Dick's attentive ear, tried to breathe to him what he would say, but his breath failed him, and he lay perfectly motionless.

Life was nearly extinct.

Tom procured some brandy, and poured a little down the dying man's throat.

But even that did not appear to take much effect.

A thrill ran through his frame.

He once breathed heavily.

Then again lay apparently lifeless.

Dick and his companion knelt side by side.

Each held a hand, that gradually grew cold and clammy.

They, in sad, earnest reverence, breathed a silent prayer, while they watched and waited for the least signs of returning life.

They watched and waited in breathless anxiety until the profound silence of their patient abandoned the slight hope they had entertained of returning life.

Dick rose, and placed his hand over the old man's heart.

There was just the slightest sign of existing life.

"He sleeps," said the boy to his companion in a whisper.

A faint groan from the old man broke the profound stillness and startled the watchers.

"Are you here ?" were the words that came very weakly from the old man.

Dick bent over him.

"Listen," said Wayne, struggling with his weakness to speak. "I would reveal all while there is yet time. Come closer, my boy."

Dick went very sadly to the old man.

Wayne looked vacantly around him.

"Tom," he said, "where are you ? Come here. I would have you bear witness to what I say."

The young man, too, bent sorrowfully over the dying man.

"Dick," began old Wayne, "you are the Earl of Aldervale, the rightful heir to the property, but you cannot press your claims without the certificate of your father's marriage; this, the countess, your mother, thought she had destroyed at the time. She thought for once she had ridden herself of your father, and committed you to the waves, but my wife, who was her nurse, secured the original, and left a forged one for the countess. It was my wife, too, who saved you from a watery grave, and brought you up in ignorance of your birth."

Here he had to pause for breath.

"Where is the original certificate?" inquired Dick eagerly.

The old man tried to speak.

He drew the boy's head close to him, and in a whisper almost inaudible, said—

"Hidden in the crevice of the rocks in an ebony box, underneath the ruins of my old house, on the Cornwall coast."

He fell back as though exhausted, and lay perfectly quiet.

Dick and his companions returned to their seats.

The boy had learned all he wanted to know.

The knowledge he had so long been secretly searching for.

When the doctor arrived and approached the bedside, they found the old man dead.

He had died without a groan.

Without the least signs of pain.

Peacefully and quiet he had quitted this world. Now he lay a quiet piece of inanimate clay.

Dick stood in a gloomy reverie, with head bowed in grief, and thought how often he had nestled for warmth to that decayed, ceaseless-throbbing breast.

. . . .

Four days later the remains of the old man was followed by the two youthful mourners to a pretty little village churchyard, where it was interred, and for ever closed from the world's light.

Our hero and his companion then started off, firstly in search of Grace, and then, when they had recovered her, they were going on the new expedition for the recovery of the hidden certificate.

We shall see how they succeeded in a chapter or two hence.

CHAPTER CX.

TOM KING FINDS A FRIEND IN LORD ERNEST DALLAS—MARIAN SYDNEY AND HER PURSUERS—A DOG'S TIMELY ASSISTANCE—GABRIEL CARNWOOD DISCLOSED IN FRESH VILLANY.

THE revelation of Captain Montrose, denouncing himself to his friend as Tom King, the highwayman, fell a heavy blow to Ernest Dallas, who loved the daring fellow with a brotherly affection.

He sat motionless for some time, as though doubting the truth of his own hearing.

"Have I heard right?" he said at length, looking at his companion with earnest seriousness.

"That I am Tom King, the highwayman?" answered the exile. "Yes, but not what I am made out."

Ernest Dallas grasped the noble fellow's hand, and held it firmly.

He could not speak for several moments, grief choked his utterance.

"You are joking," he faltered, not attempting to disguise his weakness.

The outlaw was deeply touched by the young nobleman's mark of sincerity, and felt sorry for what he had said, but he would not disown the truth.

"Unfortunately I am not jesting," he said.

"Why have you taken to this fearful life?"

"I had no other course open to me for a living."

"But you had friends."

"I knew them not, if I had. What friends could an outlawed exile, with a price upon his head, have?"

The young lord regarded him with a look of pity.

"I'm one, though perhaps you are not aware of it," he said. "You have had a friend from the first hour of our meeting though I have never had an opportunity of showing that friendship; but now I know how you are placed, let me assist you as a brother, to keep you from this terrible life."

"I am grateful, more than grateful, but it cannot be, my lord."

"Come," said Dallas, "let us be honest with each other. You want money, or you would not have stopped me, and asked for the loan of ten pounds. Take this as a loan, and pay me when you can afford it."

He held out a small roll of crisp notes.

Montrose gently pushed the hand from him.

"No, my lord," he said, "I have no prospects of ever returning them. I cannot accept your generous offer."

"Nonsense. Come, take it, or you will offend me."

"I should be very sorry to do so, but I cannot take that money. I shall be able to get what I want."

"By this degrading occupation, stopping people on the road, and threatening them with instant death if they do not give up that which is their own. No, no, Captain Montrose, such a life was not allotted for you. Let me, as a friend, prevail upon you to accept this; it is merely a trifle. You need not trouble yourself about returning it in too great a hurry, if you never have the means. I shall never expect it, and always feel too happy in assisting you whenever you require aid."

"Captain Montrose felt the sting of the first part of Lord Dallas's speech. A flush of shame mounted his handsome face, and he turned aside to hide the pain he knew his countenance exhibited.

He remained thus some minutes, lost in profound thought, and quite unconscious of his friend's presence.

The young noble took the opportunity to write on a slip of paper, roll it round the notes, and tapping the exile on the shoulder, he put out his hand, saying:—

"Adieu! I remember I have an appointment to keep; you will excuse this abrupt departure."

"I have offended you," said Tom King, hurt by the other's apparent change of manner.

"The deuce no. I hope you don't think so; but I must be off. Meet me to-night at Ranelagh."

He raised his hat with his left hand, while with the other he shook the hand of his friend and contrived to slip the roll of notes into it.

Before Montrose was aware of what he held, after releasing the nobleman's hand, Dallas had vanished from his side like a shadow.

"Most noble, generous fellow!" mentally muttered the highwayman, unrolling the little bundle, and finding he had at his command—through the generosity of Lord Ernest Dallas—bank notes to the value of two thousand pounds.

Needful as he was in want of money, he felt inclined to follow the young nobleman and return it.

That would be offering a gross insult.

No, he could not do that—offend the only friend he now, in his lonely desolation, possessed—a friend that had proved himself staunch and generous.

He rolled the notes up, and placed them in his pocket, with the determination to keep them and return them, when it would appear as though he had gathered the money and was then able to pay the debt.

Yes, it was hard that he should possess that money and live in want, because his pride would not allow him to touch it.

Again he drew it from his pocket and flipped the notes with his finger and thumb one by one; their crisp, rattling sound had an irresistible charm that many less strong-minded than the highwayman would not have been able to resist.

He looked at them longingly, and suddenly he perceived the note Ernest Dallas had written.

The night was very clear—the moon shone brightly and enabled him to read it.

"Do not be offended, my dear Montrose, with what I have done. If you want money, let me know, my purse is at your service. Call on me to-morrow, or meet me to-night at Ranelagh.—Sincerely yours,

"DALLAS."

Montrose, after reading the note carefully, placed it in his pocket, and rode away no longer with the idea of keeping the money untouched; its magnetic charm was too powerful for him, and he fell an easy victim to its enchantment.

Lord Ernest Dallas, after a brisk ride to keep clear of his companions, let his horse fall into an easy canter, while he enjoyed the peaceful quietness of the hour to meditate upon the meeting with Captain Montrose and his strange career.

The distant sound of equestrians riding swiftly down the road disturbed his reverie.

About half a mile ahead of him he could just discern the figure of a rider, followed by two others who appeared in pursuit of the first.

The foremost of the three was a lady, the other two were men—gentlemen by their rich attire and general appearance he could see as they came now in view.

One glance told the young nobleman the purpose of their ride, both were masked.

"Two ruffians in pursuit of a lady," he muttered, his proud eye flashed as his sword left its sheath. "I am wanted to the rescue."

A touch upon his rein, and his steed bounded forward. The lady was about to turn down a bye road that would have taken her in quite the opposite direction, when Dallas, seeing her danger, dashed across a ditch and hedge to overtake her. He had not taken in a view of the course before him until he suddenly came upon a five-barred gate; he waved his cap above his head, and uttered a cry as his steed cleared the gate.

The lady had now come so near, that Ernest Dallas could see her white lovely face expressive of the fear she felt at being overtaken by her dastardly pursuers.

But as her gaze fell upon the handsome features of the young nobleman a look of recognition brought a gleam of hope to her pale cheeks, and she exclaimed—

"Oh, my lord, save me! oh, save me!

"Marian Sydney," mentally ejaculated Ernest Dallas. "Save you—sweet lady, with my life."

"Oh, thanks—a thousand thanks," she said, her sweet voice tremulous with agitation, and she reined her palfrey for protection behind her gallant young defender.

"Who are these men?" he asked.

"I know them not," she answered, "but I know they mean me no good; they have followed me from my home."

"She had not time to say more.

The foremost of the two men plunged his spurs into his horse's flanks, and drawing his sword dashed furiously forward.

He did not for an instant think that the slim youth who had spoken to the lady would dare intercept him.

He did not think so until he found himself suddenly compelled to rein in.

The young nobleman drew his horse across the road, and calmly confronted him.

The other, being brought to an unexpected stand, glared fiercely upon his opposer through the holes of his mask. A wild oath burst from his lips, and raising his sword above his head, he shouted—

"Stand aside, or I will cut you down."

"Not if I know it," was the cool reply.

"Fool!" exclaimed the other, savagely. "Let me pass, or my sword shall make the way."

The youth laughed lightly.

"Not till I have seen your face," he said. "I think I have heard that pleasant voice before."

He held his sword with the point resting on his saddle, and sat regarding the two men with a look of quiet daring, which evinced a strange and calm determination to keep them back.

Marian trembled in every limb with fear for her cousin's daring lover.

The masked men standing side by side and staring furiously at the youth who kept them from the object of their pursuit, looking like two savage tigers suddenly brought to bay by a daring hunter: there stood the maiden's pursuers, eager for their prey, yet not venturing to advance one step towards her, because of her gallant defender's gleaming sword.

"May I ask, gentlemen," Lord Ernest Dallas said, at length, in a tone of biting irony, "What you want with this lady?"

"She is my wife," said the foremost of the two, speaking in an assumed tone, "and what cause she had for leaving me I really cannot say, nor have you a right to question."

"Good cause I should say if she were your wife," said Lord Dallas; "but as she is not, and I happen to know the lady, I shall endeavour to keep her from you."

"Cut him down!" yelled the other. "How dare he stand between man and wife?"

"Do not let them take me," said Marian. "I am not his wife."

"I need not your word to assert that, dear lady," said the young nobleman. "Gentlemen, stand back. Having seen this lady home safe from your clutches, I shall be at your service with my second at any appointed place."

But neither of the masked riders moved an inch.

There was a dark murderous gleam in the eyes of the elder as the dauntless youth dashed forward.

"Shoot him down!" he cried to his companion as with his own sword he crossed that of his young antagonist; "fire upon him—confound it, the girl will escape!"

Such indeed seemed a very likely occurrence.

In obedience to his companion's kind instruction, the second gentlemanly ruffian drew a pistol from his belt, and going behind the youth, took a deliberate aim at his head.

But before he could pull the trigger to complete his dastardly work, a deep fierce growl was heard from no great distance, and in another second a large black mastiff came leaping along over the hedge, and springing at the coward, fastened his fangs into his throat, and bore him to the ground.

The baffled ruffian lay stunned by the heavy

fall, with the sagacious animal standing quietly over him, growling to himself with much satisfaction.

Marian Sydney gave a glad cry at the timely deliverance.

"Jet, noble old fellow," she said.

Jet gave her an affectionate look that meant more than words could translate.

The young nobleman turned his head to see what had become of his second opponent; he knew the imminent danger he was in but a few seconds before, and wondered that the ruffian had not fired.

Seeing his dumb preserver standing over the masked man, he felt grateful, and said—

"Keep him there, old fellow."

The dog wagged his tail in a most sagacious manner.

He seemed to know that the youth was quite safe while he had but one to cope with, but he kept his eyes fixed on his master's antagonist with an expression of more than dog-like sagacity, ready at any moment to fix his teeth in the masked man's throat should the battle terminate in his favour.

It would have been difficult to say on which side glory would fall.

The contest continued with such desperation as to threaten to have a fatal termination.

Lord Dallas' opponent was a powerful man, and could use his weapon well, but the youth's supple wrist was like iron in its strength, and he held his drawn sword with a skill and coolness which in one so young was quite marvellous.

But it was not the first time that he had fought hand to hand.

On many occasions before this he had defended himself against powerful odds.

Even on the battle field, surrounded by the maddened enemy, he had stood his ground, cool and collected, while his comrades fell like reeds around him; he fought with a small company at his back, and cut his way through the opposing ranks.

With this knowledge he did not lose his confidence.

In the art of sword science he had gained a masterly knowledge through the tuition of the brave old veteran, Lord Sydney.

So cool he was, yet so quick in parring the rapid, heavy strokes of his exasperated foe that you could see his skill was inherent, like his fearlessness, and he seemed to like the peril of the excitement.

Which the other did not.

He had tried every trick of fence he had received from the most expert masters, and found himself met at every point.

"Curses!" he muttered, spitefully, between his clenched teeth. "If it were not for that confounded dog, I should not have to fight this duel by myself."

"Your arm tires," said the youth, still keeping the other actively at work.

His antagonist cursed again, and quickened his strokes with impetuous fury to end the contest.

But Ernest Dallas only laughed at his exertions.

"You would end the contest?" he said. "Well, then, it shall be so."

So saying, he drew back his sword.

Then, with one rapid thrust forward, a slight twist of the wrist, he wrenched the weapon from his opponent's grasp, and left him defenceless.

There was just the shadow of a smile on the youth's handsome face as he placed the keen point of his blade at the other's throat.

A smile of mocking sarcasm, called into life by the look of fear in the quailing eye of his adversary.

Unknown to any sense of fear himself, he could only smile thus at the man who could let such a feeling dwell within his breast.

There was a look of mischief in his eye, and all the beauty of his fine face seemed to die out, and leave such a stern, pitiless expression, that the strong man whom he held at his mercy shuddered as he saw it.

He thought that his time had come.

In truth, it would have been so with him, for the deadly weapon was breaking through his skin, and the next moment would have seen him stricken stark and bleeding from his horse but for the sweet, plaintive voice of the maiden whom he had so savagely pursued, pleaded for his life to be spared.

"Do not kill him," she said, pained, she knew not why; "do not stain your hands with his blood."

"Not kill him, lady," said the youth; "do

you know for whom you intercede? To kill him would be comparative mercy to what you would have suffered had you fallen into his power."

But the lady's gentle pleading saved the sufferer's life.

Lord Ernest Dallas sheathed his sword.

"For your gentle sake, dear," he said, "I spare his life, but let him beware should he again renew this dastardly act."

Even while he spoke thus he was not for one instant off his guard, in case of treachery. He knew the man with whom he had fought, and he wished to remove his mask before they departed, to disclose the villain to the lady.

By an imperceptible touch he made his horse leap suddenly forward, and by a touch with his hand removed the man's mask.

"Gabriel Carnwood," said Lord Dallas, as the other cowered back, ashamed at thus being discovered in his villany before the lady who was to have been his wife. "There, lady; you know now the man you were to have had for a husband."

Too much surprised and terrified at this disclosure of rascality of one of her own kinsmen, she thanked Providence for the deliverance.

"Curse you!" shouted the baffled villain at being thus exposed. "I will have your heart's blood for this! We shall meet again, and then look to it."

"Will you?" laughed the daring youth. "Well, when we meet again, see that you keep your word."

The young lord then turned to see how fared the man Jet held a captive.

He had returned to consciousness.

Once he tried to raise himself when he was again secured with the dog's teeth.

He did not try a second time.

He contented himself to lay perfectly passive beneath the huge paws of his ferocious assailant.

Barely daring to breathe, for fear that the animal should tear the windpipe from his throat, he suffered the most torturing suspense, besides the pain of his wounds.

In the scuffle with the dog his mask got dislodged.

The young nobleman knew him, too, and calling the dog off, he said—

"Ralph Carnwood, you, too, are implicated in this affair. Another account added to the many we have already got to settle. Go your way. Attempt to follow me one step, and, as sure as you do, your career will end."

The gentlemanly ruffian crawled to his feet like a beaten cur, and, mounting his horse, rode away with his brother, each strongly cursing their ill fate.

"Lady," said Ernest Dallas, 'having disposed of those two ill-looking scamps, I shall be most happy if you will suffer me to escort you safely home."

"Thanks," she said, blushing, "many thanks; in truth, I do not know how to thank you for your gallant kindness."

The youth bowed gracefully in reply, and they walked away together.

"My lord," said the gentle girl.

Then she hesitated and blushed.

"Don't you think it very strange that Captain Montrose has never called upon my uncle as he promised?"

"Perhaps," said her companion, "he has not yet had an opportunity. We must not condemn him just yet."

Marian sighed sadly.

"He seems so strange," she said, "so altered since he has been away."

"He has had much to bear, many bitter troubles and fearful wrongs."

"Do you ever see him?" she asked.

The young noble mused.

He did not like to tell a falsehood, yet, under the circumstances, how could he say he had seen him without telling her the fearful truth?

Seeing that he hesitated, she asked again.

"Once," he said, "and but for a few moments."

"Did he say anything of me?"

"He did not breathe your name at the time of our meeting. He appeared very much worried."

The girl asked no more; she seemed very sad and thoughtful.

The rest of their journey they continued in silence.

Lord Sydney, growing uneasy at his niece's

protracted absence, sent messengers out to search for her in all directions.

Gladly did her uncle own her gallant champion when they returned.

"My darling," he said, clasping to his breast the gentle girl, "what has been the cause of your long absence? Has anything occurred to frighten you?"

"Yes, uncle dear, I was pursued by two men."

"Pursued!" exclaimed the old soldier. "Who dared pursue you, my child?"

"The Carnwood brothers," said Lord Ernest Dallas.

"More of their work. They shall pay dearly for this outrage," Lord Sydney said, looking fierce as a tiger. "But how know you, my lord, they were the dastards?"

The young nobleman related the whole of his adventure.

"I thought there was something wrong," said the old veteran, "by the uneasiness of Jet. He whined and tore about the place like mad, and when the door was opened he flew out."

"Noble creature!" cried the youth, "he saved my life and that of your gentle niece; for while I was fighting with Archibald, the other took the cowardly opportunity to get behind me to shoot me, and had not Jet at the very moment when the villain's finger was on the trigger appeared and tore him from the saddle, I should not be here now."

"Did the base wretch do such a cowardly thing as that?" exclaimed Lord Sydney, foaming with rage. "Curse them! this insult shall be wiped out with their blood, if I hang for it."

He buckled on his sword, and despite the pleading of his gentle daughter, he rushed from the house in a fearful rage, to seek atonement for the outrage committed upon his fair charge.

CHAPTER CXI.

VICTOR ST. JAMES AND HIS VALET FIND THEMSELVES IN A DUNGEON—A FRIENDLY VISITOR AND A DEADLY FOE—COMBAT BETWEEN THE TWO.

WHEN Victor St. James awoke from his profound and protracted sleep, his senses were dull, and his brain seemed clouded and oppressive.

Was he really awake?

He rubbed his eyes.

He tried to pierce the heavy gloom.

But not a hand could he see before him.

Even now he must be sleeping.

Else, why this strange feeling?

To ascertain if such was the case, he pricked himself.

He started, as his cold hand touched his face.

He knew now that he slept no longer.

Where was he?

What meant this sombre gloom?

This death-like stillness?

Where was Shanks?

He asked himself these questions.

But not being able to answer any of them, he lay still lost in oblivion.

Suddenly, he made a start to rise.

He could not endure this fearful suspense any longer.

What meant this?

His limbs were cramped.

He could not move.

Horrible suspicions of the truth rushed to his mind.

He had been removed from the ante-room while he slept.

Removed to a vault, or sepulchre, where neither light nor air could penetrate.

Shut from the world, perhaps to linger out the rest of his existence.

He groaned aloud, as he thought of his wretched fate.

Had Shanks awoke just when his enemies were about to carry out their diabolical plan, fought for his master, and fell a victim to the bloodthirsty brutes?

He called upon his servant's name.

But only the echoes of his own voice answered him.

Frenzied by this fearful torture, he made one desperate effort.

He sprang to his feet.

Joy!

His sword still hung at his side.

He drew the blade with a little hope.

He groped his way around the dungeon-wall.

His foot came in contact with some soft substance lying in his path.

He fell over it.

His hand touched a cold, clammy face.

He shuddered.

"Shanks! Shanks!" he shrieked.

A groan answered him.

"'Tis he! 'tis he!" he said, frantically, and clasped a hand he found stretched forward.

Had the poor fellow been half-slain, and left there to linger in dreary agony?

Or was it the drugged wine he had drunk that had produced this lethargy?

Again and again the young nobleman called upon his faithful follower to speak—to say that he was not dying.

After some time of anxiety, Shanks said, very faintly—

"No, my dear master, I don't think I am dying."

Shanks, like his master, had lost almost all power of his limbs, through lying on the damp earth.

But he drew himself up into a sitting posture, and after several minutes' silence, he spoke.

"I should like to know where we are," he said.

"Treacherously buried alive," said his master, bitterly.

Shanks involuntarily shuddered.

"They might have left us a little light," he spoke, in a cheering voice, though his heart lay like lead with sorrowful despair. "But never mind, master; we shall get out of here as we have got out of other places."

"I hope we shall. But I have very little hope of seeing the outward world again."

"Don't despair, sir; the wicked never have it all their own way."

"Have you any idea where you are?" inquired St. James.

"It ain't the room where we had the wine and cigars. Perhaps it's one beneath it—a vault."

"A dungeon or a tomb. The wine we drank must have been drugged; and we were removed to this wretched place while we slept. That is the only way I can imagine we were brought here."

"They might have killed us had they meant us any harm," suggested Shanks.

"We then should have died without any knowledge of our fate, and such a death would have been preferable to the lingering, torturing death we shall now have to endure."

"But still," said Shanks, "while there is life there is hope."

"The hope you cherish depends upon the amount of life you possess. I cannot say am endowed with much of either."

"It's no good to despond if our time has come. We should die anywhere else as here and if it is not we shall escape and live on."

"Shanks, my good fellow," St. James said, "you speak in that brave manner to cheer me, when I know that you feel the helplessness of our situation quite as acutely as I do. But as you say, to cherish this melancholy mood will not enliven our dismal moments; so, if you are able to stand upon your feet, we will, as well as we can in the dark, examine our prison, and try for some way of exit."

"Oh, yes," said Shanks, readily, "I can stand."

He sprang to his feet, but his legs had not power enough to support him, and, swayi to and fro like an intoxicated man, he w compelled to lean against the wall for port.

Victor St. James, who had recovered little strength, took his valet's arm, and they groped their hands round the vault, tapping every inch of the wall with the pommels of their swords, and sounding the roof and ground.

But no signs of any entrance could they discover.

All had the same solid sound.

Going through this process three or four times with the same ill-success, they sank down, side by side, on the cold, damp earth, and there sat exhausted, without either food or drink to sustain their agony.

Shanks no longer maintained that vain hope of liberty now that he had ascertained how hopeless was their position.

A conviction of a slow, torturing death stared him in the face.

He imagined his last few hours of life, raving with maddening thirst, and being gnawed by the large rats that were now playing about him, as though in anticipation.

He thought of it with horror, and determined to put an end to his existence before it came to such an awful crisis.

"We can't live much longer like this," he said, in a quiet tone, that plainly showed he had resigned himself to his fate.

"You see now, then," said St. James, "how inevitable our death is; and have good cause for despair."

"Oh, no," Shanks said, "I don't despair. If death is to come, I must meet it like a coward; but—but before I die, I should like to tell you something."

"Very well, Shanks. But you won't die just yet."

"Yes I shall, very soon."

"Anyone to hear you would think you intended to kill yourself."

"So I am."

"Shanks," exclaimed his master, startled by the quiet determination of his voice, "is that talking like a brave man, to meet death half way?"

"But I can't help it," said Shanks, in a choking tone; "I can't live to be eaten by the rats."

St. James sighed.

It was a horrible contemplation to be conscious food for rats, and too weak to keep them off.

"Shanks," she said, "tell me what you would; and if by the time your revelation is done we see no hope, we will die together. We certainly could not live to be devoured."

Shanks clasped his master's hand in speechless gratitude.

It was some minutes before he could master his emotion.

Then he spoke.

"It is something awful I have got to say," he began; "but it is better you should know it, sir. But I hope you won't take on when you hear it."

"Who does it concern?" inquired the nobleman.

"Your father, sir."

"Go on. I am prepared for the worst."

"Well," began the valet, getting as close to his master as he could, "when you were lost in London, and after I had made many searches for you, I returned to your apartments to look after the things, and thinking that you would return some day."

"I knew a little about your cousin and Lady Edith's father. I knew, too, it was through them that your father—poor gentleman—lost you from his side. I also knew that they wanted to get you out of the way, to complete the villanous work they had begun. So I always kept a secret eye on their movements, when they least expected it."

"Well, sir, it was one night when I was out that I saw them walking together. They held a converse not above their breath. I knew it meant no good, so followed them to hear of what they were talking.

"I can't exactly remember every word that passed between them, but the words were to this effect: Lord Bernille said that now they had got you out of the way was their time to act. St. James, your father was next to be got out of the way. Reuben Frampton was then to take possession of your estate, and marry Lord Bernille's daughter, Lady Edith.

"Having gained so much information, I was determined to keep a sharper look upon them than I had done, and the following night I concealed myself in the shrubbery, so that I could see all that took place. It was about half-past ten o'clock when a carriage drove up in front of the door. Your father, with Lord Bernille and Reuben got in, and the vehicle was driven away. I mounted on behind, determined to watch their movements, and be at hand in case of treachery.

"The carriage was taken into a forest, and when in the very heart, from whence no cry or groan could reach the outskirts, the carriage was brought to a stop by three ruffians. I imagined this to be an arranged plan, so, to be prepared for action, I got down from my perch, and concealed myself.

"Lord Bernille put his head out of the carriage as though very much alarmed, and demanded what the ruffians wanted. The men acted their part well. They compelled every one to alight by threats to shoot them if they did not immediately comply with their demands.

"Your sire was the last to get out, and no sooner did his foot touch the ground than he received a blow from the coachman, who had dismounted. 'I suppose he was one of the gang, he having acted the most treacherous part. I thought it my duty to get him out of the way first. I fired from where I stood, and the man rolled to the earth a corpse.

"This sudden interruption started the guilty villains, and two of them fled, but the stern voice of Lord Bernille made them return, and he commanded them to look for the spy —meaning me—and let him share the fate of his victim.

"I no sooner heard this, than I retreated in an opposite direction, knowing that their search would first take place from whence the shot came. So it did, but not finding the object of their alarm, they returned to their murderous work.

"Let this job be got over," said Lord Bernille. One of the ruffians leaned over your father, who lay stunned and perfectly at their mercy. The man drew a long, gleaming dagger, and was about to plunge it into the old gentleman's heart, when I fired the second pistol. That man fell dead. I then drew my sword, and dashed among the gang of assassins."

"Ah! ah! it's you is it?" said Reuben Frampton, making a furious pass at me with his sword, " I think that will stop your firing, fool," he exclaimed, as I staggered and fell to the earth, as though badly wounded. His sword appeared to be through me, but it only pierced my clothes. I was left where I fell for dead. Then Reuben raised his sword and struck St. James. I bounded to my feet, and with my weapon, gave him a fearful cut across the head. Then I fell again."

"This will finish him," I heard someone say behind me, and the next moment I received a blow that left me stunned. When I awoke to consciousness, no traces of the murderers could I see. The place was as quiet, and the grass as green, as though not a foot had been near to disturb it. That ends my narrative," said Shanks, in conclusion.

St. James had listened to the dreaded revelation apparently unmoved.

He made no comment whatever upon the tragedy.

Shanks was astonished at his seeming calmness. The poor, faithful fellow knew little of his young master's internal sufferings, the greatest of all grief.

How silently—how intently the young nobleman prayed—prayed to be spared to seek atonement for the wrongs he had suffered —to avenge his sire's death, and rescue the gentle girl he loved from her villanous persecutor's vile grasp.

Shanks sat and wondered at his master's profound silence, fearing almost to breathe.

The stillness was suddenly broken by the noise of someone putting a key in the lock of a door that communicated with their cell.

St. James grasped his follower's arm, and, in a whisper, said—

" Shanks, they come to kill us."

In accordance with each other, they both sprang to their feet, drew their swords, and awaited in breathless anxiety to pounce upon those who entered.

Presently the lock sprang back with a grating noise, then a ponderous door was slowly opened, and a man about forty stood at the entrance with a lantern in his hand.

He raised it above his head. The dull, flickering glare fell upon the features of the prisoners.

St. James stood like a statue in the centre of the dungeon.

Not a muscle, not a sinew disturbed the placid expression of his white, handsome face.

He looked like one carved from marble, so lifeless did he appear, leaning on his sword, with the point deep in the earth, but his eyes wore a glare with a lurid light that looked dangerous.

Shanks, too, stood motionless by his master's side, awaiting the approach of the intruder.

No sooner did the man's gaze fall upon the captives, than he uttered a cry, and bounded forward.

Shanks sprang forward with drawn sword to meet him.

St. James, only in time, grasped his valet's arm, and pulled him back to prevent a thrust that would have laid the visitor a dabbled corpse at their feet.

" My prayer was heard," he cried, " and God has granted me life."

Throwing aside his weapon, he affection-ately embraced the astonished stranger.

"Jacob! Jacob!" he said, "you are our friend."

"Ready to sacrifice my life for you, my dear master," said the man.

He put down the lantern, and then, in a friendly way, shook the unbelieving Shanks cordially by the hand.

"Come, Shanks," he said, sincerely, "you have not forgotten your old friend, Jacob Martin?"

"Oh, no," replied the valet; "I ain't forgot you. But are you like the rest of 'em; be-cause if you are, why, mind my sword don't go through you."

"Like the rest?" repeated the old fellow; "no, Shanks, and I never thought that you would think so of your dear master's steward. Lord Ecclestone would have turned me ont long since could he possibly have done with-out me. Since he has had possession of this domain I have been holding the candle to the devil, as the saying is."

"Where are we?" inquired Shanks, still retaining a firm hold on his sword.

"In one of the secret dungeons, and the sooner you get out of it the better it will be for your health."

"*If they get out of it at all!*" said a deep, fierce voice.

Jacob Martin sprang round in time to see his danger.

A big, burly ruffian stood behind him with upraised sword.

A murderous gleam shot from the brute's fierce eyes.

Jacob knew his danger, and jumped aside as the gleaming weapon fell.

Fell with intent to cleave his head in twain.

The old fellow's quick movement frustrated the assassin's design.

The ponderous blade came down with fear-ful force.

But far off its intended prey.

Jacob being perfectly without a weapon of defence, bounded gladly to and secured the one St. James had cast aside.

He turned upon his assailant, who had followed him up.

Their swords met with a heavy clash.

A friend and a foe of the captives stood face to face with intent to kill.

Their was nothing scientific in their play.

Heavy blows were dealt and received un-flinchingly by both.

The fight did not last long.

The ruffian fell, pierced through the heart, and Jacob looked at him at his feet without a feeling of regret.

He cleaned his bloodstained weapon on the fallen man's garments.

"Come, my lord," he said, turning to St. James. "There is no time to be lost if you would save the lady you love."

"Is she in much danger?" inquired the youth, eagerly.

"Not so imminent but that she may be saved if not too much time is lost."

"What peril is it that threatens her?"

"A hated union with your cousin."

"Lead the way. This day shall end all. The Lord have mercy upon the base usurper! for as surely as we meet, my sword shall send him to his dread accounts. Hasten on, good Martin."

The old fellow closed the dungeon door upon the slain ruffian, and then led the way through many dark passages and stone stair-cases before they came to any of the upper apartments.

"Your arm, Shanks," said Victor St. James suddenly overtaken by a faintness that deprived him of all animation.

He leaned on his valet, and staggered into a room, where he fell, perfectly powerless, to the floor.

"Martin," he said, "bring me some power-ful stimulant, that will lend me life to rescue my dear girl, if it kills me afterwards."

Old Jacob retired to obey.

Shanks raised his young master from the floor; and lying him on the couch, knelt by his side, holding one of his small, white hands in his own, with tears rolling down his cheeks.

"My master," said the faithful fellow sob-bing like a child.

"Shanks, my good fellow," the young noble said, very feebly, "I shall be myself pre-sently. It is merely an attack of debility."

"This, my lord, will give you strength," said Jacob Martin, entering and giving to it

HE SAW AN OFFICER STOP AND SPEAK TO A MAN.

young nobleman a glass containing a potent draught of his own mixing.

Victor swallowed it without the least hesitation.

His pale cheeks instantly flushed with a hectic glow, and his eyes became strangely red, but dull, as though covered by a film.

He tried to rise, but could not.

"Heavens!" he exclaimed; "what is that you have given me? It has rendered me more weak than I was before, and yet my blood seems to be on fire."

"If you lay quiet, sir, for a few minutes,' said Jacob Martin, "you will find the benefit from it. But you must be quiet for it to take effect."

"Wait!" frantically yelled St. James; "wait while she is being dragged to a worse fate than death! All—all is now lost! While I lie here she is being sacrificed!"

He clasped his hand upon his brow.

His frame shook with a convulsive throb, and then he lay motionless as though in death.

Shanks sprang up fearfully excited.

"My master," he exclaimed, in a deep, determined tone, "shall be avenged!"

And kissing his beloved young master's cold brow, he drew his sword and dashed from the room.

"Come back, fool! You will be killed," said Martin, calling after Shanks.

A wild laugh rang through the house in answer, and the next instant the hall door closed with a tremendous bang, that announced the valet's departure.

CHAPTER CXII.

THE LUSHER COMMITS A DARING ROBBERY UPON AN OLD VICTIM—CHANGES CLOTHES WITH A PRIEST, AND BECOMES ACQUAINTED WITH SHANKS.

THE redoubtable Lusher seemed destined not to see the object of his long and hazardous journey.

When within a mile of the mansion where his adored Mary Jane lived as housemaid, his mind was fully occupied by the joyful anticipations of the meeting he so much longed for.

Thinking of the pair of soft, round arms that would entwine around his neck—the pretty, parting lips that would cling to his, and many other delicious privileges his love would bestow upon him to welcome his return, he was lost to everything, save his own reverie, until an incident occurred that brought him to himself.

He jumped round as a voice he had a slight remembrance of hearing before called out—

"Stop, you thief!"

He turned, and confronted an old enemy.

He did not lose his courage at this unexpected meeting.

"You villain!" said the old fellow, puffing and blowing, out of breath through running to overtake the Lusher. "I—I know you, you scamp!"

"I think I have seen you before," said Jack, coolly.

"Yes, you scoundrel—you—you thief!" the old fellow jerked out, foaming with rage. "You robbed me in the Cornwall mail, and now I have caught you. I—I "——

"Mean to rob you again," said Jack, producing a pistol, which he put uncomfortably close to the gentleman's nose; "so hand out your coin, old boy."

The old boy had no intentions of doing anything of the sort, nor did he think the demand was meant.

But it came again, stern and prompt, and the cold iron of the pistol touched the tip of his nose.

The old fogey fell back several paces in speechless amazement at the audaciousness of the daring highwayman's demand.

He glared like an incensed tiger into Jack's face, and suddenly blustered—

"You—you villain! Would you rob me again?"

"Of course I would," was the quiet rejoinder. "So come, hand out, or you go down dead as a boiled monkey."

"You rascally rebel! you shall hang for this!" exclaimed the old gent.

"Shut up," said Jack.

"Move that pistol directly from my face."

The Lusher did quite the reverse, for he took the other weapon from his belt, and placed one on each side of his victim's cheek.

"Now," he said, "if you don't part with every farthing of your coin in less than a minute, off goes both your ears."

"This is murderous."

"It will be."

"You villanous scamp."

"Don't call me names, or you are a dead man."

"You would shoot me?"

Jack nodded.

"Then you would kill me in cold blood because I don't choose to give you my money?"

"It ain't any good to you," said the Lusher.

"You can't do much good with it, or you would not want to rob me now, after the large amount you took from me not many days ago."

"I do more good with it than you do," Jack said, replacing one of his pistols. "I rob the rich to give to the poor. That's more than you do."

"You audacious thief," exclaimed the old gent, "how do the large institutions and churches rise if I and other gentlemen don't subscribe for their foundation?"

"No doubt," said Jack; "but I don't call that charity. What I do is the right sort."

"Not benevolence," thundered the old fellow, "to build churches for the good of the nation?"

"No," said Jack, "it ain't. A hungry man can't fill his belly on another man's sermon; but he can with a loaf, and I have filled many a poor devil's with the fruits of my profession. I have given all my money to the poor, and want some more, so out with it."

He pressed his pistol to the old fogey's face, and as he went back followed him until the gent was stopped by coming in contact with a tree.

The old fellow saw that to trifle any longer with his highwayman would be dangerous, and having no alternative to save his life but by the delivering up of his money, he re-

Instantly drew from his pocket a goodly filled purse of gold, and groaned as he saw it disappear into the Lusher's pouch.

Master Jack then cautiously advised his victim not to attempt any act of treachery after being liberated for such a trifling amount.

The old gent was only too glad to get out of range of the pistol that had kept him in such a perpetual state of fear, and caused him to submit to the robber's demand.

He turned once, when at a distance of safety, and shaking his fist at the Lusher, who had taken a circuitous route to his place of destination, to throw his pursuers off his track in case of being followed, wended his way, grumbling like a bear with a sore head.

The Lusher's manœuvre for safety did not prove so successful as he anticipated.

It had taken him a considerable distance out of his way, and being very anxious to behold his Mary Jane, he took a near cut across a private ground to shorten the space which lay between them.

He was now on the boundary of the fertile land that surrounded the Glenmorris estate.

A joyous cry escaped his lips, as his gaze fell upon his adored Mary mounted upon a ladder in the orchard, gathering fruit from the trees.

His heart momentarily bounded to his mouth, and he stood transfixed to the spot, overjoyed with happiness, gazing rapturously upon his heart's idol.

Jack's face was suddenly suffused with a glow, and calling loudly upon the name of his love, he was in the act of making his way to her, when a gruff voice fell like a death-knell upon his ears, calling for him to surrender.

He turned, filled with fearful apprehensions, and, to his inexpressible horror, saw the old gent with officers, whom he had met and informed of the robbery, coming towards him.

Jack gave vent to a most dismal howl, and took to his heels.

At that instant Mary Jane, who had heard her lover's voice, looked around with anxious eyes, and seeing the danger that threatened him, she uttered a terrified cry, and fell to the earth.

The Lusher, while flying along, saw the accident, and came to an involuntary stand.

For a few seconds he stood debating whether to confront and fight his pursuers, and go to his lover's assistance, or continue his course of flight, for he was not certain that, alone, he could vanquish the officers.

But he flattered himself that he could outstrip them in a long run, as they were not mounted, so with this thought, and the remembrance of an old maxim, which says, "self preservation is the first law of nature," he started off again like a hare before the hounds, nor did he stop until compelled to do so for want of breath.

Even then he did not feel safe, though he had gone a good five miles, but he ventured to look behind him, and not seeing his pursuers in sight he leaned against a tree to recover a little wind.

He did not long indulge ere the wind bore upon his ears the clamour of distant voices, that bore to him the tidings that the officers were still on his track.

Off again the Lusher went, at marvellous speed for his corpulent size.

Blindly, madly tearing onwards, scrambling over all impediments that barred his way, he continued flying before the wind, until suddenly brought to the earth by coming in collision with a priest, who was peacefully wending his way to fulfil some sacred calling.

For the moment Jack thought he had run into the arms of an officer, and was about to continue his run when his eyes fell upon a black robe and a clean-shaven face of the man he had felled to the earth.

A bright idea flashed to his mind.

"Well, father," he said, "what are you lying down there for?"

"Truly, my son, it was thyself who laid me low."

"Come, get up. I want to speak to you."

The holy man staggered to his feet.

The sudden concussion had somewhat shaken him.

Jack had no time to stand upon ceremonies.

Drawing one of his formidable weapons, he presented it full in the priest's face, who fell back, quailing at the sight of the deadly tube.

"Replace that murderous instrument," he faltered.

"Look here," said the Lusher. "I am pursued, and must have your robe and cowl for a disguise."

"But, my dear brother, it cannot be now, for I have the ceremonies of a wedding to perform."

"I can't help that. My life depends upon this chance alone; so you had better submit quietly."

The priest looked at him in terrified amazement.

Jack seeing that he hesitated, and having no time to lose, felt compelled to use force.

He grasped him by the nape of the neck, and hurled him to the earth.

In a moment taken the robe and cowl off him, them on his own person.

He then gagged the astonished priest, and, binding him hand and foot to a tree, left him to his wretched fate. The Lusher, while going along, felt for his handkerchief, and his hand slipped into an inner pocket of the robe. He drew forth a letter addressed to the Rev. W. Gristen.

Jack, feeling curious, opened the note, and read as follows :—

"17th August.

"Reverend Sir,—The marriage we have decided to take place to-morrow. Be at the chapel by the ruined castle by ten o'clock. The lady's father will be there, therefore you must not let any objections she may raise as an excuse deter you from fulfilling your duties. Shut your eyes and ears to any interruption that may arise, and when the ceremonies are at an end, there is a thousand pounds at your service. Be to time, at the place appointed, as delay may be dangerous. —Yours, etc., "LORD ECCLESTONE."

"Oh!" ejaculated the Lusher, folding the epistle and replacing it in his pocket. "A thousand pounds easily earned. I wonder what sort of a priest I make?"

He scanned himself, and mentally said— "I shall do."

While the Lusher is making his way to the chapel of the ruined castle to fulfil the office of the priest, the supplicating cries of a woman rang through the forest glade in distressing accents, mingled with the rumble of a chariot and four that came tearing along the quiet country road, bearing the pleading girl to a wretched fate.

"Father! father! hear me!" cried the gentle girl, in utter despair, as the carriage rolled round the bend of the road. "I beseech you, as my father, to hear me. Oh! save me from this hated man. I cannot— I will not be his wife!"

"Hush, hush, child!" commanded a stern voice. "It is my wish that you shall be Lord Ecclestone's wife, and if you do not love him you will have to learn."

"Oh, I cannot have him. Think, father, of the unhappiness you will bring upon me by forcing me to this marriage; think of my mother's last wish, when on her dying bed she asked you not to force me to marry anyone I did not like. Can you, with that remembrance, compel me to wed this man? How cruel you are to your only daughter. You seem not like my father. Speak to me, say this is a delusion. Father, father! pity your only child; this cruel silence will drive me mad!"

She sank at his feet, and buried her tearful face between his knees.

Yet he sat with sternness regarding the fair, gentle girl unmoved, with the determination to sacrifice her before the altar to the villanous usurper who sat opposite him, his crafty face beaming with savage triumph.

Edith raised her head, and looked imploringly into her father's face. But there she saw no hope.

"Father," she said, pleadingly, "do you intend to sacrifice me?"

"Edith, my child, it is for your good," he said. "Why is it that you have such an inveterate repugnance to this union?"

"Because I cannot love the man you have chosen for me," she answered, struggling to smother her emotion. "I cannot marry this man, because I love another."

"A penniless outcast," sneered her father.

"And through whom?" she said, proudly, as she rose to her feet. "He whom you have allotted for my husband; but who, I swear to Heaven, shall never be."

A taunting laugh from the coward, who thought the beautiful girl was now his helpless victim, brought an indignant flush to her fair face.

One round, alabaster arm was put out of the carriage window, her tiny white hand nervously clutched the handle of the door, and in another moment she stood on the step.

"God will forgive me," she exclaimed. "Better this than life with him."

She closed her eyes, and made a dart forward, to throw herself beneath the chariot-wheels as it rolled round the corner.

A second more, and she would have been a mangled corpse. But at that moment, when all hope seemed gone, and she had jumped from the step, her father made a clutch at her skirts, and by a desperate effort of strength, managed to pull her back into the carriage.

For a few minutes she lay at the bottom of the carriage, as though in a swoon.

Then suddenly she jumped to her feet with such a change of countenance that it started both her companions.

Her soft blue eyes gleamed with a kindling fire, and her fair cheeks blanched with inward sufferings that made her beautiful bust heave and fall as she scanned the pitiless features of her father.

"Why did you save me?" she exclaimed.

"You will know very soon," was the laconic, cruel reply.

"I cannot live! I will not live to be his wife!" she said.

Her voice was no longer gentle and pleading, but loud and determined.

She tore the long lace veil from her head, and trampled beneath her feet the wreath of orange blossoms that had been forced upon her brow.

Lord Benville and his colleague looked at each other in speechless amazement at this unexpected turn in affairs.

Just then the chariot drew up before the chapel of the ruined castle.

"We shall see now, my love, what the priest says to your objections," said Reuben Frampton, as he eagerly alighted.

"Some wretch, no doubt, whom you have bribed to complete my misery!" exclaimed the poor girl, frantically.

Driven desperate by the hopelessness of her position, she sprang after her base persecutor and caught him by the throat.

Her tiny fingers dug into the flesh of the dastardly wretch.

He was held paralysed by the sudden attack, and from strangulation his face turned purple, and his eyes protruded from their sockets.

"One of us shall die," she said, calmly.

"Fool!" hissed her father, and he dealt her a cruel blow that brought her staggering back into the coach.

Reuben, released, muttered a fierce oath, and went to the chapel.

He stamped impatiently upon the ground, and swore in a most ungentlemanly manner.

Lord Benville, thinking he had settled his daughter for a time, alighted too.

"Curse the fellow," were the first words that greeted him from the infuriated Reuben Frampton.

"What's the matter?" inquired the old man coolly.

"The matter? why that idiot has not yet come."

"It is yet five minutes to ten," said the other.

They waited in torturing suspense until five minutes past.

Every moment seemed an age while they waited and watched for the coming of their confederate in the devilish work they were so anxious to complete.

"Do you think he has misunderstood the day?" asked Lord Benville.

"The devil, no," sharply replied Reuben, "how could he be fool enough to do that when I distinctly told him in my letter of yesterday to be here to-day precisely at ten?"

"He may have had some obstruction to prevent his being here to time."

"Then why did he write back an answer to my letter, and say that he would be here at any hazard. I mean to have the girl."

"Don't be impatient."

"Impatient! I think I have waited long enough."

"He may have met with an accident on the road, perhaps."

"Confound your miserable suggestions," thundered the infuriated bridegroom, and turning upon his heel he walked to and fro spitefully kicking every little stone from his path, and tugging at his hair until his head must have been quite sore.

Presently Lord Benville said—

"Edith appears strangely quiet, see if anything is the matter with her—the fall may have stunned her."

Reuben Frampton hastened to the carriage door, but to his amazement he found that Edith had escaped.

Recovering from his amazement sufficiently to speak, he yelled out madly—

"Gone!—she has gone!"

The words fell like a thunderbolt upon her father. He made one bound from where he stood, and landed at the chariot door.

"Gone!" he iterated, his aged face blanched with rage and despair.

"Then we are ruined!"

"Not yet," said the other, with terrible vehemence. "She can't have gone far by this time."

"Without someone has followed us, and helped her to escape."

"If such is the case their minutes are numbered. Curse them! they shall both die directly I overtake them! but if she is alone, I will bring her back. She shall suffer for this daring attempt."

"Away, then, away! There is no time to be lost."

Reuben still hesitated. He wanted something to carry him faster than his legs.

"Why stand thus inactive?" yelled the old man.

"I want a horse!" thundered the other, savagely

"Take one from the chariot," suggested his companion.

Reuben could not wait for it to be unharnessed. He drew his sword and severed the traces.

A moment more he had vaulted to the back of one of the spirited steeds, and was tearing away in hot pursuit of the fair fugitive.

"Ah!" he exclaimed, with a start, which was nearly the cause of him being precipitated over his horse's head.

He placed his hand above his eyes to keep the scorching rays of the morning sun from his sight.

By following the direction of his course we see a sort of phantom form tripping quickly across the verdant fields with much haste.

As the angry pursuer gets nearer, he discerns the form to be that of a female.

It is the fair Lady Edith.

She turns her head.

A cry of terror escape her lips as her gaze falls upon the odious form of her villanous persecutor bearing down upon her.

Despair gives her strength, and she bounds forward with the fleetness of a starled fawn.

She has even broken through a thick hedge, and vanished from his sight like a vision.

An oath broke from her pursuer's lips.

Two minutes later the beautiful animal that carries the dastardly wretch has taken a graceful leap over the same hedge through which the poor girl flew to keep from the ruffian's grasp.

Reuben suddenly draws up the horse, and sits in dread terror at the scene his gaze encounters.

In the distance, standing on the brink of a silvery lake, is his intended wife.

It does not require a second look to read her intent.

Her face is beautifully calm and resigned.

Her features are lighted by an angelic smile as she raises her head and asks forgiveness of her Maker for the crime she is about to commit.

It is the only course left open to her.

She prefers such a death in preference to becoming the wife of the man whose presence she abhors.

She gives him one look of defiance. A cry of triumph escapes her lips, and in another moment the deed is done.

A heavy splash follows the plunge she has taken into the peaceful water.

A quiet smile plainly shows she does not regret the act.

Slowly she sinks, and the rich, dazzling rays of the sun play about her luxuriant golden tresses floating on the surface of the water.

She casts a last look at the blue sky, and the beautiful face sinks beneath the water.

And now the clear, rippling water flows quietly over one of nature's loveliest beings, sacrificed in the blossom of youth through the cruelty of an unjust father.

"My God!—My God! suddenly exclaimed the startled wretch, breaking the lethargy that held him powerless. "She's gone!"

Like a madman he smote his throbbing temples with his clenched hand.

His wild cries startled the timid horse he rode.

Snorting loudly, it laid its ears flat to its glossy neck, and tore off at an unmanageable speed.

Leaping another hedge, Reuben was thrown into the road, where he laid apparently lifeless.

The timid animal kept its onward, furious course.

CHAPTER CXIII.

THE THREE STRANGERS AT THE DEVIL'S REST.

THE DEVIL'S REST was a quaint, dilapidated old building, standing in a quiet part of the country, not more than thirty miles from London.

Rumour reported that it did not entirely depend upon chance customers for support, it had a select company of its own, more feared than respected, gentlemen whose presence was calculated to keep away stray customers but those they were in quest of by another fraternity in his Majesty's service, and known to most light-fingered gentlemen as Runners.

As might be imagined, the landlord, Dindle Dandy, was a curious fellow.

In stature, he measured as much in breath as in height, and that was under five feet. But, to make up for his deficiency, he had a wife, standing six feet three without her boots.

Sarah Dandy was a regular female devil when put out, and this her diminutive husband very often experienced to his cost.

Dindle Dandy was lighting the oil lamps of his primitive bar, when two well-known thief-takers walked in.

Old Dandy knew they never came his way unless they had a "plant" on.

He never saw their ill-looking faces without feeling a strong inclination to spit them to the wall with a very formidable three-pronged fork he always kept at hand behind the bar.

They had once taken off a particular favourite of his, a highwayman whom he had protected from the officers of justice, for more than two years at the risk of his good reputation.

Prudence compelled him to smother his spleen, and outwardly be civil.

"Good day, Jerry," he said to the ugliest one. "What's the game now? It's a long day since I have seen you here, and you, too, Master Billy. Still, I am glad to see you. What are you going to take?"

The officer addressed as Jerry gave his confederate a significant leer.

"Why, we'll take the cove as we are looking arter, he said. "Won't we, Bill, eh?"

"Like to," repeated the other, handing him the beer-jug.

"Well, my kiddies, and who's the unlucky bird you're after now?" inquired Dindle, leaning over the bar.

"We ain't a-goin' to tell you all our business," said Jerry. "You ain't the right sort for us."

"You can go to blazes!" exclaimed the landlord, swallowing a goblet of strong liquor.

"Old Dandy won't peach on us," said Bill. "Besides, I don't suppose he's seen or heard of our bird! he's too new."

"Peach!" said Dindle; "did you ever find me peach on you? Who's the bloke?"

"Tom King."

"Eh?" said the landlord. "Ain't seen him."

And he walked to the other end of the bar.

Feeling anxious to learn a little more about their visitation, Dandy stalked back.

"I have heard of him," he observed. "Seems a slippery sort of customer you can't hold by the nose."

"We'll hold him though, I'll bet," said Jerry, "and he'll be here to night; the road's getting too warm for him."

"What'll they do with him if they catch him?" asked Dandy.

"Scragg him, of course," said Bill; "but it ain't no business of ours what they does with him, so long as we pockets the coin. Eh, Jerry?"

"Not a bit," said that worthy. "Come, drink up; we're only losing time when we ought to be on his track."

The worthy pair of blood-hunters drank up, and departed.

Dindle watched them swagger out of sight with a peculiar ezpression of course jocularity and strong contempt.

"Toddle off, my kiddies," he soliloquised. "If ever Tom King's took by the likes of you, I'll eat my own head without salt. You catch him, you pair of sneaking varmints? I guess if you lay your paws upon him you'll find a tiger in the lady's pet, or I am much mistaken in the habits of him, and Tyburn Dick, too."

Old Dandy then drained off another goblet of wine.

At that moment one of the officers returned.

They looked curiously at one another.

"Yes; turned in to leave this here. It's his description, and caution to any one not to harbour him under their roof, or they'll hang with him."

"Harbour such villains in my house?" shouted the landlord. "Me harbour him, no!"

"It ain't very likely," said the thief-catcher; "but it's a caution. So I'll just stick it up agin the wall, if you ain't got any objection."

"Just stick it up wherever you like," exclaimed the landlord; "and another outside. It may be that it will bring me some custom, for I can tell you trade's devilish slack. Have some paste?"

"Thanks. You needn't grumble about trade. If you deals fair with us, you see the reward; and if he should give us the slip, and come here, you knows how to trap him. You understand, Dandy? There'll only be three of us to share the swag."

"Right you are, my kiddy. I am there, on a job like this."

"That's the thing, Dindle; you'll find it more profitable to stick to us. Good night."

"Good night."

The officer departed.

About an hour later, while old Dandy was quietly sipping another drop of grog, his wife came bounding into the bar in a furious rage.

Her first act was to hit him a tremendous blow with her huge fist in the pit of the stomach, and dislodged the pleasant draught he had just imbibed.

She then snatched the goblet from his hand, and drained the contents.

"Guzzling again!" she stormed. "Drink, drink, drink, all day long, you guzzling sneak of a thief. It's a wonder you don't burst, you big-bellied beast it is. I wonder when you mean to leave off drinking all the profits away."

"Gently, dame," gasped Dandy. "Don't come that ere game again, or me and you'll have a row."

"A row! There'll be a row you won't like, if I let you continue guzzling here all day, and harbouring thieves and highwaymen in my house. You big-bellied porpus! it's a wonder you ain't drank me out of house and home a long time ago. And what would you care if I was turned out, starving—and all through your drinking?"

Dandy might have said that what he drank only added a few extra gallons of water a day to the general liquor—but he didn't.

Mrs. Dandy's fierce eyes happened to alight on the proclamation.

Her indignation knew no bounds.

She turned upon him like a tigress, and seizing him by the nape of the neck, dragged him to the wall.

"Do you see that, you sneaking thief!" she roared. "I suppose you are hiding some of those sneaking villains from the lane in my house. But I will not have it. Let me tell you this, wretch that you are, if I find one of them about, I'll betray him, I will. You'd better mind; I know you will come to the gallows some of these days. And that ain't the worst; but you'll drag me there too. A pretty disgrace that will be to an honest woman's name. You shivering reptile, go from my sight before I am driven to do you some injury."

She raised him like a child in her powerful arms, and flung him over the bar.

Two strangers at that moment entered, and assisted the poor old fellow, panting, to his feet.

They were both young, and wore long cloaks that quite concealed their under garments.

The most stylish—a graceful, handsome youth—while being served with liquor, hapned to turn his head, and caught sight of the proclamation.

He sauntered towards it, and after reading the whole announcement, said, with the slightest shade of a smile playing about his well-formed mouth—

"Some desperate fellow hiding from the law. I hope we shall not find him here."

"Here!" almost shrieked Mother Dandy. "No, sir. I hope not, indeed—the desperate ruffian! I should faint at the very idea of him coming here."

"They say he is a most desperate character, an unmitigated desperado, judging from what I hear."

"He is, sir, a bloodthirsty monster. Heaven grant he may never darken my door."

Glancing across the road, our host saw an officer stop and speak to a man, and naturally concluded the enquiry was about himself.

Shortly afterwards the stranger entered, a dashing-looking young horseman; he wore a rich profusion of luxuriant whiskers and moustaches.

He glanced carelessly at the proclamation, smiled pleasantly, and winked at the cloaked stranger, who eyed him curiously.

Evidently they understood each other, for they made a silent sign, which each understood.

The younger handed the other a glass of the liquor he was imbibing, saying—

"Drink, friend. You look tired from a long journey. This is capital stuff, and will give you an appetite."

"I'faith!" said the other, taking the proffered glass. "Here's health to all. Landlord, see to my poor steed outside; she has brought me a long way, and deserves a good Samaritan to administer to her wants. Spare her nothing that you have; she is a faithful steed, and deserves a better master than I am."

Old Dindle rapidly obeyed, and when he returned in about half an hour, he joined his guest, who had adjourned to the parlour.

"Now, captain, what's the game now?" he said, taking his seat at the table.

The three strangers looked from one to the other a little astonished,

"The first game is to have some good wine," said the last comer. "The next is,

for you to take down that capital description of me you have hanging up in your shop."

"Ah, ah, ah!" laughed the landlord. "Very well, captain; but I don't think there is many of the sharks that could penetrate you so soon as I did through that disguise."

"That's a clever old cuss," said the elder of the company, when the worthy host had made his exit.

"Yes," replied one of the others, "cunning as the very devil. Don't know much about him. Had any dealings with him, Tom?"

"Oh yes, often; he's safe enough. You can trust old Dandy for being mute when the bloodhounds are after you."

Here Jerry, the thieftaker, entered.

"Beg pardon, gentlemen; didn't know you were here," he said, and turned to go.

"Nay, don't be frightened; we shan't eat you," said the one addressed as Tom.

"Feared I was intruding," he said, turning.

"No; sit down and enjoy yourself."

"Hallo, Jerry! What the devil brings you back?" shouted the landlord, coming in with two bottles of port under his arm, covered with dust and cobwebs.

"My legs," replied Jerry.

"I suppose we knows that. Can't you give a civil answer? Where's your mate?"

"Look here, Dindle," said the officer, sulkily, "you wants to know everything but your own business. Look arter that, we can look arter our own."

"I don't want any of your check, so I can tell you, my kiddy; and if you don't keep a civil tongue in your thick head I'll pitch you out, and there ain't two ways about it, don't make any mistake."

"We never wants to know your business," said Jerry, "and what is ours to do with you?"

"Confound your business!" exclaimed Dandy, banging down the wine. "Don't come here again to ransack my house, or I'll pin you to the wall."

"Come, I've got the king's warrant, and you won't stop me."

"Won't I?—won't I? Don't make any mistake."

Dandy walked after the officer, and seized him by the throat.

"Do yer s'pose I am going to stand yer cheek? Come out."

Jerry sprang to his feet, and clutched his assailant by the hair.

They glared like a pair of tigers at one another.

The landlord gave the officer a push that brought him forward, and they both rolled over a table that fell with them to the floor.

They held on to each other like grim death.

They were ripe for slaughter, each squeezed at the other's throat to extinguish his life.

One, or perhaps both, would have delivered up the ghost had not one of the guests interfered.

"What the deuce do you call this game?" he said, parting the antagonists, and assisting the landlord to his feet.

Dindle was going to make a reply, but the gentleman whispered something in his ear that kept him quiet.

Jerry got up, and cast a sneering leer at the three strangers.

He was departing, muttering something to himself, when the elder of the three pulled him back by the coat-tail.

"Don't be in a hurry to go, my friend," he said. "Sit down."

He pushed the astonished thief-taker back into a seat.

"How many of your ugly companions have you got outside?" asked the stranger.

"None," Jerry said.

"Oh, so I suppose you had an idea of doing a little bit on your own account. It won't do, Jerry, you need not look so innocent, we know each other."

"I don't know you."

"Don't lie."

"Well, I ain't said anything."

"No, nor will you now; it's too late, Jerry."

"What have I done?" said Jerry, quailing with fear.

"It's what you might do that forces me to take care of you. It's not safe for you to be at large."

The thieftaker would have spoken again, but the stranger put his hand over his mouth.

"A gag," he said, turning to one of the others.

A long silken scarf was thrown to him. He next asked for cord. The landlord brought him a long coil.

The officers then threw the trembling Jerry face downwards on the floor, put his knee upon his neck to stop his cries, and, pulling his two arms across his back, bound them securely.

Jerry was then turned over.

He took the opportunity to yell out loudly for assistance, but only for an instant; the silken scarf was twined around his mouth, and stopped his cries.

Better leave him now," said the landlord, "and come to another room."

"Better put him somewhere for safety."

"Bring him along, then," said Dandy, leading the way through a dark back door, at the farther end by the parlour.

The miserable thief-catcher was dragged along by the three strangers.

"There, push him in. He'll have plenty of rat company to amuse him till we want him."

Jerry was pushed into a dark cellar, and the landlord then conducted his guests into an upper room.

Hardly had they got comfortably seated when a loud and furious altercation with men was heard below.

"It ain't no good, old gal," said a man's voice. "We are officers of justice, and mean to search for the highwaymen who some of our mates has tracked here."

"And if you try to search here," screamed the landlady in reply, "I'll claw yer eyes and split yer ugly skulls with the poker."

"What do you mean, you she-devil?" was the reply. "I tell you it ain't any good of you harbouring highwaymen here, and trying to set us officers of justice at defiance."

Mother Dandy came bounding into the room, her eyes blazing like burning coals, and her voice thick with concentrated rage.

"Blockhead!" she shrieked at her husband. "There is a sneaking thief of an officer of justice, as he calls himself—I'll justice the varmint with the poker about his ears—says we're harbouring highwaymen, and says he'll search my house—my house."

do you hear, pot-belly? them puppies say they'll search my house for that villanous cutthroat, Tom King. Let the snivelling curs attempt it, and I'll show 'em what I can do, if you are too much of a coward to interfere."

"Well, my dear," calmly put in old Dandy, "if the curs like to make themselves officious enough, and want to search our house, why let 'em. We will give them leave to take all they find like highwaymen."

"Oh, indeed, you will, will you? Give them leave to ransack my house, turn everything upside down, and me, too, perhaps! You'll allow 'em to rummage all over the place, because you are too cowardly to stop them! A pretty landlord, you are, certainly!"

"Let 'em search, I say, if they think we are hiding away any malefactor!"

"Oh, and that's all you have to say! A pretty snivelling thief you are for a landlord! So you would allow them insignificant puppies to come prying about in every corner, and disturb these gentlemen. Surely, I am disgusted with you for a husband!"

"I assure you, my dear madam," said the youngest of the travellers, "these men will not in the least disturb us in the execution of their duty. I should let them search the place if they wished to do so.

"Of course," chimed in the landlord, "if we refuse them, they, of course, will think that we are harbouring someone here. Let 'em, I say; and find all the malefactors we have hidden."

The landlady swung open the door, and, in a shrieking voice, yelled—

"Here, you sneaking spies! come in, you pitiful automatons, you snivelling specimens of humanity, begin your dirty work! There's some gentlemen here; perhaps they're the highwaymen. Pray, come in, you skulking thieves! Come in, and see if you can find your Jerry, you crook-backed, crying jackanapes!"

The last words were a perfect squeal of fury.

"Yes, come in, you prowling alligators," seconded Dindle Dandy, why, for some reason of his own, was only making believe to be quite at his ease. "Walk in, my kiddies."

The officers entered—two lean-looking, ill-bred blood-hunters, their faces stamped with cunning greed; neither of them was Billy Jerry's companion.

"'Tain't no good of you hiding him away,' said one, in a gruff, surly voice. Dead or alive, we mean to have him."

The officers looked cautiously around.

"Don't mean to put you out of the way," said the foremost of the two, "but business is business, and we've got our duty to attend to. We've been on the trail of Tom King, and he's expected here, so is that daring young devil, Tyburn Dick. So if either of 'em ain't come, why they are on the road. So we'll just prepare, and make all safe for 'em. Won't we, Ned?"

"No mistake," retorted Ned.

"I'll break your thick skulls, I will!" shrieked Mrs. Dandy, seizing a huge flat-iron.

The officer waited for it.

"You villain! Take that, you ill-looking thief! I'll teach you to insult me in my own house!"

With a fearful crash she hurled the iron at the officer's head.

Had it struck him it must have shattered his skull to a shapeless mass; but he ducked in time to let it disappear with a crash through the partition.

The infuriated woman took up another with the same intent, and this time she would have settled the officer, but her husband got between her and the object of her rage in time to stay her upraised arm.

"Look here," he said to the officers, "you've come to look after a highwayman. Jest do that, and go your ways; but as to speakin' agin' my missus, do it, an' I'll pitch yer by the scruff of yer neck out of window!"

The officer was cowed, and said no more, to the infuriated landlady.

"These gentlemen will excuse us," one said, "but we must ax their names, and where they come from."

"Yes," squealed Mrs. Dandy, "and their mammy's names, and their grandmother's names, you sneaks, you!"

"My dear madam," observed the younger of the travellers, "these men are only obeying their orders; as an officer myself, bearing his Majesty's commission, it is part of my duty to assist them in their search; and, much as I should regret joining in any disturbance under your hospitable roof, I should be compelled, were this highwayman to show himself, to help take him prisoner. I am sure these good men will only do their duty and no more."

He drew a small packet from his breast, and displayed it open to the officers.

"You will see by this that I am an officer in the King's Guards. These gentlemen are my friends, and now, having satisfied you about ourselves, I am sure you will excuse me from accompanying you on your search. Should I be fortunate enough to help you capture him, we shall travel together; if not, I may see you some other time, when I hope to use my influence to increase your reward should you take him."

The officers touched their caps.

"We beg pardon for intruding," they began.

"Don't name it. Nay, we are all comrades under the King—drink to his health."

He filled their glasses, and refilling his to the brim, drank to the dregs.

"There!" exclaimed the irascible landlady, "perhaps now you will come bundling in upon people, looking for your highwayman, perhaps you'll say again that one of these gentlemen might be him."

"Don't never know, ma'am; he's like the devil, and takes a good many shapes. Don't he, sir? And, besides, here is the description of Tyburn Dick, and it is a little like this young gentleman."

"Pooh!" cried the landlord, knocking the document from his hand, "you're a fool!"

The young traveller smiled, displaying a handsome set of teeth.

"I hope I am not too much like him," he said, gaily; "but I heard he was a very ferocious monster, with fangs besmeared in blood."

"Oh, no, sir; he is, so they say, a perfect chick to look at; but, chick or no chick, there's a good many been a long while on the look-out for him, but now he's put his foot in it by comin' here; if me and Ned don't nab him others will—there aint no fear of his dodging off again."

"Well,"—the young officer poured out more wine—"I hope, my worthy fellows, you may get him; but I'm afraid you won't find him here—drink."

"Much obliged to you, kind sir, but we musn't take no more; afeard we shan't know him when we see him. It'll be a tough job when we nabs him; howsomdever, we'll give a look round, like. Pr'raps, ma'am, you'll show us round?"

"Show you to the devil!" screeched the landlady.

"Me show you, indeed?—catch me!"

Dandy chuckled, the young traveller laughed, and the officers left the room.

Then, and not till then, did old Dindle Dandy seem more at ease.

To observe him closely one would have thought that our hero was indeed somewhere under his roof.

The irascible hostess could not content herself with staying behind.

She followed after the officers, giving them the length of her tongue, till they had been all over the place, and had reluctantly determined to depart, when, with derisive satisfaction she hissed them off her doorway, calling all the grinning yokels from the tap-room to hoot the discomfited officers till they were out of sight.

Then she came back to the snug room with a face like a pickling cabbage.

"There!" she exclaimed, as she triumphantly squatted down in the only chair that would bear her weight, "that's the last of them!"

Old Dandy cocked his left eye to a comical expression, and a genial smile flitted about his lips.

When an hour or so had passed, the officer's young companion, taking advantage of the landlady's absence to serve customers, hinted that they had better be gone.

"Strangers," said the landlord, "if you'll take a friend's advice, you'll lay quiet where yer are, for thar's them about as is more dangerous than scotched rattlesnakes, and a 'fernal sight more cunning than vipers. I guess yer are in comfortable quarters like, and if I was yer, I'd stay till daylight afore I went further."

The same significant look beamed from the old fellow's eyes, and he did not seem surprised when the travellers decided to stay

THE STRANGER URGED HIS STEED FORWARD AS REGINALD TURNED.

The discussion of another bottle brought them to the hour of retiring, and after they had wished the hostess good night, old Dandy conducted them to their rooms.

The sleeping apartment, to which he led the younger traveller, was a large, rambling square-cornered chamber of very antique construction.

A monstrous wooden bedstead stood at one end; and all the other furniture was of the most primitive and massive construction.

A big, uncouth-looking window, with bars across, and thick shutters outside, took up nearly half of the wall on one side, an immense fire-place on the other.

"Tain't the best looking corner in the shed," the landlord observed, as if by way of apology; "but it's convenient, and you may make up your mind to sleep comfortable *till I calls you.*"

"Thanks," said the young stranger, divesting himself of his cloak and jacket, "I shall rise with cock crow."

The landlord lingered, as if he wanted to say more.

He stood opposite the noble form of his youthful guest, and looked him keenly, though respectfully, in the face.

"Friend," he said, "'taint in me to pry into your secrets, or to offer my counsel; but if yer should hear a row in the night, and shouldn't want to be seen here, yer have only to touch that knob at the back of yer head, and you'll go out of sight; only *jump off the bedstead,* arter it's done its quiet walk through the wall."

With these words, the old fellow was about to retire, but the young traveller, by a quiet, graceful movement, indicated him to say.

"Landlord," he said, in an altered, pleasing voice, that fell like magic music on the staunch old fellow's ear. "I have not mistrusted your fidelity, nor forgotten when I was last here; look at me as I am."

He removed his disguise of whiskers, eyebrows, &c., and revealed the handsome boyish features of Tyburn Dick.

Old Dindle did not seem a whit surprised; if anything, he was a little affected.

"Stranger," he said, "you're just the brave, daring, dare-devil fellow they say of you. I know'd yer the fust time I heard yer voice; for I haven't all forgot the time when I got yer out of a very ugly scrape. Wall, I reckon you're the most daring on the road. Tip us yer hand, and cuss me, I'm glad to see yer."

Dick grasped his hand warmly.

"I was sure of a welcome here," he said, "poor madame did not even suspect me."

"She? Why she ain't no more suspicion of yer than a new-born baby; and if she had, with all her ways, she'd let her flesh get torn off her back afore she'd betray you, and that's saying a good deal, it are."

"It is indeed; and now, my worthy friend, leave me. I need not conceal from you that I am pursued, and expect to be tracked here by more keen-scented blood-hunters than the precious pair who have just left."

"And if yer are, when yer hear 'em battering agin the door, you'll know where to go. I shan't be in a hurry to let 'em in, and maybe they'll knock agin summut on their way; and I shan't come to wake yer anyways, for I know yer have as quick ear as a hunter, and the spring of a young lion when you're roused. So stranger, good night, and a tough 'un yer are, as I allers said you'd be."

Once more he gripped our hero's hand.

Cheerily bidding the bold boy good-night, the landlord of the Devil's Rest quitted the apartment, and our hero threw himself on the bed, to snatch a few hours' repose.

CHAPTER CXIV.
THE LUSHER'S TIMELY DELIVERANCE—LADY EDITH RESTORED TO HAPPINESS.

THE Lusher, though in that holy disguise he had taken from the priest, did not get off so clear as he had anticipated.

He had traversed for about half-an-hour in quietness, when, to his astonishment, he was met by his pursuers with the addition of the priest in his half undress.

Jack was a little taken aback by this unexpected advent, though it did not take him long to concoct a plan for his safety.

His hunters had espied him from the distance in his unbecoming disguise, and were now bearing down rather rapidly upon him.

Jack knew it would not do to let them get too close; in fact, he had no desire to make any intimate acquaintance with them.

His surest way of getting out of such a scrape was to adopt his general plan when in such a dilemma.

That was to take to his heels, which he did most readily, firstly "taking a sight" at those who appeared most anxious of his company.

In a few minutes Jack's legs took him out of sight and hearing of his pursuers.

Again, being left to himself, he divested himself of the priestly order and cowl. He was trudging along rather uneasily. So tired had he become by this time, and his strength over-taxed, that he was compelled to throw himself down upon the sward to rest, and seek consolation in the brandy-flask he carried at his side.

He imbibed rather largely in the powerful spirit, and soon fell asleep. When he awoke he felt feverish, and parched with thirst. He glanced around to see that he was safe, and encountered a clear, beautiful stream at no great distance, and he closed his eyes again, subdued by the beautiful influence of the time and place.

He was again dozing off in a peaceful sleep, when a loud splash, as if some heavy body had fallen into the water, aroused him.

He glanced towards the lake, and there saw a female slowly sinking under the glittering water.

Forgetting the lethargic feeling, and the stiffness of his limbs, he sprang to his feet, and ran to the rescue.

Jack was not an expert swimmer, but in such a case of emergency he did not think of that. He plunged head foremost into the water after the beautiful maiden he saw sink, and in a few seconds he arose to the surface, having on his left arm the form of Lady Edith Benville. He breathed a sigh of relief when he laid the beautiful girl on the green sward.

The fair girl was quite insensible, but

after a time her bosom heaved with returning life.

A tear glistened in the Lusher's eye, like the crystal drops of water that still hung about the virgin breast of his unconscious charge.

He chafed the little hands in his own.

He bathed her placid brow with his kerchief he had dipped in the stream, and his ruddy face beamed with joyous gratification when she opened her large, languid eyes.

A slight tremor ran through her frame when she saw him kneeling by her side, and again her eyes closed with a sad expression on her pale, beautiful face.

He felt the little hand he held struggle to break from his grasp, and he wondered at this.

"My lady," he said, "you are safe now."

Edith shuddered, and again opening her eyes, she looked at her preserver in astonishment.

"Why did you save me?" she faintly murmured.

"Because," replied Jack, "you are too good to die."

"I cannot live to be that man's wife."

"Whose wife?"

"That cruel man you will take me back to."

"Don't know what you mean," said Jack, shaking his head. "I won't take you back to anyone that's cruel."

Edith looked up into his face.

The Lusher was not blessed with a very prepossessing countenance; but with all his faults he had an honest heart.

The poor girl laid her hand upon his arm, and in a sweet, murmuring voice, said—

"I will trust myself to your protection. I don't think you will betray me."

Jack took the little hand, and looked gratefully at his trusting charge.

He wanted to say something, but could not think of words to express his meaning.

Edith saw his embarassment, so to relieve him, she inquired how he became acquainted with her dangerous situation.

Jack then told her that he was lying on the grass, not far from the stream, when he heard the splash as she went in. Suspecting that something of the kind had occurred, he went to the rescue.

The gentle girl's mind was eased by what Jack said. Though she had put herself under his protection, she could not but think that he was a confederate of her rascally persecutor.

She thanked him sweetly for the risk he ran in saving her.

Seeing that he felt anxious to know the cause of the attempt to destroy her life, she related the whole of her trials.

Jack swore sudden death to anyone that should try to take the gentle girl from him.

"Can you walk?" he inquired.

"Oh, yes," she replied, "thanks to your gallant bravery. Had I risen to the surface of the water and sank again before you had come to my assistance, I should have been past all human skill."

"Well," said Jack, "that may be; but I only did my duty, the same as any other fellow would have done if he saw a lady in the water."

"You are a good, brave fellow," said Edith, "and you shall not be forgotten."

"As for that, why ——. Well, I'll leave it to yourself. But, come along, if you can walk. I don't think it's too safe to be here, if, as you say, that gentleman is after you now."

Edith rose to her feet.

She looked like a nymph just risen from a fairy stream, with the dazzling sun upon her, its enchanting beauty surrounding her in a glorious halo.

The gentle breeze playfully blew the golden threads of her rich flowing tresses about her beautiful white face.

The Lusher stood and gazed upon her in silent admiration.

He started as she laid one hand upon his arm.

"Come," she said.

Jack silently obeyed.

Lady Edith was fearfully agitated. Every moment she expected to be pounced upon by Reuben Frampton. She worked herself up to such a pitch of excitement that ere they had proceeded far she had to rest to recover strength.

"What's the matter?" inquired Jack.

"I have come over very faint," replied the lady. "I hope you will excuse my weakness, but I have such a horrid dread of meeting that man."

"Oh, you needn't fear that, he won't touch you while you are under my care," said the Lusher, with great confidence in his own powers.

"You are very brave," Edith said, with a quiet smile. "I was wrong to fear while under your protection, for it appeared as though I did not confide in you; but I do really!"

"Well," said Jack, "I can always protect a lady."

Again they walked on, but before they had got many yards they were confronted by a cloaked figure, that came running towards them.

Edith uttered a scream and fell back.

"Don't you fear, my lady," said Jack, and he drew his sword.

The cloaked figure stood mute.

"What do you want?" asked the Lusher.

"The lady," replied the stranger.

"Take your hook," said Jack, "or else I'll put this into your belly."

And he flourished his sword over his head.

The stranger did not appear very frightened by the Lusher's heroic movements. He put one hand on Jack's shoulder, and tried to push him aside.

"What do you mean?" Jack inquired, for the second time.

"The lady I've come to save," was the reply.

"I've saved her," was Jack's answer, "so you can save yourself the trouble. I shan't tell you any more to go."

The stranger went back several paces and threw off his cloak.

Lady Edith's terrified countenance brightened up with gladness.

In the long, careworn face of the stranger she recognised her lover's faithful valet.

"You know me now, my lady?" said Shanks.

"Yes. Where is your master? Is he safe?"

"Quite, my lady, but not well."

"Oh!" said Jack, "so you are a friend?"

"I am; ain't you?"

"Yes."

"Then give me your hand upon it."

Jack sheathed his sword, and shook hands with the stranger.

"I should like to know who I've spoken to," said Shanks.

"Well, I am the Lusher. Who are you?"

"Shanks."

Jack looked down at his legs.

"So it seems," he said; "blessed if you ain't all shanks!"

The valet felt the insult, and significantly shook his fist at Jack, behind their fair companion.

Jack significantly shook his head in reply.

"Come, there's good fellows," said the lady, "don't quarrel."

"Oh," said Jack, "we don't want to quarrel!" *Sotto voce*, "Wait till I get him by himself, that's all!"

Shanks took his place on the lady's left side, and between the two Edith was taken home.

Her heart sank heavily as they neared the door.

What if the dastardly coward who had watched her sink had seen the rescue, and returned home with her cruel father and the priest.

They could confine her in a room with them while the churchman went through the mock ceremonies that would for ever consign her young life to the keeping of one of the greatest villains on the earth.

She almost shrieked as these thoughts rushed like liquid fire through her brain.

Her two guides wondered why she lingered behind, and at her miserable, agitated face.

"Come, my lady," Shanks said, "you are perfectly safe now."

"Perfectly," echoed the Lusher.

She staggered up the steps, trembling in every limb, and it was as much as Jack could do to hold her while Shanks knocked at the door.

The ponderous door shook beneath the heavy strokes of the ponderous knocker.

The door was opened a little way, and a tall lacquey stood in the aperture, bewildered.

"What the devil are you making that row

for?" he shouted, clapping both hands over his ears.

Shanks made no answer, but kept up the furious knocking, even while the door swung back, and he was being dragged with it.

"Confound you!" yelled the lacquey, distracted by the noise, and, clutching Shanks by the collar, he swung him half-way down the hall.

In an instant the valet was upon his feet. He rushed at his assailant, and hitting him a fearful blow in the wind, that doubled the proud, gorgeous imp like a ball, shouted at the top of his voice—

"Victor! Master! master! we have brought her back!"

Old Jacob Martin came running out of a room awfully excited.

"What's the matter, fool?" he exclaimed, grasping Shanks by the arm.

Shanks hit him over the mouth with his hand, and then yelled out—

"Master! Master!"

"Have you gone mad?" shouted Martin, from a safe distance.

"No—o—o," bawled Shanks.

He was, though, mad by excited joy at the reunion of Lady Edith with his beloved young master.

Jacob Martin took the lady's hand, and led her to the door of an apartment.

Shanks gripped Jacob by the nape of the neck and hurled him aside, and taking Edith's hand, himself opened the door.

Victor St. James, who still reclined on a couch in a very weak state, sprang up, animated with new life, when the two entered, and saw his love standing pale and beautiful, between her two conductors like a bright, glorious star.

She ran towards her lover.

They met in silence, and wept tears of happiness.

The Lusher and Shanks blinked at each other like a pair of old owls.

The affectionate meeting of the lovers touched them.

No longer being able to master their emotion, they clung round each other's necks, and had a good blubber.

CHAPTER CXV.

THE LONE HUT ON THE HEATH—CAPTURE OF OUR HEROINE.

WE must for a time follow another thread of the story, and see what has become of Lord Merton, who, it will be remembered, was left a helpless victim in the hands of his two nephews, Percy and Reginald.

He was the only impediment that appeared to be an obstruction in their path—the only obstacle that kept them from being masters of the beautiful domain, Merton Grange. And now he lay in their power a helpless captive.

Brutal as they were, they could not find it in their hearts to kill the old man in cold blood.

In his unconscious state he was conveyed by them to a room of the Grange, and there kept a prisoner for three days, with but a scanty fare of food and drink, while the gentlemanly ruffians arranged some plan to remove him for ever from their path, without having his blood upon their heads.

The third day was drawing to a close when the poor old gentleman received a visit from two seafaring, repulsive-looking men.

They came to remove him. Hired by the base usurpers to take their noble ancestor far out on the depthless ocean and destroy him, so that their crime should not be discovered by any living being on earth.

Three months passed, and although they believed their commission had been duly carried into execution, they lived in a state of perpetual dread and misgiving that kept them from taking possession of the coveted estates.

The fourth and fifth month passed, yet they kept hidden from the world like the guilty brutes they were.

At last, when their fear had blown over, they ventured forth in their new characters, as the successors to the late Lord Merton, whom it was supposed had perished with the disastrous wreck off the Cornwall coast.

Merton Grange no longer maintained that gloomy, desolate aspect it had gradually fallen into from want of attention. It now went under thorough repair, the beautiful grounds were tastefully laid out, and the grand old mansion once more assumed its gay appearance of former days.

Grand revels were given by the new comers.

Gatherings of the noblest aristocracy were assembled there day after day.

Soon the brothers became the greatest men of the county, and were honoured by the attentions of many beautiful ladies.

Reginald had no thought for any of the fair beauties.

He had seen one—his own fair, beautiful cousin, the wronged heiress of the property he now enjoyed.

Percy wondered much at his brother's change; he had become quiet and thoughtful, and always longed to be alone. For hours together he would confine himself in his own room, buried deep in sombre thought.

Occasionally he would ride out, scouring through the country, cherishing the hope of a chance meeting with the fair girl.

Percy was a general lover. He admired and flirted with all with whom he got the chance. He could not understand that a man could be so deeply smitten with one as to lose all admiration for the many lovely beings with whom they came in contact every day. He little suspected the cause of his brother's change.

Never had Reginald breathed a syllable of his feverish love to him.

Each day that passed seemed a year of dreary suspense to the yearning passions of his heart.

One night he set out—he could wait no longer for chance to throw him in the path of his cherished idol.

He rode to the lone part of the heath, his dark brain concocting a plan to get the gentle girl in his power.

He went along at a smart gallop, anxious to put his scheme into execution. He did not notice a horseman coming towards him until the stranger pulled right across his path and looked into his face. He started then, and an involuntary shudder ran through him. It was not the first time he had seen that dark, sombre face, but he could not think where they had met before. The stranger urged his steed forward as Reginald turned to look at him, and disappeared down the road.

For a moment Reginald seemed about to follow him, but as there was very little chance of overtaking him, he went on his course

strangely troubled by the meeting, for an inward voice seemed to whisper that this mysterious man held a power over him.

Dismounting at the desolate hovel, he rapped three times on the dilapidated shutters with his knuckles.

A croaked, squealing voice from the inside inquired who it was, and what he wanted.

"Open the door, confound you?" exclaimed Reginald, in an angry, impatient tone at being interrogated.

There was, in a few seconds following the nobleman's command, the noise of huge rusty bolts being drawn back from their sockets, and the rattling of chains. A low, lumbering door was then partially opened, and an old, shrivelled form of a woman presented herself to the late visitor.

She was an old crone of about seventy, of a towering height, but slightly drooping forward with decaying age. She was miserably thin, with a huge lump on her back that rose above her shoulders.

Her dress was scant and wretched, hanging about her wasted form in a most neglected manner, that added to her wretched appearance. Her face was long and the colour of scorched parchment, puckered up in wrinkles, that bespoke a cruel, sinister nature. Her cheeks fell in under her high protruding cheek-bones. Her small, grey eyes shone a green lurid light in the darkness, like those of a ferocious cat.

"Is your son within?" inquired Reginald.

"Which?" interrogated the hag, sharply.

"Spikey," replied the visitor.

"No, he ain't."

"Will he be long?"

"Don't know."

"Then I will wait."

The old crone looked at him cunningly.

"I will wait," he repeated.

"Very well," she replied, without moving.

The nobleman glared at her spitefully.

"Who have you inside?" he asked.

"Several," was the laconic answer.

"If you have no objection, I will come in."

"Just as you like. I can't answer for the welcome you will get."

He went forward, suppressing an angry exclamation.

She slightly moved aside to let him pass, with much unwillingness.

"Tell someone to look after my horse," he said.

The woman made no answer, but followed him into a low, large room, dimly lighted by flickering lanterns that hung from the beams that supported the drooping ceiling.

The apartment was a curious-looking place, with its earthern floor and wooden walls, decorated in many places with sanguinary pictures and formidable-looking weapons.

Seated round a roughly-hewn table, on log stools, were three scowling ruffians, playing at cards.

Their game came to a conclusion when the nobleman entered, and three pairs of cynical eyes were cast curiously upon him.

The rank odour of the tobacco, and the close, unwholesome stench of the room nearly strangled the visitor on first entering from the sweet, fresh air of the country.

He drew his highly-perfumed kerchief from his pocket, and held it to his nose.

The men exchanged sneering glances of contempt among themselves.

One, to keep down his rising anger, drank off the whole tankard of liquor, another furiously kicked the burning embers, and the third, in his supreme disgust, finally upset the board, and the things upon it, into the fire.

Then the trio rose, and glanced at one another.

"I hope I have not disturbed you," said Reginald, thinking he had got into rather dangerous quarters, not that he was anyway frightened by their ill-looks; a pair of finely-chased pistols he had concealed under his cloak were trusty and serviceable companions in such a place.

They responded to his remark like so many growling bears.

The titled nobleman feigned an easy good humour, as though the ill-humour of the men had not in the least disturbed his peace of mind, when actually he was goaded to fury, and could hardly resist sending a bullet through one of their skulls.

The expectant Spikey now came in.

It was evident they had met before, by the glances exchanged between him and the nobleman, which meant silence while the others remained there.

The old crone spoke a few words in a whisper to the three scowlers, and, with savage looks, they went out.

Spikey and his titled cogitator were left alone.

"Glad to see you, my lord; hope yer are quite well," said the man, a big, burly ruffian, a perfect Colossus.

"Quite well, thank you. Have you seen anything of either of those persons?"

"Well, no, my lord, I ain't. I was down on the coast the other day, but nothing had been seen, either ship or men, since it set sail nine months ago. I've heard as how there 'ave been a great many wrecks lately, an' it is supposed that all ships that left England at the time the "Black Prince" set sail have gone down.

"And a very good go too. But how about the lady of the rocks—have you seen anything of her?"

The man turned a ghastly hue, and a slight tremor ran through his frame.

"I—I—saw something," he stammered; "but I swear before God and man, it warn't human."

"Tush! Do you believe in ghosts?"

"I used to laugh at 'em once, but what I saw took all that out of me."

"You talk like a foolish woman," said his employer, peevishly. "Did you watch where I told you, and at the time appointed?"

"I did everything you told me, to the word."

"Well, and what did you see?"

"A ghost!" gasped the man, looking suspiciously around the room, with an expression of intense terror upon his face.

"Humbug. You saw the person I told you to secure."

He clutched the man by the arm and breathed the last word into his ear in a hoarse whisper.

"I tell you, my lord," exclaimed the man, "it was no living being that I saw. I was as close to it when it passed me as you are to me. I wasn't frightened then, but when I made a grab at the long white dress my hand went clean through the form, and then it vanished into the air, and a wild, mad kind of laugh rang in my ears.

Reginald now changed colour. The steady unflinching, rigid way the man told his story caused him some uneasiness.

"However," he said, "let that affair drop. I have got a similar commission for you to undertake, but, mind you, there is no phantom here. I want you to go after a reality."

"Yes, your honour. An' you tell me who it is, you shall have them brought to you safe and sound, if you wish it."

"I do wish it, and mind how you handle the person whom I entrust to your care."

"Is it a lady, my lord?"

"It is."

"Then the pretty darling shall have all the care I 'av. But who's the lady, and where am I to find her?"

"That you will have to discover. The lady you have heard of, no doubt—the bride of Tyburn Dick, the Boy Highwayman."

"Heerd on her! Who hasn't? She's one o' the lovliest critters to be seen for many a mile's walk. An' ain't she daring? Why, I've heerd 'em say as how she'll dress up like Tyburn Dick, an' call 'Stand and deliver!' as well as any o' the high-toby men on the road."

The listener's face gleamed with a sort of pride.

He loved the beautiful girl the more for her audacious fearlessness.

"You appear to perfectly understand the person I want."

The hireling assented with a nod.

"But," he said, "there ain't no telling one from tother—so like are they when out on the road."

"Nonsense," said Reginald. "It is perfect absurdity. Do you mean to tell me you could not discover the difference between their faces?"

"Yes; but they both wear masks."

"Then the lady's hair is a bright auburn, and the boy's a dark brown. You may know one from the other by that. Listen. You must get the girl, waylay her on the road, capture her, and bring her here."

The man thought that more easily said than done. He knew by experience a silent tongue in such cases is the best counsel. He wanted

money, so he did not raise any objections to the other's plans. His master paid liberally, and always beforehand, and it paid him to consent to all his master said.

"Then it is settled," said the titled scoundrel. "I shall be here to-morrow. This purse will supply your wants until the girl is mine, and then you will want no more."

The ruffian took the heavy purse with a greedy acknowledgment.

Reginald then took his departure. He found his horse tied to a tree outside, and he rode back to Marton Grange. His mind was somewhat eased of its anxieties by the joyous anticipations he now cherished.

Barely had he been gone from the lonely hut half-an-hour when the three other ill-looking brutes returned, bringing with them an old man of three-score summers.

Spikey was too much absorbed in his own meditations to take any notice of his confederates and their pitiable captive, and even if he had not been, such scenes were too often taking place there to cause him any astonishment.

The poor, trembling old man was dragged brutally through the room, and up a rickety flight of stairs into a small room above.

It was the same night the pedlar boy had begged shelter from the cold winds, and a place to rest his weary limbs.

Anon we shall describe the scene that took place in the next one in which he retired to repose.

The reader is already acquainted with the poor lad's escape from the dark, evil hut.

The fear of being overtaken by his blood-thirsty assailant, who pursued him with murderous intent, robbed him of what little strength remained in his overtaxed body.

He must have fallen a victim to their thirsty blades; but at the very moment when he felt his legs giving way beneath him, he saw the noble form of Tyburn Dick (as he thought). Gladly uttering the name of the brave lad, he made one effort and leaped to his side, confident of being protected by the fearless youth.

"You will protect me?" the poor boy said.

"While there remains life!" replied the highwayman.

"Back!" he said, confronting the ferocious ruffians, "back, cowards, or you will share the fate of your confederate!"

The Boy Highwayman had fired a timely shot at the savage bloodhound that was in the act of springing upon the boy fugitive, and another shot maimed the foremost of his two-legged bloodhound pursuers.

"It's a woman!" yelled one of the men.

Unfortunately, such was the case—the supposed highwayman being no other than our daring heroine.

Grace changed colour, and for a few seconds stood bewildered at being thus discovered; but in a few moments more she had regained her fearless hardihood, so natural and graceful in her.

Standing at the head of her obedient, cream-coloured palfrey, her splendid figure drawn erect, her face glaring with a defiant flush, and her large blue eyes glittering like stars, she confronted the men with a pair of long barrelled pistols.

"Touch me who dares!" she said, in a stern, musical voice.

The boy pedlar, standing trembling by her side in his half nude state, could but admire her, while he felt ashamed of himself for being under the protection of that beautiful girl.

The lad was not not void of courage, but the helplessness of his condition and the feebleness of his strength compelled him, much against his proud, brave will, to put himself under the defence of the beautiful lady highwayman.

Spikey, who was with his companions, on hearing that the supposed Tyburn Dick was a female, went forward like a rocket, and called upon his mates to aid him to capture her.

Weak and helpless as was the pedlar boy, he could not stand inactive while his fair protectress was battling for her life with the murderous ruffians who had pursued him.

Desperation endowed him with a vigorous strength not his own, his blood coursed like liquid fire through his veins, he felt maddened by furious indignation at the cowardice of the ruffians who assailed the beautiful girl.

Without a word, he drew the sword from her scaobard, and like a tiger springing through a jungle, he leaped at the villanous gang.

Poor young fellow, he did but little good. His maddened fury led him but to a sorry fate. Leaping in their midst, he made a furious dig to pin one of them on his sword.

In his attempt, his foot slipped, and as he fell, one of the ruffians dealt him a blow on the head that stretched him prone at their feet.

Grace instantly fired both her pistols.

One of the men fell dangerously wounded, but there remained two powerful brutes to contend with her.

She was now entirely weaponless.

They did not make much ado ere they pounced upon her, and she was borne to the ground, and lay helpless beneath their superior strength.

She struggled bravely to resist their efforts, however, but with little success.

The pedlar boy staggered to his feet, having recovered somewhat from the effects of the blow, and although he barely had strength enough to raise an arm, he tottered towards the ill-looking villains with a determination to save the fair lady or die in the attempt.

She saw his intent, and gave him a grateful look, waving her hand to keep him back, said—

"Mount my steed and away. She will take you to the haunt. Acquaint my brother of what has occurred. Away, farewell!"

The boy got into the saddle and kissed his hand to the beautiful girl, then, giving the noble animal the reins, was soon borne away with lightning speed.

Grace being now secured hand and foot, was left while the men made an attempt to stop the fiery steed; but, like a phantom, it had vanished in the gloom with its youthful rider.

"Curses!" exclaimed Spikey.

"Curses!" iterated the other.

"Fire in the direction he has taken," said Spikey.

The other immediately acquiesced to his confederate's command, and fired.

Then they listened breathlessly to ascertain the success of the shot; but only the echo of the report resounded on their ears.

The fleeting steed had got far beyond shot range when they fired.

Our heroine was then borne away by her captors to the lone hut on the heath.

Poor girl! She little dreamed the cause of her capture; but she would not have to wait long before she learnt the bitter sorrow that was in store for her.

CHAPTER CXVI.

MIDNIGHT ATTACK UPON THE DEVIL'S REST—TOM KING MAKES A CLEVER ESCAPE, AND TYBURN DICK FALLS INTO A TRAP.

THREE o'clock—the cocks had given their first round of crowing, the last one having answered, flapped his wings, and settled down on his perch.

The church chimes died away into stillness, the cock, who had been waiting in doubt between the fading moonlight and the breaking morn, rose, and crowd lustily his morning signal, which was instantly taken up by his nearest neighbour, and answered from one to another in turn, until the crows grew fainter, and soon became almost inaudible from some far distant farm.

Then, again, all was quiet.

Amidst the peaceful hush of this silent hour the landlord of the Devil's Rest was suddenly startled from his heavy sleep by such a battering at his door that echoed through the whole neighbourhood.

The old fellow drowsily awoke, pricked up his ears, and turned towards his better half, who, till now, had been rolled up, half smothered, amongst the blankets and pillows.

She suddenly jumped up, as if a cannon had exploded at her head.

Alarm, rage, dismay were plainly stamped upon every lineament of her fiery face, while she listened with throbbing pulse; even her cap rose from her head on the ends of her wiry hair with fright. Then, with both hands, as the hammering was repeated, she seized her husband, and shook him unmercifully.

"Dandy, Dandy, Dandy!" she shrieked; "wake! Do you hear that noise?"

The landlord shot out one leg, and turning over again, drowsily mumbled—

"Don't be a fool, gal; it's ony the rats."

"The rats you ape—wake and listen. There! Is that rats, eh?—pulling the house down about our ears."

Bang, bang, bang! came violently against the door.

A giant's arm seemed to be dealing the heavy strokes with some massive club.

An excited voice bawled out—

"Open the door in the King's name!"

"There!" shrieked Mrs. Dandy, in a hoarse whisper; "that's rats, is it, you old block-headed ass, you pot-bellied elephant?—that's rats, is it?"

The landlord slid out of bed, and thrust his legs into his trousers.

Creeping quietly to the window, which swung open inwards, he noiselessly pulled it back and peered out.

He was a little astonished at what he saw. A party of officers were in front of the house battering with huge staffs at the door.

Apart from them stood a body of marines, their long steel bayonets glittering in the uncertain light.

At a loss what to do, the landlord thought it the safest plan to return to bed again.

He slid gently under the clothes, and tucked his head up to shut out the noise.

Driven frantic by the coolness of her husband, the infuriated old dame fastened her claw-like fingers around her lord's ears, and pulled him up in bed.

"You sneak!" she yelled, "you coward! What did you come into bed for again?"

"Sleep, of course."

"Sleep—sleep! you beast!" squealed his partner. "So you would sleep while the house is being pulled down! Ugh! you ugly booby!"

"Tell yer what it is, missus, if yer can't hold that 'tarnal tongue of yours, me and you will have a row."

"A row!" gasped the lady, clutching her husband's hair, and bumping his head against the head-board. "The officers are trying to knock the house down! Go and tell them we ain't got any highwaymen here."

"Blazes seize 'em! let 'em knock; they'll get tired afore the door gives way."

Bang! bang! bang!

Then followed a loud crash. It seemed as though the ponderous door fell in atoms to the floor. Even this did not disturb the landlord's mind, so confident was he in the superior strength of his door, and probably he would have dozed off again, had not his furious wife suddenly put her lank feet in the middle of his back, and shot him out of bed.

"'Say, old gal," exclaimed the good-tempered old fellow, "if you come that 'ere again, you won't catch me aside of you any more."

"Go to the window and tell them—speak to them, or I'll speak to you."

As Dindle put his head out, the shouts for him to open the door became more loud and fierce from the perspiring officers.

One voice he could detect, it was that of Billy, the thief-catcher's being most rusty amongst the officers.

"Open the door!" he bawled, "open the house! We are the King's officers, come for robbers and highwaymen. Open, I say, or the d—— old house shall be pulled down!"

"'Say, my kiddy," said a quiet voice above them.

They looked up, and saw the rough head of the landlord.

"'Say, my coons, you're making a d—— row amongst yourselves."

"Open the door!" shouted an officer, "you ugly old hound! You are doing this to give our prisoner a chance of escape. Come down and open, before we put a bullet through your cussed skull!"

"Tell yer what, if you are going to make a target of me, I'll put my head in and do for you, making such a row here about highwayman and robbers. Why, I can just tell you, you've come to the wrong house."

"It won't do," cried Billy, the thief-catcher. "Open the door, or we will burn the house down!"

"What!" shrieked the landlady, jumping out of bed and rushing to the window. "You impertinent varmints, you talk about burning my house down, do you!"

"Open the door, then," demanded a voice from amongst the group of officers.

"Open the door, indeed, and what for?—to let such scum as you in? What right have you to come and disturb respectable people at such a time, making them get out of bed to answer you? I can tell you what it is, you ill-looking dogs, if you ain't off very quickly, I'll—you grinning jackasses!"

The excited lady then disappeared.

Amidst the clamouring jests and shouts of the officers, the furious old dame made her appearance at the window again.

"Laugh—laugh!" she squealed; "laugh, you hang-dog brutes. There! you villains, take that!"

She pitched something out of window, it was not the water-jug, but one of them got it on the head, and it fitted him like a cap.

The unexpected shock brought him to the ground.

When he arose he was very wet, and his clothes smelt very unpleasantly of ammonia.

"You infernal old cat!" yelled the man, using the most horrible oaths, "you shall pay for this."

"Me pay for it, you reptile? Yes, I will. You shall see how I'll pay for it, if you ain't off."

"Shoot that woman!" shouted Billy, the thief-catcher. "'Tis she who is causing this delay."

"Billy, my boy," said the landlord, "don't ye come any of yer games with them pop-guns, or, cuss me! I'll settle the lot of yer."

"Open the door!"

"Seen you d—— first!" responded Dindle, going in, and fastening the window.

"This is all your doings, this is," commenced his wife, attacking him like a tigress. "You've brought all this on through encouraging these lounging, ill-looking, villanous companions of yours for ever infesting the house. I told you what you would do. Don't stand there making faces, you hideous specimen of humanity!"

He got a smack in the chaps from his better half's leg of mutton fist that caused him to reel round the room.

"Say, don't come——"

"Shut up!" yelled his wife. "Don't answer me, you snivelling hound. A pretty thing, indeed, that I should live to my time of life, and then be subject to the insults of such men as them outside—and all through you."

Poor old Dindle quietly shuffled out of the room while he was safe.

His partner had pulled one of the rails from the top of the bedstead, and flourished it about in a style suggestive of broken heads.

"Yes, go," she shrieked, "go and open the

door to them. Let 'em in, and see what I'll do for you!"

She followed him out of the room, but Dandy had reached the door, which he slowly began to unlock, to prevent it being shattered to pieces.

The officers were hammering away with renewed vigour. The massive door could not have resisted their furious efforts much longer. In several places the wood had flown.

The landlord knew that the officers were determined to make an entry. He also knew that they would get in, even if he refused their request. Besides, if he kept them out much longer, they would have the door down, and then he would have the expense of erecting a new one.

To prevent this, he quietly drew back the bolts.

The officers were crowding one upon the other against the door, and, when old Dandy suddenly opened it, the consequence was they all tumbled, head first, one after another into the house.

" You infernal old thief!" cried the thief-catcher, who was one of the fallen officers. " You shall pay for this."

" Don't flurry yourself," said Dindle, quietly.

" Hit him on the head! Break his jaw!" yelled his most irascible wife. " If he attempts to come this way, smash him!"

She flourished the bed-rail above her head, and glared at the officers.

" Secure that dangerous woman!" cried Bill.

" Secure me!" shrieked she. " Try it on! try it, I say!"

Her weapon whizzed around and around her head.

" We don't want to insult you, my good woman," began the thief-catcher, when she interrupted him by yelling out—

" You had better not!"

" We must do our duty," Billy went on; " we have got the King's warrant to search the house for highwaymen that are believed to be concealed here, and if you don't interrupt us in our duty, we shan't say anything to you."

" Say, Billy," exclaimed Dandy, " shall I help you to look for them?"

Billy snatched the candle from Dindle's hand he held above his head, and pushing him aside, strode upstairs.

The ireful Mrs. Dandy met him on the top of the stairs, and delivered him a terrific blow in the face from her huge fist, that sent him toppling backwards into the arms of his men, who were coming up behind him.

Billy was bent on a search, and a search he meant to have, in spite of the very devil; but he did not venture up the stairs again while the irate landlady was there.

" Men," he said, speaking to the soldiers, " have your guns ready to shoot anyone who attempts to escape while I and my men commence the search below."

The officers followed their valiant leader into the lower regions of the strange old house.

Every nook and corner of the cellars and places were carefully searched, but meeting with no success there, the thiefcatcher called his men around him for a defensive body-guard, and then ascended the stairs.

They carefully scrutinised every room, peered into cupboards, under beds, pulled out boxes and furniture that had not been disturbed for years, tapped ceilings and walls, sounded floors, banged pillows, and shook the curtains, but no sign of any highwayman could they see.

During the whole of their search the landlord was at their elbows, taunting them to madness by his goading suggestions and sarcastic sneers.

In one room they found a form, rolled up in a large cloak, soundly asleep.

He was roughly awakened, and commanded to give an account of himself. Which he did, in a very sleepy manner, to their satisfaction, and he was then left to his repose.

The sleeper was our hero's companion who had entered with him.

We need hardly say that it was young Tom who had so bravely rescued poor old Wayne from his ruffianly pursuers.

The officers then entered the big, desolate room where, not an hour before, the object of the search had been sleeping.

They found it—as the kind old host had

A PEREMPTORY DEMAND.

expected—empty. It presented no appearance of having been occupied.

Our hero had heard the first of the disturbance, and, touching the spring, had gone through the wall on the massive, sombre bedstead.

As he jumped off, about six feet square of the floor of the room in which he now stood opened as the bedstead went back into the next apartment.

He let himself down the aperture. The cards then resumed their former position, and he was now in the secret hiding-place between the floor and ceiling.

Here he was, laying in silence and darkness, when the hubbub over his head in the room which had just disappeared announced that the King's officers were gradually scenting out their prey. He did not feel quite at ease in his place of concealment. Though it was pretty secure, there remained just a chance of the officers accidentally touching

the very same spring that had put him where he was. Should they discover the spring, the bedstead would take its quiet walk through the wall.

In every probability they would walk through after it.

If such a thing should occur Tyburn Dick stood in a very critical position of being discovered.

Listening for every sound, the brave boy waited with his hand on his sword hilt, ready to spring forth or stand at bay for liberty and life.

Billy, who directed the search, evidently had his suspicions about the room, not unreasonably, for, in spite of its bareness, it looked a likely place to hide in. With a knowing look upon his ill-bred face, the thief catcher started across the room, stamping heavily with his feet.

"Sounds hollow here," he said, stopping in

the centre of the floor, and looking cunningly at the landlord.

The old fellow grinned.

"He ain't hiding in one of them cracks, is he," he asked, sneeringly.

Billy scowled.

"He's hiding here somewhere," he answered, fiercely, "and we mean to have him, or we'll pull this place down level with the ground."

Dindle laughed sarcastically.

"Men," shouted the thieftaker, beside himself with rage, "I am convinced he's hiding somewhere here. Follow me, and carefully examine the walls well. We'll soon find out if he's behind 'em."

"Is that him behind you?" exclaimed Dandy.

Billy sprang round, nearly knocking over half-a-dozen of his men.

"Look out!" bawled the landlord.

The officer jumped back again.

"Look out for the door."

The thief-catcher made a run towards that part of the room.

"He ain't behind them curtains?"

The officer tore the dusky old hangings open.

A terrified shriek left his lips.

Something had got him by the throat.

The officers, seeing their leader struggling, as they thought, with the Boy Highwayman, all rushed to his rescue at once, and got in one another's way.

Suddenly, the officers fell back amazed as a huge black cat flew across the room.

"Hallo! There he goes!" cried Dandy, as the animal sprang out of the window.

All the officers and the astounded Billy dashed there together, thinking actually that they had been assailed by the daring boy, who had now escaped.

"Clean gone!" exclaimed Dindle.

The thief-catcher being half-way out of window to inquire of the soldiers, who were below, if anyone had gone out that way, the landlord could hardly resist the temptation of hurling him out by the heels.

The thief-catcher was answered by seeing the cat writhing on the points of the bayonets.

Again he was baffled.

"Men," he yelled, "this d——d old villain is only fooling us. Follow me, and take no notice of him."

They followed him in a body round the room, tapping the wall with the butts of their pistols. But everywhere gave back the same dull sound.

The thief-catcher looked very cunningly at the large bedstead.

"Curious piece of furniture this," he remarked, "only it ain't got the prisoner."

"We'll unfold it," said the officer. "Here, men, some of you keep your eye on that old thief, and the rest of you come and help me to move this bedstead."

"Does it smell of him?" asked Dandy, laughing derisively at the officers' useless efforts to move the huge thing.

The leading officer would not give in. His suspicions were very strong concerning the bedstead.

He felt convinced, could he move it, it would lead him to the highwayman's hiding-place.

Going down on his hands and knees, he minutely examined every inch of the lumbering piece of furniture, also the flooring.

"Mind he don't hook you by the nose!" shouted Dandy. "He might come up through the cracks in the boards."

The thief-catcher turned a somersault, backwards, and struck his head severely against the bedstead-leg.

This was caused by a huge rat running along under the boards at the very moment he was peering through the crack.

He, thinking it the highwayman about to break through the flooring, moved rather more actively than was his usual custom, and thus came to grief.

"You aint got him, then?" the landlord said, with a quiet grin.

"D—— your taunts!" exclaimed the officer, fiercely.

"Have another look, my kiddy," said Dandy.

The officer meant to, despite the sarcastic jeers of the landlord, but his brother officers did not possess that persistence with which the worthy Billy was blessed. But the worthy Billy did not see the force of having

...om standing in a group, laughing at his misfortune.

"Men!" he yelled, beside himself with rage, "I command you to help me in looking for the highwayman, Tom King."

"Where the blazes can we look now?" said one, who did not hold his leader in very high esteem.

"Look, blockheads! Where do I look?"

"All in the same place," replied the man. "I think we've wasted quite enough time here."

"Never mind what you think," shouted Billy, furiously, the hard blow his head had had did not cool his temper. "What I command, you will have to do."

"Shall I. Then I'll see you d—— before I do."

The thiefcatcher looked straight at the speaker.

"Jones," he said, in a hoarse fierce voice. "You can go, to-morrow you will hear more of this."

The man laughed at the other's meaning threat. The thiefcatcher went down again upon his hands and knees to finish his examination.

All the others but the worthy Jones did likewise, and then a very minute search took place.

Just as our host had imagined, one of the officers stumbled accidentally upon the hidden spring. There was a click.

The wall opened, and the bedstead glided through.

The men stood in speechless surprise.

Not so with Billy. He made a spring, and clung on to the moving furniture.

"I say, old hoss," said Dandy, "mind you come back again."

The bed then stopped, tilted, and the officer was thrown off, down into the gap on the floor of the next room, and the boards closed over him.

The bedstead came back, and the wall closed.

Then all was still as death.

The men were dumbfounded with astonishment, but presently they were aroused by the voice of their leader, that sounded strangely hollow from beneath the boards.

"Help! help! help!"

The men searched for the hidden spring that had moved the bedstead. but they searched in vain.

The cries of the thief-catcher became louder. Then was heard a scuffle under the floor.

The officers had no doubt that their leader had encountered the highwayman, and one of the men grasped the landlord of the "Devil's Rest" by the throat.

"You," he said, pressing a pistol against Dandy's forehead, "have the power to move that bedstead. Do so, or I will send a bullet through your cussed head."

"You won't be none the nearer, my kiddy, if you do," said Dindle, struggling out of his captor's grasp.

"Pull up the boards," suggested one. "It's no good wasting time with that old thief."

Some of them began to rip the boards apart, and two or three planks were removed.

One of the officers ventured to peer down.

"Tom King," he shouted, "surrender, or I fire!"

"If you do," came a voice, "you will hit me."

It was the thief-catcher who spoke.

A few moments more, and his head appeared above the opening in the boards.

His face was blanched with terror. His eyes glared fiercely.

"I've seen him," he gasped. "He would have killed me. He got me by the throat with both hands, and his knee on my chest, but when you pulled the boards up, he let go, and vanished through a trap into a room beneath.

"Give me the lantern," said one of the officers, who wished to distinguish himself.

A companion gave him the light, and he crept down under the boards.

"Tom King," he exclaimed, "surrender. I shall fire all round, so you'd better give in."

His voice echoed strangely under the boards. There was no other sound, and the man spoke again.

"I warn you. When I have counted three, I shall fire."

There was no answer to his warning, so the officer counted slowly.

"One—two—three."

Then he fired, but when the echo of the report had died away again all was silent.

He then discharged a pistol in every direction, but with the same result.

"He can't be under the boards," he said, eeping up.

"Secure this old scoundrel!" yelled their der, "and unless he reveals the secrets nnected with this cursed old house, we will rture the words from his mouth!"

Dindle was secured to the bed-post, and a brace of pistols put in his face.

"Reveal all you know," said the thief-taker. "Where are the highwaymen you have hidden?"

"I ain't hidden any," said Dandy. "I didn't know there was any highwaymen in my house."

"Call the soldiers in," the officer said, turning to the men. "Now then, you have but three minutes to decide. Tell me where you have put Tom King."

"If you like to unbind me," said Dandy, independently, "I will show you where you may find him."

"Mind, no treachery, or I'll put a bullet through your skull."

"Well, if you think I am going to be treacherous, you'd better not release me. I don't care."

Thrown off his guard by the apparent unconcern of the innkeeper, the officer unbound his hands.

"This way. Be cautious," and Dandy, taking Billy by the wrist, led him towards the old bedstead.

They crept under there together. The officer was very watchful, but he was not watchful enough.

Dindle pointed to a small knob in the wall.

"There," he said, in a whisper, "press tnat."

The officer was about to do so, when the landlord grasped him like a vice by the throat.

The others, hearing a convulsed sob issue from under the bedstead, suspected that all was not right, and crept under, and there they found their daring leader lying strangled.

Dindle Dandy had vanished.

CHAPTER CXVIII.

THE FATE OF REUBEN FRAMPTON.

THE light of happiness once more beamed upon the lovers' faces.

Restored to each other after so long and trying a separation, their joy knew no bounds, but their happiness was not without a cloud of forebodance.

Neither Reuben Frampton nor Lord Benville had returned. This appeared very strange to St. James.

The chariot that had conveyed the lovely Lady Edith to the chapel of the ruined chateau had returned with but three horses.

The groom gave an account of the missing one, and when questioned by Victor St. James about the disappearance of the two gentlemen, he said that his master, Lord Ecclestone, had taken one of the horses to pursue the lady who had flown from the carriage. Two hours Lord Benville waited at the chapel for his return, but finding he did not come started off in quest of him. The groom and his companions were then left alone, and waited four hours, but finding neither Lord Benville or Ecclestone made any appearance, they returned.

St. James was lost in conjecture. The mystery was very strange.

The absence of his two dastardly foes troubled him much.

Alone as he was, surrounded on all sides by inveterate foes, he felt his position doubly dangerous, having to protect the lady. He could not put his trust in the servants of the house—they were all allies of his treacherous cousin; but there were three in whom he could confide, and those three were his faithful Shanks, old Jacob Martin, and the redoubtable Lusher, who still remained a guest.

He believed these to be staunch friends in his cause, and, consequently called them together to prove their fidelity and arrange some plan for their mutual safety.

He laid before them the truthful facts of his position—his fears of a premeditated attack of his enemies.

"I believe you to be true, faithful men, in whom I can place my confidence, and look for staunch protectors," he said. "The house," he went on, grateful of the willing acknowledgment he received to his compliment, "is full of my base usurper's hirelings, who, at the moment of their master's return, would take up arms against us for his cause. This must be prevented by quiet strategem. To you, Jacob, I leave the work of removing every kind of weapon of defence from out of their reach."

"It shall be done, my master," said the old man.

"As I momentarily expect an attack to be made upon us, there is no time to be lost. So you may retire to quietly execute your duty."

Old Martin retired, leaving Shanks and the Lusher with the young nobleman.

"To you," he said, addressing Jack Evans, "I owe more than my life for the restoration of the lady you bravely saved from a watery grave. By-and-by, I shall be able to prove my gratitude in more than words."

He took the Lusher's hand, and pressed it with heartfelt gratitude.

"Well, sir," said Jack, "I am fully recompensed by your kindness, and the happiness it gave me to save the sweet lady. If I can be of further service to you, command me, and to death I am yours."

"I am more than grateful to you for your generous kindness. I did not expect to find this devotion in a stranger."

"Not exactly a stranger," put in Jack.

"I have a slight remembrance of your face; but where before I have ever seen you, I cannot exactly call to mind."

"You know Captain Claude and Tyburn Dick?"

"You are one of the faithful band," said the young nobleman. "No wonder, then, that I have so true a friend."

"Nor would you want for any," said Jack, "if we were near Hampstead Heath."

"But as we cannot ensure their assistance under some great loss of time, we must prepare to meet our assailants with what strength we can muster."

He then went on to give them instructions for defence.

Shanks had not forgotten the Lusher's insulting remark about his legs, but he gave up his intended vengeance for the cause of St. James, and forgave his tormentor.

They then shook hands, became sworn

friends, and walked about the mansion, armed to the feet.

Their equanimity was suddenly disturbed by hearing a clamour of many voices, and as many more feet approaching the house.

"Jack," said Shanks, "they're com"

"Yes," replied Jack. "And we shall have to fight."

At that moment a tremendous knocking at the door startled them almost into breathless terror.

They rushed from the room, in which they were discussing a bottle of their master's wine, and called loudly upon Jacob Martin. But ere the old fellow was prepared to join his two friends, the hall door was opened by a pompous lacquey and a group of labouring men, bearing the lifeless form of Reuben Frampton on a litter, entered.

Victor St. James, who rushed out in much alarm, fell back aghast at the sight of the inanimate form of his cousin.

This was an advent he did not expect. But, nevertheless, it was an agreeable one.

The death of Reuben was not much mourned. The servants were silent and respectful in the presence of the dead, and when the day arrived for the funeral, and Lord Benville did not return, Victor paid the last tribute to his remains, forgetting the animosity which had existed between them in life, and prayed a silent prayer over the grave for the sins of his cousin to be forgiven.

Edith grew very fretful and unhappy on account of her father's protracted absence.

"It is strange," said St. James, in reply to her wondering questions one day, "but still one must not despair; he may return soon. My sire," he went on, in a tone of bitterness, "is absent under very different circumstances to those of Lord Bernille. I have but little hope of ever seeing him more, for he was cruelly, treacherously betrayed from his home, and I have cause to believe murdered by—"

He did not finish. Had he told the gentle girl at his side all he knew, it would have been a cruel death blow to her, so he kept it unsaid.

"Edith, my darling," he again said, "you must not despair. You may be certain no harm has befallen your father."

"I hope not," murmured Edith; "with

all his faults, he was my father. He had been very cruel to me of late, but I forgive him."

"Bless you, my dear," fervently exclaimed the young cavalier, "and do you forgive my bad cousin?"

"It is best that his faults be forgotten now that he is gone. But tell me, dear Victor, how it was he met his death."

"He was thrown from the horse he took to pursue you, and falling upon his head died where he fell."

"It was a shocking fate for him to meet, so unprepared to meet his Maker; but let us pray that God may forgive him his sins, as we have done."

"Now, Edith, we have no one to prevent the union I have looked forward to so long. Say, dearest, that you will be mine."

She did not reply, but he was answered by the language of her beaming eyes.

The troubles and sufferings he had gone through were rewarded now, and he felt the happiness for having gained it at such a cost.

The hour was growing late as they wandered hand-in-hand through the verdant flowery groves of the garden, and as a gloomy cloud, like a sombre pall, swept across the moon that shut the light from the earth, St. James now felt anxious to return, and they began quickly to wend their steps back, when Edith came to a dead stop, and clung, panic-stricken, to her lover.

"Save me—save me!" she shrieked, in terror.

St. James clasped her to his breast, and looked around in alarm at the cause of her fright.

"Edith—Edith, my darling, what has occurred?" he exclaimed.

She could not answer him. Her tongue now clove burning to the roof of her mouth with terror. She pointed, with trembling hand, to a clump of thick foliage.

St. James glanced in that direction, and he started. His gaze met the fierce glare of a pair of fiery orbs.

Clasping the trembling girl around the waist with his left hand, he drew his sword.

The bushes parted, and three masked ruffians leaped out upon him.

He had no chance to cope with them.

Ere he could raise his sword, a heavy blow caused him to reel backwards, half stunned, as, at the same moment, Edith, shrieking and struggling, was torn from her lover.

This was terrible for the young nobleman.

He suddenly appeared to be void of reason.

Giving vent to a cry more like a howl of a mad dog, he dashed with furious impetus into the ruffians.

They laughed at his frail efforts, and catching him like an infant, he was put in a sack, and Edith, with her lover, borne away.

CHAPTER CXIX.
MORE PLOTTING AT THE LONE HUT ON THE HEATH.

SEATED in a back apartment of the lonely hut on the heath, we see Spikey and two of his companions, deeply absorbed in low converse, and in a further corner of the dingy room are the two wounded ruffians lying on a rude couch.

"I mean to have my revenge!" exclaimed one of the maimed villains. "The girl, curse her! put a bullet in me, and I mean to have her life for it."

"If Spikey don't settle her, I will!" roared the other, "she's crippled me for life."

"Fools!" exclaimed Spikey, "do yer think I should capture the gal if I didn't want her? and if you get in the way, it's yer own fault."

"I'll have her life for what she's done to me."

"Stop your gab!" thundered Spikey, glaring furiously upon his companions."

The men growled, but were silent.

They saw by the look of Spikey, it would be dangerous to continue their threats against his fair captive.

"It ain't safe to keep the gal here," Spikey said to the two ill-looking ruffians at his side. "It was an unlucky job for us to let that boy escape. He will bring the whole gang of highwaymen down upon us, the gal will have to be removed, or we shall have to keep out of sight."

"Cuss the boy!" said one of the others. "I knowed when he comed it was only to spy. Why the furies did you let him escape out of here alive?"

"If we don't want our necks stretched—and I don't—we'd better put the old man we've got upstairs out of the way. The boy's prying spoiled us there."

"No," said Spikey, "we don't put people out of the way for nothing, an' that old man may be worth a fortune to us, since he who calls himself Lord Ecclestone has kept back with the money we was to have had for the gal. I suppose he thinks the old man's dead, and now has nothing to fear, but he shall find his mistake out. Ha! ha!"

"Better put the old cuss out of sight. There is room enough in the *Black Quarry*. He won't be the first who has found a watery grave there by many scores."

"I say, no!" exclaimed Spikey.

"Well, I can tell you he'll bring us all to the gallows, an' that ain't pleasant."

"Dan, you're the biggest funker among us. How the blazes can he bring us to the gallows?"

"Why, didn't that infernal sneaking cur of a dog put his nose in at the door just as we was going to slit the old un's wizen?"

"And who the deuce told you to slit the old man's wizen?" asked Spikey, angrily.

"Look here, Spikey, yer wants to 'ave too much yer own way. I can tell yer I ain't going to stand it."

Spikey rose to his herculean height, and took a pistol from his belt, and the man went cowering back to his seat.

"The job was entirely mine," said Spikey.

"Anyhow," replied Dan, "you didn't do the job entirely yourself; considering as how two of our mates got shot in the forest, and I got a fearful knocking about."

"You always do. You're one o' the biggest fools in the world.

"I ain't fool enough to be chiselled by you."

"Nobody wants to cheat yer. Only if yer talk about finishing the old man, you'll cheat the lot o' us."

"Leave it to me," said Spikey," and you'll all be safe enough, I'll warrant."

"I should like to know how?"

Spikey began to explain—

"Lord Ecclestone and Lord Bernille said that we should have a thousand pounds for getting the old man out of their way," he began. "Well, as you already know, we should have settled the old boy then and there, but some meddling fool interrupted us

by shooting two of our companions; but I think I settled him. We then had to cut, for the forest was alive with officers, and stuck to my prize, and, in an insensible state, brought him by the main coach here. Where the devil you got to I can't make out."

"Well, I can tell you we had to take to our heels, or we should not be here now," said Dan. "Didn't you make any arrangements with Lord Ecclestone?"

"We didn't have much time to make any arrangements, but he said he would follow, and he was here almost as soon as we, when he said he would expect to see the old man dead. I suppose he thinks the old man is dead, and now has nothing to fear, but he's made a mistake."

"What's the good of keeping the old man?" inquired Dan. "He ain't any good to us now."

"My plans are these. To keep the old man a captive, inform the *noble* Lord Ecclestone that the old fellow is in our power, and, unless he doubles the money he promised, and hands it over immediately, we shall bring the old man before a court to denounce him as the villain who attempted to assassinate him."

"Why, if you do that, the old man 'll inform agin us."

"Don't suppose I am such a fool, do you? I have too much respect for my neck. The old boy wouldn't live long when we'd got his money."

Here an interruption put a stop to their dark plotting.

The old maid of the hut came shuffling into the room.

"Spikey, you're wanted," she said.

"Who wants me?" inquired that worthy

"Reginald Merton."

The ruffian arose, and winked at his companions to keep seated.

In an adjoining apartment he found his titled visitor anxiously awaiting for him.

"Have you got the lady?" Reginald demanded, rather sternly.

"I promised to get the lady for you, and I'll do my best to fulfil my promise."

"Confound it! why don't you give me a straightforward answer!" exclaimed Reginald, with rising anger. "Is the lady here?"

"She is upstairs."

"That is well. Two hours hence, I will send a carriage for you to convey her to an old house at Richmond. You had better take the old hag to attend upon her."

Leaving Spikey a most liberal sum of money, he then took his departure, exulting with joyous anticipations.

Fortune had certainly favoured him in his dark plan against the fair, beautiful girl, whom he rejoiced to think would soon be his victim.

CHAPTER CXX.

TYBURN DICK SENTENCED TO DEATH—THE MAN OF MYSTERY PAYS THE PRISONER A VISIT, AND ARRANGES A PLAN OF ESCAPE.

So thoroughly was the King incensed by the daring of the Boy Highwayman, who had been the cause of his miserable failure with the lady captive, that he ordered him to instant death, quite forgetting, in his anger, that he had not been tried.

Of this fact he was speedily reminded by Wild Bertram. The man of mystery held the King to a degree under his control, for some reason only known between themselves.

The King, being brought back to reflection, thus determined to have the trial arranged and terminated as soon as possible.

He felt it would only end as he wished—in the boy's death.

The evidence that could be brought against him by his stern, unrelenting victims, who had been compelled to yield to his commands on the road, would bring a death-sentence, the King felt assured, to the man who had foiled him in his attempt upon the lovely maid.

So thought the King, and so perhaps, it might have been. But Tyburn Dick had no intention of awaiting any such dangerous issue.

He was visited by his devoted mistress, and to her he gave a missive, to be delivered to Bertram.

"I'll trust to you," said Grace, when she stood before her lover's dark-browed friend. "You will serve him, will you not?"

"I will make some trial to that effect," replied the man of mystery. "Something I must risk, too, but it must be done."

"Then he will be safe?"

"You think so," observed Bertram, with a smile. "Yet he has the King's enmity against him."

"But you have power."

"Greater, you think, than his?"

"I am sure of it; men, rich and great, speak of you as in fear. Even his majesty holds you in a respect brought on by fear."

"Why, so he may; for I am not one to be lightly trifled with."

"Then you will do your best for Richard!"

"Why, I can scarce do less for one who pleads so sweetly," said Bertram, smiling at the fair face before him; "trust me, Lady Grace, all that can be done I will do."

"I know not how gratefully to speak," said Grace, "but if a poor girl's thanks are aught of reward, I give you thanks from my heart."

"Why did you not plead to the King?"

"I did," replied Grace, with a vivid blush.

"You found him generous."

"As a wolf," replied the maiden, bitterly.

"I should have said as a King."

"In such a case the one word would apply to both," said Bertram. "You might purchase a hundred lives of such a King, but not without that which is more dear to a woman than aught on earth—her virtue."

Grace blushed.

"I leave him now to you," she said, "and that in confidence."

"Confidence in me!"

"You were never known to betray a trust," said Grace; "I would confide in you as deeply as a friend as I should fear you as an enemy."

"Frank at last," thought Wild Bertram.

Then, with a stately grace, he raised her hand to his lips, and said—

"Before the day of trial comes, you may hope to see your lover safe."

Grace took leave, Bertram escorting her towards the Haunt. He went to St. James's Palace.

"I would have audience with his Majesty," he said to a page.

"His Majesty gives audience within two hours," replied the page, "till then he is not to be sought or seen."

"Go with my message, and bring back the King's reply."

The page stole a furtive glance at the

speaker's deep, stern face, then went to the King's chamber.

Bertram stood immoveable till the page returned with the King's command to see him.

Bertram caught sight of a lady's robe disappearing through a door as he entered the King's chamber, and a sneering smile gathered on his lip.

"A king," he thought, "a man of boundless lust, without one redeeming virtue—a monarch, a slave to slavish passions, who would risk his soul for a night of lawless love—barter his kingdom for a wanton beauty."

Which brief soliloquy, though very strong, was very true.

"What is your business, Bertram?" asked his Majesty. "You come early."

His Majesty had been interrupted in a charming *tete-à-tete* with a lady, so he did not feel or speak graciously.

"My business, sire, is brief."

"So much the better."

"I simply want an order for the Earl of Aldervale's release from prison."

"What?"

The monarch's swarthy cheeks grew darker, and his eye flashed as he spoke.

"Bertram," said the king, biting his lips hard, to keep down his wrath, "your audacity, methinks, is over great."

"Furies," said Bertram, brusquely, "I say simply what I want. The man has done you no wrong."

"Did he not, with the assistance of one of his lawless band, try to perpetrate an outrage?"

"Granted."

"Yet you ask his release?"

"He is not the only one who has done the same," said Wild Bertram, "and that, too, without assistance of mine."

"What mean you?"

"Let that question be answered by yourself—your outrage on a girl—a child almost. Your own late attempt upon Lady Grace Merton."

"By the mass!" said his Majesty, "you know too much."

"True," said Bertram, with significant emphasis. "Enough, at least, to tell that it best to comply with my desire."

"Ha! Do you threaten?"

"Do I seem to?" said the man of mystery, quietly. "I speak for a boy, whose only faults were the sufferings of his wrongs. I cannot see him suffer alone."

"You grow chivalrous," sneered the monarch.

"You should thank me, then—that is a feeling wanted very much at Court."

The King grew still further incensed.

He stepped towards a bell, with the intention of summoning a page, and having the man of mystery shown out, when Bertram stopped him.

"Do nothing in such haste," he said, warningly. "Before I depart, I must have that order."

"Must?"

"Must. I have promised

"To whom?"

"Grace Merton," was the reply.

"Be more careful of your promises, then. The highwayman shall await the issue of the trial."

"He shall not."

"So," exclaimed the monarch, wrathfully. "You defy me?"

"To that extent—further, if necessary. If you will not give the order, I will set him free without."

"At your peril be it, then. Are we thus to be set at nought?"

"Am I?" exclaimed Bertram, growing angry in his turn. "Confusion! Am I to see a defenceless youth, for your caprice suffer? Have you not willing wantons enough but that you would kill a man because his mistress does not appreciate the honour your Majesty would bestow upon her?"

"Enough," said the king. "Retire. Once for all, I will not give the order."

"Be it so. In spite of that, the boy shall not perish."

"By the saints! Another word, and I will send you there to keep him company."

The man of mystery laughed in reckless, bold defiance.

"Do," he said. "Place me on trial, and let the judges hear such evidence as I could give."

There was a menace in his words that the king well understood.

He had gone too far, and it would be better now to make a compromise while there was time.

"I cannot set the boy free," he said. "You know that I have sent him there to await his trial, and the Lady Aldervale is resolved upon his punishment."

"Leave it, then, to me."

"Since it is your wish, and you can do it without letting it be seen that I have even wish or will in his escape, you may so contrive it."

"I will, sire."

"Enough, then."

Bertram withdrew.

He left the king by no means satisfied with the result of the interview, but he knew that he could not safely dare too much with the strange man.

Bertram went to Newgate. Bertram ruminated as he walked on, arranging a plan by which to accomplish his desire to rescue Tyburn Dick.

Arriving at Newgate, Bertram asked at once to see the governor, and was taken before him.

They were old acquaintances. The man of mystery had been there on sundry previous occasions. Not as a visitor to a prisoner, but rather as a prisoner to be visited.

"You are almost a stranger," said the governor, smiling. "To what am I indebted for this honour?"

"To the presence of a friend of mine, one Tyburn Dick, alias the Earl of Aldervale."

"A friend who will not long trouble you."

"An error," said Bertram. "I have come for him."

"On whose authority?" he asked.

"My own."

"Unrecognised in this," said his companion; "you have authority, I know; but I have duty."

"The stronger of the two," said Bertram, seeing that it was hopeless to think of bribing the governor. "Can I see the prisoner?"

"Not without an order from the King."

"Tush, man! Does his Majesty give orders at such an hour, think you?"

"I know not; my orders are strict."

"And what are they?"

"That the boy should have no visitors."

"I have the King's permission to see him," said Bertram.

"Written in trust?"

"No, by word of mouth."

The governor shook his head.

"I am sorry," he said, "but you cannot pass."

"Furies, man! would you doubt my word in such a case?"

"Why, no, if you set it in that light."

Without further word he summoned an attendant, and Wild Bertram was conducted to the apartment to which our hero had been consigned.

"Dick!" exclaimed Bertram, when they were alone, "your trial takes place to-morrow."

"I knew as much," replied the youth, gloomily.

"You will not stop to meet it, will you?"

Tyburn Dick looked at him inquiringly.

"What else should I do?"

"Escape."

"How?"

"I will tell you."

"Thanks," said the boy; "it will be welcome news."

"You must be bold and prompt," said Bertram. "It is a perilous chance."

"Not more perilous than my present risk, I can but lose my life."

"Then thus it is," said Bertram, "You must escape from here to-night."

"By what means?"

"This dagger will assist you—the blade is strong."

He took the weapon from his breast, and gave it to his companion.

Our hero secured it in his doublet.

"I will bribe the man who is stationed at the end of the corridor. Thence you can reach the window and drop into the yard."

"I shall break my neck."

"Not so. Here is a cord, you can fasten it to the bars of the window, and so lower yourself in safety."

"Thanks."

Tyburn Dick took the cord and put it with the dagger

"Then," said Bertram, "you must cross the yard, and scale the wall."

"A thing not done easily."

"That will be as occasion serves. You have a dagger and a cord. I escaped from the Bastile without the aid of anything, save my hands and teeth."

"All that is possible," said Dick, "I will do."

"That is well. Be of good heart; you will find me near to aid you."

They exchanged a grasp of hands, and Bertram departed. He ascertained the names of those men who would keep watch at midnight, and for bribes of gold they promised to be deaf and blind to anything that might transpire.

It seemed a long and weary day to our hero, and when the dark shadows of night crept on he felt relieved.

Then commenced operations; the door was bolted on the outside.

The dagger would not avail him in that instance, and he stood wondering what was to be done, when a stealthy step drew near the door.

CHAPTER CXXI.

TYBURN DICK'S PERILOUS ESCAPE FROM NEWGATE.

The daring boy stood breathless, with the gleaming dagger held firmly, ready the instant his cell-door was opened to plunge it into the gaoler's heart, and escape.

The man, hearing of the daring boy's fierceness, was very cautious how he opened the door.

He expected a dig should he apprise the prisoner of his presence too quickly, or without warning him.

Having opened the door a few inches, and keeping his foot against it to prevent the highwayman from leaping out upon him, he said, in an undertone—

"Fear nothing. I am a friend."

Dick breathed freely.

"Let me see your face," he said.

The man opened the door, and entered.

Dick was a good physiognomist. He read in the man's countenance an honest, sturdy friend.

"Bind and gag me," the sentinel said. "I will say that I heard you trying to escape, and so came in to prevent you."

Tyburn Dick gagged the man, and then bound him hand and foot, and laid him on the chamber floor. He then overturned the chamber furniture, as though a violent struggle had taken place, and finished these arrangements by breaking the man's sword. Then, armed with his dagger, he crept out.

The window was gained without interruption. Exerting all his strength, he wrenched out one of the iron bars, and threw it to the ground beneath; then he fastened the cord to the next iron bar, and lowered himself from the window.

He got down without mishap, and a sharp and sudden twitch broke the end off close to the bar which had held it. Then, taking the one which he had thrown out, he kept it ready as a weapon of defence if necessary.

He had also another use for it.

On arriving at the wall he had to pause; there the bar did good service.

He bound it strongly to the end of the cord, then, with a powerful effort, threw it over the wall.

The cord held firm. Gathering his energies, then, for the most desperate part of his enterprise, he crouched down and leaped.

He was so far successful. He had reached nearly to the top of the wall, when the rope gave way.

Our hero gave a cry of terror, and even as the rope broke he clutched at an iron spike on the wall, and saved himself from falling. But the bar fell, and struck a guard, who stood beneath the wall.

The man staggered, and looked up.

"An escape!" he shouted. "What ho! within there."

Taking aim at Tyburn Dick's breast, he fired.

Our hero gave a cry. He was wounded. At the same instant a rush of many feet was heard, and a party came from within the prison.

They had discovered the man gagged and bound, and were now looking for the prisoner, whom they saw clinging to the wall.

"Surrender!" said an officer, as the men levelled their weapons. "Surrender, or we fire."

The officer stood for a moment to see whether the boy would obey the summons to surrender.

" It was life or death.   Death if he were taken back again, life if he escaped.   The last was by far the most inviting prospect, so he suddenly let himself drop from the wall, and as he did so the men fired.

One bullet entered his neck, and he fell to the ground with a cry of pain.

The guard emerged from the gate, and went to the interior of the wall, expecting to find their prisoner lifeless on the ground.

They found him, but a tall, powerful man sprang forward, and, drawing a heavy sword, stood over the prostrate body.

" Back!" he said, sternly.   " Let the man live if he may."

" Back !" said the officer.   " He has broken out from Newgate, and we must take him in again."

" I think not," exclaimed Wild Bertram. " What ho, there !"

He beat down the weapons of the guard, who, at a word from their leader, advanced to the attack, and, when he called out, some score or so of men came out, like dark shadows, from various ways, and drove the others back with fierce determination.

Their leader was a brave man, and thought not lightly of the highwaymen whom Bertram had summoned.   He might have sounded the alarm, and obtained assistance, but preferred to trust to himself and a few men he had with him.

Wild Bertram and our hero's faithful comrades could use their weapons well, and they drove the attacking party back every time they advanced.

" Rally, comrades !" said the officer again. " Are we to be defeated by these mongrel dogs?"

Wild Bertram quietly opposed his iron frame to the speaker.

" These mongrel dogs are well trained, and can bite," he said, as their weapons crossed. " Now, my men, away with the body, some of you !   The rest bar the way with me."

The highwaymen formed in a close square, and charged the guard again, driving them back, while those of their companions in the rear raised their gallant young leader from the ground, and carried him from the spot.

. The enraged officer strove hard to cut his opponents down, and lead his men after the escaping prisoner and his rescuers; but Bertram held his ground with the cool skill acquired in many desperate encounters, and the officer strove in vain.

He was stricken down at last, stunned and bleeding, by Bertram's sword; then, seeing their leader fall, the guard sounded the alarm.

A few moments more, and the prison guard, in numbers vastly exceeding those of our hero and his companions, would have been upon the scene, so the daring man gave the order to retreat, and, fighting their way slowly back, they retired in good order.

Many of the prison guard were wounded, and many of the highwaymen lay dead upon the earth; but the loss was chiefly on the part of the officials.

Their comrades, headed by a young officer, went to the rescue, arriving just in time to see the retreating forces of the daring knights.

" Follow !" he said; " let us hunt them to their lair. We must teach these daring rogues a lesson."

He waved his men on, and marched forward, eager to avenge his comrades.

Wild Bertram looked round, and saw them coming.

" They follow well," he said; " but I do not think they will follow too far."

Then, with a grim smile, he resumed his way.

Going to our hero's side he looked at him to see how far his injuries extended.

" Two bad wounds," he said, " the neck and breast.   The poor youth is unfortunate, and the fair lady has been the cause of some trouble to him.   Perhaps he may be more successful in future."

Dick lay quite senseless in the arms of the four brave men who bore him.

They carried him with much care, giving not the slightest oscillation to his body, as the least motion caused his wounds to bleed more freely.

" Make quick progress," said their master; " the red dogs are coming closer, and I would

"LEAVE ME!" SHE CRIED, CONFRONTING HIM.

rather fight them from within than meet them here."

The men went forward with greater speed, and soon reached their haunt on Hounslow Heath.

Seeing them enter that dangerous locality, the young fellow turned to his men.

"Comrades," he said, "you are weak. We have to follow them to their very den, and the enterprise is one of peril. Are you all with me?"

A gathering close together, and the flash of every weapon, answered him.

"Then, forward!"

And away they went on the track of the highwayman, keeping them in sight.

Winding turning after turning, they passed, as Wild Bertram and his party entered the secret haunt of which such terrible tales were told.

They paused irresolutely, and their leader, brave as he was, turned slightly pale. But he did not change his purpose, though the place of the highwayman's refuge made the danger greater.

"The den of devils," he said, "the work we have to do is harder than I thought, therefore it will be the better done."

The officer tried the entrance through which the men disappeared, but to no purpose. The door was immovable.

Taking a firelock from one of his men, he swung it high above his head, and brought the butt heavily against the door.

A very hard door it was, for the weapon was broken and the door uninjured.

"Open, in the King's name!" exclaimed the officer.

No reply was given.

"Force an entrance," he said again. "These rascals defy us."

"Better let it alone," said a man who stood leaning against a tree, watching the

49

proceedings. "The master of this is a man with whom it is not wise to interfere."

"Who is the master?"

"Tyburn Dick."

"The man spoke respectfully enough. Perhaps his respect was in some sort created by the sight of half a hundred gleaming swords, in the hands of men accustomed to use them.

The young officer did not pay any heed to the warning. He instructed twenty of his men to keep guard outside while the rest forced an entry.

Further, he instructed them to shoot down all who interfered with them.

The last instructions his men prepared to obey with much seeming pleasure.

Then they rushed against the door. After repeated shocks it yielded, and went in with a crash. The officer was among the first who rushed in.

Opposite the door was a wide staircase, and on the stairs, arranged in rows one above the other, scores of the highwaymen were seated with their firelocks levelled so as to command the entire entrance-way.

On the landing at the top of the stairs stood Wild Bertram, smiling with grim satisfaction at the appearance of his own arrangements.

"Well, sir," he said, "what do you think of the position? Does it not display good generalship?"

"Excellent, but of little use in the present case. We are in, as you perceive."

"With regret. You have no space for effective action, and a single volley would sweep you down to a man. Call your men out and retire, and you shall not be molested."

"Not while a man remains."

"Your only course, and one that must be quickly taken. In five minutes every weapon here will be discharged."

"I must do my duty. You have aided the escape of a prisoner whom the King confided to my care. I must take him back, and place you under arrest."

Bertram smiled in disdain, not at the officer, but at the power he represented.

The officer looked around at his companions.

He saw no fear on any face, but knowing that he nor they had any chance of carrying out the intent with which they had come, he gave orders for a retrograde movement, and they marched out.

The officer in command smiled.

"I withdraw," he said, "but only for the sake of my men, and to avoid a needless butchery; for the disgrace into which I shall fall for letting my prisoner escape, I shall thank you in person."

"You will not suffer," said Bertram; "if you do, you will find me ready to give satisfaction. Tell the King how Tyburn Dick escaped, who aided him, and believe me, he will hold you blameless."

"He may or may not, as it pleases him. I have done my duty."

So saying, the officer left the highwaymen's haunt and marched his men back to the prison.

CHAPTER CXXII.

CONTINUES THE ADVENTURES OF OUR HERO AT THE DEVIL'S REST.

YOUNG TOM, who had watched over the safety of Tyburn Dick, was somewhat mystified when he so suddenly disappeared behind the secret panel. Apprehensive of danger befalling his gallant protector, the boy examined the wall to discover how our hero had escaped, and determining to follow him at any risk, his hand suddenly alighted upon a small iron knob.

He instantly pressed it back with his finger, and a panel slid aside.

With a glad cry, he sprang through the aperture.

His cry of joyousness was changed into a cry of horror, as the panel had slid back into its place, and he did not, as he had imagined, find himself in another chamber.

He was shut up between the two walls in total darkness; but that was not the worst. While groping his way along, his foot slipped over the verge of the flooring, and he fell forward down a gap three or four feet deep.

Fearful apprehensions of a torturing death seemed his fate unless he called for assistance. While lying in that state of fearful terror, hardly daring to breathe, he fancied he heard a slight groan.

Raising his eyes, and looking through the

oppressive gloom in the direction from whence the voice proceeded, he caught the faint glimmer of a lantern. And by that flickering light he saw two forms struggling with savage ferocity.

This sight gave him hope and joy, for he recognised in the younger combatant our hero, who had got the thieftaker with both hands by the throat.

Young Tom was crawling along towards his friend, when there was a crash as the officers tore up the boards.

A stream of light peered through the opening, and increased as more boards were pulled up.

Young Tom had to crouch back from observation.

Tyburn Dick released his foe and disappeared through a trap.

Young Tom would have followed him, but at that moment several of the officers peered down the opening of the floor and pulled their half-strangled leader out.

While waiting for an opportunity to escape, young Tom saw one of the men let himself down.

The officer came on towards him, and Young Tom drew aside, leaving an open passage for the man to pass him.

The light that came through the opening in the floor enabled him to discern the officer, while the darkness where he was concealed entirely hid him from the man's view.

When the officer had passed him, young Tom sprang upon him and pinned him in such a way as to prevent his resistance and stop his calling for help, and put a handkerchief over his mouth.

Then he made for the trap through which he had seen our hero escape.

It took him some time to discover the hidden spring, nor did he get through too quickly, for, at the very moment he made his exit, the whole flooring was taken up.

Young Tom, after going through the trap fell some ten feet into a vault beneath.

It took him some time to recover the effects of his descent, and when he rose to his feet, was no little astonished to see standing erect in a corner of the vault a man, muffled to the eyes in a long cloak, watching him

very keenly, while his finger pressed the trigger of a pistol.

It was by no means a comfortable position for any one to be in.

And Tom looked for a way of escape.

There was not any but the door, and the silent sentinel guarded that with his back, and, by way of suggestion to keep the youth at bay, he levelled his pistol in a line with his head.

The muffled man spoke.

"Surrender!" he said.

"For what?"

"To aid me to capture Tyburn Dick."

"I'll see you at the devil first."

"Do you refuse to give your services to capture the highwayman?"

"Most strongly, and on your life you had had better not stop me."

He advanced two steps towards the door.

"Back! or I scatter your brains!" said the man.

Young Tom's eyes flashed fire, and he raised his pistol. Another instant, and the man would have fallen at his feet. But he spoke in time.

"Stay, Tom! Do you know me now?" he said, and, throwing off his cloak, there stood our hero.

Dropping his weapon, with a cry of terror, Tom grasped Dick's hand.

"Why that foolish joke?" he asked. "I might innocently have sacrificed your life."

Tyburn Dick laughed.

"I did it merely to try your faith," he said. "And did you not really know me, Tom?"

"It would have puzzled the very devil to have recognised you."

"Ah!"

They both started, and Tom picked up his pistol.

"They have found the trap," exclaimed our hero.

"We must away from here. Where's Tom King?"

"I know not. He can't be far off. Come, let's leave this place before these devils make their way through."

It was too late. The officers had opened the trap in the ceiling of the vault, and the head of Billy, the thief-catcher, peeped down upon the two youthful companions.

He raised a shout for his men to follow him, and dropped through just as Dick and Tom quitted the vault.

In a few minutes the whole herd of officers were in the vault.

Loading their weapons for a desperate encounter, they set off in a body on the track of our hero.

Many places they searched without success.

Entering an underground kitchen, the whole gang came to a sudden halt.

They had not expected to meet with such a reception as awaited them.

Tom King, our hero, and his young friend stood in the centre of the room, each holding at arm's length a pair of long-barrelled pistols and a sword gripped by the blade between their teeth, for immediate use.

They looked a very formidable trio. And so they were.

The officers were astonished, though at the same time delighted—instead of Tom King alone there was the renowned Tyburn Dick, and a stranger, whom they did not know, but whom they concluded to be a highwayman, and one of the Boy King's band.

This was a glorious opportunity for making money, as they thought.

Buckling up his courage, the thief-taker shouted, in a voice of thunder—

" Highwaymen, surrender !"

" Officers," said Tyburn Dick, " that's a thing we never do."

" If you don't give in quickly we shall take you, dead or alive."

" If you are wise," said Dick, " you won't interfere with us."

" Forward, men ! Secure the prisoners !" shouted the thief-taker.

The officers rushed forward ; the highwaymen did not give an inch, and the leading officer saw at a glance they were determined to stand out till the last.

The thief-catcher was as determined to capture them as they were not to surrender.

The highwaymen were good shots he knew, and each one held in his hand two lives.

Were they to fire first six officers would fall.

Billy well knew that if six of his men were taken away the rest would stand a poor chance against their opponents. His only way of taking them was dead, and this he resolved to do.

Standing aside he gave the word to fire, and simultaneously with the command a broad sheet of flame spread along the daring knights of the road.

Shrieks and groans of dying men rent the air, and then the scene became one of terrible excitement.

Wild oaths mingled with the clash of steel, and men could be seen starting about, springing one on the other, like shadows through the volumes of circling smoke that entirely enveloped them.

When the smoke cleared away the thief-catcher stood horror-stricken to see six of his men lying dead.

It was the highwaymen who had fired, and every shot had taken deadly effect.

The officers were like so many madmen; regardless of danger they dashed at the highwaymen for revenge.

Billy, seeing the determination with which his men fought, was spirited on by their bravery and his own fury at the loss of six men.

Breaking through the combatants he attacked our hero singly. A shout of applause from his men invigorated him, and he fought like a tiger.

This turn in affairs was more than the bombastic trio had expected, and really more than they could stand against.

Dick had received a severe wound across the sword-arm, and he was consequently growing weaker, and a faintness crept slowly over him.

Dick was now compelled to fight left handed.

That he could not do for long, not being accustomed to it.

Tyburn Dick looked round, made a bound at a door, and swung it open in time to escape the volley of bullets that was fired at the highwaymen, who escaped unscratched.

The officers were soon following them through the house and into the street, where they were surprised to find the soldiers gone.

Dindle Dandy had waylaid the man the thief-catcher had sent to bring them in ; and, having made a captive of the officer, mine host fetched the soldiers in himself, under the pretence that he meant to betray the highwaymen, but in reality only to keep them out of the way until the aforesaid highwaymen escaped.

Our three friends made the most of this favourable opportunity to escape.

Putting their best leg forward, they were soon ahead of the officers.

Young Tom looking behind him, and only seeing about half the number of officers in view, said—

"Don't run; there's plenty of time."

The air at that moment was rent with the yell of voices.

"There's more than half there," said Dick.

King turned his head.

"The whole troop of lobsters," he said, "are after us."

"And the other half of the officers," put in Young Tom, turning his head.

"We shall have to run for it. Are you getting tired?" asked Dick.

At every yard the soldiers and officers gained upon our friends, and there seemed but little chance of the chase being terminated in favour of the highwaymen; in fact, there appeared no chance of them escaping.

They were fatigued by the dodging about to keep clear of their foes during the whole time they were at the Devil's Rest.

Not so with their pursuers; they were quite fresh, and in every probability would soon have made captives of the fugitives.

The highwaymen had gone as far as their strength would allow, and they felt now that they must either give in or be shot.

Tom King turned his head, and saw a sight that sent his blood chilled to ice to his very heart, and brought his comrades to a stand by a cry that left his lips.

A body of the soldiers had advanced to within a few paces of them, and raised their muskets to fire.

At the moment when the commanding officer was about to give the word to fire, our hero, pained by humiliation by having to give in, sang out only in time—

"We surrender!"

The muskets were immediately lowered,

and the soldiers advanced in quick march to surround the prisoners, while the officers got ready the handcuffs.

The worthy pair of thief-catchers were chuckling with triumph, and anticipating the heap of blood money they would receive for the apprehension of the daring knights, when an incident occurred that swept the glorious vision of glittering dross from their sight.

They had not yet come up with their intended captives, and the little distance that lay between them and the highwaymen proved the source of protection to our friends.

The clatter of many horses, and the clanking of steel heard at no great distance, announced the approach of a body of armed and mounted men, whether they were highwaymen or soldiers it could not be guessed.

Each party hoped it was friends of theirs.

A minute more settled the doubt.

A body of mounted men then came in.

Highwaymen splendidly dressed and armed for some special occasion.

Whether the present occasion was the cause of their splendid equipment it was difficult for Dick or his comrades to define.

So they remained in a state of indefinite carelessness as to the cause of their appearance.

They were delighted that they were here to assist them out of an awkward position, and they cared not for what they came.

The invincible trio could have enthusiastically shouted a welcome, but the thought that the shout might bring a shower of bullets amongst them held them quiet.

As the cavalcade of highwaymen advanced, Dick could discern amongst the foremost Captain Claude, Big Bullskin, Gallant Tom, Swig, Devil Duke, and Paul Clifford, and the pedlar boy, who was a stranger to him, and caused him to wonder why he was there.

The highwaymen raised a shout when they saw their gallant young chief and his comrades threatened by the deadly weapons of the soldiers.

The highwaymen, it was apparent to Dick, had not come with any intention to his release, as they were pursuing quite a different course before perceiving him.

It was Captain Claude who first saw him.

Every person's head was turned when the shout of recognition rang through the air.

Every sword leaped glistening from its scabbard, and every hand that held them was raised with terrible menace against the foe as they rode up and surrounded the boy chief.

The two parties regarded each other silently for a time.

The commander of the soldiers was a brave man. He could read the thoughts of his opposers by the expression of their countenances, and was determined not to give way an inch.

The highwaymen were determined to rescue their young chief.

Ie w. resolved to take him prisoner, with many others as he could ouerpower.

A grim smile flitted across Bullskin's features, making them terrible in their expression.

"Dismount, gentlemen," he said, "we can fight better on even ground.

It was done. The highwaymen slid from their saddles.

The commanding officer, seeing that something must be done promptly, gave the word to charge the highwaymen.

In an instant the soldiers advanced forward with fixed bayonets, and surrounded the three captives.

The soldiers and officers amounted to twice the number of the knights of the highway.

The highwaymen knew this, but brave men do not count odds in such a case.

The officer, seeing that the highwaymen's intention was to fight for the prisoners, said, in a determined voice—

"If one attempt is made to rescue the prisoners, we shall fire."

Captain Claude faced the soldiers.

"Though your fellows treole those of mine," he said, with his usual calmness, "there will not be a man left to tell the tale of the encounter, if you try to oppose us."

"I do my duty," said the soldier, "and these men must not yield while I have life or a comrade left."

"Then I am sorry," Claude said; "we are to fight to the death."

"To the death," replied the other.

Devil Duke, Gallant Tom, and Big Bullskin faced the armed guards, thinking nothing of the overwhelming numbers, they were fighting for life and liberty.

Like gladiator Titans, they met the charge of bayonets.

Each man fought as though for all.

The two thief-takers advanced with their ill-looking crew, and poured a volley of shot from their pistols into the heroic band of highwaymen.

This cowardly attack aroused the angry wrath of Munroe's brave nature.

Dashing amongst the thickest of the combatants, he brought out Dick and his companions, striking down with his terrible weapon any who dared to oppose him, then, in all the majesty of his heroic power, he leaped amongst the caitiff crew, and, with his ponderous weapon, he struck them down like reeds.

The officers and soldiers were stricken down, and strewed the ground, while Dick and Tom King, who had joined the other captains, kept up the work with fearful slaughter.

Step by step the foe was driven back.

The young soldier recoiled with horror, when he saw the fearful havoc that had decreased his men, and in a state of frenzy, he called out for the bloody work to stop.

Every weapon was instantly lowered, and the highwaymen drew back.

Then the fight was over. The young officer sadly gave orders for his men to carry their wounded comrades with them, and they left the highwaymen masters of the field of battle.

"I will return to the haunt," said Big Bullskin. "I may be wanted there. Claude will tell you the nature of the adventure we were on when we met you."

"Are you strong enough to ride?" inquired Dick.

"Quite, thanks. Adieu and success! He got into his saddle, and, with half a dozen of his comrades for an escort, he rode away.

Tyburn Dick, Tom King, and young Tom or rather Tom Johnson, as we shall hereafter name him—mounted three of the highwaymen's horses, whose masters had had to carry their wounded comrades to their rendezvous.

"This lad," said Captain Claude, introducing the pedlar boy to our hero, "is the bearer of very sad intelligence. He came to the haunt last night with Lilly, and informed us that Grace had been captured by a gang of ruffians."

Dick's handsome face became very white, and his brow clouded sadly.

"I expected as much!" he said. "Some more of my dastardly brother's work! By Heaven, if it is, he shall pay dearly for it." Turning to the pedlar boy, he said, "Who were the men who captured the lady?"

"I know not, nor either did she," replied the lad, and then he told Dick all he knew.

When the Black Quarry was mentioned, Tom King started involuntarily. Deeply as the boy chief was absorbed in his own reflections, he noticed the change that came over the countenance of the exile.

"You know something of that place, then," Dick observed.

"I knew some one," replied the highwayman, moodily, "who once resided there, and he—but never mind, it is best unsaid."

"What's the matter, old fellow?" asked Clifford, sympathetically.

These two gallant gentlemen were boon companions, and the other was affected by a peculiar influence.

Tom King squeezed the other's hand, his spirits were depressed by a great sorrow—the sorrow of a fearful misery and bitter sufferings.

During this conversation they had let their steeds slacken pace, and were going along without a thought of danger overtaking them, until they were suddenly apprised of the fact that some one was behind them.

Dick turned his head, and saw a cloud of dust rising and advancing behind them.

"We shall have some warm work," he said, drawing the attention of his companions to the cloud of dust that gradually grew into a body of mounted officers.

"How many are there coming?" asked Claude.

They counted twelve.

"And we are eight," Gallant Tom said. "Shall we wait for them?"

"No," Dick said; "it is no good wasting valuable time; let them come if they like. I am quite cleaned out, and want money. By Jove! here comes the very fellow; get

out of sight, comrades, and let me deal with him."

Tyburn Dick put a mask over his face, and his companions concealed themselves in a field behind a clump of trees

Dick drew his steed across the road, and took a pistol from his holster, as the horseman whom he had seen came trotting towards him.

"A fine day to you," said Dick, bringing the horseman to a sudden standstill by forcing the tube of his pistol in the astonished traveller's face; "come, give me what you have about you and go; I have no time to spare. Quick, do not hesitate, I must have your money or your life!"

It was a peremptory demand, that allowed of no denial; the traveller, seeing the officers coming in the opposite direction, would have tried to gain time, but Dick drew back the trigger of his pistol with a quiet determination that persuaded the traveller to drop a purse of gold into his hand.

Thanking the traveller for his compliance, Dick waved his hat to the officers, who had arrived in dangerous proximity, leaped the hedge and joined his companions.

The very daring of the boy to rob a person before their eyes was a proof of the contempt with which he looked upon their official authority that exasperated them to a pitch of desperation, and a determination to hunt him down.

CHAPTER CXXIII.

THE LONE HOUSE.—MARIAN SYDNEY'S PERIL.—A FRIEND IN NEED.—THE ESCAPE.

THE house to which Gabriel Carnwood bore Marian was situate in a lonely place, remote from human habitation, and well suited in every way to his felonious purpose.

It was kept by a hard-featured woman, who was known by the appellation of Gaunt Meg.

"Now, Mother Meg," exclaimed Gabriel Carnwood, as he carried the maiden in, "get a room ready for this lady. Then help her to dress; she came out in a hurry, and would not stay to do it herself."

"Ah, pretty dear!" said Gaunt Meg, looking at the helpless girl with a hideous leer. "It's the way with 'em all. They can't resist the persuasions of such gentlemen as you."

The scoundrel looked in brutal triumph at his victim, whom he still held in his strong grasp, turning a deaf ear to her appeals for mercy.

"What would you have?" he asked, savagely. "Ain't I as good as that outlaw, cut-throat, and robber?"

"Wretch!" exclaimed Marian, indignantly. "He will track you out yet, and make you suffer dearly for this outrage. Oh, Montrose! why are you not here to help me?"

"Bad thing for him, if he was," said Gabriel Carnwood, trying to look violent. "I'd give him a lesson!"

"Coward!"

"Daresay," he said, laughing, in rude derision.

"I've given a few finishing touches to the room," said Meg, "and as the pretty lady is impatient, I haven't kept you long."

"Have you no mercy?" exclaimed Marian, clasping her hands. "If you are a woman and a mother, why do you let this ruffian use me thus?"

"Woman and mother—of course I am. Ask his lordship; he knows I've two of the finest girls you ever saw, handsome as you are, for all your pink and white skin."

"So you have, Meg, as I can testify," said his lordship. "Now, my beauty, come along."

And, despite her maddened struggles, the desperate libertine bore her up the stairs and into the chamber.

"Now," he said, "let's make ourselves happy. Meg has brought us a nice supper."

He pointed to a tray, on which stood a repast, some of which he put on a plate and pushed towards her.

"Leave me!" she said, confronting him with flashing eyes as he sat with his legs crossed, and regarded her with quiet insolence. "You know that I am in your power. Why not leave me, therefore, for a little time?"

"All right, half hour, and no tricks; it won't do."

And with a longing glance at the lovely form, the libertine left the chamber.

No sooner was she alone than, with a loud cry of relief, Marian proceeded to array herself in the garments she had brought, and braided her long tresses around her fair face.

Then she ran to the window, but found it strongly barred.

She looked out, seeking in vain for aid. Nothing met her gaze but a large piece of black, barren land, and a sigh of despair broke from her lips.

"Oh! Montrose," she murmured, "dear Montrose, could you but see me now!"

She turned from the window mournfully, her cheeks scarlet with shame, as she thought of the lawless wretch who had so daringly invaded the sacred precincts of her chamber, and the flush deepened as she heard his footstep on the stairs, and thought of the purpose of his coming.

His lordship could not keep his promise.

Half an hour was too long to stay for the consummation of his purpose.

"Heaven help me!" murmured Marian as Gabriel Carnwood neared the chamber-door. "Forgive me if my thoughts are desperate, but I will not be dishonoured while I live."

So thinking, she turned and her glance fell upon a knife on the supper tray.

The presence of the weapon gave her confidence, and her eyes glistened as the libertine opened the door. She had the knife in her hand, with the blade concealed by her wrist as he came.

He only saw how beautiful she looked, with her glittering eyes and flushed cheeks, and approaching her with unsteady steps, he would have passed his arm around her waist, had she not suddenly recoiled.

"Still obstinate?" he said, preparing again to seize her. "Very well, if you will struggle you may, but it's no use."

So he went forward, grasping at her hand and laughing as she struck him back.

"Hold!" she said. "Beware, Gabriel Carnwood!"

"Of what?"

"This!"

He sprang back as the knife gleaned before his gaze; and, awed by the excited looks, shrunk away.

But only for a moment. Quick as thought he rushed forward, striking at her fair arm, thinking by this to strike the dagger from her hand, when she aimed wildly at him, and just succeeded in inflicting a slight wound on his cheek.

For an instant he closed his eyes with the pain, and that instant was enough.

She leaped past, pushing him aside with both hands; and rushed down the stairs and passed the astonished Meg, who narrowly escaped a lash with the knife, which, in her excitement, Marian brandished aloft, and so cleared the way before her.

Out and away she went, her long hair streaming over her shoulders, and her blue eyes glimmering like stars.

On she went panting like a fawn, and rushing on heedless as to who might follow.

She heard quick, heavy footsteps behind her.

Then came the voice of her persecutor, shouting for her to stop. But such was not her intention, and she kept on a pace that well-nigh left her breathless.

The excitement and exertion were too much and soon wearied her, for she began to tire. Then Gabriel Carnwood gained upon her rapidly.

Scarcely twenty yards lay between them, and Marian was about to turn again at bay, when a loud noise was heard, and a dashing-looking gentleman ran like a deer across the open space, followed by some half-dozen others.

He seemed to take things in at a glance as he ran by; and though the half-dozen gentlemen in view were officers intent upon his particular capture, he was true to the instincts of manhood, and would not leave a lady in distress.

"A lady being hunted!" he exclaimed, as he nearly overtook Gabriel Carnwood.

"Stop him!" yelled the officers to Gabriel Carnwood, who was very much astonished on seeing a stranger who had hitherto been running, stop suddenly right before him.

"Didn't you hear what they said?" exclaimed the stranger.

"Out of the way, I shall lose her."

The other dodged as his lordship tried to pass.

"Just my opinion; they want you to stop me."

"Out of the way, I say; I don't know you, I don't want to stop you."

"Don't know me, let me introduce myself—I am Dashing Ralph. Who are you?"

"Fool."

"Fool—all right. Peculiar sort of name."

"Out of the way."

"By the Lord Harry, so you said before Hallo, here they come!"

"Down you go, that's pat."

He turned and ran, having floored Gabriel Carnwood by a tremendous blow between the eyes.

"Oh!" said his lordship, becoming dimly conscious that he had lost his victim.

Dashing Ralph passed Marian; and she, seeing that he had struck her persecutor down, ran to him for protection.

"Save me!" she said, clinging to his breast; "save me from that villain!"

Dashing Ralph had a weakness for music and to him there was no music like a lady's voice.

He never could resist the wishes of a lady and finding himself suddenly called upon to act as a lovely maiden's champion, he stopped, regardless of his own peril, and, taking off his hat, bowed gracefully.

"Lady," he said, "aught that can be done in your defence, Dashing Ralph is your truest friend."

"Oh, thank you! I have been torn from my uncle's house by that ruffian whom you struck. Do not let him touch me again."

Dashing Ralph threw his arms around her, and drew her to his side as the officers drew near, and Gabriel Carnwood rose from the ground.

"Gentlemen," said Ralph, "you know I might have made good my escape; but I could not leave a lady in distress. All I ask now is time enough to take this fair young creature to a place of safety—that done, I am yours."

"What!" exclaimed the officer; "let you go now we have got you? You must think us very green."

"I think that you are a man, and eager to do your duty, but not a set of curs who would see a woman left defenceless, and be outraged by the slinking hound behind, all for the sake of a paltry reward, that is to be shared among six of you. What am I worth?"

"Only forty pounds at present."

"D—— their impudence!" muttered Ralph.

"When they set a price on me they might have made it fifty or a hundred. Here, I'll make a bargain with you. I'll give ten pounds to each of you if you forget you have seen me just for the present."

This novel proposition had the effect of causing the officers to consider; they knew that if they captured him, all the money and property found upon him would go into the hands of their superiors, whereas they could now get ten pounds each, and the forty some other time.

"What do you think?" said one.

"Just as you like. His offer's fair enough."

"Give us the ten each."

"That's the thing," said Dashing Ralph. "Nothing like a bargain, money down. Here is the cash—ten each; no flimsies or counterfeit, but good, hard gold, just as it came from someone else's pocket."

Each man pocketed his ten.

"I have not asked of you a promise," said Dashing Ralph; "but I take it for granted that you will do no sneaking tricks to try and take me unawares, or anything of that sort."

"No fear, captain. We only follow our profession for the sake of the coin. Such gentlemen as you doesn't mind dropping a little of the ready to a man as acts square."

"Whenever any of us meet," said Dashing Ralph, "and any traveller's cash should be in my pocket, I shall not forget you."

"That's the right sort, captain."

Gabriel Carnwood looked on, savagely disappointed.

"You don't mean to say that you are going to let him go?" he said.

"Don't we!" Who are you?"

"You will find out if you don't do your duty. He is a highwayman. Now arrest him."

"Do you mean to say as you knows?" said one of the officers, going close to his lordship.

"He is a peach," cried another. "Shouldn't be surprised if he was to go and tell as how we took bribes."

"He'd tell any lie," exclaimed a third. "Look at his vicious mug."

"He wanted to illuse the lady—the cur!"

"Down with him!"

"Hurrah! Yes, down with him!"

They grouped round his lordship, grasping their heavy whips.

"You are right, my good fellow," said Dashing Ralph. "He would have the audacious impudence to go and tell that you took bribes. Of course it would be a lie, but it might be believed."

"So he would! Oh! hoo!" and then followed a prolonged groan of execration.

"I would teach him a little sword exercise," said Dashing Ralph, "but you, sirs, carry good whips, and a good sword would be sullied by the stain of such carrion blood. So, suppose you teach him how to dance?"

The officers contrived to get Gabriel Carnwood in their midst, then forming a circle, commenced moving round him with much glee.

The lashed him right and left, disregarding his cries for help, and keeping at this recreative exercise till he howled with pain.

"I think he has had enough," said Ralph, when Gabriel Carnwood lay, doubled up and writhing in agony, on the ground. "Here's some loose change, just to drink my health with."

He gave them a handful of silver.

Thanking him, they replaced their whips and dispersed.

The baffled libertine crawled back to Gaunt Meg's residence, and Dashing Ralph led his fair companion away.

She had wondered much at the strange scene she had witnessed.

When the officers had gone, she said—

"I see you are in danger on my account."

"Ours is a life of danger," was the reply.

"And in the case of a fair lady there is no true knight of the road who would not dare and do much. You see I do not disguise my character or profession. It has not made me less than a man; and therefore I am not ashamed to own I am what I am."

"Whatever blame may be attached to your profession," said Marian, "you are at least generous and brave."

"I have no comrade who would not have done the same," said Dashing Ralph. "It is part of our duty to defend and protect the gentler sex. It is a pleasure, too," he added, gallantly kissing her hand; "an act that brings its own sweet reward."

"Such thanks as I can give but poorly express my gratitude," said Marian. "But my uncle will thank you for me."

"You are weary, lady. Here is a house where we may, perhaps, procure horses, and you can rest."

He led her to the house, and ordered refreshment, bidding the host prepare steeds for himself and the lady.

There was a bold free grace in Dashing Ralph's bearing that won her confidence, and made her feel that she was quite safe in his company.

While they were engaged together with their repast, Ralph rattled on in a lively flood of conversation, and so interested his companion that the remembrance of her late grief was almost banished from her mind.

"We must make the best of our journey," he said, as the landlord entered to remove the repast, and announce that the horses were ready.

Having settled the bill, he led her to the horses, and assisted her to mount.

They rode on almost in silence. It was not Ralph's usual mode when with a lady, but seeing his fair companion sad and thoughtful, and thinking perchance that she preferred her own meditations, he did not disturb her.

She was about to make some observation, when several horsemen came in view, and Marian saw that the chief was her cousin's lover, the brave young nobleman, Ernest Dallas.

"Thank heaven!" exclaimed the young nobleman as he rode up, "my dear Marian, you are found."

"For which you must thank this gentleman," said the gentle girl, taking her companion's hand. "For my danger, you must thank Gabriel Carnwood."

"The miscreant scoundrel!" exclaimed Lord Ernest, his handsome face flushed with anger.

It would have been a bad thing for either of the Carnwoods had they been within his reach just then.

The very way in which his hand fastened over the jewelled hilt of his sword was suggestive of perforated bodies.

"Rascally cowards!" he said, "I have warned them often enough. When next we meet they shall atone for this outrage with their life's blood."

"By the Lord Harry," said Ralph, "if he recovers from the cudgelling he got to-day, he must have the back of an elephant. I should say he hasn't got a sound bone in his body. By Jove, didn't they let him have it, that's all!"

"Let who have it?" asked the young nobleman.

"A lot of his Majesty's active gentlemen at Bow-street, who had taken a particular liking to me, and very much wanted to make my acquaintance, but I objected to their company, and always tried to avoid them as much as possible. But they overtook me just when I saw this lady's danger, and was going to her assistance. I asked them what they wanted. They said me. I asked wha for. They said, the reward offered for my apprehension. I asked them how much I was worth. They said forty pounds. I was disgusted. I valued myself at more than that, and gave them ten pounds each not to see me. They readily took the money, and then slipped into the sneaking hound with their whips from whom I saved this fair lady. By the Lord Harry, didn't they let him have it, that's all! The fellow capered about like an agitated monkey."

Lord Ernest laughed heartily at the novel description given by the highwayman.

"You served the scoundrel justly," he cried. "May I have the pleasure of hearing the name of the gentleman who acted so nobly in this lady's defence?"

"I am known by the appellation of Dashing Ralph," said the highwayman, raising his hat gallantly, and bowing, "a knight of the King's highway."

"A noble gentleman, indeed. Let the world say what it likes about highwaymen, and if ever you want a friend, don't forget Lord Ernest Dallas."

The young noble gave the other his hand.

"I will not," said Ralph, gratefully, "and now that I see the lady in safe hands, I'll bid you adieu."

"The deuce! You are not going like that?" said Ernest Dallas. "You will accompany us home? The lady's uncle, Lord Sydney, and Marian, will be delighted to welcome the noble protector of his fair neice, and if you do not come he will be greatly disappointed."

"Many thanks," said Ralph. "I should be happy to accept your generous welcome, but I have business which calls me to London."

"Come, sir," said Marian, giving her hand to her preserver, "Lord Sydney will give you a cordial greeting. The brave gentleman who has rescued me from danger will be a welcome guest, and my uncle will be disappointed if you do not come."

"Another time, fair lady, I shall be most happy. For the present, suffer me to congratulate you upon being safe, and say adieu."

He raised her hand to his lips, and exchange a friendly grip with his new acquaintance.

"Don't forget to give us a look up," said Lord Ernest. "At any time I shall be delighted to crack an old bottle of wine with you. Adieu!"

With this they raised their hats and parted, Lord Ernest Dallas happy that he had the pleasure to restore Marian unhurt to her uncle, Daring Ralph to seek some wild adventure on the road.

CHAPTER CXXIV.

FOR many hours the officers kept on the track of the gallant highwayman, but as the shades of evening gathered over the earth the knights of the road urged their steeds to greater speed, and finally eluded their pursuers.

When the highwaymen drew up near the lone hut on the heath, where Grace had been taken to, they were obliged to keep together because the darkness was so intense.

Had they separated, they would not have found each other again without sounding their signal, which would in all probability have warned the inmates of the cottage that they were in danger.

"Are you sure this is the place?" inquired Dick.

"Positive," replied the pedlar-boy.

"Is there more than one way of entrance?"

"Not that I am aware of."

"And you know that one?"

"I daresay I can find it."

"Gentlemen, dismount."

The gentlemen highwaymen dismounted as silently as a lot of shadows.

The horses were fastened to one tree, and the highwaymen awaited further commands.

The distant rumbling of a coach caused Dick to maintain silence. He drew his comrades back into the thickest of the gloom, out of observation.

Instinct told him that the approaching vehicle was in some way connected with their present adventure, and Dick waited, with much uneasy interest, for the approach of the coach.

With much caution the driver drew the pair of spirited horses up before the door of the cottage, and then descended from the box.

He was particularly careful to draw about him the large cloak, which enveloped him like a shroud, and in a suspicious manner he looked about to ascertain that there were no spies; and having satisfied himself on this point, he knocked at the door, which was opened by Spikey.

"What do you want?" he demanded.

"The gal," replied his coachman.

"Who sent you?"

"No names. The coach is outside, and I am to take her to the ruined castle."

Spikey made way for the man to enter, and closed the door.

Dick crept stealthily forward, and put his eye to the keyhole, with the intention of watching the proceedings of the two men.

Some one had artfully put out the light, and Dick was unable to see anything.

But he could listen, and he heard a sweet, plaintive voice pleading with the agony of despair.

For a moment Dick was almost mad, not knowing what to do, but as he had heard the coachman say he had to take the lady to the ruined castle, he concluded she would come to no harm in the hut, and so he determined to wait until they brought their captive out, but he did not wait long. The door was gently opened.

Dick got aside, out of observation. He could hear and see all that now took place

LADY GRACE, THE KING'S CAPTIVE.

He did not hear much, because little was said. But he saw that which hurried him on and took him into danger.

The two men emerged from the lone cottage, bearing the gagged and muffled form of a female.

Dick recognised the captive, and like a panther leaping through a jungle, he sprang at the foremost ruffian. He seized him by the throat: the attack was so unexpected that the man lost all power.

He was borne to the ground before his companion was aware of what had transpired.

The signal was given.

The fierce cry of execration that left his lips ere the boy's hands closed like a vice over his windpipe that stopped his respiration, brought three murderous wretches from the house, armed with huge, formidable weapons.

"Help!" shouted Tyburn Dick, as the caitiffs fell upon him.

The first that came to his rescue was the pedlar-boy; the highwaymen were not far behind.

This the ruffians saw, and not having a relish for the insertion of cold steel, they beat a quick retreat.

Dick looked round for the man who had his bride, but all had disappeared.

They could not be far off, that was evident, as the carriage still remained.

Dick was trying to think how best to proceed when a piercing shriek made him momentarily leap off his feet.

The voice was that of a female, and proceeded from the cottage.

He sprang at the door, but it was fastened on the inside, and while he was trying to force an entrance a second shriek was heard.

This time the accents were those of a man in supplicating tones. Cries for mercy and loud execrations grew louder every moment. Then was heard a scuffle, a heavy fall and a gurgling cry. Then all was quiet.

All this had taken place in a few second

—while the highwaymen were trying to batter down the door.

As soon as the cries of tho old man were heard, the pedlar boy left the gentlemen of the road, and went round to another part of the hovel.

With the strength of a lion he tore down the shutters, and battering the window in, he bounded through into the cottage.

The noise of the falling glass was followed by a prolonged shriek—a cry wrung from the very soul in death's agony.

At this moment the door gave way, and Dick leaped forward.

"Follow!" he cried, flourishing his sword above his head. "Follow, comrades! Kill all who attempt to pass—show them no mercy!"

The words had scarcely left his lips, when a mocking laugh rang in his ears, and the bleeding form of the pedlar boy was thrown in his path.

Dick fell back with a shudder. He did not expect to see that.

"Take that as a warning!" said a voice. "Go a step further, and none of you will live to see the breaking morn!"

Dick raised the boy. He was dead. The villains had done their bloody work surely. A dagger had been thrust into the poor boy's heart.

The highwaymen recoiled at the heart-rending sight.

No time was to be lost. Having so brutally butchered that poor boy, what may they do with their fair captive? Dick thought.

"Some of you go outside and surround the house," said he. "The rest follow me."

The highwaymen divided. One half went out, the rest followed their chief.

"Fools! you were warned," said the same voice that had before spoken. "You have now sought and sealed your fate."

Dick bounded in the direction whence the voice came. He saw a man spring backward, and a door closed before him. Then he turned to call his comrades, and found himself shut up within a small room. He heard the highwaymen outside, and called to let them know where he was. He was answered, and the walls were battered down.

The highwaymen searched from room to room; but no sight of the ruffians did they discover.

They were returning from their fruitless search, when a broad sheet of vivid flames arose, roaring before them.

"We are lost!" said Captain Claude, despairingly.

The room in which they were was one mass of fierce flame all round.

The gallant men stood paralysed, for their death seemed inevitable.

It appeared almost impossible to pass through without falling a victim to the leaping, tongued flame.

Above the roaring of the fire they suddenly heard the voices of their comrades.

The room door was forced open.

The highwaymen dashed forward in a body, and the men escaped unhurt, save a few burns, which they did not notice in their terror and excitement.

Tyburn Dick's plan of dividing his comrades proved wonderfully successful.

The three ruffians were caught, bearing Lady Grace, the highway queen, to the carriage.

Tyburn Dick looked at the cold-blooded brutes like an enraged tiger.

"Fiends!" he exclaimed, "you might have been spared had you not tried that hellish plan of torturing us by fire. That which you so ingeniously arranged for our destruction you shall be condemned to yourselves. It will prepare you for the next reception."

The cowering brutes shrieked and implored for mercy, but every ear was deaf to their cries.

"Hurl them into the thickest of the fire, comrades!" said the boy, in a pitiless tone.

The men struggled desperately with their captors, but they might as well have tried to escape from a herd of ferocious lions.

Despite their wild cries and furious plunging, they were driven back into the hut and the door was closed upon them.

Dick clasped his bride to his breast, and kissed her pallid brow.

"Thank God! my love, you are safe," he exclaimed.

And then they hurried out, but there they were met by a fresh danger.

Fate seemed dead set against them. The

King's guards, who had returned after their defeat by the highwaymen, had started out again with a reinforcement.

The reflection of the fire was a sort of guide to them. That aroused their suspicion, and the highwaymen were suspected of some foul work.

Arriving at this conclusion, the officer urged his men forward, and they soon arrived upon the scene of the conflagration.

The highwaymen saw how things stood.

They must either fight for life and liberty, or be taken quietly.

They preferred fighting; and soon a desperate encounter took place, in which the knights of the road were easily defeated by the soldiers.

The highwaymen had to give up their swords to their victors.

They had given up all hope, and nobly resigned themselves to their fate, when a horseman, a man of a strange, sombre appearance, rode up.

He glanced round at the many sad faces, and then went up to the commanding officer's side, and whispered something in his ear.

The commanding officer changed colour perceptibly. He was apparently in a fix; the arrival of the strange horseman slightly put out his arrangements.

"It cannot be," he said, at length.

"Then I must speak out," said the other, significantly.

"Be careful," was the warning response.

"I"—the horsemen laughed, unpleasantly—" I fear not you, although a——"

"Silence!" exclaimed the officer.

"Release those men, then."

"It is impossible."

"You alone have the power of doing so."

"But I do not choose that it shall be."

"I do, and that instantly, or the people shall know something that the King would keep to himself."

"You threaten?"

"And not idly."

The two men looked at each other, but the stranger seemed to have the greater power.

The highwaymen exchanged glances one with the other. Who could this stranger be, to take such interest in them. One alone knew—Tom King; and he soon enlightened his comrades by his superior knowledge.

The stranger was Wild Bertram, the man of mystery. And the other?

"Your Majesty, King of Great Britain," said Bertram, "takes a long time to consider!"

His Majesty foamed at the mouth like a mad dog.

He was now revealed in his disguise as an officer, and he inwardly feared that the purpose of his disguise would be revealed also, unless he quickly acquiesced to the man of mystery's wish.

Wild Bertram knew more of the King's private affairs than the King liked any one to know, and had it been possible for him to have had that dangerous man shot where he stood, without raising suspicion in the army, and among the people, he would have given the world; but he dared not.

Bertram whispered a second time in the royal ear.

"The secret will be quite safe if you do," he said, "if not, the revelation will be your own fault."

The King looked at him perplexed.

"Let it be so," he said, "all but the lady; she I will take care of. Return those men their swords."

Dick started, and looked fiercely at the King.

Bertram laid his hand on the boy's shoulder, and said a few words in his ear that quieted him.

The swords were given back to the highwaymen, and the King, having Grace put into the carriage, rode by the window as it drove away, brooding over his defeat, and trying to concoct some means by which he could quietly get Wild Bertram, the man of mystery, out of the way.

CHAPTER CXXV.

THE KING'S CAPTIVE AND THE KING—FIGHT IN THE PALACE-YARD AND CAPTURE OF TYBURN DICK.

TYBURN DICK rode with his comrades, and was lost in wonderment.

Captain Claude was the first to break the silence.

He had thought and wondered over the

strange interview between the King and Bertram, and always coming to the same point, curiosity at last compelled him to inquire to what cause they might attribute the honour of their unknown friend's noble deliverance.

"Who may we have the honour of thanking for our timely deliverance from an unpleasant situation?" Captain Claude said.

"One," replied the man of mystery, in a deep, solemn voice, "who knows the value of gallant men. My name is Bertram."

"If thanks——"

Bertram interposed by a wave of his hand.

"I want not thanks or reward in any shape," he said. "I can fully appreciate your gratitude."

"You will accompany us to the haunt," said Tom King, the only one known to him.

"With much pleasure. A terrible danger threatens you, and you will require every assistance, though I baulked the king last night. He will devise some plan of revenge which will fall upon you suddenly and secretly, without it is prevented in time."

Everyone wondered at the seeming power the man had over the king.

"His gracious majesty appears entirely under your control," remarked Tyburn Dick.

He hesitated and looked curiously at his deliverer. He would have said more, but he thought he might offend the man of mystery had he said it.

Bertram noticed his intermission.

"Go on," he said. "Say what you would."

"I would know, without meaning offence," said the boy, encouraged by the kindly voice, "why you allowed the King to take the lady, whose safety is dearer to me than my own life?"

"Merely to please his caprice without causing bloodshed. Had I opposed him, he would have ordered the soldiers to charge you, so I let her go, knowing that, had there been a battle, many of you would have fallen. But you need have no fear for her safety; I warned him, and he dares not attempt an outrage."

"She must not ramain long in his power," Dick said. "He may be tempted to dare much in spite of your warning."

"But he must not."

"He may. Passion is an irresistable power, that at times causes men to forget their rank and the danger they bring upon themselves. She must not remain in his power long."

"She shall not."

"How is she to be got out of it?"

"She will be quite safe until to-morrow," said Wild Bertram. "The King has one good quality. He is patient, and is content to wait to win by kindness before he uses more harsh means to accomplish his purpose."

This was not pleasant for Dick to hear, but he knew he could not do anything alone, and trying to master his passions, he listened, trembling with agitation.

Bertram continued—

"To-morrow, then, you must go to the palace."

"How am I to get admission without being arrested?" Dick said.

"I will give you a note that will take you through unchallenged. I would go myself, but his majesty may have got someone to arrest me unexpectedly, and quietly put me out of the way, for even in a palace there are places where one can be lodged without ever afterwards being disturbed."

Dick thought this rather cool.

He might risk the danger of which the man with the power of a king shrank from, but had he to invade Hades in the cause of his fair lady love he would have done it unflinchingly.

"I am willing to risk anything," said Dick; "but I am too well known to get admission to the palace without being recognised."

"Not if you follow my directions."

"What are they?"

"That you go in disguise as a lady to the palace, with a request to see his Majesty on private business. You will be ushered into a waiting-room, and while the lacquey's gone to announce your presence, take the opportunity to slip into another chamber, where you must remain secreted until night. The rest I will leave to you. We shall be close by if we are wanted."

"Then, to-morrow it shall be done, and if I do not make any appearance at the palace by the breaking of morn, it will be because I have been discovered."

"If you do not appear long before dawn, measures shall be taken to know the reason why."

By this time they had reached the old priory, the secret entrance to the haunt.

A signal was given by the boy chief, and a moment afterwards it was answered in a similar way; then Dick responded to it again, and on the instant, a group of dark figures stood round the mounted knights of the road.

They came forth silently, and so secretly, that it appeared as though they came from the earth.

The gallant captains dismounted, their horses were led away, and they entered the haunt.

The sentinels were changed for the night, to keep watch, a supper was prepared in the huge hall, and Wild Betram was introduced to the whole members of the gallant band.

While the above arrangement was taking place, a very different one was going on between the King and the young Lieutenant Maxwell.

"Lieutenant," began the king, when the soldier entered the royal chamber, where his Majesty was biting the tops of his nails with impatience, "Lieutenant Maxwell."

His Majesty had entirely forgotten his mental arrangement.

"Sire," responded the soldier.

"I sent for you."

His Majesty paused again.

"I should not have taken the liberty to come, my liege, had you not."

His Majesty looked curiously at the speaker.

"Lieutenant Maxwell, I sent for you to—confound it!—see if you can't help me."

"Your majesty has been insulted."

"Insulted—yes, exactly. The offender is a dangerous man—a daring, hardened fellow."

"Is it the Boy Highwayman, sire?"

"No. But he too must be taken. I entirely entrust this mission to you, and if you accomplish that which I want done, a captain's rank awaits you."

"Your Majesty is generous. Give me a warrant for their apprehension, and—"

The King interrupted.

"A warrant? no. You must ferret out this man—the stranger known as Wild Bertram; and when you have found him, give him no time to escape. Shoot him—kill him instantaneously. He should die had twenty lives. The Boy Highwayman you may afterwards apprehend. I will give you a warrant for him."

"Then I am not to shoot him if I get the chance?"

"No. Let him take his chance at his trial. It is not he who I have any fear of, but the other desperado, who has threatened my life. Even at this moment I should not be surprised did he come here to assassinate me."

"Surely, your majesty, he would not dare so much?"

"He is a desperate fellow, and would dare anything," said the king. "It would not be the first time he has entered the palace by some strange means."

"Then, sire, measures had better be taken at once for your safety, if you think he has any such murderous intentions upon your life."

"He has threatened me."

"Then, my liege, we must be prepared for him."

"What do you propose to do?" inquired his majesty, eagerly.

"I will have a dozen of my most trusty men secreted in and about the palace, so that if he does come he will be taken unawares."

"Good! good!" exclaimed the king, smacking the soldier on the back. "Lieutenant, you shall be colonel if you succeed. Ay, I will knight you if you rid me of this man."

"Leave it to me, sire. It shall be done. The man won't trouble you many hours longer. Do you know the most likely place I may find him?"

"His general rendezvous is on Hounslow Heath. I have every reason to believe he is a leader of a secret band of highwaymen, as yet unknown."

"There is a haunt of highwaymen on Hounslow Heath, of which Tyburn Dick, the boy king, is leader."

"No, no; it is not these I mean. By what I have heard, it is a band lately organised by this daring fellow. Some of his leading men are well known on the road, but lately they have been quiet. This Wild Bertram is a strange man. He has some motive in view for getting together such a band of men that may prove disastrous without it is stopped in time."

"Does your majesty know the names of any of the men connected with the new band of highwaymen?"

"Amongst them are Captain Macheath, Jack Rann, George Barrington, Will Dudley, and a lady who is to be their queen, styled STARLIGHT NELL."

The young soldier knew well these gallant men, whose daring deeds had been talked of throughout the world.

"Such men," he said, "cannot be lightly dealt with. Cautious steps must be taken to crush their powerful union. Should they rise, the terrible danger that may follow cannot be predicted."

"Kill this man—Wild Bertram—and we shall have nothing to fear from the rest."

"It shall be done, sire. By this time to-morrow I will bring you a trophy from the dead."

"His sword," said his majesty—"you will not take that from him in life?"

"His sword it shall be," the lieutenant said.

He saluted his regal master, then he retired.

"A good soldier that," cogitated his majesty. "Understands his work. Bertram, I think, will find a master in him."

His mind being eased upon this point, his second thoughts turned towards his fair captive.

He felt most anxious to press his suit upon her that night. He thought that if he encroached on her privacy he might offend her, so he retired to his royal bed with the intention of paying her a visit early on the morrow, which he did. But his patience was sorely tried by being kept from her chamber until night approached.

He coaxed, in his most wheedling tone, for admission. He made rash promises, and tapped persuasively at the panels of the door, but Grace turned a deaf ear to his pleadings.

The King at last became angry. He bit his lips to smother his wrath till blood trickled from his mouth. Then he gave vent his fury, and swore in a language totally incomprehensible to the ears of his irritating captive.

Finding that she was not to be seen, he said he would go away if she would promise he might see her to-morrow.

She told him she would consider.

Wishing her good night, he went away, but crept back to the door very quietly, thinking that the lady's maid would have an occasion to come out, and on this occasion he thought right.

And he, avoiding observation, went into the room as soon as she had gone out of sight.

On entering he saw his fair captive. She had thrown aside part of her attire, and was preparing for bed, and he went towards her, fired by the display of her beauty, but Grace threw a wrapper over her shoulders and confronted him indignantly.

"This is unjust," she said, her face crimson with shame. "It is cowardly of your majesty to take such a mean advantage."

"You were cruel," he said, his voice thick with passion. "When I came and asked for admission you kept me out."

Grace knew it would not do to be obstinate with him. She would try what stratagem would do. So throwing herself in an easy, graceful attitude upon a couch, she said, coqueetishly—

"You must own, sire, you were wrong by coming in without giving me warning."

"I did not know how I should find you," he said; "and I did not knock because I feared you would not let me in."

"You must promise to be very good if I let you stay," she said.

"As good as the time and situation will admit of, my beauty," he said.

"If you prove at all naughty, I shall send you away," Grace said, saucily.

The King was becoming terribly excited in spite of the warning. It was truly a trying position for a man of his strong passions. His cheeks glowed, his eyes grew bright, and his voice thick.

Grace saw her danger. Her eyes glittered with a light that would have warned the King, had he seen it.

But he did not. He twined both his

round her waist, and nearly squeezed out her life in his passionate embrace.

He thought only to accomplish his cruel purpose, and exerted all his strength to master his fair opponent.

"Release me!" shrieked the poor girl, beside herself with terror.

"Not if all the demons surrounded me until——"

Raising one of her hands, she smacked his face, and his Majesty went back several paces somewhat surprised.

Before he had time to recover and fall upon his captive again, the fair girl plucked a dagger from her bosom, and sprang upon him like a tigress.

He caught her descending arm in time to prevent the weapon being buried in his breast, and struck her delicate wrist a blow that caused her to release her hold.

The dagger fell to the floor, and the King laughed exultantly, and catching her up in his arms, threw her upon the bed.

Her head struck against the wall as she went back, and she lay stunned, helpless, in his power.

A shade of remorse came over his face. He had not wished for that, but it could not be helped, and now he had nothing to fear.

She was his—a resistless victim, and he stood over her anticipating, when a hand from behind grasped his throat, and he was hurled with terrific force across the chamber.

"Wretch! Cowardly villain!" exclaimed our heroine's deliverer, who was no other than Tyburn Dick disguised as a girl.

The King lay apparently lifeless, so his assailant left.

He had followed out the instructions which Wild Bertram had given him, and successfully gained admission to the palace.

The boy was not far off when he heard the voice of his love pleading for mercy. The state of his mind was not an enviable one. He could not come to her assistance, for two men stood conversing outside the door of the room in which she was concealed, but when they moved away, he lost no time in making his way to the chamber of the struggle.

He only arrived in time to save his fair mistress from the shame which would have defiled her purity.

Throwing off his woman's disguise, he turned the King over to make sure that he was beyond the power of interference, and covering the insensible girl with a large wrapper, he raised her in his arms, and drawing his sword, he muttered, as he left the royal chamber—

"Let those stop me who dare?"

It was astonishing to see how soon the King recovered. When the boy had gone, he jumped to his feet, and shook his fist spitefully at the door.

"Fool!" he hissed. "You shall pay for this."

He went to the door with the intent to summon his retainers to arrest the boy, but he came back into the room without doing so.

He thought better of it. He looked at the bed, and his face lengthened woefully. He tore his hair with baffled rage and almost howled.

"I can't have him stopped without exposing myself."

He paused.

His face brightened up.

"The girl's insensible!" he exclaimed, gleefully. "I can have him arrested for abduction. Who's to know?"

With this bright idea floating buoyantly through his mind, he gave the alarm that the palace had been broken into by highwaymen, and ordered the doors and gates to be fastened.

In a few moments the palace was in a commotion.

Retainers and guards were running about, knocking one another over in the bustle, and making a most confounded row by yelling orders one to the other.

But it was too late, Dick had escaped from the palace, but he was discovered in the palace-yard with his fair burden when he was charged to stand by a troop of soldiers under the command of Lieutenant Maxwell.

The boy's escape was unexpectedly cut short. The palace-gates were closed, and he had no hope but in the assistance of his comrades—that is, if they had arrived. This he rather doubted, as he had got out much sooner than he had expected. But he gave the signal which was to bring them to his rescue, and it was answered.

In a few seconds the band of highwaymen, under the directions of Wild Bertram, surrounded the palace-gates.

"Open the gates!" thundered Wild Bertram, "or we will pull them down!"

The King at this moment made his appearance among the excited crowd.

Catching sight of his dangerous foe, he yelled—

"That's the man, Lieutenant Maxwell! Shoot him down!"

"Some of you mind the prisoner; the rest follow me," said the soldier. "Open the gates!"

The gates were swung back.

Bertram dashed in.

"Present—fire!"

Quick as thought the soldiers fell in.

The Man of Mystery was covered with the muzzles of the weapons.

Simultaneously with the command to fire a vivid flame spread along the double line of muskets, and every weapon was discharged.

When the smoke cleared away, Wild Bertram was seen staggering. But no blood appeared about his clothes. Even as the soldiers advanced towards him he recovered, and springing into the thickest of them with the fury of a mad lion, he cut his way to where the boy chieftain stood.

The King howled with disappointment. He had expected to see the man, after the fearful volley, a mutilated corpse, and he thought he must be something more than human to stand against powder and shot. The soldiers were dumfounded too.

"Trickery! exclaimed the lieutenant. "He's shielded with chain mail! Don't let him escape."

The soldiers were coming towards him, when he turned upon them with the look of a demon.

"Save the lady!" implored Dick. "I can defend myself! Go! go! or she may be injured in the strife!"

Bertram took the insensible form from the boy, and wielded his ponderous double-handed broad sword above his head in a way suggestive of broken skulls.

The soldiers fell from his path, and at that moment they were wanted to help their comrades to keep the highwaymen from entering.

A fierce battle ensued then. The highwaymen were driven back, but Wild Bertram escaped with his fair charge.

Lieutenant Maxwell, seeing that it would be an impossibility to capture the man of mystery, now closed the gates to prevent an attempt being made to rescue Tyburn Dick.

The highwaymen on their side were baffled —as were the soldiers. Each could see the man who they wanted to capture, yet neither could get at him; and the highwaymen returned, sadly, to their haunt, leaving their beloved young chieftain a prisoner at the mercy of a disappointed and enraged monarch.

. . . .

His Majesty was in a most wretched state of mind. How devoutly he wished he had not attempted to take the life of that terrible man, Wild Bertram, especially as it had been a failure!

"My God!" he gasped, with increasing terror, and he clasped his throbbing brow, as he strode to and fro the room. "My God! this is horrible, that I who have the power of nations at my command, should be placed in this helpless position, and through a man, who, by some hellish intrigue, has learned a secret I thought no human being knew but myself."

As though fearful the walls should be secreting an eavesdropper, his Majesty lowered his voice to a whisper.

"He knows that," continued the King, "which, if revealed—even the name I mean —would not save me from an ignominious death. He must be silenced. My head is not safe while he holds that secret; but how —how is it to be done?"

His Majesty sat down and groaned, as the difficulty presented itself in full force to his imagination. He was fully bent upon destroying Wild Bertram, but he did not want to compromise himself.

That's where the difficulty arose. The man of mystery was not one easily to fall into the meshes of a hidden trap. His movements were too cautious, and his mind suspiciously inventive.

The King knew this from experience. He had made more than one secret attempt upon his life, but his attempts had proved futile.

His intended victim would laugh at his

menaces nevertheless, now, and leave him with a meaning that made his kingly blood creep with dread whenever the words flashed through his mind.

"Perhaps," thought his Majesty, "the execution of that dare-devil imp, whom they all so much worship, will strike some with surprise."

The dare-devil imp his Majesty alluded to was our hero, whom he had got lodged safely in Newgate.

"I believe," continued his Majesty, gathering courage from his own thoughts, "that if I used a little more fearless resolution with this fellow, I should bring him down. That's how it must be. I must no longer appear to have any fear from his threats. Tyburn Dick must hang to-morrow morning. Yes, yes, that's how it must be."

His Majesty laboured under a mistake, that's how it wouldn't be, which the readers were made fully aware of some time since.

Those who remember the incidents of the boy's escape from Newgate, in which he got shot, but not killed, and was carried to the haunt by the man of mystery, will please to follow us with another thread of this story in the next chapter, leaving our hero to the kind attentions of his comrades and his fair mistress until we have necessity to call upon him again.

He will be quite recovered by then, and with his usual amount of courage to take him through the many perilous scenes yet to be recorded.

CHAPTER CXXVI.

GABRIEL CARNWOOD AND HIS ALLY ARRANGE A PLOT FOR THE ABDUCTION OF MARIAN SIDNEY.

GABRIEL CARNWOOD was seated in the library of Kingston Manse, brooding over his last cowardly attempt to capture the fair Lady Marian Sydney, and the disgrace he had fallen into through the intervention of the daring highwayman, Dashing Ralph.

"Curse him!" muttered the baffled libertine between his teeth, rising and swinging the chair from him. "Curse him! She would have been mine had not that meddling fool interfered. She shall be mine, though! Though death stares me in the face, she shall be mine!"

He sat down again, and hastily wrote a note, and ringing for his valet he muttered—

"Let her escape me now, and those who stand in my way shall be warned."

The servant entered.

"Take this note to the address, and see Dashfoot personally. Tell him he must be here punctually to-morrow morning at ten."

A sardonic smile curled his cruel lip as the man withdrew to deliver the note.

The clock had scarcely finished striking the hour of ten the following morning, when Dashfoot arrived.

"I am glad you have come," said Gabriel. "Be seated, and help yourself."

He pushed wine and glasses towards his guest.

"Do you know the residence of Lord Sidney?"

"Well," answered the other.

"Are you acquainted at all with the family?"

"At one time I knew them, but now," he said, bitterly, "I am a stranger."

His interlocutor did not inquire as to the cause, nor did he appear to be at all surprised.

"You know Marian Sydney, then—the lady who was my father's *protegé*, and who was betrothed to me until some mad fool returned and claimed her as his—one who must not stand in my way much longer."

"His name?" inquired Dashfoot.

"Captain Montrose, the returned outlaw."

"I have heard of him, but I cannot say I know him by sight."

"We will talk of him by-and-by. The lady is the principal point at present. Do you know her?"

"Well."

"So much the better. No time need be lost—you understand?"

"Your meaning is not fully expressed, but I comprehend you. You want this lady abducted from her guardian's house?"

"I do. You will go to the following address."

He gave him the address of gaunt Meg—the lone house on Finchley Common

"Let it be done to-night. You can procure a post-chaise from the inn not more than a quarter of a mile from Lord Sydney's residence."

"It shall be done. But a midnight abduction is not one of the most successful enterprises. I think I can devise a safer means of getting her than that."

"I don't care what means you use, so long as you don't peril or injure the lady."

"I never fail, and the lady will be quite safe till she is conveyed to the rendezvous."

"She will be safe then," said the libertine, spitefully, taking the meaning the other's words conveyed. "I sue this lady with the honourable intention of making her my lawful wife. But I do not use the most gentle means to win her love."

"I do not doubt your honour for an instant; and it is immaterial what becomes of the lady, so long as it pays me to help you, or anyone else, in the enterprise."

"Name your price," said Gabriel. "The arrangement is settled, and I can trust you."

"You have trusted me before."

"True; and you have fulfilled previous arrangements faithfully. What money do you want?"

"You know best the value of the lady."

Gabriel made out a cheque for a thousand pounds.

"That," he said, handing it to his confederate, "will suffice you for the present; and, if you are successful in your undertaking, you shall have five thousand down. Will that pay you?"

"Most liberally," said the other, folding the piece of paper and placing it in his pocket. "We meet again to-night at the same house."

"At the same house to-night we shall meet again. Until then, adieu!"

Dashfoot withdrew to fulfil the compact, leaving the intriguing nobleman much happier then he had been for some time.

Lord Sydney had a strict watch kept over his fair charge since the last attempted outrage, never allowing her out of his sight without her maid accompanied her.

The noble old veteran thirsted for an opportunity to wreak his pent-up vengeance upon his vile kinsmen, who he knew were the instruments of the poor girl's unhappiness.

The night on which he rushed from his house in that fearful rage to seek atonement for the insult and outrage offered to his gentle niece, he made his way straight to Kingston Chase, and bravely challenged the Carnwoods to answer him at the sword's point; but, like the cowards they were, they laughed to scorn his threats; and the old soldier returned home the more incensed because he had failed to get at them. But he waited patiently for a time to come when he would efface the debt with their blood.

Regardless of her uncle's warning, Marian would walk alone through the fairy-like gardens. She loved to be alone—to dwell upon the sweet remembrance of the past.

She was seated beneath a bower of fragrant, blooming plants—her usual spot—where of an evening she sat to watch the setting sun and listen to the warbling of the feathered songsters' hymn, when she was startled from her reverie by the sound of a falling foot as it neared her sacred spot.

Looking up with a start, she saw a youth standing before her.

Turning to her as she rose, he said, politely—

"I have the pleasure, I believe, of addressing Miss Marian Sydney?"

"The same," she said, her voice trembling with agitation, she knew not why.

Handing her a note he held between his fingers, he said—

"I was requested to deliver this into your hands," and, before she had time to say a word, he had withdrawn.

With trembling fingers, Marian broke the seal, and read the following words—

"Dearest Marian,—If you still have a kind word for the companion of your youth —an affectionate thought of our early love— meet me this evening at eight, at the 'Prince.' Come alone; fear nothing, dearest. I would not seek this secret interview, but I cannot visit your uncle's through circumstances I dare not name here.   "Montrose."

Again and again she read the epistle with tear-dimmed eyes.

"A word of kindness for him!" she murmured. "Oh, how wrongly he judges me! Did he but know the unhappiness his absence has caused me, he would not stay away another hour. What—what has happened that makes him say he dare not visit my uncle? I must see him, and know all. What should I fear? He is too good—too generous—too everything that is noble in man to cause me one moment's hesitation to grant him this meeting. Yes—yes, I will see him!"

Fervently kissing the little note, she folded it with the care of a treasured gem, and placed it next to her beating heart, and then she beguiled away the time by picking the decaying leaves and drooping flowers off the plants.

It was a quarter to eight when, in her unsuspecting confidence, she innocently wended her way to the place of assignation, her gentle breast filled with the joyous hope of again seeing her noble lover.

How little she knew of the world's wickedness, and yet she had seen and suffered enough to make her suspicious; but her childish confidence, her pureness of mind, never once gave a thought contrary to the truth of the note she had received. No, she was too happy, too ready to believe that it had come from her lover, and was genuine.

With buoyant heart she hastened to the assigned place of meeting, anticipating all those dreams of fancy a mind like hers is wont to revel in.

The " Prince " was reached—a pretty, antique building, standing at the centre of the cross road, surrounded with giant trees, and thick, verdant foliage.

Marian looked about for her lover, but he was nowhere in sight.

"Perhaps," she thought, " I am too early, or he may not be able to come exactly to time. I must not be impatient."

With this generous thought she contented herself to wait for his arrival, but not without a feeling of dread creeping over her.

Her thoughts wandered from the present to bygone scenes, and in her reverie she did not hear the stealthy step that approached her; nor was she aware of anyone's presence till a hand was laid upon her shoulder.

She started, her heart bounding with hope, and she looked up, expecting to see her lover, but her hopes were crushed, and her heart sank like lead when her gaze fell upon a stranger.

She fell back from the cynical stare of the stranger's eyes; not with terror, but with disappointment and despair.

" Forgive me, fair lady," said the heartless wretch, who had drawn the innocent girl into this snare. " I did not intend to startle you."

" You are not he whom I seek," said Marian, timidly.

" Nay, lady; but I have the honour of being the bearer of a message from Captain Arthur Montrose."

" Why has he not come?" she asked.

" Through an accident he met with this afternoon."

" What accident?" she inquired, eagerly.

" He was thrown from his horse, and——"

" Do you think the injuries he has received are very dangerous?" she said, interrupting him.

" Nothing more than a severe sprain, which has prevented him from keeping his appointment. It is of the utmost importance that he wished this meeting; but, as he cannot come, it would give him infinite joy if you would honour me by placing yourself under my protection to conduct you to his residence. He has provided me with a chaise, thinking you would not refuse him in such a matter as the present."

It was hard to refuse in such a case; yet, if she went without informing her kind uncle, she knew the anxiety her absence would cause him, and she thought of returning home and acquainting Lord Sydney of her intention to visit her love. When, as though the villain read her passing thoughts, he said—

" If you will honour me with your company you will render my friend, Captain Montrose, a happiness, by granting this interview, he may never more know on this earth."

" What mean you?" exclaimed the girl, in deep distress. " Has anything serious happened?"

" I know not, my lady. Those were the words he said. He seems very unhappy. He implored me not to lose any time, if you consented, as he did not wish your uncle to miss you."

" Oh, hasten! lose not a moment! I will accompany you!" Marian Sydney exclaimed, her cheeks blanched and cold as marble with anguish. "My heart foretold this. I feared that something terrible was about to happen."

The intriguing scamp left the distressed girl with a flush of triumph on his not un-handsome face, to bring the chaise to carry off his fair prize.

He had succeeded so far in his clever plot without the aid of the three hired ruffians whom he had brought with him to the inn.

And it so happened, by a strange coinci-dence, that our hero, who had recovered from the effects of the shot, set out that day with his favourite steed, Fairy, on professional busi-ness, not that he needed the spoil, but because he loved the danger of the reckless life.

The whole day Dick had been out without meeting with an adventure of any kind, and he was passing the Prince Inn when he saw Dashfoot and his accomplices enter.

The guilty glances they now and then cast round, as though they fancied someone was following them, aroused the boy's suspicion, for he knew that when a few men of that stamp met, they were bent upon some evil purpose.

Dismounting, and giving Fairy to the ostler, with strict injunctions to have her ready in case he might want her suddenly, he followed the ill-looking gang, and took the room next to the one they occupied.

As we have often remarked on previous occasions, the walls of the rooms of an inn in those days were not made too thick, and our hero had often derived therefrom the founda-tion of a rich adventure.

In the present instance he gained much in-formation that was likely to prove very suc-cessful.

Dick heard sufficient of the scheme to put him on his guard, and he watched from the window of his room the proceedings of Dashfoot with his unsuspecting victim, but he did not disturb himself till the schemer left the lady, to get the chaise which was to carry her to her ruin.

Then he hurried to Marian's side, and warned her.

"Lady," he said, "believe not what that man has told you. It is a dark scheme—a hellish plot arranged by that heartless wretch, with three other ruffians, whom I overheard. Believe me, dear lady."

The boy spoke in a deep, earnest tone, and Marian Sydney stood bewildered.

Who was she to believe, she thought.

"Lady, if you knew but half of what I have heard," Dick said, almost imploringly, "you would not hesitate one moment to re-trace the steps that brought you here. You know not the nature of the danger—the disgrace that pitiless villain would drag you into."

Still she stood undecided how to act. Her mind was so set upon meeting her lover, that she would have risked any danger had there been the least chance of seeing him.

"Will they not take me to him—to my lover?" she asked, in a sweet, sad voice.

"Nay, lady. Your lover knows not of this subterfuge, and that intriguing man would take you to a villain—whose soul is as black as his own—for some evil purpose. Let me beseech you, as a friend," he con-tinued, "not to go, without you wish to bring sorrow upon those you love."

She could bear her trying position no longer. Bursting into a flood of tears, she sank upon the noble boy's breast, and nestled to him with child-like confidence.

Just then Dashfoot came out with the chaise, and his face changed to the expres-sion of a fiend when he saw his intended prey under the protection of the gallant youth.

"What means this?" he demanded.

"Villain!" exclaimed Dick," "it means what you see! That the lady has found a protector to save her from the vile outrage of such a villain as thou art."

"Fool!" hissed Dashfoot. "The lady has consented to accompany me to her lover, who sent for her."

"Liar!" thundered our hero, drawing his sword as the other approached. "I know the lover you would take her to. Think you I am fool enough to be gulled by such lying prate when I overheard your conversation with the three allies you have inside waiting your command to take part in this plot."

Dashfoot started as though he had been struck by a keen dagger, and turned a ghastly pallor. Taking a pistol from the inside of his coat, he fired it in the air.

It was the signal for his accomplices. And

GABRIEL STOOD OVER THE BODY OF HIS BROTHER AND WEPT.

before the report had died away, the three ruffians rushed from the inn.

"Take the lady from that interfering fool!" commanded their master.

Dick clasped the trembling girl to his side with his left arm, and drawing his stately form erect, confronted the ill-looking trio.

"Back!" he said, as they pressed upon him. "Back! the first who lays a hand upon this lady dies!"

The fellows went back, cowed by the cold glitter of his eye, and his cool stern determination.

The ostler of the "Prince" hearing the row, came out to see what it was all about.

"Bring my horse," said Dick, keeping a sharp look upon the movements of his opponents.

Fairy heard her master's voice, and before the ostler had time to get to the stable, the beautiful steed came trotting through the gates, and stood by her master's side.

Releasing his fair charge for an instant Dick vaulted into the saddle, and stooping, lifted Marian up, and placed her before him. This was done with such agility, that before the ruffians could take a step to prevent him, he was prepared to meet them.

"Pull him off his horse!" yelled Dashfoot, in a terrible rage.

He rushed with his confederates to carry out his design, when Dick wielded his sword around.

There was a cry of agony, and Dashfoot fell to the earth, his hand clasped over a deep gash on his forehead.

The others, cowed by the fall of their leader, got clear of the boy's sweeping sword.

"Don't let the lady escape," groaned Dashfoot. "Curse him! Shoot him, some of you!"

One ruffian, more daring than his companions, hurled a thick, heavy cudgel at the boy, and it struck his temple with fearful force; he reeled in the saddle, stunned by the sharp, heavy blow.

Dashfoot sprang up, and tore the clinging girl from her young protector, as the noble youth felf from the saddle, and was caught in he arms of mine host, who just then came o the door.

"You villains!" exclaimed the landlord of the "Prince." "You have killed the noble gentleman, you have."

Calling the ostler, who came on the instant at the sound of his master's voice, our hero was borne to a comfortable room of the inn.

Marian had fainted, and the ruffians bore away their lovely prize without meeting any other impediment to prevent their evil design.

CHAPTER CXXVII.

LORD ERNEST DALLAS ON THE TRACK OF MARIAN SYDNEY'S ABDUCTOR.

TYBURN DICK lost no time in informing Lord Sydney what had occurred to his niece when sufficiently recovered to leave the inn.

Ernest Dallas, who had returned, after a fruitless search for the missing girl, was at home when our hero gave the sad intelligence.

"Will you accompany me to track the villains out?" asked the young nobleman.

"With much pleasure," replied Dick, readily. "Had it not been for that treacherous blow the lady would have been restored again to her uncle's arms. But we may be too late now to save her from her persecutor."

"Let us hope not," said Ernest Dallas.

He rang a bell, and a servant entered.

"Tell the groom to saddle immediately one of the swiftest horses in the stable."

The man bowed and withdrew.

"If it is that rascal Carnwood, as I suspect," the young nobleman said, "nothing shall save him from the fate he merits."

"Don't spare them an inch," exclaimed Lord Sydney, vehemently. "Kill the villain, Ernest, kill him! He has disgraced the lady's honour, and his death shall pay for it."

"It shall," said Lord Ernest, determinedly.

A servant announced that the horse was quite ready

Taking a kindly parting of the old soldier, the two young men left the house, to hunt down the wretch who had spread desolation and unhappiness through the once happy home.

The crescent moon, in all its peaceful beauty, broke through a drift of sombre clouds, revealing by its bright lustre the faces of the gallant youths as they sped through the country.

"Look," exclaimed Dick to his titled companion. "See, here in our path, the furrows of wheels. We are on the track."

"I trust that you may be right," replied Ernest Dallas. "The cowardly scoundrel! When once I have crossed his path I will never leave him until I have stepped over his lifeless corpse, or he over mine."

Dick's attention was occupied by the distant sound of horsemen.

"My lord, if I surmise aright, I fancy I have some old acquaintances coming after me."

Ernest Dallas looked at him inquiringly.

"What do you mean?" he asked.

"Of course you know who I am?"

"I can't imagine; but if you are in danger I shall stand by you to the last. You have proved a gallant friend to our cause, and it matters not to me who you are."

Dick grasped his hand gratefully.

"We shall have an interruption, and unless we fight our way through it, we shall not save the lady to-night."

"If it is fighting they want, they shall have it."

"But it isn't fighting they want; I am the victim they are after."

"They will have to fight pretty well to take you, so let them come."

"Let them come," echoed Dick.

Both drew their swords in anticipation of a fight. They were on the track of the lady's abductor, and they did not want to be delayed.

Dick was in one of those humours, when he would have forced his way through a regiment of soldiers.

His almost effeminate companion was just in the same humour.

"We will give them a ride for it," said the Boy Highwayman.

They urged their steeds forward to greater speed than they had been going, and with gleaming swords raised above their heads, ready to strike the first person to the earth who came before them. They were carried through the air with lightning rapidity, and soon the pursuers were out-distanced, and the clatter of horses was heard no more.

"I must have made a mistake," said our hero, after an interval of twenty minutes.

"No mistake," said Lord Dallas. "The confounded idiots have made a circular route."

"The devil take them!" exclaimed Dick, as Lieutenant Maxwell and his little army confronted him.

"Tyburn Dick," said the soldier, "you are our prisoner!"

"The devil I am!"

"Here is the King's warrant for your arrest."

"And here is the King's warrant for my liberty!" Dick said, taking from his pocket the Royal document bearing the Royal seal.

"His Majesty has cancelled that!"

"Very kind of his Majesty. He can cancel that one, too."

"Will you give in quietly?" asked the young soldier.

"Not if I know it," replied Dick, recklessly, but in a tone of defiance. "You must excuse me for the present. You see I have a gentleman with me, and our business is most important. Another time I shall be most happy to consult you upon this affair."

The lieutenant could barely suppress a smile at the coolness of the observation. He admired the daring, indomitable spirit of the youth, and regretted that duty compelled him to use harsher means than persuasion to get him to accompany them.

"I am sorry," the young officer said, "but I have a duty to perform."

"There is no occasion to be sorry," Dick said, "if you will oblige me by turning your head another way, you will be doing the most honourable duty by not seeing me. You understand?"

"Perfectly. But it can't be."

"Look here, my good fellow," put in Lord Dallas. "This gentleman is a friend of mine, and as a friend I shall stand by him in honour. If it is the blood-money you crave, I will give you twice that sum not to see him."

"It is not that," said the lieutenant sadly, hurt by the other's remark. "I shall get nothing for his apprehension. I can assure you, sir," he went on in an undertone, so that his comrades should not hear him, "it was not by my wish that the duty fell upon me, but the king commanded it, and I must obey."

"Duty is a hard law, I know," said the young noble. "but can we make some arrangement? If you have any feelings of a gentleman, you would not wish to stop either of us did you know the nature of the errand we are upon. A lady dearer to me than my life has been taken from her home by a worthless villain, and this gentlemen, who nobly fought in her defence, is now accompanying me to the place where we believe she is taken."

The soldier hesitated.

"If I let him go," he said, "I shall be disgraced and lose my commission."

"You need not fear for that," said Ernest Dallas. "You shall never want if you act honourably in this case. Come, be blind for once, and take this from a future friend."

He offered the soldier a well-stocked purse, but the officer refused.

"No," he said, "I cannot take money. I owe him my life's gratitude, and by not securing him now, I only do that which is right, though I shall have to stand the consequences."

"You will never regret it."

"It would be a poor spirit, indeed, to regret any act of gratitude. No, sir, if I neglect my duty and am disgraced, I shall be happy with the consolation of having done a service to one I owe so much."

"You owe me nothing," said Dick. "It is I who will be the debtor henceforth. This is a kindness that will not be soon forgotten; and, mind you, should you be compelled to hunt me down, I shall bear you no malice."

The soldier pressed the generous boy's hand in silence, and he turned to go with his six astonished guardsmen, who were somewhat puzzled that they had not got the Boy Highwayman to escort to Newgate, when another body of horsemen were seen bearing down towards them.

"Go!" exclaimed the young officer. "Go, for God's sake! before it is too late."

Dick turned in some astonishment.

The earnest pleading of the soldier's voice touched the boy deeply.

From that moment a brotherly affection sprang up between these two young men.

They exchanged another grip of the hand and parted.

It was impossible for Dick and his companion to continue their journey. The new body of horsemen, who proved to be Bow-street officers, were coming straight towards them.

This was very annoying, as neither of our flying friends could spare any time to take a different route, to throw the officers off the scent.

"What had we better do?" asked Dick. "If we meet them, we shan't find them so generous as our late friends."

"Meet them, if you think we can stand against them."

"How many are there, do you think?"

"About twenty, I should imagine."

"Then we should not stand much chance with them, though they are not scientific; their random hits are not very pleasant

"Do you think it will be wiser if we turn our horses' heads another way?"

"I think so," said Dick. "We shan't lose so much time as if we stopped to fight them; besides, the chances are ten to one if we tried any resistance with them one of us might get a settler."

Dick was quite mistaken when he thought to throw the officers off his track, for he soon discovered they kept up a flying pursuit for more than one hour and a half.

They kept our hero and his companions in quite an opposite direction to the one they set out to take. However, suddenly, when Dick turned his head, the officers were nowhere to be seen, and he proposed that they should make their way to Finchley.

They had ridden some three or four miles without encountering any of their old enemies, when they were brought to a halt by six

of the officers pouncing upon them from behind a clump of trees.

There was no time left to argue. The thing was to act, and that promptly. The officers demanded Tyburn Dick to give in quietly, but the boy laughed, and, grasping the nearest by the throat, hurled him from his horse with lion strength.

The rest instantly closed around him, and levelled pistols at his head. Lord Ernest Dallas, though threatened—as was our hero—with instant death, unhesitatingly ran his sword through the first he could get at.

The man fell from the saddle with a melancholy howl, but he was not killed, the sword had only gone through his shoulder.

At the fall of their comrade, the men turned like savages upon the two youths, and with vile oaths fired their pieces point blank, with intent to kill.

Ernest Dallas recoiled in his saddle as a bullet grazed his cheek, and Dick staggered for a moment from the sickening pain of a fractured arm. Then both turned like ferocious tigers upon their assailants.

The officers were not prepared for this unexpected change; and, before they could draw a weapon in defence, the two infuriated youths felled two to the earth, and the others retreated for dear life.

The battle was over, and the two victors were going on their way again when the former company came in view.

Again the youths were compelled to turn, and they were driven into Richmond by their pursuers, when a strange scene met their view.

Wild Bertram, with the chosen members of the band, were there engaged in fearful combat with a gang of brutal ruffians.

Dick looked on in unutterable astonishment; but he did not stand inactive long.

Making known to his comrades his presence, he took up his position on their side with his titled companion, and took good part in the melée, though he knew not for what they were fighting. But that he learnt afterwards. The substance of it was this—

Wild Bertram had learned, by some mysterious means, that Lady Kingston, of Kingston Chase, had by some unaccountable means, been placed under the care of one of her early friends—the Duchess of Ravenborough.

The same tidings got to the ears of Lord Carawood, and his guilty conscience smote him with terror, for he knew that if his victim got again into society retribution would soon fall upon him.

He was determined not to relinquish the grand title and estate he had obtained by his fell villainy, for he had done that which he knew would sooner or later drag him to the gallows.

What was one or a dozen lives to him, so that he could enjoy his ill-gotten wealth a little longer by the silence of those who knew too much for his safety?

He had learned through the agency of the men he set to watch the movements of Lady Kingston's kind protectors, that it was her intention to take her fair charge to a fashionable ball.

This was an opportunity he had been waiting for.

Engaging a gang of ruffians—treble the quantity necessary for his evil work—he gave them instructions to waylay the Dowager Duchess's carriage, and murder the innocent lady of Kingston.

He had anticipated an interruption through an anonymous letter he had received, that warned him of his danger should he attempt any further treachery; but he only scoffed at the warning, and took the precaution to hire men enough, as he thought, to withstand any interruption.

Though the hirelings were forewarned of an interruption, they did not for a moment suppose that it would be such a one as a band of highwaymen. But they met the opposers with dogged resolution, and they fought hard to accomplish their dark work.

The contest was a long one; the brutes struggled with the gallant knights of the road with the determination not to be beaten.

The officers who had followed our hero looked on with no little amazement. They were quite puzzled what to make of the affair, and they made several attempts to learn what it was all about. But the threatening looks of the combatants warned them that it would be dangerous to interfere.

"This must come to an end," said Captain Claude to the Man of Mystery; "we shan't have a man left shortly. These fellows fight like a lot of unchained devils."

A distressing cry for help rang from the carriage, where three of the base villains had crept unobserved, and were dragging their intended victim out, to murder in cold blood.

Tom King was the first to leap to the rescue. His already blood-stained weapon swerved above his head, and descended with terrible vengeance amongst the ruffians.

One fell, his head severed in half, and the highwayman grasped another by the throat, who had got hold of the lady's delicate wrist.

Looking the quailing wretch coldly and mercilessly in the face, he deliberately ran his sword three times through his body before he touched his heart, and then he let him fall.

By this time Tyburn Dick and Wild Bertram had finished off the third. It was a horrible sight for a lady to witness, but it was a just punishment for the cold-blooded brutes, and she tendered her trembling hand in gratitude to her gallant preserver.

He detained the small white hand in a nervous clasp, and his gaze fixed upon a costly bracelet the lady wore on her wrist.

His whole aspect changed, and he became helpless with emotion as a timid child.

"Great God!" he exclaimed, falling on his knees.

In that position he remained, with his face upturned to Heaven, and he seemed as though offering up a prayer, while the moon's silvery rays fell upon his features, and at that moment they looked almost angelic, so placid and earnest was their expression.

The lady regarded him with surprised interest, and scanned his handsome face, and there she traced lineaments which brought back to her mind the sad yet sweet remembrance of bygone days.

Wild Bertram looked from one to the other with a peculiar expression, and Dick, who was more than puzzled, pinched his wounded arm, being the most sensitive part, to assure himself that he was not dreaming.

He did not wish to disturb them, but he

was most confoundedly anxious to know what it all meant.

"Can it be possible?" Tom King said, again taking the lady's hand, and fixing an intent gaze upon the brilliant jewel. "Can it be that after all these years my prayers and dearest hopes are at last realised? No, it cannot be," he added, drawing his hand across his brow. "But stay!"

He sprang to his feet, his handsome face suffused with a flush of rage.

Casting an anxious look at Bertram, he thrust his hand down his breast, and drew forth a bracelet he had kept treasured close to his heart.

"Look, Bertram," he said, in an unsteady voice. "Did you not say there was not another like it in the world but the one my mother wore?"

The strange man inclined his head in assent, and as the highwayman advanced to the carriage, with the bracelet dangling on a finger of his extended hand, Lady Kingston uttered a low cry of alarm.

"Where—where got you that?" she asked, in a trembling voice. "It is mine; there is not another like it. It went from me in a most mysterious way when——"

A shudder passed through her gentle frame and stopped her further utterance.

"Then 'tis true," exclaimed Tom King, excitedly; "thou art my mother! Thank heaven! at last I have found a parent."

He clasped the trembling lady to his manly breast in a fond embrace, and imprinted a reverent kiss upon her placid brow.

The lady was astonished into speechlessness, and, although she could not convince herself that he was her son—for she had good reasons to believe that he had been murdered by the assassin who robbed her of a loving husband—she nestled to the noble fellow by instinct of more than love.

Gently disengaging herself from his arms, she spoke in a faltering voice—

"My son," she said, struggling hard to maintain her strength to bear out the trying scene. "No, no, it cannot be. I have no son —no husband. No, no, it is a delusion, a cruel mistake."

With what terrible force these words fell upon his ears, crushing   t ray of

hope which for years had been his only guiding star, holding him back from the road of crime his desolation and reckless nature would have led to, keeping him from the path of retribution his will was good to follow up until the last of his enemies were exterminated from the face of the earth; and now that he had found and saved the being for whom he had been yearning from early childhood, was he to be abandoned from her side, her love, because he had not sufficient proofs to identify his claim upon her maternal relationhips?

The thought was maddening, and his heart sank within him like cold lead, as the fearful misgivings rushed like liquid fire through his brain.

"Madam! Mother!" he exclaimed, frantically, again falling at her feet and clasping her arms in his own, "recall those cruel words, unless you wish to distract me. Oh! I am convinced that thou art my dear mother —my bitterly wronged mother. Look into my face, and see if you cannot find there a resemblance to my dead father."

Lady Kingston's eyes filled with tears. She had already traced a likeness, in the pleading upturned face, to that of her murdered husband.

"I had a son," she said, sadly, "but he was taken from me, and murdered by my cruel kinsman."

She had suppressed her grief bravely, but it was impossible to hold it back any longer and it burst forth in a piteous flood, as she sank into the arms of the gallant highwayman.

Wild Bertram went to her side, and laid his hand kindly on her arm.

"Lady," he said, "your son lives!"

"Alas!" she said, "such happiness will never be mine, to clasp to my breast my boy I saw him in my dream murdered with his sire."

"My lady," continued Bertram, "the boy lived. He lives now. The man to whom he was given by his treacherous uncle to be murdered—brutal, cold-blooded wretch as he was—had not the heart to destroy the child who smiled up in his face and nestled to him for protection."

The lady listened to the revelation as though in a trance.

Not a muscle of her face moved, and her gaze was fixed upon the speaker as though searching him through for the truth of the words he spoke.

"The man kept the child," Bertram went on, "adopted him as his own, and guarded him from the cruel hands of his relatives until he was of an age capable to take care of himself; then the youth went abroad, leaving his father, as he thought, for he knew no other. He fought in a foreign clime for his king, and gained honours a prince would have been proud of. His uncle, the cruel Judge Carnwood, convicted him for killing a man in a duel, and outlawed him. This he did, for he suspected in Captain Arthur Montrose the heir to Kingston Chase. But the youth braved the danger of returning, and came back an exile. He sought me, his foster-father and protector."

Tom King blushed with modesty at the words of praise.

"Can this be real?" murmured the lady. "Am I dreaming a dream of happiness? This is beyond mortal power to realise. Oh, this is cruel torture! Would that I could die in this dream!"

"It is no dream, dear mother," said Tom King, touched by the plaintive tone in which she spoke. "It is no dream, but a bright, joyous truth, and your long-lamented son is restored to a mother's arms at last."

He could not say more, emotion choked his utterance.

Lady Kingston twined her arms around his neck and left a kiss upon his cheek, then her head sank on his shoulder.

"I have but little more to say," remarked the Man of Mystery. "I have lived for this—lived to atone for some of my past crimes. I told my adopted son his own father was dead. I told him his mother lived; and marked out a destiny for him to fulfil—to avenge his father's death, his mother's wrongs, and his own sufferings."

Tom King was about to seal this with a sacred oath, when such a hue and cry arose, and the combatants dashed about in every possible direction, that the oath vanished, and his only care was to guard his mother.

The fight had continued during Bertram's colloquy, with terrible fury, and this was the last grand charge made by the highwaymen.

The ruffians began to lack courage and fell back dispirited by the sight of the havoc going on amongst their companions; and when the furious onset was made, they entreated for dear life the highwaymen falling on them like so many incensed tigers.

"Arrest those men!" said Bertram in an authoritative tone, to the officers.

The whole body galloped round the retreating, beaten brutes, and charged them with drawn sword to stand.

The ruffians knew if they did, their last stand would be under the gallows. This thought made them desperate, and they fought with indomitable courage.

The officers were taken quite by surprise by the furious resistance the fellows made, but after a fierce struggle, in which many of the Bow-street gentlemen were hurled from their horses, they managed to capture four, the others having fled.

"If you value your lives," said Bertram, "do not let those men escape."

The officers looked surprised.

"But," said one, "you are highwaymen, and our prisoners."

"Fool!" said the Man of Mystery, with a warning. Be content with what you have got and go."

The men murmured their discontent. They wanted more. They would have got it had they been obstinate.

The highwaymen were mustering in a determined group.

Their resolute looks were sufficient to tell the officers that they did not intend to be taken. So the officers went away quietly with their four prisoners, who were hung at Newgate, in the reign of his most gracious majesty, anno domini—.

Of course everything that had transpired was soon made known to the gallant knights of the road. They congratulated their comrade upon his good fortune in finding a parent, and wished him success in undertakings to be mentioned as we proceed.

Tom King was then left alone with his mother and the insensible form of the dowager duchess. That venerable lady had gone off in hysterics at the first attack of the ruffians.

The highwayman knew he could not do her any good, and not being near any habitation, he let her lie where she had fallen, and then he gave the coachman instructions to drive on, and took his seat inside the dowager duchess's carriage.

Had the noble fellow seen the pair of demoniacal eyes that were fixed upon him as he alighted from the vehicle, or heard the deep malediction delivered at him in fierce hatred from the muffled person that had watched him, he would not have slept the happy sleep he did that night.

CHAPTER CXXVIII.
MARIAN SYDNEY AND HER COUSINS.

GABRIEL CARNWOOD knew that it would be quite useless for him to think of winning his fair cousin's consent without he could prove himself worthy of her.

And that was out of his power, and out of his nature, too. Knowing the hopelessness of his case, he sought the advice of his brother.

"You expect to find her at the lone house by ten o'clock?" said Ralph.

"Exactly so," replied his brother.

"And are you fool enough to suppose that she is likely to consent if you go there and persecute her? I thought you had more sense, Gab."

"Didn't I ask your advice in the matter?"

"You did."

"Then why don't you give it without preaching?"

"My advice is this—that is, if you like. Of course I don't want any hand in the affair."

"For God's sake, go on!"

"Well, I should say, let's to horse at once, and meet the carriage with the lady before it reaches the lone house, as though we had been sent in pursuit of her abductor. I will take her from Dashfoot, and convey her to an inn."

"But the lone house would do better."

"Didn't you ask for my advice?"

"Yes."

"Then be good enough to listen to it."

There was a pause, in which the brothers looked particularly spitefully at each other.

"Well," said Gabriel, "have it your way. What motive have you for taking me to her?"

"This. I am supposed to save her from her abductor. Would it do, think you, for me to take her to the lone house?"

"Not exactly."

"I must, then, win her confidence; keep her at the inn under the plea of waiting till her uncle arrives; you arrive instead. The rest you must manage."

Ralph Carnwood would not have undertaken an affair of this sort without he saw the prospects of a fine harvest.

The two scoundrels set out, Ralph took the start, and saved his cousin—as he made her believe—from the rascal who had decoyed her from her home.

He took her to an inn, under the pretext of obtaining rest and refreshment for her, but Marian, being naturally anxious to return to her guardian, would have journeyed on had not Ralph Carnwood told her that the horses were knocked up.

Though she was naturally so guileless and unsuspecting, she began to feel an instinctive sense of distrust, to which his over-heated affection only gave greater strength.

"Uncle will be dreadfully alarmed," she said. "I do not require rest, and would rather return at once."

"We will depart the first thing in the morning," said Ralph, "till then we must both remain where we are."

Marian sighed, became meditative, and thought of her lover. Ralph sat searching his mind for a plot that was then forming. The landlord brought a tray with refreshments, but not much of it was touched. Marian could not eat. Her sorrow was too great, and the excitement of the peril she had undergone quite deprived her of appetite.

Ralph could not eat, but he drank.

"Why don't Gabriel come?" he thought. "He will never get another chance, if he don't take the present one."

While he was thinking so, the object of his thoughts arrived, and inquired for his brother.

The landlord came up.

"Gentleman below for Sir Ralph," he said. "Is that you, sir?"

"Yes."

"Shall I show him up?"

"No."

"Oh!"

"Tell him to wait."

"Yes, sir."

"I will attend to him directly."

"Exactly, sir."

"Uncle Sydney!" exclaimed Marian. "It is he, perhaps."

"No," replied Ralph.

"It may be."

"How should it? He could not know whither we have come."

"But "——

She hesitated.

"But what?"

"He may have traced us out, and followed."

"I think not; however, I will see."

"I hope it is he."

"If it were, he would have come up, not stayed below."

"So he would," thought Marian, and this glad hope died sadly away.

Ralph went below.

Gabriel stood in the bar-room, awaiting him.

"So you have come at last?"

"Seems like it," said his brother, not in the most amiable tone.

"It does."

They looked at each other like the rascals they both were, then there was a pause; then Ralph spoke.

"Why did you not come before?"

"I could not."

"Why?"

"The horse wouldn't come any quicker."

"Bah! Has your fancy died out?"

The other's eyes lit up with strong, excited passion.

"I would have her, if I lost my soul."

"Pshaw! If you lost it, nobody, not the devil himself, would care to pick it up."

"Thank you!"

"Welcome; however, she is here."

"Let me see her, then."

"Fool!"

"Thank you, again."

"Fool," repeated the other. "What chance would you have here, think you?"

"All I should want."

"Why, she would call for aid."

"To whom?"

There was a sneer in his tone that the other understood.

"Not to me, but to the rest," he replied, half in angry shame at his treachery to a gentle girl of his own kindred. "That, certainly, is not our course."

"What is then?"

"I will tell you, but not now."

"Why not?"

"She must be got out of the way before we can talk together."

"Where will she go?"

"To bed, of course."

Gabriel's eyes glistened again with a villainous thought.

"Look here," he said, "couldn't we—"

"What?"

"Put something in her drink?"

"What, to make her sleep?"

"Yes."

Ralph considered.

"I do not see how."

"I do."

"How, then?"

"A drug."

"If we had any."

"I have."

He drew out a phial half-filled with a dark mixture.

"That will do it," he said; "a little drop of that."

"And she would sleep?"

"Sound enough, and unconscious of anything."

Ralph considered again.

Villain as he was, the only feeling that deterred him from joining with the idea was fear.

"She might make an outcry in the morning," he said.

"No fear," exclaimed the other. "It would be too late; she would not call in a lot of strangers to tell them what had happened. Besides, women philosophise—when a thing is done and can't be helped, they take it quietly."

"Very well, then ; we will try the effect. But she may not drink anything."

"Take a bottle of wine up with you."

"A good idea."

"Of course."

"She will not suspect then."

"No."

"Give me this drug."

Gabriel did so."

"Don't be afraid of it," he said. "It won't hurt her—the more you put in, the longer she will sleep."

He called for a bottle of wine. It was brought. The drug was poured in, and Ralph corked the bottle again.

It could not then be seen that it had been tampered with.

"Remain here," he said ; "when she has retired I will come for you."

"Do."

"You will not be slow to follow."

The libertine smiled as he thought of once again having the beautiful girl helpless before him. It was a fine anticipation, which he hoped to realise, and there did not seem much hope for her now.

In the power of two ruthless men, one of them bent upon the determination to possess her, and make her his wife even against her will; and the other resolved to assist him. She could scarcely hope to escape.

"My plan is this," said Ralph ; "if you succeed to-night——'

"And I shall not fail."

"Perhaps."

"I shall not."

"You have already done so once."

"That was——"

"I know all about it."

"What do you know ?"

"That you were attacked by a stranger."

"A highwayman !"

"How ?"

"Yes, it's a fact ; there were some officers after him, and he actually bribed them to let him go."

"And thrash you."

"Marian told you so."

"Yes."

"She shall have something else to tell before I leave her again," he said, spitefully.

"As I said before, perhaps."

"How can I fail ?"

"How did you before ?"

"Because I was an ass ; I might have had her when I went first to take her from her room. I should, too, but she woke up."

"And then '——

"I thought she was going to scream, so stopped her mouth, and got her out as soon as possible."

"Why didn't you when you had her at Mother Megg's ?"

"Because she got a knife, and cut me over the eye. However, that's not the thing."

"Scarcely. I daresay you thought so."

"Well, but your plan ?"

"Is this. If you succeed to-night, or even if you do not, we will go to some out-of-the-way place, and you shall marry her."

"Suppose she won't be married ?"

"I will manage that. There are more places than one to which you can take her, where she might shriek her heart out without gaining help. Besides, when she finds me resolute she will consent."

"Very well."

"You shall be well satisfied."

"I am."

"Such women as Marian are not seen every day."

"That I know."

He thought of her magnificent beauty as she had lain before him when he entered her chamber, and mentally agreed with his brother's words.

"In fact, you will have her much too cheaply."

"Shall I ?"

"She will cost you nothing."

"I don't know what you call nothing."

"What do you ?"

"I have had trouble enough.

"Many men have more before they can possess a mistress."

"I know that; but it will pay you very well."

"How ?"

"Am I not to give you all her fortune ?"

"But suppose Lord Sydney will not let her have it ?"

"Why shouldn't he ?"

"You are not his choice."

"You need not tell me that."

"And so he may take it into his head to disappoint you of the money."

"I don't want it."

"But I do."

"Get it, then—I only want her."

"But you don't suppose I am going to let you have her for nothing, do you?

"No."

"That is well."

"I think you have had something out of me already."

"Quite correct."

"I am glad to hear you say so."

"So am I."

"Then there is nothing more to be said. You may as well take this wine up."

"Not yet; there is something else to be considered first.

"What?"

"As I observed just now, Lord Sydney may disappoint us both, by keeping her fortune."

"That won't disappoint me."

"But it will me."

"That's your look out."

"So it must be you."

"How?"

"I will explain."

"I shall be most happy to hear you."

"Listen then. You will make Marian yours—revel in her beauty, and be her constant companion and possessor for some time before her guardian could take her away—even did he wish to do so."

"Well."

"I shall have nothing of the sort."

"You don't want it, do you?"

"No."

"Well, then?"

"But I want some money."

"Of whom?"

"You?"

"I?"

"Yes."

"Then you won't get it."

"You are hasty, my dear brother," said Ralph, coldly. "I shall."

"All right, then."

"It will be."

"Not if I know it."

"While you are perfectly conscious."

"Oh!"

He spoke doubtingly, as though he rather intended to take his brother in.

Ralph spoke confidently, as though he fully intended to take Gabriel in.

"I want ten thousand pounds," said Ralph, making this moderate demand as though it were quite a trifle.

Gabriel stared.

"And I," he said, "most heartily wish you may get it."

"I shall."

"Let me ask again from whom?"

"Let me say again from you!"

There was a pause, and the two scoundrels looked at each other again.

"Then," said Gabriel again, "you won't get it."

"Then," said his brother, "you will not get Marian.

There was another pause, longer than before.

Gabriel's face was longer, too."

"Not get her?" he said.

"No."

"The devil!"

"Precisely."

"Look here, this isn't fair, you know."

His brother smiled.

"Why?"

"Why, haven't I paid no end of debts for you, and haven't I stood your friend in everything?"

"Well?"

"Well; what the devil more do you want?"

"I have just told you."

"Ten thousand pounds."

"Which you won't get."

"Very well," said Ralph, rising; "we understand each other."

"Quite."

"And may as well separate."

"What!"

"Separate."

Gabriel looked particularly black.

"And not have her after all?"

"That's it."

"What a rank swindle."

"Like your title."

"Ah!"

"Come, now, am I to have the ten thousand?"

"Why, it's a fortune."

"Not more than she is worth."

"More than I have. But since it must be so, why it must."

"Just my opinion."

Gabriel did not intend to give in just yet.

He wanted to get his lovely bride prospective at a price somewhat cheaper.

His brother looked at him and saw him through clearly.

"The ten thousand," he said—"nothing less."

"Nothing at all, then."

"Very well."

He rose, and took the bottle of wine as though to dash it to the floor.

"This of course is of no use now," he said.

Gabriel caught his arm.

"Stop."

The other stopped.

"Don't break the bottle."

"It is no use.

"Don't be in a hurry. I didn't say I wouldn't stand something handsome."

"Ten thousand?"

"Down, no."

"Nothing less."

"What, for good and beautiful Marian?"

"That's a clever speech."

Ralph laughed.

"I could make a better."

"Could you?"

"Yes."

"Perhaps you will."

"Possibly."

"I should like to hear it."

"You shall."

"Let me, then."

"Then this it is."

He paused and looked at his scoundrel brother, with a cunning leer that made him wonder what he meant.

"What if I increase the sum?"

"You will get nothing."

"Nor you."

"Then I will go without."

"What, for the sake of twenty thousand?"

He stared aghast.

The demand was exorbitant.

So was Gabriel's desire.

"Twenty," said he, again. "Why, you said ten just now! Twenty, the idea! Why don't you say a little more?"

"I shall, unless you are satisfied with that."

"You will have to be satisfied with less."

"Than twenty?"

"Twenty be hanged! Go back to the original sum."

"Not now—too late."

"But "——

"You would not be satisfied."

"I am; quite. Come, now; go back to the original."

"What, ten thousand! Psha! Why, think of her?"

"So I do."

"Young, lovely, fair, sweet, innocent, and with the form of the Venus de Medici—that you should know, having seen her in deshabille.

The remark was well timed; it recalled the lovely figure he had seen, with her garments in disarray, and his cheeks flushed again.

"Say the ten," he said, "and I'll give you a cheque."

"Fifteen."

"No, hang it."

"Fifteen is the sum."

"Come, now, twelve."

He spoke very persuasively.

He had tried to avoid paying ten before, now he was glad to offer twelve.

Ralph smiled again.

"Fifteen," he said; "that is five less than I said."

"Five more than you said first."

"But I am quite satisfied now."

"You should have been so before. Come a cheque for fifteen, and I go with the win Within the hour you may——"

Gabriel rose, with hot cheeks and eyes that glittered with passion.

"Within an hour," he said. "Keep your word, and you shall have it.'

"I never broke my word."

"Nor I. I have just said so."

"And I have just promised myself that I should have fifteen thousand pounds from you. Ralph Carnwood never disappoints himself."

"Neither does his brother," said the libertine, drawing out his pocket-book. "She

TOM KING RECEIVES A MESSAGE FROM HIS FRIENDS.

shall be mine, though it cost me life, soul, and honour."

"Not much altogether, though they sound a great deal apart; but the first is the only one in existence."

Another sneer.

"As near the truth as possible."

"For you to go."

"Keen. However, we waste time, and Marian will wonder at my absence. You remain here while I go upstairs with this sleeping draught. We are both scoundrels, but we may as well be friends. When she has retired I will come for you."

"Do, meantime I will try to wait patiently."

"As a tiger does when the prey is in his lair. However, you will not have to wait long."

With this consolatory assurance he departed, and his brother was left alone.

Ralph went to his cousin, whom he found waiting his appearance with deep anxiety.

"Was it uncle?" she asked.

"Silly child," he said, with an effort of affection.

"Is it likely that had it been he would not have come to see you?"

"True," she said, sinking, with a sigh, into the chair from which she had risen when Ralph entered—"too true!"

"Come, my dear Marian, you shall see him early in the morning. For the present, drink a glass of wine, and go to bed."

He filled a glass from the drugged wine, and offered it to the unconscious maiden, who, so innocent herself, never suspected evil in another.

She took it, and his eyes watched her with a snake-like glitter as she drank it.

A smile lit his features as she gave the glass back.

He took it, saying—

"Retire now, Marian; you will require rest. We will start at the earliest hour in the morning."

"Thanks, cousin Ralph. How glad I shall be to see dear uncle."

The smile on Ralph's face was followed by a scowl. But he veiled the feeling, and kissed her fair brow as he said "Good night."

A Judas kiss it was—a caress like the lick of a serpent's tongue.

His gaze followed her from the room; and directly she had gone he went down to his brother.

"Now," he said, " she has gone."

"The drug—has she taken it?"

"Yes."

"Then it will work. In twenty minutes she will be mine." And during that time they sat plotting dark things against her, until, looking at his watch, Gabriel rose.

"The drug will have done its work now," he said, as he mounted the stairs that led to her chamber. "She will be mine!"

CHAPTER CXXXIV.

THE VILLAIN FOILED—A DUEL TO THE DEATH AND WRONGS REQUITED.

At the moment the reprobate thought to triumph over the insensible girl, an interruption ensued that foiled his base design.

He had entered the room of his victim, and was gloating over her delicate beauty, when the sound of a hasty step ascending the stairs stayed him in his purpose.

He was held powerless by a dread feeling of approaching danger, his limbs lost all power, and the torture he experienced was terrible.

As the door was burst open a cry of terrified despair left his lips, and he tried to retreat from the excited youth who came in time to save the lady.

"Wretch! dastardly scoundrel!" exclaimed Lord Dallas, grasping the libertine by the throat, "this is how you would serve a helpless girl!"

His eyes fell upon the insensible girl, and his face in that instant became calm; then, as he turned again to his foe, all the demoniac fire of his concentrated rage rose to his fair cheeks, and he would have remorselessly slain the trembling dastard, had not

Ralph, who had heard a scuffle, which knew could not be between his brother a his fair victim, come upon the scene.

"You, too, are then implicated in this disgraceful work," said the young nobleman, hurling Gabriel, with lion strength, across the room, and turning furiously upon the new comer.

Ralph's courage vanished when the excited youth turned upon him; and he would have much preferred being further out of his reach than in such close proximity.

"Coward!" hissed Ernest Dallas, 'were it not that I know that your days are numbered, nothing would prevent me from running my sword through your black heart; but such a death would be too good for you."

Ralph Carnwood shrank back, cowed by the determination of the young lord's words. He was skulking away, like a beaten hound, towards the door, when Ernest Dallas arrested him.

"Mark you!" he said, menacingly, "should you attempt again any treachery, or be the cause of one hour's unhappiness to this lady, whom you have so fearfully wronged, nothing will save you from my vengeance! Go, and take with you the remembrance of what I have said."

He went; but whether it was the warning he received, or a new dark plot revolving in his mind that caused his heavy brow to lower with an evil scowl, it is hard to say.

Lord Ernest remembered the oath he had sworn to avenge the wrongs of the suffering girl; he had said he would not leave his foe until he had stepped over his lifeless corpse. And he meant it.

His eyes glanced round the room for the cowardly knave. But fortunately for the coward he was not there; he had made his escape unobserved while the young nobleman attacked Ralph.

"Gone!" muttered Lord Dallas, disappointedly. "He has escaped my vengeance this time, but it will fall upon him ere long. Why did I not slay him—idiot that I am?"

He paced the chamber in an excited manner, bitterly regretting that he had spared the reprobate's life.

He had almost forgotten the purport of his

errand and the presence of the sleeping maiden.

A groan from Marian broke upon his ear. He started, and went to the bedside.

He called upon her name, but she did not appear to hear him.

The truth flashed upon his mind, and he muttered—

"She has been drugged."

How was he to get her back to her uncle's? He could not carry her on his horse in that insensible state the many miles that lay between Lord Sydney's residence and the lane.

Had the villains fled with the vehicle in which they had brought her there?—the chaise which tracks he had followed, and so discovered her abductors' retreat.

He inquired of the innkeeper.

"No, sir," replied the man; "the two gentlemen went away on horseback, and I suppose they forgot the carriage."

"Then get it ready at once."

During the interim for the departure of Marian Lord Dallas loaded his pistols, in case should be attacked on his journey.

The precaution was not taken needlessly, for, as he had anticipated, he was beset by the Carnwood brothers.

While travelling through a deserted part of the country the youth was startled by the report of a pistol, and a bullet whizzed past his head.

"Nothing more than I expected from the perfidious brutes," muttered Lord Dallas, giving the startled horses the full play of the reins to take him out of danger.

A second shot was fired.

Ernest Dallas drew up the horses and looked round for the hidden assassins.

Mentally swearing deadly vengeance against the cursed traitors, who kept out of observation, he drove on again.

He had not gone far when a third shot came hissing through the air.

The leading horse was hit—it sprang up with a loud, agonising cry, and then fell to the earth, dead.

Lord Ernest jumped from the chaise.

"Poor creature," he said, cutting the traces of the stricken horse; "this is another death they have to answer for. I wouldn't have lost you for half my fortune."

A tear stood in his eye as he mounted the carriage step. It was his favourite steed; the one he had set out in pursuit with—the one that had taken him through the ranks of the enemy unscratched in the heat of the battle.

"Cursed be the coward's hand that took thy life!" he said, sorrowfully, and again drove on.

A fourth shot followed him.

Evidently the person in pursuit was bent upon his destruction.

A dread feeling of awe crept over him. He could face any amount of danger; but the idea of being a mark for some sportive individual, or individuals, was more than any fellow could bear, especially when they had an unconscious lady to protect.

Each time Ernest looked round he could neither discover from which direction the shots came or the person who fired them.

This he thought particularly strange, and very likely to prove fatally dangerous to himself or fair charge—perhaps both, especially if the hidden persons were at all close to arm, which was not the least unlikely—so, to get as far away as possible, he lashed the horses into full gallop, and went along in splendid style.

For a time he was left alone.

Perhaps it was that the pickets had wasted all their ammunition. And Ernest Dallas heartily hoped they had. But presently he heard the clatter of horses' feet behind him.

The youth turned his head, and he saw his two cowardly enemies following him.

He drew up to wait for them.

They came on straight for the carriage.

Drawing their swords, they jumped from their steeds, and, without a word, were about to attack the young traveller.

Ernest Dallas presented his pistols at them.

The brothers went back involuntarily.

The steady hand and cold glitter of the young nobleman's eye cowed them. But only for a moment.

Thinking probably that the youth would not fire, they dashed forward. But the youth did fire both pistols, and one of the brothers fell, a bullet heavier than he weighed a minute before.

When Gabriel saw his brother fall, he
ve a despairing cry, and knelt by his side.
They loved each other in their own savage
ay, and the scene that took place between
e dying man and his brother was very touch-
g.

Gabriel put his arm round Ralph's neck,
and, supporting his body on his knee, drew
his brother's head to his own throbbing breast,
with more tenderness than might be expected
from such a man.

"Curse you!" Gabriel said, addressing the
youth. "May your coward hand that robbed
me of my brother wither to the wrist! God
grant my prayer!" he added, solemnly.

The dying man tried to stop his brother's
execrations.

A cold tremor ran through his breast, and
he fancied his hand grew benumbed.

"You shall be avenged, brother!" exclaimed Gabriel.

Then, turning to the youthful homicide, he
said—

"To-morrow meet me, if you are not
wholly a coward, at the Davenport Saloon,
and answer me with the sword for this un-
justifiable murder!"

"At what time?"

"Six o'clock."

"I shall be there," said Ernest Dallas;
"God will be on the side of the right—one of
us will fall."

He then drove on, and Ralph Carnwood
expired in his brother's arms as the carriage
rolled out of sight. The night increased in
darkness, and for hours Gabriel stood over
the body of his brother, and wept in heart-
broken sorrow.

* * * * * * *

Judge Carnwood, too, then employed the
rascal Dashfoot, he it was who had watched
Tom King conduct his mother from the carriage to the residence of the Duchess of
Downborough, and he conveyed the news of
the gallant highwayman's happy union to his
master.

The intelligence fell a heavy blow on the
old man. He might have consoled himself
with the loss of his victim—the wronged lady
whose death he had so cunningly planned—
but for her to be restored to him, with the
whole secret revealed by Bertram, was something more than a trifle to look after.

It is not to be supposed that the old villain
would relinquish the position he had held for
so long, not while he had money and ready
tools to continue his dark work with.

"Dashfoot," he said, addressing his ally,
"you must keep a sharp look out upon that
man, and at the first opportunity send a
dagger to his heart."

"You may rely upon me, my lord," said
the man. "I never failed yet."

Their arrangements were made in a few
words. Time was precious, and delay dangerous; the latter they made as little of as
possible.

Dashfoot was out again on his fell work;
his greed was glutted with gold. He was
faithful to those who served him well, and
had he to face a thousand demons to complete his work, he would not have shrunk an
inch.

He watched like a bloodhound with nervous
patience for an opportunity to spring upon his
prey.

Tom King was standing on the terrace
steps of his new home, that commanded a
view of the splendid grounds, with a young
lady friend of the dowager's by his side, when
his attention was drawn to a remote part of
the ground, where several of the female do
mestics were listening very attentively to a
pretty dark-eyed rustic young woman, who
was talking to them with much sincerity, as
she held one of the servants' hands in her
own.

"Fortune-telling, by Jove!" he muttered.
"I wonder whether she could tell me anything—of course, it is all humbug. Pshaw!
But while I have far more important matters
to think of, why should I trouble my head
with such trifles?" Turning away from the
spot, he perceived a stranger approaching,
who handed him a letter from his comrades of
Hounslow Heath.

The girl's bronzed cheeks blushed as he
stood before her, and she curtseyed politely.

The highwayman raised his hat gallantly,
and said—

"Well, my pretty juggler, and what silly
trash have you been filling the minds of these
foolish girls with?"

"What I have told them, sir, are events
forthcoming."

"Events a very long way off, eh?"

"You may laugh, sir, but I can tell you something you don't know. There is an ominous cloud of sorrow hanging over your happiness, and unless you are very cautious you will not be an inhabitant of the earth long."

The highwayman's cheeks paled.

The young woman spoke with much sincerity, and her words left an impression upon him he could not shake off dispite his gaiety.

"Indeed!" he said, smiling. "Do your prophecies ever come true?"

"I have never yet affirmed anything but what has come to pass."

"Can you foresee my future?"

"I will tell you, but you must first cross my hand with a piece of silver."

"Certainly; I wanted your information too cheap," he said, placing a sovereign in her hand.

"No, sir, it is not that I want money for telling you, but unless my hand is crossed with silver it spoils the charm."

"The gipsy girl gave him back the gold, saying, "it must be a piece of silver."

Tom King put a piece of silver in her hand; then she took his hand in her own, and for a few moments studied the lines.

"You have many enemies," she said, "many foes, of whom you must be careful. Your life is in danger. There is a lady," she went on, "of whom you think a great deal. It will be by seeing this lady that you may lose your life. Understand me rightly, it will not be by any act of hers, but it will be caused through jealousy, by a man who has a great desire to move you out of his way."

"Very kind of the man," said Tom King. "Is that all?"

"Is that not enough?"

"Plenty. I shouldn't care for much more like that."

The gipsy girl curtseyed and withdrew, leaving the highwayman gazing after her in admiration.

"It's all bosh," he mused. "Just as though one person has the power of foreseeing another person's future more than the persons themselves. It's all very well for a lot of silly women to gossip about, but I don't put any faith in it, though certainly she seemed to know a tolerable amount more than I would have given her credit for, but that she may have learnt from some one. Anyhow, I shall see how much of it comes true."

A short time after the lady left him he was riding over to Lord Sydney's residence, unconscious of the dangerous spy who was following in his track.

He was treated cordially by the grand old veteran and the young nobleman, Lord Ernest Dallas, but Marian said but little.

The poor fellow felt that she no longer cared about him, and his heart sank within him as he gazed upon her sad, beautiful face.

When they were alone, he approached her sorrowfully.

"Marian," he said, "what have I done to merit this coldness? It is no fault of mine that I have not been before, nor have I thought of you the less during my absence."

"You might have sent, if you could not come," she said, turning from him to hide her weakness rather than unkindness. "I don't believe you care for me a bit like you used to."

"Marian," he said, bending over her, and extending his hand to her, "you know not the wretchedness I have endured since we last met, or you would not reproach me thus cruelly."

The highwayman pleaded, and Marian reproached, but at last she gave way to her lover's entreaties and again they were happy— everything was forgotten, everything forgiven.

To celebrate their reunion, they were to go out for a ride together. Little thought the gentle girl, when she left her lover to prepare herself to accompany him, how soon again their happiness would be crushed.

She had hardly left the room five minutes, when a piercing cry rang through the whole house.

Lord Ernest Dallas was the first who entered the chamber, and then he beheld a spectacle that caused his blood to curdle in his veins with horror.

His brave, gallant comrade, Tom King, lay prone on the floor, with a red fountain of his life's tide oozing up around the dagger that had been driven to the hilt in his back.

Recoiling with horror, Lord Ernest stooped and plucked the bloody weapon from his stricken friend.

"I would I had the coward wretch who dealt this cruel blow within my grasp," he murmured, stooping over his comrade.

Had he not been so blind with horror when he entered, he might have seen the dark-souled monster creeping from the room.

"Help! help!" cried the voice of Lord Sydney.

Lord Ernest dashed from the chamber, still holding the dripping weapon. In the corridor he saw the old soldier struggling with the assassin.

When the villain saw the desperate young nobleman coming to the rescue of the brave old soldier, he hurled his assailant from him with brute force, and leaped from the nearest window.

But before he had time to escape Lord Dallas was upon him like a panther, and the weapon he had assassinated the gallant highwayman with was driven into his own infernal heart as he dashed through the window, and fell dead into the garden, and so ended the career of Dashfoot, the hireling.

The evening of the day on which the above cruel event occurred, Lord Ernest Dallas was to meet Gabriel Carnwood in a duel.

The young nobleman felt convinced that this last fearful tragedy was the effect of treachery by his foe, and he was doubly anxious for the time to come when he would have the chance of avenging his suffering friend.

Having had his friend put under the care of a skilful physician to restore his shattered life, he set out for the rendezvous with a determination to kill or die.

He found his opponent waiting for him, and many other gentlemen were there.

The two combatants exchanged a quiet nod.

Lord Ernest noticed that Gabriel Carnwood had wonderfully altered since they last met, the libertine's brother had certainly wrought a perceptible change on him: his face was haggard with desperate grief, his demeanour calm, but his sunken eyes were restless with a relentless fire.

"Gentlemen," he said, "I meet my opponent to avenge my brother, who he shot in cold blood. If I fall, let my request to be buried with my brother be taken to my father, Lord Carnwood, of Kingston Chase."

Many of the party unwillingly assented to acquiesce to his wish.

"Gentlemen," said Lord Dallas, "my opponent has given his reason for this meeting, now you shall have mine. Had I not accidentally shot his brother, after I was pursued by them for saving a lady from their base persecutions, I should have challenged him to such a duel, and slain him remorsely for his treachery to the lady I rescued from his violence; and the assassination of my friend, Captain Montrose, instigated by him, makes my cause doubly just."

Gabriel's face went under a complete transformation, and more than one present noticed his expression of triumph when the assassination was mentioned.

"It's a lie!" he exclaimed, in a terrible passion, glaring fiercely towards the speaker; "the murder of Captain Montrose I am innocent of."

"Then you have one sin less to answer for," replied Ernest Dallas, coolly; "if you are innocent of the crime, then your father is guilty."

"And why accuse my father? What enmity has he towards your friend?"

"Shall I tell you?"

"Speak—yes, speak!"

"Then, since you are so bold, I will. Captain Arthur Montrose is the last descendent of Lord Kingston, of Kingston Chase, the estate you and your father usurp. While my friend lived, Judge Carnwood was in danger of losing the property he suddenly became possessor of by the sudden and mysterious death of his cousin, Lord Kingston; perhaps the unexpected return of the exile gave your father and yourself a little uneasiness, and some cause for enmity; if you think I have not spoken the truth, deny it."

Gabriel stood paralysed; his lips bloodless and quivering; he did not think that the young nobleman knew so much.

The gentlemen looked at one another in surprise and then glanced scornfully at the quailing man.

Gabriel noticed, with a sickening sensation, the change of his friends towards him.

Could he, in that moment of frenzy, have killed them all, he would have kept the secret of his disgrace from spreading. But a weakness took possession of him, that made him fear he would not be able to stand against his foe.

A decanter of brandy stood on the table. This he grasped with an eager hand, and thrust it to his parched lips.

Before he had barely tasted the fiery spirit, it was dashed from his hand, and fell at his feet, shattered to atoms.

He turned like a madman upon the insulter, and would have run him through, but a pair of strong hands held him by the arms, and kept him back.

"Be not rash," said the gentleman, who kept him at bay; "it was for your own good that you were prevented from drinking. Had you swallowed that liquor it would have made you more mad than you now are, and what chance would you have had in a combat with so calm an opponent as the gentleman with whom you are going to fight?"

Gabriel acknowledged the force of the argument, and suddenly grew tame.

He seemed to see the great responsibility of the engagement he was about to enter into.

"I am ready," he said to his opponent.

In an instant both combatants were standing foot to foot, and the spectators gathered round them in a circle.

At the first onset the duel began by both with cool deliberation.

Many skilful thrusts and parries were made.

The matchless skill of Lord Dallas won undaunted admiration from the crowd of lookers on, and heavy odds were laid on him.

He kept an unceasing eye upon his combatant, and moved with that ease and grace, so natural to him each time he directed a thrust, or made a stroke.

Gabriel began the contest very calmly, and fenced with admirable skill, but after trying every trick he knew, and found himself met by the quick ready parrying of his opponent, he grew revengeful and less cautious.

With a look of desperate despair, he saw that it was impossible to cope with the young nobleman with any hope of success, and unless he could throw in a first thrust he knew that his death was inevitable.

To confuse his young combatant, he suddenly changed his play to that of the broadsword cut and thrust, but in this, like the other, he was met at every turn.

Gabriel kept his opponent at sharp work, guarding off his rapid blows which he delivered with wonderful celerity, for the purpose of throwing him off his guard; suddenly, drawing back his arm, he made a straight, furious lunge for the youth's breast, with a double step forward.

Every one held his breath in dread suspense, expecting to see the gallant youth spitted on the quivering steel.

Lord Dallas had not shifted his gaze from the other's eye, and he expected some such treachery. To the utter astonishment of everyone, he raised his sword with an easy turn of the wrist, and his antagonist's impetuous blade went over his shoulder.

The calmness of the act brought a ringing acclamation from the admiring spectators.

The frustrated duellist drew back his weapon with a fierce exclamation of anger. A second lunge he made; was leaping forward with the intention not to miss his foe this time.

Lord Ernest thought it was time the contest was ended, and as his opponent came towards him he made a point, and his sword went through his heart.

Gabriel Carnwood fell to the floor with a last earthly cry of anguish, wrung from his soul; then he expired. The young nobleman drew his weapon from the quivering body without the least remorse.

"My comrade is avenged," he said, calmly, "my destiny is fulfilled. If there are any gentlemen present who have any interest in my fallen foe, perhaps some of them will comply with his last request."

Lord Dallas sheathed his gory blade and departed.

CHAPTER CXXXV.

TYBURN DICK GOES IN SEARCH OF THE HIDDEN CERTIFICATE OF HIS BIRTH, AND DISCOVERS LORD AND LADY MERTON.

TOM JOHNSON's memory was refreshed of his

bygone scenes by the news of Lady Kingston's return. He knew her to be the same lady who had caused him so much curiosity while on board the smuggler's barque, and he thought that, as she had been released, there might be a chance of hearing something of his pretty Greek mistress whom he had left abroad.

He was determined to regain her — if perseverance would do it; and he informed our hero of his intention of going to Cornwall to commence his search.

Tyburn Dick, who had heard rumours concerning the disappearance of Lord and Lady Merton, consented to go with him.

And they went.

"The first thing we must do, Tom, on reaching Cornwall," said Dick, " is to make a search for the certificate of my birth."

That was the first thing they did do when the Cornwall coast was reached by the youthful pilgrims, but there arose some difficulty to their task.

The hut in which our hero had first learned to speak had fallen to utter decay, and there remained but few relics to show that such a habitation had ever existed on the wild coast.

Tyburn Dick felt a gloomy oppression when he viewed the distinct scene of his childhood's home.

"There is nothing now remaining to remind me of the old people who nurtured me from babyhood with all the affection of indulgent parents," he remarked, audibly. " I would have paid any amount to have had their home kept in restoration."

"Never mind, old fellow," said his companion, "you have their memory the same; nothing can destroy that!"

Dick grasped his hand gratefully for his kind sympathy.

"True," he said, " and now, Tom, we will set to work, but I would have the remnants of a once happy home moved with care."

Every piece of timber of the destroyed hut was laid aside with almost tender reverence.

The stone was reached beneath which was suffered to lie hidden the certificate of our hero's birth, and, after some exertion, the youth succeeded in throwing it aside, and in a recess they found a small iron chest containing the deed which gave Tyburn Dick the name of Earl of Aldervale.

Imagine the surprise of young Tom when his gaze fell upon the form of a female wandering along the beach, whom he recognised as the Greek slave.

With an exclamation of joy breaking from his lips he bounded from his companion's side, and Dick was left alone, bewildered, wondering whether his friend had gone mad.

He watched with deep interest the affectionate embrace of the two young people, and muttered—

" It ain't the first time they have met."

The truth of this surmise he was soon made aware of when his companion came to him and introduced the blushing girl.

"I told you I should find her," he said.

"And I am very happy you have," our hero said.

" How do you think she came here?"

" Can't imagine.'

" Why, the smuggler ship was wrecked on the coast, and that's how it was that Lady Kingston was released."

" You see, Tom, that the hand of Providence guides all things the right way. I would that I could be fortunate enough to introduce the Lord and Lady Merton; but I suppose they will be restored to their rights sooner or later."

" Let us hope so."

The Greek girl looked timidly at our hero, and then, glancing at her lover, said—

" The captain has got a lady and gentleman in his charge; he has often asked their name, but neither will tell him."

Dick put a few questions to her, which she answered, describing the captives that almost made him believe that they were the lost parents of his young bride.

The girl then conducted the anxious youth to a cave in the rocks.

The smuggler chief came forward and greeted Tom cordially.

" My boy," he said, " I never expected to see you again."

" Did you not?" replied the youth. " Then you had not the faith in Providence I had. It has been my nightly prayer that we should again meet. I have not forgotten the kindness you treated me with, and the gratitude I owe you for the care you have taken of Zelika. I shall be better able to express my thanks by helping you a little in some way, than I can in words."

"My good lad," said the smuggler, "I am delighted at having been the means of making you happy, and that for your generous thought I am grateful for, but I have sufficient wealth to keep me like a prince for the rest of my life, if I chose."

"Then why live in this miserable solitude—shut away from the world?"

"Because the bloodhounds are after me. Who is your companion?" he added, alluding to the Boy King of the Highwaymen.

Tyburn Dick was introduced, and Tom Johnson said—

"My friend has heard the description of the people whom you have living with you, and should they be those he seeks, he has the power of restoring them to the lady he loves. Would you grant him an interview with them?"

"With pleasure," readily answered the smuggler chief. And taking Dick by the hand, he led him to a sort of chamber, where sat the captives.

They were not ill, but the iron hand of sorrow had furrowed the once handsome features with lines of bitter grief.

Dick was struck by the living resemblance of the lady to Grace, and he concluded within his own mind that they were her parents.

The gentleman rose as Dick entered, and bowed gracefully to the lone occupants.

The lady looked at the young stranger sadly, and a big lump rose in Dick's throat, as he thought of the sufferings she must have endured.

"Your business, fair sir," demanded the gentleman.

"I have come on a strange mission," replied our hero. "God grant that I may be successful in my undertaking, and restore to those I seek their rights, from which they were cruelly kept, and an only child."

The lady's pale cheeks were suddenly suffused with a glow of excitement, when their visitor spoke, and she looked towards her husband inquiringly.

"I pray you speak more plainly, young sir," the gentleman said, and he seemed to

grow nervous with rising agitation; "for your words cause me some excitement."

"Then," Dick said, "I seek Lord and Lady Merton."

The gentleman started, and the lady uttered a low cry of alarm.

"What know you of them?" queried the agitated gentleman eagerly.

"This," replied the boy, "that should I be fortunate enough to find them, I shall be able to restore to their arms their only child, a fair, beautiful lady whom I rescued many years ago from a wreck on this coast."

"In Heaven's name, who art thou?" exclaimed the lady; "a fiend come to torture us, or an angel come to answer my prayers?"

"Neither, lady," said Dick. "I am a being of the earth, come to make you happy as far as lies in my power. You are, then, Lady Merton."

"Yes, yes," the gentleman answered, quickly. "We are those you sought. Where is my child?"

"Under safe protection, near London."

The poor gentleman fairly wept with joy, and the bereaved lady was so overcome by the unexpected news that she fainted.

Dick endeavoured to soothe the gentleman, and when he was calm enough to converse Dick began to lay a plan before him, showing the different courses to be taken.

In alluding to Percy and Reginald Morton the gentleman said—

"They are my brother's sons, and I would not have the law carried too far against them."

"But they have been the cause of all your unhappiness," Dick replied in astonishment; "surely you do not intend to let them go unpunished for their villainy?"

"What can I do?" said Lord Merton; "to inform against them would be signing their death warrant."

"Oh, no," said the boy, "you can punish them without condemning them to the executioner. Will you put the affair in my hands? I promise you that I will not take steps too severe against them."

"It is a painful task. I cannot undertake it, for the love of my brother's memory. I would that some stranger would do it.

"Then leave it to me."

Lord Merton assented.

When the lady had recovered from her swoon, the whole party, with the exception of the Smuggler Chief, left Cornwall.

Our hero lost no time. After seeing the Lord and Lady Morton in a splendid apartment in the fashionable part of London, he went to their solicitor's, and explained the whole matter to him.

Legal proceedings were taken against the Brothers Merton, and they were punished for their villainy.

The rightful owners were restored to Morton Grange, and there remained but one thing to complete the old people's happiness, that was done when Dick brought his fair lady-love by the hand and gave her to her parents.

The scene that took place at the meeting, our readers can better imagine than the author's pen describe.

Our hero was overwhelmed by the blessing he received from the joyous family; he never felt so happy as he did now, when he thought of the happiness he had restored to a shattered family.

Grace could only express her gratitude by her tears as she hung round his neck and wept.

Their love was told, and their marriage willingly agreed to.

"When once, darling, the holy rites of the Church have linked thy life to mine," Dick said, pressing the happy girl to his breast, "I will for ever give up the dangerous life I now lead."

A big tear stood for a moment in his eye, and then rolled down his handsome cheek, as he thought, with almost a pang of regret of for ever leaving his faithful comrades.